DON QUIXOTE

DON QUIXOTE

Miguel de Cervantes Saavedra

WORDSWORTH CLASSICS

The paper in this book is produced from pure wood
pulp, without the use of chlorine or any other substance
harmful to the environment. The energy used in its
production consists almost entirely of hydroelectricity
and heat generated from waste material, thereby
conserving fossil fuels and contributing little to the
greenhouse effect.

This edition published 1993 by
Wordsworth Editions Limited
Cumberland House, Crib Street
Ware, Hertfordshire SG12 9ET

ISBN 1 85326 036 3

REPRINTED 1995

Printed and bound in Denmark by Nørhaven
Typeset in the UK by Antony Gray

INTRODUCTION

One of the greatest and most enduring classics of European literature, *Don Quixote de la Mancha* tells the story of Don Quixote, a poor gentleman of La Mancha in central Spain, who has his senses disordered by excessive devotion to and literal reading of the tales of chivalry. He sees himself as having a mission to travel the world in rusty armour on his thin old horse, Rozinante, in search of adventure and accompanied by his rustic companion, Sancho Pança. Don Quixote chooses a good-looking maiden as his knightly belle, although she remains ignorant of this honour, naming her as Dulcinea del Taboso. There follows a series of absurd adventures, and in Part One the reader is treated to the battle with the sheep, the release of the galley slaves and the famous tilting at windmills. Thus 'quixotic' is defined in the original as absurdly directed chivalry in a combination of generosity and futility. Despite all his madness, delusion and absurdity, however, Quixote always retains an essential dignity which raises him above the level of his would-be tormentors.

The reactions to *Don Quixote* have varied largely with the taste of the period, and have ranged from mirth in the seventeenth and eighteenth centuries to a more serious interpretation in modern times. The story is almost infinitely definable, and has thus, by a supreme irony, visited a leading trait of 'quixotism' on its critics and interpreters. The genius of Cervantes' creation has inspired translations of his tragicomic hero into art (Daumier and many others), opera, cartoon and, most recently, computer games. The late-twentieth-century reader of *Don Quixote* will appreciate Cervantes' rich narrative style, and his unprecedented use of dialogue in what is one of the earliest of all novels, and one of the greatest prose works of any time in any language.

Miguel de Cervantes Saavedra was born in Alcalá de Henares in September 1547, and was baptised on 9 October that year. He was the third child of Rodrigo de Cervantes, a surgeon, and Donna Leonora de Corteñas. He was thus almost 17 years older than Shakespeare, who was born in April 1564. However, the two great authors were to die within days of each other in April 1616. Cervantes' parents were both from noble families originating from Galicia but with branches, by the time of his birth, in Toledo, Seville and Alcarria. However, although of good lineage, they were comparatively poor in their economic circumstances. He was sent early in his life to Madrid where he was placed under the instruction of a philologer and theologian – Doctor Juan Lopez de Hoyos. In the summer of 1569 Cervantes joined the entourage of Cardinal Julio Aquaviva as chamberlain, a signal honour, and travelled from Madrid to Rome.

He was, however, a man of action, and, following the treaty of combination (to combat the growing power of the Turkish fleet in the Mediterranean) between the navies of Philip II of Spain, the Papal See and the Venetian Senate, which was signed on 29 May 1571, he joined General Colonna in the Papal galleys in the fleet of Don Juan of Austria. The treaty led directly to the battle of Lepanto (immortalised for many English readers by the poem of that name by G. K. Chesterton) in which the supremacy of the Ottoman navy was successfully challenged, and in which Cervantes lost his left hand and with it the effective use of his entire left arm. He considered this a small price to have paid for the honour of being present at the great battle. Notwithstanding his wound, he sailed again with the fleet in the summer of 1572, and from 1573–5 was a soldier stationed in Naples.

In the autumn of 1575, while travelling by sea from Italy to Spain, the galley he was aboard was captured by Moorish corsairs, and he was taken to Algiers as a prisoner of the cruel Albanian apostate, Dali Mami the Lame. After a terrible time of imprisonment in the meanest conditions, escape, and recapture as a result of treachery, he was eventually freed by Ochali, tyrant of Algiers, for a ransom of 500 crowns, and returned to Spain in the spring of 1581. Thus, at the age of thirty-four, Cervantes found himself possessed of enough experiences and adventures to provide a wealth of material for a writer, but of strictly limited financial resources, and disabled from any future military career. In 1584 a daughter, Isabel, was born to Ana Franca de Rojas with whom Cervantes had had an affair. Later the same year he married Donna Catalina de Palaciosy Salazar y Vozmediano, from Esquivias, who was eighteen years younger than himself, and who brought him a modest dowry which enabled his writing to progress.

In 1585 his romance La Galatea *was published which would have established his reputation in the literature of Spain even if he had not subsequently written his masterpiece – Don Quixote. From 1585 there followed a period when Cervantes wrote poorly received plays and comedies for scant commercial advantage. During this time he lived in Madrid and Esquivias, moving to Seville in 1588 where he settled until 1604.* Don Quixote, *Part One, was published in Madrid in January 1605 and was an immediate success with a wide readership from the court downwards. It went into four editions, each of which rapidly sold out within a year of publication. He moved from Valladolid to Madrid in 1607, where he was to live for almost all of the remainder of his life, and was immediately assailed by jealous personal attacks from those who felt themselves to be the victims of his inimitable satire. Cervantes wisely largely ignored the attacks on him and his great work, being secure under the patronage, protection and support of two powerful noblemen, the Cardinal of Toledo and the Conde de Lemos. Indeed,* Don Quixote, *Part Two, published in early 1615, is inscribed to the Conde de Lemos. The new volume was another triumphant success, but Cervantes had not long to live and savour his now overwhelming literary fame. He died, a devout Catholic, in late April 1616 and is buried at the Franciscan monastery of the Holy Trinity in Madrid.*

FURTHER READING

J. Canavaggio: *Cervantes* (trans. J. R. Jones) 1990
A. J. Close: *Cervantes' Don Quixote* 1990
M. McKendrick: *Cervantes* 1980
E. C. Riley: *Don Quixote* 1986
P. E. Russell: *Cervantes* 1985

CONTENTS

PART ONE

PART TWO

PART ONE

THE AUTHOR'S PREFACE TO THE READER

You may depend upon my bare word, reader, without and further security, that I could wish this offspring of my brain were as ingenious, sprightly, and accomplished as yourself could desire; but the mischief of it is, nature will have its course: every production must resemble its author, and my barren and unpolished understanding can produce nothing but what is very dull, very impertinent, and extravagant beyond imagination. You may suppose it the child of disturbance, engendered in some dismal prison,* where wretchedness keeps its residence, and every dismal sound its habitation. Rest and ease, a convenient place, pleasant fields and groves, murmuring springs, and a sweet repose of mind, are helps that raise the fancy, and impregnate even the most barren muses with conceptions that fill the world with admiration and delight. Some parents are so blinded by a fatherly fondness, that they mistake the very imperfections of their children for so many beauties; and the folly and impertinence of the brave boy, must pass upon their friends and acquaintance for wit and sense. But I, who am only a step-father, disavow the authority of this modern and prevalent custom; nor will I earnestly beseech you, with tears in my eyes, which is many a poor author's case, dear reader, to pardon or dissemble my child's faults; for what favour can I expect from you, who are neither his friend nor relation? You have a soul of your own, and the privilege of free-will, whoever you be, as well as the proudest he that struts in a gaudy outside: you are a king by your own fireside, as much as any monarch in his throne: you have liberty and property, which set you above favour or affection, and may therefore freely like or dislike this history, according to your humour.

I had a great mind to have exposed it as naked as it was born, without the addition of a preface, or the numberless trumpery of commendatory sonnets, epigrams, and other poems that usually usher in the conceptions of authors. For I dare boldly say, that though I bestowed some time in writing the book, yet it cost me not half so much labour as this very

* The author is said to have wrote this satirical romance in a prison.

preface, I very often took up my pen, and as often laid it down, and could not for my-life think of anything to the purpose. Sitting once in a very studious posture, with my paper before me, my pen in my ear, my elbow on the table, and my cheek on my hand, considering how I should begin; a certain friend of mine, an ingenious gentleman, and of a merry disposition, came and surprised me. He asked me what I was so very intent and thoughtful upon? I was so free with him as not to mince the matter, but told him plainly I had been puzzling my brain for a preface to Don Quixote, and had made myself so uneasy about it, that I was now resolved to trouble my head no further either with preface or book, and even to let the achievements of that noble Knight remain unpublished: 'For,' continued I, 'why should I expose myself to the lash of the old legislator, the vulgar? They will say, I have spent my youthful days very finely, to have nothing to recommend my grey hairs to the world, but a dry, insipid legend, not worth a rush, wanting good language as well as invention, barren of conceits or pointed wit, and without either quotations on the margin, or annotations at the end, which other books, though never so fabulous and profane, have to set them off. Other authors can pass upon the public, by stuffing their books from Aristotle, Plato, and the whole company of ancient philosophers; thus amusing their readers into a great opinion of their prodigious reading. Plutarch and Cicero are slurred on the public for as orthodox doctors as St. Thomas, or any of the Fathers. And then the method of these moderns is so wonderfully agreeable and full of variety, that they cannot fail to please. In one line, they will describe you a whining amorous coxcomb, and the next shall be some dry scrap of a homily, with such ingenious turns as cannot choose but ravish the reader. Now I want all these embellishments and graces: I have neither marginal notes nor critical remarks; I do not so much as know what authors I follow, and consequently, can have no formal index, as it is the fashion now, methodically strung on the letters of the alphabet, beginning with Aristotle, and ending with Xenophon, or Zoilus, or Zeuxis; which last two are commonly crammed into the same piece, though one of them was a famous painter, and the other a saucy critic. I shall want also the pompous preliminaries of commendatory verses sent to me by the right honourable my Lord such a one, by the honourable the Lady such a one, or the most ingenious Master such a one; though I know I might have them at an easy rate from two or three brothers of the quill of my acquaintance, and better, I am sure, than the best quality in Spain can compose.

'In short, my friend,' said I, 'the great Don Quixote may lie buried in the musty records of La Mancha, till Providence has ordered some better hand to fit him out as he ought to be; for I must own myself altogether incapable of the task; besides, I am naturally lazy, and love my ease too well to take the pains of turning over authors for those things which I can express as well without it. And these are the considerations that made me so thoughtful when you came in.' The gentleman, after a long and loud fit of laughing, rubbing his forehead: 'O my conscience, friend,' said he, 'your discourse has freed me from a mistake that has a great while imposed upon me: I always took you for a man of sense, but now I am sufficiently convinced to the contrary. What! puzzled at so inconsiderable a trifle I a business of so little difficulty confound a man of such deep sense and searching thought as once you seemed to be!'

'I am sorry, sir, that your lazy humour and poor understanding should need the advice I am about to give you, which will presently solve all your objections and fears concerning the publishing of the Renowned Don Quixote, the luminary and mirror of all knight-errantry.' 'Pray, sir,' said I, 'be pleased to instruct me in whatever you think may remove my fears, or solve my doubts.' 'The first thing you object,' replied he, 'is your want of commendatory copies from persons of figure and quality: there is nothing sooner helped. It is but taking a little pains in writing them yourself, and clapping whose name you please to them, you may father them on Prester John of the Indies, or on the emperor of Trapizonde, whom I know to be most celebrated poets: but suppose they were not, and that some presuming pedantic critics might snarl, and deny this notorious truth, value it not two farthings; and though they should convict you of forgery you are in no danger of losing the hand with which you wrote* them.

'As to marginal notes and quotations from authors for your history, it is but dropping here and there some scattered Latin sentences that you have already by rote, or may have with little or no pains. For example, treating of liberty and slavery, clap me in, *non bene pro toto libertas venditur auro* and, at the same time, make Horace, or some other author vouch it in the margin. If you treat of the power of death, come round with this close,† *pallida mors æquo pulsat pede pauperum tabernas, regumque turres*. If of loving our enemies, as Heaven enjoins, you may, if you have the least curiosity, presently turn to the divine precept, and say, *ego autem dico vobis, diligite inimicos vestros*; or, if you discourse of bad thoughts, bring in this passage, *de corde exeunt cogitationes malæ*. If the uncertainty of friendship be your theme, Cato offers you his old couplet with all his heart; *donec eris felix multos numerabis amicos: Tempora si fuerint nubila, solus eris*: and so proceed. These scraps of latin will at least gain you the credit of a great grammarian, which, I will assure you, is no small accomplishment in this age. As to annotations or remarks at the end of your book, you may safely

---

* He lost his left hand (*izquierda*) in the sea-fight at Lepanto against the Turks.
† This quotation from Horace, and the following from Scripture, are omitted in Shelton's translation; as is also this and another ingenious preface of the author's in that of Stevens, many of whose notes indeed I have made use of.

take this course. If you have occasion for a giant in your piece, be sure you bring in Goliah, and on this very Goliah (who will not cost you one farthing) you may spin out a swinging annotation. You may say, "The giant Goliah, or Goliat, was a Philistine, whom David the shepherd slew with the thundering stroke of a pebble in the valley of Terebinthus': *Vide* "Kings," in such a chapter, and such a verse, where you may find it written. If not satisfied with this, you would appear a great humanist, and would show your knowledge in geography, take some occasion to draw the river Tagus into your discourse, out of which you may fish a most notable remark: "The river Tagus," say you, "was so called from a certain king of Spain. It takes its rise from such a place, and buries its waters in the ocean, kissing first the walls of the famous city of Lisbon; and some are of opinion that the sands of this river are gold," etc. If you have occasion to talk of robbers, I can presently give you the history of Cacus, for I have it by heart. If you would descant upon whores, or women of the town, there is the* bishop of Mondonedo, who can furnish you with Lamia, Laïs, and Flora, courtesans, whose acquaintance will add very much to your reputation. Ovid's Medea can afford you a good example of cruelty. Calypso from Homer, and Circe out of Virgil, are famous instances of witchcraft or enchantment. Would you treat of valiant commanders? Julius Cæsar has writ his Commentaries on purpose; and Plutarch can furnish you with a thousand Alexanders. If you would mention love, and have but three grains of Italian, you may find Leon the Jew ready to serve you most abundantly. But if you keep nearer home, it is but examining Fonseca of Divine Love, which you have here in your study; and you need go no further, for all that can be said on that copious subject. In short, it is but quoting these authors in your book, and let me alone to make large annotations; I will engage to crowd your margin sufficiently, and scribble you four or five sheets besides at the end of your book. And for the citation of so many authors, it is the easiest thing in nature. Find out one of those books with an alphabetical index, and without any further ceremony, remove it *verbatim* into your own: and though the world will not believe you have occasion for such lumber, yet there are fools enough to be thus drawn into an opinion of the work; at least, such a flourishing train of attendants will give your book a fashionable air, and recommend it to sale; for few chapmen will stand to examine it, and compare the authorities upon the compter, since they can expect nothing but their labour for their pains. But, after all, sir, if I know anything of the matter, you have no occasion for any of those things; for your subject being a satire on knight-errantry, is so absolutely new, that neither Aristotle, St. Basil, nor Cicero ever dreamed or heard of it. Those fabulous extravagancies

* Guevara.

have nothing to do with the impartial punctuality of true history; nor do I find any business you can have either with astrology, geometry, or logic; and I hope you are too good a man to mix sacred things with profane. Nothing but pure nature is your business; her you must consult, and the closer you can imitate, your picture is the better. And since this writing of yours aims at no more than to destroy the authority and acceptance the books of chivalry have had in the world, and among the vulgar, you have no need to go begging sentences of philosophers, passages out of holy writ, poetical fables, rhetorial orations, or miracles of saints. Do but take care to express yourself in a plain, easy manner, in well-chosen, significant, and decent terms, and to give an harmonious and pleasing turn to your periods: study to explain your thoughts, and set them in the truest light, labouring, as much as possible, not to leave them dark nor intricate, but clear and intelligible: let your diverting stories be expressed in diverting terms, to kindle mirth in the melancholic, and heighten it in the gay: let mirth and humour be your superficial design, though laid on a solid foundation, to challenge attention from the ignorant, and admiration from the judicious; to secure your work from the contempt of the graver sort, and deserve the praises of men of sense; keeping your eye still fixed on the principal end of your project, the fall and destruction of that monstrous heap of ill-contrived romances, which, though abhorred by many, have so strangely infatuated the greater part of mankind. Mind this, and your business is done.'

I listened very attentively to my friend's discourse, and found it so reasonable and convincing, that without any reply, I took his advice, and have told you the story by way of preface; wherein you may see, gentlemen, how happy I am in so ingenious a friend, to whose seasonable counsel you are all obliged for the omission of all this pedantic garniture in the history of the renowned Don Quixote de la Mancha, whose character among all the neighbours about Montiel, is, that he was the most chaste lover, and the most valiant knight, that has been known in those parts these many years. I will not urge the service I have done you by introducing you into so considerable and noble a knight's acquaintance, but only beg the favour of some small acknowledgment for recommending you to the familiarity of the famous Sancho Pança his squire; in whom, in my opinion, you will find united and described all the squire-like graces which are scattered up and down in the whole bead-roll of books of chivalry. And now I take my leave, entreating you not to forget your humble servant.

BOOK I

CHAPTER I

The quality and manner of life of the renowned Don Quixote de la Mancha

AT A CERTAIN VILLAGE in La Mancha,* which I shall not name, there lived not long ago one of those old-fashioned gentlemen who are never without a lance upon a rack, an old target, a lean horse, and a greyhound. His diet consisted more of beef than mutton; and with minced meat on most nights, lentils on Fridays, griefs and groans on Saturdays, and a pigeon extraordinary on Sundays, he consumed three quarters of his revenue: the rest was laid out in a plush coat, velvet breeches, with slippers of the same, for holidays; and a suit of the very best homespun cloth, which he bestowed on himself for working days. His whole family was a housekeeper something turned of forty, a niece not twenty, and a man that served him in the house and in the field, and could saddle a horse, and handle the pruning-hook. The master himself was nigh fifty years of age, of a hale and strong complexion, lean-bodied, and thin-faced, an early riser, and a lover of hunting. Some say his surname was Quixada, or Quesada (for authors differ in this particular): however, we may reasonably conjecture he was called Quixana (*i.e.* lanthorn-jaws) though this concerns us but little, provided we keep strictly to the truth in every point of this history.

You must know then, that when our gentleman had nothing to do (which was almost all the year round), he passed his time in reading books of knight-errantry; which he did with that application and delight, that at last he in a manner wholly left off his country sports, and even the care of his estate; nay, he grew so strangely besotted with those amusements, that he sold many acres of arable land to purchase books of that kind; by which means he collected as many of them as were to be had: but among them all, none pleased him like the works of the famous Feliciano de Silva; for the clearness of his prose, and those intricate expressions with which it is interlaced, seemed to him so many pearls of eloquence, especially when he

* A small territory, partly in the kingdom of Arragon, and partly in Castile.

came to read the challenges; and the amorous addresses, many of them in this extraordinary style. 'The reason of your unreasonable usage of my reason, does so enfeeble my reason, that I have reason to expostulate with your beauty: 'and this, 'The sublime heavens, which with your divinity divinely fortify you with the stars, and fix you the deserver of the desert that is deserved by your grandeur.' These and such-like expressions, strangely puzzled the poor gentleman's understanding, while he was breaking his brain to unravel their meaning, which Aristotle himself could never have found, though he should have been raised from the dead for that very purpose.

He did not so well like those dreadful wounds which Don Belianis gave and received; for he considered that all the art of surgery could never secure his face and body from being strangely disfigured with scars. However, he highly commended the author for concluding his book with a promise to finish that unfinishable adventure; and many times he had a desire to put pen to paper, and faithfully and literally finish it himself: which he had certainly done, and doubtless with good success, had not his thoughts been wholly engrossed in much more important designs.

He would often dispute with the curate* of the parish, a man of learning, that had taken his degrees at Ciguenza, who was the better knight, Palmerin of England, or Amadis de Gaul? but master Nicholas, the barber† of the same town, would say, that none of them could compare with the Knight of the Sun; and that if any one came near him, it was certainly Don Galaor, the brother of Amadis de Gaul; for he was a man of a most commodious temper, neither was he so cynical, nor such a puling whining lover as his brother; and as for courage, he was not a jot behind him.

In fine, he gave himself up so wholly to the reading of romances, that a-nights he would pore on until it was day, and a-days he would read on until it was night; and thus, by sleeping little and reading much, the moisture of his brain was exhausted to that degree, that at last he lost the use of his reason. A world of disorderly notions, picked out of his books, crowded into his imagination; and now his head was full of nothing but enchantments, quarrels, battles, challenges, wounds, complaints, amours, torments, and abundance of stuff and impossibilities; insomuch, that all the fables and fantastical tales which he read seemed to him now as true as the most authentic histories. He would say, that the Cid Ruydiaz was a very brave knight, but not worthy to stand in competition with the Knight of the Burning Sword, who with a single back-stroke had cut in sunder

* In Spain the curate is the head priest in the parish, and he that has the cure of souls.
† The barber in country towns in Spain is also the surgeon.

two fierce and mighty giants. He liked yet better Bernardo del Carpio, who at Roncesvalles deprived of life the enchanted Orlando, having lifted him from the ground, and choked him in the air, as Hercules did Anteus the son of the earth.

As for the giant Morgante, he always spoke very civil things of him; for, though he was one of that monstrous brood who ever were intolerably proud and brutish, he still behaved himself like a civil and well-bred person.

But of all men in the world he admired Rinaldo of Montalvan, and particularly his sallying out of his castle to rob all he met; and then again, when abroad, he carried away the idol Mahomet, which was all massy gold, as the history says: but he so hated that traitor Galalon,* that for the pleasure of kicking him handsomely, he would have given up his house-keeper, nay, and his niece into the bargain.

Having thus lost his understanding, he unluckily stumbled upon the oddest fancy that ever entered into a madman's brain; for now he thought it convenient and necessary, as well for the increase of his own honour, as the service of the public, to turn knight-errant, and roam through the whole world, armed *cap-à-pie* and mounted on his steed, in quest of adventures; that thus imitating those knights-errant of whom he had read, and following their course of life, redressing all manner of grievances, and exposing himself to danger on all occasions, at last, after a happy conclusion of his enterprises, he might purchase everlasting honour and renown. Transported with these agreeable delusions, the poor gentleman already grasped in imagination the imperial sceptre of Trapizonda; and, hurried away by his mighty expectations, he prepares with all expedition to take the field.

The first thing he did was to scour a suit of armour that had belonged to his great-grandfather, and had lain time out of mind carelessly rusting in a corner; but, when he had cleaned and repaired it as well as he could, he perceived there was a material piece wanting; for instead of a complete helmet, there was only a single head-piece: however, his industry supplied that defect; for, with some pasteboard, he made a kind of half: beaver, or vizor, which being fitted to the head-piece, made it look like an entire helmet. Then, to know whether it was cutlass-proof, he drew his sword, and tried its edge upon the pasteboard vizor; but, with the first stroke, he unluckily undid in a moment what he had been a whole week a-doing. He did not like its being broke with so much ease, and therefore to secure it from the like accident, he made it anew, and fenced it with thin plates of iron, which he fixed in the inside of it so artificially, that at last he had reason to be satisfied with the solidity of the world and so, without any

* Galalon, the Spaniards say, betrayed the French army at Roncesvalles.

experiment, he resolved it should pass to all intents and purposes for a full and sufficient helmet.

The next moment he went to view his horse, whose bones stuck out like the corners of a Spanish Real, being a worse jade than Gonela's, *qui tantum pellis et offa fuit*; however, his master thought, that neither Alexander's Bucephalus, nor the Cid's Babieca could be compared with him. He was four days considering what name to give him; for, as he argued with himself, there was no reason that a horse bestrid by so famous a knight, and withal so excellent in himself, should not be distinguished by a particular name; and therefore he studied to give him such a one as should demonstrate as well what kind of horse he had been before his master was a knight-errant, as what he was now; thinking it but just, since the owner had changed his profession, that the horse should also change his title, and be dignified with another; a sonorous word, such a one as should fill the mouth, and seem consonant with the quality and profession of his master. And thus after many names which he devised, rejected, changed, liked, disliked, and, pitched upon again, he concluded to call him Rozinante;* a name, in his opinion, lofty sounding, and significant of what he had been before, and also of what he was now; in a word, a horse before or above all the vulgar breed of horses in the world.

When he had thus given his horse a name so much to his satisfaction, he thought of choosing one for himself; and having seriously pondered on the matter eight whole days more, at last he determined to call himself Don Quixote. Whence the author of this most authentic history draws this inference, that his name was Quixada, and not Quesada, as others obstinately pretend. And observing that the valiant Amadis, not satisfied with the bare appellation of Amadis, added to it the name of his country, that it might grow more famous by his exploits, and styled himself Amadis de Gaul; so he, like a true lover of his native soil, resolved to call himself Don Quixote de la Mancha; which addition, to his thinking, denoted very plainly his parentage and country, and consequently would fix a lasting honour on that part of the world.

And now, his armour being scoured, his head-piece improved to a helmet, his horse and himself new-named, he perceived he wanted nothing but a lady, on whom he might bestow the empire of his heart; for he was sensible that a knight-errant without a mistress was a tree without either fruit or leaves, and a body without a soul. 'Should I,' said he to himself, 'by good or ill fortune chance to encounter some giant, as it is

---

* *Rozin* commonly means an 'ordinary horse'; *Ante* signifies before and formerly. Thus the word Rozinante may imply, that he was formerly an ordinary horse, and also, that he is now an horse that claims the precedence from all other ordinary horses.

common in knight-errantry, and happen to lay him prostrate on the ground, transfixed with my lance, or cleft in two, or, in short, overcome and gave him at my mercy, would it not be proper to have some lady to whom I may send him as a trophy of my valour? That, when he comes into her presence, throwing himself at her feet, he may thus make his humble submission: "Lady, I am the giant Caraculiambro, lord of the island of Malindrania, vanquished in single combat by that never-deservedly-enough-extolled knight-errant Don Quixote de la Mancha, who has commanded me to cast myself most humbly at your feet, that it may please your honour to dispose of me according to your will." ' Oh! how elevated was the Knight with the conceit of this imaginary submission of the giant; especially having bethought himself of a person on whom he might confer the title of mistress I which, it is believed, happened thus. Near the place where he lived dwelt a good likely country lass, for whom he had formerly had a sort of an inclination, though it is believed she never heard of it, nor regarded it in the least. Her name was Aldonza Lorenzo, and this was she whom he thought he might entitle to the sovereignty of his heart: upon which he studied to find her out a new name, that might have some affinity with her old one, and yet at the same time sound somewhat like that of a princess, or lady of quality: so at last he resolved to call her Dulcinea, with the addition of del Toboso, from the place where she was born; a name, in his opinion, sweet, harmonious, extraordinary, and no less significative than the others which he had devised.

CHAPTER II

Of Don Quixote's first Sally

THESE PREPARATIONS being made, he found his designs ripe for action, and thought it now a crime to deny himself any longer to the injured world, that wanted such a deliverer; the more when he considered what grievances he was to redress, what wrongs and injuries to remove, what abuses to correct and what duties to discharge. So one morning before day, in the greatest heat of July, without acquainting any one with his design, with all the secrecy imaginable, he armed himself *cap-à-pie*, laced on his ill-contrived helmet, braced on his target, grasped his lance, mounted Rozinante, and at the private door of his back-yard sallied out into the fields, wonderfully pleased to see with how much ease he had succeeded in the beginning of his enterprise. But he had not gone far ere a terrible thought alarmed him, a thought that had like to have made him renounce his great undertaking; for now it came into his mind that the honour of knighthood had not yet been conferred upon him, and therefore, according to the laws of chivalry, he neither could nor ought to appear in arms against any professed knight: nay, he also considered, that though he were already knighted, it would become him to wear white armour, and not to adorn his shield with any device, till he had deserved one by some extraordinary demonstration of his valour.

These thoughts staggered his resolution; but his folly prevailing more than any reason, he resolved to be dubbed knight by the first he should meet, after the example of several others, who, as his distracting romances informed him, had formerly done the like. As for the other difficulty about wearing white armour, he proposed to overcome it by scouring his own at leisure till it should look whiter than ermine. And having thus dismissed these busy scruples, he very calmly rode on, leaving it to his horse's discretion to go which way he pleased; firmly believing that in this consisted the very being of adventures. And as he thus went on, 'I cannot but believe,' said he to himself, 'that when the history of my famous achievements shall be given to the world, the learned author will begin it in this very manner, when he comes to give an account of this my early setting out: "Scarce had the ruddy-coloured Phœbus begun to spread the golden tresses of his lovely hair over the vast surface of the earthly globe, and scarce had those feathered poets of the grove, the pretty painted birds, tuned their little pipes, to sing their early welcomes in soft melodious strains to the beautiful Aurora, who having left her jealous husband's bed, displayed her rosy graces to mortal eyes from the gates and balconies of the Manchegan Horizon, when the renowned knight Don Quixote de la Mancha, disdaining soft repose, forsook the voluptuous down, and mounting his famous steed Rozinante entered the ancient and celebrated plains of Montiel." '* This was indeed the very road he took; and then proceeding, 'O happy age! O fortunate times!' cried he, 'decreed to usher into the world my famous achievements; achievements worthy to be engraven on brass, carved on marble, and delineated in some masterpiece of painting, as monuments of my glory, and examples for posterity! And thou, venerable sage, wise enchanter, whatever be thy name; thou whom fate has ordained to be the compiler of this rare history, forget not, I beseech thee, my trusty Rozinante, the eternal companion of all my adventures.' After this, as if he had been really in love: 'O princess Dulcinea,' cried he, 'lady of this captive heart, much sorrow and woe you have doomed me to in banishing me thus, and imposing on me your rigorous commands, never to appear before your

---

* Montiel, proper field to inspire courage, being the ground upon which Henry the Bastard slew his legitimate brother Don Pedro, whom our brave black prince Edward had set upon the throne of Spain.

beauteous face! Remember, lady, that loyal heart your slave, who for your love submits to so many miseries.' To these extravagant conceits he added a world of others, all in imitation, and in the very style of those which the reading of romances had furnished him with; and all this while he rode so softly, and the sun's heat increased so fast, and was so violent, that it would have been sufficient to have melted his brains had he had any left.

He travelled almost all that day without meeting any adventure worth the trouble of relating; which put him into a kind of despair; for he desired nothing more than to encounter immediately some person, on whom he might try the vigour of his arm.

Some authors say, that his first adventure was that of the pass called Puerto Lapice; others, that of the wind-mills; but all that I could discover of certainty in this matter, and that I meet with in the annals of La Mancha, is, that he travelled all that day; and, towards the evening, he and his horse being heartily tired, and almost famished, Don Quixote looking about him in hopes to discover some castle, or at least some shepherd's cottage, there to repose and refresh himself; at last, near the road which he kept, he espied an inn, as welcome a sight to his longing eyes, as if he had discovered a star directing him to the gate, nay, to the palace of his redemption. Thereupon hastening towards the inn with all the speed he could, he got thither just at the close of the evening. There stood by chance at the inn-door, two young female adventurers, alias common wenches, who were going to Sevil with some carriers, that happened to take up their lodgings there that very evening; and, as whatever our knight-errant saw, thought, or imagined, was all of a romantic cast, and appeared to him altogether after the manner of the books that had perverted his imagination, he no sooner saw the inn, but he fancied it to be A castle fenced with four towers and lofty pinnacles, glittering with silver, together with a deep moat, drawbridge, and all those other appurtenances peculiar to such kind of places.

Therefore when he came near it, he stopped a while at a distance from the gate, expecting that some dwarf would appear on the battlements, and sound his trumpet to give notice of the arrival of a knight; but finding that nobody came, and that Rozinante was for making the best of his way to the stable, he advanced to the inn-door, where, spying the two young doxies, they seemed to him two beautiful damsels, or graceful ladies, taking the benefit of the fresh air at the gate of the castle. It happened also at the very moment, that a swine-herd, getting together his hogs (for, without begging pardon, so they are called)* from the stubble-field,

---

* Our author here ridicules the affected delicacy of the Spaniards and Italians, who look upon it as ill manners to name the word hog or swine, as too gross an image.

winded his horn; and Don Quixote presently imagined this was the wished-for signal, which some dwarf gave to notify his approach; therefore, with the greatest joy in the world he rode up to the inn. The wenches, affrighted at the approach of a man cased in iron, and armed with a lance and target, were for running into their lodging; but Don Quixote, perceiving their fear by their flight, lifted up the pasteboard beaver of his helmet, and discovering his withered, dusty face, with comely grace and grave delivery accosted them in this manner. 'I beseech ye, ladies, do not fly, nor fear the least offence: the order of knighthood, which I profess, does not permit me to countenance or offer injuries to any one in the universe, and least of all to virgins of such high rank as your presence denotes.' The wenches looked earnestly upon him, endeavouring to get a glimpse of his face, which his ill-contrived beaver partly hid; but when they heard themselves styled virgins, a thing so out of the way of their profession, they could not forbear laughing outright; which Don Quixote resented as a great affront. 'Give me leave to tell ye, ladies,' cried he, 'that modesty and civility are very becoming in the fair sex; whereas laughter without ground is the highest piece of indiscretion: however,' added he, 'I do not presume to say this to offend you, or incur your displeasure; no, ladies, I assure you I have no other design but to do you service.' This uncommon way of expression, joined to the Knight's scurvy figure, increased their mirth; which incensed him to that degree, that this might have carried things to an extremity, had not the innkeeper luckily appeared at that juncture. He was a man whose burden of fat inclined him to peace and quietness, yet when he had observed such a strange disguise of human shape, in his old armour and equipage, he could hardly forbear keeping the wenches company in their laughter; but, having the fear of such a warlike appearance before his eyes, he resolved to give him good words, and therefore accosted him civilly: 'Sir Knight,' said he, 'if your worship be disposed to alight, you will fail of nothing here but of a bed; as for all other accommodations, you may be supplied to your mind.' Don Quixote observing the humility of the governor of the castle (for such the innkeeper and inn seemed to him), 'Senior Castellano,' said he, 'the least thing in the world suffices me; for arms are the only things I value, and combat is my bed of repose.' The innkeeper thought he had called him Castellano,* as taking him to be one of the true Castilians, whereas he was indeed of Andalusia, nay, of the neighbourhood of St. Lucar, no less thievish than Cacus, or less mischievous than a truant scholar or court page; and therefore he made him this reply: 'At this rate, Sir Knight, your bed might be a pavement, and your rest to be still awake; you may then

* Castellano signifies both a constable or governor of a castle, and an inhabitant of the kingdom of Castile in Spain.

safely alight, and I dare assure you, you can hardly miss being kept awake all the year long in this house, much less one single night.' With that he went and held Don Quixote's stirrup, who having not broke his fast that day, dismounted with no small trouble or difficulty. He immediately desired the governor (that is, the innkeeper), to take especial care of his steed, assuring him that there was not a better in the universe; upon which the innkeeper viewed him narrowly, but could not think him to be half so good as Don Quixote said: however, having set him up in the stable, he came back to the Knight to see what he wanted, and found him pulling off his armour by the help of the good-natured wenches, who had already reconciled themselves to him; but, though they had eased him of his corslet and back-plate, they could by no means undo his gorget, nor take off his ill-contrived beaver, which he had tied so fast with green ribbons, that it was impossible to get it off without cutting them; now he would by no means permit that, and so was forced to keep on his helmet all night, which was one of the most pleasant sights in the world; and while his armour was being taken off by the two kind lasses, imagining them to be persons of quality, and ladies of that castle, he very gratefully made them the following compliment (in imitation of an old romance).

> 'There never was on earth a knight
>   So waited on by ladies fair,
> As once was he, Don Quixote hight,
>   When first he left his village dear:
> Damsels to serve him ran with speed,
> And princesses to dress his steed.

'O Rozinante! for that is my horse's name, ladies, and mine Don Quixote de la Mancha; I never thought to have discovered it, till some feats of arms, achieved by me in your service, had made me better known to your ladyships; but necessity forcing me to apply to present purpose that passage of the ancient romance of Sir Lancelot, which I now repeat, has extorted the secret from me before its time; get a day will come, when you shall command, and I obey, and then the valour of my arm shall evince the reality of my zeal to serve your ladyships.'

The two females, who were not used to such rhetorical speeches, could make no answer to this; they only asked him whether he would eat anything?' That I will with all my heart,' cried Don Quixote, 'whatever it be, for I am of opinion, nothing can come to me more seasonably.' Now, as ill-luck would have it, it happened to be Friday, and there was nothing to be had at the inn but some pieces of fish, which is called Abadexo in Castile, Bacalloa in Andalusia, Curadillo in some places, and in others Truchuela or Little Trout, though, after all, it is but Poor Jack: so they asked him whether he could eat any of that Truchuela, because they had no other fish to give him. Don Quixote, imagining they meant a small trout, told them, that, provided there were more than one, it was the same thing to him, they would serve him as well as a great one; 'for,' continued he, 'it is all one to me whether I am paid a piece of eight in one single piece, or in eight small reals, which are worth as much: besides, it is probable these small trouts may be like veal, which is finer meat than beef; or like the kid, which is better than the goat. In short, let it be what it will so it comes quickly, for the weight of armour and the fatigue of travel are not to be supported without recruiting food.' Thereupon they laid the cloth at the inn-door, for the benefit of the fresh air, and the landlord brought him a piece of that salt fish, hut ill-watered and as ill dressed; and, as for the bread, it was as mouldy and brown as the Knight's armour: but it would have made one laugh to have seen him eat; for, having his helmet on, with his beaver lifted up, it was impossible for him to feed himself without help, so that one of those ladies had that office; but there was no giving him drink that way, and he must have gone without it, had not the innkeeper bored a cane, and setting one end of it to his mouth, poured the wine in at the other; all which the Knight suffered patiently, because he would not cut the ribbons that fastened his helmet.

While he was at supper, a sow-gelder happened to sound his cane-trumpet, or whistle of reeds, four or five times as he came near the inn; which made Don Quixote the more positive of his being in a famous castle, where he was entertained with music at supper, that the Poor Jack was young Trout, the bread of the finest flour, the wenches great ladies, and the innkeeper the governor of the castle; which made him applaud himself for his resolution, and his setting out on such an account. The only thing that vexed him was, that he was not dubbed a knight; for he fancied he could not lawfully undertake any adventure till he had received the order of knighthood.

CHAPTER III

An Account of the pleasant method taken by Don Quixote to be dubbed a Knight

DON QUIXOTE'S MIND being disturbed with that thought, he abridged even his short supper; and as soon as he had done, he called his host, then shut him and himself up in the stable, and falling at his feet, 'I will never rise from this place,' cried he, 'most valorous knight, till you have graciously vouchsafed to grant me a boon, which I will now beg of you, and which will redound to your honour and the good of mankind.' The landlord, strangely at a loss to find his guest at his feet, and talking at this rate, endeavoured to make him rise, but all in vain till he had promised to grant him what he asked. 'I expected no less from your great magnificence, noble sir,' replied Don Quixote, 'and therefore I make bold to tell you, that the boon which I beg, and you generously condescend to grant me, is, that tomorrow you will be pleased to bestow the honour of knighthood upon me. This night I will watch my armour in the chapel of your castle, and then in the morning you shall gratify me, as I passionately desire that I may be duly qualified to seek out adventures in every corner of the universe, to relieve the distressed, according to the laws of chivalry, and the inclinations of knights-errant like myself.' The innkeeper, who, as I said, was a sharp fellow, and had already a shrewd suspicion of the disorder in his guest's understanding, was fully convinced of it when he heard him talk after this manner; and, to make sport that night, resolved to humour him in his desires, telling him he was highly to be commended for his choice of such an employment, which was altogether worthy a knight of the first order, such as his gallant deportment discovered him to be: that he himself had in his youth followed that honourable profession, ranging through many parts of the world in search of adventures, without so much as forgetting to visit the Percheles* of Malaga, the isles of Riaran, the compass of Seville, the quicksilver house of Segovia, the olive-field of Valencia, the circle of Granada, the coast of St. Lucar, the potro of Cordova,† the hedge-taverns of Toledo, and divers other places, where he had exercised the nimbleness of his feet, and the subtilty of his hands, doing wrongs in abundance, soliciting many widows, undoing some damsels, bubbling young heirs, and, in a word, making himself famous in most of the courts of judicature in Spain, till at length he retired to this castle, where he lived on his own estate and those of others, entertaining all knights-errant of what quality or condition soever, merely for the great affection he bore them, and to partake of what they got in recompense of his good-will. He added, that his castle at present had no chapel, where the Knight might keep his vigil of arms, it being pulled down in order to be new-built; but that he knew they might lawfully be watched in any other place in a case of necessity, and therefore he might do it that night in the court-yard of the castle; and in the morning (God willing) all the necessary ceremonies should be per formed, so that he might assure himself he should be dubbed a knight, nay, as much a knight as any one in the world could be. He then asked Don Quixote, whether he had any money?' Not a cross,' replied the Knight, 'for I never read in any history

---

* These are all places noted for rogueries
† A square in the city of Cordova, where a fountain gushes out from the mouth of a horse, near which is also a whipping post.

of chivalry that any knight-errant ever carried money about him.' 'You are mistaken,' cried the innkeeper; 'for admit the histories are silent in this matter, the authors thinking it needless to mention things so evidently necessary as money and clean shirts, yet there is no reason to believe the knights went without either; and you may rest assured that all the knights-errant, of whom so many histories are full, had their purses well lined to supply themselves with necessaries, and carried also with them some shirts, and a small box of salves to heal their wounds; for they had not the conveniency of surgeons to cure them every time they fought in fields and deserts, unless they were so happy as to have some sage or magician for their friend, to give them present assistance, sending them some damsel or dwarf through the air in a cloud, with a small bottle of water of so great a virtue, that they no sooner tasted a drop of it, but their wounds were as perfectly cured as if they had never received any. But when they wanted such a friend in former ages, the knights thought themselves obliged to take care that their squires should be provided with money and other necessaries, as lint and salves to dress their wounds; and, if those knights ever happened to have no squires, which was but very seldom, then they carried those things behind them in a little bag,* as if it had been something of greater value, and so neatly fitted to their saddle that it was hardly seen; for, had it not been upon such an account, the carrying of wallets was not much allowed among knights-errant. I must therefore advise you,' continued he, 'nay, I might even charge and command you, as you are shortly to be my son in chivalry, never from this time forwards to ride without money, nor without the other necessaries of which I spoke to you, which you will find very beneficial when you least expect it.' Don Quixote promised to perform very punctually all his injunctions; and so they disposed everything in order to his watching his arms in a great yard that adjoined to the inn. To which purpose the Knight, having got them all together, laid them in a cistern close by a well in that yard; then, bracing his target and grasping his lance, just as it grew dark, he began to walk about by the horse-trough with a graceful deportment. In the meanwhile the innkeeper acquainted all those that were in the house with the extravagancies of his guest, his watching his arms, and his hopes of being made a knight. They all admired very much at so strange a kind of folly, and went on to observe him at a distance; where they saw him sometimes walk about with a great deal of gravity, and sometimes lean on his lance, with his eyes all the while fixed upon his arms. It was now undoubted night, but yet the moon did shine with such a brightness as might almost have vied with that of the luminary which lent it her; so that the Knight was wholly exposed to the spectators' view. While he was thus

* Of striped stuff, which Spaniards carry when they travel.

employed, one of the carriers who lodged in the inn came out to water his mules, which he could not do without removing the arms out of the trough. With that Don Quixote, who saw him make towards him, cried out to him aloud, 'O thou, whoever thou art, rash knight, that prepared to lay thy hands on the arms of the most valorous knight-errant that ever wore a sword, take heed; do not audaciously attempt to profane them with a touch, lest instant death be the too-sure reward of thy temerity.' But the carrier never regarded these dreadful threats; and, laying hold on the armour by the straps, without any more ado threw it a good way from him; though it had been better for him to have let it alone: for Don Quixote no sooner saw this, but lifting up his eyes to heaven, and addressing his thoughts, as it seemed, to his lady Dulcinea, 'Assist me, lady,' cried he, 'in the first opportunity that offers itself to your faithful slave; nor let your favour and protection be denied me in this first trial of my valour!' Repeating such like ejaculations, he let slip his target, and lifting up his lance with both his hands, he gave the carrier such a terrible knock on his inconsiderate pate with his lance, that he laid him at his feet in a woeful condition; and, had he backed that blow with another, the fellow would certainly have had no need of a surgeon. This done, Don Quixote took up his armour, laid it again in the horse-trough, and then walked on, backwards and forwards, with as great unconcern as he did at first.

Soon after another carrier, not knowing what had happened, came also to water his mules, while the first yet lay on the ground in a trance; but, as he offered to clear the trough of the armour, Don Quixote, without speaking a word or imploring any one's assistance, once more dropped his target, lifted up his lance, and then let it fall so heavily on the fellow's pate, that, without damaging his lance, he broke the carrier's head in three or four places. His outcry soon alarmed and brought thither all the people in the inn, and the landlord among the rest; which Don Quixote perceiving, 'Thou queen of beauty,' cried he, bracing on his shield, and drawing his sword, 'thou courage and vigour of my weakened heart, now is the time when thou must enliven thy adventurous slave with the beams of thy greatness, while this moment he is engaging in so terrible an adventure!' With this, in his opinion, he found himself supplied with such an addition of courage, that, had all the carriers in the world at once attacked him, he would undoubtedly have faced them all. On the other side, the carriers enraged to see their comrades thus used, though they were afraid to come near, gave the Knight such a volley of stones, that he was forced to shelter himself as well as he could under the covert of his target, without daring to go far from the horse-trough, lest he should seem to abandon his arms. The innkeeper called to the carriers as loud as he could to let him alone; that he had told them already that he was mad, and consequently the law would acquit him, though he should kill them. Don Quixote also made yet more noise, calling them false and treacherous villains, and the lord of the castle a base, inhospitable, and discourteous knight, for suffering a knight-errant to be so abused. 'I would make thee know,' cried he 'what a perfidious wretch thou art, had I but received the order of knighthood; but for you, base, ignominious rabble! fling on, do your worst; come on, draw nearer if you dare, and receive the reward of your indiscretion and insolence.' This he spoke with so much spirit and undauntedness, that he struck a terror into all his assailants; so that, partly through fear and partly through the innkeeper's persuasions, they gave over flinging stones at him; and he, on his side, permitted the enemy to carry off their wounded, and then returned to the guard of his arms as calm and composed as before.

The innkeeper, who began somewhat to disrelish these mad tricks of his guest, resolved to dispatch him forthwith, and bestow on him that unlucky knighthood, to prevent further mischief: so, coming to him, he excused himself for the insolence of those base scoundrels, as being done without his privity or consent; but their audaciousness, he said, was sufficiently punished. He added, that he had already told him there was no chapel in his castle; and that indeed there was no need of one to finish the rest of the ceremony of knighthood, which consisted only in the application of the sword to the neck and shoulders, as he had read in the register of the ceremonies of the order; and that this might be performed as well in a field as anywhere else. That he had already fulfilled the obligation of watching his arms, which required no more than two hours' watch, whereas he had been four hours upon the guard. Don Quixote, who easily believed him, told him he was ready to obey him, and desired him to make an end of the business as soon as possible; for, if he were but knighted, and should see himself attacked, he believed he should not leave a man alive in the castle, except those whom he should desire him to spare for his sake.

Upon this the innkeeper, lest the Knight should proceed to such extremities, fetched the book in which he used to set down the carrier's accounts for straw and barley; and having brought with him the two kind females, already mentioned, and a boy that held a piece of lighted candle in his hand, he ordered Don Quixote to kneel: then reading in his manual, as if he had been repeating some pious oration, in the midst of his devotion, he lifted up his hand, and gave him a good blow on the neck, and then a gentle slap on the back with the flat of his sword, still mumbling some words between his teeth in the tone of a prayer. After this he ordered one of the wenches to gird the sword about the Knight's waist; which she did with much solemnity, and, I may add, discretion, considering how hard a thing it was to forbear laughing at every circumstance of the ceremony. It is true, the thoughts of the Knight's late prowess did not a little contribute to the suppression of their mirth. As she girded on his sword, 'Heaven,' cried the kind lady, 'make your worship a lucky knight, and prosper you wherever you go.' Don Quixote desired to know her name, that he might understand to whom he was indebted for the favour she had bestowed upon him, and also make her partaker of the honour he was to acquire by the strength of his arm. To which the lady answered with all humility, that her name was Tolosa, a cobler's daughter, that kept a stall among the little shops of Sanchobinaya at Toledo; and that, whenever he pleased to command her, she would be his humble servant. Don Quixote begged of her to do him the favour to add hereafter the title of Lady to her name, and for his sake to be called from that time the Lady Tolosa; which she promised to do. Her companion, having buckled on his spurs, occasioned a like conference between them; and, when he had asked her name, she told him she went by the name of Miller, being the daughter of an honest miller of Antequera. Our new Knight entreated her also to style herself the Lady Miller, making her new offers of service. These extraordinary ceremonies (the like never seen before) being thus hurried over in a kind of post-haste, Don Quixote could not rest till he had taken the field in quest of adventures; therefore, having immediately saddled his Rozinante, and being mounted, he embraced the innkeeper, and returned him so many thanks at so extravagant a rate, for the obligation he had laid upon him in dubbing him a knight, that it is impossible to give a true relation of them all: to which the innkeeper, in haste to get rid of him, returned as rhetorical, though shorter answers; and, without stopping his horse for the reckoning, was glad with all his heart to see him go.

CHAPTER IV

What befell the Knight after he had left the Inn

AURORA BEGAN to usher in the morn, when Don Quixote sallied out of the inn, so well pleased, so gay, and so overjoyed to find himself knighted, that he infused the same satisfaction into his horse, who seemed ready to burst his girths for joy. But calling to mind the admonitions which the innkeeper had given him, concerning the provision of necessary accommodations in his travels, particularly money and clean shirts, he resolved to return home to furnish himself with them, and likewise get him a squire, designing to entertain, as such, a labouring man, his neighbour, who was poor and had a charge of children, but yet very fit for the office. With this resolution he took the road which led to his own village; and Rozinante, that seemed to know his will by instinct, began to carry him a round trot so briskly, that his heels seemed scarcely to touch the ground. The Knight had not travelled far, when he fancied he heard an effeminate voice complaining in a thicket on his right hand. 'I thank heaven,' said he, when he heard the cries, 'for favouring me so soon with an opportunity to perform the duty of my profession, and reap the fruit of my desires! For these complaints are certainly the moans of some distressed creature who wants my present help.' Then turning to that side with all the speed which Rozinante could make, he no sooner came into the wood but he saw a mare tied to an oak, and to another a young lad, about fifteen years of age, naked from the waist upwards. This was he who made such a lamentable outcry; and not without cause, for a lusty country-fellow was strapping him soundly with a girdle, at every stripe putting him in mind of a proverb, 'Keep your mouth shut, and your eyes open, sirrah.' 'Good master,' cried the boy, 'I'll do so no more; as I hope to be saved, I'll never do so again I Indeed, master, hereafter I'll take more care of your goods.' Don Quixote seeing this, cried, in an angry tone, 'Discourteous knight, it is an unworthy act to strike a person who is not able to defend himself: come, bestride thy steed, and take thy lance' (for the farmer had something that looked like one leaning to the same tree to which his mare was tied), 'then I'll make thee know thou hast acted the part of a coward.' The country-fellow, who gave himself for lost at the sight of an apparition in armour brandishing his lance at his face, answered him in mild and submissive words: 'Sir Knight,' cried he, 'this boy, whom I am chastising, is my servant, employed by me to look after a flock of sheep, which I have not far off; but he is so heedless, that I lose some of them every day. Now, because I correct him for carelessness or his knavery, he says I do it out of covetousness, to defraud him of his wages; but, upon my life and soul, he belies me.' 'What! the lie in my presence, you saucy clown,' cried Don Quixote; 'by the sun that shines I have a good mind to run thee through the body with my lance. Pay the boy this instant, without more words, or, by the Power that rules us all, I will immediately dispatch and annihilate thee: come, unbind him this moment.' The countryman hung down his head, and, without any further reply, unbound the boy; who, being asked by Don Quixote what his master owed him, told him it was nine months' wages, at seven reals a-month. The Knight, having cast it up, found it came to sixty-three reals in all; which he ordered the farmer to pay the fellow immediately, unless he intended to lose his life that very moment. The poor countryman, trembling for fear, told him, that, as he was on the brink of death, by the oath he had sworn (by the bye he had not sworn at all) he did not owe the lad so much: for there was to be deducted for three pair of shoes which he had bought him, and a real for his being let blood twice when he was sick. 'That may be,' replied Don Quixote; 'but, set the price of the shoes and the bleeding against the stripes which you have given him without cause: for, if he has used the leather which you paid for, you have in return misused and impaired his skin sufficiently; and, if the surgeon let him blood when he was sick, you have drawn blood from him now he is in health; so that he owes you nothing on that account.' 'The worst is, Sir Knight,' cried the farmer, 'that I have no money about me; but let Andrew go home with me, and I'll pay him every piece out of hand.' 'What! I go home with him!' cried the youngster, 'the devil a bit, sir! not I truly, I know better things; for he would no sooner have me by myself but he would flea me alive, like another St. Bartholomew.' 'He will never dare to do it,' replied Don Quixote; 'I command him, and that is sufficient to restrain him: therefore, provided he will swear by the order of knighthood which has been conferred upon him, that he will duly observe this regulation, I will freely let him go, and then thou art secure of thy money.' 'Good sir, take heed what you say,' cried the boy; 'for my master is no knight, nor ever was of any order in his life: he is John Haldudo, the rich farmer of Quintinar.' 'This signifies little,' answered Don Quixote, 'for there may be knights among the Haldudo's; besides, the brave man carves out his fortune, and every man is the son of his own works.' 'That's true, sir,' quoth Andrew; 'but of what works can this master of mine be the son, who denies me my wages, which I have earned with the sweat of my brow?' 'I do not deny to pay thee thy wages, honest Andrew,' cried the master; 'be but so kind as to go along with me, and by all the orders of knighthood in the world, I swear, I will pay thee every piece, as I said, nay, and perfumed to boot.'* 'You may spare your perfume,' said Don Quixote; 'do but pay him in reals, and I am satisfied; but be sure you perform your oath, for if you fail, I myself swear by the same oath to return and find you out, and punish you, though you should hide yourself as close as a lizard. And if you will be informed who it is that lays these injunctions on you, that you may understand how highly it concerns you to observe them; know, I am the valorous Don Quixote de la Mancha, the righter of wrongs, the revenger and redresser of grievances; and so farewell: but remember what you have promised and sworn, as you will answer the contrary at your peril.' This said, he clapped spurs to Rozinante, and quickly left the master and the man a good way behind him.

The countryman, who followed him with both his eyes, no sooner perceived that he was passed the woods and quite out of sight, but he went back to his boy Andrew. 'Come, child,' said he, 'I will pay thee what I owe thee, as that righter of wrongs and redresser of grievances has ordered me.' 'Ay,' quoth Andrew, 'on my word, you will do well to fulfil the commands of that good Knight, whom Heaven grant long to live; for he is

---

* Jarvis says this is used here as a satire on the effeminate custom of wearing everything perfumed, insomuch that the very money in their pockets was scented.

so brave a man, and so just a judge, that adad if you do not pay me he will come back and make his words good.' 'I dare swear as much,' answered the master; 'and to show thee how much I love thee, I am willing to increase the debt, that I may enlarge the payment.' With that, he caught the youngster by the arm, and tied him again to the tree; where he handled him so unmercifully, that scarce any signs of life were left in him. 'Now call your Righter of Wrongs, Mr. Andrew,' cried the farmer, 'and you shall see he will never be able to undo what I have done; though I think it is but a part of what I ought to do, for I have a good mind to flea you alive, as you said I would, you rascal.' However, he untied him at last, and gave him leave to go and seek out his judge, in order to have his decree put in execution. Andrew went his ways, not very well pleased you may be sure, yet fully resolved to find out the valorous Don Quixote de la Mancha, and give him an exact account of the whole transaction, that he might pay the abuse with sevenfold usury; in short, he crept off sobbing and weeping, while his master stayed behind laughing. And in this manner was this wrong redressed by the valorous Don Quixote de la Mancha.

In the mean time, being highly pleased with himself and what had happened, imagining he had given a most fortunate and noble beginning to his feats of arms, as he went on towards his village, 'O most beautiful of beauties,' said he with a low voice, 'Dulcinea del Toboso! well mayest thou deem thyself most happy, since it was thy good fortune to captivate and hold a willing slave to thy pleasure, so valorous and renowned a knight as is, and ever shall be, Don Quixote de la Mancha; who, as all the world knows, had the honour of knighthood bestowed on him but yesterday, and this day redressed the greatest wrong and grievance that ever injustice could design, or cruelty commit; this day has he wrested the scourge out of the hands of that tormentor, who so unmercifully treated a tender infant, without the least occasion given.' Just as he had said this, he found himself at a place where four roads met; and this made him presently bethink of those crossways which often use to put knights-errant to a stand, to consult with themselves which way they should take; and that he might follow their example, he stopped a while, and after he had seriously reflected on the matter, gave Rozinante the reins, subjecting his own will to that of his horse, who pursuing his first intent, took the way that led to his own stable.

Don Quixote had not gone above two miles, but he discovered a company of people riding towards him, who proved to be merchants of Toledo, that were going to buy silks in Murcia. They were six in all, every one screened with an umbrella, besides four servants on horseback, and three muleteers* on foot. The Knight no sooner perceived them, but he

---

* Mule-boys conduct travellers through Spain, bring back the mules, and take care of them all the way.

imagined this to be some new adventure; and, because he was resolved to imitate as much as possible the passages he had read in his books, he was pleased to represent this to himself as such a particular adventure as he had a singular desire to meet with; and so, with a dreadful grace and assurance, fixing himself in his stirrups, couching his lance, and covering his breast with his target, he posted himself in the middle of the road, expected the coming up of the supposed knights-errant. As soon as they came within hearing, with a loud voice and haughty tone, 'Hold,' cried he, 'let all mankind stand, nor hope to pass on further, unless all mankind acknowledge and confess, that there is not in the universe a more beautiful damsel than the Empress of La Mancha, the peerless Dulcinea del Toboso.' At those words they made a halt to view the unaccountable figure of their opponent; and easily conjecturing, both by his expression and disguise, that the poor gentleman had lost his senses, they were willing to understand the meaning of that strange confession which he would force from them; and therefore one of the company, who loved and understood raillery, having discretion to manage it, undertook to talk to him. 'Signior cavalier,' cried he, 'we do not know this worthy lady you talk of; but be pleased to let us see her, and then if we find her possessed of those matchless charms, of which you assert her to be the mistress, we will freely, and without the least compulsion, own the truth which you would extort from us.' 'Had I once showed you that beauty,' replied Don Quixote, 'what wonder would it be to acknowledge so notorious a truth? the importance of the thing lies in obliging you to believe it, confess it, affirm it, swear it, and maintain it, without seeing her; and therefore make this acknowledgment this very moment, or know, that it is with me you must join in battle, ye proud and unreasonable mortals. Come one by one, as the laws of chivalry require, or all at once, according to the dishonourable practice of men of your stamp; here I expect you all my single self, and will stand the encounter, confiding in the justness of my cause.' 'Sir Knight,' replied the merchant, 'I beseech you, in the name of all the princes here present, that for the discharge of our consciences, which will not permit us to affirm a thing we never heard or saw, and which, besides, tends so much to the dishonour of the Empresses and Queens of Alcaria and Estremadura, your worship will vouchsafe to let us see some portraiture of that lady, though it were no bigger than a grain of wheat; for by a small sample we may judge of the whole piece, and by that means rest secure and satisfied, and you contented and appeased. Nay, I verily believe, that we all find ourselves already so inclinable to comply with you, that though her picture should represent her to be blind of one eye, and distilling vermilion and brimstone at the other, yet to oblige you, we should be ready to say in her favour whatever your worship desires.' 'Distil, ye infamous scoundrels!' replied Don Quixote, in a burning rage, 'distil, say you? know, that nothing distils from her but amber and civit; neither is she defective in her make or shape, but more straight than a Guadaramin spindle.* But you shall all severely pay for the horrid blasphemy which thou hast uttered against the transcendent beauty of my incomparable lady.' Saying this, with his lance couched, he ran so furiously at the merchant who thus provoked him, that, had not good fortune so ordered it that Rozinante should stumble and fall in the midst of his career, the audacious trifler had paid dear for his raillery; but as Rozinante fell, he threw down his master, who rolled and tumbled a good way on the ground, without being able to get upon his legs, though he used all his skill and strength to effect it, so encumbered he was with his lance, target, spurs, helmet, and the weight of his rusty armour. However, in this helpless condition he played the hero with his tongue: 'Stay,' cried he, 'cowards, rascals, do not fly! it is not through my fault that I lie here, but through that of my horse, ye poltroons!'

One of the grooms, who was none of the best-natured creatures, hearing the overthrown Knight thus insolently treat his master, could not bear it without returning him an answer on his ribs; and therefore, coming up to him as he lay wallowing, snatched his lance, and, having broke it to pieces, he so belaboured Don Quixote's sides with one of them, that, in spite of his arms, he thrashed him like a wheat-sheaf His master indeed called to him not to lay on him so vigorously, and to let him alone; but the fellow, whose hand was in, would not give over rib-roasting the Knight, till he had tired out his passion and himself; and therefore, running to the other pieces of the broken lance, he fell to it again without ceasing, until he had splintered them all on the knight's iron enclosure. He, on his side, notwithstanding all this storm of bastinadoes, lay all the while bellowing, threatening heaven and earth, and those villainous ruffians, as he took them to be. At last the mule-driver was tired, and the merchants pursued their journey, sufficiently furnished with matter of discourse at the poor Knight's expense. When he found himself alone, he tried once more to get on his feet; but when he could not do it when he had the use of his limbs, how should he do it now, bruised and battered as he was? But yet, for all this, he esteemed himself a happy man, being still persuaded that his misfortune was one of those accidents common in knight-errantry, and such a one as he could wholly attribute to the falling of his horse; nor could he possibly get up, so sore and mortified was his body all over.

---

* 'As straight as a spindle, is a Spanish simile, and Guadarama is a noted place for making them,' says Stevens. Jarvis says, 'the rocks of this hill are so straight and perpendicular, that they are called the spindles.' Near it stands the Escurial.

CHAPTER V

A further Account of our Knight's Misfortunes

Don Quixote perceiving that he was not able to stir, resolved to have recourse to his usual remedy, which was to bethink himself what passage in his books might afford him some comfort: and presently his folly brought to his remembrance the story of Baldwin and the Marquis of Mantua, when Charlotte left the former wounded on the mountain; a story learned and known by little children, not unknown to young men and women, celebrated, and even believed by the old, and yet not a jot more authentic than the miracles of Mahomet. This seemed to him as if made on purpose for his present circumstances, and therefore he fell a-rolling and tumbling up and down, expressing the greatest pain and resentment, and breathing out, with a languishing voice, the same complaints which the wounded knight of the wood is said to have made.

> 'Alas ! where are you, lady dear
> That for my woe you do not moan?
> You little know what ails me here,
> Or are to me disloyal grown!'

Thus he went on with the lamentations in that romance, till he came to these verses:

> 'O thou, my uncle and my prince,
> Marquis of Mantua, noble lord!' –

When kind fortune so ordered it, that a ploughman, who lived in the same village, and near his house, happened to pass by, as he came from the mill with a sack of wheat. The fellow seeing a man lie at his full length on the ground, asked him who he was, and why he made such a sad complaint? Don Quixote, whose distempered brain presently represented to him the countryman for the Marquis of Mantua, his imaginary uncle, made him no answer, but went on with the romance, giving him an account of his misfortunes, and of the loves of his wife, and the emperor's son, just as the book relates them. The fellow stared, much amazed to hear a man talk such unaccountable stuff; and, taking off the vizor of his helmet, broken all to pieces with blows bestowed upon it by the muledriver, he wiped off the dust that covered his face, and presently knew the gentleman. 'Master Quixada!' cried he (for so he was properly called when he had the right use of his senses, and had not yet from a sober gentleman transformed himself into a wandering knight), 'how came you in this condition?' But the other continued his romance, and made no answers to all the questions the countryman put to him, but what followed in course in the book; which the good man perceiving, he took off the battered adventurer's armour, as well as he could, and fell a-searching for his wounds; but finding no sign of blood, or any other hurt, he endeavoured to set him upon his legs; and at last, with a great deal of trouble, he heaved him upon his own ass, as being the more easy and gentle carriage.; He also got all the Knight's arms together, not leaving behind so much as the splinters of his lance; and having tied them up, and laid them on Rozinante, which he took by the bridle, and his ass by the halter, he led them all towards the village, and trudged afoot himself very pensive, while he reflected on the extravagancies which he heard Don Quixote utter. Nor was Don Quixote himself less melancholy, for he felt himself so bruised and battered, that he could hardly sit on the ass; and now and then he breathed such grievous sighs, as seemed to pierce the very skies, which moved his compassionate neighbour once more to entreat him to declare to him the cause of his grief: but one would have imagined the Devil prompted him with stories, that had some resemblance of his circumstances; for in that instant, wholly forgetting Baldwin, he bethought himself of the Moor Abindaraez, whom Rodrigo de Narvaez, Alcayde of Antequera took and carried prisoner to his castle; so that, when the husbandman asked him how he did, and what ailed him? he answered word for word as the prisoner Abindaraez replied to Rodrigo de Narvaez, in 'The Diana' of George de Montemayor, where that adventure is related; applying it so properly to his purpose, that the countryman wished himself at the devil rather than within the hearing of such strange nonsense; and, being now fully convinced that his neighbour's brains were turned, he made all the haste he could to the village, to be rid of his troublesome impertinencies. Don Quixote in the mean time thus went on: 'You must know, Don Rodrigo de Narvaez, that this beautiful Xerifa, of whom I gave you an account, is at present the most lovely Dulcinea del Toboso, for whose sake I have done, still do, and will achieve the most famous deeds of chivalry that ever were, are, or ever shall be seen in the universe.' 'Good sir,' replied the husbandman, 'as I am a sinner, I am not Don Rodrigo de Narvaez, nor the Marquis of Mantua, but Pedro Alonzo by name, your worship's neighbour; nor are you Baldwin, nor Abindaraez, but only that worthy gentleman Signor Quixada' 'I know very well who I am,' answered Don Quixote, 'and what is more, I know, that I may not only be the persons I have named, but also the twelve peers of France, nay, and the nine worthies all in one; since my achievements will out-rival not only the famous exploits which made any of them singly illustrious, but all their mighty deeds accumulated together.'

Thus discoursing, they at last got near their village about sunset, but the countryman stayed at some distance till it was dark, that the distressed gentleman might not be seen so scurvily mounted, and then he led him home to his own house, which he found in great confusion. The curate and the barber of the village, both of them Don Quixote's intimate acquaintance, happened to be there at that juncture, as also the house-keeper, who was arguing with them. 'What do you think, pray good doctor Perez,' said she (for this was the curate's name), 'what do you think of my master's mischance? Neither he nor his horse, nor his target, lance, nor armour, have been seen these six days. What shall I do, wretch that I and I dare lay my life, and it is as sure as I am a living creature, that those cursed books of errantry, which he used to be always poring upon, have set him besides his senses; for, now I remember, I have heard him often mutter to himself, that he had a mind to turn knight-errant, and jaunt up and down the world to find out adventures. May Satan and Barabbas even take all such books that have thus cracked the best head-piece in all La Manch!' His niece said as much, addressing herself to the barber: 'You must know, Mr. Nicholas,' quoth she (for that was his name), 'that many times my uncle would read those unconscionable books of disventures for eight and forty hours together, then away he would throw his book, and, drawing his sword, he would fall a fencing against the walls, and when he had tired himself with cutting and slashing, he would cry he had killed four giants as big as any steeples; and the sweat which he put himself into, he would say, was the blood of the wounds he had received in the fight; then would he swallow a huge jug of cold water, and presently he would be as quiet and as well as ever he was in his life; and he said that this same water was a sort of precious drink brought him by the sage Esquife,* a great magician, and his special friend. Now it is I who am the cause of all this mischief, for not giving you timely notice of my uncle's raving, that you might have put a stop to it ere it was too late, and have burnt all these excommunicated books; for there are I do not know how many of them that deserve as much to be burned, as those of the rankest heretics.' 'I am of your mind,' said the curate 'and verily tomorrow shall not pass over before I have fairly brought them to a trial, and condemned them to the flames, that they may not minister occasion to such as would read them, to be perverted after the example of my good friend.' The countryman, who with Don Quixote stood without listening to all this discourse, now perfectly understood by this the cause of his neighbour's disorder, and therefore, without any more ado, he called out aloud, 'Here! house! open the gates there, for the Lord Baldwin, and the Lord Marquis of Mantua, who is coming sadly wounded; and for the Moorish Lord Abindaraez, whom the valorous Don Rodrigo de Narvaez, Alcayde of Antequera

---

* She means Alquife, a famous enchanter in 'Amadis de Gaul' and 'Don Belianis' of Greece,' husband to the no less famous Urganda the sorceress.

brings prisoner.' At which words they all got out of doors; and the one finding it to be her uncle, and the other to be her master, and the rest their friend, who had not yet alighted from the ass, because indeed he was not able, they all ran to embrace him; to whom Don Quixote, 'Forbear,' said he, 'for I am sorely hurt, by reason that my horse failed me; carry me to bed, and if it be possible, let the enchantress Urganda be sent for to cure my wounds.' 'Now, in the name of mischief,' quoth the housekeeper, 'see whether I did not guess right, on which foot my master halted! Come, get you to bed, I beseech you, and, my life for yours, we will take care to cure you without sending for that same Urganda A hearty curse, and the curse of curses, I say it again and again a hundred times, light upon those books of chivalry that have put you in this pickle.' Thereupon they carried him up to his bed, and searched for his wounds, but could find none; and then he told them he was only bruised, having had a dreadful fall from his horse Rozinante, while he was fighting ten giants, the most outrageous and audacious that ever could be found upon the face of the earth. 'How!' cried the curate, 'have we giants too in the dance?* Nay then, by the holy Sign of the Cross, I will burn them all by tomorrow night.' Then did they ask the Don a thousand questions, but to every one he made no other answer, but that they should give him something to eat, and then leave him to his repose, a thing which was to him of the greatest importance. They complied with his desires; and then the curate informed himself at large in what condition the countryman had found him; and having had a full account of every particular, as also of the knight's extravagant talk, both when the fellow found him and as he brought him home, this increased the curate's desire of effecting what he had resolved to do the next morning; at which time he called upon his friend Mr. Nicholas, the barber, and went with him to Don Quixote's house.

---

* Alluding to a passage in 'Amadis,' where several giants are mixed with ladies and knights, at Constantinople, in a dance.

CHAPTER VI

*Of the pleasant and curious scrutiny with the Curate
and the Barber made of the Library of our
ingenious Gentleman*

THE KNIGHT was yet asleep, when the curate came attended by the barber, and desired his niece to let him have the key of the room where her uncle kept his books, the author of his woes: she readily consented; and so in they went, and the housekeeper with them. There they found above a hundred large volumes neatly bound, and a good number of small ones: as soon as the housekeeper had spied them out, she ran out of the study, and returned immediately with a holy water-pot and a sprinkler: 'Here, doctor,' cried she, 'pray sprinkle every creek and corner in the room, lest there should lurk in it some one of the many sorcerers these books swarm with, who might chance to bewitch us, for the ill-will we bear them, in going about to send them out of the world.' The curate could not forbear smiling at the good woman's simplicity, and desired the barber to reach him the books one by one, that he might peruse the title-pages, for perhaps he might find some among them, that might not deserve to be committed to the flames. 'Oh, by no means,' cried the niece, 'spare none of them, they all help somehow or other to crack my uncle's brain. I fancy we had best throw them all out at the window in the yard, and lay them together in a heap, and then set them on fire, or else carry them into the back yard, and there make a pile of them, and burn them, and so the smoke will offend nobody ': the housekeeper joined with her, so eagerly bent they were both upon the destruction of those poor innocents; but the curate would not condescend to those irregular proceedings, and resolved first to read at least the title-page of every book.

The first that Mr. Nicholas put into his hands was 'Amadis de Gaul,' in four volumes. 'There seems to be some mystery in this book's being the first taken down,' cried the curate as soon as he had looked upon it, 'for I have heard it is the first book of knight-errantry that ever was printed in Spain, and the model of all the rest; and therefore I am of opinion, that, as the first teacher and author of so pernicious a sect, it ought to be condemned to the fire without mercy.' 'I beg a reprieve for him,' cried the barber, 'for I have been told it is the best book that has been written in that kind; and therefore, as the only good thing of that sort, it may deserve a pardon.' 'Well then,' replied the curate, 'for this time let him have it. Let us see that other, which lies next to him.' 'These,' said the barber, 'are the exploits of Esplandian, the lawful begotten son of Amadis de Gaul.'

'Verily,' said the curate, 'the father's goodness shall not excuse the want of it in the son; here, good mistress housekeeper, open that window, and throw it into the yard, and let it serve as a foundation to that pile we are to set a-blazing presently.' She was not slack in her obedience; and thus 'Don Esplandian 'was sent headlong into the yard, there patiently to wait the time of his fiery trial. 'To the next,' cried the curate. 'This,' said the barber, 'is "Amadis of Greece"; and I am of opinion, that all those that stand on this side are of the same family.' 'Then let them all be sent packing into the yard,' replied the curate, 'for rather than lose the pleasure of burning queen Pintiquiniestra,* and the shepherd Darinel with his eclogues, and the confounded unintelligible discourses of the author, I think I should burn my own father along with them, if I met him in the disguise of a knight-errant. 'I am of your mind,' cried the barber; 'and I too,' said the niece: 'Nay then,' quoth the old female, 'let them come, and down with them all into the yard.' They were delivered to her accordingly, and many they were; so that, to save herself the labour of carrying them down-stairs, she fairly sent them flying out at the window.

'What tun of an author have we here?' cried the curate: ' "Olivante de Laura," ' returned the barber: 'The same author wrote "The Garden of Flowers"; and, to deal ingenuously with you, I cannot well tell which of the two books has most truth in it, or, to speak more properly, less lies; but this I know for certain, that he shall march into the back yard like a nonsensical arrogant blockhead as he is.'

'The next,' cried the barber, 'is "Florismarte of Hyrcania." ' 'How! my lord Florismarte, is he here?' replied the curate, 'nay, then truly he shall even follow the rest to the yard, in spite of his wonderful birth and incredible adventures; for his rough, dull, and insipid style deserves no better usage. Come, toss him into the yard, and this other too, good mistress.' 'With all my heart,' quoth the governess; and straight she was as good as her word.

'Here is the noble "Don Platir," ' cried the barber. 'It is an old book,' replied the curate, 'and I can think of nothing in him that deserves a grain of pity; away with him, without any more words '; and down he went accordingly.

Another book was opened, and it proved to be 'The Knight of the Cross.' 'The holy title,' cried the curate, 'might in some measure atone for the badness of the book; but then, as the saying is, "The devil lurks behind the cross!" To the flames with him.'

Then the barber taking down another book, cried, 'Here is "The Mirror of Knighthood." ' 'Oh! I have the honour to know him,' replied

---

* A terrible fighting giantess in 'Amadis de Gaul,' and one of the most ridiculous characters imaginable.

the curate; 'there you will find the lord Rinaldo of Montalban, with his friends and companions, all of them greater thieves than Cacus, together with the twelve peers of France, and that faithful historian Turpin. Truly, I must needs say, I am only for condemning them to perpetual banishment, at least, because their story contains something of the famous Boyardo's invention, out of which the Christian poet Ariosto also spun his web; yet, if I happened to meet with him in this bad company, and speaking in any other language than his own, I will show him no manner of favour; but, if he talks in his own native tongue, I will then treat him with all the respect imaginable.' 'I have him at home in Italian,' said the barber, 'but I cannot understand him.' 'Neither is it any great matter whether you do or not,' replied the curate; 'and I could willingly have excused the good captain who translated it that trouble of attempting to make him speak Spanish, for he has deprived him of a great deal of his primitive graces; misfortune incident to all those who presume to translate verses, since their utmost wit and industry can never enable them to preserve the native beauties and genius that shine in the original. For this reason, I am for having not only this book, but likewise all those which we shall find here treating of French affairs, laid up and deposited to some dry vault, till we have maturely determined what ought to be done with them; yet give me leave to except "Bernardo del Carpio" and "Roncesvalles," who must be somewhere here among the rest; for whenever I meet with them, I will certainly deliver them up into the hands of the housekeeper, who shall toss them into the fire.' The barber gave his approbation to every particular, well knowing that the curate was so good a Christian, and so great a lover of truth, that he would not have uttered a falsity for all the world. Then, opening another volume, he found it to be 'Palmerin de Oliva,' and the next to that 'Palmerin of England.' 'Ha! have I found you!' cried the curate, 'here take that "Oliva," let him be torn to pieces, then burnt, and his ashes scattered in the air; but let "Palmerin of England" be preserved as a singular relic of antiquity; and let such a costly box be made for him, as Alexander found among the spoils of Darius, which he devoted to inclose Homer's works; for, I must tell you, neighbour, that book deserves particular respect for two things; first, for its own excellencies; and, secondly, for the sake of its author, who is said to have been a learned king of Portugal; then all the adventures of the Castle of Miraguarda are well and artfully managed, the dialogue very courtly and clear, and the decorum strictly observed in equal character, with equal propriety and judgment. Therefore, Mr. Nicholas,' continued he, 'with submission to your better advice, this and "Amadis de Gaul" shall be exempted from the fire; and let all the rest be condemned without any further inquiry or examination.' 'By no means, I beseech you,' returned the barber, 'for this which I have in my hands is the famous "Don Bellianis." ' 'Truly,' cried the curate, 'he with his second, third, and fourth parts, had need of a dose of rhubarb to purge his excessive choler; besides, his Castle of Fame should be demolished, and a heap of other rubbish removed, in order to which I give my vote to grant them the benefit of a reprieve; and, as they show signs of amendment, so shall mercy or justice be used towards them. In the mean time, neighbour, take them into custody, and keep them safe at home; but let none be permitted to converse with them.' 'Content,' cried the barber; and to save himself the labour of looking on any more books of that kind, he bid the housekeeper take all the great volumes and throw them into the yard. This was not spoken to one stupid or deaf, but to one who had a greater mind to be burning them than weaving the finest and largest web; so that, laying hold of no less than eight volumes at once, she presently made them leap towards the place of execution; but as she went too eagerly to work, taking more books than she could conveniently carry, she happened to drop one at the barber's feet, which he took up out of curiosity to see what it was, and found it to be the 'History of the Famous Knight Tirante the White.' 'Good-lack-a-day,' cried the curate, 'is "Tirante the White" here? Oh! pray good neighbour, give it me by all means, for I promise myself to find in it a treasure of delight and a mine of recreation. There we have the valorous knight Don Kyrie-Eleison* of Montalban, with his brother Thomas of Montalban, and the knight Fonseca; the combat between the valorous Detriente and Alano; the dainty and witty conceits of the damsel Plazerdemivida, with the loves and guiles of the widow Reposada; together with the lady Empress, that was in love with Hippolito her gentleman-usher. I vow and protest to you, neighbour,' continued he, 'that in its way there is not a better book in the world; why, here the knights eat and drink, sleep and die natural deaths in their beds, nay; and make their last wills and testaments; with a world of other things, of which all the rest of these sort of books do not say one syllable. Yet, after all, I must tell you, that for wilfully taking the pains to write so many foolish things, the worthy author fairly deserves to be sent to the galleys for all the days of his life. Take it home with you md read it, and then tell me whether I have told you the truth or no.' 'I believe you,' replied the barber, 'but what shall we do with all these smaller books that are left?' 'Certainly,' replied the curate, 'these cannot be books of knight-errantry, they are too small; you will find they are only poets: 'and so opening one, it happened to be the 'Diana' of Montemayor; which made him say (believing all the rest to be of that stamp), 'These do not deserve to be punished like the others, for they neither have done, nor can do that

---

* Most of these names are significative, and are qualities personified; as *Kyrie-Eleison*, Greek for 'Lord have mercy upon us'; *Alano* is a mastiff-dog; *Plazerdemivida*, 'pleasure of my life'; *Reposada*, sedate or quiet.

mischief which those stories of chivalry have done, being generally ingenious books, that can do nobody any prejudice.' 'Oh! good sir,' cried the niece, 'burn them with the rest, I beseech you; for should my uncle get cured of his knight-errant frenzy, and betake himself to the reading of these books, we should have him turn shepherd, and so wander through the woods and fields; nay, and what would be worse yet, turn poet, which they say is a catching and an incurable disease.' 'The gentlewoman is in the right,' said the curate, 'and it will not be amiss to remove that stumbling-block out of our friend's way; and, since we began with the "Diana" of Montemayor, I am of opinion we ought not to burn it, but only take out that part of it which treats of the Magiciao Felicia, and the enchanted water, as also all the longer poems; and let the work escape with its prose, and the honour of being the first of that kind.' 'Here is another "Diana,"' quoth the barber, 'the second of that name, by Salmantino (of Salamanca); nay, and a third too by Gil Polo.' 'Pray,' said the curate, 'let Salmantino increase the number of the criminals in the yard; but, as for that by Gil Polo, preserve it as charily as if Apollo himself had written it; and go on as fast as you can, I beseech you, good neighbour, for it grows late.' 'Here,' quoth the barber, 'I have a book called the "Ten Books of the Fortunes of Love," by Anthony de Lofraso, a Sardinian poet.' 'Now, by my holy orders,' cried the curate, 'I do not think since Apollo was Apollo, the muses muses, and the poets poets, there ever was a more comical, more whimsical book. Of all the works of the kind commend me to this, for, in its way, it is certainly the best and most singular that ever was published, and he that never read it, may safely think he never in his life read anything that was pleasant. Give it me, neighbour,' continued he, 'for I am more glad to have found it, than if any one had given me a cassock of the best Florence serge.' With that he laid it aside with extraordinary satisfaction, and the barber went on. 'These that follow,' cried he, 'are "The Shepherd of Iberia," "The Nymphs of Enares," and the "Cures of Jealousy."' 'Take them, gaoler,' quoth the curate, 'and never ask me why, for then we shall never have done.' 'The next,' said the barber,' is "The Shepherd of Filida."' 'He is no shepherd,' returned the curate, 'but a very discreet courtier; keep him as a precious jewel.' 'Here is a bigger,' cried the barber, 'called the "Treasure of Divers Poems."' 'Had there been fewer of them,' said the curate, 'they would have been more esteemed. It is fit the book should be pruned and cleared of several trifles that disgrace the rest: keep it, however, because the author is my friend, and for the sake of his other more heroic and lofty productions.' 'Here is a book of songs by Lopez Maldonado,' cried the barber. 'He is also my particular friend,' said the curate: 'his verses are well liked when he reads them himself, and his voice is so excellent, that they charm whenever he sings them. He seems indeed to be somewhat too long in his eclogues; but can we ever have too much of a good thing? Let him be preserved among the best. What is the next book?' 'The "Galatea" of Miguel de Cervantes,' replied the barber. 'That Cervantes has been my intimate acquaintance these many years,' cried the curate, 'and I know he has been more conversant with misfortunes than with poetry. His book, indeed, has I do not know what that looks like a good design; he aims at something, but concludes nothing: therefore we must stay for the second part, which he has promised us; perhaps he may make us amends, and obtain a full pardon, which is denied him for the present; till that time, keep him close prisoner at your house.' 'I will,' quoth the barber: 'but see, I have here three more for you, "The Araucana" of Don Alonso de Ercilla, "The Austriada" of Juan Rufo, a magistrate of Cordova, and the "Monserrato" of Christoval de Virves, a Valentian poet.' 'These,' cried the curate, 'are the best heroic poems we have in Spanish, and may vie with the most celebrated of Italy; reserve them as the most valuable performance which Spain has to boast of in poetry.'

At last the curate grew so tired with prying into so many volumes, that he ordered all the rest to be burnt at a venture. But the barber showed him one which he had opened by chance ere the dreadful sentence was past. 'Truly,' said the curate, who saw by the title it was 'The Tears of Angelica,' 'I should have wept myself, had I caused such a book to share the condemnation of the rest; for the author was not only one of the best poets in Spain, but in the whole world, and translated some of Ovid's fables with extraordinary success.'

CHAPTER VII

Don Quixote's second Sally in quest of Adventure

WHILE THEY WERE thus employed, Don Quixote, in a raving fit, began to talk aloud to himself: 'Here, here, valorous knights,' cried he, 'now is the time that you must exert the strength of your mighty arms; for lo, the courtiers bear away the honour of the tournament.' This amazing outcry called away the inquisitors from any further examination of the library; and therefore, the housekeeper and the niece being left to their own discretion, it is thought the 'Carolea' and 'Leon of Spain,' with the deeds of the Emperor, written by Don Louis de Avila, which to be sure were part of the collection, were committed to the flames unseen and unheard, without any legal trial; a fate which perhaps they might have escaped, had the curate been there to have weighed what might have been urged in their defence.

When they came into Don Quixote's chamber, they found him risen out of his bed as mad as ever he was, tearing his throat, and making a heavy bustle, laying about him with his sword, backstroke and forestroke, as broad awake as if he had never slept. They ran in upon him, caught him in their arms, and carried him to bed again by main force; where, after he was somewhat quiet and settled, turning himself to the curate; 'Certainly,' cried he, 'my Lord Archbishop Turpin, it is a great dishonour to us who are called the twelve peers, to suffer the knights of the court to bear away the honour of the tournament without any farther opposition, after we the knight-adventurers had carried it for three days before.' 'Be pacified, my good friend,' replied the curate; 'fortune may have yet a better success in reserve for you, and they who lose today may win tomorrow. At present think on your health, for doubtless you must needs be now extremely tired, if not very much wounded.' 'Wounded!' replied Don Quixote, 'no; but as for being bruised, I will not deny it, for that base-born knight, Don Orlando, has battered all my limbs with the trunk of an oak, out of mere envy, because he sees that I only dare rival his exploits: but, may I be no more called Rinaldo of Montaloan, if, in spite of his enchantments, I do not make him severely pay for this as soon as I can leave my bed; and therefore let my dinner be brought in, for it is what I want most at this juncture, and then let me alone to revenge this abuse.' Accordingly they brought him some victuals, which, when he had eaten, he fell asleep again; and they left him, all of them strangely amazed at his uncommon madness. That night the housekeeper burnt all the books, not only those in the yard, but all those that were in the house; and several suffered in the general calamity, that deserved to have been treasured up in everlasting archives, had not their fate and the remissness of the inquisitors ordered it otherwise. And thus they verified the proverb,' That the good often fare the worse for the bad.'

One of the expedients which the curate and the barber bethought themselves of, in order to their friend's recovery, was to stop up the door of the room where his books lay, that he might not find it, nor miss them when he rose; for they hoped the effect would cease when they had taken away the cause; and they ordered, that if he inquired about it, they should tell him, that a certain enchanter had carried away study, books and all. Two days after, Don Quixote being got up, the first thing he did was to go visit his darling books; and, as he could not find the study in the place where he had left it, he went up and down, and looked for it in every room. Sometimes he came to the place where the door used to stand, and then stood feeling and groping about a good while, then cast his eyes, and stared on every side, without speaking a word. At last, after a long deliberation, he thought fit to ask his housekeeper which was the way to his study?' What study,' answered the woman, according to her instructions, 'or rather, what nothing is it you look for? Alas! here is neither study nor books in the house now, for the devil has run away with them all.' 'No, it was not the devil,' said the niece, 'but a conjuror, or an enchanter, as they call them, who, since you went, came hither one night mounted on a dragon on the top of a cloud, and then, alighting, went into your study, where what he did, he and the devil best can tell; for, a while after he flew out at the roof of the house, leaving it full of smoke; and, when we went to see what he had done, we could neither find the books, nor so much as the very study; only the housekeeper and I very well remember, that when the old thief went away, he cried out aloud, "that out of a private grudge which he bore in his mind to the owner of those books, he had done the house a mischief, as we should soon perceive," and then, I think, he called himself the Sage Muniaton.' 'Not Muniaton, but Freston,* you should have said,' cried Don Quixote. 'Truly,' quoth the niece, 'I cannot tell whether it was Freston or Friston, but sure I am that his name ended with a ton.' 'It is so,' returned Don Quixote, 'for he is a famous necromancer, and my mortal enemy, and bears me a great deal of malice; for, seeing by his art, that, in spite of all his spells, in process of time I shall fight and vanquish in single combat a knight whose interest he espouses, therefore no endeavours to do me all manner of mischief; but, I dare assure him, he strives against the stream, nor can his power reverse the first decrees of fate.' 'Who doubts of that?' cried the niece. 'But, dear uncle, what makes you run yourself into these quarrels? Had you not better stay at home, and live in peace and quietness, than go rambling up and down like a vagabond, and seeking for better bread than is made of wheat, without once so much as considering, that many go to seek wool and come home shorn themselves?' 'Oh, good niece,' replied Don Quixote, 'how ill thou understandeth these matters! Know, that before I will suffer myself to be shorn, l will tear and pluck off the beards of all those audacious mortals that shall attempt to profane the tip of one single hair within the verge of these moustaches.' To this neither the niece nor the governess thought fit to make any reply, for they perceived the knight to grow angry. Full fifteen days did our knight remain quietly at home, without betraying the least sign of his desire to renew his rambling; during which time there passed a great deal of pleasant discourse between him and his two friends, the curate and the barber; while he maintained, that there was nothing the world stood so much in need of as knights-errant; wherefore he was resolved to revive the order. In which disputes Mr. Curate sometimes contradicted him, and sometimes submitted; for had he not now and then given way to his fancies, there would have been no conversing with him.

In the, mean time, Don Quixote earnestly solicited one of his neighbours,

* An enchanter in Don Belianis of Greece.

a country labourer, and a good honest fellow, if we may call a poor man honest, for he was poor indeed, poor in purse, and poor in brains; and, in short, the knight talked so long to him, plied him with so many arguments, and made him so many fair promises, that at last the poor silly clown consented to go along with him, and become his squire. Among other inducements to entice him to do it willingly, Don Quixote forgot not to tell him, that it was likely such an adventure would present itself, as might secure him the conquest of some island, in the time he might be picking up a straw or two, and then the squire might promise himself to be made governor of the place. Allured with these large promises, and many others, Sancho Pança (for that was the name of the fellow) forsook his wife and children to be his neighbour's squire.

This done, Don Quixote made it his business to furnish himself with money; for which purpose, selling one house, mortgaging another, and losing by all, he at last got a pretty good sum together. He also borrowed a target of a friend, and having patched up his headpiece and beaver as well as he could, he gave his squire notice of the day and hour when he intended to set out, that he might also furnish himself with what he thought necessary; but, above all, he charged him to provide himself with a wallet; which Sancho promised him to do, telling him he would also take his ass along with him, which, being a very good one, might be a great ease to him, for he was not used to travel much a-foot. The mentioning of the ass made the noble knight pause a while; he mused, and pondered whether he had ever read of any knight-errant whose squire used to ride upon an ass; but he could not remember any precedent for it: however, he gave him leave at last to bring his ass, hoping to mount him more honourably with the first opportunity, by unhorsing the next discourteous knight he should meet. He also furnished himself with shirts, and as many other necessaries as he could conveniently carry, according to the innkeeper's injunctions. Which being done, Sancho Pança, without bidding either his wife or children good-bye; and Don Quixote, without taking any more notice of his housekeeper or of his niece, stole out of the village one night, not so much as suspected by anybody, and made such haste, that by break of day they thought themselves out of reach, should they happen to be pursued. As for Sancho Pança, he rode like a patriarch, with his canvas knapsack, or wallet, and his leathern bottle, having a huge desire to see himself governor of the island, which his master had promised him.

Don Quixote happened to strike into the same road which he took the time before, that is, the plains of Montiel, over which he travelled with less inconveniency than when he went alone, by reason it was yet early in the morning; at which time the sunbeams, being almost parallel to the surface of the earth, and not directly darted down, as in the middle of the day, did not prove so offensive. As they jogged on, 'I beseech your worship, Sir Knight-errant,' quoth Sancho to his master, 'be sure you do not forget what you promised me about the island; for, I dare say, I shall make shift to govern it, let it be never so big.' 'You must know, friend Sancho,' replied Don Quixote, 'that it has been the constant practice of knights-errant, in former ages, to make their squires governors of the islands or kingdoms they conquered: now, I am not only resolved to keep up that laudable custom, but even to improve it, and outdo my predecessors in generosity: for whereas sometimes, or rather most commonly, other knights delayed rewarding their squires till they were grown old, and worn out with service, bad days, worse nights, and all manner of hard duty, and then put them off with some title, either of Count, or at least Marquis of some valley or province of great or small extent; now, if thou and I do but live, it may happen, that before we have passed six days together, I may conquer some kingdom, having many other kingdoms annexed to its imperial crown; and this would fall out most luckily for thee; and then would I presently crown thee king of one of them. Nor do thou imagine this to be a mighty matter; for so strange accidents and revolutions, so sudden and so unforeseen, attend the profession of chivalry, that I might easily give thee a great deal more than I have promised.' 'Why, should this come to pass,' quoth Sancho Pança, 'and I be made a king by some such miracle as your worship says, then happy-be-lucky, my Whither-d'ye-go Mary Gutierrez would be at least a queen, and my children infantas and princes, if it like your worship.' 'Who doubts of that?' cried Don Quixote. 'I doubt of it,' replied Sancho; 'for I cannot help believing, that though it should rain kingdoms down upon the face of the earth, not one of them would fit well upon Mary Gutierrez's head; for, I must needs tell you, she is not worth two brass jacks to make a queen of: no, Countess would be better for her, if it please you; and that too, God help her, will be as much as she can handsomely manage.' 'Recommend the matter to providence,' returned Don Quixote, 'it will be sure to give what is most expedient for thee; but yet disdain to entertain inferior thoughts, and be not tempted to accept less than the dignity of a viceroy.' 'No more I will, sir,' quoth Sancho, 'especially since I have so rare a master as your worship, who will take care to give me whatever may be fit for me, and what I may be able to deal with.'

CHAPTER VIII

*Of the good success which the valorous Don Quixote
had in the most terrifying and never-to-be-imagined
Adventure of the Wind-Mills, with other
transactions worthy to be transmitted to posterity*

As THEY WERE thus discoursing, they discovered some thirty or forty
wind-mills that are in that plain; and, as soon as the knight had spied
them, 'Fortune,' cried he, 'directs our affairs better than we ourselves
could have wished: look yonder, friend Sancho, there are at least thirty
outrageous giants, whom I intend to encounter; and, having deprived
them of life, we will begin to enrich ourselves with their spoils: for they
are lawful prize; and the extirpation of that cursed brood will be an
acceptable service to Heaven.' 'What giants?' quoth Sancho Pança.
'Those whom thou seest yonder,' answered Don Quixote, 'with their
long-extended arms; some of that detested race have arms of so immense a
size, that sometimes they reach two leagues in length.' 'Pray, look better,
sir,' quoth Sancho; 'those things yonder are no giants, but wind-mills, and
the arms you fancy, are their sails, which, being whirled about by the
wind, make the mill go.' 'It is a sign,' cried Don Quixote, 'thou art but
little acquainted with adventures. I tell thee they are giants; and therefore,
if thou art afraid, go aside and say thy prayers, for I am resolved to engage
in a dreadful, unequal combat against them all.' This said, he clapped
spurs to his horse Rozinante, without giving ear to his squire Sancho, who
bawled out to him, and assured him that they were windmills, and no
giants. But he was so fully possessed with a strong conceit of the contrary,
that he did not so much as hear his squire's outcry, nor was he sensible of
what they were, although he was already very near them; far from that.
'Stand, cowards,' cried he as loud as he could; 'stand your ground, ignoble
creatures, and fly not basely from a single knight, who dares encounter
you all.' At the same time the wind rising, the mill-sails began to move,
which, when Don Quixote spied, 'Base miscreants,' cried he, 'though you
move more arms than the giant Briareus, you shall pay for your arrogance.' He most devoutly recommended himself to his lady Dulcinea,
imploring her assistance in this perilous Adventure; and so, covering
himself with his shield, and couching his lance, he rushed with Rozinante's
utmost speed upon the first windmill he could come at, and, running his
lance into the sail, the wind whirled about with such swiftness, that the
rapidity of the motion presently broke the lance into shivers, and hurled
away both knight and horse along with it, till down he fell, rolling a good

way off in the field. Sancho Pança ran as fast as his ass could drive to help his master, whom he found lying, and not able to stir, such a blow he and Rozinante had received. 'Mercy on me!' cried Sancho, 'did I not give your worship fair warning? did not I tell you they were windmills, and that nobody could think otherwise, unless he had also wind-mills in his head?' 'Peace, friend Sancho,' replied Don Quixote: 'there is nothing so subject to the inconstancy of fortune as war. I am verily persuaded, that cursed necromancer Freston, who carried away my study and books, has transformed these giants into wind-mills, to deprive me of the honour of the victory; such is his inveterate malice against me; but, in the end, all his pernicious wiles and stratagems shall prove ineffectual against the prevailing edge of my sword.' 'Amen, say I,' replied Sancho; and so heaving him up again upon his legs, once more the knight mounted poor Rozinante, that was half shoulder-slipped with his fall.

This adventure was the subject of their discourse, as they made the best of their way towards the pass or Lapice; for Don Quixote took that road, believing he could not miss of adventures in one so mightily frequented. However, the loss of his lance was no small affliction to him; and, as he was making his complaint about it to his squire, 'I have read,' said he, 'friend Sancho, that a certain Spanish knight, whose name was Diego Perez de Vargas, having broken his sword in the heat of an engagement, pulled up by the roots a huge oaktree, or at least tore down a massy branch, and did such wonderful execution, crushing and grinding so many Moors with it that day, that he won himself and his posterity the sirname of The Pounder or Bruiser. I tell thee this, because I intend to tear up the next oak, or crab-tree we meet; with the trunk whereof I hope to perform such wondrous deeds, that thou wilt esteem thyself particularly happy in having had the honour to behold them, and been the ocular witness of achievements which posterity will scarce be able to believe.' 'Heaven grant you may,' cried Sancho. 'I believe it all, because your worship says it. But, if it please you, sit a little more upright in your saddle; you ride sidelong, methinks; but that, I suppose, proceeds from your being bruised by the fall.' 'It does so,' replied Don Quixote; 'and, if I do not complain, it is because a knight-errant must never complain of his wounds, though his bowels were dropping out through them.' 'Then I have no more to say,' quoth Sancho; 'and yet, heaven knows my heart, I should be glad to hear your worship hone a little now and then, when something ails you. For my part, I shall not fail to bemoan myself when I suffer the smallest pain, unless indeed it can be proved, that the rule of not complaining extends to the squires as well as knights.' Don Quixote could not forbear smiling at the simplicity of his squire; and told him he gave him leave to complain not only when he pleased, but as much as he pleased, whether he had any cause or no; for he had never yet read anything to the contrary in any books of chivalry. Sancho desired him, however, to consider that it was high time to go to dinner; but his master answered him, that he might eat whenever he pleased; as for himself, he was not yet disposed to do it. Sancho, having thus obtained leave, fixed himself as orderly as he could upon his ass, and, taking some victuals out of his wallet, fell to munching lustily as he rode behind his master; and ever and anon he lifted his bottle to his nose, and fetched such hearty pulls, that it would have made the best-pampered vintner in Malaga a-dry to have seen him. While he thus went on stuffing and swilling, he did not think in the least of all his master's great promises; and was so far from esteeming it a trouble to travel in quest of adventures, that he fancied it to be the greatest pleasure in the world, though they were never so dreadful.

In fine, they passed that night under some trees; from one of which Don Quixote tore a withered branch, which in some sort was able to serve him for a lance, and to this he fixed the head or spear of his broken lance. But he did not sleep all that night, keeping his thoughts intent on his dear Dulcinea, in imitation of what he had read in books of chivalry, where the knights pass that time, without sleep, in forests and deserts, wholly taken up with the entertaining thoughts of their absent mistresses. As for Sancho, he did not spend the night at that idle rate; for, having his paunch well stuffed with something more substantial than dandelion-water, he made but one nap of it; and, had not his master waked him, neither the sprightly beams which the sun darted on his face, nor the melody of the birds, that cheerfully on every branch welcomed the smiling morn, would have been able to have made him stir. As he got up to clear his eye-sight, he took two or three long-winded swigs at his friendly bottle, for a morning's draught; but he found it somewhat lighter than it was the night before; which misfortune went to his very heart, for he shrewdly mistrusted that he was not in a way to cure it of that distemper as soon as he could have wished. On the other side, Don Quixote would not break fast, having been feasting all night on the more delicate and savoury thoughts of his mistress; and therefore they went on directly towards the pass of Lapice, which they discovered about three o'clock. When they came near it, 'Here it is, brother Sancho,' said Don Quixote, 'that we may wanton, and as it were, thrust our arms up to the very elbows, in that which we call adventures. But let me give thee one necessary caution; know that though thou shouldest see me in the greatest extremity of danger, thou must not offer to draw thy sword in my defence, unless thou findest me assaulted by base plebeians and vile scoundrels; for, in such a case, thou mayest assist thy master: but if those with whom I am fighting are knights, thou must not do it; for the laws of chivalry do not allow thee to encounter a knight, till thou art one thyself.' 'Never fear,' quoth Sancho; 'I will be sure to obey your worship in that, I warrant you; for I have ever loved peace and quietness, and never cared to thrust myself into frays and quarrels; and yet I do not care to take blows at any one's hands neither; and should any knight offer to set upon me first, I fancy I should hardly mind your laws; for all laws, whether of God or man, allow one to stand in his own defence, if any offer to do him a mischief.' 'I agree to that,' replied Don Quixote; 'but, as for helping me against any knights, thou must set bounds to thy natural impulses.' 'I will be sure to do it,' quoth Sancho; 'never trust me if I do not keep your commandment as well as I do the Sabbath.'

As they were talking, they spied coming towards them two monks of the order of St. Benedict, mounted on two dromedaries, for the mules on which they rode were so high and stately, that they seemed little less. They wore riding-masks, with glasses at the eyes, against the dust, and umbrellas to shelter them from the sun. After them came a coach, with four or five men on horseback, and two muleteers on foot. There proved to be in the coach a Biscayan lady, who was going to Sevil to meet her husband, that was there in order to embark for the Indies, to take possession of a considerable post. Scarce had Don Quixote perceived the monks, who were not of the same company, though they went the same way, but he cried to his squire, 'Either I am deceived, or this will prove the most famous adventure that ever was known; for, without question, those two black things that move towards us must be some necromancers, that are carrying away by force some princess in that coach; and it is my duty to prevent so great an injury.' 'I fear me this will prove a worse job than the wind-mills,' quoth Sancho. ' 'Slife, sir, do not you see these are Benedictine friars, and it is likely the coach belongs to some travellers that are in it; therefore once more take warning, and do not you be led away by the Devil.' 'I have already told thee, Sancho,' replied Don Quixote, 'thou art miserably ignorant in matters of adventures; what I say is true, and thou shalt find it so presently.' This said, he spurred on his horse, and posted himself just in the middle of the road where the monks were to pass: and when they came within hearing, 'Cursed implements of hell,' cried he in a loud and haughty tone, 'immediately release those high-born princesses, whom you are violently conveying sway in the coach, or else prepare to meet with instant death, as the just punishment of your pernicious deeds.' The monks stopped their mules, no less astonished at the figure, than at the expressions of the speaker. 'Sir knight,' cried they, 'we are no such persons as you are pleased to term us, but religious men of the order of St. Benedict, that travel about our affairs, and are wholly ignorant whether or no there are any princesses carried away by force in that coach.' 'I am not to be deceived with fair words,' replied Don Quixote; 'I know you well enough, perfidious caitiffs'; and immediately, without expecting their reply, he set spurs to Rozinante and ran so furiously, with his lance couched, against the first monk, that, if he had not prudently flung himself off to the ground, the knight would certainly have laid him either dead or grievously wounded. The other, observing the discourteous usage of his companion, clapped his heels to his over-grown mule's flanks, and scoured over the plain as if he had been running a race with the wind. Sancho Pança no sooner saw the monk fall, but he nimbly skipped off his ass, and running to him, began to strip him immediately, but then the two muleteers, who waited on the monks, came up to him, and asked why he offered to strip him? Sancho told them that this belonged to him as lawful plunder, being the spoils won in battle by his lord and master Don Quixote. The fellows, with whom there was no jesting, not knowing what he meant by his spoils and battle, and seeing Don Quixote at a good distance in deep discourse by the side of the coach, fell both upon poor Sancho, threw him down, tore his beard from his chin, trampled on his stomach, thumped and mauled him in every part of his carcase, and there left him sprawling without breath or motion. In the meanwhile the monk, scared out of his wits, and as pale as a ghost, got upon his mule again as fast as he could, and spurred after his friend, who stayed for him at a distance, expecting the issue of this strange adventure: but, being unwilling to stay to see the end of it, they made the best of their way, making more signs of the Cross than if the Devil had been posting after them.

Don Quixote, as I said, was all that while engaged with the lady in the coach. 'Lady,' cried he, 'your discretion is now at liberty to dispose of your beautiful self as you please; for the presumptuous arrogance of those who attempted to enslave your person lies prostrate in the dust, overthrown by this my strenuous arm; and that you may not be at a loss for the name of your deliverer, know I am called Don Quixote de la Mancha, by profession a knight-errant and adventurer, captive to that peerless beauty Donna Dulcinea del Toboso: nor do I desire any other recompense for the service I have done you, but that you return to Toboso to present yourselves to that lady, and let her know what I have done to purchase your deliverance.' To this strange talk, a certain Biscainer, the lady's squire, gentleman-usher, or what you will please to call him, who rode along with the coach, listened with great attention; and perceiving that Don Quixote not only stopped the coach, but would have it presently go back to Toboso, he bore briskly up to him, and laying hold on his lance, 'Get gone,' cried he to him in bad Spanish and worse Biscayan; 'get gone, thou knight, and Devil go with thou; or, by He who me create, if thou do not leave the coach, me kill thee now so sure as me be a Biscayan.' Don Quixote, who made shift to understand him well enough, very calmly made him this answer. 'Wert thou a gentleman, as thou art not, ere this I would have chastised thy insolence and temerity, thou inconsiderable mortal.' 'What! me no gentleman?' replied the Biscainer; 'I swear thou be liar, as me be Christian. If thou throw away lance, and draw sword, me will make no more of thee than cat does of mouse, me will show thee me be Biscayan, and gentleman by land, gentleman by sea, gentleman in spite of Devil; and thou lie if thou say contrary.' 'I will try titles with you as the man said,' replied Don Quixote: and, with that, throwing away his lance, he drew his sword, grasped his target, and attacked the Biscainer, fully bent on his destruction. The Biscainer seeing him come on so furiously, would gladly have alighted, not trusting to his mule, which was one of those scurvy jades that are let out to hire; but all he had time to do was only to draw his sword, and snatch a cushion out of the coach, to serve him instead of a shield; and immediately they assaulted one another with all the fury of mortal enemies. The bystanders did all they could to prevent their fighting; but it was in vain, for the Biscainer swore in his gibberish, he would kill his very lady, and all those who presumed to hinder him, if they would not let him fight. The lady in the coach being extremely affrighted at these passages, made her coach man drive out of harm's way, and at a distance was an eyewitness of the furious combat. At the same time the Biscainer let fall such a mighty blow on Don Quixote's shoulder, over his target, that had not his armour been sword-proof, he would have cleft him down to the very waist. The knight feeling the weight of that unmeasurable blow, cried out aloud, 'Oh! lady of my soul, Dulcinea! flower of all beauty, vouchsafe to succour your champion in this dangerous combat, undertaken to set forth your worth.' The breathing out of this short prayer, the gripping fast of his sword, the covering of himself with his shield, and the charging of his enemy, was but the work of a moment; for Don Quixote was resolved to venture the fortune of the combat all upon one blow. The Biscainer, who read his design in his dreadful countenance, resolved to face him with equal bravery, and stand the terrible shock with uplifted sword, and covered with the cushion, not being able to manage his jaded mule, who defying the spur, and not being cut out for such pranks, would move neither to the right nor to the left. While Don Quixote, with his sword aloft, was rushing upon the wary Biscainer, with a full resolution to cleave him asunder, all the spectators stood trembling with terror and amazement, expecting the dreadful event of those prodigious blows which threatened the two desperate combatants: the lady in the coach, with the women, were making a thousand vows and offerings to all the images and places of devotion in Spain, that Providence might deliver them and the squire out of the great danger that threatened them.

But here we must deplore the abrupt end of this history, which the author leaves off just at the very point when the fortune of the battle is going to be decided, pretending he could find nothing more recorded of Don Quixote's wondrous achievements than what he had already related.

However, the second undertaker of this work could not believe that so curious a history could lie for ever inevitably buried in oblivion; or that the learned of La Mancha were so regardless of their country's glory, as not to preserve in their archives, or at least in their closets, some memoirs, as monuments of this famous knight; and therefore he would not give over inquiring after the continuation of this pleasant history, till at last he happily found it, as the next book will inform the reader.

BOOK II

CHAPTER I

*The event of the most stupendous Combat between
the brave Biscainer and the valorous Don Quixote*

IN THE FIRST BOOK of this history, we left the valiant Biscainer and the renowned Don Quixote with their swords lifted up, and ready to discharge on each other two furious and most terrible blows, which, had they fallen directly, and met with no opposition, would have cut and divided the two combatants from head to heel, and have split them like a pomegranate; but, as I said before, the story remained imperfect; neither did the author inform us where we might find the remaining part of the relation. This vexed me extremely, and turned the pleasure which the perusal of the beginning had afforded me into disgust, when I had reason to despair of ever seeing the rest. Yet, after all, it seemed to me no less impossible than unjust, that so valiant a knight should have been destitute of some learned person to record his incomparable exploits; a misfortune which never attended any of his predecessors, I mean the knights-adventurers, each of whom was always provided with one or two learned men, who were always at hand to write not only their wondrous deeds, but also to set down their thoughts and childish petty actions, were they never so hidden. Therefore, as I could not imagine that so worthy a knight should be so unfortunate, as to want that which had been so profusely lavished even on such a one as Platyr,* and others of that stamp; I could not induce myself to believe, that so admirable a history was ever left unfinished, and rather choose to think that time, the devourer of all things, had hid or consumed it. On the other side, when I considered that several modern books were found in his study, as 'The Cures of Jealousy,' and 'The Nymphs and Shepherds of Henares,'† I had reason to think that the history of our Knight could be of no very ancient date; and that, had it never been continued, yet his neighbours and friends could not have forgot the most remarkable passages of his life. Full of this imagination, I resolved to make it my business to make a particular and exact inquiry into the life and miracles of our renowned Spaniard Don Quixote, that refulgent glory and mirror of the knighthood of La Mancha, and the first

* A second-rate knight in 'Palmerin of England.'
† Henares runs by the University of Alcale in Old Castilo.

who in these depraved and miserable times devoted himself to the neglected profession of knight-errantry, to redress wrongs and injuries, to relieve widows, and defend the honour of damsels; such of them, I mean, who in former ages rode up and down over hills and dales, with whip in hand, mounted on their palfreys, with all their virginity about them, secure from all manner of danger; and who, unless they happened to be ravished by some boisterous villain or huge giant, were sure, at four score years of age (all which time they never slept one night under a roof) to be decently laid in their graves, as pure virgins as the mothers that bore them. For this reason and many others, I say, our gallant Don Quixote is worthy of everlasting and universal praise: nor ought I to be denied my due commendation for my indefatigable care and diligence, in seeking and finding out the continuation of this delightful History; though, after all, I must confess that, had not Providence, chance, or fortune, as I will now inform you, assisted me in the discovery. The world had been deprived of two hours' diversion and pleasure, which it is likely to afford to those who will read it with attention. One day, being in the Alcala at Toledo, I saw a young lad offer to sell a parcel of old written papers to a shopkeeper. Now I, being apt to take up the least piece of written or printed paper that lies in my way, though it were in the middle of the street, could not forbear laying my hands on one of the manuscripts, to see what it was; and I found it to be written in Arabic, which I could not read. This made me to look about, to see whether I could find ever a Morisco that understood Spanish, to read it for me and give me some account of it; nor was it very difficult to meet with an interpreter there; for, had I wanted one for a better and more ancient tongue, that place would have infallibly supplied me. It was my good fortune to find one immediately; and, having informed him of my desire, he no sooner read some lines than he began to laugh. I asked him what he laughed at. 'At a certain remark here in the margin of the book,' said he. I prayed him to explain it, whereupon, still laughing, he did it in these words: 'This Dulcinea del Toboso, so often mentioned in this history, is said to have had the best hand at salting of pork of any woman in La Mancha.' I was surprised when I heard him name Dulcinea del Toboso, and presently imagined that those old papers contained the history of Don Quixote. This made me press him to read the title of the book, which he did, turning it thus extempore out of Arabic: 'The History of Don Quixote de la Mancha, written by Cid Hamet Benengeli, an Arabian historian.' I was so overjoyed when I heard the title, that I had much ado to conceal it; and presently, taking the bargain out of the shopkeeper's hand, I agreed with the young man for the whole, and bought that for half a real, which he might have sold me for twenty times as much had he but guessed at the eagerness of his chapman. I immediately withdrew with my purchase to the cloister of the great church, taking the Moor with me, and desired him to translate to me those papers that treated of Don Quixote, without adding or omitting the least word, offering him any reasonable satisfaction. He asked me but two Arrobes* of raisins, and two bushels of wheat, and promised to do it faithfully with all expedition. In short, for the quicker dispatch and the greater security, being unwilling to let such a lucky prize go out of my hands, I took the Moor to my own house, where, in less than six weeks he finished the whole translation.

Don Quixote's fight with the Biscainer was exactly drawn on one of the leaves of the first quire, in the same posture as we left them, with their swords lifted up over their heads, the one guarding himself with his shield, the other with his cushion. The Biscainer's mule was so pictured to the life, that with half an eye you might have known it to be a hired mule. Under the Biscainer was written, 'Don Sancho de Azpetia,' and under Rozinante, 'Don Quixote.' Rozinante was so admirably delineated, so slim, so stiff, so lean, so jaded, with so sharp a ridge-bone, and altogether so like one wasted with an incurable consumption, that any one must have owned, at first sight, that no horse ever better deserved that name. Not far off stood Sancho Pança,† holding his ass by the halter, at whose feet there was a scroll, in which was written 'Sancho Canças'‡; and, if we may judge of him by his picture, he was thick and short, paunch-bellied, and long-haunched; so that, in all likelihood, for this reason he is sometimes called Pança and sometimes Cança in the History. There were some other niceties to be seen in that piece, but hardly worth observation, as not giving any light into this true history, otherwise they had not passed unmentioned; for none can be amiss, so they are authentic. I must only acquaint the reader, that if any objection is to be made as to the veracity of this, it is only that the author is an Arabian, and those of that country are not a little addicted to lying: but yet, if we consider that they are our enemies, we should sooner imagine that the author has rather suppressed the truth than added to the real worth of our Knight; and I am the more inclinable to think so, because it is plain that where he ought to have enlarged on his praises, he maliciously chooses to be silent; a proceeding unworthy of an historian, who ought to be exact, sincere, and impartial; free from passion, and not to be biassed either by interest, fear, resentment, or affection, to deviate from truth, which is the mother of history, the preserver and eterniser of great actions, the professed enemy of oblivion, the witness of things passed, and the director of future times. As for the History, I know it will afford you as great variety as you could wish,

* An Arrobe is about 32 lb. weight.
† 'Paunch.'
‡ 'Haunches,' or rather 'thigh-bones.'

in the most entertaining manner; and if in any point it falls short of your expectation, I am of opinion it is more the fault of the Infidel, its author, than the subject; and so let us go to the second book, which, according to our translation, began in this manner:

Such were the bold and formidable looks of the two enraged combatants that, with uplifted arms and with destructive steel, they seemed to threaten heaven, earth, and the infernal mansions; while the spectators seemed wholly lost in fear and astonishment. The choleric Biscainer discharged the first blow, and that with such a force and so desperate a fury that, had not his sword turned in his hand, that single stroke had put an end to the dreadful combat and all our Knight's adventures. But fate, that reserved him for greater things, so ordered it, that his enemy's sword turned in such a manner, that though it struck him on the left shoulder, it did him no other hurt than to disarm that side of his head, carrying away with it a great part of his helmet, and one half of his ear, which, like a dreadful ruin, fell together to the ground. Assist me, ye powers! – but it is in vain! The fury which then engrossed the breast of our Hero of La Mancha is not to be expressed; words would but wrong it: for what colour of speech can be lively enough to give but a slight sketch or faint image of his unutterable rage? Exerting all his valour, he raised himself upon his stirrups, and seemed even greater than himself; and, at the same instant, gripping his sword fast with both hands, he discharged such a tremendous blow full on the Biscainer's cushion and his head, that in spite of so good a defence, as if a whole mountain had fallen upon him, the blood gushed out at his mouth, nose, and ears all at once; and he tottered so in his saddle, that he had fallen to the ground immediately, had he not caught hold of the neck of his mule: but the dull beast itself, being roused out of its stupidity with that terrible blow, began to run about the fields; and the Biscainer, having lost his stirrups and his hold, with two or three winces the mule shook him off, and threw him on the ground. Don Quixote beheld the disaster of his foe with the greatest tranquillity and unconcern imaginable; and, seeing him down, slipped nimbly from his saddle, and running to him, set the point of his sword to his throat, and bid him yield, or he would cut off his head. The Biscainer was so stunned that he could make him no reply; and Don Quixote had certainly made good his threats, so provoked was he, had not the ladies in the coach, who, with great uneasiness and fear, beheld the sad transaction, hastened to beseech Don Quixote very earnestly to spare his life. 'Truly, beautiful ladies,' said the 'victorious Knight, with a deal of loftiness and gravity, 'I am willing to grant your request; but upon condition that this same knight shall pass his word of honour to go to Toboso, and there present himself, in my name, before the peerless Lady Donna Dulcinea, that she may dispose of him as she shall see convenient.' The lady, who was frightened almost out of her senses, without considering what Don Quixote enjoined, or inquiring who the lady Dulcinea was, promised in her squire' behalf a punctual obedience to the Knight's commands. 'Let him live then,' replied Don Quixote, 'upon your word, and owe to your intercession that pardon which I might justly deny his arrogance.'

CHAPTER II

What farther befell Don Quixote with the Biscainer; and of the danger he ran among a parcel of Yanguesians

SANCHO PANÇA was got up again before this, not much the better for the kicks and thumps bestowed on his carcase by the monk's grooms; and, seeing his master engaged in fight, he went devoutly to prayers, beseeching Heaven to grant him victory, that he might now win some island, in order to his being made governor of it according to his promise. At last, perceiving the danger was over, the combat at an end, and his master ready to mount again, he ran in all haste to help him; but, ere the knight put his foot in the stirrup, Sancho fell on his knees before him, and kissing his hand, 'If it please your worship,' cried he, 'my good Lord Don Quixote, I beseech you make me governor of the island you have won in this dreadful and bloody fight; for, though it were never so great, I find myself able to govern it as well as the best he that ever went about to govern an island in the world.' 'Brother Sancho,' replied Don Quixote, 'these are no adventures of islands; these are only re-encounters on the road, where little is to be got besides a broken head, or the loss of an ear: therefore have patience, and some adventure will offer itself, which will not only enable: me to prefer thee to a government but even to something more considerable.' Sancho gave him a world of thanks; and, having once more kissed his hand, and the skirts of his coat of armour, he helped him to get upon Rozinante; and then leaping on his ass, he followed the Hero, who, without taking leave of those in the coach, put on a good round pace, and rode into a wood, that was not far off. Sancho made after him as fast as his ass would trot; but, finding that Rozinante was like to leave him behind, he was forced to call to his master to stay for him. Don Quixote accordingly checked his horse, and soon gave Sancho leisure to overtake him. 'Methinks, sir,' said the fearful squire, as soon as he came up with him, 'it will not be amiss for us to betake ourselves to some church, to get out of harm's way; for, if that same man whom you have fought with should do otherwise than well, I dare lay my life they will get a warrant from the Holy Brotherhood,* and have us taken up; which if they do, on my word, it will go hard with us ere we can get out of their clutches.' 'Hold thy tongue,' cried Don Quixote: 'where didst thou ever read, or find that a knight-errant was ever brought before any judge for the homicides which he committed?' 'I cannot tell what you mean by your homilies,' replied Sancho; 'I do not know that ever I saw one in my born days, not I: but well I wot, that the law lays hold on those that go to murder one another in the fields; and, for your what-do-you-call-'ems, I have nothing to say to them.' 'Then be not afraid, good Sancho,' cried Don Quixote; 'for I would deliver thee out of the hands of the Chaldeans, and with much more ease out of those of the holy brotherhood. But come, tell me truly, dost thou believe that the whole world can boast of another knight that may pretend to rival me in valour? Didst thou ever read in history, that any other ever showed more resolution to undertake, more vigour to attack, more breath to hold out, more dexterity and activity to strike, and more art and force to overthrow his enemies.' 'Not I, by my troth,' replied Sancho. 'I never did meet anything like you in history, for I neither can read nor write; but that which I dare wager is, that I never in my life served a bolder master than your worship: pray Heaven this same boldness may not bring us to what I bid you beware of. All I have to put you in mind of now, is, that you get your ear dressed, for you lose a deal of blood; and by good luck I have here some lint and a little white salve in my wallet.' 'How needless would all this have been,' cried Don Quixote, 'had I but bethought myself of making a small bottleful of the balsam of fierabras I a single drop of which would have spared us a great deal of time and medicaments.' 'What is that same balsam, if it please you?' cried Sancho. 'A balsam,' answered Don Quixote, 'of which I have the receipt in my head; he that hath some of it may defy death itself, and dally with all manner of wounds: therefore, when I have made some of it, and given it thee, if at any time thou happenest to see my body cut in two, by some unlucky back-stroke, as it is common among us knights-errant, thou hast no more to do but to take up nicely that half of me which is fallen to the ground, and clap it exactly to the other half on the saddle, before the blood is congealed, always taking care to, lay it just in its proper place: then thou shalt give me two drops of that balsam, and thou shalt immediately see me become whole and sound as an apple.' 'If this be true,' quoth Sancho, 'I will quit you of your promise about the island this minute of an hour, and will have nothing of your worship for what service I have done, and am to do you. But the receipt of that same balsam; for, I dare say, let me go wherever I will, it will be sure to yield me three good

---

* An institution spread through all Spain, to suppress robbers, and make the roads safe to travellers.

reals an ounce; and thus I shall make shift to pick a pretty good livelihood out of it. But stay though,' continued he, 'does the making stand your worship in much, sir?' 'Three quarts of it,' replied Don Quixote, 'may be made for three reals.' 'Body of me,' cried Sancho, 'why do not you make some out of hand, and teach me how to make it?' 'Say no more, friend Sancho,' returned Don Quixote; 'I intend to teach thee much greater secrets, and design thee nobler rewards; but, in the mean time, dress my ear, for it pains me more than I could wish.' Sancho then took his lint and ointment out of his wallet; but, when Don Quixote perceived the visor of his helmet was broken, he had like to have run stark-staring mad; straight, laying hold on his sword, and lifting up his eyes to heaven, 'By the great Creator of the universe,' cried he, 'by every syllable contained in the four holy evangelists, I swear to lead a life like the great Marquis of Mantua, when he made a vow to revenge the death of his cousin Baldwin, which was never to eat bread on a tablecloth, never to lie with the dear partner of his bed, and other things, which, though they are now at present slipped out of my memory, I comprise in my vow no less than if I had now mentioned them; and this I bind myself to, till I have fully revenged myself on him that has done me this injury.'

'Good your worship,' cried Sancho (amazed to hear him take such a horrid oath), 'think on what you are doing; for if that same knight has done as you bid him, and has gone and cast himself before my Lady Dulcinea del Toboso, I do not see but you and he are quit; and the man deserves no further punishment, unless he does you some new mischief.' 'It is well observed,' replied Don Quixote; 'and therefore, as to the point of revenge, I revoke my oath; but I renew and confirm the rest, protesting solemnly to lead the life I mentioned, till I have by force of arms despoiled some knight of as good a helmet as mine was. Neither do thou fancy, Sancho, that I make this protestation lightly, or make a smoke of straw: no, I have a laudable precedent for it, the authority of which will sufficiently justify my imitation; for the very same thing happened about Mambrino's helmet, which cost Sacripante so dear.'* 'Good sir,' quoth Sancho, 'let all such cursing and swearing go to the Devil; there is nothing can be worse for your soul's health, nay, for your bodily health either. Besides, suppose we should not this good while meet any one with a helmet on, what a sad case should we then be in? Will your worship then keep your oath in spite of so many hardships, such as to lie rough for a month together, far from any inhabited place, and a thousand other idle penances which that mad old Marquis of Mantua punished himself with by his vow? Do but consider, that we may ride do not know how long upon this road without meeting any armed knight to pick a quarrel with;

* The story is in Ariosto's 'Orlando Furioso.'

for here are none but carriers and waggoners, who are so far from wearing any helmets, that it is ten to one whether they ever heard of such a thing in their lives.' 'Thou art mistaken, friend Sancho,' replied Don Quixote; 'for we shall not be two hours this way without meeting more men in arms than there were at the siege of Albraca, to carry off the fair Angelica'* 'Well then, let it be so,' quoth Sancho; 'and may we have the luck to come off well, and quickly win that island which costs me so dear, and then I do not matter what befalls me.' 'I have already bid thee not trouble thyself about this business, Sancho,' said Don Quixote; 'for should we miss an island, there is either the kingdom of Denmark, or that of Sobradisa,† as fit for thy purpose as a ring to thy finger; and, what ought to be no small comfort to thee, they are both upon *terra firma*.‡ But we will talk of this in its proper season: at this time I would have thee see whether thou hast anything to eat in thy wallet, that we may afterwards seek for some castle, where we may lodge this night, and make the balsam I told thee; for I protest my ear smarts extremely. 'I have here an onion,' replied the squire, 'a piece of cheese, and a few stale crusts of bread; but sure such coarse fare is not for such a brave knight as your worship.' 'Thou art grossly mistaken, friend Sancho,' answered Don Quixote: 'know, that it is the glory of knights-errant to be whole months without eating: and when they do, they fall upon the first thing they meet with, though it be never so homely. Hadst thou but read as many books as I have done, thou hadst been better informed as to that point; for though I think I have read as many histories of chivalry in my time as any other man, I never could find that the knights-errant ever ate, unless it were by mere accident, or when they were invited to great feasts and royal banquets; at other times they indulged themselves with little other food besides their thoughts. Though it is not to be imagined they could be without supplying the exigencies of human nature, as being after all no more than mortal men; yet it is likewise to be supposed, that, as they spent the greatest part of their lives in forests and deserts, and always destitute of a cook, consequently their usual food was but such coarse country fare as thou now offerest me. Never then make thyself uneasy about what pleases me, friend Sancho, nor pretend to make a new world, or unhinge the very constitution and ancient customs of knight-errantry.' 'I beg your worship's pardon,' cried Sancho; 'for, as I was never bred a scholar, I may chance to have missed in some main point of your laws of knighthood; but, from this time forward,

* Meaning king Marsilio, and the thirty-two kings his tributaries, with all their forces. – Ariosto.
† A fictitious kingdom in 'Amadis de Gaul.'
‡ In allusion to the famous Firm Island in 'Amadis de Gaul,' the land of promise to the faithful squires of knights-errant.

I will be sure to stock my wallet with all sorts of dry fruits for you, because your worship is a knight; as for myself, who am none, I will provide good poultry and other substantial victuals.' 'I do not say, Sancho,' replied Don Quixote, 'that a knight-errant is obliged to feed altogether upon fruit; I only mean, that this was their common food, together with some roots and herbs, which they found up and down the fields, of all which they had a perfect knowledge, as I myself have.' 'It is a good thing to know those herbs,' cried Sancho; 'for I am much mistaken, or that kind of knowledge will stand us in good stead ere long. In the mean time,' continued he, 'here is what good Heaven has sent us.' With that he pulled out the provision he bad, of which they ate heartily together. But their impatience to find out a place where they might be harboured that night, made them shorten their sorry meal and mount again, for tear of being benighted; so away they put on in search of a lodging. But the sun and their hopes failed them at once, as they came to a place where some goatherds had set up some small huts; and therefore they concluded to take up their lodging there that night. This was as great a mortification to Sancho, who was altogether for a good town, as it was a pleasure to his master, who was for sleeping in the open field, as believing, that as often as he did it, he confirmed his title to knighthood by a new act of possession.

CHAPTER III

What passed between Don Quixote and the Goatherd

THE KNIGHT was very courteously received by the goatherds, and as for Sancho, after he had set up Rozinante and his ass, as well as he could, he presently repaired to the attractive smell of some pieces of kid's flesh, which stood boiling in a kettle over the fire. The hungry squire would immediately have tried whether they were fit to be removed out of the kettle into the stomach, but was not put to that trouble; for the goatherds took them off the fire, and, spreading some sheep-skins on the ground, soon got their rural feast ready, and cheerfully invited his master and him to partake of what they had. Next, with some coarse compliment, after the country way they desired Don Quixote to sit down on a trough with the bottom upwards; and then six of them, who were all that belonged to that fold, squatted them down round the skins, while Sancho stood to wait upon his master, and gave him drink in a horn cup, which the goatherds used. But he, seeing his man stand behind, said to him, 'That thou mayest understand, Sancho, the benefits of knight-errantry, and how the meanest retainers to it have a fair prospect of being speedily esteemed and honoured by the world, it is my pleasure that they sit thee down by me in the company of those good people; and that there be no difference now observed between thee and me, thy natural lord and master, that thou eat in the same dish, and drink in the same cup; for it may be said of knight-errantry as of love, that it makes all things equal.' 'I thank your worship,' cried Sancho; 'but yet I must needs own, had I but a good deal of meat before me, I would eat it as well, or rather better, standing, and by myself, than if I sat by an emperor; and, to deal plainly and truly with you, I had rather munch a crust of brown bread and an onion in a corner, without any more ado and ceremony, than feed upon turkey at another man's table, where one is fain to sit mincing and chewing his meat an hour together, drink little, be always wiping his fingers and his chops, and never dare to cough nor sneeze, though he has never so much a mind to do it, nor do many things which a body may do freely by one's self; therefore, good sir, change those tokens of your kindness, which I have a right to by being your worship's squire, into something that may do me more good. As for these same honours, I heartily thank you as much as if I had accepted them, but yet I give up my right to them from this time to the world's end.' 'Talk no more,' replied Don Quixote, 'but sit thee down, for the humble shall be exalted'; and so, pulling him by the arm, he forced him to sit by him.

All this while the goatherds, who did not understand this jargon of knights-errant, chivalry, and squires, fed heartily and said nothing, but stared upon their guests, who very fairly swallowed while luncheons, as big as their fists, with a mighty appetite. The first course being over, they brought in the second, consisting of dried acorns, and half a cheese as hard as a brick. Nor was the horn idle all the while, but went merrily round up and down so many times, sometimes full and sometimes empty, like the two buckets of a well, that they made shift at last to drink off one of the two skins of wine which they had there. And now, Don Quixote having satisfied his appetite, he took a handful of acorns, and looking earnestly upon them: 'O happy age,' cried he, 'which our first parents called the age of gold! Not because gold, so much adored in this iron age, was then easily purchased, but because those two fatal words *mine* and *thine*, were distinctions unknown to the people of those fortunate times; for all things were in common in that holy age: men, for their sustenance, needed only to lift their hands and take it from the sturdy oak, whose spreading arms liberally invited them to gather the wholesome savoury fruit; while the clear springs, and silver rivulets, with luxuriant plenty, ordered them their pure refreshing water. In hollow trees, and in the clefts of rocks, the labouring and industrious bees erected their little commonwealths, that men might reap with pleasure and with ease the sweet and fertile harvest of their toils. The tough and strenuous cork-trees did of themselves, and without other art than their native liberality, dismiss and impart their broad light bark, which served to cover these lowly huts, propped up with rough-hewn stakes, that were first built as a shelter against the inclemencies of the air. All then was union, all peace, all love and friendship in the world; as yet no rude plough-share presumed with violence to pry into the pious bowels of our mother earth, for she, without compulsion, kindly yielded from every part of her fruitful and spacious bosom, whatever might at once satisfy, sustain, and indulge her frugal children. Then was the time when innocent, beautiful young shepherdesses went tripping over the hills and vales; their lovely hair sometimes plaited, sometimes loose and flowing, clad in no other vestment but what was necessary to cover decently what modesty would always have concealed. The Tyrian dye and the rich glossy hue of silk, martyred and dissembled into every colour, which are now esteemed so fine and magnificent, were unknown to the innocent plainness of that age; yet bedecked with more becoming leaves and flowers, they may be said to outshine the proudest of the vain-dressing ladies of our age, arrayed in the most magnificent garbs, and all the most sumptuous adornings which idleness and luxury have taught succeeding pride: lovers then expressed the passion of their souls in the unaffected language of the heart, with the native plainness and sincerity in which they were conceived, and divested of all that artificial contexture, which enervates what it labours to enforce: imposture, deceit and malice had not yet crept in and imposed themselves unbribed upon mankind in the disguise of truth and simplicity: justice, unbiassed either by favour or interest, which now so fatally pervert it, was equally and impartially dispensed; nor was the judge's fancy law, for then there were neither judges nor causes to be judged: the modest maid might walk wherever she pleased alone, free from the attacks of lewd, lascivious importuners. But, in this degenerate age, fraud and a legion of ills infecting the world, no virtue can be safe, no honour be secure; while wanton desires, diffused into the hearts of men, corrupt the strictest watches, and the closest retreats; which, though as intricate and unknown as the labyrinth of Crete, are no security for chastity. Thus that primitive innocence being vanished, the oppression daily prevailing, there was a necessity to oppose the torrent of violence: for which reason the order of knight-hood-errant was instituted to defend the honour of virgins, protect widows, relieve orphans, and assist all the distressed in general. Now I myself am one of this order, honest friends; and though all people are obliged by the law of nature to be kind to persons of my order; yet, since you, without knowing anything of this obligation, have so generously entertained me, I ought to pay you my utmost acknowledgment; and, accordingly, return you my most hearty thanks for the same.'

All this long oration, which might very well have been spared, was owing to the acorns, that recalled the golden age to our Knight's remembrance, and made him thus hold forth to the goatherds, who devoutly listened, but edified little, the discourse not being suited to their capacities. Sancho, as well as they, was silent all the while, eating acorns, and frequently visiting the second skin of wine, which, for coolness' sake, was hung upon a neighbouring cork-tree. As for Don Quixote, he was longer, and more intent upon his speech than upon his supper. When he had done, one of the goatherds, addressing himself to him, 'Sir Knight,' said he, 'that you may be sure you are heartily welcome, we will get one of our fellows to give us a song; he is just a coming: a good notable young lad he is, I will say that for him, and up to the ears in love. He is a scholar, and can read and write, and plays so rarely upon the Rebeck* that it is a charm but to hear him.' No sooner were the words out of the goatherd's mouth, but they heard the sound of the instrument he spoke of, and presently appeared a good comely young man of about two-and-twenty years of age. The goatherds asked him if he had supped, and he having told them he had, 'Then, dear Antonio,' says the first speaker, 'prithee sing us a song, to let this gentleman, our guest, see that we have those among us who know somewhat of music, for all we live amidst woods and mountains. We have told him of thee already; therefore prithee make our words good, and sing us the ditty thy uncle, the prebendary, made of thy love, that was so liked in our town.' 'With all my heart,' replied Antonio; and so, without any further entreaty, sitting down on the stump of an oak, he tuned his fiddle, and very handsomely sung the following song:

ANTONIO'S AMOROUS COMPLAINT

Tho' love ne'er prattles at your eyes,
  (The eyes those silent tongues of love)
Yet sure, Olalia, you're my prize:
  For truth with zeal ev'n Heav'n can move,
I think, my love, you only try,
  Ev'n while I fear you've seal'd my doom;
So, tho' involv'd in doubts I lie,
  Hope sometimes glimmers thro' the gloom.
A flame so fierce, so bright, so pure,
  No scorn can quench, or art improve;
Thus like a martyr I endure,
  For there's a heaven to crown my love.

* A fiddle with only three strings, used by shepherds.

In dress and dancing I have strove
  My proudest rivals to outvy;
In serenades I've breath'd my love,
  When all things slept but love and I.
I need not add, I speak your praise
  Till every nymph's disdain I move;
Tho' thus a thousand foes I raise,
  'Tis sweet to praise the fair I love.
Teresa once your charms debas'd,
  But I her rudeness soon reprov'd;
In vain her friend my anger fac'd,
  For then I fought for her I lov'd.
Dear cruel fair, why then so coy?
  How can you so much love withstand?
Alas! I crave no lawless joy,
  But with my heart would give my hand.
Soft, easy, strong is Hymen's tie;
  Oh! then no more the bliss refuse;
Oh! wed me, or I swear to die,
  Or linger wretched and recluse.

Here Antonio ended his song. Don Quixote entreated him to sing another, but Sancho Pança, who had more mind to sleep than to hear the finest singing in the world, told his master there was enough. 'Good sir,' quoth he, 'your worship had better go and lie down where you are to take your rest this night; besides, these good people are tired with their day's labour, and rather want to go to sleep, than to sit up all night to hear ballads.' 'I understand thee, Sancho,' cried Don Quixote; 'and indeed, I thought thy frequent visiting the bottle would make thee fonder of sleep than of music.' 'Make us thankful,' cried Sancho, 'we all liked the wine well enough.' 'I do not deny it,' replied Don Quixote; 'but go thou and lay thee down where thou pleasest; as for me, it better becomes a man of my profession to wake than to sleep: yet stay and dress my ear before thou goest, for it pains me extremely.' Thereupon one of the goatherds, beholding the wound as Sancho offered to dress it, desired the Knight not to trouble himself, for he had a remedy that would quickly cure him; and then fetching a few rosemary leaves, which grew in great plenty thereabout, he bruised them, and mixed a little salt among them, and having applied the medicine to the ear, he bound it up, assuring him he needed no other remedy; which, in a little time, proved very true.

CHAPTER IV

The Story which a young Goatherd told to those that were with Don Quixote

A YOUNG FELLOW, who used to bring them provisions from the next village, happened to come while this was doing, and addressing himself to the goatherds, 'Hark ye, friends,' said he, 'do you hear the news?' 'What news?' cried one of the company. 'That fine shepherd and scholar Chrysostom died this morning,' answered the other; 'and they say it was for love of that devilish untoward lass Marcella, rich William's daughter, that goes up and down the country in the habit of a shepherdess.' 'For Marcella!' cried one of the goatherds. 'I say for her,' replied the fellow, 'and what is more, it is reported, he has ordered, by his will, they should bury him in the fields like any Heathen Moor, just at the foot of the rock, hard by the cork-tree fountain, where they say he had the first sight of her. Nay, he has likewise ordered many other strange things to be done, which the heads of the parish will not allow of, for they seem to be after the way of the Pagans. But Ambrose, the other scholar, who likewise apparelled himself like a shepherd, is resolved to have his friend Chrysostom's will fulfilled in everything, just as he has ordered it. All the village is in an uproar. But after all, it is thought Ambrose and his friends will carry the day; and, tomorrow morning, he is to be buried in great state where I told you: I fancy it will be worth seeing; howsoever, be it what it will, I will ev'n go and see it, even though I should not get back again tomorrow.' 'We will all go,' cried the goatherds, 'and cast lots who shall tarry to look after the goats.' 'Well said, Peter,' cried one of the goatherds; 'but, as for casting of lots, I will save you that labour, for I will stay myself, not so much out of kindness to you neither, or want of curiosity, as because of the thorn in my toe, that will not let me go.' 'Thank you, however,' quoth Peter. Don Quixote, who heard all this, entreated Peter to tell him who the deceased was, and also to give him a short account of the shepherdess.

Peter made answer, that all he knew of the matter was, that the deceased was a wealthy gentleman, who lived not far of, that he had been several years at the university of Salamanca, and then came home mightily improved in his learning. 'But above all,' quoth he, 'it was said of him, that he had great knowledge in the stars, and whatsoever the sun and moon do in the skies; for he would tell us to a title the clip of the sun and moon.' 'We call it an Eclipse,' cried Don Quixote, 'and not a Clip, when either of these great luminaries are darkened.' 'He would also,' continued Peter, who did not stand upon such nice distinctions, 'foretell when the year would be plentiful or "Estil." ' 'You would say "sterile," ' cried Don Quixote. ' "Sterile" or "Estil," ' replied the fellow, 'that is all one to me; but this I say, that his parents and friends, being ruled by him, grew extremely rich in a short time; for he would tell them, This year sow barley, and no wheat; in this you may sow peas and no barley; next year will be a good year for oil; the three after that, you shall not gather a drop: and whatsoever he said would certainly come to pass.' 'That science,' said Don Quixote, 'is called Astrology.' 'I do not know what you call it,' answered Peter, 'but I know he knew all this, and a deal more. But, in short, within some few months after he had left the Versity, on a certain morning we saw him come dressed, for all the world like a shepherd, and driving his flock, having laid down the long gown which he used to wear as a scholar. At the same time one Ambrose, a great friend of his, who had been his fellow-scholar, also took upon him to go like a shepherd, and bear him company; which we all did not a little marvel at. I had almost forgot to tell you, how he that is dead was a mighty man for making of verses, insomuch that he commonly made the carols, which we sung on Christmas-Eve; and the plays which the young lads in our neighbourhood enacted on Corpus-Christi-day, and every one would say, that nobody could mend them. Somewhat before that time Chrysostom's father died, and left him a deal of wealth, both in land, money, cattle, and other goods, whereof the young man remained dissolute master; and in truth he deserved it all, for he was as good-natured a soul as ever trod on shoe-leather; mighty good to the poor, a main friend to all honest people, and had a face like a blessing. At last it came to be known, that the reason of his altering his garb in that fashion, was only that he might go up and down after that shepherdess Marcella, whom our comrade told you of before, for he was fallen mightily in love with her. And now I will tell you such a thing you never heard the like in your born days, and may not chance to hear of such another while you breathe, though you were to live as long as Sarah.' 'Say Sarah,' cried Don Quixote; who hated to hear him blunder thus. 'The Sarna, or the itch (for that is all one with us,' quoth Peter), 'lives long enough too; hut if you go on thus, and make me break off my tale at every word, we are not like to have done this twelvemonth.' 'Pardon me, friend,' replied Don Quixote; 'I only spoke to make thee understand that there is a difference between Sarna and Sarah: however, thou sayest well; for the Sarna (that is the itch) lives longer than Sarah; therefore pray make an end of thy story, for I will not interrupt thee any more.' 'Well then,' quoth Peter, 'you must know, good master of mine, that there lived near us one William, a yeoman, who was richer yet than Chrysostom's father; now he had no child in the versal world but a daughter; her mother died in child-bed of her (rest her soul) and was as good a woman as ever went upon two legs; methinks I see her yet standing before me, with that blessed face of hers, the sun on one side, and the moon on the other. She was a main housewife, and did a deal of good among the poor; for which I dare say she is at the minute in Paradise. Alas! her death broke poor William's heart; he soon went after her, poor man, and left all to his little daughter, that Marcella by name, giving charge of her to her uncle, the parson of our parish. Well, the girl grew such a fine child, and so like her mother, that it used to put us in mind of her every foot: however, it was thought she would make a finer woman yet; and so it happened indeed; for, by that time she was fourteen or fifteen years of age, no man set his eyes on her, that did not bless Heaven for having made her so handsome; so that most men fell in love with her, and were ready to run mad for her. All this while her uncle kept her up very close; yet the report of her great beauty and wealth spread far and near, insomuch, that she had I do not know how many sweethearts, almost all the young men in our town asked her of her uncle; nay, from I do not know how many leagues about us, there flocked whole droves of suitors, and the very best in the country too, who all begged, and sued, and teased her uncle to let them have her. But though he would have been glad to have got fairly rid of her, as soon as she was fit for a husband, yet would not he advise, or marry her against her will; for he is a good man, I will say that for him, and a true Christian every inch of him, and scorns to keep her from marrying, to make a benefit of her estate; and, to his praise be it spoken, he has been mainly commended for it more than once, when the people of our parish meet together. For, I must tell you, Sir Errant, that here in the country, and in our little towns, there is not the least thing can be said or done, but people will talk and find fault: but let busybodies prate as they please, the parson must have been a good body indeed, who could bring his whole parish to give him a good word, especially in the country.' 'Thou art in the right,' cried Don Quixote, 'and therefore go on, honest Peter, for the story is pleasant, and thou tellest it with a grace.' 'May I never want God's grace,' quoth Peter, 'for that is most to the purpose; but, for our parson, as I told you before, he was not for keeping his niece from marrying, and therefore he took care to let her know of all those that would have taken her to wife, both what they were, and what they had, and he was at her, to have her pitch upon one of them for a husband; yet would she never answer otherwise, but that she had no mind to wed as yet, as finding herself too young for the burden of wedlock. With these and such-like come-offs, she got her uncle to let her alone, and wait till she thought fit to choose for herself: for he was wont to say, that parents are not to bestow their children where they bear no liking; and, in that, he spoke like an honest man. And thus it happened, that when we least dreamed of it, that coy lass, finding herself at liberty, would needs turn shepherdess, and neither her uncle, nor all those of the village who advised her against it, could work anything upon her, but away she went to the fields, to keep her own sheep, with the other young lasses of the town. But then it was ten times worse; for no sooner was she seen abroad, when I cannot tell how many spruce gallants, both gentlemen and rich farmers, changed their garb for love of her, and followed her up and down in shepherd's guise. One of them, as I have told you, was this same Chrysostom who now lies dead, of whom it is said, he not only loved but worshipped her. However, I would not have you think or surmise, because Marcella took that course of life, and was, as it were, under no manner of keeping, that she gave the least token of naughtiness or light behaviour; for she ever was, and is still so coy, and so watchful to keep her honour pure and free from evil tongues, that among so many wooers who suitor her, there is not one can make his brags of having the least hope of ever speeding with her. For though she does not shun the company of shepherds, but uses them courteously, so far as they behave themselves handsomely; yet whensoever any one of them does but offer to break his mind to her, be it never so well meant, and only in order to marry, she casts him away from her, as with a fling, and will never have any more to say to him.

'And thus this fair maiden does more harm in this country, than the plague would do; for her courteousness and fair looks draw on everybody to love her; but then her dogged stubborn coyness breaks their hearts, and makes them ready to hang themselves; and all they can do, poor wretches, is to make a heavy complaint, and call her cruel, unkind, ungrateful, and a world of such names; whereby they plainly show what a sad condition they are in. Were you but to stay here some time, you would hear these hills and valleys ring again with the doleful moans of those she has denied, who yet cannot for the blood of them give over sneaking after her. We have a place not far off, where there are some two dozen of beech trees, and on them all you may find I do not know how many Marcellas cut in the smooth bark. On some of them there is a crown carved over the name; as much as to say that Marcella bears away the crown, and deserves the garland of beauty. Here sighs one shepherd, there another whines; here is one singing doleful ditties, there another is wringing his hands and making woeful complaints. You shall have one lay him down at night at the foot of a rock, or some oak, and there lie weeping and wailing without a wink of sleep, and talking to himself till the sun finds him the next morning; you shall have another lie stretched upon the hot sandy ground, breathing his sad lamentations to heaven, without heeding the sultry heat of the summer sun. And, all this while, the hard-hearted Marcella never minds any one of them, and does not seem to be the least concerned for them. We are all mightily at a loss to know what will be the end of all this pride and coyness, who shall be the happy man that shall at last tame her and bring her to his lure. Now, because there is nothing more certain than all this, I am the more apt to give credit to what our comrade has told us as to the occasion of Chrysostom's death; and, therefore, I would needs have you go and see him laid in his grave tomorrow; which I believe will be worth your while, for he had many friends, and it is not half a league to the place where it was his will to be buried.' 'I intend to be there,' answered Don Quixote, 'and, in the meantime, I return thee many thanks for the extraordinary satisfaction this story has afforded me.' 'Alas! Sir Knight,' replied the goatherd, 'I have not told you half the mischiefs this proud creature hath done here, but tomorrow mayhap we shall meet some shepherd by the way that will he able to tell you more. Meanwhile it will not be amiss for you to take your rest in one of the huts; for the open air is not good for your wound, though what I have put to it is so special a medicine that there is not much need to fear but it will do well enough.' Sancho, who was quite out of patience with the goatherd's long story, and wished him at the devil for his pains, at last prevailed with him to lie down in Peter's hut, where Don Quixote, in imitation of Marcella's lovers, devoted the remainder of the night to amorous expostulations with his dear Dulcinea. As for Sancho, he laid himself down between Rozinante and his ass, and slept it out, not like a disconsolate lover, but like a man that had been soundly kicked and bruised in the morning.

CHAPTER V

A continuation of the Story of Marcella

SCARCE HAD DAY BEGUN to appear from the balconies of the east, when five of the goatherds got up, and having waked Don Quixote, asked him if he held his resolution of going to the funeral, whither they were ready to bear him company. Thereupon the Knight, who desired nothing more, presently arose, and ordered Sancho to get Rozinante and the ass ready immediately; which he did with all expedition, and then they set forwards. They had not yet gone a quarter of a league, before they saw advancing towards them, out of a cross path, six shepherds clad in black skins, their heads crowned with garlands of cypress and bitter rose-bay-tree, with long holly staves in their hands. Two gentlemen on horseback, attended by three young lads on foot, came immediately after them: as they drew near, they saluted one another civilly, and after the usual question, 'Which way do ye travel?' they found they were all going the same way to see the funeral, and so they all joined company. 'I fancy, Senior Vivaldo,' said one of the gentlemen, addressing himself to the other, 'we shall not think our time misspent in going to see this famous funeral; for it must of necessity be very extraordinary, according to the account which these men have given us of the dead shepherd and his murdering mistress.' 'I am so far of your opinion,' answered Vivaldo, 'that I would not only stay one day, but a whole week rather than miss the sight.' This gave Don Quixote occasion to ask them what they had heard concerning Chrysostom and Marcella. One of the gentlemen made answer, that, having met that morning with those shepherds, they could not forbear inquiring of them, why they wore such a mournful dress. Whereupon one of them acquainted them with the sad occasion, by relating the story of a certain shepherdess, named Marcella, no less lovely than cruel, whose coyness and disdain has made a world of unfortunate lovers, and caused the death of that Chrysostom, to whose funeral they were going. In short, he repeated to Don Quixote all that Peter had told him the night before. After this, Vivaldo asked the knight why he travelled so completely armed in so peaceable a country. 'My profession,' answered the champion, 'does not permit me to ride otherwise. Luxurious feasts, sumptuous dresses, and downy ease, were invented for effeminate courtiers; but labour, vigilance, and arms are the portion of those whom the world calls knights-errant, of which number I have the honour to be one, though the most unworthy, and the meanest of the fraternity.' He needed to say no more to satisfy them his brains were out of order; however, that they might the better understand the nature of his folly, Vivaldo asked him, what he meant by a knight-errant?' Have you not read then,' cried the famous Don Quixote, 'the annals and history of Britain, where are recorded the famous deeds of King Arthur, who, according to an ancient tradition in that kingdom, never died, but was turned into a crow by enchantment, and shall one day resume his former shape, and recover his kingdom again? For which reason since that time, the people of Great Britain dare not offer to kill a crow. In this good king's time, the most noble order of the Knights of the Round Table was first instituted, and then also the amours between Sir Lancelot of the Lake and Queen Guinever were really transacted, as that history relates; they being managed and carried on by the mediation of that honourable matron the Lady Quintaniona; which produced that excellent history in verse, so sung and celebrated here in Spain:

> ' "There never was on earth a knight
>   So waited on by ladies fair
> As once was he Sir Lancelot hight,
>   When first he left his country dear."

'And the rest, which gives so delightful an account, both of his loves and feats of arms. From that time the order of knight-errantry began by degrees to dilate and extend itself into most parts of the world. Then did the great Amadis de Gaul signalise himself by heroic exploits, and so did his offspring to the fifth generation. The valorous Felixmarte of Hrycania then got immortal fame, and that undaunted knight Tirante the White, who never can be applauded to his worth. Nay, had we but lived a little sooner, we might have been blessed with the conversation of that invincible knight of our modern times, the valorous Don Belianis of Greece. And this, gentlemen, is that order of chivalry, which, as much a sinner as I am, I profess, with a due observance of the laws which those brave knights observed before me; and, for that reason I choose to wander through these solitary deserts, seeking adventures, fully resolved to expose my person to the most formidable dangers which fortune can obtrude on me, that by the strength of my arm I may relieve the weak and the distressed.'

After all this stuff, you may be sure the travellers were sufficiently convinced of Don Quixote's frenzy. Nor were they less surprised than were all those who had hitherto discovered so unaccountable a distraction in one who seemed a rational creature. However Vivaldo, who was of a gay disposition, had no sooner made the discovery, but he resolved to make the best advantage of it, that the shortness of the way would allow him.

Therefore, to give him further occasion to divert them with his whimsies, 'Methinks, Sir Knight-errant,' said he to him, 'you have taken up one of the strictest and most mortifying professions in the world. I do not think but that a Carthusian friar has a better time of it than you have.' 'Perhaps,' answered Don Quixote, 'the profession of a Carthusian may be as austere, but I am within two fingers' breadth of doubting whether it may be as beneficial to the world as ours. For, if we must speak the truth, the soldier, who puts his captain's command in execution, may be said to do as much at least as the captain who commanded him. The application is easy; for, while those religious men have nothing to do, but with all quietness and security to say their prayers for the prosperity of the world; we knights, like soldiers, execute what they do but pray for, and procure those benefits to mankind, by the strength of our arms, and at the hazard of our lives, for which they only intercede. Nor do we do this sheltered from the injuries of the air, but under no other roof than that of the wide heavens, exposed to summer's scorching heat and winter's pinching cold. So that we may justly style ourselves the ministers of Heaven, and the instruments of its justice upon earth; and as the business of war is not to be compassed without vast toil and labour, so the religious soldier must undoubtedly be preferred before the religious monk, who living still quiet and at ease, has nothing to do but to pray for the afflicted and distressed. However, gentlemen, do not imagine I would insinuate as if the profession of a knight-errant was a state of perfection equal to that of a holy recluse: I would only infer from what I have said, and what I myself endure, that ours, without question, is more laborious, more subject to the discipline of heavy blows, to maceration, to the penance of hunger and thirst, and, in a word, to rags, to want, and misery. For if you find that some knights-errant have at last, by their valour, been raised to thrones and empires, you may be sure it has been still at the expense of much sweat and blood. And had even those happier knights been deprived of those assisting sages and enchanters, who helped them in all emergencies, they would have been strangely disappointed of their mighty expectations.' 'I am of the same opinion,' replied Vivaldo, 'but one thing, among many others, which I can by no means approve in your profession, is, that when you are just going to engage in some very hazardous adventure, where your lives are evidently to be much endangered, you never once remember to commend yourselves to God, as every good Christian ought to do on such occasions, but only recommend yourselves to your mistresses, and that with as great zeal and devotion as if you worshipped no other deity; a thing which, in my opinion, strongly relishes of Paganism.' 'Sir,' replied Don Quixote, 'there is no altering that method; for, should a knight-errant do otherwise, he would too much deviate from the ancient and established customs of knight-errantry, which inviolably oblige him, just in the moment when he is rushing on, and giving birth to some dubious achievement, to have his mistress still before his eyes, still present to his mind, by a strong and lively imagine ion, and with soft, amorous, and energetic looks, imploring her favour and protection in that perilous circumstance. Nay, if nobody can overhear him, he is obliged to whisper, or speak between his teeth, some short ejaculations, to recommend himself with all the fervency imaginable to the lady of his wishes, and of this we have innumerable examples in history. Nor are you for all this to imagine, that knights-errant omit recommending themselves to Heaven, for they have leisure enough to do it even in the midst of the combat.'

'Sir,' replied Vivaldo, 'you must give me leave to tell you, I am not yet thoroughly satisfied in this point; for I have often observed in my reading, that two knights-errant, having first talked a little together, have fallen out presently, and been so highly provoked, that having turned their horses' herds, to gain room for the career, they have wheeled about, and then with all speed run full tilt at one another, hastily recommending themselves to their mistresses, in the midst of their career; and the next thing has commonly been, that one of them has been thrown to the ground, over the crupper of his horse, fairly run through and through with his enemy's lance; and the other forced to catch hold of his horse's mane to keep himself from falling. Now, I cannot apprehend how the knight that was slain had any time to recommend himself to Heaven, when his business was done so suddenly. Methinks, those hasty invocations, which in his career were directed to his mistress, should have been directed to

Heaven, as every good Christian would have done. Besides, I fancy every knight-errant has not a mistress to invoke, nor is every one of them in love.' 'Your conjecture is wrong,' replied Don Quixote; 'a knight-errant cannot be without a mistress; it is not more essential for the skies to have stars, than it is to us to be in love. Insomuch, that, I dare affirm, no history ever made mention of any knight-errant that was not a lover; for were any knight free from the impulses of that generous passion, he would not be allowed to be a lawful knight; but a misborn intruder, and one who was not admitted within the pale of knighthood at the door, but leaped the fence, and stole in like a robber and a thief.' 'Yet sir,' replied the other, 'I am much mistaken, or I have read, that Don Galaor, the brother of Amadis, never had any certain mistress to recommend himself to, and yet for all that he was not the less esteemed.' 'One swallow never makes a summer,' answered Don Quixote, 'besides, I know that knight was privately very much in love; and, as for his making his addresses wherever he met with beauty, this was an effect of his natural inclination, which he could not easily restrain. But, after all, it is an undeniable truth, that he had a favourite lady, whom he had crowned empress of his will; and to her he frequently recommended himself in private, for he did not a little value himself upon his discretion and secrecy in love.' 'Then, sir,' said Vivaldo, 'since it is so much the being of knight-errantry to be in love, I presume, you, who are of that profession, cannot be without a mistress. And therefore, if you do not set up for secrecy as much as Don Galaor did, give me leave to beg of you, in the name of all the company, that you will be pleased so far to oblige us, as to let us know the name and quality of your mistress, the place of her birth, and the charms of her person. For, without doubt, the lady cannot but esteem herself happy in being known to all the world, to be the object of the wishes of a knight so accomplished as yourself.' With that Don Quixote, breathing out a deep sigh, 'I cannot tell,' said he, 'whether this lovely enemy of my repose, is the least affected with the world's being informed of her power over my heart; all I dare say, in compliance with your request is, that her name is Dulcinea, her country La Mancha, and Toboso the happy place which she honours with her residence. As for her quality, it cannot be less than princess, seeing she is my mistress and my queen. Her beauty transcends all the united charms of her whole sex; even those chimerical perfections, which the hyperbolical imaginations of poets in love have assigned to their mistresses, cease to be incredible descriptions when applied to her, in whom all those miraculous endowments are most divinely centred. The curling locks of her bright flowing hair are purest gold; her smooth forehead the Elysian Plain; her brows are two celestial bows; her eyes two glorious suns; her cheeks two beds of roses; her lips are coral; her teeth are pearl; her neck is alabaster; her breasts marble; her hands ivory; and snow would lose its whiteness near her bosom. Then, for the parts which modesty has veiled, my imagination, not to wrong them, chooses to lose itself in silent admiration; for nature boasts nothing that may give an idea of their incomparable worth.' 'Pray, sir,' cried Vivaldo, 'oblige us with an account of her parentage, and the place of her birth, to complete the description.' 'Sir,' replied Don Quixote, 'she is not descended from the ancient Curtii, Caii, nor Scipios of Rome, nor from the more modern Colonnas, nor Ursinis; nor from the Moncadas, and Requesenes of Catalonia; nor from the Rebellas and Villanovas of Valencia; nor from the Palafoxes, Nuças, Rocabertis, Corellas, Lunas, Alagones, Urreas, Foços, or Gurreas of Arragon; nor from the Cerdas, Manriques, Mendoças, and Gusmans of Castile; nor from the Alencastros, Pallas, and Menezes of Portugal; but she derives her great original from the family of Toboso in La Mancha, a race, which, though it be modern, is sufficient to give a noble beginning to the most illustrious progenies of succeeding ages. And let no man presume to contradict me in this, unless it be upon these conditions, which Zerbin fixed at the foot of Orlando's armour:

> ' "Let none but he these arms disgrace,
>   Who dares Orlando's fury face." '

'I draw my pedigree from the Cachopines of Laredo,' replied Vivaldo, 'yet I dare not make any comparisons with the Tobosos of La Mancha; though, to deal sincerely with you, it is a family I never heard of till this moment.' 'It is strange,' said Don Quixote, 'you should never have heard of it before.'

All the rest of the company gave great attention to this discourse; and even the very goatherds and shepherds were now fully convinced that Don Quixote's brains were turned topsy turvy. But Sancho Pança believed every word that dropped from his master's mouth to be truth, as having known him from his cradle to be a man of sincerity. Yet that which somewhat staggered his faith, was this story of Dulcinea of Toboso; for he was sure he had never heard before of any such princess, nor even of the name, though he lived hard by Toboso.

As they went on thus discoursing, they saw upon the hollow road, between the neighbouring mountains, about twenty shepherds more, all accoutred in black skins with garlands on their heads, which, as they afterwards perceived, were all of yew or cyprus: six of them carried a bier covered with several sorts of boughs and flowers; which one of the goatherds espying, 'Those are they,' cried he; 'that are carrying poor Chrysostom to his grave; and it was in yonder bottom that he gave charge they should bury his corpse.' This made them all double their pace, that they might get thither in time; and so they arrived just as the bearers had set down the bier upon the ground, and four of them had begun to open the ground with their spades, just at the foot of a rock. They all saluted each other courteously, and condoled their mutual loss; and then Doll Quixote, with those who came with him, went to view the bier; where they saw the dead body of a young man in shepherd's weeds all strewed over with flowers. The deceased seemed to be about thirty years old; and, dead as he was, it is easily perceived that both his face and shape were extraordinarily handsome. Within the bier were some few books and several papers, some open, and the rest folded up. This doleful object so strangely filled all the company with sadness, that not only the beholders, but also the grave-makers, and all the mourning shepherds remained a long time silent; till at last one of the bearers, addressing himself to one of the rest: 'Look, Ambrose,' cried he, 'whether this be the place which Chrysostom meant, since you must needs have his will so punctually performed?' 'This is the very place,' answered the other: 'there it was that my unhappy friend many times told me the sad story of his cruel fortune; and there it was that he first saw that mortal enemy of mankind; there it was that he made the first discovery of his passion, no less innocent than violent; there it was that the relentless Marcella last denied, shunned him, and drove him to that extremity of sorrow and despair that hastened the sad catastrophe of his tragical and miserable life; and there it was, that, in token of so many misfortunes he desired {o be committed to the bowels of eternal oblivion.'

Then, addressing himself to Don Quixote and the rest of the travellers, 'This body, gentlemen,' said he, 'which here you now behold, was once enlivened by a soul which Heaven had enriched with the greatest part of its most valuable graces. This is the body of that Chrysostom, who was unrivalled in wit, matchless in courteousness, incomparable in gracefulness, a phœnix in friendship, generous and magnificent without ostentation, prudent and grave without pride, modest without affectation, pleasant and complaisant without meanness: in a word, the first in ever esteemable qualification, and second to none in misfortune: he loved well, and was hated; he adored, and was disdained; he begged pity of cruelty itself; he strove to move obdurate marble; pursued the wind; made his moans to solitary deserts; was constant to ingratitude; and for the recompense of his fidelity, became a prey to death in the flower of his age, through the barbarity of a shepherdess, whom he strove to immortalise by his verse; as these papers which are here deposited might testify, had he not commanded me to sacrifice them to the flames, at the same time that his body was committed to the earth.'

'Should you do so,' cried Vivaldo, 'you would appear more cruel to them than their exasperated unhappy parent. Consider, sir, it is not consistent with discretion, not even with justice, so nicely to perform the request of the dead, when it is repugnant to reason. Augustus Cæsar himself would have forfeited his title to wisdom, had he permitted that to have been effected which the divine Virgil had ordered by his will. Therefore, sir, now that you resign your friend's body to the grave, do not hurry thus the noble and only remains of that dear unhappy man to a worse fate, the death of oblivion. What though he has doomed them to perish in the height of his resentment, you ought not indiscreetly to be their executioner; but rather reprieve and redeem them from eternal silence, that they may live, and, flying through the world, transmit to all ages the dismal story of your friend's virtue, and Marcella's ingratitude, as a warning to others, that they may avoid such tempting snares and enchanting destructions; for not only to me, but to all here present, is well known the history of your enamoured and desperate friend: we are no strangers to the friendship that was between you, as also to Marcella's cruelty, which occasioned his death. Last night, being informed that he was to be buried here today, moved not so much by curiosity as pity, we are come to behold with our eyes that which gave us so much trouble to hear. Therefore, in the name of all the company, like me, deeply affected with a sense of Chrysostom's extraordinary merit and his unhappy fate, and desirous to prevent such deplorable disasters for the future, I beg that you will permit me to save some of these papers, whatever you resolve to do with the rest.' And so, without expecting an answer, he stretched out his arm, and took out those papers which lay next to his hand. 'Well, sir,' said Ambrose, 'you have found a way to make me submit, and you may keep those papers; but, for the rest, nothing shall make me alter my resolution of burning them.' Vivaldo said no more; but, being impatient to see what those papers were which he had rescued from the flames, he opened one of them immediately, and read the title of it, which was, 'The Despairing Lover.' 'That,' said Ambrose, 'was the last piece my dear friend ever wrote; and therefore, that you may all hear to what a sad condition his unhappy passion had reduced him, read it aloud, I beseech you, sir, while the grave is making.' 'With all my heart,' replied Vivaldo: and so the company, having the same desire, presently gathered round, and he read as follows.

CHAPTER VI

The unfortunate Shepherd's Verses and other unexpected matters

THE DESPAIRING LOVER

Relentless tyrant of my heart,
Attend, and hear thy slave impart
    The matchless story of his pain.
In vain I labour to conceal
What my extorted groans reveal;
    Who can be rack'd, and not complain?
But oh! who duty can express
Thy cruelty, and my distress?
    No human art, no human tongue.
Then fiends assist, and rage infuse!
A raving fury be my muse,
    And hell inspire the dismal song!
Owls, ravens, terrors of the night,
Wolves, monsters, fiends, with dire affright,
    Join your dread accents to my moans!
Join, howling winds, your sullen noise;
Thou, grumb'ling thunder, join thy voice:
    Mad seas, your roar, and hell, thy groans.
Tho' still I moan in dreary caves,
To desert rocks, and silent graves,
    My loud complaints shall wander far;
Borne, by the winds, they shall survive,
By pitying echoes kept alive,
    And fill the world with my despair.
Love's deadly cure is fierce disdain,
Distracting fear a dreadful pain,
    And jealousy a matchless woe,
Absence is death, yet while it kills,
I live with all these mortal ills,
    Scorn'd, jealous, loath'd, and absent too.
No dawn of hope e'er cheer'd my heart,
No pitying rag e'er sooth'd my smart,
    All, all the sweets of life are gone;
Then come despair, and frantic rage,

With instant fate my pain assuage,
    And end a thousand deaths by one.
But even in death let love be crown'd,
My fair destruction guiltless found.
    And I be thought with justice scorn'd:
Thus let me fall unlov'd, unbless'd,
With all my load of woes oppress'd,
    And even too wretched to he mourn'd.
O! thou, by whose destructive hate,
I'm hurry'd to this doleful fate,
    When I'm no more, thy pity spare!
I dread thy tears; oh spare 'em then –
But oh! I rave, I was too vain,
    My death can never cost a tear.
Tormented souls, on you I call,
Hear one more wretched than you all;
    Come howl as in redoubled flames.
Attend me to th' eternal night,
No other dirge, no fun'ral rite,
    A poor despairing lover claims.
And thou, my song, sad child of woe
When life is gone, and I'm below
    For thy lost parent cease to grieve:
With life and thee my woes increase
And should they not by dying cease
    Hell has no pain like these I leave.

These verses were well approved by all the company; only Vivaldo observed, that the jealousies and fears, of which the shepherd complained, did not very well agree with what he had heard of Marcella's unspotted modesty and reservedness. But Ambrose, who had been always privy to the most secret thoughts of his friend, informed him, that the unhappy Chrysostom wrote those verses when he had torn himself from his adored mistress, to try whether absence, the common cure of love, would relieve him, and mitigate his pain. And as everything disturbs an absent lover, and nothing is more usual than for him to torment himself with a thousand chimeras of his own brain, so did Chrysostom perplex himself with jealousies and suspicions, which had no ground but in his distracted imagination; and therefore whatever he said in those uneasy circumstances could never affect, or in the least prejudice, Marcella's virtuous character, upon whom, setting aside her cruelty and her disdainful haughtiness, envy itself could never fix the least reproach. Vivaldo being thus convinced, they were going to read another paper, when they were unexpectedly prevented by a kind of apparition that offered itself to their view. It was Marcella herself, who appeared at the top of the rock, at the foot of which they were digging the grave; but so beautiful, that fame seemed rather to have lessened than to have magnified her charms: those who had never seen her before, gazed on her with silent wonder and delight: nay, those who used to see her every day seemed no less lost in admiration than the rest. But scarce had Ambrose spied her, when, with anger and indignation in his heart, he cried out, 'What makest thou there, thou fierce, thou cruel basilisk of these mountains! comest thou to see whether the wounds of this murdered wretch will bleed afresh at thy presence? or comest thou, thus mounted aloft, to glory in the fatal effects of thy native inhumanity, like another Nero at the sight of flaming Rome? Or is it to trample on this unfortunate corpse, as Tarquin's ungrateful daughter did her father's? Tell us quickly why thou comest, and what thou yet desirest? For, since I know that Chrysostom's whole study was to serve and please thee while he lived, I am willing to dispose all his friends to pay thee the like obedience now he is dead.' 'I come not here to any of these ungrateful ends, Ambrose,' replied Marcella, 'but only to clear my innocence, and show the injustice of all those who lay their misfortunes and Chrysostom's death to my charge: therefore, I entreat you all, who are here at this time, to hear me a little, for I shall not need to use many words to convince people of sense of an evident truth. Heaven, you are pleased to say, has made me beautiful, and that to such a degree that you are forced, nay, as it were, compelled to love me, in spite of your endeavours to the contrary; and, for the sake of that love, you say I ought to love you again. Now, though I am sensible that whatever is beautiful is lovely, I cannot conceive, that what is loved for being handsome should be bound to love that by which it is loved, merely because it is loved. He that loves a beautiful object may happen to be ugly; and as what is ugly deserves not to be loved, it would be ridiculous to say, "I love you because you are handsome, and therefore you must love me again, though I am ugly." But suppose two persons of different sexes are equally handsome, it does not follow that their desires should be alike and reciprocal; for all beauties do not kindle love; some only recreate the sight, and never reach nor captivate the heart. Alas! should whatever is beautiful beget love, and enslave the mind, mankind's desires would ever run confused and wandering, without being able to fix their determinate choice: for, as there is an infinite number of beautiful objects, the desires would consequently be also infinite; whereas, on the contrary, I have heard that true love is still confined to one, and voluntary and unforced. This being granted, why would you have me force my inclinations for no other reason but that you say you love me? Tell me, I beseech you, had Heaven formed me as ugly as it has made me beautiful, could I justly complain of you for not loving me? Pray consider also, that I do not possess those charms by choice; such as they are, they were freely bestowed on me by Heaven: and as the viper is not to be blamed for the poison with which she kills, seeing it was assigned her by nature; so I ought not to be censured for that beauty which I derive from the same cause: for beauty in a virtuous woman is but like a distant flame, or a sharp-edged sword, and only burns and wounds those who approach too near it. Honour and virtue are the ornaments of the soul, and that body that is destitute of them cannot be esteemed beautiful, though it be naturally so. If, then, honour be one of those endowments which most adorn the body, why should she that is beloved for her beauty expose herself to the loss of it, merely to gratify the loose desires of one who, for his own selfish ends, uses all the means imaginable to make her lose it? I was born free, and that I might continue so I retired to these solitary hills and plains, where trees are my companions, and clear fountains my looking-glasses. With the trees and with the waters I communicate my thoughts and my beauty. I am a distant flame, and a sword far of: those whom I have attracted with my sight, I have undeceived with my words; and if hope be the food of desire, as I never gave any encouragement to Chrysostom, nor to any other, it may well be said it was rather his own obstinacy than my cruelty that shortened his life. If you tell me that his intentions were honest, and therefore ought to have been complied with; I answer, that when, at the very place where his grave is making, he discovered his passion, I told him I was resolved to live and die single, and that the earth alone should reap the fruit of my reservedness, and enjoy the spoils of my beauty; and if, after all the admonitions I gave him, he would persist in his obstinate pursuit, and sail against the wind, what wonder is it he should perish in the waves of his indiscretion? Had I ever encouraged him, or amused him with ambiguous words, then I had been false; and had I gratified his wishes, I had acted contrary to my better resolves. He persisted, though I had given him a due caution, and he despaired without being hated. Now I leave you to judge, whether I ought to be blamed for his sufferings? If I have deceived any one, let him complain; if I have broke my promise to any one, let him despair; if I encourage any one, let him presume; if I entertain any one, let him boast: but let no man call me cruel nor murderer, until I either deceive, break my promise, encourage, or entertain him. Heaven has not been pleased to show whether it is its will I should love by destiny, and it is vain to think I will ever do it by choice: so let this general caution serve every one of those who make their addresses to me for their own ends. And, if any one hereafter dies on my account, let not their jealousy, nor my scorn or hate, be thought the cause of their death; for she who never pretended to love, cannot make any one jealous, and a free and generous declaration of our fixed resolution ought not to be counted hate or disdain. In short, let him that calls me a tigress, and a basilisk, avoid me as a dangerous thing; and let him that calls me ungrateful, give over serving me; I assure them I will never seek nor pursue them. Therefore, let none hereafter make it their business to disturb my ease, nor strive to make me hazard among men the peace I now enjoy, which I am persuaded is not to be found with them. I have wealth enough: I neither love nor hate any one. The innocent conversation of the neighbouring shepherdesses, with the care of my flocks, help me to pass away my time, without either coquetting with this man, or practising arts to ensnare that other. My thoughts are limited by these mountains; and if they wander further, it is only to admire the beauty of Heaven, and thus, by steps, to raise my soul towards her original dwelling.'

As soon as she had said this, without expecting any answer, she left the place, and ran into the thickest of the adjoining wood, leaving all that heard her charmed with her discretion as well as with her beauty.

However, so prevalent were the charms of the latter, that some of the company, who were desperately struck, could not forbear offering to follow her, without being the least deterred by the solemn protestations which they had heard her make that very moment. But Don Quixote, perceiving their design, and believing he had now a fit opportunity to exert his knight-errantry: 'Let no man,' cried he, 'of what quality or condition soever, presume to follow the fair Marcella, under the penalty of incurring my furious displeasure. She has made it appear, by undeniable reasons, that she was not guilty of Chrysostom's death; and has positively declared her firm resolution never to condescend to the desires of any of her admirers: for which reason, instead of being importuned and persecuted, she ought to be esteemed and honoured by all good men, as being perhaps the only woman in the world that ever lived with such virtuous reservedness.' Now, whether it were that Don Quixote's threats terrified the amorous shepherds, or that Ambrose's persuasion prevailed with them to stay and see their friend interred, none of the shepherds left the place, till, the grave being made and the papers burnt, the body was deposited into the bosom of the earth, not without many tears from all the assistants. They covered the grave with a great stone till a monument was made, which Ambrose said he designed to have set up there, with the following epitaph upon it:

CHRYSOSTOM'S EPITAPH

Here of a wretched swain
The frozen body's laid,
Kill'd by the cold disdain

>   Of an ungrateful maid.
>   Here first love's pow'r he try'd,
>   Here first his pains express'd;
>   Here first he was deny'd,
>   Here first he chose to rest,
>   You who the shepherd mourn,
>   From coy Marcella fly;
>   Who Chrysostom could scorn,
>   May all mankind destroy.

The shepherds strewed the grave with many flowers and boughs; and every one, having condoled awhile with his friend Ambrose, they took their leave of him, and departed. Vivaldo and his companion did the like; as did also Don Quixote, who was not a person to forget himself on such occasions: he likewise bid adieu to the kind goatherds, that had entertained him, and to the two travellers who desired him to go with them to Seville, assuring him there was no place in the world more fertile in adventures, every street and every corner there producing some. Don Quixote returned them thanks for their kind information; but told them he neither would, nor ought to go to Seville, till he had cleared all those mountains of the thieves and robbers, which he heard very much infested all those parts. Thereupon the travellers, being unwilling to divert him from so good a design, took their leaves of him once more, and pursued their journeys, sufficiently supplied with matter to discourse on from the story of Marcella and Chrysostom, and Don Quixote's follies. As for him, he resolved to find out the shepherdess Marcella, if possible, to offer her his service to protect her to the utmost of his power: but he happened to be crossed in his designs, as you shall hear in the sequel of this true history: for here ends the second book.

BOOK III

CHAPTER I

*Giving an Account of Don Quixote's unfortunate Rencounter with certain bloody-minded and wicked Yanguesian Carriers**

THE SAGE CID HAMET BENENGELI relates, that when Don Quixote had taken leave of all those that were at Chrysostom's funeral, he and his squire went after Marcella into the wood; and, having ranged it above two hours without being able to find her, they came at last to a meadow, whose springing green, watered with a delightful and refreshing rivulet, invited, or rather pleasantly forced them to alight and give way to the heat of the day, which began to be very violent: so, leaving the ass and Rozinante to graze at large, they ransacked the wallet; and without ceremony, the master and the man fell to, and fed lovingly on what they found. Now Sancho had not taken care to tie up Rozinante, knowing him to be a horse of that sobriety and chastity, that all the mares in the pastures of Cordova could not have raised him to attempt an indecent thing. But either fortune, or the Devil, who seldom sleeps, so ordered it, that a good number of Galician mares, belonging to some Yanguesian carriers, were then feeding in the same valley, it being the custom of those men, about the hottest time of the day, to stop wherever they met with grass and water to refresh their cattle: nor could they have found a fitter place than that where Don Quixote was. Rozinante, as I said before, was chaste and modest; however, he was flesh and blood; so that, as soon as he had smelt the mares, forsaking his natural gravity and reservedness, without asking his master's leave, away he trots it briskly to make them sensible of his little necessities: but they, who it seems had more mind to feed than to be merry, received their gallant so rudely with their heels and teeth, that in a trice they broke his girths, threw down his saddle, and left him disrobed of all his equipage. And, for an addition to his misery, the carriers perceiving the violence that was offered to their mares, flew to their relief with poles and pack-staves, and so belaboured Rozinante, that he soon sank to the ground under the weight of their unmerciful blows.

Don Quixote and Sancho, perceiving at a distance the ill-usage of

* Carriers of the kingdom of Galicia.

Rozinante, ran with all speed to his rescue; and as they came near the place, panting, and almost out of breath, 'Friend Sancho,' cried Don Quixote, 'I perceive these are no knights, but only a pack of scoundrels and fellows of the lowest rank; I say it, because thus thou mayest lawfully help me to revenge the injury they have done Rozinante before our faces.' 'What a devil do ye talk of revenge?' quoth Sancho, 'we are like to revenge ourselves finely! You see they are above twenty, and we are but two; nay, perhaps but one and a half' 'I alone am worth a hundred,' replied Don Quixote; then without any more words, he drew his sword, and flew upon the Yanguesians. Sancho, encouraged by his master's example, did the like; and with the first blow which Don Quixote gave one of them, he cut through his leathern doublet, and gave him a deep slash in the shoulder. The Yanguesians, seeing themselves thus rudely handled, betook themselves to their levers and pack-staves, and then all at once, surrounding The valiant Knight and his trusty squire, they charged them and laid on with great fury. At the second round, down they settled poor Sancho, and then Don Quixote himself, who, as chance would have it, fell at the feet of Rozinante, that had not yet recovered his legs; neither could the knight's courage nor his skill avail against the fury of a number of rustical fellows armed with pack-staves. The Yanguesians, fearing the ill consequences of the mischief they had done, made all the haste they could to be gone, leaving our two adventurers in a woeful condition. The first that came to himself was Sancho Pança; who, finding himself near his master, called to him thus, with a weak and doleful voice: 'Ah, master! master! Sir, Sir Knight!' 'What is the matter, friend Sancho?' asked the Knight in the same feeble and lamentable tone. 'I could wish,' replied Sancho, 'that your worship would help me to two good draughts of the liquor you talk on, if you have any by you; perhaps it is as good to cure broken bones, as it is to heal outward wounds.' 'Oh! that I had some of it here now!' cried Don Quixote; 'we could not then be said to want anything: but I swear to thee, honest Sancho, by the faith of a knight-errant, within these two days (if no other disaster prevent me) I will have some at my disposal, or it shall hardly escape my hands.' 'Two days, sir!' replied Sancho: 'why, pray, how many days do you think it will be before we are able to stir our feet?' 'As for myself,' answered the bruised Don Quixote, 'I must own I cannot set a certain term to the days of our recovery; but it is I who am the fatal cause of all this mischief; for I ought not to have drawn my sword against a company of fellows, upon whom the honour of knighthood was never conferred; and I do not doubt but that the Lord of Hosts suffered this punishment to befall me, for transgressing thus the laws of chivalry. Therefore, friend Sancho, observe what I am going to tell thee, for it is a thing that highly concerns the welfare of us both: it is, that for the future, whenever thou perceivest us to be anyways abused by such inferior fellows, thou art not to expect I should offer to draw my sword against them; for I will not do it in the least: no, do thou then draw, and chastise them as thou thinkest fit: but if any knights come to take their parts, then will I be sure to step between thee and danger, and assault them with the utmost vigour and intrepidity. Thou hast already had a thousand proofs of the greatness of my valour, and the prevailing strength of my most dreadful arm' (so arrogant the knight was grown since his victory over the bold Biscainer); but Sancho was not so well pleased with his master's admonitions, but that he thought fit to answer him. 'Sir,' says he, 'I am a peaceful man, a harmless quiet fellow, do you see; I can make shift to pass by an injury as well as any man, as having a wife to maintain, and children to bring up; and therefore pray take this from me, by the way of advice (for I will not offer to command my master), that I will not in any wise draw my sword neither against knight nor clown, not I. I freely forgive all mankind, high and low, rich and poor, lords and beggars, whatever wrongs they ever did or may do me, without the least exception.' 'Sancho,' said his master, hearing this, 'I heartily wish I had breath enough to answer thee effectually, or that the pain which I feel in one of my short ribs would leave me but for so long as might serve to convince thee of thy error. Come, suppose, thou silly wretch, that the gale of fortune, which has hitherto been so contrary to us, should at last turn favourable, swelling the sails of our desires, so that we might with as much security as ease arrive at some of those islands which I have promised thee; what would become of thee, if after I had conquered one of them, I were to make thee lord of it? Thou wouldest certainly be found not duly qualified for that dignity, as having abjured all knighthood, all thoughts of honour, and all intention to revenge injuries, and defend thy own dominions. For thou must understand, that in kingdoms and provinces newly conquered, the hearts and minds of the inhabitants are never so thoroughly subdued, or wedded to the interests of their new sovereign, but that there is reason to fear they will endeavour to raise some commotions to change the face of affairs, and, as men say, once more try their fortune. Therefore it is necessary that the new possessor have not only understanding to govern, but also valour to attack his enemies, and defend himself on all occasions.' 'I would I had had that understanding and valour you talk of,' quoth Sancho; 'but now, sir, I must be free to tell you, I have more need of a surgeon than of a preacher. Pray, try whether you can rise, and we will help Rozinante, though he does not deserve it; for he is the chief cause of all this beating. For my part, I could never have believed the like of him before, for I always took him for as chaste and sober a person as myself In short, it is a true saying, that "a man must eat a peck of salt with his friend, before he knows him"; and I find "there is nothing sure in this world": for who would have thought, after the dreadful slashes you gave to that knight-errant, such a terrible shower of bastinadoes would so soon have fallen upon our shoulders?' 'As for thine,' replied Don Quixote, 'I doubt they are used to endure such sort of showers; but mine, that were nursed in soft linen, will most certainly be longer sensible of this misfortune; and were it not that I imagine (but why do I say imagine?), were it not that I am positively sure, that all these inconveniences are inseparable from the profession of chivalry, I would abandon myself to grief, and die of mere despair on this very spot.' 'I beseech you, sir,' quoth Sancho, 'since these rubs are the vails of your trade of knighthood, tell me whether they use to come often, or whether we may look for them at set times: for, I fancy, if we meet but with two such harvests more, we shall never be able to reap the third, unless God of His infinite mercy assist us.' 'Know, friend Sancho,' returned Don Quixote, 'that the lives of knights-errant are subject to a thousand hazards and misfortunes: but, on the other side, they may at any time suddenly become kings and emperors, as experience has demonstrated in many knights, of whose histories I have a perfect knowledge. And I could tell thee now (would my pain suffer me) of some of them, who have raised themselves to those high dignities only by the valour of their arm; and those very knights, both before and after their advancement, were involved in many calamities: for, the valorous Amadis de Gaul saw himself in the power of his mortal enemy Archelaus the enchanter, of whom it is credibly reported, that when he held him prisoner, he gave him above two hundred stripes with his horse bridle, after he had tied him to a pillar in the court-yard of his house. There is also a secret author of no little credit relates, that the Knight of the Sun, being taken in a trap in a certain castle, was hurried to a deep dungeon, where, after they had bound him hand and foot, they forcibly gave him a clyster of snow-water and sand, which would probably have cost him his life, had he not been assisted in that distress by a wise magician, his particular friend. Thus I may well bear my misfortune patiently, since those which so many greater persons have endured may be said to outdo it: for, I would have thee to know, that those wounds that are given with the instruments and tools which a man happens to have in his hand, do not really disgrace the person struck. We read it expressly in the laws of duels, "That if a shoemaker strikes another man with his last which he held in his hand, though it be of wood, as a cudgel is, yet the party who was struck with it shall not be said to have been cudgelled." I tell thee this, that thou may not think we are in the least dishonoured, though we have been horribly beaten in this rencounter: for the weapons which those men used were but instruments of their profession, and not one of them, as I very well remember, had either tuck, or sword, or dagger.' 'They gave me no leisure,' quoth Sancho, 'to examine things so narrowly; for I had no sooner laid my hand on my cutlass,* but they crossed my shoulders with such a wooden blessing, as settled me on the ground without sense or motion, where you see me lie, and where I do not trouble my head whether it be a disgrace to be mauled with cudgels or with pack-staves: let them be what they will, I am only vexed to feel them so heavy on my shoulders, where I am afraid they are imprinted as deep as they are on my mind.' 'For all this,' replied Don Quixote, 'I must inform thee, friend Sancho, that there is no remembrance which time will not deface, nor no pain to which death will not put a period.' 'Thank you for nothing!' quoth Sancho, 'what worse can befall us, than to have only death to trust to? Were our affliction to be cured with a plaster or two, a man might have some patience; but, for aught I see, all the salves in a hospital will not set us on our best legs again.' 'Come, no more of this,' cried Don Quixote; 'take courage, and make a virtue of necessity; for it is what I am resolved to do. Let us see how it fares with Rozinante; for, if I am not mistaken, the poor creature has not been the least sufferer in this adventure.' 'No wonder at that,' quoth Sancho; 'seeing he is a knight-errant too; I rather wonder how my ass has escaped so well, while we have fared so ill.' 'In our disasters,' returned Don Quixote, 'fortune leaves always some door open to come at a remedy. I say it, Sancho, because that little beast may now supply the want of Rozinante, to carry me to some castle, where I may get cured of my wounds. Nor do I esteem this kind of riding dishonourable; for I remember, that the good old Silenus, tutor and governor to the jovial God of Wine, rode very fairly on a goodly ass, when he made his entry into the city with a hundred gates.' 'Ay,' quoth Sancho, 'it will do well enough, could you ride as fairly on your ass as he did on his; but there in a deal of difference between riding and being laid across the pannel like a pack of rubbish.' 'The wounds which are received in combat,' said Don Quixote, 'rather add to our honour than deprive us of it; therefore, good Sancho, trouble me with no more replies, but, as I said, endeavour to get up, and lay me as thou pleasest upon thy ass, that we may leave this place ere night steal upon us.' 'But, sir,' cried Sancho, 'I have heard you say, that it is a common thing among you knights-errant to sleep in the fields and deserts the best part of the year, and that you look upon it to be a very happy kind of life.' 'That is to say,' replied Don Quixote, 'when we can do no better, or when we are in love; and this is so true, that there have been knights who have dwelt on rocks, exposed to the sun, and other inclemencies of the sky, for the space of two years, without their lady's knowledge: one of those was Amadis, when, assuming the name of "The Lovely Obscure," he inhabited the bare rock, either

---

* 'Tizona': the romantic name of the sword which the Spanish General, Roderick Diaz de Bivar, used against the Moors.

eight gears or eight months, I cannot now punctually tell which of the two; for I do not thoroughly remember that passage. Let it suffice that there he dwelt, doing penance, for I do not know what unkindness his Lady Oriana had showed him. But, setting these discourses aside, pray thee dispatch, lest some mischief befall the ass, as it has done Rozinante.' 'That would be the Devil indeed,' replied Sancho, and, so breathing out some thirty lamentations, threescore sighs, and a hundred and twenty plagues and poxes on those that had decoyed him thither, he at last got upon his legs, yet not so but that he went stooping, with his body bent like a Turk's bow, not being able to stand upright. Yet, in this crooked posture, he made a shift to harness his ass, who had not forgot to take his share of licentiousness that day. After this, he helped up Rozinante, who, could his tongue have expressed his sorrows, would certainly not have been behind-hand with Sancho and his master. After many bitter Ohs, and screwed faces, Sancho laid Don Quixote on the ass, tied Rozinante to its tail, and then, leading the ass by the halter, he took the nearest way that he could guess to the high road; to which he luckily came before he had travelled a short league, and then he discovered an inn; which, in spite of all he could say, Don Quixote was pleased to mistake for a castle. Sancho swore bloodily it was an inn, and his master was as positive of the contrary. In short, their dispute lasted so long, that before they could decide it they reached the inn-door, where Sancho straight went in, with all his train, without troubling himself any further about the matter.

CHAPTER II

What happened to Don Quixote in the Inn which he took for a Castle

THE INNKEEPER, seeing Don Quixote lying quite athwart the ass, asked Sancho what ailed him? Sancho answered, it was nothing, only his master had got a fall from the top of a rock to the bottom, and had bruised his sides a little. The innkeeper had a wife very different from the common sort of hostesses, for she was of a charitable nature, and very compassionate of her neighbour's affliction; which made her immediately take care of Don Quixote, and call her daughter (a good handsome girl) to set her helping hand to his cure. One of the servants in the inn was an Asturian wench, a broad-faced, flat-headed, saddle-nosed dowdy, blind of one eye, and the other almost out. However, the activity of her body supplied all other defects. She was not above three feet high from her heels to her head; and her shoulders, which somewhat loaded her, as having too much flesh upon them, made her look downwards oftener than she could have wished. This charming original likewise assisted the mistress and the daughter; and, with the latter, helped to make the Knight's bed, and a sorry one it was; the room where it stood was an old gambling cock-loft, which by manifold signs seemed to have been, in the days of yore, a repository for chopped straw. Somewhat further, in a corner of that garret, a carrier had his lodging; and, though his bed was nothing but the pannels and coverings of his mules, it was much better than that of Don Quixote, which only consisted of four rough-hewn boards laid upon two uneven tressels, a flock-bed, that, for thinness, might well have passed for a quilt, and was full of knobs and bunches, which, had they not peeped out through many a hole, and shown themselves to be of wool, might well have been taken for stones. The rest of that extraordinary bed's furniture was a pair of sheets, which rather seemed to be of leather than of linen-cloth, and a coverlet whose every individual thread you might have told, and never have missed one in the tale.

In this ungracious bed was the Knight laid to rest his belaboured carcase, and presently the hostess and her daughter anointed and plastered him all over, while Maritornes (for that was the name of the Asturian wench) held the candle. The hostess, while she greased him, wondering to see him so bruised all over: 'I fancy,' said she, 'those bumps look much more like a dry beating than a fall.' 'It was no dry beating, mistress, I promise you,' quoth Sancho, 'but the rock had I know not how many cragged ends and knobs, whereof every one gave my master a token of his kindness. And by the way, forsooth,' continued he, 'I beseech you save a little of that same tow and ointment for me too; for I do not know what is the matter with my back, but I fancy I stand mainly in want of a little greasing too.' 'What! I suppose you fell too?' quoth the landlady. 'Not I,' quoth Sancho, 'but the very fright that I took to see my master tumble down the rock has so wrought upon my body, that I am as sore as if I had been sadly mauled.' 'It may well be as you say,' cried the innkeeper's daughter, 'for I have dreamed several times that I have been falling from the top of a high tower without ever coming to the ground; and, when I waked, I have found myself as out of order, and as bruised, as if I had fallen in good earnest.' 'That is even my case, mistress,' quoth Sancho; 'only ill luck would have it so, that I should find myself even almost as battered and bruised as my lord Don Quixote, and yet all the while be as broad awake as I am now.' 'How do you call this same gentleman?' quoth Maritornes. 'He is Don Quixote de la Mancha,' replied Sancho; 'and he is a knight-errant, and one of the primest and stoutest that ever the sun shined on.' 'A knight-errant,' cried the wench, 'pray, what is that?' 'Heyday!' cried Sancho, 'does the wench know no more of the world than that comes to? Why, a knight-errant is a thing which in two words you see well cudgelled, and then an emperor. Today there is not a more wretched thing upon the earth, and yet tomorrow he will have you two or three kingdoms to give away to his squire.' 'How comes it to pass, then,' quoth the landlady, 'that thou, who art this great person's squire, hast not yet got thee at least an earldom?' 'Fair and softly goes far,' replied Sancho; 'why, we have not been a month in our gears, so that we have not yet encountered any adventure worth the naming; besides, many a time we look for one thing, and light on another. But if my lord Don Quixote happens to get well again, and I escape remaining a cripple, I will not take the best title in the land for what I am sure will fall to my share.' Here Don Quixote, who had listened with great attention to all these discourses, raised himself up in his bed with much ado, and taking the hostess in a most obliging manner by the hand, 'Believe me,' said he, 'beautiful lady, you may well esteem it a happiness that you have now the opportunity to entertain my person in your castle. Self praise is unworthy a man of honour, and therefore I shall say no more of myself, but my squire will inform you who I am; only thus much let me add, that I will eternally preserve your kindness in the treasury of my remembrance, and study all occasions to testify my gratitude: and I wish,' continued he, 'the Powers above had so disposed my fate, that I were not already love's devoted slave, and captivated by the charms of the disdainful beauty who engrosses all my softer thoughts; for then would I be proud to sacrifice my liberty to this beautiful damsel.' The hostess, her daughter, and the kind-hearted Maritornes stared on one another, quite at a loss for the meaning of this high-flown language, which they understood full as well as if it had been Greek. Yet, conceiving these were words of compliment and courtship, they looked upon him, and admired him as a man of another world: and so, having made him such returns as innkeeper's breeding could afford, they left him to his rest; only Maritornes stayed to rub down Sancho, who wanted her help no less than his master.

Now you must know, that the carrier and she had agreed to pass the night together; and she had given him her word that, as soon as all the people in the inn were in bed, she would be sure to come to him, and be at his service. And it is said of this good-natured thing, that whenever she had passed her word in such cases, she was sure to make it good, though she had made the promise in the midst of a wood, and without any witness at all: for she stood much upon her gentility, though she undervalued herself so far as to serve in an inn; often saying, that nothing but crosses and necessity could have made her stoop to it.

Don Quixote's hard, scanty, beggarly, miserable bed was the first of the four in that wretched apartment; next to that was Sancho's kennel, which consisted of nothing but a bed-mat and a coverlet, that rather seemed shorn canvas than a rug. Beyond these two beds was that of the carrier, made, as we have said, of the pannels and furniture of two of the best of twelve mules which he kept, every one of them goodly beasts, and in special good case; for he was one of the richest muleteers of Arevalo, as the Moorish author of this history relates, who makes particular mention of him, as having been acquainted with him; nay, some do not stick to say, he was somewhat of kin to him. However it be, it appears that Cid Hamet Benengeli was a very exact historian, since he takes care to give us an account of things that seem so inconsiderable and trivial. A laudable example which these historians should follow, who usually relate matters so concisely, that we have scarcely a smack of them, leaving the most essential part of the story drowned in the bottom of the ink-horn, either through neglect, malice, or ignorance. A thousand blessings then be given to the curious author of Tablante of Ricamonte, and to that other indefatigable sage who recorded the achievements of Count Tomillas; for they have described even the most minute and trifling circumstances with a singular preciseness. But, to return to our story, you must know, that, after the carrier had visited his mules, and given them their second course,* he laid himself down upon his pannels, in expectation of the most punctual Maritornes's kind visit. By this time Sancho, duly greased and anointed, had crept into his sty, where he did all he could to sleep, but his aching ribs did all they could to prevent him. As for the Knight, whose sides were in as bad circumstances as his squire's, he lay with both his eyes open like a hare. And now was every soul in the inn gone to bed, nor any light to be seen, except that of a lamp which hung in the middle of the gate-way. This general tranquillity setting Don Quixote's thoughts at work, offered to his imagination one of the most absurd follies that ever crept into a distempered brain from the perusal of romantic whimsies. Now he fancied himself to be in a famous castle (for, as we have already said, all the inns he lodged in seemed no less than castles to him) and that the innkeeper's daughter (consequently daughter to the lord of the castle) strangely captivated with his graceful presence and gallantry, had promised him the pleasure of her embraces, as soon as her father and mother were gone to rest. This chimera disturbed him, as if it had been a real truth; so that he began to be mightily perplexed, reflecting on the danger to which his honour was exposed. But at last his virtue overcame the powerful temptation, and he firmly resolved not to be guilty of the least infidelity to his lady Dulcinea del Toboso, though Queen Guinever herself, with her trusty Matron Quintaniona, should join to decoy him into the alluring snare.

While these wild imaginations worked in his brain, the gentle Maritornes

* In Spain they get up in the night to dress their cattle, and give them barley and straw, in place of oats and hay.

was mindful of her assignation, and with soft and wary steps, bare-foot, and in her smock, with her hair gathered up in a fustian coif, stole into the room, and felt about for her beloved carrier's bed: but scarce had she got to the door, when Don Quixote, whose ears were on the scout, was sensible that something was coming in: and therefore, having raised himself in his bed, sore and wrapped up in plasters as he was, he stretched out his arms to receive his fancied damsel, and caught hold of Maritornes by the wrist, as she was, with her arms stretched, groping her way to her paramour; he pulled her to him, and made her sit down by his bed's side, she not daring to speak a word all the while. Now, as he imagined her to be the lord of the castle's daughter, her smock, which was of the coarsest canvas, seemed to him of the finest holland; and the glass beads about her wrist, precious oriental pearls; her hair, that was almost as rough as a horse's mane, he took to be soft flowing threads of bright curling gold; and her breath, that had a stronger hogo than stale venison, was to him a grateful compound of the most fragrant perfumes of Arabia. In short, flattering imagination transformed her into the likeness of those romantic beauties, one of whom, as he remembered to have read, came to pay a private visit to a wounded knight, with whom she was desperately in love; and the poor gentleman's obstinate folly had so infatuated his outward sense, that his feeling and his smell could not in the least undeceive him, and he thought he had no less than a balmy Venus in his arms, while he hugged a fulsome bundle of deformities, that would have turned any man's stomach but a sharp-set carrier's. Therefore clasping her still closer, with a soft and amorous whisper: 'Oh! thou most lovely temptation,' cried he; 'oh! that I now might but pay a warm acknowledgment for the mighty blessing which your extravagant goodness would lavish on me; yes, most beautiful charmer, I would give an empire to purchase your more desirable embraces: but fortune, madam, fortune, that tyrant of my life, that unrelenting enemy to the truly deserving, has maliciously hurried and riveted me to this bed, where I lie so bruised and macerated, that, though I were eager to gratify your desires, I should at this dear unhappy minute be doomed to impotence; nay, to that unlucky bar fate has added a yet more invincible obstacle; I mean my plighted faith to the unrivalled Dulcinea del Toboso, the sole mistress of my wishes, and absolute sovereign of my heart. Oh! did not this oppose my present happiness, I could never be so dull and insensible a knight, as to lose the benefit of this extraordinary favour which you have now condescended to offer me.'

Poor Maritornes all this while sweated for fear and anxiety, to find herself thus locked in the Knight's arms; and without either understanding, or willing to understand his florid excuses, she did what she could to get from him, and sheer off without speaking a word. On the other side, the carrier, whose lewd thoughts kept him awake, having heard his trusty Lady when she first came in, and listened ever since to the Knight's discourse, began to be afraid that she had made some other assignation; and so, without any more ado he crept softly to Don Quixote's bed, where he listened a while to hear what would be the end of all this talk, which he could not understand. But perceiving at last, by the struggling of his faithful Maritornes, that it was none of her fault, and that the Knight strove to detain her against her will, he could by no means bear his familiarity; and therefore, taking it in mighty dudgeon, he up with his fist, and hit the enamoured Knight such a swinging blow on the jaws, that his face was all over blood in a moment. And, not satisfied with this, he goes on the top of the Knight, and with his splay-feet betrampled him as if he had been trampling a hay-mow. With that the bed, whose foundations were none of the best, sunk under the additional load of the carrier, and fell with such a noise, that it waked the innkeeper, who presently suspects it to be one of Maritornes's nightly skirmishes; and therefore, having called her aloud, and finding that she did not answer, he lighted a lamp, and made to the place where he heard the rustle. The wench, who heard him coming, knowing him to be of a passionate nature, was scared out of her wits, and fled for shelter to Sancho's sty, where he lay snoring to some tune: there she pigged in, and slunk under the coverlet, where she lay snug, and trussed up as round as an egg. Presently her master came in, in a mighty heat: 'Where is this damned whore?' cried he. 'I dare say, this is one of her pranks.' By this, Sancho awaked; and feeling that unusual lump, which almost overlaid him, he took it to be the night-mare, and began to lap about him with his fists, and thumped the wench so unmercifully, that at last flesh and blood were no longer able to bear it; and, forgetting the danger she was in, and her dear reputation, she paid him back his thumps as fast as her fists could lay them on, and soon roused the drowsy squire out of his sluggishness, whether he would or no: who, finding himself thus pommelled by he did not know who, bustled up in his nest, and catching hold of Maritornes, they began the most pleasant skirmish in the world. When the carrier perceiving, by the light of the innkeeper's lamp, the dismal condition that his dear mistress was in, presently took her part; and leaving the knight, whom he had more than sufficiently mauled, flew at the squire, and paid him confoundedly. On the other hand, the innkeeper, who took the wench to be the cause of all this hurly-burly, cuffed and kicked, and kicked and cuffed her over and over again: and so there was a strange multiplication of fisticuffs and drubbings. The carrier pommelled Sancho, Sancho mauled the wench, the wench belaboured the squire, and the innkeeper thrashed her again: and all of them laid on with such expedition, that you would have thought they had been afraid of losing time. But the jest was, that in the heat of the fray the lamp went out, so that being now in the dark, they plied one another at a venture: they struck and tore, all went to rack, while nails and fists flew about without mercy.

There happened to lodge that night in the inn one of the officers belonging to that society which they call the old holy brotherhood of Toledo, whose chief office is to look after thieves and robbers. Being waked with the heavy bustle, he presently jumped out of his bed, and, with his short staff in one hand, and a tin-box with his commission in it in the other, he groped out his way; and, having entered the room in the dark, cried out, 'I charge ye all to keep the peace: I am an officer of the holy brotherhood.' The first he popped his hand upon happened to be the poor battered knight, who lay upon his back at his full length, without any feeling, upon the ruins of his bed. The officer, having caught him by the beard, presently cried out, 'I charge you to aid and assist me: 'but finding he could not stir, though he gripped him hard, he presently imagined him to be dead, and murdered by the rest in the room. With that he bawled out to have the gates of the inn shut. 'Here is a man murdered,' cried he; 'look that nobody makes his escape.' These words struck all the combatants with such a terror, that as soon as they reached their ears, they gave over, and left the argument undecided. Away stole the innkeeper to his own room, the carrier to his pannels, and the wench to her kennel; only the unfortunate knight, and his as unfortunate squire, remained where they lay, not being able to stir; while the officer, having let go Don Quixote's beard, went out for a light, in order to apprehend the supposed murderers: but the innkeeper having wisely put out the lamp in the gateway, as he sneaked out of the room, the officer was obliged to repair to the kitchen-chimney, where, with much ado, puffing and blowing a long while amidst the embers, he at last made shift to get a light.

CHAPTER III

A further Account of the innumerable Hardships which the brave Don Quixote, and his worthy Squire Sancho, underwent in the Inn

DON QUIXOTE, who by his time was come to himself, began to call Sancho with the same lamentable tone as the day before, when he had been beaten by the carriers in the meadow. 'Sancho,' cried he, 'friend Sancho! art thou asleep? art thou asleep, friend Sancho?' 'Sleep!' replied Sancho, mightily out of humour, 'may Old Nick rock my cradle then: why, how the devil should I sleep, when all the imps of hell have been tormenting me to-night?' 'Nay, thou art in the right,' answered Don

Quixote, 'for either I have no skill in these matters, or this castle is enchanted. Hear what I say to thee, but first swear thou wilt never reveal it till after my death.' 'I swear it,' quoth Sancho. 'I am thus cautious,' said Don Quixote, 'because I hate to take away the reputation of any person.' 'Why,' quoth Sancho, 'I tell you again, I swear never to speak a word of the matter while you live; and I wish I may be at liberty to talk on it tomorrow.' 'Why!' cried Don Quixote, 'have I done thee so much wrong, Sancho, that you would have me die so soon?' 'Nay, it is not for that neither,' quoth Sancho; 'but because I cannot abide to keep things long, for fear they should grow mouldy.' 'Well, let it be as thou pleasest,' said Don Quixote: 'for I dare trust greater concerns to thy courtesy and affection. In short, know, that this very night there happened to me one of the strangest adventures that can be imagined; for the daughter of the lord of this castle came to me, who is one of the most engaging and most beautiful damsels that ever nature has been proud to boast of: what could I not tell thee of the charms of her shape and face, and the perfections of her mind! what could I not add of other hidden beauties, which I condemn to silence and oblivion, lest I endanger my allegiance and fidelity to my lady Dulcinea del Toboso! I will only tell thee, that the Heavens, envying the inestimable happiness which fortune had thrown into my hand; or rather, because this castle is enchanted, it happened, that in the midst of the most tender and passionate discourses that passed between us, the profane hand of some mighty giant, which I could not see, nor imagine whence it came, hit me such a dreadful blow on the jaws, that they are still embrued with blood; after which the discourteous wretch, presuming on my present weakness, did so barbarously bruise me, that I feel myself in a worse condition now than I did yesterday, after the carriers had so roughly handled me for Rozinante's incontinency: from which I conjecture, that the treasure of this damsel's beauty is guarded by some enchanted Moor, and not reserved for me.'

'Nor for me neither,' quoth Sancho; 'for I have been rib-roasted by above four hundred Moors, who have hammered my bones in such guise, that I may safely say, the assault and battery made on my body by the carrier's poles and pack-staves, were but ticklings and strokings with a feather to this.* But, sir, pray tell me, do you call this such a pleasant adventure, when we are so lamentably pounded after it? And yet your hap may well be accounted better than mine, seeing you have hugged that fair maiden in your arms. But I, what have I had, I pray you, but the heaviest blows that ever fell on a poor man's shoulders? Woe is me and the mother that bore me, for I neither am, nor ever mean to be a knight-errant; and yet, of all the misadventures, the greater part falls still to my lot.' 'What,

---

* In the original, 'were tarts and cheese-cakes to this:' *Tortas y pan pinta*.

hast thou been beaten as well as I?' said Don Quixote. 'What a plague,' cried Sancho, 'have not I been telling you so all this while!' 'Come, never let it trouble thee, friend Sancho,' replied Don Quixote; 'for I will immediately make the precious balsam, that will cure thee in the twinkling of an eye.'

By this time the officer, having lighted his lamp, came into the room, to see who it was that was murdered. Sancho seeing him enter in his shirt, a napkin wrapped about his head like a turban, and the lamp in his hand, he being also an ugly ill-looked fellow: 'Sir,' quoth the squire to his master, 'pray see whether this be not the enchanted Moor, that is come again to have the other bout with me, and try whether he has not left some place unbruised* for him now to maul as much as the rest.' 'It cannot be the Moor,' replied Don Quixote; 'for persons enchanted are to be seen by nobody.' 'If they do not suffer themselves to be seen,' quoth Sancho, 'at least they suffer themselves to be felt: if not, let my carcase bear witness.' 'So might mine,' cried Don Quixote: 'yet this is no sufficient reason to prove, that what we see is the enchanted Moor.'

While they were thus arguing, the officer advanced, and wondered to hear two men talk so calmly to one another there: yet finding the unfortunate knight lying in the same deplorable posture as he left him, stretched out like a corpse, bloody, bruised and beplastered, and not able to stir himself, 'How is it, honest fellow,' quoth he to the champion, 'how do you find yourself?' 'Were I your fellow,' replied Don Quixote, 'I would have a little more manners than you have, you blockhead, you; is that your way of approaching knights-errant in this country?' The officer could not bear such a reprimand from one who made so scurvy a figure, and lifting up the lamp, oil and all, hit Don Quixote such a blow on the head with it, that he had reason to fear he had made work for the surgeon, and therefore stole presently out of the room, under the protection of the night. 'Well, sir,' quoth Sancho, 'do you think now it was the enchanted Moor, or no? For my part, I think he keeps the treasure you talk of for others, and reserves only kicks, cuffs, thumps and knocks for your worship and myself.' 'I am now convinced,' answered Don Quixote; 'therefore let us wave that resentment of these injuries, which we might otherwise justly show; for considering these enchanters can make themselves invisible when they please, it is needless to think of revenge. But I pray thee rise, if thou canst, Sancho, and desire the governor of the castle to send me some oil, salt, wine and rosemary, that I may make my healing balsam; for truly I want it extremely, so fast the blood flows out of the wound which the phantasm gave me just now.'

---

* The new translation has it, 'Left something at the bottom of the ink-horn;' which is indeed what Cervantes literally says, *Si se dexo algo en el tintero*.

Sancho then got up as fast as his aching bones would let him, and with much ado made shift to crawl out of the room to look for the innkeeper, and stumbling by the way on the officer, who stood hearkening to know what mischief he had done. 'Sir,' quoth he to him, 'for heaven's sake, do so much as help us to a little oil, salt, wine and rosemary, to make a medicine for one of the best knights-errant that ever trod one shoe of leather, who lies yonder grievously wounded by the enchanted Moor of this inn.' The officer hearing him talk at that rate, took him to be one out of his wits; and it beginning to be daylight, he opened the inn-door, and told the innkeeper what Sancho wanted. The host presently provided the desired ingredients, and Sancho crept back with them to his master, whom he found holding his head and sadly complaining of the pain which he felt there; though, after all, the lamp had done him no more harm than only raising of two huge bumps; for that which he fancied to be blood was only sweat, and the oil of the lamp, that had liquored his hair and face.

The knight took all the ingredients, and having mixed them together, he had them set over the fire, and there kept them boiling till he thought they were enough That done, he asked for a vial to put this precious liquor in: but there being none to be got, the innkeeper presented him with an old earthen jug, and Don Quixote was forced to be contented with that. Then he mumbled over the pot above fourscore *paternosters*, and as many *ave-maries*, *salve reginas*, and *credos*, making the sign of the Cross at every word, by way of benediction. At which ceremony Sancho, the innkeeper, and the officer were present; for, as for the carrier, he was gone to look after his mules, and took no manner of notice of what was passed. This blessed medicine being made, Don Quixote resolved to make an immediate experiment of it on himself; and to that purpose he took off a good draught of the overplus, which the pot would not hold: but he had scarce gulped it down, when it set him a-vomiting so violently, that you would have thought he would have cast up his heart, liver, and guts; and his reaching and straining put him into such a sweat that he desired to be covered up warm, and left to his repose. With that they left him, and he slept three whole hours; and then waking, found himself so wonderfully eased, that he made no question but he had now the right balsam of Fierabrass; and therefore he thought he might safely undertake all the most dangerous adventures in the world, without the least hazard of his person.

Sancho, encouraged by the wonderful effect of the balsam on his master, begged that he would be pleased to give him leave to sip up what was left in the pot, which was no small quantity; and the Don having consented, honest Sancho lifted it up with both his hands, and, with a strong faith and better will, poured every drop down his throat. Now the man's stomach not being so nice as his master's, the drench did not set him a-vomiting after that manner, but caused such a wambling in his stomach, such a bitter loathing, kecking, and reaching, and such grinding pangs, with cold sweats and swoonings, that he verily believed his last hour was come, and in the midst of his agony gave both the balsam and him that made it to the Devil. 'Friend,' said Don Quixote, seeing him in that condition, 'I begin to think all this pain befalls thee, only because thou hast not received the order of knighthood; for, it is my opinion, this balsam ought to be used by no man that is not a professed knight.' 'What a plague did you mean then by letting me drink it?' quoth Sancho. 'A murrain on me and all my generation, why did not you tell me this before?' At length the dose began to work to some purpose, and forced its way at both ends so copiously, that both his bed-mat and coverlet were soon made unfit for any further use; and all the while he strained so hard, that not only himself but the standers-by thought he would have died. This dreadful hurricane lasted about two hours; and then, too, instead of finding himself as free from pain as his master, he felt himself as feeble, and so far spent, that he was not able to stand.

But Don Quixote, as we have said, found himself in an excellent temper; and his active soul loathing an inglorious repose, he presently was impatient to depart to perform the duties of his adventurous profession: for he thought those moments that were trifled away in amusements or other concerns, only a blank in life; and all delays a depriving distressed persons, and the world in general, of his needed assistance The confidence which he reposed in his balsam, heightened, if possible, his resolution; and thus, carried away by his eager thoughts, he saddled Rozinante himself, and then put the pannel upon the ass, and his squire upon the pannel, after he had helped him to huddle on his clothes: that done, he mounted his steed; and, having spied a javelin that stood in a corner, he seized and appropriated it to himself, to supply the want of his lance. Above twenty people that were in the inn stood spectators of all these transactions; and among the rest the innkeeper's daughter, from whom Don Quixote had not power to withdraw his eyes, breathing out at every glance a deep sigh from the very bottom of his heart; which those who had seen him so mortified the night before, took to proceed from the pain of his bruises.

And now, being ready to set forwards, he called for the master of the house, and with a grave delivery: 'My Lord Governor,' cried he, 'the favours I have received in your castle are so great and extraordinary, that they bind my grateful soul to an eternal acknowledgment: therefore that I may be so happy as to discharge part of the obligation, think if there be ever a proud mortal breathing on whom you desire to be revenged for some affront or other injury, and acquaint me with it now, and by my order of knighthood which binds me to protect the weak, relieve the oppressed, and punish the bad, I promise you I will take effectual care, that you shall have ample satisfaction to the utmost of your wishes.' 'Sir

Knight,' answered the innkeeper, with an austere gravity, 'I shall not need your assistance to revenge any wrong that may have been offered to my person; for I would have you to understand, that I am able to do myself justice, whenever any man presumes to do me wrong: therefore all the satisfaction I desire is, that you will pay your reckoning for horse meat and man's meat, and all your expenses in my inn.' 'How!' cried Don Quixote, 'is this an inn?' 'Yes,' answered the host, 'and one of the most noted, and of the best repute upon the road.' 'How strangely have I been mistaken then!' cried Don Quixote; 'upon my honour I took it for a castle, and a considerable one too: but, if it be an inn, and not a castle, all I have to say is, that you must excuse me from paying anything; for I would by no means break the laws which we knights-errant are bound to observe: nor was it ever known, that they ever paid in any inn whatsoever; for this is the least recompense that can be allowed them for the intolerable labours they endure day and night, winter and summer. on foot and on horseback, pinched with hunger, choked with thirst, and exposed to all the injuries of the air, and all the inconveniences in the world.' 'I have nothing to do with all this,' cried the innkeeper: 'pay your reckoning, and do not trouble me with your foolish stories of a cock and a bull: I cannot afford to keep house at that rate.' 'Thou art both a fool and a knave of an innkeeper,' replied Don Quixote: and with that, clapping spurs to Rozinante, and brandishing his javelin at his host, he rode out of the inn without any opposition, and got a good way from it, without so much as once looking behind him to see whether his squire came after him.

The Knight being marched off, there remained only the squire, who was stopped for the reckoning. However, he swore bloodily he would not pay a cross; for the self-same law that acquitted the Knight acquitted the squire. This put the innkeeper into a great passion, and made him threaten Sancho very hard, telling him, if he would not pay him by fair means, he would have him laid by the heels that moment. Sancho swore by his master's knighthood, he would sooner part with his life than his money on such an account: nor should the squires in after ages ever have occasion to upbraid him with giving so ill a precedent, or breaking their rights. But, as ill luck would have it, there happened to be in the inn four Segovia clothiers, three Cordova point-makers, and two Sevil hucksters, all brisk, gamesome, arch fellows; who, agreeing all in the same design, encompassed Sancho, and pulled him off his ass, while one of them went and got a blanket. Then they put the unfortunate squire into it, and observing the roof of the place they were in to be somewhat too low for their purpose, they carried him into the back yard, which had no limits but the sky, and there they tossed him for several times together in the blanket, as they do dogs on Shrove Tuesday. Poor Sancho made so grievous an outcry all the while, that his master heard him, and imagined those lamentations were of some person in distress, and consequently the occasion of some adventure: but, having at last distinguished the voice, he made to the inn with a broken gallop; and, finding the gates shut, he rode about to see whether he might not find some other way to get in. But he no sooner came to the back yard wall, which was none of the highest, when he was an eye-witness of the scurvy trick that was put upon his squire. There he saw him ascend and descend, and frolic and caper in the air with so much nimbleness and agility, that it is thought the Knight himself could not have forborne laughing, had he been anything less angry. He did his best to get over the wall, but alas! he was so bruised, that he could not so much as alight from his horse. This made him fume and chaff, and vent his passion in a thousand threats and curses, so strange and various, that it is impossible to repeat them. But the more he stormed, the more they tossed and laughed. Sancho, on his side, begging, and howling, and threatening, and damning to as little purpose as his master, for it was weariness alone could make the tossers give over. Then they charitably put an end to his high dancing, and set him upon his ass again, carefully wrapped in his mantle. But Maritornes's tender soul made her pity a male creature in such tribulation; and thinking he had danced and tumbled enough to be a-dry, she was so generous as to help him to a draught of water, which she purposely drew from the well that moment, that it might be the cooler. Sancho clapped the pot to his mouth, but his master made him desist: 'Hold, hold,' cried he, 'son Sancho, drink no water, child, it will kill thee: behold, I have here the most holy balsam, two drops of which will cure thee effectually.' 'Ha!' (replied Sancho, shaking his head, and looking sourly on the Knight with a side-face)' have you again forgot that I am no knight? or would you have me cast up the few guts I have left since yesternight's jobs? Keep your brewings for yourself, in the Devil's name, and let me alone.' With that he lifted up the jug to his nose., but finding it to be mere element, he squirted out again the little he had tasted, and desired the wench to help him to some better liquor: so she went and fetched him wine to make him amends, and paid for it too out of her own pocket: for, to give the devil his due, it was said of her, that though she was somewhat too free of her favours, yet she had something of Christianity in her. As soon as Sancho had tipped off his wine, he visited his ass's ribs twice or thrice with his heels; and, free egress being granted him, he trooped off mightily tickled with the thoughts of having had his ends, and got off shot-free; though at the expense of his shoulders, his usual sureties. It is true, the innkeeper kept his wallet for the reckoning; but the poor squire was so dismayed, and in such haste to be gone, that he never missed it. The host was for shutting the inn-doors after him, for fear of the worst; but the tossers would not let him, being a sort of fellows that would not have mattered Don Quixote a straw, though he had really been one of the knights of the round-table.

CHAPTER IV

Of the Discourse between the Knight and the Squire, with other matters worth relating

SANCHO OVERTOOK his master, but so pale, so dead-hearted, and so mortified, that he was hardly able to sit on his ass. 'My dear Sancho,' said Don Quixote, seeing him in that condition, 'I am now fully convinced that this castle, or inn, is enchanted; for what could they be that made themselves such barbarous sport with thee, but spirits and people of the other world? And I the rather believe this, seeing, that when I looked over the wall, I saw thee thus abused, I strove to get over it, but could not stir, nor by any means alight from Rozinante. For, by my honour, could I either have got over the wall or dismounted, I would have revenged thee so effectually on those discourteous wretches, that they should never have forgot the severity of their punishment, though for once I had infringed the laws of chivalry; which, as I have often informed thee, do not permit any knight to lay hands on one that is not knighted, unless it be in his own defence, and in case of great necessity.' 'Nay,' quoth Sancho, 'I would have paid them home myself, whether knight or no knight, but it was not in my power; and yet I dare say, those that made themselves so merry with my carcase were neither spirits nor enchanted folks, as you will have it, but mere flesh and blood as we be. I am sure they called one another by their Christian names and surnames, while they made me vault and frisk in the air: one was called Pedro Martinez, the other Tenorio Hernandez; and, as for our dog of a host, I heard them call him Juan Palomeque the Left-handed. Then pray do not you fancy, that your not being able to get over the wall, nor to alight, was some enchanter's trick. It is a folly to make many words; it is as plain as the nose in a man's face, that these same adventures which we hunt for up and down, are like to bring us at last into a peck of troubles, and such a plaguy deal of mischief, that we shall not be able to set one foot afore the other. The short and the long is, I take it to be the wisest course to jog home and look after our harvest, and not to run rambling from Ceca to Meca,* lest "we leap out of the frying-pan into the fire," or "out of God's blessing into the warm sun." ' 'Poor Sancho,' cried

---

* Ceca was a place of devotion among the Moors, in the city of Cordova, to which they used to go on pilgrimage from other places, as Meca is among the Turks: whence the proverb comes to signify, 'Sauntering about to no purpose.' A banter upon Popish pilgrimages.

Don Quixote, 'how ignorant thou art in matters of chivalry! Come say no more, and have patience. A day will come when thou shall be convinced how honourable a thing it is to follow this employment. For, tell me, what satisfaction in this world, what pleasure can equal that of vanquishing and triumphing over one's enemy? None without doubt.' 'It may be so for aught I know,' quoth Sancho, 'though I know nothing of the matter. However, this I may venture to say, that ever since we have turned knights-errant (your worship I mean, for it is not for such scrubs as myself to be named the same day with such folk) the devil of any fight you have had the better in, unless it be that with the Biscayan; and in that too you came off with the loss of one ear and the vizor of your helmet. And what have you got ever since, pray, but blows, and more blows; bruises, and more bruises? Besides this tossing in a blanket, which fell all to my share, and for which I cannot be revenged, because they were hobgoblins that served me so, though I hugely long to be even with them, that I may know the pleasure you say there is in vanquishing one's enemy.' 'I find, Sancho,' cried Don Quixote, 'thou and I are both sick of the same disease; but I will endeavour with all speed to get me a sword made with so much art, that no sort of enchantment shall be able to hurt whosoever shall wear it: and perhaps fortune may put into my hand that which Amadis de Gaul wore when he styled himself, "The Knight of the Burning Sword," which was one of the best blades that ever was drawn by knight: for besides the virtue I now mentioned, it had an edge like a razor, and would enter the strongest armour that ever was tempered or enchanted.' 'I will lay anything,' quoth Sancho, 'when you have found this sword, it will prove just such another help to me as your balsam; that is to say, it will stand nobody in any stead but your dubbed knights, let the poor devil of a squire shift how he can.' 'Fear no such thing,' replied Don Quixote; 'heaven will be more propitious to thee than thou imaginest.'

Thus they went on discoursing, when Don Quixote, perceiving a thick cloud of dust arise right before them in the road: 'The day is come,' said he, turning to his squire, 'the day is come, Sancho, that shall usher in the happiness which fortune has reserved for me: this day shall the strength of my arm be signalised by such exploits as shall be transmitted even to the latest posterity. Seest thou that cloud of dust, Sancho? It is raised by a prodigious army marching this way, and composed of an infinite number of nations.' 'Why then, at this rate,' quoth Sancho, 'there should be two armies; for yonder is as great a dust on the other side.' With that Don Quixote looked, and was transported with joy at the sight, firmly believing that two vast armies were ready to engage each other in that plain. For his imagination was so crowded with those battles, enchantments, surprising adventures, amorous thoughts, and other whimsies which he had read of in romances, that his strong fancy changed everything he saw into what he desired to see; and thus he could not conceive that the dust was only raised by two large flocks of sheep that were going the same road from different parts, and could not be discerned till they were very near. He was so positive that they were two armies that Sancho firmly believed him at last. 'Well, sir,' quoth the squire, 'what are we to do, I beseech you?' 'What shall we do,' replied Don Quixote, 'but assist the weaker and the injured side? For know, Sancho, that the army which now moves toward us is commanded by the great Alifanfaron, emperor of the vast island of Taprobana: the other that advances behind us is his enemy, the king of the Garamantians, Pentapolin with the naked arm; so called, because he always enters into battle with his right arm bare.'* 'Pray, sir,' quoth Sancho, 'why are these two great men going together by the ears?' 'The occasion of their quarrel is this,' answered Don Quixote, 'Alifanfaron, a strong Pagan, is in love with Pentapolin's daughter, a very beautiful lady and a Christian: now her father refuses to give her in marriage to the heathen prince, unless he abjure his false belief, and embrace the Christian religion.' 'Burn my beard,' said Sancho, 'if Pentapolin be not in the right on it; I will stand by him, and help him all I may.' 'I commend thy resolution,' replied Don Quixote, 'it is not only lawful, but requisite; for there is no need of being a knight to fight in such battles.' 'I guessed as much,' quoth Sancho: 'but where shall we leave my ass in the mean time, that I may be sure to find him again after the battle; for I fancy you never heard of any man that ever charged upon such a beast.' 'It is true,' answered Don Quixote, 'and therefore I would have you turn him loose, though thou wert sure never to find him again; for we shall have so many horses after we have got the day, that even Rozinante himself will be in danger of being changed for another.' Then, mounting to the top of a hillock, whence they might have seen both the flocks, had not the dust obstructed their sight, 'Look yonder, Sancho,' cried Don Quixote, 'that knight whom thou seest in the gilded arms, bearing in his shield a crowned lion couchant at the feet of a lady, is the valiant Laurealco, lord of the Silver Bridge.

'He in the armour powdered with flowers of gold, bearing three crows argent in a field azure, is the formidable Micocolembo, great duke of Quiracia. That other of a gigantic size that marches on his right, is the undaunted Brandabarbaran of Boliche, sovereign of the three Arabias; he is arrayed in a serpent's skin, and carries instead of a shield a huge gate, which they say belonged to the temple which Samson pulled down at his death, when he revenged himself upon his enemies. But cast thy eyes on this side, Sancho, and, at the head of the other army, see the ever-victorious Timonel of Carcajona, prince of New Biscay, whose armour is

* Alluding to the story of Scanderbeg, king of Epirus.

quartered azure, vert, or, and argent, and who bears in his shield a cat, or, in a field gules, with these four letters, "MIAU," for a motto, being the beginning of his mistress's name, the beautiful Miaulina, daughter to Alpheniquen, duke of Algarva. That other monstrous load upon the back of yonder wild horse, with arms as white as snow and a shield without any device, is a Frenchman, new created knight, called Pierre Papin, baron of Utrique. He whom you see pricking that pied courser's flanks with his armed heels, is the mighty duke of Nerbia Espartafilardo, of the wood, bearing in his shield a field of pure azure, powdered with asparagus (*Esparago**) with this motto in Castilian, *Rastrea mi suerte*: "Thus trails or drags my fortune." ' And thus he went on, naming a great number of others in both armies, to every one of whom his fertile imagination assigned arms, colours, impresses, and mottoes, as readily as if they had really been that moment extant before his eyes.

And then, proceeding without the least hesitation: 'That vast body,' said he, 'now just opposite to us, is composed of several nations. There you see those who drink the pleasant stream of the famous Xanthus; there the mountaineers that till the Massilian† fields; those that sift the pure gold of Arabia Fælix; those that inhabit the renowned and delightful banks of Thermodon. Yonder, those who so many ways sluice and drain the golden Pactolus for its precious sand; the Numidians, unsteady and careless of their promises; the Persians, excellent archers; the Medes and Parthians, who fight flying; the Arabs, who have no fixed habitations; the Scythians, cruel and savage, though fair complexioned; the sooty Æthiopians, that bore their lips; and a thousand other nations whose countenances I know, though I have forgotten their names. On the other side, come those whose country is watered with the crystal streams of Betis, shaded with olive trees. Those who bathe their limbs in the rich food of the golden Tagus; those whose mansions are laved by the profitable stream of the divine Genil; those who range the verdent Tartesian meadows. Those who indulge their luxurious temper in the delicious pastures of Xereza; the wealthy inhabitants of the Mancha, crowned with golden ears of corn; the ancient offspring of the Goths, cased in iron; those who wanton in the lazy current of Pisuerga; those who feed their numerous flocks in the

---

* The jingle between the duke's name Espartafilardo and Esparago (his arms) is a ridicule upon the foolish quibbles so frequent in heraldry, and probably this whole catalogue is a satire upon several great names and sounding titles in Spain, whose owners were beggars. The trailing of his fortune may allude to the word Esparto, a sort of rush they make ropes with. Or perhaps he was without a mistress, to which the asparagus may allude: for in Spain they have a proverb, *Solo comes el Esparago*: 'As solitary as asparagus,' because every one of them springs up by itself.

† An imitation of Homer's catalogue of ships.

ample plains where the Guadiana, so celebrated for its hidden course, pursues its wandering race; those who shiver with extremity of cold, on the woody Pyrenean hills, or on the hoary tops of the snowy Apennine. In a word, all that Europe includes within its spacious bounds, half a world in an army.'

It is scarce to be imagined how many countries he ran over, how many nations he enumerated, distinguishing every one by what is peculiar to them, with an incredible vivacity of mind, and that still in the puffy style of his fabulous books. Sancho listened to all this romantic muster-roll as mute as a fish, with amazement; all that he could do was now and then to turn his head on this side and the other side, to see if he could discern the knights and giants whom his master named. But at length, not being able to discover any: 'Why,' cried he, 'you had as good tell me it snows; the devil of any knight, giant, or man can I see, of all those you talk of now; who knows but all this may be witchcraft and spirits, like yesternight?' 'How,' replied Don Quixote, 'dost thou not hear their horses neigh, their trumpets sound, and their drums beat?' 'Not I,' quoth Sancho, 'I prick up my ears like a sow in the beans, and yet I can hear nothing but the bleating of sheep.' Sancho might justly say so indeed, for by this time the two flocks were got very near them. 'Thy fear disturbs thy senses,' said Don Quixote, 'and hinders thee from hearing and seeing right: but it is no matter; withdraw to some place of safety, since thou art so terrified; for I alone am sufficient to give the victory to that side which I shall favour with my assistance.' With that he couched his lance, clapped spurs to Rozinante, and rushed like a thunder-bolt from the hillock into the plain. Sancho bawled after him as loud as he could: 'Hold, sir,' cried Sancho, 'for Heaven's sake come back. What do you mean? As sure as I am a sinner, those you are going to maul are nothing but poor harmless sheep. Come back, I say. Woe be to him that begot me! Are you mad, sir? There are no giants, no knights, no cats, no asparagus gardens, no golden quarters, nor what-do-you-call-thems. Does the Devil possess you? You are leaping over the hedge before you come at the stile. You are taking the wrong sow by the ear. Oh, that I was ever born to see this day!' But Don Quixote, still riding on, deaf and lost to good advice, outroared his expostulating squire. 'Courage, brave knights,' cried he: 'march up, fall on all you who fight under the standard of the valiant Pentapolin with the naked arm: follow me, and you shall see how easily I will revenge him on that infidel Alifanfaron of Taprobana; 'and, so saying, he charged the squadron of sheep with that gallantry and resolution, that he pierced, broke, and put it to flight in an instant, charging through and through, not without a great slaughter of his mortal enemies, whom he laid at his feet, biting the ground and wallowing in their blood. The shepherds seeing their sheep go to rack, called out to him; till, finding fair means ineffectual, they unloosed their slings, and began to ply him with stones as big as their fists. But the champion, disdaining such a distant war, spite of their showers of stones, rushed among the routed sheep, trampling both the living and the slain in a most terrible manner, impatient to meet the general of the enemy, and end the war at once. 'Where, where art thou,' cried he, 'proud Alifanfaron? Appear! see here a single knight who seeks thee everywhere, to try now, hand to hand, the boasted force of thy strenuous arm, and deprive thee of life, as a due punishment for the unjust war which thou hast audaciously waged with the valiant Pentapolin.' Just as he had said this, while the stones flew about his ears, one unluckily fell upon his small ribs, and had like to have buried two of the shortest deep in the middle of his body. The Knight thought himself slain, or at least desperately wounded; and, therefore, calling to mind his precious balsam, and pulling out his earthen jug, he clapped it to his mouth: but, before he had swallowed a sufficient dose, souse comes another of those bitter almonds that spoiled his draught, and hit him so pat upon the jug, hand and teeth, that it broke the first, maimed the second, and struck out three or four of the last. These two blows were so violent, that the boisterous Knight falling from his horse, lay upon the ground as quiet as the slain; so that the shepherds fearing he was killed, got their flock together with all speed, and carrying away their dead, which were no less than seven sheep, they made what haste they could out of harm's way, without looking any further into the matter.

All this while Sancho stood upon the hill, mortified upon the sight of this mad adventure. There he stamped, swore, and banned his master to the bottomless pit; he tore his beard for madness, and cursed the moment he first knew him: but seeing him at last knocked down, and settled, the shepherds being scampered, he thought he might venture to come down; and found him in a very ill plight, though not altogether senseless. 'Ah! master,' quoth he, 'this comes of not taking my counsel. Did I not tell you it was a flock of sheep, and no army?' 'Friend Sancho,' replied Don Quixote, 'know it is an easy matter for necromancers to change the shapes of things as they please: thus that malicious enchanter, who is my inveterate enemy, to deprive me of the glory which he saw me ready to acquire, while I was reaping a full harvest of laurels, transformed in a moment the routed squadrons into sheep. If thou wilt not believe me, Sancho, yet do one thing for my sake: do but take thy ass, and follow those supposed sheep at a distance, and I dare engage thou shalt soon see them resume their former shapes, and appear such as I described them. But stay, do not go yet, for I want thy assistance: draw near, and see how many cheek-teeth and others I want; for, by the dreadful pain in my jaws and gums, I fear there is a total dilapidation in my mouth.' With that the Knight opened his mouth as wide as he could, while the squire gaped to tell his grinders, with his snout almost in his chops; but just in that fatal moment the balsam that lay wambling and fretting in Don Quixote's stomach, came up with an unlucky hickup; and, with the same violence that the powder flies out of a gun, all that he had in his stomach discharged itself upon the beard, face, eyes, and mouth of the officious squire. 'Santa Maria,' cried poor Sancho, 'what will become of me! my master is a dead man! he is vomiting his very heart's blood!' but he had hardly said this, when the colour, smell, and taste soon undeceived him; and finding it to be his master's loathsome drench, it caused such a sudden rumbling in his maw, that before he could turn his head he unladed the whole cargo of his stomach full in his master's face, and put him in as delicate a pickle as he was himself. Sancho having thus paid him in his own coin, half-blinded as he was, ran to his ass, to take out something to clean himself and his master: but when he came to look for his wallet, and found it missing, not remembering till then that he had unhappily left it in the inn, he was ready to run quite out of his wits. He stormed and stamped, and cursed him worse than before, and resolved with himself to let his master go to the Devil, and even trudge home by himself, though he was sure to lose his wages, and his hopes of being governor of the promised island.

Thereupon Don Quixote got up with much ado, and clapping his left hand before mouth, that the rest of his loose teeth might not drop out, he laid his right hand on Rozinante's bridle; (for such was the good nature of the creature, that he had not budged a foot from his master) then it crept along to squire Sancho, that stood lolling on his ass's pannel, with his face in the hollow of both his hands, in a doleful, moody, melancholy fit. 'Friend Sancho,' said he, seeing him thus abandoned to sorrow, 'learn of me, that one man is no more than another, if he do no more than what another does. All these storms and hurricanes are but arguments of the approaching calm: better success will soon follow our past calamities; good and bad fortune have their vicissitudes; and it is a maxim, that nothing violent can last long; and therefore we may well promise ourselves a speedy change in our fortune, since our afflictions have extended their reign beyond the usual stint; besides, thou oughtest not to afflict thyself so much for misfortunes, of which thou hast no share, but what friendship and humanity bid thee take.' 'How,' quoth Sancho, 'have I no other share in them? Was not he that was tossed in the blanket this morning, the son of my father? And did not the wallet, and all that was in it, which I have lost, belong to the son of my mother?' 'How,' asked Don Quixote, 'hast thou lost thy wallet?' 'I do not know,' said Sancho, 'whether it is lost or no, but I am sure I cannot tell what is become of it.' 'Nay, then,' replied Don Quixote, 'I find we must fast today.' 'Ay, marry must we,' quoth Sancho, 'unless you take care to gather in these fields some of those roots and herbs which I have heard you say you know, and which use to help such unlucky knights-errant as yourself at a dead lift.' 'For all that,' cried Don Quixote, 'I would rather have at this time a good luncheon of bread, or a cake and two pilchards heads, than all the roots and simples in Dioscorides's herbal, and Doctor Laguna's supplement and commentary: I pray thee, therefore, get upon thy ass, good Sancho, and follow me once more; for God's providence, that relieves every creature, will not fail us, especially since we are about a work so much to His service; thou seest He even provides for the little flying insects in the air, the wormlings in the earth, and the spawnlings in the water; and, in His infinite mercy, He makes His sun shine on the righteous and on the unjust, and rains upon the good and the bad.' 'Many words will not fill a bushel,' quoth Sancho, interrupting him; 'you would make a better preacher than a knight-errant, or I am plaguedly out.' 'Knights-errant,' replied Don Quixote, 'ought to know all things; there have been such in former ages, that have delivered as ingenious and learned a sermon or oration at the head of an army, as if they had taken their degrees at the University of Paris: from which we may infer, that the lance never dulled the pen, nor the pen the lance.' 'Well then,' quoth Sancho, 'for once let it be as you would have it; let us even leave this unlucky place, and seek out a lodging; where, I pray God, there may be neither blankets, nor blanket-heavers, nor hobgoblins, nor enchanted; Moors; for, before I will be hampered as I have been, may I be cursed with bell, book and candle, if I do not give the trade to the Devil.' 'Leave all things to Providence,' replied Don Quixote, 'and for once lead which way thou pleasest, for I leave it wholly to thy discretion to provide us a lodging. But first, I pray thee, feel a little how many teeth I want in mx upper jaw on the right side, for there I feel most pain.' With that Sancho feeling with his finger in the Knight's mouth: 'Pray, sir,' quoth he, 'how many grinders did your worship use to have on that side?' 'Four,' answered Don Quixote, 'besides the eye-tooth, all of them whole and sound.' 'Think well on what you say,' cried Sancho. 'I say four,' replied Don Quixote, 'if there were not five; for I never in all my life have had a tooth drawn or dropped out, or rotted by the worm, or loosened by rheum.' 'Bless me!' quoth Sancho, 'why, you have in this nether-jaw on this side but two grinders and a stump; and in that part of your upper jaw, never a stump, and never a grinder: alas! all is levelled there as smooth as the palm of one's hand.' 'Oh, unfortunate Don Quixote!' cried the Knight, 'I had rather have lost an arm, so it were not my sword-arm, for a mouth without cheek-teeth is like a mill without a mill-stone, Sancho; and every tooth in a man's head is more valuable than a diamond. But we that profess this strict order of knight-errantry, are all subject to these calamities; and therefore, since the loss is irretrievable, mount, my trusty Sancho, and go thy own pace; I will follow thee.' Sancho obeyed, and led the way, still keeping the road they were in, which being very much beaten, promised to bring him soonest to a lodging. Thus pacing along very softly, for Don Quixote's gums and ribs would not suffer him to go faster; Sancho, to divert his uneasy thoughts, resolved to talk to him all the while of one thing or other, as the next chapter will inform you.

CHAPTER V

Of the wise Discourse between Sancho and his Master; as also of the Adventure of the Dead Corpse, and other famous Occurrences

'Now, SIR,' quoth Sancho, 'I cannot help thinking but that all the mishaps that have befallen us of late, are a just judgment for the grievous sin you have committed against the order of knighthood, in not keeping the oath you swore, not to eat bread at board, nor to have a merry bout with the queen, and the Lord knows what more, until you had won what-do-you-call-him, the Moor's helmet,* I think you named him.' 'Truly,' answered Don Quixote, 'thou art much in the right, Sancho, and, to deal ingenuously with thee, I wholly forgot that: and now thou mayest certainly assure thyself, thou wert tossed in a blanket for not remembering to put me in mind of it. However, I will take care to make due atonement; for knight-errantry has ways to conciliate all sorts of matters.' 'Why,' quoth Sancho, 'did I ever swear to mind you of your vow?' 'It is nothing to the purpose,' replied Don Quixote, 'whether thou sworest or no: let it suffice that I think thou are not very clear from being accessory to the breach of my vow; and therefore to prevent the worst, there will be no harm in providing for a remedy.' 'Hark you then,' cried Sancho, 'be sure you do not forget your atonement, as you did your oath, lest those confounded hobgoblins come and maul me, and mayhap you too, for being a stubborn sinner.'

Insensibly night overtook them before they could discover any lodging; and which was worse, they were almost hunger-starved, all their provision being in the wallet which Sancho had unluckily left behind; and, to complete their distress, there happened to them an adventure, or something that really looked like one.

While our benighted travellers went on dolefully in the dark, the Knight very hungry, and the squire very sharp set, what should they see

* Melandrino.

moving towards them but a great number of lights, that appeared like so many wandering stars. At this strange apparition, down sunk Sancho's heart at once, and; even Don Quixote himself was not without some symptoms of surprise. Presently the one pulled to him his ass's halter, the other his horse's bridle? and both made a stop. They soon perceived that the lights made directly towards them, and the nearer they came the bigger they appeared. At the terrible wonder Sancho shook and shivered every joint, like one in a palsy, and Don Quixote's hair stood up on end; however, heroically shaking off the amazement which that sight stamped upon his soul, 'Sancho,' said he, 'this must doubtless be a great and most perilous adventure, where I shall have occasion to exert the whole stock of my courage and strength.' 'Woe's me,' quoth Sancho, 'should this happen to be another adventure of ghosts, as I fear it is, where shall I find ribs to endure it?' 'Come all the fiends in hell,' cried Don Quixote, 'I will not suffer them to touch a hair of thy head. If they insulted thee lately, know there was then between thee and me a wall, over which I could not climb; but now we are in the open field, where I shall have liberty to make use of my sword.' 'Ay,' quoth Sancho, 'you may talk; but, should they bewitch you as they did before, what the Devil would it avail us to be in the open field?' 'Come, Sancho,' replied Don Quixote, 'be of good cheer; the event will soon convince thee of the greatness of my valour.' 'Pray Heaven it may,' quoth Sancho; 'I will do my best.' With that they rode a little out of the way, and gazing earnestly at the lights, they soon discovered a great number of persons all in white. At the dreadful sight, all poor Sancho's shuffling courage basely deserted him. His teeth began to chatter as if he had been in an ague fit, and as the objects drew nearer his chattering increased. And now they could plainly distinguish about twenty men on horseback, all in white, with torches in their hands, followed by a hearse covered over with black, and six men in deep mourning, whose mules were also in black down to their very heels. Those in white moved slowly, murmuring from their lips something in a low and lamentable tone. This dismal spectacle, at such a time of night, in the midst of such a vast solitude, was enough to have shipwrecked the courage of a stouter squire than Sancho, and even of his master, had he been any other than Don Quixote: but as his imagination straight suggested to him, that this was one of those adventures of which he had so often read in his books of chivalry, the hearse appeared to him to be a litter, where lay the body of some knight either slain or dangerously wounded, the revenge of whose misfortunes was reserved for his prevailing arm; and so, without any more ado, couching his lance, and seating himself firm in his saddle, he posted himself in the middle of the road, where the company were to pass. As soon as they came near, 'Stand,' cried he, to them in a haughty tone, 'whoever you be, and tell me who you are, whence you come, whither you go, and what you carry in that litter? for there is all the reason in the world to believe, that you have either done or received a great deal of harm; and it is requisite I should be informed of the matter, in order either to punish you for the ill you have committed, or else to revenge you of the wrong you have suffered.' 'Sir,' answered one of the men in white, 'we are in haste; the inn is a great way off, and we cannot stay to answer so many questions;' and with that spurring his mule, he moved forwards. But Don Quixote, highly dissatisfied with the reply, laid hold on the mule's bridle and stopped him. 'Stay,' cried he, 'proud, discourteous knight, mend your behaviour, and give me instantly an account of what I asked of ye, or here I defy you all to mortal combat.' Now the mule, that was shy and skittish, being thus rudely seized by the bridle, was presently scared, and rising up on her hinder legs, threw her rider to the ground. Upon this, one of the footmen that belonged to the company gave Don Quixote ill language; which so incensed him, that being resolved to be revenged upon them all, in a mighty rage he flew at the next he met, who happened to be one of the mourners. Him he threw to the ground very much hurt; and then turning to the rest, with a wonderful agility, he fell upon them with such fury, that he presently put them all to flight. You would have thought Rozinante had wings at that time, so active and so fierce he then approved himself.

It was not indeed for men unarmed, and naturally fearful, to maintain the field against such an enemy; no wonder then if the gentlemen in white were immediately dispersed: some ran one way, some another, crossing the plain with their lighted torches: you would now have taken them for a parcel of frolicsome masqueraders, gambolling and scouring on a carnival night. As for the mourners, they, poor men, were so muffled up in their long, cumbersome cloaks, that not being able to make their party good, nor defend themselves, they were presently routed, and ran away like the rest, the rather, for that they thought it was no mortal creature, but the Devil himself, that was come to fetch away the dead body which they were accompanying to the grave.* All the while Sancho was lost in admiration and astonishment, charmed with the sight of his master's valour; and now concluded him to be the formidable champion he boasted himself.

After this the knight, by the light of a torch that lay burning upon the ground, perceiving the man who was thrown by his mule lying near it, he rode up to him, and setting his lance to his throat, 'Yield,' cried he, 'and beg thy life, or thou diest.' 'Alas, sir,' cried the other, 'what need you ask me to yield? I am not able to stir, for one of my legs is broken; and I beseech you, if you are a Christian, do not kill me. I am a master of arts, and in holy orders; it would be a heinous sacrilege to take away my life.'

* The author seems here to have intended a ridicule on those funeral solemnities.

'What a devil brought you hither then, if you are a clergyman?' cried Don Quixote. 'What else but my ill fortune,' replied the supplicant. 'A worse hovers over thy head,' cried Don Quixote, 'and threatens thee, if thou dost not answer this moment to every particular question I ask.' 'I will, I will, sir,' replied the other; 'and first I must beg your pardon for saying I was a master of arts, for I have yet but taken my bachelor's degree. My name is Alonzo Lopez: I am of Alcovendas, and came now from the town of Baeça, with eleven other clergymen, the same that now ran away with the torches. We were going to Segovia to bury the corpse of a gentleman of that town, who died at Baeça, and lies now in yonder hearse.' 'And who killed him?' asked Don Quixote. 'Heaven, with a pestilential fever,' answered the other. 'If it be so,' said Don Quixote, 'I am discharged of revenging his death. Since Heaven did it, there is no more to be said; had it been its pleasure to have taken me off so, I too must have submitted. I would have you informed, reverend sir, that I am a knight of La Mancha, my name Don Quixote; my employment is to visit an parts of the world in quest of adventures, to right and relieve injured innocence, and punish oppression.' 'Truly, sir,' replied the clergyman, 'I do not understand how you can call that to right and relieve men, when you break their legs: you have made that crooked which was right and straight before; and Heaven knows whether it can ever be set right as long as I live. Instead of relieving the injured, I fear you have injured me past relief; and while you seek adventures, you have made me meet with a very great misadventure.'* 'All things,' replied Don Quixote, 'are not blessed alike with a prosperous event, good Mr. Bachelor. You should have taken care not to have thus gone a-processioning in these desolate plains, at this suspicious time of night, with your white surplices, burning torches, and sable weeds, like ghosts and goblins, that went about to scare people out of their wits; for I could not omit doing the duty of my profession, nor would I have forborne attacking you, though you had really been all Lucifer's infernal crew; for such I took you to be, and till this moment could have no better opinion of you.' 'Well, sir,' said the Bachelor, 'since my bad fortune has so ordered it, I must desire you, as you are a knight-errant, who have made mine so ill an errand, to help me to get from under my mule, for it lies so heavy upon me that I cannot get my foot out of the stirrup.' 'Why did not you acquaint me sooner with your grievances?' cried Don Quixote. 'I might have talked on till tomorrow morning and never have thought on it.' With that he called Sancho, who made no great haste, for he was much

---

* The author's making the bachelor quibble so much, under such improper circumstances, was properly designed as a ridicule upon the younger students of the universities, who are so apt to run into an affectation that way, and to mistake it for wit; as also upon the dramatic writers, who frequently make their heroes, in their greatest distresses, guilty of the like absurdity.

better employed in rifling a load of choice provisions, which the holy men carried along with them on a sumpter-mule. He had spread his coat on the ground, and having laid on it as much food as it would hold, he wrapped it up like a bag, and laid the booty on his ass; and then away he ran to his master, and helped him to set the Bachelor upon his mule: after which he gave him his torch, and Don Quixote bade him follow his company, and excuse him for his mistake, though, all things considered, he could not avoid doing what he had done. 'And, sir,' quoth Sancho, 'if the gentlemen would know who it was that so well threshed their jackets, you may tell them it was the famous Don Quixote de la Mancha, otherwise called the Knight of the Woeful Figure.'

When the Bachelor was gone, Don Quixote asked Sancho why he called him the Knight of the Woeful Figure? 'I will tell you why,' quoth Sancho; 'I have been staring upon you this pretty while by the light of that unlucky priest's torch, and may I never stir if ever I set eyes on a more dismal figure in my born-days; and I cannot tell what should be the cause of it, unless your being tired after this fray, or the want of your worship's teeth.' 'That is not the reason,' cried Don Quixote; 'no, Sancho, I rather conjecture, that the sage who is commissioned by fate to register my achievements, thought it convenient I should assume a new appellation, as all the knights of yore: for one was called the Knight of the Burning Sword, another of the Unicorn, a third of the Phœnix, a fourth the Knight of the Damsels, another of the Griffin, and another the Knight of Death; by which by-names and distinctions they were known all over the globe. Therefore, doubtless, that learned sage, my historian, has inspired thee with the thought of giving me that additional appellation of the Knight of the Woeful Figure: and accordingly I assume the name, and intend henceforwards to be distinguished by that denomination. And, that it may seem the more proper, I will with the first opportunity have a most woeful face painted on my shield.' 'On my word,' quoth Sancho, 'you may even save the money, and instead of having a woeful face painted, you need no more but only show your own. I am but in jest, as a body may say, but what with the want of your teeth, and what with hunger, you look so queerly and so woefully, that no painter can draw you a figure so fit for your purpose as your worship's.' This merry conceit of Sancho extorted a smile from his master's austere countenance: however, he persisted in his resolution about the name and the picture; and after a pause, a sudden thought disturbing his conscience, 'Sancho,' cried he, 'I am afraid of being excommunicated for having laid violent hands upon a man in holy orders, *Juxta illud, siquis suadente diabolo*, etc.* But yet, now I think better of it, I never touched him with my hands, but only with my lance; besides, I did

---

* Canon. 72, Distinct. 134.

not in the least suspect I had to do with priests, whom I honour and revere as every good Catholic and faithful Christian ought to do, but rather took them to be evil spirits. Well, let the worst come to the worst, I remember what befell the Cid Ruy-Dias, when he broke to pieces the chair of a king's ambassador in the Pope's presence, for which he was excommunicated; which did not hinder the worthy Roderigo de Vivar from behaving himself that day like a valorous knight, and a man of honour.'

This said, Don Quixote was for visiting the hearse, to see if what was in it were only dead bones: but Sancho would not let him: 'Sir,' quoth he, 'you are come off now with a whole skin, and much better than you have done hitherto. Who knows but these same fellows that are now scampered off, may chance to bethink themselves what a shame it is for them to have suffered themselves to be thus routed by a single man, and so come back, and fall upon us all at once; then we shall have work enough upon our hands. The ass is in good case; there is a hill not far off, and our bellies cry "Cupboard." Come, let us even keep out of harm's way, "and not let the plough stand to catch a mouse," as the saying is; "to the grave with the dead, and the living to the bread." ' With that he put on a dog-trot with his ass, and his master, bethinking himself that he was in the right, put on after him without replying.

After they had rid a little way, they came to a valley that lay skulking between two hills; there they alighted, and Sancho having opened his coat and spread it on the grass, with the provision which he had bundled up in it, our two adventurers fell to; and their stomachs being sharpened with the sauce of hunger, they eat their breakfast, dinner, afternoon's luncheon, and supper, all at the same time, feasting themselves with variety of cold meats, which you may be sure were the best that could be got, the priests, who had brought it for their own eating, being like the rest of their coat, none of the worst stewards for their bellies, and knowing how to make much of themselves.

But now they began to grow sensible of a very great misfortune, and such a misfortune as was bemoaned by poor Sancho, as one of the saddest that ever could befall him; for they found they had not one drop of wine or water to wash down their meat and quench their thirst, which now scorched and choked them worse than hunger had pinched them before. However, Sancho considering they were in a place where the grass was fresh and green, said to his master what you shall find in the following chapter.

CHAPTER VI

Of a wonderful Adventure achieved by the valorous Don Quixote de la Mancha; the like never compassed with less danger by any of the most famous Knights in the World

'THE GRASS IS SO FRESH,' quoth Sancho, half choked with thirst, 'that I dare lay my life we shall light on some spring or stream hereabouts; therefore, sir, let us look, I beseech you, that we may quench this confounded thirst that plagues our throats ten times worse than hunger did our guts.' Thereupon Don Quixote, leading Rozinante by the bridle, and Sancho his ass by the halter, after he had laid up the reversion of their meal, they went feeling about, only guided by their guess; for it was so dark they scarce could see their hands. They had not gone above two hundred paces before they heard a noise of a great waterfall; which was to them the most welcome sound in the world: but then, listening with great attention to know on which side the grateful murmur came, they on a sudden heard another kind of noise that strangely allayed the pleasure of the first, especially in Sancho, who was naturally fearful and pusillanimous. They heard a terrible din of obstreperous blows, struck regularly, and a more dreadful rattling of chains and irons, which, together with the roaring of the waters, might have filled any other heart but Don Quixote's with terror and amazement. Add to this the horrors of a dark night and solitude, in an unknown place, the loud rustling of the leaves of some lofty trees under which fortune brought them at the same unlucky moment, the whistling of the wind, which concurred with the other dismaying sounds; the fall of the waters, the thundering thumps and the clinking of chains aforesaid. The worst too was, that the blows were redoubled without ceasing, the wind blowed on, and daylight was far distant. But then it was, Don Quixote, secured by his intrepidity (his inseparable companion) mounted his Rozinante, braced his shield, brandished his lance, and showed a soul unknowing fear, and superior to danger and fortune. 'Know, Sancho,' cried he, 'I was born in this iron age, to restore the age of gold, or the golden age, as some choose to call it. I am the man for whom fate has reserved the most dangerous and formidable attempts, the most stupendous and glorious adventures, and the most valorous feats of arms. I am the man who must revive the order of the round-table, the twelve peers of France, and the nine worthies, and efface the memory of your Platirs, your Tablantes, your Olivantes, and your Tirantes. Now must your Knights of the Son, your Belianises, and all the numerous throng of famous heroes, and knights-errant of former ages, see the glory of all their most dazzling actions eclipsed and darkened by more illustrious exploits. Do but observe, O thou my faithful squire, what a multifarious assemblage of terrors surrounds us! A horrid darkness, a doleful solitude, a confused rustling of leaves, a dismal rattling of chains, a howling of the winds, an astonishing noise of cataracts, that seem to fall with a boisterous rapidity from the steep mountains of the moon, a terrible sound of redoubled blows, still wounding our ears like furious thunder-claps, and a dead and universal silence of those things that might buoy up the sinking courage of frail mortality. In this extremity of danger, Mars himself might tremble with the affright: yet I, in the midst of all these unutterable alarms, still remain undaunted and unshaken. These are but incentives to my valour, and but animate my heart the more; it grows too big and mighty for my breast, and leaps at the approach of this threatening adventure, as formidable as it is like to prove. Come, girt Rozinante straighter, and then Providence protect thee: thou mayest stay for me here; but if I do not return in three days, go back to our village; and from thence, for my sake, to Toboso, where thou shalt say to my incomparable lady Dulcinea, that her faithful knight fell a sacrifice to love and honour, while he attempted things that might have made him worthy to be called her adorer.'

When Sancho heard his master talk thus, he fell a-weeping in the most pitiful manner in the world. 'Pray, sir,' cried he, 'why will you thus run yourself into mischief? Why need you go about this rueful misadventure? It is main dark, and there is never a living soul sees us; we have nothing to do but to sheer off, and get out of harm's way, though we were not to drink a drop these three days. Who is there to take notice of our flinching? I have heard our parson, whom you very well know, say in his pulpit, that he who seeks danger perishes therein: and therefore we should not tempt Heaven by going about a thing that we cannot compass but by a miracle. Is it not enough, think you, that it has preserved you from being tossed in a blanket, as I was, and made you come off safe and sound from among so many goblins that went with the dead man? If all this will not work upon that hard heart of yours, do but think of me, and rest yourself assured that when once you have left your poor Sancho, he will be ready to give up the ghost for very fear, to the next that will come for it: I left my house and home, my wife, children, and all to follow you, hoping to be the better for it, and not the worse; but as covetousness breaks the sack, so has it broke me and my hopes; for while I thought myself cocksure of that unlucky and accursed island, which you so often promised me, in lieu thereof you drop me here in a strange place. Dear master, do not be so hard-hearted; and if you won't be persuaded not to meddle with this ungracious adventure, do but put it off till daybreak, to which, according to the little skill I learned when a shepherd, it cannot be above three hours; for the muzzle of the lesser bear is just over our heads, and makes midnight in the line of the left arm.' 'How can you see the muzzle of the bear?' asked Don Quixote; 'there is not a star to be seen in the sky.' 'That is true,' quoth Sancho, 'but fear is sharpsighted, and can see things underground, and much more in the skies.' 'Let day come, or not come, it is all one to me,' cried the champion; 'it shall never be recorded of Don Quixote, that either tears or entreaties could make him neglect the duty of a knight. Then, Sancho, say no more; for Heaven, that has inspired me with a resolution of attempting this dreadful adventure, will certainly take care of me and thee: come quickly, gird my steed, and stay here for me; for you will shortly hear of me again, either alive or dead.'

Sancho, finding his master obstinate, and neither to be moved with tears nor good advice, resolved to try a trick of policy to keep him there till daylight. And accordingly, when he pretended to fasten the girths, he slily tied Rozinante's hinder legs with his ass's halter, without being so much as suspected, so that when Don Quixote thought to have moved forwards, he found his horse would not go a step without leaping, though he spurred him on smartly. Sancho, perceiving his plot took, 'Look you, sir,' quoth he, 'Heaven is on my side, and won't let Rozinante budge a foot forwards; and now, if you will still be spurring him, I dare pawn my life it will be but striving against the stream; or, as the saying is, but kicking against the pricks.' Don Quixote fretted and chafed, and raved, and was in a desperate fury, to find his horse so stubborn; but at last, observing that the more he spurred and galled his sides, the more resty he proved, and he, though unwillingly, resolved to have patience till it was light. 'Well,' said he, 'since Rozinante will not leave this place, I must tarry in it till the dawn, though its slowness will cost me some sighs.' 'You shall not need to sigh nor be melancholy,' quoth Sancho, 'for I will undertake to tell you stories, till it be day, unless your worship had rather get off your horse, and take a nap upon the green grass, as knights-errant are wont, that you may be the fresher, and the better able in the morning to go through that monstrous adventure that waits for you.' 'What dost thou mean by this alighting and sleeping?' replied Don Quixote. 'Thinkest thou I am one of those carpet-knights that abandon themselves to sleep and lazy ease, when danger is at hand? No, sleep thou, thou art born to sleep; or do what thou wilt. As for myself, I know what I have to do.' 'Good sir!' quoth Sancho, 'do not put yourself into a passion, I meant no such thing, not I; 'saying this, he clapped one of his hands upon the pummel of Rozinante's saddle, and the other upon the crupper, and thus he stood embracing his master's left thigh, not daring to budge an inch, for fear of the blows that dinned continually in his ears. Don Quixote then thought fit to claim his promise, and desired him to tell some of his stories to help to pass away the time. 'Sir,' quoth Sancho, 'I am woefully frightened, and have no heart to tell stories; however, I will do my best; and now I think on it, there is one come into my head, which, if I can but hit on it right, and nothing happen to put me out, is the best story you ever heard in your life; therefore listen, for I am going to begin. "In the days of yore, when it was as it was, good betide us all, and evil to him that evil seeks." And here, sir, you are to take notice that they of old did not begin their tales in an ordinary way; for it was a saying of a wise man whom they called Cato, the Roman Tonsor,* that said, "Evil to him that evil seeks," which is as pat for your purpose as a ring for the finger, that you may neither meddle nor make, nor seek evil and mischief for the worse, but rather get out of harm's way; for nobody forces us to run into the mouth of all the devils in hell that wait for us yonder.' 'Go on with thy story, Sancho,' cried Don Quixote, 'and leave the rest to my discretion.' 'I say then,' quoth Sancho, 'that in a country town in Estremadura, there lived a certain shepherd, goatherd I should have said; which goatherd, as the story has it, was called Lope Ruiz; and this Lope Ruiz was in love with a shepherdess, whose name was Toralva, the which shepherdess, whose name was Toralva, was the daughter of a wealthy grazier, and this wealthy grazier – ' 'If thou goest on at this rate,' cried Don Quixote, 'and makest so many needless repetitions, thou wilt not have told thy story these two days. Pray thee tell it concisely, and like a man of sense, or let it alone.' 'I tell it you,' quoth Sancho, 'as all stories are told in our country, and I cannot for the blood of me tell it any other way, nor is it fit I should alter the custom.' 'Why then, tell it how thou wilt,' replied Don Quixote, 'since my ill fortune forces me to stay and hear thee.' 'Well then, dear sir,' quoth Sancho, 'as I was saying, this same shepherd, goatherd I should have said, was extremely in love with that same shepherdess, Toralva, who was a well-trussed, round, crummy strapping wench, coy and froppish, and somewhat like a man, for she had a kind of beard on her upper lip; methinks I see her now standing before me.' 'Then I suppose thou knewest her,' said Don Quixote. 'Not I,' answered Sancho, 'I never set eyes on her in my life; but he that told me the story said this was so true, that I might vouch it for a real truth, and even swear I had seen it all myself. Well – but, as you know, days go and come, and time and straw make medlars ripe; so it happened, that after several days coming and going, the Devil, who seldom lies dead in a ditch, but will have a finger in every pie, so brought it about, that the shepherd fell out with his sweetheart, insomuch that the love he bore her turned into dudgeon and ill-will; and the cause was, by report of some mischievous tale carriers that bore no good-will to either party, for that the shepherd thought her no

---

* A mistake for Cato, the Roman Censor.

better than she should be, a little loose in the hilts, and free of her hips.*
Thereupon, being grievous in the dumps about it, and now bitterly
hating her, he even resolved to leave that country to get out of her sight:
for now, as every dog has his day, the wench perceiving he came no
longer a-suitoring her, but rather tossed his nose at her, and shunned her,
she began to love him, and doat upon him like anything.' 'That is the
nature of women,' cried Don Quixote, 'not to love when we love them,
and to love when we love them not. But go on.' 'The shepherd then gave
her the slip,' continued Sancho, 'and driving his goats before him, went
trudging through Estremadura, in his way to Portugal. But Toralva,
having a long nose, soon smelt his design; and then what does she do,
think ye, but comes after him bare-foot and bare-legged, with a pilgrim's
staff in her hand, and a wallet at her back, wherein they say she carried a
piece of looking-glass, half a comb, a broken pot with paint, and I do not
know what other trinkums-trankums, to prink herself up. But let her
carry what she would, it is no bread and butter of mine; the short and the
long is, that they say the shepherd with his goats got at last to the river
Guadiana, which happened to be overflowed at that time, and, what is
worse than ill luck, there was neither boat nor bark to ferry him over;
which vexed him the more, because he perceived Toralva at his heels, and
he feared to be teased and plagued with her weeping and wailing. At last
he spied a fisherman in a little boat, but so little it was, that it would carry
but one man and one goat at a time. Well, for all that he called to the
fisherman, and agreed with him to carry him and his three hundred goats,
over the water. The bargain being struck, the fisherman came with his
boat, and carried over one goat; then he rowed back and fetched another
goat, and after that another goat. Pray, sir,' quoth Sancho, 'be sure you
keep a good account how many goats the fisherman ferries over; for if you
happen to miss one, my tale is at an end, and the devil a word have I more
to say. Well then, whereabout was I? – Ho! I have it. – Now the landing-
place on the other side was very muddy and slippery, which made the
fisherman be a long while in going and coming; yet for all that he took
heart of grace, and made shift to carry over one goat, then another, and
then another.' 'Come,' said Don Quixote, 'we will suppose he has landed
them all on the other side of the river; for, as thou goest on by one by one,
we shall not have done these twelve months.' 'Pray let me go on in my
own way,' quoth Sancho. 'How many goats are got over already?' 'Nay,
how the devil can I tell!' replied Don Quixote. 'There it is!' quoth
Sancho: 'did I not bid you keep count? On my word the tale is at an end,

---

* In the original it runs, 'She gave him a certain quantity of little jealousies, above
measure, and within the prohibited degrees,' alluding to certain measures not
to be exceeded (in Spain) on pain of forfeiture and corporal punishment, as
swords above such a standard, etc.

and now you may go whistle for the rest.' 'Ridiculous!' cried Don Quixote: 'pray thee is there no going on with the story unless I know exactly how many goats are wafted over?' 'No, Mary is there not!' quoth Sancho, 'for as soon as you answered, that you could not tell, the rest of the story quite and clean slipped out of my head; and in truth, it is a thousand pities, for it was a special one.' 'So then,' cried Don Quixote, 'the story is ended.' 'Ah, marry is it!' quoth Sancho, 'it is no more to be fetched to life than my dead mother.' 'Upon my honour, cried Don Quixote, 'a most extraordinary story, and told and concluded in as extraordinary a manner! It is a nonsuch, I assure ye; though truly I expected no less from a man of such uncommon parts. Alas I poor Sancho, I am afraid this dreadful noise has turned thy brain.' 'That may well be,' quoth Sancho, 'but, as for my story, I am sure there is nothing more to be said, for where you lose the account of the goats, there it ends.' 'Let it be so,' replied Don Quixote, 'but now let us try whether Rozinante be in humour to march.' With that he gave Rozinante two spurs, and the high-mettled jade answered with one bound, and then stood stock-still, not having the command of his hind legs.

Much about this time, whether it was the coolness of the night, or that Sancho had eaten some loosening food at supper, or, which seems more probable, that nature, by a regular impulse, gave him notice of her desire to perform a certain function that follows the third concoction; it seems, honest Sancho found himself urged to do that which nobody could do for him; but such were his fears that he durst not for his life stir the breadth of a straw from his master; yet, to think ci bearing the intolerable load that pressed him so, was to him as great an impossibility. In this perplexing exigency (with leave be it spoken) he could find no other expedient but to take his right hand from the crupper of the saddle, and softly untying his breeches, let them drop down to his heels; having done this, he as silently took up his shirt, and exposed his posteriors, which were none of the least, to the open air: but the main point was how to ease himself of this terrible burden without making a noise; to which purpose he clutched his teeth close, screwed up his face, shrunk up his shoulders, and held in his breath as much as possible: yet see what misfortunes attend the best projected undertakings! When he had almost compassed his design, he could not hinder an obstreperous sound, very different from those that caused his fear, from unluckily bursting out. 'Hark!' cried Don Quixote, who heard it, 'what noise is that, Sancho?' 'Some new adventures, I will warrant you,' quoth Sancho, 'for ill-luck, you know, seldom comes alone.' Having passed off the thing thus, he even ventured the other strain, and did it so cleverly, that without the least rumour or noise, his business was done effectually, to the unspeakable ease of his body and mind.

But Don Quixote having the sense of smelling as perfect as that of hearing, and Sancho standing so very near, or rather tacked to him, certain fumes, that ascended perpendicularly, began to regale his nostrils with a smell not so grateful as amber. No sooner the unwelcome steams disturbed him, but, having recourse to the common remedy, he stopped his nose, and then, with a snuffling voice, 'Sancho,' said he, 'thou art certainly in great bodily fear.' 'So I am,' quoth Sancho; 'but what makes your worship perceive it now more than you did before?' 'Because,' replied Don Quixote, 'thou smellest now more unsavourily than thou didst before.' 'Ho! that may be,' quoth Sancho; 'but whose fault is that? you may even thank yourself for it. Why do you lead me a wild-goose chase, and bring me at such unseasonable hours to such dangerous places? you know I am not used to it.' 'Pray thee,' said Don Quixote, still holding his nose, 'get thee three or four steps from me; and for the future take more care, and know your distance; for I find, my familiarity with thee has bred contempt.' 'I warrant,' quoth Sancho, 'you think I have been doing something I should not have done.' 'Come, say no more,' cried Don Quixote, 'the more you stir, the worse it will be.'

This discourse, such as it was, served them to pass away the night; and now Sancho, feeling the morning arise, thought it time to untie Rozinante's feet, and do up his breeches; and he did both with so much caution that his master suspected nothing. As for Rozinante, he no sooner felt himself at liberty, but he seemed to express his joy by pawing the ground; for, with his leave be it spoken, he was a stranger to curvetting and prancing. Don Quixote also took it as a good omen, that his steed was now ready to move, and believed it was a signal given him by kind fortune, to animate him to give birth to the approaching adventure.

Now had Aurora displayed her rosy mantle over the blushing skies, and dark night withdrawn her sable veil; all objects stood confessed to human eyes, and Don Quixote could now perceive he was under some tall chestnut trees, whose thick spreading boughs diffused an awful gloom around the place, but he could not yet discover whence proceeded the dismal sound of those incessant strokes. Therefore, being resolved to find it out, once more he took his leave of Sancho, with the same injunctions as before; adding withal, that he should not trouble himself about the recompense of his services, for he had taken care of that in his will, which he had providently made before he left home; but, if he came off victorious from this adventure, he might most certainly expect to be gratified with the promised island. Sancho could not forbear blubbering again, to hear these tender expressions of his master, and resolved not to leave him till he had finished this enterprise. And from that deep concern, and this nobler resolution to attend him, the author of this history infers, that the squire was something of a gentleman by descent, or at least the offspring of the old Christians.* Nor did his good nature fail to move his master more than he was willing to show, at a time when it behoved him to shake off all softer thoughts; for now he rode towards the place whence the noise of the blows and the water seemed to come, while Sancho trudged after him, leading by the halter the inseparable companion of his good and bad fortune.

After they had gone a pretty way under a pleasant covert of chestnut trees, they came into a meadow adjoining to certain rocks, from whose top there was a great fall of waters. At the foot of those rocks they discovered certain old ill-contrived buildings, that rather looked like ruins than inhabited houses; and they perceived that the terrifying noise of the blows, which yet continued, issued out of that place. When they came nearer, even patient Rozinante himself started at the dreadful sound; but, being heartened and pacified by his master, he was at last prevailed with to draw nearer and nearer with wary steps; the knight recommending himself all the way most devoutly to his Dulcinea, and now and then also to Heaven in short ejaculations. As for Sancho, he stuck close to his master, peeping all the while through Rozinante's legs, to see if he could perceive what he dreaded to find out. When a little further, at the doubling of the point of a rock, they plainly discovered (kind reader, do not take it amiss) six huge fulling-mill hammers, which, interchangeably thumping several pieces of cloth, made the terrible noise that caused all Don Quixote's anxieties and Sancho's tribulation that night.

Don Quixote was struck dumb at this unexpected sight, and was ready to drop from his horse with shame and confusion. Sancho stared upon him, and saw him hang down his head, with a desponding, dejected countenance, like a man quite dispirited with this cursed disappointment. At the same time he looked upon Sancho, and seeing by his eyes, and his cheeks swelled with laughter, that he was ready to burst, he could not forbear laughing himself in spite of all his vexation; so that Sancho, seeing his master begin, immediately gave a loose to his mirth, and broke out into such a fit of laughing, that he was forced to hold his sides with both his knuckles, for fear of bursting his aching paunch. Four times he ceased, and four times renewed his obstreperous laughing; which sauciness Don Quixote began to resent with great indignation; and the more when Sancho, in a jeering tone, presumed to ridicule him with his own words, repeating part of the vain speech he made when first they heard the noise: 'Know, Sancho, I was born in this iron age to restore the age of gold. I am the man for whom Heaven has reserved the most dangerous and glorious adventures,' etc. Thus he went on, till his master, dreadfully enraged at his

---

* In contradistinction to the Jewish or Moorish families, of which there were many in Spain.

insolence, hit him two such blows on the shoulders with his lance, that, had they fallen upon his head, they had saved Don Quixote the trouble of paying him his wages, whatever he must have done to his heirs. Thereupon Sancho, finding his jest turn to earnest, begged pardon with all submission. 'Mercy, good your worship,' cried he, 'spare my bones, I beseech you! I meant no harm, I did but joke a little.' 'And because you joke, I do not,' cried Don Quixote. 'Come hither, good Mr. Jester, you who pretend to rally, tell me, had this been a dangerous adventure, as well as it proves only a false alarm, have I not shown resolution enough to undertake and finish it! Am I, who am a knight, bound to know the meaning of every mechanic noise, and distinguish between sound and sound? Besides, it might happen, as really it is, that I had never seen a fulling-mill before, though thou, like a base scoundrel as thou art, wert born and brought up among such mean implements of drudgery. But let the six fulling-hammers be transformed into so many giants, and then set them at me one by one, or all together; and if I do not lay them all at my feet with their heels upwards, then I will give thee leave to exercise thy ill-bred raillery as much as thou pleasest.'

'Good your worship,' quoth Sancho, 'talk no more of it, I beseech you; I confess I carried the jest too far. But now all is hushed and well; pray tell me in sober sadness, as you hope to speed in all adventures, and come off safe and sound as from this, do not you think but that the fright we were in, I mean that I was in, would be a good subject for people to make sport with?' 'I grant it,' answered Don Quixote, 'but I would not have it told; for all people are not so discreet as to place things, or look upon them in the position in which they should be considered.' 'I will say that for you,' quoth Sancho, 'you have shown you understand how to place things in their right position, when aiming at my head, you hit my shoulders; had not I ducked a little on one side, I had been in a fine condition I But let that pass, it will wash out in the bucking. I have heard my grannum say, "That man loves thee well, who makes thee to weep." Good masters may be hasty sometimes with a servant, but presently after a hard word or two they commonly give him a pair of cast breeches: what they give after a basting, Heaven knows; all I can tell is, that knights-errant, after bastinadoes, give you some cast island, or some old-fashioned kingdom upon the mainland.'

'Fortune,' said Don Quixote, 'will perhaps order everything thou hast said to come to pass; therefore, Sancho, I pray thee think no more of my severity; thou knowest a man cannot always command the first impulse of his passions. On the other side, let me advise thee not to be so saucy for the future, and not assume that strange familiarity with me which is so unbecoming in a servant. I protest, in such a vast number of books of knight-errantry as I have read, I never found that any squire was ever allowed so great a freedom of speech with his master as thou takest with me; and truly I look upon it to be a great fault in us both; in thee for disrespecting me, and in me for not making myself be more respected. Gandalin, Amadis de Gaul's squire, though he was earl of the firm island, yet never spoke to his master but with cap in hand, his head bowed, and his body half bent, after the Turkish manner. But what shall we say of Gasabal, Don Galaor's squire, who was such a strict observer of silence, that, to the honour of his marvellous taciturnity, he gave the author occasion to mention his name but once in that voluminous authentic history? From all this, Sancho, I would have thee make this observation, that there ought to be a distance kept between the master and the man, the knight and the squire. Therefore, once more I tell thee, let us live together for the future more according to the due decorum of our respective degrees, without giving one another any further vexation on this account; for, after all, it will always be the worse for you, on whatsoever occasion we happen to disagree. As for the rewards I promised you, they will come in due time; and should you be disappointed that way, you have your salary to trust to, as I have told you.'

'You say very well,' quoth Sancho; 'but now, sir, suppose no rewards should come, and I should be forced to stick to my wages, I would fain know how much a squire-errant used to earn in the days of yore? Did they go by the month, or by the day, like our labourers?' 'I do not think,' replied Don Quixote, 'they ever went by the hire, but rather that they trusted to their master's generosity. And if I have assigned thee wages in my will, which I left sealed up at home, it was only to prevent the worst, because I do not know yet what success I may have in chivalry in these depraved times; and I would not have my soul suffer in the other world for such a trifling matter; for there is no state of life so subject to dangers as that of a knight-errant.' 'Like enough,' quoth Sancho, 'when merely the noise of the hammers of a fulling-mill is able to trouble and disturb the heart of such a valiant knight as your worship! But you may be sure, I will not hereafter so much as offer to open my lips to gibe or joke at your doings, but always stand in awe of you, and honour you as my Lord and Master.' 'By doing so,' replied Don Quixote, 'thy days shall be long on the face of the earth; for next to our parents we ought to respect our masters, as if they were our fathers.'

CHAPTER VII

Of the high Adventure and Conquest of Mambrino's Helmet, with other Events relating to our invincible Knight

AT THE SAME TIME it began to rain, and Sancho would fain have taken shelter in the fulling-mills: but Don Quixote had conceived such an antipathy against them for the shame they had put upon him, that he would by no means be prevailed with to go in; and turning to the right hand, he struck into a highway, where they had not gone far before he discovered a horseman, who wore upon his head something that glittered like gold. The knight had no sooner spied him, but turning to his squire, 'Sancho,' cried he, 'I believe there is no proverb but what is true; they are all so many sentences and maxims drawn from experience, the universal mother of sciences: for instance, that saying, "That where one door shuts, another opens." Thus fortune, that last night deceived us with the false prospect of an adventure, this morning offers us a real one to make us amends; and such an adventure, Sancho, that if I do not gloriously succeed in it, I shall have now no pretence to an excuse, no darkness, no unknown sounds to impute my disappointment to: in short, in all probability yonder comes the man who wears on his head Mambrino's helmet,* and thou knowest the vow I have made.' 'Good sir,' quoth Sancho, 'mind what you say, and take heed what you do; for I would willingly keep my carcase and the case of my understanding from being pounded, mashed, and crushed with fulling-hammers.' 'Hell take the blockhead!' cried Don Quixote: 'is there no difference between a helmet and a fulling-mill?' 'I do not know,' says Sancho, 'but I am sure, were I suffered to speak my mind now as I was wont, mayhaps I would give you such main reasons, that yourself should see you are wide of the matter.' 'How can I be mistaken, thou eternal misbeliever?' cried Don Quixote. 'Dost thou not see that knight that comes riding up directly towards us upon a dapple grey steed, with a helmet of gold on his head?' 'I see what I see,' replied Sancho, 'and the devil of anything I can spy but a fellow on such another grey ass as mine is, with something that glistens on the top of his head.' 'I tell thee, that is Mambrino's helmet,' replied Don Quixote: 'do thou stand at a distance, and leave me to deal with him; thou shalt see, that without trifling away so much as a moment in needless talk, I will finish this adventure, and possess

---

* Mambrino, a Saracen of great valour, who had a golden helmet, which Rinaldo took from him. See 'Orlando Furioso,' Canto 1.

myself Or the desired helmet.' 'I shall stand at a distance, you may be sure,' quoth Sancho; 'but I wish this may not prove another blue bout, and a worse job than the fulling-mills.' 'I have warned you already, fellow,' said Don Quixote, 'not so much as to name the fulling-mills; dare but once more to do it, nay, but to think on it, and I vow to – I say no more; but I will full and pound your dogship into jelly!' These threats were more than sufficient to padlock Sancho's lips, for he had no mind to have his master's vow fulfilled at the expense of his bones.

Now the truth of the story was this: There were in that part of the country two villages; one of which was so little, that it had not so much as a shop in it, nor any barber; so that the barber of the greater village served also the smaller. And thus a person happening to have occasion to be let blood, and another to be shaved, the barber was going thither with his brass basin, which he had clapped upon his head to keep his hat, that chanced to be a new one, from being spoiled by the rain; and as the basin was newly scoured, it made a glittering show a great way off. As Sancho had well observed, he rode upon a grey ass, which Don Quixote as easily took for a dapple-grey steed, as he took the barber for a knight, and his brass basin for a golden helmet; his distracted brain easily applying every object to his romantic ideas. Therefore, when he saw the poor imaginary knight draw near, he fixed his lance, or javelin, to his thigh, and without staying to hold a parley with his thoughtless adversary, flew at him as fiercely as Rozinante would gallop, resolved to pierce him through and through; crying out in the midst of his career, 'Caitiff! wretch! defend thyself, or immediately surrender that which is so justly my due!' The barber, who as he peaceably went along saw that terrible apparition come thundering upon him at unawares, had no other way to avoid being run through with his lance, but to throw himself off from his ass to the ground; and then as hastily getting up, he took to his heels, and ran over the fields swifter than the wind, leaving his ass and his basin behind him. Don Quixote finding himself thus master of the field, and of the basin: 'The miscreant!' cried he, 'who has left this helmet, has shown himself as prudent as the beaver, who finding himself hotly pursued by the hunters, to save his life, tears and cuts off with his teeth that for which his natural instinct tells him he was followed.' Then he ordered Sancho to take up the helmet. 'On my word,' quoth Sancho, having taken it up, 'it is a special basin, and as well worth a piece of eight as a thief is worth a halter.' With that he gave it to his master, who presently clapped it on his head, turning it every way to find out the beaver or vizor; and at last, seeing it had none, 'Doubtless,' said he, 'the Pagan for whom this famous helmet was first made, had a head of a prodigious size; but the worst is, that there is at least one half of it wanting.' Sancho could not forbear smiling to hear his master call the barber's basin a helmet, and had not his fear dashed his mirth he had certainly laughed outright. 'What does the fool grin at now?' cried Don Quixote. 'I laugh,' said he, 'to think what a hugeous jolt-head he must needs have had who was the owner of this same helmet, that looks for all the world like a barber's basin.' 'I fancy,' said Don Quixote, 'this enchanted helmet has fallen by some strange accident into the hands of some person, who, not knowing the value of it, for the lucre of a little money, finding it to be of pure gold, melted one half, and of the other made this head-piece, which, as thou sayest, has some resemblance of a barber's basin. But to me, who know the worth of it, the metamorphosis signifies little; for as soon as ever I come to some town where there is an armourer, I will have it altered so much for the better, that then even the helmet which the God of Smiths made for the God of War shall not deserve to be compared with it. In the mean time I will wear it as it is; it is better than nothing, and will serve at least to save part of my head from the violent encounter of a stone.' 'Ay, that it will,' quoth Sancho, 'so it is not hurled out of a sling, as were those at the battle between the two armies, when they hit you that confounded dowse on the chops, that saluted your worship's cheek-teeth, and broke the pot about your ears in which you kept that blessed drench that made me bring up my inside.' 'True,' cried Don Quixote, 'there I lost my precious balsam indeed; but I do not much repine at it, for thou knowest I have the receipt in my memory.' 'So have I too,' quoth Sancho, 'and shall have while I have breath to draw; but if ever I make any of that stuff, or taste it again, may I give up the ghost with it. Besides, I do not intend ever to do anything that may give occasion for the use of it. For my fixed resolution is, with all my five senses, to preserve myself from hurting and from being hurt by anybody. As to being tossed in a blanket again, I have nothing to say to this for there is no remedy for accidents but patience it seems: so if it ever be my lot to be served so again, I will even shrink up my shoulders, hold my breath, and shut my eyes, and then happy be lucky, let the blanket and fortune even toss on to the end of the chapter.'

'Truly,' said Don Quixote, 'I am afraid thou art no good Christian, Sancho; thou never forgettest injuries. Let me tell thee, it is the part of noble and generous spirits to pass by trifles. Where art thou lame? which of thy ribs is broken? or what part of thy skull is bruised? that you can never think on that jest without malice. For, after all, it was nothing but a jest, a harmless piece of pastime: had I looked upon it otherwise, I had returned to that place before this time, and had made more noble mischief in revenge of the abuse than ever the incensed Grecians did at Troy, for the detention of their Helen, that famed beauty of the ancient world, who, however, had she lived in our age, or had my Dulcinea adorned hers, would have found her charms outrivalled by my mistress's perfections:' and saying this, he heaved up a deep sigh. 'Well, then,' quoth Sancho, 'I will not rip up old sores; let it go for a jest, since there is no revenging it in earnest. But what shall we do with this dapple-grey steed that is so like a grey ass? You see, that same poor devil-errant has left it to shift for itself, poor thing, and by his haste to run off, I do not think he means to come back for it, and, by my beard, the grey beast is a special one.' 'It is not my custom,' replied Don Quixote, 'to plunder those whom I overcome; nor is it usual among us knights, for the victor to take the horse of his vanquished enemy and let him go on foot, unless his own steed be killed or disabled in the combat: therefore, Sancho, leave the horse, or the ass, whatever thou pleasest to call it, the owner will be sure to come for it as soon as he sees us gone.' 'I have a huge mind to take him along with us,' quoth Sancho, 'or at least to exchange him for my own, which is not so good. What, are the laws of knight-errantry so strict, that a man must not exchange one ass for another? At least I hope they will give me leave to swop one harness for another.' 'Truly, Sancho,' replied Don Quixote, 'I am not so very certain as to this last particular, and therefore, till I am better informed, I give thee leave to exchange the furniture, if thou hast absolutely occasion for it.' 'I have so much occasion for it,' quoth Sancho, 'that though it were for my own very self I could not need it more.' So, without any more ado, being authorised by his master's leave, he made *mutatio caparum* (a change of caparisons), and made his own beast three parts in four better* for his new furniture. This done, they breakfasted upon what they left at supper, and quenched their thirst at the stream that turned the fulling-mills, towards which they took care not to cast an eye, for they abominated the very thoughts of them. Thus their spleen being eased, their choleric and melancholic humours assuaged, up they got again, and never minding their way, were all guided by Rozinante's discretion, the depository of his master's will, and also of the ass's, that kindly and sociably always followed his steps wherever he went. Their guide soon brought them again into the high road, where they kept on a slow pace, not caring which way they went.

As they jogged on thus, quoth Sancho to his master, 'Pray, sir, will you give me leave to talk to you a little; for since you have laid that bitter command upon me, to hold my tongue, I have had four or five quaint conceits that have rotted in my gizzard, and now I have another at my tongue's end that I would not for anything should miscarry.' 'Say it,' cried Don Quixote, 'but be short, for no discourse can please when too long.'

'Well, then,' quoth Sancho, 'I have been thinking to myself of late how little is to be got by hunting up and down those barren woods and strange

* Literally leaving him better by a *tierce* and a *quint*. Alluding to the game of piquet, in which a *tierce* or a *quint* may be gained by putting out bad cards, and taking in better.

places, where, though you compass the hardest and most dangerous jobs of knight-errantry, yet no living soul sees or hears of it, and so it is every bit as good as lost; and therefore methinks it were better (with submission to your worship's better judgment be it spoken) that we even went to serve some emperor, or other great prince that is at war; for there you might show how stout, and how wondrous strong and wise you be; which, being perceived by the lord we shall serve, he must needs reward each of us according to his deserts; and there you will not want a learned scholar to set down all your high deeds, that they may never be forgotten: as for mine I say nothing, since they are not to be named the same day with your worship's; and yet I dare a-vouch, that if any notice be taken in knight-errantry of the feats of squires, mine will be sure to come in for a share.'
'Truly, Sancho,' replied Don Quixote, 'there is some reason in what thou sayest; but first of all it is requisite that a knight-errant should spend some time in various parts of the world, as a probationer, in quest of adventures, that, by achieving some extraordinary exploits, his renown may diffuse itself through neighbouring climes and distant nations: so, when he goes to the court of some great monarch, his fame flying before him as his harbinger, secures him such a reception, that the knight has scarce reached the gates of the metropolis of the kingdom, when he finds himself attended and surrounded by admiring crowds, pointing and crying out, "There, there rides the Knight of the Sun (or of the Serpent, or whatever other title the knight takes upon him): that is he," they will cry, "who vanquished in single combat the huge giant Brocabruno, surnamed of the Invincible Strength; that is he that freed the great Mamaluco of Persia from the enchantment that had kept him confined for almost nine hundred years together." Thus, as they relate his achievements with loud acclamations, the spreading rumour at last reaches the king's palace, and the monarch of that country being desirous to be informed with his own eyes, will not fail to look out of his window. As soon as he sees the knight, knowing him by his arms, or by the device on his shield, he will be obliged to say to his attendants, "My lords and gentlemen, haste all of you, as many as are knights, go and receive the flower of chivalry that is coming to our court." At the king's command, away they all run to introduce him; the king himself meets him halfway on the stairs, where he embraces his valorous guest, and kisses his cheek: then, taking him by the hand, he leads him directly to the queen's apartment; where the knight finds her attended by the princess her daughter, who must be one of the most beautiful and most accomplished damsels in the whole compass of the universe. At the same time fate will so dispose of everything, that the princess shall gaze on the knight, and the knight on the princess, and each shall admire one another as persons rather angelical than human; and then, by an accountable charm, they shall both find themselves caught and

entangled in the inextricable net of love, and wonderously perplexed for want of an opportunity to discover their amorous anguish to one another. After this, doubtless, the knight is conducted by the king to one of the richest apartments in the palace; where, having taken off his armour, they will bring him a rich scarlet vestment lined with ermine; and if he looked so graceful cased in steel, how lovely will he appear in all the heightening ornaments of courtiers! Night being come, he shall sup with the king, the queen, and the princess; and shall all the while be feasting his eyes with the sight of the charmer, yet so as nobody shall perceive it; and she will repay him his glances with as much discretion; for, as I have said, she is a most accomplished person. After supper a surprising scene is unexpectedly to appear: enter first an ill-favoured dwarf, and after him a fair damsel between two giants, with the offer of a certain adventure, so contrived by an ancient necromancer, and so difficult to be performed, that he who shall undertake and end it with success, shall be esteemed the best knight in the world. Presently it is the king's pleasure that all his courtiers should attempt it; which they do, but all of them unsuccessfully; for the honour is reserved for the valorous stranger, who effects that with ease which the rest essayed in vain; and then the princess shall be overjoyed, and esteem herself the most happy creature in the world, for having bestowed her affections on so deserving an object.

'Now by the happy appointment of fate, this king, or this emperor, is at war with one of his neighbours as powerful as himself; and the knight being informed of this, after he has been some few days at court, offers the king his service, which is accepted with joy, and the knight courteously kisses the king's hand in acknowledgment of so great a favour. That night the lover takes his leave of the princess at the iron grate before her chamber window, looking into the garden, where he and she have already had several interviews, by means of the princess's confidante, a damsel who carries on the intrigue between them. The knight sighs, the princess swoons, the damsel runs for cold water to bring her to life again, very uneasy also because the morning light approaches, and she would not have them discovered, lest it should reflect on her lady's honour. At last the princess revives, and gives the knight her lovely hand to kiss through the iron grate, which he does a thousand and a thousand times, bathing it all the while with his tears. Then they agree how to transmit their thoughts with secrecy to each other, with a mutual intercourse of letters, during this fatal absence. The princess prays him to return with all the speed of a lover; the knight promises it with repeated vows, and a thousand kind protestations. At last the fatal moment being come that must tear him from all he loves, and from his very self, he seals once more his love on her soft snowy hand, almost breathing out his soul, which mounts to his lips, and even would leave its body to dwell there; and then he is hurried away by the fearful confidante. After this cruel separation he retires to his chamber, throws himself on his bed; but grief will not suffer sleep to close his eyes. Then rising with the sun, he goes to take his leave of the king and the queen: he desires to pay his compliment of leave to the princess, but he is told she is indisposed; and as he has reason to believe that his departing is the cause of her disorder, he is so grieved at the news, that he is ready to betray the secret of his heart; which the princess's confidante observing, she goes and acquaints her with it, and finds the lovely mourner bathed in tears, who tells her, that the greatest affliction of her soul is her not knowing whether her charming knight be of royal blood: but the damsel pacifies her, assuring her that so much gallantry, and such noble qualifications, were unquestionably derived from an illustrious and royal original. This comforts the afflicted fair, who does all she can to compose her looks, lest the king or the queen should suspect the cause of their alteration; and so some days after she appears in public as before. And now the knight, having been absent for some time, meets, fights, and overcomes the king's enemies, takes I do not know how many cities, wins I do not know how many battles, returns to court, and appears before his mistress laden with honour. He visits her privately as before, and they agree that he shall demand her of the king her father in marriage, as the reward of all his services; but the king will not grant his suit, as being unacquainted with his birth; however, whether it be that the princess suffers herself to be privately carried away, or that some other means are used, the knight marries her, and in a little time the king is very well pleased with the match; for now the knight appears to be the son of a mighty king, of I cannot tell you what country, for I think it is not in the map. Some time after the father dies, the princess is heiress, and thus in a trice our knight comes to be king. Having thus completed his happiness, his next thoughts are to gratify his squire, and of all those who have been instrumental in his advancement to the throne: thus he marries his squire to one of the princess's damsels, and most probably to her favourite, who had been privy to the amours, and who is daughter to one of the most considerable dukes in the kingdom.'

'That is what I have been looking for all this while,' quoth Sancho, 'give me but that, and let the world rub, there I will stick; for every tittle of this will come to pass, and be your worship's case, as sure as a gun, if you will take upon you that same nick-name of the Knight of the Woeful Figure.' 'Most certainly, Sancho,' replied Don Quixote; 'for by the same steps, and in that very manner, knights-errant have always proceeded to ascend to the throne: therefore our chief business is to find out some great potentate, either among the Christians or the Pagans, that is at war with his neighbours, and has a fair daughter. But we shall have time enough to inquire after that; for, as I have told thee, we must purchase fame in other places, before we presume to go to court. Another thing makes me more uneasy. Suppose we have found out a king and a princess, and I have filled the world with the fame of my unparalleled achievements, yet cannot I tell how to find out that I am of royal blood, though it were but second cousin to an emperor: for it is not to be expected that the king will ever consent that I should wed his daughter till I have made this out by authentic proofs, though my service deserve it never so much; and thus, for want of a punctilio, I am in danger of losing what my valour so justly merits. It is true, I am a gentleman, and of a noted ancient family, and possessed of an estate of a hundred and twenty crowns a year; nay, perhaps, the learned historiographer, who is to write the history of my life, will so improve and beautify my genealogy, that he will find me to be the fifth, or sixth, at least, in descent from a king: for, Sancho, there are two sorts of originals in the world; some who sprung from mighty kings and princes, by little and little have been so lessened and obscured, that the estates and titles of the following generations have dwindled to nothing, and ended in a point like a pyramid; others, who from mean and low beginnings, still rise and rise, till at last they are raised to the very top of human greatness: so vast the difference is, that those who were something are now nothing, and those that were nothing are now something. And therefore who knows but that I may be one of those whose original is so illustrious; which being handsomely made out, after due examination, ought undoubtedly to satisfy the king, my father-in-law. But even supposing he were still refractory, the princess is to be so desperately in love with me, that she will marry me without his consent, though I were a son of the meanest water-carrier; and if her tender honour scruples to bless me against her father's will, then it may not be amiss to put a pleasant constraint upon her, by conveying her by force out of the reach of her father, to whose persecutions either time or death will be sure to put a period.'

'Ay,' quoth Sancho, 'your rake-helly fellows have a saying that is pat to your purpose, "Never cringe nor creep for what you by force may reap;" though I think it were better said, "A leap from a hedge is better than the prayer of a good man."* No more to be said, if the king, your father-in-law, will not let you have his daughter by fair means, never stand shall I, but fairly and squarely run away with her. All the mischief that I fear is, only, that while you are making your peace with him, and waiting after a dead man's shoes, as the saying is, the poor dog of a squire is like to go long barefoot, and may go hang himself for any good you will be able to do him, unless the damsel go-between, who is to be his wife, run away too with the princess, and he solace himself with her till a better time comes: for I do not see but that the knight may clap up the match between us

---

* Better to rob than to ask charity.

without any more ado.' 'That is most certain,' answered Don Quixote. 'Why then,' quoth Sancho, 'let us even take our chance, and let the world rub.' 'May fortune crown our wishes,' cried Don Quixote, 'and let him be a wretch who thinks himself one.' 'Amen, say I,' quoth Sancho, 'for I am one of your old Christians, and that is enough to qualify me to be an earl.' 'And more than enough,' said Don Quixote, 'for though thou wert not so well descended, being a king, I could bestow nobility on thee, without putting thee to the trouble of buying it, or doing me the least service; and making thee an earl, men must call thee My Lord, though it grieves them never so much.' 'And do you think,' quoth Sancho, 'I would not become my equality main well?' 'Thou shouldest say quality,' said Don Quixote, 'and not equality.' 'Even as you will,' returned Sancho: 'but, as I was saying, I should become an earldom rarely; for I was once beadle to a brotherhood, and the beadle's gown did so become me, that everybody said, I had the presence of a warden. Then how do you think I shall look with a duke's robes on my back, all bedawbed with gold and pearl like any foreign count? I believe we shall have folks come an hundred leagues to see me.' 'Thou wilt look well enough,' said Don Quixote, 'but then thou must shave that rough bushy beard of thine at least every other day, or people will read thy beginning in thy face as soon as they see thee.' 'Why then,' quoth Sancho, 'it is but keeping a barber m my house; and, if needs be, he shall trot after me where-ever I go, like a grandee's master of the horse.' 'How camest thou to know,' said Don Quixote, 'that grandees have their masters of the horse to ride after them?' 'I will tell you,' quoth Sancho, 'some years ago I happened to be about a month among your court-folks, and there I saw a little dandi-prat riding about, who, they said, was a hugeous great lord: there was a man on horseback that followed him close where-ever he went, turning and stopping as he did; you would have thought he had been tied to his horse's tail. With that I asked why that hind man did not ride by the other, but still came after him thus, and they told me he was master of his horses, and that the grandees have always such kind of men at their tail; and I marked this so well, that I have not forgotten it since.' 'Thou art in the right,' said Don Quixote, 'and thou mayest as reasonably have thy barber to attend thee in this manner. Customs did not come up all at once, but rather started up and were improved by degrees; so thou mayest be the first earl that rode in state with his barber behind him; and this may be said to justify thy conduct, that it is an office of more trust to shave a man's beard than to saddle a horse.' 'Well,' quoth Sancho, 'leave the business of the cut-beard to me, and do but take care you be a king and I an earl.' 'Never doubt,' replied Don Quixote; and with that, looking about, he discovered – what the next chapter will tell you.

CHAPTER VIII

How Don Quixote set free many miserable creatures,
who were carrying, much against their wills, to a
place they did not like

CID HAMET BENENGELI, an Arabian and Manchegan author, relates in this most grave, high-sounding, minute, soft, and humorous history, that after this discourse between the renowned Don Quixote and his squire, Sancho Pança, which we laid down at the end of the seventh chapter, the Knight lifting up his eyes, saw about twelve men a-foot, trudging in the road, all in a row, one behind another, like beads upon a string, being linked together by the neck to a huge iron chain, and manacled besides. They were guarded by two horsemen, armed with carabines, and two men a-foot, with swords and javelins. AS soon as Sancho spied them, 'Look ye, sir,' cried he, 'here is a gang of wretches hurried away by main force to serve the king in the galleys.' 'How!' replied Don Quixote, 'is it possible the king will force anybody?' 'I do not say so,' answered Sancho; 'I mean these are rogues whom the law has sentenced for their misdeeds, to row in the kings galleys.' 'However,' replied Don Quixote, 'they are forced, because they do not go of their own free will.' 'Sure enough,' quoth Sancho. 'If it be so,' said Don Quixote, 'they come within the verge of my office, which is to hinder violence and oppression, and succour all people in misery.' 'Ay, sir,' quoth Sancho, 'but neither the king nor law offer any violence to such wicked wretches, they have but their deserts.' By this the chain of slaves came up, when Don Quixote, in very civil terms, desired the guards to inform him why these poor people were led along in that manner? 'Sir,' answered one of the horsemen, 'they are criminals condemned to serve the king in his galleys. That is all that I have to say to you, and you need inquire no further.' 'Nevertheless, sir,' replied Don Quixote, 'I have a great desire to know in few words the cause of their misfortune, and I will esteem it an extraordinary favour, if you will let me have that satisfaction.' 'We have here the copies and certificates of their several sentences,' said the other horseman, 'but we cannot stand to pull them out and read them now; you may draw near and examine the men yourself: I suppose they themselves will tell you why they are condemned; for they are such honest people, they are not ashamed to boast of their rogueries.' With this permission, which Don Quixote would have taken of himself had they denied it him, he rode up to the chain, and asked the first, for what crimes he was in these miserable circumstances? The galley-slave answered him, that it was for being in love. 'What, only for being in love!' cried Don Quixote; 'were all those that are in love to be thus used, I myself might have been long since in the galleys.' 'Ay, but,' replied the slave, 'my love was not of that sort which you conjecture: I was so desperately in love with a basket of linen, and embraced it so close, that had not the judge taken it from me by force, I would not have parted with it willingly. In short, I was taken in the fact, and so there was no need to put me to the rack, it was proved so plain upon me. So I was committed, tried, condemned, had the gentle lash; and besides that, was sent, for three years, to be an element-dasher, and there is an end of the business.' 'An element-dasher!' cried Don Quixote, 'what do you mean by that?' 'A galley-slave,' answered the criminal, who was a young fellow, about four-and-twenty years old, and said he was born at Piedra-Hita.

Then Don Quixote examined the second, but he was so sad and desponding, that we would make no answer; however, the first rogue informed the Knight of his affairs. 'Sir,' said he, 'this canary-bird keeps us company for having sung too much.' 'Is it possible!' cried Don Quixote; 'are men sent to the galleys for singing?' 'Ay, Mary are they,' quoth the arch rogue; 'for there is nothing worse than to sing in anguish.' 'How!' cried Don Quixote, 'that contradicts the saying, "Sing away sorrow, cast away care." ' 'Ay, but with us the case is different,' replied the slave, ' "he that sings in disaster, weeps all his life after." ' 'This is a riddle which I cannot unfold,' cried Don Quixote. 'Sir,' said one of the guards, 'singing in anguish, among these jail-birds, means to confess upon the rack: this fellow was put to the torture, and confessed his crime, which was stealing of cattle; and because he squeaked, or sung, as they call it, he was condemned to the galleys for six years, besides an hundred jerks with a cat-o'-nine-tails that have whisked and powdered his shoulders already. Now the reason why he goes thus mopish and out of sorts, is only because his comrogues jeer and laugh at him continually for not having had the courage to deny: as if it had not been as easy for him to say No as Yes; or, as if a fellow, taken up on suspicion, were not a lucky rogue, when there is no positive evidence can come in against him but his own tongue; and in my opinion they are somewhat in the right.' 'I think so too,' said Don Quixote.

Thence addressing himself to the third, 'And you,' said he, 'what have you done?' 'Sir,' answered the fellow, readily and pleasantly enough, 'I must mow the great meadow for five years together, for want of twice five ducats.' 'I will give twenty with all my heart,' said Don Quixote, 'to deliver thee from that misery.' 'Thank you for nothing,' quoth the slave; 'it is just like the proverb, "After meat comes mustard"; or, like money to a starving man at sea, when there are no victuals to be bought with it. Had I had the twenty ducats you offer me before I was tried, to have greased the clerk's [or recorder's] fist, and have whetted my lawyer's wit, I might have been now at Toledo in the market-place of Zocodover, and not have been thus led along like a dog in a string. But Heaven is powerful, Basta; I say no more.'

Then passing to the fourth, who was a venerable old Don, with a grey beard that reached to his bosom, he put the same question to him; whereupon the poor creature fell a-weeping, and was not able to give him an answer. So the next behind him lent him a tongue. 'Sir,' said he, 'this honest person goes to the galleys for four years, having taken his progress through the town in state, and rested at the usual stations.' 'That is,' quoth Sancho, 'as I take it, after he had been exposed to public shame.'* 'Right,' replied the slave; 'and all this he is condemned to for being a broker of human flesh: for, to tell you the truth, the gentleman is a pimp, and, besides that, he has a smack of conjuring.' 'If it were not for that addition of conjuring,' cried Don Quixote, 'he ought not to have been sent to the galleys, purely for being a pimp, unless it were to be general of the galleys: for, the profession of a bawd, pimp, or messenger of love, is not like other common employments, but an office that requires a great deal of prudence and sagacity; an office of trust and weight, and most highly necessary in a well-regulated commonwealth; nor should it be executed but by civil well-descended persons of good natural parts, and of a liberal education. Nay, it were requisite there should be a comptroller and surveyor of the profession, as there are of others; and a certain and settled number of them, as there are of exchange-brokers. This would be a means to prevent an infinite number of mischiefs that happen every day, because: the trade or profession is followed by poor ignorant pretenders, silly waiting women, young giddy-brained pages, shallow footmen, and such raw inexperienced sort of people, who in unexpected turns and emergencies stand with their fingers in their mouths, know not their right hand from their left, but suffer themselves to be surprised, and spoil all for want of quickness of invention either to conceal, carry on, or bring off a thing artificially. Had I but time I would point out what sort of persons are best qualified to be chosen professors of this most necessary employment in the commonwealth; however, at some fitter season I will inform those of it who may remedy this disorder. All I have to say now, is, that the grief I had to see those venerable grey hairs in such distress, for having followed that no less useful than ingenious vocation of pimping, is now lost in my abhorrence of his additional character of a conjurer; though I very well know that no sorcery in the world can affect or force the will, as some ignorant credulous persons fondly imagine: for our will

---

* Instead of the pillory, in Spain, they carry that sort of malefactors on an ass, and in a particular habit, along the streets, the crier going before and proclaiming their crime.

is a free faculty, and no herb nor charms can constrain it. As for philtres and such like compositions which some silly women and designing pretenders make, they are nothing but certain mixtures and poisonous preparations, that make those who take them run mad; though the deceivers labour to persuade us they can make one person love another; which, as I have said, is an impossible thing, our will being a free, uncontrollable power.' 'You say very well, sir,' cried the old coupler; 'and, upon my honour, I protest I am wholly innocent as to the imputation of witchcraft. As for the business of pimping, I cannot deny it, but I never took it to be a criminal function; for my intention was, that all the world should taste the sweets of love, and enjoy each other's society, living together in friendship and in peace, free from those griefs and jars that unpeople the earth. But my harmless design has not been so happy as to prevent my being sent now to a place whence I never expect to return, stooping as I do under the heavy burden of old age, and being grievously afflicted with the strangury, which scarce affords me a moment's respite from pain.' This said, the reverend procurer burst out afresh into tears and lamentations, which melted Sancho's heart so much, that he pulled a piece of money out of his bosom and gave it to him as an alms.

Then Don Quixote turned to the fifth, who seemed to be nothing at all concerned. 'I go to serve his majesty,' said he, 'for having been somewhat too familiar with two of my cousin-germans, and two other kind-hearted virgins that were sisters; by which means I have multiplied my kind, and begot so odd and intricate a medley of kindred, that it would puzzle a convocation of casuists to resolve their degrees of consanguinity. All this was proved upon me. I had no friends, and what was worse, no money, and so was like to have hung for it: however, I was only condemned to the galleys for six years, and patiently submitted to it. I feel myself yet young, to my comfort; so if my life but does hold out, all will be well in time. If you will be pleased to bestow something upon poor sinners, Heaven will reward you; and when we pray, we will be sure to remember you, that your life may be as long and prosperous, as your presence is goodly and noble.' This brisk spark appeared to be a student by his habit, and some of the guards said he was a fine speaker, and a good Latinist.

After him came a man about thirty years old, a clever, well-set, handsome fellow, only he squinted horribly with one eye: he was strangely loaded with irons; a heavy chain clogged his leg, and was so long, that he twisted it about his waist like a girdle: he had a couple of collars about his neck, the one to link him to the rest of the slaves, and the other, one of those iron-ruffs which they call a keep-friend, or a friend's foot; from whence two irons went down to his middle, and to their two bars were riveted a pair of manacles that gripped him by the fists, and were secured with a large padlock; so that he could neither lift his hands to his mouth, nor bend down his head towards his hands. Don Quixote inquiring why he was worse hampered with irons than the rest, 'Because he alone has done more rogueries than all the rest,' answered one of the guards. 'This is such a reprobate, such a devil of a fellow, that no gaol nor fetters will hold him; we are not sure he is fast enough, for all he is chained so.' 'What sort of crimes then has he been guilty of,' asked Don Quixote, 'that he is only sent to the galleys?' 'Why,' answered the keeper, 'he is condemned to ten years' slavery, which is no better than a civil death: but I need not stand to tell you any more of him, but that he is that notorious rogue Gines de Passamonte, alias Ginesillo de Parapilla.' 'Hark you, sir,' cried the slave, fair and softly; 'what a pox makes you give a gentleman more names than he has? Gines is my Christian name, and Passamonte my surname, and not Ginesillo, nor Parapilla, as you say. Blood! let every man mind what he says, or it may prove the worse for him.' 'Do not you be so saucy, Mr. Crack-rope,' cried the officer to him, 'or I may chance to make you keep a better tongue in your head.' 'It is a sign,' cried the slave, 'that a man is fast, and under the lash; but one day or other somebody shall know whether I am called Parapilla or no.' 'Why, Mr. Slip-string,' replied the officer, 'do not people call you by that name?' 'They do,' answered Gines, 'but I will make them call me otherwise, or I will fleece and bite them worse than I care to tell you now. But you, sir, who are so inquisitive,' added he, turning to Don Quixote, 'if you have a mind to give us anything, pray do it quickly, and go your ways; for I do not like to stand here answering questions; broil me! I am Gines de Passamonte, I am not ashamed of my name. As for my life and conversation, there is an account of them in black and white, written with this numerical hand of mine.' 'There he tells you true,' said the officer, 'for he has written his own history himself, without omitting a tittle of his roguish pranks; and he has left the manuscript in pawn in the prison for two hundred reals.' 'Ay,' said Gines, 'and will redeem it, burn me! though it lay there for as many ducats.' 'Then it must be an extraordinary piece,' cried Don Quixote. 'So extraordinary,' replied Gines, 'that it far outdoes not only Lazarillo de Tormes, but whatever has been, and shall be written in that kind: for mine is true every word, and no invented stories can compare with it for variety of tricks and accidents.' 'What is the title of the book?' asked Don Quixote. ' "The Life of Gines de Passamonte," ' answered the other. 'Is it quite finished?' asked the knight. 'How the devil can it be finished and I yet living?' replied the slave. 'There is in it every material point from my cradle, to this my last going to the galleys.' 'Then it seems you have been there before,' said Don Quixote. 'To serve God and the king, I was some four years there once before,' replied Gines: 'I already know how the biscuit and the bull's-pizzle agree with my carcase: it does not grieve me much to go there again, for there I shall have leisure to give a finishing stroke to my book. I have the devil knows what to add; and in our Spanish galleys there is always leisure and idle time enough in conscience: neither shall I want so much for what I have to insert, for I know it all by heart.'

'Thou seemest to be a witty fellow,' said Don Quixote. 'You should have said unfortunate too,' replied the slave; 'for the bitch fortune is still unkind to men of wit.' 'You mean to such wicked wretches as yourself,' cried the officer. 'Look you, Mr. Commissary.' said Gines, 'I have already desired you to use good language; the law did not give us to your keeping for you to abuse us, but only to conduct us where the king has occasion for us. Let every man mind his own business, and give good words, or hold his tongue: for by the blood – I will say no more, murder will out; there will be a time when some people's rogueries may come to light, as well as those of other folks.' With that the officer, provoked by the slave's threats, held up his staff to strike him; but Don Quixote stepped between them, and desired him not to do it, and to consider, that the slave was the more to be excused for being too free of his tongue, since he had never another member at liberty. Then addressing himself to all the slaves, 'My dearest brethren,' cried he, 'I find, by what I gather from your own words, that though you deserve punishment for the several crimes of which you stand convicted, yet you suffer execution of the sentence by constraint, and merely because you cannot help it. Besides, it is not unlikely but that this man's want of resolution upon the rack, the other's want of money, the third's want of friends and favour, and, in short, the judges' perverting and wresting the law to your great prejudice, may have been the cause of your misery. Now, as Heaven has sent me into the world to relieve the distressed, and free suffering weakness from the tyranny of oppression, according to the duty of my profession of knight-errantry, these considerations induce me to take you under my protection – but, because it is the part of a prudent man not to use violence where fair means may be effectual, I desire you, gentlemen of the guard, to release these poor men, there being people enough to serve his majesty in their places; for it is a hard case to make slaves of men whom God and nature made free; and you have the less reason to use these wretches with severity, seeing they never did you any wrong. Let them answer for their sins in the other world: Heaven is just, you know, and will be sure to punish the wicked, as it will certainly reward the good. Consider besides, gentlemen, that it is neither a Christian-like, nor an honourable action, for men to be the butchers and tormentors of one another; particularly, when no advantage can arise from it. I choose to desire this of you, with so much mildness, and in so peaceable a manner, gentlemen, that I may have occasion to pay you a thankful acknowledgment, if you will be pleased to grant so reasonable a request: but, if you provoke me by refusal, I must be obliged to tell ye, that this lance, and this sword, guided by this invincible arm, shall force you to yield that to my valour which you deny to my civil entreaties.'

'A very good jest indeed,' cried the officer, 'what a devil makes you dote at such a rate? Would you have us set at liberty the king's prisoners, as if we had authority to do it, or you to command it? Go, go about your business, good Sir Errant, and set your basin right upon your empty pate; and pray do not meddle any further in what does not concern you, for those who will play with cats must expect to be scratched.'

'Thou art a cat, and rat, and a coward also,' cried Don Quixote; and with that he attacked the officer with such a sudden and surprising fury, that before he had any time to put himself into a posture of defence, he struck him down dangerously wounded with his lance, and as fortune had ordered it, this happened to be the horseman who was armed with a carbine. His companions stood astonished at such a bold action, but at last fell upon the champion with their swords and darts, which might have proved fatal to him, had not the slaves laid hold of this opportunity to break the chain, in order to regain their liberty: for, the guards perceiving their endeavours to get loose, thought it more material to prevent them, than to be fighting a madman. But as he pressed them vigorously on one side, and the slaves were opposing them and freeing themselves on the other, the hurly-burly was so great, and the guards so perplexed, that they did nothing to the purpose. In the mean time Sancho was helping Gines de Passamonte to get off his chain, which he did sooner than can be imagined; and then that active desperado having seized the wounded officer's sword and carbine, he joined with Don Quixote, and sometimes aiming at one, and sometimes at the other, as if he had been ready to shoot them, yet still without letting off the piece, the other slaves at the same time pouring volleys of stone-shot at the guards, they betook themselves to their heels, leaving Don Quixote and the criminals masters of the field. Sancho, who was always for taking care of the main chance, was not at all pleased with this victory; for he guessed that the guards who were fled would raise a hue and cry, and soon be at their heels with the whole posse of the holy brotherhood, and lay them up for a rescue and rebellion. This made him advise his master to get out of the way as fast as he could, and hide himself in the neighbouring mountains. 'I hear you,' answered Don Quixote to this motion of his squire, 'and I know what I have to do.' Then calling to him all the slaves, who by this time had uncased the keeper to his skin, they gathered about him to know his pleasure, and he spoke to them in this manner. 'It is the part of generous spirits to have a grateful sense of the benefits they receive, no crime being more odious than ingratitude. You see, gentlemen, what I have done for your sakes, and you cannot but be sensible how highly you are obliged to me. Now all the recompense I require is only, that every one of you, loaded with that chain from which I have freed your necks, do instantly repair to the city of Toboso; and there, presenting yourselves before the Lady Dulcinea del Toboso, tell her, that her faithful votary, the Knight of the Woeful Countenance, commanded you to wait on her, and assure her of his profound veneration. Then you shall give her an exact account of every particular relating to this famous achievement, by which you once more taste the sweets of liberty; which done, I give you leave to seek your fortunes where you please.'

To this the ringleader and master-thief, Gines de Passamonte, made answer for all the rest. 'What you would have us do,' said he, 'our noble deliverer, is absolutely impracticable and impossible; for we dare not be seen all together for the world. We must rather part, and skulk some one way, some another, and lie snug in creeks and corners underground for fear of those damned man-hounds that will be after us with a hue and cry; therefore all we can, and ought to do in this case, is to change this compliment and homage which you would have us pay to the Lady Dulcinea del Toboso, into a certain number of Ave Marias and Creeds, which we will say for your worship's benefit; and this may be done by night or by day, walking or standing, and in war as well as in peace: but to imagine we will return to our flesh-pots of Egypt; that is to say, take up our chains again, and lug them the Devil knows where, is as unreasonable as to think it is night now at ten o'clock in the morning. 'Sdeath, to expect this from us, is to expect pears from an elm-tree.' 'Now, by my sword,' replied Don Quixote, 'Sir son of a whore, Sir Ginesello de Parapilla, or whatever be your name, you yourself, alone, shall go to Toboso, like a dog that has scalded his tail, with the whole chain about your shoulders.' Gines, who was naturally very choleric, judging, by Don Quixote's extravagance in freeing them, that he was not very wise, winked on his companions, who, like men that understood signs, presently fell back to the right and left, and pelted Don Quixote with such a shower of stones, that all his dexterity to cover himself with his shield was now ineffectual, and poor Rozinante no more obeyed the spur, than if he had been only the statue of a horse. As for Sancho, he got behind his ass, and there sheltered himself from the volleys of flints that threatened his bones, while his master was so battered, that in a little time he was thrown out of his saddle to the ground. He was no sooner down, but the student leaped on him, took off his basin from his head, gave him three or four thumps on the shoulders with it, and then gave it so many knocks against the stones, that he almost broke it to pieces. After this, they stripped him of his upper coat, and had robbed him of his hose too, but that his greaves hindered them. They also eased Sancho of his upper coat, and left him in his doublet:* then, having divided the spoils, they shifted every one for himself, thinking more how to avoid being taken up, and linked again in the chain, than of trudging with it to my Lady Dulcinea del Toboso. Thus the ass, Rozinante, Sancho, and Don Quixote remained indeed masters of the field, but in an ill condition: the ass hanging his head, and pensive, shaking his ears now and then, as if the volleys of stones had still whizzed about them; Rozinante lying in a desponding manner, for he had been knocked down as well as his unhappy rider; Sancho uncased to his doublet, and trembling for fear of the holy brotherhood; and Don Quixote filled with sullen regret, to find himself so barbarously used by those whom he had so highly obliged.

CHAPTER IX

What befell the renowned Don Quixote in the Sierra Morena (Black Mountains), being one of the rarest Adventures in this Authentic History

DON QUIXOTE finding himself so ill treated, said to his squire: 'Sancho, I have always heard it said, that to do a kindness to clowns is like throwing water into the sea.† Had I given ear to thy advice, I had prevented this misfortune: but, since the thing is done, it is needless to repine; this shall be a warning to me for the future.' 'That is,' quoth Sancho, 'when the Devil is blind: but, since you say you had escaped this mischief had you believed me, good sir, believe me now, and you will escape a greater; for I must tell you that those of the holy brotherhood do not stand in awe of your chivalry, nor do they care a straw for all the knights-errant in the world. Methinks I already hear their arrows whizzing about my ears.'‡ 'Thou art naturally a coward, Sancho,' cried Don Quixote; 'nevertheless, that thou mayest not say that I am obstinate, and never follow thy advice, I will take thy counsel, and for once convey myself out of the reach of this dreadful brotherhood that so strangely alarms thee; but upon this condition, that thou never tell any mortal creature, neither while I live nor after my death, that I withdrew myself from this danger through fear, but

---

* *En pelota*, which really signifies 'stark-naked,' as Sobrino explains it in French, *tout nud*. But it can hardly mean so here, as the reader will soon see, especially if, according to Stevens's Dictionary, Pelota was a sort of garment used in former times in Spain, not known at present.

† It is labour lost, because they are ungrateful.

‡ The troopers of the holy brotherhood ride with bows, and shoot arrows.

merely to comply with thy entreaties: for if thou ever presume to say otherwise, thou wilt belie me; and from this time to that time, and from that time to the world's end, I give thee the lie, and thou liest, and shalt lie in thy throat, as often as thou sayest or but thinkest to the contrary. Therefore do not offer to reply; for shouldst thou but surmise, that I would avoid any danger, and especially this, which seems to give some occasion or colour for fear, I would certainly stay here, though unattended and alone, and expect and face not only the holy brotherhood, which thou dreadest so much, but also the fraternity, or twelve heads of the tribes of Israel, the seven Maccabees, Castor and Pollux, and all the brothers and brotherhoods in the universe.' 'If it please your worship,' quoth Sancho, 'to withdraw is not to run away, and to stay is no wise action when there is more reason to fear than to hope. It is the part of a wise man to keep himself today for tomorrow, and not venture all his eggs in one basket. And though I am but a clown, or a bumpkin, as you may say, yet I would have you to know I know what is what, and have always taken care of the main chance; therefore do not be ashamed of being ruled by me, but even get on horseback if you are able: come, I will help you, and then follow me; for my mind plaguely misgives me that now one pair of heels will stand us in more stead than two pair of hands.'

Don Quixote, without any reply, made shift to mount Rozinante, and Sancho on his ass led the way to the neighbouring mountainous desert, called Sierra Morena,* which the crafty squire had a design to cross over, and get out at the furthest end, either at Viso or Almadovar del Campo, and in the mean time to lurk in the craggy and almost inaccessible retreats of that vast mountain, for fear of falling into the hands of the holy brotherhood. He was the more eager to steer this course, finding that the provision which he had laid on his ass had escaped plundering, which was a kind of miracle, considering how narrowly the galley-slaves had searched everywhere for booty. It was night before our two travellers got to the middle and most desert part of the mountain; where Sancho advised his master to stay some days, at least as long as their provisions lasted; and accordingly that night they took up their lodging between two rocks, among a great number of cork-trees: but Fortune, which, according to the opinion of those that have not the light of true faith, guides, appoints, and contrives all things as she pleases, directed Gines de Passmonte (that master rogue, who, thanks be to Don Quixote's force and folly, had been put in a condition to do him a mischief) to this very part of the mountain,

---

* Sierra, though Spanish for a mountain properly means (not a chain but) a saw, from Latin *Serra*, because of its ridges rising and falling like the teeth of a saw. This mountain (called Morena, from its Moorish or swarthy colour) parts the kingdom of Castile from the province of Andalusia.

in order to hide himself till the heat of the pursuit, which he had just cause to fear, was over. He discovered our adventurers much about the time that they fell asleep; and, as wicked men are always ungrateful, and urgent necessity prompts many to do things, at the very thoughts of which they perhaps would start at other times; Gines, who was a stranger both to gratitude and humanity, resolved to ride away with Sancho's ass; for, as for Rozinante, he looked upon him as a thing that would neither sell nor pawn: so while poor Sancho lay snoring, he spirited away his darling beast, and made such haste that before day he thought himself and his prize secure from the unhappy owner's pursuit.

Now Aurora with her smiling face returned to enliven and cheer the earth; but, alas! to grieve and affright Sancho with a dismal discovery: for he had no sooner opened his eyes, but he missed his ass, and finding himself deprived of that dear partner of his fortunes, and best comfort in his peregrinations, he broke out into the most pitiful and sad lamentations in the world; insomuch that he waked Don Quixote with his moans. 'O dear child of my bowels,' cried he, 'born and bred under my roof, my children's playfellow, the comfort of my wife, the envy of my neighbours, the ease of my burdens, the staff of my life, and, in a word, half my maintenance! for, with six-and-twenty maravedis, which were daily earned by thee, I made shift to keep half my family.' Don Quixote, who easily guessed the cause of these complaints, strove to comfort him with kind, condoling words, and learned discourses upon the uncertainty of human happiness: but nothing proved so effectual to assuage his sorrow, as the promise which his master made him of drawing a bill of exchange on his niece for three asses out of five which he had at home, payable to Sancho Pança, or his order; which prevailing argument soon dried up his tears, hushed his sighs and moans, and turned his complaints into thanks to his generous master for so unexpected a favour.

And now, as they wandered further in these mountains, Don Quixote was transported with joy to find himself where he might flatter his ambition with the hopes of fresh adventures to signalise his valour; for these vast deserts made him call to mind the wonderful exploits of other knights-errant performed in such solitudes. Filled with those airy notions, he thought on nothing else: but Sancho was for more substantial food; and now thinking himself quite out of the reach of the holy brotherhood, his only care was to fill his belly with the relics of the clerical booty; and thus, sitting sideling, as women do, upon his beast,* he slily took out now one

---

* It is scarce twenty lines since Sancho lost his ass, as Mr. Jarvis observes and here he is upon his back again. The best excuse for this evident blunder, adds that gentleman, is Horace's *aliquando bonus dormitat Homerus*. Upon which occasion the same gentleman, in his preface, asks, 'But what if Cervantes made

piece of meat, then another, and kept his grinders going faster than his feet. Thus plodding on, he would not have given a rush to have met with any other adventure.

While he was thus employed, he observed that his master endeavoured to take up something that lay on the ground with the end of his lance: this made him run to help him to lift up the bundle, which proved to be a portmanteau and the seat of a saddle, that were half, or rather quite rotten with lying exposed to the weather. The portmanteau was somewhat heavy; and Don Quixote having ordered Sancho to see what it contained, though it was shut with a chain and a padlock, he easily saw what was in it through the cracks, and pulled out four fine holland shirts, and other clean and fashionable linen, besides a considerable quantity of gold tied up in a handkerchief. 'Bless my eyesight!' quoth Sancho; 'and now, Heaven, I thank thee for sending us such a lucky adventure once in our lives: 'with that, groping further in the portmanteau, he found a table-book richly bound. 'Give me that,' said Don Quixote, 'and do thou keep the gold.' 'Heaven reward your worship,' quoth Sancho, kissing his master's hand, and at the same time clapping up the linen and the other things into the bag where he kept the victuals. 'I fancy,' said Don Quixote, 'that some person, having lost his way in these mountains, has been met by robbers who have murdered him, and buried his body somewhere hereabouts.' 'Sure your worship's mistaken,' answered Sancho; 'for had they been highwaymen, they would never have left such a booty behind them.' 'Thou art in the right,' replied Don Quixote; 'and therefore I cannot imagine what it must be. But stay, I will examine the table-book, perhaps we shall find something written in that which will help us to discover what I would know.' With that he opened it, and the first thing he found was the following rough draft of a sonnet, fairly enough written to be read with ease: so he read it aloud, that Sancho might know what was in it as well as himself.

---

this seeming slip on purpose for a bait to tempt the minor critics in the same manner as, in another place, he makes the Princess of Micomicon land at Ossuna, which is no seaport? As by that he introduced a fine satire on an eminent Spanish historian of his time, who had described it as such in his history, so by this he might have only taken occasion to reflect on a parallel incident in Ariosto where Brunelo at the siege of Albraca steals a horse from between the legs of Sacripante, king of Circassia. It is,' adds this judicious critic, 'the very defence the author makes for it himself in the fourth chapter of the second part, where, by the way, both the Italian and old English translators have preserved the excuse, though by their altering the text they had taken away the occasion of it.'

'THE RESOLVE. A SONNET

'Love is a god ne'er knows our pain,
  Or cruelty's his darling attribute;
Else he'd ne'er force me to complain,
  And to his spite my raging pain impute.
But sure, if Love's a god, he must
  Have knowledge equal to his power;
And 'tis a crime to think a god unjust:
  Whence then the pains that now my heart devour?
From Phyllis? No: why do I pause?
Such cruel ills ne'er boast so sweet I cause;
  Nor from the gods such torments we do bear,
Let death then quickly be my cure.
When thus we ills unknown endure,
  'Tis shortest to despair.'

'The devil of anything can be picked out of this,' quoth Sancho, 'unless you can tell who that same Phyllis.' 'I did not read "Phyll," but "Phyllis," ' said Don Quixote. 'Oh, then, mayhap, the man has lost his filly-foal.' 'Phyllis,' said Don Quixote, 'is the name of a lady that is beloved by the author of this sonnet, who truly seems to be a tolerable poet,* or I have but little judgment.' 'Why then,' quoth Sancho, 'belike your worship understands how to make verses, too?' 'That I do,' answered Don Quixote, 'and better than thou imaginest, as thou shalt see, when I shall give thee a letter written all in verse to carry to my Lady Dulcinea del Toboso; for I must tell thee, friend Sancho, all the knights-errant, or at least, the greatest part of them, in former times, were great poets, and as great musicians: those qualifications, or, to speak better, those two gifts or accomplishments, being almost inseparable from amorous adventures: though, I must confess, the verses of the knights in former ages are not altogether so polite, nor so adorned with words, as with thoughts and inventions.'

'Good sir,' quoth Sancho, 'look again into the pocketbook, mayhap you will find somewhat that will inform you of what you would know.' With that Don Quixote, turning over the leaf, 'Here is some prose,' cried he, 'and I think it is the sketch of a love-letter.' 'O! good your worship,' quoth Sancho, 'read it out by all means; for I mightily delight in hearing of love-stories.'

Don Quixote read it aloud, and found what follows:

* Cervantes himself

'The falsehood of your promises, and my despair, hurry me from you for ever; and you shall sooner hear the news of my death, than the cause of my complaints. You have forsaken me, ungrateful fair, for one more wealthy indeed, but not more deserving than your abandoned slave. Were virtue esteemed a treasure equal to its worth by your unthinking sex, I must presume to say, I should have no reason to envy the wealth of others, and no misfortune to bewail. What your beauty has raised, your actions have destroyed; the first made me mistake you for an angel, but the last convince me you are a very woman. However, O! too lovely disturber of my peace, may uninterrupted rest and downy ease engross your happy hours; and may forgiving Heaven still keep your husband's perfidiousness concealed, lest it should cost your repenting heart a sigh for the injustice you have done to so faithful a lover, and so I should be prompted to a revenge which I do not desire to take. Farewell.'

'This letter,' quoth Don Quixote, 'does not give us any further insight into the things we would know; all I can infer from it is, that the person who wrote it was a betrayed lover; 'and so, turning over the remaining leaves, he found several other letters and verses, some of which were legible, and some so scribbled, that he could make nothing of them. As for those he read, he could meet with nothing in them but accusations, complaints, and expostulations, distrusts and jealousies, pleasures and discontents, favours and disdain, the one highly valued, the other as mournfully resented. And while the knight was poring on the table-book, Sancho was rummaging the portmanteau and the seat of the saddle, with that exactness, that he did not leave a corner unsearched, nor a seam unripped, nor a single lock of wool unpicked; for the gold he had found, which was above a hundred ducats, had but whetted his greedy appetite, and made him wild for more. Yet though this was all he could find, he thought himself well paid for the more than Herculean labours he had undergone; nor could he now repine at his being tossed in a blanket, the straining and gripping operation of the balsam, the benedictions of pack-staves and levers, the fisticuffs of the lewd carrier, the loss of his cloak, his dear wallet, and of his dearer ass, and all the hunger, thirst, and fatigue which he had suffered in his kind master's service. On the other side, the Knight of the Woeful Figure strangely desired to know who was the owner of the portmanteau, guessing by the verses, the letter, the linen, and the gold, that he was a person of worth, whom the disdain and unkindness of his mistress had driven to despair. At length, however, he gave over the thoughts of it, discovering nobody through that vast desert; and so he rode on, wholly guided by Rozinante's discretion, which always made the grave sagacious creature choose the plainest and smoothest way;

the master still firmly believing, that in those woody, uncultivated forests he should infallibly start some wonderful adventure.

And indeed, while these hopes possessed him, he spied upon the top of a stony crag just before him, a man that skipped from rock to rock, over briers and bushes, with wonderful agility. He seemed to him naked from the waist upwards, with a thick black beard, his hair long, and strangely tangled, his head, legs, and feet bare; on his hips a pair of breeches, that appeared to be of sad-coloured velvet, but so tattered and torn, that they discovered his skin in many places. These particulars were observed by Don Quixote while he passed by: and he followed him, endeavouring to overtake him; for he presently guessed this was the owner of the portmanteau. But Rozinante, who was naturally slow and phlegmatic, was in too weak a case besides to run races with so swift an apparition: yet the Knight of the Woeful Figure resolved to find out that unhappy creature, though he were to bestow a whole year in the search; and, to that intent, he ordered Sancho to beat one side of the mountain, while he hunted the other. 'In good sooth,' quoth Sancho, 'your worship must excuse me as to that; for if I but offer to stir an inch from you, I am almost frighted out of my seven senses: and let this serve you hereafter for a warning, that you may not send me a nail's breadth from your presence.' 'Well,' said the Knight, 'I will take thy case into consideration; and it does not displease me, Sancho, to see thee thus rely upon my valour, which I dare assure thee shall never fail thee, though thy very soul should be scared out of thy body. Follow me, therefore, step by step, with as much baste as is consistent with good speed; and let thy eyes pry everywhere while we search every part of this rock, where, it is probable, we may meet with that wretched mortal, who, doubtless, is the owner of the portmanteau.'

'Odsnigs, sir,' quoth Sancho, 'I had rather get out of his way; for should we chance to meet him, and he lay claim to the portmanteau, it is a plain case I shall be forced to part with the money: and therefore I think it much better, without making so much ado, to let me keep it *bona fide*, till we can light on the right owner some more easy way, and without dancing after him; which may not happen till we spend all the money; and in that case I am free from the law, and he may go whistle for it.' 'Thou art mistaken, Sancho,' cried Don Quixote; 'for, seeing we have some reason to think that we know who is the owner, we are bound in conscience to endeavour to find him out, and restore it to him; the rather, because should we not now strive to meet him, yet the strong presumption we have that the goods belong to him, would make us possessors of them *mala fide*, and render us as guilty as if the party whom we suspect to have lost the things were really the right owner; therefore, friend Sancho, do not think much of searching for him, since if we find him out, it will extremely ease my mind.' With that he spurred Rozinante; and Sancho, not very well pleased, followed him, comforting himself, however, with the hopes of the three asses which his master had promised him. So when they had ridden over the greatest part of the mountain, they came to a brook, where they found a mule lying dead, with her saddle and bridle about her, and herself half devoured by beasts and birds of prey; which discovery further confirmed them in their suspicion, that the man who fled so nimbly from them was the owner of the mule and portmanteau. Now, as they paused and pondered upon this, they heard a whistling like that of some shepherd keeping his flocks; and presently after, upon their left hand, they spied a great number of goats, with an old herdsman after them, on the top of the mountain. Don Quixote called out to him, and desired him to come down; but the goatherd, instead of answering him, asked them in as loud a tone, how they came thither in those deserts, where scarce any living creatures resorted excepts goats, wolves, and other wild beasts? Sancho told him, they would satisfy him as to that point, if he would come where they were. With that the goatherd came down to them; and seeing them look upon the dead mule, 'That dead mule,' said the old fellow, 'has lain in that very place these six months; but pray tell me, good people, have you not met the master of it by the way?' 'We have met nobody,' answered Don Quixote; 'but we found a portmanteau and a saddle-cushion not far from this place.' 'I have seen it too,' quoth the goatherd, 'but I never durst meddle with it, nor so much as come near it, for fear of some misdemeanour, lest I should be charged with having stolen somewhat out of it: for who knows what might happen? The Devil is subtle, and sometimes lays baits in our way to tempt, or blocks to make us stumble.' 'It is just so with me, gaffer,' quoth Sancho; 'for I saw the portmanteau too, do ye see, but the devil a bit would I come within a stone's throw of it; no, there I found it, and there I left it; in faith, it shall even lie there still for me. He that steals a bellwether shall be discovered by the bell.' 'Tell me, honest friend,' asked Don Quixote, 'dost thou know who is the owner of those things?' 'All I know of the matter,' answered the goatherd, 'is, that it is now six months, little more or less, since to a certain sheepfold, some three leagues off, there came a young, well-featured, proper gentleman in good clothes, and under him the same mule that now lies dead here, with the cushion and cloak-bag, which you say you met, but touched not. He asked us which was the most desert and least frequented part of these mountains; and we told him this where we are now; and in that we spoke the plain truth, for should you venture to go but half a league further, you would hardly be able to get back again in haste; and I marvel how you could get even thus far; for there is neither highway nor footpath that may direct a man this way. Now as soon as the young gentleman had heard our answer, he turned about his mule, and made to the place we showed him, leaving us all with a hugeous liking for his comeliness, and strangely marvelling at his demand, and the haste he made towards the middle of the mountain. After that we heard no more of him for a great while, till one day by chance one of the shepherds coming by, he fed upon him, without saying why, or wherefore, and beat him without mercy: after that he went to the ass that carried our victuals, and taking away all the bread and cheese that was there, he tripped back again to the mountain with wondrous speed. Hearing this, a good number of us together resolved to find him out; and when we had spent the best part of two days in the thickest of the forest, we found him at last lurking in the hollow of a huge cork-tree, from whence he came forth to meet us as mild as could be. But then he was so altered, his face was so disfigured, wan, and sunburnt, that had it not been for his attire, which we made shift to know again, though it was all in rags and tatters, we could not have thought it had been the same man. He saluted us courteously, and told us, in few words, mighty handsomely put together, that we were not to marvel to see him in that manner, for that it behoved him so to be, that he might fulfil a certain penance enjoined him for the great sins he had committed. We prayed him to tell us who he was, but he would by no means do it: we likewise desired him to let us know where we might find him, that whensoever he wanted victuals we might bring him some, which we told him we would be sure to do; for otherwise he would be starved in that barren place; requesting him, that if he did not like that motion neither, he would, at least, come and ask us for what he wanted, and not take it by force as he had done. He thanked us heartily for our offer, and begged pardon for that injury, and promised to ask it henceforwards as an alms, without setting upon any one. As for his place of abode, he told us, he had none certain, but wherever night caught him, there he lay: and he ended his discourse with such bitter moans, that we must have had hearts of flint had we not had a feeling of them, and kept him company therein; chiefly, considering him so strangely altered from what we had seen him before: for, as I said, he was a very fine comely young man, and by his speech and behaviour we could guess him to be well-born, and a court-like sort of a body: for though we were but clowns, yet such was his genteel behaviour, that we could not help being taken with it. Now as he was talking to us, he stopped of a sudden, as if he had been struck dumb, fixing his eyes steadfastly on the ground; whereat we all stood in amaze. After he had thus stared a good while he shut his eyes, then opened them again, bit his lips, knit his brows, clutched his fists; and then rising from the ground, whereon he had thrown himself a little before, he flew at the man that stood next to him with such fury that if we had not pulled him off by main force, he would have bit and thumped him to death; and all the while he cried out, "Ah! traitor Ferdinand, here, here thou shalt pay for the wrong thou hast done me: I must rip up that false heart of thine!" And a deal more he added, all in dispraise of that same Ferdinand. After that he flung from us without saying a word, leaping over the bushes and brambles at such a strange rate, that it was impossible for us to come at him; from which we gathered that his madness comes on him by fits, and that same one called Ferdinand had done him an ill-turn that hath brought the poor young man to this pass. And this hath been confirmed since that many and many times; for when he is in his right senses he will come and beg for victuals, and thank us for it with tears. But when he is in his mad fit, he will beat us, though we proffer him meat civilly; and to tell you the truth, sirs,' added the goatherd, 'I and four others, of whom two are my men, and the other two my friends, yesterday agreed to look for him till we should find him out, either by fair means or by force to carry him to Almodover town, that is but eight leagues off; and there we will have him cured, if possible, or at least we shall learn what he is when he comes to his wits, and whether he has any friends to whom he may be sent back. This is all I know of the matter; and I dare assure you that the owner of those things which you saw in the way, is the selfsame body that went so nimbly by you;' for Don Quixote had by this time acquainted the goatherd of his having seen that man skipping among the rocks.

The Knight was wonderfully concerned when he had heard the goatherd's story, and renewed his resolution of finding out that distracted wretch, whatever time and pains it might cost him. But fortune was more propitious to his desires than he could reasonably have expected: for, just as they were speaking, they spied him right against the place where they stood, coming towards them out of the cleft of a rock, muttering somewhat to himself, which they could not well have understood had they stood close by him, much less could they guess his meaning at that distance. His apparel was such as has already been said, only Don Quixote observed, when he drew nearer, that he had on a shamoy waistcoat torn in many places, which yet the Knight found to be perfumed with amber; and by this, as also by the rest of his clothes, and other conjectures, he judged him to be a man of some quality. As soon as the unhappy creature came near them, he saluted them very civilly, but with a hoarse voice. Don Quixote returned his civilities, and, alighting from Rozinante, accosted him in a very graceful manner, and hugged him close in his arms, as if he had been one of his intimate acquaintance. The other, whom we may venture to call the Knight of the Ragged Figure, as well as Don Quixote the Knight of the Woeful Figure, having got loose from that embrace, could not forbear stepping back a little, and laying his hands on the champion's shoulders, he stood staring in his face, as if he had been striving to call to mind whether he had known him before, probably wondering as much to behold Don Quixote's countenance, armour, and strange figure, as Don Quixote did to see his tattered condition: but the first that opened his mouth after this pause was the ragged knight, as you shall find by the sequel of the story.

CHAPTER X

The Adventure of the Sierra Morena continued

THE HISTORY RELATES, that Don Quixote listened with great attention to the disastrous knight of the mountain, who made him the following compliment, 'Truly, sir, whoever you be (tor I have not the honour to know you) I am much obliged to you for your expressions of civility and friendship; and I could wish I were in a condition to convince you otherwise than by words of the deep sense I have of them! But my bad fortune leaves me nothing to return for so many favours, but unprofitable wishes.' 'Sir,' answered Don Quixote, 'I have so hearty a desire to serve you, that I was fully resolved not to depart from these mountains till I had found you out, that I might know from you whether the discontents that have urged you to make choice of this unusual course of life, might not admit of a remedy; for, if they do, assure yourself I will leave no means untried, till I have purchased you that ease which I heartily wish you: or if your disasters are of that fatal kind that exclude you for ever from the hopes of comfort or relief, then will I mingle sorrows with you, and by sharing your load of grief, help you to bear the oppressing weight of affliction: for it is the only comfort of the miserable to have partners in their woes. If then good intentions may plead merit, or a grateful requital, let me entreat you, sir, by that generous nature that shoots through the gloom with which adversity has clouded your graceful outside; nay, let me conjure you by the darling object of your wishes, to let me know who you are, and what strange misfortunes have urged you to withdraw from the converse of your fellow-creatures, to bury yourself alive in this horrid solitude, where you linger out a wretched being, a stranger to ease, to all mankind, and even to your very self. And I solemnly swear,' added Don Quixote, 'by the order of knighthood, of which I am an unworthy professor, that if you so far gratify my desires, I will assist you to the utmost of my capacity, either by remedying your disaster, if it is not past redress; or at least, I will become your partner in sorrow, and strive to ease it by a society in sadness.'

The Knight of the Wood, hearing the Knight of the Woeful Figure talk at that rate, looked upon him steadfastly for a long time, and viewed and reviewed him from head to foot; and when he had gazed a great while upon him, 'Sir,' cried he, 'if you have anything to eat, for Heaven's sake give it me, and when my hunger is abated, I shall be better able to comply with your desires, which your great civilities and undeserved offers oblige me to satisfy.' Sancho and the goatherd hearing this, presently took out some victuals, the one out of his bag, the other out of his scrip, and gave it to the ragged knight to allay his hunger, who immediately fell on with that greedy haste, that he seemed rather to devour than to feed; for he used no intermission between bite and bite, so greedily he chopped them up: and all the time he was eating, neither he, nor the by-standers, spoke the least word. When he had assuaged his voracious appetite, he beckoned to Don Quixote and the rest to follow him; and after he had brought them to a neighbouring meadow, he laid himself at his ease on the grass, where the rest of the company sitting down by him, neither he nor they having yet spoke a word since he fell to eating, be began in this manner.

'Gentlemen,' said he, 'if you intend to be informed of my misfortunes, you must promise me before-hand not to cut off the thread of my doleful narration with any questions, or any other interruption; for in the very instant that any of you do it, I shall leave off abruptly; and will not afterwards go on with the story.' This preamble put Don Quixote in mind of Sancho's ridiculous tale, which by his neglect in not telling the goats, was brought to an untimely conclusion. 'I only use this precaution,' added the ragged knight, 'because I would be quick in my relation; for the very remembrance of my former misfortune proves a new one to me, and yet I promise you I will endeavour to omit nothing that is material, that you may have as full an account of my disasters as I am sensible you desire.' Thereupon Don Quixote, for himself and the rest, having promised him uninterrupted attention, he proceeded in this manner: 'My name is Cardenio, the place of my birth one of the best cities in Andalusia; my descent noble,* my parents wealthy; but my misfortunes are so great, that they have doubtless filled my relations with the deepest of sorrows; nor are they to be remedied with wealth, for goods of fortune avail but little against the anger of Heaven. In the same town dwelt the charming Lucinda, the most beautiful creature that ever nature framed, equal in descent and fortune to myself, but more happy and less constant. I loved, nay adored her almost from her infancy; and from her tender years she blessed me with as kind a return as is suitable with the innocent freedom of that age. Our parents were conscious of that early friendship; nor did they oppose the growth of this inoffensive passion, which they perceived could have no other consequences than a happy union of our families by marriage; a thing which the equality of our births and fortunes did indeed of itself almost invite us to. Afterwards our loves so grew up with our

* In Spain all the gentry are called noble.

years, that Lucinda's father, either judging our usual familiarity prejudicial
to his daughter's honour, or for some other reasons, sent to desire me to
discontinue my frequent visits to his house: but this restraint proved but
like that which was used by the parents of that loving Thisbe, so
celebrated by the poets, and but added flames to flames, and impatience to
desires. As our tongues were now debarred their former privilege, we had
recourse to our pens, which assumed the greater freedom to disclose the
most hidden secrets of our hearts; for the presence of the beloved object
often heightens a certain awe and bashfulness, that disorders, confounds
and strikes dumb even the most passionate lover. How many letters have I
writ to that lovely charmer! how many soft moving verses have I addressed
to her I what kind, yet honourable returns have I received from her! The
mutual pledges of our secret loves, and the innocent consolations of a
violent passion. At length, languishing and wasting with desire, deprived
of that reviving comfort of my soul, I resolved to remove those bars with
which her father's care and decent caution obstructed my only happiness,
by demanding her of him in marriage. He very civilly told me, that he
thanked me for the honour I did him, but that I had a father alive, whose
consent was to be obtained as well as his, and who was the most proper
person to make such a proposal. I thanked him for his civil answer, and
thought it carried some show of reason, not doubting but my father would
readily consent to the proposal. I therefore immediately went to wait on
him, with a design to beg his approbation and assistance. I found him in
his chamber, with a letter opened before him, which, as soon as he saw
me, he put into my hand, before I could have time to acquaint him with
my business. "Cardenio," said he, "you will see by this letter the
extraordinary kindness that Duke Ricardo has for you." I suppose I need
not tell you, gentlemen, that this Duke Ricardo is a grandee of Spain,
most of whose estate lies in the best part of Andalusia. I read the letter,
and found it contained so kind and advantageous an offer, that my father
could not but accept of it with thankfulness: for the Duke entreated him
to send me to him with all speed, that I might be the companion of his
eldest son, promising withal to advance me to a post answerable to the
good opinion he had of me. This unexpected news struck me dumb; but
my surprise and disappointment were much greater, when I heard my
father say to me, "Cardenio, you must get ready to be gone in two days: in
the meantime, give Heaven thanks for opening you a way to that
preferment which I am so sensible you deserve." After this he gave me
several wise admonitions, both as a father and a man of business, and then
he left me. The day fixed for my journey quickly came; however, the night
that preceded it, I spoke to Lucinda at her window, and told her what had
happened. I also gave her father a visit, and informed him of it too,
beseeching him to preserve his good opinion of me, and defer the

bestowing of his daughter till I had been with Duke Ricardo, which he kindly promised me: and then Lucinda and I, after an exchange of vows and protestations of eternal fidelity, took our leaves of each other with all the grief which two tender and passionate lovers can feel at a separation.

'I left the town, and went to wait upon the Duke, who received and entertained me with that extraordinary kindness and civility that soon raised the envy of his greatest favourites. But he that most endearingly caressed me, was Don Ferdinand, the Duke's second son, a young, airy, handsome, generous gentleman, and of a very amorous disposition: he seemed to be overjoyed at my coming, and in a most obliging manner told me, he would have me one of his most intimate friends. In short, he so really convinced me of his affection, that though his elder brother gave me many testimonies of love and esteem, yet could I easily distinguish between their favours. Now, as it is common for bosom friends to keep nothing secret from each other, Don Ferdinand relying as much on my fidelity, as I had reason to depend on his, revealed to me his most private thoughts; and among the rest, his being in love with the daughter of a very rich farmer, who was his father's vassal. The beauty of that lovely country maid, her virtue, her discretion, and the other graces of her mind, gained her the admiration of all those who approached her; and those uncommon endowments had so charmed the soul of Don Ferdinand, that, finding it absolutely impossible to corrupt her chastity, since she would not yield to his embraces as a mistress, he resolved to marry her. I thought myself obliged by all the ties of gratitude and friendship to dissuade him from so unsuitable a match; and therefore I made use of such arguments as might have diverted any one but so confirmed a lover from such an unequal choice. At last, finding them all ineffectual, I resolved to inform the Duke, his father, with his intentions: but Don Ferdinand was too clear-sighted not to read my design in my great dislike of his resolutions; and dreading such a discovery, which he knew my duty to his father might well warrant, in spite of our intimacy, since I looked upon such a marriage as highly prejudicial to them both, he made it his business to hinder me from betraying his passion to his father, assuring me there would be no need to reveal it to him. To blind me the more effectually, he told me he was willing to try the power of absence, that common cure of love, thereby to wear out and lose his unhappy passion; and that in order to this, he would take a journey with me to my father's house, pretending to buy horses in our town, where the best in the world are bred. No sooner had I heard this plausible proposal but I approved it, swayed by the interest of my own love, that made me fond of an opportunity to see my absent Lucinda. I have heard since, that Don Ferdinand had already been blessed by his mistress with all the liberty of boundless love, upon a promise of marriage, and that he only waited an opportunity to discover it with safety, being afraid of incurring his father's indignation. But as what we call love in young men, is too often only an irregular passion, and boiling desire, that has no other object than sensual pleasure, and vanishes with enjoyment, while real love, fixing itself on the perfections of the mind, is still improving and permanent; as soon as Don Ferdinand had accomplished his lawless desires, his strong affection slackened, and his hot love grew cold: so that if at first his proposing to try the power of absence was only a pretence, to get rid of his passion, there was nothing now which he more heartily coveted, than that he might thereby avoid fulfilling his promise. And therefore, having obtained the Duke's leave, away we posted to my father's house, where Don Ferdinand was entertained according to his quality; and I went to visit my Lucinda, who, by a thousand innocent endearments, made me sensible, that her love, like mine, was rather heightened than weakened by absence, if anything could heighten a love so great and so perfect. I then thought myself obliged by the laws of friendship, not to conceal the secrets of my heart from so kind and intimate a friend, who had so generously entrusted me with his; and therefore, to my eternal ruin, I unhappily discovered to him my passion. I praised Lucinda's beauty, her wit, her virtue, and praised them so like a lover, so often, and so highly, that I raised in him a great desire to see so accomplished a lady; and, to gratify his curiosity, I showed her to him by the help of a light one evening, at a low window, where we used to have our amorous interviews. She proved but too charming, and too strong a temptation to Don Ferdinand; and her prevailing image made so deep an impression on his soul, that it was sufficient to blot out of his mind all those beauties that had till then employed his wanton thoughts: he was struck dumb with wonder and delight, at the sight of the ravishing apparition; and, in short to see her, and to love her, proved with him the same thing: and, when I say to love her, I need not add to desperation, for there is no loving her but to an extreme. If her face made him so soon take fire, her wit quickly set him all in a flame. He often importuned me to communicate to him some of her letters, which I indeed would never expose to any eyes but my own; but unhappily one day he found one, wherein she desired me to demand her of her father, and to hasten the marriage. It was penned with that tenderness and discretion that when he had read it, he presently cried out, that the amorous charms which were scattered and divided among other beauties, were all divinely centred in Lucinda, and in Lucinda alone. Shall I confess a shameful truth in Lucinda's praises, though never so deserved, did not sound pleasantly to my ears out of Don Ferdinand's mouth. I began to entertain I know not what distrusts and jealous fears, the rather, because he would be still improving the least opportunity of talking of her, and insensibly turning the discourse he held of other matters, to make her the subject, though never so far fetched, of our constant talk. Not that I was apprehensive of the least infidelity from Lucinda: far from it; she gave me daily fresh assurances of her inviolable affection; but I feared everything from my malignant stars, and lovers are commonly industrious to make themselves uneasy.

'It happened one day, that Lucinda, who took great delight in reading books of knight-errantry, desired me to lend her the "Romance of Amadis de Gaul" – '

Scarce had Cardenio mentioned knight-errantry, when Don Quixote interrupted him: 'Sir,' said he, 'had you but told me, when you first mentioned the lady Lucinda, that she was an admirer of books of knight-errantry, there had been no need of using any amplification to convince me of her being a person of uncommon sense: yet, sir, had she not used those mighty helps, those infallible guides to sense, though indulgent nature had strove to bless her with the richest gifts she can bestow, I might justly enough have doubted whether her perfections could have gained her the love of a person of your merit: but now you need not employ your eloquence to set forth the greatness of her beauty, the excellence of her worth, or the depth of her sense: for, from this account which I have of her taking great delight in reading books of chivalry, I dare pronounce her to be the most beautiful, nay, the most accomplished lady in the universe: and I heartily could have wished that with "Amadis de Gaul" you had sent her the worthy "Don Rugel of Greece"; for I am certain the lady Lucinda would have been extremely delighted with Daryda and Garaya, as also with the discreet Darinel, and those admirable verses of his Bucolics, which he sung and repeated with so good a grace: but a time may yet be found to give her the satisfaction of reading those masterpieces, if you will do me the honour to come to my house; for there I may supply you with above three hundred volumes, which are my soul's greatest delight, and the darling comfort of my life; though now I remember myself, I have just reason to fear there is not one of them left in my study, thanks to the malicious envy of wicked enchanters. I beg your pardon for giving you this interruption, contrary to my promise; but when I hear the least mention made of knight-errantry, it is no more in my power to forbear speaking, than it is in the sunbeams not to warm, or in those of the moon not to impart her natural humidity; and therefore, sir, I beseech you to go on.'

While Don Quixote was running on with this impertinent digression, Cardenio hung down his head on his breast with all the signs of a man lost in sorrow; nor could Don Quixote with repeated entreaties persuade him to look up, or answer a word. At last, after he had stood thus a considerable while, he raised his head, and suddenly breaking silence, 'I am positively convinced,' cried he, 'nor shall any man in the world ever persuade me to the contrary; and he is a blockhead who says, that great villain Mr. Elisabat* never lay with Queen Madasima.'

'It is false!' cried Don Quixote, in a mighty heat: 'by all the powers above, it is all scandal and base detraction to say this of Queen Madasima. She was a most noble and virtuous lady; nor is it to be presumed that so great a princess would ever debase herself so far as to fall in love with a quack. Whoever dares to say she did, lies like an arrant villain; and I will make him acknowledge it either on foot or horseback, armed or unarmed, by night or by day, or how he pleases.' Cardenio very earnestly fixed his eyes on Don Quixote, while he was thus defying him and taking Queen Madasima's part, as if she had been his true and lawful princess; and being provoked by these abuses into one of his mad fits, he took up a great stone that lay by him, and hit Don Quixote such a blow on his breast with it, that it beat him down backwards. Sancho seeing his lord and master so roughly handled, fell upon the mad knight with his clenched fists; but he beat him off at the first onset, and laid him at his feet with a single blow, and then fell a-trampling on his guts, like a baker in a dough-trough. Nay, the goatherd who was offering to take Sancho's part, had like to have been served in the same manner. So the ragged knight, having tumbled them one over another and beaten them handsomely, left them, and ran into the wood without the least opposition.

Sancho got up when he saw him gone, and being very much out of humour to find himself so roughly handled without any manner of reason, began to pick a quarrel with the goatherd, railing at him for not forewarning them of the ragged knight's mad fits, that they might have stood upon their guard. The goatherd answered, he had given them warning at first, and, if he could not hear, it was no fault of his. To this Sancho replied, and the goatherd made a rejoinder, till from *pro* and *con* they fell to a warmer way of disputing, and went to fisticuffs together, catching one another by the beards, and tugging, hauling, and belabouring one another so unmercifully, that has not Don Quixote parted them, they would have pulled one another's chins off. Sancho in great wrath, still keeping his hold, cried to his master, 'Let me alone, Sir Knight of the Woeful Figure. This is no dubbed knight, but an ordinary fellow like myself; that I may be revenged on him for the wrong he has done me, let me box it out, and fight him fairly hand to fist like a man.' 'Thou mayest fight him as he is thy equal,' answered Don Quixote, 'but thou oughtest not to do it, since he has done us no wrong.' After this he pacified them; and then, addressing himself to the goatherd, he asked him whether it were

* Elisabat is a skilful physician in 'Amadis de Gaul,' who performs wonderful cures; and Queen Madasima is wife to Gantasis, and makes a great figure in the aforesaid romance. They travel and lie together in woods and deserts, without any imputation on her honour.

possible to find out Cardenio again, that he might hear the end of his story? The goatherd answered that, as he already told him, he knew of no settled place he used, but that if they made any stay thereabouts, he might be sure to meet with him, mad or sober, some time or other.

CHAPTER XI

*Of the Strange Things that happened to the valiant
Knight of La Mancha in the Black Mountains: and
of the Penance he did there, in imitation of
Beltenebros, or the Lovely Obscure*

DON QUIXOTE took leave of the goatherd, and having mounted Rozinante, commanded Sancho to follow him, which he did, but with no very good will, his master leading him into the roughest and most craggy part of the mountain. Thus they travelled for a while without speaking a word to each other. Sancho, almost dead, and ready to burst for want of a little chat, waited with great impatience till his master should begin, not dairing to speak first, since his strict injunction of silence. But at last, not being able to keep his word any longer, 'Good your worship,' quoth he, 'give me your blessing and leave to begone, I beseech you, that I may go home to my wife and children, where I may talk till I am weary, and nobody can hinder me; for I must needs tell you, that for you to think to lead me a jaunt through hedge and ditch, over hills and dales, by night and by day, without daring to open my lips, is to bury me alive. Could beasts speak, as they did in Æsop's time, it would not have been half so bad with me; for then might I have communed with my ass as I pleased, and have forgot my ill-fortune:* but to trot on in this fashion all the days of my life, after adventures, and to light of nothing but thumps, kicks, cuffs, and be tossed in a blanket; and after all, forsooth, to have a man's mouth sewed up, without daring to speak one's mind, I say it again, no living soul can endure it.' 'I understand thee, Sancho,' answered Don Quixote, 'thou lingerest with impatience to exercise thy talking faculty. Well, I am willing to free thy tongue from this restraint that so cruelly pains thee, upon condition, that the time of this licence shall not extend beyond that of our continuance in these mountains.' 'A match,' quoth Sancho, 'let us make hay while the sun shines, I will talk whilst I may; what I may do hereafter Heaven knows best.' And so

---

* See note on the preceding chapter but one. The Spaniards vulgarly call Æsop 'Giosopete,' as Cervantes does here. The French too, according to Oudin, commonly call Æsop 'Isopet.'

beginning to take the benefit of his privilege, 'Pray, sir,' quoth he, 'what occasion had you to take so hotly the part of Queen Maeimasa, or what do ye call her? What a devil was it to you, whether that same master Abbot* was her friend in a corner or no? Had you taken no notice of what was said, as you might well have done, seeing it was no business of yours, the madman would have gone on with his story, you had missed a good thump on the breast, and I had escaped some five or six good dowses on the chaps, besides the trampling of my puddings.' 'Upon my honour, friend Sancho,' replied Don Quixote, 'didst thou but know, as well as I do, what a virtuous and eminent lady Queen Madasima was, thou wouldst say I had a great deal of patience, seeing I did not strike that profane wretch on the mouth, out of which such blasphemies proceeded: for, in short, it was the highest piece of detraction, to say that a queen was scandalously familiar with a barber-surgeon for the truth of the story is, that this Mr. Elisabat, of whom the madman spoke, was a person of extraordinary prudence and sagacity, and physician to that queen, who also made use of his advice in matters of importance; but to say she gave him up her honour, and prostituted herself to the embraces of a man of such an inferior degree, was an impudent, groundless, and slanderous accusation, worthy the severest punishment. Neither can I believe that Cardenio knew what he said, when he charged the queen with that debasing guilt: for, it is plain, that his raving fit had disordered the seat of his understanding.' 'Why, there it is,' quoth Sancho; 'who but a madman would have minded what a madman said? What if the flint that hit you on the breast had dashed out your brains? we had been in a dainty pickle for taking the part of that same lady, with a pease-cod in her: nay, and Cardenio would have come off too, had he knocked you on the head; for the law has nothing to do with madmen.'

'Sancho,' replied Don Quixote, 'we knights-errant are obliged to vindicate the honour of women of what quality soever, as well against madmen as against men in their senses; much more queens of that magnitude and extraordinary worth, as Queen Madasima, for whose rare endowments I have a peculiar veneration; for she was a most beautiful lady, discreet and prudent to admiration, and behaved herself with an exemplary patience in all her misfortunes. It was then that the company and wholesome counsels of Mr. Elisabat proved very useful to alleviate the burden of her afflictions: from which the ignorant and ill-meaning vulgar took occasion to suspect and rumour, that she was guilty of an unlawful commerce with him. But I say once more, they lie, and lie a thousand times, whoever they be, that shall presumptuously report, or hint, or so much as think or surmise so base a calumny.'

---

* Sancho, remembering only the latter part of Mr. Elisabat's name, pleasantly calls him 'Abad,' which is Spanish for an Abbot. Abad, Oudin observes, sounds like the end of Elisabat.

'Why,' quoth Sancho, 'I neither say nor think one way nor the other, not I: let them that say it, eat the lie, and swallow it with their bread. If they lay together, they have answered for it before now. I never thrust my nose into other men's porridge. It is no bread and butter of mine. Every man for himself, and God for us all, say I; for he that buys and lies, finds it in his purse. Let him that owns the cow take her by the tail. Naked came I into the world, and naked must I go out. Many think to find flitches of bacon, where there is not so much as the racks to lay them on: but who can hedge in a cuckoo? Little said is soon mended. It is a sin to belie the Devil, but misunderstanding brings lies to the town, and there is no padlocking of people's mouths: for a close mouth catches no flies.'

'Bless me,' cried Don Quixote, 'what a catalogue of musty proverbs hast thou run through? What a heap of frippery-ware hast thou threaded together, and how wide from the purpose! I pray thee have done, and for the future let thy whole study be to spur thy ass, nor do thou concern thyself with things that are out of thy sphere: and with all thy five senses remember this, that whatsoever I do, have done, and shall do, is no more than what is the result of mature consideration, and strictly conformable to the laws of chivalry, which I understand better than all the knights that ever professed knight-errantry.' 'Ay, ay, sir,' quoth Sancho; 'but, pray, is it a good law of chivalry that says we shall wander up and down, over bushes and briars, in this rocky wilderness, where there is neither footpath nor horse-way, running after a madman; who, if we light on him again, may chance to make an end of what he has begun, not of his tale of a roasted horse I mean, but of belabouring you and me thoroughly, and squeezing out my guts at both ends?' 'Once more, I pray thee, have done,' said Don Quixote. 'I have business of greater moment than the finding this frantic man. It is not so much that business that detains me in this barren and desolate wild, as a desire I have to perform a certain and heroic deed that shall immortalise my fame, and make it fly to the remotest regions of the habitable globe; nay, it shall seal and confirm the most complete and absolute knight-errant in the world.' 'But is not this same adventure very dangerous?' asked Sancho. 'Not at all,' replied Don Quixote; 'though, as fortune may order it, our expectations may be baffled by disappointing accidents, but the main thing consists in thy diligence.' 'My diligence?' quoth Sancho. 'I mean,' said Don Quixote, 'that if thou returnest with all the speed imaginable from the place whither I design to send thee, my pain will soon be at an end, and my glory begin. And because I do not doubt thy zeal for advancing thy master's interest, I will no longer conceal my design from thee. Know then, my faithful squire, that Amadis de Gaul was one of the most accomplished knights-errant; nay, I should not have said he was one of them, but the most perfect, the chief, and prince of them all. And let not the Belianises, nor any others, pretend to stand in competition with him for the honour of priority; for, to my knowledge, should they attempt it, they would be egregiously in the wrong I must also inform thee that when a painter studies to excel and grow famous in his art, he takes care to imitate the best originals; which rule ought likewise to be observed in all other arts and sciences that serve for the ornament of well-regulated commonwealths. Thus he that is ambitious of gaining the reputation of a prudent and patient man, ought to propose to himself to imitate Ulysses, in whose person and troubles Homer has admirably delineated a perfect pattern and prototype of wisdom and heroic patience. So Virgil, in his Æneas, has given the world a rare example of filial piety, and of the sagacity of a valiant and experienced general, both the Greek and Roman poets representing their heroes not such as they really were, but such as they should be, to remain examples of virtue to ensuing ages In the same manner, Amadis, having been the Polar star, and sun, of valorous and amorous knights it is him we ought to set before our eyes as our great example, all of us that fight under the banner of love and chivalry; for it is certain that the adventurer who shall emulate him best, shall consequently arrive nearest the perfection of knight-errantry. Now, Sancho, I find that among the things which most displayed that champion's prudence and fortitude, his constancy and love, and his other heroic virtues, none was more remarkable than his retiring from his disdainful Oriana, to do penance on the Poor Rock, changing his name into that of Beltenebros, or the Lovely Obscure, a title certainly most significant, and adapted to the life which he then intended to lead. So I am resolved to imitate him in this, the rather because I think it a more easy task than it would be to copy after his other achievements, such as cleaving the bodies of giants, cutting off the heads of dragons, killing dreadful monsters, routing armies, dispersing navies, and breaking the force of magic spells. And, since these mountainous wilds offer me so fair an opportunity, I see no reason why I should neglect it; and therefore I will lay hold on it now.' 'Very well,' quoth Sancho; 'but pray, sir, what is that you mean to do in this fag-end of the world?' ' Have I not already told thee,' answered Don Quixote, 'that I intend to copy Amadis in his madness, despair, and fury? Nay, at the same time I will imitate the valiant Orlando Furioso's extravagance, when he ran mad, after he had found the unhappy tokens of the fair Angelica's dishonourable commerce with Medoro at the fountain; at which time, in his frantic despair, he tore up trees by the roots, troubled the waters of the clear fountains, slew the shepherds, destroyed their flocks, fired their huts, demolished houses, drove their horses before him, and committed a hundred thousand other extravagancies worthy to be recorded in the eternal register of fame. Not that I intend, however, in all things to imitate Roldan, or Orlando, or Rotoland (for he had all those names), but only to make choice of such frantic effects of his amorous despair, as I shall think most essential and worthy imitation. Nay, perhaps, I shall wholly follow Amadis, who, without launching out into such destructive and fatal ravings, and only expressing his anguish in complaints and lamentations, gained nevertheless, a renown equal, if not superior, to that of the greatest heroes.'

' Sir,' quoth Sancho, 'I dare say the knights who did these penances had some reason to be mad; but what need have you to be mad too? What lady has sent you a packing or so much as slighted you? When did you ever find that my Lady Dulcinea del Toboso did otherwise than she should do, with either Moor* or Christian?' 'Why, there is the point!' cried Don Quixote. 'In this consists the singular perfection of my undertaking: for, mark me, Sancho, for a knight-errant to run mad upon any just occasion, is neither strange nor meritorious; no, the rarity is to run mad without a cause, without the least constraint or necessity. There is a refined and exquisite passion for you, Sancho! For thus my mistress must needs have a vast idea of my love, since she may guess what I should perform in the wet, if I do so much in the dry.† But, besides, I have but too just a motive to give a loose to my raving grief, considering the long date of my absence from my ever-supreme Lady Dulcinea del Toboso; for, as the shepherd in "Matthias Ambrosio" has it:

> ' "Poor lovers, absent from the darling fair,
> All ills not only dread, but bear." '

Then do not lavish any more time in striving to divert me from so rare, so happy, and so singular an imitation. I am mad, and will be mad, until thy return with an answer to the letter which thou must carry from me to the Lady Dulcinea; and, if it be as favourable as my unshaken constancy deserves, then my madness and my penance shall end; but if I find she repays my vows and services with ungrateful disdain, then will I be emphatically mad, and screw up my thoughts to such an excess of distraction, that I shall be insensible of the rigour of my relentless fair. Thus what return soever she makes to my passion, I shall be eased one way or other of the anxious thoughts that now divide my soul; either entertaining the welcome news of her reviving pity with demonstrations of sense, or else showing my insensibility of her cruelty by the height of my distraction. But, in the mean time, Sancho, tell me, hast thou carefully preserved Mambrino's helmet? I saw thee take it up the other day, after

---

* Sancho says Moor for Medoro, in his blundering way.
† A profane allusion to a text in Scripture, Luke xxiii, 31 – 'For if they do these things in a green tree, what shall be done in the dry?' So here Don Quixote's meaning is – 'My mistress may guess what I would do where occasion should he given me, since I can do so much without any.'

that monster of ingratitude had spent his rage in vain endeavours to break it; which, by the way, argues the most excellent temper of the metal.' 'Body of me,' quoth Sancho, 'Sir Knight of the Woeful Figure, I can no longer bear to hear you run on at this rate! Why, this were enough to make any man believe that all your bragging and bouncing of your knight-errantry, your winning of kingdoms, and bestowing of islands, and Heaven knows what upon your squire, are mere flim-flam stories, and nothing but shams and lies: for who the devil can hear a man call a barber's basin a helmet, nay, and stand to it, and vouch it four days together, and not think him that says it to be stark mad or without brains? I have the basin safe enough here in my pouch, and I will get it mended for my own use, if ever I have the luck to get home to my wife and children.' 'Now, as I love bright arms,' cried Don Quixote, 'I swear thou art the shallowest, silliest, and most stupid fellow of a squire that ever I heard or read of in my life. How is it possible for thee to be so dull of apprehension as not to have learnt, in all this time that thou hast been in my service, that all the actions and adventures of us knights-errant seem to be mere chimeras, follies, and impertinencies? Not that they are so, indeed, but either through the officious care, or else through the malice and envy of those enchanters that always haunt and persecute us unseen, and by their fascinations change the appearance of our actions into what they please, according to their love or hate. This is the very reason why that which I plainly perceive to be Mambrino's helmet, seems to thee to be only a barber's basin, and perhaps another man may take it to be something else. And in this I can never too much admire the prudence of the sage who espouses my interests in making that inestimable helmet seem a basin: for, did it appear in its proper shape, its tempting value would raise me as many enemies as there are men in the universe, all eager to snatch from me so desirable a prize: but so long as it shall seem to be nothing else but a barber's basin, men will not value it, as is manifest from the fellow's leaving it behind him on the ground. For, had he known what it really was, he would sooner have parted with his life. Keep it safe then, Sancho, for I have no need of it at present; far from it, I think to put off my armour, and strip myself as naked as I came out of my mother's womb, in case I determine to imitate Orlando's fury, rather than the penance of Amadis.'

This discourse brought them to the foot of a high rock, that stood by itself, as if it had been hewn out, and divided from the rest; by the skirt of it glided a purling stream, that softly took its winding course through an adjacent meadow. The verdant freshness of the grass, the number of wild trees, plants, and flowers, that feasted the eyes in that pleasant solitude, invited the Knight of the Woeful Figure to make choice of it to perform his amorous penance; and therefore, as soon as his ravished sight had roved a while over the scattered beauties of the place, he took possession of it with the following speech, as if he had utterly lost the small share of reason he had left. 'Behold, O Heavens!' cried he, 'the place which an unhappy lover has chosen to bemoan the deplorable state to which you have reduced him: here shall my flowing tears swell the liquid veins of this crystal rill, and my deep sighs perpetually move the leaves of these shady trees, in testimony of the anguish and pain that harrows up my soul! Ye rural deities, whoever you be, that make these unfrequented deserts your abode, hear the complaints of an unfortunate lover, whom a tedious absence, and some slight impressions of a jealous mistrust, have driven to these regions of despair, to bewail his rigorous destiny, and deplore the distracting cruelty of that ungrateful fair, who is the perfection of all human beauty. Ye pitying Napaean nymphs and dryades, silent inhabitants of the woods and groves, assist me to lament my fate, or at least attend the mournful story of my woes: so may no designing beastly satyrs, those just objects of your hate, ever have power to interrupt your rest. – Oh, Dulcinea del Toboso! thou sun that turnest my gloomy night to day! glory of my pain! north star of my travels, and reigning planet that controllest my heart! Pity I conjure thee, the unparalleled distress to which thy absence has reduced the faithfullest of lovers, and grant to my fidelity that kind return which it so justly claims? So may indulgent fate shower on thee all the blessings thou ever canst desire, or Heaven grant! – Ye lonesome trees, under whose spreading branches I come to linger out the gloomy shadow of a tedious being; let the soft language of your rustling leaves, and the kind nodding of your springing boughs, satisfy me that I am welcome to your shady harbours! O thou, my trusty squire, the inseparable companion of my adventures, diligently observe what thou shalt see me do in this lonely retreat, that thou mayest inform the dear cause of my ruin with every particular.' As he said this, he alighted, and presently taking off his horse's bridle and saddle, 'Go, Rozinante,' said he, giving the horse a clap on the posteriors, 'he that has lost his freedom gives thee thine; thou steed, as renowned for thy extraordinary actions, as for thy misfortunes, go, rear thy awful front wherever thou pleasest, secure that neither the Hippogryphon of Astolpho, nor the renowned Frontino, which Bradamante purchased at so high a price, could ever be thought thy equals.'

'Well fare him,' cried Sancho, 'that saved me the trouble of sending my ass to grass too: poor thing, had I him here, he should not want two or thee claps on the buttocks, nor a fine speech in his praise neither, while I took off his pannel. But stay, were he here, what need would there be to strip him of his harness: alas, he never had anything to do with these mad pranks of love, no more than myself, who was his master when fortune pleased. But do ye hear me, now I think on it, Sir Knight of the Woeful

Figure, if your worship is resolved to be mad, and send me away in good earnest, we must even clap the saddle again on Rozinante's back; for to tell you the truth, I am but a sorry footman, and if I do not ride home, I do not know when I shall be able to come back again.' 'Do as thou thinkest fit for that, Sancho,' answered Don Quixote, 'for I design thou shalt set forward about three days hence. In the meanwhile thou shalt be a witness of what I will do for my lady's sake, that thou mayest give her an account of it.' 'Bless my eyesight,' quoth Sancho, 'what can I see more than I have seen already?' 'Thou hast seen nothing yet,' answered Don Quixote; 'thou must see me throw away my armour, tear my clothes, knock my head against the rocks, and do a thousand other things of that kind, that will fill thee with astonishment.' 'For goodness' sake, sir,' quoth Sancho, 'take heed how you quarrel with those ungracious rocks; you may chance to get such a crack on the crown at the very first rap, as may spoil your penance at one dash. No, I do not like that way by no means; if you must needs be knocking your noddle, to go through-stitch with this ugly job, seeing it is all but a mockery, or as it were between jest and earnest, why cannot you as well play your tricks on something that is softer than these unconscionable stones: you may run your head against water, or rather against cotton, or the stuffing of Rozinante's saddle; and then let me alone with the rest: I will be sure to tell my lady Dulcinea, that you bebumped your pole against the point of a rock that is harder than a diamond.'

'I thank thee for thy good-will, dear Sancho,' replied Don Quixote: 'but I assure thee, that all these seeming extravagancies that I must run through, are no jests: far from it, they must all be performed seriously and solemnly; for otherwise we should transgress the laws of chivalry, that forbid us to tell lies upon pain of degradation. Now to pretend to do one thing, and effect another, is an evasion, which I esteem to be as bad as lying. Therefore the blows which I must give myself on the head, ought to be real, substantial, sound ones, without any trick, or mental reservation; for which reason I would have thee leave me some lint and salve, since fortune has deprived us of the sovereign balsam which we lost.' 'It was a worse loss to lose the ass,' quoth Sancho, 'for with him we have lost bag and baggage, lint and all; but no more of your damned drench, if you love me; the very thoughts of it are enough not only to turn my stomach, but my soul, such a rumbling I feel in my guts at the name of it. Then, as for the three days you would have me loiter here to mind your mad tricks, you had as good make account they are already over; for I hold them for done, unsight unseen, and will tell wonders to my Lady: wherefore write you your letter, and send me away with all haste; for let me be hanged if I do not long already to be back, to take you out of this purgatory wherein I leave you.'

'Dost thou only call it Purgatory, Sancho!' cried Don Quixote; 'call it

Hell rather, or something worse, if there be in nature a term expressive of a more wretched state.' 'Nay, not so neither,' quoth Sancho, 'I would not call it Hell; because, as I heard our parson say, "There is no retention* out of Hell." ' 'Retention!' cried Don Quixote, 'what dost thou mean by that word?' 'Why,' quoth Sancho, 'retention is retention: it is, that whosoever is in hell never comes, nor can come out of it; which shall not be your case this bout, if I can stir my heels, and have but spurs to tickle Rozinante's flanks, till I come to my lady Dulcinea: for I will tell her such strange things of your maggoty tricks, your folly, and your madness, for indeed they are no better, that I will lay my head to a hazel nut, I will make her as supple as a glove, though I found her at first as tough-hearted as a cork; and when I have wheedled an answer out of her, all full of sweet honey words, away will I whisk it back to you, cutting the air as swift as a witch upon a broomstick, and free you out of your purgatory; for a purgatory I will have it to be in spite of hell, nor shall you gainsay me in that fancy; for, as I have told you before, there is some hopes of your retention out of this place.'

'Well, be it so,' said the Knight of the Woeful figure: 'but how shall I do to write this letter?' 'And the order for the three asses,' added Sancho. 'I will not forget it,' answered Don Quixote; 'but, since we have here no paper, I must be obliged to write on the leaves or bark of trees, or on wax, as they did in ancient times; yet, now I consider of it, we are here as ill provided with wax as with paper: but stay, now I remember, I have Cardenio's pocket-book, which will supply that want in this exigence, and then thou shalt get the letter fairly transcribed at the first village, where thou canst meet with a schoolmaster; or, for want of a schoolmaster, thou mayest get the clerk of the parish to do it: but by no means give to any notary or scrivener to be written out; for they commonly write such confounded hands, that the Devil himself would scarce be able to read it.' 'Well,' quoth Sancho, 'but what shall I do for want of your name to it?' 'Why,' answered Don Quixote, 'Amadis never used to subscribe his letters.' 'Ay,' replied Sancho, 'but the bill of exchange for the three asses must be signed; for should I get it copied out afterwards, they would say it is not your hand, and so I shall go without the asses.' 'I will write and sign the order for them in the tablebook,' answered Don Quixote, 'and as soon as my niece sees the hand she will never scruple the delivery of the asses: and, as for the love-letter, when thou gettest it transcribed, thou must get it thus underwritten, "Yours till death, the Knight of the Woeful Figure." It is no matter whether the letter and subscription be written by the same hand or no; for, as I remember, Dulcinea can neither read nor write, nor did she ever see any of my letters, nay, not so much as any of my writing in

* No redemption, he means.

her life: for my love and hers have always been purely Platonic, never extending beyond the lawful bounds of a modest look; and that, too, so very seldom, that I dare safely swear that, though for these twelve years she has been dearer to my soul than light to my eyes, yet I never saw her four times in my life; and perhaps of those few times that I have seen her, she has scarcely perceived once that I beheld her: so strictly Lorenzo Corchuelo, her father, and Aldonza Nagales, her mother, have kept and educated her.' 'Heighday!' quoth Sancho, 'did you ever hear the like! and is my lady Dulcinea del Toboso, at last, the daughter of Lorenzo Corchuelo, she that is otherwise called Aldonza Lorenzo?' 'The same,' answered Don Quixote; 'and it is she that merits to be the sovereign mistress of the universe.' 'Udsdaggers,' quoth Sancho, 'I know her full well; she is a strapping wench, in faith, and pitches the bar with e're a lusty young fellow in our parish. By the Mass, she is a notable, strong-built, sizable, sturdy, manly lass, and one that will keep her chin out of the mire, I warrant her; nay, and hold the best knight-errant to it that wears a head, if ever he venture upon her. Body o' me, what a pair of lungs and a voice she has, when she sets up her throat! I saw her one day perched up on the top of our steeple, to call to some ploughmen that were at work in a fallow-field: and though they were half a league off, they heard her as plain as if they had been in the churchyard under her. The best of her is, that she is neither coy nor frumpish, she is a tractable lass, and fit for a courtier, for she will play with you like a kitten, and gibes and jokes with everybody. And now, in good truth, Sir Knight of the Woeful Figure, you may even play at your gambols as you please; you may run mad, you may hang yourself for her sake; there is nobody will say but you even took the wisest course, though the Devil himself should carry you away a-pick-apack. Now am I even wild to be gone, though it were for nothing else but to see her, for I have not seen her this many a day: I fancy I shall hardly know her again, for a woman's face strangely alters by her being always in the sun, and drudging and moiling in the open fields. Well, I must needs own I have been mightily mistaken all along: for I durst have sworn this lady Dulcinea had been some great princess with whom you were in love, and such a one as deserved those rare gifts you bestowed on her, as the Biscayner, the galley-slaves, and many others, that, for aught I know, you may have sent her before I was your squire. I cannot choose but laugh to think how my lady Aldonza Lorenzo (my lady Dulcinea del Toboso, I should have said) would behave herself, should any of those men which you have sent, or may send to her, chance to go and fall down on their marrow-bones before her: for it is ten to one they may happen to find her a-carding of flax, or threshing in the barn, and then how finely baulked they will be! As sure as I am alive, they must needs think the Devil owed them a shame; and she herself will but flout them, and mayhap be somewhat nettled at it.'

'I have often told thee, Sancho,' said Don Quixote, 'and I tell thee again, that thou oughtest to bridle or immure thy saucy prating tongue: for though thou art but a dull-headed dunce, yet now and then thy ill-mannered jests bite too sharp. But that I may at once make thee sensible of thy folly and my discretion, I will tell thee a short story. A handsome, brisk, young, rich widow, and withal no prude, happened to fall in love with a well-set, lusty lay-brother.* His superior hearing of it, took occasion to go to her, and said to her, by way of charitable admonition, "I mightily wonder, madam, how a lady of your merit, so admired for beauty and for sense, and withal so rich, could make so ill a choice, and dote on a mean, silly, despicable fellow, as I hear you do, while we have in our house so many masters of art, bachelors, and doctors of divinity, among whom your ladyship may pick and choose, as you would among pears, and say, 'This I like, that I do not like.' " But she soon answered the officious, grave gentleman "Sir," said she, with a smile, "you are much mistaken, and think altogether after the old out-of-fashion way, if you imagine I have made so ill a choice; for though you fancy the man is a fool, yet, as to what I take him for, he knows as much, or rather more philosophy than Aristotle himself." So, Sancho, as to the use which I make of lady Dulcinea, she is equal to the greatest princess in the world Pray thee, tell me, dost thou think the poets, who every one of them celebrate the praises of one lady or other, had all real mistresses? Or that the Amaryllises, the Phyllises, the Sylvias, the Dianas, the Galateas, the Alidas, and the like, which you shall find in so many poems, romances, songs, and ballads, upon every stage, and even in every barber's shop, were creatures of flesh and blood, and mistresses to those that did and do celebrate them? No, no, never think it; for I dare assure thee, the greatest part of them were nothing but the mere imaginations of the poets, for a groundwork to exercise their wits upon, and give to the world occasion to look on the authors as men of an amorous and gallant disposition: and so it is sufficient for me to imagine, that Aldonza Lorenzo is beautiful and chaste; as for her birth and parentage, they concern me but little for there is no need to make an inquiry about a woman's pedigree, as there is of us men, when some badge of honour is bestowed on us; and so she is to me the greatest princess in the world for thou oughtest to know, Sancho, if thou knowest it not already, that there are but two things that chiefly excite us to love a woman, an attractive beauty, and unspotted fame. Now these two endowments are happily reconciled in Dulcinea; for, as for the one, she has not her equal, and few can vie with her in the other but, to cut off all

---

* *Motillon*, a lay-brother, or servant in the convent or college, so called from *Motilo*, a cropped head; his hair being cropped short, he has no crown like those in orders.

objections at once, I imagine, that all I say of her is really so, without the least addition or diminution: I fancy her to be just such as I would have her for beauty and quality. Helen cannot stand in competition with her; Lucretia cannot rival her; and all the heroines which antiquity has to boast, whether Greeks, Romans or Barbarians, are at once out-done by her incomparable perfections. Therefore let the world say what it will; should the ignorant vulgar foolishly censure me, I please myself with the assurances I have of the approbation of men of the strictest morals, and the nicest judgment.' 'Sir,' quoth Sancho, 'I knock under: you have reason on your side in all you say, and I own myself an ass. Nay, I am an ass to talk of an ass; for it is ill talking of halters in the house of a man that was hanged. But where is the letter-will all this while, that I may be jogging?' With that Don Quixote pulled out the table-book, and retiring a little aside, he very seriously began to write the letter; which he had no sooner finished, but he called Sancho, and ordered him to listen while he read it over to him, that he might carry it as well in his memory as in his pocket-book, in case he should have the ill-luck to lose it by the way: for so cross was fortune to him, that he feared every accident. 'But, sir,' said Sancho, 'write it over twice or thrice there in the book, and give it me, and then I will be sure to deliver the message safe enough, I warrant ye: for it is folly to think I can get it by heart; alas, my memory is so bad, that many times I forget my own name! But yet, for all that, read it out to me, I beseech you, for I have a hugeous mind to hear it. I dare say, it is as fine as though it were in print.' 'Well then, listen,' said Don Quixote.

'DON QUIXOTE DE LA MANCHA, TO DULCINEA DEL TOBOSO.

'HIGH AND SOVEREIGN LADY,   He that is stabbed to the quick with the poniard of absence, and wounded to the heart with love's most piercing darts, sends you that health which he wants himself, sweetest Dulcinea del Toboso.* If your beauty reject me, if your virtue refuse to raise my fainting hopes, if your disdain exclude me from relief, I must at last sink under the pressure of my woes, though much inured to sufferings: for my pains are not only too violent, but too lasting. My trusty squire Sancho will give an exact account of the condition to which love and you have reduced me, too beautiful ingrate I If you relent at last, and pity my distress, then I may say I live, and you preserve, what is yours. But, if you abandon me to despair, I must patiently submit, and by ceasing to breathe, satisfy your cruelty and my passion.

   'Yours till death,

                                    'THE KNIGHT OF WOEFUL FIGURE'

* Dulcissima Dulcinea.

'By the life of my father,' quoth Sancho, 'if I ever saw a finer thing in my born days! How neatly and roundly you tell your mind, and how cleverly you bring in at last, "The Knight of the Woeful Figure!" Well, I say it again in good earnest, you are a devil at everything, and there is no kind of thing in the versal world but what you can turn your hand to.' 'A man ought to have some knowledge of everything,' answered Don Quixote, 'if he would be duly qualified for the employment I profess.' 'Well then,' quoth Sancho, 'do so much as write the warrant for the three asses on the other side of that leaf; and pray write it mighty plain, that they may know it is your hand at first sight.' 'I will,' said Don Quixote, and with that he wrote it accordingly, and then read it in this form:

'MY DEAR NIECE, "Upon sight of this my first bill of asses, be pleased to deliver three of the five which I left at home in your custody, to Sancho Pança my squire, for the like number received of him here in tale; and this, together with his receipt, shall be your discharge. Given* in the very bowels of Sierra Morena, the 22nd of August, in the present year." '

'It is as it should be,' quoth Sancho; 'there only wants your name at the bottom.' 'There is no need to set my name,' answered Don Quixote, 'I will only set the two first letters of it, and it will be as valid as if written at length, though it were not only for three asses, but for three hundred.' 'I dare take your Worship's word,' quoth Sancho, 'and now I am going to saddle Rozinante, and then you shall give me your blessing; for I intend to set out presently, without seeing any of your mad tricks; and I will relate, that I saw you perform so many, that she can desire no more.' 'Nay,' said Don Quixote, 'I will have thee stay a while, Sancho, and see me stark-naked; it is also absolutely necessary thou shouldest see me practice some twenty or thirty mad gambols; I shall have dispatched them in less than half an hour: and when thou hast been an eye witness of that essay, thou mayest with a safe conscience swear thou hast seen me play a thousand more; for I dare assure thee, for thy encouragement, thou never canst exceed the number of those I shall perform.' 'Good sir,' quoth Sancho, 'as you love me, do not let me stay to see you naked; it will grieve me so to the heart, that I shall cry my eyes out; and I have blubbered and howled but too much since yesternight for the loss of my ass. My head is so sore with it, I am not able to cry any longer: but, if you will needs have me see some of your antics, pray do them in your clothes out of hand, and let them be such as are most to the purpose; for the sooner I go, the sooner I shall

---

* In the original it is *Fecha*, i.e. Done; for the king of Spain writes Done at our court, etc., as the king of England does, Given, etc.

come back; and the way to be gone, is not to stay here. I long to bring you an answer to your heart's content: and I will be sure to do it, or let the Lady Dulcinea look to it; for if she does not answer as she should do, I protest solemnly I will force an answer out of her guts by dint of good kicks and fisticuffs: for it is not to be endured, that such a notable knight-errant as your Worship is, should thus run out of his wits without knowing why or wherefore, for such a – odsbobs! I know what I know; she had not best provoke me to speak it out; for, by the Lord, I shall let fly, and out with it by wholesale, though it spoil the market.'*

'I protest, Sancho,' said Don Quixote, 'I think thou art as mad as myself.' 'Nay, not so mad neither,' replied Sancho, 'but somewhat more choleric. But talk no more of that: let us see, how will you do for victuals when I am gone? Do you mean to do like the other madman yonder, rob upon the highway, and snatch the goatherds' victuals from them by main force?' 'Never let that trouble thy head,' replied Don Quixote; 'for though I had all the dainties that can feast a luxurious palate, I would feed upon nothing but the herbs and fruits which this wilderness will afford me: for the singularity of my present task consists in fasting, and half-starving myself, and in the performance of other austerities.' 'But there is another thing come into my head,' quoth Sancho; 'how shall I do to find the way hither again, it is such a by-place?' 'Take good notice of it beforehand,' said Don Quixote, 'and I will endeavour to keep hereabouts till thy return: besides, about the time when I may reasonably expect thee back, I will be sure to watch on the top of yonder high rock for thy coming. But now I bethink myself of a better expedient; thou shalt cut down a good number of boughs, and strew them in the way as thou ridest along, till thou gettest to the plains, and this will serve thee to find me again at thy return, like Perseus's clue to the labyrinth in Crete.

'I will go about it out of hand,' quoth Sancho. With that he went and cut down a bundle of boughs, then came and asked his master's blessing, and after a shower of tears shed on both sides, mounted Rozinante, which Don Quixote very seriously recommended to his care, charging him to be as tender of that excellent steed as of his own person. After that he set forward toward the plains, strewing several boughs as he rid, according to order. His master importuned him to stay and see him do two or three of his antic postures before he went, but he could not prevail with him: however, before he was got out of sight, he considered of it, and rode back: 'Sir,' quoth he, 'I have thought better of it, and believe I had best

---

* Sancho here, by threatening to blurt out something, gives a kind of sly prophecy of the Dulcinea he intended to palm upon his master's folly, and prepares the reader for that gross imposition, of enchanting the three princesses and their palfries, into three country wenches upon asses.

take your advice, that I may swear with a safe conscience I have seen you play your mad tricks; therefore I would see you do one of them at least, though I think I have seen you do a very great one already, I mean your staying by yourself in this desert.'

'I had advised thee right,' said Don Quixote; 'and therefore stay but while a man may repeat the Creed,* and I will show thee what thou wouldst see.' With that, slipping off his breeches and stripping himself naked to the waist, he gave two or three frisks in the air, and then pitching on his hands he fetched his heels over his head twice together; and as he tumbled with his legs aloft, discovered such rarities, that Sancho even made haste to turn his horse's head, that he might no longer see them, and rode away full satisfied, that he might swear his master was mad. And so we will leave him to make the best of his way till his return, which will be more speedy than might be imagined.

CHAPTER XII

A continuation of the refined Extravagancies by which the gallant Knight of La Mancha chose to express his Love in the Sierra Morena

THE HISTORY RELATES, that as soon as the Knight of the Woeful Figure saw himself alone, after he had taken his frisks and leaps naked as he was, the prelude to his amorous penance, he ascended the top of a high rock, and there began seriously to consider with himself what resolution to take in that nice dilemma, which had already so perplexed his mind; that is, whether he should imitate Orlando in his wild ungovernable fury, or Amadis in his melancholy mood. To which purpose, reasoning with himself, 'I do not much wonder,' said he, 'at Orlando's being so very valiant, considering he was enchanted in such a manner, that he could not be slain but by the thrust of a long pin through the bottom of his foot, which he sufficiently secured, always wearing seven iron soles to his shoes; and yet this availed him nothing against Bernardo del Carpio, who, knowing what he depended upon, squeezed him to death between his arms at Roncesvalles. But, setting aside his valour, let us examine his madness; for that he was mad, is an unquestionable truth; nor is it less certain, that his frenzy was occasioned by the assurances he had that the fair Angelica had resigned herself up to the unlawful embraces of Medora,

* A proverb to express brevity in Romish countries, where they huddle the Credo over so fast, that they had done before one would think they were got half through.

that young Moor with curled locks, who was page to Agramante. Now, after all, seeing he was too well convinced of his lady's infidelity, it is not to be admired he should run mad: but how can I imitate him in his furies, if I cannot imitate him in their occasion? For I dare swear my Dulcinea del Toboso never saw a downright Moor in his own garb since she first beheld light, and that she is at this present speaking as right as the mother that bore her: so that I should do her a great injury, should I entertain any dishonourable thoughts of her behaviour, and fall into such a kind of madness as that of Orlando Furioso. On the other side, I find, that Amadis de Gaul, without punishing himself with such distraction, or expressing his resentments in so boisterous and raving a manner, got as great a reputation for being a lover as any one whatsoever; for what I find in history as to his abandoning himself to sorrow, is only this: "he found himself disdained, his lady Oriana having charged him to get out of her sight, and not to presume to appear in her presence till she gave him leave; and this was the true reason why he retired to the Poor Rock with the hermit, where he gave up himself wholly to grief, and wept a deluge of tears, till pitying Heaven at last, commiserating his affliction, sent him relief in the height of his anguish." Now then, since this is true, as I know it is, what need have I to tear off my clothes, to rend and root up these harmless trees, or trouble the water of these brooks, that must give me drink when I am thirsty? No, long live the memory of Amadis de Gaul, and let him be the great example which Don Quixote de la Mancha chooses to imitate in all things that will admit of a parallel. So may it be said of the living copy, as was said of the dead original, that if he did not perform great things, yet no man was more ambitious of undertaking them than he; and though I am not disdained nor discarded by Dulcinea, yet it is sufficient that I am absent from her. Then it is resolved! And now the famous actions of the great Amadis occur to my remembrance, and be my trusty guides to follow his example.' This said, he called to mind, that the chief exercise of that hero in his retreat was prayer: to which purpose, our modern Amadis presently made himself a rosary of galls instead of beads; but he was extremely troubled for want of an hermit to hear his confession, and comfort him in his affliction. However, he entertained himself with his amorous contemplations, walking up and down the meadow, and writing some poetical conceptions in the smooth sand, and upon the barks of trees, all of them expressive of his sorrows, and the praises of Dulcinea; but unhappily none were found entire and legible, but these stanzas that follow:

> Ye lofty trees with spreading arms
>   The pride and shelter of the plain
> Ye humbler shrubs, and flow'ry charms

Which here in springing glory reign!
If my complaints may pity move,
Hear the sad story of my love,
  While with me here you pass your hours.
Should you grow faded with my cares,
  I'll bribe you with refreshing show'rs;
You shall be water'd with my tears.
    Distant, tho' present in idea,
    I mourn my absent Dulcinea
                    Del Toboso

Love's truest slave despairing chose
  This lonely wild, this desert plain,
The silent witness of the woes
  Which he, tho' guiltless, must sustain
Unknowing why those pains he bears,
He groans, he raves, and he despairs:
  With ling'ring fires love racks my soul
In vain I grieve, in vain lament;
  Like tortur'd fiends I weep, I howl
And burn, yet never can repent.
Distant, tho' present in idea
I mourn my absent Dulcinea
                    Del Toboso

While I thro' honour's thorny ways,
  In search of distant glory rove
Malignant fate my toil repays
  With endless woes, and hopeless love.
Thus I on barren rocks despair,
And curse my stars, yet bless my fair.
  Love arm'd with snakes has left his dart
And now does like a fury rave,
  And scourge and sting in every part,
And into madness lash his slave.
    Distant, tho' present in idea,
    I mourn my absent Dulcinea
                    Del Toboso.

This addition of Del Toboso to the name of Dulcinea, made those who found these verses laugh heartily; and they imagined that when Don Quixote made them, he was afraid those who should happen to read them would not understand on whom they were made, should he omit the place of his mistress's birth and residence: and this was indeed the true reason, as he himself afterwards confessed. With this employment did our disconsolate Knight beguile the tedious hours; sometimes also he expressed his sorrows in prose, sighed to the winds, and called upon the Sylvan Gods, the Fauns, the Nalades, the nymphs of the adjoining groves, and the mournful echo, imploring their attention and condolement with repeated supplications: at other times he employed himself in gathering herbs for the support of languishing nature, which decayed so fast, with his slender diet and that his studied anxiety and intenseness of thinking, that had Sancho stayed but three weeks from him, whereas by good fortune he stayed but three days, the Knight of the Woeful Figure would have been so disfigured, that his mother would never have known the child of her own womb.

But now it is necessary we should leave him a while to his sighs, his sobs, and his amorous expostulations, and see how Sancho Pança behaved himself in his embassy. He made all the haste he could to get out of the mountain; and then, taking the direct road to Toboso, the next day he arrived near the inn where he had been tossed in a blanket. Scarce had he descried the fatal walls, but a sudden shivering seized his bones, and he fancied himself to be again dancing in the air; so that he had a good mind to ride still farther before he baited, though it was dinner-time, and his mouth watered strangely at the thoughts of a hot bit of meat, the rather, because he had lived altogether upon cold victuals for a long while. This greedy longing drew him near the inn, in spite of his aversion to the place; but yet when he came to the gate he had not the courage to go in, but stopped there, not knowing whether he had best enter or no. While he sat musing, two men happened to come out, and, believing they knew him, 'Look, master doctor,' cried one to the other, 'is not that Sancho Pança whom the housekeeper told us her master had inveigled to go along with him?' 'The same,' answered the other; 'and more than that, he rides on Don Quixote's horse.' Now these two happened to be the curate and the barber, who had brought his books to a trial and passed sentence on them: therefore they had no sooner said this, but they called to Sancho, and asked him where he had left his master? The trusty squire presently knew them, and having no mind to discover the place and condition he left his master in, told them he was taken up with certain business of great consequence at a certain place which he durst not discover for his life. 'How! Sancho,' cried the barber, 'you must not think to put us off with a flim-flam story; if you will not tell us where he is, we shall believe you have murdered him, and robbed him of his horse; therefore, either satisfy us where you did leave him, or we will have you laid by the heels.'

'Look you, neighbour,' quoth Sancho, 'I am not afraid of words, do ye see: I am neither a thief nor a manslayer; I kill nobody, so nobody kills me:

I leave every man to fall by his own fortune, or by the hand of him that made him. As for my master, I left him frisking and doing penance in the midst of yonder mountain, to his heart's content.' After this, without any further entreaty, he gave them a full account of that business, and of all their adventures; how he was then going from his master to carry a letter to my lady Dulcinea del Toboso, Lorenzo Curchuelo's daughter, with whom he was up to the ears in love. The curate and barber stood amazed, hearing all these particulars: and, though they already knew Don Quixote's madness but too well, they wondered more and more at the increase of it, and at so strange a cast and variety of extravagance. Then they desired Sancho to show them the letter. He told them it was written in a pocket-book, and that his master had ordered him to get it fairly transcribed upon paper at the next village he should come at. Whereupon the curate promising to write it out very fairly himself, Sancho put his hand into his bosom to give him the table-book; but, though he fumbled a great while for it, he could find none of it. He searched and searched again, but it had been in vain though he had searched till Doomsday, for he came away from Don Quixote without it. This put him into a cold sweat, and made him turn as pale as death; he searched his clothes, turned his pockets inside outwards, and fumbled in his bosom again; but, being at last convinced he had it not about him, he fell araving and stamping, and cursing himself like a mad man: he rent his beard from his chin with both hands, befisted his own forgetful skull and his blubber cheeks, and gave himself a bloody nose in a moment. The curate and the barber asked him what was the matter with him and why he punished himself at that strange rate?' I deserve it all,' quoth Sancho, 'like a blockhead as I am, for losing at one cast no less than three asses, of which the least was worth a castle.' 'How so?' quoth the barber. 'Why,' cried Sancho, 'I have lost that same table-book, wherein was written Dulcinea's letter and a bill of exchange drawn by my master upon his niece, for three of the five asses which he has at home; 'and with that he told them how he had lost his own ass. But the curate cheered him up, and promised him to get another bill of exchange from his master written upon paper, whereas that in the table-book, not being in due form, would not have been accepted. With that Sancho took courage, and told them, if it were so, he cared not a straw for Dulcinea's letter, for he knew it almost all by rote. 'Then prithee let us hear it,' said the barber, 'and we will see and write it.' In order to this, Sancho paused, and began to study for the words. Presently he fell a scratching his head, stood first upon one leg, and then upon another, gaped sometimes upon the skies and sometimes upon the ground: at length, after he had gnawed away the top of his thumb, and quite tired out the curate and barber's patience, 'Before George,' cried he, 'Mr. Doctor, I believe the Devil is in it; for may I be choked if I remember a word of this confounded letter, but only that where was at the beginning, "High and subterrene lady." ' ' "Sovereign, or superhuman lady," you would say,' quoth the barber. 'Ay, ay,' quoth Sancho, 'you are in the right – but stay, now I think I can remember some of that which followed. Ho! I have it, I have it now – "He that is wounded, and wants sleep, sends you the dagger – which he wants himself – that stabbed him to the heart – and the hurt man does kiss your ladyship's hand;" and at last, after a hundred hums and haws, "sweetest Dulcinea del Toboso." And thus he went on rambling a good while with I do not know what more of fainting, and relief, and sinking, till at last he ended with "Yours till death, the Knight of the Woeful Figure." ' The curate and the barber were mightily pleased with Sancho's excellent memory; insomuch that they desired him to repeat the letter twice or thrice more, that they might also get it by heart, and write it down; which Sancho did very freely, but every time he made many odd alterations and additions, as pleasant as the first. Then he told them many other things of his master, but spoke not a word of his own being tossed in a blanket at that very inn. He also told them, that, if he brought a kind answer from the lady Dulcinea, his master would forthwith set out to see and make himself an emperor, or at least a king; for so they two had agreed between themselves, he said; and that, after all, it was a mighty easy matter for his master to become one, such was his prowess and the strength of his arm: which being done, his master would marry him to one of the empress's damsels; and that fine lady was to be heiress to a large country on the mainland, but not to any island, or islands, for he was out of conceit with them. Poor Sancho spoke all this so seriously and so feelingly, ever and anon wiping his nose, and stroking his beard, that now the curate and the barber were more surprised than they were before, considering the prevalent influences of Don Quixote's folly upon that silly credulous fellow. However, they did not think it worth their while to undeceive him yet, seeing this was only a harmless delusion, that might divert them a while; and therefore they exhorted him to pray for his master's health and long life, seeing it was no impossible thing, but that he might in time become an emperor, as he said, or at least an archbishop, or somewhat else equivalent to it.

'But pray, good Mr. Doctor,' asked Sancho, 'should my master have no mind to be an emperor, and take a fancy to be an archbishop, I would fain know what your archbishops-errant are wont to give their squires?' 'Why,' answered the curate, 'they used to give them some parsonage, or sinecure, or some other benefice, or church-living, which, with the profits of the altar, and other fees, brings them in a handsome revenue.' 'Ay, but,' says Sancho, 'to put in for that, the squire must be a single man, and know how to answer and assist at mass at least; and how shall I do then, seeing I have the ill-luck to be married? Nay, and besides, I do not so much as know the first letter of my Christcross-row. What will become of me, should it come into my master's head to make himself an archbishop, and not an emperor, as it is the custom of knights-errant?' 'Do not let that trouble thee, friend Sancho,' said the barber, 'we will talk to him about it, and advise him, nay, urge him to it as a point of conscience to be an emperor and not an archbishop, which will be better for him, by reason he has more courage than learning.

'Truth, I am of your mind,' quoth Sancho, 'though he is such a head-piece that I dare say he can turn himself to anything; nevertheless, I mean to make it the burden of my prayers, that Heaven may direct him to that which is best for him, and what may enable him to reward me most.' 'You speak like a wise man, and a good Christian,' said the curate, 'but all we have to do at present is, to see how we shall get your master to give over that severe unprofitable penance which he has undertaken; and therefore let us go on to consider about it, and also to eat our dinner, for I fancy it is ready by this time.' 'Do you two go in, if you please,' quoth Sancho, 'but as for me, I had rather stay without; and anon I will tell you why I do not care to go within doors; however, pray send me a piece of hot victuals to eat here, and some provender for Rozinante.' With that they went in, and a while after the barber brought him out some meat; and returning to the curate, they consulted how to compass their design. At last the latter luckily bethought himself of an expedient that seemed most likely to take, as exactly fitting Don Quixote's humour; which was that he should disguise himself in the habit of a damsel-errant, and the barber should alter his dress as well as he could, so as to pass for a squire, or gentleman-usher. 'In that equipage,' added he, 'we will go to Don Quixote, and feigning myself to be a distressed damsel, I will beg a boon of him, which he, as a valorous knight-errant, will not fail to promise me. By this means I will engage him to go with me to redress a very great injury done me by a false and discourteous knight, beseeching him not to desire to see my face, nor ask anything about my circumstances, till he has revenged me of that wicked knight. This bait will take, I dare engage, and by this stratagem we will decoy him back to his own house, where we will try to cure him of his romantic frenzy.'

CHAPTER XIII

How the Curate and Barber put their Design in execution; with other things worthy to be recorded in this important History

THE CURATE'S PROJECT was so well liked by the barber, that they instantly put it into practice. First they borrowed a complete woman's apparel of the hostess, leaving her in pawn a new cassock of the curate's; and the barber made himself a long beard with a grizzled ox's tail, in which the innkeeper used to hang his combs. The hostess being desirous to know what they intended to do with those things, the curate gave her a short account of Don Quixote's distraction, and their design. Whereupon the innkeeper and his wife presently guessed this was their romantic knight, that made the precious balsam; and accordingly they told them the whole story of Don Quixote's lodging there, and of Sancho's being tossed in a blanket. Which done, the hostess readily fitted out the curate at such a rate, that it would have pleased any one to have seen him; for she dressed him up in a cloth gown, trimmed with borders of black velvet, the breadth of a span, all pinked and jagged; and a pair of green velvet bodice, with sleeves of the same, and faced with white satin; which accoutrements probably had been in fashion in old King Bamba's* days. The curate would not let her encumber his head with a woman's headgear, but only clapped upon his crown a white quilted cap which he used to wear a-nights, and bound his forehead with one of his garters, that was of black taffety, making himself a kind of muffler and vizard mask with the other: then he half-buried his head under his hat, pulling it down to squeeze in his ears; and as the broad brim flapped down over his eyes, it seemed a kind of umbrella. This done, he wrapped his cloak about him, and seated himself on his mule sideways like a woman; then the barber clapped on his ox-tail beard, half red and half grizzled, which hung from his chin down to his waist; and, having mounted his mule, they took leave of their host and hostess, as also of the good-conditioned Maritornes, who vowed though she was a sinner, to tumble her beads, and say a rosary to the good success of so arduous and truly Christian an undertaking.

But scarce were they got out of the inn, when the curate began to be troubled with a scruple of conscience about his putting on women's

---

* An ancient Gothic king of Spain, concerning whom several fables are written, wherefore the Spaniards to express anything exceeding old, say it was in being in his time; was in England we say a thing is as old as Paul's, and the like.

apparel, being apprehensive of the indecency of the disguise in a priest, though the goodness of his intention might well warrant a dispensation from the strictness of decorum: therefore he desired the barber to change dresses, for that in his habit of a squire he should less profane his own dignity and character, to which he ought to have a greater regard than to Don Quixote; withal assuring the barber, that unless he consented to this exchange, he was absolutely resolved to go no further, though it were to save Don Quixote's soul from Hell. Sancho came up with them just upon their demur, and was ready to split his sides with laughing at the sight of these strange masqueraders. In short, the barber consented to be the damsel, and to let the curate be the squire. Now, while they were thus changing sexes, the curate offered to tutor him how to behave himself in that female attire, so as to be able to wheedle Don Quixote out of his penance; but the barber desired him not to trouble himself about that matter, assuring him, that he was well enough versed in female affairs, to be able to act a damsel without any directions; however, he said he would not now stand fiddling and managing his pins to prink himself up, seeing it would be time enough to do that when they came near Don Quixote's hermitage; and therefore, having folded up his clothes, and the curate his beard, they spurred on, while their guide Sancho entertained them with a relation of the mad, tattered gentleman whom they had met in the mountain; however, without mentioning a word of the portmanteau or the gold, for, as much a fool as he was, he loved money, and knew how to keep it when he had it, and was wise enough to keep his own counsel.

They got the next day to the place where Sancho had strewed the boughs to direct him to Don Quixote; and therefore he advised them to put on their disguises, if it were, as they told him, that their design was only to make his master leave that wretched kind of life, in order to become an emperor. Thereupon they charged him on his life not to take the least notice who they were. As for Dulcinea's letter, if Don Quixote asked him about it, they ordered him to say he had delivered it; but by reason she could neither write nor read, she had sent him her answer by word of mouth; which was, that on pain of her indignation, he should immediately put an end to his severe penance, and repair to her presence. This, they told Sancho, together with what they themselves designed to say, was the only way to oblige his master to leave the desert, that he might prosecute his design of making himself an emperor; assuring him they would take care he should not entertain the least thought of an archbishopric.

Sancho listened with great attention to all these instructions, and treasured them up in his mind, giving the curate and the barber a world of thanks for their good intention of advising his master to become an emperor, and not an archbishop; for, as he said, he imagined in his simple judgment, that an emperor-errant was ten times better than an arch-bishop-errant, and could reward his squire a great deal better.

He likewise added, that he thought it would be proper for him to go to his master somewhat before them, and give him an account of his Lady's kind answer; for, perhaps, that alone would be sufficient to fetch him out of that place, without putting them to any further trouble. They liked this proposal very well, and therefore agreed to let him go, and wait there till he came back to give them an account of his success. With that Sancho rode away, and struck into the clefts of the rock, in order to find out his master, leaving the curate and the barber by the side of a brook, where the neighbouring hills and some trees that grew along its banks, combined to make a cool and pleasant shade. There they sheltered themselves from the scorching beams of the sun, that commonly shines intolerably hot in those parts at that time, being about the middle of August, and hardly three o'clock in the afternoon. While they quietly refreshed themselves in that delightful place, where they agreed to stay till Sancho's return, they heard a voice, which, though unattended with any instrument, ravished their ears with its melodious sound: and, what increased their surprise and their admiration, was to hear such artful notes, and such delicate music in so unfrequented and wild a place, where scarce any rustics ever straggled, much less such skilful songsters, as the person whom they heard unquestionably was; for, though the poets are pleased to fill the fields and woods with swains and shepherdesses, that sing with all the sweetness and delicacy imaginable, yet it is well enough known that those gentlemen deal more in fiction than in truth, and love to embellish the descriptions they make with things that have no existence but in their own brain. Nor could our two listening travellers think it the voice of a peasant, when they began to distinguish the words of the song, for they seemed to relish more of a courtly style than a rural composition. These were the verses.

A SONG

I

What makes me languish and complain?

> Oh, 'tis disdain!

What yet more fiercely tortures me?

> 'Tis jealousy.

How have I patience lost?

> By absence crost,

Then hopes farewell, there's no relief;
I sink beneath oppressing grief;
Nor can a wretch, without despair,
Scorn, jealousy, and absence bear.

II

What in my breast this anguish drove?

                    Intruding love.

Who could such mighty ills create?

                    Blind fortune's hate.

What cruel pow'rs my fate approve?

                    The powers above.

    Then let me bear, and cease to moan;
    'Tis glorious thus to be undone:
    When these invade, who dares oppose?
    Heaven, love and fortune are my foes.

III

Where shall I find a speedy cure?

                    Death is sure.

No milder means to set me free?

                    Inconstancy.

Can nothing else my pains assuage?

                    Distracting rage.

    What die or change? Lucinda lose;
    Oh let me rather madness choose?
    But judge ye gods, what we endure
    When death or madness are a cure!

The time, the hour, the solitariness of the place, the voice and agreeable manner with which the unseen musician sung, so filled the hearers' minds with wonder and delight, that they were all attention; and when the voice was silent, they continued so too a pretty while, watching with listening ears to catch the expected sounds, expressing their satisfaction best by that dumb applause. At last, concluding the person would sing no more, they resolved to find out the charming songster; but, as they were going so to do, they heard the wished-for voice begin another air, which fixed them where they stood till it had sung the following sonnet:

A SONNET

O Sacred friendship, Heaven's delight
    Which, tir'd With man's unequal mind
Took to thy native skies thy flight
    While scarce thy shadow's left behind!

From thee, diffusive good below,
　　Peace and her train of joys we trace
But falsehood, with dissembl'd show
　　Too oft usurps thy sacred face.

Bless'd genius, then resumed thy seat!
Destroy imposture and deceit,
　　Which in thy dress confound the ball!
Harmonious peace and truth renew,
Show the false friendship from the true,
　　Or nature must to Chaos fall.

This sonnet concluded with a deep sigh, and such doleful throbs, that the curate and the barber now, out of pity as well as curiosity, resolved instantly to find out who this mournful songster was. They had not gone far, when by the side of a rock they discovered a man, whose shape and aspect answered exactly to the description Sancho had given them of Cardenio. They observed he stopped short as soon as he spied them, yet without any signs of fear; only he hung down his head, like one abandoned to sorrow, never so much as lifting up his eyes to mind what they did. The curate, who was a good and a well-spoken man, presently guessing him to be the same of whom Sancho had given them an account, went towards him, and addressing himself to him with great civility and discretion, earnestly entreated him to forsake this desert, and a course of life so wretched and forlorn, which endangered his title to a better, and from a wilful misery might make him fall into greater and everlasting woes. Cardenio was then free from the distraction that so often disturbed his senses; yet seeing two persons in a garb wholly different from that of those few rustics who frequented those deserts, and hearing them talk as if they were no strangers to his concerns, he was somewhat surprised at first; however, having looked upon them earnestly for some time, 'Gentlemen,' said he, 'whoever ye be, I find Heaven, pitying my misfortunes, has brought ye to these solitary regions, to retrieve me from this frightful retirement, and recover me to the society of men; but because you do not know how unhappy a fate attends me, and that I never am free from one affliction but to fall into a greater, you perhaps take me for a man naturally endowed with a very small stock of sense, and what is worse, for one of those wretches who are altogether deprived of reason. And indeed I cannot blame any one that entertains such thoughts of me; for even I myself am convinced, that the bare remembrance of my disasters often distracts me to that degree, that losing all sense of reason and knowledge, I unman myself for the time, and launch into those extravagancies which nothing but height of frenzy and madness would commit: and I am the more sensible of my being troubled with this distemper, when people tell me what I have done during the violence of that terrible accident, and give me too certain proofs of it. And after all, I can allege no other excuse but the cause of my misfortune, which occasioned that frantic rage, and therefore tell the story of my hard fate to as many as have the patience to hear it; for men of sense, perceiving the cause, will not wonder at the effects; and though they can give me no relief, yet at least they will cease to condemn me; for a bare relation of my wrongs must needs make them lose their resentments of the effects of my disorder into a compassion of my miserable fate. Therefore, gentlemen, if you came here with that design, I beg that before you give yourselves the trouble of reproving or advising me, you will be pleased to attend to the relation of my calamities; for perhaps, when you have heard it, you will think them past redress, and so will save yourselves the labour you would take.' The curate and the barber, who desired nothing more than to hear the story from his own mouth, were extremely glad of his proffer; and, having assured him they had no design to aggravate his miseries with pretending to remedy them, nor would they cross his inclinations in the least, they entreated him to begin his relation.

The unfortunate Cardenio then began his story, and went on with the first part of it, almost in the same words, as far as when he related it to Don Quixote and the goatherd, when the knight, out of superstitious niceness to observe the decorum of chivalry, gave an interruption to the relation, by quarrelling about master Elizabat, as we have already said. Then he went on with that passage concerning the letter sent him by Lucinda, which Don Ferdinand had unluckily found, happening to be by, to open the book of 'Amadis de Gaul' first, when Lucinda sent it back to Cardenio with that letter in it between the leaves; which Cardenio told them was as follows:

' "LUCINDA TO CARDENIO.

' "I discover in you every day so much merit, that I am obliged, or rather forced, to esteem you more and more. If you think this acknowledgment to your advantage, make that use of it which is most consistent with your honour and mine. I have a father that knows you, and is too kind a parent ever to obstruct my designs, when he shall be satisfied with their being just and honourable: so that it is now your part to show you love me, as your pretend, and I believe." '

'This letter,' continued Cardenio, 'made me resolve once more to demand Lucinda of her father in marriage, and was the same that increased Don Ferdinand's esteem for her, by that discovery of her sense and discretion, which so inflamed his soul, that from that moment he secretly resolved to destroy my hopes before I could be so happy as to crown them with success. I told that perfidious friend what Lucinda's father had advised me to do, when I had rashly asked her for my wife before, and that I durst not now impart this to my father, lest he should not readily consent I should marry yet. Not but that he knew, that her quality, beauty, and virtue were sufficient to make her an ornament to the noblest house in Spain, but because I was apprehensive he would not let me marry till he saw what the Duke would do for me. Don Ferdinand, with a pretended of officiousness, proffered me to speak to my father, and persuade him to treat with Lucinda's. Ungrateful man! deceitful friend! ambitious Marius! cruel Cataline! wicked Sylla! perfidious Galalon! faithless Vellido! malicious Julian!* treacherous, covetous Judas! thou, all those fatal hated men in one, false Ferdinand! what wrongs had that fond confiding wretch done thee, who thus to thee unbosomed all his cares, all the delights and secrets of his soul? What injury did I ever utter, or advice did I ever give, which were not all directed to advance thy honour and profit? But oh! I rave, unhappy wretch! I should rather accuse the cruelty of my stars, whose fatal influence pours mischiefs on me, which no earthly force can resist, or human art prevent. Who would have thought that Don Ferdinand, whose quality and merit entitled him to the lawful possession of beauties of the highest rank, and whom I had engaged by a thousand endearing marks of friendship and services, should forfeit thus his honour and his truth, and lay such a treacherous design to deprive me of all the happiness of my life? But I must leave expostulating, to end my story. The traitor Ferdinand, thinking his project impracticable while I stayed near Lucinda, bargained for six fine horses the same day he promised to speak to my father, and presently desired me to ride away to his brother for money to pay for them. Alas! I was so far from suspecting his treachery, that I was glad of doing him a piece of service. Accordingly I went that very evening to take my leave of Lucinda, and to tell her what Don Ferdinand had promised to do. She bid me return with all the haste of an expecting lover, not doubting but our lawful wishes might be crowned as soon as my father had spoken for me to be hers. When she had said this, I marked her trickling tears, and a sudden grief so obstructed her speech, that though she seemed to strive to tell me something more, she could not give it utterance. This unusual scene of sorrow strangely amazed and moved me; yet because I would not murder hope, I chose to attribute this to the tenderness of her affection, and unwillingness to part with me. In short,

---

* Count Julian brought the Moors into Spain, because King Roderigo had ravished his daughter. Galalon and Vellido are explained elsewhere. Marius, Cataline, etc., are well known.

away I went, buried in deep melancholy, and full of fears and imaginations, for which I could give no manner of reason. I delivered Don Ferdinand's letter to his brother, who received me with all the kindness imaginable, but did not dispatch me as I expected. For, to my sorrow, he enjoined me to tarry a whole week, and to take care the Duke might not see me, his brother having sent for money unknown to his father: but this was only a device of false Ferdinand's; for his brother did not want money, and might have dispatched me immediately, had he not been privately desired to delay my return.

'This was so displeasing an injunction, that I was ready to come away without the money, not being able to live so long absent from my Lucinda, principally considering in what condition I had left her. Yet at last I forced myself to stay, and any respect for my friend prevailed over my impatience: but, before four tedious days were expired, a messenger brought me a letter, which I presently knew to be Lucinda's hand. I opened it with trembling hands, and an aching heart, justly imagining it was no ordinary concern that could urge her to send thither to me: and before I read it, I asked the messenger who had given it him? He answered me, "that, going by accidentally in the street about noon, in our town, a very handsome lady, all in tears, had called him to her window, and with great precipitation, 'Friend,' said she, 'if you be a Christian, as you seem to be, for Heaven's sake take this letter, and deliver it with all speed into the person's own hand to whom it is directed: I assure you in this, you will do a very good action; and that you may not want means to do it, take what is wrapped up in this;' and so saying, she threw me a handkerchief, wherein I found a hundred reals, this gold ring which you see, and the letter which I now brought you: which done, I having made her signs to let her know I would do as she desired, without so much as staying for an answer, she went from the grate. This reward, but much more the beautiful lady's tears, and earnest prayers, made me post away to you that very minute, and so in sixteen hours I have travelled eighteen long leagues." While the messenger spoke, I was seized with sad apprehensions of some fatal news; and such a trembling shook my limbs, that I could scarce support my fainting body. However, taking courage, at last I read the letter, the contents of which were these:

' "Don Ferdinand, according to his promise, has desired your father to speak to mine; but he has done that for himself which you had engaged him to do for you: for he has demanded me for his wire; and my father, allured by the advantages which he expects from such an alliance, has so far consented, that two days hence the marriage is to be performed, and with such privacy, that only Heaven and some of the family are to be witnesses. Judge of the affliction of my soul by that concern which I guess fills your own; and therefore haste to me, my dear Cardenio. The issue of this business will show how much I love you: and grant, propitious Heaven, this may reach your hands before mine is in danger of being joined with his who keeps his promises so ill." '

'I had no sooner read the letter,' added Cardenio, 'but away I flew, without waiting for my dispatch: for then I too plainly discovered Don Ferdinand's treachery, and that he only sent me to his brother, to take the advantage of my absence. Revenge, love, and impatience gave me wings, so that I got home privately the next day, just when it grew duskish, in good time to speak with Lucinda; and, leaving my mule at the honest man's house who brought me the letter, I went to wait upon my mistress, whom I luckily found at the window,* the only witness of our loves. She presently knew me, and I her, but she did not welcome me as I expected, nor did I find her in such a dress as I thought suitable to our circumstances. But what man has assurance enough not to pretend to know thoroughly the riddle of a woman's mind, and who could ever hope to fix her mutable nature? "Cardenio," said Lucinda to me, "my wedding clothes are on, and the perfidious Ferdinand, with my covetous father and the rest, stay for me in the hall, to perform the marriage-rites; but they shall sooner be witnesses of my death than of my nuptials. Be not troubled, my dear Cardenio; but rather strive to be present at that sacrifice. I promise thee, if entreaties and words cannot prevent it, I have a dagger that shall do me justice; and my death, at least, shall give thee undeniable assurances of my love and fidelity." "Do, madam," cried I to her with precipitation, and so disordered that I did not know what I said, "let your actions verify your words: let us leave nothing unattempted which may serve our common interests; and I assure you, if my sword does not defend them well, I will turn it upon my own breast, rather than outlive my disappointment." I cannot tell whether Lucinda heard me, for she was called away in great haste, the bridegroom impatiently expecting her. My spirit forsook me when she left me, and my sorrows and confusion cannot be expressed. Methought I saw the sun set for ever; and my eyes and my senses partaking of my distraction, I could not so much as spy the door to go into the house, and seemed rooted to the place where I stood. But at last, the consideration of my love having roused me out of this stupefying astonishment, I got into the house without being discovered, everything there being in a hurry; and going into the hall, I hid

---

* *A la rexa*, 'at the iron grate.' In Spain, the lovers make their courtship at a low window that has a grate before it, having seldom admission into the house till the parents on both sides have agreed.

myself behind the hangings, where two pieces of tapestry met, and gave me liberty to see, without being seen. Who can describe the various thoughts, the doubts, the fears, the anguish that perplexed and tossed my soul, while I stood waiting there! Don Ferdinand entered the hall, not like a bridegroom, but in his usual habit, with only a cousin-german of Lucinda's, the rest were the people of the house: some time after came Lucinda herself, with her mother, and two waiting-women. I perceived she was as richly dressed, as was consistent with her quality, and the solemnity of the ceremony; but the distraction that possessed me, lent me no time to note particularly the apparel she had on: I only marked the colours, which were carnation and white, and the splendour of the jewels that enriched her dress in many places; but nothing equalled the lustre of her beauty, that adorned her person much more than all those ornaments. Oh, memory! thou fatal enemy of my ease, why dost thou now so faithfully represent to the eyes of my mind Lucinda's incomparable charms? Why dost thou not rather show me what she did then; that, moved by so provoking a wrong, I may endeavour to revenge it, or at least to die. Forgive me these tedious digressions, gentlemen. Alas! my woes are not such as can or ought to be related with brevity; for to me every circumstance seems worthy to be enlarged upon.'

The curate assured Cardenio that they attended every word with a mournful pleasure, that made them greedy of hearing the least passage. With that Cardenio went on. 'All parties being met,' said he, 'the priest entered, and taking the young couple by the hands, he asked Lucinda whether she were willing to take Don Ferdinand for her wedded husband? With that I thrust out my head from between the two pieces of tapestry, listening with anxious heart to hear her answer, upon which depended my life and happiness. Dull-heartless wretch that I was! why did I not then show myself? why did I not call to her aloud? "Consider what thou dost, Lucinda; thou art mine, and cannot be another man's: nor canst thou speak now the fatal Yes, without injuring Heaven, thyself, and me, and murdering thy Cardenio! And thou perfidious Ferdinand, who darest to violate all rights, both human and divine, to rob me of my treasure; canst thou hope to deprive me of the comfort of my life with impunity? Or thinkest thou that any consideration can stifle my resentments, when my honour and my love lie at stake?" Fool that I am! now that is too late, and danger is far distant; I say what I should have done, and not what I did then: after I have suffered the treasure of my soul to be stolen, I exclaim against the thief, whom I might have punished for the base attempt, had I had but so much resolution to revenge as I have now to complain. Then let me rather accuse my faint heart that durst not do me right, and let me die here like a wretch, void both of sense and honour, the outcast of society and nature. The priest stood waiting for Lucinda's answer a good while before she gave it: and all that time I expected she would have pulled out her dagger, or unloosed her tongue to plead her former engagement to me. But, alas! to my eternal disappointment, I heard her at last, with a feeble voice, pronounce the fatal Yes; and then Don Ferdinand, saying the same and giving her the ring, the sacred knot was tied which death alone can dissolve. Then did the faithless bridegroom advance to embrace his bride; but she, laying her hand upon her heart, in that very moment swooned away in her mother's arms. Oh what confusion seized me, what pangs, what torments racked me, seeing the falsehood of Lucinda's promises, all my hopes shipwrecked, and the only thing that made me wish to live, for ever ravished from me! Confounded and despairing, I looked upon myself as abandoned by Heaven to the cruelty of my destiny; and the violence of my griefs stifling my sighs, and denying a passage to my tears, I felt myself transfixed with killing anguish, and burning with jealous rage and vengeance! In the mean time, the whole company was troubled at Lucinda's swooning; and, as her mother unclasped her gown before, to give her air, a folded paper was found in her bosom, which Don Ferdinand immediately snatched; then, stepping a little aside, he opened it and read it by the light of one of the tapers: and as soon as he had done, he, as it were, let himself fall upon a chair, and there he sat with his hand upon the side of his face, with all the signs of melancholy and discontent, as unmindful of his bride as if he had been insensible of her accident. For my own part, seeing all the house thus in an uproar, I resolved to leave the hated place, without caring whether I was seen or not, and in case I were seen, I resolved to act such a desperate part in punishing the traitor Ferdinand, that the world should at once be informed of his perfidiousness, and the severity of my just resentment; but my destiny, that preserved me for greater woes (if greater can be) allowed me then the use of that small remainder of my senses, which afterwards quite forsook me: so that I left the house, without revenging myself on my enemies, whom I could easily have sacrificed to my rage in this unexpected disorder; and I chose to inflict upon myself, for my credulity the punishment which their infidelity deserved. I went to the messenger's house where I had left my mule, and without so much as bidding him adieu, I mounted, and left the town like another Lot, without turning to give it a parting look; and as I rode along the fields, darkness and silence round me, I vented my passions in execrations against the treacherous Ferdinand, and in as loud complaints of Lucinda's breach of vows and ingratitude. I called her cruel, ungrateful, false, but above all, covetous and sordid, since the wealth of my enemy was what had induced her to forget her vows to me; but then again, said I to myself, it is no strange thing for a young lady, that was so strictly educated, to yield herself up to the guidance of her father and mother, who had provided her a husband of that quality and fortune. But yet with truth and justice she might have pleaded, that she was mine before. In fine, I concluded that ambition had got the better of her love, and made her forget her promises to Cardenio. Thus abandoning myself to these tempestuous thoughts, I rode on all that night, and about break of day I struck into one of the passes that lead into these mountains; where I wandered for three days together, without keeping my road, till at last, coming to a certain valley that lies somewhere hereabouts, I met some shepherds, of whom I inquired the way to the most craggy and inaccessible part of these rocks. They directed me, and I made all the haste I could to get thither, resolved to linger out my hated life far from the converse of false ungrateful mankind. When I came among these deserts, my mule, through weariness and hunger, or rather to get rid of so useless a load as I was, fell down dead, and I myself was so weak, so tired and dejected, being almost famished, and withal destitute and careless of relief, that I soon laid myself down, or rather fainted on the ground, where I lay a considerable while, I do not know how long, extended like a corpse. When I came to myself again, I got up, and could not perceive I had any appetite to eat: I found some goatherds by me, who, I suppose, had given me some sustenance, though I was not sensible of their relief: for they told me in what a wretched condition they found me, staring, and talking to strangely, that they judged I had quite lost my senses. I have indeed since that had but too much cause to think, that my reason sometimes leaves me, and that I commit those extravagancies which are only the effects of senseless rage and frenzy; tearing my clothes, howling through these deserts, filling the air with curses and lamentations, and idly repeating a thousand times Lucinda's name; all my wishes at that time being to breathe out my soul with the dear word upon my lips; and when I come to myself, I am commonly so weak, and so weary, that I am scarce able to stir. As for my place of abode, it is usually some hollow cork-tree, into which I creep at night; and there some few goatherds, whose cattle browse on the neighbouring mountains, out of pity and Christian charity, sometimes leave some victuals for the support of my miserable life: for, even when my reason is absent, nature performs its animal functions, and instinct guides me to satisfy it. Sometimes these good people meet me in my lucid intervals, and chide me for taking that from them by force and surprise, which they are always so ready to give me willingly; for which violence I can make no other excuse, but the extremity of my distraction. Thus must I drag a miserable being, until Heaven, pitying my afflictions, will either put a period to my life, or blot out of my memory perjured Lucinda's beauty and ingratitude, and Ferdinand's perfidiousness. Could I but be so happy ere I die, I might then hope to be able, in time, to compose my frantic thoughts: but if I must despair of such a favour, I have no other way but to recommend my soul to Heaven's mercy; for I am not able to extricate my body or my mind out of that misery in which I have unhappily plunged myself.

'Thus, gentlemen, I have given you a faithful account of my misfortunes. Judge now whether it was possible I should relate them with less concern. And, pray do not lose time to prescribe remedies to a patient who will make use of none: I will, and can have no health without Lucinda; since she forsakes me, I must die: she has convinced me, by her infidelity, that she desires my ruin; and by my unparalleled sufferings to the last, I will strive to convince her I deserved a better fate. Let me then suffer on, and may I be the only unhappy creature whom despair could not relieve, while the impossibility of receiving comfort brings cure to so many other wretches!'

Here Cardenio made an end of his mournful story; and just as the curate was preparing to give him some proper consolation, he was prevented by the doleful accents of another complaint that engaged them to new attention. But the account of that adventure is reserved for the fourth book of this history; for our wise and judicious historian, Cid Hamet Benengeli, puts here a period to the third.

BOOK IV

CHAPTER I

The pleasant new Adventure the Curate and Barber met with in the Sierra Morena, or Black Mountains

MOST FORTUNATE and happy was the age, that ushered into the world that most daring knight, Don Quixote de la Mancha! for from his generous resolution to revive and restore the ancient order of knight-errantry, that was not only wholly neglected, but almost lost and abolished, our age, barren in itself of pleasant recreations, derives the pleasure it reaps from his true history, and the various tales and episodes thereof, in some respects, no less pleasing, artful, and authentic than the history itself. We told you that as the curate was preparing to give Cardenio some seasonable consolation, he was prevented by a voice, whose doleful complaints reached his ears. 'O heavens!' cried the unseen mourner, 'is it possible I have at last found out a place that will afford a private grave to this miserable body, whose load I so repine to bear? Yes, if the silence and solitude of these deserts do not deceive me, here I may die concealed from human eyes. Ah me! ah wretched creature! to what extremity has affliction driven me, reduced to think these hideous woods and rocks a kind retreat! 'Tis true indeed, I may here freely complain to Heaven, and beg for that relief which I might ask in vain of false mankind: for it is vain, I find, to seek below either counsel, ease, or remedy.' The curate and his company, who heard all this distinctly, justly conjectured they were very near the person who thus expressed his grief, and therefore rose to find him out. They had not gone above twenty paces, before they spied a youth in a country habit, sitting at the foot of a rock, behind an ash tree; but they could not well see his face, being bowed almost upon his knees, as he sat washing his feet in a rivulet that glided by. They approached him so softly that he did not perceive them: and, as he was gently paddling in the clear water, they had time to discern that his legs were as white as alabaster, and so taper, so curiously proportioned, and so fine, that nothing of the kind could appear more beautiful. Our observers were amazed at this discovery, rightly imagining that such tender feet were not used to trudge in rugged ways, or measure the steps of oxen at the plough, the common employments of people in such apparel; and therefore the curate, who went before the rest, whose curiosity was heightened by this sight, beckoned to them to step aside, and hide themselves behind some of the little rocks that were by; which they did, and from thence making a stricter observation, they found he had on a grey double-skirted jerkin, girt tight about his body with a linen towel. He wore also a pair of breeches, and gamashes of grey cloth, and a grey huntsman's cap on his head. His gamashes were now pulled up to the middle of his leg, which really seemed to be of snowy alabaster. Having made an end of washing his beauteous feet, he immediately wiped them with a handkerchief, which he pulled out from under his cap; and with that, looking up, he discovered so charming a face, so accomplished a beauty, that Cardenio could not forbear saying to the curate, that since this was not Lucinda, it was certainly no human form, but an angel. And then the youth taking off his cap, and shaking his head, an incredible quantity of lovely hair flowed down upon his shoulders, and not only covered them, but almost all his body; by which they were now convinced, that what they at first took to be a country lad, was a young woman, and one of the most beautiful creatures in the world. Cardenio was not less surprised than the other two, and once more declared that no face could vie with her's but Lucinda's. To part her dishevelled tresses, she only used her slender fingers, and at the same time discovered so fine a pair of arms and hands, so white and lovely, that our three admiring gazers grew more impatient to know who she was, and moved forwards to accost her. At the noise they made, the pretty creature started; and, peeping through her hair, which she hastily removed from before her eyes with both her hands, she no sooner saw three men coming towards her, but in a mighty fright she snatched up a little bundle that lay by her, and fled as fast as she could, without so much as staying to put on her shoes, or do up her hair. But alas I scarce had she gone six steps, when her tender feet not being able to endure the rough encounter of the stones, the poor affrighted fair fell on the hard ground; so that those from whom she fled hastening to help her: 'Stay, madam,' cried the curate, 'whoever you be, you have no reason to fly; we have no other design but to do you service.' With that, approaching her, he took her by the hand, and perceiving she was so disordered with fear and confusion, that she could not answer a word, he strove to compose her mind with kind expressions. 'Be not afraid, madam,' continued he, 'though your hair has betrayed what your disguise concealed from us, we are but the more disposed to assist you, and do you all manner of service. Then, pray, tell us how we may best do it. I imagine it was no slight occasion that made you obscure your singular beauty under so unworthy a disguise, and venture into this desert, where it was the greatest chance in the world that ever you met with us. However, we hope it is not impossible to find a remedy for your misfortunes, since there are none which reason and time will not at last surmount: and therefore, madam, if you have not absolutely renounced all human comfort, I beseech you tell us the cause of your affliction, and assure yourself we do not ask this out of mere curiosity, but a real desire to serve you, and either to condole or assuage your grief.'

While the curate endeavoured thus to remove the trembling fair one's apprehension, she stood amazed, staring, without speaking a word, sometimes upon one, sometimes upon another, like one scarce well awake, or like an ignorant clown who happens to see some strange sight. But at last, the curate having given her time to recollect herself, and persisting in his earnest and civil entreaties, she fetched a deep sigh, and then, unclosing her lips, broke silence in this manner. 'Since this desert has not been able to conceal me, and my hair has betrayed me, it would be needless now for me to dissemble with you; and, since you desire to hear the story of my misfortunes, I cannot in civility deny you, after all the obliging offers you have been pleased to make me: but yet, gentlemen, I am much afraid, what I have to say will but make you sad, and afford you little satisfaction; for you will find my disasters are not to be remedied. There is one thing that troubles me yet more; it shocks my nature to think I must be forced to reveal to you some secrets, which I had a design to have buried in my grave; but yet, considering the garb and the place you have found me in, I fancy it will be better for me to tell you all, than to give occasion to doubt of my past conduct and my present designs, by an affected reservedness.' The disguised lady having made this answer, with a modest blush and extraordinary discretion, the curate and his company, who now admired her the more for her sense, renewed their kind offers and pressing solicitations; and then they modestly let her retire a moment to some distance, to put herself in decent order. Which done, she returned, and being all seated on the grass, after she had used no small violence to smother her tears, she thus began her story.

'I was born in a certain town of Andalusia, from which a duke takes his title, that makes him a grandee of Spain. This duke has two sons, the eldest heir to his estate, and as it may be presumed, of his virtues; the youngest heir to nothing I know of; but the treachery of Vellido,* and the deceitfulness of Galalon.† My father, who is one of his vassals is but of low degree; but so very rich, that had Fortune equalled his birth to his estate, he could have wanted nothing more, and I perhaps, had never been so miserable; for I verily believe, my not being of noble blood is the chief occasion of my ruin. True it is, my parents are not so meanly born as to have any cause to be ashamed of their original, nor so high as to alter the opinion I have, that my misfortune proceeds from their lowness. It is true,

* Who murdered Sancho, King of Castile, as he was easing himself, at the siege of Camora.
† Who betrayed the French army at Roncesvalles.

they have been farmers from father to son, yet without any mixture or stain of infamous or scandalous blood. They are old rusty* Christians (as we call our true primitive Spaniards), and the antiquity of their family, together with their large possessions and the port they live in, raises them much above their profession, and has by little and little almost universally gained them the name of Gentlemen, setting them, in a manner, equal to many such in the world's esteem. As I am their only child, they ever loved me with all the tenderness of indulgent parents; and their great affection made them esteem themselves happier in their daughter, than in the peaceable enjoyment of their large estate. Now as it was my good fortune to be possessed of their love, they were pleased to trust me with their substance. The whole house and estate was left to my management, and I took such care not to abuse the trust reposed in me, that I never forfeited their good opinion of my discretion. The time I had to spare from the care of the family, I commonly employed in the usual exercise's of young women, sometimes making bone-lace, or at my needle, and now and then reading some good book, or playing on the harp; having experienced that music was very proper to recreate the wearied mind: and this was the innocent life I led. I have not descended to these particulars out of vain ostentation, but merely that, when I come to relate my misfortunes, you may observe I do not owe them to my ill-conduct. While I thus lived the life of a nun, unseen, as I thought, by anybody but our own family, and never leaving the house but to go to church, which was commonly betimes in the morning, and always with my mother, and so close hid in a veil that I could scarce find my way; notwithstanding all the care that was taken to keep me from being seen, it was unhappily rumoured abroad that I was handsome, and to my eternal disquiet, love intruded into my peaceful retirement. Don Ferdinand, second son to the Duke I have mentioned, had a sight of me – ' Scarce had Cardenio heard Don Ferdinand named, but he changed colour, and betrayed such a disorder of body and mind, that the curate and the barber were afraid he would have fallen into one of those frantic fits that often used to take him; but by good fortune it did not come to that, and he only set himself to look steadfastly on the country-maid, presently guessing who she was; while she continued her story, without taking any notice of the alterations of his countenance.

'No sooner had he seen me,' said she, 'but, as he since told me, he felt in his breast that violent passion of which he afterwards gave me so many proofs. But, not to tire you with a needless relation of every particular, I will pass over all the means he used to inform me of his love: he purchased

---

* *Ranciofos* in the original; a metaphor taken from rusty bacon, yellow and mouldy, as it were with age. It is a farmer's daughter speaks this.

the good-will of all our servants with private gifts; he made my father a thousand kind offers of service; every day seemed a day of rejoicing in our neighbourhood, every evening ushered in some serenade, and the continual music was even a disturbance in the night. He got an infinite number of love-letters transmitted to me, I do not know by what means, every one full of the tenderest expressions, promises, vows, and protestations. But all this assiduous courtship was so far from inclining my heart to a kind return, that it rather moved my indignation; insomuch that I looked upon Don Ferdinand as my greatest enemy, and one wholly bent on my ruin: not but that I was well enough pleased with his gallantry, and took a secret delight in seeing myself thus courted by a person of his quality. Such demonstrations of love are never altogether displeasing to women, and the most disdainful, in spite of all their coyness, reserve a little complaisance in their hearts for their admirers. But the disproportion between our qualities was too great to suffer me to entertain any reasonable hopes, and his gallantry too singular not to offend me. Besides, my father, who soon made a right construction of Don Ferdinand's pretensions, with his prudent admonitions concurred with the sense I ever had of my honour, and banished from my mind all favourable thoughts of his addresses. However, like a kind parent, perceiving I was somewhat uneasy, and imagining the flattering prospect of so advantageous a match might still amuse me, he told me one day he reposed the utmost trust in my virtue, esteeming it the strongest obstacle he could oppose to Don Ferdinand's dishonourable designs; yet, if I would marry, to rid me at once of his unjust pursuit, and prevent the ruin of my reputation, I should have liberty to make my own choice of a suitable match, either in our own town or the neighbourhood; and that he would do for me whatever could be expected from a loving father. I humbly thanked him for his kindness, and told him, that as I had never yet had any thoughts of marriage, I would try to rid myself of Don Ferdinand some other way. Accordingly I resolved to shun him with so much precaution, that he should never have the opportunity to speak to me: but all my reservedness, far from tiring out his passion, strengthened it the more. In short, Don Ferdinand, either hearing or suspecting I was to be married, thought of a contrivance to cross a design that was likely to cut off all his hopes. One night, therefore, when I was in my chamber, nobody with me but my maid, and the door double locked and bolted that I might be secured against the attempts of Don Ferdinand, whom I took to be a man who would stick at nothing to compass his designs, unexpectedly I saw him just before me; which amazing sight so surprised me, that I was struck dumb, and fainted away with fear. So I had not power to call for help, nor do I believe he would have given me time to have done it, had I attempted it; for he presently ran to me, and taking me in his arms, while I was sinking with the fright, he spoke to me in such endearing terms, and with so much address and pretended tenderness and sincerity, that I did not dare to cry out when I came to myself. His sighs, and yet more his tears, seemed to me undeniable proofs of his vowed integrity; and I being but young, bred up in perpetual retirement from all society but my virtuous parents, and unexperienced in those affairs, in which even the most knowing are apt to be mistaken, my reluctancy abated by degrees, and I began to have some sense of compassion, yet none but what was consistent with my honour. However, when I was pretty well recovered from my first fright, my former resolution returned; and then, with more courage than I thought I should have had, "My lord," said I, "if, at the same time that you offer me your love, and give me such strange demonstrations of it, you would also offer me poison, and leave to take my choice, I would soon resolve which to accept, and convince you, by my death, that my honour is dearer to me than my life. To be plain, I can have no good opinion of a presumption that endangers my reputation; and, unless you leave me this moment, I will so effectually make you know how much you are mistaken in me, that if you have but the least sense of honour left, you will repent the driving me to that extremity as long as you live. I was born your vassal, but not your slave; nor does the greatness of your birth privilege you to injure your inferiors, or exact from me more than the duties which all vassals pay; that excepted, I do not esteem myself less in my low degree, than you have reason to value yourself in your high rank. Do not then think to awe or dazzle me with your grandeur, or fright or force me into a base compliance; I am not to be tempted with titles, pomp and equipage; nor weak enough to be moved with vain sighs and false tears. In short, my will is wholly at my father's disposal, and I will not entertain any man as a lover, but by his appointment. Therefore, my lord, if you would have me believe you so sincerely love me, give over your vain and injurious pursuit; surfer me peaceably to enjoy the benefits of life in the free possession of my honour, the loss of which for ever embitters all life's sweets; and since you cannot be my husband, do not expect from me that affection which I cannot pay to any other." "What do you mean, charming Dorothea? "cried the perfidious lord: "cannot I be yours by the sacred title of husband? Who can hinder me, if you will but consent to bless me on those terms? Too happy if I have no other obstacle to surmount. I am yours this moment, beautiful Dorothea. See, I give you here my hand to be yours, and yours alone for ever; and let all-seeing Heaven, and this holy image here on your oratory, witness the solemn truth." '

Cardenio, hearing her call herself Dorothea, was now fully satisfied she was the person whom he took her to be: however, he would not interrupt her story, being impatient to hear the end of it; only addressing himself to her, 'Is then your name Dorothea, madam?' cried he, 'I have heard of a lady of that name, whose misfortunes have a great resemblance with yours. But proceed, I beseech you, and when you have done, I may perhaps surprise you with an account of things that have some affinity with those you relate.' With that Dorothea made a stop, to study Cardenio's face, and his wretched attire; and then earnestly desired him, if he knew anything that concerned her, to let her know it presently; telling him, that all the happiness she had left, was only the courage to bear with resignation all the disasters that might befall her, well assured that no new one could make her more unfortunate than she was already. 'Truly, madam,' replied Cardenio, 'I would tell you all I know, were I sure my conjectures were true; but, so far as I may judge by what I have heard hitherto, I do not think it material to tell it you yet, and I shall find a more proper time to do it.' Then Dorothea resuming her discourse, 'Don Ferdinand,' said she, 'repeated his vows of marriage in the most serious manner; and giving me his hand, plighted me his faith in the most binding words, and sacred oaths. But before I would let him engage himself thus, I advised him to have a care how he suffered an unruly passion to get the ascendant over his reason, to the endangering of his future happiness. "My lord," said I, "let not a few transitory and imaginary charms, which could never excuse such an excess of love, hurry you to your ruin: spare your noble father the shame and displeasure of seeing you married to a person so much below you by birth; and do not rashly do a thing of which you may repent, and that may make my life uncomfortable." I added several other reasons to dissuade him from that hasty match, but they were all unregarded. Don Ferdinand, deaf to everything but to his desires, engaged and bound himself like an inconsiderate lover, who sacrifices all things to his passion, or rather like a cheat, who does not value a breach of vows. When I saw him so obstinate, I began to consider what I had to do. I am not the first, thought I to myself, whom marriage has raised to unhoped-for greatness, and whose beauty alone has supplied her want of birth and merit; thousands besides Don Ferdinand have married merely for love, without any regard to the inequality of wealth or birth. The opportunity was fair and tempting; and as fortune is not always favourable, I thought it an imprudent thing to let it slip. Thought I to myself, while she kindly offers me a husband who assures me of an inviolable affection, why should I by an unreasonable denial make myself an enemy of such a friend? And then there was one thing more: I apprehended it would be dangerous to drive him to despair by an ill-timed refusal; nor could I think myself safe alone in his hands, lest he should resolve to satisfy his passion by force; which done, he might think himself free from performing a promise which I would not accept, and then I should be left without either honour or an excuse; for it would be no easy matter to persuade my father, and the censorious world, that this nobleman was admitted into my chamber without my consent. All these reasons, which in a moment offered themselves in my mind, shook my former resolves; and Don Ferdinand's sighs, his tears, his vows, and the sacred witnesses by which he swore, together with his graceful mien, his extraordinary accomplishments, and the love which I fancied I read in all his actions, helped to bring on my ruin, as I believe they would have prevailed with any one's heart as free and as well guarded as was mine. Then I called my maid to be witness to Don Ferdinand's vows and sacred engagements, which he reiterated to me, and confirmed with new oaths and solemn promises: he called again on Heaven, and on many particular saints, to witness sincerity, wishing a thousand curses might fall on him, in case he ever violated his word. Again he sighed, again he wept, and moved me more and more with fresh marks of affection; and the treacherous maid having left the room, the perfidious lord, presuming on my weakness, completed his pernicious design. The day which succeeded that unhappy night had not yet begun to dawn, when Don Ferdinand, impatient to be gone, made all the haste he could to leave me. For after the gratifications of brutish appetite are past, the greatest pleasure then is to get rid of that which entertained it. He told me, though not with so great a show of affection, nor so warmly as before, that I might rely on his honour, and on the sincerity of his vows and promises; and, as a further pledge, he pulled off a ring of great value from his finger, and put it upon mine. In short, he went away; and my maid, who, as she confessed it to me, let him in privately, took care to let him out into the street by break of day, while I remained so strangely concerned at the thoughts of all these passages, that I cannot well tell whether I was sorry or pleased. I was in a manner quite distracted, and either forgot, or had not the heart to chide my maid for her treachery, not knowing yet whether she had done me good or harm. I had told Don Ferdinand before he went, that, seeing I was now his own, he might make use of the same means to come again to see me, till he found it convenient to do me the honour of owning me publicly for his wife: but he came to me only the next night, and from that time I never could see him more, neither at church nor in the street, though, for a whole month together, I tired myself endeavouring to find him out: being credibly informed he was still near us, and went a-hunting almost every day, I leave you to think with what uneasiness I passed those tedious hours, when I perceived his neglect, and had reason to suspect his breach of faith. So unexpected a flight, which I looked upon as the most sensible affliction that could befall me, had like to have quite overwhelmed me. Then it was that I found my maid had betrayed me; I broke out into severe complaints of her presumption, which I had smothered till that time. I exclaimed against Don Ferdinand, and exhausted my sighs and tears without assuaging my sorrow. What was worse, I found myself obliged to set a guard upon my very looks, for fear my father and mother should inquire into the cause of my discontent, and so occasion my being guilty of shameful lies and evasions to conceal my more shameful disaster. But at last I perceived it was in vain to dissemble, and I gave a loose to my resentments; for I could no longer hold, when I heard that Don Ferdinand was married in a neighbouring town to a young lady of rich and noble parentage, and extremely handsome, whose name is Lucinda.' Cardenio, hearing Lucinda named, felt his former disorder; but, by good fortune, it was not so violent as it used to be, and he only shrugged up his shoulders, bit his lips, knit his brows, and a little while after let fall a shower of tears, which did not hinder Dorothea from going on. 'This news,' continued she, 'instead of freezing up my blood with grief and astonishment, filled me with burning rage. Despair took possession of my soul, and in the transports of my fury I was ready to run raving through the streets, and publish Don Ferdinand's disloyalty, though at the expense of my reputation. I do not know whether a remainder of reason stopped these violent motions, but I found myself mightily eased, as soon as I had pitched upon a design that presently came into my head. I discovered the cause of my grief to a young country-fellow that served my father, and desired him to lend me a suit of man's apparel, and to go along with me to the town where I heard Don Ferdinand was. The fellow used the best arguments he had to hinder me from so strange an undertaking; but, finlding I was inflexible in my resolution, he assured me he was ready to serve me. Thereupon I put on this habit, which you see, and taking with me some of my own clothes, together with some gold and jewels, not knowing but I might have some occasion for them, I set out that very night, attended with that servant and many anxious thoughts, without so much as acquainting my maid with my design. To tell you the truth, I did not well know myself what I went about; for, as there could be no remedy, Don Ferdinand being actually married to mother, what could I hope to get by seeing him, unless it were the wretched satisfaction of upbraiding him with his infidelity? In two days and a half we got to the town, where the first thing I did was to inquire where Lucinda's father lived. That single question produced a great deal more than I desired to hear: for the first man I addressed myself to showed me the house, and informed me of all that happened at Lucinda's marriage; which, it seems, was grown so public, that it was the talk of the whole town. He told me how Lucinda had swooned away as soon as she answered the priest, that she was contented to be Don Ferdinand's wife; and how, after he had approached to open her stays to give her more room to breathe, he found a letter in her own hand, wherein she declared she could not be Don Ferdinand's wife, because she was already contracted to a considerable gentleman of the same town, whose name was Cardenio; and that she had only consented to that marriage in obedience to her father. He also told me, that it appeared by the letter, and a dagger which was found about her, that she designed to have killed herself after the ceremony was over; and that Don Ferdinand, enraged to see himself thus deluded, would have killed her himself with that very dagger, had he not been prevented by those that were present. He added, it was reported, that upon this Don Ferdinand immediately left the town; and that Lucinda did not come to herself till the next day; and then she told her parents that she was really Cardenio's wife, and that he and she were contracted before she had seen Don Ferdinand. I heard also that this Cardenio was present at the wedding; and that as soon as he saw her married, which was a thing he never could have believed, he left the town in despair, leaving a letter behind him full of complaints of Lucinda's breach of faith, and to inform his friends of his resolution to go to some place where they should never hear of him more. This was all the discourse of the town when I came thither, and, soon after, we heard that Lucinda also was missing, and that her father and mother were grieving almost to distraction, not being able to learn what was become of her. For my part, this news revived my hopes, having reason to be pleased to find Don Ferdinand unmarried. I flattered myself that Heaven had perhaps prevented this second marriage to make him sensible of his violating the first, and to touch his conscience, in order to his acquitting himself of his duty like a Christian and a man of honour. So I strove to beguile my cares with an imaginary prospect of a far distant change of fortune, amusing myself with vain hopes that I might not sink under the load of affliction, but prolong life; though this was only a lengthening of my sorrows, since I have now but the more reason to wish to be eased of the trouble of living. But while I stayed in that town, not knowing what I had best to do, seeing I could not find Don Ferdinand, I heard a crier publicly describe my person, my clothes, and my age, in the open street, promising a considerable reward to any that could bring tidings of Dorothea. I also heard that it was rumoured I was run away from my father's house with the servant who attended me; and that report touched my soul as much as Don Ferdinand's perfidiousness; for thus I saw my reputation wholly lost, and that too for a subject so base and so unworthy of my nobler thoughts. Thereupon I made all the haste I could to get out of the town with my servant, who, even then, to my thinking, began by some tokens to betray a faltering in the fidelity he had promised me. Dreading to be discovered, we reached the most desert part of this mountain that night: but, as it is a common saying, that misfortunes seldom come alone, and the end of one disaster is often the beginning of a greater, I was no sooner got to that place, where I thought myself safe, but the fellow, whom I had hitherto found to be modest and respectful, now rather incited by his own villainy, than my beauty, and the opportunity which that place offered than by anything else, had the impudence to talk to me of love; and, seeing I answered him with anger and contempt, he would no longer lose time in clownish courtship, but resolved to use violence to compass his wicked design. But just Heaven, which seldom or never fails to succour just designs, so assisted mine, and his brutish passion so blinded him, that, not perceiving he was on the brink of a steep rock, I easily pushed him down; and then, without looking to see what was become of him, and with more nimbleness than could be expected from my surprise and weariness, I ran into the thickest part of the desert to secure myself The next day I met a countryman, who took me to his house amidst these mountains, and employed me ever since in quality of his shepherd. There I have continued some months, making it my business to be as much as possible in the fields, the better to conceal my sex: but, notwithstanding all my care and industry, he as last discovered I was a woman; which made him presume to importune me with beastly offers. So that, fortune not favouring me with the former opportunity of freeing myself, I left his house, and chose to seek a sanctuary among these woods and rocks, there with sighs and tears to beseech Heaven to pity me, and to direct and relieve me in this forlorn condition: or at least to put an end to my miserable life, and bury in this desert the very memory of an unhappy creature, who, more through ill fortune than ill intent, has given the idle world occasion to be too busy with her fame.'

CHAPTER II

An account of the beautiful Dorothea's Discretion, with other pleasant Passages

'THIS, GENTLEMEN,' continued Dorothea, 'is a true history of my tragical adventure; and now be you judges, whether I had reason to make the complaint you overheard, and whether so unfortunate and hopeless a creature be in a condition to admit of comfort. I have only one favour to beg of you: be pleased to direct me to some place where I may pass the rest of my life, secure from the search and inquiry of my parents; not but their former affection is a sufficient warrant for my kind reception, could the sense I have of the thoughts they must have of my past conduct permit me to return to them; but, when I think they must believe me guilty, and can now have nothing but my bare word to assure them of my innocence, I can never resolve to stand their sight.' Here Dorothea stopped, and the blushes that overspread her cheeks were certain signs of the discomposure of her thoughts, and the unfeigned modesty of her soul. Those who had heard her story were deeply moved with compassion for her hard fate, and the curate would not delay any longer to give her some charitable comfort and advice. But scarce had he begun to speak, when Cardenio, addressing himself to her, interrupted him: 'How, madam,' said he, taking her by the hand, 'are you then the beautiful Dorothea, the only daughter of the rich Cleonardo?' Dorothea was strangely surprised to hear her father named, and by one in so tattered a garb. 'And pray who are you, friend,'* said she to him, 'that know so well my father's name? for I think I did not mention it once throughout the whole relation of my afflictions?' 'I am Cardenio,' replied the other, 'that unfortunate person, whom Lucinda, as you told us, declared to be her husband: I am that miserable Cardenio, whom the perfidiousness of the man who has reduced you to this deplorable condition, has also brought to this wretched state, to rags, to nakedness, to despair, nay to madness itself, and all hardships and want of human comforts; only enjoying the privilege of reason by short intervals, to feel and bemoan my miseries the more. I am the man, fair Dorothea, who was the unhappy eyewitness of Don Ferdinand's unjust nuptials, and who heard my Lucinda give her consent to be his wife; that heartless wretch, who, unable to bear so strange a disappointment, lost in amazement and trouble, flung out of the house, without staying to know what would follow her trance, and what the paper that was taken out of her bosom would produce. I abandoned myself to despair, and, having left a letter with a person whom I charged to deliver it into Lucinda's own hands, I hastened to hide myself from the world in this desert, resolved to end there a life, which from that moment I had abhorred as my greatest enemy. But fortune has preserved me, I see, that I may venture it upon a better cause: for, from what you have told us now, which I have no reason to doubt, I am emboldened to hope that Providence may yet reserve us both to a better fate than we durst have expected; Heaven will restore to you Don Ferdinand, who cannot be Lucinda's, and to me Lucinda, who cannot be Don Ferdinand's. For my part, though my interests were not linked with yours, as they are, I have so deep a sense of your misfortunes, that I would expose myself to any dangers to see you righted by Don Ferdinand: and here, on the word of a gentleman and a Christian, I vow and promise not to forsake you till he has done you justice, and to oblige him to do it at the hazard of my life, should reason and generosity prove ineffectual to force him to be blessed with you.' Dorothea, ravished with joy, and not knowing how to express a due sense of Cardenio's obliging offers, would have thrown herself at his feet, had he not civilly hindered it. At the same time the curate, discreetly speaking for them both, highly

---

* *Y, quien sois vos hermano,* i.e. 'And pray who are you, brother?' It is the Spanish way of speaking. We say 'friend'; the French the same, *Mon ami.*

applauded Cardenio for his generous resolution, and comforted Dorothea. He also very heartily invited them to his house, where they might furnish themselves with necessaries, and consult together how to find out Don Ferdinand, and bring Dorothea home to her father; which kind offer they thankfully accepted. Then the barber, who had been silent all this while, put in for a share, and handsomely assured them, he would be very ready to do them all the service that might lie in his power. After these civilities, he acquainted them with the design that had brought the curate and him to that place; and gave them an account of Don Quixote's strange kind of madness, and of their shying there for his squire. Cardenio, hearing him mentioned, remembered something of the scuffle he had with them both, but only as if it had been a dream; so that, though he told the company of it, he could not let them know the occasion. By this time they heard somebody call, and, by the voice, knew that it was Sancho Pança, who, not finding them where he had left them, tore his very lungs with hallooing. With that they all went to meet him; which done, they asked him what was become of Don Quixote? 'Alas,' answered Sancho, 'I left him yonder, in an ill plight: I found him in his shirt, lean, pale, and almost starved, sighing and whining for his lady Dulcinea. I told him, how that she would have him come to her presently to Toboso, where she looked for him out of hand; yet for all this he would not budge a foot, but even told me he was resolved he would never set eyes on her sweet face again, till he had done some feats that might make him worthy of her goodness: So that,' added Sancho, 'if he leads this life any longer, I fear me my poor master is never like to be an emperor, as he is bound in honour to be, nay not so much as an archbishop, which is the least thing he can come off with; therefore, good sir, see and get him away by all means, I beseech you.' The curate bid him be of good cheer, for they would take care to make him leave that place whether he would or not; and then, turning to Cardenio and Dorothea, he informed them of the design which he and the barber had laid in order to his cure, or at least to get him home to his house. Dorothea, whose mind was much eased with the prospect of better fortune, kindly undertook to act the distressed lady herself, which she said she thought would become her better than the barber, having a dress very proper for that purpose; besides, she had read many books of chivalry, and knew how the distressed ladies used to express themselves when they came to beg some knight-errant's assistance. 'This is obliging, madam,' said the curate, 'and we want nothing more: so let us to work as fast as we can; we may now hope to succeed, since you thus happily facilitate the design.' Presently Dorothea took out of her bundle a petticoat of very rich stuff, and a gown of very fine green silk; also a necklace, and several other jewels out of a box; and with these in an instant she so adorned herself, and appeared so beautiful and glorious, that they all stood in admiration that

Don Ferdinand should be so injudicious, to slight so accomplished a beauty. But he that admired her most was Sancho Pança; for he thought he had never set eyes on so fine a creature, and perhaps he thought right: which made him earnestly ask the curate, who that fine dame was, and what wind had blown her thither among woods and rocks? 'Who, that fine lady, Sancho?' answered the curate; 'she is the only heiress in a direct line to the vast kingdom of Micomicon: moved by the fame of your master's great exploits, that spreads itself over all Guinea, she comes to seek him out, and beg a boon of him; that is, to redress a wrong which a wicked giant has done her.' 'Why, that is well,' quoth Sancho: 'a happy seeking and a happy finding. Now if my master be but so lucky as to right that wrong, by killing that son of a whore of a giant you tell me of, I am a made man: yes, he will kill him, that he will, if he can but come at him, and he be not a hobgoblin; for my master can do no good with hobgoblins. But, Mr. Curate, if it please you, I have a favour to ask of you: I beseech you put my master out of conceit with all archbishoprics, for that is what I dread; and therefore to rid me of my fears, put it into his head to clap up a match with this same princess: for by that means it will be past his power to make himself archbishop, and he will come to be emperor, and I a great man as sure as a gun. I have thought well of the matter, and I find it is not at all fitting he should be an archbishop for my good; for what should I get by it? I am not fit for Church preferment, I am a married man; and now for me to go trouble my head with getting a licence to hold Church-livings, it would be an endless piece of business; therefore, it will be better for him to marry out of hand this same princess, whose name I cannot tell, for I never heard it.' 'They call her the Princess Micomicona,' said the curate; 'for her kingdom being called Micomicon, it is a clear case she must be called so' 'Like enough,' quoth Sancho; 'for I have known several men in my time go by the names of the places where they were born, as Pedro de Alcala, Juan de Ubeda, Diego de Valladolid; and mayhap the like is done in Guinea, and the queens go by the name of their Kingdoms.' 'It is well observed,' replied the curate: 'as for the match, I will promote it to the utmost of my power.' Sancho was heartily pleased with this promise; and, or the other side, the curate was amazed to find the poor fellow so strangly infected with his master's mad notions, as to rely on his becoming an emperor. By this time Dorothea being mounted on the curate's mule, and the barber having clapped on his ox-tail beard, nothing remained but to order Sancho to show them the way, and to renew their admonitions to him, lest he should seem to know them, and to spoil the plot, which if he did, they told him it would be the ruin of all his hopes and his master's empire. As for Cardenio, he did not think fit to go with them, having no business there; besides, he could not tell but that Don Quixote might remember their late fray. The curate, likewise not thinking his presence necessary, resolved to stay to keep Cardenio company; so, after he had once more given Dorothea her cue, she and the barber went before with Sancho, while the two others followed on foot at a distance.

Thus they went on for about three-quarters of a league, and then, among the rocks, they spied Don Quixote, who had by this time put on his clothes, though not his armour. Immediately Dorothea, understanding he was the person, whipped her palfrey, and when she drew near Don Quixote, her squire alighted, and took her from her saddle. When she was upon her feet, she gracefully advanced towards the Knight, and, with her squire, falling on her knees before him, in spite of his endeavours to hinder her: 'Thrice valorous and invincible knight,' said she, 'never will I rise from this place, till your generosity has granted me a boon, which shall redound to your honour, and the relief of the most disconsolate and most injured damsel that the sun ever saw: and indeed if your valour and the strength of your formidable arm be answerable to the extent of your immortal renown, you are bound by the laws of honour, and the knighthood which you profess, to succour a distressed princess, who, led by the resounding fame of your marvellous and redoubted feats of arms, comes from the remotest regions, to implore your protection.' 'I cannot,' said Don Quixote, 'make you any answer, most beautiful lady, nor will I hear a word more, unless you vouchsafe to rise.' 'Pardon me, noble knight,' replied the petitioning damsel; 'my knees shall first be rooted here, unless you will courteously condescend to grant me the boon which I humbly request.' 'I grant it then, lady,' said Don Quixote, 'provided it be nothing to the disservice of my king, my country, and that beauty who keeps the key of my heart and liberty.' 'It shall not tend to the prejudice or detriment of any of these,' cried the lady. With that Sancho, closing up to his master, and whispering him in the ear, 'Grant it, sir,' quoth he, 'grant it, I tell ye; it is but a trifle next to nothing, only to kill a great booby of a giant; and she that asks this, is the high and mighty Princess Micomicona, queen of the huge kingdom of Micomicon in Ethiopia.' 'Let her be what she will,' replied Don Quixote, 'I will discharge my duty, and obey the dictates of my conscience, according to the rules of my profession.' With that, turning to the damsel, 'Rise, lady, I beseech you,' cried he; 'I grant you the boon which your singular beauty demands.' 'Sir,' said the lady, 'the boon I have to beg of your magnanimous valour, is, that you will be pleased to go with me instantly whither I shall conduct you, and promise me not to engage in any other adventure, till you have revenged me on a traitor who usurps my kingdom, contrary to all laws both human and divine.' 'I grant you all this, lady,' quoth Don Quixote; 'and therefore from this moment shake off all desponding thoughts that sit heavy upon your mind, and study to revive your drooping hopes; for, by the assistance of Heaven, and my strenuous arm, you shall see yourself restored to your kingdom, and seated on the throne of your ancestors, in spite of all the traitors that dare oppose your right. Let us then hasten our performance; delay always breeds danger; and to protract a great design is often to ruin it.' The thankful princess, to speak her grateful sense of his generosity, strove to kiss the Knight's hand; however he, who was in everything the most gallant and courteous of all knights, would, by no means, admit of such a submission; but having gently raised her up, he embraced her with an awful grace and civility, and then called to Sancho for his arms. Sancho went immediately, and having fetched them from a tree, where they hung like trophies, armed his master in a moment. And now the champion being completely accoutred, 'Come on,' said he, 'let us go and vindicate the rights of this dispossessed princess.' The barber was all this while upon his knees, and had enough to do to keep himself from laughing, and his beard from falling, which, if it had dropped off, as it threatened, would have betrayed his face and their whole plot at once. But, being relieved by Don Quixote's haste to put on his armour, he rose up, and taking the princess by the hand, they both together set her upon her mule. Then the Knight mounted his Rozinante, and the barber got on his beast. Only poor Sancho was forced to foot it, which made him fetch many a heavy sigh for the loss of his dear Dapple: however, he bore his crosses patiently, seeing his master in so fair a way of being next door to an emperor; for he did not question but he would marry that princess, and so be, at least, king of Micomicon. But yet it grieved him, to think his master's dominions where to be in the land of the negroes, and that, consequently, the people, over whom he was to he governor, were all to be black. But he presently bethought himself of a good remedy for that: 'What care I,' quoth he, 'though they be blacks? best of all; it is but loading a ship with them, and having them into Spain, where I shall find chapmen enough to take them off my hands and pay me ready money for them; and so I will raise a good round sum, and buy me a title or an office to live upon frank and easy all the days of my life. Hang him that has no shifts, say I; it is a sorry goose that will not baste herself. Why, what if I am not so book-learned as other folks, sure I have a head-piece good enough to know how to sell thirty or ten thousand slaves in the turn of a hand.* Let them even go higgledy-piggledy, little and great. What though they be as black as the Devil in hell, let me alone to turn them into white and yellow boys: I think I know how to lick my own fingers.' Big with these imaginations, Sancho trudged along so pleased and light-hearted, that he forgot his pain of travelling a-foot. Cardenio and the curate had beheld the pleasant scene through the bushes, and were at a

---

* Literally, "While one may say, 'Take away these straws:' " *en quitam ella essas pajas*, i.e. in a moment.

loss what they should do to join companies. But the curate, who had a contriving head, at last bethought himself of an expedient; and pulling out a pair of scissors, which he used to carry in his pocket, he snipped off Cardenio's beard in a trice: and having pulled off his black cloak, and a sad-coloured riding-coat, which he had on, he equipped Cardenio with them, while he himself remained in his doublet and breeches. In which new garb Cardenio was so strangely altered, that he would not have known himself in a looking-glass. This done, they made to the high-way, and there stayed till Don Quixote and his company were got clear of the rocks and bad ways, which did not permit horsemen to go so fast as those on foot. When they came near, the curate looked very earnestly upon Don Quixote, as one that was in a study whether he might not know him; and then, like one that had made a discovery, he ran towards the Knight with open arms, crying out, 'Mirror of chivalry, my noble countryman Don Quixote de la Mancha! the cream and flower of gentility! the shelter and relief of the afflicted, and quintessence of knight-errantry! how overjoyed am I to have found you!' At the same time he embraced his left leg. Don Quixote, admiring what adorer of his heroic worth this should be, looked on him earnestly; and at last calling him to mind, would have alighted to have paid him his respects, not a little amazed to meet him there. But the curate hindering him, 'Reverend sir,' cried the Knight, 'I beseech you let me not be so rude as to sit on horseback, while a person of your worth and character is on foot.' 'Sir,' replied the curate, 'you shall by no means alight: let your excellency be pleased to keep your saddle, since thus mounted you every day achieve the most stupendous feats of arms and adventures that were ever seen in our age. It will be honour enough for an unworthy priest like me, to get up behind some of your company, if they will permit me; and I will esteem it as great a happiness as to be mounted upon Pegasus, or the Zebra,* or the fleet mare of the famous Moor Musaraque, who to this hour lies enchanted in the dreary cavern of Zulema, not far distant from the great Compluto.'† 'Truly, good sir, I did not think of this,' answered Don Quixote; 'but, I suppose, my lady the princess will be so kind as to command her squire to lend you his saddle, and to ride behind himself, if his mule be used to carry double.' 'I believe it will,' cried the princess; 'and my squire, I suppose, will not stay for my commands to offer his saddle, for he is too courteous and well-bred to suffer an ecclesiastical person to go a-foot, when we may help him to a mule.' 'Most certainly,' cried the barber; and with that, dismounting, he offered the curate his saddle, which was accepted without much entreaty.

---

* Zebra, Stevens says, is a beast in Africa, shaped like a horse, hard to be tamed, wonderful fleet, and will hold its course all day.
† An university of Spain, now called Alcala de Henares.

By ill fortune the mule was a hired beast; and consequently unlucky; so, as the barber was getting up behind the curate, the resty jade gave two or three jerks with her hinder legs, that, had they met with master Nicholas's skull or ribs, he would have bequeathed his rambling after Don Quixote to the Devil. However, he flung himself nimbly off, and was more afraid than hurt: but yet, as he fell, his beard dropped off, and being presently sensible of that accident, he could not think of any better shift than to clap both his hands before his cheeks, and cry out he had broken his jaw-bone. Don Quixote was amazed to see such an overgrown bush of beard lie on the ground without jaws and bloodless. 'Bless me,' cried he, 'what an amazing miracle is this! Here is a beard as cleverly taken off by accident, as if a barber had mowed it.' The curate perceiving the danger they were in of being discovered, hastily caught up the beard, and, running to the barber, who lay all the while roaring and complaining, he pulled his head close to his own breast, and then muttering certain words, which he said were a charm appropriated to fastening on of fallen beards, he fixed it on again so handsomely, that the squire was presently then as bearded and as well as ever he was before; which raised Don Quixote's admiration, and made him engage the curate to teach him the charm at his leisure, not doubting but its virtue extended further than to the fastening on of beards, since it was impossible that such a one could be torn off without fetching away flesh and all; and, consequently, such a sudden cure might be beneficial to him upon occasion. And now, everything being set to rights, they agreed that the curate should ride first by himself, and then the other two, by turns relieving one another, sometimes riding, sometimes walking, till they came to their inn, which was about two leagues off. So Don Quixote, the princess, and the curate, being mounted, and Cardenio, the barber, and Sancho ready to move forwards on foot, the knight addressing himself to the distressed damsel: 'Now, lady,' said he, 'let me entreat your greatness to tell me which way we must go, to do you service.' The curate, before she could answer, thought fit to ask her a question, that might the better enable her to make a proper reply. 'Pray, madam,' said he, 'towards what country is it your pleasure to take your progress? is it not towards the kingdom of Micomicon? I am very much mistaken if that be not the part of the world whither you desire to go.' The lady, having got her cue, presently understood the curate, and answered that he was in the right. 'Then,' said the curate, 'your way lies directly through the village where I live, from whence we have a straight road to Carthagena, where you may conveniently take shipping; and if you have a fair wind and good weather, you may, in something less than nine years, reach the vast lake Meona, I mean the Palus Meotis, which lies somewhat more than a hundred days' journey from your kingdom.' 'Surely, sir,' replied the lady, 'you are under a mistake; for it is not quite two years since I left the place; and besides, we have had very little fair weather all the while, and yet I am already got hither, and have so far succeeded in my designs, as to have obtained the sight of the renowned Don Quixote de la Mancha, the fame of whose achievements reached my ears as soon as I landed in Spain, and moved me to find him out, to throw myself under his protection, and commit the justice of my cause to his invincible valour.' 'No more, madam, I beseech you,' cried Don Quixote; 'spare me the trouble of hearing myself praised, for I mortally hate whatever may look like adulation; and though your compliments may deserve a better name, my ears are too modest to be pleased with any such discourse; it is my study to deserve and to avoid applause. All I will venture to say, is, that whether I have any valour or no, I am wholly at your service, even at the expense of the last drop of my blood; and therefore, waving all these matters till a fit opportunity, I would gladly know of this reverend clergyman what brought him hither, unattended by any of his servants, alone, and so slenderly clothed; for I must confess, I am not a little surprised to meet him in this condition.' 'To tell you the reason in a few words,' answered the curate, 'you must know, that Mr. Nicholas, our friend and barber, went with me to Sevil, to receive some money which a relation of mine sent me from the Indies, where he has been settled these many years; neither was it a small sum, for it was no less than seventy thousand pieces of eight, and all of due weight, which is no common thing, you may well judge: but upon the road hereabouts we met four highwaymen that robbed us of all we had, even to our very beards, so that the poor barber was forced to get him a chin-periwig. And, for that young gentleman whom you see there,' continued he, pointing to Cardenio, 'after they had stripped him to his shirt, they transfigured him as you see.* Now everybody hereabouts says, that those who robbed us were certainly a pack of rogues condemned to the galleys, who, as they were going to punishment, were rescued by a single man, not far from this place, and that with so much courage, that, in spite of the king's officer and his guards, he alone set them all at liberty. Certainly that man was either mad, or as great a rogue as any of them; for would any one that had a grain of sense or honesty, have let loose a company of wolves among sheep, foxes among innocent poultry, and wasps among the honey-pots? He has hindered public justice from taking its course, broke his allegiance to his lawful sovereign, disabled the strength of his galleys, rebelled against him, opposed his officers in contempt of the law, and alarmed the holy brotherhood, that had lain quiet so long; nay, what is yet worse, he has endangered his life upon earth, and his salvation hereafter.' Sancho had given the curate an

---

* The priest had clipped off Cardenio's beard in haste.

account of the adventure of the galley-slaves, and this made him lay it on thick in the relation, to try how Don Quixote would bear it. The Knight changed colour at every word, not daring to confess he was the pious knight-errant who had delivered those worthy gentlemen out of bondage. 'These,' said the curate, by way of conclusion, 'were the men that reduced us to this condition; and may Heaven in mercy forgive him that freed them from the punishment they so well deserved.'

CHAPTER III

The pleasant Stratgems used to free the enamoured Knight from the rigorous Penance which he had undertaken

SCARCE HAD THE CURATE made an end, when Sancho, addressing himself to him, 'Faith and truth,' quoth he, 'master curate, he that did that rare job was my master his own self, and that not for want of fair warning; for I bid him have a care what he did, and told him over and over, it would be a grievous sin to put such a gang of wicked wretches out of durance, and that they all went to the galleys for their roguery.' 'You buffle-headed clown,' cried Don Quixote, 'is it for a knight-errant when he meets with people laden with chains, and under oppression, to examine whether they are in those circumstances for their crimes, or only through misfortune? We are only to relieve the afflicted, to look on their distress, and not on their crimes. I met a company of poor wretches, who went along sorrowful, dejected and linked together like the beads of a rosary; thereupon I did what my conscience and my profession obliged me to do. And what has any man to say to this? If any one dares say otherwise, saving this reverend clergyman's presence and the holy character he bears, I say, he knows little of knight-errantry, and lies like a son of a whore, and a baseborn villain; and this I will make him know more effectually with the convincing edge of my sword!' This said, with a grim look, he fixed himself in his stirrups, and pulled his helmet over his brows, for the basin, which he took to be Mambrino's helmet, hung at his saddle-bow, in order to have the damage repaired which it had received from the galley-slaves. Thereupon Dorothea, by this time well acquainted with his temper, seeing him in such a passion, and that everybody except Sancho Pança, made a jest of him, resolved, with her native sprightliness and address, to carry on the humour. 'I beseech you, sir,' cried she, 'remember the promise you have made me, and that you cannot engage in any adventure whatsoever, till you have performed that we are going about. Therefore pray assuage your anger; for had master curate known the galley-slaves were rescued by your invincible arm, I am sure he would rather have stitched up his lips, or bit off his tongue, than have spoken a word that should make him incur your displeasure.' 'Nay, I assure you,' cried the curate, 'I would sooner have twitched off one of my mustachios into the bargain.' 'I am satisfied, madam,' cried Don Quixote, 'and for your sake the flame of my just indignation is quenched; nor will I be induced to engage in any quarrel, till I have fulfilled my promise to your highness. Only in recompense of my good intentions, I beg you will give us the story of your misfortunes, if this will not be too great a trouble to you; and let me know who and what, and how many are the persons of whom I must have due and full satisfaction on your behalf.' 'I am very willing to do it,' replied Dorothea; 'but yet I fear a story like mine, consisting only of afflictions and disasters, will prove but a tedious entertainment.' 'Never fear that, madam,' cried Don Quixote. 'Since then it must be so,' said Dorothea, 'be pleased to lend me your attention. With that Cardenio and the barber gathered up to her, to hear what kind of story she had provided so soon; Sancho also hung his ears upon her side-saddle, being no less deceived in her than his master: and the lady having seated herself well on her mule, after coughing once or twice, and other preparations, very gracefully began her story.

'First, gentlemen,' said she, 'you must know my name is – ' Here she stopped short, and could not call to mind the name the curate had given her; whereupon, finding her at a non-plus, he made haste to help her out. 'It is not at all strange,' said he, 'madam, that you should be so discomposed by your disasters, as to stumble at the very beginning of the account you are going to give of them; extreme affliction often distracts the mind to that degree, and so deprives us of memory, that sometimes we for a while can scarce think on our very names: no wonder then, that the Princess Micomicona, lawful heiress to the vast kingdom of Micomicon, disordered with so many misfortunes, and perplexed with so many various thoughts for the recovery of her crown, should have her imagination and memory so encumbered; but I hope you will now recollect yourself, and be able to proceed.' 'I hope so too,' said the lady, 'and I will try to go through with my story without any further hesitation. Know then, gentlemen, that the king, my father, who was called Tinacrio the Sage, having great skill in the magic art, understood by his profound knowledge in that science, that Queen Xaramilla, my mother, should die before him, that he himself should not survive her long, and I should be left an orphan. But he often said, that this did not so much trouble him as the foresight he had by his speculations, of my being threatened with great misfortunes, which would be occasioned by a certain giant, lord of a great island near the confines of my kingdom, his name Pandafilando, surnamed of the Gloomy Aspect; because, though his eyeballs are seated in their due place, yet he affects to squint and look askew, on purpose to fright those on whom he stares My father, I say, knew that this giant, hearing of his death, would one day invade my kingdom with a powerful army, and drive me out of my territories, without leaving me so much as the least village for a retreat; though he knew withal that I might avoid that extremity, if I would but consent to marry him; but as he found out by his art, he had reason to think I never would incline to such a match. And indeed I never had any thoughts of marrying this giant, nor really any other giant in the world, unmeasurably great and mighty soever he were. My father therefore charged me to bear my misfortunes patiently, and abandon my kingdom to Pandafilando for a time, without offering to keep him out by force of arms, since this would be the best means to prevent my own death and the ruin of my subjects, considering the impossibility of withstanding the devilish force of the giant. But withal, he ordered me to direct my course towards Spain, where i should be sure to meet with a powerful champion, in the person of a knight-errant, whose fame should at that time be spread over all the kingdom; and his name, my father said, should be, if I forget not, Don Azote,* or Don Gigote.' 'And if it please you, forsooth,' quoth Sancho, 'you would say Don Quixote, otherwise called the Knight of the Woeful Figure.' 'You are right,' answered Dorothea, 'and my father also described him, and said he should be a tall thin-faced man, and that on his right side, under the left shoulder, or somewhere thereabouts, he should have a tawny mole overgrown with a tuft of hair, not much unlike that of a horse's mane.' With that Don Quixote, calling for his squire to come to him: 'Here,' said he, 'Sancho, help me off with my clothes, for I am resolved to see whether I be the knight of whom the necromantic king has prophesied.' 'Pray, sir, why would you pull off your clothes?' cried Dorothea. 'To see whether I have such a mole about me as your father mentioned,' replied the Knight. 'Your worship need not strip to know that,' quoth Sancho; 'for, to my knowledge, you have just such a mark as my lady says, on the small of your back, which betokens you to be a strong-bodied man.' 'That is enough,' said Dorothea; 'friends may believe one another without such a strict examination; and, whether it be on the shoulder or on the back-bone, it is not very material. In short, I find my father aimed right in all his predictions, and so do I in recommending myself to Don Quixote, whose stature and appearance so well agree with my father's description, and whose renown is so far spread, not only in Spain, but

---

* Don Azote, is Don Horse-whip; and Don Gigote Don Hash or Minced Meat:
  wilful mistakes upon likeness of the words.

over all La Mancha,* that I had no sooner landed at Ossuna, but the fame of his prowess reached my ears; so that I was satisfied in myself he was the person in quest of whom I came.' 'But pray, madam,' cried Don Quixote, 'how came you to land at Ossuna, since it is no seaport town?' 'Doubtless, sir,' said the curate, before Dorothea could answer for herself, 'the princess would say, that after she landed at Malaga, the first place where she heard of your feat of arms, was Ossuna.' 'That is what I would have said,' replied Dorothea. 'It is easily understood,' said the curate; 'then pray let your majesty be pleased to go on with your story.' 'I have nothing more to add,' answered Dorothea, 'but that fortune has at last so far favoured me, as to make me find the noble Don Quixote, by whose valour I look upon myself as already restored to the throne of my ancestors; since he has so courteously, and magnanimously vouchsafed to grant me the boon I begged, to go with me whithersoever I should guide him. For all I have to do is, to show him this Pandafilando of the Gloomy Aspect, that he may slay him, and restore that to me of which he has so unjustly deprived me. For all this will certainly be done with the greatest ease in the world, since it was foretold by Tinacrio the Sage, my good and royal father, who has also left a prediction written either in Chaldean or Greek characters (for I cannot read them) which denotes, that after the Knight of the prophecy has cut off the giant's head, and restored me to the possession of my kingdom, if he should ask me to marry him, I should by no means refuse him, but instantly put him in possession of my person and kingdom.' 'Well, friend Sancho,' said Don Quixote, hearing this and turning to the squire, 'what thinkest thou now? Dost thou not hear how matters go? Did not I tell thee as much before! See now, whether we have not a kingdom which we may command, and a queen whom we may espouse.' 'Ah, marry have you!' replied Sancho, 'and a pox take the son of a whore, I say, that will not wed and bed her majesty's grace as soon as master Pandafilando's windpipes are slit. Look what a dainty bit she is! Ha! would I never had a worse flea in my bed!' With that, to show his joy, he cut a couple of capers in the air; and, turning to Dorothea, laid hold on her mule by the bridle, and flinging himself down on his knees, begged she would be graciously pleased to let him kiss her hand, in token of his owning her for his sovereign lady. There was none of the beholders but was ready to burst for laughter, having a sight of the master's madness and the servant's simplicity. In short Dorothea was obliged to comply with his entreaties,

---

* 'This whimsical Anti-climax,' says Jarvis, 'puts one in mind of the instances of that figure in the "Art of sinking in Poetry," especially this:
  ' "*Under the Tropics is our language spoke,*
  And part of Flanders hath receiv'd our joke." '

  Pope and Swift's 'Miscellanies.'

and promised to make him a grandee, when fortune should favour her with the recovery of her lost kingdom. Whereupon Sancho gave her his thanks, in such a manner as obliged the company to a fresh laughter. Then going on with her relation, 'Gentlemen,' said she, 'this is my history; and among all my misfortunes, this only has escaped a recital: that not one of the numerous attendants I brought from my kingdom has survived the ruins of my fortune, but this good squire with the long beard: the rest ended their days in a great storm, which dashed our ship to pieces in the very sight of the harbour; and he and I had been sharers in the destiny, had we not laid hold of two planks, by which assistance we were driven to land, in a manner altogether miraculous, and agreeable to the whole series of my life, which seems, indeed, but one continued miracle. And if in any part of my relation I have been tedious, and not so exact as I should have been, you must impute it to what master curate observed to you, in the beginning of my story, that continual troubles oppress the senses, and weaken the memory.' 'Those pains and afflictions, be they ever so intense and difficult,' said Don Quixote, 'shall never deter me (most virtuous and high-born lady) from adventuring for your service, and enduring whatever I shall suffer in it: and therefore I again ratify the assurances I have given you, and swear that I will bear you company, though to the end of the world, in search of this implacable enemy of yours, till I shall find him; whose insulting head, by the help of Heaven, and my own invincible arm, I am resolved to cut off, with the edge of this (I will not say good) sword: a curse on Gines de Passamonte, who took away my own!' This he spoke murmuring to himself, and then prosecuted his discourse in this manner: 'And after I have divided it from the body, and left you quietly possessed of your throne, it shall be left at your own choice to dispose of your person, as you shall think convenient: for, as long as I shall have my memory full of her image, my will captivated, and my understanding wholly subjected to her, whom I now forbear to name, it is impossible I should in the least deviate from the affection I bear to her, or be induced to think of marrying, though it were a phœnix.'

The close of Don Quixote's speech, which related to his not marrying, touched Sancho so to the quick, that he could not forbear bawling out his resentments: 'Body of me, Sir Don Quixote,' cried he, 'you are certainly out of your wits, or how is it possible you should stick at striking a bargain with so great a lady as this is? Do you think, sir, fortune will put such dainty bits in your way at every corner? Is my lady Dulcinea handsomer, do you think? No, marry is she not half so handsome: I could almost say she is not worthy to tie this lady's shoe-latchets. I am likely indeed to get the earldom I have fed myself with hopes of, if you spend your time in fishing for mushrooms in the bottom of the sea. Marry, marry out of hand, or Old Nick take you for me: lay hold of the kingdom, which is ready to leap into your hands; and, as soon as you are a king, even make me a marquis, or a peer of the land; and afterwards let things go at sixes and sevens, it will be all one case to Sancho.' Don Quixote, quite divested of all patience, at the blasphemies which were spoken against his lady Dulcinea, could bear with him no longer; and therefore, without so much as a word to give him notice of his displeasure, gave him two such blows with his lance, that poor Sancho measured his length on the ground, and had certainly there breathed his last, had not the Knight desisted, through the persuasions of Dorothea. 'Thinkest thou,' said he, after a considerable pause, 'most infamous peasant, that I shall always have leisure and disposition to put up thy affronts; and that thy whole business shall be to study new offences, and mine to give thee new pardons? Dost thou not know, excommunicated traitor (for certainly excommunication is the least punishment can fall upon thee, after such profanations of the peerless Dulcinea's name), and art thou not assured, vile slave and ignominious vagabond, that I should not have strength sufficient to kill a flea, did not she give strength to my nerves, and infuse vigour into my sinews? Speak, thou villain with the viper's tongue; who doth thou imagine has restored the queen to her kingdom, cut off the head of a giant, and made thee a marquis (for I count all this is done already), but the power of Dulcinea, who makes use of my arm, as the instrument of her act in me? She fights and overcomes in me, and I live and breathe in her, holding life and being from her. Thou base-born wretch! art thou not possessed of the utmost ingratitude, thou who seest thyself exalted from the very dregs of the earth to nobility and honour, and yet dost repay so great a benefit with obloquies against the person of thy benefactress.'

Sancho was not so mightily hurt, but he could hear what his master said well enough; wherefore, getting upon his legs in all haste, he ran for shelter behind Dorothea's palfrey; and being got thither, 'Hark you, sir,' cried he to him, 'if you have no thought of marrying this same lady, it is a clear case that the kingdom will never be yours; and, if it be not, what good can you be able to do me? Then let any one judge whether I have not cause to complain. Therefore, good your worship, marry her once for all now we have her rained down, as it were, from heaven to us, and you may after keep company with my lady Dulcinea: for, I guess, you will not be the only king in the world that has kept a miss or two in a corner. As for beauty, do you see, I will not meddle nor make, for (if I must say the truth) I like both the gentlewomen well enough in conscience; though, now I think on it, I have never seen the lady Dulcinea.' 'How, not seen her, blasphemous traitor,' replied Don Quixote, 'when just now you brought me a message from her!' 'I say,' answered Sancho, 'I have not seen her so leisurely as to take notice of her features and good parts one by one; but yet, as I saw them at a blush, and all at once, methought I had no reason to find fault with them.' 'Well, I pardon thee now,' quoth Don Quixote, 'and you must excuse me for what I have done to you; for the first motions are not in our power.' 'I perceive that well enough,' said Sancho, 'and that is the reason my first motions are always in my tongue; and I cannot for my life help speaking what comes uppermost.' 'However, friend Sancho,' said Don Quixote, 'you had better think before you speak; for the pitcher goes so often to the well – I need say no more.' 'Well, what must be must be,' answered Sancho, 'there is somebody above who sees all, and will one day judge which hath most to answer for, whether I for speaking amiss, or you for doing so.' 'No more of this, Sancho,' said Dorothea, 'but run and kiss your lord's hands, and beg his pardon; and for the time to come, be more advised and cautious how you run into the praise or dispraise of any person; but especially take care you do not speak ill of that lady of Toboso, whom I do not know, though I am ready to do her any service; and, for your own part, trust in Heaven; for you shall infallibly have a lordship, which shall enable you to live like a prince.' Sancho shrugged up his shoulders, and, in a sneaking posture, went and asked his master for his hand, which he held out to him with a grave countenance; and, after the squire had kissed the back of it, the Knight gave him his blessing, and told him he had a word or two with him, bidding him come nearer, that he might have the better convenience of speaking to him. Sancho did as his master commanded, and, going a little from the company with him: 'Since thy return,' said Don Quixote, applying himself to him, 'I have neither had time nor opportunity to inquire into the particulars of thy embassy, and the answer thou hast brought; and therefore, since fortune has now befriended us with convenience and leisure, deny me not the satisfaction you may give me by the rehearsal of thy news.' 'Ask what you will,' cried Sancho, 'and you shall not want for an answer: but, good your worship, for the time to come, I beseech you do not be too hasty.' 'What occasion hast thou, Sancho, to make this request?' replied Don Quixote. 'Reason good enough, truly,' said Sancho; 'for the blows you gave me even now, were rather given me on account of the quarrel which the Devil stirred up between your worship and me the other night, than for your dislike of anything which was spoken against my lady Dulcinea.' 'I pray thee, Sancho,' cried Don Quixote, 'be careful of falling again into such irreverent expressions; for they provoke me to anger, and are highly offensive. I pardoned thee then for being a delinquent, but thou art sensible that a new offence must be attended with a new punishment.' As they were going on in such discourse as this, they saw at a distance a person riding up to them on an ass, who, as he came near enough to be distinguished, seemed to be a gipsy by his habit. But Sancho Pança, who, whenever he got sight of any asses, followed them with his eyes and his heart, as one whose thoughts were ever fixed on his own, had scarce given him half an eye, but he knew him to be Gines de Passamonte, and by the looks of the gipsy found out the visage of his ass; as really it was the very same which Gines had got under him; who, to conceal himself from the knowledge of the public, and have the better opportunity of making a good market of his beast, had clothed himself like a gipsy; the cant of that sort of people, as well as the languages of other countries, being as natural and familiar to them as their own. Sancho saw him, and knew him; and, scarce had he seen and taken notice of him, when he cried out as loud as his tongue would permit him: 'Ah! thou thief Genesillo, leave my goods and chattels behind thee; get off from the back of my own dear life: thou hast nothing to do with my poor beast, without whom I cannot enjoy a moment's ease: away from my Dapple, away from my comfort; take to thy heels thou villain; hence thou hedge-bird, leave what is none of thine!' He had no occasion to use so many words; for Gines dismounted as soon as he heard him speak, and taking to his heels, got from them, and was out of sight in an instant. Sancho ran immediately to his ass, and embraced him: 'How hast thou done?' cried he, 'since I saw thee, my darling and treasure, my dear Dapple, the delight of my eyes, and my dearest companion!' And then he stroked and slabbered him with kisses, as if the beast had been a rational creature. The ass, for his part, was as silent as could be, and gave Sancho the liberty of as many kisses as he pleased, without the return of so much as one word to the many questions he had put to him. At sight of this the rest of the company came up with him, and paid their compliments of congratulation to Sancho, for the recovery of his ass, especially Don Quixote, who told him, that though he had found his ass again, yet would not he revoke the warrant he had given him for the three asses; for which favour Sancho returned him a multitude of thanks.

While they were travelling together, and discoursing after this manner, the curate addressed himself to Dorothea, and gave her to understand, that she had excellently discharged herself of what she had undertaken, as well in the management of the history itself, as in her brevity, and adapting her style to the particular terms made use of in books of knight-errantry. She returned for answer, that she had frequently conversed with such romances, but that she was ignorant of the situation of the provinces and the sea-ports, which occasioned the blunder she had made, by saying that she landed at Ossuna. 'I perceive it,' replied the curate, 'and therefore I put in what you heard, which brought matters to rights again. But is it not an amazing thing, to see how ready this unfortunate gentleman is to give credit to these fictitious reports, only because they have the air of the extravagant stories in books of knight-errantry?' Cardenio said, that he thought this so strange a madness, that he did not believe the wit of man, with all the liberty of invention and fiction, capable of hitting so extraordinary a character. 'The gentleman,' replied the curate, 'has some qualities in him, even as surprising in a madman, as his unparalleled frenzy: for, take him but off from his romantic humour, discourse with him of any other subject, you will find him to handle it with a great deal of reason, and show himself, by his conversation, to have very clear and entertaining conceptions: insomuch, that if knight-errantry bears no relation to his discourse, there is no man but will esteem him for his vivacity of wit, and strength of judgment.' While they were thus discoursing, Don Quixote prosecuted his converse with his squire: 'Sancho,' said he, 'let us lay aside all manner of animosity, let us forget and forgive injuries;* and answer me as speedily as you can, without any remains of thy last displeasure, how, when, and where didst thou find my lady Dulcinea? What was she doing when you first paid thy respects to her? How didst thou express thyself to her? What answer was she pleased to make thee? What countenance did she put on at the perusal of my letter? Who transcribed it fairly for thee? And everything else which has any relation to this affair, without addition, lies, or flattery. On the other side, take care thou lose not a tittle of the whole matter, by abbreviating it, lest thou rob me of part of that delight, which I propose to myself from it.' 'Sir,' answered Sancho, 'if I must speak the truth, and nothing but the truth, nobody copied out the letter for me; for I carried none at all.' 'That is right,' cried Don Quixote, 'for I found the pocketbook, in which it was written, two days after thy departure, which occasioned exceeding grief in me, because I knew not what thou couldest do, when you found yourself without the letter; and I could 'not but be induced to believe that you would have returned, in order to take it with thee.' 'I had certainly done so,' replied Sancho, 'were it not for this head of mine, which kept it in remembrance ever since your worship read it to me, and helped me to say it over to a parish-clerk, who writ it out for me word for word, so purely, that he swore, though he had written out many a letter of excommunication in his time, he never in all the days of his life had read or seen anything so well spoken as it was.' 'And do you still retain the memory of it, my dear Sancho?' cried Don Quixote. 'Not I,' quoth Sancho, 'for as soon as I had given it her, and your turn was served, I was very willing to forget it. But, if I remember anything, what was on the top was thus, "High and Subterrene," I mean 'sovereign lady': and at the bottom, "Yours till death, the Knight of the Woeful Figure"; and I put between these two things, three hundred souls, and lives, and dear eyes.'

---

* In the original Spanish it is *Echemos pelillos a la mar*: i.e. literally, let us throw small hairs into the sea; but figuratively, let us renew our friendship and forget past differences.

CHAPTER IV

The pleasant Dialogue between Don Quixote and his Squire continued, with other Adventures

'ALL THIS IS MIGHTY WELL,' said Don Quixote, 'proceed, therefore: you arrived, and how was that queen of beauty then employed? On my conscience thou found her stringing of orient pearls, or embroidering some curious device in gold for me, her captive knight: was it not so, my Sancho?' 'No, faith,' answered the squire, 'I found her winnowing a parcel of wheat very seriously in the back yard.' 'Then,' said the Don, 'you may rest assured, that every corn of that wheat was a grain of pearl, since she did it the honour of touching it with her divine hand. Did you observe the quality of the wheat; was it not of the finest sort?' 'Very indifferent, I thought,' said the squire. 'Well, this at least, you must allow; it must make the finest, whitest bread, if sifted by her white hands. But go on; when you delivered my letter, did she kiss it? Did she treasure it in her bosom, or what ceremony did she use worthy such a letter? How did she behave herself?' 'Why truly, sir,' answered Sancho, 'when offered her the letter she was very busy handling her sieve; and, "Prithee, honest friend," said she, "do so much as lay that letter down upon the sack there; I cannot read it till I have winnowed out what is in my hands." ' 'O unparalleled discretion!' cried Don Quixote, 'she knew that a perusal required leisure, and therefore deferred it for her more pleasing and private hours. But oh! my squire, while she was thus employed, what conferences passed? What did she ask about her knight, and what did you reply? Say all, say all, my dearest Sancho; let not the smallest circumstance escape thy tongue; speak all that thought can frame, or pen describe.' 'Her questions were easily answered, sir,' said Sancho, 'for she asked me none at all: I told her, indeed, in what a sad pickle I had left you for her sake, naked to the waist; that you ate and slept like the brute beasts; that you would let a razor as soon touch your throat as your beard; that you were still blubbering and crying, or swearing, and cursing your fortune.' 'There you mistook,' replied Don Quixote. 'I rather bless my fortune, and always shall, while life affords me breath, since I am thought to merit the esteem of so high a lady as Dulcinea del Toboso.' 'There you hit it,' said Sancho; 'she is a high lady indeed, sir, for she is taller than I am by a foot and half.'* 'Why, how now, Sancho,' said the Knight, 'hast thou measured with her?' 'Ah, marry did I, sir,' said the squire: 'for

---

* *Coto* in Spanish is a handful. Oudin says it is the breadth of four fingers, and the height of the thumb when raised up in clenching the fist.

you must know that she desired me to lend her a hand in lifting a sack of wheat on an ass; so are buckled about it, and I came so close to her, that I found she was taller than I by a full span at least.' 'Right,' answered Don Quixote; 'but thou art also conscious that the uncommon stature of her person is adorned with innumerable graces and endowments of soul! But, Sancho, when you approached the charming she, did not an aromatic smell strike thy sense, a scent so odoriferous, pleasing, and sweet, that I want a name for it; sweet as – you understand me, as the richest fragrancy diffused around a perfumer's magazine of odours? This, at least, you must grant me.' 'I did, indeed, feel a sort of scent a little unsavoury,' said Sancho, 'somewhat vigorous or so; for I suppose she had wrought hard, and sweat somewhat plentifully.' 'It is false,' answered the Knight, 'thy smelling has been debauched by thy own scent, or some canker in thy nose; if thou couldest tell the scent of opening roses, fragrant lilies, or the choicest amber, then you might guess at hers.' 'Cry ye mercy, sir,' said Sancho, 'it may be so indeed for I remember that I myself have smelt very oft just as Madam Dulcinea did then, and that she should smell like me, is no such wondrous thing neither, since there is never a barrel the better herring of us.' 'But now,' said the Knight, 'supposing the corn winnowed and dispatched to the mill; what did she, after she had read my letter?' 'Your letter, sir,' answered Sancho, 'your letter was not read at all, sir; as for her part, she said she could neither read nor write, and she would trust nobody else, lest they should tell tales, and so she cunningly tore your letter. She said, that what I told her by word of mouth of your love and penance was enough: to make short now, she gave her service to you, and said she had rather see you than hear from you; and she prayed you, if ever you loved her, upon sight of me, forthwith to leave your madness among the bushes here, and come straight to Toboso (if you be at leisure), for she has something to say to you, and has a huge mind to see you. She had like to burst with laughing, when I called you the Knight of the Woeful Figure. She told me the Biscainer whom you mauled so was there, and that he was a very honest fellow; but that she heard no news at all of the galley-slaves.'

'Thus far all goes well,' said Don Quixote; 'but tell me, pray, what jewel did she present you at your departure, as a reward for the news you brought? for it is a custom of ancient standing among knights and ladies errant to bestow on squires, dwarfs, or damsels, who bring them good news of their ladies or servants, some precious jewel as a grateful reward of their welcome tidings.' 'Ah, sir,' said Sancho, 'that was the fashion in the days of yore, and a very good fashion I take it: but all the jewels Sancho got was a luncheon of bread and a piece of cheese, which she handed to me over the wall when I was taking my leave, by the same token (I hope there is no illluck in it), the cheese was made of sheep's milk.' 'It is strange,' said Don Quixote, 'for she is liberal, even to profuseness; and if she presented thee not a jewel, she certainly had none about her at that time; but what is deferred is not lost, sleeves are good after Easter. * I shall see her, and matters shall be accommodated. Knowest thou, Sancho, what raises my astonishment? It is thy sudden return; for, proportioning thy short absence to the length of the journey, Toboso being at least thirty leagues distant, thou must have ridden on the wind; certainly the sagacious enchanter, who is my guardian and friend (for doubtless such a one there is and ought to be, or I should not be a true knight-errant); certainly, I say, that wise magician has furthered thee on thy journey unawares: for there are sages of such incredible power, as to take up a knight-errant sleeping in his bed, and waken him next morning a thousand leagues from the place where he fell asleep. By this power knights-errant succour one another in their most dangerous exigents, when and where they please. For instance, suppose me fighting in the mountains of Armenia, with some hellish monster, some dreadful sprite, or fierce gigantic knight, where perhaps I am like to be worsted (such a thing may happen), when just in the very crisis of my fate, when I least expect it, behold on the top of a flying cloud, or riding in a flaming chariot, another knight, my friend, who but a minute before was in England perhaps; he sustains me, delivers me from death, and returns that night to his own lodging, where he sups with a very good appetite after his journey, having rid you two or three thousand leagues that day; and all this performed by the industry and wisdom of these knowing magicians, whose only business and charge is glorious knight-errantry. Some such expeditious power, I believe, Sancho, though hidden from you, has promoted so great a dispatch in your late journey.' 'I believe, indeed,' answered Sancho, 'that there was witchcraft in the case, for Rozinante went without spur all the way, and was as mettlesome as though he had been a gipsy's ass with quicksilver in his ears.' 'Quicksilver! you coxcomb,' said the Knight, 'ay, and a troop of devils besides; and they are the best horse-coursers in nature, you must know, for they must needs go whom the Devil drives; but no more of that. What is thy advice as to my lady's commands to visit her? I know her power should regulate my will; but then my honour, Sancho, my solemn promise has engaged me to the princess's service that comes with us, and the law of arms confines me to my word; love draws me one and glory the other way; on this side Dulcinea's strict commands, on the other my promised faith; but it is resolved. I will travel night and day, cut off this giant's head, and having settled the princess in her dominions, will presently return to see that sun which enlightens my senses: she will easily condescend to excuse my absence, when I convince her it was for her fame and glory; since the past,

* A proverbial expression, signifying that a good thing is always seasonable.

present, and future success of my victorious arms depends wholly on the gracious influences of her favour, and the honour of being her knight.' 'Oh sad, oh sad!' said Sancho, 'I doubt, your worship's head is much the worse for wearing: are you mad, sir, to take so long a voyage for nothing? why do not you catch at this preferment that now offers, where a fine kingdom is the portion, twenty thousand leagues round, they say; nay, bigger than Portugal and Castile both together – good your worship! hold your tongue, I wonder you are not ashamed – Take a fool's counsel for once, marry her by the first priest you meet; here is our own curate can do the job most curiously:* come, master, I have hair enough in my beard to make a counsellor, and my advice is as fit for you as your shoe is for your foot; a bird in hand is worth two in the bush, and

> ' "He that will not when he may
> When he would, he shall have nay." '

'Thou advisest me thus,' answered Don Quixote, 'that I may be able to promote thee according to my promise: but that I can do without marrying this lady; for I shall make this the condition of entering into battle; that after my victory, without marrying the princess, she shall leave part of her kingdom at my disposal, to gratify whom I please; and who can claim any such gratuity but thyself?' 'That is plain,' answered Sancho, 'but pray, sir, take care that you reserve some part near the seaside for me; that, if the air does not agree with me, I may transport my black slaves, make my profit of them, and go live somewhere else; so that I would have you resolve upon it presently; leave the lady Dulcinea for the present, and go kill this same giant, and make an end of that business first; for I dare swear it will yield you a good market.' 'I am fixed in thy opinion,' said Don Quixote; 'but I admonish thee not to whisper to any person the least hint of our conference; for, since Dulcinea is so cautious and secret, it is proper that I and mine should follow her example.' 'Why the devil, then,' said Sancho, 'should you send everybody you overcome packing to Madam Dulcinea, to fall down before her, and tell her they came from you to pay their obedience, when this tells all the world that she is your mistress as much as if they had it under your hand?' 'How dull of apprehension and stupid thou art,' said the knight; 'hast thou not sense to find that all this redounds to her greater glory? Know that, in proceedings in chivalry, a lady's honour is calculated from the number of her servants, whose services must not tend to any reward, but the favour of her acceptance, and the pure honour of performing them for her sake, and being called her servants.' 'I have heard our curate,' answered Sancho, 'preach up this

---

* 'As if it was done with pearl,' in the original: *lo hara de parlas*, i.e. to a nicety.

doctrine of loving for love's sake, and that we ought to love our Maker so for His own sake, without either hope of good, or fear of pain: though, for my part, I would love and serve Him for what I could get.' 'Thou art an unaccountable fellow,' cried Don Quixote: 'thou talkest sometimes with so much sense, that one would imagine thee to be something of a scholar.' 'A scholar, sir,' answered Sancho, 'lack-a-day, I do not know, as I am an honest man, a letter in the book.' Master Nicholas, seeing them so deep in discourse, called to them to stop and drink at a little fountain by the road: Don Quixote halted, and Sancho was very glad of the interruption, his stock of lies being almost spent, and he stood in danger besides of being trapped in his words, for he had never seen Dulcinea, though he knew she lived at Toboso. Cardenio by this time had changed his clothes for those Dorothea wore, when they found her in the mountains; and, though they made but an ordinary figure, they looked much better than those he had put off.* They all stopped at the fountain, and fell aboard the curate's provision, which was but a snap among so many, for they were all very hungry. While they sat refreshing themselves, a young lad, travelling that way, observed them, and, looking earnestly on the whole company, ran suddenly and fell down before Don Quixote, addressing him in a very doleful manner. 'Alas, good sir,' said he, 'do not you know me? do not you remember poor Andrew, whom you caused to be untied from the tree?' With that the Knight knew him; and, raising him up, turned to the company, 'That you may all know,' said he, 'of how great importance, to the redressing of injuries, punishing vice, and the universal benefit of mankind, the business of knight-errantry may be, you must understand, that riding through a desert some days ago, I heard certain lamentable shrieks and outcries: prompted by the misery of the afflicted, and borne away by the zeal of my profession, I followed the voice, and found this boy, whom you all see, bound to a great oak: I am glad he is present, because he can attest the truth of my relation. I found him, as I told you, bound to an oak, naked from the waist upwards, and a bloody-minded peasant scourging his back unmercifully with the reins of a bridle. I presently demanded the cause of his severe chastisement? The rude fellow answered, that he had liberty to punish his own servant, whom he thus used for some faults that argued him more knave than fool. "Good sir," said the boy, "he can lay nothing to my charge, but demanding my wages." His master made some reply, which I would not allow as a just excuse, and ordered him immediately to unbind the youth, and took his oath that he would take him home and pay him all his wages upon the nail, in good and lawful coin. Is not this literally true, Andrew? Did you

---

* These must be the ragged apparel Cardenio wore before he was dressed in the priest's short cassock and cloak.

not mark, besides, with face of authority I commanded, and with how much humility he promised to obey all I imposed, commanded, and desired? Answer me, boy, and tell boldly all that passed to this worthy company, that it may appear how necessary the vocation of knights-errant is up and down the high roads.'

'All you have said is true enough,' answered Andrew, 'but the business did not end after that manner you and I hoped it would.' 'How?' said the Knight, 'has not the peasant paid you?' 'Ay, he has paid me with a vengeance,' said the boy; 'for, no sooner was your back turned, but he tied me again to the same tree, and lashed me so cursedly, that I looked like St. Bartholomew flead alive; and at every blow he had some joke or another to laugh at you; and, had he not laid on me as he did, I fancy I could not have helped laughing myself. At last he left me in so pitiful a case, that I was forced to crawl to an hospital, where I have lain ever since to get cured, so woefully the tyrant had lashed me. And now I may thank you for this, for had you rid on your journey, and neither meddled nor made, seeing nobody sent for you, and it was none of your business, my master, perhaps, had been satisfied with giving me ten or twenty lashes, and after that would have paid me what he owed me; but you was so huffy, and called him so many names, that it made him mad, and so he vented all his spite against you upon my poor back, as soon: as yours was turned, insomuch that I fear I shall never be my own man again.' 'The miscarriage,' answered the Knight, 'is only chargeable on my departure before I saw my orders executed; for I might, by experience, have remembered, that the word of a peasant is regulated not by honour but by profit. But you remember, Andrew, how I swore if he disobeyed, that I would return and seek him through the universe, and find him, though hid in a whale's belly.' 'Ah, sir,' answered Andrew, 'but that is no cure for my sore shoulders.' 'You shall be redressed!' answered the Knight, starting fiercely up, and commanding Sancho immediately to bridle Rozinante, who was baiting as fast as the rest of the company. Dorothea asked what he intended to do? He answered, that he intended to find out the villain and punish him severely for his crimes, then force him to pay Andrew his wages to the last maravedi,* in spite of all the peasants in the universe. She then desired him to remember his engagements to her, which withheld him from any new achievement till that was finished; that he must therefore suspend his resentments till his return from her kingdom. 'It is but just and reasonable,' said the Knight, 'and therefore Andrew must wait with patience my return; but, when I do return, I do hereby ratify my former oath and promise, never to rest till he be fully satisfied and paid.' 'I dare not trust to that,' answered Andrew; 'but, if you will bestow on me as much money as will bear my charges to Sevil, I

---

* Near the value of a farthing.

shall thank your worship more than for all the revenge you tell me of. Give me a snap to eat, and a bit in my pocket, and so Heaven be with you and all other knights-errant, and may they prove as errant fools in their own business as they have been in mine.'

Sancho took a crust of bread and a slice of cheese, and reaching it to Andrew, 'There, friend,' said he, 'there is something for thee; on my word, we have all of us a share of thy mischance.' 'What share?' said Andrew. 'Why the curst mischance of parting with this bread and cheese to thee; for, my head to a halfpenny, I may live to want it; for thou must know, friend of mine, that we, the squires of knights-errant, often pick our teeth without a dinner, and are subject to many other things, which are better felt than told.' Andrew snatched at the provender, and seeing no likelihood of any more, he made his leg and marched off. But, looking over his shoulder at Don Quixote, 'Hark ye, you sir knight-errant,' cried he, 'if ever you meet me again in your travels, which I hope you never shall, though I were torn in pieces, do not trouble me with your plaguy help, but mind your own business; and so fare you well, with a curse upon you and all the knights-errant that ever were born.' The Knight thought to chastise him, but the lad was too nimble for any there, and his heels carried him off; leaving Don Quixote highly incensed at his story, which moved the company to hold their laughter, lest they should raise his anger to a dangerous height.

CHAPTER V

What befell Don Quixote and his Company at the Inn

WHEN THEY HAD EATEN PLENTIFULLY, they left that place, and travelled all that day and the next, without meeting anything worth notice, till they came to the inn, which was so frightful a sight to poor Sancho, that he would willingly not have gone in, but could by no means avoid it. The innkeeper, the hostess, her daughter, and Maritornes, met Don Quixote and his squire with a very hearty welcome: the Knight received them with a face of gravity and approbation, bidding them prepare him a better bed than their last entertainment afforded him. 'Sir,' said the hostess, 'pay us better than you did then, and you shall have a bed for a prince;' and, upon the Knight's promise that he would, she promised him a tolerable bed, in the large room where he lay before: he presently undressed, and being heartily crazed in body, as well as in mind, he went to bed. He was scarcely got to his chamber, when the hostess flew suddenly at the barber, and catching him by the beard, 'On my life,' said she, 'you shall use my tail no longer for a beard: pray, sir, give me my tail, my husband wants it to stick his thing into, his comb I mean, and my tail I will have, sir!' The barber held tug with her till the curate advised him to return it, telling him that he might now undisguise himself, and tell Don Quixote, that after the galley-slaves had pillaged him, he fled to that inn; and if he should ask for the princess's squire, he should pretend that he was dispatched to her Kingdom before her, to give her subjects an account of her arrival, and of the power she brought to free them all from slavery. The barber thus schooled, gave the hostess her tail, with the other trinkets which he had borrowed to decoy Don Quixote out of the desert. Dorothea's beauty, and Cardenio's handsome shape surprised everybody. The curate bespoke supper, and the host, being pretty secure of his reckoning, soon got them a tolerable entertainment. They would not disturb the knight, who slept very soundly, for his distemper wanted rest more than meat; but they diverted themselves with the hostess's account of his encounter with the carriers, and of Sancho's being tossed in a blanket. Don Quixote's unaccountable madness was the principal subject of their discourse, upon which the curate insisting, and arguing it to proceed from his reading romances, the innkeeper took him up. 'Sir,' said he, 'you cannot make me of your opinion; for, in my mind, it is the pleasantest reading that ever was. I have now in the house, two or three books of that kind and some other pieces, that really have kept me, and many others, alive. In harvest time, a great many of the reapers come to drink here in the heat of the day, and he that can read best among us takes up one of these books; and all the rest of us, sometimes thirty or more, sit round about him, and listen with such pleasure, that we think neither of sorrow nor care; as for my own part, when I hear the mighty blows and dreadful battles of those knights-errant, I have half a mind to be one myself and am raised to such a life and briskness, that I frighten away old age. I could sit and hear them from morning till night.' 'I wish you would, husband,' said the hostess, 'for then we should have some rest; for at all other times you are so out of humour, and so snappish, that we lead a hellish life with you.' 'That is true enough,' said Maritornes; 'and for my part, I think there are mighty pretty stories in those books, especially that one about the young lady who is hugged so sweetly by her knight under the orange-tree, when the damsel watches lest somebody comes, and stands with her mouth watering all the while; and a thousand such stories, which I would often forego my dinner and my supper to hear.' 'And what think you of this matter, young miss?' said the curate to the innkeeper's daughter. 'Alacka-day, sir!' said she, 'I do not understand those things, and yet I love to hear them: but I do not like that frightful ugly fighting that so pleases my father. Indeed, the sad lamentations of the poor knights for the loss of their mistresses, sometimes makes me cry like anything.' 'I suppose then, young gentlewoman,' said Dorothea, 'you will be tender-hearted, and will never let a lover die for you?' 'I do not know what may happen as to that,' said the girl; 'but this I know, that I will never give anybody reason to call me tigress and lioness, and I do not know how many other ugly names, as those ladies are often called; and I think they deserve yet worse, so they do; for they can never have soul nor conscience to let such fine gentlemen die or run mad for a sight of them. What signifies all their fiddling and coyness? If they are civil women, why do not they marry them, for that is all their knights would be at?' 'Hold your prating, mistress,' said the hostess. 'How came you to know all this? It is not for such as you to talk of these matters.' 'The gentleman only asked me a question,' said she, 'and it would be uncivil not to answer him.' 'Well,' said the curate, 'do me the favour, good landlord, to bring out these books that I may have a sight of them.'

'With all my heart,' said the innkeeper; and, with that, stepping to his chamber, he opened a little portmanteau that shut with a chain, and took out three large volumes, with a parcel of manuscripts in a fair legible letter: the title of the first was 'Don Cirongilio of Thrace;' the second 'Felixmarte of Hircania;' and the third was the 'History of the great Captain Gonçalo Hernandez de Cordova,' and the 'Life of Diego Garcia de Paredes,' bound together.* The curate, reading the titles, turned to the barber, and told him they wanted now Don Quixote's housekeeper and his niece. 'I shall do as well with the books,' said the barber, 'for I can find the way to the back yard or the chimney; there is a good fire that will do their business.' 'Business!' said the innkeeper, 'I hope you would not burn my books.' 'Only two of them,' said the curate, 'this same Don Cirongilio and his friend Felixmarte.' 'I hope, sir,' said the host, 'they are neither heretics nor flegmatics.' 'Schismatics you mean,' said the barber. 'I mean so,' said the innkeeper; 'and, if you must bum any, let it be this of Gonçalo Hernandez and Diego Garcia, for you should sooner burn one of my children than the others.' 'These books, honest friend,' said the curate, 'that you appear so concerned for, are senseless rhapsodies of falsehoods and folly; and this which you so despise is a true history, and contains a true account of two celebrated men; the first by his bravery and courage purchased immortal fame, and the name of the Great General, by the universal consent of mankind. The other, Diego Garcia de Paredes, was of noble extraction, and born in Truxillo, a town of

---

* These were such famous leaders, as the great captain who conquered Naples for King Ferdinand of Spain and Diego Garcia before him; but authors have added such monstrous fables to their true actions, that there is no more believing any of them, than the fables of Guy of Warwick, or the like romantic heroes, as may appear by what the curate speaks in their praise.

Estremadura, and was a man of singular courage, and such mighty strength, that with one of his hands he could stop a mill-wheel in its most rapid motion; and with his single force defended the passage of a bridge against a great army. Several other great actions are related in the memoirs of his life, but all with so much modesty and unbiassed truth, that they easily pronounce him his own historiographer; and, had they been written by any one else, with freedom and impartiality, they might have eclipsed your Hectors, Achilleses and Orlandos, with all their heroic exploits.' 'That is a fine jest, faith,' said the innkeeper, 'my father could have told you another tale, sir. Holding a mill-wheel? Why, is that such a mighty matter! odds fish, do but turn over a leaf of Felixmarte there; you will find how, with one single back-stroke, he cut five swinging giants off by the middle, as if they had been so many bean-cods, of which the children make little puppet-friars;* and read how, at another time, he charged a most mighty and powerful army of above a million and six hundred thousand fighting men, all armed *cap-a-pie*, and routed them all like so many sheep. And what can you say of the worthy Cirongilio of Thrace? who, as you may read there, going by water one day, was assaulted by a fiery serpent in the middle of the river; he presently leaped nimbly upon her back, and hanging by her scaly neck, grasped her throat fast with both his arms, so that the serpent, finding herself almost strangled, was forced to dive into the water to save herself and carried the knight, who would not quit his hold, to the very bottom, where he found a stately palace, and such pleasant gardens, that it was a wonder; and straight the serpent turned into a very old man, and told him such things as were never heard nor spoken. – Now a fig for your Great Captain, and your Diego Garcia.' Dorothea hearing this, said softly to Cardenio, 'that the host was capable of making a second part to Don Quixote.' 'I think so too,' cried Cardenio, 'for it is plain he believes every tittle contained in those books, nor can all the Carthusian friars in the world persuade him otherwise.' 'I tell thee, friend,' said the curate, 'there were never any such persons, as your books of chivalry mention, upon the face of tile earth: your Felixmarte of Hircania, and your Cirongilio of Thrace, are all but chimeras and fictions of idle and luxuriant wits, who wrote them for the same reason that you read them, because they had nothing else to do.' 'Sir,' said the innkeeper, 'you must angle with another bait, or you will catch no fish,† I know what is what, as well as another: I can tell where my

* Children, in Spain, we are told, make puppets resembling friars, out of bean-cods, by breaking as much of the upper end as to discover part of the first bean, which is to represent the bald head, and letting the broken cod hang back like a cowl.

† In the original, *A otro perro con esso heusso*, etc, i.e. To another dog, with this bone.

own shoe pinches me; and you must not think, sir, to catch old birds with chaff; a pleasant jest, faith, that you should pretend to persuade me now that these notable books are lies and stories; why, sir, are they not in print? are they not published according to order? licensed by authority from the privy-council? And do you think that they would permit so many untruths to be printed, and such a number of battles and enchantments, to set us all a-madding?' 'I have told you already, friend,' replied the curate, 'that this is licensed for our amusement in our idle hours, for the same reason that tennis, billiards, chess, and other recreations are tolerated, that men may find a pastime for those hours they cannot find employment for. Neither could the government foresee this inconvenience from such books that you urge, because they could not reasonably suppose any rational person would believe their absurdities. And, were this a proper time, I could say a great deal in favour of such writings, and how, with some regulations, they might be made both instructive and diverting; but I design, upon the first opportunity, to communicate my thoughts on this head to some that may redress it: in the mean time, honest landlord, you may put up your books, and believe them true if you please, and much good may they do you. And I wish you may never halt of the same foot as your guest Don Quixote. 'There is no fear of that,' said the innkeeper, 'for I never design to turn knight-errant, because I find the customs that supported that noble order are quite out of doors.'

About the middle of their discourse entered Sancho, who was very uneasy at hearing that knights-errant were out of fashion, and books of chivalry full of nothing but folly and fiction; he resolved, however (in spite of all their contempt of chivalry) still to stick by his master; and if his intended expedition failed of success, then to return to his family and plough. As the innkeeper was carrying away the books, the curate desired his leave to look over those manuscripts which appeared in so fair a character; he reached them to him, to the number of eight sheets, on one of which there was written in a large hand, 'The novel of the curious impertinent.' 'The title,' said the curate, 'promises something, perhaps it may be worth reading through.' 'Your reverence,' said the innkeeper, 'may be worse employed; for that novel has received the approbation of seven ingenious guests of mine who have read it, and who would have begged it of me; but I would by no means part with it, till I deliver it to the owner of this portmanteau, who left it here with these books and papers: I may perhaps see him again, and restore them honestly; for I am as much a Christian as my neighbours, though I am an innkeeper.' 'But I hope,' said the curate, 'if it pleases me you will not deny me a copy of it.' 'Nay, as to that matter,' said the host, 'we shall not fall out.' Cardenio, having by this perused it a little, recommended it to the curate, and entreated him to read it for the entertainment of the company. The curate would have excused himself, by urging the unseasonable time of night, and that sleep was then more proper, especially for the lady. 'A pleasant story,' said Dorothea, 'will prove the best repose for some hours to me; for my spirits are not composed enough to allow me to rest, though I want it.' Mr. Nicholas and Sancho joined in the request 'To please ye then, and satisfy my own curiosity,' said the curate, 'I will begin, if you will but give your attention.'

CHAPTER VI

The Novel of the Curious Impertinent

ANSELMO AND LOTHARIO, considerable gentlemen of Florence, the capital city of Tuscany in Italy, were so eminent for their friendship, that they were called nothing but the Two Friends. They were both young and unmarried, of the same age and humour, which did not a little concur to the continuance of their mutual affection, though, of the two, Anselmo was the most amorously inclined, and Lothario the greater lover of hunting; yet they loved one another above all other considerations, and mutually quitted their own pleasure for their friend's; and their very wills, like the different motions of a well-regulated watch, were always subservient to their unity, and still kept time with one another. Anselmo, at last, fell desperately in love with a beautiful lady of the same city; so eminent for her fortune and family, that he resolved by the consent of his friend (for he did nothing without his advice), to demand her in marriage. Lothario was the person employed in this affair, which he managed with that address, that in few days he put his friend into possession of Camilla, for that was the lady's name; and this so much to their satisfaction, that he received a thousand acknowledgments from both, for the equal happiness they derived from his endeavours. Lothario, as long as the nuptials lasted, was every day at Anselmo's, and did all he could to add to the sports and diversions of the occasion. But as soon as the new-married pair had received the congratulation of their friends, and the nuptial ceremonies were over, Lothario retired, with the rest of their acquaintance, and forbore his visits, because he prudently imagined that it was not at all proper to be so frequent at his friend's house after marriage as before: for, though true friendship entirely banishes all suspicion and jealousy, yet the honour of a married man is of so nice and tender a nature, that it has been sometimes sullied by the conversation of the nearest relations, and therefore more liable to suffer from that of a friend. Anselmo observed this remissness of Lothario; and, fond as he was of his wife, showed by his tender complaints how much it affected him. He told him that, if he could have believed he must also have left so dear a correspondence by marriage, as much as he loved, he would never have paid so great a price for the satisfaction of his passion; and that he would never, for the idle reputation of a cautious husband, suffer so tender and agreeable a name to be lost, as that of the Two Friends, which, before his marriage, they had so happily obtained; and therefore, he begged him, if that were a term lawful to be used betwixt them two, to return to his former familiarity and freedom of conversation; assuring him, that his wife's will and pleasure were entirely formed by his; and that, being acquainted with their ancient and strict friendship, she was equally surprised at so unexpected a change. Lothario replied to these endearing persuasions of his friend with such prudence and discretion, that he convinced him of the sincerity of his intentions in what he had done; and so, in conclusion, they agreed that Lothario should dine twice a week at his house, besides holy days. Yet Lothario's compliance with this resolution being only not to disoblige his friend, he designed to observe it no further than he should find it consistent with Anselmo's honour, whose reputation was as dear to him as his own; and he used to tell him, that the husband of a beautiful wife ought to be as cautious of the friends whom he carried home to her himself, as other female acquaintance and visitants. For a friend's or relation's house often renders the contrivance of those things easy, and not suspected, which could not be compassed either in the church, the markets, or at public entertainments and places of resort, which no man can entirely keep a woman from frequenting. To this Lothario said also, that every married man ought to have some friend to put him in mind of the defects of his conduct; for a husband's fondness many times makes him either not see, or at least, for fear of displeasing his wife, not command or forbid her what may be advantageous or prejudicial to his reputation. In all which, a friend's warning and advice might supply him with a proper remedy. But where shall we find a friend so qualified with wisdom and truth as Anselmo demands? I must confess I cannot tell, unless it were Lothario, whose care of his friend's honour made him so cautious as not to comply with his promised visiting days, lest the malicious observers should give a scandalous censure of the frequent admission of so well-qualified a gentleman, both for his wit, fortune, youth, and address, to the house of a lady of so celebrated as beauty as Camilla: for, though his virtue was sufficiently known to check the growth of any malignant report, yet he would not suffer his friend's honour nor his own, to run the hazard of being called in question; which made him spend the greatest part of those days, he had by promise devoted to his friend's conversation, in other places and employments; yet excusing his absence so agreeably, that Anselmo could not deny the reasonableness of what he alleged. And thus the time passed away in pathetic accusations of want of love and friendship on one side, and plausible excuses on the other.

'I know very well,' said Anselmo, walking one day in the fields with his friend, 'that of all the favours and benefits for which Heaven commands my gratitude, as the advantage of my birth, fortune and nature, the greatest and most obliging is the gift of such a wife and such a friend; being both of you pledges of so great value, that though it is impossible for me to raise my esteem and love equal to your deserts, yet is no man capable of having a greater. And yet, while I am in possession of all that can or usually does make a man happy, I live the most discontented life in the world. I am not able to tell you when my misery began, which now inwardly torments me with so strange, extravagant and singular a desire, that I never reflect on it, but I wonder at myself, and condemn and curb my folly, and would fain hide my desires even from myself: and yet I have received no more advantage from this private confusion than if I had published my extravagance to all the world. Since therefore it is evident that it will at last break out, dear Lothario, I would have it go no further than thy known fidelity and secrecy; for that and my own industry which, as my friend, thou wilt turn to my assistance) will quickly, I hope, free me from the anguish it now gives me, and restore that tranquillity of which my own folly has deprived me.'

Lothario stood in great suspense, unable to guess at the consequence of so strange and prolix an introduction. In vain he racked his imagination for the causes of his friend's affliction; the truth was the last thing he could think of: but, no longer to remain in doubt, he told Anselmo, that he did his friendship a particular injury in not coming directly to the point in the discovery of his thoughts to him, since his counsels might enable him to support, and, perhaps, to lose or compass such importunate desires.

'It is very true,' replied Anselmo, 'and with that assurance I must inform you, that the desire that gives me so much pain, is to know whether Camilla be really as virtuous as I think her. Nor can this be made evident but by such a trial, that, like gold by the fire, the standard and degree of her worth be discovered. For in my opinion, no woman has more virtue than she retains, after the force of the most earnest solicitations. *Casta est, quam nemo rogavit;** and she only may be said to be chaste, who has withstood the force of tears, vows, promises, gifts, and all the importunities of a lover, that is not easily denied: for where is the praise of a woman's virtue, whom nobody has ever endeavoured to corrupt? Where is the wonder if a wife be reserved, when she has no temptation nor opportunity of being otherwise, especially if she have a jealous husband, with whom the least suspicion goes for a reality, and who therefore punishes the least

* 'The nymph may be chaste that has never been tried.' – Prior.

appearance with death? Now I can never so much esteem her, who owes her virtue merely to fear or want of opportunity of being false, as I would one who victoriously surmounts all the assaults of a vigorous and watchful lover, and yet retains her virtue entire and unshaken. These, and many other reasons which I could urge to strengthen my opinion, make me desire that my Camilla's virtue may pass through the fiery trial of vigorous solicitations and addresses, and these offered by a gallant who may have merit enough to deserve her good opinion; and if, as I am confident she will, be able to resist so agreeable a temptation, I shall think myself the most happy man in the world, and attain to the height and utmost aim of my desires, and shall say, that a virtuous woman is fallen to my lot, of whom the Wise Man says, "Who can find her?" If she yields, I shall, at least, have the satisfaction of finding my opinion of women justified, and not be imposed on by a foolish confidence that abuses most men; which consideration will be sufficient to make me support the grief I shall derive from so expensive an experiment. And, assuring myself that nothing which you can say can dissuade me from my resolution, I desire that you yourself, my dear friend, would be the person to put my design in execution. I will furnish you with opportunities enough of making your addresses, in which I would have you omit nothing you may suppose likely to prevail with and work upon a woman of quality, who is modest, virtuous, resented, and discreet by nature. The most prevailing reason that makes me choose you for this affair above all others, is, because if she should prove so frail as to be overcome by addresses and importunities, the victory will not cost me so dear, since I am secured from your taking that advantage, of which another might make no scruple. And so my honour will remain untouched, and the intended injury a secret, in the virtue of thy silence; for I know my friend so well, that death and the grave will as soon divulge my affairs. Wherefore, if you would give me life indeed, and deliver me from the most perplexing torment of doubt, you will immediately begin this amorous assault, with all that warmth, assiduity, and courage, I expect from that confidence I put in your friendship.'

Lothario gave so great an attention to Anselmo's reasons, that he gave him no other interruption than what we mentioned. But now, finding his discourse was at an end, full of amazement at the extravagance of the proposal, he thus replied: 'Could I, my dear Anselmo, persuade myself that what you have said were any more than a piece of raillery, I should not have been so long silent; no, I should have interrupted you at the beginning of your speech. Sure you know neither yourself nor me, Anselmo, or you would never have employed me on such an affair, if you had not thought me as much altered from what I was, as you seem to be; for, as the poet has it, *usque ad aras*, a true friend ought to desire nothing of his friend that is offensive to Heaven. But should a man so far exert his friendship, as to deviate a little from the severity of religion in compliance to his friend, no trifling motives can excuse the transgression, but such only as concern at least his friend's life and honour. Which therefore of these, Anselmo, is in danger, to warrant my undertaking so detestable a thing as you desire? Neither, I dare engage: on the contrary, you would make me the assaulter of both, in which my own is included; for, to rob you of your reputation, is to take away your life, since an infamous life is worse than death; and by making me the guilty instrument of this, as you would have me, you make me worse than a dead man, by the murder of my reputation. Therefore I desire you will hear with patience what I have to urge against your extravagant desire, and I shall afterwards hear your reply without interruption.' Anselmo having promised his attention, Lothario proceeded in this manner. 'In my opinion, you are not unlike the Moors, who are incapable of being convinced of the error of their religion, by Scripture, speculative reasons, or those drawn immediately from the articles of our faith; and will yield to nothing but demonstrations as evident as those of the mathematics, and which can as little be denied, as when we say, if from two equal parts we take away two equal parts, the parts that remain are also equal. And when they do not understand this proposition, which they seldom do, we are obliged, by operation, to make it yet more plain and obvious to their senses: and yet, all this labour will at last prove ineffectual to convince them of the varieties of our religion. The same must be my method with you, since your strange desire is so very foreign to all manner of reason, that I very much fear I shall spend my time and labour in vain, in endeavouring to convince you of your own folly, for I can afford it no other name. Nay, did I not love you as I do, I should leave you to the prosecution of your own odd humour, which certainly tends to your ruin. But, to me your folly a little more open, you bid me, Anselmo, attempt a woman of honour, cautious of her reputation, and she who is not much inclined to love; for all these good qualifications you allowed her. If therefore you already know your wife is possessed of all these advantages of prudence, discretion, honour, and reservedness, what have you more to inquire after. And if you believe, as I myself do, that she will be impregnable to all my assaults, what greater and better names will you give her than she already deserves? Either you pretend to think better of her than really you do, or else you desire you know not what yourself. But then, if you do not believe her as virtuous as you pretend, why would you put it to the trial? why do you not rather use her as you think she deserves? On the other hand, if she be as good as you profess you believe her, why would you go to tempt truth and goodness itself, without any reasonable prospect of advantage? For, when the trial is over, she will be but the same virtuous woman she was before. Wherefore, it is allowed, that it is the effect of temerity, and want of reason, to attempt what is likely to produce nothing but danger and detriment to the undertaker, especially when there is no necessity for it, and when we may easily foresee the folly of the undertaking. There are but these motives to incite us to difficult attempts, religion, interest, or both together. The first makes the saints endeavour to lead angelic lives in these frail bodies: the second makes us expose ourselves to the hazards of long voyages and travels, in pursuit of riches: the third motive is compounded of both, and prompts us to act as well for the honour of God, as for our own particular glory and interests; as, for example, the daring adventures of the valiant soldier, who, urged by his duty to God, his prince, and his country, fiercely runs into the midst of a dreadful breach, unterrified with any considerations of the danger that threatens him. These are things done every day, and let them be never so dangerous, they bring honour, glory, md profit, to those that attempt them. But, by the project you design to reduce to an experiment, you will never obtain either the glory of Heaven, profit, or reputation: for, should the experiment answer your expectation, it will make no addition, either to your content, honour, or riches; but, if it disappoints your hopes, it makes you the most miserable man alive. And the imaginary advantage of no man's knowing your disgrace will soon vanish, when you consider, that, to know it yourself, will be enough to supply you perpetually with all the tormenting thoughts in the world. A proof of this is what the famous poet Ludovico Tansilo, at the end of his first part of "St. Peter's Tears,"* says, in these words:

' "Shame, grief, remorse in Peter's breast increase.
            Soon as the blushing morn his crime betrays:
    When must unseen, then most himself he sees,
            And with due horror all his soul surveys.

    "For a great spirit needs no cens'ring eyes
            To wound his soul, when conscious of a fault;
    But self-condemn'd, and e'en self-punish'd lies,
            And dreads no witness like upbraiding thought." '

So that your boasted secrecy, far from alleviating your grief, will only serve to increase it; and, if your eyes do not express it by outward tears, they will flow from your very heart in blood. So wept that simple doctor, who, as our poet tells us, made that experiment on the brittle vessel, which the more prudent Reinaldo excused himself from doing. This, indeed, is but a poetical fiction, but yet the moral which it enforces is worthy to be observed and imitated. And accordingly, I hope, you will discover the strange mistake into which you would run precipitately,

* This poem, written originally in Italian, was translated into Spanish by Juan Sedeno, and into French by Malherbe.

when you have heard what I have further to say to you.

'Suppose, Anselmo, you had a diamond, as valuable, in the judgment of the best jewellers, as such a stone could be; would you not be satisfied with their opinion, without trying its hardness on the anvil? You must own, that, should it be proof against your blows, it would not be one jot the more valuable than really it was before your foolish trial; but should it happen to break, as well it might, the jewel was then entirely lost, as well as the sense and reputation of the owner. This precious diamond, my friend, is your Camilla, for so she ought to be esteemed in all men's opinion as well as your own; why then would you imprudently put her in danger of falling, since your trial will add no greater value to her than she has already? But, if she should prove frail, reflect with yourself on the unhappiness of your condition, and how justly you might complain of your being the cause of her ruin and your own. Consider, that, as a modest and honest woman is the most valuable jewel in the world, so all women's virtue and honour consist in the opinion and reputation they maintain with other people; and, since that of your wife is perfect both in your own and all other men's opinion, why will you go, to no purpose, to call the reality of it in question? You must remember, my friend, that the nature of women is, at best, but weak and imperfect; and, for that reason, we should be so far from casting rubs in its way, that we ought, with all imaginable care, to remove every appearance that might hinder its course to that perfection it wants, which is virtue.

If you believe the naturalists, the Ermine is a very white little creature; when the hunters have found its haunts, they surround it almost with dirt and mire, toward which the Ermine being forced to fly, rather than sully its native white with dirt, it suffers itself to be taken, preferring its colour to its liberty and life. The virtuous woman is our Ermine, whose chastity is whiter than snow; but, to preserve its colour unsullied, you must observe just I contrary method: the addresses and services of an importunate lover, are the mire into which you should never drive a woman; for it is ten to one she will not be able to free herself and avoid it, being but too apt to stumble into it; arid therefore that should be always removed, and only the candour and beauty of virtue, and the charms of a good fame and reputation placed before her. A good woman is also not unlike a mirror of crystal, which will infallibly be dimmed and stained by breathing too much upon it: she must rather be used like the reliques of saints, adored, but not touched; or, like a garden of curious tender flowers, that may at a distance gratify the eye, but are not permitted by the master to be trampled on, or touched by every beholder. I shall add but a few verses out of a late new play, very fit for our present purpose, where a prudent old man advises his neighbour, that had a daughter, to lock her up close; and gives these reasons for it, besides several others:

' "Since nothing is frailer than woman and glass,
  He that wou'd expose 'em to fall is an ass:
  And sure the rash mortal is yet more unwise
  Who on bodies so ticklish experiments tries.
  With ease both are damag'd; then keep that with care,
  Which no art can restore, nor no solder repair.
  Fond man, take my counsel, watch what is so frail;
  For where Danaës lie, golden show'rs will prevail." '

All I have hitherto urged relates only to you, I may now at last be allowed to consider what regards myself; and, if I am tedious, I hope you will pardon me; for, to draw you out of the labyrinth into which you have run yourself, I am forced on that prolixity. You call me friend, yet, which is absolutely inconsistent with friendship, you would rob me of my honour; nay, you stop not here, but would oblige me to destroy yours. First, that you would rob me of mine is evident; for what will Camilla think, when I make a declaration of love to her, but that I am a perfidious villain, that makes no scruple of violating the most sacred laws of friendship, and who sacrifices the honour and reputation of my friend to a criminal passion. Secondly, that I destroy yours is as evident; for, when she sees me take such a liberty with her, she will imagine that I have discovered some weakness in her, that has given me assurance to make her so guilty a discovery, by which she esteems herself injured in her honour; you, being the principal part of her, must of necessity be affected with the affronts she receives. For this is the reason why the husband, though never so deserving, cautious and careful, suffers the infamy of a scandalous name, if his wife goes astray; whereas, in reason, he ought rather to be an object of compassion than contempt, seeing the misfortune proceeds from the vice and folly of the wife, not his own defects. But, since the reason and justice of the man's suffering for the wife's transgression may be serviceable to you, I will give you the best account of it I can; and pray do not think me tedious, since this is meant for your good. When woman was given to man, and marriage first ordained in Paradise, man and wife were made and pronounced one flesh; the husband therefore being of a piece with the wife, whatever affects her affects him, as a part of her; though, as I have said, he has been no occasion of it: for, as the whole body is affected by the pain of any part, as the head will share the pain of the foot, though it never caused that pain, so is the husband touched with his wife's infamy, because she is part of him And, since all worldly honours and dishonours are derived from flesh and blood, and the scandalous baseness of an unfaithful wife proceeds from the same principle, it necessarily follows, that the husband, though no party in the offence, and entirely ignorant and innocent of it, must have his share of the infamy. Let what I have said, my dear Anselmo, make you sensible of the danger into which you would run, by endeavouring thus to disturb the happy tranquillity and repose that your wife at present enjoys; and for how vain a curiosity, and extravagant a caprice, you would rouse and awake those peccant humours which are now lulled asleep by the power of an unattempted chastity. Reflect further, how small a return you can expect from so hazardous a voyage, and such valuable commodities as you venture; for the treasure you will lose is so great, and ought to be so dear, that all words are too inexpressive to show how much you ought to esteem it. But, if all I have said be too weak to destroy your foolish resolve, employ some other instrument of your disgrace and ruin: for, though I should lose your friendship, a loss which I must esteem the greatest in the world, I will have no hand in an affair so prejudicial to your honour.'

Lothario said no more, and Anselmo, discovering a desponding melancholy in his face, remained a great while silent and confounded. 'At last I have,' said he, 'my friend, listened to your discourse, as you might observe, with all the attention in nature, and every part of what you have said convinces me of the greatness of your wisdom and friendship; and I must own, that if I suffer my desires to prevail over your reasons, I shun the good and pursue the evil. But yet, my friend, you ought, on the other side, to reflect, that my distemper is not much unlike that of those women, who sometimes long for coals, lime, nay, some things that are loathsome to the very sight; and therefore some little arts should be used to endeavour my cure, which might easily be effected, if you would but consent to solicit Camilla, though it were but weakly and remissly; for, I am sure, she will not be so frail to surrender at the first assault, which yet will be sufficient to give me the satisfaction I desire; and in this you will fulfil the duty of our friendship, in restoring me to life, and securing my honour, by your powerful and persuasive reasons. And you are indeed bound, as my friend, to do thus much to secure me from betraying my defects and follies to a stranger, which would hazard that reputation which you have taken so much pains to preserve; since I am so bent on this experiment, that, if you refuse me, I shall certainly apply myself elsewhere: and though, awhile, your reputation may suffer in Camilla's opinion, yet, when she has once proved triumphant, you may cure that wound, and recover her good opinion by a sincere discovery of your design. Wherefore I conjure you to comply with my importunity, in spite of all the obstacles that may present themselves to you, since what I desire is so little, and the pleasure I shall derive from it so great; for, as I have promised, your very first attempt shall satisfy me as much as if you had gone through the whole experiment.'

Lothario plainly saw that Anselmo's resolution was too much fixed for anything he could say to alter it; and, finding that he threatened to betray his folly to a stranger, if he persisted in a refusal, to avoid greater inconveniences, he resolved to seem to comply with his desires, privately designing to satisfy Anselmo's caprice, without giving Camilla any trouble; and therefore he desired him to break the matter to nobody else, since he would himself undertake it, and begin as soon as he pleased. Anselmo embraced him with all the love and tenderness imaginable, and was as prodigal of his thanks, as if the very promise had been the greatest obligation that could be laid on him. They immediately agreed on the next day for the trial, at which time Anselmo should give him the opportunity of being alone with her, and gold and jewels to present her with. He advised him to omit no point of gallantry, as serenades, songs, and verses in her praise; offering to make them himself, if Lothario would not be at the trouble. But Lothario promised him to do all himself, though his design was far different from Anselmo's.

Matters being thus adjusted, they returned to Anselmo's house, where they found the beautiful Camilla sad with concern for the absence of her husband beyond his usual hour. Lothario left him there, and retired home, as pensive how to come off handsomely in this ridiculous affair, as he had left Anselmo pleased and contented with his undertaking it. But, that night, he contrived a way of imposing on Anselmo to his satisfaction, without offending Camilla. So next day he goes to Anselmo's, and was received by Camilla with a civility and respect answerable to the uncommon friendship she knew was between him and her husband. Dinner being over, Anselmo desired his friend to keep his lady company, till his return from an extraordinary affair that would require his absence about an hour and a half Camilla desired him not to go: Lothario offered to go with him; but he, pleading peculiar business, entreated his friend to stay, and enjoined his wife not to leave him alone till his return. In short, he knew so well how to counterfeit a necessity for his absence, though that necessity proceeded only from his own folly, that no one could perceive it was feigned. And so he left them together, without any one to observe their actions, all the servants being retired to dinner.

Thus Lothario found himself entered the lists, his adversary before him terribly armed with a thousand piercing beauties, sufficient to overcome all the men she should encounter, which gave him cause enough to fear his own fate. The first thing he did, in this first onset, was to lean his head carelessly on his hand, and beg her leave to take a nap in his chair till his friend came back: Camilla told him she thought he might rest with more ease on the couch* in the next room: he declared himself satisfied with the

---

* *Estrado*: a space of the visiting-rooms of ladies, raised a foot above the floor of the rest of the room, covered with carpets or mats, on which the ladies sit on cushions laid along by the wall, or low stools.

place where he was, and so slept till his friend came back. Anselmo, finding his wife in her chamber, and Lothario asleep at his return, concluded that he had given them time enough both for discourse and repose, and therefore waited with a great deal of impatience for his friend's awaking, that they might retire, and he might acquaint him with his success. Lothario at last awaked, and going out with his friend, he answered his inquiry to this purpose: That he did not think it convenient to proceed further, at that time, than in some general praise of her wit and beauty, which would best prepare his way for what he might do hereafter, and dispose her to give a more easy and willing ear to what he should say to her: as the Devil, by laying a pleasing and apparent good at first before us, insinuates himself into our inclinations, so he generally gains his point before we discover the cloven foot, if his disguise pass on us in the beginning. Anselmo was extremely satisfied with what Lothario said, and promised him every day as good an opportunity; and, though he could not go every day abroad, yet he would manage his conduct so well, that Camilla should have no cause of suspicion. He took care to do as he said. But Lothario wilfully lost the frequent opportunities he gave him; however, he soothed him still with assurances, that his lady was inflexible, her virtue not to be surmounted, and that she had threatened to discover his attempts to her husband, if ever he presumed to be so insolent again; so far was she from giving the least hope or encouragement. 'Thus far it is well,' said Anselmo, 'but yet Camilla has resisted nothing but words; we must not see what proof she has against more substantial temptations. Tomorrow I will furnish you with two thousand crowns in gold, to present her with; and, as a further bait, you shall have as much more for jewels. For women, especially if they are handsome, naturally love to go gaily and richly dressed, be they never so chaste and virtuous; and, if she has power to overcome this temptation, I will give you no further trouble.' 'Since I have begun this adventure,' replied Lothario, 'I will make an end of it, though I am sure her repulses will tire out my patience, and her virtue overcome any temptation, and baffle my endeavours.'

The next day Anselmo delivered him the four thousand crowns, and with them as many perplexing thoughts, not knowing how to supply his invention with some new story to amuse his friend. However, at last, he resolved to return the money, with assurance that Camilla was as unmoved with presents as with praise, and as untouched with promises as with vows and sighs of love; and therefore all further attempts would be but a fruitless labour. This was his intention; but fortune that meddled too much in these affairs disappointed his designs for Anselmo, having left him alone with his wife one day, as he used to do, privately conveyed himself into the closet, and through the chinks of the door set himself to observe what they did; he found, that, for one half hour, Lothario said not one word to Camilla; from whence he concluded that all the addresses, importunities, and repulses, with which he had amused him, were pure fictions. But, that he might be fully satisfied in the truth of his surmise, coming from his covert he took his friend aside, and inquired of him what Camilla had then said to him, and how he now found her inclined? Lothario replied, that he would make no further trial of her, since her answer had now been so severe and awful, that he durst not for the future venture upon a discourse so evidently her aversion.

'Ah! Lothario, Lothario!' cried Anselmo, 'is it thus that you keep your promises? Is this what I should expect from your friendship? I observed you through that door, and found that you said not a word to Camilla; and, from thence, I am very well satisfied, that you have only imposed on me all the answers and relations you have made. Why did you hinder me from employing some other, if you never intended to satisfy my desire?' Anselmo said no more, but this was enough to confound Lothario, and cover him with shame for being found in a lie. Therefore, to appease his friend, he swore to him, from that time forward to set in good earnest about the matter, and that so effectually, that he himself, if he would again give himself the trouble of observing him, should find proof enough of his sincerity. Anselmo believed him; and, to give him the better opportunity, he engaged a friend of his to send for him, with a great deal of importunity, to come to his house at a village near the city, where he meant to spend eight days, to take away all apprehension and fear from both his friend and his wife.

Was ever man so unhappy as Anselmo, who industriously contrived the plot of his own ruin and dishonour? He had a very good wife, and possessed her in quiet, without any other man's mingling in his pleasures; her thoughts were bounded with her own house, and her husband, the only earthly good she hoped or thought on, and her only pleasure and desire; his will the rule of hers, and measure of her conduct. When he possessed love, honour, beauty and discretion, without pain or toil, what should provoke him to seek, with so much danger and hazard of what he had already, that which was not to be found in nature! He that aims at things impossible, ought justly to lose those advantages which are within the bounds of possibility As the poet sings:

I

'In death I seek for life,
In a disease for health,
    For quietness in strife,
In poverty for wealth,
    And constant truth in an inconstant wife.

II

But sure the fates disdain
My mad desires to please,
Nor shall I e'er obtain
What others get with ease,
Since I demand what no man e'er cou'd gain.'

The next day Anselmo went out of town; having first informed Camilla, that his friend Lothario would look after his affairs, and keep her company in his absence, and desired her to make as much of him as of himself. His lady, like a discreet woman, begged him to consider how improper a thing it was for any other to take his place in his absence; and told him, that if he doubted her ability in managing her house, he should try her but this time, and she questioned not but he would find she had capacity to acquit herself to his satisfaction in greater matters. Anselmo replied that it was her duty not to dispute, but obey his command: to which she returned that she would comply, though much against her will. In short, her husband left the town. Lothario, the next day, was received at her house with all the respect that could be paid a friend so dear to her husband; but yet with so much caution, that she never permitted herself to be left alone with him, but kept perpetually some of her maids in the room, and chiefly Leonela, for whom she had a particular love, as having been bred in her father's house with her from her infancy.

Lothario said nothing to her the first three days, notwithstanding he might have found an opportunity when the servants were gone to dinner; for, though the prudent Camilla had ordered Leonela to dine before her, that she might have no occasion to go out of the room; yet she, who had other affairs to employ her thoughts, more agreeable to her inclinations (to gratify which that was usually the only convenient time she could find), was not so very punctually obedient to her lady's commands, but that she sometimes left them together. Lothario did not yet make use of these advantages, as I have said, being awed by the virtue and modesty of Camilla. But this silence, which she thus imposed on Lothario, had at last a quite contrary effect. For, though he said nothing, his thoughts were active, his eyes were employed to see and survey the outward charms of a form so perfect, that it was enough to fire the most cold, and soften the most obdurate heart. In these intervals of silence, he considered how much she desired to be beloved; and these considerations, by little and little, undermined and assaulted the faith which he owed to his friend. A thousand times he resolved to leave the city, and retire where Anselmo should never see him, and where he should never more behold the dangerous face of Camilla; but the extreme pleasure he found in seeing her, soon destroyed so feeble a resolve. When he was alone he would accuse his want of friendship and religion, and run into frequent comparisons betwixt himself and Anselmo, which generally concluded that Anselmo's folly and madness was greater than his breach of faith; and that, would Heaven as easily excuse his intentions as man, he had no cause to fear any punishment for the crime he was going to commit. In fine, Camilla's beauty, and the opportunity given him by the husband himself, wholly vanquished his faith and friendship. And now, having an eye only to the means of obtaining that pleasure, to which he was prompted with so much violence, after he had spent the first three days of Anselmo's absence in a conflict betwixt love and virtue, he attempted, by all means possible, to prevail with Camilla, and discovered so much passion in his words and actions, that Camilla, surprised with the unexpected assault, flung from him out of the room, and retired with haste to her chamber. Hope is always born with love, nor did this repulse in the least discourage Lothario from further attempts on Camilla, who by this appeared more charming, and more worthy his pursuit. She, on the other hand, knew not what to do upon the discovery of that in Lothario, which she never could have imagined. The result of her reflections was this, that since she could not give him any opportunity of speaking to her again, without the hazard of her reputation and honour, she would send a letter to her husband to solicit his return to his house. The letter she sent by a messenger that very night; and it was to the following purpose.

CHAPTER VII

In which the History of the Curious Impertinent is pursued

'AS IT IS VERY IMPROPER to leave an army without a general, and a garrison without its governor; so, to me, it seems much more imprudent to leave a young married woman without her husband; especially when there are no affairs of consequence to plead for his absence. I find myself so ill in yours, and so impatient, and unable to endure it any longer, that if you come not home very quickly, I shall be obliged to return to my father's, though I leave your house without any one to look after it: for the person to whom you have entrusted the care of your family, has, I believe, more regard to his own pleasure than your concerns. You are wise and prudent, and therefore I shall say no more, nor is it convenient I should.'

Anselmo was not a little satisfied at the receipt of this letter, which assured him that Lothario had begun the attempt, which she had repelled according to his hopes; and therefore he sent her word not to leave his house, assuring her it should not be long before he returned. Camilla was surprised with his answer, and more perplexed than before, being equally afraid of going to her father, and of staying at home; in the first she disobeyed her husband, in the latter ran the risk of her honour. The worst resolution prevailed, which was to stay at her own house, and not avoid Lothario's company, lest it should give some cause of suspicion to her servants. And now she repented her writing to Anselmo, lest he should suspect that Lothario had observed some indiscretion in her, that made him lose the respect due to her, and gave him assurance to offer at the corrupting her virtue: but, confiding in Heaven and her own innocence, which she thought proof against all Lothario's attempts, she resolved to make no answer to whatever he should say to her, and never more to trouble her husband with complaints, for fear of engaging him in disputes and quarrels with his friend. For that reason she considered how she might best excuse him to Anselmo, when he should examine the cause of her writing to him in that manner. With a resolution so innocent and dangerous, the next day she gave ear to all that Lothario said: and he gave the assault with such force and vigour, that Camilla's constancy could not stand the shock unmoved, and her virtue could do no more than guard her eyes from betraying that tender compassion, of which his words, and entreaties, and all his sighs and tears had made her heart sensible. Lothario discovered this with an infinite satisfaction, and no less addition to his flame; and found that he ought to make use of this opportunity, of Anselmo's absence, with all his force and importunity, to win so valuable a fortress. He began with the powerful battery of the praise of her beauty, which being directly pointed on the weakest part of woman, her vanity, with the greatest ease and facility in the world makes a breach as great as a lover would desire. Lothario was not unskilful or remiss in the attack, but followed his fire so close, that let Camilla's integrity be built on never so obdurate a rock, it must at last have fallen. He wept, prayed, flattered, promised, swore, vowed, and showed so much passion and truth in what he said, that, beating down the care of her honour, he, at last, triumphed over what he scarce durst hope, though what he most of all desired; for she, at last, surrendered, even Camilla surrendered. Nor ought we to wonder if she yielded, since even Lothario's friendship and virtue were not able to withstand the terrible assault: an evident proof that love is a power too strong to be overcome by anything but flying, and that no mortal creature ought to be so presumptuous as to stand the encounter, since there is need of something more than human, and indeed a heavenly force, to confront and vanquish that human passion. Leonela was the only confidante of this amour, which these new lovers and faithless friends could not by any means conceal from her knowledge. Lothario would not discover to Camilla, that her husband, for her trial, had designedly given him this opportunity, to which he owed so extreme a happiness; because she should not think he wanted love to solicit her himself with importunity, or that she was gained on too easy terms.

Anselmo came home in a few days, but discovered not what he had lost, though it was what he most valued and esteemed: from thence he went to Lothario, and, embracing him, begged of him to let him know his fate. 'All I call tell you, my friend,' answered Lothario, 'is that you may boast yourself of the best wife in the world, the ornament of her sex, and the pattern which all virtuous women ought to follow. Words, offers, presents, all is ineffectual, the tears I pretended to shed moved only her laughter. Camilla is not only mistress of the greatest beauty, but of modesty, discretion, sweetness of temper, and every other virtue and perfection that add to the charms of a woman of honour. Therefore, my friend, here take back your money, I have had no occasion to lay it out, for Camilla's integrity cannot be corrupted by such base and mercenary things as gifts and promises. And now, Anselmo, be at last content with the trial you have already made; and having so luckily got over the dangerous quick-sands of doubts and suspicions that are to be met with in the ocean of matrimony, do not venture out again, with another pilot, that vessel whose strength you have sufficiently experienced; but believe yourself, as you are, securely anchored in a safe harbour, at pleasure and ease, till death, from whose force no title, power, nor dignity can secure us, does come and cut the cable.' Anselmo was extremely satisfied with Lothario's discourse and believed it as firmly as if it had been an oracle; yet desired him to continue his pursuit, if it were but to pass away the time: he did not require he should press Camilla with those importunities he had before used, but only make some verses in her praise, under the name of Cloris; and he would make Camilla believe he celebrated a lady he loved under that name, to secure her honour and reputation from the censure which a more open declaration would expose her to: he added, that if Lothario would not be at the expense of so much trouble and time as to compose them himself, he would do it for him with a great deal of pleasure. Lothario told him there was no need of that, since he himself was sometimes poetically given: do you but tell Camilla of my pretended love, as you say you will, and I will make the verses as well as I call, though not so well as the excellency of the subject requires. The Curious Impertinent and his treacherous friend having thus agreed the matter, Anselmo went home, and then asked Camilla on what occasion she sent him the letter? Camilla, who wondered that this question had not been asked her before, replied, that the motive that prevailed with her to write in that manner to him, was a jealousy she had entertained that Lothario, in his absence, looked on her with more criminal and desiring eyes than he used to do when he was at home; but that, since, she had reason to believe that suspicion but wildly grounded, seeing he discovered rather an aversion than love, as avoiding all occasions of being alone with her. Anselmo told her she had nothing to apprehend from Lothario on that account, since he knew his affections engaged on one of the noblest young ladies of the city, whose praise he wrote under the name of Cloris; but, were he not thus engaged, there was no reason to suspect Lothario's virtue and friendship. Camilla, at this discourse, without doubt, would have beer; very jealous of Lothario, had he not told her his design of abusing her husband with the pretence of another love, that he might, with the greater liberty and security, express her praise and his passion. The next day, at dinner, Anselmo desired him to read some of the verses he had made on his beloved Cloris; telling him, he might say anything of her before Camilla, since she did not know who the lady was. 'Did Camilla know her,' replied Lothario, 'that should not make me pass over in silence any part of that praise which was her due; for if a lover complains of his mistress's cruelty while he is praising her perfections, she can never suffer in her reputation. Therefore, without any fear, I shall repeat a sonnet which I made yesterday on the ingratitude of Cloris:

A SONNET

' "At dead of night, when ev'ry troubl'd breast
By balmy sleep is eas'd of anxious pain,
   When slaves themselves in pleasing dreams are blest,
Of Heaven and Cloris, restless, I complain.
   The rosy morn dispels the shades of night,
The sun, the pleasures, and the day return;
   All nature's cheer'd with the reviving light,
I, only I, can never cease to mourn.

   At noon, in vain I bid my sorrow cease,
The heat increases, and my pains increase,
   And still my soul in the mild evening grieves:
The night returns, and my complaints renew,
No moment sees me free; in vain I sue,
   Heav'n ne'er relents, and Cloris ne'er relieves." '

Camilla was mightily pleased with the sonnet, but Anselmo transported; he was lavish of his commendation, and added that the lady must be barbarously cruel, that made no return to so much truth, and so violent a passion. 'What, must we then believe all that a poet in love tells us for truth?' said Camilla. 'Madam,' replied Lothario, 'though the poet may exceed, yet the lover corrects his fondness for fiction, and makes him speak truth.' Anselmo, to advance Lothario's credit with Camilla, confirmed whatever he said; but she, not minding her husband's confirmations, was sufficiently persuaded by her passion for Lothario, to an implicit faith in all he said; and therefore, pleased with this composition, and more satisfied in the knowledge she had that all was addressed to herself as the true Cloris, she desired him to repeat some other verses he had made on that subject, if he could remember any. 'I remember some,' replied Lothario; 'but, madam, in my opinion, they are not so tolerable as the former: but you shall be judge yourself:

A SONNET

I

' "I die your victim, cruel fair;
    And die without: reprieve,
If you can think your slave can bear
    Your cruelty, and live.

II

Since all my hopes of ease are vain,
    To die I now submit;
And that you may not think I feign,
    It must be at your feet.

III

Yet when my bleeding heart you view,
    Bright nymph, forbear to grieve;
For I had rather die of you,
    Than for another live.

IV

In death and dark oblivion's grave,
    Oh! let me lie forlorn,
For my poor ghost would pine and rave,
    Should you relent and mourn." '

Anselmo was not less profuse in his praise of this sonnet than he had been of the other, and so added new fuel to the fire that was to consume his reputation. He contributed to his own abuse, in commending his false friend's attempts on his honour, as the most important service he could do it; and this made him believe, that every step Camilla made down to contempt and disgrace, was a degree she mounted towards that perfection of virtue which he desired she should attain.

Sometime after, Camilla being alone with her maid, 'I am ashamed,' said she, 'my Leonela, that I gave Lothario so easy a conquest over me, and did not know my own worth enough to make him undergo some greater fatigues, before I made him so entire a surrender. I am afraid he will think my hasty consent the effect of the looseness of my temper, and not at all consider that the force and violence he used, deprived me of the power of resisting.' 'Ah! madam,' returned Leonela, 'let not that disquiet you; for the speedy bestowing a benefit of an intrinsic value, and which you design to bestow at last, can never lessen the favour; for according to the old proverb, "He that gives quickly gives twice." ' 'To answer your proverb with another,' replied Camilla, ' "That which cost little is less valued." ' 'But this has nothing to do with you,' answered Leonela, 'since it is said of love that it sometimes goes, sometimes flies; runs with one, walks gravely with another; turns a third into ice, and sets a fourth in a flame; it wounds one, another it kills: like lightning it begins and ends in the same moment: it makes that fort yield at night which it besieged but in the morning; for there is no force able to resist it. Since this is evident, what cause have you to be surprised at your own frailty? And why should you apprehend anything from Lothario, who has felt the same irresistible power, and yielded to it as soon? For love, to gain a conquest, took the short opportunity of my master's absence, which being so short and uncertain, love, that had before determined this should be done, added force and vigour to the lover, not to leave anything to time and chance, which might, by Anselmo's return, cut off all opportunities of accomplishing so agreeable a work. The best and most officious servant of love's retinue, is occasion or opportunity: this it is that love improves in all its progress, but most in the beginning and first rise of an amour. I trust not in what I have said to the uncertainty of report, but to experience, which affords the most certain and most valuable knowledge, as I will inform you, madam, some day or other; for I am like you, made of frail flesh and blood, fired by youth and youthful desires. But, madam, you did not surrender to Lothario till you had sufficient proof of his love, from his eyes, his vows, his promises, and gifts; till you had seen the merit of his person, and the beauty of his mind; all which convinced you how much he deserved to be loved. Then trouble yourself no more, madam, with these fears and jealousies; but thank your stars, that, since you were doomed a victim to love, you fell by the force of such valour and merit that cannot be doubted. You yielded to one who has not only the four S's,* which are required in every good lover, but even the whole alphabet; as, for example, he is, in my opinion, agreeable, bountiful, constant, dutiful, easy, faithful, gallant, honourable, ingenious, kind, loyal, mild, noble, officious, prudent,

---

* As if we should say, sightly, sprightly, sincere, and secret.

quiet, rich, secret, true, valiant, wise; the X indeed, is too harsh a letter to agree with him, but he is young and zealous for your honour and service.' Camilla laughed at her woman's alphabet, and thought her (as indeed she was) more learned in the practical part of love than she had yet confessed. She then informed her mistress of an affair that had been betwixt her and a young man of the town. Camilla was not a little concerned at what she said, being apprehensive that her honour might suffer by her woman's indiscretion; and therefore asked her, if the amour had passed any further than words? Leonela, without any fear or shame, owned her guilty correspondence with all the freedom in the world; for the mistress's guilt gives the servant impudence, and generally they imitate their ladies' frailties, without any fear of the public censure.

Camilla, finding her error past remedy, could only beg Leonela to disclose nothing of her affair to her lover, and manage her amour with secrecy and discretion, for fear Lothario or Anselmo should hear of it. Leonela promised to obey her; but she did it in such a manner, that Camilla was perpetually in fear of the loss of her reputation by her folly; for she grew so confident on her knowledge of her lady's transgression, that she admitted the gallant into the house, not caring if her lady knew it, being certain that she durst not make any discovery to her master; for when once a mistress has suffered her virtue to be vanquished, and admits of any criminal correspondence, it subjects her to her own servants, and makes her subservient to their lewd practices, which she is slavishly bound to conceal. Thus it was with Camilla, who was forced to wink at the visible rendezvous, which Leonela had with her lover, in a certain chamber of the house, which she thought proper for the occasion; nor was that all, she was constrained to give her the opportunity of hiding him, that he might not be seen by her husband.

But all this caution did not secure him from being seen by Lothario one morning, as he was getting out of the house by break of day. His surprise had made him think it a spirit, had not his haste away, and his muffling himself up as he did, that he might not be known, convinced him of his error, and thrown him into a fit of jealousy that had certainly undone them all, had not Camilla's wit and address prevented it. For Lothario concluded that Camilla, that had made no very obstinate resistance to him, had as easily surrendered to some other; and he fancied that the person he saw came from her house, was the new favoured lover, never remembering there was such a person as Leonela in the house, and that he might be a lover of hers. For when once a woman parts with her virtue, she loses the esteem even of the man whose vows and tears won her to abandon it; and he believes she will with as little, if not less difficulty, yield to another; he perverts the least suspicions into reality, and likes the slightest appearance for the most evident matter of fact.

Thus Lothario, distracted by the most violent jealousy in the world, without allowing himself time to consider, gave way to the transports of his rage and desire of revenge on Camilla, who had not injured him; he goes immediately to Anselmo, and having found him a-bed: 'I have, my friend,' said he to him, 'these several days undergone a most severe conflict within my mind, and used all the force and violence I was capable of to conceal an affair from you, which I can no longer forbear discovering, without an apparent wrong to justice and my friendship. Know then that Camilla is now ready to do whatsoever I shall desire of her, and the reason that most prevailed with me to delay this discovery was, that I would be satisfied whether she were in earnest, or only pretended this compliance to try me; but, had she been so virtuous as you and I believed her, she would, by this time, have informed you of that importunity which, by your desire, I used; but finding that she is silent, and takes no notice of that to you, I have reason to believe that she is but too sincere in those guilty promises she has made me, of meeting me to my satisfaction in the wardrobe, the next time your absence from the town should furnish he with an opportunity.' (This was true indeed, for that was the place of their common rendezvous.) 'Yet I would not have you,' continued he, 'take a rash and inconsiderate revenge, since it is possible, before the time of assignation, her virtue may rally, and she repent her folly. Therefore, as you have hitherto taken my advice, be ruled by me now, that you may not be imposed on, but have a sufficient conviction before you put your resolves into execution. Pretend two or three days' absence, and then privately convey yourself behind the hangings in the wardrobe, as you easily may, whence you may, without difficulty, be an eye-witness with me of Camilla's conduct; and if it be as criminal as we may justly fear, then you may with secrecy and speed punish her as the injury deserves.'

Anselmo was extremely surprised at so unexpected a misfortune, to find himself deceived in those imaginary triumphs he pleased himself with, in Camilla's supposed victory over all Lothario's assaults. A great while he was in a silent suspense, with his eyes dejected, without force, and without spirit; but, turning at last to his friend, 'You have done all,' said he, 'Lothario, that I could expect from so perfect a friendship, I will therefore be entirely guided by your advice; do therefore what you please, but use all the secrecy a thing of this nature requires.' Lothario, assuring him of that, left him, but full of repentance for the rashness he had been guilty of, in telling him so much as he had, since he might have taken a sufficient revenge by a less cruel and dishonourable way. He cursed his want of sense, and the weakness of his resolution, but could not find out any way to produce a less fatal event of his treachery, than he could justly expect from the experiment. But at last he concluded to inform Camilla of all he had done; which his freedom of access gave him opportunity to do that very day, when he found her alone; and she began thus to him: 'I am so oppressed, my Lothario, with a misfortune with I lie under, that it will certainly for ever destroy my quiet and happiness, if there be not some speedy remedy found for it. Leonela is grown so presumptuous, on her knowledge of my affairs, that she admits her lover all night to her chamber, and so exposes my reputation to the censure of any that shall see him go out at unseasonable hours from my house; and the greatest and most remediless part of my grief is, that I dare not correct or chide her for her imprudence and impudence; for, being conscious of our correspondence she obliges me to conceal her failings, which I am extremely apprehensive will in the end be very fatal to my happiness.' Lothario was at first jealous that Camilla designed cunningly thus to impose her own privado on him for Leonela's; but being convinced by her tears, and the apparent concern in her face, he began to believe her, and at the same time to be infinitely confounded and grieved for what he had done. Yet he comforted Camilla, assuring her he would take effectual care for the future, that Leonela's impudence should do her no prejudice, and therefore begged her not to torment herself any more about it. Then he told all the unhappy effects of his jealous rage, and that her husband had agreed, behind the arras, to be witness of her weakness. He asked her pardon for the folly, and her counsel how to redress and prevent the ill effect of it and bring them out of those difficulties into which his madness had plunged them.

Camilla expressed her resentment and her fears; and accused his treachery, baseness, and want of consideration; yet her anger and fears being appeased, and a woman's wit being always more pregnant in difficulties than a man's, she immediately thought of a way to deliver them from dangers that bore so dismal and helpless a face. She therefore bid him engage Anselmo to be there the next day, assuring him she did not question but by that means to get a more frequent and secure opportunity of enjoying one another than they hitherto had had. She would not make him privy to her whole design, but bid him be sure to come after her husband was hid, as soon as Leonela should call him, and that he should answer as directly to whatsoever she should ask him, as if Anselmo were not within hearing. Lothario spared no importunity to get from her her whole design, that he might act his part with the greater assurance, and the better to contribute to the imposing on her husband. 'All you have to do,' replied Camilla, 'is to answer me directly what I shall demand: 'nor would she discover any more, for fear he should not acquiesce in her opinion (which she was so well satisfied in), but raise difficulties, and by consequence, obstacles, that might hinder her design from having the desired event, or run her upon some less successful project. Lothario complied, and Anselmo in appearance left the town to retire to his friend in the country, but secretly returned to hide himself in the wardrobe, which he did with the greater ease, because Camilla and Leonela wilfully gave him opportunity. We may easily imagine the grief with which Anselmo hid himself, since it was to be a spectator of his own dishonour, and the loss of all that happiness he possessed in the embraces of his beautiful and beloved Camilla. On the other hand, she being now certain that Anselmo was hid, entered the wardrobe with Leonela, and fetching a deep and piteous sigh, thus addressed herself to her: 'Ah! my Leonela! would it not be much better that thou pierce this infamous bosom with Anselmo's dagger, before I execute what I design, which I have kept from thee that thou mightest not endeavour to disappoint me? Yet not so; for, where is the justice that I should suffer for another's offence? No, I will first know of Lothario what action of mine has given him assurance to make me a discovery of a passion so injurious to his friend and my honour. Go to the window, Leonela, and call the wicked man to me, who doubtless is waiting, in the street, the signal for his admission to accomplish his villainous design; yet, first, my resolution shall be performed, which, though it be cruel, is what my honour strictly demands of me.' 'Alas! my dear lady,' cried the cunning Leonela, 'alas! what do you intend to do with that dagger? Is your fatal design against yourself or Lothario? Alas! you can attack neither without the ruin of your fame and reputation. You had better give no opportunity to that bad man, by admitting him, while we are thus alone in the house: consider, madam, we are but two weak and helpless women, he a strong and resolute man, whose force is redoubled by the passion and desire that possess him; so that before you may be able to accomplish what you design, he may commit a crime that will be more injurious to you than the loss of your life. We have reason to curse my master Anselmo, who gives such frequent opportunities to impudence and dishonesty to pollute our house. But, madam, suppose you should kill him, as I believe you design, what shall we do with his dead body?' 'What!' said Camilla, 'why we would leave him in this place to be buried by Anselmo: for it must be a grateful trouble to him to bury with his own hand his own infamy and dishonour. Call him therefore quickly; for, methinks, every moment my revenge is deferred, I injure that loyalty I owe to my husband.'

Anselmo gave great attention to all that was said, and every word of Camilla's made a strange alteration in his sentiments, so that he could scarce forbear coming out to prevent his friend's death, when he heard her desperate resolution against his life; but his desire of seeing the end of so brave a resolve withheld him, till he saw an absolute necessity of discovering himself to hinder the mischief. Now Camilla put on a fear and weakness which resembled a swoon; and, having thrown herself on a bed in the room, Leonela began a most doleful lamentation over her: 'Alas!'

said she, 'how unfortunate should I be, if my lady, so eminent for virtue
and chastity as well as beauty, should thus perish in my arms?' This, and
much more she uttered with that force of perfect dissimulation, that
whoever had seen her would have concluded her one of the most innocent
virgins in the world, and her lady a mere persecuted Penelope. Camilla
soon came to herself, and cried to Leonela: 'Why do not you call the most
treacherous and unfaithful of friends? Go, fly, and let not thy delays waste
my revenge and anger in mere words and idle threats and curses.'
'Madam,' replied Leonela, 'I will go, but you must first give me that
dagger, lest you commit some outrage upon yourself in my absence,
which may give an eternal cause of sorrow to all your friends who love and
value you.' 'Let not those fears detain you,' said Camilla, 'but assure
yourself I will not do anything till your return; for though I shall not fear
to punish myself in the highest degree, yet I shall not, like Lucretia,
punish myself without killing him that was the principal cause of my
dishonour. If I must die, I shall not refuse it; but I will first satisfy my
revenge on him that has tempted me to come to this guilty assignation, to
make him lament his crime without being guilty of any myself.'

Camilla could scarce prevail with Leonela to leave her alone, but at last
she obeyed her, and withdrew, when Camilla entertained herself and her
husband with this following soliloquy: 'Good Heaven,' said she, 'had I not
better have continued my repulses, than by this seeming consent suffer
Lothario to think scandalously of me, till my actions shall convince him of
his error? That indeed might have been better in some respects, but then I
should have wanted this opportunity of revenge, and the satisfaction of my
husband's injured honour, if he were permitted, without any correction,
to go off with the insolence of offering such criminal assaults to my virtue.
No, no, let the traitor's life atone for the guilt of his false and unfaithful
attempts, and his blood quench that lewd fire he was not content should
burn in his own breast. Let the world be witness, if it ever comes to know
my story, that Camilla thought it not enough to preserve her virtue and
loyalty to her husband entire, but also revenged the hateful affront, and
the intended destruction of it. But it might be most convenient perhaps to
let Anselmo know of this before I put my revenge into execution; yet, on
the first attempt, I sent him word of it to the village, and I can attribute his
not resenting so notorious an abuse to nothing but his generous temper,
and confidence in his friend, incapable of believing so tried a friend could
be guilty of so much as a thought against his honour and reputation; nor is
this incredulity so strange, since I for so long together could not persuade
myself of the truth of what my eyes and ears conveyed to me; and nothing
could have convinced me of my generous error, had his insolence kept
within any bounds, and not dared to proceed to large gifts, large promises,
and a flood of tears, which he shed as the undissembled testimony of his

passion. But, to what purpose are these considerations? Or is there indeed any need of considering to persuade me to a brave resolve? Avaunt, false thoughts! Revenge is now my task, let the treacherous man approach, let him come, let him die, let him perish; let him but perish, no matter what is the fatal consequence. My dear Anselmo received me to his bosom spotless and chaste, and so shall the grave receive me from his arms. Let the event be as fatal as it will, the worst pollution I can this way suffer is of mingling my own chaste blood with the impure and corrupted blood of the most false and treacherous of friends.' Having said this, she traversed the room in so passionate a manner, with the drawn dagger in her hand, and showed such an agitation of spirits in her looks and motion, that she appeared like one distracted, or more like a murderer than a tender and delicate lady.

Anselmo, not a little to his satisfaction, very plainly saw and heard all this from behind the arras, which with the greatest reason and evidence in the world removed all his past doubts and jealousies, and he, with abundance of concern, wished that Lothario would not come, that he might by that means escape the danger that so apparently threatened him; to prevent which he had discovered himself, had he not seen Leonela at that instant bring Lothario into the room. As soon as Camilla saw him enter, she described a line with the poniard on the ground, and told him the minute he presumed to pass that, she would strike the dagger to his heart: 'Hear me,' said she, 'and observe what I say without interruption; when I have done, you shall have liberty to make what reply you please. Tell me first, Lothario, do you know my husband, and do you know me? The question is not so difficult but you may give me immediate answer; there is no need of considering; speak therefore without delay.' Lothario was not so dull as not to guess at her design in having her husband hid behind the hangings, and therefore adapted his answers so well to her questions, that the fiction was lost in the appearance of reality. 'I did never imagine, fair Camilla,' said Lothario, 'that you would make this assignation to ask questions so distant from the dear end of coming. If you had a mind still to delay my promised happiness, you should have prepared me for the disappointment; for, the nearer the hope of possession brings us to the good we desire, the greater is the pain to have those hopes destroyed. But, to answer your demands, I must own, madam, that I do know your husband, and he me; that this knowledge has grown up with us from our childhood; and, that I may be a witness against myself for the injury I am compelled by love to do him, I do also own, divine Camilla, that you too well know the tenderness of our mutual friendship: yet love is a sufficient excuse for all my errors, if they were much more criminal than they are. And, madam, that I know you is evident, and love you equal to him, for nothing but your charms could have power enough to make me forget what I owe to my own honour, and what to the holy laws of friendship, all which I have been forced to break by the resistless tyranny of love. Ah! had I known you less, I had been more innocent.' 'If you confess all this,' said Camilla, 'if you know us both, how dare you violate so sacred a friendship, injure so true a friend, and appear thus confidently before me, whom you know to be esteemed by him the mirror of his love, in which that love so often views itself with pleasure and satisfaction; and in which you ought to have surveyed yourself so far, as to have seen how small the temptation is that has prevailed on you to wrong him. But alas! this points me to the cause of your transgression, some suspicious action of mine when I have been least on my guard, as thinking myself alone; but assure yourself whatever it was, it proceeds not from looseness or levity of principle, but a negligence and liberty which the sex sometimes innocently fall into when they think themselves unobserved. If this were not the cause, say, traitor, when did I listen to your prayers, or in the least regard your tears and vows, so that you might derive from thence the smallest hope of accomplishing your infamous desires? Did I not always with the last aversion and disdain reject your criminal passion? Did I ever betray a belief in your lavish promises, or admit of your prodigal gifts? But, since, without some hope, no love can long subsist, I will lay that hateful guilt on some unhappy inadvertency of mine; and therefore will inflict the same punishment on myself that your crime deserves. And to show you that I cannot but be cruel to you, who will not spare myself, I sent for you to be a witness of that just sacrifice I shall make to my dear husband's injured honour, on which you have fixed the blackest mark of infamy that your malice could suggest, and which I, alas! have sullied too by my thoughtless neglect of depriving you of the occasion, if indeed I give any, of nourishing your wicked intentions. Once more I tell you, that the bare suspicion that my want of caution, and setting so severe a guard on my actions as I ought, has made you harbour such wild and infamous intentions, is the sharpest of my afflictions, and what with my own hands I resolve to punish with the utmost severity: for, should I leave that punishment to another, it would but increase my guilt. Yes, I will die; but first to satisfy my revenge and impartial justice, I will, unmoved, and unrelenting, destroy the fatal cause that has reduced me to this desperate condition.'

At these words she flew with so much violence, and so well acted a fury on Lothario with her naked dagger, that he could scarce think it feigned, and therefore secured himself from her blow by avoiding it and holding her hand. Thereupon, to give more life to the fiction, as in a rage at her disappointed revenge on Lothario, she cried out, 'Since my malicious fortune denies a complete satisfaction to my just desires, at least it shall not be in its power entirely to defeat my resolution.' With that, drawing back her dagger-hand from Lothario who held it, she struck it into that part of her body where it might do her the least damage, and then fell down as fainting away with the wound. Lothario and Leonela, surprised at the unexpected event, knew not yet what to think, seeing her still lie all bloody on the ground: Lothario, pale and trembling, ran to her to take out the dagger, but was delivered of his fears when he saw so little blood follow it, and more than ever admired the cunning and wit of the beautiful Camilla. Yet, to play his part as well, and show himself a friend, he lamented over Camilla's body in the most pathetic manner in the world as if she had been really dead; he cursed himself, and cursed his friend that had put him on that fatal experiment; and, knowing that Anselmo heard him, he said such things that were able to draw a greater pity for him than even for Camilla, though she seemed to have lost her life in the unfortunate adventure. Leonela removed her body to the bed, and begged Lothario to seek some surgeon, that might with all the secrecy in the world cure her lady's wound. She also asked his advice how to excuse it to her master, if he should return before it was perfectly cured. He replied, they might say what they pleased, that he was not in a humour of advising, but bid her endeavour to stanch her mistress's blood, for he would go where they should never hear more of him; and so he left them, with all the appearance of grief and concern that the occasion required. He was no sooner gone, but he had leisure to reflect, with the greatest wonder imaginable, on Camilla's and her woman's conduct in this affair, and on the assurance which this scene had given Anselmo of his wife's virtue; since now he could not but believe he had a second Portia, and he longed to meet him, to rejoice over the best dissembled imposture that ever bore away the opinion of truth. Leonela stanched the blood, which was no more than necessary for covering the cheat, and washing the wound with wine only as she bound it up, her discourse was so moving, and so well acted, that it had been alone sufficient to have convinced Anselmo that he had the most virtuous wife in the world. Camilla was not silent, but added fresh confirmations; in every word she spoke she complained of her cowardice and baseness of spirit, that denied her time and force to dispatch that life which was now so hateful to her. She asked her too, whether she should inform her husband of what had passed, or not? Leonela was for her concealing it, since the discovery must infallibly engage her husband in a revenge on Lothario, which must as certainly expose him too; for those things were never accomplished without the greatest danger; and that a good wife ought, to the best of her power, prevent involving her husband in quarrels. Camilla yielded to her reasons; but added, that they must find out some pretended cause of her wound, which he would certainly see at his return. Leonela replied, that it was a difficult task, since she was incapable even in jest to dissemble the truth.

'Am I not,' answered Camilla, 'under the same difficulty, who cannot save my life by the odious refuge of a falsehood? Had we not better then confess the real truth, than be caught in a lie?' 'Well, madam,' returned Leonela, 'let this give you no further trouble, by tomorrow morning I shall find out some expedient or other; though I hope the place where the wound is, may conceal it enough from his observation to secure us from all apprehension; leave, therefore, the whole event to Heaven, which always favours and assists the innocent.'

Anselmo saw and heard this formal tragedy of his ruined honour, with all the attention imaginable, in which all the actors performed their parts so to the life, that they seemed the truth they represented; he wished with the last impatience of the night, that he might convey himself from his hiding-place to his friend's house, and there rejoice for this happy discovery of his wife's experienced virtue. Camilla and her maid took care to furnish him with an opportunity of departing, of which he soon took hold, for fear of losing it. It is impossible to tell you all the embraces he gave Lothario, and the joy and extreme satisfaction he expressed at his good fortune, or the extravagant praises he gave Camilla. Lothario heard all this without taking a friend's share in the pleasure, for he was shocked with the concern he had to see his friend so grossly imposed on, and the guilt of his own treachery in injuring his honour. Though Anselmo easily perceived that Lothario was not touched with any pleasure at his relation, yet he believed Camilla's wound caused by him, was the true motive of his not sharing his joy and therefore assured him, he need not too much trouble himself for it, since it could not be dangerous, she and her woman having agreed to conceal it from him. This cause of his fear being removed, he desired him to put on a face of joy, since by his means he should now possess a perfect happiness and content; and therefore he would spend the rest of his life in conveying Camilla's virtue to posterity, by writing her praise in verse. Lothario approved his resolution, and promised to do the same. Thus Anselmo remained the most delightfully deceived of any man alive. He therefore carried Lothario immediately to his house, as the instrument of his glory, though he was indeed the only cause of his infamy and dishonour. Camilla received him with a face that ill-expressed the satisfaction of her mind, being forced to put on frowns in her looks, while her heart prompted nothing but smiles of joy for his presence.

For some months the fraud was concealed; but then fortune, turning her wheel, discovered to the world the wickedness they had so long and artificially disguised; and Anselmo's impertinent curiosity cost aim his life.

CHAPTER VIII

The conclusion of the Novel of the 'Curious Impertinent'; with the dreadful Battle betwixt Don Quixote and certain Wine-Skins

THE NOVEL was come near a conclusion, when Sancho Pança came running out of Don Quixote's chamber in a terrible fright, crying out 'Help! help! good people, help my master, he is just now at it, tooth and nail, with that same giant, the Princess Micomicona's foe: I never saw a more dreadful battle in my born days. He has lent him such a sliver, that whip off went the giant's head as round as a turnip.' 'You are mad, Sancho,' said the curate, interrupted in his reading; 'is thy master such a devil of a hero, as to fight a giant at two thousand leagues' distance?' Upon this, they presently heard a noise and bustle in the chamber, and Don Quixote bawling out, 'Stay villain, robber, stay; since I have thee here, the scimitar shall but little avail thee,' and, with this, they heard him strike with his sword, with all his force, against the walls. 'Good folks,' said Sancho, 'my master does not want your hearkening; why do not you run in and help him? Though I believe it is after meat mustard, for sure the giant is by this time gone to pot, and giving an account of his ill life; for I saw his blood run all about the house, and his head sailing in the middle of it: But such a head! It is bigger than any wine-skin* in Spain.' 'Death and hell,' cries the innkeeper, 'I will be cut like a cucumber, if this Don Quixote, or Don Devil, has not been hacking my wine-skins that stood filled at his bed's-head, and this coxcomb has taken the spilt liquor for blood.' Then, running with the whole company into the room, they found the poor knight in the most comical posture imaginable.

He was standing in his shirt, the fore part of it scarcely reaching to the bottom of his belly, and about a span shorter behind; this added a very peculiar air to his long lean legs, as dirty and hairy as a beast's. To make him all of a piece, he wore on his head a little red, greasy, cast nightcap of the innkeeper's; he had wrapped one of the best blankets about his left arm for a shield, and wielded his drawn sword in the right, laying about him pell-mell; with now and then a start of some military expression, as if he had been really engaged with some giant. But, the best jest of all, he was all this time fast asleep: for the thoughts of the adventure he had undertaken, had so wrought on his imagination, that his depraved fancy

---

* In Spain they keep their wines in the skin of a hog, goat, sheep, or other beast, pitched within and sewed close without.

had in his sleep represented to him the kingdom of Micomicon, and the giant: and dreaming that he was then fighting him, he assaulted the wine-skins so desperately, that he set the whole chamber a-float with good wine. The innkeeper, enraged to see the havoc, flew at Don Quixote with his fists; and, had not Cardenio and the curate taken him off, he had proved a giant indeed against the Knight. All this could not wake the poor Don, till the barber, throwing a bucket of cold water on him, wakened him from his sleep, though not from his dream.

The shortness of her champion's shirt gave Dorothea a surfeit of the battle. Sancho ran up and down the room searching for the giant's head, till, finding his labour fruitless, 'Well, well' said he, 'now I see plainly that this house is haunted, for when I was here before, in this very room was I beaten like any stock-fish, but knew no more than the man in the moon who struck me; and now the giant's head, that I saw cut off with these eyes, is vanished; and, I am sure, I saw the body spout blood like a pump.' 'What a prating and nonsense does this damned son of a whore keep about blood and a pump, and I know not what,' said the innkeeper; 'I tell you, rascal, it is my wine-skins that are slashed, and my wine that runs about the floor here, and I hope to see the soul of him that spilt it swimming in hell for his pains.' 'Well, well,' said Sancho, 'do not trouble me, I only tell you that I cannot find the giant's head, and my earldom is gone after it; and so I am undone, like salt in water.' And truly Sancho's waking dream was as pleasant as his master's when asleep. The innkeeper was almost mad to see the foolish squire harp so on the same string with his frantic master, and swore they should not come off now as before; that their chivalry should be no satisfaction for his wine, but that they should pay him sauce for the damage, and for the very leathern patches which the wounded wine-skins would want.

Don Quixote, in the meanwhile, believing he had finished his adventure,* and mistaking the curate, that held him by the arms, for the Princess Micomicona, fell on his knees before him, and with a respect due to a royal presence: 'Now may your highness,' said he, 'great and illustrious princess, live secure, free from any further apprehensions from your conquered enemy; and now am I acquitted of my engagement, since, by the assistance of Heaven and the influence of her favour by whom I live and conquer, your adventure is so happily achieved.' 'Did not I tell you so, gentlefolks?' said Sancho; 'who is drunk or mad now? See if my master has not already put the giant in pickle? Here are the bulls,† and I am an earl.'

---

* So the Knight of the burning sword dreams of finishing the adventure of disenchanting the Princess of Niquee, and wakes as much fatigued and breathless, as if it had been real. – 'Amad. de Gaul.'

† An allusion to the joy of the mob in Spain, when they see the bulls coming.

The whole company (except the innkeeper, who gave himself to the Devil) were like to split at the extravagancies of master and man. At last the barber, Cardenio, and the curate, having with much ado, got Don Quixote to bed, he presently fell asleep, being heartily tired; and then they left him, to comfort Sancho Pança for the loss of the giant's head; but it was no easy matter to appease the innkeeper, who was at his wit's end for the unexpected and sudden fate of his wine-skins.

The hostess, in the mean time, ran up and down the house crying and roaring: 'In an ill hour,' said she, 'did this unlucky knight-errant come into my house; I wish, for my part, I had never seen him, for he has been a dear guest to me. He and his man, his horse and his ass, went away last time without paying me a cross for their supper, their bed, their litter and provender; and all, forsooth, because he was seeking adventures. What, in the Devil's name, have I to do with his statutes of chivalry? If they oblige him not to pay they should oblige ham not to eat neither. It was upon this score that the other fellow took away my good tail; it is clear spoiled, the hair is all torn off, and my husband can never use it again. And now to come upon me again, with destroying my wine-skins, and spilling my liquor; may somebody spill his heart's blood for it for me: but I will be paid, so I will, to the last maravedis, or I will disown my name, and forswear the mother that bore me.' Her honest maid Maritornes seconded her fury; but Mr. Curate stopped their mouths by promising that he would see them satisfied for their wine and their skins, but especially for the tail which they kept such a clutter about. Dorothea comforted Sancho, assuring him, that whenever it appeared that his master had killed the giant, and restored her to her dominions, he should be sure of the best earldom in her disposal. With this he buckled up again, and swore that he himself had seen the giant's head, by the same token that I had a beard that reached down to his middle; and, if it could not be found, it must be hid by witchcraft; for everything went by enchantment in that house, as he had found to his cost when he was there before. Dorothea answered, that she believed him; and desired him to pluck up his spirits, for all things would be well. All parties being quieted, Cardenio, Dorothea, and the rest, entreated the curate to finish the novel, which was so near a conclusion; and he, in obedience to their commands, took up the book and read on:

Anselmo grew so satisfied in Camilla's virtue, that he lived with all the content and security in the world; to confirm which, Camilla ever in her looks seemed to discover her aversion to Lothario, which made him desire Anselmo to dispense with his coming to his house, since he found how averse his wife was to him, and how great a disgust she had to his company; but Anselmo would not be persuaded to yield to his request; and was so blind, that, seeking his content, he perpetually promoted his dishonour. He was not the only person pleased with the condition he lived in; Leonela was so transported with her amour, that, secured by her lady's connivance, she perfectly abandoned herself to the indiscreet enjoyment of her gallant: so that one night her master heard somebody in her chamber, and coming to the door to discover who it was, he found it held fast against him; but, at last forcing it open, he saw one leap out of the window the instant he entered the room: he would have pursued him, but Leonela, clinging about him, begged him to appease his anger and concern, since the person that made his escape was her husband. Anselmo would not believe her, but, drawing his dagger, threatened to kill her if she did not immediately make full discovery of the matter. Distracted with fear, she begged him to spare her life, and she would discover things that more nearly related to him than he imagined. 'Speak quickly then,' replied Anselmo, 'or you die.' ' 'Tis impossible,' returned she, 'that in this confusion and fright, I should say anything that can be understood; but give me but till tomorrow morning, and I will lay such things before you, as will surprise and amaze you: but believe me, sir, the person that leaped out of the window is a young man of this city, who is contracted to me.' This something appeased Anselmo, and prevailed with him to allow her till the next morning to make her confession: for he was too well assured of Camilla's virtue, by the past trial, to suspect that there could be anything relating to her in what Leonela had to tell him: wherefore, fastening her in her room, and threatening that she should never come out till she had done what she had promised, he returned to his chamber to Camilla, and told her all that had passed, without omitting the promise she had given him to make some strange discovery the next morning. You may easily imagine the concern this gave Camilla; she made no doubt but that the discovery Leonela had promised was of her disloyalty; and, without waiting to know whether it was so or not, that very night, as soon as Anselmo was asleep, taking with her all her jewels, and some money, she got undiscovered out of the house, and went to Lothario, informed him of all that had passed, and desired him either to put her in some place of safety, or to go with her where they might enjoy each other secure from the fears of Anselmo. This surprising relation so confounded Lothario, that for some time he knew not what he did, or what resolution to take; but at last, with Camilla's consent, he put her into a nunnery, where a sister of his was abbess, and immediately, without acquainting anybody with his departure, left the city.

Anselmo, as soon as it was day, got up, without missing his wife, and hurried away to Leonela's chamber, to hear what she had to say to him; but he found nobody there, only the sheets, tied together and fastened to the window, showed which way she had made her escape; on which he returned very sad to tell Camilla the adventure, but was extremely surprised when he found her not in the whole house, nor could hear any news of her from his servants: but finding in his search her trunks open, and most of her jewels gone, he no longer doubted of his dishonour: so, pensive and half-dressed as he was, he went to Lothario's lodging to tell him his misfortune; but, when his servants informed him that he was gone that very night, with all his money and jewels, his pangs were redoubled, and his grief increased almost to madness. To conclude, he returned home, found his house empty, for fear had driven away all his servants. He knew not what to think, say, or do: he saw himself forsaken by his friend, his wife, and his very servants, with whom he imagined that Heaven itself had abandoned him; but his greatest trouble was to find himself robbed of his honour and reputation; for Camilla's crime was but too evident from all these concurring circumstances. After a thousand distracting thoughts, he resolved to retreat to that village whither he formerly retired to give Lothario an opportunity to ruin him; wherefore, fastening up his doors, he took horse, full of despair and languishing sorrow, the violence of which was so great, that he had scarce rid half-way, when he was forced to alight, and tying his horse to a tree, he threw himself beneath it; and spent, in that melancholy posture, a thousand racking reflections, most part of the day, till a little before night he discovered a passenger coming the same road, of whom he inquired, 'What news of Florence?' The traveller replied, that the most surprising news that had been heard of late, was now all the talk of the city; which was, that Lothario had that very night carried away the wealthy Anselmo's wife Camilla, which was all confessed by Camilla's woman, who was apprehended that night as she slipped from the window of Anselmo's house by a pair of sheets. 'The truth of this story I cannot affirm,' continued the traveller, 'but everybody is astonished at the accident; for no man could ever suspect such a crime from a person engaged in so strict a friendship with Anselmo, as Lothario was; for they were called the Two Friends.' 'Is it yet known,' replied Anselmo, 'which way Lothario and Camilla are gone?' 'No! sir,' returned the traveller, 'though the governor has made as strict a search after them as is possible.' Anselmo asked no more questions, but, after they had taken their leaves of each other, the traveller left him and pursued his journey.

This mournful news so affected the unfortunate Anselmo, that he was struck with death almost that very moment; getting therefore on his horse, as well as he could, he arrived at his friend's house. He knew nothing yet of his disgrace; but seeing him so pale and melancholy, concluded that some great misfortune had befallen him. Anselmo desired to be immediately led to his chamber, and furnished with pen, ink, and paper, and to be left alone with his door locked: when, finding that his end approached, he resolved to leave in writing the cause of his sudden and unexpected death. Taking therefore the pen, he began to write; but unable to finish what he designed, he died a martyr to his impertinent curiosity. The gentleman, finding he did not call, and that it grew late, resolved to enter his chamber, and see whether his friend was better or worse; he found him half out of bed, lying on his face, with the pen in his hand, and a paper open before him. Seeing him in this posture he drew near him, called and moved him, but soon found he was dead; which made him call his servants to behold the unhappy event, and then took up the paper, which he saw was written in Anselmo's own hand, and was to this effect.

'A foolish and impertinent desire has robbed me of life. If Camilla hear of my death let her know that I forgive her; for she was not obliged to do miracles, nor was there any reason I should have desired or expected it, and since I contrived my own dishonour, there is no cause. Thus far Anselmo wrote, but life would not hold out till he could give the reasons he designed. The next day the gentleman of the house sent word of Anselmo's death to his relations, who already knew his misfortunes, as well as the nunnery whither Camilla was retired. She herself was indeed very near that death which her husband had passed, though not for the loss of him, but Lothario, of which she had lately heard a flying report. But though she was a widow now, she would neither take the veil nor leave the nunnery, till, in a few days the news was confirmed of his being slain in a battle betwixt Monsieur de Lautrec, and that great General Gonzalo Fernandez de Cordova, in the kingdom of Naples. This was the end of the offending, and too late penitent friend; the news of which made Camilla immediately profess herself, and soon after, overwhelmed with grief and melancholy, pay for her transgression with the loss of her life. This was the unhappy end of them all, proceeding from so impertinent a beginning.

'I like this novel well enough,' said the curate; 'yet, after all, I cannot persuade myself that there is anything of truth in it; and if it be purely invention, the author was in the wrong; for it is not to be imagined there could ever be a husband so foolish, as to venture on so dangerous an experiment. Had he made his husband and wife a gallant and a mistress, the fable had appeared more probable; but, as it is, it is next to impossible. However, I must confess, I have nothing to object against his manner of telling it.'

CHAPTER IX

Containing an account of many surprising accidents in the Inn

AT THE SAME TIME the innkeeper, who stood at the door, seeing company coming. 'More guests,' cried he, 'a brave jolly troop, on my word. If they stop here, we may sing "O be joyful." ' 'What are they?' said Cardenio. 'Four men,' said the host, 'on horseback, *à la Gineta*,* with black masks on their faces,† and armed with lances and targets; a lady too all in white, that rides single and masked; and two running footmen.' 'Are they near?' said the curate. 'Just at the door,' replied the innkeeper. Hearing this Dorothea veiled herself, and Cardenio had just time enough to step into the next room, where Don Quixote lay, when the strangers came into the yard. The four horsemen, who made a very genteel appearance, dismounted and went to help down the lady, whom one of them, taking in his arms, carried into the house; where he seated her in a chair by the chamber-door, into which Cardenio had withdrawn. All this was done without discovering their faces, or speaking a word; only the lady, as she sat down in the chair, breathed out a deep sigh, and let her arms sink down in a weak and fainting posture. The curate, marking their odd behaviour, which raised in him a curiosity to know who they were, went to their servants in the stable, and asked what their masters were?' Indeed, sir,'‡ said one of them, 'that is more than we can tell you; they seem of no mean quality, especially that gentleman who carried the lady into the house, for the rest pay him great respect, and his word is a law to them.' 'Who is the lady?' said the curate. 'We know no more of her than the rest,' answered the fellow, 'for we could never see her face all the time, and it is impossible we should know her or them any otherwise. They picked us up on the road, my comrade and myself, and prevailed with us to wait on them to Andalusia, promising to pay us well for our trouble; so that, bating the two days travelling in their company, they are utter strangers to us.' 'Could you not hear them name one another all this time?' asked the curate. 'No, truly, sir,' answered the footman, 'for we heard them not speak a syllable all the way: the poor lady, indeed, used to

---

* A kind of riding with short stirrups which the Spaniards took from the Arabians.

† *Antifaz*: a piece of thin black silk, which the Spaniards wear before their faces in travelling to keep off the dust and sun.

‡ It is in the original *par diez* (i.e., by ten) instead of *par Dios* (i.e., by G—d) thinking to cheat the Devil of an oath, as when we say, y-cod for by G—d.

sigh and grieve so piteously, that we are persuaded she has no stomach to this journey. Whatever may be the cause we know not; by her garb she seems to be a nun, but, by her grief and melancholy, one might guess they are going to make her one, when perhaps the poor girl has not a bit of nun's flesh about her.' 'Very likely,' said the curate; and with that leaving them, he returned to the place where he left Dorothea, who, hearing the masked lady sigh so frequently, moved by the natural pity of the soft sex, could not forbear inquiring the cause of her sorrow. 'Pardon me, madam,' said she, 'if I beg to know your grief; and assure yourself, that my request does not proceed from mere curiosity, but an earnest inclination to serve and assist you, if your misfortune be any such as our sex is naturally subject to, and in the power of a woman to cure.' The melancholy lady made no return to her compliment, and Dorothea pressed her in vain with new reasons, when the gentleman, whom the foot-boy signified to be the chief of the company, interposed: 'Madam,' said he, 'do not trouble yourself to throw away any generous offer on that ungrateful woman, whose nature cannot return an obligation; neither expect any answer to your demands, for her tongue is a stranger to truth.' 'Sir,' said the disconsolate lady, 'my truth and honour have made me thus miserable, and my sufferings are sufficient to prove you the falsest and most base of men.' Cardenio, being only parted from the company by Don Quixote's chamber-door, overheard these last words very distinctly; and immediately cried out, 'Good Heaven, what do I hear! What voice struck my ear just now?' The lady, startled at his exclamation, sprung from the chair, and would have bolted into the chamber whence the voice came; but the gentleman, perceiving it, laid hold on her, to prevent her, which so disordered the lady that her mask fell off, and discovered an incomparable face, beautiful as an angel's, though very pale and strangely discomposed, her eyes eagerly rolling on every side, which made her appear distracted. Dorothea and the rest, not guessing what her eyes sought by their violent motion, beheld her with grief and wonder. She struggled so hard, and the gentleman was so disordered by beholding her, that his mask dropped off too, and discovered to Dorothea, who was assisting to hold the lady, the face of her husband Don Ferdinand: scarce had she known him, when with a long and dismal 'Oh!' she fell in a swoon, and would have reached the floor with all her weight, had not the barber, by good fortune, stood behind and supported her. The curate ran presently to help her, and pulling off her veil to throw water in her face, Don Ferdinand presently knew her, and was struck almost as dead as she at the sight; nevertheless, he did not quit Lucinda, who was the lady that struggled so hard to get out of his hands Cardenio, hearing Dorothea's exclamation, and imagining it to be Lucinda's voice, flew into the chamber in great disorder, and the first object he met was Don Ferdinand holding Lucinda, who presently knew him. They were all struck dumb with amazement: Dorothea gazed on Don Ferdinand; Don Ferdinand on Cardenio; and Cardenio and Lucinda on one another. At last Lucinda broke silence, and, addressing Don Ferdinand, 'Let me go,' said she; 'unloose your hold, my lord: by the generosity you should have, or by your inhumanity, since it must be so, I conjure you, leave me, that I may cling like ivy to my old support; and from whom neither your threats, nor prayers, nor gifts, nor promises, could ever alienate my love. Contend not against Heaven, whose power alone could bring me to my dear husband's sight, by such strange and unexpected means: you have a thousand instances to convince you that nothing but death can make me ever forget him: let this, at least, turn your love into rage, which may prompt you to end my miseries with my life, here before my dear husband, where I shall be proud to lose it, since my death may convince him of my unshaken love and honour, till the last minute of my life.' Dorothea, by this time, had recovered, and finding by Lucinda's discourse who she was, and that Don Ferdinand would not unhand her, she made a virtue of necessity, and falling at his feet, 'My lord,' cried she, all bathed in tears, 'if that beauty which you hold in your arms has not altogether dazzled your eyes, you may behold at your feet the once happy, but now miserable Dorothea. I am the poor and humble villager, whom your generous bounty, I dare not say your love, did condescend to raise to the honour of calling you her own: I am she, who once, confined to peaceful innocence, led a contented life, till your importunity, your show of honour, and deluding words, charmed me from my retreat, and made me resign my freedom to your power. How I am recompensed, may be guessed by my grief, and my being found here in this strange place, whither I was led not through any dishonourable ends, but purely by despair and grief to be forsaken of you. It was at your desire I was bound to you by the strictest tie, and whatever you do, you can never cease to be mine. Consider, my dear lord, that my matchless love may balance the beauty and nobility of the person for whom you would forsake me; she cannot share your love, for it is only mine; and Cardenio's interest in her will not admit a partner. It is easier far, my lord, to recall your wandering desires, and fix them upon her that adores you, than to draw her to love who hates you. Remember how you did solicit my humble state, and, conscious of my meanness, you paid a veneration to my innocence, which, joined with the honourable condition of my yielding to your desires, pronounce me free from ill design or dishonour. Consider these undeniable truths: have some regard to your honour! Remember you are a Christian! Why should you then make her life end so miserably, whose beginning your favour made so happy? If I must not expect the usage and respect of a wife, let me but serve you as a slave; so I belong to you, though in the meanest rank, I never shall complain: let me not be exposed to the slandering reflections of the censorius world by so cruel a separation from my lord: afflict not the declining years of my poor parents, whose faithful services to you and yours have merited a more suitable return. If you imagine the current of your noble blood should be defiled by mixing with mine, consider how many noble houses have run in such a channel; besides, the woman's side is not essentially requisite to ennoble descent: but chiefly think on this, that virtue is the truest nobility; which, if you stain by basely wronging me, you bring a greater blot upon your family than marrying me could cause. In fine, my lord, you cannot, must not disown me for your wife: to attest which truth I call your own words, which must be true if you prize yourself for honour, and that nobility whose want you so despise in me; witness your oaths and vows, witness that Heaven which you so often invoked to ratify your promises; and, if all these should fail, I make my last appeal to your own conscience, whose sting will always represent my wrongs fresh to your thoughts, and disturb your joys amidst your greatest pleasures.'

These, with many such arguments, did the mournful Dorothea urge, appearing so lovely in her sorrow, that Don Ferdinand's friends, as well as all the rest, sympathised with her, Lucinda particularly, as much admiring her wit and beauty, as moved by the tears, the piercing sighs, and moans that followed her entreaties; and she would have gone nearer to have comforted her, had not Ferdinand's arms, that still held her, prevented it. He stood full of confusion, with his eyes fixed attentively on Dorothea a great while; at last, opening his arms, he quitted Lucinda. 'Thou hast conquered,' cried he, 'charming Dorothea, thou hast conquered me; it is impossible to resist so many united truths and charms.' Lucinda was still so disordered and weak, that she would have fallen when Ferdinand quitted her, had not Cardenio, without regard to his safety, leaped forward and caught her in his arms, and embracing her with eagerness and joy; 'Thanks, gracious Heaven,' cried he aloud, 'my dear, my faithful wife, thy sorrows now are ended; for where can you rest more safe than in my arms, which now support thee, as once they did when my blessed fortune first made thee mine?' Lucinda, then opening her eyes, and finding herself in the arms of her Cardenio, without regard to ceremony or decency, threw her arms about his neck, and laying her face to his, 'Yes,' said she, 'thou art he, thou art my lord indeed! It is even you yourself, the right owner of this poor harrassed captive. Now fortune act thy worst, nor fears nor threats shall ever part me from the sole support and comfort of my life.' This sight was very surprising to Don Ferdinand and the other spectators. Dorothea perceiving, by Don Ferdinand's change of countenance and laying his hand to his sword, that he prepared to assault Cardenio, fell suddenly on her knees; and, with an endearing embrace, held Don Ferdinand's legs so fast, that he could not stir. 'What means,' cried she, all in tears, 'the only refuge of my hope? See here thy own and dearest wife at thy feet, and her you would enjoy in her true husband's arms. Think then, my lord, how unjust is your attempt, to dissolve that knot which Heaven has tied so fast. Can you ever think or hope success in your design on her, who, contemning all dangers, and confirmed in strictest constancy and honour, before your face lies bathed in tears of joy and passion in her true lover's bosom? For Heaven's sake I entreat you, by your own words I conjure you, to mitigate your anger, and permit that faithful pair to consummate their joys, and spend their remaining days in peace: thus may you make it appear that you are generous and truly noble, giving the world so strong a proof that you have your reason at command, and your passion in subjection.' All this while Cardenio, though he still held Lucinda in his arms, had a watchful eye on Don Ferdinand; resolving, if he had made the least offer to his prejudice, to make him repent it, and all his party, if possible, though at the expense of his life. But Don Ferdinand's friends, the curate, the barber, and all the company (not forgetting honest Sancho Pança) got together about Don Ferdinand, and entreated him to pity the beautiful Dorothea's tears; that, considering what she had said, the truth of which was apparent, it would be the highest injustice to frustrate her lawful hopes; that their strange and wonderful meeting could not be attributed to chance, but the peculiar and directing Providence of Heaven; that nothing (as Mr. Curate very well urged) but death could part Cardenio from Lucinda; and that though the edge of his sword might separate them, he would make them happier by death than he could hope to be by surviving; that, in irrecoverable accidents, a submission to fate, and a resignation of our wills, showed not only the greatest prudence, but also the highest courage and generosity; that he should not envy those happy lovers what the bounty of Heaven had conferred on them, but that he should turn his eyes on Dorothea's grief; view her incomparable beauty, which, with her true and unfeigned love, made large amends for the meanness of her parentage; but principally it lay upon him, if he gloried in the titles of Nobility and Christianity, to keep his promise unviolated; that the more reasonable part of mankind could not otherwise be satisfied, or have any esteem for him: also that it was the special prerogative of beauty, if heightened by virtue and adorned with modesty, to lay claim to any dignity, without disparagement or scandal to the person that raises it; and that the strong dictates of delight having been once indulged, we are not to be blamed for following them afterwards, provided they be not unlawful. In short, to these reasons they added so many enforcing arguments, that Don Ferdinand, who was truly a gentleman, could no longer resist reason, but stooped down; and, embracing Dorothea, 'Rise, madam,' said he, 'it is not proper that she should lie prostrate at my feet, who triumphs over my soul: if I have not hitherto paid you all the respect I ought, it was perhaps so ordered by

Heaven, that having by this a stronger conviction of your constancy and goodness, I may henceforth set the greater value on your merit: let the future respects and services I shall pay you, plead a pardon for my past transgressions; and let the violent passions of my love, that first made me yours, be an excuse for that which caused me to forsake you. View the now happy Lucinda's eyes, and there read a thousand further excuses; but I promise henceforth never to disturb her quiet; and may she live long and contented with her dear Cardenio, as I hope to do with my dearest Dorothea.' Thus concluding, he embraced her again so lovingly, that it was with no small difficulty that he kept in his tears, which he endeavoured to conceal, being ashamed to discover so effeminate a proof of his remorse.

Cardenio, Lucinda, and the greatest part of the company, could not so well command their passions, but all wept for joy; even Sancho Pança himself shed tears, though, as he afterwards confessed, it was not for downright grief, but because he found not Dorothea to be the queen of Micomicona, as he supposed, and of whom he expected so many favours and preferments. Cardenio and Lucinda fell at Don Ferdinand's feet, giving him thanks, with the strongest expressions which gratitude could suggest: he raised them up, and received their acknowledgments with much modesty; then begged to be informed by Dorothea how she came to that place. She related to him all she had told Cardenio, but with such a grace, that what were misfortunes to her, proved an inexpressible pleasure to those that heard her relation. When she had done, Don Ferdinand told all that had befallen him in the city, after he found the paper in Lucinda's bosom, which declared Cardenio to be her husband; how he would have killed her, had not her parents prevented him i how afterwards, mad with shame and anger, he left the city, to wait a more commodious opportunity of revenge; how in a short time he learned that Lucinda was fled to a nunnery, resolving to end her days there, if she could not spend them with Cardenio; that, having desired those three gentlemen to go with him, they went to the nunnery, and waiting till they found the gate open, he left two of the gentlemen to secure the door, while he with the other entered the house, where they found Lucinda talking with a nun in the cloister; they forcibly brought her thence to a village, where they disguised themselves for their more convenient flight, which they more easily brought about, the nunnery being situate in the fields, distant a good way from any town. He likewise added, how Lucinda, finding herself in his power, fell into a swoon, and that, after she came to herself, she continually wept and sighed, but would not speak a syllable; and that, accompanied with silence only and tears, they had travelled till they came to that inn, which proved to him as his arrival at heaven, having put a happy conclusion to all his earthly misfortunes.

CHAPTER X

The History of the famous Princess Micomicona continued, with other pleasant Adventures

THE JOY of the whole company was unspeakable by the happy conclusion of this perplexed business; Dorothea, Cardenio, and Lucinda, thought the sudden change of their affairs too surprising to be real; and, through a disuse of good fortune, could hardly be induced to believe their happiness. Don Ferdinand thanked Heaven a thousand times for its propitious conduct, in leading him out of a labyrinth, in which his honour and virtue were like to have been lost. The curate, as he was very instrumental in the general reconciliation, had likewise no small share in the general joy; and that no discontent might sour their universal satisfaction, Cardenio and the curate engaged to see the hostess satisfied for all the damages committed by Don Quixote: only poor Sancho drooped pitifully; he found his lordship and his hopes vanished into smoke, the Princess Micomicona was changed to Dorothea, and the giant to Don Ferdinand; thus, very musty and melancholy, he slipped into his master's chamber, who had slept on, and was just wakened, little thinking of what had happened.

'I hope your early rising will do you no hurt,' said he, 'Sir Knight of the Woeful Figure; but you may now sleep on till doom's-day, if you will; nor need you trouble your head any longer about killing any giant, or restoring the princess, for all that is done to your hand.' 'That is more than probable,' answered the Knight, 'for I have had the most extraordinary the most prodigious and bloody battle with the giant, that I ever had, or shall have during the whole course of my life; yet, with one cross stroke, I laid his head thwack on the ground, whence the great effusion of blood seemed like a violent stream of water.' 'Of wine, you mean,' said Sancho, 'for you must know (if you know it not already) that your worship's dead giant is a broached wine-skin, and the blood some thirty gallons of tent, which it held in its belly, and your head so cleverly struck off, is the whore my mother; and so the Devil take both giant and head, and altogether, for Sancho.' 'What sayest thou, madman?' said the Don: 'Thou art frantic sure.' 'Rise, rise, sir,' said Sancho, 'and see what fine work you have cut out for yourself: here is the devil-and-all to pay for, and your great queen is changed into a private gentlewoman, called Dorothea, with some other such odd matters, that you will wonder with a vengeance.' 'I can wonder at nothing here,' said Don Quixote, 'where you may remember, I told you all things ruled by enchantment.' 'I believe it,' quoth Sancho, 'had my tossing in a blanket been of that kind; but sure it was the likest the tossing in a blanket of anything I ever knew in my life. And this same innkeeper, I remember very well, was one of those that tossed me into the air, and as cleverly and heartily he did it as a man could wish I will say that for him; so that after all I begin to smell a rat, and do perilously suspect, that all our enchantment will end in nothing but bruises and broken bones.' 'Heaven will retrieve all,' said the Knight: 'I will therefore dress, and march to the discovery of these wonderful transformations.' While Sancho made him ready, the curate gave Don Ferdinand and the rest an account of Don Quixote's madness, and of the device he used to draw him from the Poor Rock, to which the supposed disdain of his mistress had banished him in imagination. Sancho's adventures made also a part in the story, which proved very diverting to the strangers. He added, that since Dorothea's change of fortune had prevented their design that way, some other trick should be found to decoy him home: Cardenio offered his service in the affair, and that Lucinda should personate Dorothea: 'No, no,' answered Don Ferdinand, 'Dorothea shall humour the jest still, if this honest gentleman's habitation he not very far off.' 'Only two days' journey,' said the curate. 'I would ride twice as far,' said Don Ferdinand, 'for the pleasure of so good and charitable an action.' By this Don Quixote had sallied out, armed *cap-à-pie*, Mambrino's helmet (with a great hole in it) on his head; his shield on his left arm, and with his right he leaned on his lance. His meagre, yellow, weather-beaten face, of half a league in length,* the unaccountable medley of his armour, together with his grave and solemn port, struck Don Ferdinand and his companions dumb with admiration, while the champion, casting his eyes on Dorothea with great gravity and solidity, broke silence with these words:

'I am informed by this my squire, beautiful lady, that your greatness is annihilated, and your majesty reduced to nothing, for of a queen and mighty princess, as you used to be, you are become a private damsel. If any express order from the necromantic king your father (doubting the ability and success of my arm in the reinstating you) has occasioned this change, I must tell him that he is no conjuror in these matters, and does not know one half of his trade;† nor is he skilled in the revolutions of chivalry; for had he been conversant in the study of knight-errantry, as I have been, he

---

* Though Don Quixote was very long-visaged, yet to say his face was half a league in length, is a most extravagant hyperbole even for a Spaniard to make, but yet Cervantes does actually say it: *Fernando viendo su rostro de media legua de andadura.* Stevens is egregiously mistaken here; he says, 'Fernando seeing his countenance half a league off.'

† Literally, one half of the Mass, the saying of which is one great part of the priestly office.

might have found that, in every age, champions of less fame than Don Quixote de la Mancha have finished more desperate adventures; since the killing of a pitiful giant, how arrogant soever he may be, is no such great achievement; for, not many hours past, I encountered one myself: the success I will not mention, lest the incredulity of some people might distrust the reality; but time, the discoverer of all things, will disclose it when least expected.' 'Hold there,' said the host, 'it was with two wine-skins, but no giant that you fought.' Don Ferdinand silenced the inn-keeper, and bid him by no means interrupt Don Quixote, who thus went on: 'To conclude, most high and disinherited lady, if your father, for the causes already mentioned, has caused this metamorphosis in your person, believe him not; for there is no peril on earth, through which my sword shall not open a way; and assure yourself, that in a few days, by the overthrow of your enemy's head, it shall fix on yours that crown which is your lawful inheritance.' Here Don Quixote stopped, waiting the princess's answer. She, assured of Don Ferdinand's consent to carry on the jest, till Don Quixote was got home, and assuming a face of gravity, 'Whosoever,' answered she, 'has informed you, valorous Knight of the Woeful Figure, that I have altered or changed my condition, has imposed upon you; for I am just the same today as yesterday: it is true some unexpected, but fortunate accidents, have varied some circumstances of my fortune, much to my vantage, and far beyond my hopes; but I am neither changed in my person, nor altered in my resolution of employing the force of your redoubtable and invincible arm in my favour. I therefore apply myself to your usual generosity, to have these words spoken to my father's dishonour recalled, and believe these easy and infallible means to redress my wrongs, the pure effects of his wisdom and policy, as the good fortune I now enjoy has been the consequence of your surprising deeds, as this noble presence can testify. What should hinder us then from setting forward tomorrow morning, depending for a happy and successful conclusion on the will of Heaven, and the power of your unparalleled courage?'

The ingenious Dorothea having concluded, Don Quixote, turning to Sancho with all the signs of fury imaginable: 'Now must I tell thee, poor paltry hang-dog,' said he, 'thou art the veriest rascal in all Spain. Tell me, rogue, scoundrel, did not you just now inform me, that this princess was changed into a little private damsel, called Dorothea, and the head which I lopped from the giant's shoulders, was the whore your mother, with a thousand other absurdities? Now, by all the powers of Heaven,' looking up, and grinding his teeth together, 'I have a mind so to use thee, as to make thee appear a miserable example to all succeeding squires, that shall dare to tell a knight-errant a lie.' 'Good your worship,' cried Sancho, 'have patience, I beseech you: mayhap I am mistaken or so, about my lady princess Micomicona's concern there; but that the giant's head came off the wine-skins' shoulders, and that the blood was as good tent as ever was tipped over tongue, I will take my corporal oath on it. Gadzookers, sir, are not the skins all hacked and slashed within there, at your bed's head, and the wine all in a puddle in your chamber? But you will guess at the meat presently, by the sauce; the proof of the pudding is in the eating, master; * and if my landlord here do not let you know it to your cost, he is a very honest and civil fellow, that is all.' 'Sancho,' said the Don, 'I pronounce thee *non compos:* I therefore pardon thee and have done.' 'It is enough,' said Don Ferdinand, 'we, therefore, in pursuance of the Princess's orders, will this night refresh ourselves, and tomorrow we will all of us set out to attend the Lord Don Quixote, in prosecution of this important enterprise he has undertaken, being all impatient to be eye-witnesses of his celebrated and matchless courage.' 'I shall be proud of the honour of serving and waiting upon you, my good lord,' replied Don Quixote, 'and reckon myself infinitely obliged by the favour and good opinion of so honourable a company; which I shall endeavour to improve and confirm, though at the expense of the last drop of my blood.'

Many other compliments had passed between Don Quixote and Don Ferdinand, when the arrival of a stranger interrupted them. His dress represented him a Christian newly returned from Barbary: he was clad in a short-skirted coat of blue cloth with short sleeves, and no collar, his breeches were of blue linen, with a cap of the same colour, a pair of date-coloured stockings, and a Turkish scimitar hung by a scarf, in manner of a shoulder-belt. There rode a woman in his company, clad in a Moorish dress; her face was covered with a veil; she had on a little cap of gold tissue, and a Turkish mantle that reached from her shoulders to her feet. The man was well shaped and strong, his age about forty, his face somewhat tanned, his moustachios long, and his beard handsome: in short, his genteel mien and person were too distinguishable to let the gentleman be hid by the meanness of his habit. He called presently for a room, and being answered that all were full, seemed a little troubled: however, he went to the woman who came along with him, and took her down from her ass. The ladies, being all surprised at the oddness of the Moorish dress, had the curiosity to flock about the stranger; and Dorothea, very discreetly imagining that both she and her conductor were tired, took it ill that they could not have a chamber. 'I hope, madam, you will bear your ill fortune patiently,' said she, 'for want of room is an inconvenience incident to all public inns: but if you please, madam, to take up with us,' pointing to Lucinda, 'you may, perhaps, find that you have met with worse entertainment on the road, than what this place affords.' The

* The original runs, it will be seen in the frying of the eggs.

unknown lady made her no answer, but rising up, laid her hands across her breast, bowed her head, and inclined her body, as a sign that she acknowledged the favour. By her silence they conjectured her to be undoubtedly a Moor, and that she could not speak Spanish. Her companion was now come back from the stable, and told them, 'Ladies, I hope you will excuse this gentlewoman from answering any questions, for she is very much a stranger to our language.' 'We are only, sir,' answered Lucinda, 'making her an offer which civility obliges us to make all strangers, especially of our own sex, that she would make us happy in her company all night, and fare as we do; we will make very much of her, sir, and she shall want for nothing that the house affords.' 'I return you humble thanks, dear madam,' answered the stranger, 'in the lady's behalf and my own; and I infinitely prize the favour, which the present exigence and the worth of the donors make doubly engaging.' 'Is the lady, pray sir, a Christian or a Moor?' asked Dorothea. 'Our charity would make us hope she were the former; but, by her attire and silence, we are afraid she is the latter.' 'Outwardly, madam,' answers he, 'she appears and is a Moor, but in her heart a zealous Christian, which her longing desires of being baptised have expressly testified. I have had no opportunity of having her christened since she left Algiers, which was her habitation and native country; nor has any imminent danger of death as yet obliged her to be brought to the font, before she be better instructed in the principles of our religion; but I hope, by Heaven's assistance, to have her shortly baptised with all the decency suiting her quality, which is much above what her equipage or mine seem to promise.'

These words raised in them all a curiosity to be further informed who the Moor and her conductor were; but they thought it improper then to put them upon any more particular relation of their fortunes, because they wanted rest and refreshment after their journey. Dorothea, placing the lady by her, begged her to take off her veil. She looked on her companion, as if she required him to let her know what she said; which, when he had let her understand in the Arabian tongue, joining his own request also, she discovered so charming a face, that Dorothea imagined her more beautiful than Lucinda; she, on the other hand, fancied her handsomer than Dorothea; and most of the company believed her more beautiful than both of them. As beauty has always a prerogative, or rather charm to attract men's inclinations, the whole company dedicated their desires to serve the lovely Moor. Don Ferdinand asked the stranger her name. He answered, 'Lela Zoraida.' She, hearing him, and guessing what they asked, suddenly replied with great concern, though very gracefully, 'No, not Zoraida, Maria, Maria': giving them to understand, that her name was Maria, and not Zoraida. These words, spoken with so much eagerness, raised a concern in everybody, the ladies especially, whose natural tenderness showed itself by their tears; and, Lucinda embracing her very lovingly, 'Ay, ay,' said she, 'Maria, Maria,' which words the Moorish lady repeated by way of answer. 'Zoraida Macange,' added she; as much as to say, not Zoraida but Maria, Maria. The night coming on, and the innkeeper, by order of Don Ferdinand's friends, having made haste to provide them the best supper he could, the cloth was laid on a long table, there being neither round or square in the house. Don Quixote, after much ceremony, was prevailed upon to sit at the head; he desired the lady Micomicona to sit next to him; and the rest of the company having placed themselves according to their rank and convenience, they ate their supper very heartily. Don Quixote, to raise the diversion, never minded his meat, but, inspired with the same spirit that moved him to preach so much to the goatherds, he began to hold forth in this manner: 'Certainly, gentlemen, if we rightly consider it, those who make knight-errantry their profession, often meet with most surprising and stupendous adventures. For what mortal in the world, at this time entering within this castle, and seeing us sit together as we do, will imagine and believe us to be the same persons which in reality we are? Who is there that can judge that this lady by my side is the great queen we all know her to be, and that I am that Knight of the Woeful Figure, so universally made known by fame? It is then no longer to be doubted, but that this exercise and profession surpasses all others that have been invented by man, and is so much the more honourable, as it is more exposed to dangers. Let none presume to tell me that the pen is preferable to the sword; for be they who they will, I shall tell them they know not what they say; for the reason they give, and on which chiefly they rely, is, that the labour of the mind exceeds that of the body, and that the exercise of arms depends only on the body, as if the use of them were the business of porters, which requires nothing but much strength: or, as if this, which we who profess it call chivalry, did not include the acts of fortitude which depend very much upon the understanding. Or else, as if that warrior, who commands an army or defends a city besieged, did not labour as much with the mind as with the body. If this be not so, let experience teach us whether it be possible by bodily strength to discover or guess the intentions of an enemy. The forming designs, laying of stratagems, overcoming of difficulties, and shunning of dangers, are all works of the understanding, wherein the body has no share. It being therefore evident that the exercise of arms requires the help of the mind as well as learning, let us see in the next place, whether the scholar or the soldier's mind undergoes the greatest labour. Now this may be the better known by regarding the end and object each of them aims at; for that intention is to be most valued which makes the noblest end its object. The scope and end of learning, I mean human learning (in this place I speak not of Divinity, whose aim is to guide souls to heaven, for no other can equal a design so infinite as that), is to give a perfection to distributive justice, bestowing upon every one his due, and to procure and cause good laws to be observed; an end really generous, great, and worthy of high commendation; but yet not equal to that which knight-errantry tends to, whose object and end is peace, which is the greatest blessing man can wish for in this life. And, therefore, the first good news the world received, was that the angels brought in the night, which was the beginning of our day, when they sung in the air "Glory to God on high, peace upon earth, and to men good-will." And the only manner of salutation taught by the best Master in heaven, or upon earth, to his friends and favourites, was, that entering any house they should say, "Peace be to this house," and at other times He said to them, "My peace I give to you, My peace I leave to you, peace be among you." A jewel and legacy worthy of such a donor, a jewel so precious, that without it there can be no happiness either in earth or heaven. This peace is the true end of war; for arms and war are one and the same thing. Allowing then this truth, that the end of war is peace, and that in this it excels the end of learning, let us now weigh the bodily labours the scholar undergoes, against those the warrior suffers, and then see which are greatest.' The method and language Don Quixote used in delivering himself were such that none of his hearers at that time looked upon him as a madman. But, on the contrary, most of them being gentlemen to whom the use of arms properly appertains, they gave him a willing attention. And he proceeded in this manner: 'These, then, I say, are the sufferings and hardships a scholar endures; first, poverty (not that they are all poor, but to urge the worst that may be in this case), and having said he endures poverty, methinks nothing more need be urged to express his misery; for he that is poor enjoys no happiness, but labours under this poverty in all its parts, at one time in hunger, at another in cold, another in nakedness, and sometimes in all of them together, yet his poverty is not so great, but still he eats, though it be later than the usual hour, and of the scraps of the rich, or, which is the greatest of a scholar's misfortunes, what is called among them, 'going a sopping;'* neither can the scholar miss of some-body's stove or fire-side to sit by, where, though he be not thoroughly heated, yet he may gather warmth, and at last sleep away the night under a roof. I will not touch upon other less material circumstances, as the want of linen, and scarcity of shoes, thinness and bareness of their clothes, and their surfeiting when good fortune throws a feast in their way. This is the difficult and uncouth path they tread, often stumbling and falling, yet rising again and pushing on, till they attain the preferment they aim at; whither being arrived, we have seen many of them, who, having been

---

* The author means the sops in porridge, given at the doors of monasteries.

carried by a fortunate gale through all these quicksands, from a chair govern the world; their hunger being changed into satiety, their cold into comfortable warmth, their nakedness into magnificence of apparel, and the mat they used to lie upon into stately beds of costly silks and softest linen; a reward due to their virtue. But yet their sufferings, being compared to those the soldier endures, appear much inferior, as I shall in the next place make out.'

CHAPTER XI

A continuation of Don Quixote's curious Discourse on Arms and Learning

'SINCE SPEAKING OF THE SCHOLAR, we began with his poverty and its several parts,' continued Don Quixote, 'let us now observe whether the soldier be anything richer than he; and we shall find that poverty itself is not poorer; for he depends on his miserable pay, which he receives but seldom, or perhaps never; or else in that he makes by marauding, with the hazard of his life, and trouble of his conscience. Such is sometimes his want of apparel, that a slashed buff coat is all his holiday raiment and shirt; and in the depth of winter being in the open field, he has nothing to cherish him against the sharpness of the season, but the breath of his mouth, which, issuing from an empty place, I am persuaded is itself cold, though contrary to the rules of nature. But now see how he expects night to make amends for all these hardships in the bed prepared for him, which, unless it be his own fault, never proves too narrow; for he may freely lay out as much of the ground as he pleases, and tumble to his content, without danger of losing the sheets. But, above all, when the day shall come, wherein he is to put in practice the exercise of his profession, and strive to gain some new degree; when the day of battle shall come, then, as a mark of his honour, shall his head be dignified with a cap made of lint, to stop a hole made by a bullet, or be perhaps carried off maimed, at the expense of a leg or an arm. And if this do not happen, but that merciful Heaven preserve his life and limbs, it may fall out that he shall remain as poor as before, and must run through many encounters and battles, nay, always come off victorious, to obtain some little preferment; and these miracles too are rare: but, I pray, tell me gentlemen, if ever you made it your observation, how few are those who obtain due rewards in war in comparison of those numbers that perish? Doubtless you will answer, that there is no parity between them; that the dead cannot be reckoned up, whereas, those who live and are rewarded may be numbered

with three figures.* It is quite otherwise with scholars, not only those who
follow the law, but others also, who all either by hook or by crook get a
livelihood; so that though the soldier's sufferings be much greater, yet his
reward is much less. To this it may be answered, that it is easier to reward
two thousand scholars than thirty thousand soldiers, because the former
are recompensed at the expense of the public, by giving them employments,
which of necessity must be allowed on those of their profession, but the
latter cannot be gratified otherwise than at the cost of the master that
employs them; yet this very difficulty makes good my argument. But let us
lay this matter aside, as a point difficult to be decided, and let us return to
the preference due to arms above learning, a subject as yet in debate, each
party bringing strong reasons to make out their pretensions. Among
others learning urges, that without it warfare itself could not subsist;
because war, as other things, has its laws, and is governed by them, and
laws are the province of learning and scholars. To this objection the
soldiers make answer, that without them the laws cannot be maintained,
for it is by arms that commonwealths are defended, kingdoms supported,
cities secured, the highway made safe, and the sea delivered from pirates.
In short, were it not for them, commonwealths, kingdoms, monarchies,
cities, the roads by land and the waters of the sea, would be subject to the
ravages and confusion that attends war while it lasts, and is at liberty to
make use of its unbounded power and prerogative Besides, it is past all
controversy, that what costs dearest, is, and ought to be, most valued.
Now for a man to attain to an eminent degree of learning costs him time,
watching, hunger, nakedness, dizziness in the head, weakness in the
stomach, and other inconveniences which are the consequences of these,
of which I have already in part made mention. But the rising gradually to
be a good soldier is purchased at the whole expense of all that is required
for learning, and that in so surpassing a degree, that there is no
comparison betwixt them; because he is every moment in danger of his
life. To what danger or distress can a scholar be reduced equal to that of a
soldier, who, being besieged in some strong place, and at his post or upon
guard in some ravelin or bastion, perceives the enemy carrying on a mine
under him, and yet must upon no account remove from thence, or shun
the danger which threatens him so near? All he can do, is, to give notice to
his commander, that he may countermine, but must himself stand still
fearing and expecting, when on a sudden he shall soar to the clouds
without wings, and be again cast down headlong against his will. If this
danger seem inconsiderable, let us see whether that be not greater when
two galleys shock one another with their prows in the midst of the
spacious sea. When they have thus grappled, and are clinging together,

* i.e., do not exceed hundreds.

the soldier is confined to the narrow beak, being a board not above two feet wide and yet though he sees before him so many ministers of death threatening, as there are pieces of cannon on the other side pointing against him, and not half a pike's length from his body; and being sensible that the first slip of his feet sends him to the bottom of Neptune's dominions; still, for all this, inspired by honour, with an undaunted heart, he stands a mark to so much fire, and endeavours to make his way, by that narrow passage, into the enemy's vessel. But what is most to be admired is, that no sooner one falls, where he shall never rise till the end of the world, than another steps into the same peace; and if he also drops into the sea, which lies in wait for him like an enemy, another, and after him another, still fills up the place, without suffering any interval of time to separate their deaths; a resolution and boldness scarce to be paralleled in any other trials of war. Blessed be those happy ages that were strangers to the dreadful fury of these devilish instruments of artillery, whose inventor I am satisfied is now in Hell, receiving the reward of his cursed invention, which is the cause that very often a cowardly base hand takes away the life of the bravest gentleman, and that in the midst of that vigour and resolution which animates and inflames the bold, a chance bullet (shot perhaps by one that fled, and was frightened at the very flash the mischievous piece gave when it went off) coming nobody knows how or from whence, in a moment puts a period to the brave designs and the life of one that deserved to have survived many years. This considered, I could almost say, I am sorry at my heart for having taken upon me this profession of a knight-errant, in so detestable an age; for though no danger daunts me, yet it affects me to think, whether powder and lead may not deprive me of the opportunity of becoming famous, and making myself known throughout the world by the strength of my arm, and dint of my sword. But let Heaven order matters as it pleases, for if I compass my designs, I shall be so much the more honoured by how much the dangers I have exposed myself to are greater than those the knights-errant of former ages underwent.' All this long preamble Don Quixote made whilst the company supped, never minding to eat a mouthful, though Sancho Pança had several times advised him to mind his meat, telling him there would be time enough afterwards to talk as he thought fit. Those who heard him were afresh moved with compassion, to see a man, who seemed in all other respects to have a sound judgment and clear understanding, so absolutely mad and distracted, when any mention was made of his cursed knight-errantry. The curate told him he was much in the right in all he had said for the honour of arms; and that he, though a scholar and a graduate, was of the same opinion. Supper being ended, and the cloth taken away; whilst the innkeeper, his wife, his daughter, and Maritornes fitted up Don Quixote's loft for the ladies, that they might lie by themselves that night, Don Ferdinand entreated the slave to give them an account of his life, conscious the relation could not choose but be very delightful and surprising, as might be guessed by his coming with Zoraida. The slave answered he would most willingly comply with their desires, and that he only feared the relation would not give them all the satisfaction he could wish; but that, however, rather than disobey, he would do it as well as be could. The curate and all the company thanked him, and made fresh instances to the same effect. Seeing himself courted by so many, 'There is no need of entreaties,' said he, 'for what you may command; therefore,' continued he, 'give me your attention, and you shall hear a true relation, perhaps not to be paralleled by those fabulous stories which are composed with much art and study.' This caused all the company to seat themselves, and observe a very strict silence; and then, with an agreeable and sedate voice, he began in this manner:

CHAPTER XII

Where the Captive relates his Life and Adventures

'IN THE MOUNTAINS of Leon my family had its first original, and was more kindly dealt withal by nature than by fortune, though my father might pass for rich among the inhabitants of those parts, who are but poorly provided for; to say truth, he had been so, had he had as much industry to preserve, as he had inclination to dissipate, his income; but he had been a soldier, and the years of his youth spent in that employment, had left him in his old age a propensity to spend under the name of Liberality. War is school where the covetous grow free, and the free prodigal: to see a soldier a miser is a kind of prodigy which happens but seldom. My father was far from being one of them; for he passed the bounds of liberality, and came very near the excesses of prodigality; a thing which cannot suit well with a married life, where the children ought to succeed to the estate as well as name of the family. We were three of us, all at man's estate; and my father, finding that the only way, as he said, to curb his squandering inclination, was to dispossess himself of that which maintained it, his estate (without which Alexander himself must have been put to it), he called us one day all three to him in his chamber, and spoke to us in the following manner:

' "My sons, to persuade you that I love you, I need only tell you I am your father, and you my children; and, on the other side, you have reason to think me unkind, considering how careless I am in preserving what should one day be yours; but to convince you, however, that I have the bowels of a parent, I have taken a resolution, which I have well weighed and considered for many days. You are all now of an age to choose the kind of life each of you incline to; or, at least, to enter upon some employment that may one day procure you both honour and profit: therefore I design to divide all I have into four parts, of which I will give three among you, and retain the fourth for myself to maintain me in my old age, as long as it shall please Heaven to continue me in this life. After that each of you shall have received his part, I could wish you would follow one of the employments I shall mention to you, every one as he finds himself inclined. There is a proverb in our tongue which I take to contain a great deal of truth, as generally those sorts of sayings do, being short sentences framed upon observation and long experience. This proverb runs thus, 'Either the church, the sea, or the court.' As if it should plainly say, that whosoever desires to thrive must follow one of these three; either be a churchman, or a merchant and try his fortune at sea, or enter into the service of his Prince in the court: for another proverb says, that 'King's chaff is better than other men's corn.' I say this, because I would have one of you follow his studies, another I desire should be a merchant, and the third should serve the King in war; because it is a thing of some difficulty to get an entrance at court; and though war does not immediately procure riches, yet it seldom fails of giving honour and reputation. Within eight days' time I will give each of you your portion, and not wrong you of a farthing of it, as you shall see by experience. Now, therefore, tell me if you are resolved to follow my advice about your settling in the world." And turning to me, as the eldest, he bid me answer first. I told him, that he ought not upon our account to divide or lessen his estate or way of living; that we were young men, and could shift in the world; and at last I concluded, that for my part I would be a soldier, and serve God and the king in that honourable profession. My second brother made the same regardful offer, and chose to go to the Indies; resolving to lay out in goods the share that should be given him here. The youngest, and I believe the wisest of us all, said he would be a churchman; and, in order to it, go to Salamanca, and there finish his studies. After this, my father embraced us all three, and in a few days performed what he had promised; and, as I remember, it was three thousand ducats a-piece, which he gave us in money; for we had an uncle who bought all the estate, and paid for it in ready money, that it might not go out of the family. A little after we all took leave of my father; and at parting I could not forbear thinking it a kind of inhumanity to leave the old gentleman in so straight a condition: I prevailed with him, therefore, to accept of two thousand of my three, the remainder being sufficient to make up a soldier's equipage. My example worked upon my other brothers, and they, each of them, presented him with a thousand ducats; so that my father remained with four thousand ducats in ready money, and three thousand more in land, which he chose to keep, and not sell outright. To be short, we took our last leave of my father and the uncle I have mentioned, not without much grief and tears on all sides. They particularly recommending to us to let them know, by all opportunities, our good or ill-fortunes; we promised so to do, and having received the blessing of our old father, one of us went straight to Salamanca, the other to Sevil, and I to Alicant, where I was informed of a Genoese ship, which was loading wood for Genoa.

'This year makes two-and-twenty since I first left my father's house, and in all that time, though I have written several letters, I have not had the least news, either of him, or of my brothers. And now I will relate, in a few words, my own adventures in all that course of years. I took shipping at Alicant, arrived safe and with a good passage at Genoa, from thence I went to Milan, where I bought my equipage, resolving to go and enter myself in the army of Piedmont; but being come as far as Alexandria de la Paille, I was informed that the great duke of Alva was passing into Flanders with an army; this made me alter my first resolution. I followed him, and was present at all his engagements, as well as at the deaths of the Counts Egmont and Horne; and at last I had a pair of colours under a famous captain of Guadalajara, whose name was Diego de Urbina. Some time after my arrival in Flanders, there came news of the league concluded by Pope Pius V of happy memory, in conjunction with Spain, against the common enemy the Turk, who at that time had taken the Island of Cyprus from the Venetians; which was an unfortunate and lamentable loss to Christendom. It was also certain that the General of this holy league was the most serene Don Juan of Austria, natural brother to our good King Don Philip. The great fame of the preparations for this war excited in me a vehement desire of being present at the engagement, which was expected to follow these preparations; and although I had certain assurance, and, as it were, an earnest of my being advanced to be a captain upon the first vacancy, yet I resolved to leave all those expectations and return, as I did, to Italy. My good fortune was such that I arrived just about the same time that Don Juan of Austria landed at Genoa, in order to go to Naples and join the Venetian fleet, as he did at Messina. In short, I was at that great action of the battle of Lepanto, being a captain of foot, to which post my good fortune, more than my desert, had now advanced me; and that day, which was so happy to all Christendom (because the world was then disabused of the error they had entertained, that the Turk was invincible at sea); that day I say, in which the pride of the Ottomans was first broke, and which was so happy to all Christians, even to those who died in the fight, who were more so than those who remained alive and conquerors, I alone was the unhappy man; since, instead of a naval crown, which I might have hoped for in the time of the Romans, I found myself that very night a slave, with irons on my feet, and manacles on my hands. The thing happened thus: Vehali, king of Algiers, a brave and bold pirate, having boarded and taken the Capitana galley of Malto, in which only three knights were left alive, and those desperately wounded, the galley of John Andrea Doria bore up to succour them: in this galley I was embarked with my company, and doing my duty on this occasion; I leaped into the enemy's galley, which getting loose from ours that intended to board the Algerine, my soldiers were hindered from following me, and I remained alone among a great number of enemies; whom not being able to resist; I was taken after having received several wounds; and as you have already heard, Vehali having escaped with all his squadron, I found myself his prisoner; and was the only afflicted man among so many joyful ones, and the only captive among so many free; for, on that day above 15,000 Christians, who rowed in the Turkish galleys, obtained their long-wished for liberty. I was carried to Constantinople, where the Grand Signor Selim, made Vehali, my master, general of the sea, he having behaved himself very well in the battle, and brought away with him the great flag of the order of Malta, as a proof of his valour.

'The second year of my captivity, I was a slave in the Capitana galley at Navarino; and I took notice of the Christians' fault, in letting slip the opportunity they had of taking the whole Turkish fleet in that port; and all the Janizaries and Algerine pirates did so expect to be attacked, that they had made all in readiness to escape on shore without fighting; so great was the terror they had of our fleet: but it pleased God to order it otherwise, not by any fault of the Christian General, but for the sins of Christendom, and because it is His will we should always have some enemies to chastise us. Vehali made his way to Modon, which is an island not far from Navarino, and there landing his men, fortified the entrance of the harbour, remaining in safety there till Don Juan was forced to return home with his fleet. In this expedition, the galley called "La Presa," of which Barbarossa's own son was captain, was taken by the admiral galley of Naples, called the "Wolf," which was commanded by that thunder-bolt of war, that father of the soldiers, that happy and never-conquered captain, Don Alvaro de Bacan, Marquis of Santa Cruz; and I cannot omit the manner of taking this galley. The son of Barbarossa was very cruel, and used his slaves with great inhumanity; they perceiving that the "Wolf" galley got of them in the chase, all of a sudden laid by their oars, and, seizing on their commander, as he was walking between them on the deck and calling to them to row hard, they passed him on, from hand to hand, to one another, from one end of the galley to the other, and gave him such blows in the handling him, that before he got back to the main-mast, his soul had left his body and was fled to hell. This, as I said, was the effect of his cruelty and their hatred.

'After this we returned to Constantinople; and the next year, which was 1573, news came that Don Juan of Austria had taken Tunis and its kingdom from the Turks, and given the possession of it to Muley Hamid, having thereby defeated all the hopes of reigning of Muley Hamida, one of the cruellest, and withal one of the bravest Moors in the world. The Grand Signor was troubled at this loss, and using his wonted artifices with the Christians, he struck up a peace with the Venetians, who were much more desirous than he of it.

'The year after, which was 1574 he attacked the Goletta, and the fort which Don Juan had begun, but not above half-finished, before Tunis. All this while I was a galley-slave, without any hopes of liberty; at least, I could not promise myself to obtain it by way of ransom; for I was resolved not to write my father the news of my misfortune. La Goletta* and the fort were both taken, after some resistance; the Turkish army consisting of 75,000 Turks in pay, and above 400,000 Moors and Arabs, out of all Africa near the sea; with such provisions for war of all kinds, and so many pioneers, that they might have covered the Goletta and the fort with earth by handfuls. The Goletta was first taken, though always before reputed impregnable; and it was not lost by any fault of its defenders, who did all that could be expected from them; but because it was found by experience, that it was practicable to make trenches in that sandy soil, which was thought to have water under it within two feet, but the Turks sunk above two yards and found none; by which means, filling sacks with sand, and laying them one on another, they raised them so high, that they overtopped and commanded the fort, in which none could be safe, nor show themselves upon the walls. It has been the opinion of most men, that we did ill to shut ourselves up in the Goletta; and that we ought to have been drawn out to hinder their landing; but they who say so, talk without experience, and at random of such things; for, if in all there were not above 7,000 men in the Goletta and the fort, how could so small a number, though never so brave, take the open field against such forces as those of the enemies? And how is it possible that a place can avoid being taken, which can have no relief, particularly being besieged by such numbers, and those in their own country? But it seemed to many others, and that is also my opinion, that God Almighty favoured Spain most particularly, in suffering that sink of iniquity and misery, as well as that spunge and perpetual drain of treasure to be destroyed. For infinite sums of money were spent there to no purpose, without any other design than to preserve the memory of one of the Emperor's (Charles the Fifth's)

---

* The Goletta is a fortress in the Mediterranean; between that sea and the lake of Tunis. In 1535 Charles V took it by storm.

conquests; as if it had been necessary to support the eternity of his glory (which will be permanent) that those stones should remain in being. The fort was likewise lost, but the Turks got it foot by foot; for the soldiers who defended it sustained two and twenty assaults, and in them killed above 25,000 of those Barbarians; and when it was taken, of 300 which were left alive, there was not one man unwounded; a certain sign of the bravery of the garrison, and of their skill in defending places. There was likewise taken, by composition, a small fort in the midst of a lake, which was under the command of Don John Zanoguerra, a gentleman of Valencia and a soldier of great renown. Don Pedro Puerto Carrero, general of the Goletta, was taken prisoner, and was so afflicted at the loss of the place, that he died of grief by the way before he got to Constantinople, whither they were carrying him. They took also prisoner the commander of the fort, whose name was Gabriel Cerbellon, a Milanese, a great engineer, as well as a valiant soldier. Several persons of quality were killed in those two fortresses, and amongst the rest was Pagan Doria, the brother of the famous John Andrea Doria, a generous and noble-hearted gentleman, as well appeared by his liberality to that brother; and that which made his death more worthy of compassion, was, that he received it from some Arabs to whom he had committed his safety after the loss of the fort, they having promised to carry him disguised in a Moor's habit to Tabarca, which is a small fort held on that coast by the Genoese, for the diving for coral; but they cut off his head, and brought it to the Turkish General, who made good to them our Spanish proverb, that the treason pleases, but the traitors are odious; for he ordered them to be hanged up immediately, for not having brought him alive. Amongst the Christians which were taken in the fort, there was one Don Pedro d'Aguilar, of some place in Andalusia, and who was an ensign in the place; a very brave, and a very ingenious man, and one who had a rare talent in poetry. I mention him, because it was his fortune to be a slave in the same galley with me, and chained to the same bench. Before he left the port he made two sonnets, by way of epitaph for the Goletta and the fort, which I must beg leave to repeat here, having learned them by heart, and I believe they will rather divert than tire the company.' When the captive named Don Pedro d'Aguilar, Don Ferdinand looked upon his companions, and they all smiled; and when he talked of the sonnets, one of them said, 'Before you go on to repeat the sonnets, I desire, sir, you would tell me what became of that Don Pedro d'Aguilar, whom you have mentioned.' 'All that I know of him,' answered the slave, 'is, that after having been two years in Constantinople, he made his escape, disguised like an Arnaut,* and in company of a Greek spy; but I cannot tell whether he obtained his

---

* A trooper of Epirus, Dalmatia, or some of the adjacent countries.

liberty or no, though I believe he did, because about a year after I saw the same Greek in Constantinople, but had not an opportunity to ask him about the success of his journey.' 'Then I can tell you,' replied the gentleman, 'that the Don Pedro you speak of is my brother, and is at present at home, married rich, and has three children.' 'God be thanked,' said the slave, 'for the favours He has bestowed on him; for in my mind there is no felicity equal to that of recovering ones lost liberty.' 'And moreover,' added the same gentleman, 'I can say the sonnets you mentioned, which my brother made.' 'Pray say them then,' replied the slave, 'for I question not but you can repeat them better than I.' 'With all my heart,' answered the gentlemen. 'That upon the Goletta was thus –

CHAPTER XIII

The Story of the Captive continued

A SONNET

'Blest souls discharg'd of life's oppressive weight
　　Whose virtue proved your passport to the skies:
　You there procur'd a more propitious fate,
　　When for your faith you bravely fell to rise.

'When pious rage diffus'd thro' ev'ry vein,
　　On this ungrateful shore inflamed your blood;
　Each drop you lost, was bought with crowds of slain,
　　Whose vital purple swell'd the neighb'ring flood.

'Tho' crush'd by ruins, and by odds, you claim
　　That perfect glory, that immortal fame,
　　　Which, like true heroes, nobly you pursu'd;
　On these you seiz'd, even when of lire depriv'd,
　For still your courage even your lives surviv'd;
　　　And sure 'tis conquest, thus to be subdu'd.'

'I know it is just as you repeat it,' said the captive. 'Well, then,' said the gentleman, 'I will give you now that which was made upon the fort, if I can remember it.'

A SONNET

'Amidst these barren fields, and ruin'd towers.
  The bed of honour of the filling brave.
Three thousand champions of the Christian pow'rs
  Found a new life, and triumph in the grave.

'Long did their arms their haughty foes repel,
  Yet strew'd the fields with slaughter'd heaps in vain;
O'ercome by toils, the pious heroes fell,
  Or but surviv'd more nobly to be slain.

'This dismal soil, so famed in ills of old,
 In ev'ry age was fatal to the bold,
  The seat of horror, and the warrior's tomb!
Yet hence to Heav'n more worth was ne'er resign'd,
Than these display'd; nor has the earth combin'd,
  Resum'd more noble bodies in her womb.'

The sonnets were applauded, and the captive was pleased to hear such good news of his friend and companion; after that he pursued his relation in these terms: 'The Turks ordered the dismantling of the Goletta, the fort being razed to their hand by the siege; and yet the mines they made could not blow up the old walls, which nevertheless were always thought the weakest part of the place; but the new fortifications made by the engineer Fratin came easily down. In fine, the Turkish fleet returned in triumph to Constantinople, where not long after my master Vehali died, whom the Turks used to call Vehali Fartax, which in Turkish signifies the scabby renegade, as indeed he was; and the Turks give names among themselves, either from some virtue or some defect that is in them; and this happens, because there are but four families descended from the Ottoman family; all the rest, as I have said, take their names from some defect of the body, or some good quality of the mind. This scabby slave was at the oar in one of the Grand Signor's galleys for fourteen years, till he was four and thirty years old; at which time he turned renegade, to be revenged of a Turk who gave him a box on the ear, as he was chained to the oar; forsaking his religion for his revenge: after which he showed so much valour and conduct, that he came to be King of Algiers, and Admiral of the Turkish fleet, which was the third command in the whole empire. He was a Calabrian by birth, and of a mild disposition towards his slaves, as also of good morals to the rest of the world. He had above 3000 slaves of his own, all which after his death were divided, as he had ordered by his will, between the Grand Signor, his sons and his renegades. I fell to the share of a Venetian renegade, who was a cabin-boy in a Venetian ship which was taken by Vehali, who loved him so, that he was one of his favourite boys; and he came at last to prove one of the cruellest renegades that ever was known. His name was Azanaga, and he obtained such riches, as to rise by them to be king of Algiers; and with him I left Constantinople, with some satisfaction to think, at least, that I was in a place so near Spain, not because I could give advice to any friend of my misfortunes, but because I hoped to try whether I should succeed better in Algiers than I had done in Constantinople, where I had tried a thousand ways of running away, but could never execute any of them, which I hoped I should compass better in Algiers; for hopes never forsook me upon all the disappointments I met with in the design of recovering my liberty. By this means I kept myself alive, shut up in a prison or house, which the Turks call a Bagnio, where they keep their Christian slaves, as well those of the king as those who belong to private persons, and also those who are called the Almazen, that is, who belong to the public, and are employed by the city in works that belong to it. These latter do very difficulty obtain their liberty; for, having no particular master, but belonging to the public, they can find nobody to treat with about their ransom, though they have money to pay it. The King's slaves which are ransomable, are not obliged to go out to work as the others do, except their ransom stays too long before it comes; for then, to hasten it, they make them work, and fetch wood with the rest, which is no small labour. I was one of those who were to be ransomed; for when they knew I had been a captain, though I told them the impossibility I was in of being redeemed, because of my poverty, yet they put me among the gentlemen that were to be ransomed, and to that end put on me a slight chain, rather as a mark of distinction, than to restrain me by it; and so I passed my life in that bagnio, with several other gentlemen of quality, who expected their ransom; and though hunger and nakedness might, as it did often, afflict us, yet nothing gave us such affliction, as to hear and see the excessive cruelties with which our master used the other Christian slaves: he one day would hang one, then impale another, cut off the ears of a third; and this upon such slight occasions, that often the Turks would own, that he did it only for the pleasure of doing it, and because he was naturally an enemy to mankind. Only one Spanish soldier knew how to deal with him, his name was Saavedra; who, though he had done many things which will not easily be forgotten by the Turks, yet all to gain his liberty, his master never gave him a blow, nor used him ill, either in word or deed; and yet we were always afraid that the least of his pranks would make him be impaled; nay, he himself sometimes was afraid of it too: and, if it were not for taking up too much of your time, I could tell such passages of him, as would divert the company much better than the relation of my adventures, and cause more wonder in them. But, to go on: I say that the windows of a very rich Moor's house looked upon the court of our prison; which indeed, according to the custom of the country, were rather peeping-holes than windows, and yet they had also lattices or jalousies on the inside. It happened one day, that being upon a kind of terrace of our prison, with only three of my comrades, diverting ourselves as well as we could, by trying who could leap furthest in his chains, all the other Christians being gone out to work, I chanced to look up to those windows, and saw that out of one of them there appeared a long cane, and to it was a bit of linen tied, and the cane was moved up and down, as if it had expected that some of us should lay hold of it. We all took notice of it, and one of us went and stood just under it, to see if they would let it fall; but just as he came to it, the cane was drawn up, and shaken to and fro sideways, as if they had made the same sign as people do with their head when they deny. He retired upon that, and the same motion was made with it as before. Another of my comrades advanced, and had the same success as the former; the third man was used just as the rest; which I seeing, resolved to try my fortune too: and as I came under the cane, it fell at my feet. Immediately I untied the linen, within which was a knot, which being opened, showed us about ten Zianins, which is a sort of gold of base alloy used by the Moors, each of which is worth about two crowns of our money.

'It is not to be much questioned, whether the discovery was not as pleasant as surprising; we were in admiration, and I more particularly, not being able to guess whence this good fortune came to us, especially to me; for it was plain I was more meant than any of my comrades, since the cane was let go to me when it was refused to them. I took my money, broke the cane, and going up the terrace, saw a very white hand that opened and shut the window with haste. By this we imagined that some woman who lived in that house had done us this favour; and to return our thanks, we bowed ourselves after the Moorish fashion, with our arms across our breasts. A little after there appeared out of the same window a little cross made of cane, which immediately was pulled in again. This confirmed us in our opinion, that some Christian woman was a slave in that house, and that it was she that took pity on us; but the whiteness of the hand, and the richness of the bracelets upon the arm, which we had a glimpse of, seemed to destroy that thought again; and then we believed it was some Christian woman turned Mahometan, whom their masters often marry, and think themselves very happy; for our women are more valued by them than the women of their own country. But in all this guessing we were far enough from finding out the truth of the case: however, we resolved to be very diligent in observing the window, which was our north-star. There passed above fifteen days before we saw either the hand or cane, or any other sign whatsoever; though in all that time we endeavoured to find out who lived in that house, and if there were in it any Christian woman who was a renegade; yet all we could discover amounted only to this, that the house belonged to one of the chief Moors, a very rich man, called Agimorato, who had been Alcaide of the Pata, which is an office much valued among them. But, when we least expected our golden shower would continue, out of that window we saw on a sudden the cane appear again, with another piece of linen, and a bigger knot; and this was just at a time when the bagnio was without any other of the slaves in it. We all tried our fortunes as the first time, and it succeeded accordingly, for the cane was let go to none but me. I untied the knot, and found in it forty crowns of Spanish gold, with a paper written in Arabic, and at the top of the paper was a great cross. I kissed the cross, took the crowns, and returning to the terrace, we all made our Moorish reverences; the hand appeared again, and I having made signs that I would read the paper, the window was shut. We remained all overjoyed, and astonished at what had happened; and were extremely desirous to know the contents of the paper; but none of us understood Arabic, and it was yet more difficult to find out a proper interpreter. At last I resolved to trust a renegade of Murcia, who had shown me great proofs of his kindness. We gave one another mutual assurances, and on his side he was obliged to keep secret all that I should reveal to him; for the renegades, who have thoughts of returning to their own country, use to get certificates from such persons of quality as are slaves at Barbary, in which they make a sort of affidavit, that such a one, a renegade, is an honest man, and has always been kind to the Christians, and has a mind to make his escape on the first occasion. Some there are who procure these certificates with an honest design, and remain among Christians as long as they live; but others get them on purpose to make use of them when they go a-pirating on the Christian shores; for then if they are shipwrecked or taken, they show these certificates, and say, that thereby may be seen the intention with which they came in the Turks' company; to wit, to get an opportunity of returning to Christendom. By this means they escape the first fury of the Christians, and are seemingly reconciled to the Church without being hurt; afterwards they take their time and return to Barbary to be what they were before.

'One of these renegades was my friend, and he had certificates from us all, by which we gave him much commendation: but if the Moors had caught him with those papers about him they would have burnt him alive. I knew that not only he understood the Arabic tongue, but also that he could speak and write it currently. But yet before I resolved to trust him entirely, I bid him read me that paper, which I found by chance; he opened it, and was a good while looking upon it, and construing it to himself I asked him if he understood it? He said, "Yes, very well;" and that if I would give him pen, ink and paper, he would translate it word for word. We furnished him with what he desired, and he went to work;

having finished his translation, he said, "All that I have here put into Spanish, is word for word what is in the Arabic; only observe, that wherever the paper says Lela Marien, it means our lady the Virgin Mary." The contents were thus:

' "When I was a child, my father had a slave, who taught me in my tongue the Christian worship, and told me a great many things of Lela Marien: the Christian slave died, and I am sure she went not into the fire, but is with Alla, for I have seen her twice since; and she bid me go to the land of the Christians to see Lela Marien, who had a great kindness for me. I do not know what is the matter; but though I have seen many Christians out of this window, none has appeared to me so much a gentleman as thyself. I am very handsome and young, and can carry with me a great deal of money, and other riches; consider whether thou canst bring it to pass that we may escape together, and then thou shalt be my husband in thy own country, if thou art willing; but if thou art not, it is all one, Lela Marien will provide me a husband. I wrote this myself: have a care to whom thou givest it to read, do not trust any Moor, because they are all treacherous; and in this I am much perplexed, and could wish there were not a necessity of trusting any one; because if my father should come to know it, he would certainly throw me into a well, and cover me over with stones. I will tie a thread to a cane, and with that thou mayest fasten thy answer; and if thou canst not find any one to write in Arabic, make me understand thy meaning by signs, for Lela Marien will help me to guess it. She and Alla keep thee, as well as this cross, which I often kiss, as the Christian slave bid me to do." '

'You may imagine, gentlemen, that we were in admiration at the contents of this paper, and withal overjoyed at them, which we expressed so openly, that the renegade came to understand that the paper was not found by chance, but that it was really writ by some one among us; and accordingly he told us his suspicion, and desired us to trust him entirely, and that he would venture his life with us to procure us our liberty. Having said this, he pulled a brass crucifix out of his bosom, and with many tears, swore by the God which it represented, and in whom he, though a wicked sinner, did firmly believe, to be true and faithful to us with all secrecy, in what we should impart to him; for he guessed, that by the means of the woman who had wrote that letter, we might all of us recover our lost liberty; and he, in particular, might obtain what he had so long wished for, to be received again into the bosom of his mother the Church, from whom, for his sins, he had been cut off as a rotten member. The renegade pronounced all this with so many tears, and such signs of repentance, that we were all of opinion to trust him, and tell him the whole truth of the business. We showed him the little window out of which the cane used to appear, and he from thence took good notice of the house, in order to inform himself who lived in it. We next agreed, that it would be necessary to answer the Moorish lady's note: so immediately the renegade wrote down what I dictated to him; which was exactly as I shall relate, for I have not forgot the least material circumstance of this adventure, nor can forget them as long as I live. The words then were these:

' "The true Alla keep thee, my dear lady, and that blessed Virgin, which is the true mother of God, and has inspired thee with the design of going to the land of the Christians. Do thou pray her that she would be pleased to make thee understand how thou shalt execute what she has commanded thee; for she is so good that she will do it. On my part, and on that of the Christians who are with me, I offer to do for thee all we are able, even to the hazard of our lives. Fail not to write to me, and give me notice of thy resolution, for I will always answer thee: the great Alla having given us a Christian slave, who can read and write thy language, as thou mayst perceive by this letter; so that thou mayst, without fear, give us notice of all thy intentions. As for what thou sayst, that as soon as thou shalt arrive in the land of the Christians, thou designest to be my wife, I promise thee, on the word of a good Christian, to take thee for my wife, and thou mayst be assured that the Christians perform their promises better than the Moors. Alla, and His mother Mary, be thy guard, my dear lady."

'Having wrote and closed this note, I waited two days till the bagnio was empty, and then I went upon the terrace, the ordinary place of our conversation, to see if the cane appeared, and it was not long before it was stirring. As soon as it appeared I showed my note, that the thread might be put to the cane, but I found that was done to my hand; and, the cane being let down, I fastened the note to it. Not long after the knot was let fall, and I, taking it up, found in it several pieces of gold and silver, above fifty crowns, which gave us infinite content, and fortified our hopes of obtaining at last our liberty. That evening our renegade came to us, and told us he had found out that the master of that house was the same Moor we had been told of, called Agimorato, extremely rich, and who had one only daughter to inherit all his estate. That it was the report of the whole city, that she was the handsomest maid in all Barbary, having been demanded in marriage by several bashaws and viceroys, but that she had always refused to marry; he also told us, that he had learned she had a Christian slave who was dead: all which agreed with the contents of the letter. We immediately held a council with the renegade, about the manner we should use to carry off the Moorish lady, and go all together to Christendom; when at last he agreed to expect the answer of Zoraida, for that is the name of the lady who now desires to be called Mary; as well knowing she could best advise the overcoming all the difficulties that were in our way; and after this resolution, the renegade assured us again, that he would lose his life, or deliver us out of captivity.

'The bagnio was four days together full of people, and all that time the cane was invisible; but as soon as it returned to its solitude, the cane appeared, with a knot much bigger than ordinary; having untied it, I found in it a letter and an hundred crowns in gold. The renegade happened that day to be with us, and we gave him the letter to read; which he said contained these words:

' "I cannot tell, sir, how to contrive that we may go together for Spain; neither has Lela Marien told it me, though I have earnestly asked it of her: all I can do is to furnish you out of this window with a great deal of riches: buy your ransom and your friends with that, and let one of you go to Spain, and buy a bark there, and come and fetch the rest. As for me, you shall find me in my father's garden out of town, by the sea-side not far from Babasso gate; where I am to pass all the summer with my father and my maids, from which you may take me without fear, in the night-time, and carry me to your bark; but remember you are to be my husband: and, if thou failest in that, I will desire Lela Marien to chastise thee. If thou canst not trust one of thy friends to go for the bark, pay thy own ransom, and go thyself; for I trust thou wilt return sooner than another, since thou art a gentleman and a Christian. Find out my father's garden, and I will take care to watch when the bagnio is empty, and let thee have more money. Alla keep my dear lord."

'These were the contents of the second letter we received. Upon the reading of it, every one of us offered to be the man that should go and buy the bark, promising to return with all punctuality; but the renegade opposed that proposition, and said he would never consent that one should obtain his liberty before the rest, because experience had taught him, that people once free, do not perform what they promise when captives; and that some slaves of quality had often used that remedy, to send one either to Valencia or Majorca, with money to buy a bark, and come back for the rest; but that they never returned: because the joy of having obtained their liberty, and the fear of losing it again, made them forget what they had promised, and cancelled the memory of all obligations. To confirm which he related to us a strange story which had happened, as there often does among the slaves. After this, he said, that all that could be done, was for him to buy a bark with the money that should redeem one of us; that he could buy one in Algiers, and pretend to turn merchant, and deal between Algiers and Tetuan; by which means, he being master of the vessel, might easily find out some way of getting us out of the bagnio, and taking us on board; and especially if the Moorish lady did what she promised, and gave us money to pay all our ransoms; for, being free, we might embark even at noon-day: but the greatest difficulty would be, that the Moors do not permit renegades to keep any barks, but large ones fit to cruise upon Christians: for they believe that a renegade, particularly a Spaniard, seldom buys a bark but with a design of returning to his own country. That, however, he knew how to obviate that difficulty, by taking a Tagarin Moor for his partner both in the bark and trade, by which means he should still be master of her, and then all the rest would be easy. We durst not oppose this opinion, though we had more inclination, every one of us, to go to Spain for a bark, as the lady had advised; but were afraid, that if we contradicted him, as we were at his mercy, he might betray us, and bring our lives into danger; particularly if the business of Zoraida should be discovered, for whose liberty and life we would have given all ours: so we determined to put ourselves under the protection of God and the renegade. At the same time we answered Zoraida, telling her that we would do all she advised, which was very well, and just as if Lela Marien herself had instructed her; and that now it depended on her alone to give us the means to bring this design to pass. I promised her once more to be her husband. After this, in two days that the bagnio happened to be empty, she gave us, by means of the cane, two thousand crowns of gold; and withal a letter, in which she let us know, that the next Juma, which is their Friday, she was to go to her father's garden, and that before she went, she would give us more money; and if we had not enough, she would, upon our letting her know it, give us what we should think sufficient; for her father was so rich, that he would hardly miss it; and so much the less, because he entrusted her with the keys of all her treasure. We presently gave the renegade five hundred crowns to buy the bark, and I paid my own ransom with eight hundred crowns, which I put into the hands of a merchant at Valencia, then in Algiers, who made the bargain with the king, and had me to his house upon parole, to pay the money upon the arrival of the first bark from Valencia; for if he had paid the money immediately, the king might have suspected the money had been ready, and lain some time in Algiers, and that the merchant for his own profit had concealed it; and in short, I durst not trust my master with ready money, knowing his distrustful and malicious nature. The Thursday preceding the Friday that Zoraida was to go to the garden, she let us have a thousand crowns more; desiring me at the same time, that, if I paid my ransom, I would find out her father's garden, and contrive some way of seeing her there. I answered in few words, that I would do as she desired, and she should only take care to recommend us to Lela Marien, by those prayers which the Christian slave had taught her. Having done this, order was taken to have the ransom of my three friends paid also; lest they seeing me at liberty, and themselves not so, though there was money to set them free, should be troubled in mind, and give way to the temptation of the Devil, in doing something that might redound to the prejudice of Zoraida: for though the consideration of their quality ought to have given me security of their honour, yet I did not think it proper to run the least hazard in the matter: so they were redeemed in the same manner, and by the same merchant that I was, who had the money beforehand; but we never discovered to him the remainder of our intrigue, as not being willing to risk the danger there was in so doing.

CHAPTER XIV

The Adventures of the Captive continued

'OUR RENEGADE had in a fortnight's time bought a very good bark, capable of carrying above thirty people; and, to give no suspicion of any other design, he undertook a voyage to a place upon the coast called Sargel, about thirty leagues to the eastward of Algiers, towards Oran, where there is a great trade for dried figs. He made this voyage two or three times in company with the Tagarin Moor, his partner. Those Moors are called in Barbary Tagarins, who were driven out of Aragon; as they call those of Granada, Mudajares; and the same in the kingdom of Fez are called Elches, and are the best soldiers that prince has.

'Every time he passed with his bark along the coast, he used to cast anchor in a little bay that was not above two bow-shots from the garden where Zoraida expected us; and there used to exercise the Moors that rowed, either in making the Sala, which is a ceremony among them, or in some other employment; by which he practised in jest what he was resolved to execute in earnest. So sometimes he would go to the garden of Zoraida and beg some fruit, and her father would give him some, though he did not know him. He had a mind to find an occasion to speak to Zoraida, and tell her, as he since owned to me, that he was the man who, by my order, was to carry her to the land of the Christians, and that she might depend upon it; but he could never get an opportunity of doing it, because the Moorish and Turkish women never suffer themselves to be seen by any of their own nation, but by their husband, or by his or their father's command; but as for the Christian slaves, they let them see them, and that more familiarly than perhaps could be wished. I should have been very sorry that the renegade had seen or spoke to Zoraida, for it must needs have troubled her infinitely to see that her business was trusted to a renegade: and God Almighty, Who governed our design, ordered it so, that the renegade was disappointed. He in the mean time seeing how securely, and without suspicion, he went and came along the coast, staying where and when he pleased by the way, and that his partner the Tagarin Moor, was of his mind in all things; that I was at liberty, and there wanted nothing but some Christians to help us to row; bid me consider whom I intended to carry with me besides those who were ransomed, and that I should make sure of them for the first Friday, because he had pitched on that day for our departure. Upon notice of this resolution, I spoke to twelve lusty Spaniards, good rowers, and those who might easily get out of the city: it was a great fortune that we got so many in such a conjuncture, because there were above twenty sail of rovers gone out, who had taken aboard most of the slaves fit for the oar; and we had not got these, but that their master happened to stay at home that summer, to finish a galley he was building to cruise with, and was then upon the stocks. I said no more to them, than only they should steal out of the town in the evening upon the next Friday, and stay for me upon the way that led to Agimorato's garden. I spoke to every one by himself, and gave each of them order to say no more to any other Christian they should see, than that they stayed for me there. Having done this, I had another thing of the greatest importance to bring to pass, which was to give Zoraida notice of our design, and how far we had carried it, that she might be ready at a short warning, and not to be surprised if we came upon the house on a sudden, and even before she could think that the Christian bark could be come. This made me resolve to go to the garden, to try if it were possible to speak to her: so one day, upon pretence of gathering a few herbs, I entered the garden, and the first person I met was her father, who spoke to me in the language used all over the Turkish dominions, which is a mixture of all the Christian and Moorish languages, by which we understand one another from Constantinople to Algiers, and asked me that I looked for in his garden, and who I belonged to? I told him I was a slave of Arnaute Mami (this man I knew was his intimate friend) and that I wanted a few herbs to make up a salad. He then asked me if I were a man to be redeemed or no, and how much my master asked for me; during these questions, the beautiful Zoraida came out of the garden-house hard by, having descried me a good while before; and as the Moorish women make no difficulty of showing themselves to the Christian slaves, she drew near, without scruple, to the place where her father and I were talking; neither did her father show any dislike of her coming, but called to her to come nearer. It would be hard for me to express here the wonderful surprise and astonishment that the beauty, the rich dress, and the charming air of my beloved Zoraida put me in: she was all bedecked with pearls, which hung thick upon her head and about her neck and arms. Her feet and legs were naked, after the custom of that country, and she had upon her ankles a kind of bracelet of gold, and set with such rich diamonds that her father valued them, as she since told me, at ten thousand pistoles a pair; and those about her wrists were of the same value. The pearls were of the best sort, for the Moorish women delight much in them, and have more pearls of all sorts than any nation. Her father was reputed to have the finest in Algiers, and to be worth besides, above two hundred thousand Spanish crowns; of all which, the lady you here see was then mistress; but now is only so of me. What she yet retains of beauty after all her sufferings, may help you to guess at her wonderful appearance in the midst of her prosperity. The beauty of some ladies has its days and times, and is more or less, according to accidents or passions, which naturally raise or diminish the lustre of it, and sometimes quite extinguish it. All I can say, is, at that time she appeared to me the best-dressed and most beautiful woman I had ever seen; to which, adding the obligations I had to her, she passed with me for a goddess from Heaven, descended upon earth for my relief and happiness. As she drew near, her father told her, in his country language, that I was a slave of his friend, Arnaute Mami, and came to pick a salad in his garden. She presently took the hint, and asked me in Lingua Franca, whether I was a gentleman, and if I was, why I did not ransom myself? I told her I was already ransomed, and that by the price, she might guess the value my master set upon me, since he had bought me for one thousand five hundred pieces of eight: to which she replied, "If thou hadst been my father's slave, I would not have let him part with thee for twice as much; for," said she, "you Christians never speak truth in any thing you say, and make yourselves poor to deceive the Moors." "That may be, madam," said I, "but in truth I have dealt by my master, and do intend to deal by all those I shall have to deal with, sincerely and honourably." "And when dost thou go home? said she. "Tomorrow, madam," said I, "for here is a French bark that sails tomorrow, and I intend not to lose that opportunity." "Is it not better," replied Zoraida, "to stay till there comes some Spanish bark, and go with them, and not with the French, who, I am told, are no friends of yours?" "No," said I, "yet if the report of a Spanish bark's coming should prove true, I would perhaps stay for it, though it is more likely I shall take the opportunity of the French, because the desire I have of being at home, and with those persons I love, will hardly let me wait for any other conveniency." "Without doubt," said Zoraida, "thou art married in Spain and impatient to be with thy wife." "I am not," said I, "married, but I have given my word to a lady, to be so as soon as I can reach my own country." "And is the lady handsome that has your promise? "said Zoraida. "She is so handsome," said I, "that to describe her rightly, and tell truth, I can only say she is like you." At this her father laughed heartily, and said, "On my word, Christian, she must be very charming if she be like my daughter, who is the greatest beauty in the kingdom: look upon her well, and thou wilt say I speak truth." Zoraida's father was our interpreter for the most of what we talked, for though she understood the Lingua Franca, yet she was not used to speak it, and so explained herself more by signs than words. While we were in this conversation, there came a Moor running hastily, and cried aloud that four Turks had leaped over the fence of the garden, and were gathering the fruit, though it was not ripe. The old man started at that, and so did Zoraida, for the Moors do naturally stand in awe of the Turks, particularly of the soldiers, who are so insolent on their side, that they treat the Moors as if they were their slaves. This made the father bid his daughter go in and shut herself up close, "Whilst," said he, "I go and talk with these dogs; and for thee, Christian, gather the herbs thou wantest, and go thy ways in peace, and God conduct thee safe to thy own country." I bowed to him, and he left me with Zoraida, to go and find out the Turks: she made also as if she were going away, as her father had bid her; but she was no sooner hid from his sight by the trees of the garden, but she turned towards me with her eyes full of tears, and said in her language "*Amexi, Christiano, Amexi,*" which is, "Thou art going away, Christian, thou art going": to which I answered, "Yes, madam, I am, but by no means without you; you may expect me next Friday, and be not surprised when you see us, for we will certainly go to the land of the Christians." I said this so passionately, that she understood me; and throwing one of her arms about my neck, she began to walk softly, and with trembling towards the house. It pleased fortune, that as we were in this posture walking together (which might have proved very unlucky for us), we met Agimorato coming back from the Turks, and we perceived he had seen us as we were; but Zoraida, very readily and discreetly, was so far from taking away her arm from about my neck, that drawing still nearer to me, she leaned her head upon my breast, and letting her knees give way, was in the posture of one that swoons: I, at the same time, made as if I had much ado to bear her up against my will. Her father came hastily to us, and seeing his daughter in this condition, asked her what was the matter. But she not answering readily, he presently said, "Without a doubt, these Turks have frightened her, and she faints away'; at which he took her in his arms. She, as it were, coming to herself, fetched a deep sigh, and with her eyes not yet dried from tears, she said, "*Amexi, Christiano, Amexi*;" "Begone, Christian, begone'; to which her father replied, "It is no matter, child, whether he go or no, he has done thee no hurt, and the Turks at my request are gone." "It is they who frightened her," said I, "but since she desires I should be gone, I will come another time for my salad, by your leave; for my master says the herbs of your garden are the best of any he can have." "Thou mayest have what, and when thou wilt," said the father; "for my daughter does not think the Christians troublesome, she only wished the Turks away, and by mistake bid thee be gone too, or make haste and gather thy herbs." With this I immediately took leave of them both; and Zoraida, showing great trouble in her looks, went away with her father. I, in the mean time, upon pretence of gathering my herbs here and there, walked all over the garden, observing exactly all the places of coming in and going out, and every corner fit for my purpose, as well as what strength there was in the house, with all other conveniences to facilitate our business. Having done this I went my ways, and gave an exact account of all that had happened, to the renegade and the rest of my friends, longing earnestly for the time in which I might promise myself my dear Zoraida's company, without any fear of disturbance. At last the happy hour came, and we had all the good success we could promise ourselves, of a design so well laid; for the Friday after my discourse with Zoraida, towards the evening we came to an anchor with our ark, almost over against the place where my lovely mistress lived; the Christians, who were to be employed at the oar, were already at the rendezvous, and hid up and down thereabouts. They were all in expectation of my coming, and very desirous to seize the bark which they saw before their eyes, for they did not know our agreement with the renegade, but thought they were by main force to gain their conveyance and their liberty, by killing the Moors on board. As soon as I and my friends appeared, all the rest came from their hiding-places to us. By this time the city gates were shut, and no soul appeared in all the country near us. When we were all together, it was a question whether we should first fetch Zoraida, or make ourselves master of those few Moors in the bark. As we were in this consultation, the renegade came to us, and asking what we meant to stand idle, told us his Moors were all gone to rest, and most of them asleep. We told him our difficulty, and he immediately said that the most important thing was to secure the bark, which might easily be done, and without danger, and then we might go for Zoraida.

'We were all of his mind, and so, without more ado, he marched at the head of us to the bark, and leaping into it, he first drew a scymitar, and cried aloud in the Moorish language, "Let not a man of you stir, except he means it should cost him his life;" and while he said this, all the other Christians were got on board. The Moors, who are naturally timorous, hearing the master use this language, were frighted, and without any resistance, suffered themselves to be manacled, which was done with great expedition by the Christians, who told them at the same time, that if they made he least noise, they would immediately cut their throats. This being done, and half of our number left to guard them the remainder, with the renegade, went to Agimorato's garden; and our good fortune was such, that coming to force the gate, we found it open with as much facility as if it had not been shut at all. So we marched on with great silence to the house, without being perceived by anybody. The lovely Zoraida, who was at the window, asked softly, upon hearing us tread, whether we were Nazarani, that is Christians? I answered "Yes," and desired her to come down. As soon as she heard my voice, she stayed not a minute; but, without saying a word, came down and opened the door, appearing to us all like a goddess, her beauty and the richness of her dress not being to be described. As soon as I saw her, I took her by the hand, which I kissed, the renegade did the same, and then my friends; the rest of the company followed the same ceremony; so that we all paid her a kind of homage for our liberty. The renegade asked her in Morisco, whether her father was in the garden? She said "Yes," and that he was asleep. "Then," said he, "we must awake him, and take him with us, as also all that is valuable in the house." "No, no," said Zoraida, "my father must not be touched, and in the house there is nothing so rich as what I shall carry with me, which is enough to make you all rich and content." Having said this she stepped into the house, bid us be quiet, and she would soon return. I asked the renegade what had passed between them, and he told me what he had said: to which I replied, that by no means anything was to be done, otherwise than as Zoraida should please. She was already coming back with a small trunk so full of gold, that she could hardly carry it, when, to our great misfortune, while this was doing, her father awaked, and hearing a noise in the garden, opened a window and looked out: having perceived that there were Christians in it, he began to cry out in Arabick, "Thieves, thieves, Christians, Christians." These cries of his put us all into a terrible disorder and fear; but the renegade seeing our danger, and how much it imported us to accomplish our enterprise before we were perceived, he ran up to the place where Agimorato was, and took with him some of our company; for I durst by no means leave Zoraida, who had swooned away in my arms. Those who went up bestirred themselves so well, that they brought down Agimorato with his hands tied behind him, and his mouth stopped with a handkerchief, which hindered him from so much as speaking a word; and threatening him besides, that if he made the least attempt to speak, it should cost him his life. When his daughter, who was come to herself, saw him, she covered her eyes to avoid the sight, and her father remained the more astonished, for he knew not how willingly she had put herself into our hands. Diligence on our side being the chief thing requisite, we used it so as we came to our bark, when our men began to be in pain for us, as fearing that we had met with some ill accident: we got on board about two hours after it was dark; where the first thing we did was to untie the hands of Zoraida's father, and to unstop his mouth, but still with the same threatenings of the renegade, in case he made any noise.

When he saw his daughter there, he began to sigh most passionately, and more when he saw me embrace her with tenderness, and that she, without any resistance or struggling, seemed to endure it; he, for all this, was silent, for fear the threatenings of the renegade should be put in execution. Zoraida seeing us aboard, and that we were ready to handle our oars to be gone, bid the renegade tell me, she desired I would set her father, and the other Moors, our prisoners, on shore; or else she would throw herself into the sea, rather than see a father, who had used her so tenderly, be carried away captive for her sake, before her eyes. The renegade told me what she said, to which I agreed; but the renegade was of another opinion; saying, that if we set them on shore there, they would raise the country, and give the alarm to the city, by, which some light frigate might be dispatched in quest of us, and getting between us and the sea, it would be impossible for us to make our escape; and that all that could be done, was to set them at liberty in the first Christian land we could reach. This seemed so reasonable to us all, that Zoraida herself, being informed of the motives we had not to obey her at present, agreed to it. Immediately, with great silence and content, we began to ply our oars, recommending ourselves to Providence with all our hearts, and endeavoured to make for Majorca, which is the nearest Christian land; but the north wind rising a little, and the sea with it, we could not hold that course, but were forced to drive along shore towards Oran, not without great fear of being discovered from Sargel, upon the coast, about thirty leagues from Algiers. We were likewise apprehensive of meeting some of those galliots which come from Tetuan with merchandise. Though, to say truth, we did not so much fear these last; for, except it were a cruising galliot, we all of us wished to meet such a one, which we should certainly take, and so get a better vessel to transport us in.

'Zoraida all this while hid her face between my hands, that she might not see her father; and I could hear her call upon Lela Marien to help us. By the time we had got about thirty miles the day broke, and we found ourselves within a mile of the shore, which appeared to us a desert solitary place, but yet we rowed hard to get off to sea, for fear of being discovered by somebody. When we were got about two leagues out to sea, we proposed the men should row by turns, that some might refresh themselves; but the men at the oar said it was not time yet to rest, and that they could eat and row too, if those who did not row would assist them, and give them meat and drink; this we did, and, a little while after the wind blowing fresh, we ceased rowing, and set sail for Oran, not being able to hold any other course. We made about eight miles an hour, being in no fear of anything but meeting some cruisers. We gave victuals to our Moorish prisoners, and the renegade comforted them, and told them they were not slaves, but should be set at liberty upon the first opportunity. The same was said to Zoraida's father, who answered, "I might expect from you anything else perhaps, O Christians; but that you should give me my liberty, I am not simple enough to believe it; for you never would have run the hazard of taking it from me, if you intended to restore it me so easily; especially since you know who I am, and what you may get for my ransom; which if you will but name, I do from this moment offer you all that you can desire for me, and for that unfortunate daughter of mine, or for her alone, since she is the better part of me." When he had said this, he burst out into tears so violently, that Zoraida could not forbear looking up at him, and indeed he moved compassion in us all, but in her particularly; insomuch, as starting from my arms, she flew to her father's, and putting her head to his, they began again so passionate and tender a scene, that most of us could not forbear accompanying their grief with our tears; but her father seeing her so richly dressed, and so many jewels about her, said to her, in his language, "What is the meaning of this, daughter? for last night, before this terrible misfortune befell us, thou wert in thy ordinary dress; and now, without scarce having had time to put on such things, I see thee adorned with all the fineries I could give thee, if we were at liberty and in full prosperity. This gives me more wonder and trouble than even our sad misfortune; therefore answer me." The renegade interpreted all that the Moor said, and we saw that Zoraida answered not a word; but on a sudden, spying the little casket in which she used to put her jewels, which he thought had been left in Algiers, he remained yet more astonished, and asked her how that trunk could come into our hands, and what was in it? To which the renegade, without expecting Zoraida's answer, replied, "Do not trouble thyself to ask thy daughter so many questions, for with one word I can satisfy them all. Know then that she is a Christian, and it is she that hath filed off our chains, and given us liberty: she is with us by her own consent, and I hope well pleased, as people should be who come from darkness into light, and from death to life." "Is this true, daughter?" said the Moor. "It is," replied Zoraida. "How then," said the old man, "art thou really a Christian? and art thou she that has put thy father into the power of his enemies?" To which Zoraida replied, "I am she that is a Christian, but not she that has brought thee into this condition, for my design never was to injure my father, but only to do myself good." "And what good hast thou done thyself?" said the Moor. "Ask that of Lela Marien," replied Zoraida, "for she can tell thee best." The old man had no sooner heard this, but he threw himself with incredible fury into the sea, where without doubt he had been drowned, had not his garments, which were long and wide, kept him some time above water. Zoraida cried out to us to help him, which we all did so readily, that we pulled him out by his vest, but half drowned, and without any sense. This so troubled Zoraida, that she threw herself upon her father, and began to lament and bemoan as if he had been really dead. He turned his head downwards, and by this means having disgorged a great deal of water, he recovered a little in about two hours' time. The wind in the meanwhile was come about, and forced us toward the shore, so that we were obliged to ply our oars, not to be driven upon the land. It was our good fortune to get into a small bay, which is made by a promontory, called the Cape of the Caba Rumia; which, in our tongue, is the cape of the wicked Christian woman; and it is a tradition among the Moors, that Caba, the daughter of Count Julian, who was the cause of the loss of Spain, lies buried there; and they think it ominous to be forced into that bay, for they never go in otherwise than by necessity; but to us it was no unlucky harbour, but a safe retreat, considering how high the sea went by this time. We posted our sentries on the shore, but kept our oars ready to be plied upon occasion, taking in the mean time some refreshment of what the renegade had provided, praying heartily to God and the Virgin Mary, to protect us, and help us to bring our design to a happy conclusion. Here, at the desire of Zoraida, we resolved to set her father on shore, with all the other Moors, whom we kept fast bound; for she had not courage, nor could her tender heart suffer any longer, to see her father and her countrymen ill used before her face; but we did not think to do it before we were just ready to depart, and then they could not much hurt us, the place being a solitary one, and no habitations near it. Our prayers were not in vain; the wind fell, and the sea became calm, inviting us thereby to pursue our intended voyage: we unbound our prisoners, and set them on shore one by one, which they were mightily astonished at. When we came to put Zoraida's father on shore, who by this time was come to himself, he said, "Why do you think, Christians, that this wicked woman desires I should be set at liberty? Do you think it is for any pity she takes of me? No certainly, but it is because she is not able to bear my presence, which hinders the prosecution of her ill desires: I would not have you think neither that she has embraced your religion, because she knows the difference between yours and ours, but because she has heard that she can live more loosely in your country than at home." And then turning himself to Zoraida, while I and another held him fast by the arms, that he might commit no extravagance, he said, "O infamous and blind young woman, where art thou going in the power of these dogs, our natural enemies? Cursed be the hour in which I begot thee, and the care and affection with which I bred thee!" But I, seeing he was not like to make an end of his exclamations soon, made haste to set him on shore, from whence he continued to give us his curses and imprecations; begging on his knees of Mahomet to beg of God Almighty to confound and destroy us; and when, being under sail, we could no longer hear him, we saw his actions, which were tearing his hair and beard, and rolling himself upon the ground; but he once strained his voice so high, that we heard what he said, which was, "Come back, my dear daughter, for I forgive thee all; let those men have the treasure which is already in their possession, and do thou return to comfort thy disconsolate father, who must else lose his life in these sandy deserts." All this Zoraida heard, and shed abundance of tears, but could answer nothing, but beg that Lela Marien, who had made her a Christian, would comfort him. "God knows," said she, "I could not avoid doing what I have done; and that these Christians are not obliged to me, for I could not be at rest till I had done this, which to thee, dear father, seems so ill a thing." All this she said, when we were got so far out of his hearing, that we could scarce so much as see him. So I comforted Zoraida as well as I could, and we all minded our voyage. The wind was now so right for our purpose, that we made no doubt of being the next morning on the Spanish shore; but as it seldom happens that any felicity comes so pure, as not to be tempered and allayed by some mixture of sorrow; either our ill fortune, or the Moor's curses had such an effect (for a father's curses are to be dreaded, let the father be what he will), that about midnight, when we were under full sail, with our oars laid by, we saw by the light of the moon, hard by us, a round-sterned vessel with all her sails out, coming a-head of us, which she did so close to us, that we were forced to strike our sail not to run foul of her; and the vessel likewise seemed to endeavour to let us go by; they had come so near as to ask from whence we came, and whither we were going? But doing it in French, the renegade forbid us to answer, saying, "Without doubt these are French pirates, to whom everything is a prize." This made us all be silent; and as we sailed on, they being under the wind, fired two guns at us, both, as it appeared, with chain-shot, for one brought our mast by the board, and the other went through us, without killing anybody; but we, perceiving we were sinking, called to them to come and take us, for we were going to be drowned; they then struck their own sails, and putting out their long boat, there came about a dozen French on board us, all well armed, and with their matches lighted. When they were close to us, seeing we were but few, they took us aboard their boat, saying, that this had happened to us for not answering their questions. The renegade had time to take a little coffer or trunk, full of Zoraida's treasure, and heave it overboard, without being perceived by anybody. When we were on board their vessel, after having learned from us all they could, they began to strip us, as if we had been their mortal enemies: they plundered Zoraida of all the jewels and bracelets she had on her hands and feet; but that did not so much trouble me, as my apprehension for the rich jewel of her chastity, which she valued above all the rest. But that sort of people seldom have any desires beyond the getting of riches, which they saw in abundance before their eyes; and their covetousness was so sharpened by it, that even our slaves' clothes tempted them. They consulted what to do with us; and some were of opinion to throw us overboard, wrapped up in a sail, because they intended to put into some of the Spanish ports, under the notion of being of Britanny; and if they carried us with them, they might be punished, and their roguery come to light: but the captain, who thought himself rich enough with Zoraida's plunder, said he would not touch at any port of Spain, but make his way through the straits by night, and so return to Rochel, from whence he came. This being resolved, they bethought themselves of giving us their long boat, and what provision we might want for our short passage. As soon as it was day, and that we descried the Spanish shore (at which sight, so desirable a thing is liberty, all our miseries vanished from our thoughts in a moment), they began to prepare things, and about noon they put us on board, giving us two barrels of water, and a small quantity of biscuit; and the captain, touched with some remorse for the lovely Zoraida, gave her, at parting, about forty crowns in gold, and would not suffer his men to take from her those clothes which now she had on. We went aboard, showing ourselves rather thankful than complaining. They got out to sea, making for the straits, and we, having the land before us for our north-star, plied our oars, so that about sunset we were near enough to have landed before it was quite dark; but, considering the moon was hid in clouds, and the heavens were growing dark, and we ignorant of the shore, we did not think it safe to venture on it, though many among us were so desirous of liberty, and to be out of all danger, that they would have landed, though on a desert rock; and by that means, at least, we might avoid all little barks of the pirates of the Barbary coast, such as those of Tetuan, who come from home when it is dark, and by morning are early upon the Spanish coast; where they often make a prize, and go home to bed the same day. But the other opinion prevailed, which was to row gently on, and if the sea and shore gave leave, to land quietly where we could. We did accordingly, and about midnight came under a great hill, which had a sandy shore, convenient enough for our landing. Here we in our boat in as far as we could, and being got on land, we all kissed it for joy, and thanked God with tears for our deliverance. This done, we took out the little provision we had left, and climbed up the mountain, thinking ourselves more in safety there, for we could hardly persuade ourselves, nor believe, that the land we were upon was the Christian shore. We thought the day long a-coming, and then we got to the top of the hill, to see if we could discover any habitations; but we could nowhere descry either house, or person, or path. We resolved, however, to go further on, imagining we could not miss at last of somebody to inform us where we were: that which troubled me most was, to see my poor Zoraida go on foot among the sharp rocks, and I would sometimes have carried her on my shoulders; but she was as much concerned at the pains I took, as she could be at what she endured; so leaning upon me, she went on with much patience and content. When we were gone about a quarter of a league, we heard the sound of a little pipe, which we took to be a certain sign of some flock near us; and looking well about, we perceived, at last, at the foot of a cork tree, a young shepherd, who was cutting a stick with his knife, with great attention and seriousness. We called to him, and he having looked up, ran away as hard as he could. It seems, as we afterwards heard, the first he saw were the renegade and Zoraida, who being in the Moorish dress, he thought all the Moors in Barbary were upon him; and, running into the wood, cried all the way as loud as he could, "Moors, Moors! arm, arm! the Moors are landed!" We, hearing this outcry, did not well know what to do: but, considering that the shepherd's roaring would raise the country, and the horse-guard of the coast would be upon us, we agreed that the renegade should pull off his Turkish habit, and put on a slave's coat, which one of us lent him, though he that lent it him remained in his shirt. Thus recommending ourselves to God, we went on by the same way that the shepherd ran, still expecting when the horse would come upon us; and we were not deceived, for in less than two hours, as we came down the hills into a plain, we discovered fifty horse coming upon a half gallop towards us; when we saw that, we stood still, expecting them. As soon as they came up, and, instead of so many Moors, saw so many poor Christian captives, they were astonished. One of them asked us, if we were the occasion of the alarm that a young shepherd had given the country? "Yes," said I, and upon that began to tell him who we were, and whence we came; but one of our company knew the horseman that had asked us the question, and without letting me go on, said, "God be praised, gentlemen, for bringing us to so good a part of the country; for if I mistake not, we are near Velez Malaga: and, if the many years of my captivity have not taken my memory from me too, I think that you, sir, who ask us such questions, are my uncle Don Pedro Bustamente."

'The Christian slave had hardly said this, but the gentleman, lighting from his horse, came hastily to embrace the young slave, saying, "Dear nephew, my joy, my life, I know thee, and have often lamented thy loss, and so has thy mother and thy other relations, whom thou wilt yet find alive. God has preserved them, that they may have the pleasure of seeing thee. We had heard that thou wert in Algiers, and by what I see of thy dress, and that of all this company, you must all have had some miraculous deliverance." "It is so," replied the young man, "and we shall have time enough now to tell all our adventures." The rest of the horsemen, hearing we were Christians escaped from slavery, lighted likewise from their horses, offering them to us to carry us to the city of Velez Malaga, which was about a league and a half off. Some of them went where we had left our boat, and got it into the port, while others took us up behind them; and Zoraida rode behind the gentleman, uncle to our captive. All the people, who had already heard something of our adventure, came out to meet us;

they did not wonder to see captives at liberty, nor Moors prisoners, for in all that coast they are used to it; but they were astonished at the beauty of Zoraida, which at that instant seemed to be in its point of perfection; for, what with the agitation of travelling, and what with the joy of being safe in Christendom, without the terrible thought of being retaken, she had such a beautiful colour in her countenance, that were it not for the fear of being too partial, I durst say there was not a more beautiful creature in the world, at least that I had seen. We went straight to church, to thank God for His great mercy to us; and as we came into it, and that Zoraida had looked upon the pictures, she said there were several faces there that were like Lela Marien's; we told her they were her pictures, and the renegade explained to her as well as he could the story of them, that she might adore them, as if in reality each of them had been the true Lela Marien, who had spoke to her; and she, who has a good and clear understanding, comprehended immediately all that was said about the pictures and images. After this, we were dispersed and lodged in different houses of the town; but the young Christian slave of Velez carried me, Zoraida, and the renegade to his father's house, where we were accommodated pretty well, according to their ability, and used with as much kindness as their own son. After six days' stay at Velez, the renegade having informed himself of what was needful for him to know, went away to Granada, there to be readmitted by the holy inquisition into the bosom of the Church. The other Christians, being at liberty, went each whither he thought fit. Zoraida and I remained without other help than the forty crowns the pirate gave her, with which I bought the ass she rides on, and since we landed, have been to her a father and a friend, but not a husband. We are now going to see whether my father be alive, or if either of my brothers has had better fortune than I; though, since it has pleased Heaven to give me Zoraida, and make me her companion, I reckon no better fortune could befall me. The patience with which she bears the inconvenience of poverty, the desire she shows of being made a Christian, do give me subject of continual admiration, and oblige me to serve and love her all the days of my life. I confess the expectation of being hers is not a little allayed with the uncertainties of knowing whether I shall find in my country any one to receive us, or a corner to pass my life with her; and perhaps time will have so altered the affairs of our family, that I shall not find anybody that will know me, if my father and brothers are dead.

'This is, gentlemen, the sum of my adventures, which whether or no they are entertaining you are best judges. I wish I had told them more compendiously; and yet, I assure you, the fear of being tedious has made me cut short many circumstances of my story.'

CHAPTER XV

An Account of what happened afterwards at the Inn, with several other Occurrences worth notice

HERE THE STRANGER ended his story; and Don Ferdinand, by way of compliment in the behalf of the whole company, said, 'Truly, captain, the wonderful and surprising turns of your fortune are not only entertaining, but the pleasing and graceful manner of your relation is as extraordinary as the adventures themselves: we are all bound to pay you our acknowledgments; and I believe we could be delighted with a second recital, though it were to last till tomorrow, provided it were made by you.' Cardenio and the rest of the company joined with him in offering their utmost service in the re-establishment of his fortune, and that with so much sincerity and earnestness, that the captain had reason to be satisfied of their affection. Don Ferdinand particularly proposed to engage the Marquis his brother to stand godfather to Zoraida, if he would return with him, and further promised to provide him with all things necessary to support his figure and quality in town; but the captain, making them a very handsome compliment for their obliging favours, excused himself from accepting those kind offers at that time. It was now growing towards the dark of the evening, when a coach stopped at the inn, and with it some horsemen, who asked for a lodging. The hostess answered, they were as full as they could pack. 'Were you ten times fuller,' answered one of the horsemen, 'here must be room made for my Lord Judge, who is in this coach.' The hostess, hearing this, was very much concerned; said she, 'The case, sir, is plain, we have not one bed empty in the house; but if his Lordship brings a bed with him, as perhaps he may, he shall command my house with all my heart, and I and my husband will quit our own chamber to serve him.' 'Do so then,' said the man. And by this time a gentleman alighted from the coach, easily distinguishable for a man of dignity and office, by his long gown and great sleeves. He led a young lady by the hand, about sixteen years of age, dressed in a riding-suit; her beauty and charming air attracted the eyes of everybody with admiration, and had not the other ladies been present, any one might have thought it difficult to have matched her outward graces.

Don Quixote, seeing them come near the door, 'Sir,' said he, 'you may enter undismayed, and refresh yourselves in this castle, which though little and indifferently provided, must nevertheless allow a room, and afford accommodation to arms and learning; and more especially to arms and learning, that, like yours, bring beauty for their guide and conductor. For certainly at the approach of this lovely damsel, not only castles ought to open and expand their gates, but even rocks divide their solid bodies, and mountains bow their ambitious crests, and stoop to entertain her. Come in therefore, sir, enter this paradise, where you shall find a bright constellation worthy to shine in conjunction with that heaven of beauty which you bring: here you shall find arms in their height, and beauty in perfection.' Don Quixote's speech, mien, and garb, put the judge to a strange nonplus; and he was not a little surprised on the other hand at the sudden appearance of the three ladies, who being informed of the judge's coming and the young lady's beauty, were come out to see and entertain her. But Don Ferdinand, Cardenio, and the curate addressing him in a style very different from the Knight, soon convinced him that he had to do with gentlemen, and persons of note, though Don Quixote's figure and behaviour put him to a stand, not being able to make any reasonable conjecture of his extravagance. After the usual civilities passed on both sides, they found upon examination, that the women must all lie together in Don Quixote's apartment, and the men remain without to guard them. The judge consented that his daughter should go with the ladies, and so, what with his own bed and what with the innkeeper's, he and the gentlemen made a shift to pass the night.

The captain, upon the first sight of the judge, had a strong presumption that he was one of his brothers, and presently asked one of his servants his name and country. The fellow told him, his name was Juan Perez de Viedma, and that, as he was informed, he was born in the highlands of Leon. This, with his own observation, confirmed his opinion, that this was the brother who had made study his choice; whereupon calling aside Don Ferdinand, Cardenio, and the curate, he told them with great joy what he had learned, with what the servant further told him, that his master being made a judge of the court of Mexico, was then upon his journey to the Indies; that the young lady was his only daughter, whose mother dying in child-birth, settled her dowry upon her daughter for a portion, and that the father had still lived a widower, and was very rich. Upon the whole matter, he asked their advice, whether they thought it proper for him to discover himself presently to his brother, or by some means try how his pulse beat first in relation to his loss, by which he might guess at his reception. 'Why should you doubt of a kind one, sir?' said the curate. 'Because I am poor, sir,' said the captain, 'and would therefore by some device fathom his affections; for, should he prove ashamed to own me, I should be more ashamed to discover myself.' 'Then leave the management to me,' said the curate; 'the affable and courteous behaviour of the judge seems to me so very far from pride, that you need not doubt a welcome reception; but however, because you desire it, I will engage to find a way to sound him.' Supper was now upon the table, and all the gentlemen sat down but the captain, who ate with the ladies in the next room. When the company had half-supped, 'My Lord Judge,' said the curate, 'I remember about some years ago, I was happy in the acquaintance and friendship of a gentleman of your name, when I was a prisoner in Constantinople: he was a captain of as much worth and courage as any in the Spanish infantry, but as unfortunate as brave.' 'What was his name, pray, sir?' said the judge. 'Ruy Perez de Viedma,' answered the curate, 'of a town in the mountains of Leon. I remember he told me a very odd passage between his father, his two brothers, and himself; and truly had it come from any man of less credit and reputation, I should have thought it no more than a story: he said, that his father made an equal dividend of his estate among his three sons, giving them such advice as might have fitted the mouth of Cato; that he made arms his choice, and with such success, that within a few years (by the pure merit of his bravery) he was made captain of a foot company, and had a fair prospect of being advanced to a colonel; but his fortune forsook him, where he had most reason to expect her favour; for, in the memorable battle of Lepanto, where so many Christians recovered their liberty, he unfortunately lost his. I was taken at Goletta, and after different turns of fortune we became companions at Constantinople; thence we were carried to Algiers, where one of the strangest adventures in the world befell this gentleman.' The curate then briefly ran through the whole story of the captain and Zoraida (the judge sitting all the time more attentive than he ever did on the bench) to their being taken and stripped by the French; and that he had heard nothing of them after that, nor could ever learn whether they came into Spain, or were carried prisoners into France.

The captain stood listening in a corner and observed the motions of his brother's countenance, while the curate told his story: which, when he had finished, the judge breathing out a deep sigh, and the tears standing in his eyes: 'O sir,' said he, 'if you knew how nearly your relation touches me, you would easily excuse the violent eruption of these tears. The captain you spoke of is my eldest brother, who, being of a stronger constitution of body, and more elevated soul, made the glory and fame of war his choice, which was one of the three proposals made by my father, as your companion told you. I applied myself to study, and my younger brother has purchased a vast estate in Peru, out of which he has transmitted to my father enough to support his liberal disposition; and to me, wherewithal to continue my studies and advance myself to the rank and authority which now I maintain. My father is still alive, but dies daily for grief he can learn nothing of his eldest son, and importunes Heaven incessantly, that he may once more see him before death close his eyes. It is very strange, considering his discretion in other matters, that neither prosperity nor adversity could draw one line from him, to give his father an account of his fortunes. For had he or we had the least hint of his captivity, he needed not have stayed for the miracle of the Moorish lady's cane for his deliverance. Now am I in the greatest uneasiness in the world, lest the French, the better to conceal their robbery, may have killed him; the thoughts of this will damp the pleasure of my voyage, which I thought to prosecute so pleasantly. Could I but guess, dear brother,' continued he, 'where you might be found, I would hazard life and fortune for your deliverance! Could our aged father once understand you were alive, though hidden in the deepest and darkest dungeon in Barbary, his estate, mine, and my brother's, all should fly for your ransom! And for the fair and liberal Zoraida, what thanks, what recompense could we provide? O might I see the happy day of her spiritual birth and baptism, to see her joined to him in faith and marriage, how should we all rejoice!' These and such-like expressions the judge uttered with so much passion and vehemency, that he raised a concern in everybody.

The curate, foreseeing the happy success of his design, resolved to prolong the discovery no further; and, to free the company from suspense, he went to the ladies' room, and leading out Zoraida, followed by the rest, he took the captain by the other hand, and presenting them to the judge: 'Suppress your grief, my lord,' said he, 'and glut your heart with joy; behold what you so passionately desired, your dear brother, and his fair deliverer; this gentleman is Captain Viedma, and this the beautiful Algerine; the French have only reduced them to this low condition, to make room for your generous sentiments and liberality.' The captain then approaching to embrace the judge, he held him off with both his hands to view him well; but, once knowing him, he flew into his arms with such affection, and such abundance of tears, that all the spectators sympathised in his passions. The brothers spoke so feelingly, and their mutual affection was so moving, the surprise so wonderful, and their joy so transporting, that it must be left purely to imagination to conceive. Now they tell one another the strange turns and mazes of their fortunes, then renew their caresses to the height of brotherly love and tenderness. Now the judge embraces Zoraida, then makes her an offer of his whole fortune; next makes his daughter embrace her; then the sweet and innocent converse of the beautiful Christian, and the lovely Moor, so touched the whole company, that they all wept for joy. In the mean time Don Quixote was very solidly attentive, and wondering at these strange occurrences, attributed them purely to something answerable to the chimerical notions which are incident to chivalry. The captain and Zoraida, in concert with the whole company, resolved to return with their brother to Sevil, and thence to advise their father of his arrival and liberty, that the old gentleman should make the best shift he could to get so far to see the baptism and marriage of Zoraida, while the judge took his voyage to the Indies, being obliged to make no delay, because the Indian fleet was ready at Sevil to set sail in a month for New Spain.

Everything being now settled, to the universal satisfaction of the company, and being very late, they all agreed for bed, except Don Quixote, who would needs guard the castle whilst they slept, lest some tyrant or giant, covetous of the great treasure of beauty which it enclosed, should make some dangerous attempt. He had the thanks of the house, and the judge being further informed of his humour, was not a little pleased. Sancho Pança was very uneasy and waspish for want of sleep, though the best provided with a bed, bestowing himself on his pack-saddle; but he paid dearly for it, as we shall hear presently. The ladies being retired to their chamber, and everybody else withdrawn to rest, and Don Quixote planted sentinel at the castle-gate, a voice was heard of a sudden singing so sweetly, that it allured all their attentions, but chiefly Dorothea's, with whom the judge's daughter Donna Clara de Viedma lay. None could imagine who could make such pretty music without an instrument: sometimes it sounded as from the yard, sometimes as from the stable. With this Cardenio knocked softly at their door, 'Ladies, ladies!' said he, 'are you awake? Can you sleep when so charmingly serenaded: do not you hear how sweetly one of the footmen sings?' 'Yes, sir,' said Dorothea, 'we hear him plainly.' Then Dorothea heartening as attentively as she could, heard this song.

CHAPTER XVI

A pleasant Story of the young Muleteer, with other strange adventures that happened at the Inn

A SONG

I

'Toss'd in doubts and fears I rove
On the stormy seas of love;
Far from comfort, far from port,
Beauty's prize, and fortune's sport:
Yet my heart disclaims despair,
While I trace my leading star.

II

'But reserv'dness, like a cloud,
Does too oft her glories shroud.
Pierce the gloom, reviving sight;
Be auspicious as you're bright.
As you hide or dart your beams,
Your adorer sinks or swims.'

Dorothea thought it would not be much amiss to give Donna Clara the opportunity of hearing so excellent a voice; wherefore touching her gently, first on one side and then on the other, and the young lady waking, 'I ask your pardon, my dear,' cried Dorothea, 'for thus interrupting your repose; and I hope you will easily forgive me, since I only awake you that you may have the pleasure of hearing one of the most charming voices, that possibly you ever heard in your life.' Donna Clara, who was hardly awake, did not perfectly understand what Dorothea said, and therefore desired her to repeat what she had spoke to her. Dorothea did so; which then obliged Donna Clara also to listen; but scarce had she heard the early musician sing two verses, ere she was taken with a strange trembling, as if she had been seized with a violent fit of a quartan ague, and then closely embracing Dorothea, 'Ah! dear madam,' cried she, with a deep sigh, 'why did you wake me? Alas! the greatest happiness I could now have expected, had been to have stopped my ears: that unhappy musician!' 'How is this, my dear,' cried Dorothea, 'have you not heard, that the young lad who sung now is but a muleteer?' 'Oh no, he is no such thing,' replied Clara, 'but a young lord, heir to a great estate, and has such a full possession of my heart, that if he does not slight it, it must be his for ever.' Dorothea was strangely surprised at the young lady's passionate expressions, that seemed far to exceed those of persons of her tender years: 'You speak so mysteriously, madam,' replied she, 'that I cannot rightly understand you, unless you will please to let me know more plainly what you would say of hearts and sighs, and this young musician, whose voice has caused so great an alteration in you. However, speak no more of them now; for I am resolved I will not lose the pleasure of hearing him sing. Hold,' continued she, 'I fancy he is going to entertain us with another song.' 'With all my heart,' returned Clara, and with that she stopped her ears, that she might not hear him; at which again Dorothea could not but choose to admire; but listening to his voice she heard the following song.

HOPE

I

'Unconquer'd hope, thou bane of fear,
    And last deserter of the brave;

Thou soothing ease of mortal care
   Thou traveller beyond the grave;
Thou soul of patience, airy food,
Bold warrant of a distant good,
Reviving cordial, kind decoy:
  Tho' fortune frowns and friends depart,
Tho' Sylvia flies me, flatt'ring joy,
   Nor thou, nor love, shall leave my doting heart.

II

'The phœnix hope can wing her flight
   Thro' the vast deserts of the skies,
And still defying fortune's spite,
   Revive, and from her ashes rise.
Then soar, and promise, tho' in vain,
What reason's self despairs to gain.
Thou only, O presuming trust
   Canst feed us still yet never cloy:
And even a virtue when unjust
   Postpone our pain, and antedate our joy.

III

'No slave to lazy ease resign'd,
   E'er triumph'd over noble foes.
The monarch Fortune most is kind
   To him who bravely dares oppose.
They say Love sets his blessings high;
But who would prize an easy joy I
Then I'll my scornful fair pursue,
   Tho' the coy beauty still denies
I grovel now on earth, 'tis true
   But rais'd by her, the humble slave may rise.'

Here the voice ended, and Donna Clara's sighs began, which caused the greatest curiosity imaginable in Dorothea, to know the occasion of so moving a song, and of so sad a complaint: wherefore she again entreated her to pursue the discourse she had begun before. Then Clara, fearing Lucinda would overhear her, getting as near Dorothea as was possible, laid her mouth so close to Dorothea's ear, that she was out of danger of being understood by any other; and began in this manner: 'He who sung is a gentleman's son of Arragon, his father is a great lord, and dwelt just over against my father's at Madrid; and, though we had always canvas-windows in winter, and lattices in summer,* yet I cannot tell by what accident this young gentleman, who then went to school, had a sight of me, and whether it were at church, or at some other place, I cannot justly tell you; but, in short, he fell in love with me, and made me sensible of his passion from his own windows, which were opposite to mine, with so many signs, and such showers of tears, that at once forced me both to believe and to love him, without knowing for what reason I did so. Amongst the usual signs that he made me, one was that of joining his hands together, intimating by that his desire to marry me; which, though I heartily wished it, I could not communicate it to any one, being motherless, and having none near me whom I might trust with the management of such an affair; and was therefore constrained to bear it in silence, without permitting him any other favour, more than to let him gaze on me, by lifting up the lattice, or oiled cloth a little, when my father and his were abroad. At which he would be so transported with joy, that you would certainly have thought he had been distracted. At last my father's business called him away; yet not so soon, but that the young gentleman had notice of it some time before his departure; whence he had it I know not, for it was impossible for me to acquaint him with it. This so sensibly afflicted him, as far as I understand, that he fell sick; so that I could not get a sight of him all the day of our departure, so much as to look a farewell on him. But after two days' travel, just as we came into an inn, in a village a day's journey hence, I saw him at the inn-door, dressed so exactly like a muleteer, that it had been utterly impossible for me to have known him, had not his perfect image been stamped on my soul. Yes, yes, dear madam, I knew him, and was amazed and overjoyed at the sight of him; and he saw me unknown to my father, whose sight he carefully avoids, when we cross the ways in our journey, and when we come to any inn: and now, since I know who he is, and what pain and fatigue it must necessarily be to him to travel thus on foot, I am ready to die with the thought of what he suffers on my account; and wherever he sets his feet, there I set my eyes. I cannot imagine what he proposes to himself in this attempt; nor by what means he could thus make his escape from his father, who loves him beyond expression, both because he has no other son and heir, and because the young gentleman's merits oblige him to it; which you must needs confess when you see him: and I dare affirm, besides, that all he has sung was his own immediate composition; for, as I have heard, he is an excellent scholar, and a great poet. And now, whenever I see him, or hear him sing, I start and tremble, as at the sight of a ghost, lest my father should know him, and so be informed of our mutual affection. I

---

* Glass windows are not used in Spain; at least they are not common and formerly there were none.

never spoke one word to him in my life; yet I love him so dearly, that it is impossible I should live without him. This, dear madam, is all the account I can give you of this musician, with whose voice you have been so well entertained, and which alone might convince you that he is no muleteer, as you were pleased to say, but one who is master of a great estate, and of my poor heart, as I have already told you.'

'Enough, dear madam,' replied Dorothea, kissing her a thousand times: 'it is very well, compose yourself till daylight; and then I trust in Heaven I shall so manage your affairs, that the end of them shall be as fortunate as the beginning was innocent.' 'Alas! madam,' returned Clara, 'what end can I propose to myself; since his father is so rich, and of so noble a family, that he will hardly think me worthy to be his son's servant, much less his wife? And then again, I would not marry without my father's consent, for the universe. All I can desire is, that the young gentleman would return home, and leave his pursuit of me: happily, by a long absence, and the great distance of place, the pain, which now so much afflicts me, may be somewhat mitigated; though I fear what I now propose as a remedy would rather increase my distemper: indeed I cannot imagine whence, or by what means this passion for him seized me, since we are both so young, being much about the same age, I believe; and my father says I shall not be sixteen till Michaelmas.' Dorothea could not forbear laughing to hear the young lady talk so innocently 'My dear,' said Dorothea, 'let us repose ourselves the little remaining part of the night, and when day appears, we will put a happy period to your sorrows, or my judgment fails me.' Then they addressed themselves again to sleep, and there was a deep silence throughout all the inn; only the innkeeper's daughter and Maritornes were awake, who knowing Don Quixote's blindside very well, and that he sat armed on horseback keeping guard without doors, a fancy took them, and they agreed to have a little pastime with him, and hear some of his fine out-of-the-way speeches.

You must know then, that there was but one window in all the inn that looked out into the field, and that was only a hole out of which they used to throw their straw: to this same hole then came these two demi-ladies, whence they saw Don Quixote mounted, leaning on his lance, and often fetched such mournful and deep sighs, that his very soul seemed to be torn from him at each of them: they observed besides, that he said in a soft amorous tone, 'O my divine Dulcinea del Toboso! the heaven of all perfections! the end and quintessence of discretion! the treasury of sweet aspect and behaviour! the magazine of virtue! and, in a word, the idea of all that is profitable, modest, or delightful in the universe! What noble thing employs thy Excellency at this present? May I presume to hope that thy soul is entertained with the thoughts of thy captive-knight, who voluntarily exposes himself to so many dangers for thy sake? O thou triformed luminary, give me some account of her! Perhaps thou art now gazing with envy on her, as she is walking either through some stately gallery of her sumptuous palaces, or leaning on her happy window, there meditating how, with safety of her honour and grandeur, she may sweeten and alleviate the torture which my poor afflicted heart suffers for love of her; with what glories she shall crown my pains; what rest she shall give to my cares; what life to my death; and what reward to my services. And thou, more glorious planet, which by this time, I presume, art harnessing thy horses to pay thy earliest visit to my adorable Dulcinea; I entreat thee, as soon as thou dost see her, to salute her with my most profound respects: but take heed, that when thou lookest on her, and addressest thyself to her, that thou do not kiss her face; for if thou dost, I shall grow more jealous of thee, than ever thou wert of the swift ingrate, who made thee run and sweat so over the plains of Thessaly, or the banks of Peneus, I have forgotten through which of them thou rushed, raging with love and jealousy.' At these words the innkeeper's daughter began to call to him softly: 'Sir Knight,' said she, 'come a little nearer this way, if you please.' At these words Don Quixote turned his head, and the moon shining then very bright, he perceived somebody called him from the hole, which he fancied was a large window full of iron-bars, all richly gilt, suitable to the stately castle, for which he mistook the inn; and all on asudden, he imagined, that the beautiful damsel, daughter to the lady of the castle, overcome by the charms of his person, returned to court him, as she did once before. In this thought, that he might not appear uncivil or ungrateful, he turned Rozinante, and came to the hole; where, seeing the two lasses, 'Fair damsels,' said he, 'I cannot but pity you for your misplaced affection, since it is altogether impossible you should meet with any return from the object of your wishes, proportionable to your great merits and beauty; but yet you ought not, by any means, to condemn an unhappy knight-errant for his coldness, since love has utterly incapacitated him to become a slave to any other but to her, who, at first sight, made herself absolute mistress of his soul. Pardon me, therefore, excellent lady, and retire to your apartment. Let not, I beseech you, any further arguments of love force me to be less grateful or civil than I would: but if, in the passion you have for me, you can bethink yourself of anything else wherein I may do you any service, love alone excepted, command it freely; and I swear to you by my absent, yet most charming enemy, to sacrifice it to you immediately, though it be a lock of Medusa's hair, which are all snakes, or the very sunbeams enclosed in a glass vial.'

'My lady needs none of those things, Sir Knight,' replied Maritornes. 'What then would she command?' asked Don Quixote. 'Only the honour of one of your fair hands,' returned Maritornes, 'to satisfy in some measure, that violent passion which has obliged her to come hither with the great hazard of her honour: for if my lord her father should know it, the cutting off of one of her beautiful ears were the least thing he would do to her.' 'Oh, that he durst attempt it!' cried Don Quixote; 'but I know he dare not, unless he has a mind to die the most unhappy death that ever father suffered, for sacrilegiously depriving his amorous daughter of one of her delicate members.' Maritornes made no doubt that he would comply with her desire, and having already laid her design, got in a trice to the stable, and brought Sancho Pança's ass's halter to the hole, just as Don Quixote was got on his feet upon Rozinante's saddle, more easily to reach the barricaded window, where he imagined the enamoured lady stayed; and lifting up his hand to her, said, 'Here, madam, take the hand, or rather, as I may say, the executioner of all earthly miscreants; take, I say, that hand, which never woman touched before; no, not even she herself who has entire possession of my whole body; nor do I hold it up to you that you may kiss it, but that you may observe the contexture of the sinews, the ligament of the muscles, and the largeness and dilatation of the veins; whence you may conclude how strong that arm must be, to which such a hand is joined.' 'We shall see that presently,' replied Maritornes, and cast the noose she had made in the halter on his wrist; and then descending from the hole, she tied the other end of the halter very fast to the lock of the door. Don Quixote being sensible that the bracelet she had bestowed on him was very rough, cried, 'You seem rather to abuse than compliment my hand; but I beseech you treat it not so unkindly, since that is not the cause why I do not entertain a passion for you; nor is it just or equal you should discharge the whole tempest of your vengeance on so small a part. Consider, those who love truly can never be so cruel in their revenge.' But not a soul regarded what he said; for, as soon as Maritornes had fastened him, she and her confederate, almost dead with laughing, ran away, and left him so strongly bound, that it was impossible he should disengage himself.

He stood then, as I said, on Rozinante's saddle, with all his arm drawn into the hole, and the rope fastened to the lock, being under a fearful apprehension, that if Rozinante moved but never so little on any side, he should slip and hang by the arm, and therefore durst not use the least motion in the world, though he might reasonably have expected, from Rozinante's patience and gentle temper, that if he were not urged, he would never have moved for a whole age together of his own accord. In short, the Knight, perceiving himself fast, and that the ladies had forsaken him, immediately concluded that all this was done by way of enchantment, as in the last adventure in the very same castle, when the enchanted Moor (the carrier) did so damnably maul him. Then he began alone to curse his want of discretion and conduct, since having once made his escape out of that castle in so miserable a condition, he should venture into it a second time: for, by the way, it was an observation among all knights-errant, that if they were once foiled in an adventure, it was a certain sign it was not reserved for them, but for some other to finish; wherefore they would never prove it again. Yet, for all this, he ventured to draw back his arm, to try if he could free himself; but he was so fast bound, that his attempt proved fruitless. It is true, it was with care and deliberation he drew it, for fear Rozinante should stir: and then fain would he have seated himself in the saddle; but he found he must either stand, or leave his arm for a ransom. A hundred times he wished for Amadis's sword, on which no enchantment had power; then he fell a-cursing his stars; then reflected on the great loss the world would sustain all the time he should continue under this enchantment, as he really believed it; then his adorable Dulcinea came a-fresh into his thoughts; many a time did he call to his trusty squire Sancho Pança, who, buried in a profound sleep, lay stretched at length on his ass's pannel, never so much as dreaming of the pangs his mother felt when she bore him; then the aid of the necromancers Lirgandeo and Alquife was invoked by the unhappy Knight. And, in fine, the morning surprised him racked with despair and confusion, bellowing like a bull; for he could not hope from daylight any cure or mitigation of his pain, which he believed would be eternal, being absolutely persuaded he was enchanted, since he perceived that Rozinante moved no more than a mountain; and therefore he was of opinion, that neither he nor his horse should eat, drink, or sleep, but remain in that state till the malignancy of the stars were over-past, or till some more powerful magician should break the charm.

But it was an erroneous opinion; for it was scarce daybreak, when four horsemen, very well accoutred, their firelocks hanging at the pommels of their saddles, came thither, and finding the inn-gate shut, called and knocked very loud and hard; which Don Quixote perceiving from the post where he stood sentinel, cried out with a rough voice and a haughty mien, 'Knights or squires, or of whatsoever other degree you are, knock no more at the gates of this castle, since you may assure yourselves, that those who are within, at such an hour as this, are either taking their repose, or not accustomed to open their fortress, till Phœbus has displayed himself upon the globe: retire therefore, and wait till it is clear day, and then we will see whether it is just or no, that they should open their gates to you.' 'What a devil,' cried one of them, 'what castle or fortress is this, that we should be obliged to so long a ceremony? Pray thee, friend, if thou art the innkeeper, bid them open the door to us; for we ride post, and can stay no longer than just to bait our horses.' 'Gentlemen,' said Don Quixote, 'do I look like an innkeeper, then?' 'I cannot tell what thou art like,' replied another, 'but I am sure thou talkest like a madman, to call this inn a castle.' 'It is a castle,' returned Don Quixote, 'ay, and one of the best in the province, and contains one who has held a sceptre in her hand, and wore a crown on her head.' 'It might more properly have been said exactly contrary,' replied the traveller, 'a sceptre in her tail, and a crown in her hand: yet it is not unlikely that there may be a company of strollers within, and those do frequently hold such sceptres, and wear such crowns as thou pratest of: for certainly no person worthy to sway a sceptre, or wear a crown, would condescend to take up a lodging in such a paltry inn as this, where I hear so little noise.' 'Thou hast not been much conversant in the world,' said Don Quixote, 'since thou art so miserably ignorant of accidents so frequently met with in knight-errantry.' The companions of him that held this tedious discourse with Don Quixote, were tired with their foolish chattering so long together, and therefore they returned with greater fury to the gate, where they knocked so violently, that they waked both the innkeeper and his guests; and so the host rose to ask who was at the door.

In the mean time Rozinante, pensive and sad, with ears hanging down and motionless, bore up his outstretched lord, when one of the horses these four men rode upon, walked towards Rozinante, to smell him, and he truly being real flesh and blood, though very like a wooden block, could not but be sensible of it, nor forbear turning to smell the other, which so seasonably came to comfort and divert him; but he had hardly stirred an inch from his place, when Don Quixote's feet, that were close together, slipped asunder, and tumbling from the saddle, he had inevitably fallen to the ground, had not his wrist been securely fastened to the rope; which put him to so great a torture, that he could not imagine, but that his hand was cutting off, or his arm tearing from his body; yet he hung so near the ground, that he could just reach it with the tips of his toes, which added to his torment; for perceiving how little he wanted to the setting his feet wholly on the ground, he strove and tugged as much as he could to effect it; not much unlike those that suffer the strapado, who put themselves to greater pain in striving to stretch their limbs, deluded by the hopes of touching the ground, if they could but inch themselves out a little longer.

CHAPTER XVII

A continuation of the strange and unheard-of Adventures in the Inn

THE MISERABLE OUTCRIES of Don Quixote presently drew the inn-keeper to the door, which he hastily opening, was strangely affrighted to hear such a terrible roaring, and the strangers stood no less surprised. Maritornes, whom the cries had also roused, guessing the cause, ran straight to the loft, and slipping the halter, released the Don, who made her a very prostrate acknowledgment, by an unmerciful fall on the ground. The innkeeper and strangers crowded immediately round him to know the cause of his misfortune. He, without regard to their questions, unmanacles his wrist, bounces from the ground, mounts Rozinante, braces his target, couches his lance, and taking a large circumference in the field, came up with a handgallop: 'Whoever,' said he, 'dare affirm, assert, or declare that I have been justly enchanted, in case my Lady the Princess Micomicona will but give me leave, I will tell him he lies, and will maintain my assertion by immediate combat.' The travellers stood amazed at Don Quixote's words, till the host removed their wonder, by informing them of his usual extravagancies in this kind, and that his behaviour was not to be minded. They then asked the innkeeper if a certain youth, near the age of fifteen, had put up at this house, clad like a muleteer? Adding withal some further marks and tokens, denoting Donna Clara's lover: he told them, that among the number of his guests, such a person might pass him undistinguished; but one of them accidentally spying the coach which the judge rid in, called to his companions: 'O gentlemen, gentlemen, here stands the coach which we were told my young master followed, and here he must be, that is certain: let us lose no time, one guard the door, the rest enter the house to look for him – hold – stay,' continued he, 'ride one about to the other side of the house, lest he escape us through the back yard.' 'Agreed,' says another; and they posted themselves accordingly. The innkeeper, though he might guess that they sought the young gentleman whom they had described, was nevertheless puzzled as to the cause of their so diligent search. By this time, the daylight and the outcries of Don Quixote had raised the whole house, particularly the two ladies, Clara and Dorothea, who had slept but little, the one with the thoughts her lover was so near her, and the other through an earnest desire she had to see him. Don Quixote seeing the travellers neither regard him nor his challenge, was ready to burst with fury and indignation; and, could he have dispensed with the rules of chivalry, which oblige a knight-errant to the finishing one adventure before his embarking in another, he had assaulted them all, and forced them to answer them to their cost; but being unfortunately engaged to reinstate the Princess Micomicona, his hands were tied up, and he was compelled to desist, expecting where the search and diligence of the four travellers would terminate: one of them found the young gentleman fast asleep by a footman, little dreaming of being followed or discovered: the fellow lugging him by the arm, cries out, 'Ay, ay, Don Lewis, these are very fine clothes you have got on, and very becoming a gentleman of your quality, indeed; this scurvy bed too is very suitable to the care and tenderness your mother brought you up with.' The youth having rubbed his drowsy eyes, and fixing them steadfastly on the man, knew him presently for one of his father's servants, which struck him speechless with surprise. The fellow went on: 'There is but one way, sir, pluck up your spirits, and return with us to your father, who is certainly a dead man unless you be recovered.' 'How came my father to know,' answered Don Lewis, 'that I took this way and this disguise?' 'One of your fellow-students,' replied the servant, 'whom you communicated your design to, moved by your father's lamentation of your loss, discovered it; the good old gentleman dispatched away four of his men in search of you; And here we are all at your service, sir, and the joyfullest men alive; for our old master will give us a hearty welcome, having so soon restored him what he loved so much.' 'That, next to Heaven, is as I please,' said Don Lewis. 'What would you, or Heaven either, please, sir, but return to your father? Come, come, sir, talk no more of it, home you must go, and home you shall go.' The footman that lay with Don Lewis, hearing this dispute, rose, and related the business to Don Ferdinand, Cardenio, and the rest that were now dressed; adding withal, how the man gave him the title of Don, with other circumstances of their conference. They, being already charmed with the sweetness of his voice, were curious to be informed more particularly of his circumstances, and resolving to assist him, in case any violence should be offered him, went presently to the place where he was still contending with his father's servant.

By this Dorothea had left her chamber, and with her Donna Clara in great disorder. Dorothea beckoning Cardenio aside, gave him a short account of the musician and Donna Clara; and he told her that his father's servants were come for him. Donna Clara overhearing him, was so exceedingly surprised, that had not Dorothea run and supported her, she had sunk to the ground. Cardenio promising to bring the matter to a fair and successful end, advised Dorothea to retire with the indisposed lady to her chamber. All the four that pursued Don Lewis were now come about him pressing his return without delay, to comfort his poor father; he answered it was impossible, being engaged to put a business in execution first, on which depended no less than his honour, and his present and future happiness. They urged, that since they had found him, there was no returning for them without him, and if he would not go, he should be carried: 'Not unless you kill me,' answered the young gentleman: upon which all the company were joined in the dispute, Cardenio, Don Ferdinand and his companions, the judge, the curate, the barber, and Don Quixote, who thought it needless now to guard the castle any longer. Cardenio, who knew the young gentleman's story, asked the fellows upon what pretence, or by what authority they could carry the youth away against his will. 'Sir,' answered one of them, 'we have reason good for what we do; no less than his father's life depends upon his return.'

'Gentlemen,' said Don Lewis, 'it is not proper perhaps to trouble you with a particular relation of my affairs; only thus much, I am a gentleman, and have no dependence that should force me to anything beside my inclination.' 'Nay, but, sir,' answered the servant, 'reason, I hope, will force you; and though it cannot move you, it must govern us, who must execute our orders, and force you back; we only act as we are ordered, sir.' 'Hold,' said the judge, 'and let us know the whole state of the case.' 'O lord, sir,' answered one of the servants that knew him, 'my Lord Judge, does not your worship know your next neighbour's child? See here, sir, he has run away from his father's house, and has put on these dirty, tattered rags, to the scandal of his family, as your worship may see.' The judge then viewing him more attentively knew him, and saluting him, 'What jest is this, Don Lewis?' cried he. 'What mighty intrigue are you carrying on, young sir, to occasion this metamorphosis, so unbecoming your quality?' The young gentleman could not answer a word, and the tears stood in his eyes; the judge, perceiving his disorder, desired the four servants to trouble themselves no further, but leave the youth to his management, engaging his word to act to their satisfaction: and, retiring with Don Lewis, he begged to know the occasion of his flight.

During their conference, they heard a great noise at the inn-door, occasioned by two strangers, who, having lodged there over night, and seeing the whole family so busied in a curious inquiry into the four horsemen's business, thought to have made off without paying their reckoning; but the innkeeper, who minded no man's business more than his own, stopped them in the nick, and demanding his money, upbraided their ungenteel design very sharply: they returned the compliment with kick and cuff so roundly, that the poor host cried out for help; his wife and daughter saw none so idle as Don Quixote, whom the daughter addressing, 'I conjure you, Sir Knight,' said she, 'by that virtue delivered to you from Heaven, to succour my distressed father, whom two villains are beating to jelly.' 'Beautiful damsel,' answered Don Quixote with a slow tone and profound gravity, 'your petition cannot at the present juncture prevail, I being withheld from undertaking any new adventure, by promise first to finish what I am engaged in; and all the service you can expect is only my counsel in this important affair; go with all speed to your father, with advice to continue and maintain the battle with his utmost resolution, till I obtain permission from the Princess Micomicona to reinforce him, which once granted, you need make no doubt of his safety.' 'Unfortunate wretch that I am,' said Maritornes, who overheard him, 'before you can have this leave, my master will be sent to the other world.' 'Then, madam,' said he, 'procure me the permission I mentioned, and though he were sent into the other world, I will bring him back in spite of hell and the Devil, or at least so revenge his fall on his enemies, as shall give ample satisfaction to his surviving friends; 'whereupon, breaking off the discourse, he went and threw himself prostrate before Dorothea, imploring her, in romantic style, to grant him a commission to march and sustain the governor of that castle, who was just fainting in a dangerous engagement. The princess dispatched him very willingly; whereupon, presently buckling on his target, and taking up his sword, he ran to the inn-door, where the two guests were still handling their landlord very unmercifully; he there made a sudden stop, though Maritornes and the hostess pressed him twice or thrice to tell the cause of his delay in his promised assistance to his host. 'I make a pause,' said Don Quixote, 'because I am commanded by the law of arms to use my sword against none under the order of knighthood; but let my squire be called, this affair is altogether his province.' In the mean time drubs and bruises were incessant at the inn gate, and the poor host soundly beaten. His wife, daughter and maid, who stood by, were like to run mad at Don Quixote's hanging back, and the innkeeper's unequal combat; where we shall leave him, with a design to return to his assistance presently, though his fool-hardiness deserves a sound beating, for attempting a thing he was not likely to go through with. We now return to hear what Don Lewis answered the judge, whom we left retired with him, and asking the reason of his travelling on foot, and in so mean a disguise. The young gentleman grasping his hands very passionately, made this reply, not without giving a proof of the greatness of his sorrow by his tears:

'Without ceremony or preamble, I must tell you, dear sir, that from the instant that Heaven made us neighbours, and I saw Donna Clara, your daughter and my mistress, I resigned to her the whole command of my affections; and unless you, whom I must truly call my father, prevent it, she shall be my wife this very day; for her sake I abandoned my father's house; for her have I thus disguised my quality; her would I thus have followed through the world: she was the north star to guide my wandering course, and the mark at which my wishes flew. Her ears indeed are utter strangers to my passion; but yet her eyes may guess, by the tears she saw flowing from mine. You know my fortune and my quality: if these can plead, sir, I lay them at her feet; then make me this instant your happy son, and if my father, biassed by contrary designs, should not approve my choice, yet time may produce some favourable turn, and alter his mind.' The amorous youth having done speaking, the judge was much surprised at the handsome discovery he made of his affections, but was not a little puzzled how to behave himself in so sudden and unexpected a matter: he therefore, without any positive answer, advised him only to compose his thoughts, to divert himself with his servants, and to prevail with them to allow him that day to consider on what was proper to be done. Don Lewis expressed his gratitude by forcibly kissing the judge's hands, and bathing them with his tears, enough to move the heart of a cannibal, much more a judge's, who (being a man of the world) had presently the advantage of the match and preferment of his daughter in the wind; though he much doubted the consent of Don Lewis's father, who he knew designed to match his son into the nobility.

By this time Don Quixote's entreaties more than threats had parted the fray at the inn-door; the strangers paying their reckoning went off, and Don Lewis's servants stood expecting the result of the judge's discourse with their young master; when (as the Devil would have it) who should come into the inn but the barber whom Don Quixote had robbed of Mambrino's helmet, and Sancho of the pack-saddle. As he was leading his beast very gravely to the stable, he spies Sancho mending something about the pannel; he knew him presently, and setting upon him very roughly, 'Ay, Mr. Thief, Mr. Rogue,' said he, 'have I caught you at last, and all my ass's furniture in your hands too?' Sancho finding himself so unexpectedly assaulted, and nettled at the dishonourable terms of his language, laying fast hold on the pannel with one hand, gave the barber such a douse on the chops with the other, as set all his teeth a-bleeding; for all this the barber stuck by his hold, and cried out so loud that the whole house was alarmed at the noise and scuffle: 'I command you, gentlemen,' continued he, 'to assist me in the king's name; for this rogue has robbed me on the king's highway, and would now murder me, because I seize upon my goods!' 'That is a lie,' cried Sancho, 'it was no robbery on the king's highway, but lawful plunder, won by my Lord Don Quixote fairly in the field.' The Don himself was now come up very proud of his squire's behaviour on this occasion, accounting him thenceforth a man of spirit, and designing him the honour of knighthood on the first opportunity, thinking his courage might prove a future ornament to the order. Among other things which the barber urged to prove his claim: 'Gentlemen,' said he, 'this pack-saddle is as certainly my pack-saddle, as I hope to die in my bed; I know it as well as if it had been bred and born with me; nay, my very ass will witness for me; do but try the saddle on him, and if it does not fit him as close as can be, then call me a liar – nay, more than that, gentlemen, that very day when they robbed me of my pack-saddle, they took away a special new basin which was never used, and which cost me a crown.' Here Don Quixote could no longer contain himself; but thrusting between them, he parted them; and having caused the pack-saddle to be deposited on the ground to open view, till the method came to a final decision: 'That this honourable company may know,' cried he, 'in what a manifest error this honest squire persists, take notice how he degrades that with the name of basin, which was, is, and shall be the helmet of Mambrino, which I fairly won from him in the field, and lawfully made myself lord of by force of arms. As to the pack-saddle, it is a concern that is beneath my regard; all I have to urge in that affair, is, that my squire begged my permission to strip that vanquished coward's horse of his trappings to adorn his own; he had my authority for the deed, and he took them: and now for his converting it from a horse's furniture to a pack-saddle, no other reason can be brought, but that such transformations frequently occur in the affairs of chivalry. For a confirmation of this, dispatch, run, Sancho, and produce the helmet which this squire would maintain to be a basin.' 'On my faith, sir,' said Sancho, 'if this be all you can say for yourself, Mambrino's helmet will prove as arrant a basin, as this same man's furniture is a mere pack-saddle.' 'Obey my orders,' said Don Quixote, 'I cannot believe that everything in this castle will be guided by enchantment.' Sancho brought the basin, which Don Quixote holding up in his hand, 'Behold, gentlemen,' continued he, 'with what force can this impudent squire affirm this to be a basin, and not the helmet I mentioned? Now I swear before you all, by the order of knighthood, which I profess, that that is the same individual helmet which I won from him, without the least addition or diminution.' 'That I will swear,' said Sancho; 'for since my Lord won it, he never fought but once in it, and that was the battle wherein he freed those ungracious galley-slaves, who by the same token would have knocked out his brains with a shower of stones, had not this same honest basin-helmet saved his skull.'

CHAPTER XVIII

*The Controversy about Mambrino's Helmet and the
Pack-Saddle disputed and decided; with other
Accidents, not more strange than true*

'Pray, good gentlemen,' said the barber, 'let us have your opinion in this matter. I suppose you will grant this same helmet to be a basin.' 'He that dares grant any such thing,' said Don Quixote, 'must know that he lies plainly, if a knight; but, if a squire, he lies abominably.' Our barber (who was privy to the whole matter) to humour the jest and carry the diversion a little higher, took up the other shaver. 'Mr. Barber, you must pardon me, sir, if I do not give you your titles; I must let you understand,' said he, 'that I have served an apprenticeship to your trade, and have been a freeman in the company these thirty years, and therefore am not to learn what belongs to shaving. You must likewise know, that I have been a soldier too in my younger days, and consequently understand the differences between a helmet, a morion, and a close-helmet, with all other accoutrements belonging to a man of arms. Yet I say, with submission still to better judgment, that this piece, here in dispute before us, is as far from being a basin, as light is from darkness. Withal I affirm, on the other hand, that although it be a helmet, it is not a complete one.' 'Right,' said the Don, 'for the lower part and the beaver are wanting.' 'A clear case, a clear case,' said the curate, Cardenio, Don Ferdinand and his companions; and the judge himself (had not Lewis's concern made him thoughtful) would have humoured the matter. 'Lord, have mercy upon us all!' said the poor barber, half-distracted, 'is it possible that so many fine, honourable gentlemen should know a basin or a helmet no better than this comes to? Gadzookers, I defy the wisest university in all Spain, with their scholarship to show me the like. Well, if it must be a helmet, it must be a helmet, that is all – and by the same rule my pack-saddle must troop too, as this gentleman says.' 'I must confess,' said Don Quixote, 'as to outward appearance it is a pack-saddle; but, as I have already said, I will not pretend to determine the dispute as to that point.' 'Nay,' said the curate, 'if Don Quixote speak not, the matter will never come to a decision; because in all affairs of chivalry, we must give him the preference.' 'I swear, worthy gentlemen,' said Don Quixote, 'that the adventures I have encountered in this castle are so strange and supernatural, that I must infallibly conclude them the effects of pure magic and enchantment. The first time I ever entered its gates I was strangely embarrassed by an enchanted Moor that inhabited it, and Sancho himself had no better entertainment from his attendants; and last night I hung suspended almost two hours by this arm, without the power of helping myself, or of assigning any reasonable cause of my misfortune. So that for me to meddle, or give my opinion in such confused and intricate events, would appear presumption; I have already given my final determination as to the helmet in controversy, but dare pronounce no definitive sentence on the pack-saddle, remitting it to the discerning judgment of the company; perhaps the power of enchantment may not prevail on you that are not dubbed knights, so that your understandings may be free, and your judicial faculties more piercing to enter into the true nature of these events, and not conclude upon them from their appearances.' 'Undoubtedly,' answered Don Ferdinand, 'the decision of this process depends upon our sentiments, according to Don Quixote's opinion; that the matter therefore may be fairly discussed, and that we may proceed upon solid and firm grounds, we will put it to the vote. Let every one give me his suffrage in my ear, and I will oblige myself to report them faithfully to the board.'

To these that knew Don Quixote this proved excellent sport; but to others unacquainted with his humour, as Don Lewis and his four servants, it appeared the most ridiculous stuff in nature; three other travellers too that happened to call in by the way, and were found to be officers of the holy brotherhood, or pursuivants, thought the people were all bewitched in good earnest. But the barber was quite at his wit's end, to think that his basin, then and there present before his eyes, was become the helmet of Mambrino: and that his pack-saddle was likewise going to be changed into rich horse-furniture. Everybody laughed very heartily to see Don Ferdinand whispering each particular person very gravely to have his vote upon the important contention of the pack-saddle. When he had gone the rounds among his own faction, that were all privy to the jest, 'Honest fellow,' said he very loudly, 'I grow weary of asking so many impertinent questions; every man has his answer at his tongue's end, that it is mere madness to call this a pack-saddle, and that is positively, *nemine contradicente*, right horse-furniture, and great horse-furniture, too; besides, friend, your allegations and proofs are of no force; therefore, in spite of your ass and you too, we give it for the defendant, that this is, and will continue the furniture of a horse, nay, and of a great horse too.' 'Now the Devil take me,' said the barber,* 'if you be not all damnably deceived; and may I be hanged if my conscience does not plainly tell me, it is a downright pack-saddle: but I have lost it according to law, and so fare it well. But I am neither mad nor drunk sure, for I am fresh and fasting this morning from everything but sin.'

The barber's raving was no less diverting than Don Quixote's clamours: 'Sentence is passed,' cried he; 'and let every man take possession of his goods and chattels, and Heaven give him joy.' 'This is a jest, a mere jest,' said one of the four servants; 'certainly, gentlemen, you cannot be in earnest, you are too wise to talk at this rate: for my part, I say and will maintain it, for there is no reason the barber should be wronged, that this is a basin, and that the pack-saddle of a he-ass.' 'May not it be a she-ass's pack-saddle, friend?' said the curate. 'That is all one, sir,' said the fellow; 'the question is not, whether it be a he or a she-ass's pack-saddle, but whether it be a pack-saddle or not, that is the matter, sir.' One of the officers of the holy brotherhood, who had heard the whole controversy, very angry to hear such an error maintained: 'Gentlemen,' said he, 'this is no more a horse's saddle than it is my father; and he that says the contrary is drunk or mad.' 'You lie, like an unmannerly rascal,' said the Knight; and at the same time with his lance, which he had always ready for such occasions, he offered such a blow at the officer's head, that had not the fellow leaped aside, it would have laid him flat. The lance flew into pieces, and the rest of the officers seeing their comrade so abused, cried out for help, charging every one to aid and assist the holy brotherhood.† The

---

* In the original it is *el sobrebarbero*, i.e. the supernumerary or additional barber, in contradistinction to the other barber who appears first in the history.

† All these troops of the holy brotherhood carry wands or rods as a mark of their office.

innkeeper being one of the fraternity, ran for his sword and rod, and then joined his fellows. Don Lewis's servants got round their master, to defend him from harm, and secure him, lest he should make his escape in the scuffle. The barber seeing the whole house turned topsy-turvy, laid hold again on his pack-saddle: but Sancho, who watched his motions, was as ready as he, and secured the other end of it.

Don Quixote drew, and assaulted the officers pell-mell. Don Lewis called to his servants to join Don Quixote, and the gentlemen that sided with him; for Cardenio, Don Ferdinand and his friends, had engaged on his side. The curate cried out, the landlady shrieked, her daughter wept, Maritornes howled, Dorothea was distracted with fear, Lucinda could not tell what to do, and Donna Clara was strangely frightened; the barber pommelled Sancho, and Sancho belaboured the barber. One of Don Lewis's servants went to hold him, but he gave him such a rebuke on his jaws, that his teeth had like to have forsook their station; and then the judge took him into his protection. Don Ferdinand had got one of the officers down, and laid him on back and side. The innkeeper still cried out, 'Help the holy brotherhood,' so that the whole house was a medley of wailings, cries, shrieks, confusions, fears, terrors, disasters, flashes, buffets, blows, kicks, cuffs, battery, and bloodshed.

In the greatest of this hurly-burly, it came into Don Quixote's head, that he was certainly involved in the disorder and confusion of King Agramant's camp; and calling out with a voice that shook the whole house, 'Hold, valorous knights,' said he, 'all hold your furious hands, sheath all your swords, let none presume to strike on pain of death, but hear me speak.' The loud and monstrous voice surprised everybody into obedience, and the Don proceeded: 'I told you before, gentlemen, that this castle was enchanted, and that some legions of devils did inhabit it: now let your own eyes confirm my words: do not you behold the strange and horrid confusion of King Agramant's army removed hither, and put in execution among us? See, see how they fight for the sword, and yonder for the horse! Behold how some contend for the helmet, and here others battle it for the standard; and all fight we do not know how, nor can tell why. Let, therefore my Lord Judge, and his reverence Mr. Curate, represent one King Agramant, and the other King Sobrino, and by their wisdom and conduct appease this tumult: for, by the powers Divine, it were a wrong to honour, and a blot on chivalry, to let so many worthies, as are here met, kill one another for such trifles.'

Don Quixote's words were Hebrew to the officers, who having been roughly handled by Cardenio, Ferdinand, and his friends, would not give it over so. But the barber was content; for Sancho had demolished his beard and pack-saddle both in the scuffle; the squire dutifully retreated at the first sound of his master's voice; Don Lewis's servants were calm, finding it their best way to be quiet; but the innkeeper was refractory. He swore that madman ought to be punished for his ill-behaviour, and that every hour he was making some disturbance or another in his house. But at last, the matter was made up, the pack-saddle was agreed to be horse-furniture, the basin a helmet, and the inn a castle, till the day of judgment, if Don Quixote would have it so. Don Lewis's business came next in play. The judge, in concert with Don Ferdinand, Cardenio, and the curate, resolved that Don Ferdinand should interpose his authority on Don Lewis's behalf, and let his servants know, that he would carry him to Andalusia, where he should be entertained according to his quality by his brother the Marquis; and they should not oppose this design, seeing Don Lewis was positively resolved not to be forced to go back to his father yet. Don Ferdinand's quality, and Don Lewis's resolution prevailed on the fellows to order matters so, that three of them might return to acquaint their old master, and the fourth wait on Don Lewis. Thus this monstrous heap of confusion and disorder was digested into form, by the authority of Agramant, and wisdom of King Sobrino.

But the enemy of peace, finding his project of setting them all by the ears so eluded, resolved once again to have another trial of skill, and play the devil with them all the second bout: for though the officers, under-standing the quality of their adversaries, were willing to desist, yet one of them, whom Don Ferdinand had kicked most unmercifully, remember-ing, that among other warrants, he had one to apprehend Don Quixote for setting free the galley-slaves (which Sancho was sadly afraid would come about), he resolved to examine if the marks and tokens given of Don Quixote agreed with this person; then drawing out a parchment, and opening his warrant, he made a shift to read it, and at every other word looked cunningly in Don Quixote's face; whereupon, folding up the parchment, and taking his warrant in his left hand, he clapped his right hand fast in the Knight's collar, crying, 'You are the king's prisoner: gentlemen, I am an officer, here is my warrant. I charge you all to aid and assist the holy brotherhood.' Don Quixote, finding himself used so rudely, by one whom he took to be a pitiful scoundrel, kindled up into such a rage, that he shook with indignation, and catching the fellow by the neck, with both his hands, squeezed him so violently, that if his companions had not presently freed him, the Knight would certainly have throttled him before he had quitted his hold.

The innkeeper, being obliged to assist his brother officer, presently joined him: the hostess seeing her husband engaging a second time, raised a new outcry, her daughter and Maritornes bore the burden of the song, sometimes praying, sometimes crying, sometimes scolding: Sancho, see-ing what passed, 'By the lord,' said he, 'my master is in the right; this place is haunted, that is certain; there is no living quietly an hour together.' At last Don Ferdinand parted Don Quixote and the officer, who were both pretty well pleased to quit their bargain. However, the officers still demanded their prisoner, and to have him delivered bound into their hands, commanding all the company a second time to help and assist them to secure that public robber upon the king's high road.

Don Quixote smiled at the supposed simplicity of the fellows; at last, with solemn gravity, 'Come hither,' said he, 'you offspring of filth and extraction of dunghills, dare you call loosing the fettered, freeing the captive, helping the miserable, raising the fallen, and supplying the indigent; dare you, I say, base-spirited rascals, call these actions robbery? Your thoughts, indeed, are too grovelling and servile, to understand, or reach the pitch of chivalry, otherwise you had understood, that even the shadow of a knight-errant had claim to your adoration. You a band of officers; you are a pack of rogues indeed, and robbers on the highway by authority. What blockhead of a magistrate durst issue out a warrant to apprehend a knight-errant like me? Could not his ignorance find out that we are exempt from all courts of judicature? – that our valour is the bench, our will the common law, and our sword the executioner of justice? Could not his dulness inform him, that no rank of nobility or peerage enjoys more immunities and privileges? Has he any precedent that a knight-errant ever paid taxes, subsidy, poll-money, or so much as fare or ferry? What tailor ever had money for his clothes? or what constable ever made him a reckoning for lodging in his castle? What kings are not proud of his company? and what damsels of his love? And lastly, did you ever read of any knight-errant that ever was, is, or shall be, that could not, with his single force, cudgel four hundred such rogues as you to pieces, if they have the impudence to oppose him?'

CHAPTER XIX

The notable Adventure of the Officers of the Holy Brotherhood with Don Quixote's great ferocity and enchantment

WHILST DON QUIXOTE talked at this rate, the curate endeavoured to persuade the officers that he was distracted, as they might easily gather from his words and actions; and, therefore, though they should carry him before a magistrate, he would be presently acquitted, as being a madman. He that had the warrant made answer, that it was not his business to examine whether he were mad or not, he was an officer in commission, and must obey orders; and accordingly was resolved to deliver him up to the superior power, which once done, they might acquit him five hundred times if they would. But for all that, the curate persisted they should not carry Don Quixote away with them this time; adding, that the Knight himself would by no means be brought to it; and in short, said so much, that they had been greater fools than he, could they not have plainly seen his madness. They, therefore, not only desisted, but offered their service in compounding the difference between Sancho and the barber; their mediation was accepted, they being officers of justice, and succeeded so well, that both parties stood to their arbitration, though not entirely satisfied with their award, which ordered them to change their pannels, but not their halters nor the girths. The curate made up the business of the basin, paying the barber under-hand eight reals for it, and getting a general release under his hand of all claims or actions concerning it, and all things else. These two important differences being so happily decided, the only obstacles to a general peace were Don Lewis's servants and the innkeeper; the first were prevailed upon to accept the proposals offered, which were, that three of them should go home, and the fourth attend Don Lewis where Don Ferdinand should appoint. Thus this difference was made up, to the unspeakable joy of Donna Clara. Zoraida not well understanding anything that passed, was sad and cheerful by turns, as she observed others to be by their countenances, especially her beloved Spaniard, on whom her eyes were more particularly fixed. The innkeeper made a hideous bawling; having discovered that the barber had received money for his basin, he knew no reason, he said, why he should not be paid as well as other folks, and swore that Rozinante and Sancho's ass should pay for their master's extravagance before they should leave his stable; the curate pacified him, and Don Ferdinand paid him his bill. All things thus accommodated, the inn no longer resembled the confusion of Agramant's camp, but rather the universal peace of Augustus's reign: upon which the curate and Don Ferdinand had the thanks of the house, as a just acknowledgment for their so effectual mediation.

Don Quixote being now free from the difficulties and delays that lately embarrassed him, held it high time to prosecute his voyage, and bring to some decision the general enterprise which he had the voice and election for. He therefore fully resolved to press his departure, and fell on his knees before Dorothea, but she would not hear him in that posture, but prevailed upon him to rise: he then addressed her in his usual forms: 'Most beautiful lady,' said he, 'it is a known proverb, that "Diligence is the mother of success"; and we have found the greatest successes in war still to depend on expedition and dispatch, by preventing the enemy's design, and forcing a victory before an assault is expected. My inference from this, most high and illustrious lady, is, that our residence in this castle appears nothing conducive to our designs, but may prove dangerous; for we may reasonably suppose, that our enemy the giant may learn by spies, or some other secret intelligence, the scheme of our intentions, and consequently fortify himself in some inexpugnable fortress, against the power of our utmost endeavours, and so the strength of my invincible arm may be ineffectual. Let us therefore, dear madam, by our diligence and sudden departure hence, prevent any such his designs, and force our good fortune, by missing no opportunity that we may lay hold of.' Here he stopped, waiting the Princess's answer. She, with a grave aspect, and style suiting his extravagance replied, 'The great inclination and indefatigable desire you show, worthy knight, in assisting the injured, and restoring the oppressed, lay a fair claim to the praises and universal thanks of mankind; but your singular concern, and industrious application in assisting me, deserve my particular acknowledgments and gratification; and I shall make it my peculiar request to Heaven, that your generous designs, in my favour, may be soon accomplished, that I may be enabled to convince you of the honour and gratitude that may be found in some of our sex. As to our departure, I shall depend upon your pleasure, to whose management I have not only committed the care of my person, but also resigned the whole power of command.' 'Then by the assistance of the Divine power,' answered he, 'I will lose no opportunity of reinstating your Highness, since you condescend to humble yourself to my orders; let our march be sudden, for the eagerness of my desires, the length of the journey, and the dangers of delay, are great spurs to my dispatch; since therefore Heaven has not created, nor Hell seen the man I ever feared; fly, Sancho, saddle Rozinante harness your ass, and make ready the lady's palfrey; let us take leave of the Governor here, and these other lords, and set out from hence immediately.'

Poor Sancho hearing all that passed, shook his head, 'Lord, lord, master,' said he, 'there is always more tricks in a town than are talked of (with reverence be it spoken).' 'Ho! villain,' cried Don Quixote, 'what tricks can any town or city show to impair my credit?' 'Nay, sir,' quoth Sancho, 'if you grow angry, I can hold my tongue, if that be all; but there are some things which you ought to hear, and I should tell as becomes a trusty squire, and honest servant.' 'Say what thou wilt,' said the Knight, 'so it tend not to cowardice; for if thou art afraid, keep it to thyself, and trouble not me with the mention of fear, which my soul abhors.' 'Pshaw, hang fear,' answered Sancho, 'that is not the matter; but I must tell you, sir, that which is as certain and plain as the nose on your face. This same madam here, that calls herself the queen of the great kingdom of Micomicon, is no more a queen than my grandame. For, do but consider, sir, if she were such a fine queen as you believe, can you imagine she would always be sucking of snouts,* and kissing and slabbering a certain person, that shall be nameless in this company?' Dorothea blushed at Sancho's words, for Don Ferdinand, had indeed, sometimes, and in private, taken the freedom with his lips to reap some part of the reward his affection deserved; which Sancho spying by chance, made some constructions upon, very much to the disadvantage of her royalty; for, in short, he concluded her no better than a woman of pleasure. She would nevertheless take no notice of his aspersion, but let him go on. 'I say this, sir,' continued he, 'because after our trudging through all weathers, fair after foul, day after night, and night after day, this same person in the inn here, is like to divert himself at our expense, and to gather the fruit of our labours. I think therefore, master, there is no reason, do you see, for saddling Rozinante, harnessing my ass, or making ready the lady's palfrey; for we had better stay where we are; and let every whore brew as she bakes, and every man that is hungry go to dinner.'

Heavens! into what a fury did these disrespectful words of Sancho put the Knight? His whole body shook, his tongue faltered, his eyes glowed. 'Thou villainous, ignorant, rash, unmannerly, blasphemous, detractor,' said he, 'how darest thou entertain such base and dishonourable thoughts, much more utter thy rude and contemptible suspicions before me and this honourable presence? Away from my sight, thou monster of nature, magazine of lies, cupboard of deceits, granary of guile, publisher of follies, foe of all honour! Away, and never let me see thy face again, on pain of my most furious indignation.' Then bending his angry brows, puffing his cheeks, and stamping on the ground, he gave Sancho such a look as almost frightened the poor fellow to annihilation.

In the height of this consternation, all that the poor squire could do, was to turn his back, and sneak out of the room. But Dorothea, knowing the Knight's temper, undertook to mitigate his anger. 'Sir Knight of the Woeful Figure,' said she, 'assuage your wrath, I beseech you; it is below your dignity to be offended at those idle words of your squire; and I dare not affirm but that he has some colour of reason for what he said; for it were uncharitable to suspect his sincere understanding, and honest principles, of any false or malicious slander or accusation. We must therefore search deeper into this affair, and believe, that as you have found all transactions in this castle governed by enchantment, so some diabolical illusion has appeared to Sancho, and represented to his enchanted sight what he asserts to my dishonour.' 'Now by the powers supreme,' said the Knight, 'your Highness has cut the knot. The misdemeanor of that poor

---

* *Hocicando* in the original, from *Hocico*, the snout of any beast. *Hocico quasi Focico*, from the Latin *Fauces*, jaws. The Spanish form most Latin words by changing F into H; thus *Fenum*, hay, is *Heno*, etc.

fellow must be attributed purely to enchantment, and the power of some malicious apparition; for the good nature and simplicity of the poor wretch could never invent a lie, or be guilty of an aspersion to any one's disadvantage.' 'It is evident,' said Don Ferdinand, 'we therefore all intercede in behalf of honest Sancho, that he may be again restored to your favour, *sicut erat in principio*, before these illusions had imposed upon his sense.' Don Quixote complied, and the curate brought in poor Sancho trembling who on his knees made an humble acknowledgment of his crime, and begged to have his pardon confirmed by a gracious kiss of his master's hand. Don Quixote gave him his hand and his blessing. 'Now, Sancho,' said he, 'will you hereafter believe what I so often have told you, that the power of enchantment overrules everything in this castle?' 'I will, and like your worship,' quoth Sancho, 'all but my tossing in a blanket; for really, sir, that happened according to the ordinary course of things.' 'Believe it not, Sancho,' replied Don Quixote, 'for were I not convinced of the contrary, you should have plentiful revenge; but neither then, or now, could I ever find any object to wreak my fury or resentment on.' Every one desired to know what was the business in question; whereupon the innkeeper gave them an account of Sancho's tossing, which set them all a-laughing, and would have made Sancho angry, had not his master afresh assured him that it was only a mere illusion, which though the squire believed not, he held his tongue. The whole company having passed two days in the inn, bethought themselves of departing; and the curate and barber found out a device to carry home Don Quixote, without putting Don Ferdinand and Dorothea to the trouble of humouring his impertinence any longer. They first agreed with a waggoner that went by with his team of oxen, to carry him home: then had a kind of wooden cage made, so large that the Knight might conveniently sit, or lie in it. Presently after all the company of the inn disguised themselves, some with masks, others by disfiguring their faces, and the rest by change of apparel, so that Don Quixote should not take them to be the same persons. This done, they all silently entered his chamber, where he was sleeping very soundly after his late fatigues: they immediately laid hold on him so forcibly, and held his arms and legs so hard, that he was not able to stir, or do anything but stare on those odd figures which stood round him. This instantly confirmed him in the strange fancy that had so long disturbed his crazy understanding, and made him believe himself undoubtedly enchanted; and those frightful figures to be the spirits and demons of the enchanted castle. So far the curate's invention succeeded to his expectation. Sancho being the only person there in his right shape and senses, beheld all this very patiently; and though he knew them all very well, yet was resolved to see the end of it before he ventured to speak his mind. His master likewise said nothing, patiently expecting his fate, and waiting the event of his misfortune. They had by this lifted him out of bed, and placing him in the cage, they shut him in, and nailed the bars of it so fast, that no small strength could force them open. Then mounting him on their shoulders, as they conveyed him out of the chamber door, they heard as dreadful a voice as the barber's lungs could bellow, speak these words:

'Be not impatient, O Knight of the Woeful Figure, at your imprisonment, since it is ordained by the fates, for the more speedy accomplishment of that most noble adventure, which your incomparable valour has intended. For accomplished it shall be, when the rampant Manchegan lion* and the white Tobosian dove shall be united, by humbling their lofty and erected chests to the soft yoke of wedlock, from whose wonderful coition shall be produced and spring forth brave whelps which shall imitate the rampant paws of their valorous sire. And this shall happen before the bright pursuer of the fugitive nymph shall, by his rapid and natural course, take a double circumference in visitation of the luminous signs. An thou, the most noble and faithful squire that ever had sword on thigh, beard on face, or sense of smell in nose, be not dispirited or discontented at this captivity of the flower of all chivalry; for very speedily, by the eternal will of the world's Creator, thou shalt find thyself ennobled and exalted beyond the knowledge of thy greatness. And I confirm to thee, from the sage Mentironiana,† that thou shalt not be defrauded of the promises made by thy noble lord. I therefore conjure thee to follow closely the steps of the courageous and enchanted Knight; for it is necessarily enjoined, that you both go where you both shall stay. The fates have commanded me no more, farewell. For I now return, I well know whither.'

The barber managed the cadence of his voice so artificially towards the latter end of his prophecy, that even those who were made acquainted with the jest, had almost taken it for supernatural.

Don Quixote was much comforted at the prophecy, apprehending presently the sense of it, and applying it to his marriage with Dulcinea del Toboso, from whose happy womb should issue the cubs, signifying his sons, to the eternal glory of La Mancha; upon the strength of which belief raising his voice, and heaving a profound sigh: 'Whatsoever thou art,' said he, 'whose happy prognostication I own and acknowledge, I desire thee to implore, in my name, the wise magician, whose charge I am, that his power may protect me in this captivity, and not permit me to perish

---

* It may be translated the rampant spotted lion as well as the rampant Manchegan lion: for the Spanish word Mancha signifies both a spot, and the country La Mancha. An untranslatable double *entendre*.

† Mentironiana is a framed word from *Mentira*, 'a lie,' as if we should say *Fibberiana*.

before the fruition of these grateful and incomparable promises made to me; for the confirmation of such hopes, I would think my prison a palace, my fetters freedom, and this hard field-bed on which I lie, more easy than the softest down, or most luxurious lodgings. And as to the consolation offered my squire Sancho Pança, I am so convinced of his honesty, and he has proved his honour in so many adventures, that I mistrust not his deserting me, through any change of fortune. And though his or my harder stars should disable me from bestowing on him the island I have promised, or some equivalent, his wages at least are secured to him by my last will and testament, though what he will receive is more answerable, I confess, to my estate and ability, than to his services and great deserts.' Sancho Pança made him three or four very respectful bows, and kissed both his hands (for one alone he could not, being both tied together), and in an instant the demons hoisted up the cage, and yoked it very handsomely to the team of oxen.

CHAPTER XX

Prosecuting the course of Don Quixote's enchantment with other memorable Occurrences

DON QUIXOTE was not so much amazed at his enchantment, as at the manner of it: 'Among all the volumes of chivalry that I have turned over,' said he, 'I never read before of knights-errant drawn in carts or tugged along so leisurely, by such slothful animals as oxen. For they used to be hurried along with prodigious speed, enveloped in some dark and dusky cloud; or in some fiery chariot drawn by winged griffins, or some such expeditious creatures; but I must confess, to be drawn thus by a team of oxen, staggers my understanding not a little; though perhaps the enchanters of our times take a different method from those in former ages: or rather the wise magicians have invented some course in their proceedings for me, being the first reviver or restorer of arms, which have so long been lost in oblivion, and rusted through the disuse of chivalry. What is thy opinion, my dear Sancho?' 'Why truly, sir,' said Sancho, 'I cannot tell what to think, being not so well read in these matters as your worship; yet for all that, I am positive and can take my oath on it, that these same phantoms that run up and down here are not orthodox.' 'Orthodox, my friend,' said Don Quixote, 'how can they be orthodox, when they are devils, and have only assumed these phantastical bodies to surprise us into this condition? To convince you, are not material, but only subtile air, and outward appearance.' 'Gadzookers, sir,' said Sancho, 'I have touched them, and touched them again, sir; and I find this same busy devil here, that is fiddling about, is as plump and fat as a capon: besides, he has another property very different from a devil; for the devils, they say, smell of brimstone and other filthy things, and this spark has such a fine scent of essence about him, that you may smell him at least half a league. (Meaning Don Ferdinand, who in all probability, like other gentlemen of his quality, had his clothes perfumed.)

'Alas, honest Sancho,' answered Don Quixote, 'the cunning of these fiends is above the reach of thy simplicity; for you must know, the spirits, as spirits, have no scent at all; and if they should, it must necessarily be some unsavoury stench, because they still carry their Hell about them, and the least of a perfume or grateful odour were inconsistent with their torments; so that this mistake of yours must be attributed to some farther delusion of your sense.' Don Ferdinand and Cardenio, upon these discourses between master and man, were afraid that Sancho would spoil all, and therefore ordered the innkeeper privately to get ready Rozinante and Sancho's ass, while the curate agreed with the officers for so much a day to conduct them home. Cardenio, having hung Don Quixote's target on the pommel of Rozinante's saddle and the basin on the other side, he signified to Sancho by signs, that he should mount his ass, and lead Rozinante by the bridle; and lastly placed two officers with their firelocks on each side of the cart.

Being just ready to march, the hostess, her daughter, and Maritornes, came to the door to take their leave of the Knight, pretending unsupportable grief for his misfortune. 'Restrain your tears, most honourable ladies,' said Don Quixote, 'for these mischances are incident to those of my profession; and from these disasters it is we date the greatness of our glory and renown; they are the effects of envy, which still attends virtuous and great actions, and brought upon us by the indirect means of such princes and knights as are emulous of our dignity and fame: but, spite of all oppression, spite of all the magic that ever its first inventor Zoroastres understood, virtue will come off victorious; and, triumphing over every danger, will at last shine out in its proper lustre like the sun to enlighten the world. Pardon me, fair ladies, if through ignorance or omission of the respects due to your qualities, I have not behaved to please you; for, to the best of my knowledge, I never committed a wilful wrong. And I crave the assistance of your prayers towards my enlargement from this prison, which some malicious magician has confined me to; and the first business of my freedom shall be a grateful acknowledgment for the many and obliging favours conferred upon me in this your castle.' Whilst the ladies were thus entertained by Don Quixote, the curate and barber were busy taking their leaves of their company; and after mutual compliments and embraces, they engaged to acquaint one another with their succeeding fortunes. Don Ferdinand entreated the curate to give him a particular relation of Don Quixote's adventures, assuring him that nothing would be a greater obligation, and at the same time engaged to inform him of his own marriage and Lucinda's return to her parents; with an account of Zoraida's baptism, and Don Lewis's success in his amour.

The curate having given his word and honour to satisfy Don Ferdinand, and the last compliments being paid, was just going, when the innkeeper made him a proffer of a bundle of papers found in the folds of the same cloak-bag, where he got 'The Curious Impertinent,' telling him that they were all at his service; because, since the owner was not like to come and demand them, and he could not read, they could not better be disposed of. The curate thanked him heartily, and opening the papers, found them entitled, 'The Story of Rinconete,' and 'Cortadillo.' The title showing it to be a novel, and probably written by the author of 'The Curious Impertinent,' because found in the same wallet, he put it in his pocket, with a resolution to peruse it the very first opportunity: then, mounting with his friend the barber, and both putting on masks, they followed the procession, which marched in this order. The carter led the van, and next his cart flanked on right and left with two officers with their firelocks; then followed Sancho on his ass, leading Rozinante; and lastly the curate and the barber on their mighty mules brought up the rear of the body, all with a grave and solemn air, marching no faster than the heavy oxen allowed. Don Quixote sat leaning against the back of the cage with his hands tied, and his legs at length; but so silent and motionless, that he seemed rather statue than a man.

They had travelled about two leagues this slow and leisurely pace, when their conductor, stopping in a little valley, proposed it as a fit place to bait in; but he was prevailed upon to defer halting a little longer, being informed by the barber of a certain valley beyond a little hill in their view, better stored with grass, and more convenient for their purpose. They had not travelled much further when the curate spied coming a round pace after them six or seven men very well accoutred. They appeared, by their brisk riding, to be mounted on Churchmen's mules, not carried as the Don was by a team of sluggish oxen. They endeavoured before the heat of the day to reach their inn, which was a league further. In short, they soon came up with our slow itinerants; and one of them, that was a canon of Toledo, and master of those that came along with him, marking the formal procession of the cart, guards, Sancho, Rozinante, the curate, and the barber, but chiefly the incaged Don Quixote, could not forbear asking what meant their strange method of securing that man; though he already believed, having observed the guards, that he was some notorious criminal in custody of the holy brotherhood. One of the fraternity told him, that he could not tell the cause of that knight's imprisonment, but that he might answer for himself, because he best could tell.

Don Quixote, overhearing their discourse, 'Gentlemen,' said he, 'if you are conversant and skilled in matters of knight-errantry, I will communicate my misfortunes to you; if you are not, I have no reason to give myself the trouble.' 'Truly, friend,' answered the canon, 'I am better acquainted with books of chivalry than with Villapando's divinity; and if that be all your objection, you may safely impart to me what you please.' 'With Heaven's permission be it so,' said Don Quixote; 'you must then understand, Sir Knight, that I am borne away in this cage by the force of enchantments, through the envious spite and malice of some cursed magicians; for virtue is more zealously persecuted by ill men, than it is beloved by the good. I am by profession a knight-errant, and none of those, I assure you, whose deeds never merited a place in the records of fame; but one who in spite of envy's self, in spite of all the magi of Persia, the brahmans of India, or the gymnosophists of Ethiopia, shall secure to his name a place in the temple of immortality, as a pattern and model to following ages, that ensuing knights-errant, following my steps, may be guided to the top and highest pitch of heroic honour.' 'The noble Don Quixote de la Mancha speaks truth,' said the curate, coming up to the company, 'he is indeed enchanted in this cart, not through his own demerits or offences, but the malicious treachery of those whom virtue displeases and valour offends. This is, sir, the Knight of the Woeful Figure, of whom you have undoubtedly heard, whose mighty deeds shall stand engraved in lasting brass and time-surviving marble, till envy grows tired with labouring to deface his fame, and malice to conceal them.'

The canon hearing the prisoner and his guard talk thus in the same style, was in a maze, and blessed himself for wonder, as did the rest of the company, till Sancho Pança coming up, to mend the matter, 'Look ye, sirs,' said he, 'I will speak the truth, take it well, or take it ill. My master here is no more enchanted than my mother: he is in his sober senses, he eats and drinks, and does his needs, like other folks, and as he used to do; and yet they will persuade me that a man, who can do all this, is enchanted forsooth; he can speak too; for, if they will let him alone, he will prattle you more than thirty attorneys.' Then turning towards the curate, 'O Mr. Curate, Mr. Curate,' continued he, 'do you think I do not know you, and that I do not guess what all these new enchantments drive at! Yes, I do know you well enough, for all you do hide your face; and understand your design, for all your sly tricks, sir. But it is an old saying, There is no striving against the stream: and the weakest still goes to the wall. The Devil take the luck on it; had not your Reverence spoiled our sport, my master had been married before now to the princess Macomicona, and I had been an earl at least; nay, that I was sure of, had the worst come to the worst; but the old proverb is true again, Fortune turns round like a mill-wheel, and he that was yesterday at the top, lies today at the bottom. I wonder, Mr. Curate, you that are a clergyman should not have more conscience: consider, sir, that I have a wife and family who expect all to be great folks, and my master here is to do a world of good deeds: and do not you think, sir, that you will not be made to answer for all this one day?' 'Snuff me those candles,' said the barber, hearing Sancho talk at this rate: 'what, fool, are you brain-sick of your master's disease too? If you be, you are like to bear him company in his cage, I will assure you, friend. What enchanted island is this that floats in your skull? or what succubus has been riding thy fancy, and got it with child of these hopes?' 'With child! Sir, what do ye mean, sir?' said Sancho, 'I scorn your words, sir; the best lord in the land should not get me with child, no, not the king himself, Heaven bless him. For though I am a poor man, yet I am an honest man, and an old Christian, and do not owe any man a farthing; and though I desire islands, there are other folks not far off that desire worse things. Every one is the son of his own works; I am a man, and may be Pope of Rome, much more governor of an island; especially considering my master may gain so many as he may want persons to bestow them on. Therefore, pray, Mr. Barber, take heed what you say; for all consists not in shaving of beards; and there is some difference between a hawk and a handsaw. I say so, because we all know one another; and nobody shall put a false card upon me. As to my master's enchantment, let it stand as it is, Heaven knows best: and a stink is still worse for the stirring.' The barber thought silence the best way to quiet Sancho's impertinence; and the curate, doubting that he might spoil all, entreated the canon to move a little before, and he would unfold the mystery of the encaged knight, which perhaps he would find one of the pleasantest stories he had ever heard: the canon rode forward with him, and his men followed, while the curate made them a relation of Don Quixote's life and quality, his madness and adventures, with the original cause of his distraction, and the whole progress of his affairs, till his being shut up in the cage, to get him home in order to have him cured. They all admired at this strange account; and then the canon turning to the curate: 'Believe me, Mr. Curate,' said he, 'I am fully convinced, that those they call books of knight-errantry, are very prejudicial to the public. And though I have been led away with an idle and false pleasure to read the beginnings of almost as many of them as have been printed, I could never yet persuade myself to go through with any one to the end; for to me they all seem to contain one and the same thing; and there is as much in one of them as in all the rest. The whole composition and style resemble that of the Milesian fables, which are a sort of idle stories, designed only for diversion, and not for instruction. It is not so with those fables which are called Apologues, that at once delight and instruct. But though the main design of such books is to please; yet I cannot conceive how it is possible they should perform it, being filled with such a multitude of unaccountable extravagancies. For the pleasure which strikes the soul must be derived from the beauty and congruity it sees or conceives in those things the sight or imagination lay before it; and nothing in itself deformed or incongruous can give us any real satisfaction. Now what beauty can there be, or what proportion of the parts to the whole, or of the whole to the several parts, in a book or fable, where a stripling of sixteen years of age, at one cut of a sword, cleaves a giant as tall as a steeple through the middle, as easily as if he were made of pasteboard? Or when they give us the relation of a battle, having said the enemy's power consisted of a million of combatants, yet, provided the hero of the book be against them, we must of necessity, though never so much against our inclination, conceive that the said knight obtained the victory only by his own valour, and the strength of his powerful arm? And what shall we say of the great ease and facility with which an absolute queen or empress casts herself into the arms of an errant and unknown knight? What mortal, not altogether barbarous and unpolished, can be pleased to read, that a great tower, full of armed knights, cuts through the sea like a ship before the wind, and setting out in the evening from the coast of Italy, lands by break of day in Prester John's country, or in some other never known to Ptolemy, or seen by Marcus Paulus?* If it should be answered, that the persons who compose these books, write them as confessed lies; and therefore are not obliged to observe niceties, or to have regard to truth; L shall make this reply, that falsehood is so much the more commendable, by how much it more resembles truth; and is the more pleasing the more it is doubtful and possible. Fabulous tales ought to be suited to the reader's understanding, being so contrived, that all impossibilities ceasing, all great accidents appearing feasible, and the mind wholly hanging in suspense, they may at once surprise, astonish, please, and divert; so that pleasure and admiration may go hand in hand. This cannot be performed by him that flies from probability and imitation, which is the perfection of what is written. I have not seen any book of knight-errantry that composes an entire body of a fable with all its parts, so that the middle is answerable to tile beginning, and the end to the beginning and middle; but on the contrary, they form them of so many limbs, that they rather seem a chimera or monster, than a well propor-tioned figure. Besides all this, their style is uncouth, their exploits incredible, their love immodest, their civility impertinent, their battles tedious, their language absurd, their voyages preposterous; and in short,

---

* A Venetian, and a very great traveller. He lived in the 13th century, 1272. He had travelled over Syria, Persia, and the Indies. An account of his travels has been printed, and one of his books entitled 'De regionibus orientis.'

they are altogether void of solid ingenuity, and therefore fit to be banished a Christian commonwealth as useless and prejudicial.' The curate was very attentive, and believed him a man of sound judgment, and much in the right in all he had urged; and therefore told him, that being of the same opinion, and an enemy to the books of knight-errantry, he had burnt all that belonged to Don Quixote, which were a considerable number. Then he recounted to him the scrutiny he had made among them, what he had condemned to the flames, and what spared; at which the canon* laughed heartily, and said, 'That notwithstanding all he had spoken against those books, yet he found one good thing in them, which was the subject they furnished a man of understanding with to exercise his parts, because they allow a large scope for the pen to dilate upon without any check, describing shipwrecks, storms, skirmishes and battles; representing to us a brave commander, with all the qualifications requisite in such a one, showing his prudence in disappointing the designs of the enemy, his eloquence in persuading or dissuading his soldiers, his judgment in council, his celerity in execution, and his valour in assailing or repulsing an assault; laying before us sometimes a dismal and melancholy accident, sometimes a delightful and unexpected adventure; in one place a beautiful, modest, discreet and reserved lady; in another, a Christian-like, brave, and courteous gentleman; here a boisterous, inhuman, boasting ruffian; there an affable, warlike, and wise prince, lively expressing the fidelity and loyalty of subjects, generosity and bounty of sovereigns. He may no less, at times, make known his skill in astrology, cosmography, music, and policy; and if he pleases, he cannot want an opportunity of appearing knowing, even in necromancy. He may describe the subtlety of Ulysses, the piety of Æneas, the valour of Achilles, the misfortunes of Hector, the treachery of Sinon, the friendship of Euryalus, the liberality of Alexander, the valour of Cæsar, the clemency and sincerity of Trajan, the fidelity of Zopyrus, the prudence of Cato; and in fine, all those actions that may make up a complete hero, sometimes attributing them all to one person, and at other times dividing them among many. This being so performed in a grateful style, and with ingenious invention, approaching as much as possible to truth, will doubtless compose so beautiful and various a work, that, when finished, its excellency and perfection must attain the best end of writing, which is at once to delight and instruct, as I have said before: for the loose method practised in those books, gives the author liberty to play the epic, the lyric, and the dramatic poet, and to run through all the parts of poetry and rhetoric; for epics may be as well writ in prose† as in verse.'

---

* This canon of Toledo is Cervantes himself all along.
† The 'Adventures of Telemachus' is a proof of this.

CHAPTER XXI

Containing a continuation of the Canon's Discourse upon books of Knight-Errantry, and other curious matters

'You are much in the right, sir,' replied the curate; 'and therefore those who have hitherto published books of that kind, are the more to be blamed, for having had no regard to good sense, art, or rules, by the observation of which they might have made themselves as famous in prose, as the two princes of Greek and Latin poetry are in verse.' 'I must confess,' said the canon, 'I was once tempted to write a book of knight-errantry myself, observing all those rules; and, to speak the truth, I writ above one hundred pages, which, for the better trial whether they answered my expectation, I communicated to some learned and judicious men fond of those subjects, as well as to some of those ignorant persons, who only are delighted with extravagancies; and they all give me a satisfactory approbation. And yet I made no further progress, as well in regard I look upon it to be a thing no way agreeable with my profession, as because I am sensible the illiterate are much more numerous than the learned; and though it were of more weight to be commended by the small number of the wise, than scorned by the ignorant multitude, yet would I not expose myself to the confused judgment of the giddy vulgar, who principally are those who read such books. But the greatest motive I had to lay aside and think no more of finishing it, was the argument I formed to myself, deduced from the plays now usually acted: for, thought I, if plays now in use, as well those which are altogether of the poet's invention as those that are grounded upon history, be all of them, or, however, the greatest part, made up of most absurd extravangancies and incoherencies; things that have neither head nor foot, side nor bottom; and yet the multitude sees them with satisfaction, esteems and approves them, though they are so far from being good; and if the poets who write, and the players who act them, say they must be so contrived and no otherwise, because they please the generality of the audience; and if those which are regular and according to art, serve only to please half a score judicious persons who understand them, whilst the rest of the company cannot reach the connivance, nor know anything of the matter; and therefore the poets and actors say, they had rather get their bread by the greater number, than the applause of the less: then may I conclude the same will be the success of this book; so that, when I have racked my brains to observe the rules, I shall reap no other advantage than to be laughed at for my pains. I have sometimes endeavoured to convince the actors that they are deceived in their opinion, and that they will draw more company, and get more credit by regular plays, than by those preposterous representations now in use; but they are so positive in their humour, that no strength of reason, nor even demonstration, can beat this opinion into their heads. I remember I once was talking to one of those obstinate fellows: "Do you not remember," said I, "that within these few years, three tragedies were acted in Spain, written by a famous poet of ours, which were so excellent, that they surprised, delighted, and raised the admiration of all that saw them, as well the ignorant and ordinary people as the judicious and men of quality; and the actors got more by those three, than by thirty of the best that have been writ since?" "Doubtless, sir," said the actor, "you mean the tragedies of Isabella, Phillis, and Alexandra." "The very same," I replied, "and do you judge whether they observed the rules of the drama; and whether, by doing so, they lost anything of their esteem, or failed of pleasing all sorts of people. So that the fault lies not in the audience's desiring absurdities, but in those who know not how to give them anything else. Nor was there anything preposterous in several other plays: as for example, 'Ingratitude Revenged,' 'Numancia,' 'The Amorous Merchant,' and 'The Favourable She-enemy': nor in some others, composed by judicious poets, to their honour and credit, and to the advantage of those that acted them." Much more I added, which did indeed somewhat confound him, but no way satisfied or convinced him, so as to make him change his erroneous opinion.' 'You have hit upon a subject, sir,' said the curate, 'which has stirred up in me an old aversion I have for the plays now in use, which is not inferior to that I bear to books of knight-errantry. For whereas plays, according to the opinion of Cicero, ought to be mirrors of human life, patterns of good manners, and the very representatives of truth; those now acted are mirrors of absurdities, patterns of follies, and images of ribaldry. For instance, what can be more absurd, than for the same person to be brought on the stage a child in swaddling-bands, in the first scene of the first act; and to appear in the second grown a man? What can be more ridiculous than to represent to us a fighting old fellow, a cowardly youth, a rhetorical footman, a politic page, a churlish king, and an unpolished princess? What shall I say of their regard to the time in which those actions they represent, either might or ought to have happened, for I have seen a play, in which the first act began in Europe, the second was in Asia, and the third ended in Africa?* Probably, if there had been another act, they would have carried it into America; and thus it would have been acted in the four parts of the world. But if imitation is to be a principal part of

---

* It is to be observed, that the Spanish plays have only three *jornadas*, or acts.

the drama, how can any tolerable judgment be pleased, when representing an action that happened in the time of King Pepin or Charlemagne, they shall attribute it to the emperor Heraclius, and bring him in carrying the Cross into Jerusalem, and recovering the holy sepulchre, like Godfrey of Boulogne, there being a vast distance of time betwixt these actions? Thus they will clap together pieces of true history in a play of their own framing, and grounded upon fiction, mixing in it relations of things that have happened to different people, and in several ages. This they do without any contrivance that might make it appear probable, and with such visible mistakes as are altogether inexcusable; but the worst of it is, that there are idiots who look upon this as perfection, and think everything else to be mere pedantry. But if he look into the pious plays, what a multitude of false miracles shall we find in them? How many errors and contradictions? how often the miracles wrought by one saint attributed to another? Nay, even in the profane plays, they presume to work miracles upon the bare imagination and conceit that such a supernatural work, or a machine, as they call it, will be ornamental, and draw the common sort to see the play. These things are a reflection upon truth itself, a lessening and depreciation of history, and a reproach to all Spanish wits; because strangers, who are very exact in observing the rules of drama, look upon us as an ignorant and barbarous people, when they see the absurdities and extravagancies of our plays. Nor would it be any excuse to allege, that the principal design of all good governments, in permitting plays to be publicly acted, is to amuse the commonalty with some lawful recreation, and so to divert those ill humours which idleness is apt to breed: and since this end is attained by any sort of plays, whether good or bad, it is needless to prescribe laws to them, or oblige the poets or actors to compose and represent such as are strictly conformable to the rules. To this I would answer, that this end would be infinitely better attained by good plays than by bad ones. He who sees a play that is regular, and answerable to the rules of poetry, is pleased with the comic part, informed by the serious, surprised at the variety of accidents, improved by the language, warned by the frauds, instructed by examples, incensed against vice, and enamoured with virtue; for a good play must cause all these emotions in the soul of him that sees it, though he were never so insensible and unpolished. And it is absolutely impossible, that a play which has these qualifications, should not infinitely divert, satisfy and please beyond another that wants them, as most of them do which are now usually acted. Neither are the poets who wrote them in fault, for some of them are very sensible of their errors, and extremely capable of performing their duty; but plays being now altogether become venal, and a sort of merchandise, they say, and with reason, that the actors would not purchase them, unless they were of that stamp; and therefore the poet endeavours to suit the humour of the actors, who is to pay him for his labour. For proof of this, let any man observe, that infinite number of plays, composed by an exuberant Spanish wit,* so full of gaiety and humour, in such elegant verse and choice language, so sententious, and to conclude, in such a majestic style, that his fame is spread through the universe: yet, because he suited himself to the fancy of the actors, many of his pieces have fallen short of their due perfection, though some have reached it. Others write plays so inconsiderately, that after they have appeared on the stage, the actors have been forced to fly and abscond, for fear of being punished, as it has often happened, for having affronted kings, and dishonoured whole families. These, and many other inconsequences, which I omit, would cease, by appointing an intelligent and judicious person at court to examine all plays before they were acted, that is, not only those which are represented at court, but throughout all Spain; so that, without his licence, no magistrate should suffer any play to appear in public. Thus players would be careful to send their plays to court, and might then act them with safety, and those who wrote would be more circumspect, as standing in awe of an examiner that could judge of their works. By these means we should be furnished with good plays, and the end they are designed for would be attained, the people diverted, the Spanish wits esteemed, the actors safe, and the government spared the trouble of punishing them. And if the same person, or another, were entrusted to examine all the new books of knight-errantry, there is no doubt but some might be published with all that perfection you, sir, have mentioned, to the increase of eloquence in our language, to the utter extirpation of the old books, which would be borne down by the new; and for the innocent pastime, not only of idle persons, but even of those who have most employment; for the bow cannot always stand bent, nor can human frailty subsist without some lawful recreation.'

The canon and curate were come to this period, when the barber, overtaking them, told the latter that this was the place he had pitched on for baiting, during the heat of the day. The canon, induced by the pleasantness of the valley, and the satisfaction he found in the curate's conversation, as well as to be further informed of Don Quixote, bore them company, giving order to some of his men to ride to the next inn, and if his sumpter-mule was arrived, to send him down provisions to that valley, where the coolness of the shade, and the beauty of the prospect gave him such a fair invitation to dine; and that they should make much of themselves and their mules with what the inn could afford.

In the mean time Sancho having disengaged himself from the curate and barber, and finding an opportunity to speak to his master alone, he

---

* Lopez de Vega, who wrote an incredible number of Spanish plays.

brushed up to the cage where the knight sat. 'That I may clear my conscience, sir,' said he, 'it is fitting that I tell you the plain truth of your enchantment here. Who, would you think now, are these two fellows that ride with their faces covered? Even the parson of our parish and the barber; none else, I will assure you, sir. And they are in a plot against you, out of mere spite because your deeds will be more famous than theirs. This being supposed, it follows that you are not enchanted, but only cozened and abused; and if you will but answer me one question fairly and squarely, you shall find this out to be a palpable cheat, and that there is no enchantment in the case, but merely your senses turned topsy turvy.'

'Ask me what questions you please, dear Sancho,' said the Knight, 'and I will as willingly resolve them. But, for thy assertion that these who guard us are my old companions the curate and the barber, it is illusion all. The power of magic indeed, as it has an art to clothe any thing in any shape, may have dressed these demons in their appearances to infatuate thy sense, and draw thee into such a labyrinth of confusion that even Theseus's clue could not extricate thee out of it; and this with a design, perhaps, to plunge me deeper into doubts, and make me endanger my understanding, in searching into the strange contrivance of my enchantment, which in every circumstance is so different from all I ever read. Therefore rest satisfied that these are no more what thou imaginest, than I am a Turk. But now to thy questions; propose them, and I will endeavour to answer.'

'Bless me,' said Sancho, 'this is madness upon madness; but, since it is so, answer me one question. Tell me, as you hope to be delivered out of this cage here, and as you hope to find yourself in my Lady Dulcinea's arms, when you least think on it; as you – ' 'Conjure me no more,' answered Don Quixote, 'but ask freely, for I have promised to answer punctually.' 'That is what I want,' said Sancho, 'and you must tell me the truth, neither more nor less, upon the honour of your knighthood.' 'Pray thee, no more of your preliminaries or preambles,' cried Don Quixote, 'I tell thee I answer to a tittle.' 'Then,' said Sancho, 'I ask, with reverence be it spoken, whether your Worship, since your being caged up, or enchanted, if you will have it so, has not had a motion, more or less, as a man may say?' 'I understand not that phrase,' answered the Knight. 'Heyday,' quoth Sancho, 'do not you know what I mean?' Why there is never a child in our country, that understands the Christ-cross-row, but can tell you. I mean, have you a mind to do what another cannot do for you?' 'O, now I understand thee, Sancho,' said the Knight; 'and to answer directly to thy question, positively yes, very often; and therefore pray thee help me out of this strait; for, to be free with you, I am not altogether so sweet and clean as I could wish.'

CHAPTER XXII

A relation of the wise Conference between Sancho and his Master

'Ah! sir,' said Sancho, 'have I caught you at last? This is what I wanted to know from my heart and soul. Come, sir, you cannot deny, that when anybody is out of sorts, so as not to eat, or drink, or sleep, or do any natural occasions that you guess, then we say commonly they are bewitched or so: from whence may be gathered, that those who can eat their meat, drink their drink, speak when they are spoken to, and go to the back-side when they have occasion for it, are not bewitched or enchanted.' 'Your conclusion is good,' answered Don Quixote, 'as to one sort of enchantment, but as I said to thee, there is variety of enchantments, and the changes in them, through the alterations of times and customs, branch them into so many parts, that there is no arguing from what has been to what may be now. For my part, I am verily persuaded of my enchantment, and this suppresses any uneasiness in my conscience, which might arise on suggestion to the contrary. To see myself thus dishonourably come about in a cage, and withheld like a coward from the great offices of my function, when at this hour perhaps hundreds of wretches may want my assistance, would be unsupportable, if I were not enchanted.' 'Yet, for all that, your Worship should try to get your heels at liberty,' said Sancho. 'Come, sir, let me alone, I will set you free, I warrant you; and then get you on trusty Rozinante's back, and a fig for them all. The poor thing here jogs on as drooping and heartless, as if he were enchanted too. Take my advice for once now, and if things do not go as your heart could wish, you have time enough to creep into your cage again, and on the word of a loyal squire I will go in with you, and be content to be enchanted as long as you please.'

'I commit the care of my freedom to thy management,' said Don Quixote. 'Lay hold on the opportunity, friend Sancho, and thou shalt find me ready to be governed in all particulars; though I am still afraid thou wilt find thy cunning strangely overreached in thy pretended discovery.' The knight and squire had laid their plot. When they reached the place that the canon, curate and barber, had pitched upon to alight in, the cage was taken down, and the oxen unyoked to graze; when Sancho addressing the curate, 'Pray,' said he, 'will you do so much, as let my lord and master come out a little to slack a point, or else the prison will not be so clean as the presence of so worthy a knight as my master requires.' Tho curate understanding him, answered 'that he would comply, but that he feared Don Quixote, finding himself once at liberty,

would give them the slip.' 'I will be bail for him,' said Sancho, 'body for
body, sir'; 'And I,' said the canon, 'upon his bare parole of honour.' 'That
you shall have,' said the Knight; 'besides, you need no security beyond
the power of art, for enchanted bodies have no power to dispose of
themselves, nor to move from one place to another without permission
of the necromancer in whose charge they are: the magical charms might
rivet them for three whole centuries to one place, and fetch them back
swift as the wind, should the enchanted have fled to some other region.'
Lastly, as a most convincing argument for his release, he urged, 'that
unless they would free him, or get further off, he should be necessitated
to offend their sense of smelling.' They guessed his meaning presently,
and set him at large; and the first use he made of it was to stretch his
benumbed limbs three or four times; then marching up to Rozinante,
slapped him twice or thrice on the buttocks: 'I trust in Heaven, thou
flower and glory of horse-flesh,' said he, 'that we shall soon be restored
to our former circumstances: I mounted on thy back, and thou between
my legs, while I exercise the function for which Heaven has bestowed me
on the world.' Then walking a little aside with Sancho, he returned, after
a convenient stay, much lighter in body and mind, and very full of his
squire's project.

The canon gazed on him, admiring his unparallelled sort of madness,
the rather because in all his words and answers he displayed an excellent
judgment; and, as we have already observed, he only raved when the
discourse fell upon knight-errantry: which moving the canon to compassion, when they had all seated themselves on the grass, expecting the
coming of his sumpter-mule: 'Is it possible, sir,' said he, addressing
himself to Don Quixote, 'that the unhappy reading of books on knight-
errantry should have such an influence over you as to destroy your
reason, making you believe you are now enchanted, and many other such
extravagancies, as remote from truth as truth itself is from falsehood?
How is it possible that human sense should conceive there ever were in
the world such multitudes of famous knights-errant, so many emperors of
Trebizond, so many Amadises, Feliz-Martes of Hircania, palfreys, rambling damsels, serpents, monsters, giants, unheard-of adventures, so
many sorts of enchantments, so many battles, terrible encounters,
pompous habits and tournaments, amorous princesses, earls, squires and
jesting dwarfs, so many love-letters and gallantries, so many Amazonian
ladies, and, in short, such an incredible number of extravagant passages,
as are contained in books of knight-errantry? As for my own particular, I
confess, that while I read them, and do not reflect that they are nothing
but falsehood and folly, they give me some satisfaction; but I no sooner
remember what they are, but I cast the best of them from me, and would
deliver them up to the flames if I had a fire near me; as well deserving that

fate, because, like impostors, they act contrary to the common course of
nature. They are like broachers of new sects, and a new manner of living,
that seduce the ignorant vulgar to give credit to all their absurdities: nay,
they presume to disturb the brains of ingenious and well-bred gentlemen,
as appears by the effect they have wrought on your judgment, having
reduced you to such a condition, that it is necessary to shut you up in a
cage, and carry you in a cart drawn by oxen, like some lion or tiger that is
carried about from town to town to be shown. Have pity on yourself,
good Don Quixote, retrieve your lost judgment, and make use of those
abilities Heaven has blest you with, applying your excellent talent to some
other study, which may be safer for your conscience, and more for your
honour: but if, led away by your natural inclination, you will read books
of heroism and great exploits, read in the Holy Scripture the Book of
Judges, where you will find wonderful truths and glorious actions not to
be questioned. Lusitania had a Viratus, Rome a Cæsar, Carthage an
Hannibal, Greece an Alexander, Castile a Count Fernando Gonzalez,*
Valencia a Cid, Andalusia a Gonzalo Fernandez, Estremadura a Diego
Garcia de Paredez, Xerez a Graci Perez de Vargas, Toledo a Garcilasso,
and Sevil a Don Manuel de Leon; the reading of whose brave actions
diverts, instructs, and surprises the most judicious readers. This will be a
study worthy your talent, and by which you will become well read in
history, in love with virtue, knowing in goodness, improved in manners,
brave without rashness, and cautious without cowardice; all of which will
redound to the glory of God, your own advancement, and the honour of
the province of La Mancha, whence I understand you derive your
original.' Don Quixote listened with great attention to the canon's
discourse, and perceiving he had done, after he had fixed his eyes on him
for a considerable space: 'Sir,' said he, 'all your discourse, I find, tends to
signify to me, there never were any knights-errant; that all the books of
knight-errantry are false, fabulous, useless, and prejudicial to the public;
that I have done ill in reading, erred in believing, and been much to
blame in imitating them, by taking upon me the most painful profession
of chivalry. And you deny that ever there were any Amadises of Gaul, or
Greece, or any of those knights mentioned in those books.' 'Even as you
have said, sir,' quoth the canon. 'You also were pleased to add,' continued
Don Quixote, 'that those books had been very hurtful to me, having
deprived me of my reason, and reduced me to be carried in a cage; that
therefore it would be for my advantage, to take up in time, and apply
myself to the reading of other books, where I may find more truth, more

---

* Fernando Gonzalez, Cid, and the rest here mentioned were Spanish commanders
of note, of whom as many fables have been written, as there ever were of
knights-errant.

pleasure, and better instruction.' 'You are in the right,' said the canon. 'Then I am satisfied,' replied Don Quixote, 'you yourself are the man that raves and is enchanted, since you have thus boldly blasphemed against a truth so universally received, that whosoever presumes to contradict it, as you have done, deserves the punishment you would inflict on those books, which in reading offend and tire you. For it were as easy to persuade the world that the sun does not enlighten, the frost cool, and the earth bear us, as that there never was an Amadis, or any of the other adventurous knights, whose actions are the subjects of so many histories. What mortal can persuade another, that there is no truth in what is recorded of the Infanta Floripes, and Guy of Burgundy: as also Fierabras at the bridge of Mantible, in the reign of Charlemagne? which passages, I dare swear, are as true as that now it is day. But, if this be false, you may as well say there was no Hector, nor Achilles; nor a Trojan war, nor Twelve Peers of France, nor a King Arthur of Britain, who is now converted into a crow, and hourly expected in his kingdom. Some also may presume to say, that the history of Guarino Mezquino, and that the attempt of St. Grial are both false; that the amours of Sir Tristram and Queen Iseo are apocryphal, as well as those of Guinever and Sir Lancelot of the Lake; whereas there are people living who can almost remember they have seen the old Lady Quintanona; who had the best hand at filling a glass of wine of any woman in all Britain. This I am so well assured of, that I can remember my grandmother, by my father's side, whenever she saw an old waiting-woman with her reverend veil, used to say to me, "Look yonder, grandson, there is a woman like the old Lady Quintanona"; whence I infer she knew her, or at least had seen her picture. Now, who can deny the veracity of the history of Pierres, and the lovely Magalona, when to this day the pin, with which the brave Pierres turned his wooden horse that carried him through the air, is to be seen in the king's armoury? Which pin is somewhat bigger than the pole of a coach, by the same token it stands just by Babieca's saddle. At Roncesvalles they keep Orlando's horn, which is as big as a great beam; whence it follows, that there were Twelve Peers, that there were such men as Pierres, and the famous Cid, besides many other adventurous knights, whose names are in the mouths of all people. You may as well tell me that the brave Portuguese John de Merlo, was no knight-errant; that he did not go into Burgundy, where, in the city of Ras, he fought the famous Moses Pierre, Lord of Charney, and in the city of Basil, Moses Henry de Remestan, coming off in both victorious, and loaded with honour. You may deny the adventures and combats of the heroic Spaniards, Pedro Barba and Gutierre Quixada (from whose male-line I am lineally descended) who in Burgundy overcame the sons of the Earl of St. Paul. You may tell me that Don Ferdinand de Guevara never went into Germany to seek adventures, where he fought Sir George,* a knight of the Duke of Austria's court. You may bay the tilting of Suero de Quinones Del Paso, and the exploits of Moses Lewis de Falses, against Don Gonzalo de Guzman, a Castilian knight, are mere fables; and so of many other brave actions performed by Christian knights, as well Spaniards as foreigners; which are so authentic and true, that I say it over again, he who denies them has neither sense nor reason.' The canon was much astonished at the medley Don Quixote made of truths and fables, and no less to see how well read he was in all things relating to the achievements of knights-errant; 'And therefore I cannot deny, sir,' answered he, 'but that there is some truth in what you have said, especially in what relates to the Spanish knights-errant;† and I will grant there were Twelve Peers of France, yet I will not believe they performed all those actions Archbishop Turpin ascribes to them: I rather imagine they were brave gentlemen made choice of by the kings of France, and called Peers, as being all equal in valour and quality; or, if they were not, at least they ought to have been so; and these composed a sort of military order; like those of St. Jago, or Calatrava among us, into which all that are admitted are supposed, or ought to be, gentlemen of birth and known valour. And as now we say "a knight of St. John, or of Alcantara," so in those times they said, "a knight, one of the Twelve Peers," because there were but twelve of this military order. Nor is it to be doubted but there were such men as Bernardo del Carpio ‡ and the Cid, yet we have reason to question whether ever they performed those great exploits that are ascribed to them. As to the pin, Count Pierres's pin which you spoke of, and which you say stands by Babieca's saddle, I own my ignorance, and confess I was so short-sighted, that though I saw the saddle, yet I did not perceive the pin, which is somewhat strange, if it be so large as you describe it.' 'It is without doubt,' replied Don Quixote, 'by the same token they say it is kept in a leathern case to keep it from rusting.' 'That may very well be,' said the canon; 'but upon the word of a priest, I do not remember I ever saw it: yet grant it were there, that does not enforce the belief of so many Amadises, nor of such a multitude of knights-errant as the world talks of; nor is there any reason so worthy a person, so judicious, and so well-qualified as you are, should imagine there is any truth in the wild extravagancies contained in all the fabulous nonsensical books of knight-errantry.'

* In the original it is Micer George. Oudin says Micer is a corrupt Spanish way of spelling and pronouncing Messire, an honourable compellation in French.
† The author would impose the belief of those fabulous stories as far as there are Spaniards concerned in them, but they are ridiculous, and he that allows of Spaniards, must also allow of knights-errant of other nations.
‡ It is a great question whether there ever was such a man as Bernardo del Carpio.

CHAPTER XXIII

The notable Dispute between the Canon and Don Quixote; with other matters

'Very well,' cried Don Quixote, 'then all those books must be fabulous, though licensed by kings, approved by the examiners, read with general satisfaction, and applauded by the better sort and the meaner, rich and poor, learned and unlearned, gentry and commonalty; and, in short, by all sorts of persons of what state and condition soever; and though they carry such an appearance of truth, setting down the father, mother, country, kindred, age, place and actions to a tittle, and day by day, of the knight and knights of whom they treat? For shame, sir,' continued he, 'forbear uttering such blasphemies; and, believe me, in this I advise you to behave yourself as becomes a man of sense, or else read them and see what satisfaction you will receive. As for instance, pray tell me, can there be anything more delightful, than to read a lively description, which, as it were, brings before your eyes the following adventure? A vast lake of boiling pitch, in which an infinite number of serpents, snakes, crocodiles, and other sorts of fierce and terrible creatures, are swimming and traversing backwards and forwards, appears to a knight-errant's sight. Then from the midst of the lake a most doleful voice is heard to say these words: "O knight, whoever thou art, who gazest on this dreadful lake, if thou wilt purchase the bliss concealed under these dismal waters, make known thy valour by casting thyself into the midst of these black burning surges; for unless thou dost so, thou art not worthy to behold the mighty wonders enclosed in the seven castles of the seven fairies, that are seated under those gloomy waves." And no sooner have the last accents of the voice reached the knight's ear, but he, without making any further reflection, or considering the danger to which he exposes himself, and even without laying aside his ponderous armour, only recommending himself to Heaven and to his lady, plunges headlong into the middle of the burning lake; and when least he imagines it, or can guess where he shall stop, he finds himself on a sudden in the midst of verdant fields, to which the Elysian bear no comparison. There the sky appears to him more transparent, and the sun seems to shine with a redoubled brightness. Next he discovers a most delightful grove made up of beautiful shady trees, whose verdure and variety regale his sight, while his ears are ravished with the wild, and yet melodious notes of an infinite number of pretty, painted birds, that hop and bill, and sport themselves on the twining boughs. Here he spies a pleasant rivulet, which, through its flowery banks, glides along over the brightest sand, and remurmurs over the whitest pebbles that bedimple its smooth surface, while that other, through its liquid crystal, feasts the eye with a prospect of gold and orient pearl. There he perceives an artificial fountain, formed of parti-coloured jasper and polished marble; and hard by another, contrived in grotesque, where the small cockleshells, placed in orderly confusion among the white and yellow shells, and mixed with pieces of bright crystal and counterfeit emeralds, yield a delectable sight; so that art imitating nature, seems here to outdo her. At a distance, on a sudden, he casts his eyes upon a strong castle, or stately palace, whose walls are of massy gold, the battlements of diamonds, and gates of hyacinths; in short, its structure is so wonderful, that though all the materials are no other than diamonds, carbuncles, rubies, pearls, gold and emeralds, yet the workmanship exceed them in value. But having seen all this, can anything be so charming as to behold a numerous train of beautiful damsels come out of the castle in such glorious and costly apparel, as would be endless for me to describe, were I to relate these things as they are to be found in history? Then to see the beauty that seems the chief of all the damsels, take the bold knight, who cast himself into the burning lake, by the hand, and, without speaking one word, lead him into a sumptuous palace, where he is caused to strip naked as he was born, then put into a delicious bath, and perfumed with precious essences and odoriferous oils; after which he puts on a fine shirt, deliciously scented; and this done, another damsel throws over his shoulders a magnificent robe, worth at least a whole city, if not more. What a sight is it, when in the next place they lead him into another room of state, where he finds the tables so orderly covered, that he is surprised and astonished? There they pour over his hands water distilled from amber and odoriferous flowers: he is seated in an ivory chair; and while all the damsels that attend him observe a profound silence, such variety of dainties is served up, and all so incomparably dressed, that his appetite is at a stand, doubting on which to satisfy its desire; at the same time his ears are sweetly entertained with variety of excellent music, none perceiving who makes it, or from whence it comes. But, above all, what shall we say to see, after the dinner is ended and tables taken away, the knight left leaning back in his chair, perhaps picking his teeth, as is usual; and then another damsel, much more beautiful than any of the former, comes unexpectedly into the room, and sitting down by the knight, begins to inform him what castle that is, and how she is enchanted in it; with many other particulars, which surprise the knight, and astonish those that read his history. I will enlarge no more upon this matter, since from what has been said, it may sufficiently be inferred, that the reading of any passage in any history of knight-errantry, must be very delightful and surprising to the reader. And do you, good sir, believe me, and as I said to you before, read those books, which you may find will banish all melancholy, if you are troubled with it, and sweeten your disposition if it be harsh. This I can say for myself, that since my being a knight-errant, I am brave, courteous, bountiful, well-bred, generous, civil, bold, affable, patient, a sufferer of hardships, imprisonment and enchantments: and though I have so lately been shut up in a cage like a madman, I expect through the valour of my arm, Heaven favouring, and Fortune not opposing my designs, to be a king of some kingdom in a very few days, that so I may give proofs of my innate gratitude and liberality. For, on my word, sir, a poor man is incapable of exerting his liberality, though he be naturally never so well inclined. Now that gratitude which only consists in wishes, may be said to be dead, as faith without good works is dead. Therefore it is, I wish fortune would soon offer some opportunity for me to become an emperor, that I might give proofs of my generosity, by advancing my friends, but especially this poor! Sancho Pança my squire, who is the most harmless fellow in the world; and I would willingly give him an earldom, which I have long since promised him, but that I fear he has not sense and judgment enough to manage it.'

Sancho hearing his master's last words: 'Well, well, sir,' said he, 'never do you trouble your head about that matter; all you have to do is to get me this same earldom, and let me alone to manage it: I can do as my betters have done before me, I can put in a deputy or a servant, that shall take all trouble off my hands, while I, as a great man should, loll at my ease, receive my rents, mind no business, live merrily, and so let the world rub for Sancho.' 'As to the management of your revenue,' said the canon, 'a deputy or steward may do well, friend: but the lord himself is obliged to stir in the administration of justice, to which there is not only an honest sincere intention required, but a judicious head also to distinguish nicely, conclude justly, and choose wisely; for if this be wanting in the principal, all will be wrong in the medium and end.' 'I do not understand your philosophy,' quoth Sancho; 'all I said, and I will say it again, is, that I wish I had as good an earldom as I could govern; for I have as great a soul as another man, and as great a body as most men: and the first thing I would do in my government, I would have nobody to control me, I would be absolute: and who but I: now, he that is absolute, can do what he likes; he that can do what he likes, can take his pleasure; he that can take his pleasure, can be content; and he that can be content, has no more to desire; so the matter is over, and come what will come, I am satisfied: if an island, welcome; if no island, fare it well; we shall see ourselves in no worse condition, as one blind man said to another.' 'This is no ill reasoning of yours, friend,' said the canon, 'though there is much more to be said on this topic of earldoms, than you imagine.' 'Undoubtedly,' said Don Quixote; 'but I suit my actions to the example of Amadis de Gaul, who made his squire Gandalin earl of the Firm Island; which is a fair precedent for preferring Sancho to the same dignity to which his merit also lays an unquestionable claim.' The canon stood amazed at Don Quixote's methodical and orderly madness, in describing the adventure of the Knight of the Lake, and the impression made on him by the fabulous conceits of the books he had read; as likewise at Sancho's simplicity in so eagerly contending for his earldom, which made the whole company very good sport.

By this time the canon's servants had brought the provision, and spreading a carpet on the grass, under the shade trees, they sat down to dinner; when presently they heard the tinkling of a little bell among the copse close by them, and immediately afterwards they saw bolt out of the thicket a very pretty she-goat, speckled all over with black, white, and brown spots, and a goatherd running after it; who, in his familiar dialect, called it to stay and return to the fold; but the fugitive ran towards the company frightened and panting, and stopped close by them, as if it had begged their protection. The goatherd overtaking it, caught it by the horns, and, in a chiding way, as if the goat understood his resentments, 'You little wanton nanny,' said he, 'you spotted elf, what has made you trip it so much of late? what wolf has scared you thus, hussy? Tell me, little fool, what is the matter? But the cause is plain; thou art a female, and therefore never canst be quiet: curse on thy freakish humours, and all theirs whom thou so much resembleth; turn back, my love, turn back; and though thou canst not be content with thy fold, yet there thou mayst be safe among the rest of thy fellows; for if thou, that shouldst guide and direct the flock, lovest wandering thus, what must they do? what will become of them?' The goatherd's talk to his goat was entertaining to the company, especially to the canon, who calling to him, 'Pray thee, honest fellow,' said he, 'have a little patience, and let your goat take its liberty awhile; for since it is a female, as you say, she will follow her natural inclination the more for your striving to confine it; come then, and take a bit and a glass of wine with us, you may be better humoured after that.' He then reached him the leg of a cold rabbit, and, ordering him a glass of wine, the goatherd drank it off, and returning thanks, was pacified. 'Gentlemen,' said he, 'I would not have you think me a fool, because I talk so seriously to this senseless animal, for my words bear a mysterious meaning: I am indeed, as you see, rustical and unpolished, though not so ignorant, but that I converse with men as well as brutes.' 'That is no miracle,' said the curate; 'for I have known the woods breed learned men, and simple sheepcoats contain philosophers.' 'At least,' said the goatherd, they harbour men that have some knowledge of the world: and to make good this truth, if I thought not the offer impertinent, or my company troublesome, you should hear an accident which but too well confirms what you have said.' 'For my part,' answered Don Quixote, 'I will hear you attentively, because, methinks, your coming has something in it that looks like an adventure of knight-errantry; and I dare answer, the whole company will not so much bring their parts in question, as to refuse to hear a story so pleasing surprising and amusing, as I fancy yours will prove. Then pray thee, friend, begin, for we will all give you our attention.' 'You must excuse me for one,' said Sancho, 'I must have a word or two in private with this same pasty at yon little brook; for I design to fill my belly for tomorrow and the next day, having often heard my master Don Quixote say, that whenever a knight errant's squire finds good belly-timber, he must fall to and feed till his sides are ready to burst, because they may happen to be bewildered in a thick wood for five or six days together; so that, if a man has not his belly full beforehand, or his wallet well provided, he may chance to be crow's meat himself, as many times it falls out.' 'You are in the right, Sancho,' said the Knight; but I have, for my part, satisfied my bodily appetite, and now want only refreshment for my mind, which I hope this honest fellow's story will afford me.' All the company agreed with Don Quixote: the goatherd then stroking his pretty goat once or twice: 'Lie down. thou speckled fool,' said he, 'lie by me here; for we shall have time enough to return home.' The creature seemed to understand him; for, as soon as her master sat down, she stretched herself quietly by his side, and looked up in his face, as if she would let him know that she minded what he said; and then he began thus.

CHAPTER XXIV

The Goatherd's entertaining Tale

'ABOUT THREE LEAGUES from this valley there is a village, which, though small, yet is one of the richest hereabouts. In it there lived a farmer in very great esteem; and, though it is common for the rich to be respected, yet was this person more considered for his virtue, than for the wealth he possessed. But what he accounted himself happiest in, was a daughter of such extraordinary beauty, prudence, wit, and virtue, that all who knew or beheld her, could not but admire to see how Heaven and nature had done their utmost to embellish her. When she was but little she was handsome, till at the age of sixteen she was most completely beautiful. The fame of her beauty began to extend to the neighbouring villages; but why say I neighbouring villages? it extended to the remotest cities, and entered the palaces of kings, and the ears of all manner of persons; who from all parts flocked to see her, as something rare, or as a sort of prodigy. Her father was strictly careful of her, nor was she less careful of herself; for there are no guards, bolts or locks, which preserve a young woman like her own care and caution. The father's riches and the daughter's beauty drew a great many, as well strangers as inhabitants of that country, to sue for her in marriage; but such was tho vast number of the pretenders, as did but the more confound and divide the old man in his choice, upon whom to bestow so valuable a treasure. Among the crowd of her admirers was I; having good reason to hope for success, from the knowledge her father had of me, being a native of the same place, of a good family, and in the flower of my years, of a considerable estate, and not to be despised for my understanding. With the very same advantages, there was another person of our village who made court to her at the same time. This put the father to a stand, and held him in suspense, till his daughter should declare in favour of one of us: to bring this affair therefore to the speedier issue, he resolved to acquaint Leandra, for so was this fair one called, that since we were equals in all things, he left her entirely free to choose which of us was most agreeable to herself. An example worthy of being imitated by all parents, who have any regard for their children. I do not mean that they should be allowed to choose in things mean or mischievous; but only that proposing to them ever those things which are good, they should be allowed in them to gratify their inclination I do not know how Leandra approved of this proposal; this I only know, that her father put us both off, with the excuse of his daughter's being too young to be yet disposed of; and that he treated us both in such general terms, as could neither well please nor displease us. My rival's name is Anselmo, mine Eugenio, for it is necessary you should know the names of the persons concerned in this tragedy; the conclusion of which, though depending yet, may easily be perceived likely to be unfortunate. About that time there came to our village one Vincent de la Rosa, the son of a poor labouring man of the neighbourhood. This Vincent came out of Italy, having been a soldier there, and in other foreign parts. When he was but twelve years old, a captain that happened to pass by here with his company, took him out of this country, and at the end of other twelve years he returned hither, habited like a soldier, all gay and glorious, in a thousand various colours, bedecked with a thousand toys of crystal, and chains of steel. Today he put on one piece of finery, tomorrow another; but all false, counterfeit, and worthless. The country people, who by nature are malicious, and who, living in idleness are still more inclined to malice, observed this presently, and, counting all his fine things, they found that indeed he had but three suits of clothes, which were of a very different colour with the stockings and garters belonging to them; yet did he manage them with so many tricks and inventions, that if one had not counted them, one would have sworn he had above ten suits, and above twenty plumes of feathers. Let it not seem impertinent that I mention this particular of his clothes and trinkets, since so much of the story depends upon it. Seating himself upon a bench, under a large spreading poplar-tree, which grows in our street, he used to entertain us with his exploits, while we stood gaping and listening at the wonders he recounted: there was not that country, as he said, upon the face of the earth, which he had not seen, nor battle which he had not been engaged in; he had killed more Moors, for his own share, than were in Morocco and Tunis together; and had fought more duels than Gante, Luna, Diego, Garcia de Perede,* or a thousand others that he named, yet in all of them had the better, and never got a scratch, or lost a drop of blood. Then again he pretended to show us the scars of wounds he had received, which though they were not to be perceived, yet he gave us to understand they were so many musket-shots, which he had got in several skirmishes and encounters. In short, he treated all his equals with unparalleled arrogance; and even to those who knew the meanness of his birth, he did not stick to affirm, that his own arm was his father, his actions were his pedigree, and that except as to his being a soldier, he owed no part of his quality to the king himself, and that in being a soldier, he was as good as the king.

'Besides these assumed accomplishments, he was a piece of a musician, and could thrum a guitar a little, but what his excellency chiefly lay in was poetry; and so fond was he of showing his parts that way, that upon every trifling occasion, he was sure to make a copy of verses a league and a half long. This soldier whom I have described, this Vincent de la Rosa, this hero, this gallant, this musician, this poet, was often seen and viewed by Leandra, from a window of her house which looked into the street; she was struck with the tinsel of his dress; she was charmed with his verses, of which he took care to disperse a great many copies; her ears were pleased with the exploits he related of himself; and, in short, as the Devil would have it, she fell in love with him, before ever he had the confidence to make his addresses to her: and, as in all affairs of love, that is the most easily managed, where the lady's affection is pre-engaged; so was it here no hard thing for Leandra and Vincent to have frequent meetings to concert their matters; and before ever any one of her many suitors had the least suspicion of her inclination, she had gratified it; and leaving her father's house (for she had no mother) had run away with this soldier, who came off with greater triumph in this enterprise than in any of the rest he made his boasts of. The whole village was surprised at this accident, as was every one that heard it. I was amazed, Anselmo

* Spaniards famous for duelling.

distracted, her father in tears, her relations outrageous, justice is demanded; a party with officers is sent out, who traverse the roads, search every wood, and, at three days' end, find the poor fond Leandra in a cave of one of the mountains, naked to her shirt, and robbed of a great deal of money and jewels which she took from home. They bring and present her to her father; upon inquiry made into the cause of her misfortune, she confessed ingenuously, that Vincent de la Rosa had deceived her, and upon promise of marriage had prevailed with her to leave her father's house, with the assurance of carrying her to the richest and most delicious city of the world, which was Naples; that she foolishly had given credit to him, and robbing her father, had put herself into his hands the first night she was missed: that he carried her up a steep wild craggy mountain, and put her in that cave where she was found. In fine, she said, that though he had rifled her of all she had, yet he had never attempted her honour; but leaving her in that manner he fled. It was no easy matter to make any of us entertain a good opinion of the soldier's continence; but she affirmed it with so many repeated asseverations, that in some measure it served to comfort her father in his affliction, who valued nothing so much as his daughter's reputation. The very same day that Leandra appeared again, she also disappeared from us, for her father immediately clapped her up in a monastery, in a town not far off, in hopes that time might wear away something of her disgrace. Those who were not interested in Leandra, excused her on account of her youth. But those who were acquainted with her wit and sense, did not attribute her miscarriage to her ignorance, but to the levity and vanity of mind natural to womankind. Since the confinement of Leandra, Anselmo's eyes could never meet with an object which could give him either ease or pleasure: I too could find nothing but what looked sad and gloomy to me in the absence of Leandra. Our melancholy increased, as our patience decreased: we cursed a thousand times the soldier's finery and trinkets, and railed at the father's want of precaution; at last we agreed, Anselmo and I, to leave the village, and retire to this valley, where, he feeding a large flock of sheep, and I as large a herd of goats, all our own, we pass our time under the trees, giving vent to our passions, singing in consort the praises or reproaches of the beauteous Leandra, or else, sighing alone, make our complaints to Heaven on our misfortune. In imitation of us, a great many more of Leandra's lovers had come hither into these steep and craggy mountains, and are alike employed; and so many there are of them, that the place seems to be turned to the old Arcadia we read of. On the top of that hill there is such a number of shepherds and their cottages, that there is no part of it in which is not to be heard the name of Leandra. This man curses and calls her wanton and lascivious, another calls her light and fickle; one acquits and forgives her, another arraigns and condemns her;

one celebrates her beauty, another rails at her ill qualities; in short, all blame, but all adore her: nay, so far does this extravagance prevail, that here are those who complain of her disdain who never spoke to her; and others who are jealous of favours which she never granted to any: for, as I intimated before, her inclination was not known before her disgrace. There is not a hollow place of a rock, a bank of a brook, or a shady grove, where there is not some or other of these amorous shepherds telling their doleful stories to the air and winds. Echo has learnt to repeat the name of Leandra, Leandra all the hills resound, the brooks murmur Leandra, and it is Leandra that holds us all enchanted, hoping without hope, and fearing without knowing what we fear. Of all these foolish people, the person who shows the least, and yet has the most sense, is my rival Anselmo; who, forgetting all other causes of complaint, complains only of her absence, and to his lute, which he touches to admiration, he joins his voice in verses of his own composing, which declare the greatness of his genius. For my part, I take another course, I think a better, I am sure an easier, which is to say all the ill things I can of women's levity, inconstancy, their broken vows and vain deceitful promises, their fondness of show and disregard of merit. This, gentlemen, was the occasion of those words, which, at my coming hither, I addressed to this goat; for being a she, I hate her, though she is the best of my herd. This is the story which I promised to tell you; if you have thought it too long, I shall endeavour to requite your patience in anything I can serve you. Hard by is my cottage, where I have some good fresh milk and excellent cheese, with several sorts of fruits, which I hope you will find agreeable both to the sight and taste.'

CHAPTER XXV

Of the Combat between Don Quixote and the Goatherd: with the rare Adventure of the Penitents, which the Knight happily accomplished with the sweat of his brows

THE GOATHERD'S STORY was mightily liked by the whole company, especially by the canon, who particularly minded the manner of his relating it, that had more of a scholar and gentleman, than of a rude goatherd; which made him conclude the curate had reason to say, that even the mountains bred scholars and men of sense. They all made large proffers of their friendship and service to Eugenio, but Don Quixote exceeded them all, and addressing himself to him: 'Were I,' said he, 'at this time in a capacity of undertaking any adventure, I would certainly begin from this very moment to serve you. I would soon release Leandra out of the nunnery, where undoubtedly she is detained against her will; and, in spite of all the opposition that could be made by the lady abbess and all her adherents, I would return her to your hands, that you might have the sole disposal of her, so far, I mean, as is consistent with the laws of knighthood, which expressly forbid that any man should offer the least violence to a damsel; yet (I trust in Heaven) that the power of a friendly magician will prevail against the force of a malicious enchanter; and, whenever this shall happen, you may assure yourself of my favour and assistance, to which I am obliged by my profession, that enjoins me to relieve the oppressed.'

The goatherd, who till then had not taken the least notice of Don Quixote in particular, now looking earnestly on him, and finding his dismal countenance and wretched habit were no great encouragement for him to expect a performance of such mighty matters, whispered to the barber who sat next him: 'Pray, sir,' said he, 'who is this man that talks so extravagantly? For I protest I never saw so strange a figure in all my life.' 'Whom can you imagine it should be,' replied the barber, 'but the famous Don Quixote de la Mancha, the establisher of justice, the avenger of injuries, the protector of damsels, the terror of giants, and the invincible gainer of battles.' 'The account you give of this person,' returned the goatherd, 'is much like what we read in romances and books of chivalry of those doughty Dons, who, for their mighty prowess and achievements, were called knights-errant; and therefore I dare say you do but jest, and that this gentleman's brains have deserted their quarters.' 'Thou art an impudent, insolent varlet,' cried Don Quixote. 'it is thy paper skull is full of empty rooms: I have more brains than the prostitute thy mother had about her when she carried thy lump of nonsense in her womb.' With that, snatching up a loaf that was near him, he struck the goatherd so furious a blow with it, that he almost levelled his nose with his face. The other, not accustomed to such salutations, no sooner perceived how scurvily he was treated, but without any respect to the tablecloth, napkins, or to those who were eating, he leaped furiously on Don Quixote, and grasping him by the throat with both his hands, had certainly strangled him, had not Sancho Pança come in that very nick of time, and seizing him fast behind, pulled him backwards on the table, bruising dishes, breaking glasses, spilling and overturning all that lay upon it. Don Quixote seeing himself freed, fell violently again upon the goatherd, who, all besmeared with blood, and trampled to pieces under Sancho's feet, groped here and there for some fork or knife to take a fatal revenge; but the canon and curate took care to prevent his purpose, and, in the meanwhile, by the barber's contrivance, the goatherd got Don Quixote under him, on whom he let fall such a tempest of blows, as caused as great a shower of blood to pour from the poor Knight's face as had streamed from his own. The canon and curate were ready to burst with laughing, the officers danced and jumped at the sport, every one cried 'Hullo!' as men do when two dogs are snarling or fighting; Sancho Pança alone was vexed, fretted himself to death, and raved like a madman because he could not get from one of the canon's serving-men, who kept him from assisting his master. In short, all were exceedingly merry, except the bloody combatants, who were mauling one another most miserably, when on a sudden they heard the sound of a trumpet, so doleful that it made them to turn and listen towards that part from whence it seemed to come: but he who was most troubled at this dismal alarm, was Don Quixote; therefore, though he lay under the goatherd, very much against his will, and was most lamentably bruised and battered, 'Friend devil,' cried he to him, 'for sure nothing less could have so much valour and strength as to subdue my forces, let us have a cessation of arms but for a single hour; for the dolorous sound of that trumpet strikes my soul with more horror than thy hard fists do my ears with pain, and methinks excites me to some new adventure.' With that the goatherd, who was as weary of beating, as of being beaten, immediately gave him a truce; and the Knight once more getting on his feet, directed his then not hasty steps to the place whence the mournful sound seemed to come, and presently saw a number of men all in white, like penitents, descending from a rising ground. The real matter was this: the people had wanted rain for a whole year together, wherefore they appointed rogations, processions and disciplines throughout all that country, to implore Heaven to open its treasury, and shower down plenty upon them; and to this end, the inhabitants of a village near that place came in procession to a devote hermitage, built on one of the hills which surrounded that valley.

Don Quixote taking notice of the strange habit of the penitents, and never reminding himself that he had often seen the like before, fancied it was some new adventure, and he alone was to engage in it, as he was obliged by the laws of knight-errantry; and that which the more increased his frenzy, was his mistaking an image which they carried (all covered with black) for some great lady, whom those miscreant and discourteous knights, he thought, were carrying away against her will. As soon as this whimsy took him in the head, he moved with what expedition he could towards Rozinante, who was feeding up and down upon the plains, and whipping off his bridle from the pommel, and his target, which hung hard by, he bridled him in an instant; then, taking his sword from Sancho, he got in a trice on Rozinante's back; where, bracing his target, and addressing himself aloud to all there present: 'O valorous company,' cried he, 'you shall now perceive of how great importance it is to mankind, that such illustrious persons as those who profess the order of knight-errantry should exist in the world; now, I say, you shall see by my freeing that noble lady, who is there basely and barbarously carried away captive, that knight-adventurers ought to be held in the highest and greatest estimation.' So saying, he punched Rozinante with his heels for want of spurs; and forcing him to a hand gallop (for it was never read in any part of this history that Rozinante did ever run full speed) he posted to encounter the penitents, in spite of all the curate, canon, and barber could do to hinder him; much less could Sancho Pança's outcries detain him. 'Master! Sir! Don Quixote!' bawled out the poor squire: 'whither are you posting? Are you bewitched? Does the Devil drive and set you on, thus to run against the Church? Ah, wretch that I am! See, sir, this is a procession of penitents, and the lady they carry is the image of the immaculate Virgin, our Blessed Lady. Take heed what you do, for at this time it may be certainly said you are out of your wits.' But Sancho might as well have kept his breath for another use, for the Knight was urged with so vehement a desire to encounter the white men, and release the mourning lady, that he heard not a syllable that he said, or, if he had, he would not have turned back, even at the king's express command. At last, being come near the procession, and stopping Rozinante, that already had a great desire to rest a little, in a dismal tone, and with a hoarse voice, 'Ho!' cried he, 'you there, who cover your faces, perhaps, because you are ashamed of yourselves, and of the crime you are now committing, give heed and attention to what I have to say.' The first who stopped at this alarm, were those who carried the image; when one of the four priests that sung the litanies, seeing the strange figure Don Quixote made, and the leanness of Rozinante, with other circumstances which he observed in the Knight sufficient to have forced laughter, presently made him this answer:

'Good sir, if you have anything to say to us, speak it quickly; for these poor men whom you see are very much tired, therefore we neither can, nor is it reasonable we should stand thus in pain to hear anything that cannot be delivered in two words.' 'I will say it in one,' replied Don Quixote, 'which is: I charge you immediately to release that beautiful lady, whose tears and looks, full of sorrow, evidently show you carry her away by violence, and have done her some unheard-of injury. This do, or I, who was born to punish such outrages, will not suffer you to advance one step with her, till she is entirely possessed of that liberty she so earnestly desires, and so justly deserves.' This last speech made them all conclude that the Knight was certainly distracted, and caused a general laughter; but this proved like oil to fire, and so inflamed Don Quixote, that laying his hand on his sword, without more words, he presently assaulted those who carried the image. At the same time, one of them quitting his post, came to encounter our hero with a wooden fork, on which he supported the bier when they made a stand, and warding with it a weighty blow which Don Quixote designed and aimed at him, the fork was cut in two; but the other, who had the remaining piece in his hand, returned the Knight such a whack on his left shoulder, that his target not being able to resist such rustic force, the poor unfortunate Don Quixote was struck to the ground, and miserably bruised.

Sancho Pança, who had followed him as fast as his breath and legs would permit, seeing him tall, cried out to his adversary to forbear striking him, urging, that he was a poor enchanted knight, and one who in his whole life had never done any man harm. But it was not Sancho's arguments that held the country fellow's hands; the only motive was, that he feared he had killed him, since he could not perceive he stirred either hand or foot; wherefore, tucking his coat up to his girdle, with all possible expedition, he scoured over the fields like a greyhound. Meanwhile Don Quixote's companions hastened to the place where he lay, when those of the procession seeing them come running towards them, attended by the officers of the holy brotherhood with their crossbows along with them, began to have apprehensions of some disaster from the approaching party, wherefore, drawing up in a body about the image, the disciplinants lifting up their hoods, and grasping fast their whips, as the priests did their tapers, they expected the assault with the greatest bravery, resolving to defend themselves and repel their enemy as long and as much as possible: but Providence had ordered the matter much better than they could hope; for, while Sancho, who had thrown himself on his master's body, was lamenting his loss, and the supposed death of so noble and generous a lord, in the most ridiculous manner that ever was heard, the curate of the Knight's party was come up with the other who came in the procession, and was immediately known by him, so that their acquaintance put an end to the fears which both sides were in of an engagement. Don Quixote's curate in few words acquainted the other with the Knight's circumstances; whereupon he and the whole squadron of penitents went over to see whether the unfortunate Knight were living or dead, and heard Sancho Pança, with tears in his eyes, bewailing over his master: 'O flower of knighthood,' cried he, 'that with one single perilous knock art come to an untimely end! Thou honour of thy family, and glory of all La Mancha! nay, and of the whole world besides; which, now that it has lost thee, will be over-run by miscreants and outlaws, who will no longer be afraid to be mauled for their misdeeds. O bountiful above all the Alexanders in the world! thou who hast rewarded me but for poor eight months' service with the best island that is washed by salt water! Thou who wert humble to the proud, and haughty to the humble! Thou who durst undertake perils, and patiently endure affronts! Thou who wert in love, nobody knows why! True patron of good men, and scourge of the wicked, sworn foe to all reprobates; and, to say all at once that man can say, thou knight-errant!'

The woeful accents of the squire's voice at last recalled Don Quixote to himself; when, after a deep sigh, the first thing he thought of was his absent Dulcinea. 'O charming Dulcinea,' cried he, 'the wretch that lingers, banished from thy sight, endures far greater miseries than this!' And then looking on his faithful squire, 'Good Sancho,' said he, 'help me once more into the enchanted car: for I am not in a condition to press the back of Rozinante: this shoulder is all broke to pieces.' 'With all my heart, my good lord,' replied Sancho, 'and pray let me advise you to go back to our village with these gentlemen, who are your special friends. At home we may think of some other journey that may be more profitable and honourable than this.' 'With reason hast thou spoken, Sancho,' replied Don Quixote: 'it will become our wisdom to be inactive, till the malevolent aspects of the planets, which now reign, be over.' This grave resolution was highly corn mended by the canon, curate, and barber, who had been sufficiently diverted by Sancho Pança's ridiculous lamentation. Don Quixote was placed in the wagon as before, the processioners recovered their former order, and passed on about their business. The goatherd took his leave of the whole company. The curate satisfied the officers for their attendance, since they could stir no further. The canon desired the curate to send him an account of Don Quixote's condition from that time forward, having a mind to know whether his frenzy abated or increased; and then took his leave to continue his journey. Thus the curate, the barber, Don Quixote, and Sancho Pança were left together; as also the good Rozinante, that bore all those passages as patiently as his master. The wagoner then yoked his oxen, and having set Don Quixote on a truss of hay, jogged on after his slow accustomed pace the way the curate directed. In six days' time they reached the Knight's village. It was about noon when they entered the town; and as it happened to be on a Sunday, all the people were assembled in the market-place, through the middle of which Don Quixote must of necessity pass. Everybody was curious to know what was in it; and the people were strangely surprised when they saw and knew their townsman. While they were gaping and wondering, a little boy ran to the Knight's house, and gave intelligence to the housekeeper and niece, that their master and uncle was returned, and very lean, pale, and frightful as a ghost, stretched out at length on a bundle of hay, in a wagon, and drawn along by a team of oxen.

It was a piteous thing to hear the wailings of these two poor creature; the thumps too which they gave their faces, with the curses and execrations they thundered out against all books of chivalry, were almost as numerous as their sighs and tears: but the height of their lamenting was when Don Quixote entered the door. Upon the noise of his arrival Sancho Pança's wife made haste thither to inquire after her husband, who, she was informed, went a-squiring with the Knight. As soon as ever she set eyes on him, the question she asked him was this: 'Is the ass in health, or no?' Sancho answered, he was come back in better health than his master. 'Well,' said she, 'Heaven be praised for the good news. But hark you, my friend,' continued she, 'what have you got by this new squireship? Have you brought me home ever a gown or petticoat, or shoes for my children?' 'In truth, sweet wife,' replied Sancho, 'I have brought thee none of those things; I am loaded with better things.' 'Ay,' said his wife, 'that is well. I pray thee let me see some of them fine things; for I vow I have a hugeous mind to see them; the sight of them will comfort my poor heart, which has been like to burst with sorrow and grief ever since you went away.' 'I will show them to thee when we come home,' returned Sancho: 'in the mean time rest satisfied; for if Heaven see good that we should once again go abroad in search of other adventures, within a little time after, at my return, thou shalt find me some earl, or the governor of some island; ay, of one of the best in the world.' 'I wish with all my heart this may come to pass,' replied the good wife; 'for, by my troth, husband, we want it sorely. But what do you mean by that same word island? for believe me, I do not understand it.' 'All in good time, wife,' said Sancho; 'honey is not made for an ass's mouth: I will tell thee what it is hereafter. Thou wilt be amazed to hear all thy servants and vassals never speak a word to thee without, "If it please you, madam, if it like your ladyship, and your honour." ' 'What dost thou mean, Sancho, by ladyship, islands and vassals?' quoth Joan Pança, for so she was called, though her husband and she were nothing a-kin, only it is a custom in La Mancha, that the wives are there called by their husband's surnames. 'Prithee, Joan,' said Sancho, 'do not trouble thy head to know these matters all at once, and in a heap, as a body may say: it is enough, I tell thee the truth, therefore hold thy tongue.* Yet, by the way, one thing I will assure thee, that nothing in the versal world is better for an honest man, than to be squire to a knight-errant while he is hunting of adventures? It is true, most adventures he goes about does not answer a man's expectations so much as he could wish: for of a hundred that are met with, ninety-nine are wont to be crabbed and unlucky ones. This I know to my cost: I myself have got well kicked and tossed in some of them, and soundly drubbed and belaboured in others; yet, for all that, it is rare sport to be a-watching for strange chances, to cross forests, to search and beat up and down in woods, to scramble over rocks, to visit castles,

* *Cose la boca*, i.e. sew up thy mouth.

and to take up quarters in an inn at pleasure, and all the while the devil a cross to pay.'

These were the discourses with which Sancho Pança and his wife Joan entertained one another, while the housekeeper and niece undressed Don Quixote and put him into his bed; where he lay looking asquint on them, but could not imagine where he was. The curate charged the niece to be very careful and tender of her uncle, and to be very watchful lest he should make another sally; telling her the trouble and charge he had been at to get him home. Here the women began their outcries again: here the books of knight-errantry were again execrated, and damned to the bottomless pit. Here they begged those bewitching chimeras and lies might be thrown down into the very centre, to the hellish father of them! For, they were still almost distracted with the fear of losing their master and uncle again, so soon as ever he recovered; which indeed fell out according to their fear. But, though the author of this history has been very diligent in his inquiry after Don Quixote's achievements in his third expedition in quest of adventures, yet he could never learn a perfect account of them, at least from any author of credit: fame and tradition alone have preserved some particulars of them in the memoirs and antiquities of La Mancha; as, that after the Knight's third sally, he was present at certain famous tilts and tournaments made in the city of Saragossa, where he met with occasions worthy the exercise of his sense and valour: but how the Knight died, our author neither could or ever should have learned, if by good fortune he had not met with an ancient physician, who had a leaden box in his possession, which, as he averred, was found in the ruins of an old hermitage, as it was rebuilding. In this box were certain scrolls of parchment written in Gothic characters, but containing verses in the Spanish tongue, in which many of his noble acts were sung, Dulcinea del Toboso's beauty celebrated, Rozinante's figure described, and Sancho Pança's fidelity applauded. They likewise gave an account of Don Quixote's sepulchre, with several epitaphs and encomiums on his life and conversation. These that could be thoroughly read and transcribed, are here added by the faithful author of this new and incomparable history; desiring no other recompense or reward of the readers, for all his labour and pains, in searching all the numerous and old records of La Mancha to perfect this matchless piece, but that they will be pleased to give it as much credit as judicious men use to give to books of knight-errantry, which are nowadays so well received. This is the utmost of his ambition, and will be sufficient satisfaction for him, and likewise encourage him to furnish them with other matter of entertainment; which, though possibly not altogether so true as this, yet it may be as well contrived and diverting. The first words in the parchment found in the leaden box are these:

MONICONGO, ACADEMIAN OF ARGAMASILLA, ON DON QUIXOTE'S MONUMENT

EPITAPH

'Here lies a doughty knight,
   Who, bruised, and ill in plight,
Jogg'd over many a track
   On Rozinante's back.

'Close by him Sancho's laid;
   Whereat let none admire:
He was a clown, 'tis said,
   But ne'er the worse a squire.'

PANIAGUADO, ACADEMIC OF ARGAMASILLA, ON DULCINEA DEL TOBOSO'S MONUMENT

EPITAPH

'Here Dulcinea lies,
   Once brawny, plump, and lusty;
But now to death a prize,
   And somewhat lean and musty.

'For her the country-fry,
   Like Quixote, long stood steady.
Well might she carry't high;
   Far less has made a lady.'

These were the verses that could be read: as for the rest, the characters being defaced, and almost eaten away, they were delivered to a university student, in order that he might give us his conjectures concerning their meaning. And we are informed, that after many lucubrations and much pains, he has effected the work, and intends to oblige the world with it, giving us at the same time some hopes of Don Quixote's third sally.

Forsi altro cantera con miglior plectro.

PART TWO

THE AUTHOR'S PREFACE

BLESS ME! reader, gentle or simple, or whatever you be, how impatiently by this time must you expect this preface, supposing it to be nothing but revengeful invectives against the author of the second* Don Quixote. But I must beg your pardon: for I shall say no more of him than everybody says, that Tordesillas is the place where he was begotten, and Tarragona the place where he was born; and though it be universally said, that even a worm when trod upon, will turn again, yet I am resolved for once to cross the proverb. You perhaps now would have me call him coxcomb, fool, and madman; but I am of another mind; and so let his folly be its own punishment. But there is something which I cannot so silently pass over: he is pleased to upbraid me with my age: indeed, had it been in the power of man to stop the career of time, I would not have suffered the old gentleman to have laid his fingers on me. Then he reflectingly tells me of the loss of one of my hands: as if that maim had been got in a scandalous or drunken quarrel in some tavern, and not upon the most memorable† occasion that either past or present ages have beheld, and which perhaps futurity will never parallel. If my wounds do not redound to my honour in the thoughts of some of those that look upon them, they will at least secure me the esteem of those that know how they were gotten. A soldier makes a nobler figure as he lies bleeding in the bed of honour, than safe in an inglorious flight; and I am so far from being ashamed of the loss of my hand, that were it possible to recall the same opportunity, I should think my wounds but a small price for the glory of sharing in that prodigious action. The scars in a soldier's face and breast, are the stars that by a laudable imitation guide others to the port of honour and glory. Besides, it is not the hand, but the understanding of a man, that may be said to write; and those years, that he is pleased to quarrel with, always improve the latter.

* A person, who wrote himself a native of Tordesillas, published an impertinent book by that name, printed at Tarragona, while our author was preparing his second part for the press.
† The battle of Lepanto.

I am not wholly insensible of his epithets of ignorant and envious; but I take Heaven to witness, I never was acquainted with any branch of envy beyond a sacred, generous, and ingenuous emulation, which could never engage me to abuse a clergyman, especially if made more reverend by a post in the inquisition: and if any such person thinks himself affronted, as that author seems to hint, he is mightily mistaken; for I have a veneration for his parts,* admire his works, and have an awful regard for the efficacious virtue of his office.

I must return this fine dogmatic gentleman my hearty thanks for his criticism upon my novels: he is pleased very judiciously to say, that they have more of satire than of morality; and yet owns, that the novels are good. Now I thought that if a thing was good, it must be so in every respect.

Methinks, reader, I hear you blame me for showing so little resentment, and using him so gently; but pray, consider, it is not good to bear too hard upon a man that is so over-modest, and so much in affliction: for certainly this must be a miserable soul. He has not the face, poor man! to appear in public; but, conscious of his wretched circumstances, conceals his name, and counterfeits his country, as if he had committed treason, or some other punishable crime. Well then, if ever you should happen to fall into his company, pray in pity tell him from me, that I have not the least quarrel in the world with him: for I am not ignorant of the temptations of Satan, and of all his imps. The scribbling devil is the most irresistible. When that demon is got into a man's head, he takes the possession for inspiration, and, full of his false ability, falls slapdash to writing and publishing, which gets him as much fame from the world as he has money from the booksellers, and as little money from the booksellers as he has fame from the world. But if he will not believe what you say, and you be disposed to be merry, pray tell him this story:

Once upon a time, there was a madman in Seville that hit upon one of the prettiest out-of-the-way whims that ever madman in this world was possessed withal. He gets him a hollow cane, small at one end, and catching hold of a dog in the street, or anywhere else, he clapped his foot on one of the cur's legs, and holding up his hind legs in his hand, he fitted his cane to the dog's anatomy, and blew him up as round as a ball: then giving him a thump or two on the guts, and turning to the by-standers, who are always a great many upon such occasions: 'Well, gentleman,' said he, 'what do you think, is it such an easy matter to blow up a dog? And what think you, sir, is it such an easy matter to write a book?' But if this picture be not like him, pray, honest reader, tell him this other story of a dog and a madman.

* He means Lopez de Vega.

There was a madman at Cordova, who made it his business to carry about the streets, upon his head, a huge stone of a pretty conscionable weight; and whenever he met with a dog without a master, especially such a surly cur as would stalk up to his nose, he very fairly dropped his load all at once, souse upon him: the poor beast would howl, and growl, and clapping his tail between his legs, limped away without so much as looking behind him, for two or three streets' length at least. The madman, mightily pleased with his new device, served every dog, that had courage to look him in the face, with the same sauce; till one day it was his fortune to meet with a sportsman's dog, a cap-maker by trade, though that is neither here nor there. The dog was mightily valued by his master, but that was more than the madman knew; so slap went the stone upon the poor dog. The animal being almost crushed to death, set up his throat, and yelped most piteously; insomuch that his master knowing it was his dog by the howl, runs out, and, touched with the injury, whips up a stick that was at hand, lets drive at the madman, and belabours him to some purpose, crying out at every blow, 'You son of a bitch, abuse my spaniel! You inhuman rascal, did not you know that my dog was a spaniel?' And so thwacked the poor lunatic till he had not a whole bone in his skin. At last he crawled from under his clutches, and it was a whole month before he could lick himself whole again. Nevertheless out he came once more with his invention, and heavier than the former; but coming by the same dog again, though he had a month's mind to give him the other dab; yet recollecting himself, and shrugging up his shoulders; 'No,' quoth he, 'I must have a care, this dog is a spaniel' In short, all dogs he met, whether mastiffs or hounds were downright spaniels to him ever after. Now the moral of the fable is this: this author's wit is the madman's stone, and it is likely he will be cautious how he lets it fall for the future.

One word more, and I have done with him. Pray tell the mighty man, that as to his menaces of taking the bread out of my mouth, I shall only answer him with a piece of an old song, 'God prosper long our noble king, our lives and safeties all.' – And so peace be with him. Long live the great Conde de Lemos, whose humanity and celebrated liberality sustain me under the most severe blows of fortune! And may the eminent charity of the Cardinal of Toledo, make an eternal monument to his fame! Had I never published a word, and were as many books published against me, as there are letters in Mingo Revulgo's poems; yet the bounty of these two princes, that have taken charge of me, without any soliciting or adulation, were sufmcient in my favour: and I think myself richer and greater in their esteem, than I would in any profitable honour that can be purchased at the ordinary rate of advancement. The indigent men may attain their favour, but the vicious cannot. Poverty may partly eclipse a gentleman, but cannot totally obscure him; and those glimmerings of ingenuity that peep through the chinks of a narrow fortune, have always gained the esteem of the truly noble and generous spirits.

Now, reader, I have done with him and you; only give me leave to tell you, that this Second Part of Don Quixote, which I now present you, is cut by the same hand, and of the same piece with the first. Here you have the Knight once more fitted out, and at last brought to his death, and fairly laid in his grave; that nobody may presume to raise any more stories of him. He has committed extravagancies enough already, he is sorry for it, and that is sufficient. Too much of one thing clogs the appetite, but scarcity makes everything go down.

I forgot to tell you, that my 'Persiles' is almost finished, and expects to kiss your hands in a little time; and the second part of the 'Galatea' will shortly put in for the same honour.

PART TWO

CHAPTER I

What passed between the Curate, the Barber, and Don Quixote, concerning his Indisposition

CID HAMET BENENGELI relates in the second part of this history, and Don Quixote's third sally, that the curate and the barber were almost a whole month without giving him a visit; lest, calling to mind his former extravagancies, he might take occasion to renew them. However, they failed not every day to see his niece and his housekeeper, whom they charged to treat and cherish him with great care, and to give him such diet as might be most proper to cheer his heart, and comfort his brain, whence in all likelihood his disorder wholly proceeded. They answered, that they did so, and would continue it to their utmost power; the rather because they observed, that sometimes he seemed to be in his right senses. This news was very welcome to the curate and the barber, who looked on this amendment as an effect of their contrivance in bringing him home in the enchanted wagon, as it is recorded in the last chapter of the first part of this most important, and no less punctual history. Thereupon they resolved to give him a visit, and make trial themselves of the progress of a cure, which they thought almost impossible. They also agreed not to speak a word of knight-errantry, lest they should endanger a wound so lately closed and so tender. In short, they went to see him, and found him sitting up in his bed in a waistcoat of green baize, and a red Toledo cap on his head; but the poor gentleman was so withered and wasted, that he looked like a mere mummy. He received them very civilly, and when they required of his health, gave them an account of his condition, expressing himself very handsomely, and with a great deal of judgment. After they had discoursed a while of several matters, they fell at last on state affairs, and forms of government, correcting this grievance, and condemning that, reforming one custom, rejecting another, and establishing new laws, as if they had been the Lycurguses or Solons of the age; till they had refined and new modelled the commonwealth at such a rate, that they seemed to have clapped it into a forge, and drawn it out wholly different from what it was before. Don Quixote reasoned with so much discretion on every subject, that his two visitors now undoubtedly believed him in his right senses.

His niece and housekeeper were present at these discourses; and, hearing him give so many marks of sound understanding, thought they could never return Heaven sufficient thanks for so extraordinary a blessing. But the curate, who wondered at this strange amendment, being resolved to try whether Don Quixote was perfectly recovered, thought fit to alter the resolution he had taken, to avoid entering into any discourse of knight-errantry; and therefore began to talk to him of news, and among the rest that it was credibly reported at court, that the Grand Signior was advancing with a vast army, and nobody knew where the tempest would fall; that all Christendom was alarmed, as it used to be almost every year; and that the king was providing for the security of the coasts of Sicily and Naples, and the island of Malta. 'His majesty,' said Don Quixote, 'acts the part of a most prudent warrior, in putting his dominions betimes in a posture of defence; for by that precaution he prevents the surprises of the enemy: but yet, if my counsel were to be taken in this matter, I would advise another sort of preparation, which I fancy his majesty little thinks of at present.' 'Now Heaven assist thee, poor Don Quixote,' said the curate to himself, hearing this, 'I am afraid thou art now tumbling from the top of thy madness to the very bottom of simplicity.' Thereupon the barber, who had presently made the same reflection, desired Don Quixote to communicate to them this mighty project of his: 'For,' said he, 'who knows but, after all, it may be one of those that ought only to find a place in the list of impertinent admonitions usually given to princes.' 'No, good Mr. Trimmer,' answered Don Quixote, my project is not impertinent, but highly advisable.' 'I mean no harm in what I said, sir,' replied the barber, 'only we generally find, most of these projects that are offered to the king are either impracticable or whimsical, or tend to the detriment of the king or kingdom.' 'But mine,' said Don Quixote, 'is neither impossible nor ridiculous; far from that, it is the most easy, the most thoroughly weighed, and the most concise, that ever can be devised by man.' 'Methinks you are too long before you let us know it, sir,' said the curate. 'To deal freely with you,' replied Don Quixote, 'I should be loth to tell it you here now, and have it reach the ear of some privy-counsellor tomorrow, and so afterwards see the fruit of my invention reaped by somebody else.' 'As for me,' said the barber, 'I give you my word here, and in the face of Heaven, never to tell it, either to king, queen, rook, pawn, or knight,* or any earthly man: an oath I learned out of the romance of the curate, in the preface to which he tells the king who it was that robbed him of his hundred doublons, and his ambling mule.' 'I know nothing of the story,' said Don Quixote; 'but I have reason to be satisfied with the oath, because I am confident Master Barber is an honest man.' 'Though he were not,' said the curate, 'I will be his surety in this matter, and will engage for him, that

* In allusion to the game at Chess, so common then in Spain.

he shall no more speak of it, than if he were dumb, under what penalty you please.' 'And who shall answer for you, Mr. Curate?' answered Don Quixote. 'My profession,' replied the curate, 'which binds me to secrecy.' 'Body of me then!' cried Don Quixote, 'what has the king to do more, but to cause public proclamation to be made enjoining all the knights-errant that are dispersed in this kingdom, to make their personal appearance at court upon a certain day. For though but half-a-dozen should meet, there may be some one among them, who even alone might be able to destroy the whole united force of Turkey. For, pray observe well what I say, gentlemen, and take me along with ye. Do you look upon it as a new thing for one knight-errant alone to rout an army of two hundred thousand men, with as much ease as if all of them joined together had but one throat, or were made of sugar paste? You know how many histories are full of these wonders. Were but the renowned Don Belianis living now, with a vengeance on me (for I will curse nobody else), or some knight of the innumerable race of Amadis de Gaul, and if he met with these Turks, what a woeful condition would they be in! However, I hope Providence will in pity look down upon His people, and raise up, if not so prevalent a champion as those of former ages, at least some one who may perhaps rival them in courage: Heaven knows my meaning; I say no more.' 'Alas!' said the niece, hearing this, 'I will lay my life my uncle has still a hankering after knight-errantry.' 'I will die a knight-errant,' cried Don Quixote, 'and so let the Turks land where they please, and when they please, and with all the forces they can muster: once more I say, Heaven knows my meaning.' 'Gentlemen,' said the barber, 'I beg leave to tell you a short story of somewhat that happened at Sevile: indeed it falls out as pat as if it had been made for our present purpose, and so I have a great mind to tell it.' Don Quixote gave consent, the curate and the rest of the company were willing to hear; and thus the barber begun:

'A certain person being distracted, was put into the madhouse at Sevile by his relations. He had studied the civil law, and taken his degrees at Ossuna; though, had he taken them at Salamanca, many are of opinion he would have been mad too. After he had lived some years in this confinement, he was pleased to fancy himself in his right senses, and upon this conceit wrote to the archbishop, beseeching him with great earnestness and all the colour of reason imaginable, to release him out of his misery by his authority, since by the mercy of Heaven he was wholly freed from any disorder in his mind; only his relations, he said, kept him in still to enjoy his estate, and designed in spite of truth, to have him mad to his dying day. The archbishop, persuaded by many letters which he wrote to him on that subject, all penned with sense and judgment, ordered one of his chaplains to inquire of the governor of the house into the truth of the matter, and also to discourse with the party, that he might set him at large, in case he found him free from distraction. Thereupon the chaplain went, and having asked the governor what condition the graduate was in was answered, that he was still mad; that, sometimes indeed, he would talk like a man of excellent sense, but presently after he would relapse into his former extravagancies which at least balanced all his rational talk, as he himself might find, if he pleased to discourse him. The chaplain, being resolved to make the experiment, went to the madman, and conversed with him above an hour, and in all that time could not perceive the least disorder in his brain; far from that, he delivered himself with so much sedateness, and gave such direct and pertinent answers to every question, that the chaplain was obliged to believe him sound in his understanding: nay, he went so far, as to make a plausible complaint against his keeper, alleging that, for the lucre of those presents which his relations sent him, he represented him to those who came to see him as one who was still distracted, and had only now and then lucid intervals; but that, after all, his greatest enemy was his estate, the possession of which his relations, being unwilling to resign, they would not acknowledge the mercy of Heaven, that had once more made him a rational creature. In short, he pleaded in such a manner, that the keeper was suspected, his relations were censured as covetous and unnatural, and he himself was thought master of so much sense, that the chaplain resolved to take him along with him, that the archbishop might be able to satisfy himself of the truth of the whole business. In order to do this, the credulous chaplain desired the governor to give the graduate the habit which he had brought with him at his first coming. The governor used all the arguments which he thought might dissuade the chaplain from his design, assuring him, that the man was still frantic and disordered in his brain. But he could not prevail with him to leave the madman there any longer, and therefore was forced to comply with the archbishop's order, and returned the man his habit, which was neat and decent.

'Having now put off his madman's weeds, and finding himself in the garb of rational creatures, he begged of the chaplain, for charity's sake, to permit him to take leave of his late companions in affliction. The chaplain told him he would bear him company, having a mind to see the mad folks in the house. So they went upstairs, and with them some other people that stood by. Presently the graduate came to a kind of a cage, where lay a man that was outrageously mad, though at that instant still and quiet; and addressing himself to him, "Brother," said he, "have you any service to command me? I am just going to my own house, thanks be to Heaven, which, of its infinite goodness and mercy, has restored me to my senses. Be of good comfort, and put your trust in the Father of Wisdom, who will, I hope, be as merciful to you as he has been to me. I will be sure to send you some choice victuals, which I would have you eat by all means; for I must needs tell you, that I have reason to imagine, from my own experience, that all our madness proceeds from keeping our stomachs empty of food, and our brains full of wind. Take heart then, my friend, and be cheerful; for this desponding in misfortunes impairs our health, and hurries us to the grave." Just over against that room lay another madman, who, having listened with an envious attention to all this discourse, starts up from an old mat, on which he lay stark naked: "Who is that," cried he aloud, "that is going away so well recovered and so wise?" "It is I, brother, that am going," replied the graduate; "I have now no need to stay here any longer; for which blessing I can never cease to return my humble and hearty thanks to the infinite goodness of Heaven." "Doctor," quoth the madman, "have a care what you say, and let not the Devil delude you. Stir not a foot, but keep snug in your old lodging, and save yourself the cursed vexation of being brought back to your kennel." "Nay," answered the other, "I will warrant you there will be no occasion for my coming hither again; I know I am perfectly well.'* "You well!" cried the madman, "we shall soon see that. Farewell: but by the sovereign Jupiter, whose majesty I represent on earth, for this very crime alone that Sevile has committed, in setting thee at large, affirming that thou art sound in thy intellects, I will take such a severe revenge on the whole city, that it shall be remembered with terror from age to age, for ever and ever: Amen. Dost thou not know, my poor brainless thing in a gown, that this in my power? I that am the thundering Jove, that grasp in my hands the red-hot bolts of heaven, with which I keep the threatened world in awe, and might reduce it all to ashes. But stay, I will commute the fiery punishment, which this ignorant town deserves, into another; I will only shut up the flood-gates of the skies, so that there shall not fall a drop of rain upon this city, nor on all the neighbouring country round about it, for three years together, to begin from the very moment that gives date to this my inviolable execration. Thou free! thou well! and in thy senses! and I here mad, distempered, and confined! By my thunder, I will no more indulge the town with rain, than I would hang myself." As every one there was attentive to these loud and frantic threats, the graduate turned to the chaplain, and, taking him by the hand, "Sir," said he, "let not that madman's threats trouble you. Never mind him; for, if he be Jupiter, and will not let it rain, I am Neptune, the parent and god of the waters, and it shall rain as often as I please, wherever necessity shall require it." "However," answered the chaplain, "good Mr. Neptune, it is not convenient to provoke Mr. Jupiter; therefore be pleased to stay here a

---

* In the original, *tornar a andar estationes*: *i.e.* to visit the station-churches again: certain churches, with indulgences, appointed to be visited, either for pardon of sins or for procuring blessings. Madmen, probably in their lucid intervals, were obliged to this exercise.

little longer, and some other time, at convenient leisure, I may chance to find a better opportunity to wait on you, and bring you away." The keeper and the rest of the company could not forbear laughing, which put the chaplain almost out of countenance. In short, Mr. Neptune was disrobed again, stayed where he was, and there is an end of the story.'

'Well, Mr. Barber,' said Don Quixote, 'and this is your tale, which you said came so pat to the present purpose that you could not forbear telling it! Ah, Goodman Cutbeard, Goodman Cutbeard! how blind must he be that cannot see through a sieve! Is it possible your pragmatical worship should not know that the comparisons made between wit and wit, courage and courage, beauty and beauty, birth and birth, are always odious and ill-taken? I am not Neptune, the god of the waters, good Mr. Barber; neither do I pretend to set up for a wise man when I am not so. All I aim at, is only to make the world sensible how much they are to blame, in not labouring to revive those most happy times, in which the order of knight-errantry was in its full glory. But, indeed, this degenerate age of ours is unworthy the enjoyment of so great a happiness which former ages could boast, when knights-errant took upon themselves the defence of kingdoms, the protection of damsels, the relief of orphans, the punishment of pride and oppression, and the reward of humility. Most of your knights, now-a-days, keep a greater rustling with their sumptuous garments of damask, gold-brocade, and other costly stuffs, than with the coats of mail which they should glory to wear. No knight now will lie on the hard ground in the open field, exposed to the injurious air, from head to foot enclosed in ponderous armour: where are those now, who, without taking their feet out of the stirrups, and only leaning on their lances, like the knights-errant of old, strive to disappoint invading sleep, rather than indulge it? Where is that knight, who, having first traversed a spacious forest, climbed up a steep mountain, and journeyed over a dismal barren shore, washed by a turbulent, tempestuous sea, and finding on the brink a little skiff, destitute of sails, oars, mast, or any kind of tackling, is yet so bold as to throw himself into the boat with an undaunted resolution, and resign himself to the implacable billows of the main, that now mount him to the skies, and then hurry him down to the most profound recesses of the waters; till, with his insuperable courage, surmounting at last the hurricane, even in its greatest fury, he finds himself above three thousand leagues from the place where he first embarked, and leaping ashore in a remote and unknown region, meets with adventures that deserve to be recorded, not only on parchment but on Corinthian brass. But now, alas! sloth and effeminacy triumph over vigilance and labour; idleness over industry; vice over virtue; arrogance over valour, and the theory of arms over the practice, that true practice, which only lived and flourished in those golden days, and among these professors of chivalry. For where shall we hear of a knight more valiant and more honourable than the renowned Amadis de Gaul? Who more discreet than Palmerin of England? Who more affable and complaisant than Tirante the White? Who more gallant than Lisuarte of Greece? Who more cut and hacked, or a greater cutter and hacker than Don Belianis? Who more intrepid than Perion of Gaul? Who more daring than Felixmarte of Hyrcania? Who more sincere than Esplandian? Who more courteous than Ciriongillo of Thrace? Who more brave than Rodomont? Who more prudent than King Sobrino? Who more desperate than Rinaldo? Who more invincible than Orlando? And who more agreeable, or more affable, than Rogero, from whom (according to Turpin in his "Cosmography"), the dukes of Ferrara are descended? All these champions, Mr. Curate, and a great many more that I could mention, were knights-errant, and the very light and glory of chivalry; now, such as these are the men I would advise the king to employ; by which means his majesty would be effectually served, and freed from a vast expense, and the Turk would tear his very beard for madness. For my part, I do not design to stay where I am, because the chaplain will not fetch me out; though, if Jupiter, as Mr. Barber said, will send no rain, here stands one that will, and can rain, when he pleases. This I say, that Goodman Basin here may know I understand his meaning.' 'Truly, good sir,' said the barber, 'I meant no ill. Heaven is my witness, my intent was good, and therefore, I hope your worship will take nothing amiss.' 'Whether I ought to take it amiss or no,' replied Don Quixote, 'is best known to myself.' 'Well,' said the curate, 'I have hardly spoken a word yet; and before I go, I would gladly be eased of a scruple, which Don Quixote's words have started within me, and which grates and gnaws my conscience.' 'Mr. Curate may be free with me in great matters,' said Don Quixote, 'and so may well tell his scruple; for it is no pleasure to have a burden upon one's conscience.' 'With your leave then, sir,' said the curate, 'I must tell you, that I can by no means prevail with myself to believe, that all this multitude of knights-errant, which your worship has mentioned, were ever real men of this world, and true substantial flesh and blood; but rather, that whatever is said of them, is all fable and fiction, lies and dreams, related by men rather half asleep than awake.' 'This is indeed another mistake,' said Don Quixote, 'into which many have been led, who do not believe there ever were any of those knights in the world. And in several companies, I have many times had occasion to vindicate that manifest truth from the almost universal error that is entertained to its prejudice. Sometimes my success has not been answerable to the goodness of my cause, though at others it has; being supported on the shoulders of truth, which is so apparent, that I dare almost say, I have seen Amadis de Gaul with these very eyes. He was a tall, comely personage, of a good and lively complexion, his beard well ordered, though black, his aspect at once awful and affable: a man of few words, slowly provoked, and quickly pacified. And as I have given you the picture of Amadis, I fancy I could readily delineate all the knights-errant that are to be met with in history; for once apprehending as I do, that they were just such as their histories report them, it is an easy matter to guess their features, statures, and complexions, by the rules of ordinary philosophy, and the account we have of their achievements, and various humours.' 'Pray, good sir,' quoth the barber, 'how tall then might the giant Morgante be?' 'Whether there ever were giants or no,' answered Don Quixote, 'is a point much controverted among the learned. However, the Holy Writ, that cannot deviate an atom from truth, informs us there were some, of which we have an instance in the account it gives us of that huge Philistine, Goliah, who was seven cubits and a half high, which is a prodigious stature. Besides, in Sicily, thigh-bones and shoulder-bones have been found of so immense a size, that from thence of necessity we must conclude by the certain rules of geometry, that the men to whom they belonged were giants, as big as huge steeples. But, for all this, I cannot positively tell you how big Morgante was; though I am apt to believe he was not very tall, and that which makes me inclinable to believe so, is, that in the history which gives a particular account of his exploits, we read, that he often used to lie under a roof. Now, if there were any house that could hold him, it is evident he could not be of an immense bigness.' 'That must be granted,' said the curate, who took some pleasure in hearing him talk at that strange rate, and therefore asked him what his sentiments were of the faces of Rinaldo of Montalban, Orlando, and the rest of the Twelve Peers of France, who had all of them been knights-errant?' As for Rinaldo,' answered Don Quixote, 'I dare venture to say, he was broad-faced, of a ruddy complexion, his eyes sparkling and large, very captious, extremely choleric, and a favourer of robbers and profligate fellows. As for Rolando, Rotolando, or Orlando (for all these several names are given him in history) I am of opinion and assure myself, that he was of the middling stature, broad-shouldered, somewhat bandy-legged, brown-visaged, red-bearded, very hairy on his body, surly-looked, no talker, but yet very civil and good-humoured.' 'If Orlando was no handsomer than you tell us,' said the curate, 'no wonder the fair Angelica slighted him, and preferred the brisk, pretty, charming, downy-chinned young Moor before him; neither was she to blame to neglect the roughness of the one for the soft embraces of the other.' 'That Angelica, Mr. Curate,' said Don Quixote, 'was a dissolute damsel, a wild, flirting, wanton creature and somewhat capricious besides. She left the world as full of her impertinencies as of the fame of her beauty. She despised a thousand princes, a thousand of the most valiant and discreet knights in the whole world, and took up with a paltry beardless page, that had neither estate nor honour, and who could lay claim to no other reputation, but that of being grateful, when he gave a proof of his affection to his friend Dardinel. And indeed, even that great extoller of her beauty, the celebrated Ariosto, either not desiring to rehearse what happened to Angelica, after she had so basely prostituted herself (which passages doubtless could not be very much to her reputation), that very Ariosto, I say, dropped her character quite, and left her with these verses:

"Perhaps some better lyre shall sing
How love and she made Cataya king."

And without doubt that was a kind of a prophecy; for the denomination of Vates, which signifies a prophet, is common to those whom we otherwise call poets. Accordingly indeed this truth has been made evident; for in process of time, a famous Andalusian poet* wept for her, and celebrated her tears m verse; and another eminent and choice poet of Castile† made her beauty his theme.' 'But, pray, sir,' said the barber, 'among so many poets that have written in that lady Angelica's praise, did none of them ever write a satire upon her?' 'Had Sacripante, or Orlando been poets,' answered Don Quixote, 'I make no question but they would have handled her to some purpose; for there is nothing more common than for cast poets, when disdained by their feigned or false mistresses, to revenge themselves with satires and lampoons; a proceeding certainly unworthy a generous spirit. However, I never yet did hear of any defamatory verses on the lady Angelica, though she made so much mischief in the world.' 'That is a miracle indeed,' cried the curate. But here they were interrupted by a noise below in the yard, where the niece and the housekeeper, who had left them some time before, were very obstreperous, which made them all hasten to know what was the matter.

CHAPTER II

Of the memorable Quarrel between Sancho Pança, and Don Quixote's Niece and Housekeeper; with other pleasant passages

THE HISTORY INFORMS US, that the occasion of the noise which the niece and housekeeper made, was Sancho Pança's endeavouring to force his way into the house, while they at the same time held the door against him to keep him out. 'What have you to do in this house, ye paunch-gutted squob?' cried one of them. 'Go, go, keep to your own home, friend.

* Luis Barahona de Solo. † Lopez de Vega.

It is all along by you, and nobody else, that my poor master is distracted, debauched, and carried a-rambling, all the country over.' 'The housekeeper for the Devil,' replied Sancho, 'it is I that am distracted, debauched, and carried a-rambling, and not your master. It was he led me the jaunt; so you are wide of the matter. It was he that inveigled me from my house and home with his colloguing, and saying he would give me an island; which is not come yet, and I still wait for.' 'Mayest thou be choked with thy plaguey islands,' cried the niece, 'thou cursed paunch! And what are your islands! anything to eat, good man greedy-gut, ha?' 'Hold you there!' answered Sancho, 'they are not to eat, but to govern; and better governments than any four cities, or as many heads of the king's best corporations.' 'For all that,' quoth the housekeeper, 'thou comest not within these doors, thou bundle of wickedness, and sackful of roguery! Go, govern your own house! Work, you lazy rogue! To the plough, and never trouble your jolter-head about islands or islets.' The curate and the barber took a great deal of pleasure to hear this dialogue. But Don Quixote fearing lest Sancho should not keep within bounds, but blunder out something prejudicial to his reputation, while he ripped up a pack of little foolish slander, called him in, and enjoined the women to be silent. Sancho entered, and the curate and the barber took leave of Don Quixote, despairing of his cure, considering how deep his folly was rooted in his brain, and how bewitched he was with his silly knight-errantry. 'Well, neighbour,' said the curate to the barber, 'now do I expect nothing better of our gentleman, than to hear shortly he is gone upon another ramble.' 'Nor I neither,' answered the barber; 'but I do not wonder so much at the Knight's madness, as at the silliness of the squire, who thinks himself so sure of the island, that I fancy all the art of man can never beat it out of his skull.' 'Heaven mend them,' said the curate. In the mean time let us observe them; we shall find what will be the event of the extravagance of the Knight, and the foolishness of the squire: one would think they had been cast in one mould; and indeed the master's madness without the man's impertinence, were not worth a rush. 'Right,' said the barber, 'and now they are together, methinks I long to know what passes between them. I do not doubt but the two women will be able to give an account of that, for they are not of a temper to withstand the temptation of listening.' Meanwhile Don Quixote having locked himself up with his squire, they had the following colloquy. 'I take it very ill,' said he, 'Sancho, that you should report, as you do, that I enticed you out of your paltry hut, when you know, that I myself left my own mansion house. We set out together, continued together, and travelled together. We ran the same fortune, and the same hazards together. If thou hast been tossed in a blanket once, I have been battered and bruised a hundred times; and that is all the advantage I have had above thee.' 'And reason good,' answered Sancho;

'for you yourself use to say, that ill luck and cross-bitings are oftener to lighten the knights than on their squires.' 'Thou art mistaken, Sancho,' replied Don Quixote; 'for the proverb will tell thee, that *Quando caput dolet,*' etc. 'Nay,' quoth Sancho, 'I understand no language but my own.' 'I mean,' said Don Quixote, 'that when the head aches, all the members partake of the pain: so then, as I am thy master, I am also thy head; and as thou art my servant, thou art one of my members; it follows therefore, that I cannot be sensible of pain, but thou too oughtest to be affected with it; and likewise, that nothing of ill can befall thee, but I must bear a share.' 'Right,' quoth Sancho, 'but when I, as a limb of you, was tossed in a blanket, my head was pleased to stay at the other side of the wall, and saw me striking in the air, without going snacks in my bodily trouble.' 'Thou art greatly mistaken, Sancho,' answered Don Quixote, 'if thou thinkest I was not sensible of thy sufferings: for I was then more tortured in mind, than thou wast tormented in body; but let us adjourn this discourse till some other time, which doubtless will afford us an opportunity to redress past grievances. I pray thee tell me now what does the town say of me? What do the neighbours, what do the people think of me? What say the gentry, and the better sort? How do the knights discourse of my valour, my high feats of arms, and my courteous behaviour? What thoughts do they entertain of my design, to raise from the grave of oblivion the order of knight-errantry, and restore it to the world? In short tell me freely and sincerely whatever thou hast heard; neither enlarged with flattering commendations, nor lessened by any omission of my dispraise; for it is the duty of faithful servants to lay truth before their masters in its honourable nakedness. And I would have thee know, Sancho, that if it were to appear before princes, in its native simplicity, and disrobed of the odious disguise of flattery, we should see happier days; this age would be changed into an age of gold, and former times, compared to this, would be called the Iron Age. Remember this, and be advised, that I may hear thee impart a faithful account of these matters.' 'That I will, with all heart,' answered Sancho, 'so your worship will not take it amiss, if I tell what I have heard, just as I heard it, neither better nor worse.' 'Nothing shall provoke me to anger,' answered Don Quixote; 'speak freely, and without any circumlocution.' 'Why then,' quoth Sancho, 'first and foremost you are to know, that the common people take you for a downright madman, and me for one that has not much guts in his brains. The gentry say, that not being content to keep within the bounds of gentility, you have taken upon you to be a Don, and set up for a knight, and a right worshipful, with a small vineyard, and two acres of land, a tatter before, and another behind. The knights, forsooth, take pepper in the nose, and say, they do not like to have your small gentry think themselves as good as they, especially your old-fashioned country squires that mend and lamp-black their own shoes, and darn their old black stockings themselves with a needleful of green silk.' 'All this does not affect me,' said Don Quixote, 'for I always wear good clothes, and never have them patched. It is true, they may be a little torn sometimes, but that is more with my armour than my long wearing.' 'As for what relates to your prowess,' said Sancho, proceeding, 'together with your feats of arms, your courteous behaviour, and your undertaking, there are several opinions about it. Some say he is mad, but a pleasant sort of a madman; others say, he is valiant, but his luck is naught; others he is courteous, but damned impertinent. And thus they spend so many verdicts upon you, and take us both so to pieces, that they leave neither you nor me a sound bone in our skins.' 'Consider, Sancho,' said Don Quixote, 'that the more eminently virtue shines, the more it is exposed to the persecution of envy. Few or none of those famous heroes of antiquity, could escape the venomous arrows of calumny. Julius Cæsar, that most courageous, prudent, and valiant captain, was marked, as being ambitious, and neither so clean in his apparel, nor in his manners, as he ought to have been. Alexander, whose mighty deeds, gained him the title of the Great, was charged with being addicted to drunkenness. Hercules, after his many heroic labours, was accused of voluptuousness and effeminacy. Don Galaor, the brother of Amadis de Gaul, was taxed with being quarrelsome, and his brother himself with being a whining, blubbering lover. And therefore, my Sancho, since so many worthies have not been free from the assaults of detraction, well may I be content to bear my share of that epidemical calamity, if it be no more than thou hast told me now.' 'Body of my father!' quoth Sancho, 'there is the business; you say well, if this were all: but they do not stop here.' 'Why,' said Don Quixote, 'what can they say more?' 'More,' cried Sancho, 'oddsnigs! we are still to flea the cat's tail. You have had nothing yet but apple-pies and sugar-plums. But if you have a mind to hear all those slanders and backbitings that are about town concerning your worship, I will bring you one anon that shall tell you every kind of thing that is said of you, without bating you an ace of it! Bartholomew Carrasco's son I mean, who has been a scholard at the Versity of Salamanca, and is got to be a bachelor of arts. He came last night, you must know, and as I went to bid him welcome home, he told me, that your worship's history is already in books, by the name of the most renowned Don Quixote de la Mancha. He says I am in too, by my own name of Sancho Pança, and eke also my Lady Dulcinea del Toboso; nay, and many things that passed betwixt nobody but us two, which I was amazed to hear, and could not for my soul imagine, how the devil he that set them down could come by the knowledge of them.' 'I dare assure thee, Sancho,' said Don Quixote, 'that the author of our history must be some sage enchanter, and one of those from whose universal knowledge none of the things which they have a mind to record can be concealed.' 'How should he be a sage and an enchanter?' quoth Sancho. 'The bachelor Samson Carrasco, for that is the name of my tale master, tells me, he that wrote the history is called Cid Hamet Berengenas.'* 'That is a Moorish name,' said Don Quixote. 'Like enough,' quoth Sancho, 'your Moors are main lovers of Berengenas.' 'Certainly, Sancho,' said Don Quixote 'thou art mistaken in the surname of that Cid, that lord, I mean; for Cid in Arabic signifies lord.' 'That may very well be,' answered Sancho. 'But if you will have me fetch you the young scholard, I will fly to bring him hither.' 'Truly, friend,' said Don Quixote, 'thou wilt do me a particular kindness; for what thou hast already told me, has so filled me with doubts and expectations, that I shall not eat a bit that will do me good till I am informed of the whole matter.' 'I will go and fetch him,' said Sancho. With that, leaving his master, he went to look for the bachelor, and having brought him along with him awhile after, they all had a very pleasant dialogue.

CHAPTER III

The pleasant Discourse between Don Quixote, Sancho Pança, and the Bachelor Carrasco

DON QUIXOTE remained strangely pensive, expecting the bachelor Carrasco, from whom he hoped to hear news of himself, recorded and printed in a book, as Sancho had informed him: he could not be persuaded that there was such a history extant, while yet the blood of those enemies he had cut off, had scarce done reeking on the blade of his sword; so that they could not have already finished and printed the history of his mighty feats of arms. However, at last, he concluded, that some learned sage had, by way of enchantment, been able to commit them to the press, either as a friend, to extol his heroic achievements above the noblest performances of the most famous knights-errant; or as an enemy, to sully and annihilate the lustre of his great exploits, and debase them below the most inferior actions that ever were mentioned of any of the meanest squires. Though, thought he to himself, the actions of squires were never yet recorded; and, after all, if there were such a book printed, since it was the history of a knight-errant, it could not choose but be pompous, lofty, magnificent, and

---

* A sort of fruit in Spain, which they boil with or without flesh, it was brought over by the Moors. Sancho makes this blunder, being more used to this fruit than hard names. He meant Benengeli.

authentic. This thought yielded him awhile some small consolation; but then he relapsed into melancholic doubts and anxieties, when he considered that the author had given himself the title of Cid, and consequently must be a Moor. A nation from whom no truth could be expected, they all being given to impose on others with lies and fabulous stories, to falsify and counterfeit, and very fond of their own chimeras. He was not less uneasy, lest that writer should have been too lavish in treating of his amours, to the prejudice of his lady Dulcinea del Toboso's honour. He earnestly wished, that he might find his own inviolable fidelity celebrated in the history, and the reservedness and decency which he had always so religiously observed in his passion for her; slighting queens, empresses, and damsels of every degree for her sake, and suppressing the dangerous impulses of natural desire. Sancho and Carrasco found him thus agitated and perplexed with a thousand melancholic fancies, which yet did not hinder him from receiving the stranger with a great deal of civility.

This bachelor, though his name was Samson, was none of the largest in body, but a very great man at all manner of drollery; he had a pale and bad complexion, but good sense. He was about four and twenty years of age, round visaged, flat nosed, and wide mouthed, all signs of a malicious disposition, and of one that would delight in nothing more than in making sport for himself, by ridiculing others; as he plainly discovered when he saw Don Quixote. For, falling on his knees before him, 'Admit me to kiss your honour's hand,' cried he, 'most noble Don Quixote; for, by the habit of St. Peter, which I wear (though indeed I have as yet taken but the four first of the holy orders), you are certainly one of the most renowned knights-errant that ever was, or ever will be, through the whole extent of the habitable globe. Blessed may the sage Cid Hamet Benengeli be, for enriching the world with the history of your mighty deeds; and more than blessed, that curious virtuoso, who took care to have it translated out of the Arabic into our vulgar tongue, for the universal entertainment of mankind!' 'Sir,' said Don Quixote, making him rise, 'is it then possible that my history is extant, and that it was a Moor, and one of the sages that penned it?' 'It is so notorious a truth,' said the bachelor, 'that I do not in the least doubt but at this day there have already been published above twelve thousand copies of it. Portugal, Barcelona, and Valencia, where they have been printed, can witness that, if there were occasion. It is said, that it is also now in the press at Antwerp. And I verily believe there is scarce a language into which it is not to be translated.' 'Truly, sir,' said Don Quixote, 'one of the things that ought to yield the greatest satisfaction to a person of eminent virtue, is to live to see himself in good reputation in the world, and his actions published in print. I say, in good reputation, for otherwise there is no death but would be preferable to such a life.' 'As for a good name and reputation,' replied

Carrasco, 'your worship has gained the palm from all the knights-errant that ever lived: for the Arabian in his history, and the Christian in his version, have been very industrious to do justice to your character; your peculiar gallantry; your intrepidity and greatness of spirit in confronting danger; your constancy in adversities, your patience in suffering wounds and afflictions, your modesty and continence in that amour, so very platonic, between your worship and my Lady Donna Dulcinea del Toboso.' 'Odsbobs!' cried Sancho, 'I never heard her called so before; that Donna is a new kick; for she used to be called only my Lady Dulcinea del Toboso; in that, the history is out already.' 'That is no material objection,' said Carrasco. 'No, certainly,' added Don Quixote: 'but pray, good Mr. Bachelor, on which of all my adventures does the history seem to lay the greatest stress of remark?' 'As to that,' answered Carrasco, 'the opinions of men are divided according to their tastes: some cry up the adventure of the wind-mills, which appeared to your worship so many Briareuses and giants. Some are for that of the fulling-mills: others stand up for the description of the two armies, that afterwards proved two flocks of sheep. Others prize most the adventure of the dead corpse that was carrying to Segovia. One says, that none of them can compare with that of the galley-slaves; another, that none can stand in competition with the adventure of the Benedictine giants, and the valorous Biscainer.' 'Pray, Mr. Bachelor,' quoth Sancho, 'is there nothing said of that of the Yanguesians, if it please you, when our precious Rozinante was so mauled for offering to take a little carnel recreation with the mares?' 'There is not the least thing omitted,' answered Carrasco; 'the sage has inserted all with the nicest punctuality imaginable: so much as the capers which honest Sancho fetched in the blanket.' 'I fetched none in the blanket,' quoth Sancho, 'but in the air; and that too, oftener than I could have wished, the more my sorrow.' 'In my opinion,' said Don Quixote, 'there is no manner of history in the world, where you shall not find variety of fortune, much less any story of knight-errantry, where a man cannot always be sure of good success.' 'However,' said Carrasco, 'some who have read your history, wish that the author had spared himself the pains of registering some of that infinite number of drubs which the noble Don Quixote received.' 'There lies the truth of the history,' quoth Sancho. 'Those things in human equity,' said Don Quixote, 'might very well have been omitted; for actions that neither impair nor alter the history, ought rather to be buried in silence than related, if they redound to the discredit of the hero of the history. Certainly Æneas was never so pious as Virgil represents him, nor Ulysses so prudent as he is made by Homer.' 'I am of your opinion,' said Carrasco; 'but it is one thing to write like a poet, and another thing to write like an historian. It is sufficient for the first to deliver matters as they ought to have been, whereas the last must relate them as they were really transacted, without adding or omitting anything, upon any pretence whatever.' 'Well,' quoth Sancho, 'if this same Moorish lord be once got into the road of truth, a hundred to one but among my master's rib-roastings, he has not forgot mine: for they never took measure of his worship's shoulders, but they were pleased to do as much for my whole body: but it was no wonder; for it is his own rule, that if once his head aches, every limb must suffer too.' 'Sancho,' said Don Quixote, 'you are an arch unlucky knave; upon my honour you can find memory when you have a mind to have it.' 'Nay,' quoth Sancho, 'though I were minded to forget the rubs and drubs I have suffered, the bumps and tokens that are yet fresh on my ribs would not let me.' 'Hold your tongue,' said Don Quixote, 'and let the learned bachelor proceed, that I may know what the history says of me.' 'And of me too,' quoth Sancho, 'for they tell me I am one of the top parsons in it.' 'Persons, you should say, Sancho,' said Carrasco, 'and not parsons.' 'Hey-day!' quoth Sancho, 'have we got another corrector of hard words? If this be the trade, we shall never have done.' 'May I be cursed,' said Carrasco, 'if you be not the second person in the history, honest Sancho; nay, and some there are who had rather hear you talk than the best there; though some there are again that will say you were horribly credulous, to flatter yourself with having the government of that island, which your master here present promised you.' 'While there is life there is hope,' said Don Quixote. 'When Sancho is grown mature with time and experience, he may be better qualified for a government than he is yet.' 'Odsbodikins, sir!' quoth Sancho, 'if I be not fit to govern an island at these years, I shall never be a governor, though I live to the years of Methusalem; but there the mischief lies, we have brains enough, but we want the island.' 'Come, Sancho,' said Don Quixote, 'hope for the best; trust in providence; all will be well, and perhaps better than you imagine: but know, there is not a leaf on any tree that can be moved without the permission of Heaven.' 'That is very true,' said Carrasco; 'and I dare say, Sancho shall not want a thousand islands to govern, much less one; that is, if it be Heaven's will.' 'Why not?' quoth Sancho. 'I have seen governors in my time, who, to my thinking, could not come up to me passing the sole of my shoes, and yet forsooth, they call them "your Honour," and they eat their victuals all in silver.' 'Ay,' said Carrasco, 'but these were none of your governors of islands, but of other easy governments: why man, these ought, at least, to know their grammar.' 'Gramercy, for that,' quoth Sancho, 'give me but a grey mare* once, and I shall know her well enough, I will warrant ye. But, leaving the government in the hands of him that will best provide for me,

* This jingle of the words grammar, gramercy, and grey mare, is done in conformity to the original, which would not admit of a literal translation.

I must tell you, master bachelor Samson Carrasco, I am huge glad, that as your author has not forgot me, so he has not given an ill character of me; for by the faith of a trusty squire, had he said anything that did not become an old Christian* as I am, I had rung him such a peal, that the deaf should have heard me.' 'That were a miracle,' said Carrasco. 'Miracle me no miracles,' cried Sancho; 'let every man take care how he talks, or how he writes of other men, and not set down at random, higgle-de-piggledy, whatever comes into his noddle.' 'One of the faults found with this history,' said Carrasco, 'is, that the author has thrust into it a novel, which he calls, "The Curious Impertinent"; not that it is ill writ, or the design of it to be disliked; but because it is not in its right place, and has no coherence with the story of Don Quixote.' 'I will lay my life,' quoth Sancho, 'the son of a mongrel has made a gallimawfry of it all.' 'Now,' said Don Quixote, 'I perceive that he who attempted to write my history, is not one of the sages, but some ignorant prating fool, who would needs be meddling and set up for a scribbler, without the least grain of judgment to help him out; and so he has done like Orbaneja, the painter of Ubeda; who being asked what he painted, answered, as it may hit; and when he had scrawled out a mis-shapen cock, was forced to write underneath in Gothic letters, "This is a Cock." At this rate I believe he has performed in my history, so that it will require a commentary to explain it.' 'Not at all,' answered Carrasco; 'for he has made everything so plain, that there is not the least thing in it but what any one may understand. Children handle it, youngsters read it, grown men understand it, and old people applaud it. In short, it is universally so thumbed, so gleaned, so studied, and so known, that if the people do but see a lean horse, they presently cry, there goes Rozinante. But none apply themselves to the reading of it more than your pages: there is never a nobleman's anti-chamber where you shall not find a Don Quixote. No sooner has one laid it down, but another takes it up. One asks for it here, and there it is snatched up by another. In a word, it is esteemed the most pleasant and least dangerous diversion that ever was seen, as being a book that does not betray the least indecent expression, nor so much as a profane thought.' 'To write after another manner,' said Don Quixote, 'were not to write truth but falsehood; and those historians who are guilty of that, should be punished like those who counterfeit the lawful coin.† But I cannot conceive what could move the author to stuff his history with foreign novels and adventures not at all to the purpose; while there was a sufficient number of my own to have exercised his pen. But without

---

* A name by which the Spaniards desire to be distinguished from the Jews and Moors.
† Clippers and coiners in Spain are burnt.

doubt we may apply the proverb, With hay or with straw,* etc., for verily, had he altogether confined himself to my thoughts, my sighs, my tears, my laudable designs, my adventures, he might yet have swelled his book to as great a bulk, at least, as all Tostatus's† works. I have also reason to believe, Mr. Bachelor, that to compile a history, or write any book whatsoever, is a more difficult task than men imagine. There is need of a vast judgment, and a ripe understanding. It belongs to none but great geniuses to express themselves with grace and elegance, and draw the manners and actions of others to the life. The most artful part in a play is the fool's, and therefore a fool must not pretend to write it. On the other side, history is in a manner a sacred thing, so far as it contains truth; for where truth is, the Supreme Father of it may also be said to be, at least, in as much as concerns truth. However, there are men that will make you books, and turn them loose into the world, with as much dispatch as they would do a dish of fritters.' 'There is no book so bad,' said the bachelor, 'but something good may be found in it.' 'That is true,' said Don Quixote; 'yet it is a common thing for men, who have gained a very good reputation by their writings, before they printed them, to lose it afterwards quite, or, at least, the greatest part.' 'The reason is plain,' said Carrasco; 'their faults are more easily discovered, after their books are printed, as being then more read, and more narrowly examined, especially if the author had been much cried up before, for then the severity of the scrutiny is so much the greater. All those that have raised themselves a name by their ingenuity, great poets, and celebrated historians, are most commonly, if not always, envied by a sort of men who delight in censuring the writings of others, though they never publish any of their own.' 'That is no wonder,' said Don Quixote, 'for there are many divines, that could make but very dull preachers, and yet are quick at finding faults and superfluities in other men's sermons.' 'All this is truth,' replied Carrasco; 'and therefore I could wish these censurers would be more merciful and less scrupulous, and not dwell ungenerously upon small spots, that are in a manner but so many atoms on the face of the clear sun which they murmur at. And if *aliquando bonus dormitat Homerus*, let them consider how many nights he kept himself awake to bring his noble works to light, as little darkened with defects as might be. Nay, many times it may happen that what is censured for a fault, is rather an ornament, like moles that sometimes add to the beauty of the face. And when all is said, he that publishes a book runs a very great hazard, since nothing can be more impossible than to compose one that may secure the approbation of every reader.' 'Sure,' said Don

---

* The proverb entire is, *De paja o de heno jergon ileno*: *i.e.* The bed or tick full of hay or straw, so it be filled no matter with what.
† A famous Spaniard, who wrote many volumes of divinity.

Quixote, 'that which treats of me can have pleased but few.' 'Quite contrary,' said Carrasco; 'for as *Stultorum infinitus est numerus*, so an infinite number has admired your history. Only some there are who have taxed the author with want of memory or sincerity; because he has forgot to give an account who it was that stole Sancho's Dapple; for that particular is not mentioned there; only we find by the story that it was stolen; and yet, by and by, we find him riding the same ass again, without any previous light given us into the matter. Then they say, that the author forgot to tell the reader, what Sancho did with those hundred pieces of gold he found in the portmanteau in Sierra Morena; for there is not a word said of them more; and many people have a great mind to know what he did with them, and how he spent them; which is one of the most material points in which the work is defective.' 'Master Samson,' quoth Sancho, 'I am not now in a condition to cast up the accounts, for I am taken ill of a sudden with such a wambling in the stomach, and find myself so maukish, that if I do not see and fetch it up with a sup or two of good old bub, I shall waste like the snuff of a farthing candle.* I have that cordial at home, and my chuck stays for me. When I have had my dinner, I am for you, and will satisfy you, or any man that wears a head, about anything in the world, either as to the loss of the ass, or the laying out of those same pieces of gold.' This said, without a word more, or waiting for a reply, away he went. Don Quixote desired and entreated the bachelor to stay and do penance with him. The bachelor accepted his invitation, and stayed. A couple of pigeons were got ready to mend their commons. All dinner-time they discoursed about knight-errantry, Carrasco humouring him all the while. After they had slept out the heat of the day, Sancho came back, and they renewed their former discourse.

CHAPTER IV

Sancho Pança satisfies the Bachelor Samson Carrasco in his doubts and queries; with other passages fit to be known and related

SANCHO RETURNED to Don Quixote's house, and beginning where he left off; 'Now,' quoth he, 'as to what Master Samson wanted to know; that is, when, where, and by whom my ass was stolen: I answer, that the very night

---

* 'I shall be stuck upon St. Lucia's thorn,' supposed to be a cant phrase for the rack; for which the royal Spanish dictionary produces no other voucher but this passage.

that we marched off to the Sierra Morena, to avoid the hue and cry of the holy brotherhood, after the rueful adventure of the galley-slaves, and that of the dead body that was carrying to Segovia, my master and I slunk into a wood; where he leaning on his lance, and I, without alighting from Dapple, both sadly bruised and tired with our late skirmishes, fell fast asleep, and slept as soundly as if we had four feather-beds under us; but I especially was as serious at it as any dormouse; so that the thief, whoever he was, had leisure enough to clap four stakes under the four corners of the pack-saddle, and then leading away the ass from between my legs, without being perceived by me in the least, there he fairly left me mounted.' 'This is no new thing,' said Don Quixote, 'nor is it difficulty be done: with the same stratagem Sacripante had his steed stolen from under him by that notorious thief Brunelo, at the siege of Albraca.' 'It was broad day,' said Sancho, going on, 'when I, half awake and half asleep, began to stretch myself in my pack-saddle; but with my stirring, down came the stakes, and down came I souse, with a confounded squelch on the ground. Presently I looked for my ass, but no ass was to be found. O how thick the tears trickled from my eyes, and what a piteous moan I made; if he that made our history has forgot to set it down word for word, I would not give a rush for his book, I will tell him that. Some time after that, I cannot just tell you how long it was, as we were going with my lady the Princess Micomicona, I knew my ass again, and he that rid him, though he went like a gipsy; and who should it be, do you think, but Gines de Passamonte, that son of mischief, that crack-rope, whom my master and I saved, from the gallies.' 'The mistake does not lie there,' said Carrasco, 'but only that the author sets you upon the same ass that was lost, before he gives an account of his being found.' 'As to that,' replied Sancho, 'I do not know well what to say. If the man made a blunder, who can help it? But mayhaps it was a fault of the printer.' 'I make no question of that,' said Carrasco: but pray, what became of the hundred pieces? Were they sunk?' I fairly spent them on myself,' quoth Sancho, 'and on my wife and children; they helped me to lay my spouse's clack, and made her take so patiently my rambling and trotting after my master Don Quixote; for, had I come back with my pockets empty, and without my ass, I must have looked for a rueful greeting. And now, if you have any more to say to me, here am I, ready to answer the king himself. For what has anybody to meddle or make whether I found or found not, or spent or spent not? If the knocks and swaddlings that have been bestowed on my carcase in our jaunts, were to be rated but at three Maravedis a-piece, and I to be satisfied ready cash for every one, a hundred pieces of gold more would not pay for half of them; and therefore let every man lay his finger on his mouth, and not run hand over head, and mistake black for white, and white for black; for every man is as Heaven made him, and sometimes a great deal worse.' 'Well,' said the bachelor, 'if the author print another edition of the history, I will take special care he shall not forget to insert what honest Sancho has said, which will make the book as good again.' 'Pray, good Mr. Bachelor,' asked Don Quixote, ' are there any other emendations requisite to be made in this History?' 'Some there are,' answered Carrasco, 'but none of so much importance as those already mentioned.' 'Perhaps the author promises a second part?' said Don Quixote. 'He does,' said Carrasco; 'but he says he cannot find it, neither can he discover who has it: so that we doubt whether it will come out or not, as well for this reason, as because some people say that second parts are never worth anything; others cry, there is enough of Don Quixote already: however, many of those that love mirth better than melancholy, cry out, give us more Quixotery; let but Don Quixote appear, and Sancho talk, be it what it will, we are satisfied.' 'And how stands the author affected?' said the Knight. 'Truly,' answered Carrasco, 'as soon as ever he can find out the history, which he is now looking for with all imaginable industry, he is resolved to send it immediately to the press, though more for his own profit than through any ambition of applause.' 'What,' quoth Sancho, 'does he design to do it to get a penny by it? Nay, then we are like to have a rare history indeed; we shall have him botch and whip it up, like your tailors on Easter-eve, and give us a huddle of flim-flams that will never hang together; for your hasty work can never be done as it should be. Let Mr. Moor take care how he goes to work; for, my life for his, I and my master will stock him with such a heap of matter of adventures and odd chances, that he will have enough not only to write one second part, but an hundred. The poor fellow, belike, thinks we do nothing but sleep on a hay-mow; but let us once put foot into the stirrup, and he will see what we are about: this at least I will be bold to say, that if my master would be ruled by me, we had been in the field by this time, undoing of misdeeds and righting of wrongs, as good knights-errant use to do.' Scarce had Sancho made an end of his discourse, when Rozinante's neighing reached their ears. Don Quixote took it for a lucky omen, and resolved to take another turn within three or four days. He discovered his resolutions to the bachelor, and consulted him to know which way he should steer his course. The bachelor advised him to take the road of Saragossa in the kingdom of Arragon, a solemn tournament being shortly to be performed at that city on St. George's festival; where, by worsting all the Arragonian champions, he might win immortal honour, since to out-tilt them would be to outrival all the knights in the universe. He applauded his noble resolution, but withal admonished him not to be so desperate in exposing himself to dangers, since his life was not his own, but theirs who in distress stood in want of his assistance and protection. 'That is it now,' quoth Sancho, 'that makes me sometimes ready to run mad, Mr. Bachelor; for my master makes no more to set upon an hundred armed men, than a young hungry tailor to guttle down half-a-dozen of cucumbers. Body of me! master Bachelor, there is a time to retreat as well as a time to advance; Saint Jago and Close Spain,* must not always be the cry: for, I have heard somebody say, and, if I am not mistaken, it was my master himself, that valour lies just half-way between rashness and cow-heartedness; and if it be so, I would not have him run away without there is a reason for it, nor would I have him fall on when there is no good to be got by it. But above all things I would have him to know, if he has a mind I should go with him, that the bargain is, he shall fight for us both, and that I am tied to nothing but to look after him and his victuals and clothes: so far as this comes to, I will fetch and carry like any water-spaniel; but to think I will lug out my sword, though it be but against poor rogues, sorry shirks, and hedge-birds, yet troth I must beg his diversion. For my part, Mr. Bachelor, it is not the fame of being thought valiant that I aim at, but that of being deemed the very best and trustiest squire that ever followed the heels of a knight-errant: and if, after all my services, my master Don Quixote will be so kind as to give me one of those many islands which his worship says he shall light on, I shall be much beholden to him; but if he does not, why then I am born, do ye see, and one man must not live to rely on another, but on his Maker. Mayhaps the bread I shall eat without government, will go down more savourily than if I were a governor; and what do I know but that the Devil is providing me one of these governments for a stumbling-block, that I may stumble and fall, and so break my jaws, and ding out my butter-teeth. I was born Sancho, and Sancho I mean to die; and yet for all that, if fairly and squarely, with little trouble, and less danger, Heaven would bestow on me an island, or some such-like matter, I am no such fool neither, do ye see, as to refuse a good thing when it is offered me. No, I remember the old saying, when the ass is given thee, run and take him by the halter; and when good luck knocks at the door let him in, and keep him there.' 'My friend Sancho,' said Carrasco, 'you have spoken like any university professor: however, trust in Heaven's bounty, and the noble Don Quixote, and he may not only give thee an island, but even a kingdom.' 'One as likely as the other,' quoth Sancho; 'and yet, let me tell you, Mr. Bachelor, the kingdom which my master is to give me, you shall not find it thrown into an old sack; for I have felt my own pulse, and find myself sound enough to rule kingdoms and govern islands: I have told my master as much before now.' 'Have a care, Sancho,' said Carrasco, 'honours change manners; perhaps when you come to be a governor, you will scarce know the mother that bore you.' 'This,' said Sancho, 'may happen to those that were born in a ditch, but not to those whose souls are covered, as mine is,

---

* *Santiago y cierra Espana* is the cry of the Spanish soldiers when they fall on in battle, encouraging one another to close with the enemy: *Cerrar con el enemigo.*

four fingers thick with good old Christian fat!: no, do but think how good conditioned I be, and then you need not fear I should do dirtily by any one.' 'Grant it, good Heaven!' said Don Quixote, 'we shall see when the government comes; and methinks I have it already before my eyes.' After this he desired the bachelor, if he were a poet, to oblige him with some verses on his designed departure from his mistress Dulcinea del Toboso, every verse to begin with one of the letters of her name, so that joining every first letter of every verse together, they might make Dulcinea del Toboso. The bachelor told him, that though he were none of the famous poets of Spain, who, they say, were but three and a half,* he would endeavour to make that acrostic; though he was sensible this would be no easy task, there being seventeen letters in the name; so that if he made four stanzas of four verses a-piece, there would be a letter too much; and if he made his stanza of five lines, so as to make a double Decima or a Redondilla, there would be three letters too little; however, he would strive to drown a letter, and so take in the whole name in sixteen verses. 'Let it be so by any means,' said Don Quixote; 'for no woman will believe that those verses were made for her where her name is not plainly to be discerned.' After this, it was agreed they should set out within a week. Don Quixote charged the bachelor not to speak a word of all this, especially to the curate, Mr. Nicolas the barber, his niece, and his housekeeper, lest they should obstruct his honourable and valorous design. Carrasco gave him his word, and having desired Don Quixote to send an account of his good or bad success at his conveniency, took his leave! and left him; and Sancho went to get everything ready for his journey.

CHAPTER V

The wise and pleasant Dialogue between Sancho Pança, and Teresa Pança his Wife; together with other passages worthy of happy memory

THE TRANSLATOR OF THIS HISTORY, being come to this fifth chapter, thinks fit to inform the reader, that he holds it to be apocryphal; because it introduces Sancho speaking in another style than could be expected from his slender capacity, and saying things of so refined a nature, that it seems

---

* The first Alonzo de Ercilla, author of 'The Araucana'; the second, Juan Rufo of Cordova, author of 'The Austriada'; and the third, Christopher Vervis, of Valencia, author of 'The Monserrate.' By the half-poet, Don Gregorio thinks Cervantes means himself.

impossible he could do it. However, he thought himself obliged to render it into our tongue, to maintain the character of a faithful translator, and therefore he goes on in this manner.

Sancho came home so cheerful and so merry that his wife read his joy in his looks, as far as she could see him. Being impatient to know the cause, 'My dear,' cried she, 'what makes you so merry?' 'I should be more merry, my chuck,' quoth Sancho, 'would but Heaven so order it, that I were not so well pleased as I seem to be.' 'You speak riddles, husband,' quoth she; 'I do not know what you mean by saying you should be more merry if you were not so well pleased; for, though I am silly enough, I cannot think a man can take pleasure in not being pleased.' 'Look ye, Teresa,' quoth Sancho, 'I am merry because I am once more going to serve my master, Don Quixote, who is resolved to have the other frolic, and go a-hunting after adventures, and I must go with him; for he needs must, whom the Devil drives. What should I lie starving at home for? The hopes of finding another parcel of gold like that we spent, rejoices the cockles of my heart. But then it grieves me to leave thee, and those sweet babes of ours; and would Heaven but be pleased to let me live at home dry-shod, in peace and quietness, without gadding over hill and dale, through brambles and briars (as Heaven might do well with small cost, if it would, and with no manner of trouble, but only to be willing it should be so), why then it is a clear case that my mirth would be more firm and sound, since my present gladness is mingled with a sorrow to part with thee. And so I think I have made out what I have said, that I should be merrier if I did not seem so well pleased.' 'Look you, Sancho,' quoth the wife, 'ever since you have been a member of a knight-errant, you talk so round about the bush that nobody can understand you.' 'It is enough,' quoth Sancho, 'that he understands me who understands all things; and so scatter no more words about it, spouse. But be sure you look carefully after Dapple for these three days, that he may be in good case, and fit to bear arms; double his pittance, look for his pannel, and all his harness, and let everything be set to rights; for we are not going to a wedding, but to roam about the world, and to make our party good with giants, and dragons, and hobgoblins, and to hear nothing but hissing, and yelling, and roaring, and bowling, and bellowing; all which would yet be but sugar-plums if we were not to meet with the Yanguesian carriers,* and enchanted Moors.' 'Nay, as for that, husband,' quoth Teresa, 'I am apt enough to think you squires-errant do not eat their masters' bread for nothing; and therefore it shall be my daily prayer, that you may quickly be freed from that plaguy trouble.' 'Troth, wife,' quoth Sancho, 'were not I in hopes to see myself, ere it be long, governor of an island, on my conscience I should drop down dead on the

---

* Who beat the master and man before in the preceding volume.

spot.' 'Not so, my chicken,' quoth the wife, ' "let the hen live, though it be with pip"; do thou live, and let all the governments in the world go to the Devil. Thou camest out of thy mother's belly without government, thou hast lived hitherto without government, and thou mayest be carried to thy long home without government, when it shall please the Lord. How many people in this world live without government yet do well enough, and are well looked upon? There is no sauce in the world like hunger; and as the poor never want that, they always eat with a good stomach. But look ye, my precious, if it should be thy good luck to get a government, pray thee do not forget your wife and children. Take notice that little Sancho is already full fifteen, and it is high time he went to school, if his uncle the abbot mean to leave him something in the church. Then there is Mary Pança, your daughter: I dare say the burden of wedlock will never be the death of her, for I shrewdly guess, she longs as much for a husband, as you do for a government; and when all comes to all, better my daughter ill married, than well kept.' 'In good sooth I wife,' quoth Sancho, 'if it be Heaven's blessed will that I get anything by government, I will see and match Mary Pança so well, that she shall, at least, be called "My Lady." ' 'By no means, husband,' cried the wife; 'let her match with her match: if from clouted shoes you set her upon high heels, and from her coarse russet-coat you put her into a farthingale, and from plain "Moll" and "thee" and "thou," go to call her "Madam," and "Your Ladyship," the poor girl will not know how to behave herself, but will every foot make a thousand blunders, and show her homespun country breeding.' 'Tush! fool,' answered Sancho, 'it will be but two or three years' 'prenticeship; and then you will see how strangely she will alter; "Your Ladyship" and keeping of state will become her as if they had been made for her; and suppose they should not, what is it to anybody? Let her but be a lady, and let what will happen.' 'Good Sancho,' quoth the wife, 'do not look above yourself; I say, keep to the proverb, that says, "Birds of a feather flock together." It would be a fine thing, troth, for us to go and throw away our child on one of your lordlings, or right worshipfuls, who, when the toy should take him in the head, would find new names for her, and call her country Joan, plough-jobber's bairn, and spinner's web. No, no, husband, I have not bred the girl up as I have done, to throw her away at that rate, I will assure you. Do thou but bring home money, and leave me to get her a husband. Why there is Lope Tocho, old Joan Tocho's son, a hale, jolly young fellow, and one whom we all know; I have observed he casts a sheep's eye at the wench, he is one of our inches, and will be a good match for her; then we shall always have her under our wings, and be all as one, father and mother, children and grandchildren, and Heaven's peace and blessing will always be with us. But never talk to me of marrying her at your courts and great men's houses, where she will understand nobody,

and nobody will understand her.' 'Why, thou beast,' cried Sancho, 'thou
wife for Barabbas, why dost thou hinder me from marrying my daughter
to one that will get me grandchildren that may be called "Your Honour"
and "Your Lordship"? Have not I always heard my betters say, that "he
who will not when he may, when he will he shall have nay": When good
luck is knocking at our door, is it fit to shut him out? No, no, let us make
hay while the sun shines, and spread our sails before this prosperous gale.'
[This mode of locution, and the following huddle of reflections and
apophthegms, said to have been spoken by Sancho, made the translator of
this History say, he held this chapter apocryphal.] 'Canst thou not
perceive, thou senseless animal,' said Sancho, going on, 'that I ought to
venture over head and ears to light on some gainful government, that may
free our ankles from the clogs of necessity, and marry Mary Pança to
whom we please? Then thou wilt see how folks will call thee my Lady
Teresa Pança, and thou will sit in the church with thy carpets and
cushions and lean and loll in state, though the best gentlewoman in the
town burst with spite and envy. No, no, remain as you are, still in the same
posture, neither higher nor lower, like a picture in the hangings. Go to, let
us have no more of this; little Sanchica shall be a countess in spite of thy
teeth, I say.' 'Well, well, husband,' quoth the wife, 'have a care what you
say, for I fear me these high kicks will be my Molly's undoing. Yet do what
you will, make her a duchess or a princess, but I will never give my
consent. Look ye, yoke-fellow, for my part, I ever love to see everything
upon the square, and cannot abide to see folks take upon them when they
should not: I was christened plain Teresa, without any fiddle-faddle, or
addition of "Madam" or "Your Ladyship." My father's name was Cascajo;
and because I married you, they call me Teresa Pança, though, indeed, by
right I should be called Teresa Cascajo.* But where the kings are, there
are the laws, and I am even contented with that name without a flourish
before it, to make it longer and more tedious than it is already: neither will
I make myself anybody's laughing-stock. I will give them no cause to cry
(when they see me go like a countess, or a governor's madam), "Look,
look, how Madam Hog-wash struts along! It was but the other day she
would tug ye a distaff, capped with hemp, from morning till night, and
would go to mass with her coat over her head for want of a hood; yet now,
look, how she goes in her farthingale, and her rich trimmings and fallals,
no less than a whole tradesman's shop about her mangy back, as if
everybody did not know her." No, husband, if it please Heaven but to
keep me in my seven senses, or my five, or as many as I have, I will take
care to tie up people's tongues from setting me out at this rate You may

---

* The custom of Spain is ever to call women, though married, by their maiden
   names, which makes Teresa say what she does.

go, and be a governor, or an islander, and look as big as bull-beef if you will; but by my grandmother's daughter, neither I nor my girl will budge a foot from our thatched house. For the proverb says:

"The wife that expects to have a good name
Is always at home as if she were lame:
And the maid that is honest, her chiefest delight,
Is still to be doing from morning to night."*

'March you and your Don Quixote together, to your islands and adventures, and leave us here to our sorry fortune: I will warrant you Heaven will better it, if we live as we ought to do. I wonder though who made him a Don; neither his father nor his grandsire ever had that feather in their caps.' 'The Lord help thee, woman!' quoth Sancho, 'what a heap of stuff hast thou twisted together, without head or tail! What have thy Cascajos, thy farthingales and fallals, thy old saws, and all this tale of a roasted horse, to do with what I have said? Hark thee me, Gammar Addlepate (for I can find no better name for thee, since thou art such a blind buzzard as to miss my meaning, and stand in thy own light), should I have told thee that my girl was to throw herself head foremost from the top of some steeple, or to trot about the world like a gipsy, or, as the Infanta Donna Urraca† did, then thou mightest have some reason not to be out of my mind. But if in the twinkling of an eye, and while one might toss a pancake, I clap you a Don and a Ladyship upon the back of her; if I fetch her out of her straw, to sit under a stately bed's tester; and squat her down on more velvet cushions, than all the Almohadas‡ of Morocco had Moors in their generation, why shouldest thou be against it, and not be pleased with what pleases me?' 'Shall I tell you why, husband?' answered Teresa: 'it is because of the proverb, "He that covers thee, discovers thee." A poor man is scarce minded, but every one's eyes will stare upon the rich; and if that rich man has formerly been poor, this sets others a-grumbling and backbiting; and your evil tongues will never have done, but swarm about the streets like bees, and buzz their stories into people's ears.' 'Look you, Teresa,' said Sancho, 'mind what I say to thee, I will tell thee things that perhaps thou never heardest of in thy life: nor do I speak of my own

---

* *La Muger honrada, / La pierna quebrada, y en casa; / La Douzeila honesta / El hazer algo es su siesta.*

† A Spanish princess.

‡ *Almohada* signifies a cushion, and was also the surname of a famous race of the Arabs in Africa, and from thence introduced among the Moors in Spain. So that here is a sort of pun or allusion to the name, and the women in Spain sit all upon cushions on the ground, which is the cause there is so much mention made of them.

head, but what I heard from that good father who preached in our town all last Lent. He told us, if I am not mistaken, that all those things which we see before our eyes, do appear, hold and exist in our memories much better, and with a greater stress than things past.' [All these reasons which are here offered by Sancho, are another argument to persuade the translator to hold this chapter for apocryphal, as exceeding the capacity of Sancho.] 'From thence it arises,' said Sancho, going on, 'that when we happen to see a person well dressed, richly equipped, and with a great train of servants, we find ourselves moved and prompted to pay him respect, in a manner, in spite of our teeth, though at that very moment our memory makes us call to remembrance some low circumstances, in which we had seen that person before. Now this ignominy, be it either by reason of his poverty, or mean parentage, as it is already passed, is no more, and only that which we see before our eyes remains. So then, if this person, whom fortune has raised to that height out of his former obscurity, by his father's means, be well bred, generous, and civil to all men, and does not affect to vie with those that are of noble descent; assure thyself, Teresa, nobody will remember what he was, but look upon him as what he is, unless it be your envious spirits, from whose taunts no prosperous fortune can be free.' 'I do not understand you, husband,' quoth Teresa, 'even follow your own inventions, and do not puzzle my brains with your harangues and rhetoric If you are so devolved to do as ye say,' – ' "Resolved" you should say, wife,' quoth Sancho, 'and not "devolved." ' 'Pray thee, husband,' said Teresa, 'let us have no words about that matter: I speak as Heaven's pleased I should; and for hard words, I give my share to the curate. All I have to say now, is this: if you hold still in the mind of being a governor, pray even take your son Sancho along with you; and henceforth train him up to your trade of governing; for it is but fitting that the son should be brought up to the father's calling.' 'When once I am a governor,' quoth Sancho, 'I will send for him by the post, and I will send thee money withal; for I dare say, I shall want none; there never wants those that will lend governors money when they have none. But then be sure you clothe the boy so, that he may look, not like what he is, but like what he is to be.' 'Send you but money,' quoth Teresa, and I will make him as fine as a May-day garland.'* 'So then, wife,' quoth Sancho, 'I suppose we are agreed that our Moll shall be a Countess?' 'The day I see her a Countess,' quoth Teresa, 'I reckon I lay her in her grave. However, I tell you again, even follow your own inventions; you men will be masters, and we poor women are born to bear the clog of obedience, though our

---

* *Como un palmito*, in the original; *i.e.* as fine as a palm-branch. In Italy and Spain they carry in procession, on Palm Sunday, a palm-branch the leaves of which are plaited and interwoven with great art and nicety.

husbands have no more sense than a cuckoo.' Here she fell a-weeping as heartily as if she had seen her daughter already dead and buried. Sancho comforted her, and promised her, that though he was to make her a Countess, yet he would see and put it off as long as he could. Thus ended their dialogue, and he went back to Don Quixote, to dispose everything for a march.

CHAPTER VI

What passed between Don Quixote, his Niece, and the Housekeeper: being one of the most important chapters in the whole History

WHILE SANCHO PANÇA, and his wife Teresa Cascajo, had the foregoing impertinent* dialogue, Don Quixote's niece and housekeeper were not idle, guessing by a thousand signs that the Knight intended a third sally. Therefore they endeavoured by all possible means to divert him from his foolish design; but all to no purpose; for this was but preaching to a rock, and hammering cold stubborn steel. But among other arguments: 'In short, sir,' quoth the housekeeper, 'if you will not be ruled, but will needs run wandering over hill and dale, like a stray soul between heaven and hell, seeking for mischief, for so I may well call the hopeful adventures which you go about, I will never leave complaining to Heaven and the king till there is a stop put to it some way or other.' 'What answer Heaven will vouchsafe to give thee, I know not,' answered Don Quixote, 'neither can I tell what return his majesty will make to thy petition; but, were I king, I would excuse myself from answering the infinite number of impertinent memorials that disturb the repose of princes. I tell thee, woman, among the many other fatigues which royalty sustains, it is one of the greatest to be obliged to hear every one, and to give answer to all people. Therefore pray trouble not his majesty with anything concerning me.' 'But, pray, sir, tell me,' replied she, 'are there not many knights in the king's court?' 'I must confess,' said Don Quixote, 'that for the ornament, the grandeur, and the pomp of royalty, many knights are, and ought to be maintained there.' 'Why then,' said the woman, 'would it not be better for your worship to be one of those brave knights, who serve the king their master on foot in his

---

* So it is in the original, viz. *impertinente platica*: but Mr. Jarvis, very justly, suspects the irony to be here broke by the transcriber or printer and not by the author himself, and that it should be (*importante*) important, which carries on the grave ridicule of the history.

court?' 'Hear me, sweetheart,' answered Don Quixote, 'all knights cannot be courtiers, nor can all courtiers be knights-errant. There must be of all sorts in the world; and though we were all to agree in the common appellation of knights, yet there would be a great difference between the one and the other. For your courtiers, without so much as stirring out of their chambers, or the shade and shelter of the court, can journey over all the universe in a map, without the expense and fatigue of travelling, without suffering the inconveniences of heat, cold, hunger, and thirst; while we who are the true knights-errant, exposed to those extremities, and all the inclemencies of Heaven, by night and by day, on foot as well as on horseback, measure the whole surface of the earth with our own feet. Nor are we only acquainted with the pictures of our enemies, but with their very persons, ready upon all occasions and at all times to engage them, without standing upon trifles, or the ceremony of measuring weapons, stripping, or examining whether our opponents have any holy relics, or other secret charms about them, whether the sun be duly divided, or any other punctilios and circumstances observed among private duelists; things which thou understandest not, but I do: and must further let thee know, that the true knight-errant, though he meets ten giants, whose tall aspiring heads not only touch but overtop the clouds, each of them stalking with prodigious legs like huge towers, their sweeping arms like masts of mighty ships, each eye as large as a mill-wheel, and more fiery than a glass-furnace; yet he is so far from being afraid to meet them, that he must encounter them with a gentle countenance, and an undaunted courage, assail them, close with them, and if possible vanquish and destroy them all in an instant; nay, though they came armed with the scales of a certain fish, which they say is harder than adamant, and instead of swords had dreadful sabres of keen Damascan steel, or mighty maces with points of the same metal, as I have seen them more than a dozen times. I have condescended to tell thee thus much, that thou mayest see the vast difference between knights and knights; and I think it were to be wished that all princes knew so far how to make the distinction, as to give the pre-eminence to this first species of knights-errant, among whom there have been some whose fortitude has not only been the defence of our kingdom, but of many more, as we read in their histories.' 'Ah! sir,' said the niece, 'have a care what you say; all the stories of knights-errant are nothing but a pack of lies and fables, and if they are not burnt, they ought at least to wear a Sanbenito,* the badge of heresy, or some other mark of infamy, that the world may know them to be wicked, and perverters of good manners.' 'Now, by the powerful sustainer of my being,' cried Don Quixote, 'wert thou not so nearly related to me,

* A coat of black canvas, painted over with flames and devils, worn by heretics when going to be burnt, by order of the Inquisition.

wert thou not my own sister's daughter, I would take such revenge for the blasphemy thou hast uttered, as would resound through the whole universe. Who ever heard of the like impudence? That a young baggage, who scarce knows her bobbins from a bodkin, should presume to put in her oar, and censure the histories of knights-errant! What would Sir Amadis have said, had he heard this? But he undoubtedly would have forgiven thee, for he was the most courteous and complaisant knight of his time, especially to the fair sex, being a great protector of damsels; but thy words might have reached the ears of some, that would have sacrificed thee to their indignation; for all knights are not possessed of civility or good-nature; some are rough and revengeful; and neither are all those that assume the name, of a disposition suitable to the function; some indeed were of the right stamp, but others are either counterfeit, or of such an allay as cannot bear the touchstone, though they deceive the sight. Inferior mortals they are, who aim at knighthood, and strain to reach the height of honour; and high-born knights there are, who seem fond of grovelling in the dust, and being lost in the crowd of inferior mortals. The first raise themselves by ambition or by virtue; the last debase themselves by negligence or by vice; so that there is need of a distinguishing understanding to judge between these two sorts of knights, so nearly allied in name, and so different in actions.' 'Bless me! dear uncle,' cried the niece, 'that you should know so much, as to be able, if there was occasion, to get up into a pulpit, or preach* in the streets, and yet be so strangely mistaken, so grossly blind of understanding, as to fancy a man of your years and infirmity can be strong and valiant; that you can set everything right, and force stubborn malice to bend, when you yourself stoop beneath the burden of age; and what is yet more odd, that you are a knight, when it is well known you are none! For though some gentlemen may be knights, a poor gentleman can hardly be so, because he cannot buy it' 'You say well, niece,' answered Don Quixote; 'and as to this last observation, I could tell you things that you would admire at, concerning families; but because I will not mix sacred things with profane, I waive the discourse. However, listen both of you, and for your further instruction know, that all the lineages and descents of mankind, are reducible to these four heads: first, of those who, from a very small and obscure beginning, have raised themselves to a spreading and prodigious magnitude. Secondly, of those who, deriving their greatness from a noble spring, still preserve the dignity and character of their original splendour. A third, are those who, though they had large foundations, have ended in a point like a pyramid, which by

---

* A common thing in Spain and Italy, for the friars and young Jesuits, in an extraordinary fit of zeal, to get upon a bulk, and hold forth in the streets or market place.

little and little dwindles as it were into nothing, or next to nothing, in comparison of its basis. Others there are (and those are the bulk of mankind), who have neither had a good beginning, nor a rational continuance, and whose ending shall therefore be obscure; such are the common people, the plebeian race. The Ottoman family is an instance of the first sort, having derived their present greatness from the poor beginning of a base-born shepherd. Of the second sort, there are many princes who, being born such, enjoy their dominions by inheritance, and leave them to their successors without addition or diminution. Of the third sort, there is an infinite number of examples: for all the Pharaohs and Ptolomies of Egypt, your Cæsars of Rome, and all the swarm (if I may use that word) of princes, monarchs, lords, Medes, Assyrians, Persians, Greeks, and Barbarians, – all these families and empires have ended in a point, as well as those who gave rise to them: for it were impossible at this day to find any of their descendants, or if we could find them, it would be in a poor grovelling condition. As for the vulgar, I say nothing of them, more than that they are thrown in as ciphers to increase the number of mankind, without deserving any other praise. Now, my good-natured souls, you may at least draw this reasonable inference from what I have said of this promiscuous dispensation of honours, and this uncertainty and confusion of descent, that virtue and liberality in the present possessor are the most just and undisputable titles to nobility; for the advantages of pedigree, without these qualifications, serve only to make vice more conspicuous. The great man that is vicious will be greatly vicious, and the rich miser is only a covetous beggar; for, not he who possesses, but that spends and enjoys his wealth, is the rich and the happy man; nor he neither who barely spends, but who does it with discretion. The poor knight indeed cannot show he is one by his magnificence; but yet by his virtue, affability, civility, and courteous behaviour, he may display the chief ingredients that enter into the composition of the knighthood; and though he cannot pretend to liberality, wanting riches to support it, his charity may recompense that defect; for an alms of two maravedies cheerfully bestowed upon an indigent beggar, by a man in poor circumstances speaks him as liberal as the larger donative of a vain-glorious rich man before a fawning crowd. These accomplishments will always shine through the clouds of fortune, and at last break through them with splendour and applause. There are two paths to dignity and wealth: arts and arms. Arms I have chosen; and the influence of the planet Mars that presided at my nativity, led me to that adventurous road. So that all your attempts to shake my resolution are in vain: for in spite of all mankind, I will pursue what Heaven has fated, fortune ordained, what reason requires, and (which is more) what my inclination demands. I am sensible of the many troubles and dangers that attend the prosecution of knight-errantry, but I also know what infinite honours and rewards are the consequences of the performance. The path of virtue is narrow, and the way of vice easy and open; but their ends and resting-places are very different. The latter is a broad road indeed, and down-hill all the way but death and contempt are always met at the end of the journey; whereas the former leads to glory and life, not a life that soon must have an end, but an immortal being. For I know, as our great Castilian* poet expresses it, that

> ' "Thro' steep ascents, thro' straight and rugged ways,
>   Ourselves to glory's lofty seats we raise:
>   In vain he hopes to reach the bless'd abode,
>   Who leaves the narrow path, for the more easy road." '

'Alack-a-day!' cried the niece, 'my uncle is a poet, too! He knows everything. I will lay my life he might turn mason in case of necessity. If he would but undertake it, he could build a house as easy as a bird-cage.' 'Why truly, niece,' said Don Quixote, 'were not my understanding wholly involved in thoughts relating to the exercise of knight-errantry, there is nothing which I durst not engage to perform, no curiosity should escape my hands, especially bird-cages and tooth-pickers.'† By this somebody knocked at the door, and being asked who it was, Sancho answered, it was he. Whereupon the housekeeper slipped out of the way, not willing to see him, and the niece let him in. Don Quixote received him with open arms, and, locking themselves both in the closet, they had another dialogue as pleasant as the former.

CHAPTER VII

An account of Don Quixote's Conference with his Squire, and other most famous passages

The housekeeper no sooner saw her master and Sancho locked up together, but she presently surmised the drift of that close conference, and concluding that no less than villainous knight-errantry and another sally would prove the result of it, she flung her veil over her head, and quite cast down with sorrow and vexation, trudged away to seek Samson Carrasco, the bachelor of arts; depending on his wit and eloquence to dissuade his

---

* Boscan, one of the first reformers of the Spanish poetry.
† *Palillo de dientes*, i. e. a little stick for the teeth. Tooth-pickers in Spain are made of long shavings of boards, split and reduced to a straw's breadth and wound up like small wax-lights.

friend Don Quixote from his frantic resolution. She found him walking in the yard of his house, and fell presently on her knees before him in a cold sweat, and with all the marks of a disordered mind. 'What is the matter, woman,' said he (somewhat surprised at her posture and confusion), 'what has befallen you that you look as if you were ready to give up the ghost?' 'Nothing,' said she, 'dear sir, but that my master's departing; he is departing, that is most certain.' 'How' cried Carrasco; 'what do you mean? Is his soul departing out of his body?' 'No,' answered the woman, 'but all his wits are quite and clean departing. He means to be gadding again into the wide world, and is upon the spur now the third time to hunt after "ventures"* as he calls them, though I do not know why he calls those chances so. The first time he was brought home, was athwart an ass, and almost cudgelled to pieces. The other bout he was forced to ride home in a wagon, cooped up in a cage, where he would make us believe he was enchanted; and the poor soul looked so dismally, that the mother that bore him would not have known the child of her bowels; so meagre, wan, and withered, and his eyes so sunk and hid in the utmost nook and corner of his brain, that I am sure I spent about six hundred eggs to cocker him up again; ay, and more too, as Heaven and all the world is my witness, and the hens that laid them cannot deny it.' 'That I believe,' said the bachelor, 'for your hens are so well bred, so fat, and so good, that they will not say one thing and think another for the world. But is this all? Has no other ill-luck befallen you besides this of your master's intended ramble?' 'No other, sir,' quoth she. 'Then trouble your head no further,' said he, 'but get you home, and as you go, say me the prayer of St. Appollonia, if you know it; then get me some warm bit for breakfast, and I will come to you presently, and you shall see wonders.' 'Dear me,' quoth she, 'the prayer of St. Polonia! Why, it is only good for the toothache; but his ailing lies in his skull.' 'Mistress,' said he, 'do not dispute with me: I know what I say. Have I not commenced bachelor of arts at Salamanca, and do you think there is any bachelorising beyond that?' With that away she goes, and he went presently to find the curate, to consult with him about what shall be declared in due time.

When Sancho and his master were locked up together in the room, there passed some discourse between them, of which the history gives a very punctual and impartial account. 'Sir,' quoth Sancho to his master, 'I have at last reluced my wife to let me go with your worship wherever you will have me.' ' "Reduced," you would say, Sancho,' said Don Quixote, 'and not "reluced." 't 'Look you, sir,' quoth Sancho, 'if I am not mistaken,

---

* *Ventura* signifies both good luck and also adventures.

† But just now Sancho corrected his wife for saying 'devolved' instead of 'resolved.'

I have wished you once or twice not to stand correcting my words, if you understand my meaning: if you do not, why then do but say to me, "Sancho, devil," or what you please, "I understand thee not"; and if I do not make out my meaning plainly, then take me up; for I am so focible' – 'I understand you not,' said Don Quixote, interrupting him, 'for I cannot guess the meaning of your "focible." ' 'Why, so focible,' quoth Sancho, 'is as much as to say – focible. That is, I am so and so, as it were.' 'Less and less do I understand thee,' said the Knight. 'Why, then,' quoth Sancho, 'there is an end of the matter; it must even stick there for me, for I can speak no better.' 'O! now,' quoth Don Quixote, 'I fancy I guess your meaning; you mean "docible," I suppose, implying that you are ready and apprehensive, that you will presently observe what I shall teach you.' 'I will lay any even wager now,' said the squire, 'you understood me well enough at first, but you had a mind to put me out, merely to hear me put your fine words out-a-joint.' 'That may be,' said Don Quixote, 'but pray thee tell me, what says Teresa?' 'Why, if it please you,' quoth Sancho, 'Teresa bids me make sure work with your worship, and that we may have less talking and more doing; that a man must not be his own carver; that he who cuts does not shuffle; that it is good to be certain; that paper speaks when beards never wag; that a bird in hand is worth two in the bush. One "hold fast" is better than two "I will give thee." Now, I say, a woman's counsel is not worth much, yet he that despises it is no wiser than he should be.' 'I say so, too,' said Don Quixote, 'but pray, good Sancho, proceed; for thou art in an excellent strain; thou talkest most sententiously today.' 'I say,' quoth Sancho, 'as you know better yourself than I do, that we are all mortal men, here today and gone tomorrow; as soon goes the young lamb to the spit, as the old wether; no man can tell the length of his days; for Death is deaf, and when he knocks at the door, mercy on the porter. He is in post-haste, neither fair words nor foul, crowns nor mitres, can stay him, as the report goes, and as we are told from the pulpit.' 'All this I grant,' said Don Quixote; 'but what would you infer from hence?' 'Why, sir,' quoth Sancho, 'all I would be at is, that your worship allow me so much a month* for my wages, whilst I stay with you, and that the aforesaid wages be paid me out of your estate. For I will trust no longer to rewards, that mayhaps may come late, and mayhaps not at all. I would be glad to know what I get, be it more or less. A little in one's own pocket is better than much in another man's purse. It is good to keep a nest-egg. Every little makes a mickle; while a man gets he can never lose. Should it happen indeed that your worship should give me this same island which you promised me, though it is what I dare not so much as hope for, why then I am not such an ungrateful, nor so unconscionable a muck-worm,

---

* The custom of Spain is to pay their servants wages by the month.

but that I am willing to strike off upon the income, for what wages I receive, cantity for cantity.' 'Would not quantity have been better than "cantity"?' asked Don Quixote. 'Ho! I understand you now,' cried Sancho; 'I dare lay a wager I should have said "quantity," and not "cantity"; but no matter for that, since you knew what I meant.' 'Yes, Sancho,' quoth the Knight, 'I have dived to the very bottom of your thought, and understand now the aim of all your numerous shot of proverbs. Look you, friend Sancho, I should never scruple to pay thee wages, had I any example to warrant such a practice. Nay, could I find the least glimmering of a precedent through all the books of chivalry that ever I read, for any yearly or monthly stipend, your request should be granted. But I have read all, or the greatest part of the histories of knights-errant, and find that all their squires depended purely on the favour of their masters for a subsistence; till by some surprising turn in the knight's fortune the servants were advanced to the government of some island, or some equivalent gratuity; at least, they had honour and a title conferred on them as a reward. Now, friend Sancho, if you will depend on these hopes of preferment, and return to my service, it is well; if not, get you home, and tell your impertinent wife that I will not break through all the rules and customs of chivalry to satisfy her sordid diffidence and yours; and so let there be no more words about the matter, but let us part friends: and remember this, that if there be vetches in my dove-house, it will want no pigeons Good arrears are better than ill-pay; and a fee in reversion is better than a farm in possession. Take notice, too, there is proverb for proverb, to let you know that I can pour out a volley of them as well as you. In short, if you will not go along with me upon courtesy, and run the same fortune with me, Heaven be with you, and make you a saint; I do not question but I shall get me a squire, more obedient, more careful, and less saucy and talkative than you.'

Sancho, hearing his master's firm resolution, it was cloudy weather with him in an instant; he was struck dumb with disappointment, and down sunk at once his heart to his girdle; for he verily thought he could have brought him to any terms, through a vain opinion, that the Knight would not for the world go without him. While he was thus dolefully buried in thought, in came Samson Carrasco, and the niece, very eager to hear the bachelor's arguments to dissuade Don Quixote from his intended sally. But Samson, who was a rare comedian, presently embracing the Knight, and beginning in a high strain, soon disappointed her. 'O flower of chivalry,' cried he, 'refulgent glory of arms, living honour, and mirror of our Spanish nation, may all those who prevent the third expedition which thy heroic spirit meditates be lost in the labyrinth of their perverse desires, and find no thread to lead them to their wishes.' Then turning to the housekeeper: 'You have no need now to say the prayer of St. Apollonia,' said he, 'for I find it written in the stars, that the illustrious champion must no longer delay the prosecution of glory; and I should injure my conscience should I presume to dissuade him from the benefits that shall redound to mankind, by exerting the strength of his formidable arm, and the innate virtues of his heroic soul. Alas! his stay deprives the oppressed orphans of a protector, damsels of a deliverer, champions of their honour, widows of an obliging patron, and married women of a vigorous comforter; nay, also delays a thousand other important exploits and achievements, which are the duty and necessary consequences of the honourable order of knight-errantry. Go on then, my graceful, my valorous Don Quixote, rather this very day than the next; let your greatness be upon the wing, and if anything be wanting towards the completing of your equipage, I stand forth to supply you with my life and fortune, and ready, if it be thought expedient, to attend your Excellence as a squire, an honour which I am ambitious to attain.' 'Well, Sancho,' said Don Quixote, hearing this and turning to his squire, 'did not I tell thee I should not want squires; behold who offers me his service, the most excellent bachelor of arts, Samson Carrasco, the perpetual darling of the muses, and glory of the Salamanca schools; sound and active of body, patient of labour, inured to abstinence, silent in misfortune, and, in short, endowed with all the accomplishments that constitute a squire. But, forbid it, Heaven, that to indulge my private inclinations I should presume to weaken the whole body of learning, by removing from it so substantial a pillar, so vast a repository of sciences, and so eminent a branch of the liberal arts. No, my friend, remain thou another Samson in thy country, be the honour of Spain, and the delight of thy ancient parents: I shall content myself with any squire, since Sancho does not vouchsafe to go with me.' 'I do, I do,' cried Sancho, relenting with tears in his eyes; 'I do vouchsafe; it shall never be said of Sancho Pança, no longer pipe no longer dance. Nor have I a heart of flint, sir; for all the world knows, and especially our town, what the whole generation of the Pança's has ever been: besides, I well know and have already found by many good turns, and more good words, that your worship has had a goodwill towards me all along; and if I have done otherwise than I should, in standing upon wages, or so, it was merely to humour my wife, who, when once she is set upon a thing stands digging and hammering at a man like a cooper at a tub, till she clinches the point. But, hang it, I am the husband, and will be her husband, and she is but a wife, and shall be a wife. None can deny but I am a man every inch of me, wherever I am, and I will be a man at home in spite of anybody; so that you have no more to do but to make your will and testament; but be sure you make the conveyance so firm that it cannot be rebuked, and then let us be gone as soon as you please, that Master Samson's soul may be at rest; for he says his conscience will not let him be quiet till he has set you upon another journey through the world; and I here again offer myself to follow your worship, and promise to be faithful and loyal, as well, nay, and better, than all the squires that ever waited on knights-errant.' The bachelor was amazed to hear Sancho Pança express himself after that manner; and, though he had read much of him in the first part of his history, he could not believe him to be so pleasant a fellow as he is there represented. But hearing him now talk of 'rebuking' instead of 'revoking' testaments and conveyances, he was induced to credit all that was said of him, and to conclude him one of the oddest compounds of the age; nor could he imagine that the world ever saw before so extravagant a couple as the master and the man.

Don Quixote and Sancho embraced, becoming as good friends as ever, and so with the approbation of the grand Carrasco, who was then the Knight's oracle, it was decreed that they should set out at the expiration of three days; in which time all necessaries should be provided, especially a whole helmet, which Don Quixote said he was resolved by all means to purchase. Samson offered him one which he knew he could easily get of a friend, and which looked more dull with the mould and rust, than bright with the lustre of the steel. The niece and the housekeeper made a woeful outcry; they tore their hair, scratched their faces, and howled like common mourners at funerals, lamenting the Knight's departure as it had been his real death; and cursing Carrasco most unmercifully, though his behaviour was the result of a contrivance plotted between the curate, the barber, and himself. In short, Don Quixote and his squire having got all things in readiness, the one having pacified his wife, and the other his niece and housekeeper; towards the evening, without being seen by anybody but the bachelor, who would needs accompany them about half a league from the village, they set forward for Toboso. The knight mounted his Rozinante, and Sancho his trusty Dapple, his wallet well stuffed with provisions, and his purse with money, which Don Quixote gave him to defray expenses. At last Samson took his leave, desiring the champion to give him, from time to time, an account of his success, that according to the laws of friendship, he might sympathise in his good or evil fortune. Don Quixote made him a promise, and then they parted; Samson went home, and the Knight and the squire continued their journey for the city of Toboso.

CHAPTER VIII

Don Quixote's success in his Journey to visit the
Lady Dulcinea del Toboso

'BLESSED BE THE MIGHTY ALLA,'* says Hamet Benengeli, at the beginning of his eighth chapter; 'blessed be Alla!' Which ejaculation he thrice repeated, in consideration of the blessing that Don Quixote and Sancho had once more taken the field again; and that from this period the readers of their delightful history may date the Knight's achievements, and the squire's pleasantries; and he entreats them to forget the former heroical transactions of the wonderful Knight, and fix their eyes upon his future exploits, which take birth from his setting out for Toboso, as the former began in the fields of Montiel. Nor can so small a request be thought unreasonable, considering what he promises, which begins in this manner.

Don Quixote and his squire were no sooner parted from the bachelor, but Rozinante began to neigh, and Dapple to bray; which both the Knight and the squire interpreted as good omens, and most fortunate presages of their success; though the truth of the story is, that as Dapple's braying exceeded Rozinante's neighing, Sancho concluded that his fortune should outrival and eclipse his master's; which inference I will not say he drew from some principles in judicial astrology, in which he was undoubtedly well grounded, though the history is silent in that particular: however, it is recorded of him, that oftentimes upon the falling or stumbling of his ass, he wished he had not gone abroad that day, and from such accidents prognosticated but dislocation of joints, and breaking of ribs; and, notwithstanding his foolish character, this was no bad observation. 'Friend Sancho,' said Don Quixote to him, 'I find the approaching night will overtake us ere we can reach Toboso, where, before I enter upon any expedition I am resolved to pay my vows, receive my benediction, and take my leave of the peerless Dulcinea; being assured after that of happy events, in the most dangerous adventures; for nothing in this world inspires a knight-errant with so much valour as the smiles and favourable aspects of his mistress.' 'I am of your mind,' quoth Sancho; 'but I am afraid, sir, you will hardly come at her, to speak with her, at least not meet her in a place where she may give you her blessing, unless she throw it you

* The Moors call God 'Alla.'

over the mud-wall of the yard, where I first saw her, when I carried her news of your mad pranks in the midst of Sierra Morena.' 'Mud-wall, dost thou say!' cried Don Quixote. 'Mistaken fool, that wall could have no existence but in thy muddy understanding: it is a mere creature of thy dirty fancy; for that never-duly-celebrated paragon of beauty and gentility was then undoubtedly in some court, in some stately gallery, or walk, or as it is properly called, in a sumptuous and royal palace.' 'It may be so,' said Sancho, 'though, so far as I can remember, it seemed to me neither better nor worse than a mud-wall.' 'It is no matter,' replied the Knight, 'let us go thither; I will visit my dear Dulcinea; let me but see her, though it be over a mud-wall, through a chink of a cottage, or the pales of a garden, at a lattice, or anywhere; which way soever the least beam from her bright eyes reaches mine, it will so enlighten my mind, so fortify my heart, and invigorate every faculty of my being, that no mortal will be able to rival me in prudence and valour.' 'Troth, sir,' quoth Sancho, 'when I beheld that same sun of a lady, methought it did not shine so bright as to cast forth any beams at all; but mayhaps the reason was, that the dust of the grain she was winnowing raised a cloud about her face, and made her look somewhat dull.' 'I tell thee again, fool,' said Don Quixote, 'thy imagination is dusty and foul; will it never be beaten out of thy stupid brain, that my lady Dulcinea was winnowing? Are such exercises used by persons of her quality, whose recreations are always noble, and such as display an air of greatness suitable to their birth and dignity? Canst thou not remember the verses of our poet, when he recounts the employments of the four nymphs at their crystal mansions, when they advanced their heads above the streams of the lovely Tagus, and sat upon the grass, working those rich embroideries, where silk and gold, and pearl embossed, were so curiously interwoven, and which that ingenious bard so artfully describes? So was my princess employed when she blessed thee with her sight; but the envious malice of some base necromancer fascinated thy sight, as it represents whatever is most grateful to me in different and displeasing shapes. And this makes me fear, that if the history of my achievements, which they tell me is in print, has been written by some magician who is no well-wisher to my glory, he has undoubtedly delivered many things with partiality, misrepresented my life, inserting a hundred falsehoods for one truth, diverting himself with the relation of idle stories, foreign to the purpose, and unsuitable to the continuation of a true history. O envy! envy! thou gnawing worm of virtue, and spring of infinite mischiefs! there is no other vice, my Sancho, but pleads some pleasure in its excuse; but envy is always attended by disgust, rancour, and distracting rage.' 'I am much of your mind,' said Sancho, 'and I think, in the same book which neighbour Carrasco told us he had read of our lives, the story makes bold with my credit, and has handled it at a strange rate, and has dragged it about the kennels, as a body may say. Well, now as I am an honest man, I never spoke an ill word of a magician in my born days; and I think they need not envy my condition so much. The truth is, I am somewhat malicious; I have my roguish tricks now and then; but I was ever counted more fool than knave for all that, and so indeed I was bred and born; and if there was nothing else in me but my religion (for I firmly believe whatever our holy Roman Catholic Church believes, and I hate the Jews mortally), these same historians should take pity on me, and spare me a little in their books. But let them say on to the end of the chapter; naked I came into the world, and naked must go out. It is all a case to Sancho: I can neither gain nor lose by the bargain; if so my name be in print, and handed about, I care not a fig for the worst they can say of me.' 'What thou sayest, Sancho,' answered Don Quixote, 'reminds me of a story. A celebrated poet of our time wrote a very scurrilous and abusive lampoon upon all the intriguing ladies of the Court, forbearing to name one, as not being sure whether she deserved to be put into the catalogue or not; but the lady not finding herself there, was not a little affronted at the omission, and made a great complaint to the poet, asking him what he had seen in her, that he should leave her out of his list? desiring him at the same time to enlarge his satire, and put her in, or expect to hear further from her. The author obeyed her commands, and gave her a character with a vengeance, and, to her great satisfaction, made her as famous for infamy as any woman about the town. Such another story is that of Diana's Temple, one of the seven wonders of the world, burnt by an obscure fellow merely to eternise his name; which, in spite of an edict that enjoined all people never to mention it, either by word of mouth, or in writing, yet is still known to have been Erostratus. The story of the great emperor Charles the Fifth, and a Roman knight, upon a certain occasion, is much the same. The emperor had a great desire to see the famous temple once called the Pantheon, but now more happily the Church of All Saints. It is the only entire edifice remaining of heathen Rome, and that which best gives an idea of the glory and magnificence of its great founders. It is built in the shape of a half orange, of a vast extent and very lightsome, though it admits no light but at one window, or, to speak more properly, at a round aperture on the top of the roof. The emperor being got up thither, and looking down from the brink upon the fabric, with a Roman knight by him, who showed all the beauties of that vast edifice: after they were gone from the place, says the knight, addressing the emperor, "It came into my head a thousand times, sacred sir, to embrace your majesty, and cast myself with you, from the top of the church to the bottom, that I might thus purchase an immortal name." "I thank you," said the emperor, "for not doing it; and for the future, I will give you no opportunity to put your loyalty to such a test. Therefore I banish you my presence for ever;" which done, he bestowed some considerable favour on him. I tell thee, Sancho, this desire of honour is a strange bewitching thing. What dost thou think made Horatius, armed at all points, plunge headlong from the bridge into the rapid Tiber? What prompted Curtius to leap into the profound flaming gulf? What made Mutius burn his hand? What forced Cæsar over the Rubicon, in spite of all the omens that dissuaded his passage? And, to instance a more modern example, what made the undaunted Spaniards sink their ships when under the most courteous Cortez, but that scorning the stale honour of this so often conquered world, they sought a maiden glory in a new scene of victory? These, and a multiplicity of other great actions, are owing to the immediate thirst and desire of fame, which mortals expect as the proper price and immortal recompense of their great actions. But we that are Christian Catholic knights-errant, must fix our hopes upon a higher reward, placed in the eternal and celestial regions, where we may expect a permanent honour and complete happiness; not like the vanity of fame, which at best is but the shadow of great actions, and must necessarily vanish, when destructive time has eaten away the substance which it followed. So, my Sancho, since we expect a Christian reward, we must suit our actions to the rules of Christianity. In giants we must kill pride and arrogance: but our greatest foes, and whom we must chiefly combat, are within. Envy we must overcome by generosity and nobleness of soul; anger by a reposed and easy mind; riot and drowsiness by vigilance and temperance; lasciviousness by our inviolable fidelity to those who are mistresses of our thoughts; and sloth, by our indefatigable peregrinations through the universe, to seek occasions of military, as well as Christian honours. This, Sancho, is the road to lasting fame, and a good and honourable renown.' 'I understand passing well every tittle you have said,' answered Sancho; 'but pray now, sir, will you dissolve me of one doubt, that is just come into my head?' ' "Resolve" thou wouldst say, Sancho,' replied Don Quixote; 'well, speak, and I will endeavour to satisfy thee.' 'Why then,' quoth Sancho, 'pray tell me these same Julies, and these Augusts, and all the rest of the famous knights you talk of that are dead, where are they now?' 'Without doubt,' answered Don Quixote, 'the heathens are in hell. The Christians, if their lives were answerable to their profession, are either in purgatory or in heaven.' 'So far, so good,' said Sancho; 'but pray tell me the tombs of these lordlings, have they any silver lamps still burning before them, and are their chapel-walls hung about with crutches, winding-sheets, old periwigs, legs and wax eyes, or with what are they hung?' 'The monuments of the dead heathens,' said Don Quixote, 'were for the most part sumptuous pieces of architecture. The ashes of Julius Cæsar were deposited on the top of an obelisk, all of one stone of a prodigious bigness, which is now called Aguglia di San Pietro, St. Peter's Needle. The emperor Adrian's sepulchre was a vast structure, as big as an ordinary village, and called Moles Adriani, and now the castle of St. Angelo in Rome. Queen Artemisia buried her husband Mausolus in so curious and magnificent a pile, that his monument was reputed one of the seven wonders of the world. But none of these, nor any other of the heathen sepulchres, were adorned with any winding-sheets, or other offering, that might imply the persons interred were saints.' 'Thus far we are right,' quoth Sancho; 'now, sir, pray tell me, which is the greatest wonder, to raise a dead man, or kill a giant?' 'The answer is obvious,' said Don Quixote, 'to raise a dead man, certainly.' 'Then, master, I have nicked you,' saith Sancho, 'for he that raises the dead, makes the blind see, the lame walk, and the sick healthy, who has lamps burning night and day before his sepulchre, and whose chapel is full of pilgrims, who adore his relics on their knees; that man, I say, has more fame in this world and in the next, than any of your heathenish emperors or knights-errant ever had, or will ever have.' 'I grant it,' said Don Quixote. 'Very good,' quoth Sancho, 'I will be with you anon. This fame, these gifts, these rights, privileges, and what do ye call them, the bodies and relics of these saints have; so that, by the consent and good-liking of our holy mother the Church, they have their lamps, their lights, their winding-sheets, their crutches, their pictures, their heads of hair, their legs, their eyes, and the Lord knows what, by which they stir up people's devotion, and spread their Christian fame. Kings will vouchsafe to carry the bodies of saints, or their relics on their shoulders, they will kiss you the pieces of their bones, and spare no cost to set off and deck their shrines and chapels.' 'And what of all this?' said Don Quixote, 'what is your inference?' 'Why, truly, sir,' quoth Sancho, 'that we turn saints as fast as we can, and that is the readiest and cheapest way to get this same honour you talk of. It was but yesterday or the other day, or I cannot tell when; I am sure it was not long since, that two poor bare-footed friars were sainted; and you cannot think what a crowd of people there is to kiss the iron chains they wore about their waists, instead of girdles, to humble the flesh. I dare say, they are more reverenced than Orlando's sword, that hangs in the armoury of our sovereign lord the king, whom Heaven grant long to reign! So that for aught I see, better it is to be a friar, though but of a beggarly order, than a valiant errant-knight; and a dozen or two of sound lashes, well meant, and as well laid on, will obtain more of heaven than two thousand thrusts with a lance; though they be given to giants, dragons, or hobgoblins.' 'All this is very true,' replied Don Quixote, 'but all men cannot be friars; we have different paths allotted us, to mount to the high seat of eternal felicity. Chivalry is a religious order, and there are knights in the fraternity of saints in heaven.' 'However,' quoth Sancho, 'I have heard say there are more friars there than knights-errant.' 'That is,' said Don Quixote, 'because there is a greater number of friars than of knights.' 'But are there not a great many knights-errant, too?' said Sancho. 'There are many indeed,' answered Don Quixote, 'but very few that deserve the name.' In such discourses as these, the Knight and the squire passed the night and the whole succeeding day, without encountering any occasion to signalise themselves; at which Don Quixote was very much concerned. At last, towards evening the next day, they discovered the goodly city of Toboso, which revived the Knight's spirits wonderfully, but had a quite contrary effect on his squire, because he did not know the house where Dulcinea lived, no more than his master. So that the one was mad till he saw her, and the other very melancholic and disturbed in mind, because he had never seen her; nor did he know what to do, should his master send him to Toboso. However, as Don Quixote would not make his entry in the daytime, they spent the evening among some oaks not far distant from the place, till the prefixed moment came; then they entered the city, where they met with adventures indeed.

CHAPTER IX

Which gives an account of things which you will know when you read it

THE SABLE NIGHT had spun out half her course, when Don Quixote and Sancho descended from a hill, and entered Toboso. A profound silence reigned over all the town, and all the inhabitants were fast asleep, and stretched out at their ease. The night was somewhat clear, though Sancho wished it dark, to hide his master's folly and his own. Nothing disturbed the general tranquillity, but now and then the barking of dogs, that wounded Don Quixote's ears, but more poor Sancho's heart. Sometimes an ass brayed, hogs grunted, and cats mewed; which jarring mixture of sounds was not a little augmented by the stillness and serenity of the night, and filled the enamoured champion's head with a thousand inauspicious chimeras. However, turning to his squire: 'My dear Sancho,' said he, 'show me the way to Dulcinea's palace, perhaps we shall find her still awake.' 'Body of me,' cried Sancho, 'what palace do you mean? When I saw her Highness, she was in a little paltry cot.' 'Perhaps,' replied the Knight, 'she was then retired into some corner of the palace, to divert herself in private with her damsels, as great ladies and princesses sometimes do.' 'Well, sir,' said Sancho, 'since it must be a palace whither I will or no, yet can you think this is a time of night to find the gates open, or a seasonable hour to thunder at the door, till we raise the house and alarm the whole town? Are we going to a bawdy-house, think you, like your wenchers, that can rap at a door any hour of the night, and knock people up when they list?' 'Let us once find the palace,' said the Knight, 'and then I will tell thee what we ought to do: but stay, either my eyes delude me, or that lofty gloomy structure, which I discover yonder, is Dulcinea's palace.' 'Well, lead on, sir,' said the squire, 'and yet though I were to see it with my eyes, and feel it with my ten fingers, I shall believe it even as much as I believe it is now noonday.' The Knight led on, and having rode about two hundred paces, came at last to the building which he took for Dulcinea's palace; but found it to be the great church of the town. 'We are mistaken, Sancho,' said he, 'I find this is a church.' 'I see it is,' said the squire; 'and I pray the Lord we have not found our graves; for it is a plaguy ill sign to haunt churchyards at this time of night, especially when I told you, if I am not mistaken, that this lady's house stands in a little blind alley, without any thoroughfare!' 'A curse on thy distempered brain!' cried Don Quixote, 'where, blockhead, where didst thou ever see royal edifices and palaces built in a blind alley, without a thoroughfare?' 'Sir,' said Sancho, 'every country has its several fashions; and, for aught you know, they may build their great houses and palaces in blind alleys at Toboso: and therefore, good your worship, let me alone to hunt up and down in what by-lanes and alleys I may strike into; mayhap in some nook or corner we may light upon this same palace: would Old Nick had it for me, for leading us such a jaunt, and plaguing a body at this rate.' 'Sancho,' said Don Quixote, 'speak with greater respect of my mistress's concerns; be merry and wise, and do not throw the helve after the hatchet.' 'Cry mercy, sir,' quoth Sancho, 'but would it not make one mad, to have you put me upon finding readily our Dame's house at all times, which I never saw but once in my life? Nay, and to find it at midnight when you yourself cannot find it, that has seen it a thousand times!' 'Thou wilt make me desperately angry,' said the Knight: 'Hark you, heretic, have I not repeated it a thousand times, that I never saw the peerless Dulcinea, nor ever entered the portals of her palace; but that I am in love with her purely by hearsay, and upon the great fame of her beauty and rare accomplishments?' 'I hear you say so now,' quoth Sancho; 'and since you say you never saw her, I must needs tell you I never saw her neither.' 'That is impossible,' said Don Quixote; 'at least you told me you saw her winnowing wheat when you brought me an answer to the letter which I sent by you.' 'That is neither here nor there, sir,' replied Sancho; 'for, to be plain with you, I saw her but by hearsay too, and the answer I brought you was by hearsay as well as the rest, and I know the Lady Dulcinea no more than the man in the moon.' 'Sancho, Sancho,' said Don Quixote, 'there is a time for all things; unseasonable mirth always turns to sorrow: what, because I declare that I have never seen nor spoken to the mistress of my soul, is it for you to trifle and say so too, when you are so sensible of the contrary?'

Here their discourse was interrupted, a fellow with two mules happening to pass by them, and by the noise of the plough which they drew along they guessed it might be some country labourer going out before day to his husbandry; and so indeed it was. He went singing the doleful ditty of the defeat of the French at Roncesvalles*; 'Ye Frenchmen all must rue the woeful day.' 'Let me die,' said Don Quixote, hearing what the fellow sung, 'if we have any good success tonight; dost thou hear what this peasant sings, Sancho?' 'Ay, marry do I,' quoth the squire; 'but what is the rout at Roncesvalles to us? It concerns us no more than if he had sung the ballad, "Colly my Cow"; we shall speed neither the better nor the worse for it.' By this time the ploughman being come up to them: 'Good-morrow, honest friend,' cried Don Quixote to him: 'pray, can you inform me which is the palace of the peerless princess, the Lady Dulcinea del Toboso?' 'Sir,' said the fellow, 'I am a stranger, and but lately come into this town; I am ploughman to a rich farmer: but here, over against you, lives the curate and the sexton, they are the likeliest to give you some account of that Lady Princess, as having a list of all the folks in town, though I fancy there is no princess at all lives here; there be indeed a power of gentle-folk, and each of them may be a princess in her own house for aught I know.' 'Perhaps, friend,' said Don Quixote, 'we shall find the lady for whom I inquire among those.' 'Why truly, master,' answered the ploughman, 'as you say, such a thing may be, and so speed you well! It is break of day.' With that, switching his mules, he stopped for no more questions.

Sancho perceiving his master in suspense, and not very well satisfied: 'Sir,' said he, 'the day comes on apace, and I think it will not be handsome for us to stay, be stared at, and sit sunning ourselves in the street. We had better slip out of the town, and betake ourselves to some wood hard by, and then I will come back, and search every hole and corner in town for this same house, castle, or palace of my Lady's, and it will go hard if I do not find it out at long-run; then will I talk to her Highness, and tell her how you do, and how I left you hard by, waiting her orders and instructions about talking with her in private, without bringing her name in question.' 'Dear Sancho,' said the Knight, 'thou hast spoke and included a thousand sentences in the compass of a few words: I approve, and lovingly accept thy advice. Come, my child, let us go, and in some neighbouring grove find out a convenient retreat; then, as thou sayest, thou shalt return to seek, to see, and to deliver my embassy to my Lady, from whose discretion and most courteous mind I hope for a thousand favours, that may be counted more than wonderful.' Sancho sat upon

* 'The battle of Roncesvalles,' is a doleful melancholy song, like our 'Chevy-Chase,' which is the reason why it is looked upon as ominous by superstitious people.

thorns till he had got his master out of town, lest he should discover the falsehood of the account he brought him in Sierra Morena, of Dulcinea's answering his letter; so hastening to be gone, they were presently got two miles from the town into a wood, where Don Quixote took covert, and Sancho was dispatched to Dulcinea. In which negotiation some accidents fell out, that require new attention and a fresh belief.

CHAPTER X

How Sancho cunningly found out a way to enchant the Lady Dulcinea; with other passages no less certain than ridiculous

THE AUTHOR of this important history being come to the matters which he relates in this chapter, says he would willingly have left them buried in oblivion, in a manner despairing of his reader's belief: for Don Quixote's madness flies here to so extravagant a pitch, that it may he said to have out-stripped, by two bow-shots, all imaginable credulity. However, not-withstanding this mistrust, he has set down every particular, just as the same was transacted, without adding or diminishing the least atom of truth through the whole history; not valuing in the least such objections as may be raised to impeach him of breach of veracity. A proceeding which ought to be commended; for truth indeed rather alleviates than hurts, and will always bear up against falsehood, as oil does above water. And so continuing his narration, he tells us, that when Don Quixote was retired into the wood or forest, or rather into the grove of oaks near the grand Toboso, he ordered Sancho to go back to the city, and not to return to his presence till he had had audience of his lady; beseeching her that it might please her to be seen by her captive knight, and vouchsafe to bestow her benediction on him, that by the virtue of that blessing he might hope for a prosperous event in all his onsets and perilous attempts and adventures. Sancho undertook the charge, engaging him as successful a return of this as of his former message.

'Go then, child,' said the Knight, 'and have a care of being daunted when thou approachest the beams of that refulgent sun of beauty. Happy, thou, above all the squires of the universe! Observe and engrave in thy memory the manner of thy reception; mark whether her colour changes upon the delivery of thy commission; whether her looks betray any emotion or concern when she hears my name; whether she does not seem to sit on her cushion with a strange uneasiness, in case thou happenest to find her seated on the pompous throne of her authority. And if she be standing, mind whether she stands sometimes upon one leg, and sometimes on another; whether she repeats three or four times, the answer which she gives thee, or changes it from kind to cruel, and then again from cruel to kind; whether she does not seem to adjust her hair, though every lock appears in perfect order. In short, observe all her actions, every motion, every gesture; for by the accurate relation which thou givest of these things, I shall divine the secrets of her breast, and draw just inferences in relation to my amour. For I must tell thee, Sancho, if thou dost not know it already, that the outward motions of lovers are the surest indications of their inward affections; they are the most faithful intelligencers in an amorous negotiation. Go then, my trusty squire, thy own better stars, not mine, attend thee; and meet with a more prosperous event, than that which in this doleful desert, tossed between hopes and fears, I dare expect.' 'I will go, sir,' quoth Sancho, 'and I will be back in a trice: meanwhile cheer up, I beseech you; come, sir, comfort that little heart of yours, no bigger than a hazelnut! Do not be cast down, I say; remember the old saying, "Faint heart never won fair lady": where there is no hook, to be sure there will hang no bacon: the hare leaps out of the bush where we least look for her. I speak this, to give you to understand, that though we could not find my Lady's castle in the night, I may light on it when I least think on it now it is day; and when I have found it, let me alone to deal with her.' 'Well, Sancho,' said the Knight, 'thou hast a rare talent in applying thy proverbs; Heaven give thee better success in thy designs!' This said, Sancho turned his back, and switching his Dapple, left the Don on horseback, leaning on his lance, and resting on his stirrups, full of melancholy and confused imaginations. Let us leave him too, to go along with Sancho, who was no less uneasy in his mind.

No sooner was he got out of the grove, but turning about, and perceiving his master quite out of sight, he dismounted, and laying himself down at the foot of a tree, thus began to hold a parley with himself. 'Friend Sancho,' quoth he, 'pray let me ask you whither your worship is a-going? Is it to seek some ass you have lost? No, by my troth. What is it then thou art hunting after? Why I am looking, you must know, for a thing of nothing, only a princess, and in her the sun of beauty, forsooth, and all heaven together. Well, and where dost thou think to find all this, friend of mine? Where! why in the great city of Toboso. And pray, sir, who set you to work? Who set me to work? there is a question! why, who but the most renowned Don Quixote de la Mancha, he that rights the wronged, that gives drink to the hungry, and meat to those that are dry. Very good, sir, but pray, dost thou know where she lives? Not I, efackins! but my master says it is somewhere in a king's palace, or stately castle. And hast thou ever seen her trow? No, marry have not I: why, my master himself never set eyes on her in his life. But tell me, Sancho, what if the people of Toboso should know that you are come to inveigle their princesses, and make their ladies run astray, and should baste your carcase handsomely, and leave you never a sound rib, do you not think they would be mightily in the right of it? Why, troth, they would not be much in the wrong; though methinks they should consider too, that I am but a servant, and sent on another body's errand, and so I am not at all in fault. Nay, never trust to that, Sancho, for your people of La Mancha are plaguy hot and toucheous, and will endure no tricks to be put upon them: Body of me! if they but smoke thee, they will mawl thee after a strange rate. No, no, forewarned forearmed: why do I go about to look for more feet than a cat has, for another man's maggot? Besides, when all is done, I may perhaps as well look for a needle in a bottle of hay, or for a scholar at Salamanca, as for Dulcinea all over the town of Toboso. Well, it is the Devil, and nothing but the Devil, has put me upon this troublesome piece of work.' This was the dialogue Sancho had with himself; and the consequence of it was the following soliloquy. 'Well, there is a remedy for all things but death, which will be sure to lay us flat one time or other. This master of mine, by a thousand tokens I have seen, is a downright madman, and I think I come within an inch of him; nay, I am the greatest cod's-head of the two, to serve and follow him as I do, if the proverb be not a liar, "Show me thy company, I will tell thee what thou art"; and the other old saw, "Birds of a feather flock together." Now then my master being mad, and so very mad as to mistake sometimes one thing for another, black for white, and white for black; as when he took the windmills for giants, the friars' mules for dromedaries, and the flocks of sheep for armies, and much more to the same tune; I guess it will be no hard matter to pass upon him the first country wench I shall meet with, for the Lady Dulcinea. If he will not believe it, I will swear it; if he swear again, I will out-swear him; if he be positive, I will be more positive than he; and stand to it, and out-face him in it, come what will of it: so that when he finds I will not flinch, he will either resolve never to send me more of his sleeveless errands, seeing what a lame account I bring him, or he will think some one of those wicked wizards, who, he says, owes him a grudge, has transmogrified her into some other shape out of spite.' This happy contrivance helped to compose Sancho's mind, and now he looked on his grand affair to be as good as done. Having therefore stayed till the evening, that his master might think he had employed so much time in going and coming, things fell out very luckily for him; for as he arose to mount his Dapple, he spied three country wenches coming towards him from Toboso, upon three young asses; whether male or female the author has left undetermined, though we may reasonably suppose they were she-asses, such being most frequently used to ride on by country lasses in those parts. But this being no very material circumstance, we need not dwell any longer upon the decision of that point. It is sufficient they were asses, and discovered by Sancho; who thereupon made all the haste he could to get to his master, and found him breathing out a thousand sighs and amorous lamentations. 'Well, my Sancho,' said the Knight, immediately upon his approach, 'what news? Are we to mark this day with a white or a black stone?' 'Even mark it rather with red oker,' answered Sancho, 'as they do church chairs, that everybody may know who they belong to.' 'Why then,' said Don Quixote, 'I suppose thou bringest good news?' 'Ay, marry do I,' quoth Sancho, 'you have no more to do but to clap spurs to Rozinante, and get into the open fields, and you will see my Lady Dulcinea del Toboso, with a brace of her damsels, coming to see your worship.' 'Blessed heavens!' cried Don Quixote, 'what art thou saying, my dear Sancho? Take heed, and do not presume to beguile my real grief with a delusive joy.' 'Adsookers! sir,' said Sancho, 'what should I get by putting a trick upon you, and being found out the next moment? Seeing is believing all the world over. Come, sir, put on, put on, and you will see our Lady Princess coming, dressed up and bedecked like her own sweet self indeed. Her damsels and she are all one spark of gold; all pearls, all diamonds, all rubies, all cloth of gold above ten inches high. Their hair spread over their shoulders like so many sunbeams, and dangling and dancing in the wind; and what is more, they ride upon three flea-bitten gambling hags; there is not a piece of horse-flesh can match them in three kingdoms.' ' "Ambling nags" thou meanest, Sancho,' said Don Quixote. ' "Ambling hags" or "ambling nags," ' quoth Sancho, 'there is no such difference methinks; but be they what they will, I am sure, I never set eyes on finer creatures than those that ride upon their backs, especially my Lady Dulcinea; it would make one swoon away but to look upon her.' 'Let us move, then, my Sancho,' said Don Quixote: 'and as a gratification for these unexpected happy tidings, I freely bestow on thee the best spoils the next adventure we meet with shall afford; and if that content thee not, take the colts which my three mares thou knowest of, are now ready to foal on our town common.' 'Thank you for the colts,' said Sancho; 'but as for the spoils, I am not sure they will be worth anything.' They were now got out of the wood, and discovered the three country lasses at a small distance. Don Quixote casting his eyes towards Toboso, and seeing nobody on the road but the three wenches, was strangely troubled in mind, and turning to Sancho, asked him, whether the princess and her damsels were come out of the city when he left them. 'Out of the city,' cried Sancho, 'why, where are your eyes? are they in your heels, in the name of wonder, that you cannot see them coming towards us, shining as bright as the sun at noon-day?' 'I see nothing,' returned Don Quixote, 'but three wenches upon as many asses.' 'Now Heaven deliver me from the Devil,' quoth Sancho. 'Is it possible your worship should mistake three what-d'ye-call-ems, three ambling nags I mean, as white as driven snow, for three ragged ass colts? Body of me! I will even pull off my beard by the roots, if it be so.' 'Take it from me, friend Sancho,' said the Knight, 'they are either he or she asses, as sure as I am Don Quixote, and thou Sancho Pança; at least, they appear to be such.' 'Come, sir,' quoth the squire, 'do not talk at that rate, but snuff your eyes, and go pay your homage to the mistress of your soul; for she is near at hand'; and so saying, Sancho hastens up to the three country wenches, and alighting from Dapple, took hold of one of the asses by the halter, and falling on his knees, 'Queen, and princess, and duchess of beauty,' quoth he, 'if it please your Haughtiness, and Greatness, vouchsafe to take into your good grace and liking, yonder Knight, your prisoner and captive, who is turned of a sudden into cold marble stone, and struck all of a heap, to see himself before your High and Mightiness. I am Sancho Pança, his squire, and he himself the wandering weather-beaten knight, Don Quixote de la Mancha, otherwise called the Knight of the Woeful Figure.' By this time, Don Quixote, having placed himself down on his knees by Sancho, gazed with dubious and disconsolate eyes on the creature, whom Sancho called Queen and Lady; and perceiving her to be no more than a plain country wench, so far from being well-favoured, that she was blubber-cheeked, and flat-nosed, he was lost in astonishment, and could not utter one word. On the other side, the wenches were no less surprised, to see themselves stopped by two men in such different outsides, and on their knees. But at last she whose ass was held by Sancho took courage, and broke silence in an angry tone. 'Come,' cried she, 'get out of our way with a murrain, and let us go about our business; for we are in haste.' 'O Princess! and universal Lady of Toboso,' answered Sancho, 'why does not that great heart of yours melt, to see the post and pillar of knight-errantry fall down before your high and mighty presence?' 'Heyday,' quoth another of the females, hearing this, 'what is here to do? Look how your small gentry come to jeer and flout poor country girls, as if we could not give them as good as they bring. Go, get about your business, and let us go about ours, and speed you well.' 'Rise, Sancho,' said Don Quixote, hearing this, 'for I am now convinced, that my malicious stars, not yet satisfied with my past misfortunes, still shed their baleful influence, and have barred all the passages that could convey relief to my miserable soul, in this frail habitation of animated clay. O! thou extremity of all that is valuable, masterpiece of all human perfection, and only comfort of this afflicted heart, thy adorer; though now a spiteful enchanter persecutes me, and fascinates my sight, hiding with mists and cataracts from me, and me alone, those peerless beauties under the foul disguise of rustic deformity, if he has not transformed thy faithful Knight into some ugly shape to make me loathsome to thy sight, look on me with a smiling amorous eye; and in the submission and genuflexion which I pay to thy beauty, even under the fatal cloud that obscures it, read the humility with which my soul adores thee.' 'Tittle-tattle,' quoth the country wench, 'spare your breath to cool your porridge, and rid me of your idle gibberish. Get you on, sir, and let us go; and we shall think it a kindness.' This said, Sancho made way for her, and let her pass, overjoyed his plot had succeeded so well. The imaginary Dulcinea was not sooner at liberty, but punching her ass with the end of a staff which she had in her hand, she began to scour along the plain: but the angry beast not being used to such smart instigations, fell a-kicking and wincing at such a rate, that down came my Lady Dulcinea. Presently Don Quixote ran to help her up, and Sancho to resettle and gird her pack-saddle, that hung under the ass's belly. Which being done, the Knight very courteously was going to take his enchanted mistress in his arms, to set her on her saddle; but she being now got on her legs, took a run, and clapping her hands upon the ass's crupper, at one jump leaped into her pannel, as swift as a hawk, and there she sat with her legs astride like a man. 'By the lord Harry!' quoth Sancho, 'our lady mistress is as nimble as an eel. Let me be hanged, if I do not think she might teach the best jockey in Cordova or Mexico to mount a horse-back. At one jump she was vaulted into the saddle, and, without spurs, makes her nag smoke it away like a greyhound; her damsels are notable whipsters too; adad! they do not come much short of her, for they fly like the wind.' Indeed, he said true, for when Dulcinea was once mounted, they both made after her full speed, without so much as looking behind them for above half a league. Don Quixote followed them as far as he could with his eyes; and when they were quite out of sight, turning to his squire, 'Now, Sancho,' saith he, 'what thinkest thou of this matter? Are not these base enchanters inexorable? How extensive is their spite, thus to deprive me of the happiness of seeing the object of my wishes in her natural shape and glory? Sure I was doomed to be an example of misfortunes, and the mark against which those caitiffs are employed to shoot all the arrows of their hatred. Note, Sancho, that these traitors were not content to turn and transform my Dulcinea, but they must do it into the vile and deformed resemblance of that country wench; nay, they even took from her that sweet scent of flagrant flowers and amber, those grateful odours, so essential to ladies of her rank; for, to tell the truth, when I went to help her upon her nag, as thou callest it (for to me it seemed nothing but an ass), such a whiff, such a rank hogo of raw garlic invaded my nostrils, as had like to have overcome me, and put me into a convulsion.' 'O ye vile wretches!' cried Sancho. 'O ye wicked and ill-minded enchanters! O that I might but once see the whole nest of ye threaded together on one string, and hung up a-smoking by the gills like so many pilchards! You know a deal, you can do a deal, and you make a deal of mischief. One would have thought you might have been contented, like a pack of rogues as you are, with having changed the pearls of my Lady's eyes into gall nuts, and her most pure golden locks into a red cow's tail; but you must be meddling with her breath, by which we might have guessed what lay hid under that coarse disguise; though for my part I must needs own, she did not appear to be deformed at all, but rather fair and beautiful; by the same token that she had a mole on the side of the upper lip, like a whisker, whence sprouted seven or eight red hairs, each about a span in length, looking like so many threads of gold wire.' 'As the moles on the body,' said Don Quixote, 'are generally answerable to those on the face, Dulcinea should have such another mole on the brawn of her thigh, opposite to that side of her face where that beauty-spot is seated: but methinks, Sancho, the hairs thou talkest of, are of a length somewhat extraordinary for moles.' 'That is neither here nor there,' quoth Sancho; 'there they were, I will assure you, and they looked too as if she had brought them with her into the world.' 'That I believe,' said Don Quixote, 'for every part of Dulcinea must be naturally perfect and complete; so that though a hundred moles were scattered over her fair outside, and as conspicuous too as that which thou didst see, they would be no deformities in her; but so many moons and stars, an additional lustre to her beauty. But tell me, Sancho, that saddle which appeared to me to be the pannel of an ass, was it a pillion or side-saddle?' 'It was a pad-saddle,' answered Sancho, 'with a field-covering, and so rich that it might purchase half a kingdom.' 'And could not I see all this?' cried Don Quixote. 'Well, I have said it, and must repeat it a thousand times, I am the most unfortunate man in the universe.' The cunning rogue of a squire, hearing his master talk at that rate, could hardly keep his countenance, and refrain from laughing to see how admirably he had fooled him. At last, after a great deal of discourse of the same nature, they both mounted again, and took the road for Saragossa, designing to be present at the most celebrated festivals and sports that are solemnised every year in that noble city. But they met with many accidents by the way, and those so extraordinary, and worthy the reader's information, that they must not be passed over unrecorded nor unread; as shall appear from what follows.

CHAPTER XI

*Of the stupendous Adventure that befell the valorous
Don Quixote, with the Chariot or Cart of the Court
or Parliament of Death*

DON QUIXOTE RODE on very melancholic; the malice of the magicians,
in transforming his Lady Dulcinea, perplexed him strangely, and set his
thoughts upon the rack, how to dissolve the enchantment, and restore
her to her former beauty. In this disconsolate condition, he went on
abandoned to distraction, carelessly giving Rozinante the reins: and the
horse finding himself at liberty, and tempted by the goodness of the
grass, took the opportunity to feed very heartily. Which Sancho perceiving, 'Sir,' said he, rousing him from his waking dream, 'sorrow was never
designed for beasts, but men; but yet let me tell you, if men give way to it
too much, they make beasts of themselves. Come, sir, awake, awake, by
any means, pull up the reins, and ride like a man; cheer up, and show
yourself a knight-errant. What the devil ails you? Was ever a man so
moped? Are we here, or are we in France, as the saying is? Let all the
Dulcineas in the world be doomed to the pit of hell, rather than one
single knight-errant be cast down at this rate.' 'Hold, Sancho,' cried Don
Quixote, with more spirit than one would have expected; 'hold, I say; not
a blasphemous word against that beauteous enchanted Lady; for all her
misfortunes are chargeable on the unhappy Don Quixote, and flow from
the envy which those necromancers bear to me.' 'So say I, sir,' replied
the squire; 'for would it not vex any one that had seen her before, to see
her now as you saw her?' 'Ah, Sancho,' said the Knight, 'thy eyes were
blessed with a view of her perfections in their entire lustre, thou hast
reason to say so. Against me, against my eyes only is the malice of her
transformation directed. But now I think on it, Sancho, thy description
of her beauty was a little absurd in that particular, of comparing her eyes
to pearls; sure such eyes are more like those of a whiting, or a sea bream,
than those of a fair lady; and in my opinion Dulcinea's eyes are rather
like two verdant emeralds railed in with two celestial arches, which
signify her eye-brows. Therefore, Sancho, you must take your pearls
from her eyes, and apply them to her teeth, for I verily believe you
mistook the one for the other.' 'Troth, sir, it might be so,' replied
Sancho, 'for her beauty confounded me, as much as her ugliness did you.
But let us leave all to Heaven, that knows all things that befall us in this
vale of misery, this wicked, troublesome world, where we can be sure of
nothing without some spice of knavery or imposture. In the mean time,

there is a thing comes into my head that puzzles me plaguily. Pray, sir, when you get the better of any giant or knight, and send them to pay homage to the beauty of your Lady and Mistress, how the devil will the poor knight or giant be able to find this same Dulcinea? I cannot but think how they will be to seek, how they will saunter about, gaping and staring all over Toboso town, and if they should meet her full butt in the middle of the king's highway, yet they will know her no more than they knew the father that begot me.' 'Perhaps, Sancho,' answered Don Quixote, 'the force of her enchantment does not extend so far as to debar vanquished knights and giants from the privilege of seeing her in her unclouded beauties; I will try the experiment on the first I conquer, and will command them to return immediately to me, to inform me of their success.' 'I like what you say main well,' quoth Sancho; 'we may chance to find out the truth by this means: and if so be, my Lady is only hid from your worship, she has not so much reason to complain as you may have; but when all comes to all, so our mistress be safe and sound, let us make the best of a bad market, and e'en go seek adventures. The rest we will leave to time, which is the best doctor in such cases, nay, in worse diseases.' Don Quixote was going to return an answer, but was interrupted by a cart that was crossing the road. He that drove it was a hideous devil, and the cart being open, without either tilt or boughs, exposed a parcel of the most surprising and different shapes imaginable. The first figure that appeared to Don Quixote, was no less than Death itself, though with a human countenance; on the one side of Death stood an angel with large wings of different colours; on the other side was placed an emperor with a crown that seemed to be of gold; at the feet of Death lay Cupid with his bow, quiver, and arrows, but not blindfold. Next to these a knight appeared completely armed except his head, on which, instead of a helmet, he wore a hat; whereon was mounted a large plume of parti-coloured feathers. There were also several other persons in strange and various dresses.

This strange appearance at first somewhat surprised Don Quixote, and frightened the poor squire out of his wits; but presently the Knight cleared up on second thoughts, imagining it some rare and hazardous adventure that called on his courage. Pleased with this conceit, and armed with a resolution able to confront any danger, he placed himself in the middle of the road, and with a loud and menacing voice, 'You carter, coachman, or devil,' cried he, 'or whatever you be, let me know immediately whence you come, and whither you go, and what strange figures are those who load that carriage, which by the freight rather seems to be Charon's boat, than any terrestrial vehicle.' 'Sir,' answered the devil very civilly, stopping his cart, 'we are strolling players, that belong to Angulo's company, and it being Corpus Christi-tide, we have this morning acted a tragedy, called "The Parliament of Death," in a town yonder behind the mountain, and this afternoon we are to play it again in the town you see before us, which being so near, we travel to it in the same clothes we act in, to save the trouble of new dressing ourselves. That young man plays Death; that other an angel: this woman, sir, our poet's bed-fellow, plays the queen; there is one acts a soldier; he next to him an emperor; and I myself play the devil; and you must know the devil is the best part of the play. If you desire to be satisfied in anything else, do but ask and I will resolve you, for the devil knows everything.' 'Now by the faith of my function,' said Don Quixote, 'I find we ought not to give credit to appearances, before we have made the experiment of feeling them; for at the discovery of such a scene, I would have sworn some great adventure had been approaching. I wish you well, good people; drive on to act your play, and if I can be serviceable to you in any particular, believe me to be ready to assist you with all my heart; for in my very childhood I loved shows, and have been a great admirer of dramatic representations, from my youthful days.' During this conversation, it unluckily fell out, that one of the company anticly dressed, being the fool of the play, came up striking with his morrice bells, and three full-blown cows' bladders fastened to the end of a stick. In this odd appearance he began to flourish his stick in the air, and bounce his bladders against the ground just at Rozinante's nose. The jingling of the bells, and the rattling noise of the bladders so startled and affrighted the quiet creature, that Don Quixote could not hold him in; and having got the curb betwixt his teeth, away the horse hurried his unwilling rider up and down the plain, with more swiftness than his feeble bones seemed to promise. Sancho considering the danger of his master's being thrown, presently alighted, and ran as fast as he could to his assistance; but before he could come up to him, Rozinante had made a false step, and laid his master and himself on the ground; which was indeed the common end of Rozinante's mad tricks and presumptuous racing. On the other side, the fool no sooner saw Sancho slide off to help his master, but he leapt upon poor Dapple, and rattling his bladders over the terrified animal's head, made him fly through the field towards town where they were to play. Sancho beheld his master's fall, and his ass's flight at the same time, and stood strangely divided in himself, not knowing which to assist first, his master or his beast. At length the duty of a good servant and a faithful squire prevailing, he ran to his master, though every obstreperous bounce with his bladders upon Dapple's hindquarters, struck him to the very soul, and he could have wished every blow upon his own eyeballs, rather than on the least hair of his ass's tail. In this agony of spirits, he came to Don Quixote, whom he found in far worse circumstances than the poor Knight could have wished; and helping him to remount: 'O! sir,' cried he, 'the devil is run away with

Dapple.' 'What devil?' asked Don Quixote. 'The devil with the bladders,' answered Sancho. 'No matter,' said Don Quixote, 'I will force the traitor to restore him, though he were to lock him up in the most profound and gloomy caverns of hell. Follow me, Sancho; we may easily overtake the wagon, and the mules shall atone for the loss of the ass.' 'You need not be in such haste now,' quoth Sancho; 'for I perceive the devil has left Dapple already, and is gone his ways.' What Sancho said was true, for both ass and devil tumbled for company, in imitation of Don Quixote and Rozinante; and Dapple having left his new rider to walk on foot to the town, now came himself running back to his master. 'All this,' said Don Quixote, 'shall not hinder me from revenging the affront put upon us by that unmannerly devil, at the expense of some of his companions, though it were the emperor himself.' 'O good your worship!' cried Sancho, 'never mind it; I beseech you take my counsel, sir; never meddle with players, there is never anything to be got by it; they are a sort of people that always find many friends. I have known one of them taken up for two murders, yet escape the gallows. You must know, that as they are a parcel of merry wags, and make sport wherever they come, everybody is fond of them, and is ready to stand their friend, especially if they be the king's players, or some of the noted gangs, who go at such a tearing rate, that one night mistake some of them for gentlemen or lords.' 'I care not,' said Don Quixote 'though all mankind unite to assist them, that buffooning devil shall never escape unpunished, to make his boast that he has affronted me.' Whereupon riding up to the wagon, which was now got pretty near the town: 'Hold, hold!' he cried; 'stay, my pretty sparks, I will teach you to be civil to the beasts that are entrusted with the honourable burden of a squire to a knight-errant.' This loud salutation having reached the ears of the strolling company, though at a good distance; and resolving to be ready to entertain him, Death presently leaped out of the cart; the emperor, the devil-driver, and the angel immediately followed; and even the queen, and the god Cupid, as well as the rest, having taken up their shares of flints, stood ranked in battle array ready to receive their enemy, as soon as he should come within stone-shot. Don Quixote seeing them drawn up in such an excellent order, with their arms lifted up, and ready to let fly at him a furious volley of shot, made a halt to consider in what quarter he might attack this dreadful battalion with least danger to his person. Thus pausing, Sancho overtook him, and seeing him ready to charge, 'For goodness' sake,' cried he, 'what do ye mean? Are you mad, sir? There is no fence against the beggars' bullets, unless you could fight with a brazen bell over you. Is it not rather rashness than true courage, think you, for one man to offer to set upon a whole army? where Death is too, and where emperors fight in person, nay, and where good and bad angels are against you? But if all this weighs nothing with you, consider, I beseech you, that though they seem to be kings, princes, and emperors, yet there is not so much as one knight-errant among them all.' 'Now thou hast hit upon the only point,' said Don Quixote, 'that could stop the fury of my arm: for indeed, as I have often told thee, Sancho, I am bound up from drawing my sword against any below the order of knighthood. It is thy business to fight in this cause, if thou hast a just resentment of the indignities offered to thy ass; and I from this post will encourage and assist thee with salutary orders and instructions.' 'No, I thank you, sir,' quoth Sancho, 'I hate revenge; a true Christian must forgive and forget: and as for Dapple, I do not doubt but to find him willing to leave the matter to me, and stand to my verdict in the case, which is to live peaceably and quietly as long as Heaven is pleased to let me.' 'Nay then,' said Don Quixote, 'if that be thy resolution, good Sancho, prudent Sancho, Christian Sancho, downright Sancho, let us leave these idle apparitions, and proceed in search of more substantial and honourable adventures, of which, in all probability, this part of the world will afford us a wonderful variety.' So saying, he wheeled off, and Sancho followed him. On the other side, Death with all his flying squadron returned to their cart, and went on their journey. Thus ended the most dreadful adventure of the chariot of death, much more happily than could have been expected, thanks to the laudable counsels which Sancho Pança gave his master; who the day following had another adventure no less remarkable, with one that was a knight-errant and a lover too.

CHAPTER XII

The valorous Don Quixote's strange Adventure with the Knight of the Mirrors

Don Quixote passed the night, that succeeded his encounter with Death, under the cover of some lofty trees; where, at Sancho's persuasion, he refreshed himself with some of the provisions which Dapple carried. As they were at supper, 'Well, sir,' quoth the squire, 'what a rare fool I had been, had I chosen for my good news the spoils of your first adventure, instead of the breed of the three mares! Troth, commend me to the saying, "A bird in hand is worth two in the bush." ' 'However,' answered Don Quixote, 'hadst thou let me fall on, as I would have done, thou mightest have shared, at least, the emperor's golden crown, and Cupid's painted wings; for I would have plucked them off, and put them into thy power.' 'Ah, but,' says Sancho, 'your strolling emperor's crowns and sceptres are not of pure gold, but tinsel and copper.' 'I grant it,' said Don

Quixote; 'nor is it fit the decorations of the stage should be real, but rather imitations, and the resemblance of realities, as the plays themselves must be; which, by the way, I would have you love and esteem, Sancho, and consequently those that write, and also those that act them; for they are all instrumental to the good of the commonwealth, and set before our eyes those looking-glasses that reflect a lively representation of human life; nothing being able to give us a more just idea of nature, and what we are or ought to be, than comedians and comedies. Prithee tell me, hast thou never seen a play acted, where kings, emperors, prelates, knights, ladies, and other characters, are introduced on the stage? One acts a ruffian, another a soldier; this man a cheat, and that a merchant; one plays a designing fool, and another a foolish lover: but the play done, and the actors undressed, they are all equal, and as they were before.' 'All this I have seen,' quoth Sancho. 'Just such a comedy,' said Don Quixote, 'is acted on the great stage of the world, where some play the emperors, others the prelates, and, in short, all the parts can be brought into a dramatic piece; till death, which is the catastrophe, and end of the action, strips the actors of all their marks of distinction, and levels their quality in the grave.' 'A rare comparison,' quoth Sancho, 'though not so new, but that I have heard it over and over. Just such another is that game at chess, where, while the play lasts, every piece has its particular office; but when the game's over, they are all mingled and huddled together, and clapped into a bag, just as when life is ended, we are laid up in the grave.' 'Truly, Sancho,' said Don Quixote, 'thy simplicity lessens, and thy sense improves every day.' 'And good reason why,' quoth Sancho; 'some of your worship's wit must needs stick to me; for your dry unkindly land, with good dunging and tilling, will in time yield a good crop. I mean, sir, that the dung and muck of your conversation being thrown on the barren ground of my wit, together with the time I have served your worship, and kept you company – which is, as a body may say, the tillage – I must needs bring forth blessed fruit at last, so as not to shame my master, but keep in the paths of good manners, which you have beaten into my sodden understanding.' Sancho's affected style made Don Quixote laugh, though he thought his words true in the main; and he could not but admire at his improvement. But the fellow never discovered his weakness so much as by endeavouring to hide it, being most apt to tumble when he strove to soar too high. His excellence lay chiefly in a knack at drawing proverbs into his discourse, whether to the purpose or not, as any one that has observed his manner of speaking in this history must have perceived.

In such discourses they passed a great part of the night, till Sancho wanted to drop the portcullises of his eyes, which was his way of saying he had a mind to go to sleep. Thereupon he unharnessed Dapple, and set him a-grazing: but poor Rozinante was condemned to stand saddled all night, by his master's injunction and prescription, used of old by all knights-errant, who never unsaddled their steeds in the field, but took off their bridles, and hung them at the pommel of the saddle. However, he was not forsaken by faithful Dapple, whose friendship was unparalleled and inviolable, that unquestioned tradition has handed it down from father to son, that the author of this true history composed particular chapters of the united affection of these two beasts; though, to preserve the decorum due to so heroic a history, he would not insert them in the work. Yet sometimes he cannot forbear giving us some new touches on that subject; as when he writes, that the two friendly creatures took a mighty pleasure in being together to scrub and lick one another; and when they had had enough of that sport, Rozinante would gently lean his head at least half a yard over Dapple's neck, and so they would stand very lovingly together, looking wistfully on the ground for two or three days; except somebody made them leave that contemplative posture, or hunger compelled them to a separation. Nay, I cannot pass by what is reported of the author, how he left in writing, that he had compared their friendship to that of Nysus and Eurialus, and that of Pylades and Orestes, which if it were so, deserves universal admiration; the sincere affection of these quiet animals being a just reflection on men, who are so guilty of breaking their friendship to one another. From hence came the saying, 'There is no friend: all friendship is gone: now men hug, then fight anon.' And that other, 'Where you see your friend, trust to yourself.' Neither should the world take it ill, that the cordial affection of these animals was compared by our author to that of men; since many important principles of prudence and morality have been learned from irrational creatures; as, the use of clysters from the stork, and the benefit of vomiting from the dog. The crane gave man an example of vigilance, the ant of Providence, the elephant of honesty, and the horse of loyalty. At last Sancho fell asleep at the root of a cork-tree, and his master fetched a slumber under a spacious oak. It was not long ere he was disturbed by a noise behind him, and starting up, he looked and hearkened on the side whence he thought the voice came, and discovered two men on horseback; one of whom letting himself carelessly slide down from the saddle, and calling to the other, 'Alight, friend,' said he, 'and unbridle the horse; for methinks this place will supply them plentifully with pasture, and me with silence and solitude to indulge my amorous thoughts.' While he said this, he laid himself down on the grass; in doing which, the armour he had on made a noise, a sure sign, that gave Don Quixote to understand he was some knight-errant. Thereupon going to Sancho, who slept on, he plucked him by the arm; and having awakened him with much ado, 'Friend Sancho,' said he, whispering in his ear, 'here is an adventure.' 'Heaven grant it be a good one!' quoth Sancho. 'But where is that same lady adventure's worship?'

'Where! dost thou ask, Sancho? why, turn thy head, man, and look yonder. Dost thou not see a knight-errant there lying on the ground? I have reason to think he is in melancholy circumstances, for I saw him fling himself from off his horse, and stretch himself on the ground in a disconsolate manner, and his armour clashed as he fell.' ' What of all that?' quoth Sancho. ' How do you make this to be an adventure?' 'I will not yet affirm,' answered Don Quixote, ' that it is an adventure; but a very fair rise to one as ever was seen. But hark! he is tuning some instrument, and, by his coughing and spitting, he is clearing his throat to sing.' 'Troth now, sir,' quoth Sancho, 'it is even so in good earnest; and I fancy it is some knight that is in love.' ' All knights-errant must be so,' answered Don Quixote; ' but let us hearken, and if he sings, we will know more of his circumstances presently, for out of the abundance of the heart the mouth speaketh.' Sancho would have answered; but the Knight of the Wood's voice, which was but indifferent, interrupted him with the following

SONG

I

'Bright queen, how shall your loving slave
Be sure not to displease?
Some rule of duty let him crave;
He begs no other ease.

II

'Say, must I die, or hopeless live
I'll act as you ordain:
Despair a silent death shall give,
Or Love himself complain.

III

'My heart, tho' soft as wax, will prove
Like diamonds firm and true:
For, what th' impression can remove
That's stamp'd by love and you?'

The Knight of the Wood concluded his song with a sigh, that seemed to be fetched from the very bottom of his heart; and after some pause, with a mournful and disconsolate voice: 'O the most beautiful, but most ungrateful of womankind,' cried he, ' how is it possible, most serene Casildea de Vandalia, your heart showed consent that a knight, who idolises your charms, should waste the flower of his youth, and kill himself with continual wanderings and hard fatigues? Is it not enough, that I have made you to be acknowledged the greatest beauty in the world, by all the knights of Navarre, all the knights of Leon, all the Tartesians, all the Castilians, and, in fine, by all the knights of La Mancha?' 'Not so neither,' said Don Quixote then; 'for I myself am of La Mancha, and never acknowledged, nor ever could, nor ought to acknowledge a thing so injurious to the beauty of my mistress; therefore, Sancho, it is a plain case, this knight is out of his senses. But let us hearken, perhaps we shall discover something more.' 'That you will, I will warrant you,' quoth Sancho, 'for he seems in tune to hoan a month together.' But it happened otherwise; for the Knight of the Wood, overhearing them, ceased his lamentation, and raising himself on his feet, in a loud but courteous tone called to them, 'Who is there? What are ye? Are ye of the number of the happy or miserable?' 'Of the miserable,' answered Don Quixote. 'Repair to me then,' said the Knight of the Wood, 'and be assured you have met misery and affliction itself.' Upon so moving and civil an invitation, Don Quixote and Sancho drew near to him; and the mournful knight, taking Don Quixote by the hand, 'Sit down,' said he, 'Sir Knight; for that your profession is chivalry, I need no other conviction than to have found you in this retirement, where solitude and the cold night-dews are your companions, and the proper stations and reposing places of knights-errant.' 'I am a knight,' answered Don Quixote, 'and of the order you mention; and though my sorrows, disasters, and misfortunes usurp the seat of my mind, I have still a heart disposed to entertain the affliction of others. Yours, as I gather by your complaints, is derived from love and, I suppose, owing to the ingratitude of that beauty you now mentioned.' While they were thus parleying together, they sat close by one another on the hard ground, very peaceably and lovingly, and not like men that by break of day were to break one another's heads. 'And is it your fortune to be in love?' asked the Knight of the Wood. 'It is my misfortune,' answered Don Quixote; 'though the pleasant reflection of having placed our affections worthily, sufficiently balances the weight of our disasters, and turns them to a blessing.' 'This might be true,' replied the Knight of the Wood, 'if the disdain of some of the mistresses were not often so galling to our tempers, as to inspire us with something like the spirit of revenge.' 'For my part,' said Don Quixote, 'I never felt my mistress's disdain.' 'No truly,' quoth Sancho, who was near them; 'for my lady is as gentle as a lamb, and as soft as butter.' 'Is that your squire?' said the Knight of the Wood. 'It is,' answered Don Quixote. 'I never saw a squire,' said the Knight of the Wood, 'that durst presume to interrupt his master, when he is speaking himself. There is my fellow yonder; he is as big as his father, and yet no man can say he was ever so saucy as to open his lips when I spoke.' 'Well, well,' quoth Sancho, 'I have talked, and may talk again, and before as, and perhaps – but I have done; the more ye stir, the more it will stink.' At the same time the Squire of the Wood, pulling Sancho by the arm, 'Come, brother,' said he, 'let us two go where we may chat freely by ourselves, like downright squires as we are, and let our masters get over head and ears in the stories of their loves: I will warrant ye they will be at it all night, and will not have done by that time it is day.' 'With all my heart,' quoth Sancho; 'and then I will tell you who I am, and what I am, and you shall judge if I am not fit to make one among the talking squires.' With that the two squires withdrew, and had a dialogue, as comical as that of their masters was serious.

CHAPTER XIII

The Adventure with the Knight of the Wood continued; with the wise and pleasant Discourse that passed between the two Squires

THE KNIGHTS AND THEIR SQUIRES thus divided, the latter to tell their lives, and the former to relate their amours; the story begins with the Squire of the Wood. 'Sir,' said he to Sancho, 'this is a troublesome kind of life, that we squires of knights-errant lead: well may we say, we eat our bread with the sweat of our brows; which is one of the curses laid on our first parents.' 'Well may we say too,' quoth Sancho, 'we eat it with a cold shivering of our bodies; for there are no poor creatures that suffer more by heat or cold than we do. Nay, if we could but eat at all, it would never vex one; for good fare lessens care; but sometimes we shall go ye a day or two, and never so much as breakfast, unless it be upon the wind that blows.' 'After all,' said the Squire of the Wood, 'we may bear with this, when we think of the reward we are to expect; for that same knight-errant must be excessively unfortunate, that has not some time or other the government of some island, or some good handsome earldom, to bestow on his squire.' 'As for me,' quoth Sancho, 'I have often told my master, I would be contented with the government of any island; and he is so noble and free-hearted, that he has promised it me over and over.' 'For my part,' quoth the other squire, 'I should think myself well paid for my services with some good canonry, and I have my master's word for it too.' 'Why then,' quoth Sancho, 'belike your master is some church-knight, and may bestow such livings on his good squires. But mine is purely laic; some of his wise friends indeed (no thanks to them for it), once counselled him to be an archbishop: I fancy they wished him no good, but he would not, for he will be nothing but an emperor. I was plaguily afraid he might have a hankering after the Church, and so have spoiled my preferment, I not being gifted that way; for between you and I, though I look like a man in a doublet, I should make but an ass in a cassock.' 'Let me tell you, friend,' quoth the Squire of the Wood, 'that you are out in your politics; for these island-governments bring more cost than worship; there is a great cry, but little wool; the best will bring more trouble and care than they are worth, and those that take them on their shoulders are ready to sink under them. I think it were better for us to quit this confounded slavery, and even jog home, where we may entertain ourselves with more delightful exercises, such as fishing, and hunting, and the like; for he is a sorry country squire indeed, that wants his horse, his couple of hounds, or his fishing-tackle to live pleasantly at home.' 'All this I can have at will,' quoth Sancho; 'indeed, I have never a nag; but I have an honest ass here, worth two of my master's horses any day in the year. A bad Christmas be my lot, and may it be the next, if I would swop beasts with him, though he gave me four bushels of barley to boot, no marry would not I: laugh as much as you will at the value I set on my Dapple; for Dapple, you must know, is his colour. Now, as for hounds, we have enough to spare in our town; and there is no sport like hunting at another man's cost.' 'Faith and troth! brother squire,' quoth the Squire of the Wood, 'I am fully set upon it. These vagrant knights may even seek their mad adventures by themselves for me, I will home, and breed up my children as it behoves me; for I have three, as precious as three orient pearls.' 'I have but two,' quoth Sancho; 'but they might be presented to the Pope himself, especially my girl, that I breed up to be a countess (Heaven bless her!), in spite of her mother's teeth.' 'And how old, pray,' said the Squire of the Wood, 'may this same young lady countess be?' 'Why, she is about fifteen,' answered Sancho, 'a little over or a little under; but she is as tall as a pike, as fresh as an April morning, and strong as a porter.' 'With those parts,' quoth the other, 'she may set up not only for a countess, but for one of the wood-nymphs! Ah, the young buxom whore's brood! what a spring the mettlesome queen will have with her!' 'My daughter is no whore,' quoth Sancho, in a grumbling tone, 'and her mother was an honest woman before her: and they shall be honest, by Heaven's blessing, while I live and do well: so, sir, pray keep your tongue between your teeth, or speak as you ought. Methinks your master should have taught you better manners; for knights-errant are the very pink of courtesy.' 'Alas,' quoth the Squire of the Wood, 'how you are mistaken! how little you know the way of praising people nowadays! Have you never observed when any gentleman at a bull-feast gives the bull a home thrust with his lance, or when anybody behaves himself cleverly upon any occasion, the people will cry out, "What a brisk son of a whore that is! – a clever dog, I will warrant him." So what seems to be slander in that sense is notable commendation: and be advised by me, do not think those children worth the owning, who will not do that which may make their parents be commended in that fashion.' 'Nay, if it be so,' quoth Sancho, 'I will disown them if they do not, and henceforth you may call my wife and daughter all the whores and bawds you can think on, and welcome; for they do a thousand things that deserves all these fine names. Heaven send me once more to see them, and deliver me out of this mortal sin of squire-erranting, which I have been drawn into a second time, by the wicked bait of a hundred ducats, which the Devil threw in my own way in Sierra Morena, and which he still haunts me with, and brings before my eyes here and there and everywhere. Oh that plaguy purse, it is still running in my head; methinks I am counting such another over and over! Now I hug it, now I carry it home, now I am buying land with it; now I let leases, now I am receiving my rents, and live like a prince.

'Thus I pass away the time, and this lulls me on to drudge on to the end of the chapter, with this dunder-headed master of mine, who to my knowledge is more a madman than a knight.' 'Truly,' said the Squire of the Wood, 'this makes the proverb true covetousness breaks the sack. And now you talk of madmen, I think my master is worse than yours; for he is one of those, of whom the proverb says, "Fools will be meddling; and, who meddles with another man's business, milks his cows into a sieve." In searching after another knight's wits, he loses his own; and hunts up and down for that which may make him rue the finding.' 'And is not the poor man in love?' quoth Sancho. 'Ay marry,' said the other, 'and with one Casildea de Vandalia, one of the oddest pieces in the world; she will neither roast nor boil, and is neither fish, flesh, nor good red-herring. But that is not the thing that plagues his noddle now. He has some other crotchets in his crown, and you will hear more of it ere long.' 'There is no way so smooth,' quoth Sancho, 'but it has a hole or rub in it to make a body stumble. In some houses they boil beans, and in mine are whole kettles full. So madness has more need of good attendants than wisdom. But if this old saying be true, that it lightens sorrow to have companions in our grief, you are the fittest to comfort me; you serve one fool and I another.' 'My master,' quoth the Squire of the Wood, 'is more stout than foolish, but more knave than either.' 'Mine is not like yours then,' quoth Sancho, 'he has not one grain of knavery in him; he is as dull as an old cracked pitcher, hurts nobody, does all the good he can to everybody: a child may persuade him it is night at noonday, and he is so simple, that I cannot help loving him with all my heart and soul, and cannot leave him in spite of all his follies.' 'Have a care, brother,' said the Squire of the Wood, 'when the blind leads the blind both may fall into the ditch. It is better to wheel about fairly and softly, and steal home again to our own firesides; for those who follow their nose are often led into a stink.' Here the Squire of the Wood, observing that Sancho spit very often and very dry, – ' I fancy, brother,' said he, 'that our tongues stick to the palates of our mouths with talking, but to cure that disease I have something that hangs to the pommel of my saddle, as good as ever was tipped over tongue.' Then he went and took down a leather bottle of wine, and a cold pie, at least half a yard long; which is no fiction, for Sancho himself, when he laid his hands on it, took it rather for a baked goat than a kid, though it was indeed but an overgrown rabbit. 'What!' said Sancho, at the sight, 'did you bring this too abroad with you?' 'What do you think?' said the other. 'Do you take me for one of your fresh-water squires? I would have you know, I carry as good provision at my horse's crupper, as any general upon his march.' Sancho did not stay for an invitation, but fell to in the dark, cramming down morsels as big as his fist. 'Ay marry, sir,' said he, 'you are a squire every inch of you, a true and trusty, round and sound, noble and free-hearted squire. This good cheer is a proof of it, which I do not say jumped hither by witchcraft; but one would almost think so. Now, here sits poor wretched I, that have nothing in my knapsack but a crust of cheese, so hard, a giant might break his grinders in it, and a few acorns, walnuts and filberts; a shame on my master's niggardly temper, and his cursed maggot, in fancying that all the knights-errant must live on dried fruit and salads.' 'Well, well, brother,' replied the Squire of the Wood, 'our masters may diet themselves by rules of chivalry, if they please; your thistles, and your herbs and roots do not at all agree with my stomach, I must have good meat, i'faith! and this bottle here still at the pommel of my saddle. It is my joy, my life, the comfort of my soul. I hug and kiss it every moment, and now recommend, it to you as the best friend in the world.' Sancho took the bottle, and rearing it to his thirsty lips, with his eyes fixed upon the stars, kept himself in that happy contemplation for a quarter of an hour together. At last, when he had taken his draught with a deep groan, a nod on one side, and a cunning leer, – ' O! the son of a whore! what a rare and catholic bub this is!' 'Oh ho!' quoth the Squire of the Wood, 'have I caught you at your son of a whore! Did I not tell you, that it was a way of commending a thing?' 'I knock under,' quoth Sancho, 'and own it is no dishonour to call one a son of a whore, when we mean to praise him. But now, by the remembrance of her you love best, pray thee, tell me, is not this your right Ciudad Real wine?'* 'Thou hast a rare palate,' answered the Squire of the Wood, 'it is the very same, and of a good age too.' 'I thought so,' said Sancho, 'but is it not strange now, that but turn me loose among a parcel of wines I shall find the difference? Adad! sir, I no sooner clap my nose to a taster of wine, but I can tell the place, the grape, the flavour, the age, the strength, and all the qualities of

* Cindad Real is a city of Spain, noted for good wine.

the parcel: and all this is natural to me, sir, for I had two relations by the father's side that were the nicest tasters that were known of a long time in La Mancha; of which two I will relate you a story that makes good what I said. It fell out on a time, that some wine was drawn fresh out of a hogshead, and given to these same friends of mine to taste; and they were asked their opinions of the condition, the quality, the goodness, the badness of the wine, and all that. The one tried it with the tip of his tongue, the other only smelled it; the first said the wine tasted of iron; the second said, it rather had a taste of goats' leather. The vintner swore his vessel was clean, and the wine neat, and so pure that it could have no taste of any such thing. Well, time ran on, the wine was sold, and when the vessel came to be emptied, what do you think, sir, was found in the cask? A little key, with a bit of leather thong tied to it. Now, judge you by this, whether he that comes of such a generation, has not reason to understand wine?' 'More reason than to understand adventures,' answered the other; 'therefore, since we have enough, let us not trouble ourselves to look after more, but even jog home to our little cots, where Heaven will find us, if it be its will.' 'I intend,' said Sancho, 'to wait on my master till we come to Saragossa, but then I will turn over a new leaf.' To conclude: the two friendly squires having talked and drank, and held out almost as long as their bottle, it was high time that sleep should lay their tongues, and assuage their thirst, for to quench it was impossible. Accordingly they had no sooner filled their bellies, but they fell fast asleep, both keeping their hold on their almost empty bottle. Where we shall for a while leave them to their rest, and see what passed between their masters.

CHAPTER XIV

A continuation of the Adventure of the Knight of the Wood

MANY WERE THE DISCOURSES that passed between Don Quixote and the Knight of the Wood: amongst the rest, 'You must know, Sir Knight,' said the latter, 'that by the appointment of fate, or rather by my own choice, I became enamoured of the peerless Casildea de Vandalia I call her peerless, because she is singular in the greatness of her stature, as well as in that of her state and beauty. But this lady has been pleased to take no other notice of my honourable passion, than employing me in many perilous adventures, like Hercules's step-mother; still promising me, after I had put a happy end to one, that the performance of the next should put me in possession of my desires. But after a succession of numberless labours, I do not know which of her commands will be the last, and will crown my lawful wishes. Once, by her particular injunction, I challenged that famous giantess La Giralda of Seville,* who is as strong and undaunted as one that is made of brass, and who, without changing place, is the most changeable and unconstant woman in the world; I went, I saw, and overcame: I made her stand still, and fixed her in a constant point, for the space of a whole week; no wind having blown in the skies during all that time but the north. Another time she enjoined me to remove the ancient stones of the sturdy bulls of Guisando;† a task more suitable to the arms of porters than those of knights. Then she commanded me to descend and dive into the cavern or den of Cabra‡ (a terrible and unheard-of attempt), and to bring her an account of all the wonders in that dismal profundity. I stopped the motion of La Giralda, I weighed the bulls of Guisando, and with a precipitated fall plunged and brought to light the darkest secrets of Cabra's black abyss. But still, ah! still my hopes are dead. How dead? How because her disdain still lives, lives to enjoin me new labours, new exploits. For, lastly, she has ordered me to traverse the remotest provinces of Spain, and exact a confession from all the knights-errant that roam about the land, that her beauty alone excels that of all other women, and that I am the most valiant and most enamoured knight in the world. I have already journeyed over the greatest part of Spain on this expedition, and overcome many knights who had the temerity to contradict my assertion: but the perfection of my glory, is the result of my victory over the renowned Don Quixote de la Mancha, whom I conquered in single combat, and compelled to submit his Dulcinea's to my Casildea's beauty. And now I reckon the wandering knights of the whole universe all vanquished by my prowess: their fame, their glory, and their honours being all vested in this great Don Quixote, who had before made them the spoils of his valorous arm; though now they must attend the triumphs of my victory, which is the greater, since the reputation of the victor rises in proportion to that of the vanquished; and all the latter's laurels are transferred to me.'

Don Quixote was amazed to hear the knight run on at this rate, and had the lie ready at his tongue's end to give him a thousand times; but designing to make him own his falsity with his own mouth, he strove to contain his choler: and arguing the matter very calmly, 'Sir Knight,' said he, 'that your victories have extended over all the knights in Spain, and

---

* Giralda is a brass statue, on a steeple in Seville; which serves instead of a weathercock.
† The bulls of Guisando are two vast statues remaining in that town ever since the time of the Romans. Supposed to be set up by Metellus.
‡ A place like some of the caverns in the Peak in Derbyshire.

perhaps over the whole world, I will not dispute, but that you have vanquished Don Quixote de la Mancha, you must give me leave to doubt: it might be somebody like him; though he is a person whom but very few can resemble.' 'What do you mean?' answered the Knight of the Wood. 'By yon spangled canopy of the skies, I fought Don Quixote hand to hand, vanquished him, and made him submit; he is a tall wither-faced, leathern-jaw fellow, scragged, grizzle-haired, hawk-nosed, and wears long, black, lank mustachios: he is distinguished in the field by the title of the Knight of the Woeful Figure: he has for his squire one Sancho Pança, a labouring man; he bestrides and manages that far-famed courser Rozinante; and has for the mistress of his affection one Dulcinea del Toboso, sometimes called Aldonsa Lorenzo; as mine, whose name was Casildea, and who is of Andalusia, is now distinguished by the denomination of Casildea de Vandalia; and if all these convincing marks be not sufficient to prove this truth, I wear a sword that shall force even incredulity to credit it.' 'Not so fast, good Sir Knight,' said Don Quixote; 'pray attend to what I shall deliver upon this head: you must know that this same Don Quixote is the greatest friend I have in the world; insomuch that I may say I love him as well as I do myself. Now the tokens that you have described him by, are so agreeable to his person and circumstances, that one would think he should be the person you subdued. On the other hand, I am convinced by the more powerful argument of undeniable sense, that it cannot be he. But thus far I will allow you, as there are many enchanters that are his enemies, especially one whose malice hourly persecutes him, perhaps one of them has assumed his likeness, thus by a counterfeit conquest, to defraud him of the glory contracted by his signal chivalry over all the universe. In confirmation of which I can further tell you, it is but two days ago that these envious magicians transformed the figure and person of the beautiful Dulcinea del Toboso into the base and sordid likeness of a rustic wench. And if this will not convince you of your error, behold Don Quixote himself in person, that here stands ready to maintain his words with his arms, either on foot or on horseback, or in what other manner you may think convenient.' As he said this, up he started, and laid his hand to his sword, expecting the motions and resolutions of the Knight of the Wood. But with a great deal of calmness, 'Sir,' said he, 'a good paymaster grudges no surety; he that could once vanquish Don Quixote when transformed, needs not fear him in his proper shape. But since darkness is not proper for the achievements of knights, but rather for robbers and ruffians, let us expect the morning light, that the sun may be witness of our valour. The conditions of our combat shall be: "That the conquered shall be wholly at the mercy of the conqueror, who shall dispose of him at discretion; provided always he abuses not his power, by commanding anything unworthy the honour of knighthood." ' 'Content,' said Don

Quixote, 'I like these terms very well.' With that they both went to look out their squires, whom they found snoring very soundly in just the same posture as when they first fell asleep. They roused them up, and ordered them to get their steeds ready; for the first rays of the rising sun must behold them engage in a bloody and unparalleled single combat. This news thunderstruck Sancho, and put him to his wits-end for his master's danger; having heard the Knight of the Wood's courage strangely magnified by his squire. However, without the least reply, he went with his companion to seek their beasts, who by this time had smelled out one another, and were got lovingly both together. 'Well, friend,' said the squire to Sancho, as they went, 'I find our masters are to fight; so you and I are like to have a brush too; for it is the way among us Andalusians, not to let the seconds stand idly by, with arms across, while their friends are at it.' 'This,' said Sancho, 'may be a custom in your country; but let me tell you, it is a damned custom, Sir Squire, and none but ruffians and bloody-minded fellows would stand up for it. But there is no such practice among squire-errants, else my master would have minded me of it ere this; for he has all the laws of knight-errantry by heart. But suppose there be such a law, I will not obey it, that is flat; I will rather pay the penalty that is laid on such peaceable squires: I do not think the fine can be above two pounds of wax,* and that will cost me less than the lint would to make tents for my skull, which methinks is already cleft down to my chin. Besides, how would you have me fight? I have never a sword, nor ever wore any.' 'No matter,' quoth the Squire of the Wood, 'I have a cure for that sore. I have got here a couple of linen bags, both of a size, you shall take one, and I the other, and so we will let drive at one another with these weapons, and fight at bag-blows.' 'Ay, ay, with all my heart,' quoth Sancho, 'this will dust our jackets purely, and will not hurt our skins.' 'Not so neither,' replied the Squire of the Wood; 'for we will put half a dozen of smooth stones into each bag, that the wind may not blow them to and fro, and they may play the better, and we may brush one another's coat cleverly, and yet do ourselves no great hurt.' 'Body of my father!' quoth Sancho, 'what soft sable fur, what dainty carded cotton and lamb's wool he crams into the bags, to hinder our making pap of our brains and touchwood of our bones: but I say again and again, I am not in a humour to fight, though they were only full of silk balls. Let our masters fight, and hear of it in another world; but let us drink and live while we may, for why should we strive to end our lives before their time and season, and be so eager to gather the plums that will drop off themselves when they are ripe?' 'Well,' said the squire of the Wood, 'for all that, we must fight half an hour or so.'

---

* A custom in Spain of fining small offenders to pay a small quantity of wax for the use of some church.

'Not a minute,' replied Sancho: 'I have not the heart to quarrel with a gentleman with whom I have been eating and drinking. I am not angry with you in the least, and were I to be hanged for it, I could never fight in cold blood.' 'Nay, if that be all,' said the Squire of the Wood, 'you shall be angry enough, I will warrant you; for, before we go to it, do you see, I will walk up very handsomely to you, and lend your worship three or four sound slaps on the chaps, and knock you down; which will be sure to waken your choler, though it slept as sound as a dormouse.' 'Nay then,' quoth Sancho, 'I have a trick for your trick, if that be all, and you shall have as good as you bring; for I will take me a pretty meddling lever (you understand me), and before you can awaken my choler, will I lay yours asleep so fast that it shall never wake more, unless in the other world; where it is well known I am one who will let no man's fist dust my nose. Let every man look before he leaps. Many come for wool, that go home shorn. No man knows what another can do: so, friend, let every man's choler sleep with him: blessed are the peace-makers, and cursed are the peace-breakers. A baited cat may turn as fierce as a lion. Who knows then what I, that am a man, may turn to, if I am provoked? Take it therefore for a warning from me, squire, that all the mischief you may be hatching, in this manner shall lie at your door.' 'Well,' said the other, 'it will be day anon, and then we shall see what is to be done.'

And now a thousand sorts of pretty birds began to warble in the trees, and with their various cheerful notes seem to salute the fresh Aurora, who then displayed her rising beauty through the gates and arches of the east, and gently shook from her dewy locks a shower of liquid pearls, sprinkling and enriching the verdant meads with that reviving treasure, which seemed to spring and drop from the bending leaves. The willows distilled their delicious manna, the rivulets fondly murmured, the fountains smiled, the woods were cheered, the fields enriched at her approach. But no sooner the dawning light recalled distinction, than the first thing that presented itself to Sancho's view, was the Squire of the Wood's nose, which was so big that it overshadowed almost his whole body. In short, it is said to have been of a monstrous size, crooked in the middle, studded with warts and carbuncles, tawny as a russet pippin, and hanging down some two fingers below his mouth. The unreasonable bulk, dismal hue, protuberancy, and crookedness of that nose, so disfigured the squire, that Sancho was seized with a trembling at the sight, like a child in convulsions, and resolved now to take two hundred cuffs, before his choler should awaken to encounter such an hobgoblin. As for Don Quixote, he fixed his eyes upon his antagonist; but as his helmet was on, and he had pulled down the beaver, his face could not be seen, however, he observed him to be strong limbed, though not very tall. Over his armour he wore a coat that looked like cloth of gold, overspread with looking-glasses (mirrors) cut into half moons, which made a very glittering show: a large plume of yellow, green, and white feathers waved about his helmet; and his lance, which he had set up against a tree, was very thick and long, with a steel head a foot in length. Don Quixote surveyed every particular, and from his observations, judged him to be a man of great strength. But all this was so far from daunting his courage, like Sancho, that, with a gallant deportment, 'Sir Knight of the Mirrors,' said he, 'if your eager desire of combat has not made you deaf to the entreaties of civility, be pleased to lift up your beaver a while, that I may see whether the gracefulness of your face equals that of your body.' 'Whether you be vanquished or victorious in this enterprise,' answered the Knight of the Mirrors, 'you shall have leisure enough to see my face: I cannot at present satisfy your curiosity; for every moment of delay from combat is, in my thoughts, a wrong done to the beautiful Casildea de Vandalia.' 'However,' replied Don Quixote, 'while we get a-horseback, you may tell me whether I be the same Don Quixote whom you pretend to have overcome?' 'To this I answer you,' said the Knight of the Mirrors, 'you are as like the knight I vanquished as one egg is like another. But considering what you tell me, that you are persecuted by enchanters, I dare not affirm that you are the same.' 'It is enough for me,' said Don Quixote, 'that you believe you may be in an error; but that I may entirely rid your doubts, let us to horse; for if providence, my mistress, and my arm assist me, I will see your face in less time than it would have cost you to have lifted up your beaver, and make you know that I am not that Don Quixote whom you talked of having vanquished.' This said, without any more words they mounted. Don Quixote wheeled about with Rozinante, to take ground for the career; the Knight of the Mirrors did the like. But before Don Quixote had ridden twenty paces, he heard him call to him: so meeting each other halfway, 'Remember, Sir Knight,' cried he, 'the conditions on which we fight; the vanquished, as I told you before, shall be at the mercy of the conqueror.' 'I grant it,' answered Don Quixote, 'provided the victor imposes nothing on him that derogates from the laws of chivalry.' 'I mean no otherwise,' replied the Knight of the Mirrors. At the same time Don Quixote happened to cast his eye on the squire's strange nose, and wondered no less at the sight of it than Sancho, taking him to be rather a monster than a man. Sancho seeing his master set out to take so much distance as was fit to return on his enemy with greater force, would not trust himself alone with Squire Nose, fearing the greater should be too hard for the less, and either that or fear should strike him to the ground. This made him run after his master, till he had taken hold of Rozinante's stirrup leathers; and when he thought him ready to turn back to take his career, 'Good your worship,' cried he, 'before you run upon your enemy, help me to get up into yon cork-tree, where I may better, and much more to my liking, see your brave battle with the knight.' 'I rather believe,' said Don Quixote, "thou wantest to be perched up yonder as on a scaffold, to see the bull-baiting without danger.' 'To tell you the truth,' quoth Sancho, 'that fellow's unconscionable nose has so frightened me, that I dare not stay within his reach.' 'It is indeed such a sight,' said Don Quixote, 'as might affect with fear, any other but myself; and therefore come, I will help thee up.' Now while Sancho was climbing up the tree, with his master's assistance, the Knight of the Mirror took as much ground as he thought proper for his career; and imagining Don Quixote had done the same, he faced about, without expecting the trumpet's sound, or any other signal for a charge, and with his horse's full speed, which was no more than a middling trot (for he was neither more promising, nor a better performer than Rozinante), he went to encounter his enemy. But seeing him busy in helping up his squire, he held in his steed, and stopped in the middle of the career, for which the horse was mightily obliged to him, being already scarce able to stir a foot further. Don Quixote, who thought his enemy was flying upon him, set spurs to Rozinante's hinder flank vigorously, and so wakened his mettle, that the story says, this was the only time he was known to gallop a little, for at all others, downright trotting was his best. With this unusual fury, he soon got to the place where his opponent was striking his spurs into his horse's sides up to the rowels, without being able to make him stir an inch from the spot. Now while he was thus goading him on, and at the same time encumbered with his lance, either not knowing how to set it in the rest, or wanting time to do it, Don Quixote, who took notice of his disorder, encountered him without danger so furiously, that the Knight of the Mirrors was hurried, in spite of his teeth, over his horse's crupper, and was so hurt with falling to the ground, that he lay without motion, or any sign of life. Sancho no sooner saw him fallen, but down he comes sliding from the tree, and runs to his master; who having dismounted, was got upon the Knight of the Mirrors, and was unlacing his helmet, to see if he were dead or alive, and give him air. But who can relate what he saw, when he saw the face of the Knight of the Mirrors, with raising wonder, amazement, or astonishment in those that shall hear it; he saw, says the history, in that face, the very visage, the very aspect, the very physiognomy, the very make, the very features, the very effigy of the bachelor Samson Carrasco. 'Come, Sancho,' cried he, as he saw it, 'come hither, look and admire what thou mayest see, yet not believe. Haste, my friend, and mark the power of magic; what sorcerers and enchanters can do!' Sancho drew near, and seeing the bachelor Samson Carrasco's face, began to cross himself a thousand times, and bless himself as many more. The poor defeated knight all this while gave no sign of life: 'Sir,' quoth Sancho to his master, 'if you will be ruled by me, make sure work: right or wrong, even thrust your sword down this fellow's throat that is so like the bachelor Samson Carrasco; and so mayhaps in him you may chance to murder one of those bitter dogs, those enchanters that haunt you so.' 'That thought is not amiss,' said Don Quixote; and with that drawing his sword, he was going to put Sancho's advice in execution, when the knight's squire came running, without the nose that so disguised him before; and calling to Don Quixote, 'Hold, noble Don Quixote!' cried he. 'Take heed! Beware! It is your friend Samson Carrasco, that now lies at your worship's mercy, and I am his squire.' 'And where is your nose?' quoth Sancho, seeing him now without disguise. 'Here in my pocket,' answered the squire, and so saying, he pulled out the nose of a varnished pasteboard vizard, such as it has been described. Sancho having more and more stared him in the face with great earnestness, 'Blessed Virgin defend me!' quoth he. 'Who is this? Thomas Cecial, my friend and neighbour?' 'The same, friend Sancho,' quoth the squire. 'I will tell you anon by what tricks and wheedles he was inveigled to come hither. Meanwhile desire your master not to misuse, nor slay, nor meddle in the least with the Knight of the Mirrors, that now lies at his mercy; for there is nothing more sure than that it is our ill-advised countryman Samson Carrasco, and nobody else.'

By this time the Knight of the Mirrors began to come to himself; which when Don Quixote observed, setting the point of his sword to his throat, 'Thou diest, knight,' cried he, 'if thou refuse to confess that the peerless Dulcinea del Toboso excels thy Casildea de Vandalia in beauty. Besides this, thou shalt promise (if thou escape with life from this combat) to go to the city of Toboso; where, as for me, thou shalt present thyself before the mistress of my desires, and resign thy person to her disposal: if she leaves thee to thy own, then thou shalt come back to me (for the tract of my exploits will be thy guide), and thou shalt give me an account of the transaction between her and thee. These conditions are conformable to our agreement before the combat, and do not transgress the rules of knight-errantry.' 'I do confess,' said the discomfited knight, 'that the lady Dulcinea del Toboso's ripped and dirty shoe is preferable to the clean, though ill-combed locks of Casildea; and I promise to go to her, and come from her presence to yours, and bring you a full and true relation of all you have enjoined me.' 'You shall also confess and believe,' added Don Quixote, 'that the knight you vanquished neither was nor could be Don Quixote de la Mancha, but somebody else in his likeness; as I, on the other side, do confess and believe, that though you seem to be the bachelor Samson Carrasco, you are not he, but some other whom my enemies have transformed into his resemblance, to assuage the violence of my wrath, and make me entertain with moderation the glory of my victory.' 'All this I confess, believe, and allow,' said the knight; 'and now I beseech you let me rise, if the hurt I have received by my fall will give me leave, for I find myself very much bruised.' Don Quixote helped him to rise, by the aid of his squire Thomas Cecial, on whom Sancho fixed his eyes all the while, asking him a thousand questions; the answers to which convinced him, that he was the real Thomas Cecial, as he said, though the conceit of what was told him by his master, that the magicians had transformed the Knight of the Mirrors into Samson Carrasco, had made such an impression on his fancy, that he could not believe the testimony of his own eyes. In short, the master and the man persisted in their error. The Knight of the Mirrors and his squire, much out of humour, and much out of order, left Don Quixote, to go to some town where he might get some ointments and plasters for his ribs. Don Quixote and Sancho continued their progress for Saragossa; where the history leaves them, to relate who the Knight of the Mirrors and his squire were.

CHAPTER XV

Giving an account who the Knight of the Mirrors and his Squire were

DON QUIXOTE WENT ON extremely pleased, and joyful, priding himself, and glorying in the victory he had got over so valiant a knight as the Knight of the Mirrors, and relying on his parole of honour, which he could not violate, without forfeiting his title to chivalry, that he would return to give him an account of his reception, by which means he expected to hear whether his mistress continued under the bonds of enchantment. But Don Quixote dreamed of one thing, and the Knight of the Mirrors thought of another. His only care for the present was how to get cured of his bruises.

Here the history relates, that when the bachelor Carrasco advised Don Quixote to proceed in his former profession of knight-errantry, it was the result of a conference which he had with the curate and the barber, about the best means to prevail with Don Quixote to stay quietly at home, and desist from rambling after his unlucky adventures. For Carrasco thought, and so did the rest, that it was in vain to pretend to hinder him from going abroad again; and therefore the best way would be to let him go, and that he should meet him by the way, equipped like a knight-errant, and should take an opportunity to fight, and overcome him, which he might easily do; first making an agreement with him, that the vanquished should submit to the victor's discretion: so, that after the bachelor had vanquished him, he should command him to return to his house and village, and not offer to depart from thence in two years, without permission; which it was not doubted Don Quixote would religiously observe, for fear of infringing the laws of chivalry; and in this time they hoped he might be weaned of his frantic imaginations, or they might find some means to cure him of his madness. Carrasco undertook this task, and Thomas Cecial, a brisk, pleasant fellow, Sancho's neighbour and gossip, proffered to be his squire. Samson equipped himself as you have heard, and Thomas Cecial fitted a huge pasteboard nose to his own, that his gossip Sancho might not know him when they met. Then they followed Don Quixote so close, that they had like to have overtaken him in the midst of his adventure with the chariot of death; and at last, they found him in the wood, that happened to be the scene of their encounter, which might have proved more fatal to the bachelor, and had spoiled him for ever from taking another degree, had not Don Quixote been so obstinate, in not believing him to be the same man.

And now Thomas Cecial, seeing the ill success of their journey: 'By my troth,' said he, 'Mr. Carrasco, we have been served well enough. It is easy to begin a business, but a hard matter to go through. Don Quixote is mad, and we think ourselves wise; yet he is gone away sound, and laughing in his sleeve; and your worship is left here well banged, and in the dumps: now, pray, who is the greatest madman, he that is so because he cannot help it, or he that is so for his pleasure?' 'The difference is,' answered the bachelor, 'that he that cannot help being mad, will always be so; but he that only plays the fool for his fancy, may give over when he pleases.' 'Well, then,' quoth Cecial, 'I, who was pleased to play the fool in going a squire-erranting with your worship, for the self-same reason will give it over now, and even make the best of my way home again.' 'Do as you will,' replied Carrasco, 'but it is a folly to think I ever will go home, till I have swingingly paid that unaccountable madman. It is not that he may recover his wit neither: no, it is pure revenge now, for the pain in my bones will not give me leave to have any manner of charity for him.' Thus they went on discoursing, till at last they got to a town, where, by good fortune, they met with a bone setter, who gave the bruised bachelor some ease. Thomas Cecial left him, and went home, while the other stayed to meditate revenge. In due time the history will speak of him again, but must not forget to entertain you now with Don Quixote's joy.

CHAPTER XVI

What happened to Don Quixote, with a sober Gentleman of La Mancha

DON QUIXOTE PURSUED his journey, full, as we said before, of joy and satisfaction; his late victory made him esteem himself the most valiant knight-errant of the age. He counted all his future adventures as already finished, and happily achieved. He defied all enchantments and enchanters. No longer did he remember the innumerable blows he had received in the course of his errantry, nor the shower of stones that had dashed out half of his teeth, nor the ingratitude of the galley-slaves, nor the insolence of the Yanguesian carriers, that had so abominably battered his ribs with their pack-staves. In short, he concluded with himself, that if he could but by any manner of means dissolve the enchantment of his adored Dulcinea, he should have no need to envy the greatest felicity that ever was, or ever could be attained by the most fortunate knight in the habitable globe. While he was wholly employed in these pleasing imaginations, 'Sir,' quoth Sancho to him 'is it not a pleasant thing that I cannot for the blood of me put out of my mind that huge unconscionable nose, and whapping nostrils of Thomas Cecial, my gossip?' 'How! Sancho,' answered Don Quixote, 'dost thou still believe, that the Knight of the Mirrors was the bachelor Carrasco, and that Thomas Cecial was his squire?' 'I do not know what to say to it,' quoth Sancho; 'but this I am sure of, that no one but he could give me those items of my house, and of my family as he did. Besides, when his hugeous nose was off, he had Tom Cecial's face to a hair. I ought to know it, I think: I have seen it a hundred and a hundred times, for we are but next-door neighbours; and then he had his speech to a tittle.' 'Come on,' returned Don Quixote; 'let us reason upon this business. How can it enter into any one's imagination, that the bachelor Samson Carrasco should come armed at all points like a knight-errant, on purpose to fight with me? Have I ever been his enemy, or given him any occasion to be mine? Am I his rival? or has he taken up the profession of arms, in envy of the glory which I have purchased by my sword?' 'Ay, but then,' replied Sancho, 'what shall we say to the resemblance between this same knight, whoever he be, and the bachelor Carrasco, and the likeness between his squire and my gossip? If it is an enchantment, as your worship says, were there no other people in the world but they two, to make them like?' 'All, all,' cried Don Quixote, 'is the artifice and delusion of those malevolent magicians that persecute me, who, foreseeing that I should get the victory, disguised their vanquished property under the resemblance of my friend the bachelor; that at the sight, my friendship might interpose between the edge of my sword, and moderate my just resentment, and so rescue him from death, who basely had attempted on my life. But thou, Sancho, by experience, which could not deceive thee, knowest how easy a matter it is for magicians to transmute the face of any one into another resemblance fair into foul, and foul in fair; since not two days ago, with thy own eyes thou beheldest the peerless Dulcinea in her natural state of beauty and proportion: when I, the object of their envy, saw her in the homely disguise of a blear-eyed, fetid, ugly country wench. Why then shouldst thou wonder so much at the frightful transformation of the bachelor and thy neighbour Cecial: but, however, this is a comfort to me, that I got the better of my enemy, whatsoever shape he assumed.' 'Well,' quoth Sancho, 'Heaven knows the truth of all things.' This was all the answer he thought fit to make; for as he knew that the transformation of Dulcinea was only a trick of his own, he was willing to wave the discourse, though he was the less satisfied in his master's chimeras; but feared to drop some word that might have betrayed his roguery.

While they were in this conversation, they were overtaken by a gentleman, mounted on a very fine flea-bitten mare. He had on a riding-coat of fine green cloth, faced with murry-coloured velvet, and a hunter's cap of the same. The furniture of his mare was country-like, and after the jennet-fashion, and also murry and green. By his side hung a Moorish scimitar, in a large belt of green and gold. His buskins were of the same work with his belt: his spurs were not gilt, but burnished so well with a certain green varnish that they looked better to suit with the rest of his equipage, than if they had been of pure gold. As he came up with them, be very civilly saluted them, and clapping spurs to his mare, began to leave them behind. Thereupon Don Quixote called to him: 'Sir,' cried he, 'if you are not in too much haste, we should be glad of the favour of your company, so far as you travel this road.' 'Indeed,' answered the gentleman, 'I had not thus rid by you, but that I am afraid your horse may prove unruly with my mare.' 'If that be all,' quoth Sancho, 'you may hold in your mare; for our horse here is the honestest and soberest horse in the world; he is not in the least given to do any naughty thing on such occasions. Once upon a time indeed he happened to forget himself, and go astray; but then he, and I, and my master rued for it, with a vengeance. I tell you again, sir, you may safely stay if you please, for if your mare were to be served up to him in a dish, I will lay my life he would not so much as touch her.' Upon this the traveller stopped his mare, and did not a little gaze at the figure and countenance of our Knight, who rode without his helmet, which, like a wallet, hung at the saddle-bow of Sancho's ass. If the gentleman in green gazed on Don Quixote, Don Quixote looked no less upon him, judging him to be some man of consequence. His age seemed about fifty; he had some grey hairs, a sharp look, and a grave, yet pleasing aspect. In short, his mien and appearance spoke him a man of quality. When he looked on Don Quixote, he thought he had never beheld before such a strange appearance of a man. He could not but admire at the lankness of his horse; he considered then the long-backed, raw-boned thing that bestrid him; his wan, meagre face, his air, his gravity, his arms, and equipage; such a figure as, perhaps, had not been seen in that country time out of mind. Don Quixote observed how intent the travelling gentleman had been in surveying him, and reading his desire in his surprise, as he was the very pink of courtesy, and fond of pleasing every one, without staying till he should question him he thought fit to prevent him, 'Sir,' said he, 'that you are surprised at this figure of mine, which appears so new and exotic, I do not wonder in the least; but your admiration will cease when I have informed you, that I am one of those knights who go in quest of adventures. I have left my country, mortgaged my estate, quitted my pleasures, and thrown myself into the arms of Fortune. My design was to give a new life to knight-errantry, that so long has been lost to the world; and thus, after infinite toils and hardships; sometimes stumbling, sometimes falling; casting myself headlong in one place, and rising again in another. I have compassed a great part of my desire, relieving widows, protecting damsels, assisting married women and orphans, the proper and natural office of knights-errant; and so, by many valorous and Christian-like achievements, I have merited the honour of the press in almost all the nations of the world. Thirty thousand volumes of my history have been printed already, and thirty millions more are like to be printed, if Heaven prevent not. In short, to sum up all in one word, know I am Don Quixote de la Mancha, otherwise called the Knight of the Woeful Figure; I own it lessens the value of praise to be the publisher of it one's self; yet it is what I am forced to when there is none present to do me justice. And now, good sir, no longer let this steed, this lance, this shield, this armour, nor this squire, nor the paleness of my looks, nor my exhausted body, move your admiration, since you know who I am, and the profession I follow.'

Having said this, Don Quixote was silent, and the gentleman in green, by his delaying to answer him, seemed as if he did not intend to make any return. But at last, after some pause: 'Sir Knight,' said he, 'you were sensible of my curiosity by my looks, and were pleased to say my wonder would cease when you had informed me who you were; but I must confess, since you have done that, I remain no less surprised and amazed than ever. For is it possible there should be at this time any knights-errant in the world, or that there should be a true history of a living knight-errant in print? I cannot persuade myself there is anybody now upon earth that relieves widows, protects damsels, or assists married women and orphans; and I should still have been of the same mind, had not my eyes afforded me a sight of such a person as yourself. Now, Heaven be praised, for this history of your true and noble feats of arms, which you say is in print, will blot out the memory of all those idle romances of pretended knights-errant that have so filled and pestered the world, to the detriment of good education, and the prejudice and dishonour of true history.' 'There is a great deal to be said,' answered Don Quixote, 'for the truth of histories of knight-errantry, as well as against it.' 'How!' returned the gentleman in green, 'is there anybody living who makes the least scruple but that they are false?' 'Yes, sir, myself for one,' said Don Quixote; 'but let that pass: if we continue any time together on the road, I hope to convince you that you have been to blame in suffering yourself to be carried away with the stream of mankind that generally disbelieves them.' The traveller, at this discourse, began to have a suspicion that Don Quixote was distracted, and expected the next words would confirm him in that opinion: but before they entered into any further conversation, Don Quixote begged him to acquaint him who he was, since he had given him some account of his own life and condition. 'Sir Knight of the Woeful Figure,' answered the other, 'I am a gentleman, born at a village, where, God willing, we shall dine by and by. My name is Don Diego de Miranda. I have a reasonable competency; I pass my time contentedly with my wife, my children, and my friends; my usual diversions are hunting and fishing; yet I keep neither hawks nor hounds, but some tame partridges and a ferret. I have about three or four score books, some Spanish, some Latin; some of history, and others of divinity. But for books of knight-errantry, none ever came within my doors. I am more inclinable to read those that are profane than those of devotion, if they be such as yield an innocent amusement, and are agreeable for their style, and surprising for their invention, though we have but few of them in our language. Sometimes I eat with my neighbours and friends, and often I invite them to do the like with me. My treats are clean and handsome, neither penurious nor superfluous. I am not given to murmur and backbite, nor do I love to hear others do it. I am no curious inquirer into the lives and actions of other people. Every day I hear divine service, and give to the poor, without making a show of it, or presuming on my good deeds, lest I should give way to hypocrisy and vain-glory; enemies that too easily possess themselves of the best-guarded hearts. I endeavour to reconcile those that are at variance. I pay my devotions to the Blessed Virgin, and ever trust in Heaven's infinite mercy.' Sancho listened with great attention to this relation of the gentleman's way of living; and believing that a person who had led so good and pious a life was able to work miracles, he jumped in haste from his ass, and catching hold of his right stirrup, with tears in his eyes, and devotion in his heart, fell a-kissing his foot. 'What is the matter, friend?' cried the gentleman, wondering at his proceeding; 'what is the meaning of this kissing?' 'Oh! good sir,' quoth Sancho, 'let me kiss that dear foot of yours, I beseech you; for you are certainly the first saint on horseback I ever saw in my born days.' 'Alas!' replied the gentleman, 'I am no saint, but a great sinner: you indeed, friend, I believe are a good soul, as appears by your simplicity.' With that Sancho returned to his pack-saddle, having by this action provoked the profound gravity of his master to smile, and caused new admiration in Don Diego. And now Don Quixote inquires of him, how many children he had, telling him at the same time, that among the things in which the ancient philosophers, who had not the true knowledge of God, made happiness consist, as the advantages of nature and fortune, one was, to have many friends and a numerous and virtuous offspring. 'I have a son, Sir Knight,' answered the gentleman; 'and perhaps if I had him not, I should not think myself the more unhappy; not that he is so bad neither: but because he is not so good as I would have him. He is eighteen years of age; the last six he has spent at Salamanca to perfect himself in his Latin and Greek: but, when I would have him to have proceeded to the study of other sciences, I found him so engaged in that of poetry, if it may be called a science, that it was impossible to make him look either to the study of the law, which I intended him for, or of divinity, the noblest part of all learning. I was in hopes he might have become an honour to his family, living in an age in which good and virtuous literature is highly favoured and rewarded by princes; for learning without virtue, is like a pearl upon a dunghill. He now spends whole days in examining, whether Homer, in such a verse of his "Iliad," says well or no? Whether such an epigram in Martial ought not to be expunged for obscenity? and whether such and such verses in Virgil are to be taken in such a sense, or otherwise? In short, his whole converse is with the celebrated poets, with Horace and Persius, Juvenal, and Tibullus. But as for modern rhymers, he has but an indifferent opinion of them. And yet for all this disgust of Spanish poetry, he is now breaking his brain upon a paraphrase or gloss on four verses that were sent him from the university, and which I think are designed for a prize.' 'Sir,' replied Don Quixote, 'children are the flesh and blood of their parents, and, whether good or bad, are to be cherished as part of ourselves. It is the duty of a father, to train them up from their tenderest years in the paths of virtue, in good discipline and Christian principles, that when they advance in years they may become the staff and support of their parents' age, and the glory of their posterity. But as for forcing them to this or that study, it is a thing I do not so well approve. Persuasion is all, I think, that is proper in such a case; especially when they are so fortunate as to be above studying for bread, as having parents that can provide for their future subsistence; they ought, in my opinion, to be indulged in the pursuit of that science to which their own genius gives them the most inclination. For though the art of poetry is not so profitable as delightful, yet it is none of those that disgrace the ingenious professor. Poetry, sir, in my judgment, is like a tender virgin in her bloom, beautiful and charming to amazement: all the other sciences are so many virgins, whose care it is to enrich, polish, and adorn her, and as she is to make use of them all, so are they all to have from her a grateful acknowledgment. But this virgin must not be roughly handled, nor dragged along the streets, nor exposed to every marketplace, and corner of great men's houses. A good poet is a kind of an alchemist, who can turn the matter he prepares into the purest gold, and an inestimable treasure. But he must keep his muse within the rules of decency, and not let her prostitute her excellency in lewd satires and lampoons, nor in licentious sonnets. She must not be mercenary, though she need not give away the profits she may claim from heroic poems, deep tragedies, and pleasant and artful comedies. She is not to be attempted by buffoons, nor by the ignorant vulgar, whose capacity can never reach to a due sense of the treasures that are locked up in her. And know, sir, that when I mention the vulgar, I do not mean only the common rabble; for whoever is ignorant, be he lord or prince, is to be listed in the number of the vulgar. But whoever shall apply himself to the muses with those qualifications, which, as I said, are essential to the character of a good poet, his name shall be famous, and valued in all the polished nations of the world. And as to what you say, sir, that your son does not much esteem our modern poetry; in my opinion, he is somewhat to blame; and my reason is this: Homer never wrote in Latin, because he was a Grecian; nor did Virgil write in Greek, because Latin was the language of his country. In short, all your ancient poets wrote in their mother-tongue, and did not seek other languages to express their lofty thoughts. And thus, it would be well that custom should extend to every nation; there being no reason that a German poet should be despised, because he writes in his own tongue; or a Castilian or Biscainer, because they write in theirs. But, I suppose, your son does not mislike modern poetry, but such modern poets as have no tincture of any other language or science that may adorn, awaken, and assist their natural impulse though even in this too there may be error. For, it is believed, and not without reason, that a poet is naturally a poet from his mother's womb, and that, with the talent which Heaven has infused into him, without the help of study or art, he may produce these compositions that verify that saying, *Est Deus in nobis*, etc. Not but that a natural poet, that improves himself by art, shall be much more accomplished, and have the advantage of him that has no title to poetry but by his knowledge in the art; because art cannot go beyond nature, but only adds to its perfection. From which it appears, that the most perfect poet is he whom nature and art combine to qualify.

Let then your son proceed, and follow the guidance of his stars; for being so good a student as I understand he is and already got up the first step of the sciences, the knowledge of the learned tongues, he will easily ascend to the pinnacle of learning, which is no less an honour and an ornament to a gentleman, than a mitre is to a bishop, or the long robe to the civilian. Should your son write satires to lessen the reputation of any person, do you take him to task, and tear his defamatory rhymes; but if he studies to write such discourses in verse, to ridicule and explode vice in general, as Horace so elegantly did, then encourage him: for a poet's pen is allowed to inveigh against envy and envious men; and so against other vices, provided it aim not at particular persons. But there are poets so abandoned to the itch of scurrility, that rather than lose a villainous jest, they will venture being banished to the islands of Pontus* If a poet is modest in his manners, he will be so in his verses. The pen is the tongue of the mind; the thoughts that are formed in the one, and those that are traced by the other, will bear a near resemblance. And when kings and princes see the wonderful art of poetry shine in prudent, virtuous, and solid subjects, they honour, esteem, and enrich them, and even crown them with leaves of that tree, which is never offended by the thunderbolt, as a token that nothing shall offend those whose brows are honoured and adorned with such crowns.' The gentleman hearing Don Quixote express himself in this manner, was struck with so much admiration, that he began to lose the bad opinion he had conceived of his understanding. As for Sancho, who did not much relish this fine talk, he took an opportunity to slink aside in the middle of it, and went to get a little milk of some shepherds that were hard by keeping their sheep. Now when the gentleman was going to renew his discourse, mightily pleased with these judicious observations, Don Quixote lifting up his eyes, perceived a wagon on the road, set round with little flags, that appeared to be the king's colours; and believing it to be some new adventure, he called out to Sancho to bring him his helmet. Sancho hearing him call aloud, left the shepherds, and clapping his heels vigorously to Dapple's sides, came trotting up to his master, to whom there happened a most terrifying and desperate adventure.

* As Ovid was.

CHAPTER XVII

*Where you will find set forth the highest and utmost
proof that the great Don Quixote ever gave, or could
give of his incredible courage, with the successful issue
of the Adventure of the Lions*

THE HISTORY RELATES, that Sancho was chaffering for some curds,
when Don Quixote called to him; and finding that his master was in haste,
he did not know what to do with them, nor what to bring them in; yet loth
to lose his purchase (for he had already paid for them) he bethought
himself at last of clapping them into the helmet, where having them safe,
he went to know his master's pleasure. As soon as he came up to him,
'Give me that helmet, friend,' said the Knight, 'for if I understand
anything of adventures I descry one yonder that obliges me to arm.' The
gentleman in green hearing this, looked about to see what was the matter,
but could perceive nothing but a wagon, which made towards them, and
by the little flags about it, he judged it to be one of the King's carriages,
and so he told Don Quixote. But his head was too much possessed with
notions of adventures to give any credit to what the gentleman said. 'Sir,'
answered he, 'forewarned, forearmed; a man loses nothing by standing on
his guard. I know by experience that I have enemies visible and invisible,
and I cannot tell when, nor where, nor in what shape they attack me.' At
the same time he snatched the helmet out of Sancho's hands, before he
could discharge it of the curds, and clapped it on his head, without
examining the contents. Now the curds being squeezed between his bare
crown and the iron, the whey began to run all about his face and beard;
which so surprised him, that calling to Sancho in great disorder, 'What is
this?' cried he, 'Sancho! What is the matter with me? Sure my skull is
growing soft, or my brains are melting, or else I sweat from head to foot!
But if I do, I am sure it is not for fear. This certainly must be a very
dreadful adventure that is approaching. Give me something to wipe me if
thou canst, for I am almost blinded with the torrent of sweat.' Sancho did
not dare to say a word, but giving him a cloth, blessed his stars that his
master had not found him out. Don Quixote dried himself, and taking off
the helmet to see what it should be that felt so cold on his head, perceiving
some white stuff, and putting it to his nose, soon found what it was. 'Now,
by the life of my Lady Dulcinea del Toboso,' cried he, 'thou hast put
curds in my helmet, vile traitor, and unmannerly squire!' 'Nay,' replied
Sancho cunningly, and keeping his countenance, 'if they be curds, good
your worship give them me hither, and I will eat them: but hold, now I

think on it, the Devil eat them for me; for he himself must have put them there. What! I offer to do so beastly a trick! Do you think I have no more manners? As sure as I am alive, sir, I have got my enchanters too that owe me a grudge, and plague me as a limb of your worship; and I warrant have put that nasty stuff there on purpose to set you against me, and make you fall foul on my bones. But I hope they have missed their aim this time, in troth! My master is a wise man, and must needs know that I had neither curds nor milk, or anything of that kind; and if I had met with curds, I should sooner have put them in my belly than his helmet.' 'Well,' said Don Quixote, 'there may be something in that.' The gentleman had observed these passages, and stood amazed, but especially at what immediately followed: for the knight-errant having put on the helmet again, fixed himself well in the stirrups, tried whether his sword were loose enough in his scabbard, and rested his lance. 'Now,' cried he, 'come what will come; here am I, who dare encounter the Devil himself in *propria persona*!' By this time the wagon was come up with them, attended only by the carter, mounted on one of the mules, and another man that sat on the fore part of the wagon. Don Quixote making up to them, 'Whither go ye, friends?' said he. 'What wagon is this? What do you convey in it? And what is the meaning of these colours?' 'The wagon is mine,' answered the wagoner; 'I have there two brave lions, which the General of Oran is sending to the King our master, and these colours are to let people understand that what goes here belongs to him.' 'And are the lions large?' inquired Don Quixote. 'Very large,' answered the man in the fore-part of the wagon; 'there never came bigger from Africa into Spain. I am their keeper,' added he, 'and have had charge of several others, but I never saw the like of these before. In the foremost cage is a he-lion, and in the other behind, a lioness. By this time they are cruel hungry, for they have not eaten today; therefore pray, good sir, ride out of the way, for we must make haste to get to the place where we intend to feed them.' 'What!' said Don Quixote, with a scornful smile, 'lion-whelps against me! Against me those puny beasts! And at this time of day? Well, I will make those gentlemen, that sent their lions this way, know whether I am a man to be scared with lions. Get off, honest fellow; and since you are the keeper, open their cages, and let them both out; for maugre and in despite of those enchanters that have sent them to try me, I will make the creatures know, in the midst of this very field, who Don Quixote de la Mancha is.' So, thought the gentleman to himself, now has our poor Knight discovered what he is; the curds, I find, have softened his skull, and mellowed his brains. While he was making this reflection, Sancho came up to him and begged him to dissuade his master from his rash attempt. 'O, good dear sir!' cried he, 'for pity's sake hinder my master from falling upon these lions, by all means, or we shall be torn in pieces.' 'Why,' said this gentleman, 'is your master so arrant a madman then, that you should fear he would set upon such furious beasts?' 'Ah, sir,' said Sancho, 'he is not mad, but woundy venturesome 'Well,' replied the gentleman, 'I will take care there shall be no harm done '; and with that advancing up to Don Quixote, who was urging the lion-keeper to open the cage; 'Sir,' said he, 'knights-errant ought to engage in adventures, from which there may be some hopes of coming off with safety, but not in such as are altogether desperate; for that courage which borders on temerity, is more like madness than true fortitude. Besides, these lions are not come against you, but sent as a present to the King, and therefore it is not the best way to detain them, or stop the wagon.' 'Pray, sweet sir,' replied Don Quixote, 'go and amuse yourself with your tame partridges and your ferrets, and leave every one to his own business. This is mine, and I know best whether these worthy lions are sent against me or no.' Then, turning about to the keeper, 'Sirrah! you rascal you,' said he, 'either open the cages immediately, or I vow to* — I will pin thee to the wagon with this lance.' 'Good sir,' cried the wagoner, seeing this strange apparition in armour so resolute, 'for mercy's sake do but let me take out our mules first, and get out of harm's way with them as fast as I can, before the lions get out; for if they should once set upon the poor beasts, I should be undone for ever; for alas! that cart and they are all I have in the world to get a living with.' 'Thou man of little faith,' said Don Quixote, 'take them out quickly then, and go with them where thou wilt; though thou shalt presently see that thy precaution was needless, and thou mightest have spared thy pains.' The wagoner upon this made all the haste he could to take out his mules, while the keeper cried out as loud as he was able, 'Bear witness all ye that are here present, that it is against my will I am forced to open the cages and let loose the lions; and that I protest to this gentleman here, that he shall be answerable for all the mischief and damage they may do; together with the loss of my salary and fees. And now, sirs, shift for yourselves as fast as you can before I open the cages: for, as for myself, I know the lions will do me no harm.' Once more the gentleman tried to dissuade Don Quixote from doing so mad a thing, telling him, that he tempted Heaven, in exposing himself without reason to so great a danger. To this Don Quixote made no other answer, but that he knew what he had to do. 'Consider, however, what you do,' replied the gentleman, 'for it is most certain that you are very much mistaken.' 'Well, sir,' said Don Quixote, 'if you care not to be spectator of an action, which you think is like to be tragical, even set spurs to your mare, and provide for your safety.' Sancho hearing this, came up to his master with tears in his eyes, and begged him

---

* In Spanish, it is *Voto a tal*, which is an offer to swear, but our Knight stops without going on with the oath.

not to go about this fearful undertaking, to which the adventure of the wind-mills, and the fulling-mills, and all the brunts he had ever borne in his life, were but children's play. 'Good your worship,' cried he, 'do but mind, here is no enchantment in the case, nor anything like it. Alack-a-day! sir, I peeped even now through the grates of the cage, and I am sure I saw the claw of a true lion, and such a claw as makes me think the lion that owns it must be as big as a mountain.' 'Alas, poor fellow!' said Don Quixote, 'thy fear will make him as big as half the world. Retire, Sancho, and leave me, and if I chance to fall here, thou knowest our old agreement; repair to Dulcinea, I say no more.' To this he added some expressions, which cut off all hopes of his giving over his mad design. The gentleman in the green would have opposed him, but considering the other was much better armed, and that it was not prudence to encounter a madman, he even took the opportunity while Don Quixote was storming at the keeper, to march off with his mare, as Sancho did with Dapple, and the carter with his mules, every one making the best of their way to get as far as they could from the wagon, before the lions were let loose. Poor Sancho at the same time made sad lamentations for his master's death; for he gave him up for lost, not questioning but the lions had already got him into their clutches. He cursed his ill-fortune, and the hour he came again to his service; but for all his wailing and lamenting, he punched on poor Dapple, to get as far as he could from the lions. The keeper, perceiving the persons who fled to be at a good distance, fell to arguing and entreating Don Quixote as he had done before. But the Knight told him again, that all his reasons and entreaties were but in vain, and bid him say no more, but immediately dispatch. Now while the keeper took time to open the foremost cage, Don Quixote stood debating with himself, whether he had best make his attack on foot or on horseback; and upon mature deliberation, he resolved to do it on foot, lest Rozinante, not used to lions, should be put into disorder. Accordingly he quitted his horse, threw aside his lance, grasped his shield, and drew his sword; then advancing with a deliberate motion, and an undaunted heart, he posted himself just before the door of the cage, commending himself to Heaven, and afterwards to his Lady Dulcinea. Here the author of this faithful history could not forbear breaking the thread of his narration, and, raised by wonder to rapture and enthusiasm, makes the following exclamation: 'O thou most magnanimous hero! Brave and unutterably bold Don Quixote de la Mancha! Thou mirror and grand exemplar of valour! Thou second, and new Don Emanuel de Leon, the late glory and honour of all Spanish cavaliers! What words, what colours shall I use to express, to paint in equal lines, this astonishing deed of thine! What language shall I employ to convince posterity of the truth of this thy more than human enterprise! What praises can be coined, and eulogies invented, that will not be outvied by thy superior merit, though hyperboles were piled on hyperboles! Thou, alone, on foot, intrepid and magnanimous, with nothing but a sword, and that none of the sharpest, with thy single shield, and that none of the brightest, stoodest ready to receive and encounter the savage force of two vast lions, as fierce as ever roared within the Lybian deserts. Then let thy own unrivalled deeds, that best can speak thy praise, amaze the world, and fill the mouth of fame, brave champion of La Mancha: while I am obliged to leave off the high theme, for want of vigour to maintain the flight.' Here ended the author's exclamation, and the history goes on.

The keeper observing the posture Don Quixote had put himself in, and that it was not possible for him to prevent letting out the lions, without incurring the resentment of the desperate knight, set the door of the foremost cage quite open; where, as I have said, the male lion lay, who appeared of a monstrous bigness, and of a hideous frightful aspect. The first thing he did was to roll and turn himself round in his cage; in the next place he stretched out one of his paws, put forth his claws, and roused himself. After that he gaped and yawned for a good while, and showed his dreadful fangs, and then thrust out half a yard of a broad tongue, and with it licked the dust out of his eyes and face. Having done this, he thrust his head out of his cage, and stared about with his eyes that looked like two live coals of fire; a sight and motion enough to have struck terror into temerity itself. But Don Quixote only regarded it with attention, wishing his grim adversary would leap out of his hold, and come within his reach, that he might exercise his valour, and cut the monster piecemeal. To this height of extravagance had his folly transported him; but the generous lion, more gentle than arrogant, taking no notice of his vapouring and bravadoes, after he had looked about him awhile, turned his tail, and showing Don Quixote his posteriors, very contentedly lay down again in his apartment. Don Quixote seeing this, commanded the keeper to rouse him with his pole, and force him out whether he would or no. 'Not I, indeed, sir,' answered the keeper; 'I dare not do it for my life; for, if I provoke him, I am sure to be the first he will tear to pieces. Let me advise you, sir, to be satisfied with your day's work. It is as much as the bravest he that wears a head can pretend to do. Then pray go no further, I beseech you: the door stands open, the lion is at his choice, whether he will come out or no. You have waited for him, you see he does not care to look you in the face, and since he did not come out at the first, I dare engage he will not stir out this day. You have shown enough the greatness of your courage. No man is obliged to do more than challenge his enemy, and wait for him in the field. If he comes not, that is his own fault, and the scandal is his, as the honour is the challenger's.' 'It is true,' replied Don Quixote. 'Come, shut the cage-door, honest friend, and give me a certificate under thy hand, in the amplest form thou canst devise, of what thou hast seen me perform; how thou didst open the cage for the lion; how I expected his coming, and he did not come out. How, upon his not coming out then, I stayed his own time, and instead of meeting me, he turned tail and lay down. I am obliged to do no more. So, enchantments avaunt! and Heaven prosper truth, justice, and knight-errantry! Shut the door, as I bid thee, while I make signs to those that ran away from us, and get them to come back, that they may have an account of this exploit from thy own mouth:' The keeper obeyed, and Don Quixote clapping on the point of his lance the handkerchief, with which he had wiped off the curds from his face, waved it in the air, and called as loud as he was able to the fugitives, who fled nevertheless, looking behind them all the way, and trooped on in a body with the gentleman in green at the head of them. At last, Sancho observed the signal of the white flag, and calling out to the rest, 'Hold,' cried he, 'my master calls us; I will be hanged if he has not got the better of the lions.' At this they all faced about, and perceived Don Quixote flourishing his ensign; whereupon recovering a little from their fright, they leisurely rode back, till they could plainly distinguish Don Quixote's voice; and then they came up to the wagon. As soon as they were come near it, 'Come on friend,' said he to the carter; 'put thy mules into the wagon again, and pursue thy journey; and Sancho, do thou give him two ducats for the lion-keeper and himself, to make them amends for the time I have detained them.' 'Ay, that I will with all my heart,' quoth Sancho; 'but what is become of the lions? Are they dead or alive?' Then the keeper very formally related the whole action, not failing to exaggerate, to the best of his skill, Don Quixote's courage; how at his sight alone the lion was so terrified, that he neither would nor durst quit his stronghold, though for that end his cage door was kept open for a considerable time; and how at length, upon his remonstrating to the knight, who would have had the lion forced out, that it was presuming too much upon Heaven, he had permitted, though with great reluctancy, that the lion should be shut up again. 'Well, Sancho,' said Don Quixote to his squire, 'what dost thou think of this? Can enchantment prevail over true fortitude? No, these magicians may perhaps rob me of success, but never of my invincible greatness of mind.' In short, Sancho gave the wagoner and the keeper the two pieces. The first harnessed his mules, and the last thanked Don Quixote for his noble bounty, and promised to acquaint the king himself with his heroic action when he came to court. 'Well,' said Don Quixote, 'if his majesty should chance to inquire who the person was that did this thing, tell him it was the Knight of the Lions; a name I intend henceforth to take up, in lieu of that which I hitherto assumed, of the Knight of the Woeful Figure; in which proceeding I do but conform to the ancient custom of knights-errant, who changed their names as often as they pleased, or as it suited with their advantage.' After this, the wagon made the best of its way, as Don Quixote, Sancho, and the gentleman in green did of theirs. The latter for a great while was so taken up with making his observations on Don Quixote, that he had not time to speak a syllable; not knowing what opinion to have of a person, in whom he discovered such a mixture of good sense and extravagance. He was a stranger to the first part of his history; for had he read it, he could not have wondered either at his words or actions: but not knowing the nature of his madness, he took him to be wise and distracted by fits, since in his discourse he still expressed himself justly and handsomely enough; but in his actions all was wild, extravagant and unaccountable. 'For,' said the gentleman to himself, 'can there be anything more foolish, than for this man to put on his helmet full of curds, and then believe them conveyed there by enchanters; or anything more extravagant than forcibly to endeavour to fight with lions?' In the midst of this soliloquy, Don Quixote interrupted him. 'Without doubt, sir,' said he, 'you take me for a downright madman, and indeed my actions seem to speak me no less. But for all that, give me leave to tell you, I am not so mad, nor is my understanding so defective, as I suppose you may fancy. What a noble figure does the gallant knight make, who in the midst of some spacious place transfixes a furious bull* with his lance in the view of his prince! What a noble figure makes the knight, who before the ladies, at a harmless tournament, comes prancing through the lists enclosed in shining steel; or those court champions, who in exercises of martial kind, or that at least are such in appearance, show their activity: and though all they do is nothing but for recreation, are thought the ornament of a prince's court! But a much nobler figure is the knight-errant, who, fired with the thirst of glorious fame, wanders through deserts,-through solitary wildernesses, through woods, through crossways, over mountains and valleys, in quest of perilous adventures, resolved to bring them to a happy conclusion. Yes, I say, a nobler figure is a knight-errant, succouring a widow in some depopulate place, than the court knight making his addresses to the city dames. Every knight has his particular employment. Let the courtier wait on the ladies; let him with splendid equipage adorn his prince's court, and with a magnificent table support poor gentlemen. Let him give birth to feasts and tournaments and show his grandeur, liberality, and munificence, and especially his piety; in all these things he fulfils the duties of his station.

'But as for the knight-errant, let him search into all the corners of the world, enter into the most intricate labyrinths, and every hour be ready to attempt impossibility itself. Let him in desolate wilds bame the rigour of

---

* The manner of riding at and killing bulls in the bull feasts in Spain.

the weather, the scorching heat of the sun's fiercest beams, and the inclemency of winds and snow: let lions never fright him, dragons daunt him, nor evil spirits deter him. To go in quest of these, to meet, to dare, to conflict, and to overcome them all, is his principal and proper office. Since then my stars have decreed me to be one of these adventurous knights, I think myself obliged to attempt everything that seems to come within the verge of my profession. This, sir, engaged me to encounter those lions just now, judging it to be my immediate business, though I was sensible of the extreme rashness of the undertaking. For well I know, that valour is a virtue situated between the two vicious extremes of cowardice and temerity. But certainly it is not so ill for a valiant man to rise to a degree of rashness, as it is to fall short and border upon cowardice. For as it is easier for a prodigal to become liberal, than a miser; so it is easier for the hardy and rash person to be reduced to true bravery, than for the coward ever to rise to that virtue: and therefore in thus attempting adventures believe me, Signor Don Diego, it is better to exceed the bounds a little, and overdo, rather than underdo the thing; because it sounds better in people's ears to hear it said, how that such a knight is rash and hardy, than such a knight is dastardly and timorous.' 'For my part, sir,' answered Don Diego, 'I think all you have said and done is agreeable to the exactest rules of reason; and I believe, if the laws and ordinances of knight-errantry were lost, they might be all recovered from you, your breast seeming to be the safe repository and archive where they are lodged. But it grows late, let us make a little more haste to get to our village, and to my habitation, where you may rest yourself after the fatigues which doubtless you have sustained, if not in body, at least in mind, whose pains often afflict the body too.' 'Sir,' answered Don Quixote, 'I esteem your offer as a singular favour;' and so putting on a little faster than they had done before, about two in the afternoon they reached the village, and got to the house of Don Diego, whom now Don Quixote called the Knight of the Green Coat.

CHAPTER XVIII

How Don Quixote was entertained at the Castle or House of the Knight of the Green Coat, with other extravagant passages

DON QUIXOTE FOUND that Don Diego de Miranda's house was spacious, after the country manner; the arms of the family were over the gate in rough stone, the buttery in the foreyard, the cellar under the porch, and all around several great jars of that sort commonly made at Toboso; the sight of which bringing to his remembrance his enchanted and transformed Dulcinea, he heaved a deep sigh, and neither minding what he said, nor who was by, broke out into the following exclamation:

> 'O pledges* once my comfort and relief,
> Though pleasing still, discovered now with grief.

O ye Tobosian urns, that awaken in my mind the thoughts of the sweet pledge of my most bitter sorrows!' Don Diego's son, who, as it has been said, was a student, and poetically inclined, heard these words as he came with his mother to welcome him home; and, as well as she, was not a little surprised to see what a strange creature his father had brought with him. Don Quixote alighted from Rozinante, and very courteously desiring to kiss her ladyship's hand, 'Madam,' said Don Diego, 'this gentleman is the noble Lion Quixote de la Mancha, the wisest and most valiant knight-errant in the world; pray let him find a welcome suitable to his merit, and your usual civility.' Thereupon Donna Christina (for that was the lady's name) received him very kindly, and with great marks of respect; to which Don Quixote made a proper and handsome return; and then almost the same compliments passed between him and the young gentleman, whom Don Quixote judged by his words to be a man of wit and sense.

Here the author inserts a long description of every particular in Don Diego's house, giving us an inventory of all the goods and chattels, and every circumstance peculiar to the house of a rich country gentleman: but the translator presumed that it would be better to omit these little things, and suchlike insignificant matters, being foreign to the main subject of this history, which ought to be more grounded on material truth, than cold and insipid digressions.

Don Quixote was brought into a fair room, where Sancho took off his armour, and then the knight appeared in a pair of close breeches, and a doublet of chamois leather, all besmeared with the rust of his armour. About his neck he wore a plain band, unstarched, after the manner of a student; about his legs sad-coloured spatter-dashes, and on his feet a pair of wax leather shoes. He hung his trusty sword by his side in a belt of a sea-wolf's skin; which makes many of opinion he had been long troubled with a pain in the kidneys. Over all this he clapped on a long cloak of good russet-cloth: but first of all he washed his head and face in five kettles full of water, if not in six: for as to the exact number there is some dispute. And it is observable, that the water still retained a tincture of whey: thanks to Sancho's gluttony, that had made him clap into his master's helmet those dismal curds that so contaminated his awful head and face. In this

---

* *O dulces prendas*, the beginning of a sonnet in the 'Diana' of Montemayor.

dress the Knight, with a graceful and sprightly air, walked into another room, where Don Lorenzo the young gentleman whom we have already mentioned, waited his coming, to keep him company till the cloth was laid; the mistress of the house being gone in the mean time to provide a handsome entertainment, that might convince her guest she understood how to make those welcome that came to her house. But before the Knight was ready, Don Lorenzo had leisure to discourse his father about him. 'Pray, sir,' said he, 'who is this gentleman you have brought with you? Considering his name, his aspect, and the title of knight-errant, which you give him, neither my mother nor I can tell what to think of him.' 'Truly, son,' answered Don Diego, 'I do not know what to say to you; all that I can inform you of, is, that I have seen him play the maddest pranks in the world, and yet say a thousand sensible things that contradict his actions. But discourse him yourself, and feel the pulse of his under-standing; make use of your sense to judge of his; though to tell you the truth, I believe his folly exceeds his discretion.' Don Lorenzo then went to entertain Don Quixote, and after some discourse had passed between them, 'Sir,' said the Knight, 'I am not wholly a stranger to your merit; Don Diego de Miranda, your father, has given me to understand you are a person of excellent parts, and especially a great poet.'

'Sir,' answered the young gentleman, 'I may perhaps pretend to poetry, but never to be a great poet: it is true, I am somewhat given to rhyming, and love to read good authors but I am very far from deserving to be thought one of their number.' 'I do not mislike your modesty,' replied Don Quixote; 'it is a virtue not often found among poets, for almost every one of them thinks himself the greatest in the world.' 'There is no rule without an exception,' said Don Lorenzo; 'and it is not impossible but there may be one who may deserve the name, though he does not think so himself.' 'That is very unlikely,' replied Don Quixote. 'But pray, sir, tell me what verses are those that your father says you are so puzzled about? If it should be what we call a gloss or a Don Quixote de la Mancha paraphrase, I understand something of that way of writing, and should be glad to see it. If the composition be designed for a poetical prize, I would advise you only to put in for the second; for the first always goes by favour, and is rather granted to the great quality of the author than to his merit; but, as to the next, it is adjudged to the most deserving; so that the third may in a manner be esteemed the second, and the first no more than the third, according to the methods used in our universities of giving degrees. And yet, after all, it is no small matter to gain the honour of being called the first.' 'Hitherto all is well,' thought Don Lorenzo to himself, I cannot think thee mad yet; let us go on.' With that addressing himself to Don Quixote, 'Sir,' said he, 'you seem to me to have frequented the schools; pray what science has been your particular study?'

'That of knight-errantry,' answered Don Quixote, 'which is as good as that of poetry, and somewhat better too.' 'I do not know what sort of a science that is,' said Don Lorenzo, 'nor indeed did I ever hear of it before.' 'It is a science,' answered Don Quixote 'that includes in itself all the other sciences in the world, or at the least the greatest part of them: whoever professes it, ought to be learned in the laws, and understand distributive and communative justice, in order to right all mankind. He ought to be a divine, to give a reason of his faith, and vindicate his religion by dint of argument. He ought to be skilled in physic, especially in the botanic part of it, that he may know the nature of simples, and have recourse to those herbs that can cure wounds; for a knight-errant must not expect to find surgeons in the woods and deserts. He must be an astronomer, to understand the motions of the celestial orbs, and find out by the stars the hour of the night, and the longitude and latitude of the climate on which fortune throws him; and he ought to be well instructed in all the other parts of the mathematics, that science being of constant use to a professor of arms, on many accounts too numerous to be related. I need not tell you, that all the divine and moral virtues must centre in his mind. To descend to less material qualifications; he must be able to swim like a fish, know how to shoe a horse, mend a saddle or a bridle: and, returning to higher matters, he ought to be inviolably devoted to Heaven and his mistress, chaste in his thoughts, modest in words, and liberal and valiant in deeds; patient in afflictions, charitable to the poor; and finally, a maintainer of truth, though it cost him his life to defend it. These are the endowments to constitute a good knight-errant; and now, sir, be you a judge, whether the professors of chivalry have an easy task to perform, and whether such a science may not stand in competition with the most celebrated and best of those that are taught in colleges?' 'If it be so,' answered Don Lorenzo, 'it deserves the pre-eminence over all other sciences.' 'What do you mean, sir by that, "If it be so"?' cried Don Quixote. 'I mean, sir,' replied Don Lorenzo, 'that I doubt whether there are now, or ever were, any knights-errant, especially with so many rare accomplishments.' 'This makes good what I have often said,' answered Don Quixote; 'most people will not be persuaded there ever were any knights-errant in the world. Now, sir, because I verily believe, that unless Heaven will work some miracle to convince them that there have been, and still are knights-errant, those incredulous persons are too much wedded to their opinion to admit such a belief: I will not now lose time to endeavour to let you see how much you and they are mistaken; all I design to do, is only to beseech Heaven to convince you of your being in an error, that you may see how useful knights-errant were in former ages, and the vast advantages that would result in ours from the assistance of men of that profession. But now effeminacy, sloth, luxury, and ignoble pleasures, triumph, for the punishment of our sins.' 'Now,' said Don Lorenzo to himself, 'our gentleman has already betrayed his blind side; but yet he gives a colour of reason to his extravagance, and I were a fool should I think otherwise.' Here they were called to dinner, which ended the discourse: and at that time Don Diego taking his son aside, asked him what he thought of the stranger. 'I think, sir,' said Don Lorenzo, 'that it is not in the power of all the physicians in the world to cure his distemper. He is mad past recovery, but yet he has lucid intervals.' In short, they dined and their entertainment proved such as the old gentleman had told the Knight he used to give his guests, neat, plentiful, and well ordered. But that which Don Quixote most admired, was, the extraordinary silence he observed through the whole house, as if it had been a monastery of mute Carthusians. The cloth being removed, grace said, and hands washed, Don Quixote earnestly desired Don Lorenzo to show him the verses he had wrote for the poetical prize. 'Well, sir,' answered he, 'because I will not be like those poets that are unwilling to show their verses when entreated to do it; but will tire you with them when nobody desires it, I will show you my gloss or paraphrase, which I did not write with a design to get a prize, but only to exercise my muse.' 'I remember,' said Don Quixote, 'a friend of mine, a man of sense, once told me, he would not advise any one to break his brains about that sort of composition; and he gave me this reason for it, that the gloss or comment could never come up to the theme; so far from it, that most commonly it left it altogether, and run contrary to the thought of the author. Besides, he said, that the rules to which custom ties up the composers of those elaborate amusements are too strict, allowing no interrogations, no such interjections as "said he," or "shall I say"; no changing of nouns into verbs; nor any altering of the sense: besides several other confinements that cramp up those who puzzle their brains with such a crabbed way of glossing, as you yourself, sir, without doubt, must know.' 'Really, Signor Don Quixote,' said Don Lorenzo, 'I would fain catch you tripping, but you still slip from me like an eel.' 'I do not know, sir,' replied Don Quixote, 'what you mean by your slipping.' 'I will tell you another time,' answered the young gentleman; in the meanwhile be pleased to hear the Theme and Paraphrase, which is this:

THE THEME

'Cou'd I recall departed joy,
    Tho' barr'd the hopes of greater gain,
Or now the future hours employ,
    That must succeed my present pain!'

THE GLOSS OR PARAPHRASE

I

'All fortune's blessings disappear,
    She's fickle as the wind;
And now I find her as severe,
    As once I thought her kind.
How soon the fleeting pleasure's past!
How long the ling'ring sorrows last!
    Unconstant goddess, thro' thy hate,
Do not thy prostrate slave destroy,
    I'd ne'er complain, but bless my fate,
Could I recall departed joy.

II

'Of all thy gifts I beg but this,
    Glut all mankind with more;
Transport 'em with redoubled bliss,
    But only mine restore.
With thought of pleasure once possess'd,
I'm now as curs'd as I was bless'd
    Oh wou'd the charming hour return
How pleas'd I'd live, how free from pain!
    I ne'er wou'd pine, I ne'er wou'd mourn,
Tho' barr'd the hopes of greater gain.

III

'But oh! the blessing I implore,
    Not fate itself can give!
Since time elaps'd exists no more,
    No power can bid it live.
Our days soon vanish into nought,
And have no being but in thought
    Whate'er began must end at last -
In vain we twice would youth enjoy;
    In vain wou'd we recall the past,
Or now the future hours employ.

IV

'Deceiv'd by hope, and rack'd by fear
    No longer life can please;

I'll then no more its torments bear,
   Since death so soon can ease.
This hour I'll die – But let me pause –
A rising doubt my courage awes.
   Assist ye pow'rs, that rule my fate,
Alarm my thoughts, my rage refrain,
   Convince my soul there's yet a state
That must succeed my present pain.'

As soon as Don Lorenzo had read over his paraphrase, Don Quixote rose from his seat, and taking him by the hand, 'By the highest mansions in the skies,' cried the Knight aloud 'noble youth, you are the best poet in the world, and deserve to be crowned with laurel, not at Cyprus or Gaeta, as a certain poet said, whom Heaven forgive, but at the university of Athens were it still in being, and at those of Paris, Bologna, and Salamanca. May those judges, that deny you the honour of the first prize, be shot with arrows by the god of verse, and may the muses abhor to come within their houses. Pray, sir, if I may beg that favour, let me hear you read one of your loftiest productions, for I desire to have a full taste of your admirable genius.' I need not tell you that Don Lorenzo was mightily pleased to hear himself praised by Don Quixote, though he believed him to be mad. So bewitching and welcome a thing is adulation, even from those we at other times despise. Don Lorenzo verified this truth, by his ready compliance with Don Quixote's request, and recited to him the following sonnet, on the story of Pyramus and Thisbe:

PYRAMUS AND THISBE   A SONNET

'See how, to bless the loving boy,
   The nymph for whom he burns with equal fires
Pierces the wall that parts 'em from their joy,
   While hovering love prompts, gazes, and admires!
The trembling maid in whispers and in sighs
   Dares hardly breathe the passion she betrays:
But silence speaks, and love thro' ravish'd eyes,
   Their thoughts, their flames their very souls conveys.
Wild with desires, they sally out at last,
But quickly find their ruin in their haste:
   And rashly lose all pleasure in despair.
O strange mischance! but do not fortune blame;
Love join'd 'em first, then death, the grave, and fame:
   What loving wretch a nobler fate would share!'

'Now Heaven be praised!' said Don Quixote, when Don Lorenzo had made an end. Among the infinite number of insipid men of rhyme, I have at last found a man of rhyme and reason, and, in a word, an absolute poet.

Don Quixote stayed four days at Don Diego's house, and, during all that time, met with a very generous entertainment. However, he then desired his leave to go, and returned him a thousand thanks for his kind reception; letting him know, that the duty of his profession did not admit of his staying any longer out of action; and therefore he designed to go in quest of adventures, which he knew were plentifully to be found in that part of Spain; and that he would employ his time in that, till the tilts and tournaments began at Saragossa, to which place it was his chief intent to go However, he would first go to Montesino's cave, about which so many wonderful stories were told in those parts; and there he would endeavour to explore and discover the source and original springs of the seven lakes, commonly called the Lakes of Ruydera. Don Diego and his son highly commended his noble resolution, and desired him to command whatever their house afforded, assuring him he was sincerely welcome to do it; the respect they had for this honourable profession, and his particular merit, obliging them to do him all manner of service. In short, the day of his departure came, a day of joy and gladness to Don Quixote, but of grief and sadness to poor Sancho, who had no mind to change his quarters, and liked the good cheer and plenty at Don Diego's house much better than his short hungry commons in forests and deserts, the sorry pittance of his ill-stored wallets, which he however crammed and stuffed with what he thought would best make the change of his condition tolerable. And now Don Quixote taking his leave of Don Lorenzo, 'Sir,' said he, 'I do not know whether I have already said it to you, but, if I have, give me leave to repeat it once more, that if you are ambitious of climbing up the difficult, and in a manner inaccessible, summit of the temple of fame, your surest way is to leave on one hand the narrow path of poetry, and follow the narrower track of knight-errantry, which in a trice may raise you to an imperial throne.' With these words Don Quixote seemed to have summed up the whole evidence of his madness. However, he could not conclude without adding something more: 'Heaven knows,' said he, 'how willingly I would take Lorenzo with me, to instruct him in those virtues that are annexed to the employment I profess, to spare the humble, and crush the proud and haughty. But since his tender years do not qualify him for the hardships of that life, and his laudable exercises detain him, I must rest contented with letting you know, that one way to acquire fame in poetry, is to be governed by other men's judgments more than your own: for it is natural to fathers and mothers not to think their own children ugly; and this error is nowhere so common as in the offspring of the mind.' Don Diego and his son were again surprised to hear this medley of good sense and extravagance, and to find the poor gentleman so strongly bent on the quest of his unlucky adventures, the only aim and object of his desires. After this, and many compliments and mutual reiterations of offers of service, Don Quixote having taken leave of the lady of the castle, he on Rozinante, and Sancho on Dapple, set out, and pursued their journey.

CHAPTER XIX

The Adventure of the amorous Shepherd, and other comical passages

DON QUIXOTE had not travelled far, when he was overtaken by two men that looked like students or ecclesiastics, with two farmers, all mounted upon asses. One of the scholars had behind him a small bundle of linen, and two pairs of stockings, trussed up in green buckram, like a portmanteau; the other had no other luggage but a couple of foils and a pair of fencing pumps. And the husbandmen had a parcel of other things, which showed, that having made their market at some adjacent town, they were now returning home with their ware. They all admired (as indeed all others did that ever beheld him) what kind of a fellow Don Quixote was, seeing him make a figure so different from anything they had ever seen. The Knight saluted them, and perceiving their road lay the same way, offered them his company, entreating them however to move an easier pace, because their asses went faster than his horse; and to engage them the more, he gave them a hint of his circumstances and profession; that he was a knight-errant travelling round the world in quest of adventures; that his proper name was Don Quixote de la Mancha, but his titular denomination, the 'Knight of the Lions.' All this was Greek, or pedlar's French to the countrymen; but the students presently found out his blind side. However, with a respectful distance, 'Sir Knight,' said one, 'if you are not fixed to any set stage, as persons of your function seldom are, let us beg the honour of your company; and you shall be entertained with one of the finest and most sumptuous weddings that ever was seen, either in La Mancha, or many leagues round it.' 'The nuptials of some young prince, I presume?' said Don Quixote. 'No, sir,' answered the other, 'but of a yeoman's son, and a neighbour's daughter; he the richest in all this country, and she the handsomest you ever saw. The entertainment at the wedding will be new and extraordinary, it is to be kept in a meadow near the village where the bride lives. They call her "Quiteria the handsome," by reason of her beauty, and the bridegroom "Comacho the rich," on account of his wealth. They are well matched as to age, for she draws towards eighteen, and he is about two and twenty, though some nice folks, that have all the pedigrees in the world in their heads, will tell ye, that the bride comes of a better family than he; but that is not minded nowadays, for money you know will hide many faults. And indeed, this same Comacho is as free as a prince, and designs to spare no cost upon his wedding. He has taken a fancy to get the meadow shaded with boughs, that are to cover it like an arbour, so that the sun will have much ado to peep through, and visit the green grass underneath. There are also provided for the diversion of the company several sorts of antics and morrice-dancers, some with swords, and some with bells; for there are young fellows in his village can manage them cleverly. I say nothing of those that play tricks with the soles of their shoes when they dance, leaving that to the judgment of the guests. But nothing that I have told or might tell you of this wedding is like to make it so remarkable as the things which I imagine poor Basil's despair will do. This Basil is a young fellow, that lives next door to Quiteria's father. Hence love took occasion to give birth to an amour, like that of old between Pyramus and Thisbe; for Basil's love grew up with him from a child, and she encouraged his passion with all the kind return that modesty could grant; insomuch, that the mutual affection of the two little ones was the common talk of the village. But Quiteria coming to years of maturity, her father began to deny Basil the usual access to his house; and to cut off his further pretence, declared his resolution of marrying her to Camacho, who is indeed his superior in estate, though far short of him in all other qualifications; for Basil, to give the Devil his due, is the cleverest fellow we have; he will pitch ye a bar, wrestle, or play at tennis with the best he in the country; he runs like a stag, leaps like a buck, plays at ninepins so well, you would think he tips them down by witchcraft; sings like a lark; touches a guitar so rarely, that he even makes it speak; and to complete his perfections, he handles a sword like a fencer.' 'For that very single qualification,' said Don Quixote, 'he deserves not only "Quiteria the handsome," but a princess; nay, Queen Guinever herself, were she now living, in spite of Sir Lancelot and all that would oppose it.' 'Well,' quoth Sancho, who had been silent, and listening all the while, 'my wife used to tell me she would have every one marry with their match. Like to like, quoth the Devil to the collier, and every sow to her own trough, as the other saying is: as for my part, all I would have is, that honest Basil even marry her. For methinks I have a huge liking to the young man, and so Heaven bless them together, say I, and a murrain seize those that will spoil a good match between those that love one another!' 'Nay,' said Don Quixote, 'if marriage should be always the consequence of mutual love, what would become of the prerogative of parents, and their authority over their children? If young girls might always choose their own husbands, we should have the best families intermarry with coachmen and grooms; and young heiresses would throw themselves away upon the first wild young fellows, whose promising outsides and assurance make them set up for fortunes, though all their stock consists in impudence. For the understanding, which alone should distinguish and choose in these cases as in all others, is apt to be blinded or biassed by love and affection; and matrimony is so nice and critical a point, that it requires not only our own cautious management, but even the direction of a superior power to choose right. Whoever undertakes a long journey, if he be wise, makes it his business to find out an agreeable companion. How cautious then should he be, who is to take a journey for life, whose fellow traveller must not part with him but at the grave; his companion at bed and board and sharer of all the pleasures and fatigues of his journey; as the wife must be to the husband! She is no such sort of ware, that a man can be rid of when he pleases: when once that is purchased, no exchange, no sale, no alienation can be made: she is an inseparable accident to man: marriage is a noose, which, fastened about the neck, runs the closer, and fits more uneasy by our struggling to get loose: it is a Gordian knot which none can untie, and being twisted with our thread of life, nothing but the scythe of death can cut it.

'I could dwell longer on this subject, but that I long to know from the gentleman, whether he can tell us anything more of Basil?' 'All I can tell you,' said the student, 'is, that he is in the case of all desperate lovers; since the moment he heard of this intended marriage, he has never been seen to smile or talk rationally; he is in a deep melancholy, that might indeed rather be called a dozing frenzy; he talks to himself, and seems out of his senses; he hardly eats or sleeps, and lives like a savage in the open fields; his only sustenance a little fruit, and his only bed the hard ground; sometimes he lifts up his eyes to Heaven, then fixes them on the ground, and in either posture stands like a statue. In short, he is reduced to that condition, that we, who are his acquaintance, verily believe, that the consummation of this wedding tomorrow will be attended by his death.' 'Heaven forbid; marry, and amen!' cried Sancho; 'who can tell what may happen? he that gives a broken head can give a plaster. This is one day, but to morrow is another, and strange things may fall out in roasting of an egg. After a storm comes a calm. Many a man that went to bed well, has found himself dead in the morning when he awaked. Who can put a spoke in fortune's wheel? nobody here, I am sure. Between a woman's "yea" and "nay" I would not engage to put a pin's point, so close they be one to another. If Mrs. Quiteria love Mr. Basil, she will give Camacho the bag to hold; for this same love, they say, looks through spectacles, that makes copper look like gold, a cart like a coach, and a shrimp like a lobster.' 'Whither in the name of ill-luck art thou running now, Sancho?' said Don Quixote. 'When thou fallest to threading thy proverbs and old wives' sayings, the Devil (who I wish had thee) cannot stop thee. What dost thou know, poor animal, of fortune, or her wheel, or anything else?' 'Why truly, sir,' quoth Sancho, 'if you do not understand me, no wonder if my sentences be thought nonsense. But let that pass, I understand myself; and I am sure I have not talked so much like a ninny. But you forsooth are so sharp a cricket.' 'A critic, blockhead,' said Don Quixote, 'thou confounded corrupter of human speech!' 'By yea, and by nay,' quoth Sancho, 'what makes you so angry, sir? I was never brought up at school nor 'varsity, to know when I murder a hard word. I was never at court to learn to spell, sir. Some are born in one town, some in another; one at St. Jago, another at Toledo; and even there all are not so nicely spoken.' 'You are in the right, friend,' said the student; 'those natives of that city, who live among the tanners, or about the market of Zocodover, and are confined to mean conversation, cannot speak so well as those that frequent the polite part of the town, and yet they are all of Toledo. But propriety, purity, and elegance of style, may be found among men of breeding and judgment; let them be born where they will, for their judgment is the grammar of good language, though practice and example will go a great way. As for my part, I have had the happiness of good education; it has been my fortune to study the civil law at Salamanca, and I have made it my business all along to express myself properly, neither like a rustic nor a pedant.' 'Ay, ay, sir,' said the other student, 'your parts might have qualified you for a Master-of-Arts degree, had you not misemployed them in minding so much those foolish foils you carry about with you, and that make you lag behind your juniors.' 'Look you, good Sir Bachelor,' said the other, 'your mean opinion of these foils is erroneous and absurd; for I can deduce the usefulness of the art of fencing from several undeniable axioms.' 'Pshaw,' said Corchuelo, for so was the other called, 'do not tell me of axioms; I will fight you, sir, at your own weapons. Here am I that understand neither quart nor tierce; but I have an arm, I have strength, and I have courage. Give me one of your foils, and in spite of all your distances, circles, falsifies, angles, and all other terms of your art, I will show you there is nothing in it, and will make reason glitter in your eyes. That man breathes not vital air, that I will turn my back on. And he must have more than human force, that can stand his ground against me.' 'As for standing ground,' said the artist, 'I will not be obliged to it. But have a care, sir, how you press upon a man of skill, for, ten to one, at the very first advance, but he is in your body up to the hilt.' 'I will try that presently,' said Corchuelo; and springing briskly from his ass, snatched one of the foils which the student carried. 'Hold, hold, sir,' said Don Quixote, 'I will stand judge of the field, and see fair play on both sides,' and interposing with his lance, he alighted, and gave the artist time to put himself in his posture, and take his distance. Then Corchuelo flew at him like a fury, helter-skelter, cut and thrust, backstroke and forestroke, single and double, and laid on like any lion. But the student stopped him in the middle of his career with such a dab in the teeth, that he made Corchuelo foam at the mouth. He made him kiss the button of his foil, as if it had been a relic, though not altogether with so much devotion. In short, he told all the buttons of his short cassock with pure clean thrusts, and made the skirts of it hang about him in rags like fish tails. Twice he struck off his hat, and in fine, so mauled and tired him, that through perfect vexation Corchuelo took the foil by the hilt, and hurled it from him with such violence, that one of the countrymen that were by, happening to be a notary-public, has it upon record to this day, that he threw it almost three-quarters of a league; which testimony has served, and yet serves to let posterity know that strength is overcome by art. At last Corchuelo, puffing and blowing, sat down to rest himself, and Sancho, coming up to him, 'Mr. Bachelor,' quoth he, 'henceforwards take a fool's advice, and never challenge a man to fence, but to wrestle or pitch the bar; you seem cut out for those sports: but this fencing is a ticklish point, sir, meddle no more with it; for I have heard some of your masters of the science say, they can hit the eye of a needle with the point of a sword.' Corchuelo acknowledged himself convinced of an error by experience, and embracing the artist, they became the better friends for this tilting. So, without staying for the notary that went for the foil, and could not be back in a great while, they put on to the town where Quiteria lived, they all dwelling in the same village. By the way, the student held forth upon the excellency of the noble science of defence, with so many plain and convincing reasons, drawn from expressive figures and mathematical demonstrations, that all were satisfied of the excellency of the art, and Corchuelo was reclaimed from his incredulity.

It was now pretty dark; but, before they got to the village, there appeared an entire blazing constellation: their ears were entertained with the pleasing, but confused sounds of several sorts of music, drums, fiddles, pipes, tabours and bells; and as they approached nearer still, they found a large arbour at the entrance of the town, stuck full of lights, which burnt undisturbed by the least breeze of wind. The musicians, which are the life and soul of diversion at a wedding, went up and down in bands about the meadow. In short, some danced, some sung, some played, and mirth and jollity revelled through that delicious seat of pleasure. Others were employed in raising scaffolds for the better view of the shows and entertainments prepared for the happy Camacho's wedding, and likewise to solemnise poor Basil's funeral. All the persuasions and endeavours of the students and countrymen could not move Don Quixote to enter the town; urging for his reason the custom of knights-errant, who chose to lodge in fields and forests under the canopy of heaven, rather than in soft beds under a gilded roof; and therefore he left them, and went a little out of the road, full sore against Sancho's will, who had not yet forgot the good lodging and entertainment he had at Don Diego's house or castle.

CHAPTER XX

An account of rich Camacho's Wedding, and what befell poor Basil

SCARCE HAD THE FAIR AURORA given place to the refulgent ruler of the day, and allowed him time, with the heat of his prevailing rays, to dry the liquid pearls on his golden locks, when Don Quixote, shaking off sluggish sleep from his drowsy limbs, arose and called his squire: but finding him still snoring, 'O thou most happy mortal upon earth,' said he, 'how sweet is thy repose! envied by none, and envying no man's greatness, secure thou sleepest, thy soul composed and calm! no power of magic persecutes thee, nor are thy thoughts affrighted by enchantments. Sleep on, sleep on, a hundred times sleep on. Those jealous cares that break a lover's heart do not extend to thee; neither the dread of craving creditors, nor the dismal foresight of inevitable want, or care of finding bread for a helpless starving family, keep thee waking. Ambition does not make thee uneasy, the pomp and vanity of this world do not perplex thy mind; for all thy cares extant reaches but to thy ass. Thy person and thy welfare thou hast committed to my charge, a burthen imposed on masters by nature and custom, to weigh and counterpoise the offices of servants. Which is the greatest slave? The servant's business is performed by a few manual duties, which only reconcile him more to rest, and make him sleep more sound; while the anxious master has not leisure to close his eyes, but must labour day and night to make provision for the subsistence of his servant; not only in the time of abundance, but even when the heavens deny those kindly showers that must supply this want.'

To this fine expostulation Sancho answered not a word; but slept on, and was not to be waked by his master's calling, or otherwise, till he pricked him in the buttocks with the sharp end of his lance. At length, opening his eyelids halfway, and rubbing them, after he had gaped and yawned, and stretched his drowsy limbs, he looked about him, and snuffing up his nose, 'I am much mistaken,' quoth he, 'if from this same arbour there come not a pure steam of a good broiled rasher, that comforts my nostrils more than all the herbs and rushes hereabouts. And, by my Holy Dame, a wedding that begins so savourly must be a dainty one.' 'Away, cormorant,' said Don Quixote, 'rouse and let's go see it, and learn how it fares with the disdained Basil.' 'Fire!' quoth Sancho; 'why if he be poor, he must even be so still, and not think to marry Quiteria. It is a pretty fancy i'faith! for a fellow who has not a cross to run madding after what is meet for his betters. I will lay my neck that Camacho covers this same Basil from head to foot with white sixpences, and will spend ye more at a breakfast than the other is worth, and never be the worse. And do you think that Madam Quiteria will quit her fine rich gowns and petticoats, her necklaces of pearl, her jewels, her finery and bravery, and all that Camacho has given her, and may afford to give her, to marry a fellow with whom she must knit or spin for her living? What signifies his bar-pitching and fencing? Will that pay for a pint of wine at the tavern? If all those rare parts will not go to market, and make the pot boil, the deuce take them for me; though were they to light on a man that has wherewithal, may I never stir if they do not set him off rarely. With good materials, on a good foundation, a man may build a good house, and money is the best foundation in the world.' 'For Heaven's sake, dear Sancho,' said Don Quixote, 'bring thy tedious harangue to a conclusion. For my part, I believe, wert thou alone when thy clack is once set a-going, thou wouldst scarce allow thyself time to eat or sleep, but wouldst prate on to the end of the chapter.' 'Troth, master,' replied Sancho, 'your memory must be very short, not to remember the articles of our agreement before I came this last journey with you. I was to speak what I would, and when I would, provided I said nothing against my neighbour, or your worship's authority; and I do not see that I have broken my indentures yet.' 'I remember no such article,' said Don Quixote; 'and though it were so, it is my pleasure you now be silent, and attend me; for the instruments we heard last night begin to cheer the valleys, and doubtless the marriage will be solemnised this morning, ere the heat of the day prevent the diversion.' Thereupon Sancho said no more, but saddled Rozinante, and clapped his pack-saddle on Dapple's back; then, both mounting, away they rode fair and softly into the arbour. The first thing that blessed Sancho's sight there, was a whole steer spitted on a large elm, before a mighty fire made of a pile of wood, that seemed a flaming mountain. Round this bonfire were placed six capacious pots, cast in no common mould, or rather six ample coppers, every one containing a whole shamble of meat, and entire sheep were sunk and lost in them, and soaked as conveniently as pigeons. The branches of the trees around were garnished with an infinite number of cased hares, and plucked fowls of several sorts; and then for drink, Sancho told above threescore skins of wine, each of which contained above two arrobas,* and, as it afterwards proved, sprightly liquor. A

---

* In Spain they reckon the quantity of wine by the weight, an arroba being 28 pounds, so that two of them make seven gallons.

goodly pile of white loaves made a large rampart on the one side, and a stately wall of cheeses, set up like bricks, made a comely bulwark on the other. Two pans of oil, each bigger than a dyer's vat, served to fry their pancakes, which they lifted out with two strong peels when they were fried enough, and then they dipped them in as large a kettle of honey, prepared for that purpose. To dress all this provision there were above fifty cooks, men and women, all cleanly, diligent, and cheerful. In the ample belly of the steer they had sewed up twelve little suckling pigs embowelled, to give it the more savoury taste. Spices of all sorts lay about in such plenty, that they appeared to be bought by wholesale. In short, the whole provision was indeed country-like, but plentiful enough to feast an army. Sancho beheld all this with wonder and delight. The first temptation that captivated his senses was the goodly pots; his bowels yearned, and his mouth watered at the dainty contents: by and by he falls desperately in love with the skins of wine; and lastly, his affections were fixed on the frying-pans, if such honourable kettles may accept of the name. The scent of the fried meat put him into such a commotion of spirit that he could hold out no longer, but accosting one of the busy cooks with all the smooth and hungry reasons he was master of, he begged his leave to sop a luncheon of bread in one of the pans. 'Friend,' quoth the cook, 'no hunger must be felt near us today (thanks to the founder). 'Light, 'light, man, and if thou canst find ever a ladle there, skim out a pullet or two, and much good may it do you.' 'Alack-a-day,' quoth Sancho, 'I see no ladle, sir.' 'Blood and suet,' cried the cook, 'what a silly helpless fellow thou art! Let me see.' With that he took a kettle, and sousing into one of the pots, he fished out three hens and a couple of geese at one heave. 'Here, friend,' said he to Sancho, 'take this, and make shift to stay your stomach with that *scum* till dinner be ready.' 'Heaven reward you,' cried Sancho, 'but where shall I put it?' 'Here,' answered the cook, 'take ladle and all, and thank the founder once more, I say; nobody will grudge it thee.' While Sancho was thus employed, Don Quixote saw twelve young farmer's sons, all dressed very gay, enter upon stately mares, as richly and gaudily equipped as the country could afford, with little bells fastened to their furniture. These in a close body made several careers up and down the meadow, merrily shouting and crying out, 'Long live Camacho and Quiteria, he as rich as she fair, and she the fairest in the world!' 'Poor ignorants,' thought Don Quixote, overhearing them, 'you speak as you know; but had you even seen my Dulcinea del Toboso, you would not be so lavish of your praises here.' In a little while, at several other parts of the spacious arbour entered a great number of dancers, and amongst the rest twenty-four young active country lads in their fine holland shirts, with their handkerchiefs wrought with several colours of fine silk, wound about their heads, each of them with sword in hand. They danced a military dance, and skirmished with one another, mixing and intermixing with their naked swords, with wonderful flight and activity, without hurting each other in the least. This dance pleased Don Quixote mightily, and though he was no stranger to such sort of dances, he thought it the best he had ever seen. There was another he also liked very well, performed all by the most beautiful young maids, between fourteen and eighteen years of age, clad in slight green, with their hair partly filleted up with ribbons, and partly hanging loose about their shoulders, as bright and lovely as the sun's golden beams. Above all they wore garlands of roses, jessamine, amaranth, and honey-suckles. They were led up by a reverend old man and a matronly woman, both much more light and active than their years seemed to promise. They danced to the music of Zamora bagpipes; and such was the modesty of their looks, and the agility of their feet, that they appeared the prettiest dancers in the world. After these came in an artificial dance, or masque, consisting of eight nymphs, cast into two divisions, of which Love led one, and Wealth the other; one with his wings, his bow, his arrows, and his quiver; the other arrayed in several gaudy colours of gold and silk. The nymphs of Cupid's party had their names inscribed in large characters behind their backs. The first was Poesy, Prudence was the next, the third Nobility, and Valour was the fourth. Those that attended Wealth were Liberality, Reward, Treasure, and Peaceable Possession. Before them came a pageant representing a Castle, drawn by four savages clad in green, covered over with ivy, and grim surly vizards on their faces, so to the life, that they had almost frightened Sancho. On the frontispiece, and on every quarter of the edifice, was inscribed, 'The Castle of Wise Reservedness.' Four expert musicians played to them on pipe and tabour. Cupid began the dance, and, after two movements, he cast up his eyes, and bent his bow against a virgin that stood upon the battlements of the castle, addressing himself in this manner:

THE MASQUE

LOVE

'My name is Love, supreme my sway,
    The greatest good and greatest pain,
  Air, earth, and seas, my power obey,
    And gods themselves must drag my chain.

'In every heart my throne I keep,
    Fear ne'er could daunt my daring soul;
  I fire the bosom of the deep,
    And the profoundest hell control.'

Having spoken these verses, Cupid shot an arrow over the castle, and retired to his station. Then Wealth advanced, and performed two movements; after which the music stopped, and he expressed himself thus:

WEALTH

'Love's my incentive and my end,
    But I'm a greater power than Love:
Tho' earthly born I earth transcend,
    For Wealth's a blessing from above.

'Bright maid, with me receive and bless
    The surest pledge of all success;
Desir'd by all, us'd right by few,
    But best bestow'd when grac'd by you.'

Wealth withdrew, and Poesy came forward, and after she had performed her movements like the rest, fixing her eyes upon the lady of the castle, repeated these lines:

POESY

'Sweet Poesy in moving lays
    Love into hearts, sense into souls conveys;
With sacred rage can tune to bless or woe,
    Sways all the man, and gives him heav'n below.

'Bright nymph with every grace adorn'd,
    Shall noble verse by thee be scorn'd?
'Tis wit can best thy beauty prize;
    Then raise the muse, and thou by her shalt rise.'

Poesy retired, and Liberality advanced from Wealth's side, and after the dance spoke thus:

LIBERALITY

'Behold that noble golden mean
    Betwixt the sparing and profuse;
Good sense and merit must be seen
    Where Liberality's in use.

'But I for thee will lavish seem;
    For thee profuseness I'll approve:
For, where the merit is extreme,
    Who'd not be prodigal of love?'

In this manner all the persons of each party advanced and spoke their verses, of which some were pretty, and some foolish enough. Among the rest, Don Quixote, though he had a good memory, remembered only those here set down. Then the two divisions joined into a very pretty country dance; and still as Cupid passed by the castle he shot a flight of arrows, and Wealth battered it with golden balls; then drawing out a great purse of Roman cat's-skin, that seemed full of money, he threw it against the castle, the boards of which were presently disjointed, and fell down, leaving the virgin discovered without any defence. Thereupon Wealth immediately entered with his party, and throwing a golden chain about her neck, made a show of leading her prisoner: but then Cupid with his attendants came to her rescue; and both parties engaging, were parted by the savages, who, joining the boards together, enclosed the virgin as before; and all was performed with measure, and to the music, that played all the while; and so the show ended, to the great content of the spectators. When all was over, Don Quixote asked one of the nymphs who it was that composed the entertainment? She answered, that it was a certain clergyman who lived in their town, that had a rare talent that way. 'I dare lay a wager,' said Don Quixote, 'he was more a friend to Basil than to Camacho, and knows better what belongs to a play than a prayer-book: he has expressed Basil's parts and Camacho's estate very naturally in the design of your dance.' 'God bless the King and Camacho, say I,' quoth Sancho, who heard this. 'Well, Sancho,' says Don Quixote, 'thou art a white-livered rogue, to change parties as thou dost; thou art like the rabble, which always cry, "Long live the conqueror." ' 'I know not what I am like,' replied Sancho; 'but this I know, that this kettleful of geese and hens is a bribe for a prince. Camacho has filled my belly, and therefore has won my heart. When shall I ladle out such dainty *scum* out of Basil's porridge-pots,' added he, showing his master the meat and falling on lustily; 'therefore a fig for his abilities, say I. As he sows so let him reap, and as he reaps so let him sow. My old grannum (rest her soul) was wont to say, there were but two families in the world Have-much and Have-little; and she had ever a great kindness for the family of the Have-much. A doctor gives his advice by the pulse of your pocket; and an ass covered with gold, looks better than a horse with a pack-saddle: so once more I say, Camacho for my money.' 'Hast thou not done yet?' said Don Quixote. 'I must have done,' answered Sancho 'because I find you begin to be in a passion, else I had work cut out for three days and a half.' 'Well,' said Don Quixote, 'thou wilt never be silent till thy mouth is full of clay; when thou art dead, I hope I shall have some rest.' 'Faith and troth now, master,' quoth Sancho, 'you did ill to talk of death, Heaven bless us, it is no child's play; you have e'en spoiled my dinner; the very thought of raw bones and lanthorn jaws make me sick. Death eats up all things, both the young lamb and old sheep; and I have heard our parson say, death values a prince no more than a clown; all is fish that comes to his net; he throws at all, and sweeps stakes; he is no mower that takes a nap at noon-day, but drives on, fair weather or foul, and cuts down the green grass as well as the ripe corn: he is neither squeamish nor queasy-stomached, for he swallows without chewing, and crams down all things into his ungracious maw; and though you can see no belly he has, he has a confounded dropsy, and thirsts after men's lives, which he guzzles down like mother's milk.' 'Hold, hold,' cried the Knight, 'go no further, for thou art come to a very handsome period; thou hast said as much of death in thy home-spun cant, as a good preacher could have done: thou hast got the knack of preaching, man! I must get thee a pulpit and benefice, I think.' 'He preaches well that lives well,' quoth Sancho; 'that is all the divinity I understand.' 'Thou hast divinity enough,' said the Don; 'only I wonder at one thing: it is said the beginning of wisdom proceeds from the fear of Heaven; how happens it then that thou, who fearest a lizard more than Omnipotence, shouldst be so wise?' 'Pray, sir,' replied Sancho, 'judge you of your knight errantry, and do not meddle with other men's fears, for I am as pretty a fearer of Heaven as any of my neighbours; and so let me dispatch this *scum* (and much good may it do thee, honest Sancho); consider, sir, we must give an account of our idle words another day; I must have the other pluck at the kettle.' With that he attacked it with so courageous an appetite, that he sharpened his master's, who would certainly have kept him company had he not been prevented by that which necessity obliges me to relate this instant.

CHAPTER XXI

The progress of Camacho's Wedding, with other delightful accidents

WHILE DON QUIXOTE AND SANCHO were discoursing, as the former chapter has told, they were interrupted by a great noise of joy and acclamations raised by the horsemen, who shouting and galloping went to meet the young couple, who, surrounded by a thousand instruments and devices, were coming to the arbour, accompanied by the curate, their relations, and all the better sort of the neighbourhood, set out in their holiday-clothes. 'Hey-day!' quoth Sancho, as soon as he saw the bride, 'what have we here? Adzookers, this is no country lass, but a fine court lady, all in her silks and satins, by the mass! Look, look ye, master, see if instead of glass-necklaces, she has not on fillets of rich coral; and instead of green serge of Cuencha, a thirty-piled velvet. I will warrant her lacing is white linen too; but hold, may I never squint if it be not satin. Bless us! see what rings she has on her fingers, no jet, no pewter baubles, pure beaten gold, as I am a sinner, and set with pearls too! If every pearl be not as white as a syllabub, and each of them as precious as an eye! How she is bedizened, and glistens from top to toe! And now yonder again, what fine long locks the young slut has got! If they be not false, I never saw longer in my born days: ah jade! what a fine stately person she is! What a number of trinkets and glaring gewgaws are dangling in her hair and about her neck! Cudsniggers, she puts me in mind of an overloaden date-tree! On my conscience, she is a juicy bit, a mettled wench, and well might pass muster in Flanders. Well! I say no more, but happy is the man that has thee!' Don Quixote could not help smiling to hear Sancho set forth the bride after his rustic way, though at the same time he beheld her with admiration, thinking her the most beautiful woman he had ever seen except his mistress Dulcinea. However, the fair Quiteria appeared somewhat pale, probably with the ill rest which brides commonly have the night before they are married, in order to dress themselves to advantage. There was a large scaffold erected on one side of the meadow, and adorned with carpets and boughs, for the marriage ceremony, and the more convenient prospect of the shows and entertainments. The procession was just arrived to this place, when they heard a piercing outcry, and a voice calling out, 'Stay, rash and hasty people, stay: 'upon which all turning about, they saw a person coming after them in a black coat, bordered with crimson, powdered with flames of fire. On his head he wore a garland of mournful cypress, and a large truncheon in his hand, headed with an iron spike. As soon as he drew near, they knew him to be the gallant Basil, and the whole assembly began to fear some mischief would ensue, seeing him come thus unlooked for, and with such an outcry and behaviour. He came up tired and panting before the bride and bridegroom; then leaning on his truncheon, he fixed his eyes on Quiteria, turning pale and trembling at the same time, and with a fearful hollow voice, 'Too well you know,' cried he, 'unkind Quiteria, that, by the ties of truth, and law of that Heaven which we all revere, while I have life you cannot be married to another. You may remember, too, that all the while I stayed, hoping that time and industry might better my fortune, and render me a match more equal to you, I never offered to transcend the bounds of honourable love, by soliciting favours to the prejudice of your virtue. But you, forgetting all the ties between us, are going now to break them, and give my right to another, whose large possessions, though they can procure him all other blessings, I had never envied, could they not have purchased you. But no more, the fates have ordained it, and I will further their design, by removing this unhappy obstacle out of your way. Live, rich Camacho, live happy with the ungrateful Quiteria many years, and let the poor, the miserable Basil die, whose poverty has clipped the wings of his felicity, and laid him in the grave!' Saying these last words, he drew out of his supposed truncheon a short tuck that was concealed in it, and setting the hilt of it to the ground, he fell upon the point in such a manner that it came out all bloody at his back, the poor wretch weltering on the ground in blood. His friends, strangely confounded by this sad accident, ran to help him, and Don Quixote, forsaking Rozinante, made haste to his assistance, and taking him up in his arms, found there was still life in him. They would have drawn the sword out of his body, but the curate urged it was not convenient till he made confession, and prepared himself for death, which would immediately attend the effusion of blood, upon pulling the tuck out of his body. While they were debating this point, Basil seemed to come a little to himself, and calling on the bride: 'Oh! Quiteria,' said he with a faint and doleful voice, 'now, now, in this last and departing minute of my life, even in this dreadful agony of death, would you but vouchsafe to give me your hand, and own yourself my wife, I should think myself rewarded for the torments I endure; and pleased to think this desperate deed made me yours, though but for a moment, I would die contented.' The curate hearing this, very earnestly recommended to him the care of his soul's health, which at the present juncture was more proper than any gratification of his outward man; that his time was but short, and he ought to be very earnest with Heaven, in imploring its mercy and forgiveness for all his sins, but especially for this last desperate action. To which Basil answered, 'That he could think of no happiness till Quiteria yielded to be his; but if she would do it, that satisfaction would calm his spirits, and dispose him to confess himself heartily.' Don Quixote hearing this, cried out aloud that Basil's demand was just and reasonable, and that Signior Camacho might as honourably receive her as the worthy Basil's widow, as if he had received her at her father's hands. 'Say but the word, madam,' continued he, 'pronounce it once to save a man from despair and damnation; you will not be long bound to it, since the nuptial bed of this bridegroom must be the grave.' Camacho stood all this while strangely confounded, till at last he was prevailed on, by the repeated importunities of Basil's friends to consent that Quiteria should humour the dying man, knowing her own happiness would thereby be deferred but a few minutes longer. Then they all bent their entreaties to Quiteria, some with tears in their eyes, others with all the engaging arguments their pity could suggest. She stood a long time inexorable, and did not return any answer, till at last the curate came to her, and bid her resolve what she would do; for Basil was just ready to give up the ghost. But then the poor virgin, trembling and dismayed, without speaking a word, came to poor Basil, who lay gasping for breath, with his eyes fixed in his head as if he were just expiring; she kneeled down by him, and with the most manifest signs of grief beckoned to him for his hand. Then Basil opening his eyes, and fixing them in a languishing posture on hers, 'Oh! Quiteria,' said he, 'your heart at last relents when your pity comes too late. Thy arms are now extended to relieve me, when those of death draws me to their embraces; and they, alas! are much too strong for thine. All I desire of thee, O fatal beauty, is this, let not that fair hand deceive me now, as it has done before, but confess, that what you do is free and voluntary, without constraint, or in compliance to any one's commands; declare me openly thy true and lawful husband: thou wilt not sure dissemble with one in death, and deal falsely with his departing soul, that all his life has been true to thee.' In the midst of all this discourse he fainted away, and all the by-standers thought him gone. The poor Quiteria, with a blushing modesty, a kind of violence upon herself, took him by the hand with a great deal of emotion: 'No force,' said she, 'could ever work upon my will to this degree, therefore believe it purely my own free will and inclination, that I here publicly declare you my only lawful husband: here is my hand in pledge, and I expect yours in return, if your pains and this sudden accident have not yet bereft you of all sense.' 'I give it you,' said Basil, with all the presence of mind imaginable, 'and here I own myself thy husband.' 'And I thy wife,' said she, 'whether thy life be long, or whether from my arms they bear thee this instant to the grave.' 'Methinks,' quoth Sancho, 'this young man talks too much for a man in his condition; pray advise him to leave off his wooing, and mind his soul's health. I am afraid his death is more in his tongue than between his teeth.'

Now when Basil and Quiteria had thus plighted their faith to each other, while yet their hands were joined together, the tender-hearted curate, with tears in his eyes, poured on them both the nuptial blessing, beseeching Heaven, at the same time, to have mercy on the new-married man's soul, and in a manner mixing the burial service with the matrimonial. As soon as the benediction was pronounced, up starts Basil briskly from the ground, and with an unexpected activity whips the sword out of his body, and caught his dear Quiteria close in his arms. All the spectators stood amazed, and some of the simpler sort stuck not to cry out, 'A miracle, a miracle!' 'No, no,' cried Basil, 'no miracle, no miracle, but a stratagem, a stratagem!' The curate, more astonished and concerned than all the rest, came with both his hands to feel the wound, and discovered that the sword had nowhere passed through the cunning Basil's body, but only through a tin pipe full of blood artfully fitted to his body, and, as it was afterwards known, so prepared that the blood could not congeal. In short, the curate, Camacho, and the company, found they had all been egregiously imposed upon. As for the bride, she was far from being displeased, that hearing it urged that the marriage could not stand good in law, because it was fraudulent and deceitful, she publicly declared that she again confirmed it to be just, and by the free consent of both parties.

Camacho and his friends, judging by this that the trick was premeditated, and that she was privy to the plot, enraged at this horrid disappointment, had recourse to a stronger argument, and drawing their swords, set furiously on Basil, in whose defence as many were immediately unsheathed. Don Quixote immediately mounting, with his lance couched and covered with his shield, led the van of Basil's party, and falling in with the enemy, charged clear through the gross of their battalia. Sancho, who never liked any dangerous work, resolved to stand neuter, and so retired under the walls of the mighty pot whence he had got the precious skimmings, thinking that would be respected whatever side gained the battle. Don Quixote addressing himself to Camacho's party, 'Hold, gentlemen,' cried he, 'it is not just thus with arms to redress the injuries of love. Love and war are the same thing, and stratagems and policy are as allowable in the one as in the other. Quiteria was designed for Basil, and he for her, by the unalterable decrees of Heaven. Camacho's riches may purchase him a bride, and more content elsewhere; and "those whom Heaven has joined let no man put asunder." Basil had but this one lamb, and the lamb of his bosom, let none therefore offer to take his single delight from him, though presuming on his power; for here I solemnly declare, that he who first attempts it must pass through me, and this lance through him.' At which he shook his lance in the air with such vigour and dexterity, that he cast a sudden terror into those that beheld him, who did not know the threatening champion. In short, Don Quixote's words, the good curate's diligent mediation, together with Quiteria's inconstancy brought Camacho to a truce; and he then discreetly considered that since Quiteria loved Basil before marriage, it was probable she would love him afterwards, and that therefore he had more reason to thank Heaven for so good a riddance, than to repine at losing her. This thought, improved by some other considerations, brought both parties to a fair accommodation; and Camacho to show he did not resent the disappointment, blaming rather Quiteria's levity than Basil's policy, invited the whole company to stay, and take share of what he had provided. But Basil, whose virtues, in spite of his poverty, had secured him many friends, drew away part of the company to attend him and his bride to her own town; and among the rest Don Quixote, whom they all honoured as a person of extraordinary worth and bravery. Poor Sancho followed his master with a heavy heart; he could not be reconciled to the thoughts of turning his back so soon upon the good cheer and jollity at Camacho's feast, that lasted till night; and had a strange hankering after those dear fleshpots of Egypt, which though he left behind in reality, he carried along with him in mind. The beloved *scum* which he had, that was nigh glutted already, made him view with sorrow the almost empty kettle, the dear casket where his treasure lay: so that stomaching mightily his master's defection from Camacho's feast, he sullenly paced on after Rozinante, very much out of humour, though he had just filled his belly.

CHAPTER XXII

An account of the great Adventure of Montesinos' Cave, situated in the heart of La Mancha, which the valorous Don Quixote successfully achieved

THE NEW-MARRIED COUPLE entertained Don Quixote very nobly, in acknowledgment of his readiness to defend their cause, they esteemed his wisdom equal to his valour, and thought him both a Cid in arms, and a Cicero in arts. Honest Sancho, too, recruited himself to the purpose, during the three days his master stayed, and so came to his good humour again. Basil then informed them, that Quiteria knew nothing of his stratagem: but being a pure device of his own, he had made some of his nearest friends acquainted with it, that they should stand by him if occasion were, and bring him off upon the discovery of the deceit. 'It deserves a handsomer name,' said Don Quixote, 'since conducive to so good and honourable an end, as the marriage of a loving couple. By the way, sir, you must know that the greatest obstacle to love is want, and a narrow fortune: For the continual bands and cements of mutual affection are mirth, content, satisfaction, and jollity. These, managed by skilful hands, can make variety in the pleasures of wedlock, preparing the same thing always with some additional circumstance, to render it new and delightful. But when pressing necessity and indigence deprive us of those pleasures that prevent satiety, the yoke of matrimony is often found very galling, and the burden intolerable.' These words were chiefly directed by Don Quixote to Basil, to advise him by the way to give over those airy sports and exercises, which indeed might fill his youth with praise, but not his old age with bread, and to bethink himself of some grave and substantial employment, that might afford him a competency, and something of a stock for his declining years. Then pursuing his discourse: 'The honorable poor man,' said he, 'if the poor can deserve that epithet, when he has a beautiful wife, is blessed with a jewel: he that deprives him of her, robs him of his honour, and may be said to deprive him of his life. The woman that is beautiful, and keeps her honesty when her husband is poor, deserves to be crowned with laurel, as the conquerors were of old. Beauty is a tempting bait, that attracts the eyes of all beholders, and the princely eagles, and the most high-flown birds stoop to its pleasing lure. But when they find it in necessity, then kites and crows, and other ravenous birds, will all be grappling with the alluring prey. She that can withstand these dangerous attacks, well deserves to be the crown of her husband. However, sir, take this along with you, as the opinion of a wise man, whose name I have forgot; he said there was but one good woman in the world, and his advice was, that every married man should think his own wife was she, as being the only way to live contented. For my own part, I need not make the application to myself, for I am not married, nor have I as yet any thoughts that way; but if I had, it would not be a woman's fortune, but her character, should recommend her; for public reputation is the life of a lady's virtue, and the outward appearance of modesty is in one sense as good as the reality; since a private sin is not so prejudicial in this world, as a public indecency. If you bring a woman honest to your bosom, it is easy keeping her so, and perhaps you may improve her virtues. If you take an unchaste partner to your bed, it is hard mending her; for the extremes of vice and virtue are so great in a woman, and their points so far asunder, that it is very improbable, I will not say impossible, they should ever be reconciled.' Sancho, who had patiently listened so far, could not forbear making some remarks on his master's talk. 'This master of mine,' thought he to himself, 'when I am talking some good things, full of pith and marrow, as he may be now, was wont to tell me that I should tie a pulpit at my back, and stroll with it about the world to retail my rarities: but I might as well tell him that when once he begins to tack his sentences together, a single pulpit is too little for him; he had need have two for every finger, and go peddling about the market and cry, "Who buys my ware?" Old Nick take him for a knight-errant! I think he is one of the seven wise masters. I thought he knew nothing but his knight-errantry, but now I see the devil a thing can escape him; he has an oar in every man's boat, and a finger in every pie.' As he muttered this somewhat loud, his master overheard him. 'What is that thou art grumbling about, Sancho?' said he. 'Nothing, sir, nothing,' quoth Sancho. 'I was only wishing I had heard your worship preach this doctrine before I married, then mayhap I might have with the old proverb said, "A sound man needs no physician." ' 'What is Teresa so bad, then?' asked Don Quixote. 'Not so very bad neither,' answered Sancho; 'nor yet so good as I would have her.' 'Fie, Sancho,' said Don Quixote, 'thou dost not do well to speak ill of thy wife, who is a good mother to thy children.' 'There is no love lost, sir,' quoth Sancho, 'for she speaks as ill of me, when the fit takes her, especially when she is in one of her jealous moods, for then Old Nick himself could not hear her maundering.'

Don Quixote, having tarried three days with the young couple, and been entertained like a prince, he entreated the student, who fenced so well, to help him to a guide that might conduct him to Montesinos' cave, resolving to go down into it, and prove by his own eyesight the wonders that were reported of it round the country. The student recommended a cousin-german of his for his conductor, who, he said, was an ingenious lad, a pretty scholar, and a great admirer of books of knight-errantry, and could show him the famous lake of Ruydera too: adding, that he would be very good company for the Knight, as being one that wrote books for the booksellers, in order to dedicate them to great men. Accordingly, the learned cousin came, mounted on an ass with foal; his pack-saddle covered with an old carpet, or coarse packing-cloth. Thereupon Sancho having got ready Rozinante and Dapple, well stuffed his wallet and the student's knapsack to boot, they all took their leave, steering the nearest course to Montesinos' cave. To pass the time on the road, Don Quixote asked the guide, to what course of study he chiefly applied himself. 'Sir,' answered the scholar, 'my business is writing, and copy-money my chief study. I have published some things with the general approbation of the world, and much to my own advantage. Perhaps, sir, you may have heard of one of my books, called "The Treatise of Liveries and Devices"; in which I have obliged the public with no less than seven hundred and three sorts of liveries and devices, with their colours, mottoes, and ciphers; so that any courtier may furnish himself there upon any extraordinary appearance, with what may suit his fancy or his circumstances, without racking his own invention to find what is agreeable to his inclination. I can furnish the jealous, the forsaken, the disdained, the absent, with what will fit them to a hair. Another piece which I now have on the anvil, I design to call the "Metamorphosis," or "The Spanish Ovid"; an invention very new and extraordinary. It is, in short, "Ovid burlesqued"; wherein I discover who the Giralda* of Seville was; who the angel of the Magdalen: I tell ye what was the pipe of Vicenguerra of Cordova, what the bulls of Guisando, the Sierra Morena, the fountains of Leganitos, and Lavapies at Madrid; not forgetting that of Piojo, nor those of the golden pipe, and the abbey; and I embellish the fables with allegories, metaphors, and translations, that will both delight and instruct. Another work, which I soon design for the press, I call a supplement to "Polydore Virgil," concerning the invention of things, a piece I will assure you, sir, that shows the great learning of the compiler, and perhaps in a better style than the old author. For example, he has forgot to tell us, who was the first that was troubled with a catarrh in the world, and who was the first that was fluxed for the French disease. Now, sir, I immediately resolve it, and confirm my assertion by the testimony of at least four-and-twenty authentic writers; by which quotations

* All these are noted things, or places in Spain, on which many fabulous stories are grounded.

alone you may guess, sir, at what pains I have been to instruct and benefit
the public.'

Sancho having hearkened with great attention all this while, 'Pray, sir,'
quoth he to him, 'so Heaven guide your right hand in all you write, let me
ask you, who was the first man that scratched his head?' 'Scratched his
head, friend,' answered the author. 'Ay, sir, scratched his head,' quoth
Sancho: 'sure you that know all things can tell me that, or the devil is in it!
What think you of old father Adam?' 'Old father Adam!' answered the
scholar; 'let me see – father Adam had a head, he had hair, he had hands,
and he could scratch: but father Adam was the first man, *ergo*, Father
Adam was the first man that scratched his head. It is plain you are in the
right.' 'Oh ho, am I so, sir,' quoth Sancho. 'Another question by your
leave, sir: who was the first tumbler in the world?' 'Truly, friend,'
answered the student, 'that is a point I cannot resolve you without
consulting my books; but as soon as ever I get home, I will study night and
day to find it out.' 'For two fair words,' quoth Sancho, 'I will save you that
trouble. 'Can you resolve that doubt,' asked the author?' 'Ay, marry, can
I,' said Sancho: 'the first tumbler in the world was Lucifer; when he was
cast out of heaven, he tumbled into hell.' 'You are positively in the right,'
said the scholar. 'Where did you get that, Sancho?' said Don Quixote, 'for
I dare swear it is none of your own.' 'Mum,' quoth Sancho; 'in asking of
foolish questions, and selling of bargains, let Sancho alone, quoth l; I do
not want the help of my neighbours.' 'Truly,' said Don Quixote, 'thou
hast given thy question a better epithet than thou art aware of: for there
are some men who busy their heads, and lose a world of time in making
discoveries, the knowledge of which is good for nothing upon the earth,
unless it be to make the discoverers laughed at.'

With these, and such diverting discourses, they passed their journey, till
they came to the cave the next day, having lain the night before in an
inconsiderable village on the road. There they bought an hundred fathom
of cordage to hang Don Quixote by, and let him down to the lowest part
of the cave; he being resolved to go to the very bottom, were it as deep as
hell. The mouth of it was inaccessible, being quite stopped up with weeds,
bushes, brambles, and wild fig-trees, though the entrance was wide and
spacious. Don Quixote was no sooner come to the place but he prepared
for his expedition into that under world, telling the scholar, that he was
resolved to reach the bottom, though deep as the profound abyss; and all
having alighted, the squire and his guide accordingly girt him fast with a
rope. While this was doing, 'Good sweet sir,' quoth Sancho, 'consider
what you do. Do not venture into such a cursed black hole! Look before
you leap, sir, and be not so wilful as to bury yourself alive. Do not hang
yourself like a bottle or a bucket, that is let down to be soused in a well.
Alack-a-day, sir, it is none of your business to pry thus into every hole, and

go down to the pit of hell for the nonce!' 'Peace, coward,' said the Knight, 'and bind me fast; for surely for me such an enterprise as this is reserved.' 'Pray, sir,' said the student, 'when you are in be very vigilant in exploring and observing all the rarities in the place. Let nothing escape your eyes, perhaps you may discover there some things worthy to be inserted in my "Metamorphosis." ' 'Let him alone,' quoth Sancho, 'he will go through stitch with it; he will make a hog or a dog of it, I will warrant you.' Don Quixote being well bound, not over his armour but his doublet, bethought himself of one thing they had forgot. 'We did ill,' said he, 'not to provide ourselves of a little bell, that I should have carried down with me, to ring for more or less rope, as I may have occasion for, and inform you of my being alive. But since there is no remedy, Heaven prosper me.' Then kneeling down, he in a low voice recommended himself to the Divine Providence for assistance and success in so strange, and so dangerous an adventure. Then raising his voice, 'O thou mistress of my life and motions,' cried he, 'most illustrious and peerless Dulcinea del Toboso, if the prayers of an adventurous absent lover may reach the ears of the far-distant object of his wishes, by the power of thy unspeakable beauty I conjure thee to grant me thy favour and protection, in this plunge and precipice of my fortune. I am now going to engulf and cast myself into this dismal profundity, that the world may know nothing can be impossible to him, who, influenced by thy smiles, attempts under the banner of thy beauty the most difficult task.' This said, he got up again, and approaching the entrance of the cave, he found it stopped up with brakes and bushes, so that he must be obliged to make his way by force. Whereupon, drawing his sword, he began to cut and slash the brambles that stopped up the mouth of the cave, when presently an infinite number of overgrown crows and daws came rushing and fluttering out of the cave about his ears, so thick, and with such impetuosity, as overwhelmed him to the ground. He was not superstitious enough to draw any ill omen from the flight of the birds; besides, it was no small encouragement to him, that he spied no bats or owls, nor other ill-boding birds of night among them: he therefore rose again with an undaunted heart, and committed himself to the black and dreadful abyss. But Sancho first gave him his benediction, and making a thousand crosses over him, 'Heaven be thy guide,' quoth he, 'and our Lady of the Rock in France, with the Trinity of Gaeta,* thou flower and cream, and scum of all knights-errant! Go thy ways, thou hackster of the world, heart of steel, and arms of brass! And mayest thou come back sound, wind and limb, out of this dreadful hole, which thou art running into, once more to see the warm sun which thou art now leaving.'

The scholar too prayed to the same effect for the Knight's happy

* Particular places of devotion.

return. Don Quixote then called for more rope, which they gave him by
degrees, till his voice was drowned in the windings of the cave, and their
cordage was run out. That done they began to consider whether they
should hoist him up again immediately or no; however, they resolved to
stay half-an-hour, and then they began to draw up the rope, but were
strangely surprised to find no weight upon it; which made them conclude
the poor gentleman was certainly lost. Sancho, bursting out in tears, made
a heavy lamentation, and fell a-hauling up the rope as fast as he could, to
be thoroughly satisfied. But after they had drawn up about four score
fathoms, they felt a weight again, which made them take heart; and at
length they plainly saw Don Quixote. 'Welcome,' cried Sancho to him, as
soon as he came in sight; 'welcome, dear master, I am glad you are come
again; we were afraid you had been pawned for the reckoning.' But
Sancho had no answer to his compliment; and when they had pulled the
Knight quite up, they found that his eyes were closed as if he had been fast
asleep. They laid him on the ground, and unbound him, yet he made no
sign of waking; and all their turning and shaking was little enough to make
him come to himself. At last he began to stretch his limbs, as if he had
wakened out of the most profound sleep, and staring wildly about him:
'Heaven forgive you, friends,' cried he, 'for you have raised me from one
of the sweetest lives that ever mortal led, and most delightful sights that
ever eyes beheld. Now I perceive how fleeting are all the joys of this
transitory life; they are but an imperfect dream, they fade like a flower,
and vanish like a shadow. Oh, ill-fated Montesinos! Oh, Durandarte,
unfortunately wounded! Oh, unhappy Belerma! Oh, deplorable Guadiana!
and you, the distressed daughters of Ruydera, whose flowing waters show
what streams of tears once trickled from your lovely eyes!' These
expressions, uttered with great passion and concern, surprised the scholar
and Sancho, and they desired to know his meaning, and what he had seen
in that hell upon earth. 'Call it not hell,' answered Don Quixote, 'for it
deserves a better name, as I shall soon let you know. But first give me
something to eat, for I am prodigiously hungry.' They then spread the
scholar's coarse saddle-cloth for a carpet; and examining their old cup
board, the knapsack, they all three sat down on the grass, and ate heartily
together, like men that were a meal or two behind-hand. When they had
done, 'Let no man stir,' said Don Quixote; 'sit still and hear me with
attention.'

CHAPTER XXIII

Of the wonderful things that the unparalleled Don Quixote declared he had seen in the deep Cave of Montesinos, the greatness and impossibility of which makes this Adventure pass for apocryphal

IT WAS NOW FOUR in the afternoon, and the sun was opportunely hid behind the clouds, which interposing between his rays, invited Don Quixote, without heat or trouble, to relate to his illustrious auditors the wonders he had seen in Montesinos' cave.

'About twelve or fourteen men's depth,' said he, 'in the profundity of this cavern, on the right hand, there is a concavity wide enough to contain a large wagon, mules and all. This place is not wholly dark, for through some chinks and narrow holes, that reach to the distant surface of the earth, there comes a glimmering light. I discovered this recess, being already weary of hanging by the loins, discouraged by the profound darkness of the region below me, destitute of a guide, and not knowing whither I went: resolving therefore to rest myself there a while, I called to you to give me no more rope, but it seems you did not hear me. I therefore entered, and coiling up the cord, sat upon it very melancholy, and thinking how I should most conveniently get down to the bottom, having nobody to guide or support me. While thus I sat pensive, and lost in thought, insensibly, without any previous drowsiness, I found myself surprised by sleep; and after that, not knowing how, nor. which way I wakened, I unexpectedly found myself in the finest, the sweetest, and most delightful meadow that ever nature adorned with her beauties, or the most inventive fancy could ever imagine. Now, that I might be sure this was neither a dream nor illusion, I rubbed my eyes, blowed my nose, and felt several parts of my body, and convinced myself that I was really awake, with the use of all my senses, and all the faculties of my understanding sound and active as at this moment.

'Presently I discovered a royal and sumptuous palace, of which the walls and battlements seemed all of clear and transparent crystal. At the same time, the spacious gates opening, there came out towards me a venerable old man, clad in a sad-coloured robe, so long that it swept the ground; on his breast and shoulders he had a green satin tippet, after the manner of those worn in colleges. On his head he wore a black Milan cap, and his broad hoary beard reached down below his middle. He had no kind of weapon in his hands, but a rosary of beads about the bigness of walnuts, and his credo-beads appeared as large as ordinary ostrich eggs. The awful and grave aspect, the pace, the port and goodly presence of this old man, each of them apart, and much more altogether, struck me with veneration and astonishment. He came up to me, and without any previous ceremony embracing me close, "It is a long time," said he, "most renowned Knight, Don Quixote de la Mancha, that we who dwell in this enchanted solitude` have hoped to see you here; that you may inform the upper world of the surprising prodigies concealed from human knowledge in this subterranean hollow, called the Cave of Montesinos; an enterprise reserved alone for your insuperable heart and stupendous resolution. Go with me then, thou most illustrious Knight, and behold the wonders enclosed within this transparent castle, of which I am the perpetual governor and chief warden, being the same individual Montesinos from whom this cavern took its name."

'No sooner had the reverend old man let me know who he was, but I entreated him to tell me whether it was true or no, that, at his friend Durandarte's dying request, he had taken out his heart with a small dagger, the very moment he expired, and carried it to his mistress, Belerma, as the story was current in the world? "It is literally true," answered the old gentleman, "except that single circumstance of the dagger; for I used neither a small nor a large dagger on this occasion, but a well-polished poniard, as sharp as an awl." ' 'I will be hanged,' quoth Sancho, 'if it was not one of your Seville poniards of Raymond de Hoze's making.' 'That cannot be,' said Don Quixote, 'for that cutler lived but the other day, and the battle of Roncesvalles, where this accident happened, was fought many years ago: but this is of no importance to the story.' 'You are in the right, sir,' said the student, 'and pray go on, for I hearken to your relation with the greatest satisfaction imaginable.' 'That, sir,' said the Knight, 'increases my pleasure in telling it. But, to proceed: the venerable Montesinos, having conducted me into the crystal palace, led me into a spacious ground-room, exceeding cool, and all of alabaster. In the middle of it stood a stately marble tomb, that seemed a masterpiece of art; upon which lay a knight extended all at length, not of stone or brass, as on other monuments, but pure flesh and bones: he covered the region of his heart with his right hand, which seemed to me somewhat hairy, and very full of sinews, a sign of the great strength of the body to which it belonged. Montesinos observing that I viewed this spectacle with surprise, "Behold," said he, "the flower and mirror of all the amorous and valiant knights of his age, my friend Durandarte, who, together with me and many others of both sexes, are kept here enchanted by Merlin that British magician, who, they say was the son of the Devil; though I cannot believe it, only his knowledge was so great, that he might be said to know more than the Devil. Here I say we are enchanted, but how, and for what cause no man can tell, though time I hope will shortly reveal it. But the most wonderful part of my fortune is this, I am as certain as that the sun now shines, that Durandarte died in my arms; and that with these hands I took out his heart, by the same token that it weighed above two pounds, a sure mark of his courage; for, by the rules of natural philosophy, the most valiant men have still the biggest hearts. Nevertheless, though this knight really died, he still complains and sighs sometimes, as if he were alive." Scarce had Montesinos spoke these words, but the miserable Durandarte cried out aloud, "Oh! cousin Montesinos, the last and dying request of your departing friend, was to take my heart out of my breast with a poniard or a dagger, and carry it to Belerma."

'The venerable Montesinos hearing this fell on his knees before the afflicted knight, and with tears in his eyes, "Long, long ago," said he, "Durandarte, thou dearest of my kinsmen, have I performed what you enjoined me on that bitter, fatal day when you expired. I took out your heart with all imaginable care, not leaving the least particle of it in your breast: I gently wiped it with a laced handkerchief, and posted away with it to France, as soon as I had committed your dear remains to the bosom of the earth, having shed tears enough to have washed my hands clear of the blood they had gathered by plunging in your entrails. To confirm this truth yet further, at the first place where I stopped from Roncesvalles, I laid a little salt upon your heart, to preserve it from putrefaction, and keep it, if not fresh, at least free from any ill smell, till I presented it into the hands of Belerma, who with you and me, and Guadiana* your squire, as also Ruydera (the lady's woman) with her seven daughters, her two nieces, and many others of your friends and acquaintance, is here confined by the necromantic charms of the magician Merlin; and though it be now above five hundred years since we were first conveyed to this enchanted castle, we are still alive, except Ruydera, her daughters and nieces, who by the favour of Merlin, that pitied their tears, were turned into so many lakes, still extant in the world of the living, and in the province of La Mancha, distinguished by the names of the lakes of Ruydera; seven of them belong to the kings of Spain, and the two nieces to the knights of the most noble order of St. John. Your squire Guadiana, lamenting his hard fate, was in like manner metamorphosed into a river that bears his name; yet still so sensible of your disaster, that when he first arose out of the bowels of the earth to flow along its surface, and saw the sun in a strange hemisphere, he plunged again underground, striving to hide his melting sorrows from the world; but the natural current of his waters forcing a passage up again, he is compelled to appear where the sun and mortals may see him. Those lakes mixing their waters in his bosom, he swells, and glides along in

---

* Guadiana, a river in Spain, that sinks into the earth and rises again a great distance off.

sullen state to Portugal, often expressing his deep melancholy by the muddy and turbid colour of his streams; which, as they refuse to please the sight, so likewise they deny to indulge mortal appetite, by breeding such fair and savoury fish as may be found in the golden Tagus. All this I have often told you, my dearest Durandarte; and since you return me no answer, I must conclude you believe me not, or that you do not hear me; for which (witness it, Heaven) I am extremely grieved. But now I have other news to tell ye, which, though perhaps it may not assuage your sorrows, yet I am sure it will not increase them. Open your eyes, and behold in your presence that mighty Knight, of whom Merlin the sage has foretold so many wonders: that Don Quixote de la Mancha, I mean, who has not only restored to the world the function of knight-errantry, that has lain so long in oblivion, but advanced it to greater fame than it could boast in former ages, the nonage of the world. It is by his power we may expect to see the fatal charm dissolved, that keeps us here confined; for great performances are properly reserved for great personages." "And should it not be so?" answered the grieving Durandarte, with a faint and languishing voice. "Should it not be so, I say? Oh! cousin, 'patience, and shuffle the cards.' "* Then turning on one side, without speaking a word more, he relapsed into his usual silence. After this I was alarmed with piteous howling and crying, which, mixed with lamentable sighs and groans, obliged me to turn about, to see whence it proceeded. Then through the crystal wall I saw a mournful procession of most beautiful damsels, all in black, marching in two ranks, with turbans on their heads after the Turkish fashion; and last of all came a majestic lady, dressed also in mourning, with a long white veil, that reached from her head down to the ground. Her turban was twice as big as the biggest of the rest: she was somewhat beetle-browed, her nose was flattish, her mouth wide, but her lips red; her teeth, which she sometimes discovered, seemed to be thin and snaggy, but indeed as white as blanched almonds. She held a fine handkerchief, and within it I could perceive a heart of flesh, so dry and withered, that it looked like mummy. Montesinos informed me, that the procession consisted of Durandarte's and Belerma's servants, who were enchanted there with their master and mistress: but that the last was Belerma herself, who with her attendants used four days in the week constantly thus to sing, or rather howl their dirges over the heart and body of his cousin; and that though Belerma appeared a little haggard at that juncture, occasioned by the grief she bore in her own heart, for that which she carried in her hand, yet, had I seen her before her misfortunes had

---

* 'Patience and shuffle' is a Spanish proverb, like our 'patience perforce'; used by them, because those that lose at cards commonly used to shuffle them afterwards very much.

sunk her eyes and tarnished her complexion, worse than the diseases of her sex, from which she was free, I must have owned, that even the celebrated Dulcinea del Toboso, so famous in La Mancha, and over the whole universe, could scarce have vied with her in gracefulness and beauty. "Hold there, good Signior Don Montesinos," said I; "you know that comparisons are odious, therefore no more comparing, I beseech you; but go on with your story. The peerless Dulcinea del Toboso is what she is, and the Lady Belerma is what she is, and has been: so no more upon that subject."

' "I beg your pardon," answered Montesinos, "Signior Don Quixote, I might have guessed indeed that you were the lady Dulcinea's knight, and therefore I ought to have bit my tongue off, sooner than to have compared her to anything lower than Heaven itself." This satisfaction, which I thought sufficient from the great Montesinos, stifled the resentment I else had shown, for hearing my mistress compared to Belerma.' 'Nay, Mary,' quoth Sancho, 'I wonder you did not catch the old doating huncks by the weasond, and maul, and thrash him thick and threefold! How could you leave one hair on his chin!' 'No, no, Sancho,' answered Don Quixote, 'there is always a respect due to our seniors, though they be no knights; but most when they are such, and under the oppression of enchantment. However, I am satisfied, that in what discourse passed between us, I took care not to have anything that looked like an affront fixed upon me.' 'But, sir,' asked the scholar, 'how could you see and hear so many strange things in so little time? I cannot conceive how you could do it.' 'How long,' said Don Quixote, 'do you reckon that I have been in the cave?' 'A little above an hour,' answered Sancho. 'That is impossible,' said Don Quixote, 'for I saw morning and evening, evening and morning, three times since; so that I could not be absent less than three days from this upper world.' 'Ay, ay,' quoth Sancho, 'my master is in the right; for these enchantments, that have the greatest share in all his concerns, may make that seem three days and three nights to him, which is but an hour to other people.' 'It must be so,' said Don Quixote. 'I hope, sir,' said the scholar, 'you have eaten something in all that time?' 'Not one morsel,' replied Don Quixote, 'neither have I had the least desire to eat, or so much as thought of it all the while.' 'Do not they that are enchanted sometimes eat?' asked the scholar. 'They never do,' answered Don Quixote, 'and consequently they are never troubled with exonerating the dregs of food; though it is unlikely that their nails, their beards and hair still grow.' 'Do they never sleep neither?' said Sancho. 'Never' said Don Quixote; 'at least they never closed their eyes while I was among them.' 'Nor I neither,' quoth Sancho. 'This makes good the saying, "Tell me thy company, and I will tell thee what thou art." Troth, you have all been enchanted together. No wonder if you neither eat nor slept, since you were in the land of those that always watch and fast. But, sir, would you have me speak as I think! and pray do not take it in ill part, for I do not believe one word you have said – ' 'What do you mean, friend?' said the student. 'Do you think the noble Don Quixote would be guilty of a lie? And if he had a mind to stretch a little, could he, think you, have had leisure to frame such a number of stories in so short a time?' 'I do not think that my master would lie neither,' said Sancho. 'What do ye think, sir?' said Don Quixote. 'Why truly, sir,' quoth Sancho, 'I do believe that this same cunning man, this Merlin, that bewitched, or enchanted, as you call it, all that rabble of people you talk of, may have crammed and enchanted some way or other, all that you have told us, and have yet to tell us, into your noddle' 'It is not impossible but such a thing may happen,' said Don Quixote, 'though I am convinced it was otherwise with me; for I am positive that I saw with these eyes, and felt with these hands, all I have mentioned. But what will you think when I tell you, among many wonderful things, that I saw three country wenches leaping and skipping about those pleasant fields, like so many wild goats; and at first sight knew one of them to be the peerless Dulcinea, and the other two the very same we spoke to not far from Toboso. I asked Montesinos if he knew them? He answered in the negative; but imagined them some enchanted ladies, who were newly come, and that the appearance of strange faces was no rarity among them, for many of the past ages and the present were enchanted there, under several disguises; and that, among the rest, he knew Queen Guinever, and her woman Quintaniona, that officiated as Sir Lancelot's cup-bearer, as he came from Britain.'

Sancho hearing his master talk at that rate, had like to have forgot himself, and burst out a-laughing; for he well knew that Dulcinea's enchantment was a lie, and that he himself was the chief magician, and raiser of the story; and thence concluding his master stark mad: 'In an ill hour,' quoth he, 'dear master of mine, and in a woeful day, went your worship down to the other world, and in a worse hour met you with that plagued Montesinos, that has sent you back in this rueful pickle. You went hence in your right senses; could talk prettily enough now and then; had your handsome proverbs and wise sayings at every turn, and would give wholesome counsel to all that would take it: but now, bless me! you talk as if you had left your brains in the Devil's cellar.' 'I know thee, Sancho,' said Don Quixote, 'and therefore I regard thy words as little as possible.' 'And I yours,' replied Sancho. 'Nay, you may cripple, lame, or kill me, if you please, either for what I have said, or mean to say, I must speak my mind though I die for it. But before your blood's up, pray, sir, tell me, how did you know it was your mistress? Did you speak to her? What did she say to you? And what did you say to her?' 'I knew her again,' said Don Quixote, 'by the same clothes she wore when you showed her to me. I spoke to her; but she made no answer, but suddenly turned away, and fled from me like a whirlwind. I intended to have followed her, had not Montesinos told me it would be to no purpose; warning me besides, that it was high time to return to the upper air: and changing the discourse, he told me that I should hereafter be made acquainted with the means of disenchanting them all. But while Montesinos and I were thus talking together, a very odd accident, the thoughts of which trouble me still, broke off our conversation. For as we were in the height of our discourse, who should come to me but one of the unfortunate Dulcinea's companions, and before I was aware, with a faint and doleful voice, "Sir," said she, "my Lady Dulcinea del Toboso gives her service to you, and desires to know how you do; and being short of money at present, desires you, of all love and kindness, to lend her six reals upon this new fustian petticoat, or more or less as you can spare it, sir, and she will take care to redeem it very honestly in a little time." The message surprised me strangely, and therefore, turning to Montesinos, "Is it possible, sir," said I, "that persons of quality, when enchanted, are in want?" "Oh, very possible, sir," said he; "poverty ranges everywhere, and spares neither quality enchanted nor unenchanted; and therefore since the lady Dulcinea desires you to lend her these six reals, and the pawn is good, let her have the money; for sure it is very low with her at this time." "I scorn to take pawns," said I, "but my misfortune is, that I cannot answer the full request; for I have but four reals about me," and that was the money thou gavest me the other day, Sancho, to distribute among the poor. However, I gave her all I had, and desired her to tell her mistress, I was very sorry for her wants; and that if I had all the treasures which Crœsus possessed, they should be at her service; and withal, that I died every hour for want of her reviving company; and made it my humble and earnest request, that she would vouchsafe to see and converse with her captive servant, and weather-beaten knight: "tell her," continued I, "when she least expects it, she will come to hear how I made an oath, as the Marquis of Mantua did, when he found his nephew Baldwin ready to expire on the mountain, never to eat upon a table-cloth, and several other particulars which he swore to observe, till he had revenged his death; so in the like solemn manner will I swear, never to desist from traversing the habitable globe, and ranging through all the seven parts of the world, more indefatigable than ever was done by Prince Pedro of Portugal,* till I have freed her from her enchantment." "All this and more you owe my mistress," said the damsel; and then having got the four reals, instead of

---

* Prince Pedro of Portugal was a great traveller for the time he lived in, which gave occasion to the spreading of many fables concerning him, and which made the ignorant vulgar say, 'He travelled over the seven parts of the world.'

dropping me a courtesy, she cut me a caper in the air two yards high.'
'Now Heaven defend us!' cried Sancho. 'Who could ever have believed
that these devilish enchanters and enchantments should have so much
power as to bewitch my master at this rate, and craze his sound
understanding in this manner? Alas! sir, for the love of Heaven take care
of yourself. What will the world say of you? Rouse up your dozing senses,
and do not dote upon those whimsies, that have so wretchedly cracked
that rare head-piece of yours.' 'Well,' said Don Quixote, 'I cannot be
angry at thy ignorant tittle-tattle, because it proceeds from thy love
towards me. Thou thinkest, poor fellow, that whatever is beyond the
sphere of thy narrow comprehension must be impossible: but, as I have
already said, there will come a time when I shall give thee an account of
some things I have seen below, that will convince thee of the reality of
those I told thee now; the truth of which admits of no dispute.'

CHAPTER XXIV

Which gives an account of a thousand flimflams and
stories, as impertinent as necessary to the right
understanding of this grand History

THE TRANSLATOR of the famous history declares, that at the beginning
of the chapter, which treats of the adventure of Montesinos' cave, he
found a marginal annotation, written with the Arabian author's own hand,
in these words:

'I cannot be persuaded, nor believe, that all the wonderful accidents said
to have happened to the valorous Don Quixote in the cave, so punctually
befell him as he relates them: for, the course of his adventures hitherto has
been very natural, and bore the face of probability; but in this there
appears no coherence with reason, and nothing but monstrous incongrui-
ties. But, on the other hand, if we consider the honour, worth, and
integrity of the noble Don Quixote, we have not the least reason to
suspect he would be guilty of a lie; but rather that he would sooner have
been transfixed with arrows. Besides, he has been so particular in his
relation of that adventure, and given so many circumstances, that I dare
not declare it absolutely apocryphal; especially when I consider, that he
had not time enough to invent such a cluster of fables. I therefore insert it
among the rest, without offering to determine whether it is true or false;
leaving it to the discretion of the judicious reader. Though I must
acquaint him by the way, that Don Quixote, upon his death-bed, utterly
disowned this adventure, as a perfect fable, which he said he had invented

purely to please his humour, being suitable to such as he had formerly read in romances :' and so much by way of digression.

The scholar thought Sancho the most saucy servant, and his master the calmest madman that ever he saw; though he attributed the patience of the latter to a certain good humour and easiness of temper infused into him by the sight of his mistress Dulcinea, even under enchantment. Otherwise he would have thought his not checking Sancho a greater sign of madness than his discourse. 'Noble Don Quixote,' said he, 'for four principal reasons I am extremely pleased with having taken this journey with you. First, it has procured me the honour of your acquaintance, which I shall always esteem a singular happiness. In the second place, sir, the secrets of Montesinos' cave, and the transformations of Guadiana, and Ruydera's lakes, have been revealed to me, which may look very great in my "Spanish Ovid." My third advantage is, to have discovered the antiquity of card-playing, which I find to have been a pastime in use even in the Emperor Charles the Great's time, as may be collected from the words of Durandarte, who, after a long speech of Montesinos', said as he waked, "Patience and shuffle the cards,"* which vulgar expression he could never have learned in his enchantment: it follows therefore that he must have heard it when he lived in France, which was in the reign of that emperor; which observation is nicked, I think, very opportunely, for my supplement to "Polydore Virgil," who, as I remember, has not touched upon card-playing: I will insert it in my work, I will assure you, sir, as a matter of great importance, having the testimony of so authentic and ancient an author as Sir Durandarte. The fourth part of my good fortune, is to know the certain and true source of the river Guadiana, which has hitherto disappointed all human inquiries.' 'There is a great deal of reason in what you say,' answered Don Quixote: 'but, under favour, sir, pray tell me, should you happen to get a licence to publish your book, which I somewhat doubt, whom will you pitch upon for your patron?' 'Oh, sir,' answered the author, 'there are grandees† enough in Spain, sure, that I may dedicate to.' 'Truly, not many,' said Don Quixote; 'there are, indeed, several whose merits deserve the praise of a dedication, but very few, whose generosity will reward the pains and civility of the author. I must confess, I know a prince whose generosity may make amends for what is wanting in the rest; and that to such a degree, that should I make bold to come to particulars, and speak of his great merits, it would be enough to stir up a noble emulation in above four generous breasts; but more of this some other time, it is late now, and therefore convenient to think of a

---

* See this proverb explained in the preceding chapter.
† Grandees are such of the nobility as have the privilege of being covered before the king.

lodging.' 'Hard by us here, sir,' said the author, 'is an hermitage, the retirement of a devout person, who, as they say, was once a soldier, and is looked upon as a good Christian, and so charitable, that he has built there a little house at his own expense, purely for the entertainment of strangers.' 'But does he keep hens there trow?' asked Sancho. 'Few hermits in this age are without them,' said Don Quixote; 'for their way of living now falls short of the strictness and austerity of those in the deserts of Egypt, who went clad only with palm-leaves, and fed on the roots of the earth. Now because I speak well of those of old, I would not have you think I reflect on the others. No, I only mean that their penances are not so severe as in former days; yet this does not hinder but that the hermits of the present age may be good men. I look upon them to be such; at least their dissimulation secures them from scandal; and the hypocrite that puts on the form of holiness, does certainly less harm than the barefaced sinner.' As they went on in their discourse, they saw a man following them a great pace on foot, and switching up a mule laden with lances and halberts. He presently overtook them, gave them the time of the day, and passed by. 'Stay, honest fellow,' cried Don Quixote, seeing him go so fast, 'make no more haste than is consistent with good speed.' 'I cannot stay, sir,' said the man, 'for these weapons that you see, must be used tomorrow morning; so, sir, I am in haste, good-bye, I shall lodge the night at the inn beyond the hermitage; if you chance to go that way, there you may find me, and I will tell you strange news: so fare ye well.' Then whipping his mule, away he moved forwards, so fast that Don Quixote had not leisure to ask him any more questions. The Knight who had always an itching ear after novelties, to satisfy his curiosity immediately proposed their holding straight on to the inn without stopping at the hermitage, where the scholar designed to have stayed all night. Well, they all consented, and made the best of their way: however, when they came near the hermitage, the scholar desired Don Quixote to call with him for a moment, and drink a glass of wine at the door. Sancho no sooner heard this proposed, but he turned Dapple that way, and rode thither before; but to his great grief, the hospitable hermit was abroad, and nobody at home but the hermit's companion, who being asked whether he had any strong liquor within? made answer, that he could not come at any, but as for small water he might have his belly-full. 'Body of me!' quoth Sancho, 'were mine a water-thirst, or had I a liking to your cold comfort, there are wells enough upon the road, where I might have swilled my skin-full: oh, the good cheer at Don Diego's house, and the savory scum at Camacho's wedding, when shall I find your fellow!' They now spurred on towards the inn, and soon overtook on the road a young fellow beating it on the hoof pretty leisurely. He carried his sword over his shoulder with a bundle of clothes hanging upon it; which, to all outward appearance, consisted of a pair of breeches, a cloak, and a shirt or two. He had on a tattered velvet-jerkin, with a ragged satin lining; his shirt hung out, his stockings were of silk, and his shoes square at the toes, after the court fashion. He seemed about eighteen or nineteen years of age, a good pleasant-looked lad, and of a lively and active disposition. To pass the fatigue of his journey the best he could, he sung all the way, and as they came near him, was just ending the last words of a ballad which the scholar got by heart, and were these:

'A plague on ill luck! Now my ready's all gone,
  To the wars poor pilgarlic must trudge:
Though had I but money to rake as I've done
  The devil a foot would I budge.'

'So, young gentleman,' said Don Quixote to him, 'methinks you go very light and airy. Whither are you bound, I pray you, if a man may be so bold?' 'I am going to the wars, sir,' answered the youth; 'and for my travelling thus, heat and poverty will excuse it.' 'I admit the heat,' replied Don Quixote; 'but why poverty, I beseech you?' 'Because I have no clothes to put on,' replied the lad, 'but what I carry in this bundle; and if I should wear them out upon the road, I should have nothing to make a handsome figure within any town; for I have no money to buy new ones till I overtake a regiment of foot that lies about some twelve leagues off, where I design to 'list myself, and then I shall not want a conveniency to ride with the baggage till we come to Carthagena, where, I hear, they are to embark; for I had rather serve the king abroad, than any beggarly courtier at home.' 'But pray,' said the scholar, 'have not you laid up something while you were there?' 'Had I served any of your grandees or great persons,' said the young man, 'I might have done well enough, and have had a commission by this time, for their foot-boys are presently advanced to be captains and lieutenants, or some other good post: but a plague on it, sir, it was always my ill-fortune to serve pitiful upstarts and younger brothers, and my allowance was commonly so ill paid, and so small, that the better half was scarce enough to wash my linen; how then should a poor devil of a page, who would make his fortune come to any good in such a miserable service?' 'But,' said Don Quixote, 'how comes it about that in all this time you could not get yourself a whole livery?' 'Alack-a-day, sir,' answered the lad, 'I had a couple, but my masters dealt with me as they do with novices in monasteries, if they go off before they profess the fresh habit is taken from them, and they return them their own clothes. For you must know, that such as I served, only buy liveries for a little ostentation; so when they have made their appearance at court, they sneak down into the country, and then the poor servants are stripped, and must even betake themselves to their rags again.' 'A sordid trick,' said Don Quixote, 'or, as the Italians call it, a notorious *espilorcheria*.* Well, you need not repine at leaving the court, since you do it with so good a design; for there is nothing in the world more commendable than to serve God in the first place, and the king in the next, especially in the profession of arms, which if it does not procure a man so much riches as learning, may at least entitle him to more honour. It is true, that more families have been advanced by the gown, but yet your gentlemen of the sword, whatever the reason of it is, have always I know not what advantage above the men of learning; and something of glory and splendour attends them, that makes them outshine the rest of mankind. But take my advice along with you, child; if you intend to raise yourself by military employment, I would not have you be uneasy with the thoughts of what misfortunes may befall you; the worst can be but to die, and if it be an honourable death, your fortune is made, and you are certainly happy. Julius Cæsar, that valiant Roman emperor, being asked what kind of death was best? "That which is sudden and unexpected," said he; and though his answer had a relish of paganism, yet, with respect to human infirmities, it was very judicious: for, suppose you should be cut off at the very first engagement by a cannon-ball, or the spring of a mine; what matters it? It is all but dying, and there is an end of the business. As Terence says, "A soldier makes a better figure dead in the field of battle, than alive and safe in flight." The more likely he is to rise in fame and preferment, the better discipline he keeps, the better he obeys, the better he will know how to command: and pray observe, my friend, that it is more honourable for a soldier to smell of gunpowder than of musk and amber; or, if old age overtakes you in this noble employment, though all over scars, though maimed and lame, you will still have honour to support you, and secure you from the contempt of poverty; nay, from poverty itself; for there is care taken, that veteran and disabled soldiers may not want: neither are they to be used as some men do their negro slaves, who when they are old and past service, are turned naked out of doors, under pretence of freedom, to be made greater slaves to cold and hunger; a slavery from which nothing but death can set the wretches free. But I will say no more to you on this subject at this time. Get up behind me, and I will carry you to the inn, where you shall sup with me, and tomorrow morning make the best of your way; and may Heaven prosper your good designs.'

The page excused himself from riding behind the Knight, but accepted of his invitation to supper very willingly. Sancho who had all the while given ear to his master's discourse, is said to have been more than usually surprised, hearing him talk so wisely. 'Now blessing on thee, master of mine,' thought he to himself; 'how comes it about that a man who says so many good things, should relate such ridiculous stories and whimsies, as

* *Espilorcheria*, a beggarly mean action.

he would have us believe of Montesinos' cave. Well, Heaven knows best, and the proof of the pudding is in the eating.' By this time, it began to grow dark, and they arrived at the inn, where, Don Quixote alighting, asked presently for the man with the lances and halberts. The innkeeper answered that he was rubbing down his mule in the stable. Sancho was very well pleased to be at his journey's end, and the more, that his master took the house for a real inn, and not for a castle, as he used to do. He and the scholar then set up the asses, giving Rozinante the best manger and standing in the stable.

CHAPTER XXV

Where you find the grounds of the Braying Adventures, that of the Puppet-Player, and the memorable divining of the fortune-telling Ape

DON QUIXOTE was on thorns to know the strange story that the fellow upon the road engaged to tell him; so that going into the stable he minded him of his promise, and pressed him to relate the whole matter to him that moment. 'My story will take up some time,' quoth the man, 'and is not to be told standing; have a little patience, master of mine, let me make an end of serving my mule, then I will serve your worship, and tell you such things as will make you stare.' 'Do not let that hinder,' replied Don Quixote, 'for I will help you myself,' and, so saying, he lent him a helping hand, cleansing the manger, and sifting the barley; which humble compliance obliged the fellow to tell his tale the more willingly: so that, seating himself upon a bench with Don Quixote, the scholar, the page, Sancho, and the innkeeper about him, for his full auditory, he began in this manner:

'It happened on a time, that in a borough about some four leagues and a half from this place, one of the aldermen* lost his ass: they say it was by the roguery of a waggish jade that was his maid; but that is neither here nor there, the ass was lost and gone, that is certain; and, what is more, it could not be found neither high nor low. This same ass had been missing about a fortnight, some say more, some less, when another alderman of the same town, meeting this same losing alderman in the market-place, "Brother," quoth he, "pay me well, and I will tell you news of your ass." "Troth!" quoth the other, "that I will; but then let me know where the poor beast is?" "Why," answered the other, "this morning what should I

* Rigidor.

meet upon the mountains yonder but he, without either pack-saddle or furniture, and so lean that it grieved my heart to see him; but yet so wild and skittish, that when I would have driven him home before me, he ran away as the Devil were in him, and got into the thickest of the wood. Now, if you please, we will both go together and look for him; I will but step home first and put up this ass, then I will come back to you, and we will about it out of hand." "Truly, brother," said the other, "I am mightily beholden to you, and will do as much for you another time." The story happened neither more nor less, but such as I tell you, for so all that know it relate it word for word. In short, the two aldermen went hand in hand, a-foot trudged up the hills, and hunted up and down; but after many a weary step, no ass was to be found. Upon which, quoth the alderman that had seen him, to the other, "Hark you me, brother, I have a device in my noddle to find out this same ass of yours, though he were underground, as you shall hear. You must know, I can bray to admiration, and if you can but bray never so little, the job is done." "Never so little," cried the other, "body of me! I will not veil my bonnet at braying to ever an ass or alderman in the land." "Well, we shall try that," quoth the other, "for my contrivance is that you shall go on one side of the hill, and I on the other; sometimes you shall bray, and sometimes I; so, that, if your ass be but thereabouts, my life for yours, he will be sure to answer his kind, and bray again." "Gramercy, brother," quoth the other, "a rare device, i'faith! let you alone for plotting." At the same time they parted according to agreement, and when they were far enough off they both fell a-braying so perfectly well, that they cheated one another; and meeting, each in hopes to find the ass, "Is it possible, brother," said the owner of the ass, "that it was not my ass that brayed?" "No, marry, that it was not; it was I," answered the other alderman. "Well, brother," cried the owner, "then there is no manner of difference between you and an ass, as to matter of braying; I never heard anything so natural in my life." "O fie! sir," quoth the other, "I am nothing to you: you shall lay two to one against the best brayer in the kingdom, and I will go you halves. Your voice is lofty, and of a great compass; you keep excellent time, and hold out a note rarely, and your cadence is full and ravishing. In short, sir, I knock under the table, and yield you the bays." "Well then, brother," answered the owner, "I shall always have the better opinion of myself for this one good quality; for though I knew I brayed pretty well, I never thought myself so great a master before." "Well," quoth the other, "thus you see what rare parts may be lost for want of being known, and a man never knows his own strength, till he puts it to a trial." "Right, brother," quoth the owner, "for I should never have found out this wonderful gift of mine, had it not been for this business in hand, and may we speed in it, I pray!" After these compliments they parted again, and went braying, this on one side of the hill, and that one the other. But all to no purpose, for they still deceived one another with their braying, and, running to the noise, met one another as before.

'At last they agreed to bray twice, one after another, that by that token they might be sure it was not the ass, but they that brayed. But all in vain, they almost brayed their hearts out, but no answer from the ass. And indeed how could it, poor creature? when they found him at last in the wood, half eaten by the wolves. "Alack-a-day, poor Grizzle," cried the owner, "I do not wonder now he took so little notice of his loving master; had he been alive, as sure as he was an ass, he would have brayed again. But let him go, this comfort I have at least, brother, though I have lost him I have found out that rare talent of yours, that has hugely solaced me under this affliction." "The glass is in a good hand, Mr. Alderman," quoth the other, "and if the abbot sings well, the young monk is not much behind him."

'With this, these same aldermen, very much down in the mouth, and very hoarse, went home and told all their neighbours the whole story, word for word, one praising the other's skill in braying, and the other returning the compliment. In short, one got it by the end, and the other got it by the end; the boys got it, and all the idle fellows got it, and there was such a brawling, and such a braying in our town, that one would have thought hell broke loose among us. But to let you see now how the Devil never lies dead in a ditch, but catches at every foolish thing to set people by the ears, our neighbouring towns had it up, and when they saw any of our townsfolk they fell a-braying, hitting us in the teeth with the braying of our aldermen. This made ill-blood between us, for we took it in mighty dudgeon, as well we might, and came to words upon it, and from words to blows; for the people of our town are well known by this, as the beggar knows his dish, and are apt to be jeered wheresoever they go; and then to it they go, ding-dong, hand over head, in spite of law or gospel. And they have carried the jest so far, that I believe tomorrow or next day the men of our town, the brayers, will be in the field against those of another town about two leagues off, that are always plaguing us. Now, that we should be well provided, I have brought these lances and halberts that ye saw me carry. So this is my story, gentlefolks, and if it be not a strange one, I am woundily mistaken.'

Here the honest man ended, when presently enters a fellow dressed in trowsers and doublet, all of chamois leather, and calling out as if he were somebody, 'Landlord,' cried he, 'have you any lodgings? For here comes the fortune-telling ape, and the puppet-show of "Melisandra's deliverance." ' 'Body of me,' cried the innkeeper, 'who is here, Master Peter? We shall have a merry night, faith! Honest Master Peter, you are welcome with all my heart. But where is the ape, and the show, that I cannot see them?' 'They will be here presently,' said Peter. 'I only came before to see if you had any lodgings.' 'Lodging, man,' said the innkeeper, 'zookers! I would turn out the Duke of Alva himself, rather than Mr. Peter should want room. Come, come, bring in your things, for here are guests in the house to-night that will be good customers to you, I warrant you.' 'That is a good hearing,' said Peter, 'and to encourage them I will lower my prices; and if I can but get my charges to-night, I will look for no more; so I will hasten forward the cart.' This said, he ran out of the door again.

I had forgot to tell you, that this same Master Peter wore over his left eye, and half his cheek, a patch of green taffeta, by which it was to be supposed that something ailed that side of his face. Don Quixote inquired who this Master Peter was, and what his ape and his show?' 'Why, sir,' answered the innkeeper, 'he has strolled about this country this great while with a curious puppet-show, which represents the play of Melisandra and Don Gayferos, one of the best shows that has been acted time out of mind in this kingdom. Then he has an ape! Bless us, sir, it is such an ape! But I will say no more; you shall see, sir: it will tell you everything you ever did in your life. The like was never seen before. Ask him a question, it will listen to you, and then whip, up it leaps on its master's shoulder, and whispers first in his ear what it knows, and then Master Peter tells you. He tells you what is to come, as well as what is past: it is true, he does not always hit so pat as to what is to come; but, after all, he is seldom in the wrong, which makes us apt to think, the Devil helps him at a dead lift. Two reals is the price for every question he answers, or his master for him, which is all one, you know; and that will amount to money at the year's end, so that it is thought the rogue is well to pass; and indeed much good may it do him, for he is a notable fellow, and a boon companion, and leads the merriest life in the world, talks for six men, and drinks for a dozen, and all this he gets by his tongue, his ape, and his show.'

By this time Master Peter came back with his puppet-show and his ape, in a cart. The ape was pretty lusty, without any tail, and his buttocks bare as a felt. Yet he was not very ugly neither. Don Quixote no sooner saw him, but coming up to him, 'Mr. Fortune-teller,' said he, 'will you be pleased to tell us what fish we shall catch, and what will become of us? and here is your fee.' Saying this, he ordered Sancho to deliver Mr. Peter two reals. 'Sir,' answered Peter, 'this animal gives no account of things to come, he knows something indeed of matters past, and a little of the present.' 'Odds bobs!' quoth Sancho, 'I would not give a brass jack to know what is past; for who knows that better than myself; I am not so foolish as to pay for what I know already: but since you say he has such a knack at guessing the present, let goodman ape tell me what my wife Teresa is doing, and what she is about, and here is my two reals.' 'I will have nothing of you beforehand,' said Master Peter; so clapping himself on his left shoulder, up skipped the ape thither, at one frisk, and laying his mouth to his ear grated his teeth; and having made apish grimaces and a chattering noise for a minute or two, with another skip down he leaped upon the ground. Immediately upon this, Master Peter ran to Don Quixote, and fell on his knees, and embracing his legs, 'Oh glorious restorer of knight-errantry,' cried he, 'I embrace these legs, as I would the pillars of Hercules. Who can sufficiently extol the great Don Quixote de la Mancha, the reviver of drooping hearts, the prop and stay of the falling, the raiser of the fallen, and the staff of comfort to the weak and afflicted!' At these words Don Quixote stood amazed, Sancho quaked, the page wondered, the brayer blessed himself; the innkeeper stared, and the scholar was in a brown study, all astonished at Master Peter's speech; who then turning to Sancho, 'And thou honest Sancho Pança,' said he, 'the best squire to the best knight in the world, bless thy kind stars, for thy good spouse Teresa is a good housewife, and is at this instant dressing a pound of flax, by the same token, she has standing by her, on her left hand, a large broken-mouth jug, which holds a pretty scantling of wine, to cheer up her spirits.' 'By yea and nay,' quoth Sancho, 'that is likely enough, for she is a true soul, and a jolly soul; were it not for a spice of jealousy that she has now and then, I would not change her for the giantess Andondona herself, who, as my master says, was as clever a piece of woman's flesh as ever went upon two legs. Well, much good may it do thee, honest Teresa; thou art resolved to provide for one, I find, though thy heirs starve for it.' 'Well,' said Don Quixote, 'great is the knowledge procured by reading, travel, and experience; what on earth but the testimony of my own eyes could have persuaded me that apes had the gift of divination! I am indeed the same Don Quixote de la Mancha, mentioned by this ingenious animal, though I must confess somewhat undeserving of so great a character as it has pleased him to bestow on me: but nevertheless I am not sorry to have charity and compassion bear so great a part in my commendation, since my nature has always disposed me to do good to all men, and hurt to none.'

'Now had I but money,' said the page, 'I would know of Mr. Ape what luck I shall have in the wars.' 'I have told you already,' said Master Peter, who was got up from before Don Quixote, 'that this ape does not meddle with what is to come; but if he could, it should cost you nothing, for Don Quixote's sake, whom to oblige I would sacrifice all the interest I have in the world; and, as a mark of it, gentlemen, I freely set up my show, and give all the company in the house some diversion gratis.' The innkeeper hearing this, was overjoyed, and ordered Master Peter a convenient room to set up his motion, and he immediately went about it.

In the mean time, Don Quixote, who could not bring himself to believe that an ape could do all this, taking Sancho to a corner of the stable: 'Look

ye, Sancho,' said he, 'I have been weighing and considering the wonderful
gifts of this ape, and find, in short, Master Peter must have made a secret
compact with the Devil.' 'Nay,' quoth Sancho, misunderstanding the
word 'compact,' 'if the Devil and he have packed anything together in
hugger-mugger, it is a pack of roguery to be sure, and they are a pack of
rogues for their pains, and let them even pack together, say I.' 'Thou dost
not apprehend me,' said Don Quixote; 'I mean the Devil and he must
have made an agreement together, that Satan should infuse this knowledge into the ape, to purchase the owner an estate; and in return, the last
has certainly engaged his soul to this destructive seducer of mankind. For
the ape's knowledge is exactly of the same proportion with the Devil's,
which only extends to the discovery of things past and present, having no
insight into futurity, but by such probable conjectures and conclusions as
may be deduced from the former working of antecedent causes; true
prescience and prediction being the sacred prerogative of God, to whose
all-seeing eyes all ages, past, present, and to come, without the distinction
of succession and termination, are always present. From this, I say, it is
apparent, this ape is but the organ through which the Devil delivers his
answers to those that ask it questions, and this same rogue should be put
into the inquisition, and have the truth pressed out of his bones. For sure
neither the master nor his ape can lay any pretence to judicial astrology;
nor is the ape so conversant in the mathematics, I suppose, as to erect a
scheme: though I must confess, that creatures of less parts, as foolish
illiterate women, footmen, and cobblers, pretend nowadays to draw
certainties from the stars, as easily and readily as they shuffle a pack of
cards, to the disgrace of the sublime science, which they have the
impudence to profess. I knew a lady that asked one of these figure-casters,
if a little foisting bitch she had should have puppies, and how many, and of
what colour? My conjurer, after he had scrawled out his scheme, very
judiciously pronounced, that the pretty creature should have three puppies, one green, one red, and another mixed-coloured, provided she would
take dog between eleven and twelve at night, or noon, either on a Monday
or a Saturday; and the success happened as exactly as could be expected
from his art; for the bitch some days after died very fairly of a surfeit, and
Master Figure-flinger was reputed a special conjurer all the town over, as
most of these fellows are.' 'For all that,' said Sancho, 'I would have you ask
Master Peter's ape, whether the passages you told us concerning
Montesinos' cave be true or no? For, saving the respect I owe your
worship, I take them to be no better than fibs, and idle stories, or dreams
at least.' 'You may think what you will,' answered Don Quixote, 'however
I will do as you would have me, though I confess my conscience somewhat
scruples to do such a thing.' While they were thus engaged in discourse,
Master Peter came and told Don Quixote the show was ready to begin,

and desired him to come and see it, for he was sure his worship would like it. The Knight told him, he had a question to put to his ape first, and desired he might tell him, whether certain things that happened to him in Montesinos' cave were dreams or realities? for he doubted they had something of both in them. Master Peter fetched his ape immediately, and placing him just before the Knight and his squire, 'Look you,' says he, 'Mr. Ape, this worthy Knight would have you tell him, whether some things which happened to him in Montesinos' cave were true or no?' Then, upon the usual signal, the ape jumping upon Master Peter's left shoulder, chattered his answer into his ear, which the interpreter delivered thus to the inquirer. 'The ape, sir, says, that part of those things are false, and part of them true, which is all he can resolve ye as to this question; and now his virtue has left him, and will not return till Friday next. If you would know any more, you must stay till then, and he will answer as many questions as you please.' 'Law you there now,' quoth Sancho, 'did not I tell you that all you told us of Montesinos' cave would not hold water?' 'That the event will determine,' replied the Knight, 'which we must leave to process of time to produce; for it brings everything to light, though buried in the bowels of the earth. No more of this at present, let us now see the puppet-show: I fancy we shall find something in it worth seeing.' 'Something!' said Master Peter, 'sir, you shall see a thousand things worth seeing. I tell you, sir, I defy the world to show such another. I say no more, *Operibus credite, et non verbis*. But now let us begin, for it grows late, and we have much to do, say, and show.' Don Quixote and Sancho complied, and went into the room where the show stood, with a good number of small wax-lights glimmering round about, that made it shine gloriously. Master Peter got to his station within, being the man that was to move the puppets; and his boy stood before to tell what the puppets said, and, with a white wand in his hand, to point at the several figures as they came in and out, and explain the mystery of the show. Then all the audience having taken their places, Don Quixote, Sancho, the scholar, and the page, being preferred to the rest; the boy, who was the mouth of the motion, began a story, that shall be heard or seen by those who will take the pains to read or hear the next chapter.

CHAPTER XXVI

A pleasant account of the Puppet-Play, with other good things truly

THE TYRIANS AND THE TROJANS were all silent; that is, the ears of all the spectators hung on the mouth of the interpreter of the show, when in the first place they had a loud flourish of kettle-drums and trumpets within the machine, and then several discharges of artillery; which prelude being soon over, 'Gentlemen,' cried the boy, raising his voice, 'we present you here with a true history taken out of the chronicles of France, and the Spanish ballads, sung even by the boys about the streets, and in everybody's mouth; it tells you how Don Gayferos delivered his wife Melisandra, that was a prisoner among the Moors in Spain, in the city of Sansuena, now called Saragossa. Now, gallants, the first figure we present you with is Don Gayferos playing at Tables, according to the ballad:

> ' "Now Gayferos the livelong day
> Oh arrant shame at draughts does play
> And, as at Court most husbands do
> Forgets his lady fair and true."

'Gentlemen, in the next place, mark that personage that peeps out there with a crown on his head and a sceptre in his hand. It is the Emperor Charlemagne, fair Melisandra's reputed father, who, vexed at the idleness and negligence of his son-in-law, comes to chide him; and pray observe with what passion and earnestness he rates him, as if he had a mind to lend him half-a-dozen sound raps over the pate with his sceptre. Nay, some authors do not stick to tell ye, he gave him as many, and well laid on too; and after he had told him how his honour lay a-bleeding, till he had delivered his wife out of durance, among many other pithy sayings, "Look to it," quoth he to him as he went, "I will say no more." Mind how the emperor turns his back upon him, and how he leaves Don Gayferos nettled and in the dumps. Now see how he starts up, and in a rage throws the tables one way, and whirls the men another; and calling for his arms with all haste, borrows his cousin-german Orlando's sword, Durindana, who withal offers to go along with him in this difficult adventure, but the valorous enraged knight will not let him, and says, he is able to deliver his wife himself, without his help, though they kept her down in the very centre of the earth. And now he is going to put on his armour in order to begin his journey.

'Now, gentlemen, cast your eyes upon yon tower; you are to suppose it one of the towers of the castle of Saragossa, now called the Aljaferia. That lady, whom you see in the balcony there, in a Moorish habit, is the peerless Melisandra, that casts many a heavy look towards France, thinking of Paris and her husband, the only comfort in her imprisonment. But now, silence, gentlemen, pray silence; here is an accident wholly new, the like perhaps never heard of before: do not you see that Moor who comes a-tiptoe creeping and stealing along with his finger in his mouth behind Melisandra? Hear what a smack he gives on her sweet lips, and see how she spits and wipes her mouth with her white smock sleeve: see how she takes on and tears her lovely hair for very madness, as if it were to blame for this affront. Next pray observe that grave Moor that stands in the open gallery: that is Marsilius, the king of Sansuena, who having been an eye-witness of the sauciness of the Moor, ordered him immediately to be apprehended, though his kinsman and great favourite, to have two hundred lashes given him, then to be carried through the city, with criers before to proclaim his crime, the rods of justice behind. And look how all this is put in execution sooner almost than the fact is committed: for your Moors, you must know, do not use any form of indictment as we do, neither have they any legal trials.' 'Child, child,' said Don Quixote, 'go on directly with your story, and do not keep us here with your excursions and ramblings out of the road: I tell you there must be a formal process and legal trial to prove matters of fact.' 'Boy,' said the master from behind the show, 'do as the gentleman bids you. Do not run so much upon flourishes, but follow your plain song, without venturing on counter-points, for fear of spoiling all.' 'I will, sir,' quoth the boy, and so proceeding: 'Now, sirs, he that you see there a-horseback, wrapt up in the Gascoigne cloak, is Don Gayferos himself, whom his wife, now revenged on the Moor for his impudence, seeing him from the battlements of the tower, takes him for a stranger, and talks with him as such, according to the ballad:

> ' "Quoth Melisandra, if perchance
> Sir Traveller, you go for France
> For pity's sake ask, when you're there,
> For Gayferos, my husband dear."

'I omit the rest, not to tire you with a long story. It is sufficient, that he makes himself known to her, as you may guess by the joy she shows; and accordingly now see how she lets herself down from the balcony, to come at her loving husband, and get behind him; but unhappily, alas, one of the skirts of her gown is caught upon one of the spikes of the balcony, and there she hangs and hovers in the air miserably, without being able to get down. But see how Heaven is merciful, and sends relief in the greatest distress! Now Don Gayferos rides up to her, and not fearing to tear her rich gown, lays hold of it, and at one pull brings her down; and then at one lift sets her astride upon his horse's crupper, bidding her to sit fast, and clasp her arms about him, that she might not fall, for the lady Melisandra was not used to that kind of riding.

'Observe now, gallants, how the horse neighs, and shows how proud he is of the burden of his brave master and fair mistress. Look now how they turn their backs, and leave the city, and gallop it merrily away towards Paris. Peace be with you, for a peerless couple of true lovers! may ye get safe and sound into your own country, without any let or ill chance in your journey, and live as long as Nestor in peace and quietness among your friends and relations.' 'Plainness, boy,' cried Mr. Peter, 'none of your flights, I beseech you, for affectation is the Devil.' The boy answered nothing, but going on: 'Now sirs,' quoth he, 'some of those idle people, that love to pry into everything, happened to spy Melisandra as she was making her escape, and ran presently and gave Marsilius notice of it: whereupon he straight commanded to sound an alarm; and now mind what a din and hurly-burly there is, and how the city shakes with the ring of the bells backwards in all the mosques!' 'There you are out, boy,' said Don Quixote: 'the Moors have no bells, they only use kettle-drums, and a kind of shawms like our waits or hautboys; so that your ringing of bells in Sansuena is a mere absurdity, good Mr. Peter.' 'Nay, sir,' said Mr. Peter, 'giving over ringing; if you stand upon trifles with us, we shall never please you. Do not be so severe a critic: are there not a thousand plays that pass with great success and applause, though they have many greater absurdities, and nonsense in abundance? On, boy, on, let there be as many impertinences as moats in the sun; no matter, so I get the money.' 'Well said,' answered Don Quixote. 'And now, sirs,' quoth the boy, 'observe what a vast company of glittering horse comes pouring out of the city, in pursuit of the Christian lovers; what a dreadful sound of trumpets, and clarions, and drums, and kettle-drums there is in the air. I fear they will overtake them, and then will the poor wretches be dragged along most barbarously at the tails of their horses, which would be sad indeed.' Don Quixote, seeing such a number of Moors, and hearing such an alarm, thought it high time to assist the flying lovers; and starting up, 'It shall never be said while I live,' cried he aloud, 'that I suffered such a wrong to be done to so famous a knight and so daring a lover as Don Gayferos. Forbear then your unjust pursuit, ye base rascals: stop, or prepare to meet my furious resentment.' Then drawing out his sword, to make good his threats, at one spring he gets to the show, and with a violent fury lays at the Moorish puppets, cutting and slashing in a most terrible manner; some he overthrows, and beheads others; maims this, and cleaves that in pieces. Among the rest of his merciless strokes, he thundered one down with a mighty force, that had not Mr. Peter luckily ducked and squatted down, it had certainly chopped off his head as easily as one might cut an apple. 'Hold, hold, sir,' cried the puppet-player, after the narrow escape, 'hold for pity's sake. What do you mean, sir? These are no real Moors that you cut and hack so, but poor harmless puppets made of pasteboard. Think of what you do, you ruin me for ever. Oh that ever I was born! you have broke me quite.' But Don Quixote, without minding his words, doubled and redoubled his blows so thick, and laid about him so outrageously, that in less than two credos he had cut all the strings and wires, mangled the puppets, and spoiled and demolished the whole motion. King Marsilius was in a grievous condition. The Emperor Charlemagne's head and crown were cleft in two. The whole audience was in a sad consternation. The ape scampered off to the top of the house. The scholar was frightened out of his wits; the page was very uneasy; and Sancho himself was in a terrible fright; for, as he swore after the hurricane was over, he had never seen his master in such a rage before.

The general rout of the puppets being over, Don Quixote's fury began to abate; and with a more pacified countenance turning to the company, 'Now,' said he, 'could I wish all those incredulous persons here who slight knight-errantry, might receive conviction of their error, and behold undeniable proofs of the benefit of that function: for how miserable had been the condition of poor Don Gayferos and the fair Melisandra by this time, had not I been there and stood up in their defence! I make no question but those infidels would have apprehended them, and used them barbarously. Well, when all is done, long live knight-errantry, long let it live, I say, above all things whatsoever in this world.' 'Ay, ay,' said Mr. Peter in a doleful tone, 'let it live long for me, so I may die; for why should I live so unhappy, as to say with King Rodrigo,* "Yesterday I was a lord in Spain, today have not a foot of land I can call mine"? It is not half-an-hour, nay scarce a moment, since I had kings and emperors at command. I had horses in abundance, and chests and bags full of fine things; but now you see me a poor sorry undone man, quite and clean broke and cast down, and in short a mere beggar. What is worst of all, I have lost my ape too, who I am sure will make me sweat ere I catch him again; and all through the rash fury of this Sir Knight here, who they say protects the fatherless, redresses wrongs, and does other charitable deeds but has failed in all these good offices to miserable me, Heaven be praised for it! Well may I call him the Knight of the Woeful Figure, for he has put me and all that belongs to me in a woeful case.' The puppet-player's lamentations moving Sancho's pity, 'Come,' quoth he, 'do not cry, Mr. Peter, thou breakest my heart to hear thee lament so; do not be cast down, man, for my master is a better Christian, I am sure, than to let any poor man come to loss by him: when he comes to know he has done you wrong, he will

* The last king of the Goths that reigned in Spain, conquered by the Moors.

pay you for every farthing of damage, I will engage.' 'Truly,' said Mr. Peter, 'if his worship would but pay me for the fashion of my puppets he has spoiled, I will ask no more, and he will discharge a good conscience; for he that wrongs his neighbour, and does not make restitution, can never hope to be saved, that is certain.' 'I grant it,' said Don Quixote; 'but I am not sensible how I have in the least injured you, good Mr. Peter!' 'No, sir! not injured me!' cried Mr. Peter. 'Why these poor relics that lie here on the cold ground, cry out for vengeance against you. Was it not the invincible force of that powerful arm of yours that has scattered and dismembered them so? And whose were those bodies, sir, but mine? and by whom was I maintained, but by them?' 'Well,' said Don Quixote, 'I am now thoroughly convinced of a truth, which I have had reason to believe before, that those cursed magicians that daily persecute me, do nothing but delude me, first drawing me into dangerous adventures by the appearances of them as they really are, and then presently after changing the face of things as they please. Really and truly, gentlemen, I vow and protest before ye all that hear me, that all that was acted here, seemed to be really transacted *ipso facto* as appeared. To me Melisandra appeared to be Melisandra, Don Gayferos was Don Gayferos, Marsilius Marsilius, and Charlemagne was the real Charlemagne. Which being so, I could not contain my fury, and acted according to the duties of my function, which obliges me to take the injured side. Now, though what I have done proves to he quite contrary to my good design, the fault ought not to be imputed to me, but to my persecuting foes; yet I own myself sorry for the mischance, and will condemn myself to pay the costs. Let Mr. Peter see what he must have for the figures that are damaged, and I will pay it now in good and lawful money on the nail.' 'Heaven bless your worship,' cried Mr. Peter, with a profound cringe; 'I could expect no less from the wonderful Christianity of the valorous Don Quixote de la Mancha, the sure relief and bulwark of all miserable wanderers. Now let my landlord and the great Sancho be mediators and appraisers between your worship and myself, and I will stand to their award.' They agreed: and presently Mr. Peter taking up Marsilius, King of Saragossa, that lay by on the ground with his head off: 'You see, gentlemen,' said he, 'it is impossible to restore this king to his former dignity; and therefore, with submission to your better judgments, I think that for his destruction, and to get him a successor, seven and twenty pence* is little enough of conscience.' 'Proceed,' said Don Quixote. 'Then for this that is cleft in two,' said Mr. Peter, taking up the Emperor Charlemagne, 'I think he is richly worth one and thirty pence half-penny.'† 'Not so richly neither,' quoth Sancho. 'Truly,' said the innkeeper, 'I think it is pretty reasonable; but we will

---

* Four reals and a half.   † Five reals and a quarter.

make it even money, let the poor fellow have half-a-crown.' 'Come,' said Don Quixote, 'let him have his full price, we will not stand haggling for so small a matter in a case like this: so make haste, Mr. Peter, for it is near supper-time, and I have some strong presumptions that I shall eat heartily.' 'Now,' said Mr. Peter, 'for this figure here that is without a nose, and blind of one eye, being the fair Melisandra, I will be reasonable with you; give me fourteen pence,* I would not take less from my brother.' 'Nay,' said Don Quixote, 'the Devil is in it if Melisandra be not by this time with her husband, upon the frontiers of France at least; for the horse that carried them seemed to me rather to fly than to gallop; and now you tell me of a Melisandra here without a nose forsooth, when it is ten to one but she is now in her husband's arms in a good bed in France. Come, come, friend, God help every man to his own; let us have fair dealing, so proceed.' Mr. Peter finding that the Knight began to harp upon the old string, was afraid he would fly off; and making as if he had better considered of it, 'Cry y'e mercy, sir,' said he, 'I was mistaken, this could not be Melisandra indeed, but one of the damsels that waited on her; and so I think fivepence will be fair enough for her.' In this manner he went on, setting his price upon the dead and wounded, which the arbitrators moderated to the content of both parties; and the whole sum amounted to forty reals and three-quarters, which Sancho paid him down; and then Mr. Peter too demanded two reals more, for the trouble of catching his ape. 'Give it him,' said Don Quixote, 'and set the monkey to catch the ape; and now would I give two hundred more to be assured that Don Gayferos and the lady Melisandra were safely arrived in France among their friends.' 'Nobody can better tell than my ape,' said Mr. Peter, 'though the Devil himself will hardly catch him, if hunger, or his kindness for me, do not bring us together again to-night. However, tomorrow will be a new day, and when it is light we will see what is to be done.'

The whole disturbance being appeased, to supper they went lovingly together, and Don Quixote treated the whole company, for he was liberality itself. Before day the man with the lances and halberts left the inn, and some time after the scholar and the page came to take leave of the Knight, the first to return home, and the second to continue his journey, towards whose charges Don Quixote gave him twelve reals. As for Master Peter, he knew too much of the Knight's humour to desire to have anything to do with him, and therefore having picked up the ruins of the puppet-show, and got his ape again, by break of day he packed off to seek his fortune. the innkeeper, who did not know Don Quixote, was as much surprised at his liberality as at his madness. In fine, Sancho paid him very honestly by his master's order, and mounting a little before eight o'clock,

* Two reals and twelve maravedis.

they left the inn, and proceeded on their journey; where we will leave them, that we may have an opportunity to relate some other matters very requisite for the better understanding of this famous history.

CHAPTER XXVII

Wherein is discovered who Master Peter was, and his Ape; as also Don Quixote's ill success in the Braying Adventure, which did not end so happily as he desired and expected

CID HAMET, THE AUTHOR of this celebrated history, begins this chapter with this asseveration, 'I swear as a true Catholic!' which the translator illustrates and explains in this manner: that historian's swearing like a true Catholic, though he was a Mahometan Moor, ought to be received in no other sense, than that, as a true Catholic, when he affirms anything with an oath, does or ought to swear truth, so would he relate the truth as impartially as a Christian would do, if he had taken such an oath, in what he designed to write of Don Quixote; especially as to the account that is to be given us of the person who was known by the name of Master Peter, and the fortune-telling ape, whose answers occasioned such a noise, and created such an amazement all over the country. He says then, that any one who has read the foregoing part of this history, cannot but remember one Gines de Passamonte, whom Don Quixote had rescued, with several other galley slaves, in Sierra Morena; a piece of service for which the Knight was not over-burdened with thanks, and which that ungrateful pack of rogues repaid with a treatment altogether unworthy such a deliverance. This Gines de Passamonte, or, as Don Quixote called him, Ginesillo de Parapilla, was the very man that stole Sancho's ass; the manner of which robbery, and the time when it was committed being not inserted in the first part, has been the reason that some people have laid that, which was caused by the printer's neglect, to the inadvertency of the author. But it is beyond all question, that Gines stole the ass while Sancho slept on his back, making use of the same trick and artifice which Brunelo practised when he carried off Sacripante's horse from under his legs, at the siege of Albraca. However, Sancho got possession again, as has been told you before.

Gines, it seems, being obnoxious to the law, was apprehensive of the strict search that was made after him, in order to bring him to justice for his repeated villainies, which were so great and numerous, that he himself had wrote a large book of them; and therefore he thought it advisable to make the best of his way into the kingdom of Aragon, and having clapped a plaister over his left eye, resolved in that disguise to set up a puppet-show, and stroll with it about the country; for you must know, he had not his fellow at anything that could be done by sleight of hand. Now it happened, that in his way he fell into the company of some Christian slaves who came from Barbary, and struck a bargain with them for this ape, whom he taught to leap on his shoulder at a certain sign, and to make as if he whispered something in his ear. Having brought his ape to this, before he entered into any town he informed himself in the adjacent parts as well as he could, of what particular accidents had happened to this or that person; and having a very retentive memory, the first thing he did was to give them a sight of his show, that represented sometimes one story and sometimes another, which were generally well known and taking among the vulgar. The next thing he had to do, was to commend the wonderful qualities of his ape, and tell the company, that the animal had the gift of revealing things past and present; but that in things to come, he was altogether uninstructed. He asked two reals* for every answer, though now and then he lowered his price as he felt the pulse of his customers. Sometimes when he came to the houses of people, of whose concerns he had some account, and who would ask the ape no questions, because they did not care to part with their money, he would notwithstanding be making signs to his ape, and tell them, the animal had acquainted him with this or that story, according to the information he had before; and by that means he got a great credit among the common people, and drew a mighty crowd after him. At other times, though he knew nothing of the person, the subtilty of his wit supplied his want of knowledge, and brought him handsomely off: and nobody being so inquisitive or pressing as to make him declare by what means his ape attained to this gift of divination, he imposed on every one's understanding, and got almost what money he pleased.

He was no sooner come to the inn, but he knew Don Quixote, Sancho, and the rest of the company: but he had like to have paid dear for his knowledge, had the Knight's sword fallen but a little lower when he made King Marsilius's head fly, and routed all his Moorish horse, as the reader may have observed in the foregoing chapter. And this may suffice in relation to Mr. Peter and his ape.

Now let us overtake our Champion of La Mancha. After he had left the inn, he resolved to take a sight of the River Ebro, and the country about it, before he went to Saragossa, since he was not straitened for time, but might do that, and yet arrive soon enough to make one at the justs and tournaments at that city. Two days he travelled without meeting with

* About a shilling.

anything worth his notice or the reader's, when on the third, as he was riding up a hill, he heard a great noise of drums, trumpets, and guns. At first he thought some regiment of soldiers was on its march that way, which made him spur up Rozinante to the brow of the hill, that he might see them pass by; and then he saw in a bottom above two hundred men, as near as he could guess, armed with various weapons, as lances, cross-bows, partisans, halberts, pikes, some few firelocks, and a great many targets. Thereupon he descended into the vale, and made his approaches towards the battalion, so near as to be able to distinguish their banners, judge of their colours, and observe their devices; more especially one that was to be seen on a standard of white satin, on which was represented to the life a little jackass, much like a Sardinian ass-colt, holding up his head, stretching out his neck, and thrusting out his tongue, in the very posture of an ass that is braying, with this distich written in fair characters about it:

> ' 'Twas something more than nothing which one day
> Made one and t'other worthy bailiff bray.'

Don Quixote drew this inference from the motto, that those were the inhabitants of the braying town, and he acquainted Sancho with what he had observed, giving him also to understand, that the man who told them the story of the two braying aldermen was apparently in the wrong, since, according to the verses on the standard, they were two bailiffs, and not two aldermen.* 'It matters not one rush what you call them,' quoth Sancho; 'for those very aldermen that brayed might in time come to be made bailiffs of the town, and so both those titles might have been given them well enough. But what is it to you or me, or the story, whether the two brayers were aldermen or bailiffs, so they but brayed as we are told? As if a bailiff were not as likely to bray as an alderman?'

In short, both master and man plainly understood, that the men who were thus up in arms, were those that were jeered for braying, got together to fight the people of another town, who had indeed abused them more than was the part of good neighbours; thereupon Don Quixote advanced towards them, to Sancho's great grief, who had no manner of liking to such kind of adventures. The multitude soon got about the Knight, taking him for some champion, who was come to their assistance. But Don Quixote, lifting up his vizor, with a graceful deportment, rode up to the standard, and there all the chief leaders of the army got together about him, in order to take a survey of his person, no less amazed at this strange appearance than the rest. Don Quixote seeing them look so earnestly on him, and no man offer so much as a word or question,

---

* The Spanish word *alcade* answers nearly to our bailiff of a corporation, as *rigidor* does to that of alderman.

took occasion from their silence to break his own; and raising his voice, 'Good gentlemen,' cried he, 'I beseech you with all the endearments imaginable, to give no interruption to the discourse I am now delivering to you, unless you find it distasteful or tedious; which if I am unhappy enough to occasion, at the least hint you shall give me, I will clap a seal on my lips, and a padlock on my tongue.' They all cried that he might speak what he pleased, and they would hear him with all their hearts. Having this licence, Don Quixote proceeded. 'Gentlemen,' said he, 'I am a knight-errant: arms are my exercise; and my profession is to show favour to those that are in necessity of favour, and to give assistance to those that are in distress. I have for some time been no stranger to the cause of your uneasiness, which excites you to take arms to be revenged on your insulting neighbours; and having often busied my intellectuals, in making reflections on the motives which have brought you together, I have drawn this inference from it, that according to the laws of arms, you really injure yourselves, in thinking yourselves affronted; for no particular person can give an affront to a whole town and society of men, except it be by accusing them all of high treason in general, for want of knowing on which of them to fix some treasonable action, of which he supposes some of them to be guilty. We have an instance of this nature, in Don Diego Ordonnez de Lara, who sent a challenge to all the inhabitants of Zamora, not knowing that Vellido de Olsos had assassinated the King his master in that town, without any accomplices; and so accusing and defying them all, the defence and revenge belonged to them all in general. Though it must be owned, that Don Diego was somewhat unreasonable in his defiance, and strained the point too far: for, it was very little to the purpose to defy the dead, the waters, the bread, those that were yet unborn, with many other trifling matters mentioned in the challenge. But let that pass; for when once the choler boils over, the tongue grows unruly, and knows no moderation. Taking it for granted, then, that no particular person can affront a whole kingdom, province, city, commonwealth, or body politic, it is but just to conclude, that it is needless to revenge such a pretended affront; since such an abuse is no sufficient provocation, and indeed, positively, no affront. It would be a pretty piece of wisdom, truly, should those out of the town of Reloxa sally out every day on those who spend their ill-natured breaths miscalling them everywhere. It would be a fine business indeed, if the inhabitants of those several famous towns that are nicknamed by our rabble, and called the one cheese-mongers, the other coster-mongers, these fishmongers, and those soap-boilers, should know no better than to think themselves dishonoured, and in revenge, be always drawing out their swords at the least word for every idle insignificant quarrel. No, no, Heaven forbid! Men of sagacity and wisdom, and well-governed commonwealths are never induced to take up arms, nor endanger their persons, and estates, but on the four following occasions. In the first place, to defend the Holy Catholic faith. Secondly, for the security of their lives, which they are commanded to preserve by the laws of God and nature. Thirdly, the preservation of their good name, the reputation of their family, and the conservation of their estates. Fourthly, the service due to their prince in a just war; and if we please we may add a fifth, which indeed may be referred to the second, the defence of our country. To these five capital causes may be subjoined several others, which may induce men to vindicate themselves, and have recourse even to the way of arms: but to take them up for mere trifles, and such occasions as rather challenge our mirth and contemptuous laughter, than revenge, shows the person who is guilty of such proceedings to labour under a scarcity of sense. Besides, to seek after an unjust revenge (and indeed no human revenge can be just) is directly against the holy law we profess, which commands us to forgive our enemies, and to do good to those that hate us. An injunction, which, though it seems difficult in the implicit obedience we should pay to it, yet is only so to those who have less of heaven than of the world, and more of the flesh than of the spirit. For, the Redeemer of mankind, whose words never could deceive, said, "that His yoke was easy, and His burthen light"; and according to that, He could prescribe nothing to our practice which was impossible to be done. Therefore, gentlemen, since reason and religion recommend love and peace to you, I hope you will not render yourselves obnoxious to all laws, both human and divine, by a breach of the public tranquillity.' 'The Devil fetch me,' quoth Sancho to himself, 'if this master of mine must not have been bred a parson, if not, he is as like one as one egg is like another.' Don Quixote paused a while, to take breath; and perceiving his auditory still willing to give him attention, had proceeded in his harangue, had not Sancho's good opinion of his parts made him lay hold on this opportunity to talk in his turn. 'Gentlemen,' quoth he, 'my master Don Quixote de la Mancha, once called the "Knight of the Woeful Figure," and now the "Knight of the Lions," is a very judicious gentleman, and talks Latin and his own mother tongue as well as any of your 'varsity doctors. Whatever discourse he takes in hand, he speaks ye to the purpose, and like a man of mettle; he has ye all the laws and rules of that same thing you call duel and punctilio of honour, at his fingers' end; so that you have no more to do but to do as he says, and if in taking his counsel you ever tread awry, let the blame be laid on my shoulders. And indeed, as you have already been told, it is a very silly fancy to be ashamed to hear one bray; for I remember when I was a boy, I could bray as often as I listed, and nobody went about to hinder me; and I could do it so rarely, and to the life, without vanity be it spoken, that all the asses in our town would fall a-braying when they heard me bray; yet for all this, I was an honest body's child, and came of good parentage, do you see; it is true indeed, four of the best young men in our parish envied me for this great ability of mine; but I cared not a rush for their spite. Now, that you may not think I tell you a flam, do but hear me, and then judge; for this rare art is like swimming, which, when once learned, is never to be forgotten.' This said, he clapped both the palms of his hands to his nose, and fell a-braying so obstreperously, that it made the neighbouring valleys ring again. But while he was thus braying, one of those that stood next to him, believing he did it to mock them, gave him such a hearty blow with a quarterstaff on his back, that down he brought him to the ground. Don Quixote seeing what a rough entertainment had been given to his squire, moved with his lance in a threatening posture towards the man that had used poor Sancho thus; but the crowd thrust themselves in such a manner between them, that the Knight found it impracticable to pursue the revenge he designed. At the same time, finding that a shower of stones began to rain about his ears, and a great number of cross-bows and muskets were getting ready for his reception, he turned Rozinante's reins, and galloped from them as fast as four legs would carry him, sending up his hearty prayers to Heaven to deliver him from this danger, and, being under grievous apprehension at every step, that he should be shot through the back, and have the bullet come out at his breast, he still went fetching his breath, to try if it did any ways fail him. But the country battalion were satisfied with seeing him fly, and did not offer to shoot at him.

As for Sancho, he was set upon his ass before he had well recovered his senses, which the blow had taken from him, and then they suffered him to move off; not that the poor fellow had strength enough to guide him, but Dapple naturally followed Rozinante of his own accord, not being able to be a moment from him. The Don being at a good distance from the armed multitude, faced about, and seeing Sancho pacing after him without any troublesome attendants, stayed for his coming up. As for the rabble, they kept their posts till it grew dark, and their enemies not having taken the field to give them battle, they marched home, so overjoyed to have shown their courage, without danger, that had they been so well bred as to have known the ancient custom of the Greeks, they would have erected a trophy in that place.

CHAPTER XXVIII

Of some things which Benengeli tells us so that he that reads shall know, if he reads them with attention

WHEN THE VALIANT MAN flies, he must have discovered some foul play, and it is the part of prudent persons to reserve themselves for more favourable opportunities. This truth is verified in Don Quixote, who, rather than expose himself to the fury of an incensed and ill-designing multitude, betook himself to flight, without any thoughts of Sancho, till he found himself beyond the reach of those dangers in which he had left his trusty squire involved. Sancho came after him, as we have told you before, laid across his ass, and having recovered his senses overtook him at last, and let himself drop from his packsaddle at Rozinante's feet, all battered and bruised, and in a sorrowful condition. Don Quixote presently dismounted to search his wounds, and finding no bones broken, but his skin whole from head to feet, 'You must bray,' cried he angrily, 'you must bray, with a pox, must you! It is a piece of excellent discretion to talk of halters in the house of a man whose father was hanged. What counterpart could you expect to your music, blockhead, but a thorough-bass of bastinadoes? Thank Providence, sirrah! that as they gave you a dry benediction with a quarter-staff, they did not cross you with a cutlass.' 'I have not breath to answer you at present,' quoth Sancho, 'but my back and shoulders speak enough for me. Pray let us make the best of our way from this cursed place, and whenever I bray again, may I get such another pelt on my kidneys. Yet I cannot help saying, that your knights-errant can betake themselves to their heels to save one upon occasion, and leave their trusty squires to be beaten like stock-fish, in the midst of their enemies.' 'A retreat is not to be accounted a flight,' replied Don Quixote; 'for know, Sancho, that courage which has not wisdom for its guide, falls under the name of temerity; and the rash man's successful actions are rather owing to his good fortune than to his bravery. I own I did retire, but I deny that I fled; and in such a retreat I did but imitate many valiant men, who, not to hazard their persons indiscreetly, reserved themselves for a more fortunate hour. Histories are full of examples of this nature, which I do not care to relate at present, because they would be more tedious to me, than profitable to thee.'

By this time Don Quixote had helped Sancho to bestride his ass, and being himself mounted on Rozinante, they paced softly along, and got into a grove of poplar-trees, about a quarter of a league from the place where they mounted. Yet, as softly as they rid, Sancho could not help now and then heaving up deep sighs and lamentable groans. Don Quixote asked him, why he made such a heavy moan. Sancho told him, that from his rump to his poll, he felt such grievous pains that he was ready to sink. 'Without doubt,' said Don Quixote, 'the intenseness of thy torments is by reason the stick with which thou wert struck was broad and long, and so having fallen on those parts of thy back, caused a contusion there, and affects them all with pain; and had it been of a greater magnitude, thy grievances had been so much the greater.' 'Truly,' quoth Sancho, 'you have cleared that in very pithy words, of which nobody made any doubt. Body of me! was the cause of my ailing so hard to be guessed, that you must tell me that so much of me was sore as was hit by the weapon? Should my anklebone ache, and you scratch your head till you had found out the cause of it, I would think that something; but for you to tell me, that place is sore where I was bruised, every fool could do as much. Faith and troth, sir master of mine, I grow wiser and wiser every day: I find you are like all the world, that lay to heart nobody's harms but their own. I find whereabouts we are, and what I am like to get by you; for even as you left me now in the lurch to be well belaboured and rib-roasted, and the other day to dance the caper-galliard in the blanket you wot of; so I must expect a hundred and a hundred more of these good vails in your service; and as the mischief has now lighted on my shoulders, next bout I look for it to fly at my eyes. A plague of my jolter-head, I have been a fool and sot all along, and am never like to be wiser while I live. Would it not be better for me to trudge home to my wife and children, and look after my house with that little wit that Heaven has given me, without galloping after your tail high and low, through confounded cross-roads and by-ways, and wicked and crooked paths, that the ungodly themselves cannot find out; and then most commonly to have nothing to moisten one's weasand that is fitting for a Christian to drink, nothing but mere element and dogs' porridge; and nothing to stuff one's puddings that is worthy of a catholic stomach? Then after a man has tired himself off his legs, when he would be glad of a good bed, to have a master cry, "Here, are you sleepy? Lie down, Mr. Squire, your bed is made: take six feet of good hard ground, and measure your corpse there; and if that will not serve, take as much more and welcome; you are at rack and manger, spare not, I beseech your dogship, there is room enough." Old Nick roast and burn to a cinder that unlucky son of mischief that first set people a-madding after this whim of knight-errantry, or at least the first ninny-hammer that had so little forecast as to turn squire to such a parcel of madmen, as were your knights-errant – in the days of yore I mean; I am better bred than to speak ill of those in our time; no, I honour them, since your worship has taken up this blessed calling; for you have a long nose, the Devil himself could not out-reach you, you can see further into a millstone than he.' 'I durst lay a wager,' said Don Quixote, 'that now thou art suffered to prate without interruption, thou feelest no manner of pain in the whole body. Pr'ythee talk on, my child, for anything that comes uppermost to thy mouth, or is burdensome to thy brain; so it but alleviates thy pain thy impertinences will rather please than offend me; and if thou hast such a longing desire to be at home with thy wife and children, Heaven forbid I should be against it. Thou hast money of mine in thy hands; see how long it is since we sallied out last from home, and cast up thy wages by the month, and pay thyself.' 'If it like your worship,' quoth Sancho, 'when I served my master Carrasco, father to the bachelor, your worship's acquaintance, I had two ducats a month besides my victuals; I do not know what you will give me, though I am sure there is more trouble in being squire to a knight-errant, than in being servant to a farmer; for truly we that go to plough and cart in a farmer's service, though we moil and sweat so a-days as not to have a dry thread to our backs, let the worst come to the worst, are sure of a bellyful at night out of the pot, and to snore in a bed. But I do not know when I had a good meal, or a good night's rest in all your whole service, unless it were that short time when we were at Don Diego's house, and when I made a feast on the flavoury skimming of Camacho's cauldron, and eat, drank, and lay at Mr. Basil's. All the rest of my time I have had my lodging on the cold ground, and in the open fields, subject to the inclemency of the sky, as you call it; living on the rinds of cheese, and crusts of mouldy bread; drinking sometimes ditch-water, sometimes spring, as we chanced to light upon it in our way.' 'Well,' said Don Quixote, 'I grant all this, Sancho, then how much more dost thou expect from me, than thou hadst from thy master Carrasco?' 'Why, truly,' quoth Sancho 'if your worship will pay me twelve-pence a month more than Thomas Carrasco gave me, I shall think it very fair, and tolerable wages; but then, instead of the island which you know you promised me, I think you cannot in conscience give me less than six and thirty-pence a month more, which will make in all thirty reals, neither more nor less.' 'Very well,' said Don Quixote, 'let us see, then, it is now twenty-five days since we set out from home, reckon what this comes to, according to the wages thou hast allowed thyself, and be thy own paymaster.' 'Odsdiggers!' quoth Sancho, 'we are quite out in our account; for as to the governor of an island's place, which you promised to help me to, we ought to reckon from the time you made the promise, to this very day.' 'Well, and pray how long is it?' asked Don Quixote. 'If I remember rightly,' quoth Sancho, 'it is about some twenty years ago, two or three days more or less.' With that Don Quixote, hitting himself a good clap on the forehead, fell a-laughing heartily. 'Why,' cried he, 'we have hardly been out two months from the very beginning of our first expedition, and in all that time we were in Sierra Morena, and our whole progress: and hast thou the impudence to affirm it is twenty years since I promised the grant of the island? I am now convinced thou hast a mind to make all the money which thou hast of mine in thy keeping go for the payment of thy wages. If this be thy meaning, well and good, even take it, and much good may it do thee; for rather than be troubled any longer with such a varlet, I would contentedly see myself without a penny. But tell me, thou perverter of the laws of chivalry that relate to squires, where didst thou ever see or read, that any squire to a knight-errant stood capitulating with his master, as thou hast done with me, for so much, or so much a month? Launch, unconscionable wretch, thou cut-throat scoundrel! launch, launch, thou base spirit of mammon, into the vast ocean of their histories, and if they canst show me a precedent of any squire that ever dared to say, or but to think, as much as thou hast presumed to tell me, then will I give leave to affix it on my forehead, and hit me four fillips on the nose. Away, then, pack off with thy ass this moment, and get thee home, for thou shalt never stay in my service any longer. Oh how much bread, how many promises have I now ill-bestowed on thee! Vile grovelling wretch, that hast more of the beast than of the man! When I was just going to prefer thee to such a post, that in spite of thy wife thou hadst been called "My Lord," thou sneakest away from me. Thou art leaving me when I had resolved, without any more delay to make thee lord of the best island in the world, sordid clod! Well mightest thou say indeed, that honey is not for the chaps of an ass. Thou art indeed a very ass, an ass thou wilt live, and an ass thou wilt die; for I dare say, thou wilt never have sense enough while thou livest to know thou art a brute.' While Don Quixote thus upbraided and railed at Sancho, the poor fellow, all dismayed, and touched to the quick, beheld him with a wistful look; and the tears standing in his eyes for grief. 'Good sweet sir,' cried he with a doleful and whining voice; 'I confess I want nothing but a tail to be a perfect ass; if your worship will be pleased but to put one to my backside, I shall deem it well set on, and be your most faithful ass all the days of my life. But forgive me, I beseech you, and take pity on my youth. Consider I have but a dull headpiece of my own and if my tongue runs at random sometimes, it is because I am more fool than knave, sir: "Who errs and mends, to Heaven himself commends." ' 'I should wonder much,' said Don Quixote, 'if thou shouldest not interlard thy discourse with some pretty proverb. Well, I will give thee my pardon for this once, provided thou correct those imperfections that offend me, and showest thyself of a less craving temper. Take heart, then, and let the hopes which thou mayest entertain of the performance of my promise, raise in thee a nobler spirit. The time will come, do not think it impossible because delayed.' Sancho promised to do his best, though he could not rely on his own strength.

Matters being thus amicably adjusted, they put into the grove, where the Don laid himself at the foot of an elm, and his squire at the foot of a beech; for every one of those trees, and such others, has always a foot, though never a hand. Sancho had but an ill night's rest of it, for his bruises made his bones more than ordinarily sensible of the cold. As for Don Quixote, he entertained himself with his usual imaginations. However, they both slept, and by break of day continued their journey towards the river Ebro, where they met – what shall be told in the next chapter.

CHAPTER XXIX

The famous Adventure of the Enchanted Park

FAIR AND SOFTLY, step by step, Don Quixote and his squire got in two days' time to the banks of the river Ebro, which yielded a very entertaining prospect to the Knight. The verdure of its banks, and the abounding plenty of the water, which, clear like liquid crystal, flowed gently along within the spacious channel, awaked a thousand amorous chimeras in his roving imagination, and more especially the thoughts of what he had seen in Montesinos' cave; for though Master Peter's ape had assured him that it was partly false as well as partly true, he was rather inclined to believe it all true; quite contrary to Sancho, who thought it every tittle as false as hell.

While the Knight went on thus agreeably amused, he spied a little boat without any oars or tackle, moored by the riverside to the stump of a tree; thereupon looking round about him, and discovering nobody, he presently alighted, and ordered Sancho to do the like, and tie their beasts fast to some of the elms or willows thereabouts. Sancho asked him what was the meaning of all this. 'Thou art to know,' answered Don Quixote, 'that most certain this boat lies here for no other reason but to invite me to embark in it, for the relief of some knight, or other person of high degree, that is in great distress: for thus, according to the method of enchanters in the books of chivalry, when any knight whom they protect happens to be involved in some very great danger, from which none but some other valorous knight can set him free; then, though they be two or three thousand leagues at least distant from each other, up the magician snatches the auxiliary champion in a cloud, or else provides him a boat, and in the twinkling of an eye, in either vehicle, through the airy fluid, or the liquid plain, he wafts him to the place where his assistance is wanted. Just to the same intent does this very bark lie here; it is as clear as the day, and therefore, before it be too late, Sancho, tie up Rozinante and Dapple, let us commit ourselves to the guidance of Providence, for embark I will, though barefooted friars should beg me to desist.' 'Well, well,' quoth Sancho, 'if I must, I must. Since you will every foot run hazard into these – I don't know how to call them, these confounded vagaries, I have no more to do but to make a leg, and submit my neck to the collar; for, as the saying is, "Do as thy master bids thee, though it be to sit down at his table." But for all that, fall back, fall edge, I must and will discharge my conscience, and tell you plainly, that, as blind as I am, I can see with half an eye that it is no enchanted bark, but some fisherman's boat; for there are many in this river, whose waters affords the best shads in the world.' This caution did Sancho give his master while he was tying the beasts to a tree, and going to leave them to the protection of enchanters, full sore against his will. Don Quixote bid him not be concerned at leaving them there, for the sage who was to carry them through in a journey of such an extent and longitude, would be sure to take care of the animals. 'Nay, as for that matter,' quoth Sancho, 'I do not understand your longitude, I never heard such a cramp word in my born days.' 'Longitude,' said Don Quixote, 'is the same as length: I do not wonder that thou dost not understand the word, for thou art not obliged to understand Latin. Yet you shall have some forward coxcombs pretend to be knowing when they are ignorant.' 'Now the beasts are fast sir,' quoth Sancho, 'what is next to be done?' 'Why now,' answered Don Quixote, 'let us recommend ourselves to Providence and weigh anchor; or, to speak plainly, embark and cut the cable.' With that, leaping in, and Sancho following, he cut the rope, and so by degrees the stream carried the boat from the shore. Now when Sancho saw himself towards the middle of the river, he began to quake for fear; but nothing grieved his heart so much as to hear Dapple bray, and to see Rozinante struggle to get loose. 'Sir,' quoth he, 'hark how my poor Dapple brays, to bemoan our leaving of him; and see how poor Rozinante tugs hard to break his bridle, and is even wild to throw himself after us. Alack and alack! my poor dear friends, peace be with you where you are, and when this mad freak, the cause of our doleful parting, is ended in repentance, may we be brought back to your sweet company again." This said, he fell a-blubbering, and set up such a howl, that non Quixote had no patience with him, but looking angrily on him, 'What dost thou fear,' cried he, 'thou great white-livered calf? What dost thou cry for? Who pursues thee? Who hurts thee, thou dastardly craven, thou cowardly mouse, thou soul of a milk-sop, thou heart of butter? Dost want for anything, base unsatisfied wretch? What wouldest thou say, wert thou to climb barefoot the rugged Riphaen mountains: thou that sittest here in state like an archduke, plenty and delight on each side of thee, while thou glidest gently down the calm current of this delightful river, which will soon convey us into the main ocean? We have already flowed down some seven or eight hundred leagues. Had I but an astrolabe here to take the altitude of the pole, I could easily tell thee how far we have proceeded to an inch: though either I know but little, or we have just passed, or shall presently pass, the Equinoctial Line, that divides and cuts the two opposite poles at equal distances.'

'And when we come to this same line you speak of,' quoth Sancho, 'how far have we gone then?' 'A mighty way,' answered Don Quixote. 'When we come under the line I speak of, we shall have measured the other half of the terraqueous globe, which according to the system and computation of Ptolemy, who was the greatest cosmographer in the world, contains three hundred and sixty degrees.' 'Osbodikins,' quoth Sancho, 'you have brought me now a notable fellow to be your voucher, goodman Tollme, with his "amputation" and "cistern," and the rest of your gibberish!' Don Quixote smiled at Sancho's blunders, and going on, 'The Spaniards,' said he, 'and all those that embark at Cadiz for the East Indies, to know whether they have passed the Equinoctial Line, according to an observation that has been often experienced, need do no more than look whether there be any lice left alive among the ship's crew; for, if they have passed it, not a louse is to be found in the ship, though they would give his weight in gold for him. Look therefore, Sancho, and if thou findest any such vermin still creeping about thee, then we have not yet passed the line; but if thou doest not, then we have surely passed it.' 'The devil a word I believe of all this,' quoth Sancho. 'However I will do as you bid me. But hark you me, sir, now I think on it again, where is the need of trying the quirks; do not I see with my two eyes that we are not five rods length from the shore? Look you there stands Rozinante and Dapple, upon the very spot where we left them; and now I look closely into the matter, I will take my corporal oath that we move no faster than a snail can gallop, or an ant can trot.' 'No more words,' said Don Quixote, 'but make the experiment as I bid you, and let the rest alone. Thou dost not know what belongs to colures, lines, parallels, zodiacs, ecliptics, poles, solstices, equinoctials, planets, signs, points, and measures, of which the spheres celestial and terrestrial are composed; for didst thou know of all these things, or some of them at least, thou mightest plainly perceive what parallels we have cut, what signs we have passed, and what constellations we have left, and are now leaving behind us. Therefore I would wish thee once again to search thyself; for I cannot believe but thou art as clear from vermin as a sheet of white paper.' Thereupon Sancho advancing his hand very gingerly towards the left side of his neck, after he had groped a while, lifted up his head; and staring in his master's face, 'Look you, sir,' quoth he, pulling out something, 'either your rule is not worth this, or we are many a fair league from the place you spoke of.' 'How!' answered Don Quixote, 'hast thou found something then, Sancho?' 'Ay, marry have I,' quoth Sancho; 'and more things than one too,' and so saying he shook and snapped his fingers, and then washed his whole hand in the river; down whose stream the boat drove gently along, without being moved by any secret influence or hidden enchantment, but only by the help of the current, hitherto calm and smooth.

By this time they descried two great water-mills in the middle of the river, which Don Quixote no sooner spied, but calling to his squire, 'Look, look, my Sancho!' cried he, 'seest thou yon city or castle there! This is the place where some knight lies in distress, or some queen or princess is detained, for whose succour I am conveyed hither.' 'What a devil do you mean with your city or castle?' cried Sancho. 'Body of me! sir, do not you see, as plain as the nose on your face, they are nothing but water-mills, in the midst of the river, to grind corn?' 'Peace, Sancho,' replied Don Quixote, 'they look like water-mills, I grant you, but they are no such things: how often, have I not told thee already, do these magicians change and overturn everything as they please; not that they can change their very being, but they disguise and alter the appearances of them; of which we have an instance in the unhappy transformation of Dulcinea, the only refuge of my hope.'

The boat being now got into the very strength of the stream, began to move less slowly than it did before. The people in the mills perceiving the boat to come adrift full upon the mill-wheels, came running out with their long poles to stop it: and as their faces and clothes were powdered all over with meal dust, they made a very odd appearance. 'So ho! there,' cried they as loud as they could bawl, 'is the Devil in the fellows! are ye mad in the boat there! Hold! you will be drowned, or ground to pieces by the mill-wheels.' Don Quixote having cast his eyes on the millers, 'Did I not tell thee, Sancho,' said he, 'that we should arrive where I must exert the strength of my arm? Look what hang-dogs, what horrid wretches come forth to make head against me! How many hobgoblins oppose my passage! Do but see what deformed physiognomies they have: mere bugbears! But I shall make ye know, scoundrels, how insignificant all your efforts must prove.' Then, standing up in the boat, he began to threaten the millers in a haughty tone: 'Ye paltry slaves!' cried he, 'base and ill-advised scum of the world, release instantly the captive person who is injuriously detained and oppressed within your castle or prison, be they of high or low degree; for I am Don Quixote de la Mancha, otherwise called the Knight of the Lions, for whom the happy achievement of this adventure is reserved, by the decree of Heaven.' This said, he unsheathed his sword, and began to fence with the air, as if he had been already engaging the millers; who hearing, but not understanding, his mad words, stood ready with their poles to stop the boat, which was now near the mill-dam and just entering the rapid stream and narrow channel of the wheels.

In the mean time, Sancho was devoutly fallen on his knees, praying Heaven for a happy deliverance out of this mighty plunge but this one time. And indeed his prayers met with pretty good success; for the millers so bestirred themselves with their poles that they stopped the boat, yet not so cleverly but they overset it, tipping Don Quixote and Sancho over into the river. It was well for the Knight that he could swim like a duck; and yet the weight of his armour sunk him twice to the bottom; and had it not been for the millers, who jumped into the water, and made shift to pull out both the master and the man, in a manner craning them up, there had been an end of them both.

When they were both hauled ashore, more over-drenched than thirsty, Sancho betook himself to his knees again, and with uplifted hands and eyes made a long and hearty prayer that Heaven might keep him from this time forwards clear of his master's rash adventures.

And now came the fishermen who owned the boat, and finding it broken to pieces, fell upon Sancho, and began to strip him, demanding satisfaction both of him and his master for the loss of their bark. The Knight with a great deal of gravity and unconcern, as if he had done no manner of harm, told both the millers and the fishermen, that he was ready to pay for the boat, provided they would fairly surrender the persons that were detained unjustly in their castle. 'What persons, or what castle, you mad oaf?' said one of the millers. 'Marry guep, would you carry away the folk that come to grind their corn at our mills?' 'Well,' said Don Quixote to himself, 'man had as good preach to a stone-wall, as to expect to persuade with entreaties such dregs of human kind to do a good and generous action. Two sage enchanters certainly clash in this adventure, and the one thwarts the other: one provided me a bark, the other overwhelmed me in it. Heaven send us better times! There is nothing but plotting and counter-plotting, undermining and counter-mining in this world. Well, I can do no more.' Then raising his voice, and casting a fixed eye on the water-mills, 'My dear friends,' cried he, 'whoever you are that are immured in this prison, pardon me, I beseech ye; for so my ill-fate and yours ordains, that I cannot free you from your confinement: the adventure is reserved for some other knight.' This said, he came to an agreement with the fishermen, and ordered Sancho to pay them fifty reals for the boat. Sancho pulled out the money with very ill-will, and parted with it with a worse, muttering between his teeth, that two voyages like that would sink their whole stock.

The fishermen and the millers could not forbear admiring at two such figures of human offsprings, that neither spoke nor acted like the rest of mankind: for they could not so much as guess what Don Quixote meant by all his extravagant speeches; so taking them for madmen, they left them, and went, the millers to their mills, and the fishermen to their huts.

Don Quixote and Sancho returned to their beasts like a couple of senseless animals; and thus ended the adventure of the enchanted bark.

CHAPTER XXX

What happened to Don Quixote with the fair Huntress

WITH WET BODIES and melancholy minds, the Knight and squire went back to Rozinante and Dapple; though Sancho was the more cast down and out of sorts of the two; for it grieved him to the very soul to see the money dwindle; being as chary of that as of his heart's blood, or the apples of his eyes. To be short, to horse they went, without speaking one word to each other, and left the famous river: Don Quixote buried in his amorous thoughts, and Sancho in those of his preferment, which he thought far enough off yet; for as much a fool as he was, he plainly perceived that all, or most of his master's actions, tended only to folly: therefore he but waited an opportunity to give him the slip and go home, without coming to any further reckoning, or taking a formal leave. But fortune provided for him much better than he expected.

It happened that the next day about sunset, as they were coming out of a wood, Don Quixote cast his eyes around a verdant meadow, and at the further end of it descried a company, whom upon nearer view he judged to be persons of quality, that were taking the diversion of hawking; approaching nearer yet, he observed among them a very fine lady upon a white pacing mare, in green trappings, and a saddle-cloth of silver. The lady herself was dressed in green, so rich and so gay, that nothing could be finer. She rode with a goss-hawk on her left fist, by which Don Quixote judged her to be of quality, and mistress of the train that attended; as indeed she was. Thereupon calling to his squire, 'Son Sancho,' cried he, 'run and tell that lady on the palfrey with the goss-hawk on her fist, that I the "Knight of the Lions" humbly salute her highness; and that if she pleases to give me leave, I should be proud to receive her commands, and have the honour of waiting on her, and kissing her fair hands. But take special care, Sancho, how thou deliverest thy message, and be sure do not lard my compliments with any of thy proverbs.' 'Why this to me?' quoth Sancho. 'Marry, you need not talk of larding, as if I had never went ambassador before to a high and mighty dame.' 'I do not know that ever thou didst,' replied Don Quixote, 'at least on my account, unless it were when I sent thee to Dulcinea.' 'It may be so,' quoth Sancho; 'but a good paymaster needs no surety; and where there is plenty the guests cannot be empty: that is to say, I need none of your telling, nor tutoring about that matter: for, as silly as I look, I know something of everything.' 'Well, well, I believe it,' said Don Quixote; 'go then in a good hour, and Heaven inspire and guide thee.'

Sancho put on, forcing Dapple from his old pace to a gallop; and approaching the fair huntress, he alighted, and falling on his knees, 'Fair lady,' quoth he, 'that knight yonder, called "the Knight of the Lions," is my master: I am his squire, Sancho Pança by name. This same "Knight of the Lions," who but the other day was called "the Knight of the Woeful Figure," has sent me to tell you, that, so please your Worship's Grace to give him leave, with your good liking, to do as he has a mind; which, as he says, and as I believe, is only to serve your high-flown beauty, and be your 'ternal vassal; you may chance to do a thing that would be for your own good, and he would take it for a hugeous kindness at your hands.' 'Indeed, honest squire,' said the lady, 'you have acquitted yourself of your charge with all the graceful circumstances which such an embassy requires: rise, pray rise; for it is by no means fit the squire to so great a knight as "the Knight of the Woeful Figure," to whose name and merit we are no strangers, should remain on his knees. Rise then, and desire your master, by all means to honour us with his company, that my Lord Duke and I may pay him our respects at a house we have hard by.'

Sancho got up, no less amazed at the lady's beauty than her affability, but much more because she told him they were no strangers to his master, 'the Knight of the Woeful Figure.' Nor did he wonder why she did not call him by his title of 'Knight of the Lions'; considering he had but lately assumed it.

'Pray,' said the Duchess (whose particular title we do not yet know), 'is not this master of yours the person, whose history came out in print, by the name of "The renowned Don Quixote de la Mancha," the mistress of whose affections is a certain lady called Dulcinea del Toboso?' 'The very same, if it please your worship,' said Sancho; 'and that squire of his that is or should be in the book, Sancho Pança by name, is my own self, if I was not changed in my cradle; I mean, changed in the press.' 'I am mighty glad to hear all this,' said the Duchess. 'Go then, friend Pança, and tell your master, that I congratulate him upon his arrival in our territories, to which he is welcome; and assure him from me, that this is the most agreeable news I could possibly have heard.'

Sancho, overjoyed with this gracious answer, returned to his master, to whom he repeated all that the great lady had said to him; praising to the skies, in his clownish phrase, her great beauty and courteous nature.

Don Quixote, pleased with this good beginning, seated himself handsomely in the saddle, fixed his toes in his stirrups, set the bever of his helmet as he thought best became his face, roused up Rozinante's mettle, and with a graceful assurance moved forwards to kiss the Duchess's hand. As soon as Sancho went from her, she sent for the Duke her husband and gave him an account of Don Quixote's embassy. Thereupon they both attended his coming with a pleasant impatience; for having read the first part of his history, they were no less desirous to be acquainted with his person; and resolved, as long as he stayed with them, to give him his own way, and humour him in all things, treating him still with all the forms essential to the entertainment of a knight-errant; which they were the better able to do, having been much conversant with books of that kind.

And now Don Quixote drew nigh with his vizor up; and Sancho, seeing him offer to alight, made all the haste he could to be ready to hold his stirrup: but, as ill-luck would have it, as he was throwing his leg over his pack-saddle to get off, he entangled his foot so strangely in the rope which served him instead of a stirrup, that not being able to get it out, he hung by the heel with his nose to the ground. On the other side Don Quixote, who was used to have his stirrup held when he dismounted, thinking Sancho had hold of it already lifted up his right leg over the saddle to alight; but as it happened to be ill-girt, down he brought it with himself to the ground, confounded with shame, and muttering between his teeth many a hearty curse against Sancho, who was all the while with his foot in the stocks. The Duke seeing them in that condition, ordered some of his people to help them; and they raised Don Quixote, who was in a very bad case with his fall: however, limping as well as he could, he went to pay his duty to the lady, and would have fallen on his knees at her horse's feet: but the Duke alighting, would by no means permit it; and embracing Don Quixote, 'I am sorry,' said he, 'Sir Knight of the Woeful Figure, that such a mischance should happen to you at your first appearance on my territories; the negligence of squires is often the cause of worse accidents.' 'Most generous prince,' said Don Quixote, 'I can think nothing bad that befalls me here, since I have had the happiness of seeing your Grace: for though I had fallen low as the very centre, the glory of this interview would raise me up again. My squire indeed, a vengeance seize him for it, is much more apt to give his saucy idle tongue a loose, than to gird a saddle well; but prostrate or erect, on horseback or on foot, in any posture I shall always be at your Grace's command, and no less at her Grace's, your worthy consort's service. Worthy did I say; yes, she is worthy to be called the queen of beauty, and sovereign lady of all courtesy.' 'Pardon me there,' said the Duke, 'noble Don Quixote de la Mancha; where the peerless Dulcinea is remembered, the praise of all other beauties ought to be forgot.'

Sancho was now got clear of the noose, and standing near the Duchess, 'If it please your Worship's Highness,' quoth he, before his master could answer, 'it cannot be denied, nay, I dare vouch it in any ground in Spain, that my Lady Dulcinea del Toboso is woundy handsome and fair: but "where we least think, there starts the hare." I have heard your great scholars say, that she you call Dame Nature, is like a potter, and he that makes one handsome pipkin may make two or three hundred. So, do ye see, you may understand by this, that my lady Duchess here does not a jot come short of my lady Dulcinea del Toboso.' Don Quixote, upon this addressed himself to the Duchess, 'Your Grace must know,' said he, 'that no knight-errant ever had such an eternal babbler, such a bundle of conceit for a squire, as I have; and if I have the honour to continue for some time in your service, your Grace will find it true.' 'I am glad,' answered the Duchess, 'that honest Sancho has his conceits, it is a shrewd sign he is wise; for merry conceits, you know, sir, are not the offspring of a dull brain, and therefore if Sancho be jovial and jocose, I will warrant him also a man of sense.' 'And a prater, madam,' added Don Quixote. 'So much the better,' said the Duke; 'for a man that talks well, can never talk too much. But not to lose our time here, come on, Sir Knight of the Woeful Figure' – ' "Knight of the Lions," your Highness should say,' quoth Sancho; 'the "Woeful Figure" is out of date: and so pray let the "Lions" come in play.' 'Well, then,' said the Duke, 'I entreat the Knight of the Lions to vouchsafe us his presence at a castle I have hard by, where he shall find such entertainment, as is justly due to so eminent a personage, such honours as the Duchess and myself are not wont to pay to all knights-errant that travel this way.'

Sancho having by this time got Rozinante ready, and girded the saddle tight, Don Quixote mounted his steed, and the Duke a stately horse of his own; and, the Duchess riding between them both, they moved towards the castle: she desired that Sancho might always attend near her, for she was extremely taken with his notable sayings. Sancho was not hard to be entreated, but crowded in between them, and made a fourth in their conversation, to the great satisfaction of both the Duke and the Duchess, who esteemed themselves very fortunate, in having an opportunity to entertain at their castle such a knight-errant and such an erring squire.

CHAPTER XXXI

Which treats of many and great matters

SANCHO WAS OVERJOYED to find himself so much in the Duchess's favour, flattering himself that he should fare no worse at her castle than he had done at Don Diego's and Basil's houses; for he was ever a cordial friend to a plentiful way of living, and therefore never failed to take such opportunities by the foretop, wherever he met them. Now the history tells us, that before they got to the castle, the Duke rode away from them, to instruct his servants how to behave themselves towards Don Quixote; so that no sooner did the Knight come near the gates, but he was met by two of the Duke's lacqueys or grooms in long vests, like nightgowns, of fine crimson satin. These suddenly took him in their arms, and lifting him from his horse without any further ceremony, 'Go, great and mighty sir,' said they, 'and help my Lady Duchess down.' Thereupon Don Quixote went and offered to do it; and many compliments and much ceremony passed on both sides: but in conclusion the Duchess's earnestness prevailed; for she would not alight from her palfrey but in the arms of her husband, excusing herself from incommoding so great a knight with so insignificant a burden. With that the Duke took her down. And now, being entered into a large courtyard, there came two beautiful damsels, who threw a long mantle of fine scarlet over Don Quixote's shoulders. In an instant, all the galleries about the courtyard were crowded with men and women, the domestics of the Duke, who cried, 'Welcome, welcome, the flower and cream of knight-errantry!' Then most, if not all of them, sprinkled bottles of sweet water upon Don Quixote, the Duke, and Duchess: all which agreeably surprised the Don, and this was indeed the first day he knew and firmly believed himself to be a real knight-errant, and that his knighthood was more than fancy; finding himself treated just as he had read the brothers of the order were entertained in former ages.

Sancho was so transported, that he even forsook his beloved Dapple, to keep close to the Duchess, and entered the castle with the company: but his conscience flying in his face for leaving that dear companion of his alone, he went to a reverend old waiting-woman, who was one of the Duchess's retinue, and whispering her in the ear, 'Mrs Gonzales, or Mrs – pray forsooth may I crave your name?' 'Donna Rodriguez de Grijalva is my name,' said the old duenna; 'what is your business with me, friend?' 'Pray now, mistress,' quoth Sancho, 'do so much as go out at the castle-gate, where you will find a dapple ass of mine; see him into the stable, or else put him in yourself; for, poor thing, it is main fearful and timersome, and cannot abide to be alone in a strange place.' 'If the master,' said she pettishly, 'has no more manners than the man, we shall have a fine time of it. Get you gone, you saucy jack, the Devil take thee and him that brought you hither to affront me. Go seek somewhere else for ladies to look to your ass, you lolpoop! I would have you to know, that gentlewomen like me are not used to such drudgeries.' 'Do not take pepper in your nose at it,' replied Sancho, 'you need not be so frumpish, mistress. As good as you have done it. I have heard my master say (and he knows all the histories in the world), that when Sir Lancelot came out of Britain, damsels looked after him, and waiting-women after his horse. Now, by my troth! whether you believe it or no, I would not swop my ass for Sir Lancelot's horse, I will tell you that.' 'I think the fool rides the fellow,' quoth the waiting-woman; 'hark you, friend, if you be a buffoon, keep your stuff for those chapmen that will bid you fairer. I would not give a fig for all the jests in your budget.' 'Well enough yet,' quoth Sancho, 'and a fig for you too, if you go to that. Adad! should I take thee for a fig, I might be sure of a ripe one, your fig is rotten ripe, forsooth; say no more: if sixty is the game, you are a peep-out.' 'You rascally son of a whore,' cried the waiting-woman, in a pelting chafe, 'whether I am old or no, Heaven best knows, I shall not stand to give an account to such a ragamuffin as thou, thou garlic-eating stinkard.' She spoke this so loud that the Duchess overheard her; and seeing the woman so altered, and as red as fire, asked what was the matter. 'Why, madam,' said the waiting-woman, 'here is a fellow would have me put his ass in the stable: telling me an idle story of ladies that looked after one Lancelot, and waiting-women after his horse; and because I will not be his ostler, the rake-shame very civilly calls me old.' 'Old,' said the Duchess, 'that is an affront no woman can well bear. You are mistaken, honest Sancho, Rodriguez is very young, and the long veil she wears, is more for authority and fashion-sake, than upon account of her years.' 'May there be never a good one in all those days I have to live,' quoth Sancho, 'if I meant her any harm, only I have such a natural love for my ass, if it like your worship, that I thought I could not recommend the poor tilt to a more charitable body than this same Madam Rodriguez.' 'Sancho,' said Don Quixote, with a sour look, 'does this talk befit this place? Do you know where you are?' 'Sir,' quoth Sancho, 'every man must tell his wants, be he where he will. Here I bethought myself of Dapple, and here I spoke of him: had I called him to mind in the stable, I would have spoken of him there.'

'Sancho has reason on his side,' said the Duke; 'and nobody ought to chide him for it. But let him take no further care, Dapple shall have as much provender as he will eat, and be used as well as Sancho himself.'

These small jars being over, which yielded diversion to all the company, except Don Quixote, he was led up a stately staircase, and then into a noble hall sumptuously hung with rich gold brocade. There his armour was taken off by six young damsels, that served him instead of pages, all of them fully instructed by the Duke and Duchess how to behave themselves so towards Don Quixote, that he might look on his entertainment as conformable to those which the famous knights-errant received of old.

When he was unarmed, he appeared in his close breeches and chamois doublet, raw-boned and meagre, tall and lank, with a pair of lantern jaws that met in the middle of his mouth; in short, he made so very odd a figure, that notwithstanding the strict injunction the Duke had laid on the young females who waited on him, to stifle their laughter, they were hardly able to contain. They desired he would give them leave to take off his clothes, and put on him a clean shirt. But he would by no means permit it, giving them to understand, that modesty was as commendable a virtue in a knight as valour; and therefore he desired them to leave the shirt with Sancho; and then retiring to an adjacent chamber, where there was a rich bed, he locked himself up with his squire, pulled off his clothes, shifted himself, and then while they were alone he began to take him to task.

'Now,' said he, 'modern buffoon and jolter-head of old, what canst thou say for thyself? Who learned you to abuse such a venerable ancient gentlewoman, one so worthy of respect as Donna Rodriguez? Was that a proper time to think of your Dapple? Or can you think persons of quality, who nobly entertain the masters, forget to provide for their beasts? For Heaven's sake, Sancho, mend thy behaviour, and do not betray thy homespun breeding, lest thou be thought a scandal to thy master. Dost not thou know, saucy rustic, that the world often makes an estimate of the master's discretion by that of his servant, and that one of the most considerable advantages the great have over their inferiors, is to have servants as good as themselves? Art thou not sensible pitiful fellow as thou art, the more unhappy I, that if they find thee a gross clown, or a mad buffoon, they will take me for some hedge knight or a paltry shifting rook? Pray thee, therefore, dear Sancho, shun these inconveniences; for he that aims too much at jests and drolling, is apt to trip and tumble and is at last despised as an insipid ridiculous buffoon. Then curb thy tongue, think well, and ponder thy words before they get loose; and take notice we are come to a place, whence by the assistance of Heaven, and the force of this puissant arm we may depart better five to one in fortune and reputation.' Sancho promised to behave himself better for the future, and to sew up his mouth or bite out his tongue, rather than speak one word which was not duly considered, and to the purpose; so that his master need not fear any one should find out what they were. Don Quixote then dressed himself, put on his belt and sword, threw his scarlet cloak over his shoulders, and clapped on a monteer cap of green velvet, which had been left him by the damsels. Thus accoutred, he entered the stateroom, where he found the damsels ranged in two rows, attending with water, and all necessaries to wash him in state; and having done him that office, with many humble courtesies and solemn ceremonies, immediately twelve pages with the gentleman-sewer at the head of them, came to conduct him to supper, letting him know that the Duke and Duchess expected him. Accordingly, they led him in great pomp, some walking before and some behind, into another room, where a table was magnificently set out for four people.

As soon as he approached, the Duke and the Duchess came as far as the door to receive him, and with them a grave clergyman, one of those that assume to govern great men's houses, and who, not being nobly born themselves, do not know how to instruct those that are, but would have the liberality of the great measured by the narrowness of their own souls, making those whom they govern stingy, when they pretend to teach them frugality. One of these in all likelihood was this grave ecclesiastic, who came with the Duke to receive Don Quixote.

After a thousand courtly compliments on all sides, Don Quixote at last approached the table, between the Duke and the Duchess, and here arose a fresh contest; for the Knight, being offered the upper end of the table, thought himself obliged to decline it. However he could not withstand the Duke's pressing importunities, but was forced at last to comply. The parson sat right against him, and the Duke and the Duchess on each side.

Sancho stood by all the while, gaping with wonder to see the honour done his master; and observing how many ceremonies passed, and what entreaties the Duke used to prevail with him to sit at the upper end of the table: 'With your worship's good leave,' quoth he, 'I will tell you what once happened in our town, in reference to this stir and ado that you have had now about places.' The words were scarce out of his mouth, when Don Quixote began to tremble, having reason to believe he was going to throw up some impertinent thing or other. Sancho had his eyes upon him, and presently understanding his motions, 'Sir,' quoth he, 'do not fear; I will not be unmannerly, I warrant you. I will speak nothing but what shall be pat to the purpose: I have not so soon forgot the lesson you gave me about talking sense or nonsense, little or much.' 'I do not know what thou meanest,' said Don Quixote; 'say what thou wilt, so thou do it quickly.' 'Well,' quoth Sancho, turning to the Duke, 'what I am going to tell you is every tittle true. Should I trip never so little in my story, my master is here to take me up, and give me the lie.' 'Pr'ythee,' said Don Quixote, 'lie as much as thou wilt, for all me; I will not be thy hindrance. But take heed however what thou sayest.' 'Nay, nay,' quoth Sancho, 'let me alone for that: I have heeded it and reheeded it over and over, and that you shall see, I warrant you.' 'Truly, my lord,' said Don Quixote, 'it were convenient, that your Grace should order this fellow to be turned out of the room; for he will plague you with a thousand impertinences.' 'Oh, as for that you must excuse us,' said the Duchess, 'for by the Duke's life* I swear, Sancho must not stir a step from me; I will engage for him he shall say nothing but what is very proper.' 'Many and many proper years,' quoth Sancho, 'may your holiness live, Madam Duchess, for your good opinion of me; though it is more your goodness than my desert. Now then for my tale.

'Once upon a time a gentleman in our town, of a good estate and family,

---

* A custom in Spain to swear by the life of those they love and honour.

for he was of the blood of the Alamos of Medina del Campo, and married one Donna Mencia de Quinones, who was the daughter of Don Alonzo de Maranon, a knight of the order of St. Jago, the very same that was drowned in the Herradura, about whom that quarrel happened formerly in our town, in which I heard say that my master, Don Quixote, was embroiled, and little Tom the mad-cap, who was the son of old Balvastro the farrier, happened to be sorely hurt. Is not all this true now, master? Speak the truth and shame the Devil, that their Worships' Graces may know that I am neither a prater nor a liar.' 'Thus far,' said the clergyman, 'I think thou art the first rather than the latter; I cannot tell what I shall make of thee by and by.' 'Thou producest so many witnesses, Sancho,' said Don Quixote, 'and mentionest so many circumstances, that I must needs own, I believe what thou sayest to be true. But go on, and shorten the story; for, as thou beginnest, I am afraid thou wilt not have done these two days.' 'Pray do not let him shorten it,' said the Duchess; 'let him go on his own way, though he were not done these six days: I shall hear him with pleasure, and think the time as pleasantly employed as any I ever passed in my life.' 'I say then, my masters,' quoth Sancho, 'that this same gentleman I told you of at first, and I know him as well as I know my right hand from my left, for it is not a bow-shot from my house to his; this gentleman invited a husbandman to dine with him, who was a poor man, but main honest.' 'On, friend,' said the chaplain; 'at the rate you proceed you will not have made an end before you come to the other world.' 'I shall stop short of half-way,' quoth Sancho, 'if it be Heaven's blessed will: a little more of your Christian patience, good doctor! Now this same husbandman, as I said before, coming to this gentleman's house, who had given him the invitation, Heaven rest his soul, poor heart, for he is now dead and gone; and more than that, they say he died the death of an angel. For my part, I was not by him when he died; for I was gone to harvest work at that very time, to a place called Temblique.' 'Pr'ythee, honest friend,' said the clergyman, 'leave your harvest work, and come back quickly from Temblique, without staying to bury the gentleman, unless you have a mind to occasion more funerals; therefore pray make an end of your story.' 'You must know, then,' quoth Sancho, 'that as they two were ready to sit down at table – I mean the husbandman and the gentleman – methinks I see them now before my eyes, plainer than ever I did in my born days.' The Duke and the Duchess were infinitely pleased to find how Sancho spun out his story, and how the clergyman fretted at his prolixity, and Don Quixote spent himself with anger and vexation. 'Well,' quoth Sancho, 'to go on with my story, when they were going to sit down, the husbandman would not sit till the gentleman had taken his place; but the gentleman made him a sign to put himself at the upper end; "By no means, sir," quoth the husbandman. "Sit down," said the other. "Good your worship – " quoth the husbandman. "Sit where I bid thee," said the gentleman. Still the other excused himself and would not; and the gentleman told him he should, as meaning to be master in his own house. But the over-mannerly looby, fancying he should be huge well bred and civil in it, scraped and cringed, and refused; till at last the gentleman, in a great passion, even took him by the shoulders, and forced him into the chair. "Sit there, Clodpate," cried he, "for let me sit wherever I will, that still will be the upper end, and the place of worship to thee." And now you have my tale, and I think I have spoke nothing but what is to the purpose.'

Don Quixote's face was in a thousand colours that speckled its natural brown; so that the Duke and Duchess were obliged to check their mirth, when they perceived Sancho's roguery, that Don Quixote might not be put too much out of countenance. And therefore to turn the discourse, that Sancho might not run into other fooleries, the Duchess asked Don Quixote, what news he had of the Lady Dulcinea, and how long it was since he had sent her any giants or robbers for a present, not doubting but that he had lately subdued many such? 'Alas! madam,' answered he, 'my misfortunes have had a beginning but, I fear, will never have an end. I have vanquished giants, elves, and cut-throats, and sent them to the mistress of my soul, but where shall they find her? She is enchanted, madam, and transformed to the ugliest piece of rusticity that can be imagined.' 'I do not know, sir,' quoth Sancho; 'when I saw her last she seemed to be the finest creature in the "versal" world; thus far, at least, I can safely vouch for her upon my own knowledge, that for activity of body, and leaping, the best tumbler of them all does not go beyond her. Upon my honest word, madam Duchess, she will vault from the ground upon her ass like a cat.' 'Have you seen her enchanted?' said the Duke. 'Seen her!' quoth Sancho; 'and who the devil was the first that hit upon this trick of her enchantment, think you, but I? She is as much enchanted as my father.'

The churchman hearing them talk of giants, elves, and enchantments, began to suspect this was Don Quixote de la Mancha, whose history the Duke so often used to read, though he had several times reprehended him for it; telling him, it was a folly to read such follies. Being confirmed in his suspicion, he addressed himself very angrily to the Duke. 'My Lord,' said he, 'your Grace will have a large account to give one day, for soothing this poor man's follies. I suppose this same Don Quixote, or Don Quite Sot, or whatever you are pleased to call him, cannot be quite so besotted as you endeavour to make him, by giving him such opportunities to run on in his fantastical humours.' Then, directing his discourse to Don Quixote, 'Hark ye,' said he; 'goodman Addlepate, who has put it into your crown that you are a knight-errant, that you vanquish giants and robbers? Go, go, get you home again, look after your children, if you have any, and what honest business you have to do, and leave wandering about the world, building castles in the air, and making yourself a laughing-stock to all that know you, or know you not. Where have you found, in the name of mischief, that there ever has been, or are now, any such thing as knights-errant? Where will you meet with giants in Spain, or monsters in La Mancha? Where shall one find your enchanted Dulcineas, and all those legions of whimsies and chimeras that are talked of on your account, but in your own empty skull?'

Don Quixote gave this reverend person the hearing with great patience. But at last, seeing him silent, without minding his respect to the Duke and Duchess, up he started with indignation and fury in his looks, and said – but his answer deserves a chapter by itself.

CHAPTER XXXII

Don Quixote's answer to his Reprover, with other grave and merry accidents

DON QUIXOTE being thus suddenly got up, shaking from head to foot for madness, as if he had quicksilver in his bones, cast an angry look on his indiscreet censor, and with an eager delivery, sputtering and stammering with choler, 'This place,' cried he, 'the presence of these noble persons, and the respect I have always had for your function, check my just resentment, and tie up my hands from taking the satisfaction of a gentleman. For these reasons, and since every one knows that you gownmen, as well as women, use no other weapon but your tongues, I will fairly engage you upon equal terms, and combat you at your own weapon. I should rather have expected sober admonitions from a man of your cloth, than infamous reproaches. Charitable and wholesome correction ought to be managed at another rate, and with more moderation. The least that can be said of this reproof which you have given me here so bitterly, and in public, is, that it has exceeded the bounds of Christian correction, and a gentle one had been much more becoming. Is it fit, that without any insight into the offence which you reprove, you should, without any more ado, call the offender fool, sot, and addlepate? Pray, sir, what foolish action have you seen me do, that should provoke you to give me such ill language, and bid me so magisterially go home to look after my wife and children, before you know whether I have any? Do not you think those deserve as severe a censure, who screw themselves into other men's houses, and pretend to rule the master? A fine world it is truly, when a poor pedant, who has seen no more of it than lies within twenty or thirty leagues about him, shall take upon him to prescribe laws to knight-errantry, and judge of those who profess it! You, forsooth, esteem it an idle undertaking, and time lost, to wander through the world, though scorning its pleasures, and sharing the hardships and toils of it, by which the virtuous aspire to the high seat of immortality. If persons of honour, knights, lords, gentlemen, or men of any birth, should take me for a fool or a coxcomb, I should think it an irreparable affront. But for mere scholars, that never trod the paths of chivalry, to think me mad, I despise and laugh at it. I am a knight, and a knight will I die, if so it please Omnipotence. Some choose the high road of haughty ambition; others the low ways of base servile flattery; a third sort take the crooked path of deceitful hypocrisy; and a few, very few, that of true religion. I, for my own part, guided by my stars, follow the narrow track of knight-errantry; and, for the exercise of it, I despise riches, but not honour. I have redressed grievances, and righted the injured, chastised the insolent, vanquished giants, and trod elves and hobgoblins under my feet! I am in love, but no more than the profession of knight-errantry obliges me to be; yet I am none of this age's vicious lovers, but a chaste Platonic. My intentions are all directed to virtuous ends, and to do no man wrong, but good to all the world. And now let your Graces judge, most excellent Duke and Duchess, whether a person who makes it his only study to practise all this, deserves to be upbraided for a fool.'

'Well said, i'faith!' quoth Sancho, 'say no more for yourself, my good lord and master, stop when you are well, for there is not the least matter to be added more on your side, either in word, thought, or deed. Besides, since Mr. Parson has had the face to say point-blank as one may say, that there neither are, nor ever were, any knights-errant in the world, no marvel he does not know what he says.' 'What,' said the clergyman, 'I warrant you are that Sancho Pança, to whom they say your master has promised an island?' 'Ay, marry am I,' answered Sancho, 'and I am he that deserves it as well as another body; and I am one of those of whom they say, Keep with good men, and thou shalt be one of them; and of those of whom it is said again, Not with whom thou wert bred, but with whom thou hast fed; as also, Lean against a good tree, and it will shelter thee. I have leaned and stuck close to my good master, and kept him company this many a month; and now he and I are all one; and I must be as he is, if it be Heaven's blessed will; and so he lives and I live, he will not want kingdoms to rule, nor shall I want islands to govern.'

'That thou shalt not, honest Sancho,' said the Duke; 'for I, on the great Don Quixote's account, will now give thee the government of an odd one of my own of no small consequence.' 'Down, down on thy knees, Sancho,' cried Don Quixote, 'and kiss his Grace's feet for this favour.' Sancho did accordingly: but when the clergyman saw it, he got up in a great heat. 'By the habit which I wear,' cried he, 'I can scarce forbear telling your Grace, that you are as mad as these sinful wretches. Well may they be mad, when such wise men as you humour and authorise their frenzy; you may keep them here and stay with them yourself, if your Grace pleases; but, for my part, I will leave you and go home, to save myself the trouble of reprehending what I cannot mend.' With that, leaving the rest of his dinner behind him, away he flung; the Duke and the Duchess not being able to pacify him: though indeed the Duke could not say much to him, for laughing at his impertinent passion. When he had done laughing, 'Sir Knight of the Lions,' said he, 'you have answered so well for yourself and your profession, that you need no further satisfaction of the angry clergyman; especially if you consider, that whatever he might say, it was not in his power to fix an affront on a person of your character, since women and churchmen cannot give an affront.' 'Very true, my Lord,' said Don Quixote, 'and the reason is, because he that cannot receive an affront, consequently can give none. Women, children, and churchmen, as they cannot vindicate themselves when they are injured, so neither are they capable of receiving an affront. For there is this difference betwixt an *affront* and an *injury*, as your Grace very well knows; an *affront* must come from a person that is both able to give it, and maintain it when he has given it: an *injury* may be done by any sort of people whatsoever. For example, a man walking in the street about his business is set upon by ten armed men, who cudgel him; he draws his sword to revenge the injury, but the assailants overpowering him, he cannot have the satisfaction he desired. This man is injured, but not affronted. But, to confirm it by another instance, suppose a man comes behind another's back, hits him a box on the ear, and then runs away, the other follows him, but cannot overtake him. He that has received the blow has received an injury, it is true, but not an affront; because, to make an affront, it should have been justified. But if he that gave it, though he did it basely, stands his ground, and faces his adversary, then he that received it is both injured and affronted: injured, because he was struck in a cowardly manner; affronted, because he that struck him stood his ground to maintain what he had done. Therefore, according to the settled laws of duelling, I may be injured, but am not affronted. Children can have no resentment, and women cannot fly, nor are they obliged to stand it out; and it is the same thing with the clergy, for they carry neither arms, either offensive or defensive. Therefore, though they are naturally bound by the laws of self-preservation to defend themselves, yet are they not obliged to offend others. Upon second thoughts, then, though I said just now I was injured, I think now I am not; for he that can receive no affront, can give none. Therefore I ought not to have any resentment for what that good man said, neither indeed have I any. I only wish he would have stayed a little longer, that I might have convinced him of his error, in believing there were never any knights-errant in the world. Had Amadis or any one of his innumerable race but heard him say anything like this, I can assure his reverence it would have gone hard with him.' 'I will be sworn it would,' quoth Sancho, 'they would have undone him, as you would undo an oyster; and have cleft him from head to foot, as one would slice a pomegranate, or a ripe musk-melon, take my word for it. They were a parcel of tough blades, and would not have swallowed such a pill. By the mackins, I verily believe, had Rinaldo of Montalban but heard the poor toad talk at this rate, he would have laid him on such a poult over the chaps with his shoulder-of-mutton fist, as would have secured him from prating these three years. Ay, ay, if he had fallen into their clutches, see how he would have got out again!'

The Duchess was ready to die with laughing at Sancho, whom she thought a more pleasant fool, and a greater madman than his master; and she was not the only person at that time of this opinion. In short, Don Quixote being pacified, they made an end of dinner, and then, while the servants took away the cloth, there came in four damsels, one carrying a silver basin, another an ewer of the same metal; a third some fine towels over her arm, and the fourth, with her sleeves tucked above her elbows, held in her lily-white hand (for exceeding white it was) a large wash-ball of Naples soap. Presently she that held the basin, went very civilly, and clapped it under Don Quixote's chin, while he, wondering at this extraordinary ceremony, yet fancying it was the custom of the country to wash the face instead of the hands, thrust out his long chin, without speaking a word, and then the ewer began to rain on his face, and the damsel that brought the wash-ball fell to work, and belathered his beard so effectually, that the suds, like huge flakes of snow, flew all over the passive Knight's face; insomuch, that he was forced to shut his eyes.

The Duke and Duchess, who knew nothing of the matter, stood expecting where this extraordinary scouring would end. The female barber, having thus laid the Knight's face a-soaking a handful high in suds, pretended she wanted water, and sent another with the ewer for more, telling her the gentleman would stay for it. She went and left him in one of the most odd ridiculous figures that can be imagined. There he sat exposed to all the company, with half a yard of neck stretched out, his bristly beard and chaps all in a white foam, which did not at all mend his walnut complexion, insomuch that it is not a little strange how those, that had so comical a spectacle before them, could forbear laughing outright. The malicious damsels, who had a hand in the plot, did not dare to look up, nor let their eyes meet those of their master or mistress, who stood strangely divided between anger and mirth, not knowing what to do in the case, whether they should punish the girls for their boldness, or reward them for the diversion they took in seeing the Knight in that posture.

At last the maid came back with the water, and the other having rinsed off the soap, she that held the linen gently wiped and dried the Knight's beard and face; after which all four, dropping a low courtesy, were going out of the room. But the Duke, that Don Quixote might not smell the jest, called to the damsel that carried the basin, and ordered her to come and wash him too, but be sure she had water enough. The wench, being sharp and cunning, came and put the basin under the Duke's chin, as she had done to Don Quixote, but with a quicker dispatch; and then having dried him clean, they all made their honours, and went off. It was well they understood their master's meaning, in serving him as they did the Knight; for as it was afterwards known, had they not done it, the Duke was resolved to have made them pay dear for their frolic.

Sancho took great notice of all the ceremonies at this washing. 'S'life!' quoth he, 'I would fain know whether it is not the custom of this country to scrub the squire's beard, as well as the Knight's: for on my conscience mine wants it not a little. Nay, if they would run it over with a razor too, so much the better.' 'What are thou talking to thyself, Sancho?' said the Duchess. 'Why, an't like your Grace's Worship,' quoth Sancho, 'I am only saying, that I have been told in other houses, when the cloth is taken away, they used to give folks water to wash their hands, and not suds to scour their beards. I see now it is good to live and learn. There is a saying indeed, He that lives long suffers much. But I have a huge fancy, that to suffer one of these same scourings is rather a pleasure than a pain.' 'Well, Sancho,' said the Duchess, 'trouble thyself no further, I shall see that one of my maids shall wash thee, and if there be occasion, lay thee a-bucking too.' 'My beard is all I want to have scrubbed at present,' quoth Sancho; 'as for the rest, we will think on it another time.' 'Here, steward,' said the Duchess, 'see that Sancho has what he has a mind to, and be sure do just as he would have you.' The steward told her Grace, that Signior Sancho should want for nothing; and so he took Sancho along with him to dinner.

Meanwhile Don Quixote stayed with the Duke and Duchess, talking of several matters, but all relating to arms and knight-errantry. The Duchess then took an opportunity to desire the Knight to give a particular description of the Lady Dulcinea del Toboso's beauty and accomplishments, not doubting but his good memory would enable him to do it well; adding withal, that, according to the voice of fame, she must needs be the finest creature in the whole world, and consequently in all La Mancha.

With that, Don Quixote, fetching a deep sigh, 'Madam,' said he, 'could I rip out my heart, and expose it to your Grace's view in a dish on this table, I might save my tongue the labour of attempting that which it cannot express, and you can scarce believe; for there your Grace would see her beauty painted to the life. But why should I undertake to delineate, and copy one by one each several perfection of the peerless Dulcinea! That burden must be sustained by stronger shoulders than mine: that talk were worthy of the pencils of Parrhasius, Timantes, and Apelles, or the graving tools of Lysippus. The hands of the best painters and statuaries should indeed be employed to give in speaking paint, in marble; and Corinthian brass, an exact copy of her beauties; while Ciceronian and Demosthenian eloquence laboured to reach the praise of her endowments.' 'Pray, sir,' asked the Duchess, 'what do you mean by that word "Demosthenian"?' 'Demosthenian eloquence, madam,' said Don Quixote, 'is as much as to say, the eloquence of Demosthenes, and the Ciceronian that of Cicero, the two greatest orators that ever were in the world.' 'It is true,' said the Duke; 'and you but showed your ignorance, my dear, in asking such a question. Yet the noble Don Quixote would highly oblige us, if he would but be pleased to attempt her picture now; for, even in a rude draught of her lineaments, I question not but she will appear so charming, as to deserve the envy of the brightest of her sex.' 'Ah, my lord,' said Don Quixote, 'it would be so indeed, if the misfortune which lately befell her, had not in a manner razed the idea out of the seat of my memory; and as it is, I ought rather to bewail her change, than describe her person: for your Grace must know, that, as I lately went to kiss her hands, and obtain her benediction and leave for my intended absence in quest of new adventures, I found her quite another creature than I expected. I found her enchanted, transformed from a princess to a country wench, from beauty to ugliness, from courtliness to rusticity, from a reserved lady to a jumping Joan, from sweetness itself to the stench of a pole-cat, from light to darkness, from an angel to a devil; in short, from Dulcinea del Toboso, to a peasantess of Sayago.'* 'Bless us!' cried the Duke with a loud voice, 'what villain has done the world such an injury? Who has robbed it not only of the beauty that was its ornament, but of those charming graces that were its delight, and that virtue which was its honour?' 'Who should it be,' replied Don Quixote, 'but one of those damned enchanters, one of those numerous envious fiends, that without cessation persecute me? That wicked brood of hell, spawned into the world to eclipse the glory of good and valiant men, and blemish their exploits, while they labour to exalt and magnify the actions of the wicked. These cursed magicians have persecuted me, and persecute me now, and will continue till they have sunk me and my lofty deeds of chivalry into the profound abyss of oblivion. Yes, yes, they choose to wound me in that part which they well know is most sensible: well knowing, that to deprive a

---

* Villanos de Sayago are properly peasants of Galicia, which are accounted the most uncouth in all Spain, whence all rude people come to be compared with them.

knight-errant of his lady, is to rob him of those eyes with which he sees, of the sun that enlightens him, and the food that sustains him. For, as I have often said, a knight-errant without a lady, is like a tree without leaves, a building without mortar, or a shadow without a body that causes it.'

'I grant all this,' said the Duchess; 'yet if we may believe the history of your life, which was lately published with universal applause, it seems to imply, to the best of my remembrance, that you never saw the Lady Dulcinea, and that there is no such lady in the world; but rather that she is a mere notional creature, engendered and brought forth by the strength and heat of your fancy, and there endowed with all the charms and good qualifications which you are pleased to ascribe to her.'

'Much may be said upon this point,' said Don Quixote; 'Heaven knows whether there be a Dulcinea in the world or not, and whether she be a notional creature or not. These are mysteries not to be so narrowly inquired into. Neither have I engendered, or begot that lady. I do indeed make at her the object of my contemplations, and as I ought, look on her as a lady endowed with all those qualifications that may raise the character of a person to universal fame. She is to me beautiful without blemish, reserved without pride, amorous with modesty, agreeable for her courteous temper, and courteous, as an effect of her generous education, and, in short, of an illustrious parentage. For beauty displays its lustre to a higher degree of perfection when joined with noble blood, than it can in those that are meanly descended.'

'The observation is just,' said the Duke; 'but give me leave, sir, to propose to you a doubt, which the reading of that history hath started in my mind. It is, that allowing there be a Dulcinea at Toboso, or elsewhere, and as beautiful as you describe her, yet I do not find she can any way equal in greatness of birth the Orianas, the Alastrajareas, the Madasimas,* and a thousand others of whom we read in those histories with which you have been so conversant.' 'To this,' said Don Quixote, 'I answer, that Dulcinea is the daughter of her own actions, and that virtue ennobles the blood. A virtuous man of mean condition, is more to be esteemed than a vicious person of quality. Besides, Dulcinea is possessed of those other endowments that may entitle her to crowns and sceptres, since beauty alone has raised many of her sex to a throne. Where merit has no limits, hope may well have no bounds; and to be fair and virtuous is so extensive an advantage, that it gives, though not a *formal*, at least a *virtual* claim to larger fortunes.' 'I must own, sir,' said the Duchess, 'that in all your discourse, you, as we say, proceed with the plummet of reason, and fathom all the depths of controversy. Therefore I submit, and from this time I am resolved to believe, and will make all my domestics, nay, my

* The names of great ladies in romances.

husband too, if there be occasion, believe and maintain, that there is a Dulcinea del Toboso extant, and living at this day; that she is beautiful and of good extraction; and to sum up all in a word, altogether deserving the services of so great a knight as the noble Don Quixote; which I think is the highest commendation I can bestow on her. But yet I must confess, there is still one scruple that makes me uneasy, and causes me to have an ill opinion of Sancho. It is that the history says, that when Sancho Pança carried your letter to the lady Dulcinea, he found her winnowing a sack of corn, by the same token it was the worst sort of wheat, which makes me much doubt her quality.'

'Your Grace must know,' answered Don Quixote, 'that almost everything that relates to me, is managed quite contrary to what the affairs of other knights-errant used to be. Whether it be the unfathomable will of destiny, or the implacable malice of some envious enchanter orders it so, or no, I cannot well tell. For it is beyond all doubt, that most of us knights-errant still have had something peculiar in our fates. One has had the privilege to be above the power of enchantments, another invulnerable, as the famous Orlando, one of the Twelve Peers of France, whose flesh, they tell us, was impenetrable everywhere but in the sole of his left foot, and even there too he could be wounded with no other weapon than the point of a great pin; so that when Bernardo del Carpio killed him at Roncesvalles, finding he could not wound him with his sword, he lifted him from the ground, and squeezed him to death in his arms; remembering how Hercules killed Anteus, that cruel giant, who was said to be the son of the earth. Hence I infer, that probably I may be secured in the same manner, under the protection of some particular advantage, though it is not that of being invulnerable; for I have often found by experience, that my flesh is tender, and not impenetrable. Nor does any private prerogative free me from the power of the enchantment; for I have found myself clapped into a cage, where all the world could not have locked me up, but the force of necromantic incantations. But since I got free again, I believe that even the force of magic will never be able to confine me thus another time. So that these magicians finding they cannot work their wicked ends directly on me, revenge themselves on what I most esteem, and endeavour to take away my life by persecuting that of Dulcinea, in whom, and for whom I live. And therefore I believe, when my squire delivered my embassy to her, they transformed her into a country dowdy, poorly busied in the low and base employment of winnowing wheat. But I do aver, that it was neither rye, nor wheat, but oriental pearl: and to prove this, I must acquaint your Graces, that passing the other day by Toboso, I could not so much as find Dulcinea's palace; whereas my squire went the next day, and saw her in all her native charms, the most beautiful creature in the world! yet when I met her presently after, she appeared to me in the shape of an ugly, coarse, country mawkin, boorish, and ill bred, though she really is discretion itself. And therefore because I cannot be enchanted, the unfortunate lady must be thus enchanted, misused, disfigured chopped, and changed. Thus my enemies wreaking their malice on her, have revenged themselves on me, which makes me abandon myself to sorrow, till she be restored to her former perfections.

'I have been the more large in this particular, that nobody might insist on what Sancho said, of her sifting of corn; for if she appeared changed to me, what wonder is it if she seemed so to him? In short, Dulcinea is both illustrious and well born, being descended of the most ancient and best families in Toboso, of whose blood I am positive she has no small share in her veins; and now that town will be no less famous in after ages for being the place of her nativity, than Troy for Helen, or Spain for Cava,* though on a more honourable account.

'As for Sancho Pança's part, I assure your Grace he is one of the most pleasant squires that ever waited on a knight-errant. Sometimes he comes out with such sharp simplicities, that one is pleasantly puzzled to judge, whether he be more knave or fool. The varlet indeed is full of roguery enough to be thought a knave; but then he has yet more ignorance, and may better be thought a fool. He doubts of everything, yet he believes everything; and when one would think he had entangled himself in a piece of downright folly, beyond recovery, he brings himself off of a sudden so cleverly, that he is applauded to the skies. In short, I would not change him for the best squire that wears a head, though I might have a city to boot; and therefore I do not know whether I had best let him go to the government which your Grace has been pleased to promise him. Though I must confess, his talent seems to lie pretty much that way: for, give never so little a whet to his understanding, he will manage his government as well as the king does his customs. Then experience convinces us, that neither learning nor any other abilities, are very material to a governor. Have we not a hundred of them that can scarce read a letter, and yet they govern as sharp as so many hawks? Their main business is only to mean well, and to be resolved to do their best; for they cannot want able counsellors to instruct them. Thus those governors who are men of the sword, and no scholars, have their assessors on the bench to direct them. My counsel to Sancho shall be, that he neither take bribes, nor lose his privileges, with some other little instructions, which I have in my head for him, and which at a proper time I will communicate, both for

---

* The nickname of Count Julian's daughter, who having been ravished by King Roderigo, occasioned the bringing in of the Moors into Spain. Her true name was Florinda, but as she was the occasion of Spain's being betrayed to the Moors, the name is left off among the women, and commonly given to bitches.

his private advantage, and the public good of the island he is to govern.'

So far had the Duke, the Duchess, and Don Quixote been discoursing together, when they heard a great noise in the house, and by and by Sancho came running unexpectedly into the room where they sat, in a terrible fright, with a dish-clout before him instead of a bib. The scullions, and other greasy rabble of the kitchen were after him, one of them pursuing him with a little kneading-trough full of dish-water, which he endeavoured by any means to put under his chin, while another stood ready to have washed the poor squire with it. 'How now, fellow!' said the Duchess, 'what is the matter here? What would you do with this good man? Do not you consider he is a governor-elect?' 'Madam,' quoth the barber-scullion, 'the gentleman will not let us wash him according to custom, as my Lord Duke and his master were.' 'Yes, marry but I will,' quoth Sancho, in a mighty huff, 'but then it shall be with cleaner suds, cleaner towels, and not quite so slovenly paws; for there is no such difference between my master and me neither, that he must be washed with angel-water, and I with the Devil's lye: so far the customs of great men's houses are good as they give no offence. But this same beastly washing in a puddle, is worse penance than a friar's flogging. My beard is clean enough, and wants no such refreshing. Stand clear, you had best; for the first that comes to wash me, or touch a hair of my head (my beard, I would say), sir, reverence of the company, I will take him such a dowse on the ear, he shall feel it a twelve-month after: for these kind of ceremonies and soapings, do you see, look more like flouts and jeers, than like a civil welcome to strangers!' The Duchess was like to have burst her sides with laughing, to see Sancho's fury, and hear how he argued for himself. But Don Quixote did not very well like to see him with such a nasty dish-clout about his neck, and made the sport of the kitchen pensioners. Therefore, after he had made a deep bow to the Duke, as it were desiring leave to speak, looking on the scullions: 'Hark ye, gentlemen,' cried he, very gravely, 'pray let the young man alone, and get you gone as you came, if you think fit. My squire is as cleanly as another man; that trough will not do; you had better have brought him a dram cup. Away; be advised by me, and leave him: for neither he nor I can abide such slovenly jesting.' 'No, no,' quoth Sancho, taking the words out of his master's mouth, 'let them stay, and go on with their show. I will pay my barbers, I will warrant ye. They had as good take a lion by the beard, as meddle with mine. Let them bring a comb hither, or what they will, and curry-comb it, and if they find anything there that should not be there, I will give them leave to cut and mince me as small as a horse.' 'Sancho is in the right,' said the Duchess, still laughing, 'and will be in the right, in all he says; he is as clean and neat as can be, and needs none of your scouring, and if he does not like our way of washing, let him do as he pleases. Besides, you who pretend to make others clean, have shown yourselves now very careless and idle, I do not know whether I may not say impudent too, to offer to bring your kneading-trough and your dish-clouts to such a person, and such a beard, instead of a golden basin and ewer, and fine diaper towels. But you are a pack of unmannerly varlets, and like saucy rascals as you are, cannot help showing your spite to the squires of knights-errant.'

The greasy regiment, and even the steward, who was with them, thought verily the Duchess had been in earnest. So they took the cloth from Sancho's neck, and sneaked off quite out of countenance. Sancho, seeing himself delivered from his apprehension of danger, ran and threw himself on his knees before the Duchess. 'Heaven bless your Worship's Grace,' quoth he, 'Madam Duchess! great persons are able to do great kindnesses. For my part, I do not know how to make your worship amends for this you have done me now. I can only wish I might see myself an armed knight-errant for your sake, that I might spend all the days of my life in the service of so high a lady. I am a poor countryman, my name is Sancho Pança, children I have, and serve as a squire. If in any of these matters, I can do you any good, you need but speak; I will be nimbler in doing, than your worship shall be in ordering.' 'It is evident, Sancho,' said the Duchess, 'that you have learned civility in the school of courtesy itself, and have been bred up under the wings of Don Quixote, who is the very cream of compliment, and the flower of ceremonies. All happiness attend such a knight and such a squire; the one the North Star of chivalry-errant, the other the bright luminary of squire-like fidelity. Rise, my friend Sancho, and assure yourself, that, for the recompense of your civilities, I will persuade my Lord Duke to put you in possession of the government he promised you as soon as he can.' After this Don Quixote went to take his afternoon's sleep. But the Duchess desired Sancho, if he were not very sleepy, he would pass the afternoon with her and her women in a cool room. Sancho told her Grace, that indeed he did use to take a good sound nap, some four or five hours long, in a summer's afternoon; but to do her good honour a kindness, he would break an old custom for once, and do his best to hold up that day, and wait on her worship. The Duke, on his side, gave fresh orders, that Don Quixote should be entertained exactly like a knight-errant, without deviating the least step from the road of chivalry, such as is observable in books of that kind.

CHAPTER XXXIII

The relishing Conference which the Duchess and her women held with Sancho Pança, worth your reading and observation

THE STORY AFTERWARDS informs us, that Sancho slept not a wink all that afternoon, but waited on the Duchess as he had promised. Being mightily taken with his comical discourse, she ordered him to take a low chair and sit by her; but Sancho, who knew better things, absolutely declined it, till she pressed him again to sit as he was a governor, and speak as he was a squire; in both which capacities he deserved the very seat of Cid Ruy Dias, the famous champion. Sancho shrugged up his shoulders and obeyed, and all the Duchess's women standing round about her to give her silent attention, she began the conference.

'Now that we are private,' said she, 'and nobody to overhear us, I would desire you, my Lord Governor, to resolve me of some doubts in the printed history of the great Don Quixote, which puzzle me very much. First, I find that the good Sancho had never seen Dulcinea, the Lady Dulcinea del Toboso, I should have said, nor carried her his master's letter, as having left the table-book behind him in Sierra Morena; how then durst he feign an answer, and pretend he found her winnowing wheat? A fiction and banter so injurious to the reputation of the peerless Dulcinea, and so great a blemish on the character of a faithful squire!' Here Sancho got up without speaking a word, laid his finger on his lips, and with his body bent, crept cautiously round the room, lifting up the hangings, and peeping in every hole and corner: at last, finding the coast clear, he returned to his seat. 'Now,' quoth he, 'Madam Duchess, since I find there is nobody here but ourselves, you shall even hear, without fear or favour, the truth of the story, and what else you will ask of me; but not a word of the pudding. First and foremost, I must tell you, I look on my master Don Quixote to be no better than a downright madman, though sometimes he will stumble on a parcel of sayings so quaint and so tightly put together, that the Devil himself could not mend them; but in the main, I cannot beat it out of my noddle but that he is as mad as a March hare. Now, because I am pretty confident of knowing his blind side, whatever crotches come into my crown, though without either head or tail, yet can I make them pass upon him for gospel. Such was the answer to his letter, and another sham that I put upon him but the other day, and is not in print yet, touching my Lady Dulcinea's enchantment; for you must know, between you and I, she is no more enchanted than the man in the

moon.' With that, at the Duchess's request, he related the whole passage
of the late pretended enchantment very faithfully, to the great diversion of
the hearers.

'But, sir,' said the Duchess, 'I have another scruple in this affair no less
unaccountable than the former; for I think I hear something whisper me
in the ear, and say, if Don Quixote de la Mancha be such a shallow-brain,
why does Sancho Pança, who knows him to be so, wait upon this madman,
and rely thus upon his vain extravagant promises? I can only infer from
this, that the man is more a fool than the master; and if so will not Madam
Duchess be thought as mad as either of them, to bestow the government
of an island, or the command of others, on one who cannot govern
himself?' 'By our Lady,' quoth Sancho, 'your scruple comes in pudding-
time. But it need not whisper in your ear, it may even speak plain, and as
loud as it will. I am a fool, that is certain, for, if I had been wise, I had left
my master many a fair day since; but it was my luck and my vile errantry,
and that is all that can be said of it. I must follow him through thick and
thin. We are both town-born children; I have eaten his bread, I love him
well, and there is no love lost between us. He pays me very well, he has
given me three colts, and I am so very true and trusty to him, that nothing
but death can part us. And if your High and Mightiness does not think fit
to let me have this same government, why, so be it; with less was I born,
and with less shall I die; it may be for the good of my conscience to go
without it. I am a fool, it is true, but yet I understand the meaning of the
saying, The pismire had wings to do her hurt; and Sancho the squire may
sooner get to heaven than Sancho the governor. There is as good bread
baked here as in France, and Joan is as good as my lady in the dark. In the
night all cats are grey. Unhappy is he that wants his breakfast at two in the
afternoon. It is always good fasting after a good breakfast. There is no
man has a stomach a yard bigger than another, but let it be never so big,
there will be hay and straw enough to fill it. A bellyful is a bellyful. The
sparrow speeds as well as the sparrow-hawk. Good serge is fine, but coarse
cloth is warm; and four yards of the one are as long as four yards of the
other. When the hour is come we must all be packed off; the prince and
the prick-louse go the same way at last: the road is no fairer for the one
than the other. The Pope's body takes up no more room than the sexton's,
though one be taller; for when they come to the pit, all are alike, or made
so in spite of our teeth,* and so good-night or good-morrow, which you
please. And let me tell you again, if you do not think fit to give me an
island, because I am a fool, I will be so wise not to care whether you do or

---

* The common sort in Spain are buried without coffins, which is the reason
Sancho is made to suppose, if the grave be not long enough they bow the body,
and cram it in: a clownish ignorant notion, but never practised.

no. It is an old saying, The Devil lurks behind the cross. All is not gold that glitters. From the tail of the plough, Bamba was made king of Spain; and from his silks and riches was Roderigo cast to be devoured by snakes, if the old ballads say true; and sure they are too old to tell a lie.' 'That they are indeed,' said Donna Rodriguez, the old waiting-woman, who listened among the rest; 'for I remember one of the ballads tells us, how Don Roderigo was shut up alive in a tomb full of toads, snakes, and lizards; and how after two days he was heard to cry out of the tomb in a low and doleful voice, "Now they eat me, now they gnaw me in the part where I sinned most": and, according to this, the gentleman is in the right, in saying, he had rather be a poor labourer than a king, to be gnawed to death by vermin.' Sancho's proverbial aphorisms, and the simple waiting-woman's comment upon the text, were no small diversion to the Duchess. 'You know,' said she, 'honest Sancho, that the promise of a gentleman or knight must be as precious and sacred to him as his life; I make no question, then, but that my Lord Duke, who is also a knight, though not of your master's order, will infallibly keep his word with you in respect of your government. Take courage, then, Sancho, for when you least dream of it, in spite of all the envy and malice of the world, you will suddenly see yourself in full possession of your government, and seated in your chair of state in your rich robes, with all your marks and ornaments of power about you. But be sure to administer true justice to your vassals, who by their loyalty and discretion will merit no less at your hands.'

'As for the governing part,' quoth Sancho, 'let me alone, I was ever charitable and good to the poor, and scorn to take the bread out of another man's mouth. On the other side, by our Lady, they shall play me no foul play. I am an old cur at a crust, and can sleep dog-sleep when I list. I can look sharp as well as another, and let me alone to keep the cob-webs out of my eyes. I know where the shoe wrings me. I will know who and who is together. Honesty is the best policy. I will stick to that. The good shall have my hand and heart, but the bad neither foot nor fellowship. And in my mind, the main point in this post of governing, is to make a good beginning. I will lay my life, that as simple as Sancho sits here, in a fortnight's time he will manage ye this same island as rightly as a sheaf of barley.' 'You say well, Sancho,' said the Duchess, 'for time ripens all things. No man is born wise; bishops are made of men, and not of stones. But to return once more to the Lady Dulcinea; I am more than half persuaded that Sancho's design of putting the trick upon his master was turned into a greater cheat upon himself: for I am well assured that the creature whom you fancied to be a country wench, and took so much pains to persuade your master that she was Dulcinea del Toboso, was really the same Dulcinea del Toboso, and really enchanted, as Don Quixote thought; and the magicians that persecute your master first invented that story, and put it into your head. For you must know, that we have our enchanters here that have a kindness for us, and give us an account of what happens in the world faithfully and impartially, without any tricks or equivocations; and, take my word for it, the jumping country wench was, and is still, Dulcinea del Toboso, who is as certainly enchanted as the mother that bore her; and when we least expect it, we shall see her again in her true shape, and in all her native lustre, and then Sancho will find it was he himself was bubbled.' 'Troth, madam,' quoth Sancho, 'all this might well be: and now I am apt to believe what my master tells me of Montesinos' cave; where, as he says, he saw my Lady Dulcinea del Toboso in the self-same garb, and as handsome as I told him I had seen her, when it came into my noddle to tell him she was enchanted. Ay, my lady, it must be quite contrary to what I weened, as your Worship's Grace well observes; for, Lord bless us! who the devil can imagine that such a numskull as I should have it in him to devise so cunning a trick of a sudden? Besides, who can think that my master is such a goose as to believe so unlikely a matter upon the single vouching of such a dunderhead-fellow as I? But for all that, my good lady, I hope you know better things than to think me a knave; alack-a-day, it cannot be expected that such an ignoramus as I am, should be able to divine into the tricks and wiles of wicked magicians. I invented that flam only, because my master would never leave teasing me; but I had no mind to abuse him, not I; and if it fell out otherwise than I meant, who can help it? Heaven knows my heart.'

'That is honestly said,' answered the Duchess, 'but pray tell me, Sancho, what was it you were speaking of Montesinos' cave? I have a great mind to know that story.' Thereupon Sancho, having related the whole matter to the Duchess, 'Look you,' said she, 'this exactly makes out what I said to you just now; for since the great Don Quixote affirms he saw there the same country wench that Sancho met coming from Toboso, it is past all doubt it was Dulcinea; and this shows the enchanters are a subtle sort of people, that will know everything, and give a quick and sure information.' 'Well,' quoth Sancho, 'if my Lady Dulcinea del Toboso be enchanted, it is the worse for her: what have I to do to quarrel with all my master's enemies? They cannot be few for aught I see, and they are plaguy fellows to deal withal. Thus much I dare say, she I saw was a country wench; a country wench I took her to be, and a country wench I left her. Now, if that same dowdy was Dulcinea in good earnest, how can I help it? I ought not to be called to an account for it. No, let the saddle be set upon the right horse, or we shall never have done. Sancho told me this, cries one, Sancho told me that, cries the other; Sancho on this side, Sancho on that side; Sancho did this, and Sancho did that; as if Sancho were I do not know who, and not the same Sancho that goes already far and near through the world in books, as Samson Carrasco tells me, and he is no less than a bachelor of arts at Salamanca 'varsity, and such folks as he cannot tell a lie, unless they be so disposed, or it stands them in good stead. So let nobody meddle or make, nor offer to pick a quarrel with me about the matter, since I am a man of reputation; and, as my master says, a good name is better than riches. Clap me but into this government* once, and you shall see wonders. He that has been a good servant, will make a good master; a trusty squire will make a rare governor, I will warrant you.' 'Sancho speaks like an oracle,' said the Duchess, 'everything he says is a sentence like those of Cato, or at least the very marrow of Michael Verino†: *Florentibus occidit annis*; that is, he died in his spring: in short, to speak after his way, "Under a bad cloak look for a good drinker." '

'Faith and troth, Madam Duchess,' quoth Sancho, 'I never drank out of malice in my born days; for thirst perhaps I may; for I have not a bit of hypocrisy in me, I drink when I have occasion, and sometimes when I have no occasion: I am no proud man, do ye see, and when the liquor is offered me I whip it off, that they may not take me for a churl or a sneaksby, or think I do not understand myself nor good manners; for when a friend or good fellow drinks and puts the glass to one, who can be so hard-hearted as to refuse, to pledge him, when it costs nothing but to open one's mouth. However, I commonly look before I leap, and take no more than needs must. And truly there is no fear that we poor squires to knights-errant should be great trespassers that way. Alack-a-day! mere element must be our daily beverage, ditch-water, for want of better, in woods and deserts, on rocks and mountains, without lighting on the blessing of one merciful drop of wine, though you would give one of your eyes for a single gulp.'

'I believe it, Sancho,' said the Duchess; 'but now it grows late, and therefore go and take some rest; after that we will have a longer conversation, and will take measures about "clapping" you suddenly into this government, as you are pleased to word it.' Sancho kissed the Duchess's hand once more, and begged her Worship's Grace that special care might be taken of his Dapple, for that he was the light of his eyes. 'What is that Dapple?' asked the Duchess. 'My beast, if it like your honour,' answered Sancho; 'my ass I would say, saving your presence; but because I will not call him ass, which is so common a name among men, I

---

* In the original *encaxenme esse govierno*, i.e. case me but in this same government.
† A young Florentine of exceeding great hopes, who died young, and whose loss was lamented by all the poets of *his* time. His fables and distichs, in imitation of Cato's, are preserved and esteemed. He died at seventeen, rather than take his physician's advice, which was a wife. Politian made the following epitaph on this very learned youth and excellent moral poet of Florence. '*Sola Venus poterat lento succurere morbo*: / *Ne se pollueret, maluit ille mori*.' 'Venus alone his slow disease could cure: / But he chose death, rather than life not pure.'

call him Dapple. It is the very same beast I would have given charge of to that same gentlewoman when I came first to this castle; but her back was up presently, and she flew out as if I had called her ugly face, old witch, and what not. However, I will be judged by any one, whether such-like sober grave bodies as she and other *duenas* are, be not fitter to look after asses, than to sit with a prim countenance to grace a fine state-room? Passion of my heart! what a deadly grudge a certain gentleman of our town, that shall be nameless, had to these creatures! I mean these old waiting-gentlewomen.' 'Some filthy clown, I dare engage,' said Donna Rodriguez the *duena**; 'had he been a gentleman, or a person of good breeding, he would have praised them up to the skies.'

'Well,' said the Duchess, 'let us have no more of that; let Donna Rodriguez hold her tongue, and Signior Sancho Pança go to his repose, and leave me to take care of his Dapple's good entertainment; for since I find him to be one of Sancho's moveables, I will place him in my esteem above the apple of my eye.' 'Place him in the stable, my good lady,' replied Sancho, 'that is as much as he deserves; neither he nor I are worthy of being placed a minute of an hour where you said; Odsbods! I would sooner be stuck in the guts with a butcher's knife, than you should be served so; I am better bred than that comes to; for though my lord and master has taught me, that in point of behaviour one ought rather to overdo than underdo, yet when the case lies about an ass and the ball of one's eye, it is best to think twice, and go warily about the matter.' 'Well,' said the Duchess, 'your ass may go with you to the government, and there you may feed, and pamper him, and make as much of him as you please.' 'Adad! my lady,' quoth Sancho, 'do not let your worship think this will be a strange matter neither. I have seen more asses than one go to a government before now: and if mine goes too, it will be no new thing I trow.'

Sancho's words again set the Duchess a-laughing; and so sending him to take his rest, she went to the Duke, and gave him an account of the pleasant discourse between her and the squire. After this they resolved to have some notable contrivance to make sport with Don Quixote, and of such a romantic cast as should humour his knight-errantry. And so successful they were in their management of that interlude, that it may well be thought one of the best adventures in this famous history.

---

* The Spanish word is *duenas*, which are old women, kept by ladies for state only, and to make up the number of their attendants, as likewise to have an eye over the young maids, for women of quality keep many. By the maids they are hated as spies on their actions, and by others are accounted no better than bawds, so that by this means they become odious to all.

CHAPTER XXXIV

Containing ways and means for disenchanting the peerless Dulcinea del Toboso, being one of the most famous Adventures in the whole book

THE DUKE AND DUCHESS were extremely diverted with the humours of their guests: resolving therefore to improve their sport, by carrying on some pleasant design, that might bear the appearance of an adventure, they took the hint from Don Quixote's account of Montesinos' cave, as a subject from which they might raise an extraordinary entertainment; the rather, since, to the Duchess's amazement, Sancho's simplicity was so great, as to believe that Dulcinea del Toboso was really enchanted, though he himself had been the first contriver of the story, and her only enchanter.

Accordingly, having given directions to their servants that nothing might be wanting, and proposed a day for hunting the wild boar, in five or six days they were ready to set out, with a train of huntsmen and other attendants not unbecoming the greatest prince. They presented Don Quixote with a hunting suit, but he refused it, alleging it superfluous, since he was in a short time to return to the hard exercise of arms, and could carry no sumpters or wardrobes along with him: but Sancho readily accepted one of fine green cloth, with design to sell it the first opportunity.

The day prefixed being come, Don Quixote armed, and Sancho equipped himself in his new suit, and mounting his ass, which he would not quit for a good horse that was offered him, he crowded in among the train of sportsmen. The Duchess also, in a dress both odd and gay, made one of the company. The Knight, who was courtesy itself, very gallantly would needs hold the reins of her palfrey, though the Duke seemed unwilling to let him. In short, they came to the scene of their sport, which was in a wood between two very high mountains, where alighting, and taking their several stands, the Duchess with a pointed javelin in her hand, attended by the Duke and Don Quixote, took her stand in a place where they knew the boars were used to pass through. The hunters posted themselves in several lanes and paths, as they most conveniently could: but as for Sancho, he chose to stay behind them all with his Dapple, whom he would by no means leave a moment, for fear the poor creature should meet with some sad accident.

And now the chase began with full cry, the dogs opened, the horns sounded, and the huntsmen hallooed in so loud a consort, that there was no hearing one another. Soon after, a hideous boar, of a monstrous size, came on, gnashing his teeth and tusks, and foaming at the mouth; and, being baited hard by the dogs and followed close by the huntsmen, made furiously towards the pass which Don Quixote had taken. Whereupon the Knight grasping his shield, and drawing his sword, moved forward to receive the raging beast. The Duke joined him with a boar-spear, and the Duchess would have been foremost, had not the Duke prevented her. Sancho alone, seeing the furious animal, resolved to shift for once, and leaving Dapple, away he scudded as fast as his legs would carry him towards an high oak, to the top of which he endeavoured to clamber: but as he was getting up, one of the boughs unluckily broke, and down he was tumbling, when a snag or stump of another bough caught hold of his new coat, and stopped his fall, flinging him in the air by the middle, so that he could neither get up nor down. His fine green coat was torn, and he fancied every moment the wild boar was running that way with foaming chaps and dreadful tusks to tear him to pieces; which so disturbed him, that he roared and bellowed for help, as if some wild beast had been devouring him in good earnest.

At last the tusky boar was laid at his length with a number of pointed spears fixed in him; and Don Quixote being alarmed by Sancho's noise, which he could distinguish easily, looked about, and discovered him swinging from the tree with his head downwards, and close by him poor Dapple, who, like a true friend, never forsook him in his adversity; for Cid Hamet observes, that they were such true and inseparable friends, that Sancho was seldom seen without Dapple, or Dapple without Sancho. Don Quixote went and took down his squire, who, as soon as he was at liberty, began to examine the damage his fine hunting-suit had received, which grieved him to the soul; for he valued it as much as if it had made him heir to an estate.

Meanwhile, the boar being laid across a large mule, and covered with branches of rosemary and myrtle, was carried in triumph by the victorious huntsmen to a large field-tent, pitched in the middle of the wood, where an excellent entertainment was provided, suitable to the magnificence of the founder.

Sancho drew near the Duchess, and showing her his torn coat, 'Had we been hunting the hare now, or catching of sparrows,' quoth he, 'my coat might have slept in a whole skin. For my part, I wonder what pleasure there can be in beating the bushes for a beast, which, if it does but come at you, will run its plaguy tusks in your guts, and be the death of you: I have not forgot an old song to this purpose:

' "May Fabila's sad fate be thine
    And make thee food for bears or swine." '

'That Fabila,' said Don Quixote, 'was a king of the Goths, who going a-hunting once, was devoured by a bear.' 'That is it, I say,' quoth Sancho; 'and therefore why should kings and other great folk run themselves into harm's way when they may have sport enough without it: mercy on me! what pleasure can you find, any of you all, in killing a poor beast that never meant any harm?' 'You are mistaken, Sancho,' said the Duke, 'hunting wild beasts is the most proper exercise for knights and princes; for in the chase of a stout noble beast, may be represented the whole art of war stratagems, policy, and ambuscades, with all other devices usually practised to overcome an enemy with safety. Here we are exposed to the extremities of heat and cold; ease and laziness can have no room in this diversion: by this we are inured to toil and hardship, our limbs are strengthened, our joints made supple, and our whole body hale and active: in short, it is an exercise that may be beneficial to many, and can be prejudicial to none, and the most enticing property is its rarity, being placed above the reach of the vulgar, who may indeed enjoy the diversion of other sorts of games, but not this nobler kind, nor that of hawking, a sport also reserved for kings and persons of quality. Therefore, Sancho, let me advise you to alter your opinion before you become a governor for then you will find the great advantage of these sports and diversions.' 'You are out, far wide, sir,' quoth Sancho, 'it were better that a governor had his legs broken, and be laid up at home, than to be gadding abroad at this rate. It would be a pretty business, forsooth, when poor people come weary and tired to wait on the governor about business, that he should be rambling about the woods for his pleasure! There would be a sweet government truly! Good faith, sir, I think these sports and pastimes are fitter for those that have nothing to do than for governors. No, I intend my recreation shall be a game at whist at Christmas, and ninepins on Sundays and holidays; but for your hunting, as you call it, it goes mightily against my calling and conscience.' 'I wish with all my heart,' said the Duke, 'that you prove as good as you promise; but saying and doing are different things.' 'Well, well,' quoth Sancho, 'be it how it will, I say that an honest man's word is as good as his bond. Heaven's help is better than early rising. It is the belly makes the feet amble, and not the feet the belly. My meaning is, that with Heaven's help and my honest endeavours, I shall govern better than any goss-hawk. Do put your finger in my mouth and try if I can bite.' 'A curse on thee and thy impertinent proverbs,' said Don Quixote: 'shall I never get thee to talk sense, without a string of that disagreeable stuff! I beseech your Graces, do not countenance this eternal dunce, or he will tease your very souls with a thousand unseasonable and insignificant proverbs, for which I wish his mouth stitched up, and myself a mischief, if I hear him.' 'Oh, sir,' said the Duchess, 'Sancho's proverbs will always please for their sententious brevity, though they were as numerous as a printed collection; and I assure you, I relish them more than I would do others, that might be better, and more to the purpose.'

After this and suchlike diverting talk, they left the tent, and walked into the wood to see whether any game had fallen into their nets. Now, while they were thus intent upon their sport, the night drew on apace, and more cloudy and overcast than was usual at that time of the year, which was about midsummer; but it happened very critically for the better carrying on the intended contrivance. A little while after the close of the evening, when it grew quite dark, in a moment the wood seemed all on fire, and blazed in every quarter. This was attended by an alarming sound of trumpets, and other warlike instruments, answering one another from all sides, as if several parties of horse had been hastily marching through the wood: then presently was heard a confused noise of Moorish cries, such as are used in joining battle, which, together with the rattling of the drums, the loud sound of the trumpets, and other instruments of war, made such a hideous and dreadful consort in the air, that the Duke was amazed, the Duchess astonished, Don Quixote was surprised, and Sancho shook like a leaf, and even those that knew the occasion of all this were affrighted.

This consternation caused a general silence, and by and by, one riding post, equipped like a devil, passed by the company, winding a huge hollow horn, that made a horrible hoarse noise. 'Hark you, post,' said the Duke, 'whither so fast? What are you? and what parties of soldiers are these that march across the wood?' 'I am the Devil,' cried the post, in a horrible tone, 'and go in quest of Don Quixote de la Mancha; and those that are coming this way are six bands of necromancers, that conduct the peerless Dulcinea del Toboso, enchanted in a triumphant chariot. She is attended by that gallant French knight, Montesinos, who comes to give information how she may be freed from enchantment.' 'Wert thou as much a devil,' said the Duke, 'as thy horrid shape speaks thee to be, thou wouldst have known this knight here before thee to be that Don Quixote de la Mancha whom thou seekest.' 'Before Heaven, and on my conscience,' replied the Devil, 'I never thought on it; for I have so many things in my head that it almost distracts me: I had quite and clean forgot my errand.' 'Surely,' quoth Sancho, 'this Devil must be a very honest fellow, and a good Christian; for he swears as devoutly by Heaven and his conscience, as I should do; and now I am apt to believe there be some good people even in hell.' At the same time the Devil, directing himself to Don Quixote, without dismounting: 'To thee, O Knight of the Lions,' cried he, '(and I wish thee fast in their claws), to thee am I sent by the valiant but unfortunate Montesinos, to bid thee attend his coming in this very place, whither he brings one whom they call Dulcinea del Toboso, in order to give thee instructions touching her disenchantment. Now I have delivered my message, I must fly, and the devils that are like me be with thee, and angels guard the rest.' This said, he winded his monstrous horn, and, without staying for an answer, disappeared.

This increased the general consternation, but most of all surprised Don Quixote and Sancho; the latter, to find, that, in spite of truth, they still would have Dulcinea to be enchanted; and the Knight to think that the adventures of Montesinos' cave were turned to reality. While he stood pondering these things in his thoughts: 'Well, sir,' said the Duke to him; 'what do you intend to do? will you stay?' 'Stay!' cried Don Quixote, 'shall I not? I will stay here, intrepid and courageous, though all the infernal powers enclose me round.' 'So you may if you will,' quoth Sancho, 'but if any more devils or horns come hither, they shall as soon find me in Flanders as here.'

Now the night grew darker and darker, and several shooting lights were seen glancing up and down the wood, like meteors or glaring exhalations from the earth. Then was heard a horrid noise, like the creaking of the ungreased wheels of heavy wagons, from which piercing ungrateful sound, bears and wolves themselves are said to fly. This odious jarring was presently seconded by a greater, which seemed to be the dreadful din and shocks of four several engagements in each quarter of the wood, with all the sounds and hurry of so many joined battles. On one side were heard several peals of cannon; on the other the discharging of numerous volleys of small shot; here the shouts of the engaging parties that seemed to be near at hand; there cries of the Moors that seemed at a great distance. In short, the strange, confused intermixture of drums, trumpets, cornets, horns, the thundering of the cannon, the rattling of the small shot, the creaking of the wheels, and the cries of the combatants, made the most dismal noise imaginable, and tried Don Quixote's courage to the uttermost. But poor Sancho was annihilated, and fell into a swoon upon the Duchess's coats, who taking care of him, and ordering some water to be sprinkled in his face, at last recovered him, just as the foremost of the creaking carriages came up, drawn by tour heavy oxen covered with mourning, and carrying a large lighted torch upon each horn. On the top of the cart or wagon was an exalted seat, on which sat a venerable old man, with a beard as white as snow, and so long that it reached down to his girdle. He was clad in a long gown of black buckram, as were also two devils that drove the wagons, both so very monstrous and ugly, that Sancho, having seen them once, was forced to shut his eyes, and would not venture upon a second look. The cart, which was stuck full of lights within, being approached to the place, the reverend old man stood up, and cried with a loud voice, 'I am the sage Lirgandeo;' and the cart passed on without one word more being spoken. Then followed another cart with another grave old man, who making the cart stop at a convenient distance, rose up from his high seat, and in as deep a tone as the first, cried, 'I am the sage Alquife, great friend to Urganda the Unknown;' and so went forward. He was succeeded by a third cart, that moved in the same solemn pace, and bore a person not so ancient as the rest, but a robust and sturdy, sour-looked, ill-favoured fellow, who rose from his throne like the rest, and with a more hollow and diabolical voice, cried out, 'I am Arcalaus the Enchanter, the mortal enemy of Amadis de Gaul, and all his race;' which said, he passed by, like the other carts; which, taking a short turn, made a halt, and the grating noise of the wheels ceasing, an excellent consort of sweet music was heard, which mightily comforted poor Sancho; and passing with him for a good omen, 'My Lady,' quoth he to the Duchess, from whom he would not budge an inch, 'there can be no mischief sure where there is music.' 'Very true,' said the Duchess, 'especially when there is brightness and light.' 'Ay, but there is no light without fire,' replied Sancho, 'and brightness comes most from flames; who knows but those about us may burn us? But music I take to be always a sign of feasting and merriment.' 'We shall know presently what this will come to,' said Don Quixote; and he said right, for you will find it in the next chapter.

CHAPTER XXXV

Wherein is contained the Information given to Don Quixote how to disenchant Dulcinea, with other wonderful passages

WHEN THE PLEASANT MUSIC drew near, there appeared a stately triumphant chariot, drawn by six dun mules covered with white, upon each of which sat a penitent clad also in white, and holding a great lighted torch in his hand. The carriage was twice or thrice longer than any of the former, twelve other penitents being placed at the top and sides all in white, and bearing likewise each a lighted torch, which made a dazzling and surprising appearance. There was a high throne erected at the further end, on which sat a nymph arrayed in cloth of silver, with many golden spangles glittering all about her, which made her dress, though not rich, appear very glorious: her face was covered with transparent gauze, through the flowing folds of which might be descried a most beautiful face; and by the great light which the torches gave, it was easy to discern, that as she was not less than seventeen years of age, neither could she be thought above twenty. Close by her was a figure clad in a long gown like that of a magistrate, reaching down to its feet, and its head covered with a black veil. When they came directly opposite to the company, the shawms or hautboys, that played before, immediately ceased, and the Spanish harps and lutes, that were in the chariot, did the like; then the figure in the gown stood up, and opening its garments, and throwing away its mourning veil, discovered a bare and frightful skeleton, that represented the deformed figure of death; which startled Don Quixote, made Sancho's bones rattle in his skin for fear, and caused the Duke and the Duchess to seem more than commonly disturbed. This living death being thus got up, in a dull heavy sleeping tone, as if its tongue had not been well awake, began in this manner:

MERLIN'S SPEECH

'Behold old Merlin, in romantic writ,
Miscall'd the spurious progeny of hell;
A falsehood current with the stamp of age:
I reign the Prince of Zoroastic science
That oft evokes and rates the rigid pow'rs:
Archive of Fate's dread records in the skies
Coëvous with the chivalry of yore;
All brave knights-errant still I've deem'd my charge,
Heirs of my love, and fav'rites of my charms.

While other magic seers averse from good,
Are dire and baleful like the seat of woe,
My nobler soul, where power and pity join,
Diffuses blessings, as they scatter plagues.

Deep in the nether world, in dreary caves
Where my retreated soul, in silent state,
Forms mystic figures and tremendous spells,
I heard the peerless Dulcinea's moans.

Appris'd of her distress, her frightful change,
From princely state, and beauty near divine
To the vile semblance of a rustic queen,
The dire misdeed of necromantic hate:
I sympathis'd, and awfully revolv'd
Twice fifty-thousand scrolls, occult and loath'd
Some of my art, hell's black philosophy
Then clos'd my soul within this bony trunk
This ghastly form, the ruins of a man;
And rise in pity to reveal a cure
To woes so great, and break the cursed spell.

O glory thou of all that e'er could grace
A coat of steel, and fence of adamant!
Light, lantern, path, and polar star and guide
To all who dare dismiss ignoble care
And downy sleep for exercise of arms
For toils continual, perils, wounds and blood!

Knight of unfathom'd worth, abyss of praise
Who blend'st in one the prudent and the brave:
To thee, great Quixote! I this truth declare
That to restore her to her state and form
Toboso's pride, the peerless Dulcinea
'Tis Fate's decree that Sancho, thy good squire
On his bare brawny buttocks should bestow
Three thousand lashes, and eke three hundred more
Each to afflict, and sting, and gall him sore.
So shall relent the authors of her woes
Whose awful will I for her ease disclose.'

'Body o' me,' quoth Sancho, 'three thousand lashes! I will not give myself three; I will as soon give myself three stabs in the guts. May you and your disenchanting go to the Devil. What a plague have my buttocks to do with the black art? Passion of my heart! Master Merlin, if you have no better way for disenchanting the Lady Dulcinea, she may even lie bewitched to her dying-day for me.'

'How now, opprobrious rascal!' cried Don Quixote, 'stinking garlic eater! Sirrah, I will take you and tie your dogship to a tree, as naked as your mother bore you; and there I will not only give you three thousand three hundred lashes, but six thousand six hundred, ye varlet! and so smartly, that you shall feel them still though you rub your backside three thousand times, scoundrel! Answer me a word, you rogue, and I will tear out your soul.' 'Hold, hold!' cried Merlin, hearing this, 'this must not be; the stripes inflicted on honest Sancho, must be voluntary, without compulsion, and only laid on when he thinks most convenient. No set time is for the task fixed, and if he has a mind to have abated one half of this atonement, it is allowed; provided the remaining stripes be struck by a strange hand, and heavily laid on.'

'Hold you there,' quoth Sancho, 'neither a strange hand nor my own, neither heavy nor light shall touch my bum. What a pox, did I bring Madam Dulcinea del Toboso into the world, that my hind-parts should pay for the harm her eyes have done: let my master Don Quixote whip himself, he is a part of her; he calls her, every foot, my life, my soul, my sustenance, my comfort, and all that. So even let him jerk out her enchantment at his own bum's cost, but as for any whipping of me, I deny and pronounce* it flat and plain.'

No sooner had Sancho thus spoke his mind, but the nymph that sat by Merlin's ghost in the glittering apparel, rising, and lifting up her thin veil, discovered a very beautiful face; and with a masculine grace, but no very

* A blunder of Sancho's, for 'renounce.'

agreeable voice, addressing Sancho: 'O thou disastrous squire,' said she, 'thou lump with no more soul than a broken pitcher, heart of cork, and bowels of flint! hadst thou been commanded, base sheep-stealer, to have thrown thyself headlong from the top of a high tower to the ground; hadst thou been desired, enemy of mankind, to have swallowed a dozen of toads, two dozen of lizards, and three dozen of snakes; or hadst thou been requested to have butchered thy wife and children, I should not wonder that it had turned thy squeamish stomach: but to make such a hesitation at three thousand three hundred stripes, which every puny schoolboy makes nothing of receiving every month, it is amazing, nay astonishing to the tender and commiserating bowels of all that hear thee, and will be a blot in thy escutcheon to all futurity. Look up, thou wretched and marble-hearted animal; look up, and fix thy huge lowering goggle eyes upon the bright luminaries of my sight: behold these briny torrents, which, streaming down, furrow the flowery meadows of my cheeks: relent, base and inexorable monster, relent; let thy savage breast confess at last a sense of my distress; and, moved with the tenderness of my youth, that consumes and withers in this vile transformation, crack this sordid shell of rusticity that envelopes my blooming charms. In vain has the goodness of Merlin permitted me to reassume a while my native shape, since neither that, nor the tears of beauty in affliction, which are said to reduce obdurate rocks to the softness of cotton, and tigers to the tenderness of lambs, are sufficient to melt thy haggard breast. Scourge, scourge that brawny head of thine, stubborn and unrelenting brute, that coarse enclosure of thy coarser soul, and rouse up thus thyself from that base sloth, that makes thee live only to eat and pamper thy lazy flesh, indulging still thy voracious appetite. Restore me the delicacy of my skin, the sweetness of my disposition, and the beauty of my face. But, if my entreaties and tears cannot work thee into a reasonable compliance, if I am not yet sufficiently wretched to move thy pity, at least let the anguish of that miserable Knight, thy tender master, mollify thy heart. Alas! I see his very soul just at his throat, and sticking not ten inches from his lips, waiting only thy cruel or kind answer, either to fly out of his mouth, or to return into his breast.'

Don Quixote, hearing this, clapped his hand upon his gullet, and turning to the Duke: 'By Heavens, my Lord,' said he, 'Dulcinea is in the right; for I find my soul traversed in my windpipe like a bullet in a crossbow.' 'What is your answer now, Sancho?' said the Duchess. 'I say as I said before,' quoth Sancho; 'as for the flogging I pronounce it flat and plain.' 'Renounce, you mean,' said the Duke. 'Good your worship,' quoth Sancho, 'this is no time for me to mind niceties, and spelling of letters: I have other fish to fry. This plaguy whipping-bout makes me quite distracted. I do not know what I say or do. But I would fain know of my Lady Dulcinea del Toboso, where she picked up this kind of breeding, to beg thus like a sturdy beggar? Here she comes to desire me to lash my backside, as raw as a piece of beef, and the best word she can give, is, soul of a broken pitcher, monster, brute, sheep-stealer, with a ribble-rabble of saucy nicknames, that the Devil himself would not bear. Do you think, mistress of mine, that my skin is made of brass? Or shall I get anything by your disenchantment? Beshrew her heart, where is the fine present she has brought along with her to soften me? A basket of fine linen, holland shirts, caps and socks (though I wear none) had been somewhat like. But to fall upon me, and bespatter me thus with dirty names, do you think that will do? No, in faith: remember the old sayings, a golden load makes the burthen light; gifts will enter stone walls; scratch my breech and I will claw your elbow; a bird in hand is worth two in the bush. Nay, my master too, who, one should thank, would tell me a fine story, and coax me up with dainty sugar-plum words, talks of tying me to a tree, forsooth, and of doubling the whipping. Odsbobs! methinks those trouble-some people should know who they prate to. It is not only a squire-errant they would have to whip himself, but a governor; and there is no more to do, think they, but up and ride. Let them even learn manners, with a pox. There is a time for some things; and a time for all things; a time for great things, and a time for small things. Am I now in the humour to hear petitions, do you think? Just when my heart is ready to burst, for having torn my new coat; they would have me tear my own flesh too in the Devil's name, when I have no more stomach to it, than to be among the men-eaters.'* 'Upon my honour, Sancho,' said the Duke, 'if you do not relent, and become as soft as a ripe fig, you shall have no government. It would be a fine thing indeed, that I should send among my islanders a merciless, hard-hearted tyrant, whom neither the tears of distressed damsels, nor the admonitions of wise, ancient, and powerful enchanters, can move to compassion. In short, sir, no stripes, no government.' 'But,' quoth Sancho, 'may not I have a day or two to consider on it?' 'Not a minute,' cried Merlin, 'you must declare now, and in this very place, what you resolve to do, for Dulcinea must be again transformed into a country wench, and carried back immediately to Montesinos' cave; or else she shall go as she is now to the Elysian fields, there to remain till the number of the stripes be made out.' 'Come, come, honest Sancho,' said the Duchess, 'pluck up a good courage, and show your gratitude to your master, whose bread you have eaten, and to whose generous nature, and high feats of chivalry we are all so much obliged: come, child, give your consent, and make a fool of the Devil: hang fear, faint heart never won fair lady; fortune favours the brave, as you know better than I can tell you.' 'Hark you, Mr Merlin,' quoth

* In the original, to turn Cazique; Bolverme Cazique. Caziques are petty kings in the West Indies.

Sancho, without giving the Duchess an answer, 'pray, will you tell me one thing? How comes it about, that this same post-devil that came before you, brought my master word from Signior Montesinos, that he would be here, and give him directions about this disenchantment, and yet we hear no news of Montesinos all this while?' 'Pshaw,' answered Merlin, 'the Devil is an ass, and a lying rascal; he came from me, and not from Montesinos: for he, poor man, is still in his cave, expecting the dissolution of the spell that confines him there yet, so that he is not quite ready to be free, and the worst is still behind.* But if he owes you any money, or you have any business with him, he shall be forthcoming, when and where you please. But now pray make an end, and undergo this small penance, it will do you a world of good; for it will not only prove beneficial to your soul, as an act of charity, but also to your body, as a healthy exercise; for you are of a very sanguine complexion, Sancho, and losing a little blood will do you no harm.' 'Well,' quoth Sancho, 'there is like to be no want of physicians in this world, I find; the very conjurers set up for doctors too. Well, then, since everybody says as much (though I can hardly believe it), I am content to give myself the three thousand three hundred stripes, upon condition that I may be paying them off as long as I please; observe, that though I will be out of debt as soon as I can, that the world may not be without the pretty face of the lady Dulcinea del Toboso, which, I must own, I could never have believed to have been so handsome. Item, I shall not be bound to fetch blood, that is certain; and if any stroke happens to miss me, it shall pass for one, however. Item, Mr. Merlin (because he knows all things), shall be obliged to reckon the lashes, and take care I do not give myself one more than the tale.' 'There is no fear of that,' said Merlin; 'for at the very last lash the Lady Dulcinea will be disenchanted, come straight to you, make you a courtesy, and give you thanks. Heaven forbid I should wrong any man of the least hair of his head.' 'Well,' said Sancho, 'what must be, must be: I yield to my hard luck, and on the aforesaid terms, take up with my penance.'

Scarce had Sancho spoke, when the music struck up again, and a congratulatory volley of small shot was immediately discharged. Don Quixote fell on Sancho's neck, hugging and kissing him a thousand times. The Duke, the Duchess, and the whole company seemed mightily pleased. The chariot moved on, and, as it passed by, the fair Dulcinea made the Duke and Duchess a bow, and Sancho a low courtesy.

And now the jolly morn began to spread her smiling looks in the eastern quarter of the skies, and the flowers of the field to disclose their bloomy folds, and raise their fragrant heads. The brooks, now cool and clear, in

* *Aun le falta la cola por desollar*, i. e. the tail still remains to be flayed: which is the most troublesome and hard to be done.

gentle murmurs, played with the grey pebbles, and flowed along to pay their liquid crystal tribute to the expecting rivers. The sky was clear, the air serene, swept clean by brushing winds for the reception of the shining light, and everything, not only jointly but in its separate gaiety, welcomed the fair Aurora, and, like her, foretold a fairer day. The Duke and Duchess, well pleased with the management and success of the hunting, and the counterfeit adventure, returned to the castle; resolving to make a second essay of the same nature, having received as much pleasure from the first, as any reality could have produced.

CHAPTER XXXVI

The strange and never-thought-of Adventure of the disconsolate Matron, alias the Countess Trifaldi, with Sancho Pança's Letter to his wife Teresa Pança

THE WHOLE CONTRIVANCE of the late adventure was plotted by the Duke's steward, a man of wit, and a facetious and quick fancy: he made the verses, acted Merlin himself, and instructed a page to personate Dulcinea. And now, by his master's appointment, he prepared another scene of mirth, as pleasant and as artful and surprising as can be imagined.

The next day, the Duchess asked Sancho whether he had begun his penitential task to disenchant Dulcinea? 'Ay, marry have I,' quoth Sancho, 'for I have already lent myself five lashes on the buttocks.' 'With what, friend?' asked the Duchess. 'With the palm of my hand,' answered Sancho. 'Your hand!' said the Duchess, 'those are rather claps than lashes, Sancho; I doubt Father Merlin will not be satisfied at so easy a rate; for the liberty of so great a lady is not to be purchased at so mean a price. No, you should lash yourself with something that may make you smart: a good friar's scourge, a cat-of-nine-tails, or penitent's whip, would do well; for letters written in blood stand good; but works of charity, faintly and coldly done, lose their merit, and signify nothing.' 'Then, madam,' quoth he, 'will your worship's Grace do so much as help me to a convenient rod, such as you shall think best; though it must not be too smarting neither; for faith, though I am a clown, my flesh is as soft as any lady's in the land, no disparagement to anybody's buttocks.' 'Well, well, Sancho,' said she, 'it shall be my care to provide you a whip, that shall suit your soft constitution, as if they were twins.' 'But now, my dear madam,' quoth he, 'you must know I have written a letter to my wife Teresa Pança, to give her to understand how things are with me. I have it in my bosom, and it is just ready to send away; it wants nothing but the direction on the outside.

Now I would have your wisdom to read it, and see if it be not written like a governor; I mean, in such a style as governors should write.' 'And who penned it?' asked the Duchess. 'What a question there is now,' quoth Sancho. 'Who should pen it but myself, sinner as I am.' 'And did you write it too?' said the Duchess. 'Not I,' quoth Sancho, 'for I can neither write nor read, though I can make my mark.' 'Let me see the letter,' said the Duchess; 'for I dare say your wit is set out in it to some purpose.' Sancho pulled the letter out of his bosom unsealed, and the Duchess having taken it, read what follows:

'SANCHO PANÇA TO HIS WIFE TERESA PANÇA.   If I am well-lashed, yet I am whipped into a government: I have got a good government, and it cost me many a good lash. Thou must know, my Teresa, that I am resolved thou shalt ride in a coach; for now, any other way of going, is to me, but creeping on all fours, like a kitten. Thou art now a governor's wife, guess whether any one will dare to tread on thy heels. I have sent thee a green hunting-suit of *reparel*, which my Lady Duchess gave me. Pray see and get it turned into a petticoat and jacket for our daughter. The folks in this country are very ready to talk little good of my master, Don Quixote. They say he is a mad-wise-man, and a pleasant mad-man, and that I am not a jot behindhand with him. We have been in Montesillos' cave, and Merlin the wizard has pitched on me to disenchant Dulcinea, the same who among you is called Aldonza Lorenzo. When I have given myself three thousand three hundred lashes, lacking five, she will be as disenchanted as the mother that bore her. But not a word of the pudding; for if you tell your case among a parcel of tattling gossips, you will never have done; one will cry it is white, and others it is black. I am to go to my government very suddenly, whither I go with a huge mind to make money, as I am told all new governors do. I will first see how matters go, and then send thee word whether thou hadst best come or no. Dapple is well, and gives his humble service to you. I will not part with him, though I were to be made the Great Turk. My Lady Duchess kisses thy hands a thousand times over; pray return her two thousand for her one: for there is nothing cheaper than fair words, as my master says. Heaven has not been pleased to make me light on another cloak-bag, with a hundred pieces of gold in it, like those you wot of. But all in good time; do not let that vex thee, my jug, the government will make it up, I will warrant thee. Though after all, one thing sticks plaguily in my gizzard: they tell me, that when once I have tasted of it, I shall be ready to eat my very fingers after it, so savoury is the sauce. Should it fall out so, I should make but an ill hand of it; and yet your maimed and crippled alms-folks pick up a pretty livelihood, and make their begging as good as a prebend. So that one way or other, old girl, matters will go swimmingly, and thou wilt be rich and happy. Heaven make thee so, as well as it may; and keep me for thy sake. From this castle, the twentieth of June, 1614.

'Thy husband the Governor,
'SANCHO PANÇA.'

'Methinks, Mr. Governor,' said the Duchess, having read the letter, 'you are out in two particulars; first, when you intimate that this government was bestowed on you for the stripes you are to give yourself; whereas, you may remember it was allotted you before this disenchantment was dreamed of. The second branch that you failed in, is the discovery of your avarice, which is the most detestable quality in governors; because their self-interest is always indulged at the expense of justice. You know the saying, covetousness breaks the sack, and that vice always prompts a governor to fleece and oppress the subject.' 'Truly, my good lady,' quoth Sancho 'I meant no harm, I did not well think of what I wrote, and if your Grace's worship does not like this letter, I will tear it and have another; but remember the old saying, "Seldom comes a better." I shall make but sad work of it, if I must pump my brains for it.' 'No, no,' said the Duchess, 'this will do well enough, and I must have the Duke see it.'

They went into the garden, where they were to dine that day, and there she showed the Duke the learned epistle, which he read over with a great deal of pleasure.

After dinner, Sancho was entertaining the company very pleasantly, with some of his savoury discourse, when suddenly, they were surprised with the mournful sound of a fife, which played in consort with a hoarse, unbraced drum. All the company seemed amazed and discomposed at the unpleasing noise; but Don Quixote especially was so alarmed with this solemn martial harmony, that he could not compose his thoughts. Sancho's fear undoubtedly wrought the usual effects, and carried him to crouch by the Duchess.

During this consternation, two men in deep mourning-cloaks trailing on the ground entered the garden, each of them beating a large drum covered also with black, and with these a third playing on a fife, in mourning like the rest. They ushered in a person of gigantic stature, to which the long black garb in which he was wrapped up, was no small addition: it had a trail of prodigious length, and over the cassock was girt a broad black belt, which slung a scimitar of a mighty size. His face was covered with a thin black veil, through which might be discerned a beard of a vast length, as white as snow. The solemnity of his pace kept exact time to the gravity of the music: in short, his stature, his motion, his black hue, and his attendance were every way surprising and astonishing. With this state and formality he approached, and fell on his knees at a convenient distance, before the Duke; who not suffering him to speak till he arose, the monstrous spectre erected his bulk, and throwing off his veil, discovered the most terrible, hugeous, white, broad, prominent, bushy beard, that ever mortal eyes were frightened at. Then fixing his eyes on the Duke, and with a deep sonorous voice, roaring out from the ample cavern of his spreading lungs, 'Most High and Potent Lord,' cried he, 'my name is Trifaldin with the white beard, squire to the Countess Trifaldi, otherwise called the Disconsolate Matron, from whom I am ambassador to your Grace, begging admittance for her ladyship to come and relate, before your magnificence, the unhappy and wonderful circumstances of her misfortune. But first, she desires to be informed whether the valorous and invincible knight, Don Quixote de la Mancha, resides at this time in your castle; for it is in quest of him that my Lady has travelled without coach or palfrey, hungry and thirsty; and, in short, without breaking her fast, from the kingdom of Candaya, all the way to these your Grace's territories: a thing incredibly miraculous, if not wrought by enchantment. She is now without the gate of this castle, waiting only for your Grace's permission to enter.' This said, the squire coughed, and with both his hands, stroked his unwieldy beard from the top to the bottom, and with a formal gravity expected the Duke's answer.

'Worthy Squire Trifaldin with the White Beard,' said the Duke, 'long since have we heard of the misfortunes of the Countess Trifaldi, whom enchanters have occasioned to be called the Disconsolate Matron; and therefore, most stupendous squire, you may tell her that she may make her entry; and that the valiant Don Quixote de la Mancha is here present, on whose generous assistance she may safely rely for redress. Inform her also from me, that, if she has occasion for my aid, she may depend on my readiness to do her service, being obliged, as I am a knight, to be aiding and assisting, to the utmost of my power, to all persons of her sex in distress, especially widowed matrons, like her Ladyship.'

Trifaldin hearing this, made his obeisance with the knee, and beckoning to the fife and drums to observe his motion, they all marched out in the same solemn procession as they entered, and left all the beholders in a deep admiration of his proportion and deportment.

Then the Duke, turning to Don Quixote, 'Behold, Sir Knight,' said he, 'how the light and glory of virtue dart their beams through the clouds of malice and ignorance, and shine to the remotest parts of the earth: it is hardly six days since you have vouchsafed to honour this castle with your presence, and already the afflicted and distressed flock hitherto from the uttermost regions, not in coaches or on dromedaries, but on foot, and without eating by the way; such is their confidence in the strength of that arm, the fame of whose great exploits flies and spreads everywhere, and makes the whole world acquainted with your valour.'

'What would I give, my lord,' said Don Quixote, 'that the same holy pedant were here now, who, the other day at your table would have run down knight-errantry at such a rate; that the testimony of his own eyes might convince him of the absurdity of his error, and let him see that the comfortless and afflicted do not in enormous misfortunes, and uncommon adversity, repair for redress to the doors of droning churchmen, or your little parish priests of villages; nor to the fireside of your country gentlemen, who never travels beyond his landmark; nor to the lolling, lazy courtier, who rather hearkens after news which he may relate, than endeavours to perform such deeds as may deserve to be recorded and related. No, the protection of damsels, the comfort of widows, the redress of the injured, and the support of the distressed, are nowhere so perfectly to be expected as from the generous professors of knight-errantry. Therefore I thank Heaven a thousand times, for having qualified me to answer the necessities of the miserable by such a function. As for the hardships and accidents that may attend me, I look upon them as no discouragements, since proceeding from so noble a cause. Then let this matron be admitted to make known her request, and I will refer her for redress to the force of my arm, and the intrepid resolution of my courageous soul.'

CHAPTER XXXVII

The famous Adventure of the disconsolate Matron * continued

THE DUKE AND DUCHESS were mightily pleased to find Don Quixote wrought up to a resolution so agreeable to their design. But Sancho, who made his observations, was not so well satisfied. 'I am in a bodily fear,' quoth he, 'that this same Mistress Waiting-woman will be a baulk to my preferment. I remember I once knew a Toledo apothecary that talked like a canary-bird, and used to say, "wherever come old waiting-women, good luck can happen there to no man." Body o' me, he knew them too well, and therefore valued them accordingly. He could have eaten them all with a grain of salt. Since then the best of them are so plaguy troublesome and impertinent, what will those be that are in doleful dumps, like this same Countess Threefolds, three skirts, or three tails,† what do you call her?' 'Hold your tongue, Sancho,' said Don

---

* The Spanish is *duena*, which signifies an old waiting-woman, or *governante*, as it is rendered in Quevedo's Visions.

† Trifaldi, the name of the Countess, signifies three skirts, or three tails.

Quixote: 'this matron that comes so far in search of me, lives too remote to lie under the lash of the apothecary's satire. Besides, you are to remember she is a countess; and when ladies of that quality become governantes, or waiting-women, it is only to queens or empresses; and in their own houses they are as absolute ladies as any others, and attended by other waiting-women.' 'Ay, ay,' cried Donna Rodriguez, who was present, 'there are some that serve my Lady Duchess here in that capacity, that might have been countesses too had they had better luck. But we are not all born to be rich, though we are all born to be honest. Let nobody then speak ill of waiting-gentlewomen, especially of those that are ancient and maidens; for though I am none of those, I easily conceive the advantage that a waiting-gentle-woman, who is a maiden, has over one that is a widow. When all is said, whoever will offer to meddle with waiting-women will get little by it. Many go out for wool, and come home shorn themselves.' 'For all that,' quoth Sancho, 'your waiting-women are not so bare, but that they may be shorn, if my barber spoke truth: so that they had best not stir the rice, though it sticks to the pot.' 'These squires, forsooth,' answered Donna Rodriguez, 'must be always cocking up their noses against us: as they are always haunting the ante-chambers, like a parcel of evil spirits as they are, they see us whisk in and out at all times; so when they are not at their devotion, which, Heaven knows, is almost all the day long, they can find no other pastime than to abuse us, and tell idle stories of us, unburying our bones, and burying our reputation. But their tongues are no slander, and I can tell those silly rakeshames, that, in spite of their flouts, we shall keep the upper hand of them, and live in the world in the better sort of houses, though we starve for it, and cover our flesh, whether delicate or not, with black gowns, as they cover a dunghill with a piece of tapestry when a procession goes by. S'life, sir, were this a proper time, I would convince you and all the world, that there is no virtue but is enclosed within the stays of a waiting-woman.' 'I fancy,' said the Duchess, 'that honest Rodriguez is much in the right: but we must now choose a fitter time for this dispute, to confound the ill opinion of that wicked apothecary, and to rout out that which the great Sancho Pança has fixed in his breast.' 'For my part,' quoth Sancho, 'I will not dispute with her; for since the thoughts of being a governor have steamed up into my brains, all my concern for the squire is vanished into smoke; and I care not a wild fig for all the waiting-women in the world.'

This subject would have engaged them longer in discourse, had they not been cut short by the sound of the fife and drums that gave them notice of the Disconsolate Matron's approach. Thereupon the Duchess asked the Duke how it might be proper to receive her. And how far ceremony was due to her quality as a countess? 'Look you,' quoth Sancho, striking in before the Duke could answer, 'I would advise you to meet her Countess-ship halfway, but for the waiting-womanship do not stir a step.'

'Who bids you trouble yourself?' said Don Quixote. 'Who bid me?' answered Sancho, 'why I myself did. Have not I been squire to your worship, and thus served a 'prenticeship to good manners? And have not I had the flower of courtesy for my master, who has often told me, a man may as well lose at one and thirty, with a card too much, as a card too little? Good wits jump; a word to the wise is enough.' 'Sancho says well,' said the Duke; 'to decide the matter, we will first see what kind of a countess she is, and behave ourselves accordingly.'

Now the fife and the drums entered, as before. But here the author ends this short chapter, and begins another, prosecuting the same adventure, which is one of the most notable in the history.

CHAPTER XXXVIII

The account which the disconsolate Matron gives of her Misfortune

THE DOLEFUL DRUMS and fife were followed by twelve elderly waiting-women that entered the garden, ranked in pairs, all clad in large mourning habits, that seemed to be of milned serge, over which they wore veils of white calico, so long, that nothing could be seen of their black dress, but the very bottom. After them came the Countess Trifaldi, handed by her squire Trifaldin, with the white beard. The lady was dressed in a suit of the finest baize; which, had it been napped, would have had tufts as big as Rouncival peas. Her train, or tail, which you will, was mathematically divided into three equal skirts or angles, and borne up by three pages in mourning; and from this pleasant triangular figure of her train, as every one conjectured, was she called Trifaldi; as who should say, the Countess of Threefolds, or Three Skirts. Benengeli is of the same opinion, though he affirms that her true title was the Countess of Lobuna,* or of Wolf-Land, from the abundance of wolves bred in her country; and had they been foxes, she had, by the same rule, been called the Countess Zorrunna,† or of Fox-Land; it being a custom in those nations, for great persons to take their denominations from the commodity with which their country most abounds. However, this countess chose to borrow her title from this new fashion of her own invention, and leaving her name of Lobuna, took that of Trifaldi.

Her twelve female attendants approached with her in a procession pace, with black veils over their faces, not transparent, like that of

* *Lobo* is Spanish for a 'wolf.'
† *Zorro* is Spanish for a 'he-fox'; whence these two words are derived.

Trifaldin, but thick enough to hinder altogether the sight of their countenances. As soon as the whole train of waiting-women was come in, the Duke, the Duchess, and Don Quixote stood up, and so did all those who were with them. Then the twelve women ranging themselves in two rows, made a lane for the Countess to march up between them, which she did, still led by Trifaldin, her squire. The Duke, the Duchess, and Don Quixote, advancing about a dozen paces to meet her, she fell on her knees, and with a voice, rather hoarse and rough than clear and delicate, 'May it please your Highnesses,' said she, 'to spare yourselves the trouble of receiving with so much ceremony and compliment a man (woman, I would say) who is your devoted servant. Alas! the sense of my misfortunes has so troubled my intellectuals, that my responses cannot be supposed able to answer the critical opinion of your presence. My understanding has forsook me, and is gone a-wool-gathering, and sure it is far remote; for the more I seek it, the more unlikely I am to find it again.' 'The greatest claim, madam,' answered the Duke, 'that we can lay to sense, is a due respect, and decent deference to the worthiness of your person, which, without any further view, sufficiently bespeaks your merit and excellent qualifications.' Then begging the honour of her hand, he led her up, and placed her in a chair by his Duchess, who received her with all the ceremony suitable to the occasion.

Don Quixote said nothing all this while, and Sancho was sneaking about, and peeping under the veils of the lady's women; but to no purpose; for they kept themselves very close and silent, until she at last thus began: 'Confident* I am, thrice potent lord, thrice beautiful lady, and thrice intelligent auditors, that my most unfortunate miserableness shall find, in your most generous and compassionate bowels, a most misericordial sanctuary; my miserableness, which is such as would liquefy marble, malleate steel, and mollify adamantine rocks. But before the rehearsal of my ineffable misfortunes enter, I will not say your ears, but the public mart of your hearing faculties, I earnestly request, that I may have cognisance, whether the cabal, choir, or conclave of this illustrissimous appearance, be not adorned with the presence of the adjutoriferous Don Quixote de la Manchissima, and his squirissimous Pança?' 'Pança is at your elbowissimus,' quoth Sancho, before anybody else could answer, 'and Don Quixotissimo likewise: therefore, most dolorous medem, you may tell out your teale; for we are all ready to be your Ladyship's servitorissimous to the best of our cepecities, and so forth.' Don Quixote then advanced, and, addressing the Countess, 'If your misfortunes, embarrassed Lady,' said he, 'may hope any redress from the power and assistance of knight-errantry, I offer you my force and courage; and, such as they are, I dedicate them to your service. I

---

* A fustian speech contrived on purpose, and imitated by Sancho.

am Don Quixote de la Mancha, whose profession is a sufficient obligation to succour the distressed, without the formality of preambles, or the elegance of oratory to circumvent my favour. Therefore, pray, madam, let us know, by a succinct and plain account of your calamities, what remedies should be applied; and, if your griefs are such as do not admit of a cure, assure yourself at least, that we will comfort you in your afflictions, by sympathising in your sorrow.'

The lady hearing this, threw herself at Don Quixote's feet, in spite of his kind endeavours to the contrary; and striving to embrace them, 'Most invincible Knight,' said she, 'I prostrate myself at these feet, the foundations and pillars of chivalry errant, the supporters of my drooping spirits, whose indefatigable steps alone can hasten my relief, and the cure of my afflictions. O valorous knight-errant, whose real achievements eclipse and obscure the fabulous legend of the Amadises, Esplandians, and Belianises!' Then, turning from Don Quixote, she laid hold on Sancho, and squeezing his hands very hard, 'And thou, the most loyal squire that ever attended on the magnanimity of knight-errantry, whose goodness is more extensive than the beard of my usher Trifaldin! how happily have thy stars placed thee under the discipline of the whole martial college of chivalry professors, centred and epitomised in the single Don Quixote! I conjure thee, by thy love of goodness and thy unspotted loyalty to so great a master, to employ thy moving and interceding eloquence in my behalf, that eftsoons his favour may shine upon this humble, and most disconsolate countess.'

'Look you, Madam Countess,' quoth Sancho, 'as for measuring my goodness by your squire's beard, that is neither here nor there; so my soul go to heaven when I depart this life, I do not matter the rest; for, as for the beards of this world, it is not what I stand upon, so that without all this pawing and wheedling, I will put in a word for you to my master. I know he loves me, and besides, at this time, he stands in need of me about a certain business, and he shall do what he can for you. But pray discharge your burthened mind; unload, and let us see what griefs you bring, and then leave us to take care of the rest.'

The Duke and Duchess were ready to burst with laughing, to find the adventure run in this pleasant strain; and they admired, at the same time, the rare cunning and management of Trifaldi, who, resuming her seat, thus began her story.

'The famous kingdom of Candaya, situated between the Great Tabrobana and the South Sea, about two leagues beyond Cape Comorin, had, for its queen, the Lady Donna Maguntia, whose husband, King Archipelo, dying, left the Princess Antonomasia, their only child, heiress to the crown. This princess was educated, and brought up under my care and direction; I being the eldest and first lady of the bed-chamber to the queen, her mother. In process of time, the young princess arrived at the age of fourteen years, and appeared so perfectly beautiful, that it was not in the power of nature to give any addition to her charms: what is yet more, her mind was no less adorned than her body. Wisdom itself was but a fool to her: she was no less discreet than fair, and the fairest creature in the world; and so she is still, unless the fatal knife, or unrelenting shears of the envious and inflexible sisters have cut her thread of life. But sure the heavens would not permit such an injury to be done to the earth, as the untimely lopping off the loveliest branch that ever adorned the garden of the world.

'Her beauty, which my unpolished tongue can never sufficiently praise, attracting all eyes, soon got her a world of adorers, many of them princes, who were her neighbours, and more distant foreigners. Among the rest, a private knight, who resided at Court, was so audacious as to raise his thoughts to that heaven of beauty. This young gentleman was indeed master of all gallantries that the air of his courtly education could inspire; and so confiding in his youth, his handsome mien, his agreeable air and dress, his graceful carriage, and the charms of his easy wit, and other qualifications, he followed the impulse of his inordinate and most presumptuous passion. I must needs say, that he was an extraordinary person, he played to a miracle on the guitar, and made it speak not only to the ears, but to the very soul. He danced to admiration, and had such a rare knack at making of bird-cages, that he might have got an estate by that very art; and, to sum up all his accomplishments, he was a poet. So many parts and endowments were sufficient to have moved a mountain, and much more the heart of a young tender virgin. But all his fine arts and soothing behaviour had proved ineffectual against the virtue and reserved-ness of my beautiful charge, if the damned cunning rogue had not first conquered me. The deceitful villain endeavoured to seduce the keeper, so to secure the keys of the fortress: in short, he so plied me with pleasing trifles, and so insinuated himself into my soul, that at last he perfectly bewitched me, and made me give way before I was aware, to what I should never have permitted. But that which first wrought me to his purpose, and undermined my virtue, was a cursed copy of verses he sung one night under my window, which, if I remember right, began thus:

A SONG

' "A secret fire consumes my heart;
    And to augment my raging pain,
  The charming foe that rais'd the smart.
    Denies me freedom to complain.
But sure 'tis just, we should conceal
The bliss and woe in love we feel:
For oh! what human tongue can tell
The joys of heaven, or pains of hell."

'The words were to me so many pearls of eloquence, and his voice sweeter to my ears than sugar to the taste. The reflection on the misfortune which these verses brought on me, has often made me applaud Plato's design of banishing all poets from a good and well-governed commonwealth, especially those who write wantonly or lasciviously. For, instead of composing lamentable verses, like those of the Marquis of Mantua, that make the women and children cry by the fireside, they try their utmost skill on such soft strokes as enter the soul, and wound it, like that thunder which hurts and consumes all within, yet leaves the garment sound. Another time he entertained me with the following song:

A SONG

' "Death, put on some kind disguise,
  And at once my heart surprise;
  For 'tis such a curse to live,
    And so great a bliss to die;
  Shouldst thou any warning give,
  I'd relapse to life for joy."

'Many other verses of this kind he plied me with, which charmed when read, but transported when sung. For you must know, that when our eminent poets debase themselves to the writing a sort of composure called love-madrigals, and roundelays, now much in vogue in Candaya, those verses are no sooner heard, but they presently produce a dancing of souls, tickling of fancies, emotion of spirits, and, in short, a pleasing distemper in the whole body, as if quicksilver shook it in every part.

'So that once more I pronounce these poets very dangerous, and fit to be banished to the Isles of Lizards. Though truly, I must confess, the fault is rather chargeable on these foolish people that commend, and the silly wenches that believe them. For, had I been as cautious as my place required, his amorous serenades could never have moved me, nor would I have believed his poetical cant, such as, "I dying live," "I burn in ice," "I shiver in flames," "I hope in despair," "I go, yet stay"; with a thousand such contradictions, which make up the greater part of those kind of compositions. As ridiculous are their promises of the Phœnix of Arabia, Ariadne's crown, the coursers of the sun, the pearls of the Southern Ocean, the gold of Tagus, the balsam of Panchaya, and Heaven knows what! By the way, it is observable, that these poets are very liberal of their gifts, which they know they never can make good.

'But whither, woe's me, whither do I wander, miserable woman? What madness prompts me to accuse the faults of others, having so long a score of my own to answer for! Alas! Not his verses, but my own inclination; not his music, but my own levity; not his wit, but my own folly, opened a passage, and levelled the way for Don Clavijo (for that was the name of the knight). In short, I procured him admittance, and by my connivance, he very often had natural familiarity with Antonomasia, who, poor lady, was rather deluded by me, than by him. But, wicked as I was, it was upon the honourable score of marriage; for had he not been engaged to be her husband, he should not have touched the very shadow of her shoe-string. No, no; matrimony, matrimony, I say, for without that, I will never meddle in any such concern. The greatest fault in this business, was the disparity of their conditions: he being but a private knight, and she heiress to the crown Now this intrigue was kept very close for some time by my cautious management; but at last a certain kind of swelling in Antonomasia's belly began to tell tales; so that, consulting upon the matter, we found there was but one way; Don Clavijo should demand the young lady in marriage before the curate,* by virtue of a promise under her hand, which I dictated for the purpose, and so binding, that all the strength of Samson himself could not have broke the tie. The business was put in execution, the note was produced before the priest, who examined the lady, and finding her confession to agree with the tenor of the contract, put her in custody of a very honest serjeant.' 'Bless us,' quoth Sancho, 'serjeants too; and poets, and songs, and verses in your country! O my conscience, I think the world is the same all the world over! But go on, Madam Trifaldi, I beseech you, for it is late, and I am upon thorns till I know the end of this long-winded story.' 'I will,' answered the Countess.

---

* In Spain, when a young couple have promised each other marriage, and the parents obstruct it, either party may have recourse to the Vicar who, examining the case, has full power to bring them together, and this it is the Countess ridiculously alludes to in her story.

CHAPTER XXXIX

Where Trifaldi continues her stupendous and memorable Story

IF EVERY WORD that Sancho spoke gave the Duchess new pleasure, everything he said put Don Quixote to as much pain; so that he commanded him silence, and gave the matron opportunity to go on. 'In short,' said she, 'the business was debated a good while, and after many questions and answers, the princess firmly persisting in her first declaration, judgment was given in favour of Don Clavijo, which Queen Maguntia, her mother, took so to heart, that we buried her about three days after.' 'Then without doubt she died,' quoth Sancho. 'That is a clear case,' replied Trifaldin, 'for in Candaya they do not use to bury the living, but the dead.' 'But with your good leave, Mr. Squire,' answered Sancho, 'people that were in a swoon have been buried alive before now, and methinks Queen Maguntia should only have swooned away, and not have been in such haste to have died in good earnest; for while there is life there is hopes, and there is a remedy for all things but death. I do not find the young lady was so much out of the way neither, that the mother should lay it so grievously to heart. Indeed, had she married a footman, or some other servant in the family, as I am told many others have done, it had been a very bad business, and past curing; but for the queen to make such a heavy outcry when her daughter married such a fine-bred young knight, faith and troth, I think the business had been better made up. It was a slip, but not such a heinous one, as one would think: for as my master here says, and he will not let me tell a lie, as of scholars they make bishops, so of your knights (chiefly if they be errant) one may easily make kings and emperors.'

'That is most certain,' said Don Quixote, 'turn a knight-errant loose into the wide world with two pennyworth of good fortune, and he is in *potentia propinqua* (*proxima*, I would say) the greatest emperor in the world. But let the lady proceed, for hitherto her story has been very pleasant, and I doubt the most bitter part of it is still untold.' 'The most bitter truly, sir,' answered she; 'and so bitter, that wormwood, and every bitter herb, compared to it, are as sweet as honey.

'The queen being really dead,' continued she, 'and not in a trance, we buried her, and scarce had we done her the last offices, and taken our last leaves; when (*quis talia fando temperet à lachrymis?* who can relate such woes and not be drowned in tears?) the giant Malambruno, cousin-german to the deceased queen, who, besides his native cruelty, was also a magician, appeared upon her grave, mounted on a wooden horse, and, by his dreadful angry looks, showed he came thither to revenge the death of his relation, by punishing Don Clavijo for his presumption, and Antonomasia for her oversight. Accordingly, he immediately enchanted them both upon the very tomb, transforming her into a brazen female monkey, and the young knight into a hideous crocodile of an unknown metal; and between them both he set an inscription in the Syriac tongue, which we have got since translated into the Candayan, and then into Spanish, to this effect:

' "These two presumptuous lovers shall never recover their natural shapes, till the valorous Knight of la Mancha enter into a single combat with me; for, by the irrevocable decrees of fate, this unheard-of adventure is reserved for his unheard-of courage."

'This done, he drew a broad scimitar of a monstrous size, and, catching me fast by the hair, made an offer to cut my throat, or to whip off my head. I was frightened almost to death, my hair stood on end, and my tongue cleaved to the roof of my mouth. However, recovering myself as well as I could, trembling and weeping, I begged mercy in such a moving accent, and in such tender, melting words, that at last my entreaties prevailed on him to stop the cruel execution. In short, he ordered all the waiting-women at Court to be brought before him, the same that you see here at present; and after he had aggravated our breach of trust, and railed against the deceitful practices, mercenary procuring, and what else he could urge in scandal of our profession, and its very being, reviling us for the fact of which I alone stood guilty. "I will not punish you with instant death," said he, "but inflict a punishment which shall be a lasting and eternal mortification." Now, in the very instant of his pronouncing our sentence, we felt the pores of our faces to open, and all about them perceived an itching pain, like the pricking of pins and needles. Thereupon clapping our hands to our faces, we found them as you shall see them immediately:' saying this, the Disconsolate Matron and her attendants, throwing off their veils, exposed their faces all rough with bristly beards; some red, some black, some white, and others motley. The Duke and Duchess admired, Don Quixote and Sancho were astonished, and the standers-by were thunderstruck. 'Thus,' said the Countess proceeding, 'has that murthering and bloody-minded Malambruno served us, and planted these rough and horrid bristles on our faces, otherwise most delicately smooth. Oh! that he had chopped off our heads with his monstrous scimitar, rather than to have disgraced our faces with these brushes upon them! For, gentlemen, if you rightly consider it, and truly, what I have to say should be attended with a flood of tears; but such rivers and oceans have fallen from me already upon this doleful subject, that my eyes are as dry as chaff; and therefore, pray let me speak without tears at this time. Where, alas! shall a waiting-woman dare to show her head with such a furze-bush upon her chin? What charitable person will entertain her? What relations will own her! At the best, we can scarcely make our faces passable, though we torture them with a thousand slops and washes, and even thus we have much ado to get the men to care for us. What will become of her then that wears a thicket upon her face! Oh, ladies, and companions of my misery! in an ill hour were we begot, and in a worse came we into the world!' With these words the Disconsolate Matron seemed to faint away.

CHAPTER XL

Of some things which relate to the Adventure, and appertain to this memorable History

ALL PERSONS that love to read histories of the nature of this, must certainly be very much obliged to Cid Hamet, the original author, who has taken such care in delivering every minute particular distinctly entire, without concealing the least circumstances that might heighten the humour, or, if omitted, have obscured the light and the truth of the story. He draws lively pictures of the thoughts, discovers the imaginations, satisfies curiosity in secrets, clears doubts, resolves arguments; and, in short, makes manifest the least atoms of the most inquisitive desire. O most famous author! O fortunate Don Quixote! O renowned Dulcinea! O facetious Sancho! jointly and severally may you live, and continue to the latest posterity, for the general delight and recreation of mankind—but the story goes on :

'Now, on my honest word,' quoth Sancho, when he saw the Matron in a swoon, 'and by the blood of all the Panças, my forefathers, I never heard nor saw the like, neither did my master ever tell me, or so much as conceive in that working head-piece of his, such an adventure as this. Now all the devils in hell (and I would not curse anybody) run away with thee for an enchanting son of a whore, thou damned giant Malambruno! Couldst thou find no other punishment for these poor sinners, but by clapping scrubbing-brushes about their muzzles, with a pox to you? Had it not been much better to slit their nostrils halfway up their noses, though they had snuffled for it a little, than to have planted these quick-set hedges over their chops? I will lay any man a wager now, the poor devils have not money enough to pay for their shaving.'

'It is but too true, sir,' said one of them, 'we have not wherewithal to pay for taking our beards off; so that some of us, to save charges, are forced to lay on plaisters of pitch that pull away roots and all, and leave our chins as smooth as the bottom of a stone-mortar. There is indeed a sort of women in Candaya, that go about from house to house, to take off the down or hairs that grow about the face,* trim the eyebrows, and do twenty other little private jobs for the women; but we here, who are my lady's duennas, would never have anything to do with them, for they have an ill report; for though, formerly, they got free access, and passed for relations, now they are looked upon to be no better than bawds. So, if my Lord Don Quixote do not relieve us, our beards will stick by us as long as we live.' 'I will have mine plucked off hair by hair among the Moors,' answered Don Quixote, 'rather than not free you from yours.' 'Ah, valorous Knight!' cried the Countess Trifaldi, recovering that moment from her fit; 'the sweet sound of your promise reached my hearing in the very midst of my trance, and has perfectly restored my senses. I beseech you therefore once again, most illustrious sir, and invincible knight-errant, that your gracious promise may soon have the wished-for effect.' 'I will be guilty of no neglect, madam,' answered Don Quixote; 'point out the way, and you shall soon be convinced of my readiness to serve you.'

'You must know then, sir,' said the Disconsolate Lady, 'from this place to the kingdom of Candaya, by computation, we reckon is about five thousand leagues, two or three more or less: but if you ride through the air in a direct line, it is not above three thousand two hundred and twenty-seven. You are likewise to understand that Malambruno told me, that when fortune should make me find out the knight who is to dissolve our enchantment, we would send him a famous steed, much easier and less resty and full of tricks, than those jades that are commonly let out to hire, as being the same wooden horse that carried the valorous Peter of Provence, and the fair Magalona, when he stole her away. It is managed by a wooden peg in its forehead, instead of a bridle, and flies as swiftly through the air as if all the devils in hell were switching him, or blowing fire in his tail. This courser tradition delivers to have been the handiwork of the sage Merlin, who never lent him to any but particular friends, or when he was paid sauce for him. Among others, his friend Peter of Provence borrowed him, and by the help of his wonderful speed, stole away the fair Magalona, as I said, setting her behind on the crupper; for

---

* There are a sort of women-barbers in Spain, that take the down off women's faces, and sell them washes, and these are commonly reputed to be given to bawding. This down the Spaniards call *bello* from the Latin *vellus* (I suppose), which means a 'fleece' (or 'fell,' from the same *vellus*). *Bello* is also Spanish for 'handsome,' from *bellus*, Latin. In old Spanish books *bello* is 'riches'; to intimate there is nothing handsome, without being rich. Accordingly Horace says, *Formam regina pecunia donat.*

you must know he carries double, and so towering up in the air, he left the people that stood near the place whence he started, gaping, staring, and amazed.

'Since that journey, we have heard of nobody that has backed him. But this we know, that Malambruno since that got him by his art; and has used him ever since, to post about to all parts of the world. He is here today, and tomorrow in France, and the next day in America: and one of the best properties of the horse is, that he costs not a farthing in keeping; for he neither eats nor sleeps, neither needs he any shoeing; besides, without having wings, he ambles so very easily through the air, that you may carry in your hand a cup full of water a thousand leagues, and not spill a drop; so that the fair Magalona loved mightily to ride him.'

'Nay,' quoth Sancho, 'as for an easy pacer, commend me to my Dapple. Indeed he is none of your high flyers, he cannot gallop in the air: but on the king's highway, he shall pace ye with the best ambler that ever went on four legs.' This set the whole company a-laughing. But then, the Disconsolate Lady going on: 'This horse,' said she, 'will certainly be here within half-an-hour after it is dark, if Malambruno designs to put an end to our misfortunes, for that was the sign by which I should discover my deliverer.' 'And pray, forsooth,' quoth Sancho, 'how many will this same horse carry upon occasion?' 'Two,' answered she, 'one on the saddle, and the other behind on the crupper: and those two are commonly the knight and the squire, if some stolen damsel be not to be one.' 'Good disconsolate madam,' quoth Sancho, 'I would fain know the name of this same nag.' 'The horse's name,' answered she, 'is neither Pegasus, like Bellephoron's; nor Bucephalus, like Alexander's; nor Brilladoro, like Orlando's; nor Bayard, like Rinaldo's; nor Frontin, like Rogero's; nor Bootes, nor Pyrithous, like the horses of the Sun; neither is he called Orelia, like the horse which Rodrigo, the last king of Spain of the Gothic race, bestrode that unfortunate day when he lost the battle, the kingdom, and his life.' 'I will lay you a wager,' quoth Sancho, 'since the horse goes by none of those famous names, he does not go by that of Rozinante neither, which is my master's horse, and another guess-beast than you have reckoned up.' 'It is very right,' answered the bearded lady: 'however, he has a very proper and significant name; for he is called Clavileno, or Wooden Peg the Swift, from the wooden peg in the forehead; so that for the significancy of name at least he may be compared with Rozinante.' 'I find no fault with his name,' quoth Sancho; 'but what kind of bridle or halter do you manage him with?' 'I told you already,' replied she, 'that he is guided with the peg, which being turned this way or that way, he moves accordingly, either mounting aloft in the air, or almost brushing and sweeping the ground, or else flying in the middle region, the way which ought indeed most to be chosen in all affairs of life.' 'I should be glad to see this notable tit,' quoth Sancho, 'but do not desire to get on his back, either before or behind. No, by my Holy Dame, you may as well expect pears from an elm. It were a petty jest, I trow, for me that can hardly sit my own Dapple, with a pack-saddle as soft as silk, to suffer myself to be horsed upon a hard wooden thing, without either cushion or pillow under my buttocks. Before George! I will not gall my backside to take off the best lady's beard in the land. Let them that have beards wear them still, or get them whipped off as they think best; I will not take such a long jaunt with my master, not I. There is no need of me in this shaving of beards, as there was in Dulcinea's business.' 'Upon my word, dear sir, but there is,' replied Trifaldi, 'and so much, that without you nothing can he done.' 'God save the king!' cried Sancho, 'what have we squires to do with our master's adventures? We must bear the trouble forsooth, and they run away with the credit! Body o' me, it were something, would those that write their stories, but give the squires their due share in their books: as thus, "Such a knight ended such an adventure; but it was with the help of such a one his squire, without which the devil a bit could he ever have done it." But they shall barely tell you in their histories, "Sir Paralipomenon, knight of the three stars, ended the adventure of the six hobgoblins"; and not a word all the while of his squire's person, as if there were no such man, though he was by all the while, poor devil. In short, good people, I do not like it; and once more I say, my master may even go by himself for Sancho, and joy betide him. I will stay and keep Madam Duchess company here, and mayhap by that time he comes back, he will find his Lady Dulcinea's business pretty forward; for I mean to give my bare breech a jirking till I brush off the very hair, at idle times, that is, when I have nothing else to do.'

'Nevertheless, honest Sancho,' said the Duchess, 'if your company be necessary in this adventure, you must go; for all good people will make it their business to entreat you; and it would look very ill, that, through your vain fears, these poor gentlewomen should remain thus with rough and bristly faces.' 'God save the King, I cry again,' said Sancho, 'were it a piece of charity for the relief of some good sober gentlewomen, or poor innocent hospital-girl, something might be said: but to gall my backside, and venture my neck, to unbeard a pack of idling, trolloping chamber-jades, with a murrain! not I, let them go elsewhere for a shaver: I wish I might see the whole tribe of them wear beards from the highest to the lowest, from the proudest to the primmest, all hairy like so many she-goats.' 'You are very angry with waiting-women, Sancho,' said the Duchess: 'that apothecary has inspired you with this bitter spirit. But you are to blame, friend, for I will assure you there are some in my family that may serve for patterns of discretion to all those of their function; and Donna Rodriguez here will let me say no less.' 'Ay, ay, madam,' said

Donna Rodriguez, 'your Grace may say what you please: this is a censorious world we live in, but Heaven knows all; and whether good or bad, bearded or unbearded, we waiting-gentlewomen had mothers as well as the rest of our sex; and since Providence has made us as we are, and placed us in the world, it knows wherefore, and so we trust in its mercy, and nobody's beard.' 'Enough, Donna Rodriguez,' said Don Quixote: 'as for you, Lady Trifaldi, and other distressed matrons, I hope that Heaven will speedily look with a pitying eye on your sorrows, and that Sancho will do as I shall desire. I only wish Clavileno would once come, that I may encounter Malambruno; for I am sure no razor should be more expeditious in shaving your ladyship's beard, than my sword to shave that giant's head from his shoulders: Heaven may a while permit the wicked, but not for ever.'

'Ah! most valorous champion,' said the Disconsolate Matron, 'may all the stars in the celestial regions shed their most propitious influence on your generous valour, which thus supports the cause of our unfortunate office, so exposed to the poisonous rancour of apothecaries, and so reviled by fancy grooms and squires. Now all ill-luck attend the low-spirited queen, who, in the flower of her youth, will not rather choose to turn nun, than waiting-woman! Poor forlorn contemned creatures as we are! though descended in a direct line from father to son, from Hector of Troy himself; yet would not our ladies find a more civil way to speak to us, than thee and thou, though it were to gain them a kingdom. O giant Malambruno! thou, who, though an enchanter, art always most faithful to thy word, send us the peerless Clavileno, that our misfortunes may have an end. For if the weather grows hotter than it is, and these shaggy beards still sprout about our faces, what a sad pickle will they be in!'

The disconsolate lady uttered these lamentations in so pathetic a manner, that the tears of all the spectators waited on her complaints; and even Sancho himself began to water his plants, and condescended at last to share in the adventure, and attend his master to the very fag-end of the world, so he might contribute to the clearing away the weeds that overspread those venerable faces.

CHAPTER XLI

Of Clavileno's* (alias *Wooden Peg's) arrival, with the conclusion of this tedious Adventure*

THOSE DISCOURSES brought on the night, and with it the appointed time for the famous Clavileno's arrival. Don Quixote, very impatient at his delay, began to fear, that either he was not the knight for whom this adventure was reserved, or else that the giant Malambruno had not courage to enter into a single combat with him. But, unexpectedly, who should enter the garden but four savages covered with green ivy, bearing on their shoulders a large wooden horse, which they set upon his legs before the company; and then one of them cried out, 'Now let him that has the courage, mount this engine'—'I am not he,' quoth Sancho, 'for I have no courage, nor am I a knight,'—'and let him take his squire behind him, if he has one,' continued the savage; 'with this assurance from the valorous Malambruno, that no foul play shall be offered, nor will he use anything but his sword to offend him. It is but only turning the peg before him, and the horse will transport him through the air to the place where Malambruno attends their coming. But let them blindfold their eyes, lest the dazzling and stupendous height of their career should make them giddy; and let the neighing of the horse inform them that they are arrived at their journey's end.' Thus having made his speech, the savage turned about with his companions, and, leaving Clavileno, marched out handsomely the same way they came in.

The Disconsolate Matron seeing the horse, almost with tears, addressed Don Quixote: 'Valorous knight,' cried she, 'Malambruno is a man of his word, the horse is here, our beards bud on; therefore I and every one of us conjure you by all the hairs on our chins, to hasten our deliverance; since there needs no more, but that you and your squire get up, and give a happy beginning to your intended journey.' 'Madam,' answered Don Quixote, 'I will do it with all my heart, nor will I so much as stay for a cushion, or to put on my spurs, but mount instantly; such is my impatience to disbeard your Ladyship's face, and restore ye all to your former gracefulness.' 'That is more than I should do,' quoth Sancho. 'I am not in such plaguy haste, not I; and if the quickset hedges on their snouts cannot be lopped off without my riding on that hard crupper, let my master furnish himself with another squire, and these gentlewomen get

---

* A name derived from two Spanish words, *clavo* a 'nail,' and *leno* 'wood.'

some other barber. I am no witch sure, to ride through the air at this rate on a broomstick! What will my islanders say, think ye, when they hear their governor is flying like a paper-kite? Besides, it is three or four thousand leagues from hence to Candaya, and what if the horse should tire upon the road; or the giant grow humorsome? what would become of us then? We may be seven years a-getting home again; and Heaven knows by that time what would become of my government: neither island nor dry land would know poor Sancho again. No, no, I know better things; what says the old proverb? Delays breed danger; and when a cow is given thee, run and halter her. I am the gentlewoman's humble servant, but they and their beards must excuse me, faith! St. Peter is well at Rome, that is to say, here I am much made of, and, by the master of the house's good-will, I hope to see myself a governor.' 'Friend Sancho,' said the Duke, 'as for your island, it neither floats nor stirs, so there is no fear it should run away before you come back; the foundations of it are fixed and rooted in the profound abyss of the earth. Now, because you must needs think I cannot but know, that there is no kind of office of any value that is not purchased with some sort of bribe or gratification, of one kind or other, all that I expect for advancing you to this government, is only that you wait on your master in this expedition, that there may be an end of this memorable adventure: and I here engage my honour, that whether you return on Clavileno with all the speed his swiftness promises, or that it should be your ill-fortune to be obliged to foot it back like a pilgrim, begging from inn to inn and door to door, still whenever you come, you will find your island where you left it, and your islanders as glad to receive you for their governor as ever. And for my own part, Signor Sancho, I will assure you, you would very much wrong my friendship should you in the least doubt my readiness to serve you.' 'Good your worship, say no more,' cried Sancho, 'I am but a poor squire, and your goodness is too great a load for my shoulders. But hang baseness; mount, master, and blindfold me, somebody; wish me a good voyage, and pray for me. But hark ye, good folks, when I am got up, and fly in the skies, may not I say my prayers, and call on the angels myself to help me through?' 'Yes, yes,' answered Trifaldi; 'for Malambruno, though an enchanter, is nevertheless a Christian, and does all things with a great deal of sagacity, having nothing to do with those he should not meddle with.' 'Come on then,' quoth Sancho, 'God and the most Holy Trinity of Gaeta* help me!' 'Thy fear, Sancho,' said Don Quixote, 'might by a superstitious mind be thought ominous: since the adventure of the fulling-mills, I have not seen thee possessed with such a panic terror. But, hark ye, begging this noble company's leave, I must have a word with you in private.' Then, withdrawing into a distant

---

* A church in Italy, of special devotion to the Blessed Trinity.

part of the garden, among some trees: 'My dear Sancho,' said he, 'thou seest we are going to take a long journey; thou art no less sensible of the uncertainty of our return, and Heaven alone can tell what leisure or conveniency we may have in all that time: let me therefore beg thee to slip aside to thy chamber, as if it were to get thyself ready for our journey; and there presently dispatch me only some five hundred lashes, on the account of the three thousand three hundred thou standest engaged for; it will soon be done, and a business well begun, you know, is half ended.' 'Stark mad, before George!' cried Sancho. 'I wonder you are not ashamed, sir. This is just as they say, You see me in haste, and ask me for a maidenhead! I am just going to ride the wooden horse, and you would have me flay my backside. Truly, truly, you are plaguely out this time. Come, come, sir, let us do one thing after another; let us get off these women's whiskers, and then I will feague it away for Dulcinea: I have no more to say on the matter at present.' 'Well, honest Sancho,' replied Don Quixote, 'I will take thy word for once, and I hope thou wilt make it good; for I believe thou art more fool than knave.' 'I am what I am,' quoth Sancho; 'but whatever I be, I will keep my word, never fear it.'

Upon this they returned to the company; and just as they were going to mount, 'Blind thy eyes, Sancho,' said Don Quixote, 'and get up. Sure he that sends so far for us, can have no design to deceive us; since it would never be to his credit, to delude those that rely on his word of honour; and though the success should not be answerable to our desires, still the glory of so brave an attempt will be ours, and it is not in the power of malice to eclipse it.' 'To horse then, sir,' cried Sancho, 'to horse: the tears of those poor bearded gentlewomen have melted my heart, and methinks I feel the bristles sticking in it. I shall not eat a bit to do me good, till I see them have as pretty dimpled smooth chins and soft lips as they had before. Mount then, I say, and blindfold yourself first; for if I must ride behind, it is a plain case you must get up before me.' 'That is right,' said Don Quixote; and with that pulling a handkerchief out of his pocket, he gave it to the Disconsolate Matron to hoodwink him close. She did so; but presently after, uncovering himself, 'If I remember right,' said he, 'we read in Virgil, of the Trojan Palladium, that wooden horse which the Greeks offered Pallas, full of armed knights, who afterwards proved the total ruin of that famous city. It were prudent therefore, before we get up, to probe this steed, and see what he has in his guts.' 'You need not,' said the Countess Trifaldi. 'I dare engage there is no ground for any such surmise; for Malambruno is a man of honour, and would not so much as countenance any base or treacherous practice; and whatever accidents befall ye, I dare answer for it.' Upon this Don Quixote mounted, without any reply, imagining that what he might further urge concerning his security, would be a reflection on his valour. He then began to try the pin, which was easily turned; and as he sat with his long legs stretched at length for want of stirrups, he looked like one of those antique figures in the Roman triumph, woven in some old piece of arras.

Sancho very leisurely and unwillingly was made to climb up behind him; and fixing himself as well as he could on the crupper, felt it somewhat hard and uneasy. With that looking on the Duke, 'Good my Lord,' quoth he, 'will you lend me something to clap under me; some pillow from the page's bed, or the Duchess's cushion of state, or anything; for this horse's crupper is so confounded hard, I fancy it is rather marble than wood.' 'It is needless,' said the Countess, 'for Clavileno will bear no kind of furniture upon him; so that, for your greater ease, you had best sit sideways like a woman.' Sancho took her advice; and then, after he had taken his leave of the company, they bound a cloth over his eyes. But presently after uncovering his face, with a pitiful look on all the spectators, 'Good tender-hearted Christians,' cried he with tears in his eyes, 'bestow a few Pater-nosters and Ave-Mary's on a poor departing brother, and pray for my soul, as you expect the like charity yourselves in such a condition.' 'What! you rascal,' said Don Quixote, 'do you think yourself at the gallows, and at the point of death, that you hold forth in such a lamentable strain? Dastardly wretch without a soul, dost thou not know that the fair Magalona once sat in thy place, and alighted from thence, not into the grave, thou chicken-hearted varlet, but into the throne of France, if there is any truth in history? And do not I sit by thee, that I may vie with the valorous Peter of Provence, and press the seat that was once pressed by him? Come, blindfold thy eyes, poor spiritless animal, and let me not know thee betray the least symptom of fear, at least not in my presence.' 'Well,' quoth Sancho, 'hoodwink me then among ye: but it is no marvel one should be afraid, when you will not let one say his prayers, nor be prayed for, though, for ought I know, we may have a legion of imps about our ears, to clap us up in the devil's pound* presently.'

Now both being hoodwinked, and Don Quixote perceiving everything ready for their setting out, began to turn the pin; and no sooner had he set his hand to it, but the waiting women and all the company set up their throats, crying out, 'Speed you, speed you well, valorous Knight, Heaven be your guide, undaunted squire! Now, now, you fly aloft. See how they cut the air more swiftly than an arrow! Now they mount, and tower, and

---

* In the original it is to carry us to Peralvillo, *i.e.* to hang us first, and try us afterwards as Jarvis translates it. Stevens's Dictionary says, 'Peralvillo is a village near Ciudad-Real in Castile, where the holy brotherhood, or officers for apprehending highwaymen, dispatch those they take in the act, without bringing them to trial; like what we call hanging a man first, and trying him afterwards.'

soar, while the gazing world wonders at their course. Sit fast, sit fast, courageous Sancho; you do not sit steady; have a care of falling; for should you now drop from that amazing height, your fall would be greater than the aspiring youth's that misguided the chariot of the sun his father. All this Sancho heard, and girting his arms fast about his master's waist, 'Sir,' quoth he, 'why do they say we are so high, since we can hear their voices? Truly I hear them so plainly, that one would think they were close by us.' 'Never mind that,' answered Don Quixote; 'for in those extraordinary kind of flights, we must suppose our hearing and seeing will be extraordinary also. But do not hold me so hard, for you will make me tumble off. What makes thee tremble so? I am sure I never rode easier in all my life; our horse goes as if he did not move at all. Come then, take courage; we make swinging way, and have a fair merry gale.' 'I think so too,' quoth Sancho, 'for I feel the wind puff as briskly upon me here, as if I do not know how many pairs of bellows were blowing wind in my tail.' Sancho was not altogether in the wrong; for two or three pairs of bellows were indeed levelled at him then, which gave air very plentifully; so well had the plot of this adventure been laid by the Duke, the Duchess, and their steward, that nothing was wanting to further the diversion.

Don Quixote at last feeling the wind, 'Sure,' said he, 'we must be risen to the middle region of the air, where the winds, hail, snow, thunder, lightning, and other meteors are produced; so that if we mount at this rate, we shall be in the region of fire presently, and, what is worst, I do not know how to manage this pin, so as to avoid being scorched and roasted alive.' At the same time some flax, with other combustible matter, which had been got ready, was clapped at the end of a long stick, and set on fire at a small distance from their noses, and the heat and smoke affecting the knight and the squire; 'May I be hanged,' quoth Sancho, 'if we be not come to this fireplace you talk of, or very near it; for the half of my beard is singed already. I have a huge mind to peep out, and see whereabouts we are. 'By no means,' answered Don Quixote: 'I remember the strange but true story of Doctor Torralva, whom the Devil carried to Rome hoodwinked, and bestriding a reed, in twelve hours' time, setting him down on the tower of Nona, in one of the streets of that city. There he saw the dreadful tumult, assault, and death of the Constable of Bourbon; and the next morning he found himself at Madrid, where he related the whole story. Among other things, he said, as he went through the air, the Devil bid him open his eyes, which he did, and then he found himself so near the moon, that he could touch it with his finger; but durst not look towards the earth, lest the distance should make his brains turn round. So, Sancho, we must not unveil our eyes, but rather wholly trust to the care and providence of him that has charge of us; and fear nothing, for we only mount high, to come souse down like a hawk, upon the kingdom of

Candaya, which we shall reach presently: for though it appears not half an hour to us since we left the garden, we have, nevertheless, travelled over a vast tract of air.' 'I know nothing of the matter,' replied Sancho, 'but this I am very certain, that if your Madam Magulane, or Magalona (what do ye call her?) could sit this damned wooden crupper without a good cushion under her tail, she must have a harder pair of buttocks than mine.'

This dialogue was certainly very pleasant all this while to the Duke and Duchess, and the rest of the company; and now at last, resolving to put an end to this extraordinary adventure, which had so long entertained them successfully, they ordered one of their servants to give fire to Clavileno's tail; and the horse being stuffed full of squibs, crackers, and other fireworks, burst presently into pieces, with a mighty noise, throwing the knight one way, and the squire another, both sufficiently singed. By this time, the Disconsolate Matron, and bearded regiment, were vanished out of the garden, and all the rest counterfeiting a trance, lay flat upon the ground; Don Quixote and Sancho sorely bruised, made shift to get up, and looking about, were amazed to find themselves in the same garden whence they took horse, and see such a number of people lie dead, as they thought, on the ground. But their wonder was diverted by the appearance of a large lance stuck in the ground, and a scroll of white parchment fastened to it by two green silken strings, with the following inscription upon it in golden characters.

'The renowned knight, Don Quixote de la Mancha, achieved the venture of the Countess Trifaldi, otherwise called the Disconsolate Matron, and her companions in distress, by barely attempting it. Malambruno is fully satisfied. The waiting gentlewomen have lost their beards: King Clavijo and Queen Antonomasia have resumed their pristine shapes; and when the squire's penance shall be finished, the white dove shall escape the pounces of the pernicious hawks that pursue her, and her pining lover shall lull her in his arms. This is preordained by the Sage Merlin, proto-enchanter of enchanters.'

Don Quixote having read this oracle, and construing it to refer to Dulcinea's disenchantment, rendered thanks to Heaven for so great a deliverance; and approaching the Duke and Duchess, who seemed as yet in a swoon, he took the Duke by the hand: 'Courage, courage, noble sir,' cried he, 'there is no danger; the adventure is finished without blood-shed, as you may read it registered in that record.'

The Duke, yawning and stretching, as if he had been waked out of a sound sleep, recovered himself by degrees, as did the Duchess, and the rest of the company; all of them acting the surprise so naturally, that the jest could not be discovered. The Duke, rubbing his eyes, made a shift to read the scroll; then, embracing Don Quixote, he extolled his valour to the skies, assuring him, he was the bravest knight the earth had ever possessed. As for

Sancho, he was looking up and down the garden for the Disconsolate
Matron, to see what sort of a face she had got, now her furze-bush was off.
But he was informed, that as Clavileno came down flaming in the air, the
Countess with her women, vanished immediately, but not one of them
chin-bristled, nor so much as a hair upon their faces.

Then the Duchess asked Sancho, how he had fared in his long voyage:
'Why truly, madam,' answered he, 'I have seen wonders; for you must
know, that though my master would not suffer me to pull the cloth from
my eyes, yet as I have a kind of itch to know everything, and a spice of the
spirit of contradiction, still hankering after what is forbidden me; so when,
as my master told me, we were flying through the region of fire, I shoved
my handkerchief a little above my nose, and looked down; and what do
you think I saw? I spied the earth a hugeous way afar off below me
(Heaven bless us!) no bigger than a mustard-seed; and the men walking to
and fro upon it not much larger than hazel nuts. Judge now if we were not
got up woundy high.' 'Have a care what you say, my friend,' said the
Duchess; 'for if the men were bigger than hazel nuts, and the earth no
bigger than a mustard-seed, one man must be bigger than the whole
earth, and cover it so that you could not see it.' 'Like enough,' answered
Sancho; 'but for all that, do you see, I saw it with a kind of a side-look
upon one part of it, or so.' 'Look you, Sancho,' replied the Duchess, 'that
will not bear; for nothing can be wholly seen by any part of it.' 'Well, well,
madam,' quoth Sancho, 'I do not understand your parts and wholes: I saw
it, and there is an end of the story. Only you must think, that as we flew by
enchantment, so we saw by enchantment; and thus I might see the earth,
and all the men, which way soever I looked. I will warrant, you will not
believe me neither when I tell you that when I thrust up the 'kerchief
above my brows, I saw myself so near heaven, that between the top of my
cap and the main sky there was not a span and a half. And, Heaven bless
us! forsooth, what a hugeous great place it is! And we happened to travel
that road where the seven* she-goat stars were; and faith and troth, I had
such a mind to play with them (having been once a goatherd myself), that
I fancy I would have cried myself to death, had I not done it. So soon as I
spied them, what does me I, but sneaks down very soberly from behind
my master, without telling any living soul, and played and leaped about
for three quarters of an hour by the clock, with the pretty nanny-goats,
who are as sweet and fine as so many marigolds or gillyflowers; and honest
Wooden Peg stirred not one step all the while.' 'And while Sancho
employed himself with the goats,' asked the Duke, 'how was Don Quixote
employed?' 'Truly,' answered the knight, 'I am sensible all things were
altered from their natural course; therefore what Sancho says, seems the

* The *Pleiades*, vulgarly called in Spanish, the 'Seven Young She-Goats.'

less strange to me. But, for my own part, I neither saw heaven nor hell, sea nor shore. I perceived indeed we passed through the middle region of the air, and were pretty near that of fire, but that we came so near heaven as Sancho says, is altogether incredible; because we then must have passed quite through the fiery region, which lies between the sphere of the moon and the upper region of the air. Now it was impossible for us to reach that part, where are the Pleiades, or the Seven Goats, as Sancho calls them, without being consumed in the elemental fire; and therefore since we escaped those flames, certainly we did not soar so high, and Sancho either lies or dreams.' 'I neither lie nor dream,' replied Sancho. 'Uds precious! I can tell you the marks and colour of every goat among them: if you do not believe me, do but ask and try me. You will easily see whether I speak truth or no.' 'Well,' said the Duchess, 'prithee tell them to me, Sancho.' 'Look you,' answered Sancho, 'there were two of them green, two carnation, two blue, and one parti-coloured.' 'Truly,' said the Duke, 'that is a new kind of goats you have found out. Sancho, we have none of those colours upon earth.' 'Sure, sir,' replied Sancho, 'you will make some sort of difference between heavenly she-goats, and the goats of this world?' 'But, Sancho,' said the Duke, 'among these she-goats, did you see never a he?* Not one horned beast of the masculine gender?' 'Not one, sir. I saw no other horned thing but the moon: and I have been told, that neither he-goats, nor any other cornuted tups are suffered to lift their horns beyond those of the moon.'

They did not think fit to ask Sancho any more questions about his airy voyage; for, in the humour he was in, they judged he would not stick to ramble all over the heavens, and tell them news of whatever was doing there, though he had not stirred out of the garden all the while.

Thus ended, in short, the adventure of the Disconsolate Matron, which afforded sufficient sport to the Duke and Duchess, not only for the present, but for the rest of their lives. And might have supplied Sancho with matter of talk from generation to generation, for many ages, could he have lived so long. 'Sancho,' said Don Quixote, whispering him in the ear, 'since thou wouldst have us believe what thou hast seen in heaven, I desire thee to believe what I saw in Montesinos' cave. Not a word more.'

---

* *Cabron*: A jest on the double meaning of that word which signifies both a he-goat and a cuckold.

CHAPTER XLII

The instructions which Don Quixote gave Sancho Pança, before he went to the Government of his island, with other matters of moment

THE SATISFACTION which the Duke and Duchess received by the happy success of the adventure of the Disconsolate Matron, encouraged them to carry on some other pleasant project, since they could with so much ease impose on the credulity of Don Quixote and his squire. Having therefore given instructions to their servants and vassals how to behave themselves towards Sancho in his government; the day after the scene of the wooden horse, the Duke bid Sancho prepare, and be in a readiness to take possession of his government; for now his islanders wished as heartily for him, as they did for rain in a dry summer. Sancho made an humble bow, and looking demurely on the Duke, 'Sir,' quoth he, 'since I came down from heaven, whence I saw the earth so very small, I am not half so hot as I was for being a governor. For what greatness can there be in being at the head of a puny dominion, that is but a little nook of a tiny mustard seed? and what dignity and power can a man be reckoned to have, in governing half a dozen men no bigger than hazel-nuts? For I could not think there were any more in the whole world. No, if your Grace would throw away upon me never so little a corner in heaven, though it were but half a league, or so, I would take it with better will than I would the largest island on earth.' 'Friend Sancho,' answered the Duke, 'I cannot dispose of an inch of heaven; for that is the province of God alone; but what I am able to bestow, I give you; that is, an island tight and clever, round and well proportioned, fertile and plentiful to such a degree, that if you have but the art and understanding to manage things right, you may hoard there both of the treasure of this world, and the next.'

'Well then,' quoth Sancho, 'let me have this island, and I will do my best to be such a governor, that, in spite of rogues, I shall not want a small nook in heaven one day or other. It is not out of covetousness neither, that I would leave my little cot, and set up for somebody, but merely to know what kind of thing it is to be a governor.' 'Oh! Sancho,' said the Duke, 'when once you have had a taste of it, you will never leave licking your fingers, it is so sweet and bewitching a thing to command and be obeyed. I am confident, when your master comes to be an Emperor (as he cannot fail to be, according to the course of his affairs) he will never by any consideration be persuaded to abdicate; his only grief will be, that he was one no sooner.'

'Troth, sir,' replied Sancho, 'I am of your mind; it is a dainty thing to command, though it were but a flock of sheep.' 'Oh! Sancho,' cried the Duke, 'let me live and die with thee: for thou hast an insight into everything. I hope thou wilt prove as good a governor as thy wisdom bespeaks thee. But no more at this time, – tomorrow, without further delay, you may set forward to your island, and shall be furnished this afternoon with equipage and dress answerable to your post, and all other necessaries for your journey.'

'Let them dress me as they will,' quoth he, 'I shall be the same Sancho Pança still.' 'That is true,' said the Duke, 'yet every man ought to wear clothes suitable to his place and dignity; for a lawyer should not go dressed like a soldier, nor a soldier like a priest. As for you, Sancho, you are to wear the habit both of a captain and a civil magistrate; so your dress shall be a compound of those two; for on the government that I bestow on you, arms are as necessary as learning, and a man of letters as requisite as a swordsman.' 'Nay, as for letters,' quoth Sancho, 'I cannot say much for myself: for as yet I scarce know my A, B, C; but yet, if I can but remember my Christ's-cross,* it is enough to make me a good governor: as for my arms, I will not quit my weapon as long as I can stand, and so Heaven be our guard.' 'Sancho cannot do amiss,' said the Duke, 'while he remembers these things.'

By this time Don Quixote arrived, and hearing how suddenly Sancho was to go to his government, with the Duke's permission, he took him aside to give him some good instructions for his conduct in the discharge of his office.

Being entered Don Quixote's chamber, and the door shut, he almost forcibly obliged Sancho to sit by him; and then, with a grave deliberate voice, he thus began.

'I give Heaven infinite thanks, friend Sancho, that before I have the happiness of being put in possession of my hopes, I can see thine already crowned: fortune hastening to meet thee with thy wishes. I, who had assigned the reward of thy services upon my happy success, am yet but on the way to preferment; and thou, beyond all reasonable expectation, art arrived at the aim and end of thy desires. Some are assiduous, solicitous, importunate, rise early, bribe, entreat, press, will take no denial, obstinately persist in their suit and yet at last never obtain it. Another comes on, and by a lucky hit or chance, bears away the prize, and jumps into the preferment which so many had pursued in vain; which verifies the saying,

' "The happy have their days, and those they choose;
The unhappy have but hours, and those they lose."

---

* He means the Christ's-cross-row; so called from the cross being put at the beginning of the A, B, C.

Thou, who seems to me a very blockhead, without sitting up late, or rising early, or any manner of fatigue or trouble, only the air of knight-errantry being breathed on thee, art advanced to the government of an island in a trice, as if it were a thing of no moment, a very trifle. I speak this, my dear Sancho, not to upbraid thee, nor out of envy, but only to let thee know, thou art not to attribute all this success to thy own merit, while it is entirely owing to the kind heavenly disposer of human affairs, to whom thy thanks ought to be returned. But, next to Heaven, thou art to ascribe thy happiness to the greatness of the profession of knight-errantry, which includes within itself such stores of honour and preferment.

'Being convinced of what I have already said, be yet attentive, O my son, to what I, thy Cato, have further to say: listen, I say, to my admonitions, and I will be thy north star, and pilot to steer and bring thee safe into the port of honour, out of the tempestuous ocean, into which thou art just going to launch; for offices and great employments are no better than profound gulfs of confusion.

'First of all, O my son, fear God; for the fear of God is the beginning of wisdom, and wisdom will never let thee go astray.

'Secondly, consider what thou wert, and make it thy business to know thyself, which is the most difficult lesson in the world. Yet from this lesson thou wilt learn to avoid the frog's foolish ambition of swelling to rival the bigness of the ox; else the consideration of your having been a hog-driver, will be, to the wheel of your fortune, like the peacock's ugly feet.'

'True,' quoth Sancho, 'but I was then but a little boy; for when I grew up to be somewhat bigger, I drove geese, and not hogs, but methinks that is nothing to the purpose; for all governors cannot come from kings and princes.'

'Very true,' pursued Don Quixote; 'therefore those who want a noble descent, must allay the severity of their office with mildness and civility, which, directed by wisdom, may secure them from the murmurs and malice, from which no state nor condition is exempt.

'Be well-pleased with the meanness of thy family, Sancho, nor think it a disgrace to own thyself derived from labouring men; for, if thou art not ashamed of it thyself, nobody else will strive to make thee so. Endeavour rather to be esteemed humble and virtuous, rather than proud and vicious. The number is almost infinite of those who, from low and vulgar births, have been raised to the highest dignities, to the papal chair, and the imperial throne; and this I could prove by examples enough to tire thy patience.

'Make virtue the medium of all thy actions, and thou wilt have no cause to envy those whose birth gives them the titles of great men, and princes; for nobility is inherited, but virtue acquired: and virtue is worth more in itself, than nobleness of birth.

'If any of thy poor relations come to see thee, never reject or affront them; but, on the contrary, receive and entertain them with marks of favour; in this thou wilt display a generosity of nature, and please Heaven that would have nobody to despise what it has made.

'If thou sendest for thy wife, as it is not fit a man in thy station should be long without his wife, and she ought to partake of her husband's good fortune, teach her, instruct her, polish her the best thou canst, till her native rusticity is refined to a handsomer behaviour; for often an ill-bred wife throws down all that a good and discreet husband can build up.

'Shouldst thou come to be a widower (which is not impossible) and thy post recommend thee to a bride of a higher degree, take not one that shall, like a fishing-rod, only serve to catch bribes. For, take it from me, the judge must, at the general and last court of judicature, give a strict account of the discharge of his duty, and must pay severely at his dying-day for what he has suffered his wife to take.

'Let never obstinate self-conceit be thy guide; it is the vice of the ignorant, who vainly presume on their understanding.

'Let the tears of the poor find more compassion, though not more justice, than the informations of the rich.

'Be equally solicitous to find out the truth, where the offers and presents of the rich, and the sobs and importunities of the poor are in the way.

'Wherever equity should, or may take place, let not the extent or rigour of the law bear too much on the delinquent; for it is not a better character in a judge to be rigorous, than to be indulgent.

'When the severity of the law is to be softened, let pity, not bribes, be the motive.

'If thy enemy has a cause before thee, turn away thy eyes from thy prejudice, and fix them on the matter or fact.

'In another man's cause, be not blinded by thy own passions, for those errors are almost without remedy; or their cure will prove expensive to thy wealth and reputation.

'When a beautiful woman comes before thee, turn away thy eyes from her tears, and thy ears from her lamentations; and take time to consider sedately her petition, if thou wouldst not have thy reason and honesty lost in her sighs and tears.

'Revile not with words those whom their crimes oblige thee to punish in deed; for the punishment is enough to the wretches, without the addition of ill language.

'In the trial of criminals, consider as much as thou canst without prejudice to the plaintiff, how defenceless and open the miserable are to the temptations of our corrupt and depraved nature, and so far show thyself full of pity and clemency; for though God's attributes are equal, yet His mercy is more attractive and pleasing in our eyes, than His justice.

'If thou observest these rules, Sancho, thy days shall be long, thy fame eternal, thy recompense full, and thy felicity unspeakable. Thou shalt marry thy children and thy grandchildren to thy heart's desire; they shall want no titles: beloved of all men, thy life shall be peaceable, thy death in a good and venerable old age, and the offspring of thy grandchildren, with their soft youthful hands shall close thy eyes.

'The precepts I have hitherto given thee regard the good and ornament of thy mind; now give attention to those directions that relate to the adorning of thy body.'

CHAPTER XLIII

The second part of Don Quixote's advice to Sancho Pança

WHO WOULD NOT have taken Don Quixote for a man of extraordinary wisdom, and as excellent morals, having heard him documentise his squire in this manner; only, as we have often observed in this history, the least talk of knight-errantry spoiled all, and made his understanding muddy: but in everything else, his judgment was very clear, and his apprehension very nice, so that every moment his actions used to discredit his judgment, and his judgment his actions. But in these economical precepts which he gave Sancho, he showed himself master of a pleasant fancy, and mingled his judgment and extravagance in equal proportions. Sancho lent him a great deal of attention, in hopes to register all those good counsels in his mind, and put them in practice; not doubting but by their means he should acquit himself of his duty like a man of honour.

'As to the government of thy person and family,' pursued Don Quixote, 'my first injunction is cleanliness. Pare thy nails, nor let them grow as some do, whose folly persuades them that long nails add to the beauty of the hand; till they look more like casterils' claws, than a man's nails. It is foul and unsightly.

'Keep thy clothes tight about thee; for a slovenly looseness is an argument of a careless mind; unless such a negligence, like that of Julius Cæsar, be affected for some cunning design.

'Prudently examine what thy income may amount to in a year: and if sufficient to afford thy servants' liveries, let them be decent and lasting, rather than gaudy and for show; and for the overplus of thy good husbandry, bestow it on the poor. That is, if thou canst keep six footmen, have but three; and let what would maintain three more, be laid out in charitable uses. By that means thou wilt have attendants in Heaven as well as on earth, which our vain-glorious great ones, who are strangers to this practice, are not like to have.

'Lest thy breath betray thy peasantry, defile it not with onions and garlic.

'Walk with gravity, and speak with deliberation, and yet not as if thou didst hearken to thy own words; for all affectation is a fault.

'Eat little at dinner, and less at supper; for the stomach is the storehouse, whence health is to be imparted to the whole body.

'Drink moderately; for drunkenness neither keeps a secret, nor observes a promise.

'Be careful not to chew on both sides, that is, fill not thy mouth too full, and take heed not to eruct before company.'

'Eruct,' quoth Sancho, 'I do not understand that cramp word.' 'To eruct,' answered Don Quixote, 'is as much as to say, to belch; but this being one of the most disagreeable and beastly words in our language, though very expressive and significant, the more polite, instead of belching, say eructing, which is borrowed from the Latin. Now though the vulgar may not understand this, it matters not much; for use and custom will make it familiar and understood. By such innovations are languages enriched, when the words are adopted by the multitude, and naturalised by custom.'

'Faith and troth,' quoth Sancho, 'of all your counsels, I will be sure not to forget this, for I have been mightily given to belching.' 'Say eructing,' replied Don Quixote, 'and leave off belching.' 'Well,' quoth Sancho, 'be it as you say, eruct, I will be sure to remember.'

'In the next place, Sancho,' said the Knight, 'do not overlard your common discourse with that glut of proverbs, which you mix in it continually; for though proverbs are properly concise and pithy sentences, yet as thou bringest them in, in such a huddle, by the head and shoulders, thou makest them look like so many absurdities.' 'Alas! sir,' quoth Sancho, 'this is a disease that Heaven alone can cure; for I have more proverbs than will fill a book; and when I talk, they crowd so thick and fast to my mouth, that they quarrel which shall get out first; so that my tongue is forced to let them out as fast, first come first served, though nothing to my purpose. But henceforwards I will set a watch on my mouth, and let none fly out, but such as shall befit the gravity of my place. For in a rich man's house the cloth is soon laid: where there is plenty the guests cannot be empty. A blot's no blot till it is hit. He is safe who stands under the bells: you cannot eat your cake and have your cake: and store's no sore.'

'Go on, go on, friend,' said Don Quixote, 'thread, tack, stitch on, heap proverb upon proverb, out with them, man, spew them out! there is nobody coming. My mother whips me, and I whip the gig. I warn thee to forbear foisting in a rope of proverbs everywhere, for thou blunderest out a whole litany of old saws, as much to the purpose as the last year's snow. Observe me, Sancho, I condemn not the use of proverbs, but it is most certain, that such a confusion and hodge-podge of them, as you throw out and drag in by the hair together, make conversation fulsome and poor.

'When you do ride, cast not thy body all on the crupper nor hold thy legs stiff down, and straddling from the horse's belly; nor yet so loose, as if thou wert still on Dapple; for the air and gracefulness of sitting a horse, distinguishes sometimes a gentleman from a groom. Sleep with moderation; for he that rises not with the sun, loses so much day. And remember this, Sancho, that diligence is the mother of good fortune: sloth, on the contrary, never effected any thing that sprung from a good and reasonable desire.

'The advice which I shall conclude with, I would have thee to be sure to fix in thy memory, though it relate not to the adorning thy person; for I am persuaded, it will redound as much to thy advantage, as any I have yet given thee. And this it is:

'Never undertake to dispute, or decide any controversies concerning the pre-eminence of families; since, in the comparison, one must be better than the other; for he that is lessened by thee will hate thee, and the other whom you prefer, will not think himself obliged to thee.

'As for thy dress, wear close breeches and hose, a long coat, and a cloak a little longer. I do not advise thee to wear wide-kneed breeches, or trunk-hose, for they become neither swordsmen, nor men of business.

'This is all the advice, friend Sancho, I have to give thee at present. If you take care to let me hear from thee hereafter, I shall give thee more, according as the occasions and emergencies require.'

'Sir,' said Sancho, 'I see very well that all you have told me is mighty good, wholesome, and to the purpose: but what am I the better, if I cannot keep it in my head? I grant you, I shall not easily forget that about paring my nails, and marrying again, if I should have the luck to bury my wife. But for all that other gallimaufry, and heap of stuff, I can no more remember one syllable of it, than the shapes of last year's cloud. Therefore let me have it in black and white, I beseech you. It is true, I can neither write nor read, but I will give it to my father-confessor, that he may beat and hammer it into my noddle, as occasion serves.' 'O Heaven,' cried Don Quixote, 'how scandalous it looks in a governor not to be able to write or read! I must needs tell thee, Sancho, that for a man to be so illiterate, or to he left-handed, implies that either his parents were very poor and mean, or that he was of so perverse a nature, he could not receive the impressions of learning, or any thing that is good. Poor soul, I pity thee! this is indeed a very great defect. I would have thee at least learn to write thy name.' 'Oh! as for that,' quoth Sancho, 'I can do well enough: I can set my name; for when I served offices in our parish, I learned to scrawl a sort of letters, such as they mark bundles of stuff with, which they told me spelt my name. Besides, I can pretend my right hand is lame, and so another shall sign for me; for there is a remedy for all things but death. And since I have the power, I will do what I list; for, as the saying is, he whose father is judge, goes safe to his trial.* And, as I am a governor, I hope I am somewhat better than a judge. New lords, new laws. Ay, ay, any, let them come as they will, and play at bo-peep. Let them back-bite me to my face, I will bite-back the biters. Let them come for wool, and I will send them home shorn. Whom God loves, his house happy proves. The rich man's follies pass for wise sayings in this world. So I, being rich, do you see, and a governor, and free-hearted too into the bargain, as I intend to be, I shall have no faults at all. It is so, daub yourself with honey, and you will never want flies. What a man has, so much he is sure of, said my old grannam: and who shall hang the bell about the cat's neck?'

'Confound thee,' cried Don Quixote, 'for an eternal proverb-voiding swag-belly. Threescore thousand Belzebubs take thee, and thy damned nauseous rubbish. Thou hast been this hour stringing them together, like so many ropes of onions, and poisoning and racking† me with them. I dare say, these wicked proverbs will one day bring thee to the gallows; they will provoke thy islanders to pull thee down, or at least make them shun thee like a common nuisance. Tell me, thou essence of ignorance, where dost thou rake them up? and who taught thy cod's-head to apply them? For it makes me sweat, as if I were delving and threshing, to speak but one, and apply it properly.'

'Udsprecious! my good master,' quoth Sancho, 'what a small matter puts you in a pelting chase! why the devil should you grudge me the use of my own goods and chattels? I have no other estate. Proverbs on proverbs are all my stock. And now I have four ready to pop out, as pat to the purpose as pears to a panier; but mum for that.‡ Now silence is my name.'§ 'No,' replied Don Quixote, 'rather prate-roast and sauce-box I

---

* The new translation has it, 'He whose father is mayor – ' with a break, and this note at bottom, viz. 'Sancho hints at some well-known proverb.' The proverb may be found in Stevens's dictionary: *Quien padre Quien padre tiene Alcalde seguro va al juicio.* The original indeed does break off in the middle, as being a well-known proverb, applicable to all that have powerful friends.

† The original is, 'draughts of the rack.' It alludes to a particular kind of torture in Spain; namely, a thin piece of gauze, moistened, and put to the lips of a person dying with thirst, who swallows it down by degrees, and then it is pulled up again by the end the executioner holds in his hand.

‡ Pears sent to Madrid, from Daroca, in March, when they are scarce, and made up nicely, to prevent bruising.

§ In the original, 'to keep silence well is called Sancho.' The proverb is, 'To keep silence well is called (*santo*) holy:' but Sancho, out of archness or ignorance, changes *santo* to his own name Sancho.

should call thee; for thou art all tittle-tattle and obstinacy. Yet methinks I would fain hear these four notable proverbs that come so pat to the purpose. I thank Heaven I have a pretty good memory, and yet I cannot for my soul call one to mind.' 'Why, sir,' quoth Sancho, 'what proverbs would you have better than these? Between two cheek-teeth never clap thy thumbs. And when a man says, Get out of my house; what would you with my wife? there is no answer to be made. And again, Whether the pitcher hit the stone, or the stone the pitcher, it is bad for the pitcher. All these fit to a hair, sir; that is, let nobody meddle with his governor, or his betters, or he will rue for it, as sure as a gun; as he must expect who runs his finger between two cheek-teeth (and though they were not cheek-teeth, if they be but teeth, that is enough). In the next place, let the governor say what he will there is no gainsaying him; it is as much as when one says, Get out of my house; what would you with my wife? And as for the stone and the pitcher, a blind man may see through it. And so he that sees a mote in another man's eye, should do well to take the beam out of his own; that people may not say, The pot calls the kettle black-arse, and the dead woman is afraid of her that is fleaed. Besides, your worship knows, that a fool knows more in his own house, than a wise body in another man's.' 'That is a mistake, Sancho,' replied Don Quixote; 'for the fool knows nothing, neither in his own house, nor in another man's; for no substantial knowledge can be erected on so bad a foundation as folly. But let us break off this discourse: if thou dost not discharge the part of a good governor, thine will be the fault, though the shame and discredit will be mine. However, this is my comfort, I have done my duty in giving thee the best and most wholesome advice I could: and so Heaven prosper and direct thee in thy government, and disappoint my fears of thy turning all things upside down in that poor island; which I might indeed prevent, by giving the Duke a more perfect insight into thee, and discovering to him, that all that gorbellied paunch-gutted little corpse of thine is nothing but a bundle of proverbs, and sack-full of knavery.'

'Look you, sir,' quoth Sancho, 'if you think me not fit for this government, I will think no more on it. Alas! the least snip of my soul's nails (as a body may say) is dearer to me than my whole body: and I hope I can live plain Sancho still, upon a luncheon of bread and a clove of garlic, as contented as Governor Sancho upon capons and partridges. Death and sleep makes us all alike, rich and poor, high and low. Do but call to mind what first put this whim of government into my noddle, you will find it was your own self; for, as for me, I know no more what belongs to islands and governors than a blind buzzard.

'So if you fancy the Devil will have me for being a governor, let me be plain Sancho still, and go to heaven, rather than my Lord Governor and go to hell.'

'These last words of thine, Sancho,' said Don Quixote, 'in my opinion, prove thee worthy to govern a thousand islands. Thou hast naturally a good disposition, without which all knowledge is insufficient. Recommend thyself to the Divine Providence, and be sure never to depart from uprightness of intention; I mean, have still a firm purpose and design to be thoroughly informed in all the business that shall come before thee, and act upon just grounds, for Heaven always favours good desires: and so let us go to dinner, for I believe now the Duke and Duchess expect us.'

CHAPTER XLIV

How Sancho Pança was carried to his Government, and of the strange Adventures that befell Don Quixote in the Castle

WE HAVE IT from the traditional account of this History, that there is a manifest difference between the translation and the Arabic in the beginning of this chapter; Cid Hamet having in the original taken an occasion of criticising on himself, for undertaking so dry and limited a subject, which must confine him to the bare history of Don Quixote and Sancho, and debar him the liberty of launching into episodes and digressions that might be of more weight and entertainment. To have his fancy, his hand, and pen bound up to a single design, and his sentiments confined to the mouths of so few persons, he urged as an insupportable toil, and of small credit to the undertaker; so that, to avoid this inconveniency, he has introduced into the first part some novels, as 'The Curious Impertinent,' and that of the 'Captive,' which were in a manner distinct from the design, though the rest of the stories which he brought in there, fall naturally enough in with Don Quixote's affairs, and seem of necessity to claim a place in the work. It was his opinion likewise, as he has told us, that the adventures of Don Quixote, requiring so great a share of the reader's attention, his novels must expect but an indifferent reception, or, at most, but a cursory view, not sufficient to discover their artificial contexture, which must have been very obvious, had they been published by themselves without the interludes of Don Quixote's madness or Sancho's impertinence. He has therefore in this second part avoided all distinct and independent stories, introducing only such as have the appearance of episodes, yet flow naturally from the design of the story, and those but seldom, and with as much gravity as can be expressed. Therefore, since he has tied himself up to such narrow bounds, and confined his understanding and parts, otherwise capable of the most copious subjects, to the pure matter of this present undertaking, he begs it may add a value to his work; and that he may be commended, not so much for what he has written, as what he has forborne to write. And then he proceeds in his history as follows:

After dinner Don Quixote gave Sancho, in writing, the copy of his verbal instructions, ordering him to get somebody to read them to him. But the squire had no sooner got them, but he dropped the paper, which fell into the Duke's hands; who, communicating the same to the Duchess, they found a fresh occasion of admiring the mixture of Don Quixote's good sense and extravagance: and so carrying on the humour, they sent Sancho that afternoon, with a suitable equipage, to the place he was to govern, which, wherever it lay, was to be an island to him.

It happened that the management of this affair was committed to a steward of the Duke's, a man of a facetious humour, and who had not only wit to start a pleasant design, but discretion to carry it on; two qualifications which make an agreeable consort when they meet, nothing being truly agreeable without good sense. He had already personated the Countess Trifaldi very successfully, and, with his master's instructions, in relation to his behaviour towards Sancho, could not but discharge his trust to a wonder. Now it fell out, that Sancho no sooner cast his eyes on the steward, but he fancied he saw the very face of Trifaldi; and, turning to his master, 'The Devil fetch me, sir,' quoth he, 'if you don't own that this same steward of the Duke's, here, has the very phiz of my Lady Trifaldi.' Don Quixote looked very earnestly on the steward; and having perused him from top to toe, 'Sancho,' said he, 'thou needest not give thyself to the Devil to confirm this matter: I see their faces are the very same; yet for all that the steward and the disconsolate lady cannot be the same person; for that would imply a very great contradiction, and might involve us in more abstruse and difficult doubts than we have conveniency now to discuss or examine. Believe me, friend, our devotion cannot be too earnest, that we may be delivered from the power of these cursed enchantments.' 'Adad, sir,' quoth Sancho, 'you may think I am in jest; but I heard him open just now, and I thought the very voice of Madam Trifaldi sounded in my ears: but mum is the word: I say nothing, though I shall watch his waters to find out whether I am right or wrong in my suspicion.' 'Well, do so,' said Don Quixote; 'and fail not to acquaint me with all the discoveries thou canst make in this affair, and other occurrences in thy government.'

At last Sancho set out, with a numerous train. He was dressed like a man of the long robe, and wore over his other clothes a white sad-coloured coat or gown of watered camblet, and a cap of the same stuff. He was mounted on a he mule, and rid short after the Gineta fashion. Behind him, by the Duke's order, was led his Dapple, bridled and saddled like a horse of state, in gaudy trappings of silk; which so delighted Sancho, that every now and then he turned his head about to look upon him, and thought himself so happy, that now he would not have changed fortunes with the Emperor of Germany. He kissed the Duke and Duchess's hand at parting, and received his master's benediction, while the Don wept, and Sancho blubbered abundantly.

Now, reader, let the noble governor depart in peace, and speed him well. His administration in his government may perhaps make you laugh to some purpose, when it comes in play. But in the meantime let us observe the fortune of his master the same night; for though it do not make you laugh outright, it may chance to make you draw in your lips, and show your teeth like a monkey; for it is the property of his adventures, to create always either surprise or merriment.

It is reported then, that immediately upon Sancho's departure, Don Quixote found the want of his presence; and had it been in his power, he would have revoked his authority, and deprived him of his commission. The Duchess, perceiving his disquiet and desiring to understand the cause of his melancholy, told him, that if it was Sancho's absence made him uneasy, she had squires enough and damsels in her house, that should supply his place in any service he would be pleased to command them. 'It is true, madam,' answered Don Quixote, 'I am somewhat concerned for the absence of Sancho; but there is a more material cause of my present uneasiness; and I must beg to be excused, if among the many obligations your Grace is pleased to confer on me, I decline all but the good intention that has offered them. All I have further to crave, is your Grace's permission to be alone in my apartment, and to be my own servant.' 'Your pardon, sir,' replied the Duchess; 'I cannot consent you should be alone: I have four damsels, blooming as so many roses, that shall attend you.' 'They will be no roses to me,' returned Don Quixote,' but so many prickles to my conscience; and if they come into my chamber, they must fly in at the window. If your Grace would crown the many favours you have heaped on this worthless person, I beseech you to leave him to himself, and the service of his own hands. No desires, madam, must enter my doors; for the walls of my chamber have always been a bulwark to my chastity, and I shall not infringe my rule, for all the bounty you can lavish on me. In fine, rather than think of being undressed by any mortal, I would lie rough the whole night.' 'Enough, enough, noble sir,' said the Duchess; 'I desist, and will give orders that not so much as the buzzing of a fly, much less the impertinence of a damsel, shall disturb your privacy. I am far from imposing anything, sir, that should urge Don Quixote to a transgression in point of decency; for, if I conjecture right, among the many virtues that adorn him, his modesty is the most distinguishable. Dress, therefore, and undress by yourself,

how you please, when you will, and nobody shall molest you: nay, that
you may not be obliged to open your doors upon the account of any
natural necessity, care shall be taken that you may find in your room
whatever you may have occasion for in the night. And may the great
Dulcinea del Toboso live a thousand ages, and her fame be diffused all
over the habitable globe, since she has merited the love of so valorous, so
chaste, and loyal a knight; and may the indulgent heavens incline the
heart of our governor Sancho Pança, to put a speedy end to his discipline,
that the beauties of so great a lady may be restored to the view of the
admiring world!' 'Madam,' returned Don Quixote, 'your Grace has
spoken like yourself; so excellent a lady could utter nothing but what
denotes the goodness and generosity of her mind: and certainly it will be
Dulcinea's peculiar happiness to have been praised by you; for it will raise
her character more to have had your Grace for her panegyrist, than if the
best orators in the world had laboured to set it forth.' 'Sir,' said the
Duchess, waving this discourse, 'it is supper-time, and my Lord expects
us: come then, let us to supper, that you may go to bed betimes; for you
must needs be weary still with the long journey you took to Candaya
yesterday.' 'Indeed, madam,' answered Don Quixote, 'I feel no manner of
weariness, for I can safely swear to your Grace, that I never rid an easier
beast, nor a better goer than Clavileno. For my part, I cannot imagine
what could induce Malambruno to part with so swift and gentle a horse,
nay, and to burn him too in such a manner.' 'It is to be supposed,' said the
Duchess, 'that being sorry for the harm he had done, not only to the
Countess Trifaldi and her attendants, but to many others, and repenting
of the bad deeds which, as a wizard and a necromancer, he doubtless had
committed, he had a mind to destroy all the instruments of his wicked
profession, and accordingly he burned Clavelino as the chief of them, that
engine having served him to rove all over the world; or perhaps he did
not think any man worthy of bestriding him after the great Don Quixote,
and so with his destruction, and the inscription which he has caused to be
set up, he has eternised your valour.'

Don Quixote returned his thanks to the Duchess, and after supper
retired to his chamber, not suffering anybody to attend him; so much he
feared to meet some temptation that might endanger the fidelity which he
had consecrated to his Dulcinea, keeping always the eyes of his mind fixed
on the constancy of Amadis, the flower and mirror of knight-errantry. He
therefore shut the door of his chamber after him, and undressed himself
by the light of two wax-candles. But oh! the misfortune that befell him,
unworthy such a person. As he was straining to pull off his hose, there fell
not sighs, or anything that might disgrace his decent cleanliness, but about
four and twenty stitches of one of his stockings, which made it look like a
lattice-window. The good Knight was extremely afflicted, and would have

given then an ounce of silver for a drahm of green silk; green silk, I say, because his stockings were green.

Here Benengeli could not forbear exclaiming: 'O poverty! poverty! what could induce that great Cordova poet to call thee a Holy Thankless Gift! Even I that am a Moor, have learned by the converse I have had with Christians, that holiness consists in charity, in humility, in faith, in obedience, and in poverty: but sure he who can be contented when poor, had need to be strengthened by God's peculiar grace; unless the poverty which is included among these virtues, be only that poorness in spirit, which teaches us to use the things of this world, as if we had them not. But thou, second poverty, fatal indigence, of which I now am speaking, why dost thou intrude upon gentlemen, and affect well-born souls more than other people? Why dost thou reduce them to cobble their shoes, and wear some silk, some hair, and some glass buttons on the same tattered waistcoat, as if it were only to betray variety of wretchedness? Why must their ruffs be of such a dismal hue, in rags, dirty, rumpled, and ill starched? (And by this you may see how ancient is the use of starch and ruffs.) How miserable is a poor gentleman who, to keep up his honour, starves his person, fares sorrily, or fasts unseen within his solitary narrow apartment; then, putting the best face he can upon the matter, comes out picking his teeth, though it is but an honourable hypocrisy, and though he has eaten nothing that requires that nice exercise! Unhappy he, whose honour is in continual alarms, who thinks that at a mile's distance every one discovers the patch in his shoe, the sweat of his forehead soaked through his old rusty hat, the bareness of his clothes, and the very hunger of his famished stomach.'

All these melancholy reflections are renewed in Don Quixote's mind, by the rent in his stocking. However, for his consolation, he bethought himself that Sancho had left him a pair of light boots, which he designed to put on the next day.

In short, to bed he went, with a pensive, heavy mind, the thoughts of Sancho's absence, and the irreparable damage that his stocking had received, made him uneasy: he would have darned it, though it had been with silk of another colour, one of the greatest tokens of want a poor gentleman can show, during the course of his tedious misery.

At last he put out the lights, but it was sultry hot, and he could not compose himself to rest. Getting up, therefore, he opened a little shutter of a barred window that looked into a fine garden, and was presently sensible that some people were walking and talking there: he listened, and as they raised their voices, he easily overheard their discourse.

'No more, dear Emerenia,' said one to the other: 'do not press me to sing; you know that from the first moment this stranger came to the castle, and my unhappy eyes gazed on him, I have been too conversant with tears and sorrow, to sing or relish songs. Alas! all music jars when the soul's out of tune. Besides, you know the least thing wakens my lady, and I would not for the world she should find us here. But grant she might not wake, what will my singing signify, if this new Æneas, who is come to our habitation to make me wretched, should be asleep, and not hear the sound of my complaints?' 'Pray, my dear Altisidora,' said the other, 'do not make yourself uneasy with those thoughts; for without doubt the Duchess is fast asleep, and everybody in the house but we and the lord of thy desires; he is certainly awake, I heard him open his window just now; then sing, my poor grieving creature, sing and join the melting music of thy lute, to the soft accents of thy voice. If my lady happens to hear us, we will pretend we came out for a little air. The heat within doors will be our excuse.' 'Alas! my dear,' replied Altisidora, 'it is not that frights me most: I would not have my song betray my thoughts; for those that do not know the mighty force of love will be apt to take me for a light and indiscreet creature; but yet since it must be so I will venture: better shame on the face, than sorrow in the heart!' This said, she began to touch her lute so sweetly, that Don Quixote was ravished. At the same time an infinite number of adventures of this nature, such as he had read of in his idle books of knight-errantry, windows, grates, gardens, serenades, amorous meetings, parleys, and fopperies, all crowded into his imagination, and he presently fancied that one of the Duchess's damsels was fallen in love with him, and struggled with her modesty to conceal her passion. He began to be apprehensive of the danger to which his fidelity was exposed, but yet firmly determined to withstand the powerful allurement; and so recommending himself with a great deal of fervency to his Lady Dulcinea del Toboso, he resolved to hear the music; and, to let the serenading ladies know he was awake, he feigned a kind of a sneeze, which did not a little please them; for it was the only thing they wanted, to be assured their jest was not lost. With that, Altisidora having tuned her lute afresh, after a flourish, began the following song:

THE MOCK SERENADE

'Wake, Sir Knight, now love's invading,
　　Sleep in Holland sheets no more;
When a nymph is serenading,
　　'Tis an errant shame to snore.

Hear a damsel, tall and tender,
　　Honing in most rueful guise,
With heart almost burn'd to cinder,
　　By the sunbeams of thy eyes.

To free damsels from disaster,
 Is, they say, your daily care:
Can you then deny a plaster,
 To a wounded virgin here?

Tell me, doughty youth, who curs'd thee
 With such humours and ill-luck?
Was't some sullen bear dry-nurs'd thee,
 Or she-dragon gave thee suck?

Dulcinea, that virago,
 Well may brag of such a kid:
Now her name is up, and may go
 From Toledo to Madrid.

Would she but her prize surrender,
 (Judge how on thy face I dote!)
In exchange I'd gladly send her
 My best gown and petticoat.

Happy I, would fortune doom thee
 But to have me near thy bed,
Stroke thee, pat thee, curry-comb thee,
 And hunt o'er thy solid head.

But I ask too much sincerely,
 And I doubt I ne'er must do't,
I'd but kiss thy toe, and fairly
 Get the length thus of thy foot.

How I'd rig thee, and what riches
 Should be heap'd upon thy bones;
Caps and sock, and cloaks and breeches,
 Matchless pearls, and precious stones.

Do not from above, like Nero,
 See me burn, and slight my woe!
But to quench my fires, my hero,
 Cast a pitying eye below.

I'm a virgin-pullet truly;
 One more tender ne'er was seen,
A mere chicken, fledg'd but newly;
 Hang me if I'm yet fifteen.

Wind and limb, all's tight about me,
   My hair dangles to my feet,
I am straight too, if you doubt me,
   Trust your eyes, come down and see't.

I've a bob nose has no fellow,
   And a sparrow's mouth as rare,
Teeth like topazes all yellow;
   Yet I'm deem'd a beauty here.

You know what a rare musician,
   (If you hearken) courts your choice:
I can say my disposition
   Is as taking as my voice.

Those and suchlike charms I've plenty,
   I'm a damsel of this place:
Let Altisidora tempt ye;
   Or she's in a woeful case.'

Here the courting damsel ended her song, and the courted Knight began his expostulation. 'Why,' said he, with a sigh heaved from the bottom of his heart, 'why must I be so unhappy a knight, that no damsel can gaze on me without falling in love? Why must the peerless Dulcinea del Toboso be so unfortunate, as not to be permitted the single enjoyment of my transcendent fidelity? Queens, why do you envy her? Empresses, why do you persecute her? Damsels of fifteen, why do you attempt to deprive her of her right? Leave! oh, leave the unfortunate fair! let her triumph, glory, and rejoice in the quiet possession of the heart which love has allotted her, and the absolute sway which she bears over my yielding soul. Away, unwelcome crowd of loving impertinents: Dulcinea alone can soften my manly temper, and mould me as she pleases. For her I am all sweetness, for you I am bitterness itself. There is to me no beauty, no prudence, no modesty, no gaiety, no nobility among your sex, but in Dulcinea alone. All other women seem to be deformed, silly, wanton, and base-born, when compared with her. Nature brought me forth only that I might be devoted to her service. Let Altisidora weep or sing: let the lady despair on whose account I have received so many blows in the disastrous castle of the enchanted Moor;* still I am Dulcinea's, and hers alone, dead or alive, dutiful unspotted, and unchanged, in spite of all the necromantic

* Alluding to the story of Maritornes and the carrier, in the former part of the
  history.

powers in the world.' This said, he hastily clapped down the window, and flung himself into his bed, with as high an indignation as if he had received some great affront. There let us leave him awhile, in regard the great Sancho Pança calls upon us to see him commence his famous government.

CHAPTER XLV

How the great Sancho Pança took possession of his Island, and in what manner he began to govern

O THOU PERPETUAL SURVEYOR of the Antipodes, bright luminary of the world, and eye of heaven, sweet ferventer of liquids,* here Timbrius called, there Phœbus, in one place an archer, in another a physician! Parent of poesy, and inventor of music, perpetual mover of the universe, who, though thou seemest sometimes to set, art always rising? O sun, by whose assistance man begets man, on thee I call for help! inspire me, I beseech thee, warm and illumine my gloomy imagination, that my narration may keep pace with the great Sancho Pança's actions throughout his government; for without thy powerful influence, I feel myself benumbed, dispirited, and confused. Now I proceed.

Sancho, with all his attendants, came to a town that had about a thousand inhabitants, and was one of the best where the Duke had any power: they gave him to understand, that the name of the place was the island of Barataria, either because the town was called Barataria, or because the government cost him so cheap.† As soon as he came to the gates (for it was walled) the chief officers and inhabitants, in their formalities, came out to receive him, the bells rung, and all the people gave general demonstrations of their joy. The new governor was then carried in mighty pomp to the great church, to give Heaven thanks; and after some ridiculous ceremonies, they delivered him the keys of the gates, and received him as a perpetual governor of the island of Barataria. In the meantime, the garb, the port, the huge beard, and the short and thick shape of the new Governor, made every one who knew nothing of the jest wonder, and even those who were privy to the plot, who were many, were not a little surprised.

---

* Sweat motive of wine cooling bottles, so Jarvis has it, with the following note, viz. *Cantimplora* is a sort of bottle for keeping wine cool, with a very long neck, and very broad and flat below, that the ice may lie conveniently upon it in the pail, and a broad cork fitted to the pail, with a hole in the middle to let the neck of the bottle through.'
† *Barato* signifies 'cheap.'

In short, from the church they carried him to the court of justice; where, when they had placed him in his seat, 'My Lord Governor,' said the Duke's steward to him, 'it is an ancient custom here, that he who takes possession of this famous island, must answer to some difficult and intricate question that is propounded to him; and by the return he makes, the people feel the pulse of his understanding, and by an estimate of his abilities, judge whether they ought to rejoice, or to be sorry for his coming.'

All the while the steward was speaking, Sancho was staring on an inscription in large characters on the wall over against his seat, and as he could not read, he asked, what was the meaning of that which he saw painted there upon the wall. 'Sir,' said they, 'it is an account of the day when your Lordship took possession of this island, and the inscription runs thus: "This day, being such a day of this month, in such a year, the Lord Don Sancho Pança took possession of this island, which may he long enjoy."' 'And who is he,' asked Sancho, 'whom they call Don Sancho Pança?' 'Your Lordship,' answered the steward; 'for we know of no other Pança in this island but yourself, who now sits in this chair.' 'Well, friend,' said Sancho, 'pray take notice, that Don does not belong to me, nor was it borne by any of my family before me. Plain Sancho Pança is my name; my father was called Sancho, my grandfather Sancho; and all of us have been Panças, without any Don or Donna added to our name. Now do I already guess your Dons are as thick as stones in this island. But it is enough that Heaven knows my meaning; if my government happens but to last four days to an end, it shall go hard but I will clear the island of those swarms of Dons that must needs be as troublesome as so many flesh-flies.* Come, now for your question, good Mr. Steward, and I will answer it as well as I can, whether the town be sorry or pleased.'

At the same instant two men came into the court, the one dressed like a country fellow, the other looked like a tailor, with a pair of shears in his hand. 'If it please you, my Lord,' cried the tailor, 'I and this farmer here are come before your worship. This honest man came to my shop yesterday; for, saving your presence, I am a tailor, and Heaven be praised free of my company: so my Lord, he showed me a piece of cloth: "Sir," quoth he, "is there enough of this to make me a cap?"† Whereupon I measured the stuff, and answered him, "Yes, if it like your worship." Now as I imagined, do ye see, he could not but imagine (and perhaps he imagined right enough) that

---

* A severe satire on the Spanish pride and affectation of gentility. Don is a title properly belonging only to families of note, but of late it has grown very common, which is the abuse which Sancho would here redress.

† *Caperuza* in the original, which means a countryman's cap: though Stevens translates it in this place, a cloak: but he is mistaken, as the reader will soon see.

I had a mind to cabbage some of his cloth; judging hard of us honest tailors. "Prithee," quoth he, "look there be not enough for two caps." Now I smelt him out, and told him there was. Whereupon the old knave (if it like your worship) going on to the same tune, bid me look again and see whether it would not make three; and at last if it would not make five. I was resolved to humour my customer, and said it might. So we struck a bargain; just now the man is come for his caps, which I give him, but when I asked him for my money, he will have me give him his cloth again, or pay him for it.' 'Is this true, honest man?' said Sancho to the farmer. 'Yes, if it please you,' answered the fellow; 'but pray let him show the five caps he has made me.' 'With all my heart,' cried the tailor; and with that, pulling his hand from under his cloak, he held up five little tiny caps, hanging upon his four fingers and thumb, as upon so many pins. 'There,' quoth he, 'you see the five caps this good gaffer asks for; and may I never whip a stitch more, if I have wronged him of the least snip of his cloth, and let any workman be judge.' The sight of the caps, and the oddness of the cause set the whole court a-laughing. Only Sancho sat gravely, considering a while, and then, 'Methinks,' said he, 'this suit here needs not be long depending, but may be decided without any more ado, with a great deal of equity; and therefore the judgment of the court is, that the tailor shall lose his making, and the countryman his cloth, and that the caps be given to the poor prisoners, and so let there be an end of the business.'

If this sentence provoked the laughter of the whole court, the next no less raised their admiration. For after the Governor's order was executed, two old men appeared before him, one of them with a large cane in his hand, which he used as a staff. 'My Lord,' said the other, who had none, 'some time ago I lent this man ten gold crowns to do him a kindness; which money he was to repay me on demand. I did not ask him for it again in a good while, lest it should prove a greater inconveniency to him to repay me than he laboured under when he borrowed it: however, perceiving that he took no care to pay me, I have asked him for my due; nay, I have been forced to dun him hard for it. But still he did not only refuse to pay me again, but denied he owed me anything, and said, that if I lent him so much money, he certainly returned it. Now, because I have no witnesses of the loan, nor he of the pretended payment, I beseech your Lordship to put him to his oath; and if he will swear he has paid me, I will freely forgive him before God and the world.' 'What say you to this, old gentleman with the staff?' asked Sancho. 'Sir,' answered the old man, 'I own he lent me the gold; and since he requires my oath, I beg you will be pleased to hold down your rod of justice,* that I may swear upon it, how I

---

* The way of swearing in Spain in some cases, is to hold down the rod of justice, and making a cross on it, swear by that.

have honestly and truly returned him his money.' Thereupon the
Governor held down his rod, and in the mean time, the defendant gave
his cane to the plaintiff to hold, as if it hindered him, while he was to
make a cross, and swear over the judge's rod: this done, he declared, that
it was true the other had lent him the ten crowns: but that he had really
returned him the same sum into his own hands: and that because he
supposed the plaintiff had forgot it, he was continually asking him for it.
The great Governor hearing this, asked the creditor what he had to reply.
He made answer, that since his adversary had sworn it, he was satisfied;
for he believed him to be a better Christian than to offer to forswear
himself, and that perhaps he had forgot he had been repaid. Then the
defendant took his cane again, and having made a low obeisance to the
judge, was immediately leaving the court. Which when Sancho perceived, reflecting on the passage of the cane, and admiring the creditor's
patience, after he had studied a while with his head leaning over his
stomach, and his forefinger on his nose, on a sudden he ordered the old
man with the staff to be called back. When he was returned, 'Honest
man,' said Sancho, 'let me see that cane a little: I have a use for it.' 'With
all my heart,' answered the other; 'sir, here it is'; and with that he gave it
him. Sancho took it; and giving it the other old man, 'There,' said he, 'go
your ways, and Heaven be with you; for now you are paid.' 'How so, my
Lord?' cried the old man. 'Do you judge this cane to be worth ten gold
crowns?' 'Certainly,' said the Governor, 'or else I am the greatest dunce
in the world. And now you shall see whether I have not a headpiece fit to
govern a whole kingdom upon a shift.' This said, he ordered the cane to
be broken in open court, which was no sooner done, but out dropped the
ten crowns. All the spectators were amazed, and began to look on their
governor as a second Solomon. They asked him how he could conjecture
that the ten crowns were in the cane. He told them, that having observed
how the defendant gave it to the plaintiff to hold while he took his oath,
and then swore he had returned him the money in his own hands, after
which he took his cane again from the plaintiff; this considered, it came
into his head that the money was lodged within the reed. From whence
may be learned, that though sometimes those that govern are destitute of
sense, yet it often pleases God to direct them in their judgment. Besides,
he had heard the curate of his parish tell of such another business; and he
had so special a memory, that were it not that he was so unlucky as to
forget all he had a mind to remember, there could not have been a better
in the whole island. At last the two old men went away, the one to his
satisfaction, the other with eternal shame and disgrace; and the beholders
were astonished, insomuch that the person, who was commissioned to
register Sancho's words and actions, and observe his behaviour, was not
able to determine, whether he should not give him the character of a wise

man, instead of that of a fool, which he had been thought to deserve.

No sooner was this trial over, but in came a woman, hauling along a man that looked like a good substantial grazier. 'Justice, my Lord Governor, justice!' cried she, aloud; 'and if I cannot have it on earth, I will have it from Heaven! Sweet Lord Governor, this wicked fellow met me in the middle of a field, and has had the full use of my body; he has handled me like a dish-clout. Woe is me, he has robbed me of that which I had kept these three and twenty years. Wretch that I am, I had guarded it safe from natives and foreigners, Christians and infidels! I have been always as tough as cork; no salamander ever kept itself more entire in fire, nor no wool among the briers, than did poor I, till this lewd man, with nasty fists, handled me at this rate.' 'Woman, woman,' quoth Sancho, 'no reflections yet; whether your gallant's hands were nasty or clean, that is not to the purpose.' Then turning to the grazier, 'Well friend,' said he, 'what have you to say to this woman's complaint?' 'My Lord,' answered the man, looking as if he had been frightened out of his wits, 'I am a poor drover, and deal in swine; so this morning I was going out of this town, after I had sold* (under correction be it spoken) four hogs, and what with the duties and the sharping tricks of the officers, I hardly cleared anything by the beasts. Now, as I was trudging home, whom should I pick up by the way, but this hedge-madam here; and the Devil, who has a finger in every pie, being powerful, forced us to yoke together. I gave her that which would have contented any reasonable woman; but she was not satisfied, and wanted more money; and would never leave me till she had dragged me hither. She will tell you I ravished her; but, by the oath I have taken, or mean to take, she lies, like a drab as she is, and this is every tittle true.' 'Fellow,' quoth Sancho, 'hast thou any silver about thee?' 'Yes, if like your worship,' answered the drover, 'I have some twenty ducats in silver, in a leathern purse here in my bosom.' 'Give it the plaintiff, money and all,' quoth Sancho. The man, with a trembling hand, did as he was commanded: the woman took it, and dropped a thousand courtesies to the company, wishing, on her knees, as many blessings to the good Governor, who took such special care of poor fatherless and motherless children, and abused virgins; and she then nimbly tripped out of court, holding the purse fast in both her hands; though first she took care to peep into it, to see whether the silver was there. Scarce was she gone, when Sancho, turning to the fellow, who stood with tears in his eyes, and looked as if he

---

* In the original, *Esta Manana salia deste lugar de vender*, etc., which the new translation turns thus: 'This morning I was going out of this town to sell,' etc, not 'after I had sold,' etc. The critics must judge which is right. I do not mention this to depreciate that performance, which I must own I admire for its accuracy, no less than the prints for their beauty.

had parted with his blood as well as his money; 'Friend,' said he, 'run and overtake the woman, and take the purse from her whether she will or no, and bring it hither.' The drover was neither so deaf nor so mad as to be twice bid; away he flew like lightning after his money. The whole court was in mighty expectation, and could not tell what would be the end of the matter. But a while after, the man and the woman came back, he pulling, and she tugging; she with her petticoat tucked up, and the purse in her bosom, and he using all the strength he had to get it from her. But it was to no purpose; for the woman defended her prize so well, that all his manhood little availed. 'Justice,' cried she, 'for Heaven's sake, justice, gentlemen! Look you, my Lord, see this impudent ruffian, that on the king's highway, nay, in the face of the court, would rob me of my purse, the very purse you condemned him to give me.' 'And has he got it from you?' asked the Governor. 'Got it,' quoth the woman; 'I will lose my life before I lose my purse. I were a pretty baby then, to let him wipe my nose thus. No, you must set other dogs upon me than this sorry sneaking mangy whelp: pincers, hammers, mallets, and chisels, shall not wrench it out of my clutches; no, not the claws of a lion; they shall sooner have my soul than my money.' 'She says the truth, my Lord,' said the fellow, 'for I am quite spent: the jade is too strong for me; I cannot grapple with her.' Sancho then called to the female. 'Here,' quoth he, 'honesty! you she dragon, let me see the purse.' The woman delivered it to him; and then he returned it to the man. 'Hark you, mistress,' said he to her, 'had you showed yourself as stout and valiant to defend your body (nay, but half so much), as you have done to defend your purse, the strength of Hercules could not have forced you. Hence, Impudence, get out of my sight. Away, with a pox to you; and do not offer to stay in this island, nor within six leagues of it, on pain of two hundred lashes. Out, as fast as you can, you tricking, brazen-faced, brimstone hedge-drab, away!' The wench was in a terrible fright, and sneaked away hanging down her head as shamefully as if she had been catched in the deed of darkness. 'Now friend,' said the Governor to the man, 'get you home with your money, and Heaven be with you: but another time, if you have not a mind to come off worse, be sure you do not yoke with such cattle.' The drover thanked him as well as he could, and away he went; and all the people admired afresh their new Governor's judgment and sentences. An account of which was taken by him that was appointed to be his historiographer, and forthwith transmitted to the Duke, who expected it with impatience. Now let us leave honest Sancho here; for his master, with great earnestness, requires our attendance, Altisidora's serenade having strangely discomposed his mind.

CHAPTER XLVI

Of the dreadful alarms given to Don Quixote by the Bells and Cats, during the course of Altisidora's amours

WE LEFT the great Don Quixote profoundly buried in the thoughts into which the enamoured Altisidora's serenade had plunged him. He threw himself into his bed; but the cares and anxieties which he brought thither with him, like so many fleas, allowed him no repose, and the misfortune of his torn stocking added to his affliction. But as time is swift, and no bolts nor chains can bar his rapid progress, posting away on the wings of the hours, the morning came on apace. At the return of light, Don Quixote, more early than the sun, forsook his downy bed, put on his chamois apparel, and drawing on his walking boots, concealed in one of them the disaster of his hose: he threw his scarlet cloak over his shoulder, and clapped on his valiant head his cap of green velvet edged with silver lace. Over his right shoulder he hung his belt,* the sustainer of his trusty executing sword. About his wrist he wore the rosary, which he always carried about him. And thus accoutred, with a great deal of state and majesty, he moved towards the antechamber, where the Duke and Duchess were ready dressed, and, in a manner, expecting his coming. As he went through a gallery he met Altisidora and her companion, who waited for him in the passage; and no sooner did Altisidora espy him, but she dissembled a swooning fit, and immediately dropped into the arms of her friend, who presently began to unlace her stays. Which Don Quixote perceiving, he approached, and turning to the damsel, 'I know the meaning of all this,' said he, 'and whence these accidents proceed.' 'You know more than I do,' replied the assisting damsel. 'But this I am sure of, that hitherto there is not a damsel in this house, that has enjoyed her health better than Altisidora: I never knew her make the least complaint before. A vengeance seize all the knights-errant in the world, if they are all so ungrateful. Pray, my Lord Don Quixote, retire; for this poor young creature will not come to herself as long as you are by.' 'Madam,' answered the Knight, 'I beg that a lute may be left in my chamber this evening, that I may assuage this lady's grief as well as I can; for in the beginning of an amour, a speedy and free

---

* Here his belt, according to the true signification of Tahali, is one hung on his shoulders: at Diego de Mirandas it seemed to be a belt girded about his loins, and was made of a skin proper for the weakness he was supposed to have in them.

discovery of our aversion or pre-engagement, is the most effectual cure.'
This said, he left them, that he might not be found alone with them by
those that might happen to go by. He was scarce gone, but Altisidora's
counterfeited fit was over; and, turning to her companion, 'By all means,'
said she, 'let him have a lute; for, without doubt, the Knight has a mind to
give us some music, and we shall have sport enough.' Then they went and
acquainted the Duchess with their proceeding, and Don Quixote's desiring
a lute. Whereupon, being overjoyed at the occasion, she plotted with the
Duke and her woman a new contrivance, to have a little harmless sport
with the Don. After this they expected, with a pleasing impatience, the
return of night, which stole upon them as fast as had done the day, which
the Duke and Duchess passed in agreeable converse with Don Quixote.
The same day she dispatched a trusty page of hers, who had personated
Dulcinea in the wood, to Teresa Pança, with her husband's letter, and the
bundle of clothes which he had left behind, charging him to bring her back
a faithful account of every particular between them.

At last, it being eleven o'clock at night, Don Quixote retired to his
apartment, and finding a lute there, he tuned it, opened the window, and
perceiving there was somebody walking in the garden, he ran over the
strings of the instrument; and, having tuned it again as nicely as he could,
he coughed and cleared his throat, and then with a voice somewhat
hoarse, yet not unmusical, he sang the following song, which he had
composed himself that very day:

THE ADVICE

'Love, a strong designing foe
    Careless hearts with ease deceives;
Can that breast resist his blow,
    Which your sloth unguarded leaves?

'If you're idle, you're destroy'd,
    All his arts on you he tries;
But be watchful and employ'd,
    Straight the baffled tempter flies.

'Maids for modest grace admir'd,
    If they would their fortunes raise,
Must in silence live retir'd,
    'Tis their virtue speaks their praise.

'Prudent men in this agree,
    Whether alms or courts they use;
They may trifle with the free,
    But for wives the virtuous chuse.

'Wanton loves, which in their way
    Roving travellers put on,
In the morn are fresh and gay,
    In the evening cold and gone.

'Loves that come with eager haste,
    Still with equal haste depart;
For an image ill imprest,
    Soon is vanish'd from the heart.

'On a picture fair and true
    Who would paint another face?
Sure no beauty can subdue,
    While a greater holds the place.

'The divine Tobosan, fair
    Dulcinea, claims me whole;
Nothing can her image tear;
    'Tis one substance with my soul.

'Then let fortune smile or frown,
    Nothing shall my faith remove;
Constant truth, the lover's crown,
    Can work miracles in love.'

No sooner had Don Quixote made an end of his song, to which the Duke, Duchess, Altisidora, and almost all the people in the castle listened all the while; but on a sudden, from an open gallery, that was directly over the Knight's window, they let down a rope, with at least a hundred little tinkling bells hanging about it. After that came down a great number of cats, poured out of a huge sack, all of them with smaller bells tied to their tails. The jangling of the bells, and the squalling of the cats made such a dismal noise, that the very contrivers of the jest themselves were scared for the present, and Don Quixote was strangely surprised and quite dismayed. At the same time, as ill-luck would have it, two or three frightened cats leaped in through the bars of his chamber-window, and running up and down the room like so many evil spirits, one would have thought a whole legion of devils had been flying about the chamber. They put out the candles that stood lighted there, and endeavoured to get out. Meanwhile the rope, with the bigger bells about it, was pulled up and down, and those who knew nothing of the contrivance were greatly surprised. At last, Don Quixote, recovering from his astonishment, drew his sword, and fenced and laid about him at the window, crying aloud, 'Avaunt, ye wicked enchanters! hence infernal scoundrels! for I am Don Quixote de la Mancha, and all your damned devices cannot work their ends against me.' And then, running after the cats that frisked about the room, he began to thrust and cut at them furiously, while they strove to get out. At last they made their escape at the window, all but one of them, who finding himself hard put to it, flew in his face; and laying hold on his nose with his claws and teeth, put him to such pain, that the Don began to roar as loud as he could. Thereupon the Duke and Duchess, imagining the cause of his outcry, ran to his assistance immediately; and having opened the door of his chamber with a master-key, found the poor Knight struggling hard with the cat, that would not quit its hold. By the light of candles which they had with them, they saw the unequal combat: the Duke offered to interpose, and take off the animal; but Don Quixote would not permit him. 'Let nobody take him,' cried he; 'let me alone hand to hand with this devil, this sorcerer, this necromancer! I'll make him know what it is to deal with Don Quixote de la Mancha' But the cat, not minding his threats, growled on, and still held fast; till at length the Duke got its claws unhooked from the Knight's flesh, and flung the beast out at the window. Don Quixote's face was hideously scratched, and his nose in no very good condition. Yet nothing vexed him so much as that they had rescued out of his hands that villainous necromancer. Immediately some ointment was sent for, and Altisidora herself, with her own lily-white hands, applied some plasters to his sores, and whispered him in the ear, as she was dressing him, 'Cruel hard-hearted Knight,' said she, 'all these disasters are befallen thee, as a just punishment for thy obdurate stubbornness and disdain. May thy Squire Sancho forget to whip himself, that thy darling Dulcinea may never be delivered from her enchantment, nor thou be ever blessed with her embraces, at least so long as I thy neglected adorer lives.' Don Quixote made no answer at all to this, only he heaved up a profound sigh, and then went to take his repose, after he had returned the Duke and Duchess thanks, not so much for their assistance against that rascally crew of caterwauling and jangling enchanters, for he defied them all, but for their kindness and good intent. Then the Duke and Duchess left him, not a little troubled at the miscarriage of their jest, which they did not think would have proved so fatal to the Knight, as to oblige him, as it did, to keep his chamber five days. During which time, there happened to him another adventure, more pleasant than the last; which, however, cannot be now related; for the historian must return to Sancho Pança, who was very busy, and no less pleasant in his government.

CHAPTER XLVII

A further account of Sancho Pança's behaviour in his Government

The history informs us, that Sancho was conducted from the court of justice to a sumptuous palace; where, in a spacious room, he found the cloth laid, and a most neat and magnificent entertainment prepared. As soon as he entered, the wind music played, and four pages waited on him, in order to the washing his hands; which he did with a great deal of gravity. And now the instruments ceasing, Sancho sat down at the upper end of the table; for there was no seat but there, and the cloth was only laid for one. A certain personage, who afterwards appeared to be a physician, came and stood at his elbow, with a whalebone wand in his hand. Then they took off a curious white cloth that lay over the dishes on the table, and discovered great variety of fruit, and other eatables. One that looked like a student, said grace; a page put a laced bib under Sancho's chin; and another, who did the office of sewer, set a dish of fruit before him.* But he had hardly put one bit into his mouth, before the physician touched the dish with his wand, and then it was taken away by a page in an instant. Immediately another with meat was clapped in the place; but Sancho no sooner offered to taste it, but the doctor with the wand conjured it away as fast as the fruit. Sancho was amazed at this sudden removal, and looking about him on the company, asked them whether they used to tantalise people at that rate, feeding their eyes, and starving their bellies. 'My Lord Governor,' answered the physician, 'you are to eat here no otherwise than according to the use and custom of other islands where there are governors. I am a doctor of physic, my Lord, and have a salary allowed me in this island, for taking charge of the Governor's health, and I am more careful of it than of my own; studying night and day his constitution, that I may the better know what to prescribe when he falls sick. Now the chief thing I do, is to attend him always at his meals, to let him eat what I think convenient for him, and to prevent his eating what I imagine to be prejudicial to his health, and offensive to his stomach. Therefore I now ordered the fruit to be taken away, because it is too cold and moist; and the other dish, because it is as much too hot, and overseasoned with spices, which are apt to increase thirst; and he that drinks much, destroys and consumes the radical moisture, which is the fuel of life.' 'So then,' quoth Sancho, 'this dish of

---

* The Spaniards and Italians begin dinner with fruit, as we end it.

roasted partridges here can do me no manner of harm.' 'Hold,' said the physician, 'the Lord Governor shall not eat of them, while I live to prevent it.' 'Why so?' cried Sancho. 'Because,' answered the doctor, 'our great master, Hippocrates, the north star and luminary of physic, says in one of his aphorisms, *Omnis saturatio mala, perdicis autem pessima*: that is, all repletion is bad, but that of partridges is worst of all.' 'If it be so,' said Sancho, 'let Mr. Doctor see which of all these dishes on the table will do me most good and least harm, and let me eat my belly full of that, without having it whisked away with his wand. For, by my hopes, and the pleasures of government, as I live, I am ready to die with hunger; and not to allow me to eat any victuals (let Mr. Doctor say what he will) is the way to shorten my life, and not to lengthen it.' 'Very true, my Lord,' replied the physician, 'however, I am of opinion, you ought not to eat of these rabbits, as being a hairy, furry sort of food; nor would I have you taste of that veal: indeed if it were neither roasted nor pickled, something might be said; but as it is, it must not be.' 'Well then,' said Sancho, 'what think you of that huge dish yonder that smokes so? I take it to be an *olla-podrida*;* and that being a hodge-podge of so many sorts of victuals, sure I cannot but light upon something there that will nick me, and be both wholesome and toothsome.' '*Absit*,' cried the doctor, 'far be such an ill thought from us: no diet in the world yields worse nutriment than those mish-mashes do. No, leave that luxurious compound to your rich monks and prebendaries, your masters of colleges, and lusty feeders at country weddings. But let them not encumber the tables of governors, where nothing but delicate unmixed viands in their prime, ought to make their appearance. The reason is, that simple medicines are generally allowed to be better than compounds; for in a composition there may happen a mistake by the unequal proportion of the ingredients; but simples are not subject to that accident. Therefore what I would advise at present, as a fit diet for the Governor, for the preservation and support of his health, is a hundred of small wafers, and a few thin slices of marmalade, to strengthen his stomach, and help digestion.' Sancho hearing this, leaned back upon his chair, and looking earnestly in the doctor's face, very seriously asked him, what his name was, and where he had studied?' My Lord,' answered he, 'I am called Doctor Pedro Rezio de Aguero. The name of the place where I was born is Tirteafuera, and lies between Caraquel and Almodabar del Campo, on the right hand; and I took my degree of doctor in the university of Osuna.† 'Hark you,' said Sancho, in a mighty chafe, 'Mr. Dr. Pedro Rezio de Aguero, born at Tirteafuera,

---

* It is what we corruptly call an *olio*, all sorts of meats stewed together.
† The doctor's name and birthplace are fictitious; *Rezio de Aguero* signifies 'positive of the omen'; and *Tirteafuera*, 'take yourself away.'

that lies between Caraquel and Almodabar del Campo, on the right hand, and who took your degree of doctor at the university of Osuna, and so forth, take yourself away! Avoid the room this moment, or by the sun's light, I'll get me a good cudgel, and beginning with your carcase, will so belabour and rib-roast all the physic-mongers in the island, that I will not leave therein one of the tribe of those, I mean that are ignorant quacks; for, as for learned and wise physicians, I will make much of them, and honour them like so many angels. Once more Pedro Rezio, I say, get out of my presence. Avaunt! or I will take the chair I sit upon, and comb your head with it to some purpose; and let me be called to an account about it when I give up my office; I do not care, I will clear myself by saying, I did the world good service, in ridding it of a bad physician, the plague of a commonwealth. Body of me! let me eat, or let them take their government again; for an office that will not afford a man his victuals, is not worth two horse beans.' The physician was terrified, seeing the Governor in such a heat, and would that moment have slunk out of the room, had not the sound of a post-horn in the street been heard that moment; whereupon the steward immediately looking out of the window, turned back, and said, there was an express come from the Duke, doubtless with some dispatch of importance. Presently the messenger entered sweating, with haste and concern in his looks, and pulling a packet out of his bosom, delivered it to the Governor. Sancho gave it to the steward, and ordered him to read the direction, which was this: 'To Don Sancho Pança, Governor of the island of Barataria, to be delivered into his own hands, or those of his secretary.' 'Who is my secretary?' cried Sancho. 'It is I, my Lord,' answered one that was by, 'for I can write and read, and am a Biscainer.' 'That last qualification is enough to make thee set up for secretary to the emperor himself,' said Sancho. 'Open the letter then, and see what it says.' The new secretary did so, and having perused the dispatch by himself, told the Governor, that it was a business that was to be told only in private: Sancho ordered every one to leave the room except the steward and the carver, and then the secretary read what follows:

'I have received information, my Lord Don Sancho Pança, that some of our enemies intend to attack your island with great fury, one of these nights: You ought therefore to be watchful, and stand upon your guard, that you may not be found unprovided. I have also had intelligence from faithful spies, that there are four men got into the town in disguise, to murder you; your abilities being regarded as a great obstacle to the enemies' designs. Look about you, take heed how you admit strangers to speak with you, and eat nothing that is laid before you. I will take care to send you assistance, if you stand in need of it: And in everything I rely on your prudence. From our castle, the 16th of August, at four in the morning.

'Your friend,

'THE DUKE.'

Sancho was astonished at the news, and those that were with him seemed no less concerned. But at last, turning to the steward, 'I will tell you,' said he, 'what is first to be done in this case, and that with all speed; clap me that same Doctor Rezio in a dungeon; for if anybody has a mind to kill me, it must be he, and that with a lingering death, the worst of deaths, hunger-starving.' 'However,' said the carver, 'I am of opinion, your Honour ought not to eat any of the things that stand here before ye; for they were sent in by some of the convents; and it is a common saying, The Devil lurks behind the cross.' 'Which nobody can deny,' quoth Sancho; 'and therefore let me have for the present but a luncheon of bread, and some four pound of raisins; there can be no poison in that. For, in short, I cannot live without eating; and if we must be in readiness against those battles, we had need be well victualled; for it is the belly keeps up the heart, and not the heart the belly. Meanwhile, secretary, do you send my Lord Duke an answer, and tell him, his order shall be fulfilled in every part without fail. Remember me kindly to my Lady Duchess, and beg of her not to forget to send one on purpose, with my letter and bundle, to Teresa Pança my wife; which I shall take as a special favour; and I will be mindful to serve her to the best of my power: and when your hand is in, you may crowd in my service to my Master Don Quixote de la Mancha, that he may see I am neither forgetful nor ungrateful; the rest I leave to you; put in what you will, and do your part like a good secretary, and a staunch Biscainer. Now take away here, and bring me something to eat; and then you shall see I am able to deal with all the spies, wizards, and cut-throat dogs that dare to meddle with me and my island.'

At that time a page entering the room; 'My Lord,' said he, 'there is a countryman without desires to speak with your Lordship about business of great consequence.' 'It is a strange thing,' cried Sancho, 'that one must be still plagued with these men of business! Is it possible they should be such sots, as not to understand this is not a time for business? Do they fancy, that the governors and distributers of justice are made of iron and marble, and have no need of rest and refreshment like other creatures of flesh and blood? Well, before Heaven, and on my conscience, if my government does but last, as I shrewdly guess it will not, I will get some of these men of business laid by the heels. Well, for once let the fellow come in – but take heed he be not one of the spies or ruffian rogues that would murder me.' 'As for that,' said the page, 'I dare say he had no hand in the plot; poor soul, he looks as if he could not help it; there's no more harm in him, seemingly, than in a piece of good bread.'* 'There is no need to fear,' said the steward, 'since we are all here by you.' 'But hark you,' quoth Sancho, 'now Dr. Rezio is gone, might not I eat something that has some substance in it, though it were but a crust and an onion?' 'At night,' answered the carver, 'your Honour shall have no cause to complain: supper shall make amends for the want of your dinner.' 'Heaven grant it may,' said Sancho.

Now the countryman came in, and by his looks seemed to be a good harmless silly soul. As soon as he entered the room. 'Which is my Lord Governor?' quoth he. 'Who but he that sits in the chair,' answered the secretary. 'I humble myself to his Worship's presence,' quoth the fellow; and with that, falling on his knees, begged to kiss his hand; which Sancho refused, but bid him rise and tell him what he had to say. The countryman then got up; 'My Lord,' quoth he, 'I am a husbandman of Miguel Turra, a town about two leagues from Ciudad-Real.' 'Here is another Tirteafuera,' quoth Sancho; 'well, go on friend, I know the place full well; it is not far from our town.' 'If it please you,' said the countryman, 'my business is this: I was married by Heaven's mercy, in the face of our Holy Mother the Roman Catholic Church; and I have two boys that take their learning at the college; the youngest studies to become a Bachelor, and the eldest to be a Master of Arts. I am a widower, because my wife is dead; she died, if it please you, or to speak more truly, she was killed, as a body may say, by a damned doctor, that gave her a purge when she was with child. Had it been Heaven's blessed will that she had been brought to bed of a boy, I would have sent him to study to have been a doctor, that he might have had no cause to envy his brothers.' 'So then,' quoth Sancho, 'had not your wife died, or had they not made her die, you had not been a widower.' 'Very true,' answered the man. 'We are much the nearer,' cried Sancho; 'go on, honest friend, and prithee dispatch; for it is rather time to take an afternoon's nap, than to talk of business.' 'Now, sir, I must tell you,' continued the farmer, 'that that son of mine the Bachelor of Arts, that is to be, fell in love with a maiden of our town, Clara Perlerina by name, the daughter of Andrew Perlerina, a mighty rich farmer; and Perlerino is not the right name neither; but because the whole generation of them is troubled with the palsy,† they used to be called from the name of that ailing, Perlaticos, but now they go by that of Perlerino; and truly it fits the young woman rarely, for she is a precious pearl for beauty, especially if you stand on her right side, and

---

* *Bueno como el pan.* When the country people would define an honest good-natured man, they say, 'He is as good as bread itself.'

† *Perlesia*, in Spanish, is the palsy; and those who have it the Spaniards call *perlaticos*; whence this name.

view her, she looks like a flower in the fields. On the left indeed she does not look altogether so well; for there she wants an eye, which she lost by the small pox, that has digged many pits somewhat deep all over her face; but those that wish her well, say, that's nothing; and that those pits are but so many graves to bury lovers' hearts in. She is so cleanly, that because she will not have her nose drop upon her lips, she carries it cocked up, and her nostrils are turned up on each side, as if they shunned her mouth, that is somewhat of the widest; and for all that she looks exceedingly well; and were it not for some ten or dozen of her butter teeth and grinders, which she wants, she might set up for one of the cleverest lasses in the country. As for her lips, I do not know what to say of them, for they are so thin and so slender, that were it the fashion to wind lips as they do silk, one might make a skein of hers; besides, they are not of the ordinary hue of common lips; no, they are of the most wonderful colour that ever was seen, as being speckled with blue, green, and orange-tawny. I hope my Lord Governor will pardon me, for dwelling thus on the picture, and several rare features of her that is one day to be my daughter, seeing it is merely out of my hearty love and affection for the girl.' 'Prithee paint on as long as thou wilt,' said Sancho; 'I am mightily taken with this kind of painting; and if I had but dined, I would not desire a better desert than thy original.' 'Both myself and that are at your service,' quoth the fellow: 'or at least we may be in time, if we are not now. But, alas! sir, that is nothing; could I set before your eyes her pretty carriage, and her shape, you would admire. But that is not to be done; for she is so crooked and crumpled up together, that her knees and her chin meet, and yet any one may perceive that if she could but stand upright, her head would touch the very ceiling; and she would have given her hand to my son the Bachelor, in the way of matrimony before now, but that she is not able to stretch it forth, the sinews being quite shrunk up. However, the broad long-guttered nails add no small grace to it, and may let you know what a well made hand she has.'

'So far so good,' said Sancho; 'but let us suppose you have drawn her from head to foot: what is it you would be at now? Come to the point, friend, without so many windings and turnings, and going round about the bush.' 'Sir,' said the farmer, 'I would desire your Honour to do me the kindness to give me a letter of recommendation to the father of my daughter-in-law, beseeching him to be pleased to let the marriage be fulfilled; seeing we are not unlike, neither in estate nor in bodily concerns. For, to tell you the truth, my Lord Governor, my son is bewitched, and there is not a day passes over his head, but the foul fiends torment him three or four times; and having once had the ill-luck to fall into the fire, the skin of his face is shrivelled up like a piece of parchment, and his eyes are somewhat sore and full of rheum. But when all is said, he has the temper of an angel; and were he not apt to thump and belabour himself now and then in his fits, you would take him to be a saint.'

'Have you anything else to ask, honest man?' said Sancho. 'Only one thing more,' quoth the farmer; 'but I am somewhat afraid to speak it: yet I cannot find in my heart to let it rot within me; and therefore, fall back fall edge, I must out with it. I would desire your Worship to bestow on me some three hundred or six hundred ducats towards my Bachelor's portion, only to help him to begin the world, and furnish him with a house; for in short, they would live by themselves, without being subject to the impertinencies of a father-in-law.' 'Well,' said Sancho, 'see if you would have anything else; if you would, do not let fear or bashfulness be your hindrance. Out with it man.' 'No, truly,' quoth the farmer; and he had hardly spoke the words, when the Governor starting up, and laying hold of the chair he sat on: 'You brazen-faced silly impudent country booby,' cried he, 'get out of my presence this moment, or, by the blood of the Panças, I will crack your jolter head with this chair, you whore-son raggamuffin, painter for the Devil; dost thou come at this time of the day to ask me for six hundred ducats! Where should I have them, mangy clod pate? And, if I had them, why should I give them to thee, thou old doting scoundrel? What a pox care I for Miguel Turra, or all the generation of Perlerinos? Avoid the room I say, or by the life of the Duke, I'll be as good as my word, and knock out thy cuckoo brains. Thou art no native of Miguel Turra, but some imp of the Devil, sent on his master's errand to tempt my patience. It is not a day and half that I have been Governor, and thou wouldst have me have six hundred ducats already, dunder-headed sot.'

The steward made signs to the farmer to withdraw, and he went out accordingly, hanging down his head, and to all appearance very much afraid, lest the Governor should make good his angry threats; for the cunning knave knew very well how to act his part. But let us leave Sancho in his angry mood, and let there be peace and quietness, while we return to Don Quixote, whom we left with his face covered over with plasters, the scratches which he had got when the cat so clapper-clawed him, having obliged him to no less than eight days' retirement: during which time there happened that to him, which Cid Hamet promises to relate with the same punctuality and veracity with which he delivers the particulars of this History, how trivial soever they may be.

CHAPTER XLVIII

What happened to Don Quixote with Donna Rodriguez, the Duchess's woman; as also other passages worthy to be recorded, and had in eternal remembrance

DON QUIXOTE, thus unhappily hurt, was extremely sullen and melancholy, his face wrapped up and marked, not by the hand of a Superior Being, but the paws of a cat, a misfortune incident to knight-errantry. He was six days without appearing in public; and one night, when he was thus confined to his apartment, as he lay awake, reflecting on his misfortunes, and Altisidora's importunities, he perceived somebody was opening his chamber door with a key, and presently imagined that the amorous damsel was coming to make an attempt on his chastity, and expose him to the danger of forfeiting that loyalty which he had vowed to his Lady Dulcinea del Toboso. Prepossessed with that conceit, 'No,' said he, loud enough to be heard, 'the greatest beauty in the universe shall never remove the dear idea of the charming fair, that is engraved and stamped in the very centre of my heart, and the most secret recesses of my breast. No, thou only mistress of my soul, whether transformed into a rank country wench, or into one of the nymphs of the golden Tagus, that weave silk and gold in the loom: whether Merlin or Montesinos detain thee where they please, be where thou wilt, thou still art mine; and wherever I shall be, I must and will be thine': just as he ended his speech, the door opened. Up he got in the bed, wrapped from head to foot in a yellow satin quilt, with a woollen cap on his head, his face and his mustachios bound up; his face to heal his scratches, and his mustachios to keep them from hanging down: in which posture, he looked like the strangest apparition that can be imagined. He fixed his eyes towards the door, and when he expected to have seen the yielding and doleful Altisidora, he beheld a most reverend matron approaching in a white veil, so long that it covered her from head to foot. Betwixt her left-hand fingers she carried half a candle lighted, and held her right before her face to keep the blaze of the taper from her eyes, which were hidden by a huge pair of spectacles. All the way she trod very softly, and moved a very slow pace. Don Quixote watched her motions, and observing her garb and her silence, took her for some witch or enchantress that came in that dress to practise her wicked sorceries upon him; and began to make the sign of the cross as fast as he could. The vision advanced all the while, and being got to the middle of the chamber, lifted up its eyes, and saw Don Quixote thus making a thousand crosses on his breast. But if he was astonished at the sight of such a figure, she was no less affrighted at his; so that, as soon as she spied him thus wrapped up in yellow, so lank, bepatched and muffled up; 'Bless me,' cried she, 'what is this!' With the sudden fright she dropped the candle; and now, being in the dark, as she was running out, the length of her coats made her stumble, and down she fell in the middle of the chamber: Don Quixote at the same time was in great anxiety: 'Phantom,' cried he, 'or whatever thou art, I conjure thee to tell me who thou art, and what thou requirest of me? If thou art a soul in torment, tell me, and I will endeavour thy ease to the utmost of my power; for I am a Catholic Christian, and love to do good to all mankind; for which reason I took upon me the order of knight-errantry, whose extensive duties engage me to relieve the souls in Purgatory.' The poor old woman hearing herself thus conjured, judged Don Quixote's fears by her own; and therefore, with a low and doleful voice, 'My Lord Don Quixote,' said she ('if you are he), I am neither a phantom nor a ghost, nor a soul in Purgatory, as I suppose you fancy; but Donna Rodriguez, my Lady Duchess's matron of honour, who come to you about a certain grievance, of the nature of those which you use to redress.' 'Tell me, Donna Rodriguez,' said Don Quixote, 'are not you come to manage some love intrigue? If you are, take it from me, you will lose your labour: it is all in vain, thanks to the peerless beauty of my Lady Dulcinea del Toboso. In a word, madam, provided you come not on some such embassy, you may go light your candle and return, and we will talk of anything you please; but remember I bar all dangerous insinuations, all amorous enticements.' 'What do I procure for others,' cried the matron! 'I find you do not know me, sir. I am not so stale yet, to be reduced to such poor employments. I have good flesh still about me, Heaven be praised, and all my teeth in my head, except some few, which the rheums, so plenty in this country of Arragon, have robbed me of. But stay a little, I will go light my candle, and then I will tell you my misfortunes, for it is you that sets to rights everything in the world.' This said, away she went, without staying for an answer.

Don Quixote expected her a while quietly, but his working brain soon started a thousand chimeras concerning this new adventure; and he fancied he did ill in giving way, though but to a thought of endangering his faith to his mistress. 'Who knows,' said he to himself,' but that the Devil is now endeavouring to circumvent me with an old governante, though it has not been in his power to do it with countesses, marchionesses, duchesses, queens, nor empresses. I have often heard say, and that by persons of great judgment, that if he can, he will rather tempt a man with an ugly object, than with one that is beautiful.* Who knows but this

* In the original 'with a flat-nosed rather than a hawk-nosed woman.'

solitude, this occasion, the stillness of the night, may rouse my sleeping desires, and cause me in my latter age to fall, where I never stumbled before? In such cases it is better to fly than to stay to face the danger. But why do I argue so foolishly? Sure it is impossible that an antiquated waiting-matron, in a long white veil, like a winding-sheet, with a pair of spectacles over her nose, should create, or waken, an unchaste thought in the most abandoned libertine in the world. Is there any of these duenas, or governantes, that has good flesh? Is there one of these implements of antichambers that is not impertinent, affected, and intolerable? Avaunt then, all ye idle crowd of wrinkled female waiters, unfit for any human recreation! How is that lady to be commended, who, they tell us, set up only a couple of mawkins in her chamber, exactly representing two waiting-matrons, with their work before them! The state and decorum of her room was as well kept with those statues, as it would have been with real duenas. So saying, he started from the bed, to lock the door, and shut out Donna Rodriguez; but in that very moment she happened to come in with a wax candle lighted; at what time spying the Knight near her, wrapped in his quilt, his face bound up, and a woollen cap on his head; she was frightened again, and started two or three steps back. 'Sir Knight,' said she, 'is my honour safe? for I do not think it looks handsomely in you to come out of your bed.' 'I ought to ask you the same question, madam,' said Don Quixote; 'and, therefore, tell me whether I shall be safe from being assaulted and ravished.' 'Whom are you afraid of, Sir Knight?' cried she. 'Of you,' replied Don Quixote. 'For, in short, I am not made of marble, nor you of brass; neither is it now the noon of day, but that of night, and a little later too, if I am not mistaken; beside, we are in a place more close and private than the cave must have been, where the false and presumptuous Æneas enjoyed the beautiful and tender-hearted Dido. However, give me your hand, madam; for I desire no greater security than that of my own continence and circumspection.' This said, he kissed his own right hand, and with it took hold of hers, which she gave him with the same ceremony.

Here Cid Hamet (making a parenthesis) swears by Mahomet, he would have given the best coat of two that he had, only to have seen the Knight and the Matron walk thus hand-in-hand from the chamber-door to the bed-side. To make short, Don Quixote went to bed again, and Donna Rodriguez sat down in a chair at some distance, without taking off her spectacles, or setting down the candle. Don Quixote crowded up together, and covered himself close, all but his face, and after they had both remained a while in silence, the first that broke it was the Knight. 'Now, madam,' said he, 'you may freely unburden your heart, sure of attention to your complaints from chaste ears, and assistance in your distress from a compassionate heart.' 'I believe as much,' said the matron, 'and promised myself no less charitable an answer from a person of so graceful and pleasing a presence. The case then is, noble sir, that, though you see me sitting in this chair, in the middle of Arragon, in the habit of an insignificant, unhappy duena, I am of Asturias de Oviedo, and one of the best families in that province. But my hard fortune, and the neglect of my parents, who fell into decay too soon, I cannot tell how, brought me to Madrid; where, because they could do no better, for fear of the worst, they placed me with a court-lady, to be her chambermaid. And though I say it, for all manner of plain work, I was never outdone by any one in all my life. My father and mother left me at service, and returned home; and some few years after they both died and went to heaven, I hope; for they were very good and religious Catholics. Then was I left an orphan, and wholly reduced to the sorrowful condition of such court-senants, wretched wages, and a slender allowance. About the same time the gentleman-usher fell in love with me, before I dreamt of any such thing, Heaven knows. He was somewhat stricken in years, had a fine beard, was a personable man, and what is more, as good a gentleman as the King; for he was of the mountains We did not carry matters so close in our love, but it came to my Lady's ears; and so to hinder people's tongues, without any more ado, she caused us to be married in the face of our Holy Mother the Catholic Church; which matrimony produced a daughter, that made an end of my good fortune, if I had any. Not that I died in child-bed; for I went my full time, and was safely delivered; but because my husband (rest his soul) died a while after of a fright; and had I but time to tell you how it happened, I dare say you would wonder.' Here she began to weep piteously: 'Good sir,' cried she, 'I must beg your pardon, for I cannot contain myself. As often as I think of my poor husband, I cannot forbear shedding of tears. Bless me, how he looked! and with what stateliness he would ride, with my Lady behind him, on a stout mule as black as jet, for coaches and chairs were not used then as they are nowadays, but the ladies rode behind the gentlemen-ushers. And now my tongue is in, I cannot help telling you the whole story, that you may see what a fine well-bred man my dear husband was, and how nice in every punctilio.

'One day, at Madrid, as he came into St. James's Street, which is somewhat narrow, with my Lady behind him, he met a Judge of the court, with two officers before him; whereupon, as soon as he saw him, to show his respect, my husband turned about his mule, as if he designed to have waited on him. But my Lady, whispering him in the ear, "What do you mean?" said she, "blockhead! do not you know I am here." The Judge, on his side, was no less civil; and, stopping his horse, "Sir," said he, "pray keep your way; you must not wait on me, it becomes me rather to wait on my Lady Gasilda (for that was my Lady's name)." However, my husband, with his hat in his hand, persisted in his civil intentions. But, at last, the

Lady being very angry with him for it, took a great pin, or rather, as I am apt to believe, a bodkin out of her case, and run it into his back; upon which, my husband suddenly starting, and crying out, fell out of the saddle, and pulled down my Lady after him. Immediately two of her footmen ran to help her, and the Judge and his officers did the like. The gate of Guadalajara was presently in a hubbub (the idle people about the gate I mean). In short, my Lady returned home a-foot, and my husband went to a surgeon, complaining that he was pricked through the lungs. And now this civility of his was talked of everywhere, insomuch that the very boys in the streets would flock about him and jeer him: for which reason, and because he was somewhat short-sighted, my Lady dismissed him her service; which he took so to heart, poor man, that it cost him his life soon after. Now was I left a poor helpless widow, and with a daughter to keep, who still increased in beauty as she grew up, like the foam of the sea. At length, having the name of an excellent work-woman at my needle, my Lady Duchess, who was newly married to his Grace, took me to live with her here in Arragon, and my daughter, as well as myself. In time the girl grew up, and became the most accomplished creature in the world. She sings like a lark, dances like a fairy, trips like a wild buck, writes and reads like a schoolmaster, and casts accompts like an usurer. I say nothing of her neatness; but certainly the purest spring-water that runs is not more cleanly; and then for her age, she is now, if I mistake not, just sixteen years, five months, and three days old. Now, who should happen to fall in love with this daughter of mine, but a mighty rich farmer's son, that lives in one of my Lord Duke's villages not far off; and, indeed, I cannot tell how he managed matters, but he plied her so close, that upon a promise of marriage he wheedled her into a consent, and, in short, got his will of her, and now refuses to make his word good. The Duke is no stranger to the business; for I have made my complaint to him about it many and many times, and begged of him to enjoin the young man to wed my daughter; but he turns his deaf ear to me, and cannot endure I should speak to him of it, because the young knave's father is rich, and lends the Duke money, and is bound for him upon all occasions, so that he would by no means disoblige him.

'Therefore, sir, I apply myself to your Worship, and beseech you to see my daughter righted, either by entreaties, or by force, seeing everybody says you were sent into the world to redress grievances, and assist those in adversity. Be pleased to cast an eye of pity on my daughter's orphan state, her beauty, her youth, and all her other good parts; for, on my conscience, of all the damsels my Lady has, there is not one can come up to her by a mile; no, not she that is cried up as the airiest and finest of them all, whom they call Altisidora: I am sure she is not to be named the same day: for, let me tell you, sir, all is not gold that glitters. This same Altisidora, after all, is a hoity-toity, that has more vanity than beauty, and less modesty than confidence: besides, she is none of the soundest neither; for her breath is so strong, that nobody can endure to stand near her for a moment. Nay, my Lady Duchess too – but I must say no more, for as they say, walls have ears.' 'What of my Lady Duchess?' said Don Quixote. 'By all that is dear to you, Donna Rodriguez, tell me, I conjure you.' 'Your entreaties,' said the matron, 'are too strong a charm to be resisted, dear sir, and I must tell you the truth. Do you observe, sir, that beauty of my Lady's, that softness, that clearness of complexion, smooth and shining, like a polished sword; those cheeks, all milk and vermilion, fair like the moon, and glorious like the sun; that air when she treads, as if she disdained to touch the ground; and, in short, that look of health that enlivens all her charms; let me tell you, sir, she may thank Heaven for it in the first place, and next to that, two issues in both her legs, which she keeps open to carry off the ill humours, with which the physicians say her body abounds.' 'Blessed virgin,' cried Don Quixote, 'is it possible the Duchess should have such drains? I should not have believed it from anybody but you, though a barefoot friar had sworn it. But yet certainly from so much perfection, no ill humours can flow, but rather liquid amber. Well, I am now persuaded such sluices may be of importance to health.'

Scarce had Don Quixote said those words, when at one bounce the chamber door flew open; whereupon Donna Rodriguez was seized with such a terrible fright, that she let fall her candle, and the room remained as dark as a wolf's mouth* as the saying is; and presently the poor duena felt somebody hold her by the throat, and squeeze her weasand so hard, that it was not in her power to cry out. And another having pulled up her coats, laid on her so unmercifully, upon her bare buttocks with a slipper, or some such thing, that it would have moved any one but those that did it, to pity. Don Quixote was not without compassion, yet he did not think fit to stir from the bed, but lay snug and silent all the while, not knowing what the meaning of this bustle might be, fearing lest the tempest that poured on the matron's posteriors, might also light upon his own; and not without reason; for, indeed, after the mute executioners had well cured the old gentlewoman, who durst not cry out, they came to Don Quixote, and turning up the bedclothes, pinched him so hard, and so long, that, in his own defence, he could not forbear laying about him with his fists as well as he could; till at last, after the scuffle had lasted about half an hour, the invisible phantoms vanished. Donna Rodriguez set her coats to rights; and lamenting her hard fortune, left the room, without speaking a word to the Knight. As for him, he remained where he was, sadly pinched and tired, and very moody and thoughtful, not knowing who this wicked

* Because a wolf's mouth is black, say the dictionaries.

enchanter should be, that had used him in that manner: but we shall know that in its proper time. Now let us leave him, and return to Sancho Pança, who calls upon us, as the order of our History requires.

CHAPTER XLIX

What happened to Sancho Pança as he went his rounds in his Island

WE LEFT our mighty Governor much out of humour, and in a pelting chase with that saucy knave of a countryman, who, according to the instructions he had received from the steward, and the steward from the Duke, had bantered his worship with his impertinent description. Yet as much a dunce and a fool as he was, he made his party good against them all. At last, addressing himself to those about him, among whom was Dr. Pedro Rezio, who had ventured into the room again, after the consultation about the Duke's letter was over. 'Now,' said he, 'do I find in good earnest, that judges and governors must be made of brass, or ought to be made of brass, that they may be proof against the importunities of those that pretend business, who at all hours, and at all seasons, would be heard and dispatched, without regard to anybody but themselves, let what will become of the rest, so their turn is served. Now, if a poor Judge does not hear them, and dispatch them presently, either because he is otherwise busy and cannot, or because they do not come at a proper season, then do they grumble, and give him their blessing backwards, rake up the ashes of his forefathers, and would gnaw his very bones. But with your leave, good Mr. Busy-body, with all your business, you are too hasty; pray have a little patience, and wait a fit time to make your application. Do not come at dinner-time, or when a man is going to sleep, for we judges are flesh and blood, and must allow nature what she naturally requires; unless it be poor I, who am not to allow mine any food, thanks to my friend Mr. Doctor Rezio Tirteafuera, here present, who is for starving me to death, and then swears it is for the preservation of my life. Heaven grant him such a life, I pray, and all the gang of such physic-mongers as he is; for the good physicians deserve palms and laurels.'

All that knew Sancho wondered to hear him talk so sensibly, and began to think that offices and places of trust inspired some men with understanding, as they stupefied and confounded others. However, Dr. Pedro Rezio Auguero de Tirteafuera promised him he should sup that night, though he trespassed against all the aphorisms of Hippocrates. This pacified the Governor for the present, and made him wait with a mighty impatience for the evening, and supper. To his thinking, the hour was so long a-coming, that he fancied time stood still, but yet at last the wished-for moment came, and they served him up some minced beef with onions, and some calves'-feet somewhat stale. The hungry Governor presently began with more eagerness and appetite than if they had given him Milan godwits, Roman pheasants, Sorrento veal, Moron partridges, or Lavajos green geese. And after he had pretty well taken off the sharp edge of his stomach, turning to the physician, 'Look you,' quoth he, 'Mr. Doctor, hereafter never trouble yourself to get me dainties or tit-bits to humour my stomach; that would but quite take it off the hinges; by reason it has been used to nothing but good beef, bacon, pork, goats'-flesh, turnips and onions; and if you ply me with your kick-shaws, your nice courtiers' fare, it will but make my stomach squeamish and untoward, and I should perfectly loath them one time or other. However, I shall not take it amiss, if master sewer will now and then get me one of those *ollapodridas*; and the stronger they are the better;* where all sorts of rotten things are stewed, and as if they were lost in one another: and the more they are thus rotten, and like their name, the better the smack; and there you may make a jumble of what you will, so it be eatable; and I shall remember him, and make him amends one of those days. But let nobody put tricks upon travellers, and make a fool of me; for either we are or we are not. Let us be merry and wise; when God sends His light He sends it to all; I will govern this island fair and square, without underhand dealings, or taking of bribes; but take notice, I will not beat an inch of my right; and, therefore, let every one carry an even hand, and mind their hits, or else I would have them to know there is rods in piss for them. They that urge me too far shall rue for it; make yourself honey, and the flies will eat you.' 'Indeed, my Lord Governor,' said the steward, 'your Lordship is much in the right in all you have said; and I dare engage for the inhabitants of this island, that they will obey and observe your commands, with diligence, love, and punctuality; for your gentle way of governing, in the beginning of your administration, does not give them the least opportunity to act, or but to design, anything to your Lordship's disadvantage.' 'I believe as much,' answered Sancho, 'and they would be silly wretches, should they offer to do or think otherwise. Let me tell you, too, it is my pleasure you take care of me and my Dapple, that we may both have our food as we ought, which

* A dish consisting of a great number of ingredients, as flesh, fowl, &c., all stewed together. *Olla* signifies a pot, and *podrida*, 'putrified,' 'rotten'; as if the stewing them together was supposed to have the same effect, as to making them tender, as rottenness would have. But Covarruvias, in his 'Etymologies,' derives it from *poderoso*, 'powerful'; because all the ingredients are substantial and nourishing: and this is confirmed by Sancho's adding, 'the stronger they are the better.'

is the most material business. Next, let us think of going the rounds, when it is time for me to do it; for I intend to clear this island of all filth and rubbish, of all rogues and vagrants, idle knaves and sturdy beggars. For I would like you to know, my good friends, that your slothful, lazy, lewd people in a commonwealth, are like drones in a bee-hive, that waste and devour the honey which the labouring bees gather. I design to encourage husbandmen, preserve the privileges of the gentry, reward virtuous persons, and, above all things, reverence religion, and have regard to the honour of religious men. What think you of this, my good friends? Do I talk to the purpose, or do I talk idly?' 'You speak so well, my Lord Governor,' answered the steward, 'that I stand in admiration to hear a man so unlettered as you are (for I believe your Lordship cannot read at all) utter so many notable things, and in every word a sentence; far from what they who sent you hither, and they who are here present, ever expected from your understanding. But every day produces some new wonder, jests are turned into earnest, and those who designed to laugh at others, happened to be laughed at themselves.'

It being now night, and the Governor having supped, with Doctor Rezio's leave, he prepared to walk the rounds, and set forward, attended by the steward, the secretary, the gentleman-waiter, the historiographer, who was to register his acts, several serjeants and other limbs of the law, so many in number, that they made a little battalion, in the middle of which the great Sancho marched, with his rod of justice in his hand, in a notable manner. They had not walked far in the town, before they heard the clashing of swords, which made them hasten to the place whence the noise came. Being come thither, they found only two men fighting, who gave over, perceiving the officers. 'What,' cried one of them at the same time, 'do they suffer folks to be robbed in this town in defiance of Heaven and the king? Do they let men be stripped in the middle of the street?' 'Hold, honest man,' said Sancho, 'have a little patience, and let me know the occasion of this fray, for I am the Governor.' 'My Lord,' said the other party, 'I will tell you in few words. Your Lordship must know that this gentleman, just now, at a gaming ordinary over the way, won above a thousand reals, Heaven knows how: I stood by all the while, and gave judgment for him in more than one doubtful cast, though I could not tell how to do it in conscience. He carried off his winnings, and when I expected he would have given me a crown gratuity,* as it is a claim among

---

* *Barato*. It originally signifies cheap; but amongst gamesters, *dar barato* is, when a winning gamester, by way of courtesy, or for some other reason, gives something to a stander-by. And this in Spain is a common practice among all ranks of people, and many live upon it; for it is expected as due, and sometimes, to make the reward the greater, these rascals give judgment wrongfully for the winner.

gentlemen of my fashion, who frequent gaming ordinaries, from those that play high and win, for preventing quarrels, being at their backs, and giving judgment right or wrong, nevertheless he went away without giving me anything: I ran after him not very well pleased with his proceeding, yet very civilly desired him to consider I was his friend, that he knew me to be a gentleman, though fallen to decay, that had nothing to live upon, my friends having brought me up to no employment; and therefore, I entreated him to be so kind as to give me eight reals; but the stingy soul, a greater thief than Cacus, and a worse sharper than Andradilla, would give me but sneaking four reals. And now, my Lord, you may see how little shame and conscience there is in him. But in faith, had not your Lordship come just in the nick, I would have made him disgorge his winnings, and taught him the difference between a rook and a jack-daw.' 'What say you to this?' cried Sancho to the other. The other made answer, 'That he could not deny what his antagonist had said, that he would give him but four reals, because he had given him money several times before; and they who expect the benevolence, should be mannerly, and be thankful for what is given them, without haggling with those who have won, unless they know them to be common cheats, and the money not won fairly; and that to show he was a fair gamester, and no sharper, as the other said, there needed no better proof than his refusal to give him anything, since the sharpers are always in fee with these bully-rocks who know them, and wink at their cheats.' 'That is true,' said the steward. 'Now what would your Lordship have us to do with these men?' 'I will tell you,' said Sancho. 'First, you that are the winner, whether by fair play or by foul, give your bully-back here a hundred reals immediately, and thirty more for the poor prisoners: and you that have nothing to live on, and were brought up to no employment, and go sharping up and down from place to place, pray take your hundred reals, and be sure by tomorrow to go out of this island, and not to set foot in it again these ten years and a day, unless you have a mind to make an end of your banishment in another world; for if I find you here, I will make you swing on a gibbet, with the help of the hangman. Away, and let nobody offer to reply, or I will lay him by the heels.' Thereupon the one disbursed, and the other received; the first went home and the last went out of the island; and then the Governor going on, 'Either I shall want of my will,' said he, 'or I will put down these disorderly gaming-houses; for I have a fancy they are highly prejudicial.' 'As for this house in question,' said one of the officers, 'I suppose it will be a hard matter to put it down, for it belongs to a person of quality, who loses a great deal more by play at the year's end, than he gets by his cards. You may show your authority against other gaming-houses of less note, that do more mischief, and harbour more dangerous people than the houses of gentlemen and persons of quality, where your notorious sharpers dare not use their sleights of hand. And since gaming is a vice that is become a common practice, it is better to play in good gentlemen's houses, than in those of under-officers, where they shall draw you in a poor bubble; and, after they have kept him playing all the night long, send him away stripped naked to the skin.' 'Well, all in good time,' said Sancho: 'I know there is a great deal to be said in this matter.' At the same time one of the officers came holding a youth, and having brought him before the Governor: 'If it please your Worship,' said he, 'this young man was coming toward us, but as soon as he perceived it was the rounds, he sheered off, and set a-running as fast as his legs would carry him; a sign he is no better than he should be. I ran after him, but had not he happened to fall, I had never come up with him.' 'What made you run away, friend?' said Sancho. 'Sir,' answered the young man, 'it was only to avoid the questions one is commonly teased with by the watch.' 'What business do you follow?' asked Sancho. 'I am a weaver by trade,' answered the other. 'A weaver of what?' asked the Governor. 'Of steel heads for lances, with your Worship's good leave,' said the other. 'Oh, ho!' cried Sancho, 'you are a wag, I find, and pretend to pass your jests upon us. Very well. And pray whither are you going at this time of night?' 'To take the air, if it please your Worship,' answered the other. 'Good,' said Sancho, 'and where do they take the air in this island?' 'Where it blows,' said the youth. 'A very proper answer,' cried Sancho. 'You are a very pretty impudent fellow, that is the truth of it. But pray make account that I am the air, or the wind, which you please, and that I blow in your poop, and drive you to the roundhouse. Here, take and carry him away thither directly: I will take care the youngster shall sleep out of the air to-night; he might catch cold else by lying abroad.' 'Before George,' said the young man, 'you shall as soon make me a king as make me sleep out of the air to-night.' 'Why, you young slip-string,' said Sancho, 'is it not in my power to commit thee to prison, and fetch thee out again, as often as it is my will and pleasure?' 'For all your power,' answered the fellow, 'you shall not make me sleep in prison.' 'Say you so?' cried Sancho; 'here, away with him to prison, and let him see to his cost who is mistaken, he or I; and, lest the gaoler should be greased in the fist to let him out, I will fine him in two thousand ducats if he let thee stir a foot out of prison.' 'All that is jest,' said the other; 'for I defy all mankind to make me sleep this night in a prison.' 'Tell me, Devil incarnate,' said Sancho, 'hast thou some angel to take off the irons which I will have thee clapped in, and get thee out?' 'Well, now, my good Lord Governor,' said the young man very pleasantly, 'let us talk reason, and come to the point. Suppose your Lordship should send me to gaol, and get me laid by the heels in the dungeon, shackled and manacled, and lay a heavy penalty on the gaoler in case he let me out; and suppose your orders be strictly obeyed; yet for all that, if I have no mind to sleep, but will keep awake all night, without so much as shutting my eyes, pray can you with all the power you have, make me sleep whether I will or no?' 'No, certainly,' said the secretary, 'and the young man has made out his meaning.' 'Well,' said Sancho, 'but I hope you mean to keep yourself awake, and only forbear sleeping to please your own fancy, and not to thwart my will. Why then go home and sleep,' quoth Sancho, 'and Heaven send thee good rest. I will not be thy hindrance. But have a care another time of sporting with justice; for you may meet with some in an office, that may chance to break your head, while you are breaking your jest.' The youth went his way, and the Governor continued his rounds.

A while after came two of the officers, bringing a person along with them. 'My Lord Governor,' said one of them, 'we have brought here one that is dressed like a man, yet is no man, but a female, and no ugly one neither.' Thereupon they lifted up to her eyes two or three lanterns, and by their light discovered the face of a woman about sixteen years of age, beautiful to admiration, with her hair put up in a net-work caul of gold and green silk. They examined her dress from head to foot, and found that her stockings were of carnation silk, and her garters of white taffeta, fringed with gold and pearls. Her breeches were of gold tissue, upon a green ground, and her coat upon the same stuff; under which she wore a doublet of very fine stuff gold and white. Her shoes were white, and made like men's. She had no sword, but only a very rich dagger, and several costly rings on her fingers. In a word, the young creature seemed very lovely to them all, but not one of them knew her. Those of the company who lived in the town, could not imagine who she was; and those who were privy to all the tricks that were to be put upon Sancho, were more at a loss than the rest, well knowing that this adventure was not of their own contriving; which put them in great expectation of the event. Sancho was surprised at her beauty, and asked her who she was, whither she was going, and upon what account she had put on such a dress?' Sir,' said she, casting her eyes on the ground with a decent bashfulness, 'I cannot tell you before so many people, what I have so much reason to wish may be kept a secret. Only this one thing I do assure you, I am no thief, nor evil-minded person; but an unhappy maid, whom the force of jealousy has constrained to transgress the laws of maiden decency.' The steward hearing this, 'My Lord Governor,' said he, 'be pleased to order your attendants to retire, that the gentlewoman may more freely tell her mind.' The Governor did accordingly, and all the company removed at a distance, except the steward, the gentleman-waiter, and the secretary, and then the young lady thus proceeded:

'I am the daughter of Pedro Perez Mazorca, farmer of the wool in this town, who comes very often to my father's house.' 'This will hardly pass, madam,' said the steward, 'for I know Pedro Perez very well, and I am sure he has neither son nor daughter: besides, you tell us he is your father, and at the same time that he comes very often to your father's house. 'I observed as much,' said Sancho. 'Indeed, gentlemen,' said she, 'I am now so troubled in mind that I know not what I say; but the truth is, I am the daughter of Diego de la Llana, whom I suppose you all know.' 'Now this may pass,' said the steward, 'for I know Diego de la Llana, who is a very considerable gentleman, has a good estate, and a son and a daughter. But since his wife died, nobody in this town can say he ever saw that daughter, for he keeps her so close, that he hardly suffers the sun to look on her; though indeed the common report is, that she is an extraordinary beauty.' 'You say very true, sir,' replied the young lady, 'and I am that very daughter; as for my beauty, if fame has given a wrong character of it, you will now be undeceived, since you have seen my face'; and with this she burst into tears. The secretary perceiving this, whispered the gentleman-waiter in the ear: 'Sure,' said he, 'some extraordinary matter must have happened to this poor young lady, since it could oblige one of her quality to come out of doors in this disguise, and at this unseasonable hour.' 'That is without question,' answered the other; 'for her tears too confirm the suspicion.' Sancho comforted her with the best reasons he could think on; and bid her not be afraid, but tell them what had befallen her, for they would all really do whatever lay in their power to make her easy.

'You must know, gentlemen,' said she, 'that it is now ten years that my father has kept me close, ever since my mother died. We have a small chapel richly adorned in the house, where we hear mass; and in all that time I have seen nothing but the sun by day, and the moon and stars by night; neither do I know what streets, squares, market-places, and churches are, no nor men, except my father, my brother, and that Pedro Perez the wool-farmer, whom I at first would have passed upon you for my father, that I might conceal the right. This confinement (not being allowed to stir abroad, though but to go to church), has made me uneasy this great while, and made me long to see the world, or at least the town where I was born, which I thought was no unlawful or unseemly desire. When I heard them talk of bull-feasts, prizes, acting of plays, and other public sports, I asked my brother, who is a year younger than I, what they meant by those things, and a world of others, which I have not seen; and he informed me as well as he could; but that made me but the more eager to be satisfied by my own eyes. In short I begged of my brother – I wish I never had done it – ' and here she relapsed into tears. The steward perceiving it; 'Come, madam,' said he, 'pray proceed, and make an end of telling us what has happened to you; for your words and your tears keep us all in suspense.' 'I have but few words more to add,' answered she, 'but many more tears to shed; for they are commonly the fruit of such imprudent desires.'

That gentleman of the Duke's, who acted the part of Sancho's sewer, or gentleman-waiter, and was smitten with the young lady's charms, could not forbear lifting up his lanthorn to get another look; and as he viewed her with a lover's eye, the tears that trickled down her cheeks, seemed to him so many pearls, or some of the heavenly dew on a fair drooping flower, precious as oriental gems. This made him wish that the misfortune might not be so great as her sighs and tears bespoke it. As for the Governor, he stood fretting to hear her hang so long upon her story; and therefore bid her make an end, and keep them no longer thus, for it was late, and they had a great deal of ground to walk over yet. Thereupon, with broken sobs, and half-fetched sighs, 'Sir,' said she, 'all my misfortune is, that I desired my brother to lend me some of his clothes, and that he would take me out some night or another to see all the town, while our father was asleep. Importuned by my entreaties, he consented; and having lent me his clothes, he put on mine, which fit him as if they had been made for him; for he has no beard at all, and makes a mighty handsome woman. So this very night, about an hour ago, we got out; and being guided by my father's foot-boy, and our own unruly desires, we took a ramble over the whole town; and as we were going home, we perceived a great number of people coming our way; whereupon, said my brother, "Sister, this is certainly the watch; follow me, and let us not only run, but fly as fast as we can; for if we should be known, it will be the worse for us." With that he began to run as fast as if he had wings to his feet. I made haste too, but was so frighted, that I fell down before I had gone half a dozen steps, and then a man overtook me, and brought me before you, and this crowd of people, by whom, to my shame, I am taken for an ill creature; a bold indiscreet night-walker.' 'And has nothing befallen you but this?' cried Sancho. 'You talked at first of some jealousy, that had set you a gadding.' 'Nothing else indeed,' answered the damsel; 'though I pretended jealousy; I ventured out on no other account but a little to see the world, and that too no further than the streets of this town.' All this was afterwards confirmed by her brother, who now was brought by some of the watch, one of whom had at last overtaken him, after he had left his sister. He had nothing on but a very rich petticoat, and a blue damask manteau, with a gold galloon; his head without any ornament but his own hair, that hung down in natural curls like so many rings of gold. The Governor, the steward, and the gentleman-waiter took him aside; and after they had examined him apart, why he had put on that dress, he gave the same answer his sister had done, and with no less bashfulness and concern, much to the satisfaction of the-gentleman-waiter, who was much smitten with the young lady's charms.

As for the Governor, after he had heard the whole matter, 'Truly, gentlefolks,' said he, 'here is a little piece of childish folly: and to give an account of this wild frolic, and slip of youth, there needed not all those sighs and tears, nor those hems and haws, and long excuses. Could not you, without any more ado, have said, our names are so and so, and we stole out of our father's house for an hour or two, only to ramble about the town, and satisfy a little curiosity, and there had been an end of the story, without all this weeping and wailing?' 'You say very well,' said the young damsel, 'but you may imagine, that, in the trouble and fright I was in, I could not behave myself as I should have done.' 'Well,' said Sancho, 'there is no harm done; go along with us, and we will see you home to your father's, perhaps you may not yet be missed. But have a care how you gad abroad to see fashions another time. Do not be too venturesome. An honest maid should be still at home as if she had one leg broken. A hen and a woman are lost by rambling; and she that longs to see, longs also to be seen. I need say no more.'

The young gentleman thanked the Governor for his civility, and then went home under his conduct. Being come to the house, the young spark threw a little stone against one of the iron-barred windows; and presently a maid-servant, who sat up for them, came down, opened the door, and let him and his sister in.

The Governor, with his company, then continued his rounds, talking all the way they went of the genteel carriage and beauty of the brother and sister, and the great desire these poor children had to see the world by night.

As for the gentleman-waiter, he was so passionately in love, that he resolved to go the next day, and demand her of her father in marriage, not doubting but the old gentleman would comply with him, as he was one of the Duke's principal servants. On the other side, Sancho had a great mind to strike a match between the young man and his daughter Sanchica; and he resolved to bring it about as soon as possible; believing no man's son could think himself too good for a Governor's daughter. At last his round ended for that night, and his government two or three days after; which also put an end to all his great designs and expectations, as shall be seen hereafter.

CHAPTER L

*Who the Enchanters and Executioners were that
whipped the Duenna, and pinched and scratched Don
Quixote; with the success of the Page that carried
Sancho's letter to his wife Teresa Pança*

CID HAMET, the most punctual inquirer into the minutest particles of
this authentic history, relates, that when Donna Rodriguez was going
out of her chamber to Don Quixote's apartment, another old waiting-
woman that lay with her perceived it; and as one of the chief pleasures of
all those female implements consists in inquiry, prying, and running
their noses into everything, she presently watched her fellow-servant's
motions and followed her so cautiously, that the good woman did not
discover it. Now Donna Rodriguez was no sooner got into the Knight's
chamber, but the other, lest she should forfeit her character of a true
tattling waiting-woman, flew to tell the Duchess in her ear, that Donna
Rodriguez was in Don Quixote's chamber. The Duchess told the Duke,
and having got his leave to take Altisidora with her, and go to satisfy her
curiosity about this night-visit, they very silently crept along in the dark,
till they came to Don Quixote's door; and, as they stood listening there,
overheard very easily every word they said within. So that when the
Duchess heard her leaky woman expose the fountains* of her issues, she
was not able to contain, nor was Altisidora less provoked. Full of rage
and greedy revenge, they rushed into the chamber, beat the Duenna, and
pinched the Knight, as has been related. For those affronting expressions
that are levelled against the beauty of women, or the good opinion of
themselves, raise their anger and indignation to the highest degree, and
incense them to a desire of revenge.

The Duchess diverted the Duke with an account of what had passed;
and, having a great desire to continue the merriment which Don
Quixote's extravagancies afforded them, the page that acted the part of
Dulcinea, when it was proposed to end her enchantment, was dispatched
away to Teresa Pança, with a letter from her husband (for Sancho having
his head full of his government, had quite forgot to do it), and at the same
time the Duchess sent another from herself, with a large costly string of
coral, as a present.

* *El aranjuez*, in the original. It is a royal garden, near Madrid, famous for its
fountains and water-works. The metaphor is too far fetched for an English
translation.

Now the story tells us, that the page was a sharp and ingenious lad; and being very desirous to please his Lord and Lady, made the best of his way to Sancho's village. When he came near the place, he saw a company of females washing at a brook, and asked them, whether they could inform him, if there lived not in that town a woman whose name was Teresa Pança, wife to one Sancho Pança, squire to a Knight called Don Quixote de la Mancha? He had no sooner asked the question, but a young wench, that was washing among the rest, stood up: 'That Teresa Pança is my mother,' quoth she; 'that Gaffer Sancho is my own father, and the same Knight our master.' 'Well then, damsel,' said the page, 'pray go along with me, and bring me to your mother; for I have a letter and a token here for her from your father.' 'That I will with all my heart, sir,' said the girl, who seemed to be about fourteen years of age, little more or less; and with that, leaving the clothes she was washing, to one of her companions, without staying to dress her head, or put on her shoes, away she sprung before the page's horse, bare-legged, and with her hair about her ears. 'Come along, if it please you,' quoth she, 'our house is hard by; it is but just as you come into the town, and my mother is at home, but brimful of sorrow, poor soul, for she has not heard from my father I do not know how long.' 'Well,' said the page, 'I bring those tidings that will cheer her heart, I warrant her.' At last, what with leaping, running, and jumping, the girl being come to the house, 'Mother, mother,' cried she as loud as she could, before she went in, 'come out, mother, come out! here is a gentleman has brought letters and tokens from my father.' At that summons, out came the mother, spinning a lock of coarse flax, with a russet petticoat about her, so short, that it looked as if it had been cut off at the placket; a waistcoat of the same, and her smock hanging loose about it. Take her otherwise she was none of the oldest, but looked somewhat turned of forty, strong built, sinewy, hale, vigorous, and in good case. 'What is the matter, girl?' quoth she, seeing her daughter with the page. 'That gentleman is that?' 'A servant of your Ladyship's, my Lady Teresa Pança,' answered the page; and at the same time alighting, and throwing himself at her feet with the most humble submission, 'My noble Lady Donna Teresa,' said he, 'permit me the honour to kiss your Ladyship's hand, as you are the only legitimate wife of my Lord Don Sancho Pança, proper Governor of the island of Barataria.' 'Alack-a-day, good sir,' quoth Teresa, 'what do you do? by no means: I am none of your Court-dames, but a poor silly country body, a ploughman's daughter, the wife indeed of a Squire-errant, but no Governor.' 'Your ladyship,' replied the page, 'is the most worthy wife of a thrice worthy Governor; and for proof of what I say, be pleased to receive this letter, and this present.' With that he took out of his pocket a string of coral beads set in gold, and putting it about her neck: 'This letter,' said he,' is from his Honour the Governor; and another that I have for you, together with these beads, are from her Grace the Lady Duchess, who sends me now to your Ladyship.'

Teresa stood amazed, and her daughter was transported. 'Now I will be hanged,' quoth the young baggage, 'if our Master, Don Quixote, be not at the bottom of this. Ay, this is his doing, he has given my father that same government or earldom he has promised him so many times.' 'You say right,' answered the page: 'it is for the Lord Don Quixote's sake that the Lord Sancho is now Governor of the island of Barataria, as the letter will inform you.' 'Good sir,' quoth Teresa, 'read it to me, if it like your worship; for though I can spin, I cannot read a jot.' 'Nor I neither, i'fackins,' cried Sanchica; 'but do but stay a little, and I will go and fetch one that shall, either the Bachelor Sampson Carrasco, or our parson himself, who will come with all their hearts, to hear news of my father.' 'You may spare yourself the trouble,' said the page; 'for though I cannot spin, yet I can read; and I will read it to you.' With that he read the letter which is now omitted, because it has been inserted before. That done, he pulled out another from the Duchess, which runs as follows:

'FRIEND TERESA, Your husband Sancho's good parts, his wit, and honesty, obliged me to desire the Duke my husband, to bestow on him the government of one of his islands. I am informed he is as sharp as a hawk in his office; for which I am very glad, as well as my Lord Duke, and return Heaven many thanks, that I have not been deceived in making choice of him for that preferment. For you must know, Signiora Teresa, it is a difficult thing to meet with a good Governor in this world; and may Heaven make me as good as Sancho proves in his government.

'I have sent you, my dear friend, a string of coral beads, set in gold; I could wish they were oriental pearls for your sake; but a small token may not hinder a great one. The time will come when we shall be better acquainted; and when we have conversed together, who knows what may come to pass? Commend me to your daughter Sanchica, and bid her from me to be in a readiness; for I design to marry her greatly when she least thinks of it.

'I understand you have fine large acorns in your town; pray send me a dozen or two of them; I shall set a greater value upon them, as coming from your hands. And, pray, let me have a good long letter, to let me know how you do; and if you have occasion for anything, it is but ask and have; I shall even know your meaning by your gaping. So Heaven preserve you.

'Your loving Friend,

'From this castle. THE DUCHESS.'

'Bless me,' quoth Teresa, when she had heard the letter, 'what a good Lady is this! not a bit of pride in her! Heaven grant me to be buried with such ladies, and not with such proud madams as we have in our town; who, because they are gentle-folks forsooth, think the wind must not blow upon them, but come flaunting to church, as stately as if they were queens. It seems they think it scorn to look upon a poor country woman: but, la you I here is a good lady, who, though she be a Duchess, calls me her friend, and uses me as if I were as high as herself. Well, may I see her as high as the highest steeple in the whole country: as for the acorns she writes, master of mine, I will send her good Ladyship a whole peck, and such swinging acorns, that everybody shall come to admire them far and near. And now, Sanchica, see that the gentleman be made welcome, and want for nothing. Take care of his horse. Run to the stable, get some eggs, cut some bacon; he shall fare like a prince: the rare news he has brought us, and his good looks deserve no less. Meanwhile I will among my neighbours; I cannot hold. I must run and tell them the news; our good curate, too, shall know it, and Mr. Nicholas the barber; for they have all along been thy father's friends.' 'Ay, do, mother,' said the daughter; 'but, hark you, you must give me half the beads; for, I dare say, the great Lady knows better things than to give them all to you.' 'It is all thy own, child,' cried the mother; 'but let me wear it a few days about my neck; for thou canst not think how it rejoices the very heart of me.' 'You will rejoice more presently,' said the page, 'when you see what I have got in my portmanteau; a fine suit of green cloth, which the Governor wore but one day a-hunting, and has here sent to my Lady Sanchica.' 'Oh! the Lord love him,' cried Sanchica, 'and the fine gentleman that brings it me!'

Presently, away ran Teresa with the beads about her neck, and the letters in her hand, all the while playing with her fingers on the papers as if they had been a timbrel, and meeting by chance the curate and the bachelor Carrasco, she fell to dancing and frisking about: 'Faith and troth,' cried she, 'we are all made now. Not one small body in all our kindred. We have got a poor thing called a government. And now let the proudest of them all toss up her nose at me, and I will give her as good as she brings. I will make her know her distance. 'How now, Teresa?' said the curate. 'What mad fit is this? What papers are those in your hands?' 'No mad fit at all,' answered Teresa; 'but these are letters from Duchesses and Governors; and those beads about my neck are right coral, the Ave-Maries I mean; and the Pater Nosters are of beaten gold, and I am a Madam Governess, I will assure you.' 'Verily,' said the curate, 'there is no understanding you. Teresa, we do not know what you mean.' 'There is what will clear the riddle,' quoth Teresa, and with that she gave them the letters. Thereupon the curate having read them aloud, that Samson Carrasco might also be informed, they both stood and looked on one another, and were more at a loss than before. The bachelor asked her who brought the letter? Teresa told them they might go home with her and see: it was a fine, handsome young man, as fine as anything; and that he had brought her another present worth twice as much. The curate took the string of beads from her neck, and viewed it several times over, and finding that it was a thing of value, he could not conceive the meaning of all this. 'By the habit that I wear,' cried he, 'I cannot tell what to think of this business. In the first place, I am convinced these beads are right coral, and gold; and in the next, here is a Duchess sends to beg a dozen or two of acorns.' 'Crack that nut if you can,' said Samson Carrasco. 'But come, let us go see the messenger, and probably he will clear our doubts.'

Thereupon going with Teresa, they found the page sifting a little corn for his horse, and Sanchica cutting a rasher* of bacon to be fried with eggs for his dinner. They both liked the page's mien and his garb, and after the usual compliments, Samson desired him to tell them some news of Don Quixote and Sancho Pança; for, though they had read a letter from the latter to his wife, and another from the Duchess, they were no better than riddles to them, nor could they imagine how Sancho should come by a government, especially of an island, well knowing that all the islands in the Mediterranean, or the greatest part of them, were the king's.

'Gentlemen,' answered the page, 'it is a certain truth, that Signior Sancho Pança is a governor, but whether it be of an island or not, I do not pretend to determine: but this I can assure you, that he commands in a town that has above a thousand inhabitants. And as for my Lady Duchess sending to a country-woman for a few acorns, that is no such wonder; for she is so free from pride, that I have known her send to borrow a comb of one of her neighbours. You must know, our ladies of Arragon, though they are as noble as those of Castile, do not stand so much upon formalities and punctilios; neither do they take so much state upon them, but treat people with more familiarity.'

While they were thus discoursing, in came Sanchica skipping, with her lap full of eggs; and turning to the page, 'Pray sir,' said she, 'tell me, does my father wear trunk breeches† now he is a governor?' 'Truly,' said the page, 'I never minded it, but without doubt he does.' 'Oh, Gemini!' cried the young wench, 'what would I not give to see my father in his trunk breeches! Is it not a strange thing, that ever since I can remember myself, I have wished to see my father in trunk breeches?' 'You will see him as you would have him,' said the page, 'if your Ladyship does but live. Odsfish, if

---

* In the original it is, 'cutting a rasher to fry, and to pave it with eggs,' *i.e.* eggs laid as close together in the frying-pan, as pebbles in a pavement.

† In the original *calças atacadas*. They are breeches and stockings all in one, and laced, or clasped, or tied to the girdle.

his government holds but two months, you will see him go with an umbrella over his head.'

The curate and the bachelor plainly perceived that the page did but laugh at the mother and daughter; but yet the costly string of beads, and the hunting-suit, which by this time Teresa had let them see, confounded them again. In the mean while, they could not forbear smiling at Sanchica's odd fancy, and much less at what her mother said. 'Good master curate,' quoth she, 'do so much as inquire whether any of our neighbours are going to Madrid or Toledo. I would have them buy me a hugeous farthingale of the newest and most courtly fashion, and the very finest that can be got for money; for, by my Holy Dame, I mean to credit my husband's government as much as I can; and if they vex me, I will hie me to that same court, and ride in my coach too, as well as the best of them; for she that is a Governor's Lady, may very well afford to have one.' 'O, rare mother,' cried Sanchica, 'would it were to-night before tomorrow. Mayhap when they saw me sitting in our coach by my lady mother, they would jeer and flout: "Look, look," would they say, "yonder is goody trollop, the plough jobber's child! How she flaunts it, and goes on lolling in her coach like a little Pope Joan!"* But what would I care? Let them trudge on in the dirt, while I ride in my coach. Shame and ill-luck go along with all your little backbiting scrubs. Let them laugh that win; the cursed fox thrives the better. Am I not in the right, mother?' 'Ay, marry art thou, child,' quoth Teresa; 'and indeed my good honest Sancho has often told me all those good things, and many more would come to pass; and thou shalt see, daughter, I will never rest till I get to be a countess. There must be a beginning in all things, as I have heard it said by thy father, who is also the father of proverbs. When a cow is given thee, run and take her with a halter. When they give thee a government, take it; when an earldom, catch it; and when they whistle† to thee with a good gift, snap at it. That which is good to give, is good to take, girl. It were a pretty fancy, troth, to lie snoring a-bed, and when good luck knocks, not to rise and open the door.' 'Ay,' quoth Sanchica, 'what is it to me, though they should say all they have a mind to say. When they see me so tearing fine, and so woundy great, let them spit their venom, and say, "Set a beggar on horseback," and so forth.' 'Who would not think,' said the curate, hearing this, 'but that the whole race of the Panças came into the

---

* *Papesa.* A she-pope. 'Our translators,' says Jarvis, 'have rendered this Pope Joan.' 'But,' adds he, 'there is more humour in making the country-people so ignorant, as to believe the Pope had, if not a wife, a concubine, as many of the great clergy had, than in supposing they had ever heard of Pope Joan.'

† In the original, 'when they cry, *Tus, Tus,' i.e.* as people call dogs to their porridge.

world with their paunches stuffed with proverbs? I never knew one of the name but threw them out at all times, let the discourse be what it would.' 'I think so too,' said the page; 'for his Honour the Governor blunders them out at every turn, many times, indeed, wide from the purpose; however, always to the satisfaction of the company, and with high applause from my Lord and my Lady.' 'Then, sir, you assure us still,' said Carrasco, 'that Sancho is really a Governor: and that a Duchess sends these presents and letters upon his account? for though we see the things, and read the letters, we can scarce prevail with ourselves to believe it; but are apt to run into our friend Don Quixote's opinion, and look on all this as the effect of some enchantment: so that I could find in my heart to feel and try whether you are a visionary messenger, or a creature of flesh and blood.' 'For my part, gentlemen,' answered the page, 'all I can tell you, is, that I am really the messenger I appear to be, that the Lord Sancho Pança is actually a Governor, and that the Duke and the Duchess, to whom I belong, are able to give, and have given him that government, where I am credibly informed he behaves himself most worthily. Now if there be any enchantment in the matter, I leave you to examine that; for, by the life of my parents, one of the greatest oaths I can utter, for they are both alive, and I love them dearly, I know no more of the business.' 'That may be,' said the bachelor, 'but yet *dubitat Augustinus*.' 'You may doubt if you please,' replied the page; 'but I have told you the truth; which will always prevail over falsehood, and rise uppermost, as oil does above water. But if you will *operibus credite, et non verbis*, let one of ye go along with me, and you shall see with your eyes, what you will not believe by the help of your ears.' 'I will go with all my heart,' quoth Sanchica; 'take me up behind you, sir; I have a huge mind to see my father.' 'The daughters of governors,' said the page, 'must not travel thus unattended, but in coaches or litters, and with a handsome train of servants.' 'Cod's my life,' quoth Sanchica, 'I can go a journey as well on an ass, as in one of your coaches. I am none of your tender squeamish things, not I.' 'Peace, chicken,' quoth the mother, 'thou dost not know what thou sayest, the gentleman is in the right: times are altered. When it was plain Sancho, it was plain Sanchica; but now he is a governor, thou art a Lady. I cannot well tell whether I am right or no.' 'My Lady Teresa says more than she is aware of,' said the page. 'But now,' continued he, 'give me a mouthful to eat as soon as you can, for I must go back this afternoon.' 'Be pleased then, sir,' said the curate, 'to go with me, and partake of a slender meal at my house; for my neighbour Teresa is more willing than able to entertain so good a guest.' The page excused himself a while, but at last complied, being persuaded it would be much for the better; and the curate, on his side, was glad of his company, to have an opportunity to inform himself at large about Don Quixote and his proceedings. The bachelor offered Teresa to write her answers to her letters; but as she looked upon him to be somewhat waggish, she would not permit him to be of her counsel; so she gave a roll, and a couple of eggs, to a young noviciate of the church, who could write, and he wrote two letters for her; one to her husband, and the other to the Duchess, all of her own inditing, and perhaps not the worst in this famous history, as hereafter may be seen.

CHAPTER LI

A continuation of Sancho Pança's Government, with other passages, such as they are

THE MORNING OF THAT DAY arose, which succeeded the Governor's rounding night, the remainder of which the gentleman-waiter spent not in sleep, but in the pleasing thoughts of the lovely face, and charming grace of the disguised virgin; on the other side, the steward bestowed that time in writing to his Lord and Lady what Sancho did and said; wondering no less at his actions than at his expressions, both which displayed a strange intermixture of discretion and simplicity.

At last the Lord Governor was pleased to rise; and, by Dr. Pedro Rezio's order, they brought him for his breakfast a little conserve, and a draught of fair water, which he would have exchanged with all his heart for a good luncheon of bread, and a bunch of grapes; but seeing he could not help himself, he was forced to make the best of a bad market, and seem to be content, though full sore against his will and appetite; for the doctor made him believe, that to eat but little, and that which was dainty, enlivened the spirits, and sharpened the wit, and consequently such a sort of diet was most proper for persons in authority and weighty employments, wherein there is less need of the strength of the body than of that of the mind. This sophistry served to famish Sancho, who, half-dead with hunger, cursed in his heart both the government and him that had given it him. However, hungry as he was, by the strength of his slender breakfast, he failed not to give audience that day; and the first that came before him was a stranger, who put the following case to him, the steward and the rest of the attendants being present.

'My Lord,' said he, 'a large river divides in two parts one and the same lordship. I beg your honour to lend me your attention, for it is a case of great importance, and some difficulty. Upon this river there is a bridge; at one end of which there stands a gallows, and a kind of court of justice, where four judges used to sit, for the execution of a certain law made by the lord of the land and river, which runs thus:

' "Whoever intends to pass from one end of this bridge to the other, must first upon his oath declare whither he goes, and what his business is. If he swear truth, he may go on; but if he swear false, he shall be hanged, and die without remission upon the gibbet at the end of the bridge."

'After due promulgation of this law, many people, notwithstanding its severity, adventured to go over this bridge, and as it appeared they swore true, the judges permitted them to pass unmolested. It happened one day that a certain passenger being sworn, declared, that by the oath he had taken, he was come to die upon that gallows, and that was all his business.

'This put the judges to a nonplus; "for," said they, "if we let this man pass freely, he is forsworn, and according to the letter of the law he ought to die; if we hang him, he has sworn truth, seeing he swore he was to die on that gibbet; and then by the same law we should let him pass."

'Now your Lordship's judgment is desired what the judges ought to do with this man. For they are still at a standing, not knowing what to determine in this case; and having been informed of your sharp wit, and great capacity in resolving difficult questions, they sent me to beseech your Lordship, in their names, to give your opinion in so intricate and knotty a case.'

'To deal plainly with you,' answered Sancho; 'those worshipful judges that sent you hither might as well have spared themselves the labour; for I am more inclined to dulness I assure you than sharpness: however, let me hear your question once more, that I may thoroughly understand it, and perhaps I may at last hit the nail on the head.' The man repeated the question again and again; and when he had done, 'To my thinking,' said Sancho, 'this question may be presently answered, as thus: the man swore he came to die on the gibbet, and if he dies there, he swore true, and according to the law he ought to be free, and go over the bridge. On the other side, if you do not hang him, he swore false, and by the same law he ought to be hanged.' 'It is as your Lordship says,' replied the stranger, 'you have stated the case right.' 'Why then,' said Sancho, 'even let that part of the man that swore true freely pass; and hang the other part of the man that swore false, and so the law will be fulfilled.' 'But then, my Lord,' replied the stranger, 'the man must be divided into two parts, which if we do, he certainly dies, and the law, which must every tittle of it be observed, is not put in execution.'

'Well, hark you me, honest man,' said Sancho, 'either I am a very dunce, or there is as much reason to put this same person you talk of to death as to let him live and pass the bridge; for if the truth saves him, the lie condemns him. Now the case stands thus, I would have you tell those gentlemen that sent you to me, since there is as much reason to bring him off, as to condemn him, that they even let him go free; for it is always more commendable to do good than hurt. And this I would give you under my own hand, if I could write. Nor do I speak this of my own head; but I remember one precept, among many others, that my master Don Quixote gave me the night before I went to govern this island, which was, that when the scale of justice is even, or a case is doubtful, we should prefer mercy before rigour; and it has pleased God I should call it to mind so luckily at this juncture.' 'For my part,' said the steward, 'this judgment seems to me so equitable, that I do not believe Lycurgus himself, who gave laws to the Lacedæmonians, could ever have decided the matter better than the great Sancho has done.

'And now, sir, sure there is enough done for this morning; be pleased to adjourn the court, and I will give order that your Excellency may dine to your heart's content.' 'Well said,' cried Sancho, 'that is all I want, and then a clear stage, and no favour. Feed me well, and then ply me with cases and questions thick and threefold; you shall see me untwist them, and lay them open as clear as the sun.'

The steward was as good as his word, believing it would be a burthen to his conscience to famish so wise a governor: besides, he intended the next night to put in practice the last trick which he had commission to pass upon him.

Now Sancho having plentifully dined that day, in spite of all the aphorisms of Dr. Tirteafuera, when the cloth was removed, in came an express with a letter from Don Quixote to the Governor. Sancho ordered the secretary to read it to himself, and if there was nothing in it for secret perusal, then to read it aloud. The secretary having first run it over accordingly, 'My Lord,' said he, 'the letter may not only be publicly read, but deserves to be engraved in characters of gold; and thus it is:

DON QUIXOTE DE LA MANCHA, TO SANCHO PANÇA, GOVERNOR OF THE ISLAND OF BARATARIA

' "When I expected to have had an account of thy carelessness and impertinences, friend Sancho, I was agreeably disappointed with news of thy wise behaviour; for which I return particular thanks to Heaven, that can raise the lowest from their poverty, and turn the fool into a man of sense. I hear thou governest with all the discretion of a man; and that, while thou approvest thyself one, thou retainest the humility of the meanest creature. But I desire thee to observe, Sancho, that it is many times very necessary and convenient to thwart the humility of the heart, for the better support of the authority of a place. For the ornament of a person that is advanced to an eminent post, must be answerable to its greatness, and not debased to the inclination of his former meanness. Let thy apparel be neat and handsome; even a stake well dressed, does not look like a stake. I would not have thee wear foppish, gaudy things: nor affect the garb of a soldier, in the circumstances of a magistrate; but let thy dress be suitable to thy degree, and always clean and decent.

' "To gain the hearts of thy people, among other things, I have two chiefly to recommend: one is, to be affable, courteous, and fair to all the world: I have already told thee of that. And the other, to take care that plenty of provisions be never wanting, for nothing afflicts, or urges more the spirits of the poor, than scarcity and hunger.

' "Do not put out many new orders, and if thou dost put out any, see that they be wholesome and good, and especially that they be strictly observed, for laws not well obeyed, are no better than if they were not made, and only show that the prince who had the wisdom and authority to make them, had not the resolution to see them executed; and laws that only threaten, and are not kept, become like the log that was given to the frogs to be their king, which they feared at first, but soon scorned and trampled on.

' "Be a father to virtue, but a father-in-law to vice. Be not always severe, nor always merciful; choose a mean between these two extremes; for that middle point is the centre of discretion.

' "Visit the prisons, the shambles, and the public markets, for the governor's presence is highly necessary in such places.

' "Comfort the prisoners that hope to be quickly dispatched.

' "Be a terror to the butchers, that they may be fair in their weights, and keep hucksters and fraudulent dealers in awe, for the same reason.

' "Shouldst thou unhappily be inclined to be covetous, given to women, or a glutton, as I hope thou art not, avoid showing thyself guilty of those vices; for when the town, and those that come near thee have discovered thy weakness, they will be sure to try thee on that side, and tempt thee to thy everlasting ruin.

' "Read over and over, and seriously consider the admonitions and documents I gave thee in writing before thou wentest to thy government, and thou wilt find the benefit of it, in all those difficulties and emergencies that so frequently attend the function of a governor.

' "Write to thy Lord and Lady, and show thyself grateful; for ingratitude is the offspring of pride, and one of the worst corruptions of the mind; whereas he that is thankful to his benefactors, gives a testimony that he will be so to God, who has done, and continually does him so much good.

' "My Lady Duchess dispatched a messenger on purpose to thy wife Teresa, with thy hunting-suit, and another present. We expect his return every moment.

' "I have been somewhat out of order, by a certain catencounter I had lately, not much to the advantage of my nose; but all that is nothing, for if there are necromancers that misuse me, there are others ready to defend me.

' "Send me word whether the steward that is with thee, had any hand in the business of the Countess of Trifaldi, as thou wert once of opinion; and let me also have an account of whatever befalls thee, since the distance between us is so small. I have thoughts of leaving this idle life ere long; for I was not born for luxury and ease.

' "A business has offered, that I believe will make me lose the Duke and Duchess's favour; but though I am heartily sorry for it, that does not alter my resolution; for, after all, I owe more to my profession than to complaisance; and as the saying is, *Amicus Plato, sed magis amica veritas*. I send thee this scrap of Latin, flattering myself that since thou camest to be a governor, thou mayest have learned something of that language. Farewell, and Heaven keep thee above the pity of the world.

'Thy friend,

' "DON QUIXOTE DE LA MANCHA." '

Sancho gave great attention to the letter, and it was highly applauded both for sense and integrity, by everybody that heard it. After that he rose from table, and calling the secretary, went without any further delay, and locked himself up with him in his chamber to write an answer to his master Don Quixote. He ordered the scribe to set down word for word what he dictated, without adding or diminishing the least thing. Which being strictly observed, this was the tenor of the letter.

SANCHO PANÇA, TO DON QUIXOTE DE LA MANCHA

'I am so taken up with business, that I have not time to scratch my head, or pare my nails, which is the reason they are so long. God help me! I tell you this, dear master of mine, that you may not marvel, why I have not yet let you know whether it goes well or ill with me in this same government, where I am more hunger-starved than when you and I wandered through woods and wildernesses.

'My Lord Duke wrote to me the other day, to inform me of some spies that were got into this island to kill me: but as yet I have discovered none but a certain doctor, hired by the islanders to kill all the governors that came near it. They call him Dr. Pedro Rezio de Auguero, and he was born at Tirteafuera, his name is enough to make me fear he will be the death of me. This same doctor says of himself, that he does cure diseases when you have them; but when you have them not he only pretends to keep them from coming. The physic he uses, is fasting upon fasting, till he turns a body to a mere skeleton; as if to be wasted to skin and bones were not as bad as a fever. In short, he starves me to death; so that when I thought, as being a governor, to have a bellyful of good hot victuals, and cool liquor, and to refresh my body in holland-sheets, and on a soft feather bed, I am come to do penance like a hermit; and as I do it unwillingly, I am afraid the Devil will have me at last.

'All this while I have not as yet so much as fingered the least penny of money, either for fees, bribes, or anything; and how it comes to be no better with me, I cannot for my soul imagine; for I have heard by the bye, that the governors who come to this island are wont to have a very good gift, or at least a very round sum lent them by the town before they enter: and they say too that this is the usual custom, not only here, but in other pieces.

'Last night, going my rounds, I met with a mighty handsome damsel in boy's clothes, and a brother of hers in woman's apparel. My gentleman-waiter fell in love with the girl, and intends to make her his wife, as he says. As for the youth, I have pitched on him to be my son-in-law. Today we both design to discourse the father, one Diega de la Llana, who is a gentleman, and an old Christian every inch of him.

'I visit the markets, as you advised me, and yesterday found one of the hucksters, selling hazel-nuts; she pretended they were all new, but I found she had mixed a whole bushel of old, empty, rotten nuts among the same quantity of new. With that I judged them to be given to the hospital-boys, who knew how to pick the good from the bad, and gave sentence against her that she should not come into the market in fifteen days; and people said, I did well. What I can tell you is, that if you will believe the folks of this town, there is not a more rascally sort of people in the world than these market women, for they are all a saucy, foul-mouthed, impudent, hellish rabble; and judge them to be so, by those I have seen in other places.

'I am mighty well pleased that my Lady Duchess has writ to my wife Teresa Pança, and sent her the token you mention. It shall go hard but I shall requite her kindness one time or other. Pray give my service to her, and tell her from me, she has not cast her gift in a broken sack, as something more than words shall show.

'If I might advise you, and had my wish, there should be no falling out between your worship and my Lord and Lady; for if you quarrel with them, it is I that must come by the worst for it. And since you mind me of being grateful, it will not look well in you not to be so to those who have made so much of you at their castle.

'As for your cat-affair I can make nothing of it, only I fancy you are still haunted after the old rate. You will tell me more when we meet.

'I would fain have sent you a token, but I do not know what to send, unless it were some lithe glister-pipes, which they make here very curiously, and fix most cleverly to the bladders. But if I stay in my place, it shall go hard but I will get something worth the sending, be it what it will.

'If my wife Teresa Pança writes to me, pray pay the postage, and send me the letter; for I mightily long to hear how it is with her, and my house and children.

'So Heaven preserve you from ill-minded enchanters, and send me safe and sound out of this government, which I am as much afraid of, as Dr. Pedro Rezio diets me.

'Your worship's servant,

'SANCHO PANÇA, the Governor.'

The secretary made up the letter, and immediately dispatched the express. Then those who carried on the plot against Sancho combined together, and consulted how to remove him from the government: and Sancho passed that afternoon in making several regulations, for the better establishment of that which he imagined to be an island. He published an order against the higglers and forestallers of the markets; and another to encourage the bringing in of wines from any part whatever, provided the owners declared of what growth they were, that they might be rated according to their value and goodness; and that they who should adulterate wine with water, or give it a wrong name, should be punished with death. He lowered the price of all kinds of apparel, and particularly that of shoes, as thinking it exorbitant. He regulated servants' wages, that were unlimited before, and proportioned them to the merit of their service. He laid severe penalties upon all those that should sing or vend lewd and immoral songs and ballads, either in the open day, or in the dusk of the evening; and also forbid all blind people the singing about miracles in rhymes, unless they produced authentic testimonies of their truth; for it appeared to him, that most of those that were sung in such manner were false, and a disparagement to the true.

He appointed a particular officer to inspect the poor, not to persecute, but to examine them, and know whether they were truly such; for under pretence of counterfeit lameness, and artificial sores, many canting vagabonds impudently rob the true poor of charity, to spend it in riot and drunkenness.

In short, he made so many wholesome ordinances, that, to this day they are observed in that place, and called, 'The Constitutions of the great Governor Sancho Pança.'

CHAPTER LII

*A relation of the Adventures of the second
disconsolate or distressed Matron, otherwise
called Donna Rodriguez*

CID HAMET RELATES, that Don Quixote's scratches being healed, he
began to think the life he led in the castle not suitable to the order of
knight-errantry which he professed; he resolved therefore to take leave of
the Duke and Duchess, and set forwards for Saragossa; where, at the
approaching tournament, he hoped to win the armour, the usual prize at
the festivals of that kind. Accordingly, as he sat at table with the lord and
lady of the castle, he began to acquaint them with his design, when
behold two women entered the great hall, clad in deep mourning from
head to foot: one of them, approaching Don Quixote, threw herself at his
feet, where lying prostrate, and in a manner kissing them, she fetched
such deep and doleful sighs, and made such sorrowful lamentations, that
all those who were by, were not a little surprised. And though the Duke
and the Duchess imagined it to be some new device of their servants
against Don Quixote, yet perceiving with what earnestness the woman
sighed and lamented, they were in doubt, and knew not what to think; till
the compassionate champion raising her from the ground, engaged her to
lift up her veil, and discover, what they least expected, the face of Donna
Rodriguez, the duenna of the family: and the other mourner proved to be
her daughter, whom the rich farmer's son had deluded. All those that
knew them were in great admiration, especially the Duke and the
Duchess; for though they knew her simplicity and indiscretion, they did
not believe her so far gone in madness. At last the sorrowful matron,
addressing herself to the Duke and the Duchess, 'May it please your
Graces,' said she, 'to permit me to direct my discourse to this Knight, for
it concerns me to get out of an unlucky business, into which the
impudence of a treacherous villain has brought us.' With that the Duke
gave her leave to say what she would; then applying herself to Don
Quixote: 'It is not long,' said she, 'valorous Knight, since I gave your
worship an account how basely and treacherously a graceless young
farmer had used my dear child, the poor undone creature here present;
and then you promised me to stand up for her, and see her righted; and
now I understand you are about to leave this castle, in quest of the good
adventures Heaven shall send you. And therefore before you are gone
nobody knows whither, I have this boon to beg of your worship, that you
would do so much as challenge this sturdy clown, and make him marry

my daughter, according to his promise before he was concerned with her. For, as for my Lord Duke, it is a folly to think he will ever see me righted, for the reason I told you in private. And so Heaven preserve your worship, and still be our defence.' 'Worthy matron,' answered Don Quixote, with a great deal of gravity and solemn form, 'moderate your tears, or, to speak more properly, dry them up, and spare your sighs; for I take upon me to see your daughter's wrongs redressed; though she had done much better, had not her too great credulity made her trust the protestations of lovers, which generally are readily made, but most uneasily performed. Therefore, with my Lord Duke's permission, I will instantly depart, to find out this ungracious wretch, and as soon as he is found, I will challenge him, and kill him if he persists in his obstinacy; for the chief end of my profession is to pardon the submissive, and to chastise the stubborn; to relieve the miserable, and destroy the cruel.' 'Sir Knight,' said the Duke, 'you need not give yourself the trouble of seeking the fellow, of whom that good matron complains; nor need you ask me leave to challenge him; for I already engage that he shall meet you in person to answer it here in this castle, where safe lists shall be set up for you both, observing all the laws of arms that ought to be kept in affairs of this kind, and doing each party justice, as all princes ought to do, that admit of single combats within their territories.' 'Upon that assurance,' said Don Quixote, 'with your Grace's leave, I for this time wave my punctilios of gentility, and debasing myself to the meanness of the offender qualify him to measure lances with me; and so let him be absent or present, I challenge and defy him, as a villain, that has deluded this poor creature, that was a maid, and now, through his baseness, is none; and he shall either perform his promise of making her his lawful wife, or die in the contest.' With that, pulling off his glove, he flung it down into the middle of the hall, and the Duke took it up, declaring, as he had already done, that he accepted the challenge in the name of his vassal: fixing the time for combat to be six days after, and the place to be the castle-court. The arms to be such as are usual among knights, as lance, shield, armour of proof, and all other pieces, without fraud, advantage, or enchantment, after search made by the judges of the field.

'But in the first place,' added the Duke, 'it is requisite, that this true matron, and this false virgin, commit the justice of their cause into the hands of their champion, for otherwise there will be nothing done, and the challenge is void in course.' 'I do,' answered the matron. 'And so do I,' added the daughter, all ashamed, blubbering, and in a crying tone. The preliminaries being adjusted, and the Duke having resolved with himself what to do in the matter, the mourning petitioners went away, and the Duchess ordered they should no longer be looked upon as her domestics, but as ladies-errant, that came to demand justice in her castle; and accordingly there was a peculiar apartment appointed for them, where they were served as strangers to the amazement of the other servants, who could not imagine what would be the end of Donna Rodriguez and her forsaken daughter's ridiculous confident undertaking.

Presently after this, to complete their mirth, and as it were for the last course, in came the page that had carried the letters and the presents to Teresa Pança. The Duke and Duchess were overjoyed to see him returned, having a great desire to know the success of his journey. They inquired of him accordingly; but he told them that the account he had to give them could not well be delivered in public, nor in few words; and therefore begged their Graces would be pleased to take it in private, and in the mean time entertain themselves with those letters. With that, taking out two, he delivered them to her Grace. The superscription of the one was, 'These for my Lady Duchess of I do not know what place'; and the direction on the other thus, 'To my husband Sancho Pança, Governor of the island of Barataria, whom Heaven prosper as many or more years than me.'

The Duchess sat upon thorns till she had read her letter; so having opened it, and run it over to herself, finding there was nothing of secrecy in it, she read it out aloud, that the whole company might hear what follows.

TERESA PANÇA'S LETTER TO THE DUCHESS

'MY LADY, The letter your Honour sent me pleased me hugeously; for troth it is what I heartily longed for. The string of coral is a good thing, and my husband's hunting-suit may come up to it. All our town takes it mighty kindly, and is very glad that your Honour has made my spouse a Governor, though nobody will believe it, especially our curate, Master Nicholas the barber, and Samson Carrasco the bachelor. But what care I, whether they do or no? So it be true, as it is, let every one have their saying. Though it is a folly to lie, I had not believed it neither, but for the coral and the suit; for every one here takes my husband to be a dolt, and cannot for the blood of them imagine what he can be fit to govern, unless it be a herd of goats. Well, Heaven be his guide, and speed him as he sees best for his children. As for me, my dear Lady, I am resolved, with your good liking, to make hay while the sun shines, and go to Court, to loll it along in a coach, and make a world of my back friends, that envy me already, stare their eyes out. And therefore, good your Honour, pray bid my husband send me store of money; for I believe it is dear living at Court; one can have but little bread there for sixpence, and a pound of flesh is worth thirty maravedies, which would make one stand amazed. And if he is

Dot for my coming, let him send me word in time, for my feet itch to be jogging; for my gossips and neighbours tell me, that if I and my daughter go about the Court as we should, spruce and fine, and at a tearing rate, my husband will be better known by me, than I by him; for many cannot choose but ask, "What ladies are these in the coach?" With that one of my servants answers, "The wife and daughter of Sancho Pança, Governor of the island of Barataria; and thus shall my husband be known, and I honoured far and near; and so have at all; Rome has everything."*

'You cannot think how I am troubled that we have gathered no acorns hereaway this year; however, I send your Highness about half a peck, which I have culled one by one: I went to the mountains on purpose, and got the biggest I could find. I wish they had been as big as ostrich-eggs.

'Pray, let not your pomposity forget to write to me, and I will be sure to send you an answer, and let you know how I do; and send you all the news in our village, where I am waiting and praying the Lord to preserve your Highness, and not to forget me. My daughter Sanchica, and my son, kiss your Worship's hands.

'She that wishes rather to see you than write to you,

'Your servant,

'TERESA PANÇA.'

This letter was very entertaining to all the company, especially to the Duke and Duchess; insomuch that her Grace asked Don Quixote, whether it would be amiss to open the Governor's letter, which she imagined was a very good one? The Knight told her, that, to satisfy her curiosity, he would open it; which being done, he found what follows.

TERESA PANÇA'S LETTER TO HER HUSBAND SANCHO PANÇA

'I received thy letter, dear honey Sancho, and I vow and swear to thee, as I am a Catholic Christian, I was within two fingers' breadth of running mad for joy. Look you, my chuck, when I heard you was made a Governor, I was so transported, I had like to have fallen down dead with mere gladness; for thou knowest sudden joy is said to kill as soon as great sorrow. As for thy daughter Sanchica, she scattered her water about, before she was aware, for very pleasure. I had the suit thou sentest me before my eyes, and the Lady Duchess's corals about my neck, held the letter in my hands, and had him that brought them

* As head of the world, formerly in temporals, as now in spirituals.

standing by me; and for all that, I thought what I saw and felt was but a dream. For who could have thought a goatherd should ever come to be a Governor of islands? But what said my mother, "Who a great deal would see, a great deal must live." I speak this because if I live longer, I mean to see more; for I shall never be at rest till I see thee a farmer or receiver of the customs; for though they be offices that send many to the Devil, for all that they bring grist to the mill. My Lady Duchess will tell thee how I long to go to Court. Pray think of it, and let me know thy mind; for I mean to credit thee there, by going in a coach.

'Neither the curate, the barber, the bachelor, nor the sexton, will believe thou art a Governor; but say, it is all juggling or enchantment, as all thy Master Don Quixote's concerns used to be; and Samson threatens to find thee out, and put this maggot of a government out of thy pate, and Don Quixote's madness out of his coxcomb. For my part, I do but laugh at them, and look upon my string of coral, and contrive how to fit up the suit thou sentest me into a gown for thy daughter.

'I sent my Lady the Duchess some acorns; I would they were beaten gold. I prithee send me some strings of pearl, if they be in fashion in thy island.

'The news here is, that Berreuca has married her daughter to a sorry painter, that came hither, pretending to paint anything. The township set him to paint the King's arms over the town-hall: he asked them two ducats for the job, which they paid him: so he fell to work; and was eight days a-daubing, but could make nothing of it at last; and said he could not hit upon such piddling kind of work, and so gave them their money again. Yet for all this he married with the name of a good workman. The truth is, he has left his pencil upon it, and taken the spade, and goes to the field like a gentleman. Pedro de Lobo's son has taken orders, and shaved his crown, meaning to be a priest. Minguilla, Mingo Salvato's granddaughter, heard of it, and sues him upon a promise of marriage: ill tongues do not stick to say she has been with child by him, but he stiffly denies it. We have no olives this year, nor is there a drop of vinegar to be got for love or money. A company of soldiers went through this place, and carried along with them three wenches out of the town: I do not tell thee their names, for mayhaps they will come back, and there will not want some that will marry them, for better for worse. Sanchica makes bone-lace, and gets three-halfpence a day clear, which she saves in a box with a slit, to go towards buying household-stuff. But now she is a Governor's daughter, she has no need to work, for thou wilt give her a portion. The fountain in the market is dried up. A thunderbolt lately fell upon the pillory: there may they all light. I expect thy answer to this, and thy resolution concerning my going to Court: so Heaven send thee long to live, longer than myself, or rather as long; for I would not willingly leave thee behind me in this world.

'Thy wife,

'TERESA PANÇA.'

These letters were admired, and caused a great deal of laughter and diversion; and to complete the mirth, at the same time the express returned that brought Sancho's answer to Don Quixote, which was likewise publicly read, and startled all the hearers, who took the Governor for a fool! Afterwards the Duchess withdrew, to know of the page what he had to relate of his journey to Sancho's village; of which he gave her a full account, without omitting the least particular. He also brought her the acorns, and a cheese, which Teresa had given him for a very good one, and better than those of Troncheon, and which the Duchess gratefully accepted. Now let us leave her, to tell the end of the government of great Sancho Pança, the flower and mirror of all island-governors.

CHAPTER LIII

The toilsome end and conclusion to Sancho Pança's Government

To THINK the affairs of this life are always to remain in the same state, is an erroneous fancy. The face of things rather seems continually to change and roll with circular motion; summer succeeds the spring, autumn the summer, winter the autumn, and then spring again; so time proceeds in this perpetual round; only the life of man is ever hastening to its end, swifter than time itself, without hopes to be renewed unless in the next, that is unlimited and infinite. This says Cid Hamet, the Mahometan philosopher. For even by the light of nature, and without that of faith, many have discovered the swiftness and instability of this present being, and the duration of the eternal life which is expected. But this moral reflection of our author is not here to be supposed as meant by him in its full extent; for he intended it only to show the uncertainty of Sancho's fortune, how soon it vanished like a dream, and how from his high preferment he returned to his former low station.

It was now but the seventh night, after so many days of his government, when the careful Governor had betaken himself to his repose, sated not with bread and wine, but cloyed with hearing causes, pronouncing sentences, making statutes, and putting out orders and proclamations: scarce was sleep, in spite of wakeful hunger, beginning to close his eyes, when, of a sudden, he heard a great noise of bells, and most dreadful outcries, as if the whole island had been sinking. Presently he started, and sat up in his bed, and listened with great attention, to try if he could learn how far this uproar might concern him. But while he was thus hearkening in the dark, a great number of drums and trumpets were heard, and that sound being added to the noise of the bells and the cries, gave so dreadful an alarm, that his fear and terror increased, and he was in a sad consternation. Up he leaped out of his bed, and put on his slippers, the ground being damp, and without anything else in the world on but his shirt, ran and opened his chamber-door, and saw about twenty men come running along the galleries with lighted links in one hand, and drawn swords in the other, all crying out, 'Arm! my Lord Governor, arm! a world of enemies are got into the island, and we are undone, unless your valour and conduct relieve us.' Thus bawling and running with great fury and disorder, they got to the door where Sancho stood quite scared out of his senses. 'Arm, arm, this moment, my Lord!' cried one of them, 'if you have not a mind to be lost with the whole island.' 'What would you have me arm for?' quoth Sancho. 'Do I know anything of arms or fighting, think ye? why do not ye rather send for Don Quixote, my Master, he will dispatch your enemies in a trice? Alas! as I am a sinner to Heaven, I understand nothing of this hasty service.' 'For shame, my Lord Governor,' said another, 'what a faint-heartedness is this! See, we bring you here arms offensive and defensive; arm yourself, and march to the market-place. Be our leader and captain as you ought, and show yourself a Governor.' 'Why then, arm me, and good luck attend me,' quoth Sancho; with that they brought him two large shields, which they had provided, and without letting him put on his other clothes, clapped them over his shirt, and tied the one behind upon his back, and the other before upon his breast, having got his arms through some holes made on purpose. Now the shields being fastened to his body, as hard as cords could bind them, the poor Governor was cased up and immured as straight as an arrow, without being able so much as to bend his knees, or stir a step. Then, having put a lance into his hand for him to lean upon, and keep himself up, they desired him to march, and lead them on, and put life into them all, telling him that they did not doubt of victory, since they had him for their commander. 'March!' quoth Sancho, 'how do you think I am able to do it, squeezed as I am? These boards stick so plaguy close to me, I cannot so much as bend the joints of my knees; you must even carry me in your arms, and lay me across or set me upright, before some passage, and I will make good that spot of ground, either with this lance or my body.' 'Fie, my Lord Governor,' said another, 'it is more your fear than your armour that stiffens your legs, and hinders you from moving. Move, move, march on, it is high time, the enemy grows stronger, and the danger presses.' The poor Governor, thus urged and upbraided, endeavoured to go forwards; but the first motion he made, threw him to the ground at his full length, so heavily, that he gave over all his bones for broken; and there he lay like a huge tortoise in his shell, or a flitch of bacon clapped between two boards, or like a boat overturned upon a flat, with the keel upwards. Nor had those drolling companions the least compassion upon him as he lay; quite contrary, having put out their lights, they made a terrible noise, and clattered with their swords, and trampled to and again upon the poor Governor's body, and laid on furiously with their swords upon his shields, insomuch, that if he had not shrunk his head into them for shelter, he had been in a woeful condition. Squeezed up in his narrow shell, he was in a grievous fright, and a terrible sweat, praying from the bottom of his heart, for deliverance from the cursed trade of governing islands. Some kicked him, some stumbled and fell upon him, and one among the rest jumped full upon him, and there stood for some time, as on a watch-tower, like a general encouraging his soldiers, and giving orders, crying out, 'There boys, there! the enemies charge most on that side, make good that breach, secure that gate, down with those scaling ladders, fetch fire-balls, more granadoes, burning pitch, rosin, and kettles of scalding oil. Intrench yourselves, get beds, quilts, cushions, and barricade the streets;' in short, he called for all the instruments of death, and all the engines used for the defence of a city that is besieged and stormed. Sancho lay snug, though sadly bruised, and while he endured all quietly, 'Oh that it would please the Lord,' quoth he to himself, 'that this island were but taken, or that I were fairly dead, or out of this peck of troubles.' At last Heaven heard his prayers; and, when he least expected it, he heard them cry, 'Victory! victory! the enemy is routed. Now, my Lord Governor, rise, come and enjoy the fruits of conquest, and divide the spoils taken from the enemy, by the valour of your invincible arms.' 'Help me up,' cried poor Sancho in a doleful tone; and when they had set him on his legs, 'Let all the enemy I have routed,' quoth he, 'be nailed to my forehead: I will divide no spoils of enemies: but if I have one friend here, I only beg he would give me a draught of wine to comfort me, and help me to dry up the sweat that I am in; for I am all over water.' Thereupon they wiped him, gave him wine and took off his shields: after that, as he sat upon his bed, what with his fright, and what with the toil he had endured, he fell into a swoon, insomuch that those who acted this scene, began to repent they had carried it so far. But Sancho recovering from his fit in a little time, they also recovered from their uneasiness. Being come to himself, he asked what it was o'clock? They answered, it was now break of day. He said nothing; but, without any words, began to put on his clothes.

While this was doing, and he continued seriously silent, all the eyes of the company were fixed upon him, wondering what could be the meaning of his being in such haste to put on his clothes. At last, he made an end of dressing himself, and creeping along softly (for he was too much bruised to go along very fast), he got to the stable, followed by all the company; and coming to Dapple, he embraced the quiet animal, gave him a loving kiss on the forehead, and, with tears in his eyes, 'Come hither,' said he 'my friend, thou faithful companion, and fellow-sharer in my travels and miseries; when thee and I consorted together, and all my cares were but to mend thy furniture, and feed thy little carcase, then happy were my days, my months, and years. But since I forsook thee, and clambered up the towers of ambition and pride, a thousand woes, a thousand torments, and four thousand tribulations have haunted and worried my soul.' While he was talking thus, he fitted on his pack-saddle, nobody offering to say anything to him. This done, with a great deal of difficulty he mounted his ass, and then addressing himself to the steward, the secretary, the gentleman-waiter, and Dr. Pedro Rezio, and many others that stood by, 'Make way, gentlemen,' said he, 'and let me return to my former liberty. Let me go that I may seek my old course of life, and rise again from that death that buries me here alive. I was not born to be a Governor, nor to defend islands nor cities from enemies that break in upon them. I know better what belongs to ploughing, delving, pruning, and planting of vineyards, than how to make laws, and defend countries and kingdoms. St. Peter is very well at Rome; which is as much as to say, let every one stick to the calling he was born to. A spade does better in my hand than a Governor's truncheon; and I had rather fill my belly with a mess of plain porridge,* than lie at the mercy of a coxcombly physic-monger that starves me to death. I had rather solace myself under the shade of an oak in summer, and wrap up my corpse in a double sheep-skin in the winter at my liberty, than lay me down with the slavery of a government in fine holland-sheets, and case my hide in furs and richest sables. Heaven be with you, gentle-folks, and pray tell my Lord Duke from me, that naked I was born, and naked I am at present. I have neither won nor lost, which is as much as to say, without a penny I came to this government, and without a penny I leave it, quite contrary to what governors of islands use to do, when they leave them. Clear the way, then, I beseech you, and let me pass; I must get myself wrapped up all over in cerecloth; for I do not think I have a sound rib left, thanks to the enemies that have walked over me all night long.' 'This must not be, my Lord Governor,' said Dr. Rezio, 'for I will give your Honour a balsamic drink, that is a specific against falls,

---

* *Gaspacho*: it is made of oil, vinegar, water, salt, and spice, with toasted bread. A sort of *soupe maigre*, says Stevens's Dictionary.

dislocations, contusions, and all manner of bruises, and that will presently restore you to your former health and strength. And then for your diet, I promise to take a new course with you, and to let you eat abundantly of whatsoever you please.' 'It is too late, Mr. Doctor,' answered Sancho; 'you should as soon make me turn Turk, as hinder me from going. No, no, these tricks shall not pass upon me again, you shall as soon make me fly to heaven without wings, as get me to stay here, or ever catch me nibbling at a government again, though it were served up to me in a covered dish. I am of the blood of the Panças, and we are all wilful and positive. If once we cry Odd, it shall be odd in spite of all mankind, though it be even. Go to, then: let the pismire leave behind him in this stable, those wings that lifted him up in the air to be a prey to martlets and sparrows. Fair and softly. Let me now tread again on plain ground; though I may not wear pinked Cordovan leather-pumps, I shall not want a pair of sandals* to my feet. Every sheep to her mate. Let not the cobbler go beyond his last; and so let me go, for it is late.' 'My Lord Governor,' said the steward, 'though it grieves us to part with your Honour, your sense and Christian behaviour engaging us to covet your company, yet we would not presume to stop you against your inclination: but you know that every Governor, before he leaves the place he has governed, is bound to give an account of his administration. Be pleased therefore to do so for the ten days† you have been among us, and then peace be with you.' 'No man has power to call me to an account,' replied Sancho, 'unless it be by my Lord Duke's appointment. Now to him it is that I am going, and to him I will give a fair and square account. And indeed, going away so bare as I do, there needs no greater signs that I have governed like an angel.' 'In truth,' said Dr. Rezio, 'the great Sancho is in the right; and I am of opinion, we ought to let him go; for certainly the Duke will be very glad to see him.' Thereupon they all agreed to let him pass, offering first to attend him, and supply him with whatever he might want in his journey, either for entertainment or conveniency. Sancho told them, that all he desired was a little corn for his ass, and half a cheese, and half a loaf for himself; having occasion for no other provisions in so short a journey. With that they all embraced him, and he embraced them all, not without tears in his eyes, leaving them in admiration of the good sense which he discovered both in his discourse and unalterable resolution.

---

* A sort of flat sandal or shoe, made of hemp, or of bulrushes, artfully plaited, and fitted to the foot; worn by the poor people in Spain and Italy.

† How comes the steward to say ten days, when it is plain Sancho governed only seven days? 'It is,' says Jarvis, 'either owing to forgetfulness in the author, or perhaps is a new joke of the steward's, imagining Sancho to be as ignorant of reckoning as of writing.' And in effect, Sancho, by not denying it, allows the ten days.

CHAPTER LIV

Which treats of matters that relate to this History, and no other

THE DUKE AND DUCHESS resolved that Don Quixote's challenge against their vassal should not be ineffectual; and the young man being fled into Flanders, to avoid having Donna Rodriguez to his mother-in-law, they made choice of a Gascoon lacquey, named Tosilos, to supply his place, and gave him instructions how to act his part. Two days after, the Duke acquainted Don Quixote, that within four days his antagonist would meet him in the lists, armed at all points like a knight, to maintain that the damsel lied through the throat, and through the beard, to say that he had ever promised her marriage. Don Quixote was mightily pleased with this news promising himself to do wonders on this occasion; and esteeming it an extraordinary happiness to have such an opportunity to show before such noble spectators, how extensive were his valour and his strength. Cheered and elevated with these hopes, he waited for the end of those four days, which his eager impatience made him think so many ages.

Well, now letting them pass, as we do other matters, let us a while attend Sancho, who divided betwixt joy and sorrow, was now on his Dapple, making the best of his way to his master, whose company he valued more than the government of all the islands in the world. He had not gone far from his island, or city, or town (or whatever you will please to call it, for he never troubled himself to examine what it was), before he met upon the road six pilgrims, with their walking-staves, foreigners as they proved, and such as used to beg alms singing. As they drew near him, they placed themselves in a row, and fell a-singing all together in their language something that Sancho could not understand, unless it were one word, which plainly signified alms; by which he guessed that charity was the burthen and intent of their song. Being exceeding charitable, as Cid Hamet reports him, he opened his wallet, and having taken out the half-loaf and half-cheese, gave them those, making signs withal, that he had nothing else to give them. They took the dole with a good will, but yet, not satisfied, they cried, 'Guelte, Guelte.'* 'Good people,' quoth Sancho, 'I do not understand what you would have.' With that, one of them pulled out a purse that was in his bosom, and showed it to Sancho, by which he understood, that it was money they wanted. But he, putting his thumb to his mouth, and wagging his hand with his four fingers upwards, made a

* Guelte, in Dutch, is money.

sign that he had not a cross; and so clapping his heels to Dapple's sides, he began to make way through the pilgrims; but at the same time one of them, who had been looking on him very earnestly, laid hold on him, and throwing his arms about his middle, 'Bless me!' cried he in very good Spanish, 'what do I see? Is it possible? Do I hold in my arms my dear friend, my good neighbour Sancho Pança? Yes, sure it must be he, for I am neither drunk nor dreaming.' Sancho wondering to hear himself called by his name, and to see himself so lovingly hugged by the pilgrim, stared upon him without speaking a word; but, though he looked seriously in his face a good while, he could not guess who he was. The pilgrim observing his amazement, 'What,' said he, 'friend Sancho, do not you know your old acquaintance, your neighbour Ricote the Morisco, that kept a shop in your town?' Then Sancho looking wistly on him again, began to call him to mind; at last he knew him again perfectly, and clapping him about the neck without alighting, 'Ricote,' cried he, 'who the devil could ever have known thee transmogrified in this mumming dress! Pr'ythee who has frenchified thee at this rate? And how durst thou offer to come again into Spain? Shouldst thou come to be known, adad I would not be in thy coat for all the world.' 'If thou dost not betray me,' said the pilgrim, 'I am safe enough, Sancho; for nobody can know me in this disguise. But let us get out of the road, and make to yonder elm-grove: my comrades and I have agreed to take a little refreshment there, and thou shalt dine with us. They are honest souls, I will assure thee. There I shall have an opportunity to tell thee how I have passed my time, since I was forced to leave the town in obedience to the king's edict, which, as thou knowest, so severely threatens these of our unfortunate nation.' Sancho consented, and Ricote having spoken to the rest of the pilgrims, they went all together to the grove, at a good distance from the road. There they laid by their staves, and taking off their pilgrims' weeds, remained in jackets; all of them young handsome fellows, except Ricote, who was somewhat stricken in years. Every one carried his wallet, which seemed well furnished, at least with savoury and high-seasoned bits, the provocative to the turning down good liquor. They sat down on the ground, and making the green grass their table-cloth, presently there was a comfortable appearance of bread, salt, knives, nuts, cheese, and some bacon bones, on which there were still some good pickings left, or which at least might be sucked. They had also a kind of black meat called *caviere*, made of the roes of fish, a certain charm to keep thirst awake. They also had good store of olives, though none of the moistest; but the chief glory of the feast, was six leather bottles of wine, every pilgrim exhibiting one for his share; even honest Ricote himself was now transformed from a Morisco to a German, and clubbed his bottle, his quota making as good a figure as the rest. They began to eat like men that liked mighty well their savoury fare; and as it was very relishing, they went leisurely to work, to continue the longer, taking but a little of every one at a time on the point of a knife. Then all at once they lifted up their arms, and applying their own mouths to the mouths of the bottles, and turning up their bottoms in the air, with their eyes fixed on heaven, like men in an ecstasy, they remained in that posture a good while, transfusing the blood and spirit of the vessels into their stomachs, and shaking their heads, as in a rapture, to express the pleasure they received. Sancho admired all this extremely; he could not find the least fault with it, quite contrary; he was for making good the old proverb, 'When thou art at Rome, do as they do at Rome,' so he desired Ricote to lend him his bottle, and taking his aim as well as the rest, and with no less satisfaction, showed them he wanted neither method nor breath. Four times they caressed the bottles in that manner, but there was no doing it the fifth; for they were quite exhausted, and the life and soul of them departed, which turned their mirth into sorrow. But while the wine lasted, all was well. Now and then one or other of the pilgrims would take Sancho by the right hand, Spaniard and German all one now, and cried, '*Bon campagno*.' 'Well said, i'faith,' answered Sancho; ' "*Bon campagno, perdie*." ' And then he would burst out a-laughing for half an hour together, without the least concern for all his late misfortunes, or the loss of his government; for anxieties use to have but little power over the time that men spend in eating or drinking. In short, as their bellies were full, their bones desired to be at rest, and so five of them dropt asleep, only Sancho and Ricote, who had indeed eat more, but drank less, remained awake, and removed under the cover of a beech at a small distance, where, while the other slept, Ricote in good Spanish spoke to Sancho to this purpose.

'Thou well knowest, friend Sancho Pança, how the late edict, that enjoined all those of our nation to depart the kingdom, alarmed us all; at least me it did; insomuch that the time limited for our going was not yet expired, but I thought the law was ready to be executed upon me and my children. Accordingly I resolved to provide betimes for their security and mine, as a man does that knows his habitation will be taken away from him, and so secures another before he is obliged to remove. So I left our town by myself, and went to seek some place beforehand, where I might convey my family, without exposing myself to the inconveniency of a hurry, like the rest that went; for the wisest among us were justly apprehensive, that the proclamations issued out for the banishment of our Moorish race were not only threats, as some flattered themselves, but would certainly take effect at the expiration of the limited time. I was the rather inclined to believe this, being conscious that our people had very dangerous designs; so I could not but think the king was inspired by Heaven to take so brave a resolution, and expel those snakes out of the bosom of the kingdom: not that we were all guilty, for there were some sound and real Christians among us; but their number was so small, that they could not be opposed to those that were otherwise, and it was not safe to keep enemies within doors. In short, it was necessary we should be banished; but though some might think it a mild and pleasant fate, to us it seems the most dreadful thing that could befall us: wherever we are, we bemoan with tears our banishment from Spain; for, after all, there we were born, and it is our native country. We find nowhere the entertainment our misfortune requires; and even in Barbary, and all other parts of Africa, where we expected to have met with the best reception and relief, we find the greatest inhumanity, and the worst usage. We did not know our happiness till we had lost it; and the desire which most of us have to return to Spain, is such, that the greatest part of those that speak the tongue as I do, who are many, come back hither, and leave their wives and children there in a forlorn condition; so strong is their love for their native place; and now I know by experience the truth of the saying, "Sweet is the love of one's own country." For my part, having left our town, I went into France, and though I was very well received there, yet I had a mind to see other countries; and so, passing through it, I travelled into Italy, and from thence into Germany, where methought one might live with more freedom, the inhabitants being a good-humoured sociable people, that love to live easy with one another, and everybody follows his own way. For there is liberty of conscience allowed in the greatest part of the country. There, after I had taken a dwelling in a village near Augsburg, I struck into the company of these pilgrims, and got to be one of their number, finding they were some of those that make it their custom to go to Spain, many of them every year to visit the places of devotion, which they look upon as their Indies, their best market, and surest means to get money. They travel almost the whole kingdom over, nor is there a village where they are not sure to get meat and drink, and sixpence at least in money. And they manage matters so well, that at the end of their pilgrimage they commonly carry off about a hundred crowns clear gain, which they change into gold, and hide either in the hollow of their staves, or the patches of their clothes, and either thus, or some other private way, convey it usually into their own country, in spite of all searches at their going out of the kingdom. Now, Sancho, my design in returning hither is to fetch the treasure that I left buried when I went away, which I may do with the less inconveniency, by reason it lies in a place quite out of the town. That done, I intend to write or go over myself from Valencia to my wife and daughter, who I know are in Algiers, and find one way or other to get them over to some port of France, and from thence bring them over into Germany, where we will stay, and see how providence will dispose of us. For I am sure my wife Francisca and my daughter are good Catholic

Christians; and though I cannot say I am as much a believer as they are, yet I have more of the Christian than of the Mahometan, and make it my constant prayer to the Almighty, to open the eyes of my understanding, and let me know how to serve Him. What I wonder at is, that my wife and daughter should rather choose to go for Barbary than for France, where they might have lived like Christians.'

'Look you, Ricote,' answered Sancho, 'mayhaps, that was none of their fault, for to my knowledge John Tiopieyo, thy wife's brother, took them along with him, and he, belike, being a rank Moor, would go where he thought best. And I must tell thee further, friend, that I doubt thou wilt lose thy labour in going to look after thy hidden treasure; for the report was hot among us, that thy brother-in-law and thy wife had a great many pearls, and a deal of gold taken away from them, which should have been interred.' 'That may be,' replied Ricote, 'but I am sure, friend of mine, they have not met with my hoard; for I never would tell them where I had hid it, for fear of the worst: and therefore, if thou wilt go along with me, and help me to carry off this money, I will give thee two hundred crowns, to make thee easier in the world. Thou knowest I can tell it is but low with thee.' 'I would do it,' answered Sancho, 'but I am not at all covetous. Were I in the least given to it, this morning I quitted an employment, which had I but kept, I might have got enough to have made the walls of my house of beaten gold; and, before six months had been at an end, I might have eaten my victuals in plate. So that as well for this reason, as because I fancy it would be a piece of treason to the king, in abetting his enemies, I will not go with thee, though thou wouldst lay me down twice as much.' 'And prithee,' said Ricote, 'what sort of employment is it thou hast left?' 'Why,' quoth Sancho, 'I have left the government of an island, and such an island as i'faith you will scarce meet with the like in haste within a mile of an oak.' 'And where is this island?' said Ricote. 'Where,' quoth Sancho, 'why some two leagues off, and it is called the island of Barataria.' 'Pr'ythee do not talk so,' replied Ricote; 'islands lie a great way off in the sea; there are none of them on the main land.' 'Why not?' quoth Sancho. 'I tell thee, friend Ricote, I came from thence but this morning, and yesterday I was there governing it at my will and pleasure like any dragon; yet, for all that, I even left it, for this same place of a governor seemed to me but a ticklish and perilous kind of an office.' 'And what didst thou get by thy government?' asked Ricote. 'Why,' answered Sancho, 'I have got so much knowledge, as to understand that I am not fit to govern anything, unless it be a herd of cattle; and that the wealth that is got in these kind of governments costs a man a great deal of labour and toil, watching and hunger; for in your islands, governors must eat next to nothing; especially if they have physicians to look after their health.' 'I can make neither head nor tail of all this,' said Ricote; 'it seems to me all madness; for who would be such a simpleton as to give thee islands to govern? Was the world quite bare of abler men, that they could pick out nobody else for a governor? Pr'ythee say no more, man, but come to thy senses, and consider whether thou wilt go along with me and help me to carry off my hidden wealth, my treasure, for I may well give it that name, considering how much there is of it, and I will make a man of thee, as I have told thee.' 'Hark you me, Ricote,' answered Sancho, 'I have already told thee my mind: let it suffice that I will not betray thee, and so a God's name go thy way, and let me go mine; for full well I wot, "That what is honestly got may be lost, but what is ill got will perish and the owner too." ' 'Well, Sancho,' said Ricote, 'I will press thee no further. Only, pr'ythee tell me, wert thou in the town when my wife and daughter went away with my brother-in-law?' 'Ay, marry was I,' quoth Sancho, 'by the same token, thy daughter looked so woundy handsome, that there was old crowding to see her, and everybody said she was the finest creature on God's earth. She wept bitterly all the way, poor thing, and embraced all her she-friends and acquaintance, and begged of all those that flocked about her to pray for her, and that in so earnest and piteous a manner, that she even made me shed tears, though I am none of the greatest blubberers. Faith and troth, many there had a good mind to have got her away from her uncle upon the road, and have hid her; but the thoughts of the king's proclamation kept them in awe. But he that showed himself the most concerned, was Don Pedro de Gregorio, that young rich heir that you know. They say he was up to the ears in love with her, and has never been seen in the town since she went. We all thought he was gone after her, to steal her away, but hitherto we have heard no more of the matter.' 'I have all along had a jealousy,' said Ricote, 'that this gentleman loved my daughter. But I always had too good an opinion of my Ricote's virtue, to be uneasy with his passion; for thou knowest, Sancho, very few, and hardly any of our women of Moorish race, ever married with the old Christians on the account of love; and so I hope that my daughter, who, I believe, minds more the duties of religion than anything of love, will but little regard this young heir's courtship.' 'Heaven grant she may,' quoth Sancho, 'for else it would be the worse for them both. And now, honest neighbour, I must bid thee good-bye, for I have a mind to be with my master Don Quixote this evening.' 'Then Heaven be with thee, friend Sancho,' said Ricote: 'I find my comrades have fetched out their naps, and it is time we should make the best of our way.' With that, after a kind embrace, Sancho mounted his Dapple, Ricote took his pilgrim's staff, and so they parted.

CHAPTER LV

What happened to Sancho by the way, with other matters, which you will have no more to do than to see

SANCHO STAYED so long with Ricote, that the night overtook him within half a league of the Duke's castle. It grew dark; however, as it was summer time, he was not much uneasy, and chose to go out of the road, with a design to stay there till the morning. But, as ill-luck would have it, while he was seeking some place where he might rest himself, he and Dapple tumbled of a sudden into a very deep hole, which was among the ruins of some old buildings. As he was falling, he prayed with all his heart, fancying himself all the while sinking down into the bottomless pit; but he was in no such danger, for by that time he had descended somewhat lower than eighteen feet, Dapple made a full stop at the bottom, and his rider found himself still on his back, without the least hurt in the world. Presently Sancho began to consider the condition of his bones, held his breath, and felt all about him, and finding himself sound, wind and limb, and in a whole skin, he thought he could never give Heaven sufficient thanks for his wondrous preservation; for at first he gave himself over for lost, and broke into a thousand pieces. He groped with both hands about the walls of the pit, to try if it were possible to get out without help; but he found them all so plain, and so steep, that there was not the least hold or footing to get up. This grieved him to the soul; and, to increase his sorrow, Dapple began to raise his voice in a very piteous and doleful manner, which pierced his master's very heart; nor did the poor beast make such moan without reason; for, to say the truth, he was but in a woeful condition. 'Woe's me,' cried Sancho, 'what sudden and unthought-of mischances every foot befall us poor wretches that live in this miserable world! Who would have thought that he, who but yesterday saw himself seated in the throne of an island governor, and had servants and vassals at his back, should today find himself buried in a pit, without the least soul to help him, or come to his relief!' Here we are like to perish with deadly hunger, I and my ass, if we do not die before, he of his bruises, and I of grief and anguish: at least, I shall not be so lucky as was my master Don Quixote, when he went down into the cave of the enchanter Montesinos. He found better fare there than he could have at his own house, the cloth was laid, and his bed made, and he saw nothing but pleasant visions: but I am like to see nothing here but toads and snakes: unhappy creature that I am! what have my foolish designs and whimsies brought me to? If ever it is Heaven's blessed will that my bones be found, they will be taken out of this dismal place, bare, white, and smooth, and those of my poor Dapple with them; by which, perhaps it will be known whose they are, at least by those who shall have taken notice that Sancho Pança never stirred from his ass, nor his ass from Sancho Pança. Unhappy creatures that we are, I say again! Had we died at home among our friends, though we had missed of relief, we should not have wanted pity, and some to close our eyes at the last gasp. Oh! my dear companion and friend,' said he to his ass, 'how ill have I requited thy faithful services! Forgive me, and pray to fortune the best thou canst to deliver us out of this plunge, and I here promise thee to set a crown of laurel on thy head, that thou mayest be taken for no less than a poet laureate, and thy allowance of provender shall be doubled.' Thus Sancho bewailed his misfortune, and his ass hearkened to what he said, but answered not a word, so great was the grief and anguish which the poor creature endured at the same time.

At length, after a whole night's lamenting and complaining at a most miserable rate, the day came on, and its light having confirmed Sancho in his doubts of the impossibility of getting out of that place without help, he set up his throat again, and made a vigorous outcry, to try whether anybody might not hear him. But alas! all his calling was in vain,* for all around there was nobody within hearing, and then he gave himself over for dead and buried. He cast his eyes on Dapple, and seeing him extended on the ground, and sadly down in the mouth, he went to him, and tried to get him on his legs, which, with much ado, by means of his assistance, the poor beast did at last, being hardly able to stand. Then he took a luncheon of bread out of his wallet, that had run the same fortune with them, and giving it to the ass, who took it not at all amiss, and made no bones of it. 'Here,' said Sancho, as if the beast had understood him, 'a fat sorrow is better than a lean.' At length he perceived on one side of the pit a great hole wide enough for a man to creep through stooping: he drew to it, and having crawled through on all-fours, found that it led into a vault that enlarged itself the further it extended, which he could easily perceive, the sun shining in towards the top of the concavity. Having made this discovery, he went back to his ass, and like one that knew what belonged to digging, with a stone, began to remove the earth that was about the hole, and laboured so effectually, that he soon made a passage for his companion. Then taking him by the halter, he led him along fair and softly through the cave, to try if he could not find a way to get out on the other side. Sometimes he went in the dark, and sometimes without light, but never without fear. 'Heaven defend me,' said he to himself, 'what a

---

* In the original, 'All his cries were in the desert,' *i.e.* thrown away; alluding, perhaps, to the Scripture character of John the Baptist, that he was *Vox clamantis in deserto*, 'the voice of one crying in the wilderness, or desert.'

heart of a chicken have I! This now, which to me is a sad disaster, to my master Don Quixote would be a rare adventure. He would look upon these caves and dungeons as lovely gardens, and glorious palaces, and hope to be led out of these dark narrow cells into some fine meadow; while I, luckless, helpless, heartless wretch that I am, every step I take, expect to sink into some deeper pit than this, and go down I do not know whither. Welcome ill-luck, when it comes alone.' Thus he went on, lamenting and despairing, and thought he had gone somewhat more than half a league, when, at last, he perceived a kind of confused light like that of daybreak in at some open place, but which, to poor Sancho, seemed a prospect of a passage into another world.

But here Cid Hamet Benengeli leaves him a while, and returns to Don Quixote, who entertained and pleased himself with the hopes of a speedy combat between him and the dishonourer of Donna Rodriguez's daughter, whose wrongs he designed to see redressed on the appointed day.

It happened one morning, as he was riding out to prepare and exercise against the time of battle, as he was practising with Rozinante, the horse, in the middle of his *ménage*, pitched his feet near the brink of a deep cave; insomuch that if Don Quixote had not used the best of his skill, he must infallibly have tumbled into it. Having escaped that danger, he was tempted to look into the cave without alighting, and wheeling about, rode up to it. Now while he was satisfying his curiosity, and seriously musing, he thought he heard a noise within, and thereupon listening, he could distinguish these words, which in a doleful tone arose out of the cavern: 'Ho! above there! Is there no good Christian that hears me, no charitable knight or gentleman that will take pity of a sinner buried alive, a poor governor without a government.' Don Quixote fancied he heard Sancho's voice, which did not a little surprise him; and for his better satisfaction, raising his voice as much as he could, 'Who is that below,' cried he; 'who is that complains?' 'Who should it be, to his sorrow,' cried Sancho, 'but the most wretched Sancho Pança, Governor, for his sins and for his unlucky errantry, of the island of Barataria, formerly squire to the famous Knight, Don Quixote de la Mancha?' The words redoubled Don Quixote's admiration, and increased his amazement; for he presently imagined that Sancho was dead, and that his soul was there doing penance. Possessed with that fancy, 'I conjure thee,' said he, 'by all that can conjure thee, as I am a Catholic Christian, to tell me who thou art? And, if thou art a soul in pain, let me know what thou wouldst have me to do for thee? For since my profession is to assist and succour all that are afflicted in this world, it shall also be so to relieve and help those who stand in need of it in the other, and who cannot help themselves.' 'Surely, sir,' answered he from below, 'you that speak to me should be my master Don Quixote: by the tone of your voice it can be no man else.' 'My name is Don Quixote,' replied the Knight, 'and I think it my duty to assist not only the living but the dead in their necessities. Tell me then who thou art, for thou fillest me with astonishment. And if thou art my squire Sancho Pança, and dead, if the Devil has not got thee, and through Heaven's mercy thou art in Purgatory, our holy mother, the Roman Catholic Church, has sufficient suffrages to redeem thee from the pains thou endurest, and I myself will solicit her on thy behalf, as far as my estate will go; therefore proceed, and tell me quickly who thou art.' 'Why then,' replied the voice, 'by whatever you will have me swear by, I make oath that I am Sancho Pança your squire, and that I never was dead yet in my life. But only having left my government, for reasons and causes which I have not leisure yet to tell you, last night unluckily I fell into this cave, where I am still, and Dapple with me, that will not let me tell a lie; for, as a further proof of what I say, he is here.' Now, what is strange, immediately, as if the ass had understood what his master said, to back his evidence, he fell a-braying so obstreperously, that he made the whole cave ring again. 'A worthy witness!' cried Don Quixote; 'I know his bray, as if I were the parent of him, and I know thy voice too, my Sancho. I find thou art my real squire; stay, therefore, till I go to the castle, which is hard by, and fetch more company to help thee out of the pit into which thy sins, doubtless, have thrown thee.' 'Make haste, I beseech you, sir,' quoth Sancho, 'and for Heaven's sake come again as fast as you can, for I can no longer endure to be here buried alive, and I am even dying with fear.'

Don Quixote went with all speed to the castle, and gave the Duke and Duchess an account of Sancho's accident, whilst they did not a little wonder at it, though they conceived he might easily enough fall in at the mouth of the cave, which had been there time out of mind. But they were mightily surprised to hear he had abdicated his government before they had an account of his coming away.

In short, they sent ropes, and other conveniences by their servants to draw him out, and at last, with much trouble and labour, both he and his Dapple were restored from that gloomy pit, to the full enjoyment of the light of the sun. At the same time a certain scholar standing by, and seeing him hoisted up: 'Just so,' said he, 'should all bad governors come out of their governments; just as this wretch is dragged out of this profound abyss, pale, half-starved, famished, and, as I fancy, without a cross in his pocket.' 'Hark you, good man Slander,' replied Sancho, 'it is now eight or ten days since I began to govern the island that was given me, and in all that time I never had my belly full but once; physicians have persecuted me, enemies have trampled over me, and bruised my bones, and I have had neither leisure to take bribes, nor to receive my just dues. Now all this considered, in my opinion I did not deserve to come out in this fashion. But man appoints, and God disappoints. Heaven knows best what is best for us all.

We must take time as it comes, and our lot as it falls. Let no man say, I will drink no more of this water. Many count their chickens before they are hatched, and where they expect bacon meet with broken bones. Heaven knows my mind, and I say no more though I might.' 'Never trouble thyself, Sancho,' said Don Quixote, 'nor mind what some will say, for then thou wilt never have done. So thy conscience be clear, let the world talk at random, as it uses to do. One may as soon tie up the winds, as the tongues of slanderers. If a governor returns rich from his government, they say he has fleeced and robbed the people; if poor, then they call him idle fool, and ill-husband.' 'Nothing so sure then,' quoth Sancho, 'but this bout they will call me a shallow fool, but for a fleecer or a robber, I scorn their words, and defy all the world.' Thus discoursing as they went, with a rabble of boys, and idle people about them, they at last got to the castle, where the Duke and Duchess waited in the gallery for the Knight and squire. As for Sancho, he would not go up to see the Duke, till he had seen his ass in the stable, and provided for him; for he said, the poor beast had but very sorry entertainment in his last night's lodging: this done, away he went to wait on his Lord and Lady; and, throwing himself on his knees, 'My Lord and Lady,' said he, 'I went to govern your island of Barataria, such being your will and pleasure, though it was your goodness more than my desert. Naked I entered into it, and naked I came away. I neither won nor lost. Whether I governed well or ill, there are those not far off can tell, and let them tell, if they please, that can tell better than I. I have resolved doubtful cases, determined law-suits, and all the while ready to die for hunger; such was the pleasure of Dr. Pedro Rezio of Tirteafuera, that physician-in-ordinary to island governors. Enemies set upon us in the night, and after they had put us in great danger, the people of the island say they were delivered, and had the victory by the strength of my arm; and may Heaven prosper them as they speak truth, say I. In short, in that time, I experienced all the cares and burdens this trade of governing brings along with it, and I found them too heavy for my shoulders. I never was cut out for a ruler, and I am too clumsy to meddle with edge-tools, and so before the government left me, I even resolved to leave the government: and accordingly, yesterday morning I quitted the island as I found it, with the same streets, the same houses, and the same roofs to them, as when I came to it. I have asked for nothing by way of loan, and made no hoard against a rainy day. I designed, indeed, to have issued out several wholesome orders, but did not for fear they should not be kept, in which case it signifies no more to make them than if one made them not. So, as I said before, I came away from the island without any company but my Dapple: I fell into a cave, and went a good way through it, till this morning, by the light of the sun, I spied the way out, yet not so easy, but that had not Heaven sent my master Don Quixote to help me, there I might have stayed till Doomsday. And now, my Lord Duke, and my Lady Duchess, here is your Governor Sancho Pança again, who, by a ten days' government, has only picked up so much experience, as to know he would not give a straw to be governor, not only of an island, but of the universal world. This being allowed, kissing your Honour's hands, and, doing like the boys, when they play at trusse or saille, who cry "Leap you, and then let me leap;" so I leap from the government to my old master's service again. For, after all, though with him I often eat my bread in bodily fear, yet still I fill my belly; and, for my part, so I have but that well stuffed, no matter whether it be with carrots or with partridges.'

Thus Sancho concluded his long speech, and Don Quixote, who all the while dreaded he would have said a thousand impertinencies, thanked Heaven in his heart, finding him end with so few. The Duke embraced Sancho, and told him he was very sorry he had quitted his government so soon, but that he would give him some other employment that should be less troublesome, and more profitable. The Duchess was no less kind, giving orders he should want for nothing, for he seemed sadly bruised and out of order.

CHAPTER LVI

Of the extraordinary and unaccountable Combat between Don Quixote de la Mancha, and the Lacquey, Tosilos, in vindication of the Matron Donna Rodriguez's daughter

THE DUKE AND DUCHESS were not sorry that the interlude of Sancho's government had been played, especially when the steward, who came that very day, gave them a full and distinct account of everything the Governor had done and said, during his administration, using his very expressions, and repeating almost every word he had spoken, concluding with a description of the storming of the island, and Sancho's fear and abdication, which proved no unacceptable entertainment.

And now the History relates, that the day appointed for the combat was come, nor had the Duke forgot to give his lacquey, Tosilos, all requisite instructions how to vanquish Don Quixote, and yet neither kill nor wound him; to which purpose he gave orders that the spears or steel heads of their lances should be taken off, making Don Quixote sensible that Christianity, for which he had so great a veneration, did not admit that such conflicts should so much endanger the lives of the combatants, and that it was enough he granted him free lists in his territories, though it was against the decree of the holy council, which forbids such challenges; for which reason he desired him not to push the thing to the utmost rigour. Don Quixote replied, that his Grace had the sole disposal of all things, and it was only his duty to obey.

And now, the dreadful day being come, the Duke caused a spacious scaffold to be erected for the judges of the field of battle, and for the matron and her daughter, the plaintiffs.

An infinite number of people flocked from all the neighbouring towns and villages to behold this wonderful new kind of combat, the like to which had never been seen, or so much as heard of in those parts, either by the living or the dead. The first that made his entrance at the barriers, was the marshal of the field, who came to survey the ground, and rode all over it, that there might be no foul play, nor private holes, or contrivance to make one stumble or fall. After that entered the matron and her daughter, who seated themselves in their places all in deep mourning, their veils close to their eyes, and over their breasts, with no small demonstration of sorrow. Presently, at one end of the listed field, appeared the peerless champion, Don Quixote de la Mancha: a while after, at the other, entered the grand lacquey Tosilos, attended with a great number of trumpets, and mounted on a mighty steed, that shook the very earth. The vizor of his helmet was down, and he was armed *cap-à-pie* in shining armour of proof. His courser was a flea-bitten horse, that seemed of Friesland breed, and had a quantity of wool about each of his fetlocks. The valorous combatant came on, well tutored by the Duke, his master, how to behave himself towards the valorous Don Quixote de la Mancha, being warned to spare his life by all means, and therefore, to avoid a shock in his first career, that might otherwise prove fatal, should he encounter him directly; Tosilos fetched a compass about the barrier, and at last made a stop right against the two women, casting a leering eye upon her that had demanded him in marriage. Then the marshal of the field called to Don Quixote, and, in the presence of Tosilos, asked the mother and the daughter, whether Don Quixote de la Mancha, should vindicate their right, and whether they would stand or fall by the fortune of their champion. They said they did, and allowed of whatever he should do in their behalf, as good and valid. The Duke and Duchess by this time were seated in a gallery that was over the barriers, which were surrounded by a vast throng of spectators, all waiting to see the vigorous and never-before-seen conflict. The conditions of the combat were those, that if Don Quixote were the conqueror, his opponent should marry Donna Rodriguez's daughter; but if the Knight were overcome, then the victor should be discharged from his promise, and not bound to give her any other satisfaction. Then the marshal of the field placed each of them on the spot whence they should start, dividing equally between them the advantage of the ground, that neither of them might have the sun in his eyes. And now the drums beat, and the clangor of the trumpets resounded through the air; the earth shook under them, and the hearts of the numerous spectators were in suspense, some fearing, others expecting the good or bad issue of the battle. Don Quixote recommending himself with all his soul to Heaven, and his Lady Dulcinea del Toboso, stood expecting when the precise signal for the onset should be given. – But our lacquey's mind was otherwise employed, and all his thoughts were upon what I am going to tell you.

It seems, as he stood looking on his female enemy, she appeared to him the most beautiful woman he had ever seen in his whole life; which, being perceived by the little blind archer, to whom the world gives the name of love, he took his advantage, and, fond of improving his triumphs, though it were but over the soul of a lacquey;* he came up to him softly, and without being perceived by any one, he shot an arrow two yards long into the poor footman's side so smartly, that his heart was pierced through and through: a thing which the mischievous boy could easily do; for love is invisible, and has free ingress or egress where he pleases, at a most unaccountable rate. You must know then, that when the signal for the onset was given, our lacquey was in an ecstasy, transported with the thoughts of the beauty of his lovely enemy, insomuch that he took no manner of notice of the trumpet's sound; quite contrary to Don Quixote, who no sooner heard it, but clapping spurs to his horse, he began to make towards his enemy with Rozinante's best speed. At the same time his good squire Sancho Pança, seeing him start, 'Heaven be thy guide,' cried he aloud, 'thou cream and flower of chivalry-errant, Heaven give thee the victory, since thou hast right on thy side.' Tosilos saw Don Quixote coming towards him; yet, instead of taking his career to encounter him; without leaving the place, he called as loud as he could to the marshal of the field, who thereupon rode up to him to see what he would have. 'Sir,' said Tosilos, 'is not this duel to be fought, that I may marry yonder young lady, or let it alone?' 'Yes,' answered the marshal. 'Why then,' said the lacquey, 'I feel a burden upon my conscience, and am sensible I should have a great deal to answer for, should I proceed any further in this combat; and, therefore, I yield myself vanquished, and desire I may marry the lady this moment.' The marshal of the field was surprised; and, as he was privy to the Duke's contrivance of that business, the lacquey's unexpected submission put him to such a nonplus, that he knew not what to answer. On the other side, Don Quixote stopped in the middle of his career, seeing his adversary did not put himself in a posture of defence. The Duke could not imagine why the business of the field was at a stand; but the marshal having informed him, he was amazed, and in a great

* *Lacayuna*, a Lacquean soul. A word made for the purpose.

passion. In the mean time, Tosilos, approaching Donna Rodriguez: 'Madam,' he cried, 'I am willing to marry your daughter, there is no need of lawsuits, nor of combats in the matter, I had rather make an end of it peaceably, and without the hazard of body and soul.' 'Why then,' said the valorous Don Quixote, hearing this, 'since it is so, I am discharged of my promise; let them even marry in God's name, and Heaven bless them, and give them joy.' At the same time the Duke coming down within the lists, and applying himself to Tosilos, 'Tell me, Knight,' said he, 'is it true, that you yield without fighting, and that, at the instigation of your timorous conscience, you are resolved to marry this damsel?' 'Yes, if it please your grace,' answered Tosilos. 'Marry, and I think it is the wisest course,' quoth Sancho; 'for what says the proverb, What the mouse would get, give the cat, and keep thyself out of trouble.' In the meanwhile Tosilos began to unlace his helmet, and called out that somebody might help him off with it quickly, as being so choked with his armour, that he was scarce able to breathe. With that they took off his helmet with all speed, and then the lacquey's face was plainly discovered. Donna Rodriguez and her daughter perceiving it presently, 'A cheat! a cheat!' cried they: 'they have got Tosilos, my Lord Duke's lacquey, to counterfeit my lawful husband; justice of Heaven and the King! This is a piece of malice and treachery not to be endured.' 'Ladies,' said Don Quixote, 'do not vex yourselves, there is neither malice nor treachery in the case; or if there be, the Duke is not in the fault: no, those evil-minded necromancers that persecute me are the traitors, who, envying the glory I should have got by this combat, have transformed the face of my adversary into this, which you see is the Duke's lacquey. But take my advice, madam,' added he to the daughter, 'and, in spite of the baseness of my enemies, marry him; for I dare engage it is the very man you claim as your husband.' The Duke hearing this, angry as he was, could hardly forbear losing all his indignation in laughter. 'Truly,' said he, 'so many extraordinary accidents every day befall the great Don Quixote, that I am inclinable to believe this is not my lacquey, though he appears to be so. But for our better satisfaction, let us defer the marriage but a fortnight, and in the meanwhile keep in close custody this person that has got us into this confusion; perhaps by that time he may resume his former looks; for, doubtless, the malice of these mischievous magicians against the noble Don Quixote, cannot last so long, especially when they find all these tricks and transformations so little avail.' 'Alack-a-day! sir,' quoth Sancho, 'those plaguy imps of the Devil are not so soon tired as you think; for where my master is concerned, they used to form and deform, and chop and change this into that, and that into the other. It is but a while ago that they changed the Knight of the Mirrors, whom he had overcome, into a special acquaintance of ours, the Bachelor Samson Carrasco of our village; and as for the Lady Dulcinea del Toboso, our

Mistress, they have bewitched and be-deviled her into the shape of a mere country-blouze; and so I verily think this saucy fellow here is like to die a footman, and will live a footman all the days of his life.' 'Well,' cried the daughter, 'let him be what he will, if he will have me I will have him. I ought to thank him, for I had rather be a lacquey's wife, than a gentleman's cast-off mistress; besides, he that deluded me is no gentleman neither.' To be short, the sum of the matter was, that Tosilos should be confined, to see what his transformation would come to. Don Quixote was proclaimed victor by general consent; and the people went away, most of them very much out of humour because the combatants had not cut one another to pieces to make them sport; according to the custom of the young rabble, to be sorry, when, after they have stayed, in hopes to see a man hanged, he happens to be pardoned, either by the party he has wronged, or the magistrate. The crowd being dispersed, the Duke and Duchess returned with Don Quixote into the castle; Tosilos was secured, and kept close: as for Donna Rodriguez and her daughter, they were very well pleased to see, one way or other, that the business would end in marriage; and Tosilos flattered himself with the like expectation.

CHAPTER LVII

How Don Quixote took his leave of the Duke, and what passed between him and the witty wanton Altisidora, the Duchess's damsel

DON QUIXOTE thought it now time to leave the idle life he led in the castle, believing it a mighty fault, thus to shut himself up, and indulge his sensual appetite among the tempting varieties of dainties and delights, which the Lord and Lady of the place provided for his entertainment, as a knight-errant; and he thought he was to give a strict account to Heaven for a course of life so opposite to his active profession. Accordingly, one day he acquainted the Duke and Duchess with his sentiments, and begged their leave to depart. They both seemed very unwilling to part with him, but yet at last yielded to his entreaties. The Duchess gave Sancho his wife's letters, which he could not hear read without weeping. 'Who would have thought,' cried he, 'that all the mighty hopes with which my wife swelled herself up at the news of my preferment, should come to this at last, and now I should be reduced again to trot after my master, Don Quixote de la Mancha, in search of hunger and broken bones! However, I am glad to see my Teresa was like herself, in sending the Duchess the acorns; which if she had not done, she had showed herself a dirty, ungrateful sow, and I should have been confounded mad with her. My comfort is, that no man can say the present was a bribe; for I had my government before she sent it, and it is fit those who have a kindness done them, should show themselves grateful, though it be with a small matter. In short, naked I came into the government, and naked I went out of it; and so I may say for my comfort with a safe conscience, naked I came into the world, and naked I am still; I neither won nor lost; that is no easy matter, as times go, let me tell you.' These were Sancho's sentiments at his departure.

Don Quixote, having taken his solemn leave of the Duke and Duchess over-night, left his apartment the next morning, and appeared in his armour in the courtyard, the galleries all round about being filled at the same time with the people of the house; the Duke and Duchess being also got thither to see him: Sancho was upon his Dapple, with his cloak-bag, his wallet, and his provision, very brisk and cheerful; for the steward that acted the part of Trafaldi, had given him a purse, with two hundred crowns in gold to defray expenses, which was more than Don Quixote knew at that time. And now, while everybody looked to see them set forward, on a sudden the arch and witty Altisidora started from the rest of the Duchess's damsels and attendants, that stood by among the rest, and in a doleful tune, addressed herself to him in the following doggerel rhymes:

THE MOCK FAREWELL

I

'Stay, cruel Don,
　Do not be gone,
Nor give thy horse the rowels;
　For every jag
　Thou giv'st thy nag,
Does prick me to the bowels.

　Thou dost not shun
　Some butter'd bun,
Or drab without a rag on:
　Alas! I am
　A very lamb,
Yet love like any dragon.

　Thou didst deceive
　And now dost leave
A lass, as tight as any
　That ever stood,
　In hill or wood
Near Venus and Diana.

    Since thou, false fiend,
      When nymph's thy friend,
Æneas-like dost bob her
      Go rot, and die,
      Boil, roast, or fry,
With Barrabas the robber.

II

    Thou tak'st thy flight,
      Like ravenous kite,
That holds within his pounces
      A tender bit ,
      A poor Tom-tit,
Then whist away he flounces.

    The heart of me
      And night-coifs three,
With garters twain you plunder,
      From legs of hue,
      White, black, and blue,
So marbl'd o'er you wonder.

    Two thousand groans,
      And warm ahones,
Are stuff'd within thy pillion:
      The least of which,
      Like flaming pitch,
Might have burn'd down old Ilion.

    Since thou, false fiend,
      When nymph's thy friend,
Æneas-like dost bob her;
      Go, rot, and die,
      Boil, roast, or fry,
With Barrabas the robber.

III

    As sour as crab,
      Against thy drab,
May be thy Sancho's gizzard:
      And he ne'er thrum
      His brawny bum,
To free her from the wizard.

May all the flouts,
And sullen doubts,
Be scor'd upon thy dowdy;
And she ne'er freed,
For thy misdeed,
From rusty phiz, and cloudy.

May fortune's curse
From bad to worse,
Turn all thy best adventures;
Thy joys to dumps
Thy brags to thumps,
And thy best hopes to banters

Since thou, false fiend,
When nymph's thy friend,
Æneas like dost bob her;
Go, rot, and die,
Boil, roast, or fry,
With Barrabas the robber.

IV

May'st thou incog.
Sneak like a dog,
And o'er the mountains trudge it
From Spain to Cales,*
From Usk to Wales,
Without a cross in budget.

If thou'rt so brisk
To play at whisk,
In hopes of winning riches;
For want of strump
Stir ev'n thy rump,
And lose thy very breeches.

May thy corns ache,
Then pen-knife take,
And cut thee to the raw bone:
With toothache mad,
No ease be had,
Though quakes pull out thy jaw bone.

* Good Spanish geography.

> Since thou, false fiend,
> When nymph's thy friend,
> Æneas-like dost bob her;
> Go, rot, and die
> Boil, roast, or fry,
> With Barrabas the robber.'

Thus Altisidora expressed her resentments, and Don Quixote, who looked on her seriously all the while, would not answer a word; but turning to Sancho: 'Dear Sancho,' said he, 'by the memory of thy forefathers, I conjure thee to tell me one truth: say, hast thou any night-coifs or garters that belong to this love-sick damsel?' 'The three night-coifs I have,' quoth Sancho; 'but as for the garters, I know no more of them than the man in the moon.' The Duchess, being wholly a stranger to this part of Altisidora's frolic, was amazed to see her proceed so far in it, though she knew her to be of an arch and merry disposition. But the Duke, being pleased with the humour, resolved to carry it on. Thereupon addressing himself to Don Quixote, 'Truly, Sir Knight,' said he, 'I do not take it kindly, that after such civil entertainment as you have had here in my castle, you should offer to carry away three night-coifs, if not a pair of garters besides, the proper goods and chattels of this damsel here present. This was not done like a gentleman, and does not make good the character you would maintain in the world: therefore, restore her garters, or I challenge you to a mortal combat, without being afraid that your evil-minded enchanters should alter my face, as they did my footman's.' 'Heaven forbid,' said Don Quixote, 'that I should draw my sword against your most illustrious person, to whom I stand indebted for so many favours. No, my lord, as for the night-coifs I will cause them to be restored, for Sancho tells me he has them; but as for the garters, it is impossible, for neither he nor I ever had them; and if this damsel of yours will look carefully among her things, I daresay she will find them. I never was a pilferer, my Lord, and while Heaven forsakes me not, I never shall be guilty of such baseness. But this damsel, as you may perceive, talks like one that is in love, and accuses me of that whereof I am innocent; so that not regarding her little revenge, I have no need to ask pardon either of her or your Grace. I only beg you will be pleased to entertain a better opinion of me, and once more permit me to depart.' 'Farewell, noble Don Quixote,' said the Duchess; 'may Providence so direct your course, that we may always be blessed with the good news of your exploits; and so Heaven be with you, for the longer you stay, the more you increase the flames in the hearts of the damsels that gaze on you. As for this young indiscreet creature, I will take her to task so severely, she shall not misbehave herself so much as in a word or look for the future.' 'One word more I beseech you, O, valorous Don Quixote,' cried Altisidora: 'I beg your pardon for saying you had stolen my garters, for on my conscience I have them on: but my thoughts ran a-woolgathering; and I did like the countryman, who looked for his ass while he was mounted on his back.' 'Marry come up,' cried Sancho, 'whom did they take me for, trow, a concealer of stolen goods? no, indeed; had I been given that way, I might have had opportunities enough in my government.'

Then Don Quixote bowed his head, and after he had made a low obeisance to the Duke, the Duchess, and all the company, he turned about with Rozinante, and Sancho following him on Dapple, they left the castle, and took the road for Saragossa.

CHAPTER LVIII

How Adventures crowded so thick and threefold on Don Quixote, that they trod upon one another's heels

DON QUIXOTE no sooner breathed the air in the open field free from Altisidora's amorous importunities, but he fancied himself in his own element; he thought he felt the spirit of knight-errantry reviving in his breast: and turning to Sancho: 'Liberty,' said he, 'friend Sancho, is one of the most valuable blessings that Heaven has bestowed on mankind. Not all the treasures concealed in the bowels of the earth, nor those in the bosom of the sea, can be compared with it. For liberty, a man may, nay, ought to, hazard even his life, as well as for honour, accounting captivity the greatest misery he can endure. I tell thee this, my Sancho, because thou wert a witness of the good cheer and plenty which we met with in the castle; yet in the midst of those delicious feasts, among those tempting dishes, and those liquors cooled with snow, methought I suffered the extremity of hunger, because I did not enjoy them with that freedom as if they had been my own: for the obligations that lie upon us to make suitable returns for kindnesses received, are ties that will not let a generous mind be free. Happy the man whom Heaven has blessed with bread, for which he is obliged to thank kind Heaven alone!' 'For all these fine words,' quoth Sancho, 'it is not proper for us to be unthankful for two good hundred crowns in gold, which the Duke's steward gave me in a little purse, which I have here, and cherish in my bosom, as a relic against necessity, and a comforting cordial next my heart against all accidents; for we are not like always to meet with castles, where we shall be made much of. A pease-cods on it! We are more like to meet with damned inns, where we shall be rib-roasted.'

As the wandering knight and squire went discoursing of this and other matters, they had not rode much more than a league, ere they espied about a dozen men, who looked like country-fellows sitting at their victuals, with their cloaks under them, on the green grass, in the middle of a meadow. Near them they saw several white cloths or sheets, spread out and laid close to one another, that seemed to cover something. Don Quixote rode up to the people, and after he had civilly saluted them, asked what they had got under that linen. 'Sir,' answered one of the company, 'they are some carved images that are to be set up at an altar we are erecting in our town. We cover them lest they should be sullied, and carry them on our shoulders for fear they should be broken.' 'If you please,' said Don Quixote, 'I should be glad to see them; for considering the care you take of them, they should be pieces of value.' 'Ay, marry are they,' quoth another, 'or else we are damnably cheated; for there is never an image among them that does not stand us in more than fifty ducats; and, that you may know I am no liar, do but stay, and you shall see with your own eyes.' With that, getting up on his legs, and leaving his victuals, he went and took off the cover from one of the figures, that happened to be St. George on horseback, and under his feet a serpent coiled up, his throat transfixed with a lance, with the fierceness that is commonly represented in the piece; and all, as they use to say, spick and span new, and shining like beaten gold. Don Quixote having seen the image, 'This,' said he, 'was one of the best knights-errant the divine warfare or Church Militant ever had: his name was Don St. George, and he was an extraordinary protector of damsels. What is the next?' The fellow having uncovered it, it proved to be St. Martin on horseback. 'This knight too,' said Don Quixote at the first sight, 'was one of the Christian adventurers, and I am apt to think he was more liberal than valiant; and thou mayst perceive it, Sancho, by his dividing his cloak with a poor man; he gave him half, and doubtless it was winter-time, or else he would have given it him whole, he was so charitable.' 'Not so neither, I fancy,' quoth Sancho, 'but I guess he stuck to the proverb: To give and keep what is fit, requires a share of wit.' Don Quixote smiled, and desired the men to show him the next image, which appeared to be that of the Patron of Spain on horseback, with his sword bloody, trampling down Moors, and treading over heads. 'Ay, this is a knight, indeed,' cried Don Quixote, when he saw it, 'one of those that fought in the squadrons of the Saviour of the world: he is called Don St. Jago, Mata Moros, or Don St. James the Moor-killer, and may be reckoned one of the most valorous saints and professors of chivalry that the earth then enjoyed, and Heaven now possesses.' Then they uncovered another piece, which showed St. Paul falling from his horse, with all the circumstances usually expressed in the story of his conversion, and represented so to the life, that he looked as if he had been answering the voice that spoke to him from Heaven. 'This,' said Don Quixote, 'was the greatest enemy the Church Militant had once, and proved afterwards the greatest defender it will ever have. In his life a true knight-errant, and in death a steadfast saint; an indefatigable labourer in the vineyard of the Lord, a teacher of the Gentiles, who had Heaven for his school, and Christ Himself for his master and instructor.' Then Don Quixote, perceiving there were no more images, desired the men to cover those he had seen: 'And now, my good friends,' said he to them, 'I cannot but esteem the sight that I have had of those images as a happy omen; for these saints and knights were of the same profession that I follow, which is that of arms: the difference only lies in this point, that they were saints, and fought according to the rules of holy discipline; and I am a sinner, and fight after the manner of men. They conquered Heaven by force, for Heaven is taken by violence; but I, alas cannot yet tell what I gain by the force of my labours! Yet were my Dulcinea del Toboso but free from her troubles, by a happy change in my fortune, and an improvement in my understanding, I might perhaps take a better course than I do.' 'Heaven grant it,' quoth Sancho, 'and let the Devil do his worst.'

All this while the men wondered at Don Quixote's figure as well as his discourse; but could not understand one half of what he meant. So that, after they had made an end of their dinner, they got up their images, took their leaves of Don Quixote, and continued their journey.

Sancho remained full of admiration, as if he had never known his master; he wondered how he should come to know all these things; and fancied there was not that history or adventure in the world, but he had it at his fingers' end. 'Faith and troth, master of mine,' quoth he, 'if what has happened to us today may be called an adventure, it is one of the sweetest and most pleasant we ever met with in all our rambles; for we are come off without a dry basting, or the least bodily fear. We have not so much as laid our hands upon our weapons, nor have we beaten the earth with our carcases; but here we be safe and sound, neither a-dry nor a-hungry. Heaven be praised, that I have seen all this with my own eyes!' 'Thou sayest well, Sancho,' said Don Quixote, 'but I must tell thee, that seasons and times are not always the same, but often take a different course. And what the vulgar call forebodings and omens, for which there are no rational grounds in nature, ought only to be esteemed happy encounters by the wise. One of these superstitious fools, going out of his house betimes in the morning, meets a friar of the blessed order of St. Francis, and starts as if he had met a griffin, turns back, and runs home again. Another wiseacre happens to throw down the salt on the tablecloth, and thereupon is sadly cast down himself, as if nature were obliged to give tokens of ensuing disasters, by such slight and inconsiderable accidents as these. A wise and truly religious man ought never to pry into the secrets of

Heaven. Scipio, landing in Africa, stumbled and fell down as he leaped ashore: presently his soldiers took this for an ill omen, but he, embracing the earth, cried, "I have thee fast, Africa; thou shalt not escape me." In this manner Sancho, I think it a very happy accident, that I met these images.' 'I think so too,' quoth Sancho; 'but I would fain know why the Spaniards call upon that same St. James the destroyer of Moors; just when they are going to give battle, they cry, "Sant Jago, and close Spain." Pray is Spain open, that it wants to be closed up? What do you make of that ceremony?' 'Thou art a very simple fellow, Sancho,' answered Don Quixote. 'Thou must know that Heaven gave to Spain this mighty champion of the Red-cross for its patron and protector, especially in the desperate engagements which the Spaniards had with the Moors; and, therefore, they invoke him in all their martial encounters, as their protector; and many times he has been personally seen cutting and slaying, overthrowing, trampling and destroying the Hagarene squadrons;* of which I could give thee many examples, deduced from authentic Spanish histories.'

Here Sancho changing the discourse, 'Sir,' quoth he, 'I cannot but marvel at the impudence of Altisidora, the Duchess's damsel. I warrant you, that same mischief-monger they call Love has plaguely mauled her, and run her through without mercy. They say he is a little blind urchin, and yet the dark youth, with no more eyesight than a beetle, will hit your heart as sure as a gun, and bore it through and through with his dart, if he undertakes to shoot at it. However, I have heard say, that the shafts of love are blunted and beaten back by the modest and sober carriage of young maidens. But upon this Altisidora their edge seems rather to be whetted than made blunt.' 'You must observe, Sancho,' said Don Quixote, 'that love is void of consideration, and disclaims the rules of reason in his proceedings. He is like death, and equally assaults the lofty palaces of kings, and the lowly cottages of shepherds. Wherever he takes entire possession of a soul, the first thing he does, is to banish thence all bashfulness and shame. So these being banished from Altisidora's breast, she confidently discovered her loose desires, which, alas! rather filled me with confusion than pity.' 'If so,' quoth Sancho, 'you are confoundedly cruel; how could you be so hardhearted and ungrateful? Had the poor thing but made love to me, I dare say I should have come to at the first word, and have been at her service. Beshrew my midriff, what a heart of marble, bowels of brass, and soul of plaster you have! But I cannot for the blood of me imagine, what the poor creature saw in your worship, to make her dote on you, and play the fool at this rate! Where the Devil was the sparkling appearance, the briskness, the fine carriage, the sweet face that

---

* Hagarene squadrons, *i.e.* Moorish, because they have a tradition that the Moors are descended from Hagar.

bewitched her? Indeed and indeed, I often survey your worship from the tip of your toe to the topmost hair on your crown; and, not to flatter you, I can see nothing in you, but what is more likely to scare one, than to make one fall in love. I have heard that beauty is the first and chief thing that begets love; now you not having any, if it like your worship, I cannot guess what the poor soul was smitten with.' 'Take notice, Sancho,' answered Don Quixote, 'that there are two sorts of beauty, the one of the soul, and the other of the body. That of the soul lies and displays itself in the understanding, in principles of honour and virtue, in a handsome behaviour, in generosity and good breeding; all which qualities may be found in a person not so accomplished in outward features. And when this beauty, and not that of the body, is the object of love, then the assaults of that passion are much more fierce, more surprising and effectual. Now, Sancho, though I am sensible I am not handsome, I know at the same time I am not deformed; and provided an honest man be possessed of the endowments of the mind which I have mentioned, and nothing appears monstrous in him, it is enough to entitle him to the love of a reasonable creature.'

Thus discoursing, they got into a wood quite out of the road, and on a sudden Don Quixote, before he knew where he was, found himself entangled in some nets of green thread, that were spread across among the trees. Not being able to imagine what it was: 'Certainly, Sancho,' cried he, 'this adventure of the nets must be one of the most unaccountable that can be imagined. Let me die now if this be not a stratagem of the evil-minded necromancers that haunt me, to entangle me so that I may not proceed, purely to revenge my contempt of Altisidora's addresses. But let them know, that though these nets were adamantine chains, as they are only made of green thread, and though they were stronger than those in which the jealous god of blacksmiths caught Venus and Mars, I would break them with as much ease as if they were weak rushes, or fine cotton yarn.' With that the Knight put briskly forwards, resolved to break through, and make his words good; but in the very moment there sprung from behind the trees two most beautiful shepherdesses, at least they appeared to be so by their habits, only with this difference, that they were richly dressed in gold brocade. Their flowing hair hung down about their shoulders in curls, as charming as the sun's golden rays, and circled on their brows with garlands of green bays and red-flower-gentle interwoven. As for their age, it seemed not less than fifteen, nor more than eighteen years. This unexpected vision dazzled and amazed Sancho, surprised Don Quixote, made even the gazing sun stop short in his career, and held the surprised parties a while in the same suspense and silence; till at last one of the shepherdesses opening her coral lips, 'Hold, sir,' she cried; 'pray do not tear those nets which we have spread here, not to offend you, but to divert ourselves; and because it is likely you will inquire why they are spread here, and who we are, I shall tell you in few words.

'About two leagues from this place lies a village, where there are many people of quality and good estates; among these, several have made up a company, all of friends, neighbours, and relations, to come and take their diversion in this place, which is one of the most delightful in these parts. To this purpose we design to set up a new Arcadia. The young men have put on the habit of shepherds, and ladies the dress of shepherdesses. We have got two eclogues by heart; one out of the famous Garcilasso, and the other out of Camoens, the most excellent Portuguese poet; though the truth is, we have not yet repeated them, for yesterday was but the first day of our coming hither. We have pitched some tents among the trees, near the banks of a large brook that waters all these meadows. And last night we spread these nets, to catch such simple birds as our calls should allure into the snare. Now, sir, if you please to afford us your company, you shall be made very welcome, and handsomely entertained; for we are all disposed to pass the time agreeably, and for a while banish melancholy from this place.' 'Truly, fair lady,' answered Don Quixote, 'Actaeon could not be more lost in admiration and amazement, at the sight of Diana bathing herself, than I have been at the appearance of your beauty. I applaud the design of your entertainment, and return you thanks for your obliging offers; assuring you, that if it lies in my power to serve you, you may depend on my obedience to your commands: for my profession is the very reverse of ingratitude, and aims at doing good to all persons, especially those of your merit and condition; so that were these nets spread over the surface of the whole earth, I would seek out a passage throughout new worlds, rather than I would break the smallest thread that conduces to your pastime: and that you may give some credit to this seeming exaggeration, know that, he who makes this promise is no less than Don Quixote de la Mancha, if ever such a name has reached your ears.' 'Oh, my dear,' cried the other shepherdess, 'what good fortune this is! You see this gentleman before us: I must tell you, he is the most valiant, the most amorous, and the most complaisant person in the world, if the history of his exploits, already in print, does not deceive us. I have read it, my dear, and I hold a wager, that honest fellow there by him is one Sancho Pança, his squire, the most comical creature that ever was.' 'You have nicked it,' quoth Sancho, 'I am that comical creature, and that very squire you wot of, and there is my Lord and Master, the selfsame historified, and aforesaid Don Quixote de la Mancha.' 'Oh, pray, my dear,' said the other, 'let us entreat him to stay; our father, and our brothers will be mighty glad of it; I have heard of his valour and his merit, as much as you now tell me; and what is more, they say he is the most constant and faithful lover in the world; and that his mistress, whom they call Dulcinea del Toboso, bears the prize from all the beauties in Spain.' 'It is not without justice,' said Don Quixote; 'if your peerless charms do not dispute her that glory. But, ladies, I beseech you do not endeavour to detain me; for the indispensable duties of my profession will not suffer me to rest in one place.'

At the same time came the brother of one of the shepherdesses, clad like a shepherd, but in a dress as splendid and gay as those of the young ladies. They told him that the gentleman, whom he saw with them, was the valorous Don Quixote de la Mancha, and that other, Sancho Pança, his squire, of whom he had read the history. The gallant shepherd having saluted him, begged of him so earnestly to grant them his company to their tents, that Don Quixote was forced to comply, and go with them.

About the same time the nets were drawn and filled with divers little birds, who, being deceived by the colour of the snare, fell into the danger they would have avoided. Above thirty persons, all gaily dressed like shepherds and shepherdesses, got together there, and being informed who Don Quixote and his squire were, they were not a little pleased, for they were already no strangers to his history. In short, they carried them to their tents, where they found a clean, sumptuous, and plentiful entertainment ready. They obliged the Knight to take the place of honour; and while they sat at table, there was not one that did not gaze on him, and wonder at so strange a figure. At last, the cloth being removed, Don Quixote, with a great deal of gravity, lifting up his voice: 'Of all the sins that men commit,' said he, 'none, in my opinion, is so great as ingratitude, though some think pride a greater; and I ground my assertion on this, that hell is said to be full of the ungrateful. Ever since I have had the use of reason, I have employed my utmost endeavours to avoid this crime; and if I am not able to repay the benefits I receive in their kind, at least I am not wanting in real intentions of making suitable returns; and if that be not sufficient I make my acknowledgments as public as I can; for he that proclaims the kindnesses he has received, shows his disposition to repay them if he could; and those that receive are generally inferior to those that give. The Supreme Being, that is infinitely above all things, bestows His blessings on us so much beyond the capacity of all other benefactors, that all the acknowledgments we can make can never hold proportion with His goodness. However, a thankful mind in some measure supplies its want of power with hearty desires, and unfeigned expressions of a sense of ingratitude and respect. I am in this condition as to the civilities I have been treated with here; for I am unable to make an acknowledgment equal to the kindnesses I have received. I shall, therefore, only offer ye what is within the narrow limits of my own abilities; which is to maintain, for two whole days together, in the middle of the road that leads to Saragossa, that these ladies here disguised in the habit of shepherdesses, are the fairest and most courteous damsels in the world, excepting only the peerless Dulcinea del Toboso, sole mistress of my thoughts; without offence to all that hear me be it spoken.'

Here Sancho, who had with an uncommon attention all the while given ear to his master's compliment, thought fit to put in a word or two. 'Now, in name of wonder,' quoth he, 'can there be anybody in the world so impudent as to offer to swear, or but to say, this master of mine is a madman? Pray tell me, ye gentlemen shepherds, did you ever know any of your country parsons, though never so wise, or so good scholars, that could deliver themselves so finely? Or is there any of your knights-errant, though never so famed for prowess, that can make such an offer as he here has done?' Don Quixote turned towards Sancho, and beholding him with eyes full of fiery indignation: 'Can there be anybody in the world,' cried he, 'that can say thou art not an incorrigible blockhead, Sancho; a compound of folly and knavery, wherein malice also is no small ingredient? Who bids thee meddle with my concerns, fellow, or busy thyself with my folly or discretion? Hold your saucy tongue, scoundrel! Make no reply, but go and saddle Rozinante, if he is unsaddled, that I may immediately perform what I have offered; for, in so noble and so just a cause, thou mayest reckon all those who shall presume to oppose me, subdued and overthrown.' This said, up he started, in a dreadful fury, and with marks of anger in his looks, to the amazement of all the company, who were at a loss whether they should esteem him a madman, or a man of sense: they endeavoured to prevail with him to lay aside his challenges, telling him, they were sufficiently assured of his grateful nature, without exposing him to the danger of such demonstrations; and as for his valour, they were so well informed by the history of his numerous achievements, that there was no need of any new instance to convince them of it. But all these representations could not dissuade him from his purpose; and, therefore, having mounted Rozinante, braced his shield, and grasped his lance, he went and posted himself in the middle of the highway, not far from the verdant meadow, followed by Sancho on his Dapple, and all the pastoral society, who were desirous to see the event of that arrogant and unaccountable resolution. And now the champion having taken his ground, made the neighbouring air ring with the following challenge: 'O ye, whoever you are, knights, squires, on foot or on horseback, that now pass, or shall pass this road within these two days, know that Don Quixote de la Mancha, knight-errant, stays here, to assert and maintain, that the nymphs, who inhabit these groves and meadows, surpass in beauty and courteous disposition, all those in the universe, setting aside the sovereign of my soul, the Lady Dulcinea del Toboso. And he that dares uphold the contrary, let him appear, for here I expect his coming.' Twice he repeated these lofty words, and twice they were repeated in vain, not being heard by any adventurer. But his old friend, Fortune, that had a strange hand at managing his concerns, and always mended upon it, showed him a jolly sight; for by and by he discovered on the road a great number of people on horseback, many of them with lances in their hands, all trooping together very fast. The company that watched Don Quixote's motions, no sooner spied such a squadron, driving the dust before them, but they got out of harm's way, not judging it safe to be so near danger; and as for Sancho, he sheltered himself behind Rozinante's crupper; only Don Quixote stood fixed with an undaunted courage. When the horsemen came near, one of the foremost bawling to the champion, 'So hey!' cried he; 'get out of the way, and be hanged. The Devil is in the fellow! Stand off, or the bulls will tread thee to pieces.' 'Go to, ye scoundrels,' answered Don Quixote, 'none of your bulls are anything to me, though the fiercest that ever were fed on the banks of Xamara.* Acknowledge, hang-dogs, all in a body, what I have proclaimed here to be truth, or else stand combat with me.' But the herdsmen had not time to answer, neither had Don Quixote any to get out of the way, if he had been inclined to it; for the herd of wild bulls were presently upon him, as they poured along, with several tame cows,† and a huge company of drivers and people, that were going to a town where they were to be baited the next day. So bearing all down before them, Knight and squire, horse and man, they trampled them under feet at an unmerciful rate. There lay Sancho mauled, Don Quixote stunned, Dapple bruised, and Rozinante in very indifferent circumstances. But for all this, after the whole route of men and beasts were gone by, up started Don Quixote, ere he was thoroughly come to himself; and staggering, and stumbling, falling, and getting up again, as fast as he could, he began to run after them: 'Stop, scoundrels, stop,' cried he aloud, 'stay, it is a single knight defies ye all, one who scorns the humour of making a golden bridge for a flying enemy.' But the hasty travellers did not stop nor slacken their speed for all his loud defiance; and minded it no more than the last year's snow.

At last weariness stopped Don Quixote: so that with all his anger, and no prospect of revenge, he was forced to sit down in the road, till Sancho came up to him with Rozinante and Dapple. Then the master and man made a shift to remount, and, ashamed of their bad success, hastened their journey, without taking leave of their friends of the New Arcadia.

---

* The bulls of Xamara are accounted the fiercest in Spain.
† *Mansus Cabestros.* According to the 'Royal Dictionary,' they are the old tame oxen, with bells about their necks.

CHAPTER LIX

*Of an extraordinary accident that happened to Don
Quixote, which may well pass for an Adventure*

A CLEAR FOUNTAIN, which Don Quixote and Sancho found among some
verdant trees, served to refresh them, besmeared with dust, and tired as
they were, after the rude encounter of the bulls. There by the brink,
leaving Rozinante and Dapple, unbridled and unhaltered, to their own
liberty, the two forlorn adventurers sat down. Sancho washed his mouth,
and Don Quixote his face. The squire then went to his old cupboard, the
wallet; and having taken out of it what he used to call belly timber, laid it
before the Knight: but Don Quixote would eat nothing for pure vexation,
and Sancho durst not begin for pure good-manners, expecting that he
would first show him the way. However, finding him so wrapped in his
imaginations, as to have no thoughts of lifting his hands up to his mouth,
the squire, without letting one word come out of his, laid aside all kind of
good breeding, and began to stuff his hungry maw with what bread and
cheese he had before him: 'Eat, friend Sancho,' cried Don Quixote, 'repair
the decays of nature, and sustain life, which thou hast more reason to
cherish than I; leave me to die abandoned to my sorrows, and the violence
of my misfortunes. I was born, Sancho, to live dying, and thou to die
eating. And, that thou mayest be convinced I tell thee truth, do but reflect
upon me, famous in history, dignified with the honour of the press,
renowned for feats of arms, courteous in behaviour, respected by princes,
beloved and importuned by damsels; yet after all this, when I at last
flattered myself with hopes of laurels, triumphs, and crowns, the reward
merited by my valorous achievements, behold me trod under foot,
trampled like the highway dirt, kicked and bruised by the hoofs of vile and
filthy beasts. The thought dulls the edge of my teeth, and my appetite;
unhinges my jaws, benumbs my hands, and stupefies my senses; and
fearing more to live than to die, I am resolved almost to starve myself;
though to die with hunger be the most cruel of all deaths.' 'So that belike,'
quoth Sancho, without losing any time in chewing, 'you will not make
good the saying, "It is good to die with a full belly." For my part, I am not
so simple yet as to kill myself. No, I am like the cobbler, that stretches his
leather with his teeth: I am for lengthening my life by eating; and I will
stretch it with my grinders as far as Heaven will let it run. Faith and troth,
master, there is no greater folly in the world than for a man to despair, and
throw the helve after the hatchet. Therefore, take my advice, fall to, and
eat as I do, and when you have done, lie down and take a nap; the fresh

grass here will do as well as a feather-bed. I dare say, by that time you awake, you will find yourself better in body and mind.'

Don Quixote followed Sancho's counsel; for he was convinced the squire spoke good natural philosophy at that time. However, in the meanwhile, a thought coming into his mind, 'Ah! Sancho,' said he, 'if thou wouldest but do something that I am now going to desire thee, my cares would sit more easy on me, and my comfort would be more certain. It is only this; while, according to thy advice, I try to compose my thoughts with sleep, do thou but step aside a little, and exposing thy back-parts bare in the open air, take the reins of Rozinante's bridle, and give thyself some three or four hundred smart lashes, in part of the three thousand and odd thou art to receive to disenchant Dulcinea; for, in truth, it is a shame, and a very great pity that poor lady should remain enchanted all this while, through thy carelessness and neglect.' 'There is a great deal to be said as to that,' quoth Sancho; 'but that will keep cold, first let us go to sleep, and then come what will come: Heaven knows what will be done. Do you think, sir, it is nothing for a man to flog himself in cold blood? I would have you to know, it is a cruel thing, especially when the lashes must light upon a body, so weak, and so horribly lined within as mine is. Let my Lady Dulcinea have a little patience; one of these days, when she least dreams of it, she shall see my skin pinked and jagged like a slashed doublet with lashes. There is nothing lost that comes at last; while there is life there is hopes; which is as good as to say, I live with an intent to make good my promise.' Don Quixote gave him thanks, ate a little, and Sancho a great deal; and then both betook themselves to their rest, leaving those constant friends and companions, Rozinante and Dapple to their own discretion, to repose or feed at random on the pasture that abounded in that meadow.

The day was now far gone, when the Knight and the squire awaked: they mounted, and held on their journey, making the best of their way to an inn, that seemed to be about a league distant. I call it an inn, because Don Quixote himself called it so, contrary to his custom, it being a common thing with him to take inns for castles.

Being got thither, they asked the innkeeper whether he had got any lodgings. 'Yes,' answered he, 'and as good accommodation as you could expect to find even in the city of Saragossa.' They alighted, and Sancho put up his baggage in a chamber, of which the landlord gave him the key; and after he had seen Rozinante and Dapple well provided for in the stable, he went to wait on his master, whom he found sitting upon a seat made in the wall, the squire blessing himself more than once, that the Knight had not taken the inn for a castle. Supper-time approaching, Don Quixote retired to his apartment, and Sancho, staying with his host, asked him what he had to give them for supper?' What you will,' answered he, 'you may pick and choose, fish or flesh, butchers' meat or poultry, wild-fowl and what not: whatever land, sea, and air afford for food, it is but ask and have, everything is to be had in this inn.' 'There is no need of all this,' quoth Sancho, 'a couple of roasted chickens will do our business; for my master has a nice stomach, and eats but little; and as for me, I am none of your unreasonable trencher-men.' 'As for chickens,' replied the inn-keeper, 'truly we have none, for the kites have devoured them.' 'Why then,' quoth Sancho, 'roast us a good handsome pullet with eggs, so it be young and tender.' 'A pullet, master!' answered the host, 'faith and troth, I sent above fifty yesterday to the city to sell; but, setting aside pullets, you may have anything else.' 'Why then,' quoth Sancho, 'even give us a good joint of veal or kid.' 'Cry you mercy,' replied the innkeeper, 'now I remember me, we have none left in the house, the last company that went cleared me quite, but by next week we will have enough and to spare.' 'We are finely holped up!' quoth Sancho. 'Now, will I hold a wager, all these defects must be made up with a dish of eggs and bacon.' 'Hey dey!' cried the host, 'my guest has a rare knack at guessing i'faith, I told him I had no hens nor pullets in the house, and yet he would have me to have eggs! Think on something else, I beseech you, and let us talk no more of that.' 'Body of me,' cried Sancho, 'let us come to something; tell me what thou hast, good Mr. Landlord, and do not put me to trouble my brains any longer.' 'Why then, do you see,' quoth the host, 'to deal plainly with you, I have a delicate pair of cow-heels that look like calves' feet, or a pair of calves' feet that look like cow-heels, dressed with onions, pease and bacon; a dish for a prince, they are just ready to be taken off, and by this time they cry, "Come eat me, come eat me." ' 'Cow-heels!' cried Sancho, 'I set my mark on them: let nobody touch them. I will give more for them than anybody else shall. There is nothing I love better.' 'Nobody else shall have them,' answered the host; 'you need not fear, for all the guests I have in the house besides yourselves, are persons of quality, that carry their steward, their cook, and their provisions along with them.' 'As for quality,' quoth Sancho, 'my master is a person of as good quality as the proudest he of them all, if you go to that; but his profession allows of no larders nor butteries. We commonly clap us down in the middle of a field, and fill our bellies with acorns or medlars.' This was the discourse that passed betwixt Sancho and the innkeeper; for as to the host's interrogatories, concerning his master's profession, Sancho was not then at leisure to make him any answer.

In short, supper-time came, Don Quixote went to his room, the host brought the dish of cow-heels, such as it was, and sat him down fairly to supper. But at the same time, in the next room, which was divided from that where they were by a slender partition, the Knight overheard somebody talking: 'Dear Don Jeronimo,' said the unseen person, 'I beseech you, till supper is brought in, let us read another chapter of the "Second Part of Don Quixote." ' The champion no sooner heard himself named, but up he started, and listened with attentive ears to what was said of him, and then he heard that Don Jeronimo answer, 'Why would you have us read nonsense, Signor Don John? Methinks that any one who has read the "First Part of Don Quixote," should take but little delight in reading the Second.' 'That may be,' replied Don John; 'however, it may not be amiss to read it; for there is no book so bad, as not to have something that is good in it. What displeases me most in this part, is, that it represents Don Quixote no longer in love with Dulcinea del Toboso.' Upon these words, Don Quixote, burning with anger and indignation, cried out: 'Whoever says that Don Quixote de la Mancha has forgot, or can forget, Dulcinea del Toboso, I will make him know with equal arms that he departs wholly from the truth; for the peerless Dulcinea del Toboso cannot be forgotten, nor can Don Quixote be guilty of forgetfulness. "Constancy" is his motto; and to preserve his fidelity with pleasure, and without the least constraint, is his profession.' 'Who is that answers us?' cries one of those in the next room. 'Who should it be,' quoth Sancho, 'but Don Quixote de la Mancha his own self, the same that will make good all he has said, and all that he has to say, take my word for it: for a good pay-master never grudges to give security.'

Sancho had no sooner made that answer, but in came the two gentlemen (for they appeared to be no less), and one of them throwing his arms about Don Quixote's neck, 'Your presence, Sir Knight,' said he, 'does not belie your reputation, nor can your reputation fail to raise a respect for your presence. You are certainly the true Don Quixote de la Mancha, the north-star, and luminary of chivalry-errant, in despite of him that has attempted to usurp your name, and annihilate your achievements, as the author* of this book, which I here deliver into your hand, has presumed to do.' With that he took the book from his friend, and gave it to Don Quixote. The Knight took it, and, without saying a word, began to turn over the leaves; and then returning it a while after: 'In the little I have seen,' said he, 'I have found three things in this author that deserve reprehension. First, I find fault with some words in his preface. In the second place, his language is Arragonian, for sometimes he writes without articles: and the third thing I have observed, which betrays most his ignorance, is, he is out of the way in one of the principal parts of the history: for there he says, that the wife of my Squire Sancho Pança is

---

* An Arragonian published a book, which he called the 'Second Part of Don Quixote,' before our author had printed this. See the preface of this Second Part, and the account of the life of Cervantes; who brings this in by way of invective against that Arragonian.

called Mary Gutierrez, which is not true; for her name is Teresa Pança; and he that errs in so considerable a passage may well be suspected to have committed many gross errors through the whole history.' 'A pretty impudent fellow is this same history-writer!' cried Sancho. 'Sure he knows little what belongs to our concerns, to call my wife Teresa Pança, Mary Gutierrez! Pray take the book again, if it like your worship, and see whether he says anything of me, and whether he has not changed my name too.' 'Sure, by what you have said, honest man,' said Don Jeronimo, 'you should be Sancho Pança, Squire to Signor Don Quixote!' 'So I am,' quoth Sancho, 'and I am proud of the office.' 'Well,' said the gentleman, 'to tell you the truth, the last author does not treat you so civilly as you seem to deserve. He represents you as a glutton and a fool, without the least grain of wit or humour, and very different from the Sancho we have in the first part of your master's history.' 'Heaven forgive him,' quoth Sancho; 'he might have left me where I was, without offering to meddle with me. Every man's nose will not make a shoeing horn. Let us leave the world as is. St. Peter is very well at Rome.' Presently the two gentlemen invited Don Quixote to sup with them in their chamber; for they knew there was nothing to be got in the inn fit for his entertainment. Don Quixote, who was always very complaisant, could not deny their request, and went with them. Sancho stayed behind with the flesh-pot, *cum mero mixto imperio*:* he placed himself at the upper end of the table, with the innkeeper for his mess-mate; for he was no less a lover of cow-heels than the squire. While Don Quixote was at supper with the gentlemen, Don John asked him when he heard of the Lady Dulcinea del Toboso? whether she were married? whether she had any children, or were with child or no? or whether, continuing still in her maiden-state, and preserving her honour and reputation unstained, she had a grateful sense of the love and constancy of Signor Don Quixote. 'Dulcinea is still a virgin,' answered Don Quixote, 'and my amorous thoughts more fixed than ever; our correspondence after the old rate, not frequent, but her beauty transformed into the homely appearance of a female rustic.' And with that, he told the gentlemen the whole story of her being enchanted, what had befallen him in the cave of Montesinos, and the means that the sage Merlin had prescribed to free her from enchantment, which was Sancho's penance of three thousand three hundred lashes. The gentlemen were extremely pleased to hear from Don Quixote's own mouth the strange passages of his history, equally wondering at the nature of his extravagancies, and his elegant manner of relating them. One minute they

---

* That is, with a deputed or subordinate power. *Merum imperium*, according to the Civilians, is that residing in the sovereign; *Merum mixtum imperium*, is that delegated to vassals or magistrates in causes civil or criminal.

looked upon him to be in his senses, and the next, they thought he had lost them all; so that they could not resolve what degree to assign him between madness and sound judgment.

By this time Sancho having eaten his supper, and left his landlord, moved to the room where his master was with the two strangers, and as he bolted in, 'Hang me,' quoth he, 'gentlemen, if he that made the book your worships have got, could have a mind that he and I should ever take a loving cup together: I wish, as he calls me Greedy-gut, he does not set me out for a drunkard too.' 'Nay,' said Don Jeronimo, 'he does not use you better as to that point; though I cannot well remember his expressions. Only this I know, they are scandalous and false, as I perceive by the physiognomy of sober Sancho here present.' 'Take my word for it, gentlemen,' quoth the squire, 'the Sancho, and the Don Quixote in your book, I do not know who they be, but they are not the same men as those in Cid Hamet Benengeli's history, for we two are they, just such as Benengeli makes us; my master valiant, discreet, and in love; and I a plain, merry-conceited fellow, but neither a glutton nor a drunkard.' 'I believe you,' said Don John, 'and I could wish, were such a thing possible, 'that all other writers whatsoever were forbidden to record the deeds of the great Don Quixote, except Cid Hamet, his first author; as Alexander forbad all other painters to draw his picture, except Apelles.' 'Let any one draw mine, if he pleases,' said Don Quixote; 'but let him not abuse the original; for when patience is loaded with injuries, many times it sinks under its burden.' 'No injury,' replied Don John, 'can be offered to Signor Don Quixote but what he is able to revenge, or at least ward off with the shield of his patience, which, in my opinion, is very great and powerful.'

In such discourse they spent a good part of the night; and though Don John endeavoured to persuade Don Quixote to read more of the book, to see how the author had handled his subject, he could by no means prevail with him, the Knight giving him to understand, he had enough of it, and as much as if he had read it throughout, concluding it to be all of a piece, and nonsense over all; and that he would not encourage the scribbler's vanity so far as to let him think he had read it, should it ever come to his ears that the book had fallen into his hands; well knowing we ought to avoid defiling our thoughts, and much more our eyes, with vile and obscene matters.

They asked him, which way he was travelling? He told them he was going for Saragossa, to make one at the tournaments held in that city once a year, for the prize of armour. Don John acquainted him, that the pretended Second Part of his history gave an account how Don Quixote, whoever he was, had been at Saragossa at a public running at the ring, the description of which was wretched and defective in the contrivance, mean and low in the style and expression, and miserably poor in devices, all made up of foolish, idle stuff. 'For that reason,' said Don Quixote, 'I will not set a foot in Saragossa, and so the world shall see what a notorious lie this new historian is guilty of, and all mankind shall perceive I am not the Don Quixote he speaks of.' 'You do very well,' said Don Jeronimo, 'besides, there is another tournament at Barcelona, where you may signalise your valour.' 'I design to do so,' replied Don Quixote: 'and so, gentlemen, give me leave to bid you good-night, and permit me to go to bed, for it is time; and pray place me in the number of your best friends, and most faithful servants.' 'And me too,' quoth Sancho; 'for mayhap you may find me good for something.'

Having taken leave of one another, Don Quixote and Sancho retired to their chamber, leaving the two strangers in admiration, to think what a medley the Knight had made of good sense and extravagance: but fully satisfied, however, that these two persons were the true Don Quixote and Sancho, and not those obtruded upon the public by the Arragonian author.

Early in the morning Don Quixote got up, and knocking at a thin wall that parted his chamber from that of the gentlemen, he took his leave of them. Sancho paid the host nobly, but advised him either to keep better provisions in *his* inn, or to commend it less.

CHAPTER LX

What happened to Don Quixote in Barcelona

THE MORNING WAS COOL, and seemed to promise a temperate day? when Don Quixote left the inn, having first informed himself, which was the readiest way to Barcelona; for he was resolved he would not so much as see Saragossa, that he might prove that new author a liar, who (as he was told) had so misrepresented him in the pretended Second Part of his history. For the space of six days he travelled without meeting any adventure worthy of memory; but the seventh, having lost his way, and being overtaken by the night, he was obliged to stop in a thicket, either of oaks or cork-trees, for in this Cid Hamet does not observe the same punctuality he has kept in other matters. There both master and man dismounted, and laying themselves down at the foot of the trees; Sancho, who had handsomely filled his belly that day, easily resigned himself into the arms of sleep. But Don Quixote, whom his chimeras kept awake much more than hunger, could not so much as close his eyes; his working thoughts being hurried to a thousand several places. This time he fancied himself in Montesinos' cave; fancied he saw his Dulcinea, perverted as she was into a country wench, jump at a single leap upon her ass colt. The next moment he thought he heard the sage Merlin's voice, heard him in awful words relate the means required to effect her disenchantment. Presently a fit of despair seized him: he was stark mad to think on Sancho's remissness and want of charity; the squire having not given himself above five lashes, a small and inconsiderable number in proportion to the quantity of the penance still behind. This reflection so nettled him, and so aggravated his vexation, that he could not forbear thinking on some extraordinary methods. If Alexander the Great, thought he, when he could not untie the Gordian knot, said, it is the same thing to cut, or to undo, and so lashed it asunder, and yet became the sovereign of the world, why may not I free Dulcinea from enchantment, by whipping Sancho myself, whether he will or no? For, if the condition of this remedy consists in Sancho's receiving three thousand and odd lashes, what does it signify to me, whether he gives himself those blows, or another give them him, since the stress lies upon his receiving them, by what means soever they are given? Full of that conceit he came up to Sancho, having first taken the reins of Rozinante's bridle, and fitted them to his purpose of lashing him with them. He then began to untruss Sancho's points; and it is a received opinion, he had but one that was used before, which held up his breeches; but he no sooner fell to work, but Sancho started out of his sleep, and was thoroughly awake in an instant. 'What is here?' cries he, 'who is that fumbles about me, and untrusses my points?' 'It is I,' answered Don Quixote, 'I am come to repair thy negligence, and to seek the remedy of my torments. I come to whip thee, Sancho, and to discharge, in part at least, that debt for which though standest engaged. Dulcinea perishes, whilst thou livest careless of her fate, and I die with desire. Untruss, therefore, freely and willingly; for I am resolved, while we are here alone in this recess, to give thee at least two thousand stripes.'

'Hold you there,' quoth Sancho, 'pray be quiet, will you! Body of me, let me alone, or I protest deaf men shall hear us! The jirks I am bound to give myself, are to be voluntary, and not forced; and at this time I have no mind to be whipped at all: let it suffice, that I promise you to sirk and scourge myself, when the humour takes me.' 'No,' said Don Quixote, 'there is no standing to thy courtesy, Sancho; for thou art hardhearted; and though a clown, yet thou art tender of thy flesh;' and so saying, he strove with all his force to untie the squire's points. Which, when Sancho perceived, he started upon his legs, and setting upon his master, closed with him, tripped up his heels, threw him fairly upon his back; and then set his knee upon his breast, and held his hands fast, so that he could hardly stir, or fetch his breath. Don Quixote, overpowered thus, cried, 'How now, traitor! what, rebel against thy master, against thy natural lord, against him that gives thee bread!' 'I neither mar king, nor make king,'* quoth Sancho; 'I do but defend myself, that am naturally my own lord. If your worship will promise to let me alone, and give over the thoughts of whipping me at this time, I will let you rise, and will leave you at liberty; if not, here thou diest, traitor to Donna Sancho.' Don Quixote gave his parole of honour, and swore by the life of his best thoughts, not to touch so much as a hair of Sancho's coat,† but entirely leave it to his discretion to whip himself when he thought fit. With that, Sancho got up from him, and removed his quarters to another place at a good distance, but as he went to lean against a tree, he perceived something bobbing at his head, and, lifting up his hands, found it to be a man's feet, with shoes and stockings on: quaking for fear, he moved off to another tree, where the like impending horror dangled over his head. Straight he called out to Don Quixote for help. Don Quixote came, and inquiring into the occasion of his fright, Sancho answered, that all those trees were full of men's feet and legs. Don Quixote began to search and grope about, and, falling presently into the account of the business, 'Fear nothing, Sancho,' said he, 'there is no danger at all: for what thou feelest in the dark are certainly the feet and legs of some banditti and robbers, that have been hanged upon those trees; for here the officers of justice hang them up by twenties and thirties in clusters, by which I suppose we cannot be far from Barcelona;' and indeed he guessed right.

And now day breaking, they lifted up their eyes and saw the bodies of the highwaymen hanging on the trees: but if the dead surprised them, how much more were they disturbed at the appearance of about forty live banditti, who poured upon them, and surrounded them on a sudden, charging them in the Catalan tongue, to stand till their captain came.

Don Quixote found himself on foot, his horse unbridled, his lance against a tree at some distance, and, in short, void of all defence; and therefore he was forced to put his arms across, hold down his head, and shrug up his shoulders, reserving himself for a better opportunity. The robbers presently fell to work, and began to rifle Dapple, leaving on his back nothing of what he carried, either in the wallet or the cloak-bag; and it was very well for Sancho, that the Duke's pieces of gold, and those he

---

* Henry the Bastard, afterwards King of Castile, being about to murder Pedro, the lawful king; as they struggled, he fell under him, when Beltan Claquin, a Frenchman that served Henry, coming to assistance, turned him a-top of Pedro, speaking at the same time those words that Sancho repeats.

† *Ropa* in the original, which signifies 'all that belongs to a man's clothing.' Stevens translates it 'Hair of his head.' The French translator has it right, *Poil de la robe*. How Jarvis has it, I know not; but I make no doubt of its being right, as having been supervised by the learned and polite Dr. O—d and Mr. P—.

brought from home, were hid in a girdle about his waist; though for all that, those honest gentlemen would certainly have taken the pains to have searched and surveyed him all over, and would have had the gold, though they had stripped him of his skin to come at it; but by good fortune their captain came in the interim. He seemed about four and thirty years of age, his body robust, his stature tall, his visage austere, and his complexion swarthy. He was mounted on a strong horse, wore a coat of mail, and no less than two pistols on each side. Perceiving that his squires (for so they called men of that profession in those parts) were going to strip Sancho, he ordered them to forbear, and was instantly obeyed, by which means the girdle escaped. He wondered to see a lance reared up against a tree, a shield on the ground, and Don Quixote in armour and pensive, with the saddest, most melancholy countenance that despair itself could frame. Coming up to him, 'Be not so sad, honest man,' said he; 'you have not fallen into the hands of some cruel Osiris, but into those of Roque Guinart, a man rather compassionate than severe.' 'I am not sad,' answered Don Quixote, 'for having fallen into thy power, valorous Roque, whose boundless fame spreads through the universe, but for having been so remiss as to be surprised by thy soldiers with my horse unbridled; whereas, according to the order of chivalry-errant, which I profess, I am obliged to live always upon my guard, and at all hours be my own sentinel; for, let me tell thee, great Roque, had they met me mounted on my steed, armed with my shield and lance, they would have found it no easy task to make me yield; for, know, I am Don Quixote de la Mancha, the same whose exploits are celebrated through all the habitable globe.'

Roque Guinart found out immediately Don Quixote's blind side, and judged there was more madness than valour in the case: now, though he had several times heard him mentioned in discourse, he could never believe what was related of him to be true, nor could he be persuaded that such a humour should reign in any man; for which reason he was very glad to have met him, that experience might convince him of the truth. Therefore, addressing himself to him, 'Valorous knight,' said he, 'vex not yourself, nor tax fortune with unkindness, for it may happen, that what you look upon now as a sad accident, may redound to your advantage: for Heaven, by strange and unaccountable ways, beyond the reach of human imagination, uses to raise up those that are fallen, and fill the poor with riches.' Don Quixote was going to return him thanks, when from behind them they heard a noise like the trampling of several horses, though it was occasioned but by one, on which came full speed a person that looked like a gentleman about twenty years of age. He was clad in green damask edged with gold-galloon suitable to his waistcoat, a hat turned up behind, strait wax-leather boots, his spurs, sword, and dagger gilt, a light bird-piece in his hand, and a case of pistols before him. Roque having turned his head at the noise, discovered the handsome apparition, which approaching nearer, spoke to him in this manner.

'You are the gentleman I looked for, valiant Roque; for with you I may perhaps find some comfort, though not a remedy, in my affliction. In short, not to hold you in suspense, for I am sensible you do not know me, I will tell you who I am. My name is Claudia Jeronima; I am the daughter of your particular friend Simon Forte, sworn foe to Clauquel Torrelas, who is also your enemy, being one of your adverse faction. You already know, this Torrelas had a son whom they call Don Vincente Torrelas, at least he was called so within these two hours. That son of his, to be short in my sad story, I will tell you in four words what sorrow he has brought me to. He saw me, courted me, was heard, and was beloved. Our amour was carried on with so much secrecy, that my father knew nothing of it; for there is no woman, though ever so retired and closely looked to, but can find time enough to compass and fulfil her unruly desires. In short, he made me a promise of marriage, and I the like to him, but without proceeding any further. Now yesterday I understood, that, forgetting his engagements to me, he was going to wed another, and that they were to be married this morning; a piece of news that quite distracted me, and made me lose all patience. Therefore, my father being out of town, I took the opportunity of equipping myself as you see, and by the speed of this horse overtook Don Vincente about a league hence, where, without urging my wrongs, or staying to hear his excuses, I fired at him, not only with this piece, but with both my pistols, and, as I believe, shot him through the body, thus with his heart's blood washing away the stains of my honour. This done, there I left him to his servants, who neither dared nor could prevent the sudden execution; and came to seek your protection, that by your means I may be conducted into France, where I have relations to entertain me; and withal to beg of you to defend my father from Don Vincente's party, who might otherwise revenge his death upon our family.'

Roque admiring at once the resolution, agreeable deportment, and handsome figure of the beautiful Claudia: 'Come, madam,' said he, 'let us first be assured of your enemy's death, and then consider what is to be done for you.' 'Hold,' cried Don Quixote, who had hearkened with great attention to all this discourse, 'none of you need trouble yourselves with this affair, the defence of the lady is my province. Give me my horse and arms, and stay for me here: I will go and find out this knight, and, dead or alive, force him to perform his obligations to so great a beauty.' 'Ay, ay,' quoth Sancho, 'you may take his word for it, my master has a rare stroke at making matches; it is but the other day he made a young rogue yield to marry a maid whom he would have left in the lurch, after he was promised to her; and had it not been for the enchanters that plague his worship, who transmogrified the bridegroom into a footman, and broke off the match, the said maid had been none by this time.'

Roque was so much taken up with the thoughts of Claudia's adventure, that he little minded either master or man; but ordering his squires to restore what they had taken from Dapple to Sancho, and to retire to the place where they had quartered the night before, he went off upon the spur with Claudia, to find the expiring Don Vincente. They got to the place where Claudia met him, and found nothing but the marks of blood newly spilt; but looking round about them, they discovered a company of people at a distance on the side of a hill, and presently judged them to be Don Vincente carried by his servants either to his cure or burial. They hastened to overtake them, which they soon effected, the others going but slowly; and they found the young gentleman in the arms of his servants, desiring them with a spent and fainting voice to let him die in that place, his wounds paining him so that he could not bear going any further. Claudia and Roque dismounting, hastily came up to him. The servants were startled at the appearance of Roque, and Claudia was troubled at the sight of Don Vincente; and, divided between anger and compassion, 'Had you given me this, and made good your promise,' said she to him, laying hold of his hand, 'you had never brought this misfortune upon yourself.' The wounded gentleman, lifting up his languishing eyes, and knowing Claudia, 'Now do I see,' said he, 'my fair deluded mistress, it is you that has given me the fatal blow, a punishment never deserved by the innocent unfortunate Vincente, whose actions and desires had no other end but that of serving his Claudia.' 'What, sir,' answered she, presently, 'can you deny that you went this morning to marry Leonora, the daughter of wealthy Balvastro?' 'It is all a false report,' answered he, 'raised by my evil stars to spur up your jealousy to take my life, which since I leave in your fair hands, I reckon well disposed of; and to confirm this truth, give me your hand, and receive mine, the last pledge of love and life, and take me for your husband: it is the only satisfaction I have to give for the imaginary wrong you suspect I have committed.' Claudia pressed his hand, and being pierced at once to the very heart, dropped on his bloody breast into a swoon, and Don Vincente fainted away into a deadly trance.

Roque's concern struck him senseless, and the servants ran for water to throw in the faces of the unhappy couple; by which at last Claudia came to herself again, but Don Vincente never waked from his trance, but breathed out the last remainder of his life. When Claudia perceived this, and could no longer doubt but that her dear husband was irrecoverably dead, she burst the air with her sighs, and wounded the heavens with her complaints. She tore her hair, scattered it in the wind, and with her merciless hands disfigured her face, showing all the lively marks of grief that the first sallies of despair can discover. 'Oh, cruel and inconsiderate woman,' cried she, 'how easily wast thou set on this barbarous execution! Oh, madding sting of jealousy, how desperate are thy motions, and how tragic the effects! Oh, my unfortunate husband, whose sincere love and fidelity to me have thus, for his nuptial bed, brought me to the cold grave!' Thus the poor lady went on in so sad and moving a strain, that even Roque's rugged temper now melted into tears, which on all occasions had still been strangers to his eyes. The servants wept and lamented, Claudia relapsed into her swooning as fast as they found means to bring her to life again; and the whole appearance was a most moving scene of sorrow. At last Roque Guinart bid Don Vincente's servants carry his body to his father's house, which was not far distant, in order to have it buried. Claudia communicated to Roque her resolution of retiring into a monastery, where an aunt of hers was abbess, there to spend the rest of her life, wedded to a better and an immortal bridegroom. He commended her pious resolution, offering to conduct her whither she pleased, and to protect her father and family from all assaults and practices of their most dangerous enemies. Claudia made a modest excuse for declining his company, and took leave of him weeping. Don Vincente's servants carried off the dead body, and Roque returned to his men. Thus ended Claudia Jeronima's amour, brought to so lamentable a catastrophe by the prevailing force of a cruel and desperate jealousy.

Roque Guinart found his crew where he had appointed, and Don Quixote in the middle of them, mounted on Rozinante, and declaiming very copiously against their way of living, at once dangerous to their bodies, and destructive to their souls; but his auditory being chiefly composed of Gascoigns, a wild, unruly kind of people, all his morality was thrown away upon them. Roque, upon his arrival, asked Sancho if they had restored him all his things. 'Everything, sir,' answered Sancho, 'but three night-caps, that are worth a king's ransom.' 'What says the fellow' cried one of the robbers. 'Here they be, and they are not worth three reals.' 'As to the intrinsic value,' replied Don Quixote, 'they may be worth no more, but it is the merit of the person that gave them me that raises their value to that price.'

Roque ordered them to be restored immediately; and commanding his men to draw up in a line, he caused all the clothes, jewels, money, and all the other booty they had got since the last contribution, to be brought before him; then readily apprising every particular, and reducing into money what could not be divided, he cast up the account of the whole, and then made a just dividend into parts, paying to every man his exact and due proportion with so much prudence and equity, that he failed not in the least point of distributive justice. The booty thus shared to the general satisfaction, 'If it were not for this punctual management,' said Roque, turning to Don Quixote, 'there would be no living among us.'

'Well,' quoth Sancho, 'justice must needs be a good thing, and the old proverb still holds good, "Thieves are never rogues among themselves." ' One of the banditti overhearing him, cocked his gun, and would certainly have shot him through the head, had not the captain commanded him to hold. Poor Sancho was struck as mute as a fish, and resolved not to open his lips once more, till he got into better company.

By this time, came one or two of their scouts that were posted on the road, and informed their captain that they had discovered a great company of travellers on the way to Barcelona. 'Are they such as we look for,' asked Roque, 'or such as look for us?' 'Such as we look for, sir,' answered the fellow. 'Away then,' cried Roque, 'all of ye, my boys, and bring them me hither straight; let none escape.' The squires presently obeyed the word of command, and left Don Quixote, Roque, and Sancho to wait their return. In the mean time Roque entertained the Knight with some remarks on his way of living. 'I should not wonder,' said he, 'Signor Don Quixote, that our life should appear to you a restless complication of hazards and disquiets; for it is no more than what daily experience has made me sensible of. You must know, that this barbarity and austere behaviour which I affect to show is a pure force upon my nature, being urged to this extremity by the resentment of some severe injuries, which I could not put up without a satisfactory revenge, and now I am in, I must go through; one sin draws on another, in spite of my better designs; and I am now involved in such a chain of wrongs, factions, abetters, and engagements, that no less than the divine power of providence can free me from this maze of confusion: nevertheless, I despair not still of a successful end of my misfortunes.'

Don Quixote, being surprised to hear such sound sense, and sober reflection, come from one whose disorderly profession was so opposite to discretion and politeness. 'Signor Roque,' said he, 'it is a great step to health for a man to understand his distemper, and the compliance of the patient to the rules of physic is reckoned half the cure. You appear sensible of the malady, and therefore may reasonably expect a remedy, though your disease, being fixed by a long inveteracy, must subject you, I am afraid, to a tedious course. The Almighty Physician will apply effectual medicines: therefore be of good heart, and do your part towards the recovery of your sick conscience. If you have a mind to take the shortest road to happiness, immediately abandon the fatal profession you now follow, and come under my tuition, to be instructed in the rules of knight-errantry, which will soon expiate your offences, and entitle you to honour, and true felicity.' Roque smiled to hear Don Quixote's serious advice, and changing the discourse, gave him an account of Claudia Jeronima's tragical adventure, which grieved Sancho to the heart; for the beauty, life, and spirit of the young damsel, had not a little wrought upon his affections.

By this time Roque's party had brought in their prize, consisting of two gentlemen on horseback, and two pilgrims on foot, and a coach full of women, attended by some half a dozen servants on foot and on horseback, besides two muleteers that belonged to the two gentlemen. They were all conducted in solemn order, surrounded by the victors, both they and the vanquished being silent, and expecting the definitive sentence of the grand Roque. He first asked the gentlemen who they were, whither bound, and what money they had about them. They answered, that they were both captains of Spanish foot, and their companies were at Naples; and they designed to embark on the four galleys, which they heard were bound for Sicily, and their whole stock amounted to two or three hundred crowns, which they thought a pretty sum of money for men of their profession, who seldom use to hoard up riches. The pilgrims being examined in like manner, said, they intended to embark for Rome, and had about some threescore reals between them both. Upon examining the coach, he was informed by one of the servants, that my Lady Donna Guiomar de Quinones, wife to a judge of Naples, with her little daughter, a chamber-maid, and an old duena, together with six other servants, had among them all about six hundred crowns. 'So then,' said Roque, 'we have got here in all nine hundred crowns and sixty reals. I think I have got about threescore soldiers here with me. Now among so many men how much will fall to each particular share? Let me see, for I am none of the best accountants. Cast it up, gentlemen.' The highwaymen hearing this, cried, 'Long live Roque Guinart, and damn the dogs that seek his ruin.' The officers looked simply, the Lady was sadly dejected, and the pilgrims were no less cast down, thinking this a very odd confiscation of their little stock. Roque held them a while in suspense to observe their humours, which he found all very plainly agree in that point, of being melancholy for the loss of their money: then turning to the officers, 'Do me the favour, captains,' said he, 'to lend me threescore crowns; and you, madam, if your Ladyship pleases, shall oblige me with fourscore, to gratify these honest gentlemen of my squadron: it is our whole estate and fortune; and you know, the abbot dines on what he sings for. Therefore I hope you will excuse our demands, which will free you from any more disturbance of this nature, being secured by a pass, which I shall give you, directed to the rest of my squadrons that are posted in these parts, and who, by virtue of my order, will let you go unmolested; for I scorn to wrong a soldier, and I must not fail in my respects, madam, to the fair sex, especially to ladies of your quality.'

The captains, with all the grace they could, thanked him for his great civility and liberality, for so they esteemed his letting them keep their own money. The Lady would have thrown herself out of the coach at his feet, but Roque would not suffer it, rather excusing the presumption of his demands, which he was forced to, in pure compliance with the necessity of his fortune. The Lady then ordered one of her servants to pay immediately the fourscore crowns. The officers disbursed their quota, and the pilgrims made an oblation of their mite; but Roque ordering them to wait a little, and turning to his men, 'Gentlemen,' said he, 'here are two crowns a-piece for each of you, and twenty over and above. Now let us bestow ten of them on these poor pilgrims, and the other ten on this honest squire, that he may give us a good word in his travels.' So calling for pen, ink, and paper, of which he always went provided, he wrote a passport for them, directed to the commanders of his several parties, and taking his leave, dismissed them, all wondering at his greatness of soul, that spoke rather an Alexander than a professed highwayman. One of his men began to mutter in his Catalan language: 'This captain of ours is plaguy charitable, he would make a better friar than a pad; come, come, if he has a mind to be so liberal forsooth, let his own pocket, not ours, pay for it.' The wretch spoke not so low, but he was overheard by Roque, who, whipping out his sword, with one stroke almost cleft his skull in two. 'Thus it is I punish mutiny,' said he. All the rest stood motionless, and durst not mutter one word, so great was the awe they bore him. Roque then withdrew a little, and wrote a letter to a friend of his in Barcelona, to let him know that the famous knight-errant Don Quixote, of whom so many strange things were reported, was with him; that he might be sure to find him on Midsummerday on the great quay of that city, armed at all points, mounted on Rozinante, and his squire on an ass; that he was a most pleasant, ingenious person, and would give great satisfaction to him and his friends the Niarri, for which reason he gave them this notice of the Don's coming; adding, that he should by no means let the Cadelli, his enemies, partake of this pleasure, as being unworthy of it: but how was it possible to conceal from them, or anybody else, the folly and discretion of Don Quixote, and the buffoonery of Sancho Pança? He delivered the letter to one of his men, who changing his highway clothes to a countryman's habit, went to Barcelona, and gave it as directed.

CHAPTER LXI

Don Quixote's entry into Barcelona, with other Accidents that have less ingenuity in them than truth

DON QUIXOTE stayed three days and three nights with Roque, and had he tarried as many hundred years, he might have found subject enough for admiration in that kind of life. They slept in one place, and eat in another, sometimes fearing they knew not what, then lying in wait for they knew not whom. Sometimes forced to steal a nap standing, never enjoying a sound sleep. Now in this side the country, then presently in another quarter; always upon the watch, spies hearkening, scouts listening, carbines presenting; though of such heavy guns they had but few, being armed generally with pistols. Roque himself slept apart from the rest, making no man privy to his lodgings; for so many were the proclamations against him from the Viceroy of Barcelona, and such were his disquiets and fears of being betrayed by some of his men for the price of his head, that he durst trust nobody. A life most miserable and uneasy. At length, by cross-roads and by-ways, Roque, Don Quixote, and Sancho attended by six other squires, got to the strand of Barcelona on Midsummer-eve at night; where Roque, having embraced Don Quixote, and presented Sancho with the ten crowns he had promised him, took his leave of them both, after many compliments on both sides. Roque returned to his company, and Don Quixote stayed there waiting the approach of day, mounted as Roque left him. Not long after the fair Aurora began to peep through the balconies of the east, cheering the flowery fields, while at the same time a melodious sound of hautboys and kettle-drums cheered the ears, and presently was joined with jingling of morice-bells, and the trampling and cries of horsemen coming out of the city. Now Aurora ushered up the jolly sun, who looked big on the verge of the horizon, with his broad face as ample as a target. Don Quixote and Sancho, casting their looks abroad, discovered the sea, which they had never seen before. To them it made a noble and spacious appearance, far bigger than the Lake Ruydera, which they saw in La Mancha. The galleys in the port taking in their awnings, made a pleasant sight with their flags and streamers, that waved in the air, and sometimes kissed and swept the water. The trumpets, hautboys, and other warlike instruments that resounded from on board, filled the air all round with reviving and martial harmony. A while after, the galleys moving, began to join on the calm sea in a counterfeit engagement; and at the same time a vast number of gentlemen marched out of the city, nobly equipped with rich liveries, and gallantly mounted, and in like manner did their part on the land, to complete the warlike entertainment. The marines discharged numerous volleys from the galleys, which were answered by the great guns from the battlements of the walls and forts about the city, and the mighty noise echoed from galleys again by a discharge of the long pieces of ordnance on their forecastles. The sea smiled and danced, the land was gay, and the sky serene in every quarter, but where the clouds of smoke dimmed it a while: fresh joy sat smiling in the looks of men, and gladness and pomp were displayed in their glory. Sancho was mightily puzzled though, to discover how these huge bulky things that moved on the sea could have so many feet.

By this time the gentlemen that maintained the sports on the shore, galloping up to Don Quixote with loud acclamations, the Knight was not a little astonished: one of them amongst the rest, who was the person to whom Roque had written, cried out aloud: 'Welcome, the mirror, the light, and north-star of knight-errantry! Welcome, I say, valorous Don Quixote de la Mancha, not the counterfeit and apocryphal, shown us lately in false histories, but the true, legitimate and identic He, described by Cid Hamet, the flower of historiographers!' Don Quixote made no answer, nor did the gentleman stay for any, but wheeling about with the rest of his companions, all prancing round him in token of joy, they encompassed the Knight and the squire. Don Quixote, turning about to Sancho, 'It seems,' said he, 'these gentlemen know us well. I dare engage they have read our history, and that which the Arragonian lately published.' The gentleman that spoke to the Knight, returning, 'Noble Don Quixote,' said he, 'we entreat you to come along with the company, being all your humble servants, and friends of Roque Guinart.' 'Sir,' answered Don Quixote, 'your courtesy bears such a likeness to the great Roque's generosity, that could civility beget civility, I should take yours for the daughter or near relation of his: I shall wait on you where you please to command, for I am wholly at your devotion.' The gentleman returned his compliment, and so all of them enclosing him in the middle of their brigade, they conducted him towards the city, drums beating, and hautboys playing before them all the way. But as the Devil and ill-luck would have it, or the boys, who are more unlucky than the Devil himself, two mischievous young bastards made a shift to get through the crowd of horsemen, and one of them lifting up Rozinante's tail, and the other that of Dapple, they thrust a handful of briers under each of them. The poor animals feeling such unusual spurs applied to their posteriors, clapped their tails close, and increased their pain and began to wince, and flounce, and kick so furiously, that at last they threw their riders, and laid both master and man sprawling in the street. Don Quixote, out of countenance, and nettled at his disgrace, went to disengage his horse from his new plumage, and Sancho did as much for Dapple, while the gentlemen turned to chastise the boys for their rudeness. But the young rogues were safe enough, being presently lost among a huge rabble that followed. The Knight and squire then mounted again, and the music and procession went on, till they arrived at their conductor's house, which, by its largeness and beauty, bespoke the owner master of a great estate; where we leave him for the present, because it is Cid Hamet's will and pleasure it should be so.

CHAPTER LXII

*The Adventure of the Enchanted Head, with other
impertinences not to be omitted*

THE PERSON who entertained Don Quixote, was called Don Antonio
Moreno, a gentleman of good parts, and plentiful fortune, loving all those
diversions that may innocently be obtained without prejudice to his
neighbours, and not of the humour of those, who would rather lose their
friend than their jest. He therefore resolved to make his advantage of Don
Quixote's follies without detriment to his person.

In order to this, he persuaded the Knight to take off his armour, and in
his strait-laced chamois-clothes (as we have already shown him) to stand
in a balcony that looked into one of the principal streets of the city, where
he stood exposed to the rabble that were got together, especially the boys,
who gaped and stared on him, as if he had been some overgrown baboon.
The several brigades and cavaliers in their liveries, began afresh to fetch
their careers about him, as if the ceremony were rather performed in
honour of Don Quixote than any solemnity of the festival. Sancho was
highly pleased, fancying he had chopped upon another Camachio's
wedding, or another house like that of Don Diego de Miranda, or some
castle like the Duke's.

Several of Don Antonio's friends dined with him that day, and all of
them honouring and respecting Don Quixote as a knight-errant, they
puffed up his vanity to such a degree that he could scarce conceal the
pleasure he took in their adulation. As for Sancho, he made such sport to
the servants of the house, and all that heard him, that they watched every
word that came from his mouth. Being all very merry at table, 'Honest
Sancho,' said Don Antonio, 'I am told you admire capons and sausages so
much, that you cannot be satisfied with a bellyful, and when you can eat no
more, you cram the rest into your breeches against the next morning.' 'No,
sir, if it like you,' answered Sancho, 'it is all a story, I am more cleanly than
greedy: I would have you know; here is my master can tell you, that many
times he and I use to live for a week together upon a handful of acorns and
walnuts. The truth is, I am not overnice; in such a place as this, I eat what is
given me; for a gift-horse should not be looked in the mouth. But
whosoever told you I was a greedy-gut and a sloven, has told you a fib; and
were it not for respect to the company, I would tell him more of my mind,
so I would.' 'Verily,' said Don Quixote, 'the manner of Sancho's feeding
ought to be delivered to succeeding ages on brazen monuments, as a future
memorial of his abstinence, and cleanliness, and an example to posterity. It
is true, when he satisfies the call of hunger, he seems to do it somewhat

ravenously; indeed he swallows apace, uses his grinders very notably, and chews with both jaws at once. But, in spite of the charge of slovenliness now laid upon him, I must declare, he is so nice an observer of neatness, that he ever makes a clear conveyance of his food; when he was governor, his nicety in eating was remarkable, for he would eat grapes, and even pomegranate-seeds with the point of his fork.' 'How,' cried Antonio, 'has Sancho then been a governor?' 'Ay, marry has he,' answered Sancho, 'governor of the island of Barataria. Ten days I governed, and who but I! But I was so broken of my rest all the time, that all I got by it was to learn to hate the trade of governing from the bottom of my soul. So that I made such haste to leave it, I fell into a deep hole, where I was buried alive, and should have lain till now, had not Providence pulled me out of it.' Don Quixote then related the circumstances of Sancho's government; and the cloth being taken away, Don Antonio took the Knight by the hand, and carried him into a private chamber, wherein there was no kind of furniture, but a table that seemed to be of jasper, supported by feet of the same, with a brazen head set upon it, from the breast upwards, like the effigies of one of the Roman emperors. Don Antonio having walked with Don Quixote several turns about the room, 'Signor Don Quixote,' said he, 'being assured that we are very private, the door fast, and nobody listening, I shall communicate to you one of the most strange and wonderful adventures that ever was known, provided you treasure it up as a secret in the closest apartment of your breast.' 'I shall be secret as the grave,' answered the Knight, 'and will clap a tombstone over your secret, for further security; besides, assure yourself, Don Antonio,' continued he (for by this time he had learned the gentleman's name), 'you converse with a person whose ears are open to receive what his tongue never betrays. So that whatever you commit to my trust, shall be buried in the depth of bottomless silence, and fie as secure as in your own breast.'

'In confidence of your honour,' said Don Antonio, 'I doubt not to raise your astonishment, and disburden my own breast of a secret, which has long lain upon my thoughts, having never found hitherto any person worthy to be made a confidant in matters to be concealed.' This cautious proceeding raised Don Quixote's curiosity strangely; after which Don Antonio led him to the table, and made him feel and examine all over the brazen head, the table and jasper supporters 'Now, sir,' said he, 'know, that this head was made by one of the greatest enchanters or necromancers in the world. If I am not mistaken, he was a Polander by birth, and the disciple of the celebrated Escotillo,* of whom so many prodigies are

* Or, Little Scot. Cervantes means Michael Scotus, who, being more knowing in natural and experimental philosophy than was common in the dark ages of ignorance, passed for a Magician; as Friar Bacon and Albert the Great did; of the first of whom (Friar Bacon) a like story of a brazen head is told.

related. This wonderful person was here in my house, and by the intercession of a thousand crowns, was wrought upon to frame me this head, which has the wonderful property of answering in your ear to all questions. After long study, erecting of schemes, casting of figures, consultations with the stars, and other mathematical operations, this head was brought to the aforesaid perfection; and tomorrow (for on Fridays it never speaks) it shall give you proof of its knowledge, till when you may consider of your most puzzling and important doubts, which will have a full and satisfactory solution.' Don Quixote was amazed at this strange virtue of the head, and could hardly credit Don Antonio's account; but, considering the shortness of the time that deferred his full satisfaction in the point, he was content to suspend his opinion till next day; and only thanked the gentleman for making him so great a discovery. So out of the chamber they went, and Don Antonio having locked the door very carefully, they returned into the room, where the rest of the company were diverted by Sancho's relating to them some of his master's adventures.

That afternoon they carried Don Quixote abroad without his armour, mounted, not on Rozinante, but on a large easy mule, with genteel furniture, and himself dressed after the city fashion, with a long coat of tawny-coloured cloth, which with the present heat of the season, was enough to put frost itself into a sweat. They gave private orders that Sancho should be entertained within doors all that day, lest he should spoil their sport by going out. The Knight being mounted, they pinned to his back, without his knowledge, a piece of parchment, with these words written in large letters: 'This is Don Quixote de la Mancha.' As soon as they began their walk, the sight of the parchment drew the eyes of everybody to read the inscription; so that the Knight hearing so many people repeat the words, 'This is Don Quixote de la Mancha,' wondered to hear himself named and known by every one that saw him: thereupon, turning to Don Antonio, that rode by his side: 'How great,' said he, 'is this single prerogative of knight-errantry, by which its professors are known and distinguished through all the confines of the universe! Do not you hear, sir,' continued he, 'how the very boys in the street, who have never seen me before, know me?' 'It is very true, sir,' answered Don Antonio, 'like fire that always discovers itself by its own light, so virtue has that lustre that never fails to display itself, especially that renown which is acquired by the profession of arms.'

During this procession of the Knight and his applauding followers, a certain Castilian reading the scroll at Don Quixote's back, cried out aloud, 'Now the Devil take thee for Don Quixote de la Mancha! Who would have thought to have found thee here, and still alive, after so many hearty drubbings that have been laid about thy shoulders? Cannot you be mad in private, and among your friends, with a pox to you, but you must run about the world at this rate, and make everybody that keeps you company as errant-coxcombs as yourself? Get you home to your wife and children, blockhead, look after your house, and leave playing the fool, and distracting thy senses at this rate with a parcel of nonsensical whimsies.' 'Friend,' said Don Antonio, 'go about your business, and keep your advice for them that want it. Signor Don Quixote is a man of too much sense, not to be above your counsel, and we know our business without your intermeddling. We only pay the respect due to virtue. So in the name of ill-luck, go your ways, and do not meddle where you have no business.' 'Truly,' said the Castilian, 'you are in the right, for it is but striving against the stream to give him advice, though it grieves me to think this whim of knight-errantry should spoil all the good parts which they say this madman has. But ill-luck light on me, as you would have it, and all my generation, if ever you catch me advising him or any one else again, though I were desired, and were to live to the years of Methusalem.' So saying, the adviser went his ways, and the cavalcade continued; but the rabble pressed so very thick to read the inscription, that Don Antonio was forced to pull it off, under pretence of doing something else.

Upon the approach of night they returned home, where Don Antonio's wife, a lady of quality, and every way accomplished, had invited several of her friends to a ball, to honour her guest, and share in the diversion his extravagance afforded. After a noble supper, the dancing begun about ten o'clock at night. Among others were two ladies of an airy, waggish disposition, such as though virtuous enough at the bottom, would not stick to strain a point of modesty for the diversion of good company. These two made their court chiefly to Don Quixote, and plied him so with dancing one after another, that they tired not only his body but his very soul. But the best was to see what an unaccountable figure the grave Don made, as he hopped and stalked about, a long, sway-backed, starved-looked, thin-flanked, two-legged thing, wainscot-complexioned, stuck up in his close doublet, awkward enough a-conscience, and certainly none of the lightest at a saraband. The ladies gave him several private hints of their inclinations to his person, and he was not behind hand in intimating to them as secretly, that they were very indifferent to him; till at last, being almost teased to death, '*Fugite partes adversae,*' cried he, aloud, 'and avaunt temptation! Pray, ladies, play your amorous pranks with somebody else, leave me to the enjoyment of my own thoughts, which are employed and taken up with the peerless Dulcinea del Toboso, the sole queen of my affection;' and so saying, he sat himself down on the ground in the midst of the hall to rest his wearied bones. Don Antonio gave order that he should be taken up and carried to bed; and the first who was ready to lend a helping hand was Sancho, and as he was lifting him up, 'By our Lady, sir, master of mine, you have shook your heels most cleverly. Do you think we, who are stout and valiant, must be caperers, and that every knight-errant must be a snapper of castanets? If you do, you are woundily deceived, let me tell you. Gadzookers, I know those who would sooner cut a giant's windpipe, than a caper. Had you been for the shoe-jig,* I had been your man; for I slap it away like any jerfaulcon; but as for regular dancing, I cannot work a stitch at it.' This made diversion for the company, till Sancho led out his master, in order to put him to bed, where he left him covered over head and ears, that he might sweat out the cold he had caught by dancing.

The next day Don Antonio resolving to make his intended experiment on the enchanted head, conducted Don Quixote into the room where it stood, together with Sancho, a couple of his friends, and the two ladies that had so teased the Knight at the ball, and who had stayed all night with his wife; and having carefully locked the door, and enjoined them secrecy, he told them the virtue of the head, and that this was the first time he ever made proof of it; and except his two friends, nobody did know the enchantment, and, had they not been told of it before, they had been drawn into the same error with the rest; for the contrivance of the machine was so artful and so cunningly managed, that it was impossible to discover the cheat. Don Antonio himself was the first that made his application to the ear of the head, close to which speaking in a voice just loud enough to be heard by the company: 'Tell me, O head,' said he, 'by that mysterious virtue wherewith thou art endued, what are my thoughts at present?' The head in a distinct and intelligible voice, though without moving the lips, answered, 'I am no judge of thoughts.' They were all astonished at the voice, being sensible nobody was in the room to answer. 'How many of us are there in the room?' said Don Antonio again. The voice answered in the same key, 'Thou and thy wife, two of thy friends, and two of hers, a famous knight called Don Quixote de la Mancha, and his squire, Sancho Pança by name.' Now their astonishment was greater than before, now they wondered indeed, and their hair stood on end with amazement. 'It is enough,' said Antonio, stepping aside from the head, 'I am convinced it was no impostor sold thee to me, sage head, discoursing head, oraculous, miraculous head! Now let somebody else try their fortunes.' As women are generally most curious and inquisitive, one of the ladies venturing up to it, 'Tell me, head,' said she, 'what shall I do to be truly beautiful.' 'Be honest,' answered the head. 'I have done,' replied the lady. Her companion then came on, and with the same curiosity, 'I would know,' said she, 'whether my husband loves me or no.' The head answered, 'Observe his usage, and that will tell thee.' 'Truly,' said the

---

* Shoe jig, in which the dancers slap the sole of their shoe with the palm of their hand in time and measure.

married lady to herself as she withdrew, 'that question was needless; for indeed a man's actions are the surest tokens of the dispositions of his mind.' Next came up one of Don Antonio's friends and asked, 'Who am I?' The answer was, 'Thou knowest.' 'That is from the question,' replied the gentleman, 'I would have thee tell me whether thou knowest me.' 'I do,' answered the head, 'thou art Don Pedro Norris.' 'It is enough, O head,' said the gentleman, 'thou hast convinced me, that thou knowest all things.' So making room for somebody else, his friend advanced, and asked the head what his eldest son and heir desired. 'I have already told thee,' said the head, 'that I was no judge of thoughts; however, I will tell thee, that what thy heir desires is to bury thee.' 'It is so,' replied the gentleman; 'what I see with my eye, I mark with my finger; I know enough.'

Don Antonio's lady asked the next question: 'I do not well know what to ask thee,' said she to the head, 'only tell me whether I shall long enjoy my dear husband.' 'Thou shalt,' answered the head, 'for his healthy constitution and temperance promise length of days, while those who live too fast are not like to live long.' Next came Don Quixote: 'Tell me, thou oracle,' said he, 'was what I reported of my adventures in Montesinos' cave, a dream or reality? Will Sancho my squire fulfil his promise, and scourge himself effectually? and shall Dulcinea be disenchanted?' 'As for the adventures in the cave,' answered the head, 'there is much to be said: they have something of both; Sancho's whipping shall go on but leisurely; however, Dulcinea shall at last be really freed from enchantment.' 'That is all I desire to know,' said Don Quixote, 'for the whole stress of my good fortune depends on Dulcinea's disenchantment.' Then Sancho made the last application, 'An't please you, Mr. Head,' quoth he, 'shall I chance to have another government? Shall I ever get clear of this starving, squire-erranting? And shall I ever see my own fireside again?' The head answered, 'Thou shalt be a governor in thine own house; if thou goest home, thou mayest see thy own fireside again; and if thou leavest off thy service, thou shalt get clear of thy squireship.' 'Gadzookers,' cried Sancho, 'that is a very good one, I vow! a horse-head might have told all this; I could have prophesied thus much myself.' 'How now, brute,' said Don Quixote, 'what answers wouldst thou have, but what are pertinent to thy questions?' 'Nay' quoth Sancho, 'since you will have it so, it shall be so; I only wish Mr. Head would have told me a little more concerning the matter.'

Thus the questions proposed, and the answers returned, were brought to a period, but the amazement continued among all the company, except Don Antonio's two friends, who understood the mystery, which Benengeli is resolved now to discover, that the world should be no longer amazed with an erroneous opinion of any magic or witchcraft operating in the head. He therefore tells you, that Don Antonio Moreno, to divert himself, and surprise the ignorant, had this made in imitation of such another device, which he had seen contrived by a statuary at Madrid.

The manner of it was thus; the table and the frame on which it stood, the feet of which resembled four eagle's claws, were of wood, painted and varnished like jasper. The head, which looked like the bust of a Roman emperor, and of a brass colour, was all hollow, and so were the feet of the table, which answered exactly to the neck and breast of the head; the whole so artificially fixed, that it seemed to be all of a piece; through this cavity ran a tin pipe, conveyed into it by a passage through the ceiling of the room under the table. He that was to answer set his mouth to the end of the pipe in the chamber underneath, and by the hollowness of the trunk received their questions, and delivered his answers in clear and articulate words, so that the imposture could scarcely be discovered. The oracle was managed by a young ingenious gentleman, Don Antonio's nephew, who, having his instructions beforehand from his uncle, was able to answer readily and directly to the first questions, and by conjectures or evasions, make a return handsomely to the rest, with the help of his ingenuity. Cid Hamet informs us further, that during ten or twelve days after this, the wonderful machine continued in mighty repute; but at last the noise of Don Antonio's having an enchanted head in his house, that gave answers to all questions, began to fly about the city; and as he feared this would reach the ears of the watchful sentinels of our faith, he thought fit to give an account of the whole matter to the reverend inquisitors, who ordered him to break it to pieces lest it should give occasion of scandal among the ignorant vulgar. But still the head passed for an oracle, and a piece of enchantment with Don Quixote and Sancho, though the truth is, the Knight was much better satisfied in the matter than the squire.

The gentry of the city, in complaisance to Don Antonio, and for Don Quixote's more splendid entertainment, or rather to make his madness a more public diversion, appointed a running at the ring about six days after, but this was broken off upon an occasion that afterwards happened.

Don Quixote had a mind to take a turn in the city on foot, that he might avoid the crowd of boys that followed him when he rode. He went out with Sancho and two of Don Antonio's servants, that attended him by their master's order; and passing through a certain street, Don Quixote looked up, and spied written over a door, in great letters, these words, 'Here is a printing-house.' This discovery pleased the Knight extremely, having now an opportunity of seeing a printing-press, a thing he had never seen before: and, therefore, to satisfy his curiosity, in he went with all his train. There he saw some working off the sheets, others correcting the formes, some in one place picking of letters out of the cases, in another some looking over a proof; in short, all the variety that is to be seen in great printing-houses. He went from one workman to another, and was very inquisitive to know what everybody had in hand; and they were not backward to satisfy his curiosity. At length coming to one of the compositors, and asking him what he was about: 'Sir,' said the printer, 'this gentleman here' (showing a likely sort of a man, something grave, and not young), 'has translated a book out of Italian into Spanish, and I am setting some of it here for the press.' 'What is the name of it pray?' said Don Quixote. 'Sir,' answered the author, 'the title of it in Italian is "*Le Bagetelle*."' 'And pray, sir,' asked Don Quixote, 'what is the meaning of that word in Spanish?' 'Sir,' answered the gentleman, '*Le Bagetelle* is as much as to say, Trifles; but though the title promises so little, yet the contents are matters of importance.' 'I am a little conversant in the Italian,' said the Knight, 'and value myself upon singing some stanzas of Ariosto; therefore, sir, without any offence, and not doubting of your skill, but merely to satisfy my curiosity, pray tell me, have you ever met with such a word as *Pignata* in Italian?' 'Yes, very often, sir,' answered the author. 'And how do you render it, pray?' said Don Quixote. 'How should I render it, sir,' replied the translator, 'but by the word Porridge-pot?' 'Body of me,' cried Don Quixote, 'you are master of the Italian idiom. I dare hold a good wager, that where the Italian says *Piace*, you translate it Please; where it says, *Piu*, you render it More; *Su*, Above, and *Giu*, Beneath.' 'Most certainly, sir,' answered the other, 'for such are their proper significations.' 'What rare parts,' said Don Quixote, 'are lost to mankind for want of their being exerted and known! I dare swear, sir, that the world is backward in encouraging your merit. But it is the fate of all ingenious men: how many of them are cramped up and discountenanced by a narrow fortune? and how many, in spite of the most laborious industry, discouraged? Though, by the way, sir, I think this kind of version from one language to another, except it be from the noblest of tongues, the Greek and Latin, is like viewing a piece of Flemish tapestry on the wrong side, where though the figures are distinguishable yet there are so many ends and threads, that the beauty and exactness of the work is obscured, and not so advantageously discerned as on the right side of the hangings. Neither can this barren employment of translating out of easy languages show either wit or mastery of style, no more than copying a piece of writing by a precedent; though still the business of translating wants not its commendations, since men very often may be worse employed. As a further proof of its merits, we have Dr. Christoval de Figuero's translation of "Pastor Fido," and Don Juan de Xaurigui's "Aminta," pieces so excellently well done, that they have made them purely their own, and left the reader in doubt which was the translation, and which the original. But tell me, pray, sir, do you print your book at your own charge, or have you sold the copy to a bookseller?' 'Why truly, sir,' answered the translator, 'I publish it upon my own account, and I hope to clear at least a thousand crowns by this first edition; for I design to print off two thousand books, and they will go off at six reals apiece in a trice.' 'I am afraid you will come short of your reckoning,' said Don Quixote; 'it is a sign you are still a stranger to the tricks of these booksellers and printers, and the juggling there is among them. I dare engage you will find two thousand books lie heavy upon your hands, especially if the piece be somewhat tedious, and wants spirit.' 'What, sir,' replied the author, 'would you have me sell the profit of my labour to a bookseller for three maravadis a sheet? for that is the most they will bid, nay, and expect too I should thank them for the offer. No, no, sir, I print not my works to get fame in the world, my name is up already; profit, sir, is my end, and without it what signifies reputation?' 'Well, sir, go on and prosper,' said Don Quixote, and with that moving to another part of the room, he saw a man correcting a sheet of a book called 'The Light of the Soul.' 'Ay, now, this is something,' cried the Knight, 'these are the books that ought to be printed, though there are a great many of that kind; for the number of sinners is prodigious in this age, and there is need of an infinite quantity of lights for so many dark souls as we have among us.' Then passing on, and inquiring the title of a book, of which another man was correcting a sheet, they told him it was the Second Part of that ingenious gentleman 'Don Quixote de la Mancha,' written by a certain person, a native of Tordesillas. 'I have heard of that book,' said Don Quixote, 'and really thought it had been burnt, and reduced to ashes for a foolish impertinent libel; but all in good time. Execution day will come at last.* For made stories are only so far good and agreeable, as they are profitable, and bear the resemblance of truth; and true history the more valuable, the further it keeps from the fabulous.' And so saying, he flung out of the printing-house in a huff.

That very day Don Antonio would needs show Don Quixote the galleys in the road, much to Sancho's satisfaction, because he had never seen any in his life. Don Antonio therefore gave notice to the commander of the galleys, that in the afternoon he would bring his guest, Don Quixote de la Mancha, to see them, the commander and all the people of the town being by this time no strangers to the Knight's character. But what happened in the galleys, must be the subject of the next chapter.

---

* Martimas, or about the feast of St. Martin, is the time for making bacon for winter. Hence this Spanish proverb.

CHAPTER LXIII

Of Sancho's Misfortune on board the Galleys, with the strange Adventures of the beautiful Morisca (Moorish lady)

MANY AND SERIOUS were Don Quixote's reflections on the answer of the enchanted head, though none hit on the deceit, but centred all in the promise of Dulcinea's disenchantment; and expecting it would speedily be effected, he rested joyfully satisfied. As for Sancho, though he hated the trouble of being a governor, yet still he had an itching ambition to rule, to be obeyed, and appear great; for even fools love authority.

In short, that afternoon Don Antonio, his two friends, Don Quixote, and Sancho, set out for the galleys. The commander being advertised of their coming, upon their appearance on the quay, ordered all the galleys to strike sail; the music played, and a pinnace spread with rich carpets and crimson-velvet cushions was presently hoisted out, and sent to fetch them on board. As soon as Don Quixote set his foot into it, the admiral galley discharged her forecastle piece, and the rest of the galleys did the like. When Don Quixote got over the gunnel of the galley on the starboard side, the whole crew of slaves, according to their custom of saluting persons of quality, welcomed him with three 'hu, hu, huz,' or huzzas. The general (for so we must call him) by birth a Valencian, and a man of quality, gave him his hand, and embraced him. 'This day,' said he, 'will I mark as one of the happiest I expect to see in all my life, since I have the honour now to see Signor Don Quixote de la Mancha; this day, I say, that sets before my eyes the summary of wandering chivalry collected in one person.' Don Quixote returned his compliment with no less civility, and appeared overjoyed to see himself so treated like a grandee. Presently they all went into the state-room, which was handsomely adorned, and there they took their places. The boatswain went to the forecastle, and, with his whistle or call gave the sign to the slaves to strip, which was obeyed in a moment. Sancho was scared to see so many fellows in their naked skins, but most of all, when he saw them hoist up the sails so incredibly fast, as he thought could never have been done but by so many devils. He had placed himself amidship, next the aftmost rower on the starboard side; who, being instructed what to do, caught hold of him, and giving him a hoist, handed him to the next man, who tossed him to a third; and so the whole crew of slaves, beginning on the starboard side, made him fly so fast from bench to bench, that poor Sancho lost the very sight of his eyes, and verily believed all the devils in hell were carrying him away to rights. Nor did the slaves give over bandying him about, till they had handed him in the same manner over all the larboard side; and then they did set him down where they had taken him up, but strangely disordered, out of breath, in a cold sweat, and not truly sensible what it was that happened to him.

Don Quixote seeing his squire fly at this rate without wings, asked the general if that were a ceremony used to all strangers aboard the galleys; for, if it were, he must let him know, that as he did not design to take up his residence there, he did not like such entertainment; and vowed to Heaven, that if any of them came to lay hold on him, to toss him at that rate, he would spurn their souls out of their bodies; and, with this, starting up, he lays his hand on his sword.

At the same time they lowered their sails, and, with a dreadful noise, let down the mainyard; which so frightened Sancho, who thought the sky was flying off its hinges, and falling upon him, that he ducked and thrust his head between his legs for fear. Don Quixote was a little out of sorts too, he began to shiver, and shrug up his shoulders, and changed colour. The slaves hoisted the mainyard again with the same force and noise that they had lowered it withal. But all this with such silence on their parts, as if they had neither voice nor breath. The boatswain then gave the word to weigh anchor; and leaping atop of the forecastle among the crew, with his whip or bull's-pizzle, he began to dust and fly-flap their shoulders, and by little and little to put off to sea.

When Sancho saw so many coloured feet moving at once, for he took the oars to be such: 'Beshrew my heart,' quoth he, 'here is enchantment in good earnest; all our adventures and witchcrafts have been nothing to this. What have these poor wretches done, that their hides must be curried at this rate? And how dares this plaguy fellow go whistling about here by himself, and maul thus so many people? Well, I say this is hell, or purgatory at least.'

Don Quixote observing how earnestly Sancho looked on these passages: 'Ah! dear Sancho,' said he, 'what an easy matter now were it for you to strip to the waist, and clap yourself among these gentlemen, and so complete Dulcinea's disenchantment; among so many companions in affliction, you would not be so sensible of the smart; and besides, the sage Merlin perhaps might take every one of these lashes, being so well laid on, for ten of those which you must certainly one day inflict on yourself.' The general of the galleys was going to ask what he meant by these lashes, and Dulcinea's disenchantment, when a mariner cried out, 'They make signs to us from Monjoui* that there is a vessel standing under the shore to the

---

* Monjoui is a high tower at Barcelona, on which always stands a sentinel who by signs gives notice what vessels he discovers at sea.

westward.' With that, the general leaping upon the coursey, cried, 'Pull away, my hearts, let her not escape us; this brigantine is an Algerine, I warrant her.' Presently the three other galleys came up with the admiral to receive orders, and he commanded two of them to stand out to sea, while he with the other would keep along the shore, that so they might be sure of their prize.

The rowers tugged so hard that the galleys scudded away like lightning, and those that stood to sea discovered, about two miles off, a vessel with fourteen or fifteen oars, which, upon sight of the galleys, made the best of her way off, hoping by her lightness to make her escape, but all in vain; for the admiral's galley being one of the swiftest vessels in those seas, gained so much way upon her, that the master of the brigantine, seeing his danger, was willing the crew should quit their oars, and yield, for fear of exasperating their general. But fate ordered it otherwise; for upon the admiral's coming up with the brigantine so near as to hail her, and bid them strike, two Toraquis, that is, two drunken Turks, among twelve others that were on board the vessel, discharged a couple of muskets, and killed two soldiers that were upon the prow of the galley. The general seeing this, vowed he would not leave a man of them alive; and coming up with great fury to grapple with her, she slipped away under the oars of the galley. The galley ran ahead a good way, and the little vessel finding herself clear for the present, though without hopes to get off, crowded all the sail she could, and with oars and sails, began to make the best of their way, while the galley tacked about. But all their diligence did not do them so much good as their presumption did them harm; for the admiral coming up with her, after a short chase, clapped his oars in the vessel, and so took her, and every man in her alive.

By this time the other galleys were come up, and all four returned with their prize into the harbour, where great numbers of people stood waiting, to know what prize they had taken. The general came to an anchor near the land, and perceiving the viceroy was on the shore, he manned his pinnace to fetch him aboard, and gave orders to lower the mainyard, to hang up the master of the brigantine, with the rest of the crew, which consisted of about six and thirty persons, all proper lusty fellows, and most of them Turkish musketeers. The general asked, who commanded the vessel; whereupon one of the prisoners, who was afterwards known to be a Spaniard, and a renegado, answered him in Spanish. 'This was our master, my Lord,' said he, showing him a young man not twenty years of age, and one of the handsomest persons that could be imagined. 'You inconsiderate dog,' said the general, 'what made you kill my men, when you saw it was not possible for you to escape? Is this the respect due to an admiral? Do not you know that rashness is no courage? While there is any hope, we are allowed to be bold, but not to be desperate.' The master was offering to reply, but the general could not stay to hear his answer, being obliged to go and entertain the viceroy, who was just come on board with his retinue and others of the town. 'You have had a lucky chase, my Lord,' said the viceroy; 'what have you got?' 'Your Excellency shall see presently,' answered the general. 'I will show them you immediately hanging at the mainyard arm.' 'How so?' replied the viceroy. 'Because,' said he, 'they have killed, contrary to all law of arms, reason, and custom of the sea, two of the best soldiers I had on board; for which I have sworn to hang them every mother's son, especially this young rogue, the master.' Saying thus, he showed him a person with his hands already bound, and the halter about his neck, expecting nothing but death. His youth, beauty, and resignation began to plead much in his behalf with the viceroy, and made him inclinable to save him: 'Tell me, captain,' said he, 'art thou born a Turk, or a Moor, or art thou a renegado?' 'None of all these,' answered the youth in good Spanish. 'What then?' said the viceroy. 'A Christian woman,' replied the youth; 'a woman, and a Christian, though in these clothes, and in such a post; but it is a thing rather to be wondered at, than believed. I humbly beseech ye, my lords,' continued the youth, 'to defer my execution till I give you the history of my life, and I can assure ye, the delay of your revenge will be but short.' This request was urged so piteously that nobody could deny it; whereupon the general bade him proceed, assuring him, nevertheless, that there was no hopes of pardon for an offence so great as was that of which he was guilty. Then the youth began.

'I am one of that unhappy and imprudent nation, whose miseries are fresh in your memories. My parents being of the Morisco race: the current of their misfortunes, with the obstinacy of two uncles, hurried me out of Spain into Barbary. In vain I professed myself a Christian, being really one, and not such a secret Mahometan as too many of us were; this could neither prevail with my uncles to leave me in my native country, nor with the severity of those officers that had ordered us to evacuate Spain, to believe it was not a pretence. My mother was a Christian, my father, a man of discretion, professed the same belief, and I sucked the Catholic faith with my milk. I was handsomely educated, and never betrayed the least mark of the Morisco breed, either in language or behaviour. With these endowments, as I grew up, that little beauty I had, if ever I had any, began to increase; and for all my retired life, and the restraint upon my appearing abroad, a young gentleman, called Don Gasper Gregorio, got a sight of me: he was son and heir to a knight that lived in the next town. It were tedious to relate, how he got an opportunity to converse with me, fell desperately in love, and affected me with a sense of his passion. I must be short, lest this halter cut me off in the middle of my story. I shall only tell you, that he would needs bear me company in my banishment, and accordingly, by the help of the Morisco language, of which he was a perfect master, he mingled with the exiles, and getting acquainted with my two uncles that conducted me, we all went together to Barbary, and took up our residence at Algiers, or rather hell itself.

'My father, in the mean time, had very prudently, upon the first news of the proclamation to banish us, withdrawn to seek a place of refuge for us in some foreign country, leaving a considerable stock of money and jewels hidden in a private place, which he discovered to nobody but me, with orders not to move it till his return.

'The king of Algiers, understanding I had some beauty, and also that I was rich, which afterwards turned to my advantage, sent for me, and was very inquisitive about my country, and what jewels and gold I had got. I satisfied him as to the place of my nativity, and gave him to understand, that my riches were buried in a certain place where I might easily recover them, were I permitted to return where they lay.

'This I told him, that in hopes of sharing in my fortune, his covetousness should divert him from injuring my person. In the midst of these questions, the king was informed, that a certain youth, the handsomest and loveliest in the world, had come over in company with us. I was presently conscious that Don Gregorio was the person, his beauty answering so exactly their description. The sense of the young gentleman's danger was now more grievous to me than my own misfortunes, having been told that those barbarous Turks are much fonder of a handsome youth, than the most beautiful woman. The king gave immediate orders he should be brought into his presence, asking me whether the youth deserved the commendations they gave him. I told him, inspired by some good angel, that the person they so much commended was no man, but of my own sex, and withal begged his permission to have her dressed in a female habit, that her beauty might shine in its natural lustre, and so prevent her blushes, if she should appear before His Majesty in that unbecoming habit. He consented, promising withal, to give order next morning for my return to Spain, to recover my treasure. I spoke with Don Gasper, represented to him the danger of appearing a man, and prevailed with him to wait on the king that evening in the habit of a Moorish woman. The king was so pleased with her beauty, that he resolved to reserve her as a present for the Grand Seignior; and fearing the malice of his wives in the Seraglio, and the solicitations of his own desires, he gave her in charge to some of the principal ladies of the city, to whose house she was immediately conducted.

'This separation was grievous to us both, for I cannot deny that I love him. Those who have ever felt the pangs of a parting love can best imagine the affliction of our souls. Next morning, by the king's order, I embarked for Spain in this vessel, accompanied by these two Turks that killed your men, and this Spanish renegado that first spoke to you, who is a Christian in his heart, and came along with me with a greater desire to return to Spain than to go back to Barbary. The rest are all Moors and Turks, who serve for rowers. Their orders were to set me on shore with this renegado, in the habits of Christians, on the first Spanish ground they should discover; but these two covetous and insolent Turks, would needs, contrary to their order, first cruise upon the coast, in hopes of taking some prize; being afraid, that if they should first set us ashore, some accident might happen to us, and make us discover that the brigantine was not far off at sea, and so expose them to the danger of being taken, if there were galleys upon the coast. In the night we made this land, not mistrusting any galley lying so near, and so we fell into your hands.

'To conclude, Don Gregorio remains in women's habit among the Moors, nor can the deceit long protect him from destruction; and here I stand expecting, or rather fearing my fate, which yet cannot prove unwelcome, I being now weary of living. Thus, gentlemen, you have heard the unhappy passages of my life; I have told you nothing but what is true, and all I have to beg is, that I may die as a Christian, since I am innocent of the crimes of which my unhappy nation is accused.' Here she stopped, and with her story and her tears melted the hearts of many of the company.

The viceroy being moved with a tender compassion, was the first to unbind the cords that manacled her fair hands, when an ancient pilgrim, who came on board with the viceroy's attendants, having with a fixed attention minded the damsel during her relation, came suddenly, and throwing himself at her feet, 'Oh! Anna Felix,' cried he, 'my dear unfortunate daughter! Behold thy father, Ricote, that returned to seek thee, being unable to live without thee, who art the joy and support of my age.' Upon this, Sancho, who had all this while been sullenly musing, vexed at the usage he had met with so lately, lifting up his head, and staring the pilgrim in the face, knew him to be the same Ricote he had met on the road the day he left his government, and was likewise fully persuaded, that this was his daughter, who being now unbound, embraced her father, and joined with him in his joy and grief. 'My lords,' said the old pilgrim, 'this is my daughter, Anna Felix, more unhappy in fortune than in name, and famed as much for her beauty as for her father's riches. I left my country to seek a sanctuary for my age, and having fixed upon a residence in Germany, returned in this habit with other pilgrims to dig up and regain my wealth, which I have effectually done; but I little thought thus unexpectedly to have found my greatest treasure, my dearest daughter. My lords, if it can consist with the integrity of your justice, to pardon our small offence, I join my prayers and tears with hers, to implore your mercy on our behalf; since we never designed you any injury, and are innocent of those crimes for which our nation has justly been banished.' 'Ay, ay,' cried Sancho, putting in, 'I know Ricote as well as the beggar knows his dish; and so far as concerns Anna Felix's being his daughter, I know that is true too; but for all the story of his goings-out and comings-in, and his intentions, whether they were good or whether they were bad, I will neither meddle nor make, not I.'

So uncommon an accident filled all the company with admiration; so that the general turning to the fair captain, 'Your tears,' said he, 'are so prevailing, madam, that they compel me now to be forsworn. Live, lovely Anna Felix, live as many years as Heaven has decreed you: and let those rash and insolent slaves, who alone committed the crimes, bear the punishment of it.' With that he gave order to have the two delinquent Turks hanged up at the yard-arm: but at the intercession of the viceroy, their fault showing rather madness than design, the fatal sentence was revoked; the general considering at the same time, that their punishment in cold blood would look more like cruelty than justice.

Then they began to consider how they might retrieve Don Gisper Gregorio from the danger he was in; to which purpose Raote offered to the value of above a thousand ducats, which he had about him in jewels, to purchase his ransom. But the readiest expedient was thought to be the proposal of the Spanish renegado, who offered, with a small bark and half-a-dozen oars manned by Christians, to return to Algiers, and set him at liberty, as best knowing when and where to land, and being acquainted with the place of his confinement. The general and the viceroy demurred to this motion, through a distrust of the renegado's fidelity, since he might perhaps betray the Christians that were to go along with him. But Anna Felix engaging for his truth, and Ricote obliging himself to ransom the Christians if they were taken, the design was resolved upon.

The viceroy went ashore, committing the Morisca and her father to Don Antonio Moreno's care, desiring him at the same time to command his house for anything that might conduce to their entertainment; such sentiments of kindness and good nature had the beauty of Anna Felix infused into his breast.

CHAPTER LXIV

Of an unlucky Adventure, which Don Quixote laid most to heart of any that had yet befallen him

DON ANTONIO'S LADY was extremely pleased with the company of the fair Morisca, whose sense being as exquisite as her beauty, drew all the most considerable persons in the city to visit her. Don Quixote told Don Antonio that he could by no means approve the method they had taken to release Don Gregorio, it being full of danger, with little or no probability of success; but that their surest way would have been to set him ashore in Barbary, with his horse and arms, and leave it to him to deliver the gentleman in spite of all the Moorish power, as Don Gayseros had formerly rescued his wife Melissandra. 'Good your worship,' quoth Sancho, hearing this, 'look before your leap. Don Gayseros had nothing but a fair race for it on dry land, when he carried her to France. But here, if it please you, though we should deliver Don Gregorio, how the devil shall we bring him over to Spain cross the broad sea?' 'There is a remedy for all things but death,' answered Don Quixote, 'it is but having a bark ready by the seaside, and then let me see what can hinder our getting into it.' 'Ah! master, master!' quoth Sancho, 'there is more to be done than a dish to wash. Saying is one thing, and doing is another, and for my part, I like the renegado very well, he seems to me a good honest fellow, and cut out for the business.' 'Well,' said Don Antonio, 'if the renegado fails, then the great Don Quixote shall embark for Barbary.'

In two days the renegado was dispatched away in a fleet cruiser of six oars on each side, manned with brisk, lusty fellows, and two days after that, the galleys with the general left the port, and steered their course eastwards. The general having first engaged the viceroy to give him an account of Don Gregorio's and Anna Felix's fortune.

Now it happened one morning that Don Quixote going abroad to take the air upon the seashore, armed at all points, according to his custom (his arms, as he said, being his best attire, as combat was his refreshment), he spied a knight riding towards him, armed like himself from head to foot, with a bright moon blazoned on his shield, who coming within hearing, called out to him, 'Illustrious, and never-sufficiently extolled Don Quixote de la Mancha, I am the Knight of the White Moon, whose incredible achievements, perhaps, have reached thy ears. Lo, I am come to enter into combat with thee, and to compel thee by dint of sword, to own and acknowledge my mistress, by whatever name and dignity she be distinguished, to be without any degree of comparison, more beautiful than thy

Dulcinea del Toboso. Now if thou wilt fairly confess this truth, thou freest thyself from certain death, and me from the trouble of taking or giving thee thy life. It not, the conditions of our combat are these: if victory be on my side, thou shalt be obliged immediately to forsake thy arms, and the quest of adventures, and to return to thy own home, where thou shalt engage to live quietly and peaceably for the space of one whole year, without laying hand on thy sword, to the improvement of thy estate, and the salvation of thy soul. But if thou comest off conqueror, my life is at thy mercy, my horse and arms shall be thy trophy, and the fame of all my former exploits, by the lineal descent of conquest, be vested in thee as victor. Consider what thou hast to do, and let thy answer be quick, for my dispatch is limited to this very day.'

Don Quixote was amazed and surprised as much at the arrogance of the Knight of the White Moon's challenge, as at the subject of it; so with a solemn and austere address, 'Knight of the White Moon,' said he, 'whose achievements have as yet been kept from my knowledge, it is more than probable, that you have never seen the illustrious Dulcinea; for had you ever viewed her perfections, you had there found arguments enough to convince you, that no beauty past, present, or to come, can parallel hers; and therefore, without giving you directly the lie, I only tell thee, knight, thou art mistaken, and this position I will maintain by accepting your challenge on your conditions, except that article of your exploits descending to me; for, not knowing what character your actions bear, I shall rest satisfied with the fame of my own, by which, such as they are, I am willing to abide. And since your time is so limited, choose your ground, and begin your career as soon as you will, and expect to be met with a fair field and no favour: to whom God shall give her,* St. Peter give his blessing.' While the two knights were thus adjusting the preliminaries of combat, the viceroy, who had been informed of the Knight of the White Moon's appearance near the city walls, and his parleying with Don Quixote, hastened to the scene of battle, not suspecting it to be anything but some new device of Don Antonio Moreno, or somebody else. Several gentlemen, and Don Antonio among the rest, accompanied him thither. They arrived just as Don Quixote was wheeling Rozinante to fetch his career; and seeing them both ready for the onset, he interposed, desiring to know the cause of the sudden combat. The Knight of the White Moon told him there was a lady in the case, and briefly repeated to his Excellency what passed between him and Don Quixote. The viceroy whispered Don Antonio, and asked him whether he knew that Knight of the White Moon, and whether their combat was not some jocular device to impose upon Don Quixote. Don Antonio answered positively, that he neither

---

* Meaning victory.

knew the knight, nor whether the combat were in jest or earnest. This put
the Viceroy to some doubt whether he should not prevent their engagement; but being at last persuaded that it must be jest at the bottom, he
withdrew. 'Valorous knights,' said he, 'if there be no medium between
confession and death, but Don Quixote be still resolved to deny, and you,
the Knight of the White Moon, as obstinately to urge, I have no more to
say; the field is free, and the Lord have mercy on ye.'

The Knights made their compliments to the Viceroy for his gracious
consent; and Don Quixote making some short ejaculations to Heaven and
his mistress, as he always used upon these occasions, began his career,
without either sound of trumpet or any other signal. His adversary was no
less forward; for setting spurs to his horse, which was much the swifter, he
met Don Quixote before he had run half his career, so forcibly, that
without making use of his lance, which it is thought he lifted up on
purpose, he overthrew the Knight of la Mancha and Rozinante, both
coming to the ground with a terrible fall.

The Knight of the White Moon got immediately upon him, and
clapping the point of his lance to his face, 'Knight,' cried he, 'you are
vanquished, and a dead man, unless you immediately fulfil the conditions
of your combat.' Don Quixote, bruised and stunned with his fall, without
lifting up his beaver, answered in a faint hollow voice, as if he had spoken
out of a tomb, 'Dulcinea del Toboso is the most beautiful woman in the
world, and I the most unfortunate knight upon the earth. It were unjust
that such perfection should suffer through my weakness. No, pierce my
body with thy lance, Knight, and let my life expire with my honour.' 'Not
so rigorous neither,' replied the conqueror, 'let the fame of the Lady
Dulcinea del Toboso remain entire and unblemished; provided the great
Don Quixote return home for a year, as we agreed before the combat, I
am satisfied.' The Viceroy and Don Antonio, with many other gentlemen
were witnesses to all these passages, and particularly to this proposal; to
which Don Quixote answered, that upon condition he should be enjoined
nothing to the prejudice of Dulcinea, he would, upon the faith of a true
knight, be punctual in the performance of everything else. This acknowledgment being made, the Knight of the White Moon turned about his
horse, and saluting the Viceroy, rode at a hand-gallop into the city,
whither Don Antonio followed him, at the Viceroy's request, to find who
he was, if possible.

Don Quixote was lifted up, and upon taking off his helmet, they found
him pale, and in a cold sweat. As for Rozinante he was in so bad a plight,
that he could not stir for the present. Then, as for Sancho, he was in so
heavy a taking, that he knew not what to do, nor what to say; he was
sometimes persuaded he was in a dream, sometimes he fancied this rueful
adventure was all witchcraft and enchantment. In short, he found his

master discomfited in the face of the world, and bound to good behaviour, and to lay aside his arms for a whole year. Now he thought his glory eclipsed, his hopes of greatness vanished into smoke, and his master's promises like his bones, put out of joint by that cursed fall, which he was afraid had at once crippled Rozinante and his master. At last, the vanquished knight was put into a chair, which the Viceroy had sent for, for that purpose, and they carried him into town, accompanied likewise by the Viceroy, who had a great curiosity to know who this Knight of the White Moon was, that had left Don Quixote in so sad a condition.

CHAPTER LXV

An account of the Knight of the White Moon, Don Gregorio's enlargement, and other Passages

DON ANTONIO MORENO followed the Knight of the White Moon to his inn, whither he was attended by a troublesome rabble of boys. The knight being got to his chamber, where his squire waited to take off his armour, Don Antonio came in, declaring he would not be shook off, till he had discovered who he was. The knight finding that the gentleman would not leave him: 'Sir,' said he, 'since I lie under no obligation of concealing myself, if you please, while my man disarms me, you shall hear the whole truth of the story.'

'You must know, sir, I am called the Bachelor Carrasco: I live in the same town with this Don Quixote, whose unaccountable frenzy has moved all his neighbours, and me among the rest, to endeavour by some means to cure his madness; in order to which, believing that rest and ease would prove the surest remedy, I bethought myself of this present stratagem; and about three months ago, in all the equipage of a knight-errant, under the title of the Knight of the Mirrors, I met him on the road, fixed a quarrel upon him, and the conditions of our combat were as you have heard already. But fortune then declared for him, for he unhorsed and vanquished me, and so I was disappointed: he prosecuted his adventures, and I returned home shamefully, very much hurt with my fall. But, willing to retrieve my credit, I made this second attempt, and now have succeeded. For I know him to be so nicely punctual in whatever his word and honour is engaged for, that he will undoubtedly perform his promise. This, sir, is the sum of the whole story, and I beg the favour of you to conceal me from Don Quixote, that my project may not be ruined the second time, and that the honest gentleman, who is naturally a man of good parts, may recover his understanding.' 'Oh! sir,' replied Don

Antonio, 'what have you to answer for, in robbing the world of the most diverting folly, that ever was exposed among mankind? Consider, sir, that his cure can never benefit the public half so much as his distemper. But I am apt to believe, Sir Bachelor, that his madness is too firmly fixed for your art to remove, and (Heaven forgive me) I cannot forbear wishing it may be so; for by Don Quixote's cure we not only lose his good company, but the drolleries and comical humours of Sancho Pança too, which are enough to cure melancholy itself of the spleen. However, I promise to say nothing of the matter, though I confidently believe, sir, your pains will be to no purpose.' Carrasco told him, that having succeeded so far, he was obliged to cherish better hopes. And, asking Don Antonio if he had any further service to command him, he took his leave, and, packing up his armour on a carriage mule, presently mounted his charging horse; and, leaving the city that very day, posted homewards, meeting no adventure on the road worth a place in this faithful history.

Don Antonio gave an account of the discourse he had had with Carrasco to the Viceroy, who was vexed to think that so much pleasant diversion was like to be lost to all those that were acquainted with the Don's follies.

Six days did Don Quixote keep his bed, very dejected, sullen, and out of humour, and full of severe and black reflections on his fatal overthrow. Sancho was his comforter, and among other his crumbs of comfort, 'My dear master,' quoth he, 'cheer up, come pluck up a good heart, and be thankful for coming off no worse. Why, a man has broke his neck with a less fall, and you have not so much as a broken rib. Consider, sir, that they that game, sometimes must lose; we must not always look for bacon where we see the hooks. Come, sir, cry a fig for the doctor, since you will not need him this bout; let us jog home fair and softly, without thinking any more of sauntering up and down, nobody knows whither, in quest of adventures and bloody noses. Why, sir, I am the greatest loser, if you go to that, though it is you that are in the worst pickle. It is true, I was weary of being a governor, and gave over all thoughts that way; but yet I never parted with my inclination of being an earl; and now, if you miss being a king, by casting off your knight-errantry, poor I may go whistle for my earldom.' 'No more of that, Sancho,' cried Don Quixote; 'I shall only retire for a year, and then reassume my honourable profession, which will undoubtedly secure me a kingdom, and thee an earldom.' 'Heaven grant it may,' quoth Sancho, 'and no mischief betide us: Hope well, and have well, says the proverb.'

Don Antonio coming in, broke off the discourse, and with great signs of joy calling to Don Quixote, 'Reward me, sir,' cried he, 'for my good news; Don Gregorio and the renegado are safe arrived, they are now at the Viceroy's palace, and will be here this moment.' The Knight was a little revived at this news: 'Truly, sir,' said he to Antonio, 'I could almost be sorry for his good fortune, since he has forestalled the glory I should have acquired, in releasing, by the strength of my arm, not only him, but all the Christian slaves in Barbary. But whither am I transported, wretch that I am! Am I not miserably conquered, shamefully overthrown! forbidden the paths of glory for a whole long tedious year? What should I boast, who am fitter for a distaff than a sword!' 'No more of that,' quoth Sancho: 'better my hog-dirty at home, than no hog at all. Let the hen live, though she have the pip. Today for thee, and tomorrow for me. Never lay this ill-fortune to heart; he that is down today, may be up tomorrow, unless he has a mind to lie a-bed. Hang bruises; so rouse, sir, and bid Don Gregorio welcome to Spain; for by the hurry in the house, I believe he is come': and so it happened; for Don Gregorio having paid his duty to the Viceroy, and given him an account of his delivery, was just arrived at Don Antonio's with the renegado, very impatient to see Anna Felix. He had changed the female habit he wore when he was freed, for one suitable to his sex, which he had from a captive who came along with him in the vessel, and appeared a very amiable and handsome gentleman, though not above eighteen years of age. Ricote and his daughter went out to meet him, the father with tears, and the daughter with a joyful modesty. Their salutation was reserved, without an embrace, their love being too refined for any loose behaviour: but their beauties surprised everybody: silence was emphatical in their joys, and their eyes spoke more love than their tongues could express. The renegado gave a short account of the success of his voyage; and Don Gregorio briefly related the shifts he was put to among the women in his confinement, which showed his wit and discretion to be much above his years. Ricote gratified the ship's crew very nobly, and particularly the renegado, who was once more received into the bosom of the Church, having with due penance and sincere repentance purified himself from all his former uncleanness.

Some few days after, the viceroy, in concert with Don Antonio, took such measures as were expedient, to get the banishment of Ricote and his daughter repealed, judging it no inconvenience to the nation, that so just and orthodox persons should remain among them. Don Antonio being obliged to go to court about some other matters, offered to solicit in their behalf, hinting to him, that through the intercession of friends, and more powerful bribes, many difficult matters were brought about there, to the satisfaction of the parties. 'There is no relying upon favour and bribes in our business,' said Ricote, who was by, 'for the great Don Bernardo de Velasco, Count de Salazar, to whom the king gave the charge of our expulsion, is a person of too strict and rigid justice to be moved either by money, favour, or affection; and though I cannot deny him the character of a merciful judge in other matters, yet his piercing and diligent policy finds the body of our Moriscan race to be so corrupted, that amputation is the only cure. He is an Argus in his ministry, and by his watchful eyes has discovered the most secret springs of their machinations, and resolving to prevent the danger which the whole kingdom was in, from such a powerful multitude of inbred foes, he took the most effectual means; for, after all, lopping off the branches may only prune the tree, and make the poisonous fruit spring faster; but to overthrow it from the root, proves a sure deliverance; nor can the great Philip the Third be too much extolled; first, for his heroic resolution in so nice and weighty an affair, and then for his wisdom in entrusting Don Bernardo de Velasco with the execution of this design.' 'Well, when I come to court,' said Don Antonio to Ricote, 'I will, however, use the most advisable means, and leave the rest to Providence. Don Gregorio shall go with me to comfort his parents, that have long mourned for his absence. Anna Felix shall stay here with my wife, or in some monastery; and as for honest Ricote, I dare engage the viceroy will be satisfied to, let him remain under his protection till he sees how I succeed.' The viceroy consented to all this; but Don Gregorio, fearing the worst, was unwilling to leave his fair mistress; however, considering that he might return to her after he had seen his parents, he yielded to the proposal, and so Anna Felix remained with Don Antonio's Lady, and Ricote with the viceroy.

Two days after, Don Quixote, being somewhat recovered, took his leave of Don Antonio, and having caused his armour to be laid on Dapple, he set forwards on his journey home: Sancho thus being forced to trudge after him on foot. On the other side, Don Gregorio bid adieu to Anna Felix, and their separation, though but for a while, was attended with floods of tears, and all the excess of passionate sorrow. Ricote offered him a thousand crowns, but he refused them, and only borrowed five of Don Antonio, to repay him at court.

CHAPTER LXVI

Which treats of that which shall be seen by him who reads it, and heard by him who listens when it is read

Don Quixote, as he went out of Barcelona, cast his eyes on the spot of ground where he was overthrown. 'Here once Troy stood,' said he; 'here my unhappy fate, and not my cowardice, deprived me of all the glories I had purchased. Here Fortune, by an unexpected reverse, made me sensible of her unconstancy and fickleness. Here my exploits suffered a total eclipse; and, in short, here fell my happiness never to rise again.'

Sancho hearing his master thus dolefully paraphrasing on his misfortunes, 'Good sir,' quoth he, 'it is as much the part of great spirits to have patience when the world frowns upon them, as to be joyful when all goes well: and I judge of it by myself; for if when I was a governor, I was merry, now I am but a poor squire afoot I am not sad. And indeed I have heard say, that this same she thing they call Fortune, is a whimsical freakish drunken queen, and blind into the bargain; so that she neither sees what she does, nor knows whom she raises, nor whom she casts down.' 'Thou art very much a philosopher, Sancho,' said Don Quixote, 'thou talkest very sensibly. I wonder how thou camest by all this; but I must tell thee there is no such thing as fortune in the world; nor does anything that happens here below of good or ill come by chance, but by the particular providence of Heaven; and this makes good the proverb, That every man may thank himself for his own fortune. For my part I have been the maker of mine, but for want of using the discretion I ought to have used, all my presumptuous edifice sunk, and tumbled down at once. I might well have considered, that Rozinante was too weak and feeble to withstand the Knight of the White Moon's huge and strong-built horse. However, I would needs adventure: I did the best I could, and was overcome. Yet though it has cost me my honour, I have not lost, nor can I lose, my integrity to perform my promise. When I was a knight-errant, valiant and bold, the strength of my hands and my actions gave a reputation to my deeds; and now I am no more than a dismounted squire, the performance of my promise shall give a reputation to my words. Trudge on then, friend Sancho, and let us get home, to pass the year of our probation. In that retirement we shall recover new vigour, to return to that which is never to be forgotten by me, I mean the profession of arms.' 'Sir,' quoth Sancho, 'it is no such pleasure to beat the hoof, as I do, that I should be for large marches. Let us hang up this armour of yours upon some tree, in the room of one of those highwaymen that hang hereabouts in clusters; and when I am got upon Dapple's back, we will ride as fast as you please; for to think I can mend my pace, and foot it all the way, is what you must excuse me in.' 'Thou hast spoken to purpose, Sancho,' said Don Quixote; 'let my arms be hung for a trophy, and underneath, or about them, we will carve on the bark of the trees the same inscription which was written near the trophy of Orlando's arms:

> 'Let none but he those arms displace,
>   Who dares Orlando's fury face.'

'Why, this is as I would have it,' quoth Sancho; 'and were it not that we shall want Rozinante upon the road, it were not amiss to leave him hanging too.' 'Now I think better on it,' said Don Quixote, 'neither the armour nor the horse shall be served so. It shall never be said of me: "For good service, bad reward." ' 'Why, that is well said,' quoth Sancho, 'for indeed it is a saying among wise men, that the fault of the ass must not be laid on the packsaddle; and therefore, since in this last job, you yourself were in fault, even punish yourself, and let not your fury wreak itself upon your poor armour, bruised and battered with doing you service, nor upon the tameness of Rozinante, that good-conditioned beast, nor yet upon the tenderness of my feet, requiring them to travel more than they ought.'

They passed that day, and four more after that, in such kind of discourse, without meeting anything that might interrupt their journey; but, on the fifth day, as they entered into a country town, they saw a great company of people at an inn door, being got together for pastime, as being a holiday. As soon as Don Quixote drew near, he heard one of the countrymen cry to the rest, 'Look ye, we will leave it to one of these two gentlemen that are coming this way, they know neither of the parties: let either of them decide the matter.' 'That I will with all heart,' said Don Quixote, 'and with all the equity imaginable, if you will but state the case right to me.' 'Why, sir,' said the countryman, 'the business is this; one of our neighbours here in town, so fat and so heavy, that he weighs eleven arrobas,* or a eleven quarters of a hundred (for that is the same thing), has challenged another man of this town, that weighs not half so much, to run with him a hundred paces with equal weight. Now he that gave the challenge, being asked how they should make equal weight, demands that the other who weighs but five quarters of a hundred, should carry a hundred and a half of iron, and so the weight, he says, will be equal.' 'Hold, sir,' cried Sancho, before Don Quixote could answer, 'this business belongs to me, that came so lately from being a governor, and judge, as all the world knows: I ought to give judgment in this doubtful case.' 'Do then, with all my heart, friend Sancho,' said Don Quixote, 'for I am not fit to give crumbs to a cat,† my brain is so disturbed, and out of order.' Sancho having thus got leave, and all the countrymen standing about him, gaping to hear him give sentence, 'Brothers,' quoth he, 'I must tell you, that the fat man is in the wrong box, there is no manner of reason in what he asks; for if, as I always heard say, he that is challenged may choose his weapons, there is no reason that he should choose such as may encumber him, and hinder him from getting the better of him that defied him. Therefore it is my judgment, that he who gave the challenge, and is so big and so fat, shall cut, pare, slice, or shave off a hundred and fifty pounds of his flesh, here and there, as he thinks fit; and then being reduced to the

---

* An arroba is a quarter of a hundredweight.
† Alluding to the custom in Spain, of an old or disabled soldier's carrying offals of tripe or liver about the streets to feed the cats.

weight of the other, both parties may run their race upon equal terms.'
'Before George,' quoth one of the country people, that had heard the
sentence, 'this gentleman has spoken like one of the saints in heaven; he
has given judgment like a casuist; but I warrant the fat squab loves his flesh
too well to part with the least sliver of it, much less will he part with a
hundred and a half.' 'Why then,' quoth another fellow, 'the best way will
be not to let them run at all; for then Lean need not venture to sprain his
back by running with such a load; and Fat need not cut out his pampered
sides into collops: so let half the wager be spent in wine, and let us take
these gentlemen to the tavern that has the best, "and lay the cloak upon
me when it rains." ' 'I return ye thanks, gentlemen,' said Don Quixote,
'but I cannot stay a moment, for dismal thoughts and disasters force me to
appear unmannerly, and to travel at an uncommon rate;' and, so saying, he
clapped spurs to Rozinante, and moved forwards, leaving people to
descant on his strange figure, and the rare parts of his groom, for such
they took Sancho to be. 'If the man be so wise,' quoth another of the
country fellows to the rest, 'bless us! what shall we think of the master?' 'I
will hold a wager, if they be going to study at Salamanca, they will come to
be Lord Chief Justices in a trice; for there is nothing more easy, it is but
studying and studying again, and having a little favour and good luck; and
when a man least dreams of it, slap, he shall find himself with a judge's
gown upon his back, or a bishop's mitre upon his head.'

That night the master and the man took up their lodging in the middle
of a field, under the roof of the open sky; and the next day, as they were
on their journey, they saw coming towards them, a man a-foot with a
wallet about his neck, and a javelin or dart in his hand, just like a foot-
post: the man mended his pace when he came near Don Quixote, and
almost running, came, with a great deal of joy in his looks, and embraced
Don Quixote's right thigh, for he could reach no higher. 'My lord Don
Quixote de la Mancha,' cried he, 'oh! how heartily glad my lord Duke will
be when he understands you are coming again to his castle, for there he is
still with my lady Duchess.' 'I do not know you, friend,' answered Don
Quixote, 'nor can I imagine who you should be, unless you tell me
yourself.' 'My name is Tosilos, if it please your honour; I am my lord
Duke's footman, the same who would not fight with you about Donna
Rodriguez's daughter.' 'Bless me!' cried Don Quixote, 'is it possible you
should be the man whom those enemies of mine, the magicians,
transformed into a lacquey, to deprive me of the honour of that combat?'
'Softly, good sir,' replied the footman, 'there was neither enchantment
nor transformation in the case. I was as much a footman when I entered
the list, as when I went out; and it was because I had a mind to marry the
young gentlewoman, that I refused to fight. But I was sadly disappointed;
for when you were gone, my lord Duke had me soundly banged, for not

doing as he ordered me in that matter; and the upshot was this, Donna Rodriguez is packed away to seek her fortune, and the daughter is shut up in a nunnery. As for me, I am going to Barcelona, with a packet of letters from my lord to the Viceroy. However, sir, if you please to take a sup, I have here a calabash full of the best. It is a little hot, I must own, but it is neat, and I have some excellent cheese, that will make it go down I warrant ye.' 'I take you at your word,' quoth Sancho; 'I am no proud man, leave ceremonies to the Church, and so let us drink, honest Tosilos, in spite of all the enchanters in the Indies.' 'Well, Sancho,' said Don Quixote, 'thou art certainly the veriest glutton that ever was, and the silliest blockhead in the world, else thou wouldst consider that this man thou seest here, is enchanted, and a sham-lacquey. Then stay with him if thou thinkest fit, and gratify thy voracious appetite; for my part, I will ride softly on before.' Tosilos smiled, and laying his bottle and his cheese upon the grass, he and Sancho sat down there, and like sociable messmates, never stirred till they had quite cleared the wallet of all that was in it fit for the belly; and this with such an appetite, that when all was consumed, they licked the very packet of letters, because it smelt of cheese. While they were thus employed, 'Hang me,' quoth Tosilos, 'if I know what to make of this master of yours: doubtless he ought to be reckoned a madman.' 'Why ought?'* replied Sancho; 'he owes nothing to anybody; for he pays for everything, especially where madness is current: there he might be the richest man in the kingdom, he has such a stock of it. I see it full well, and full well I tell him of it; but what boots it? especially now he is in the dumps, for having been worsted by the Knight of the White Moon.' Tosilos begged of Sancho to tell him that story; but Sancho said it would not be handsome to let his master stay for him, but that next time they met he would tell him the whole matter. With that they got up, and after the squire had brushed his clothes, and shaking off the crumbs from his beard, he drove Dapple along; and with a 'Good-bye to ye,' left Tosilos, in order to overtake his master, who stayed for him under the cover of a tree.

---

* A double entendre upon the word 'dove,' which is put for 'must,' the sign of a mood, or for owing a debt.

CHAPTER LXVII

*How Don Quixote resolved to turn Shepherd, and lead
a rural life, for the year's time he was obliged not to
bear arms; with other passages truly good and diverting*

IF DON QUIXOTE was much disturbed in mind before his overthrow, he was much more disquieted after it. While he stayed for his squire under the tree, a thousand thoughts crowded into his head, like flies into a honey-pot; sometimes he pondered on the means to free Dulcinea from enchantment, and at others, on the life he was to lead during his involuntary retirement. In this brown study, Sancho came up to him, crying up Tosilos as the honestest fellow and the most gentleman-like footman in the world. 'Is it possible, Sancho,' said Don Quixote, 'thou shouldst still take that man for a real lacquey? Hast thou forgot how thou sawest Dulcinea converted and transformed into the resemblance of a rustic wench, and the Knight of the Mirrors into the bachelor Carrasco; and all this by the necromantic arts of those evil-minded magicians, that persecute me? But laying this aside, pray thee tell me, didst thou not ask Tosilos what became of Altisidora; whether she bemoaned my absence, or dismissed from her breast those amorous sentiments that disturbed her when I was near her?' 'Faith and troth,' quoth Sancho, 'my head ran on something else, and I was too well employed to think of such foolish stuff. Body of me! sir, are you now in a mood to ask about other folks' thoughts, especially their love thoughts too?' 'Look you,' said Don Quixote, 'there is a great deal of difference between those actions that proceed from love, and those that are the effect of gratitude. It is possible a gentleman should not be at all amorous, but, strictly speaking, he cannot be ungrateful. It is very likely that Altisidora loved me well; she presented me, as thou knowest, with three night-caps; she wept and took on when I went away; cursed me, abused me, and, in spite of modesty, gave a loose to her passion: all tokens that she was deeply in love with me, for the anger of lovers commonly vents itself in curses. It was not in my power to give her any hopes, nor had I any costly present to bestow on her; for all I have reserved is for Dulcinea; and the treasures of a knight-errant are but fairy-gold, and a delusive good: so all I can do, is only to remember the unfortunate fair, without prejudice however to the rights of my Dulcinea, whom thou greatly injurest, Sancho, by delaying the accomplishment of the penance that must free the poor lady from misery. And since thou art so ungenerously sparing of that pampered hide of thine, may I see it devoured by wolves, rather than see it kept so charily for the worms.' 'Sir,' quoth Sancho, 'to deal plainly with you, it cannot for the blood of me, enter into my head, that jerking my backside will signify a straw to the disenchanting of the enchanted. Sir, it is as if we should say, if your head aches anoint your shins. At least I dare be sworn that in all the stories of knight-errantry you have thumbed over, you never knew flogging unbewitched anybody. However, when I can find myself in the humour, do ye see, I will about it when time serves, I will chastise myself, never fear.' 'I wish thou wouldest,' answered Don Quixote, 'and may Heaven give thee grace at least to understand how much it is thy duty to relieve thy mistress; for as she is mine, by consequence she is thine, since thou belongest to me.'

Thus they went on talking till they came near the place where the bulls had run over them; and Don Quixote knowing it again, 'Sancho,' said he, 'yonder's that meadow where we met the fine shepherdesses, and the gallant shepherds, who had a mind to renew or imitate the pastoral Arcadia. It was certainly a new and ingenious conceit. If thou thinkest well of it, we will follow their example, and turn shepherds too, at least for the time I am to lay aside the profession of arms; I will buy a flock of sheep, and everything that is fit for a pastoral life, and so calling myself the shepherd Quixotis, and thee the shepherd Pansino, we will range the woods, the hills and meadows, singing and versifying. We will drink the liquid crystal, sometimes out of the fountains, and sometimes from the purling brooks, and the swift gliding streams. The oaks, the cork-trees, and chestnut-trees will afford us both lodging and diet, the willows will yield us their shade; the roses present us their inoffensive sweets; and the spacious meads will be our carpets, diversified with colours of all sorts; blessed with the purest air, and unconfined alike, we shall breathe that and freedom. The moon and stars, our tapers of the night, shall light our evening walks. Light hearts will make us merry, and mirth will make us sing. Love will inspire us with a theme and wit, and Apollo with harmonious lays. So shall we become famous, not only while we live, but make our loves eternal as our songs.' 'As I live,' quoth Sancho, 'this sort of life nicks me to a hair, * and I fancy, that, if the bachelor, Samson Carrasco and Master Nicholas have but once a glimpse of it, they will even turn shepherds too; nay, it is well if the curate does not put in for one among the rest, for he is a notable joker, and merrily inclined.' 'That was well thought on,' said Don Quixote; 'and then if the bachelor will make one among us, as I doubt not but he will, he may call himself the shepherd Samsonino, or Carrascon; and Master Nicholas Niculoso, as formerly old Boscan called himself Nemoroso.† For the curate, I do not well know what name we shall give

* This kind of life squares and corners with me exactly, *Quadrado y esquinado*: alluding to the corner-stone of a building, which answers both ways.
† In plain English, as if Mr. Wood (for so Bosque signifies) should call himself Mr. Grove, so *Nemus* signifies in Latin.

him, unless we should call him the shepherd Curiambro. As for the shepherdesses, with whom we must fall in love, we cannot be at a loss to find them names, there are enough for us to pick and choose; and since my mistress's name is not improper for a shepherdess, any more than for a princess, I will not trouble myself to get a better; thou mayest call thine as thou pleasest.' 'For my part,' quoth Sancho, 'I do not think of any other name for mine, but Teresona, that will fit her fat sides full well, and is taken from her Christian name too: so, when I come to mention her in my verses, everybody will know her to be my wife, and commend my honesty, as being one that is not for picking another man's lock: as for the curate, he must be contented without a shepherdess, for good example's sake. And for the bachelor, let him take his own choice, if he means to have one.' 'Bless me,' said Don Quixote, 'what a life we shall lead! What a melody of oaten reeds, and Zamora bagpipes* shall we have resounding in the air! what intermixture of tabours, morrice-bells, and fiddles! And if, to all the different instruments, we add the albogues, we shall have all manner of pastoral music.' 'What are the albogues?' quoth Sancho, 'for I do not remember I have seen or ever heard of them in my life.' 'They are,' said Don Quixote, 'a sort of instruments made of brass plates, rounded like candlesticks: the one shutting into the other, there arises through the holes or stops, and the trunk or hollow, an odd sound, which if not very grateful, or harmonious, is however not altogether disagreeable, but does well enough with the rusticity of the bagpipe and tabour. You must know the word is Moorish, as indeed are all those in our Spanish, that begin with an "Al," as Almoaza, Almorsar, Alhombra, Alguasil, Alucema, Almacen, Alcanzia, and the like, which are not very many. And we have also but three Moorish words in our tongue that end in "I"; and they are Borcequi, Zaquicami, and Maravedi; for as to Alheli and Alfaqui, they are as well known to be Arabic by their beginning with "Al" as their ending in "I." I could not forbear telling thee so much by the bye, thy inquiry about Albogue having brought it into my head. There is one thing more that will go a great way towards making us complete in our new kind of life, and that is poetry; thou knowest I am somewhat given that way, and the bachelor Carrasco is a most accomplished poet, to say nothing of the curate; though I will hold a wager he is a dabbler in it too, and so is Master Nicholas, I dare say; for all your barbers are notable scrapers and songsters. For my part, I will complain of absence, thou shalt celebrate thy own loyalty and constancy; the shepherd Carrascon shall expostulate on his shepherdess's disdain, and the pastor Curiambro choose what subject he likes best; and so all will be managed to our hearts' content.' 'Alas!' quoth

---

* Zamora is a city in Spain, famous for that sort of music, as Lancashire is in England for the bagpipe.

Sancho, 'I am so unlucky, that I fear me, I shall never live to see these blessed days. How shall I lick up the curds and cream! I will never be without a wooden spoon in my pocket! Oh, how many of them will I make! What garlands and what pretty pastoral fancies will I contrive! which, though they may not recommend me for wisdom, will make me pass at least for an ingenious fellow. My daughter Sanchica shall bring us our dinner afield. But hold, have a care of that! She is a young likely wench, and some shepherds are more knaves than fools; and I would not have my girl go out for wool, and come home shorn; for love and wicked doings are to be found in the fields, as well as in cities; and in a shepherd's cot, as well as in a king's palace. Take away the cause, and the effect ceases; what the eye never sees, the heart never rues. One pair of heels is worth two pair of hands; and we must watch as well as pray.' 'No more proverbs, good Sancho,' cried Don Quixote; 'any one of these is sufficient to make us know thy meaning. I have told thee often enough not to be so lavish of thy proverbs; but it is all lost upon thee: I preach in a desert: My mother whips me, and I whip the top.' 'Faith and troth,' quoth Sancho, 'this is just as the saying is, the porridge-pot calls the kettle black-arse. You chide me for speaking proverbs, and yet you bring them out two at a time.' 'Look you, Sancho, those I spoke, are to the purpose, but thou fetchest thine in by head and shoulders, to their utter disgrace, and thy own. But no more at this time, it grows late, let us leave the road a little, and take up our quarters yonder in the fields; tomorrow will be a new day.' They did accordingly, and made a slender meal, as little to Sancho's liking as his hard lodging; which brought the hardships of knight-erranting fresh into his thoughts, and made him wish for the better entertainment he had sometimes found, as at Don Diego's, Camacho's, and Don Antonio's houses: but he considered after all, that it could not be always fair weather, nor was it always foul; so he betook himself to his rest till morning, and his master to the usual exercise of his roving imaginations.

CHAPTER LXVIII

The Adventure of the Hogs

THE NIGHT WAS PRETTY DARK, though the moon still kept her place in the sky; but it was in such a part, as obliged her to be invisible to us; for now and then Madam Diana takes a turn to the antipodes, and then the mountains in black, and the valleys in darkness, mourn her ladyship's absence. Don Quixote, after his first sleep, thought nature sufficiently refreshed, and would not yield to the temptation of a second. Sancho indeed did not enjoy a second, but from a different reason: for he usually made but one nap of the whole night, which was owing to the soundness of his constitution, and his unexperience of cares, that lay so heavy upon Don Quixote.

'Sancho,' said the Knight, after he had pulled the squire till he had waked him too, 'I am amazed at the insensibility of thy temper. Thou art certainly made of marble or solid brass, thou liest so without either motion or feeling: thou sleepest while I wake; thou singest while I mourn; and while I am ready to faint for want of sustenance, thou art lazy and unwieldy with mere gluttony. It is the part of a good servant, to share in the afflictions of his master. Observe the stillness of the night, and the solitary place we are in. It is a pity such an opportunity should be lost in sloth and unactive rest; rouse for shame, step a little aside, and with a good grace, and a cheerful heart, score me up some three or four hundred lashes upon thy back, towards the disenchanting of Dulcinea This I make my earnest request, being resolved never to be rough with thee again upon this account; for I must confess thou canst lay a heavy hand on a man upon occasion. When that performance is over, we will pass the remainder of the night in chanting, I of absence, and thou of constancy, and so begin those pastoral exercises, which are to be our employment at home.' 'Sir,' answered Sancho, 'do you take me for a monk or friar, that I should start up in the middle of the night, and discipline myself at this rate? Or, do you think it such an easy matter to scourge and clapper-claw my back one moment, and fall a-singing the next? Look you, sir, say not a word more of this whipping; for as I love my flesh, you will put me upon making some rash oath or other that you will not like, and then if the bare brushing of my coat would do you any good, you should not have it, much less the currying of my hide, and so let me go to sleep again.' 'Oh, obdurate heart!' cried Don Quixote; 'oh, impious squire! Oh, nourishment and favours ill bestowed! Is this my reward for having got thee a government, and my good intentions to get thee an earldom, or an equivalent at least, which I dare engage to do when this year of our obscurity is elapsed; for, in short, *post tenebras spero lucem*.' 'That I do not understand,' quoth Sancho, 'but this I very well know, that while I am asleep, I feel neither hope nor despair; I am free from pain and insensible of glory. Now blessings light on him that first invented this same sleep: it covers a man all over, thoughts and all, like a cloak; it is meat for the hungry, drink for the thirsty, heat for the cold, and cold for the hot. It is the current coin that purchases all the pleasures of the world cheap; and the balance that sets the king and the shepherd, the fool and the wise man even. There is only one thing, which somebody once put into my head, that I dislike in sleep; it is, that it resembles death; there is very little difference between a man in his first sleep, and a man in his last sleep.'

'Most elegantly spoken,' said Don Quixote; 'thou hast much outdone anything I ever heard thee say before, which confirms me in the truth of one of thy own proverbs: birth is much, but breeding more.' 'Cod's me! master of mine,' cried Sancho, 'I am not the only he now that threads proverbs, for you tack them together faster than I do, I think: I see no difference, but that yours come in season, mine out of season; but for all that, they are all but proverbs.'

Thus they were employed, when their ears were alarmed with a kind of a hoarse and grunting noise, that spread itself over all the adjacent valleys. Presently Don Quixote started upon his legs, and laid his hand to his sword: as for Sancho, he immediately set up some entrenchments about him, clapping the bundle of armour on one side, and fortifying the other with the ass's pack-saddle, and then gathering himself up of a heap, squatted down under Dapple's belly, where he lay panting, as full of fears as his master of surprise; while every moment the noise grew louder, as the cause of it approached, to the terror of the one, at least; for as for the other, it is sufficiently known what his valour was.

Now the occasion was this: some fellows were driving a herd of above six hundred swine to a certain fair; and with their grunting and squeaking, the filthy beasts made such a horrible noise, that Don Quixote and Sancho were almost stunned with it, and could not imagine whence it proceeded. But at length the Knight and squire standing in their way, the rude, bristly animals came thronging up all in a body, and without any respect of persons, some running between the Knight's legs, and some between the squire's, threw down both master and man, having not only insulted Sancho's intrenchments, but also thrown down Rozinante: and having thus broke in upon them, on they went, and bore down all before them, overthrowing pack-saddle, armour, Knight, squire, horse and all; crowding, treading, and trampling over them all at a horrid rate. Sancho was the first that made a shift to recover his legs; and having by this time found out what the matter was, he called to his master to lend him his sword, and swore he would stick at least half-a-dozen of those rude porkers immediately. 'No, no, my friend,' said Don Quixote, 'let them even go; Heaven inflicts this disgrace upon my guilty head; for it is a just punishment that dogs should devour, hornets sting, and vile hogs trample on a vanquished Knight-errant.' 'And belike,' quoth Sancho, 'that Heaven sends the fleas to sting, the lice to bite, and hunger to famish us poor squires, for keeping these vanquished knights company. If we squires were the sons of those knights, or any ways related to them, why then something might be said for our bearing a share of their punishment, though it were to the third and fourth generation. But what have the Panças to do with the Quixotes? Well, let us to our old places again, and sleep out the little that is left of the night. Tomorrow is a new day.' 'Sleep, Sancho,' cried Don Quixote, 'sleep, for thou wert born to sleep: but I, who was designed to be still waking, intend before Aurora ushers in the sun, to give a loose to my thoughts, and vent my conceptions in a madrigal, that I made last night unknown to thee.' 'Methinks,' quoth Sancho, 'a man cannot be in great affliction, when he can turn his brain to the making of verses. Therefore, you may versify on as long as you please, and I will sleep it out as much as I can.' This said, he laid himself down on the ground, as he thought best, and hunching himself close together, fell fast asleep, without any disturbance from either debts, suretiships, or any care whatsoever. On the other side, Don Quixote, leaning against the trunk of a beech, or a cork-tree (for it is not determined by Cid Hamet which it was) sang, in concert with his sighs, the following composition:

A SONG TO LOVE

'Whene'er I think what mighty pain
    The slave must bear who drags thy chain,
Oh! Love, for ease to death I go,
    The cure of thee, the cure of life and woe.

But when, alas! I think I am sure
    Of that which must by killing cure,
The pleasure that I feel ill death,
    Proves a strong cordial to restore my breath.

Thus life each moment makes me die,
    And death itself new life can give;
I hopeless and tormented lie,
    And neither truly die nor live.'

The many tears as well as sighs that accompanied this musical complaint, were a sign that the Knight had deeply laid to heart his late defeat, and the absence of his Dulcinea.

Now day came on, and the sun darting his beams on Sancho's face, at last awakened him: whereupon, rubbing his eyes, and yawning and stretching his drowsy limbs, he perceived the havoc that the hogs had made in his baggage, which made him wish not only the herd but somebody else too at the Devil for company. In short, the Knight and the squire both set forward on their journey, and about the close of the evening, they discovered some half a score horsemen, and four or five fellows on foot, making directly towards them. Don Quixote at the sight, felt a strange emotion in his breast, and Sancho fell a-shivering from head to foot; for they perceived that these strangers were provided with spears and shields, and other warlike implements: whereupon the Knight turning to the squire, 'Ah! Sancho,' said he, 'were it lawful for me at this time to bear arms, and had I my hands at liberty and not tied up by my promise, what a joyful sight should I esteem this squadron that approaches! But perhaps, notwithstanding my present apprehensions, things may fall out better than we expect.'

By this time the horsemen with their lances advanced, came close up to them without speaking a word, and encompassing Don Quixote in a menacing manner, with their points levelled to his back and breast; one of the footmen, by laying his finger upon his mouth, signified to Don Quixote, that he must be mute; then taking Rozinante by the bridle, he led him out of the road, while the rest of the footmen secured Sancho and Dapple, and drove them silently after Don Quixote, who attempted twice or thrice to ask the cause of this usage; but he no sooner began to open, but they were ready to run the heads of their spears down his throat. Poor Sancho fared worse yet; for as he offered to speak, one of the foot-guards gave him a jag with a goad, and served Dapple as bad, though the poor beast had no thought of saying a word.

As it grew night, they mended their pace, and then the darkness increased the fears of the captive Knight and squire, especially when every minute their ears were tormented with these or such like words; 'On, on, ye Troglodytes; silence, ye Barbarian slaves; vengeance, ye Anthropophagi; grumble not, ye Scythians; be blind, ye murdering Polyphemuses, ye devouring lions.' Bless us (thought Sancho) what names do they call us here! Trollopites, Barber's slaves, and Andrew Hodgepodgy, City-Cans, and Burframes; I do not like the sound of them. Here is one mischief on the neck of another. When a man is down, down with him: I would compound for a good dry beating, and glad to escape so too Don Quixote was no less perplexed, not being able to imagine the reason either of their hard usage or scurrilous language, which hitherto promised but little good. At last, after they had rode about an hour in the dark, they came to the gates of the castle, which Don Quixote, presently knowing to be the Duke's, where he had so lately been; 'Heaven bless me,' he cried, 'what do I see? Was not this the mansion of civility and humanity? But thus the vanquished are doomed to see everything frown upon them.' With that the two prisoners were led into the great court of the castle, and found such strange preparations made there, as increased at once their fear, and their amazement; as we shall find in the next chapter.

CHAPTER LXIX

Of the most singular and strange Adventure that befell Don Quixote in the whole course of this famous History

ALL THE HORSEMEN alighted, and the footmen snatching up Don Quixote and Sancho in their arms, hurried them into the courtyard, that was illuminated with above a hundred torches, fixed in huge candlesticks; and about all the galleries round the court, were placed above five hundred lights; insomuch, that all was day in the midst of the darkness of the night. In the middle of the court there was a tomb, raised some two yards from the ground, with a large pall of black velvet over it, and round about it a hundred tapers of virgin wax stood burning in silver candlesticks. Upon the tomb lay the body of a young damsel, who, though to all appearance dead, was yet so beautiful, that death itself seemed lovely in her face. Her head was crowned with a garland of fragrant flowers, and supported by a pillow of cloth of gold, and in her hands, that were laid across her breast, was seen a branch of that yellow palm, that used of old to adorn the triumphs of conquerors. On the one side of the court there was a kind of a theatre erected, on which two personages sat in chairs, who by the crowns upon their heads, and sceptres in their hands were, or at least appeared to be kings. By the side of the theatre, at the foot of the steps by which the kings ascended, two other chairs were placed, and thither Don Quixote and Sancho were led, and caused to sit down; the guards that conducted them continuing silent all the while, and making their prisoners understand, by awful signs, that they must also be silent. But there was no great occasion for that caution; for their surprise was so great, that it had tied up their tongues without it.

At the same time two other persons of note ascended the stage with a numerous retinue, and seated themselves on two stately chairs by the two theatrical kings. These Don Quixote presently knew to be the Duke and Duchess, at whose palace he had been so nobly entertained. But what he discovered as the greatest wonder, was, that the corpse upon the tomb was the body of the fair Altisidora.

As soon as the Duke and Duchess had ascended, Don Quixote and Sancho made them a profound obeisance, which they returned with a short inclining of their heads. Upon this a certain officer entered the court, and coming up to Sancho, he clapped over him a black buckram frock, all figured over with flames of fire, and taking off his cap, he put on his head a kind of mitre, such as is worn by those who undergo public penance by the inquisition; whispering him in the ear at the same time, that if he did but offer to open his lips, they would put a gag in his mouth, or murder him outright. Sancho viewed himself over from head to foot, and was a little startled to see himself all over in fire and flames; but yet since he did not feel himself burn, he cared not a farthing. He pulled off his mitre, and found it pictured over with devils; but he put it on again, and bethought himself, that since neither the flames burned him, nor the devils ran away with him, it was well enough. Don Quixote also steadfastly surveyed him, and in the midst of all his apprehensions, could not forbear smiling to see what a strange figure he made. And now in the midst of that profound silence, while everything was mute, and expectation most attentive, a soft and charming symphony of flutes, that seemed to issue from the hollow of the tomb, agreeably filled their ears. Then there appeared at the head of the monument, a young man, extremely hand-some, and dressed in a Roman habit, who to the music of a harp, touched by himself, sung the following stanzas with an excellent voice:

ALTISIDORA'S DIRGE

'While slain, the fair Altisidora lies,
    A victim to Don Quixote's cold disdain;
Here all things mourn, all pleasure with her dies,
    And weeds of woe disguise the graces' train.

I'll sing the beauties of her race and mind,
    Her hopeless passion, her unhappy fate;
Not Orpheus' self in numbers more refin'd,
    Her charms, her love, her suff'ring could relate.

Nor shall the fair alone in life be sung,
    Her boundless praise is my immortal choice;
In the cold grave, when death benumbs my tongue,
    For thee, bright maid, my soul shall find a voice.

When from this narrow cell my spirit's free,
    And wanders grieving with the shades below,
Ev'n o'er oblivion's waves I'll sing to thee;
    And hell itself shall sympathise in woe.'

'Enough,' cried one of the two kings; 'no more, divine musician; it were an endless task to enumerate the perfections of Altisidora, or give us the story of her fate. Nor is she dead, as the ignorant vulgar surmises; no, in the mouth of fame she lives, and once more shall revive, as soon as Sancho has undergone the penance that is decreed to restore her to the world.

Therefore, O Rhadamanthus; thou who sittest in joint commission with me in the opacous shades of Dis, tremendous judge of hell! thou to whom the decrees of fate, inscrutable to mortals, are revealed, in order to restore this damsel to life, open and declare them immediately, nor delay the promised felicity of her return, to comfort the drooping world.'

Scarce had Minos finished his charge, but Rhadamanthus started up: 'Proceed,' said he, 'ye ministers and officers of the household, superior and inferior, high and low; proceed one after another, and mark me Sancho's chin with twenty-four twitches, give him twelve pinches, and run six pins into his arms and backside; for Altisidora's restoration depends on the performance of this ceremony.' Sancho hearing this could hold out no longer, but bawling out, 'Body of me!' cried he, 'I will as soon turn Turk, as give you leave to do all this. You shall put no chin or countenance of mine upon any such mortification. What the devil can the spoiling of my face signify to the restoring of this damsel? I may as soon turn up my broad end, and awaken her with a gun. Dulcinea is bewitched, and I forsooth must flog myself, to free her from witchcraft! and here is Altisidora too drops off of one distemper or other, and presently poor Sancho must be pulled by the handle of his face, his skin filled with oiled holes, and his arms pinched black and blue, to save her from the worms! No, no, you must not think to put tricks upon travellers. An old dog understands trap.'* 'Relent,' cried Rhadamanthus aloud, 'thou tiger, submit proud Nimrod, suffer and be silent, or thou diest: no impossibility is required from thee; and therefore pretend not to expostulate on the severity of thy doom. Thy face shall receive the twitches, thy skin shall be pinched, and thou shalt groan under the penance. Begin, I say, ye ministers of justice, execute my sentence, or, as I am an honest man, ye shall curse the hour ye were born.' At the same time six old duenas, or waiting-women, appeared in the court, marching in a formal procession one after another, four of them wearing spectacles, and all with their right hands held aloft, and their wrists, according to the fashion, about four inches bare, to make their hands seem the longer. Sancho no sooner spied them, but, roaring out like a bull, 'Do with me what you please,' cried he; 'let a sackful of mad cats lay their claws on me, as they did on my master in this castle, drill me through with sharp daggers, tear the flesh from my bones with red-hot pinchers, I will bear it with patience, and serve your worships: but the Devil shall run away with me at once, before I will suffer old waiting-women to lay a finger upon me.' Don Quixote upon this broke silence: 'Have patience, my son,' cried he, 'and resign thyself to these potentates, with thanks to Heaven, for having endowed thy person with such a gift, as to release the enchanted, and raise the dead from the grave.'

* *Tus, tus*, in the original. See this explained elsewhere (page 656).

By this time the waiting-women were advanced up to Sancho, who, after much persuasion, was at last wrought upon to settle himself in his seat, and submit his face and beard to the female executioners; the first that approached gave him a clever twitch, and then dropped him a courtesy. 'Less courtesy, and less sauce, good Mrs. Governante,' cried Sancho; 'for, by the life of Pharaoh, your fingers stink of vinegar.' In short, all the waiting-women, and most of the servants came and twitched and pinched him decently, and he bore it all with unspeakable patience. But when they came to prick him with pins, he could contain no longer; but starting up in a pelting chase, snatched up one of the torches that stood near him, and swinging it round, put all the women and the rest of his tormentors to their heels. 'Avaunt,' cried he, 'ye imps of the Devil, do ye think my backside is made of brass, or that I intend to be your master's martyr, with a pox to ye?'

At the same time Altisidora, who could not but be tired with lying so long upon her back, began to turn herself on one side, which was no sooner perceived by the spectators, but they all set up the cry, 'She lives, she lives! Altisidora lives!' And then Rhadamanthus addressing himself to Sancho, desired him to be pacified, for now the wonderful recovery was effected. On the other side, Don Quixote, seeing Altisidora stir, went and threw himself on his knees before Sancho: 'My dear son,' cried he, 'for now I will not call thee squire, now is the hour for thee to receive some of the lashes that are incumbent upon thee for the disenchanting Dulcinea. This, I say, is the auspicious time, when the virtue of thy skin is most mature and efficacious for working the wonders that are expected from it.' 'Out of the frying-pan into the fire,' quoth Sancho: 'I have brought my hogs to a fair market truly; after I have been twinged and tweaked by the nose, and everywhere, and my buttocks stuck all over, and made a pin-cushion of, I must now be whipped like a top, must I? If you have a mind to be rid of me, cannot you as well tie a good stone about my neck, and tip me into a well? Better make an end of me at once than have me loaded so every foot like a pack-horse with other folks' burdens. Look ye, say but one word more to me of any such thing, and on my soul all the fat shall be in the fire.'

By this time Altisidora sat on the tomb, and presently the music struck up, all the instruments being joined with the voices of the spectators, who cried aloud, 'Live, live, Altisidora live!' The Duke and Duchess got up, and with Minos and Rhadamanthus, accompanied by Don Quixote and Sancho, went all in a body to receive Altisidora, and hand her down from the tomb. She pretending to faint, bowed to the Duke and Duchess, and also to the two kings; but after looking askew upon Don Quixote, 'Heaven forgive that hard-hearted lovely Knight,' said she, 'whose barbarity has made me an inhabitant of the other world for ought I know a thousand years. But to thee,' said she, turning to Sancho, 'to thee, the most compassionate squire that the world contains, I return my thanks for my change from death to life; in acknowledgment of which, six of the best smocks I have shall be changed into shirts for thee; and if they are not spick and span new, yet they are all as clean as a penny.' Sancho pulled off his mitre, put his knee to the ground, and kissed her hand. The Duke commanded that they should return him his cap, and, instead of his flaming frock, to give him his gaberdine; but Sancho begged of his Grace, that he might keep the frock and mitre, to carry into his own country, as a relic of that wonderful adventure. The Duchess said he should have them, for he knew she was always one of his best friends. Then the Duke ordered the company to clear the court, and retire to their respective lodgings, and that Don Quixote and Sancho should be conducted to their apartments.

CHAPTER LXX

Which comes after the sixty-ninth, and contains several particulars necessary for the illustration of this History

THAT NIGHT SANCHO LAY in a truckle-bed in Don Quixote's chamber, a lodging not much to the squire's liking, being very sensible that his master would disturb him with impertinent chat all night long; and this entertainment he found himself not rightly disposed for; his late penance having taken him quite off the talking-pin; and a hovel, with good sound sleep, had been more agreeable to his circumstances, than the most stately apartments in such troublesome company; and indeed his apprehensions proved so right, that his master was scarcely laid when he began to open.

'Sancho,' said he, 'what is your opinion of this night's adventure? Great and mighty is the force of love when heightened by disdain, as the testimony of your own eyes may convince you in the death of Altisidora. It was neither a dart, a dagger, nor any poison that brought her to her end, but she expired through the mere sense of my disdain of her affection.' 'I had not cared a pin,' answered Sancho, 'though she had died of the pip, so she had but let me alone; I never courted her, nor slighted her in my born days; and, for my part, I must still think it strange that the life and well-doing of Altisidora, a whimsical, maggoty gentlewoman, should depend upon the plaguing of Sancho Pança. But there are such things as enchanters and witchcrafts that is certain, from which good Heaven deliver me! For it is more than I can do myself. But now, sir, let me sleep, I beseech you; for, if you trouble me with any more questions, I am resolved to leap out of the window.' 'I will not disturb thee, honest Sancho,' said Don Quixote, 'sleep, if the smart of thy late torture will let thee.' 'No pain,' answered Sancho, 'can be compared to the abuse my face suffered, because it is done by the worst of ill-natured creatures, I mean old waiting-women; the Devil take them, say I, and so good-night; I want a good nap to set me to rights, and so once again, pray let me sleep.' 'Do so,' said Don Quixote, 'and Heaven be with thee.' Thereupon they both fell asleep, and while they are asleep Cid Hamet takes the opportunity to tell us the motives that put the Duke and Duchess upon this odd compound of extravagancies, that has been last related. He says that the Bachelor Carrasco meditating revenge for having been defeated by Don Quixote, when he went by the title of the Knight of the Mirrors, resolved to make another attempt in hopes of better fortune; and therefore, having understood where Don Quixote was, by the page that brought the letters and present to Sancho's wife, he furnished himself with a fresh horse and arms, and had a white moon painted on his shield; his accoutrements were all packed up on a mule, and, lest Thomas Cecial, his former attendant, should be known by Don Quixote or Sancho, he got a country fellow to wait on him as a squire. Coming to the Duke's castle, he was informed that the Knight was gone to the tournament at Saragossa, the Duke giving the bachelor an account also how pleasantly they had imposed upon him with the contrivance for Dulcinea's disenchantment, to be effected at the expense of Sancho's posteriors. Finally, he told him how Sancho had made his master believe that Dulcinea was transformed into a country wench by the power of magic; and how the Duchess had persuaded Sancho that he was deluded himself, and Dulcinea enchanted in good earnest. The bachelor, though he could not forbear laughing, was nevertheless struck with wonder at this mixture of cunning and simplicity in the squire, and the uncommon madness of the master. The Duke then made it his request that if he met with the Knight he should call at the castle as he returned, and give him an account of his success, whether he vanquished him or not. The bachelor promised to obey his commands; and departing in search of Don Quixote, he found him not at Saragossa, but travelling farther, met him at last, and had his revenge, as we have told you. Then taking the Duke's castle in his way home, he gave him an account of the circumstances and conditions of the combat, and how Don Quixote was repairing homewards to fulfil his engagements of returning to and remaining in his village for a year, as it was incumbent on the honour of chivalry to perform; and in this space, the bachelor said, he hoped the poor gentleman might recover his senses; declaring withal that the concern he had upon him to see a man of his parts in such a distracted condition was the only motive that could put him upon such an attempt.

Upon this he returned home, there to expect Don Quixote, who was coming after him. This information engaged the Duke, who was never to be tired with the humours of the Knight and the squire, to take this occasion to make more sport with them; he ordered all the roads thereabouts, especially those that Don Quixote was most likely to take, to be watched by a great many of his servants, who had orders to bring him to the castle, right or wrong.

They met him accordingly, and sent their master an account of it; whereupon all things being prepared against his coming, the Duke caused the torches and tapers to be all lighted round the court, and Altisidora's tragi-comical interlude was acted, with the humours of Sancho Pança, the whole so to the life, that the counterfeit was hardly discernible. Cid Hamet adds, that he believed those that played all these tricks were as mad as those they were imposed upon: and that the Duke and Duchess were within a hair's breadth of being thought fools themselves, for taking so much pains to make sport with the weakness of two poor silly wretches.

To return to our two adventurers; the morning found the one fast asleep, and the other broad awake, transported with his wild imaginations. They thought it time to rise, especially the Don; for the bed of sloth was never agreeable to him, whether vanquished or victorious.

Altisidora, whom Don Quixote supposed to have been raised from the dead, did, that day (to humour her lord and lady) deck her head with the same garland she wore upon the tomb, and in a loose gown of white taffeta, flowered with gold, her dishevelled locks flowing negligently on her shoulders, she entered Don Quixote's chamber, supporting herself with an ebony staff.

The Knight was so surprised and amazed at this unexpected apparition, that he was struck dumb; and not knowing how to behave himself, he slunk down under the bed-clothes, and covered himself over head and ears. However, Altisidora placed herself in a chair close by his bed's-head, and after a profound sigh: 'To what an extremity of misfortune and distress,' said she in a soft and languishing voice, 'are young ladies of my virtue and quality reduced, when they thus trample upon the rule of modesty, and without regard to virgin-decency, are forced to give their tongues a loose, and betray the secrets of their hearts! Alas! noble Don Quixote de la Mancha, I am one of those unhappy persons overruled by my passion, but yet so reserved and patient in my sufferings, that silence broke my heart, and my heart broke in silence. It is now two days, most inexorable and marble-hearted man, since the sense of your severe usage and cruelty brought me to my death, or something so like it, that every one that saw me judged me to be dead. And had not love been compassionate, and assigned my recovery on the sufferings of this kind squire, I had ever remained in the other world.' 'Truly,' quoth Sancho, 'love might even as well have made choice of my ass for that service, and he would have obliged me a great deal more. But pray, good mistress, tell me one thing now, and so Heaven provide you a better natured sweetheart than my master; what did you see in the other world? What sort of folks are there in hell? for there I suppose you have been; for those that die of despair must needs go to that summer-house.' 'To tell you the truth,' replied Altisidora, 'I fancy I could not be dead outright, because I was not got so far as hell; for had I been once in, I am sure I should never have been allowed to have got out again. I got to the gates indeed, where I found a round dozen of devils in their breeches and waistcoats, playing at tennis with flaming rackets; they wore flat-bands with scolloped Flanders lace and ruffles of the same; four inches of their wrists bare, to make their hands look the longer; in which they held rackets of fire. But what I most wondered at, was, that instead of tennis-balls, they made use of books that were every whit as light, and stuffed with wind and flocks, or such kind of trumpery. This was indeed most strange and wonderful; but, what still amazed me more, I found, that, contrary to the custom of gamesters, among whom the winning party at least is in good humour, and the losers only angry, these hellish tossers of books of both sides did nothing but fret, fume, stamp, curse, and swear most horribly, as if they had been all losers.'

'That is no wonder at all,' quoth Sancho; 'for your devils, whether they play or no, win or lose, they can never be contented.' 'That may be,' said Altisidora, 'but another thing that I admire (I then admired I would say) was, that the ball would not bear a second blow, but at every stroke they were obliged to change books, some of them new, some old, which I thought very strange. And one accident that happened upon this I cannot forget: they tossed up a new book fairly bound, and gave it such a smart stroke, that the very guts flew out of it, and all the leaves were scattered about. Then cried one of the devils to another, "Look, look, what book is that?" "It is the Second Part of the History of Don Quixote," said the other; "not that which was composed by Cid Hamet, the author of the first, but by a certain Arragonian, who professes himself a native of Tordesillas." "Away with it," cried the first devil, "down with it, plunge it to the lowest pit of hell, where I may never see it more." "Why, is it such sad stuff?" said the other. "Such intolerable stuff," cried the first devil, "that if I and all the devils in hell should set their heads together to make it worse, it were past our skill." The devils continued their game, and shattered a world of other books, but the name of Don Quixote that I so passionately adored, confined my thoughts only to that part of the vision which I have told you.' 'It could be nothing but a vision to be sure,' said Don Quixote, 'for I am the only person of the name now in the universe, and that very book is tossed about here at the very same rate, never resting in a place, for everybody has a fling at it. Nor am I concerned that any phantom assuming my name, should wander in the shades of darkness, or in the light of this world, since I am not the person of whom that history treats. If it be well writ, faithful, and authentic, it will live ages; but if it be bad, it will have a quick journey from its birth to the grave of oblivion.' Altisidora was then going to renew her expostulations and complaints against Don Quixote, had not he thus interrupted her: 'I have often cautioned you, madam,' said he, 'of fixing your affections upon a man who is absolutely incapable of making a suitable return. It grieves me to have a heart obtruded upon me, when I have no entertainment to give it but bare cold thanks. I was only born for Dulcinea del Toboso, and to her alone the Destinies (if such there be) have devoted my affection: so it is presumption for any other beauty to imagine she can displace her, or but share the passion she holds in my soul. This I hope may suffice to take away all foundation from your hopes, to recall your modesty, and re-instate it in its proper bounds, for impossibilities are not to be expected from any creature upon earth.'

At hearing of this, 'Death of my life!' cried Altisidora, putting on a violent passion, 'thou lump of lead, who hast a soul of mortar, and a heart as little and as hard as the stone of an olive, more stubborn than a common plough-jobber, or a carrier's horse that will never go out of his road; I have a good mind to tear your eyes out, as deep as they are in your head. Why, thou beaten swash-buckler, thou rib-roasted Knight of the cudgel, hast thou impudence to think that I died for love of thy lantern-jaws? No, no, sir Tiffany, all that you have seen this night has been counterfeit, for I would not suffer the pain of a flea-bite, much less that of dying, for such a dromedary as thou art.' 'Troth, lass, I believe thee,' quoth Sancho; 'for all these stories of people dying for love are mere tales of a roasted horse. They tell you they will die for love, but the devil a-bit. Trust to that, and be laughed at.'

Their discourse was interrupted by the coming in of the harper, singer, and composer of the stanzas that were performed in the court the night before. 'Sir Knight,' said he to Don Quixote, making a profound obeisance, 'let me beg the favour of being numbered among your most humble servants; it is an honour which I have long been ambitious to receive, in regard of your great renown, and the value of your achieve-ments.' 'Pray, sir,' said Don Quixote, 'let me know who you are, that I may proportion my respects to your merits.' The spark gave him to understand, he was the person that made and sung the verses he heard the last night. 'Truly, sir,' said Don Quixote, 'you have an excellent voice; but I think your poetry was little to the purpose; for what relation pray have the stanzas of Garcilasso to this lady's death?' 'Oh! sir, never wonder at that,' replied the musician, 'I do but as other brothers of the quill; all the upstart poets of the age do the same, and every one writes what he pleases, how he pleases, and steals from whom he pleases, whether it be to the purpose or no; for let them write and set to music what they will, though never so impertinent and absurd, there is a thing called poetical licence, that is our warrant, and a safeguard and refuge for nonsense, among all the men of jingle and metre.'

Don Quixote was going to answer, but was interrupted by the coming of the Duke and Duchess, who improving the conversation, made it very pleasant for some hours; and Sancho was so full of his odd conceits and arch wipes, that the Duke and Duchess were at a stand which to admire most, his wit, or his simplicity. After that, Don Quixote begged leave for his departure that very day, alleging that knights in his unhappy circumstances were rather fitter to inhabit an humble cottage than a kingly palace. They freely complied with his request, and the Duchess desired to know if Altisidora had yet attained to any share of his favour. 'Madam,' answered Don Quixote,

'I must freely tell your Grace, that I am confident all this damsel's disease proceeds from nothing else in the world but idleness. So nothing in nature can be better physic for her distemper, than to be continually employed in some innocent and decent things. She has been pleased to inform me, that bone-lace is much worn in hell; and since, without doubt, she knows how to make it, let that be her task, and I will engage the tumbling of her bobbins to and again will soon toss her love out of her head: now this is my opinion, madam, and my advice.' 'And mine too,' quoth Sancho, 'for I never knew any of our bone-lace makers die of love, nor any other young wench, that had anything else to do: I know it by myself; when I am hard at work, with a spade in my hand, I no more think of pig'snyes (my own dear wife I mean) than I do of my dead cow, though I love her as the apple of my eye.' 'You say well, Sancho,' answered the Duchess, 'and I will take care that Altisidora shall not want employment for the future; she understands her needle, and I am resolved she shall make use of it.' 'Madam,' said Altisidora, 'I shall have no occasion for any remedy of that nature; for the sense of the severity and ill-usage that I have met with from that vagabond monster, will, without any other means, soon raze him out of my memory. In the mean time, I beg your Grace's leave to retire, that I may no longer behold, I will not say his woeful figure, but his ugly and abominable countenance.' 'These words,' said the Duke, 'put me in mind of the proverb, After railing comes forgiving.' Altisidora putting her handkerchief to her eyes, as it were to dry her tears, and then making her honours to the Duke and Duchess, went out of the room. 'Alack-a-day! poor girl,' cried Sancho 'I know what will be the end of thee, since thou art fallen into the hands of that sad soul, that merciless master of mine, with a crab-tree heart, as tough as any oak.

Woe be to thee, a-faith! hadst thou fallen in love with this sweet face of mine, body of me, thou hadst met with the cock of the game.' The discourse ended here. Don Quixote dressed, dined with the Duke and Duchess, and departed that afternoon.

CHAPTER LXXI

What happened to Don Quixote, and his Squire, in their way home

THE VANQUISHED KNIGHT-ERRANT continued his journey, equally divided between grief and joy; the thought of his overthrow sometimes sunk his spirits, but then the assurance he had of the virtue lodged in Sancho, by Altisidora's resurrection, raised them up again; and yet, after all, he had much ado to persuade himself that the amorous damsel was really dead. As for Sancho, his thoughts were not at all of the pleasing kind; on the contrary, he was mightily upon the sullen, because Altisidora had bilked him of the smocks she promised him; and his head running upon that, 'Faith and troth, sir,' quoth he, 'I have the worst luck of any physician under heaven; other doctors kill their patients, and are paid for it too, and yet they are at no further trouble than scrawling two or three cramp words for some physical slip-slop, which the apothecaries are at the pains to make up. Now here am I, that save people from the grave at the expense of my own hide, pinched, clapper-clawed, run through with pins, and whipped like a top, and yet the devil a cross I get by the bargain. But if ever they catch me a-curing anybody in this fashion, unless I have my fee beforehand, may I be served as I have been for nothing. Odsdiggers! they shall pay sauce for it; no money, no cure; the monk lives by his singing; and I cannot think Heaven would make me a doctor, without allowing me my fees.' 'You are in the right, Sancho,' said Don Quixote 'and Altisidora has done unworthily in disappointing you of the smocks. Though you must own, that the virtue by which thou workest these wonders was a free gift, and cost thee nothing to learn, but the art of patience. For my part, had you demanded your fees for disenchanting Dulcinea, you should have received them already; but I am afraid there can be no gratuity proportionable to the greatness of the cure; and therefore I would not have the remedy depend upon a reward; for who knows whether my proffering it, or thy acceptance of it, might not hinder the effect of penance? However, since we have gone so far, we will put it to a trial. Come, Sancho name your price, and down with your breeches. First pay your hide, then pay yourself out of the money of mine that you have in your custody.' Sancho, opening his eyes and ears above a foot wide at this fair offer, leaped presently at the proposal. 'Ay, ay, sir, now you say something,' quoth he. 'I will do it with a jerk now, since you speak so feelingly. I have a wife and children to maintain, sir, and I must mind the main chance. Come then, how much will you give me by the lash?' 'Were your payment,' said Don Quixote, 'to be answerable to the greatness and merits of the cure, not all the wealth of Venice, nor the Indian mines were sufficient to reward thee. But see what cash you have of mine in your hands, and set what price you will on every stripe.' 'The lashes,' quoth Sancho, 'are in all three thousand three hundred and odd, of which I have had five; the rest are to come, let those five go for the odd ones, and let us come to the three thousand three hundred. At a quartillo, or three-halfpence, apiece; and I would not bate a farthing, if it were to my brother. They will make three thousand three hundred three-halfpences. Three thousand three-halfpences, make fifteen hundred threepences, which amounts to seven hundred and fifty reals, or sixpences. Now the three hundred remaining three halfpences, make an hundred and fifty threepences, and threescore and fifteen sixpences; put that together, and it comes just to eight hundred and twenty-five reals, or sixpences, to a farthing. This money, sir, if you please, I will deduct from yours that I have in my hands, and then I will reckon myself well paid for my jerking, and go home well pleased, though well whipped; but that is nothing, something has some savour; he must not think to catch fish, who is afraid to wet his feet. I need say no more.' 'Now blessings on thy heart, my dearest Sancho,' cried Don Quixote; 'oh! my friend, how shall Dulcinea and I be bound to pray for thee, and serve thee while it shall please Heaven to continue us on earth! If she recover her former shape and beauty, as now she infallibly must, her misfortune will turn to her felicity, and I shall triumph in my defeat. Speak, dear Sancho, when wilt thou enter upon thy task, and a hundred reals more shall be at thy service, as a gratuity for thy being expeditious?' 'I will begin this very night,' answered Sancho, 'do but order it so that we may lie in the fields, and you shall see how I will lay about me; I shall not be sparing of my flesh, I will assure you.' Don Quixote longed for night so impatiently, that, like all eager expecting lovers, he fancied Phœbus had broken his chariot-wheels, which made the day of so unusual a length; but at last it grew dark, and they went out of the road into a shady wood, where they both alighted, and being sat down upon the grass, they went to supper upon such provision as Sancho's wallet afforded.

And now having satisfied himself, he thought it time to satisfy his master, and earn his money. To which purpose he made himself a whip of Dapple's halter, and having stripped himself to the waist, retired further up into the wood at a small distance from his master. Don Quixote, observing his readiness and resolution, could not forbear calling after him,

'Dear Sancho,' cried he, 'be not too cruel to thyself neither. Have a care, do not hack thyself to pieces: make no more haste than good speed: go more gently to work, soft and fair goes furthest; I mean, I would not have thee kill thyself before thou gettest to the end of the tally; and that the reckoning may be fair on both sides, I will stand at a distance, and keep an account of the strokes by the help of my beads; and so Heaven prosper thy pious undertaking.' 'He is an honest man,' quoth Sancho, 'who pays to a farthing; I only mean to give myself a handsome whipping, for do not think I need kill myself to work miracles.' With that he began to exercise the instrument of penance, and Don Quixote to tell the strokes. But by that time Sancho had applied seven or eight lashes on his bare back, he felt the jest bite him so smartly, that he began to repent him of his bargain: whereupon, after a short pause, he called to his master, and told him, that he would be off with him, for such lashes as these, laid on with such a confounded lick-back, were modestly worth threepence apiece of any man's money; and truly he could not afford to go on at three-halfpence a lash. 'Go on, friend Sancho,' answered Don Quixote, 'take courage and proceed, I will double thy pay, if that be all.' 'Say you so?' quoth Sancho, 'then have at all; I will lay it on thick and threefold. Do but listen!' With that, slap went the scourge; but the cunning knave left persecuting his own skin, and fell foul of the trees, fetching such dismal groans every now and then, that one would have thought he had been giving up the ghost. Don Quixote, who was naturally tender-hearted, fearing he might make an end of himself before he could finish his penance, and so disappoint the happy effects of it: 'Hold,' cried he, 'hold my friend, as thou lovest thy life, hold I conjure thee, no more at this time. This seems to be a very sharp sort of physic. Therefore pray do not take it all at once, make two doses of it. Come, come, all in good time, Rome was not built in a day. If I have told right, thou hast given thyself above a thousand stripes; that is enough for one beating; for, to use a homely phrase, the ass will carry his load, but not a double load; ride not a free horse to death.' 'No, no,' quoth Sancho, 'it shall never be said of me, the eaten bread is forgotten, or that I thought it working for a dead horse, because I am paid beforehand. Therefore stand off, I beseech you; get out of the reach of my whip, and let me lay on the other thousand, and then the heart of the work will be broke: such another flogging bout, and the job will be over.' 'Since thou art in the humour,' replied Don Quixote, 'I will withdraw, and Heaven strengthen and reward thee.' With that, Sancho fell to work afresh, and beginning upon a new score, he lashed the trees at so unconscionable a rate, that he fetched off their skins most unmercifully. At length, raising his voice, seemingly resolved to give himself a sparing blow, he lets drive at a beech tree with might and main: 'There!' cried he; 'down with thee, Sampson, and all that are about thee!' This dismal cry, with the sound of the dreadful strokes that attended it, made Don Quixote run presently to his squire, and laying fast hold on the halter, which Sancho had twisted about and managed like a bull's-pizzle, 'Hold,' cried he, 'friend Sancho, stay the fury of thy arm: dost thou think I will have thy death, and the ruin of thy wife and children to be laid at my door? Forbid it, Fate! Let Dulcinea stay a while, till a better opportunity offers itself. I myself will be contented to live in hopes, that when thou hast recovered new strength, the business may be accomplished to everybody's satisfaction.' 'Well, sir,' quoth Sancho,' if it be your worship's will and pleasure it should be so, so let it be, quoth I. But, for goodness' sake do so much as throw your cloak over my shoulders; for I am all in a muck-sweat, and I have no mind to catch cold; we novices are somewhat in danger of that when we first undergo the discipline of flogging.' With that Don Quixote took off his cloak from his own shoulders, and putting it over those of Sancho, chose to remain in cuerpo; and the crafty squire being lapped up warm, fell fast asleep, and never stirred till the sun waked him.

In the morning they went on their journey, and after three hours' riding, alighted at an inn, for it was allowed by Don Quixote himself to be an inn, and not a castle, with moats, towers, portcullices, and draw-bridges, as he commonly fancied; for now the Knight was mightily off the romantic pin to what he used to be, as shall be showed presently more at large. He was lodged in a ground-room, which, instead of tapestry, was hung with a coarse painted stuff, such as is often seen in villages. One of the pieces had the story of Helen of Troy, when Paris stole her away from her husband Menelaus, but scrawled out after a bungling rate by some wretched dauber or other. Another had the story of Dido and Æneas, the Lady on the top of a turret, waving a sheet to her fugitive guest, who was in a ship at sea, crowding all the sails he could to get from her. Don Quixote made this observation upon the two stories, that Helen was not at all displeased at the force put upon her, but rather leered and smiled upon her lover: whereas, on the other side, the fair Dido showed her grief by her tears; which, because they should be seen, the painter had made as big as walnuts. 'How unfortunate,' said Don Quixote, 'were these two ladies that they lived not in this age, or rather how much more unhappy am I for not having lived in theirs! I would have met and stopped those gentlemen, and saved both Troy and Carthage from destruction; nay, by the death of Paris alone all these miseries had been prevented.' 'I will lay you a wager,' quoth Sancho, 'that before we be much older there will not be an inn, a hedge-tavern, a blind victualling-house, nor a barber's shop in the country, but will have the story of our lives and deeds pasted and painted along the walls. But I could wish with all my heart though that they may be done by a better hand than the bungling son of a whore that drew these.' 'Thou art in the right, Sancho; for the fellow that did these puts me in mind of Orbaneja, the painter of Uveda, who, as he sat at work, being asked what he was about, made answer, anything that comes uppermost; and if he chanced to draw a cock he underwrit, "This is a cock," lest people should take it for a fox. Just such a one was he that painted or that wrote (for they are much the same), the history of this new Don Quixote, that has lately peeped out, and ventured to go a-strolling; for his painting or writing is all at random, and anything that comes uppermost. I fancy he is also not much unlike one Mauleon, a certain poet, who was at court some years ago, and pretended to give answers *extempore* to any manner of questions: somebody asked what was the meaning of *Deum de Deo*. Whereupon my gentleman answered very pertly in Spanish, "*De donde diére*," that is, Hab-nab at a venture.

'But to come to our own affairs. Hast thou an inclination to have the other brush to-night? What think you of a warm house; would it not do better for that service than the open air?' 'Why truly,' quoth Sancho, 'a whipping is but a whipping either abroad or within doors, and I could like a close, warm place well enough, so it were among trees; for I love trees hugely, do you see, methinks they bear me company, and have a sort of fellow-feeling of my sufferings.' 'Now I think on it,' said Don Quixote, 'it shall not be to-night, honest Sancho, you shall have more time to recover, and we will let the rest alone till we get home; it will not be above two days at most.' 'Even as your worship pleases,' answered Sancho; 'but if I might have my will, it were best making an end of the job, now my hand is in and my blood up. There is nothing like striking while the iron is hot, for delay breeds danger: it is best grinding at the mill before the water is past; ever take while you may have it: a bird in hand is worth two in the bush.' 'For Heaven's sake, good Sancho,' cried Don Quixote, 'let alone thy proverbs; if once thou goest back to *Sicut erat*, or, as it was in the beginning, I must give thee over. Canst thou not speak as other folks do, and not after such a tedious round-about manner? How often have I told thee of this? Mind what I tell you, I am sure you will be the better for it.' 'It is an unlucky trick I have got,' replied Sancho, 'I cannot bring you in three words to the purpose without a proverb, nor bring you any proverb but what I think to the purpose; but I will mend if I can.' And so for this time their conversation broke off.

CHAPTER LXXII

How Don Quixote and Sancho got home

THAT WHOLE DAY Don Quixote and Sancho continued in the inn, expecting the return of night, the one to have an opportunity to make an end of his penance in the fields, and the other to see it fully performed, as being the most material preliminary to the accomplishment of his desires.

In the mean time, a gentleman with three or four servants came riding up to the inn, and one of them calling him that appeared to be the master, by the name of Don Alvaro Tarfe, 'Your worship,' said he, 'had as good stop here till the heat of the day be over. In my opinion, the house looks cool and cleanly.' Don Quixote, overhearing the name of Tarfe, and presently turning to his squire, 'Sancho,' said he, 'I am much mistaken if I had not a glimpse of this very name of Don Alvaro Tarfe in turning over that pretended second part of my history.' 'As likely as not,' quoth Sancho; 'but first let him alight, and then we will question him about the matter.'

The gentleman alighted, and was showed by the landlady into a ground-room that faced Don Quixote's apartment, and was hung with the same sort of coarse painted stuff. A while after the stranger had undressed for coolness, he came out to take a turn, and walked into the porch of the house, that was large and airy: there he found Don Quixote, to whom addressing himself, 'Pray, sir,' said he, 'which way do you travel?' 'To a country town, not far off,' answered Don Quixote, 'the place of my nativity. And pray, sir, which way are you bound?' 'To Granada, sir,' said the knight 'the country where I was born.' 'And a fine country it is,' replied Don Quixote. 'But pray, sir, may I beg the favour to know your name, for the information I am persuaded will be of more consequence to my affairs than I can well tell you.' 'They call me Don Alvaro Tarfe,' answered the gentleman. 'Then, without dispute,' said Don Quixote, 'you are the same Don Alvaro Tarfe, whose name fills a place in the Second Part of Don Quixote de la Mancha's history, that was lately published by a new author?' 'The very man,' answered the knight; 'and that very Don Quixote, who is the principal subject of that book was my intimate acquaintance: I am the person that enticed him from his habitation so far at least, that he had never seen the tournament at Saragosa, had it not been through my persuasions, and in my company; and indeed, as it happened, I proved the best friend he had, and did him a singular piece of service; for had I not stood by him, his intolerable impudence had brought him to some shameful punishment.' 'But pray, sir,' said Don Quixote, 'be pleased to tell me one thing; am I anything like that Don Quixote of yours?' 'The farthest from it in the world, sir,' replied the other. 'And had he,' said our Knight, 'one, Sancho Pança, for his squire?' 'Yes,' said Don Alvaro, 'but I was the most deceived in him that could be; for, by common report, that same squire was a comical, witty fellow; but I found him a very great blockhead.' 'I thought no less,' quoth Sancho; 'for, it is not in everybody's power to crack a jest, or say pleasant things; and that Sancho you talk of must be some paultry raggamuffin, some guttling mumper, or pilfering crack-rope, I warrant him. For it is I that am the true Sancho Pança, it is I that am the merry, conceited squire, that have always a tinker's budget full of wit and waggery, that will make gravity grin in spite of its teeth. If you will not believe me, do but try me; keep me company but for a twelvemonth or so, you will find what a shower of jokes and notable things drop from me every foot. Adad! I set everybody a-laughing many times, and yet I wish I may be hanged if I designed it in the least. And then for the true Don Quixote de la Mancha, here you have him before you. The staunch, the famous, the valiant, the wise, the loving Don Quixote de la Mancha, the righter of wrongs, the punisher of wickedness, the father to the fatherless, the bully-rock of widows, the murderer* of damsels and maidens; he whose only dear and sweetheart is the peerless Dulcinea del Toboso; here he is, and here am I, his squire. All other Don Quixotes, and all Sancho Panças, besides us two, are but shams, and tales of a tub.' 'Now, by the sword of St. Jago, honest friend,' said Don Alvaro, 'I believe as much; for the little thou hast uttered now, has more of the humour than all I ever heard come from the other. The blockhead seemed to carry all his brains in his guts, there is nothing a jest with him but filling his belly, and the rogue is too heavy to be diverting. For my part, I believe the enchanters that persecute the good Don Quixote, sent the bad one to persecute me too. I cannot tell what to make of this matter; for though I can take my oath, I left one Don Quixote under the surgeon's hands at the nuncio's house in Toledo, yet here starts up another Don Quixote quite different from mine.' 'For my part,' said our Knight, 'I dare not avow myself the good, but I may venture to say I am not the bad one; and, as a proof of it, sir, be assured, that in the whole course of my life, I never saw the city of Saragosa; and, so far from it, that hearing this usurper of my name had appeared there at the tournament, I declined coming near it, being resolved to convince the world that he was an impostor. I directed my course to Barcelona, the seat of urbanity, the sanctuary of strangers, the refuge of the distressed, the mother of men of valour, the redresser of the injured, the residence of true friendship, and the first city in the world for beauty and situation. And though some accidents that befel me there

* In the original, *el Matador de las Donzellas*. A blunder of Sancho's – 'murderer' of damsels, instead of 'maintainer.'

are so far from being grateful to my thoughts, that they are a sensible mortification to me, yet in my reflection of having seen that city, I find pleasure enough to alleviate my misfortune. In short, Don Alvaro, I am that Don Quixote de la Mancha whom fame has celebrated, and not the pitiful wretch who has usurped my name, and would arrogate to himself the honour of my designs. Sir, you are a gentleman, and I hope will not deny me the favour to depose before the magistrate of this place, that you never saw me in all your life till this day, and that I am not the Don Quixote mentioned in that second part, nor was this Sancho Pança my squire the person you knew formerly.' 'With all my heart,' said Don Alvaro, 'though I must own myself not a little confounded to find at the same time two Don Quixotes, and two Sancho Panças, as different in their behaviour as they are alike in name; for my part, I do not know what to think of it, and I am sometimes apt to fancy my senses have been imposed upon.'* 'Ay, ay,' quoth Sancho, 'there has been foul play to be sure. The same trick that served to bewitch my Lady Dulcinea del Toboso has been played you; and if three thousand and odd lashes laid on by me on the hinder part of my belly, would disenchant your worship as well as her, they should be at your service with all my heart; and what is more, they should not cost you a farthing.' 'I do not understand what you mean by those lashes,' said Don Alvaro. 'Thereby hangs a tale,' quoth Sancho, 'but that is too long to relate at a minute's warning; but if it be our luck to be fellow-travellers, you may chance to hear more of the matter.'

Dinner-time being come, Don Quixote and Don Alvaro dined together; and the mayor, or bailiff of the town, happening to come into the inn with a public notary, Don Quixote desired him to take the deposition which Don Alvaro Tarfe there present was ready to give, confessing and declaring, that the said deponent had not any knowledge of the Don Quixote there present, and that the said Don Quixote was not the same person that he, this deponent, had seen mentioned in a certain printed history, intituled, or called, 'The Second Part of Don Quixote de la Mancha,' written by Avellaneda, a native of Tordefillas. In short, the notary drew up and engrossed the affidavit in due form; and the testimonial wanted nothing to make it answer all the intentions of Don Quixote and Sancho, who were as much pleased as if it had been a matter of the last consequence, and that their words and behaviour had not been enough to make the distinction apparent between the two Don Quixotes and the two Sanchos.

The compliments and offers of service that passed after that between Don Alvaro and Don Quixote were not a few; and our Knight of La

---

* In the original, it is, 'I am now assured that I have not seen what I have seen, nor, in respect to me, has that happened which has happened.'

Mancha behaved himself therein with so much discretion, that Don Alvaro was convinced he was mistaken; for he thought there was some enchantment in the case, since he had thus met with two knights and two squires of the same names and professions, and yet so very different.

They set out towards the evening, and about half a league from the town, the road parted into two, one way led to Don Quixote's habitation, and the other to that which Don Alvaro was to take. Don Quixote in that little time let him understand the misfortune of his defeat, with Dulcinea's enchantment, and the remedy prescribed by Merlin; all which was new matter of wonder to Don Alvaro, who having embraced Don Quixote and Sancho, left them on their way, and he followed his own.

Don Quixote passed that night among the trees, to give Sancho a fair occasion to make an end of his discipline, when the cunning knave put it in practice just after the same manner as the night before. The bark of the trees paid for all, and Sancho took such care of his back, that a fly might have rested there without any disturbance.

All the while his abused master was very punctual in telling the strokes, and reckoned that, with those of the foregoing night, they amounted just to the sum of three thousand and twenty-nine. The sun, that seemed to have made more than ordinary haste to rise and see this human sacrifice, gave them light however to continue their journey; and, as they went on, they descanted at large upon Don Alvaro's mistake, and their own prudence, in relation to the certificate before the magistrate, in so full and authentic a form.

Their travels all that day, and the ensuing night, afforded no occurrence worth mentioning except that Sancho that night put the last hand to his whipping-work, to the inexpressible joy of Don Quixote, who waited for the day with as great impatience, in hopes he might light on his Lady Dulcinea in her disenchanted state; and all the way he went, he made up to every woman he spied, to see whether she were Dulcinea del Toboso or not; for he so firmly relied on Merlin's promises, that he did not doubt of the performance.

He was altogether taken up with these hopes and fancies, when they got to the top of a hill, that gave them a prospect of their village. Sancho had no sooner blessed his eyes with the sight, but down he fell on his knees, and, 'O my long, long-wished for home!' cried he, 'open thy eyes, and here behold thy child, Sancho Pança, come back to thee again, if not very full of money, yet very full of whipping: open thy arms, and receive thy son Don Quixote too, who, though he got the worst of it with another, he nevertheless got the better of himself, and that is the best kind of victory one can wish for; I have his own word for it. However, though I have been swingingly flogged, yet I have not lost all by the bargain, for I have whipped some money into my pocket.' 'Forbear thy impertinence,' said Don Quixote, 'and let us now in a decent manner make our entry into the place of our nativity, where we will give a loose to our imaginations, and lay down the plan that is to be followed in our intended pastoral life.' With these words they came down the hill, and went directly to their village.

CHAPTER LXXIII

Of the ominous Accidents that crossed Don Quixote as he entered his village, with other Transactions that illustrate and adorn this memorable History

WHEN THEY were entering into the village, as Cid Hamet relates, Don Quixote observed two little boys contesting together, in an adjoining field; and says one to the other: 'Never fret thy gizzard about it, for thou shalt never see her while thou hast breath in thy body.' Don Quixote overhearing this, 'Sancho,' said he, 'did you mind the boy's words, "Thou shalt never see her while thou hast breath in thy body." ' 'Well,' answered Sancho, 'and what is the great business though the boy did say so?' 'How,' replied Don Quixote, 'dost thou not perceive, that applying the words to my affairs, they plainly imply that I shall never see my Dulcinea?' Sancho was about to answer again, but was hindered by a full cry of hounds and huntsmen pursuing a hare, which was put so hard to her shifts, that she came and squatted down for shelter just between Dapple's feet. Immediately Sancho laid hold of her without difficulty, and presented her to Don Quixote; but he, with a dejected look, refusing the present, cried out aloud, *Malum signum, malum signum,* an ill omen, an ill omen, a hare runs away, hounds pursue her, and Dulcinea is not started.' 'You are a strange man,' quoth Sancho. 'Cannot we suppose now, that poor puss here is Dulcinea, the greyhounds that followed her, are those dogs the enchanters, that made her a country lass. She scouts away, I catch her by the scut, and give her safe and sound into your worship's hands; and pray make much of her now you have her; for my part, I cannot, for the blood of me, see any harm nor any ill luck in this matter.'

By this time the two boys that had fallen out came up to see the hare; and Sancho having asked the cause of their quarrel, he was answered by the boy that spoke the ominous words, that he had snatched from his play-fellow a little cage full of crickets, which he would not let him have again. Upon that, Sancho put his hand in his pocket, and gave the boy a threepenny piece for his cage; and giving it to Don Quixote, 'There, sir,' quoth he, 'here are all the signs of ill-luck come to nothing. You have them in your own hands; and though I am but a dunder-head, I dare swear these things are no more to us than the rain that falls at Christmas. I am much mistaken if I have not heard the parson of our parish advise all sober Catholics against heeding such fooleries; and I have heard you yourself, my dear master, say, that all such Christians as troubled their heads with those fortune-telling follies, were neither better nor worse than downright numskulls: so let us even leave things as we found them, and get home as fast as we can.'

By this time, the sportsmen were come up, and demanding their game, Don Quixote delivered them their hare. They passed on, and just at their coming into the town, they perceived the curate and the Bachelor Carrasco at their devotions in a small field adjoining. But we must observe by the way, that Sancho Pança, to cover his master's armour, had, by way of sumpter-cloth, laid over Dapple's back the buckram-frock figured with flames of fire, which he wore at the Duke's the night that Altisidora rose from the dead, and he had no less judiciously clapped the mitre on the head of the ass, which made so odd and whimsical a figure, that it might be said, never four-footed ass was so bedizened before. The curate and the bachelor presently knowing their old friends, ran to meet him with open arms; and while Don Quixote alighted and returned their embraces, the boys, who are ever so quick-sighted that nothing can escape their eyes, presently spying the mitred ass, came running and flocking about them: 'Oh law!' cried they one to another, 'look ye there, boys! here is Gaffer Sancho Pança's ass as fine as a lady! and Don Quixote's beast leaner than ever.' With that they ran hooping and hollowing about them through the town, while the two adventurers, attended by the curate and the bachelor, moved towards Don Quixote's house, where they were received at the door by his housekeeper and his niece, that had already got notice of their arrival. The news having also reached Teresa Pança, Sancho's wife, she came running half naked, with her hair about her ears, to see him; leading by the hand all the way her daughter Sanchica, who hardly wanted to be lugged along. But when she found that her husband looked a little short of the state of a governor, 'Mercy on me,' quoth she, 'what is the meaning of this, husband? You look as though you had come all the way on foot, nay, and tired off your legs too! Why, you come liker a shark than like a governor.' 'Mum, Teresa,' quoth Sancho, 'it is not all gold that glitters, and every man was not born with a silver spoon in his mouth. First let us go home, and then I will tell thee wonders. I have taken care of the main chance. Money I have, old girl, and I came honestly by it, without wronging anybody.' 'Hast got money, old boy? nay, then it is well enough, no matter which way, let it come by hook or by crook, it is but what your betters have done before you.' At the same time, Sanchica hugging her father, asked him what he had brought her home, for she had gaped for him as the flowers do for the dew in May. Thus Sancho, leading Dapple by the halter on one side, his wife taking him by the arm on the other, and his daughter fastening upon the waistband of his breeches, away they went together to his cottage, leaving Don Quixote at his own house, under the care of his niece and housekeeper, with the curate and bachelor to keep him company.

That very moment Don Quixote took the two last aside, and, without mincing the matter, gave them a short account of his defeat, and the obligations he lay under of being confined to his village for a year, which, like a true knight-errant, he was resolved punctually to observe: he added, that he intended to pass that interval of time in the innocent functions of a pastoral life; and therefore he would immediately commence shepherd, and entertain his amorous passion solitarily in fields and woods; and begged, if business of greater importance were not an obstruction, that they would both please to be his companions, assuring them he would furnish them with such a number of sheep, as might entitle them to such a profession. He also told them, that he had already in a manner fitted them for the undertaking; for he had provided them all with names the most pastoral in the world. The curate being desirous to know the names, Don Quixote told him, he would himself be called the shepherd Quixotis; that the bachelor should be called the shepherd Carrascone; the curate, pastor Curiambro; and Sancho Pança, Pansino the shepherd.

They were struck with amazement at this new strain of folly; but considering this might be a means of keeping him at home, and hoping at the same time, that, within the year, he might be cured of his mad knight-errantry, they came into his pastoral folly, and, with great applause to his project, freely offered their company in the design. 'We shall live the most pleasant wife imaginable,' said Samson Carrasco; 'for, as everybody knows I am a most celebrated poet, I will write pastorals in abundance. Sometimes too I may raise my strain, as occasion offers, to divert us, as we range the groves and plains. But one thing, gentlemen, we must not forget, it is absolutely necessary that each of us choose a name for the shepherdess he means to celebrate in his lays; nor must we forget the ceremony used by the amorous shepherds, of writing, caning, notching or engraving on every tree the names of such shepherdesses, though the bark be ever so hard.' 'You are much in the right,' replied Don Quixote, 'though, for my part, I need not be at the trouble of devising a name for any imaginary shepherdess, being already captivated by the peerless Dulcinea del Toboso, the nymph of these streams, the ornament of these meads, the primrose of beauty, the cream of gracefulness, and, in short, the subject that can merit all the praises that hyperbolical eloquence can bestow.' 'We grant all this,' said the curate, 'but we who cannot pretend to such perfections, must make it our business to find out some shepherdess of a lower form, that will be good-natured, and meet a man half-way upon occasion.' 'We shall find enough, I will warrant you,' replied Carrasco: 'and though we meet with none, yet will we give those very names we find in books, such as Phyllis, Amaryllis, Diana, Florinda, Galatea, Belisarda, and a thousand more, which are to be disposed of publicly in the open market; and when we have purchased them, they are our own. Besides, if my mistress (my shepherdess I should have said) be called Anne, I will name her in my verses Anarda; if Frances, I will call her Francenia; and if Lucy be her name, then Lucinda shall be my shepherdess, and so forth: and if Sancho Pança makes one of our fraternity, he may celebrate his wife Teresa by the name of Teresania.' Don Quixote could not forbear smiling at the him given to that name. The curate again applauded his laudable resolution, and repeated his offer of bearing him company all the time that his other employment would allow him; and then they took their leaves, giving him all the good advice that they thought might conduce to his health and welfare.

No sooner were the curate and bachelor gone, but the housekeeper and niece, who, according to custom, had been listening to all their discourse, came both upon Don Quixote: 'Bless me, uncle,' cried the niece, 'what is here to do! What new maggot has got into your head? When we thought you were come to stay at home, and live like a sober, honest gentleman in your own house, are you hearkening after new inventions, and running a wool-gathering after sheep, forsooth! By my troth, sir, you are somewhat of the latest: the corn is too old to make oaten pipes of.' 'Lord, sir,' quoth the housekeeper, 'how will your Worship be able to endure the summer's sun, and the winter's frost in the open fields? And then the howlings of the wolves, Heaven bless us! Pray, good sir, do not think of it: it is a business fit for nobody but those that are bred and born to it, and as strong as horses. Let the worst come to the worst, better be a knight-errant still, than a keeper of sheep. Troth, master, take my advice; I am neither drunk nor mad, but fresh and fasting from everything but sin, and I have fifty years over my head; be ruled by me; stay at home, look after your concerns, go often to confession, do good to the poor, and if ought goes ill with you, let it lie at my door.' 'Good girls,' said Don Quixote, 'hold your prating: I know best what I have to do: only help to get me to bed, for I find myself somewhat out of order. However, do not trouble your heads, whether I be a knight-errant, or an errant-shepherd, you shall always find that I will provide for you.' The niece and maid, who, without doubt, were good-natured creatures, undressed him, put him to bed, brought him something to eat, and tended him with all imaginable care.

CHAPTER LXXIV

How Don Quixote fell sick, made his last will, and died

As ALL HUMAN THINGS, especially the lives of men, are transitory, their very beginnings being but steps to their dissolution; so Don Quixote, who was no way exempted from the common fate, was snatched away by death, when he least expected it. Whether his sickness was the effect of his melancholy reflections, or whether it was so pre-ordained by Heaven, most certain it is, he was seized with a violent fever, that confined him to his bed six days.

All that time his good friends, the curate, bachelor, and barber, came often to see him, and his trusty squire Sancho Pança never stirred from his bed-side.

They conjectured that his sickness proceeded from the regret of his defeat, and his being disappointed of Dulcinea's disenchantment; and accordingly they left nothing unessayed to divert him. The bachelor begged him to pluck up a good heart, and rise, that they might begin their pastoral life, telling him that he had already writ an eclogue to that purpose, not inferior to those of Sanazaro, and that he had bought with his own money, of a shepherd of Quintanar, two tearing dogs to watch their flock, the one called Barcino, and the other Butron; but this had no effect on Don Quixote, for he still continued dejected. A physician was sent for, who, upon feeling his pulse, did not very well like it; and therefore desired him of all things to provide for his soul's health, for that of his body was in a dangerous condition. Don Quixote heard this with much more temper than those about him; for his niece, his housekeeper, and his squire fell a-weeping as bitterly as if he had been laid out already. The physician was of opinion, that mere melancholy and vexation had brought him to his approaching end. Don Quixote desired them to leave him a little, because he found himself inclinable to rest; they retired, and he had a hearty sleep of about six hours' which the maid and niece were afraid had been his last.

At length he waked, and with a loud voice, 'Blessed be the Almighty,' cried he, 'for this great benefit He has vouchsafed to do me! Infinite are His mercies; they are greater, and more in number than the sins of men.' The niece hearkening very attentively to these words of her uncle, and finding more sense in them than there was in his usual talk, at least since he had fallen ill: 'What do you say, Sir,' said she, 'has any thing extraordinary happened? What mercies are these you mention?'

'Mercies,' answered he, 'that Heaven has this moment vouchsafed to show me, in spite of all my iniquities. My judgment is returned clear and undisturbed and that cloud of ignorance is now removed, which the continual reading of those damnable books of knight-errantry had cast over my understanding. Now, I perceive their nonsense and impertinence, and am only sorry the discovery happens so late, when I want time to make amends by those studies that should enlighten my soul, and prepare me for futurity. I find, niece, my end approaches; but I would have it such, that though my life has got me the character of a madman I may deserve a better at my death. Dear child,' continued he, 'send for my honest friend the curate, the bachelor Carrasco, and Mr. Nicholas the barber, for I intend to make my confession and my will.' His niece was saved the trouble of sending, for presently they all three came in; which Don Quixote perceiving, 'My good friends,' said he, 'I have happy news to tell you; I am no longer Don Quixote de la Mancha, but Alonso Quixano, the same whom the world for his fair behaviour has been formerly pleased to call the Good. I now declare myself an enemy to Amadis de Gaul, and his whole generation; all profane stories of knight-errantry, all romances I detest. I have a true sense of the danger of reading them, and of all my past follies, and through Heaven's mercy, and my own experience, I abhor them.' His three friends were not a little surprised to hear him talk at this rate, and concluded some new frenzy had possessed him. 'What now?' said Sampson to him. 'What is all this to the purpose, Signor Don Quixote? We have just had the news that the Lady Dulcinea is disenchanted; and now we are upon the point of turning shepherds, to sing, and live like princes, you are dwindled down to a hermit.'

'No more of that, I beseech you,' replied Don Quixote; 'all the use I shall make of these follies at present, is to heighten my repentance; and though they have hitherto proved prejudicial, yet, by the assistance of Heaven, they may turn to my advantage at my death: I find it comes fast upon me; therefore, pray, gentlemen, let us be serious. I want a priest to receive my confession, and a scrivener to draw up my will. There is no trifling at a time like this; I must take care of my soul; and therefore pray let the scrivener be sent for, while Mr. Curate prepares me by confession.'

Don Quixote's words put them all into such admiration, that they stood gazing upon one another; they thought they had reason to doubt of the return of his understanding, and yet they could not help believing him. They were also apprehensive he was near the point of death, considering the sudden recovery of his intellects; and he delivered himself after that with so much sense, discretion, and piety, and showed himself so resigned, to the will of Heaven, that they made no scruple to believe him restored to his perfect judgment at last. The curate thereupon cleared the room of all the company but himself and Don Quixote, and then confessed him. In the mean time the bachelor ran for the scrivener, and presently brought him with him; and Sancho Pança being informed by the bachelor how ill his master was, and finding his niece and housekeeper all in tears, began to make wry faces, and fall a-crying. The curate having heard the sick person's confession, came out and told them, that the good Alonso Quixano was very near his end, and certainly in his senses; and therefore, they had best go in, that he might make his will. These dismal tidings opened the sluices of the housekeeper's, the niece's, and the good squire's swollen eyes, so that a whole inundation of tears burst out of those flood-gates, and a thousand sighs from their hearts; for indeed, either as Alonso Quixano, or as Don Quixote de la Mancha, as it has been observed, the sick gentleman had always showed himself such a good-natured man, and of so agreeable a behaviour, that he was not only beloved by his family, but by every one that knew him.

The scrivener, with the rest of the company, then went into the chamber, and the preamble and former part of the will being drawn, and the testator having recommended his soul to Heaven, and bequeathed his body to the earth, according to custom, he came to the legacies, as follows:

'Item, I give and bequeath to Sancho Pança, whom in my madness I made my squire, whatever money he has, or may have of mine in his hands; and whereas there are reckonings and accounts to be adjusted between us, for what he has received and disbursed; my will and pleasure is, that whatever may remain due to me, which can be but small, be enjoyed by him as my free gift, without any let or molestation, and much good may it do him. And as, when I was mad, he was through my means made governor of an island, I would now, in my right senses, give him the government of a kingdom, were it in my power, in consideration of his integrity and faithfulness. And now, my friend,' said he, turning to Sancho, 'pardon me that I have brought upon thee, as well as myself, the scandal of madness, by drawing thee into my own errors, and persuading thee that there have been and still are knights-errant in the world.' 'Woe's me, my dear master's worship!' cried Sancho, all in tears, 'do not die this bout, but even take my counsel, and live on many years; it is the maddest trick a man can ever play in his whole life, to let his breath sneak out of his body without any more ado, and without so much as a rap over the pate, or a kick on the guts; to go out like the snuff of a farthing candle, and die merely of the mulligrubs, or the sullens. For shame, sir, do not give way to sluggishness, but get out of your doleful dumps, and rise. Is this a time to lie honing and groaning a-bed, when we should be in the fields in our shepherd's clothing, as we had resolved? Ten to one but behind some bush, or under some hedge, we may find the Lady Madam Dulcinea, stripped of her enchanted rags, and as fine as a queen. Mayhaps you take it to heart, that you were unhorsed, and a little crupper-scratched the other day; but if that be all, lay the blame upon me, and say it was my fault, in not girting Rozinante tight enough. You know too, there is nothing more common in your errantry-books, than for the knights to be every foot jostled out of the saddle. There is nothing but ups and downs in this world, and he that is cast down today, maybe a cock-a-hoop tomorrow.' 'Even so,' said Samson, 'honest Sancho has a right notion of the matter.' 'Soft and fair, gentleman,' replied Don Quixote, 'never look for birds of this year in the nests of the last: I was mad, but I am now in my senses; I was once Don Quixote de la Mancha but am now, as I said before, the plain Alonso Quixano, and I hope the sincerity of my words, and my repentance, may restore me to the same esteem you have had for me before; and so, Mr. Scrivener, pray go on.'

'Item, I constitute and appoint Antonia Quixano, my niece here present, sole heiress of all my estate both real and personal after all my just debts and legacies, bequeathed by these presents, shall have been payed, satisfied, and deducted, out of the best of my goods and chattels; and the first of that kind to be discharged shall be the salary due to my housekeeper, together with twenty ducats over and above her wages; which said sum I leave and bequeath her to buy her mourning.

'Item, I appoint Mr. Curate, and Mr. Samson Carrasco the bachelor, here present, to be the executors of this my last will and testament.

'Item, it is my will, that if my niece Antonia Quixano be inclinable to marry, it be with none but a person, who, upon strict inquiry, shall be found never to have read a book of knight-errantry in his life; and in case it appears, that he has been conversant in such books, and that she persists in her resolution to marry him, she is then to forfeit all right and title to my bequest, which in such case, my executors are hereby empowered to dispose of to pious uses, as they shall think most proper.

'Item, I entreat the said executors, that if at any time they happen to meet with the author of a book now extant, entitled, "The Second Part of the Achievements of Don Quixote de la Mancha," they would from me most heartily beg his pardon for my being undesignedly the occasion of his writing such a parcel of impertinences as is contained in that book; for it is the greatest burthen to my departing soul, that ever I was the cause of his making such a thing public.'

Having finished the will he fell into a swooning fit, and extended his body to the full length in the bed. All the company were troubled and alarmed, and ran to his assistance: however, he came to himself at last; but relapsed into the like fits almost every hour, for the space of three days that he lived after he had made his will.

The whole family was in grief and confusion; and yet, after all, the niece continued to eat, the housekeeper drank, and washed down sorrow; and Sancho Pança made much of himself: for there is a strange charm in the thoughts of a good legacy, or the hopes of an estate, which wondrously removes, or at least alleviates, the sorrow that men would otherwise feel for the death of friends.

In short, Don Quixote's last day came, after he had made those preparations for death which good Christians ought to do; and by many fresh and weighty arguments showed his abhorrence of books of knight-errantry. The scrivener, who was by, protested he had never read in any books of that kind of any knight-errant who ever died in his bed so quietly, and like a good Christian, as Don Quixote did. In short, amidst the tears and lamentations of his friends, he gave up the ghost, or, to speak more plainly, died; which, when the curate perceived, he desired the scrivener to give him a certificate, how Alonso Quixano, commonly called the Good, and sometimes known by the name of Don Quixote de la Mancha, was departed out of this life into another, and died a natural death. This he desired, lest any other author but Cid Hamet Benengeli should take occasion to raise him from the dead, and presume to write endless histories of his pretended adventures.

Thus died that ingenious gentleman Don Quixote de la Mancha, whose native place Cid Hamet has not thought fit directly to mention, with design that all the towns and villages in La Mancha should contend for the honour of giving him birth, as the seven cities of Greece did for Homer. We shall omit Sancho's lamentations, and those of the niece and the housekeeper, as also several epitaphs that were made for his tomb, and will only give you this which the Bachelor Carrasco caused to be put over it.

DON QUIXOTE'S EPITAPH

'The body of a knight lies here,
    So brave, that to his latest breath
Immortal glory was his care,
    And makes him triumph over death.

His looks spread terror every hour;
    He strove oppression to control;
Nor cou'd all Hell's united pow'r
    Subdue, or daunt his mighty soul.

Nor has his death the world deceiv'd
    Less than his wondrous life surpris'd
For if he like a madman liv'd,
    At least he like a wise one dy'd.'

Here the sagacious Cid Hamet addressing himself to his pen, 'O thou my slender pen,' says he, 'thou, of whose nib, whether well or ill cut, I dare not speak my thoughts! Suspended by this brass-wire, remain upon this spit-rack where I lodge thee. There mayest thou claim a being many ages, unless presumptuous and wicked historians take the down to profane thee. But ere they lay their heavy hands on thee, bid them beware, and, as well as thou can'st in their own style, tell them,

' "Avaunt, ye scoundrels, all and some!*
I'm kept for no such thing;
Defile me not; but hang yourselves;
And so, God save the king."

'For me alone was the great Quixote born, and I alone for him. Deeds were his task, and to record them, mine. We two, like tallies for each other struck, are nothing when apart. In vain the Spurious Scribe of Tordesillas, dared with his blunt and bungling ostrich-quill invade the deeds of my most valorous knight: His shoulders are unequal to the attempt: The task is superior to his frozen genius.

'And thou, reader, if ever thou canst find him out in his obscurity, I beseech thee advise him likewise to let the wearied, mouldering bones of Don Quixote rest quiet in the earth that covers them. Let him not expose them in Old Castile, against the sanctions of death, impiously raking him out of the vault where he lies stretched out beyond a possibility of taking a third ramble through the world. The two sallies that he has made already, which are the subject of these two volumes, and have met with such universal applause in this and other kingdoms are sufficient to ridicule the pretended adventures of knights-errant. Thus advising him for the best, thou shalt discharge the duty of a Christian, and do good to him that wishes thee evil. As for me, I must esteem myself happy, to have been the first that rendered those fabulous nonsensical stories of knight-errantry, the object of the public aversion. They are already going down, and I do not doubt but they will drop and fall all together in good earnest, never to rise again. Adieu.'

* *Tatè tatè sollonzicos* – these seem to be words borrowed from an old romance.

WORDSWORTH CLASSICS

General Editors: Marcus Clapham & Clive Reynard

JANE AUSTEN
Emma
Mansfield Park
Northanger Abbey
Persuasion
Pride and Prejudice
Sense and Sensibility

ARNOLD BENNETT
Anna of the Five Towns

R. D. BLACKMORE
Lorna Doone

ANNE BRONTË
Agnes Grey
The Tenant of
Wildfell Hall

CHARLOTTE BRONTË
Jane Eyre
The Professor
Shirley
Villette

EMILY BRONTË
Wuthering Heights

JOHN BUCHAN
Greenmantle
Mr Standfast
The Thirty-Nine Steps

SAMUEL BUTLER
The Way of All Flesh

LEWIS CARROLL
Alice in Wonderland

CERVANTES
Don Quixote

G. K. CHESTERTON
Father Brown:
Selected Stories
The Man who was
Thursday

ERSKINE CHILDERS
The Riddle of the Sands

JOHN CLELAND
Memoirs of a Woman of
Pleasure: Fanny Hill

WILKIE COLLINS
The Moonstone
The Woman in White

JOSEPH CONRAD
Heart of Darkness
Lord Jim
The Secret Agent

J. FENIMORE COOPER
The Last of the
Mohicans

STEPHEN CRANE
The Red Badge of
Courage

THOMAS DE QUINCEY
Confessions of an English
Opium Eater

DANIEL DEFOE
Moll Flanders
Robinson Crusoe

CHARLES DICKENS
Bleak House
David Copperfield
Great Expectations
Hard Times
Little Dorrit
Martin Chuzzlewit
Oliver Twist
Pickwick Papers
A Tale of Two Cities

BENJAMIN DISRAELI
Sybil

THEODOR DOSTOEVSKY
Crime and Punishment

SIR ARTHUR CONAN
DOYLE
The Adventures of
Sherlock Holmes
The Case-Book of
Sherlock Holmes
The Lost World &
Other Stories
The Return of
Sherlock Holmes
Sir Nigel

GEORGE DU MAURIER
Trilby

ALEXANDRE DUMAS
The Three Musketeers

MARIA EDGEWORTH
Castle Rackrent

GEORGE ELIOT
The Mill on the Floss
Middlemarch
Silas Marner

HENRY FIELDING
Tom Jones

F. SCOTT FITZGERALD
A Diamond as Big as the
Ritz & Other Stories
The Great Gatsby
Tender is the Night

GUSTAVE FLAUBERT
Madame Bovary

JOHN GALSWORTHY
In Chancery
The Man of Property
To Let

ELIZABETH GASKELL
Cranford
North and South

KENNETH GRAHAME
The Wind in the
Willows

GEORGE & WEEDON
GROSSMITH
Diary of a Nobody

RIDER HAGGARD
She

THOMAS HARDY
Far from the
Madding Crowd
The Mayor of Casterbridge
The Return of the
Native
Tess of the d'Urbervilles
The Trumpet Major
Under the Greenwood
Tree

NATHANIEL HAWTHORNE
The Scarlet Letter

O. HENRY
Selected Stories

HOMER
The Iliad
The Odyssey

E. W. HORNUNG
Raffles: The Amateur Cracksman

VICTOR HUGO
The Hunchback of Notre Dame
Les Misérables: volume 1
Les Misérables: volume 2

HENRY JAMES
The Ambassadors
Daisy Miller & Other Stories
The Golden Bowl
The Turn of the Screw & The Aspern Papers

M. R. JAMES
Ghost Stories

JEROME K. JEROME
Three Men in a Boat

JAMES JOYCE
Dubliners
A Portrait of the Artist as a Young Man

RUDYARD KIPLING
Captains Courageous
Kim
The Man who would be King & Other Stories
Plain Tales from the Hills

D. H. LAWRENCE
The Rainbow
Sons and Lovers
Women in Love

SHERIDAN LE FANU
(edited by M. R. James)
Madam Crowl's Ghost & Other Stories

JACK LONDON
Call of the Wild & White Fang

HERMAN MELVILLE
Moby Dick
Typee

H. H. MUNRO
The Complete Stories of Saki

EDGAR ALLAN POE
Tales of Mystery and Imagination

FREDERICK ROLFE
Hadrian the Seventh

SIR WALTER SCOTT
Ivanhoe

WILLIAM SHAKESPEARE
All's Well that Ends Well
Antony and Cleopatra
As You Like It
A Comedy of Errors
Hamlet
Henry IV Part 1
Henry IV part 2
Henry V
Julius Caesar
King Lear
Macbeth
Measure for Measure
The Merchant of Venice
A Midsummer Night's Dream
Othello
Richard II
Richard III
Romeo and Juliet
The Taming of the Shrew
The Tempest
Troilus and Cressida
Twelfth Night
A Winter's Tale

MARY SHELLEY
Frankenstein

ROBERT LOUIS STEVENSON
Dr Jekyll and Mr Hyde

BRAM STOKER
Dracula

JONATHAN SWIFT
Gulliver's Travels

W. M. THACKERAY
Vanity Fair

TOLSTOY
War and Peace

ANTHONY TROLLOPE
Barchester Towers
Dr Thorne
Framley Parsonage
The Last Chronicle of Barset
The Small House at Allington
The Warden

MARK TWAIN
Tom Sawyer & Huckleberry Finn

JULES VERNE
Around the World in 80 Days & Five Weeks in a Balloon
20,000 Leagues Under the Sea

VOLTAIRE
Candide

EDITH WHARTON
The Age of Innocence

OSCAR WILDE
Lord Arthur Savile's Crime & Other Stories
The Picture of Dorian Gray

VIRGINIA WOOLF
Orlando
To the Lighthouse

P. C. WREN
Beau Geste

Distribution

AUSTRALIA, BRUNEI
& MALAYSIA
Reed Editions
22 Salmon Street, Port Melbourne
Vic 3207, Australia
Tel: (03) 245 7111
Fax (03) 245 7333

DENMARK
BOG-FAN
St. Kongensgade 61A
1264 København K

BOGPA SIKA
Industrivej 1, 7120 Vejle Ø

FRANCE
Bookking International
60 Rue Saint-André-des-Arts
75006 Paris

GERMANY, AUSTRIA
& SWITZERLAND
Swan Buch-Marketing GmbH
Goldscheuerstrabe 16
D-7640 Kehl Am Rhein, Germany

GREAT BRITAIN & IRELAND
Wordsworth Editions Ltd
Cumberland House, Crib Street,
Ware, Hertfordshire SG12 9ET

Selecta Books
The Selectabook
Distribution Centre
Folly Road, Roundway, Devizes
Wiltshire SN10 2HR

HOLLAND & BELGIUM
Uitgeverlj en Boekhandel
Van Gennep BV, Spuistraat 283
1012 VR Amsterdam, Holland

INDIA
OM Book Service
1690 First Floor
Nai Sarak, Delhi – 110006
Tel: 3279823-3265303 Fax: 3278091

ITALY
Magis Books
Piazza Della Vittoria l/C
42100 Reggio Emilia
Tel: 0522-452303 Fax: 0522-452845

NEW ZEALAND
Whitcoulls Limited
Private Bag 92098, Auckland

NORWAY
Norsk Bokimport AS
Bertrand Narvesensvei 2
Postboks 6219, Etterstad, 0602 Oslo

PORTUGAL
Isabel Leao **Editorial Noticias**
Rua da Cruz da Carreira, 4B
1100 Lisboa
Tel: 01-570051 Fax: 01-3522066

SINGAPORE
Book Station
18 Leo Drive, Singapore
Tel: 4511998 Fax: 4529188

CYPRUS & GREECE
Huckleberry Trading
4 Isabella, Anavargos, Pafos, Cyprus
Tel: 06-231313

SOUTH AFRICA
Struik Book Distributors (Pty) Ltd
Graph Avenue, Montague Gardens,
7441 P O Box 193 Maitland 7405
South Africa
Tel: (021) 551-5900 Fax: (021) 551-1124

SPAIN
Ribera Libros, S.L.
Poligono Martiartu, Calle 1 – no 6
48480 Arrigorriaga, Vizcaya
Tel: 34-4-6713607 (Almacen)
     34-4-4418787 (Libreria)
Fax: 34-4-6713608 (Almacen)
     34-4-4418029 (Libreria)

USA, CANADA & MEXICO
Universal Sales & Marketing
230 Fifth Avenue, Suite 1212
New York, N Y 10001 USA
Tel: 212-481-3500 Fax: 212-481-3534

DIRECT MAIL
Redvers
Redvers House, 13 Fairmile,
Henley-on-Thames, Oxfordshire RG9 2JR
Tel: 0491 572656 Fax: 0491 573590